DRUMS OF AUTUMN

Diana Gabaldon is the author of the international bestselling Outlander novels and Lord John Grey series.

She says that the Outlander series started by accident: 'I decided to write a novel for practice in order to learn what it took to write a novel, and to decide whether I really wanted to do it for real. I did - and here we all are trying to decide what to call books that nobody can describe, but that fortunately most people seem to enjoy.'

And enjoy them they do - in their millions, all over the world. Published in 42 countries and 38 languages, in 2014 the Outlander novels were made into an acclaimed TV series starring Sam Heughan as Jamie Fraser and Caitriona Balfe as Claire. Seasons three and four are currently in production.

Diana lives with her husband and dogs in Scottsdale, Arizona, and is currently at work on her ninth Outlander novel.

For further information, please see Diana's website at
www.DianaGabaldon.com, or talk to her on
Twitter (@Writer_DG) or
Facebook: AuthorDianaGabaldon

OUTLANDER SERIES

Outlander (previously published as *Cross Stitch*)
Claire Randall leaves her husband for an afternoon walk in the
Highlands, passes through a circle of standing stones and finds
herself in Jacobite Scotland, pursued by danger and forcibly married
to another man – a young Scots warrior named Jamie Fraser.

Dragonfly in Amber

For twenty years Claire Randall has kept the secrets of an ancient
battle and her daughter's heritage. But the dead don't sleep, and the
time for silence is long past.

Voyager

Jamie Fraser died on the battlefield of Culloden – or did he? Claire
seeks through the darkness of time for the man who once was her
soul – and might be once again.

Drums of Autumn

How far will a daughter go, to save the life of a father she's never
known?

The Fiery Cross

The North Carolina backcountry is burning and the long fuse of
rebellion is lit. Jamie Fraser is a born leader of men – but a passionate
husband and father as well. How much will such a man sacrifice for
freedom?

A Breath of Snow and Ashes

1772, and three years hence, the shot heard round the world will be
fired. But will Jamie, Claire, and the Frasers of Fraser's Ridge be still
alive to hear it?

An Echo in the Bone

Jamie Fraser is an 18th-century Highlander, and ex-Jacobite traitor,
and a reluctant rebel. His wife, Claire Randall Fraser, is a surgeon –
from the 20th century. What she knows of the future compels him to
fight; what she doesn't know may kill them both.

Written in My Own Heart's Blood

Jamie Fraser returns from a watery grave to discover that his best
friend has married his wife, his illegitimate son has discovered (to
his horror) who his father really is, and his nephew wants to marry
a Quaker. The Frasers can only be thankful that their daughter and
her family are safe in 20th-century Scotland. Or not...

DIANA GABALDON
DRUMS OF AUTUMN

arrow books

9 10

Arrow Books
20 Vauxhall Bridge Road
London SW1V 2SA

Arrow Books is part of the Penguin Random House group of companies
whose addresses can be found at global.penguinrandomhouse.com.

Penguin
Random House
UK

First published in Great Britain by Arrow Books in 1994

www.penguin.co.uk

A CIP catalogue record for this book
is available from the British Library.

ISBN 9781784751340

Typeset by Intype, London Ltd
Printed and bound by Clays Ltd, St Ives plc

Penguin Random House is committed to a sustainable future for
our business, our readers and our planet. This book is made from
Forest Stewardship Council® certified paper.

MIX
Paper from
responsible sources
FSC® C018179

This book turned out to have a lot to do with fathers, and so it's for my own father, Tony Gabaldon, who also tells stories

ACKNOWLEDGMENTS

The author's grateful thanks to:

My editor, Jackie Cantor, who said, when informed that there was (ahem) actually another book in this series, 'Why am I not surprised to hear this?'

Susan Schwartz and her loyal minions – the copyeditors, typesetters, and book designers – without whom this book would not exist; I hope they fully recover from the experience.

My husband, Doug Watkins, who said, 'I don't know how you go on getting away with this; you don't know *anything* about men!'

My daughter Laura, who generously allowed me to steal two lines of her eighth-grade essay for my Prologue; my son Samuel, who said, 'Aren't you *ever* going to finish writing that book?' and (without pausing for breath), 'Since you're still busy writing, can we have McDonalds again?' and my daughter Jennifer, who said, 'You *are* going to change clothes before you come talk to my class, aren't you? Don't worry, Mommy, I have an outfit all picked out for you.'

The anonymous sixth grader who handed back a sample chapter passed around during a talk at his school and said, 'That was kind of gross, but really interesting. People don't really *do* that, do they?'

Iain MacKinnon Taylor and his brother Hamish, for Gaelic translations, idioms, and colourful invective. Nancy Bushey, for Gaelic tapes. Karl Hagen, for general advice on Latin grammar. Susan Martin and Reid Snider, for Greek epigrams and rotting pythons. Sylvia Petter, Elise Skidmore, Janet Kieffer Kelly, and Karen Pershing for help with the French bits.

Janet MacConnaughey and Keith Sheppard, for Latin love poetry, macaronics, and the original lyrics of 'To Anacreon in Heaven'.

Mary Campbell Toerner and Ruby Vincent, for the loan of an unpublished historical manuscript about the Highlanders of the Cape Fear. Claire Nelson for the loan of the Encyclopaedia Britannica, 1771 edition. Esther and Bill Schindler, for the loan of the books on Eastern forests.

Ron Wodaski, Karl Hagen, Bruce Woods, Rich Hamper, Eldon Garlock, Dean Quarrel, and several other gentlemen members of the CompuServe Writers Forum, for expert opinions on what it feels like to be kicked in the testicles.

Marte Brengle, for detailed descriptions of sweat lodge ceremonials and suggestions on sports cars. Merrill Cornish, for his stunning description of redbuds in bloom. Arlene and Joe McCrea, for saints' names and descriptions of plowing with a mule. Ken Brown, for details of the Presbyterian Baptismal rite (much abridged in the text). David Stanley, Scotland's next great writer, for advice on anoraks, jackets and the difference between them.

Babara Schnell, for German translations, error-checking, and sympathetic reading.

Dr. Ellen Mandell, for medical opinions, close reading, and useful suggestions for dealing with inguinal hernias, abortion, and other forms of harrowing bodily trauma.

Dr. Rosina Lippi-Green, for details of Mohawk life and customs, and notes on Scots linguistics and German grammar.

Mac Beckett, for his notion of new and ancient spirits.

Jack Whyte, for his memoirs of life as a Scottish folksinger, including the proper response to kilt jokes.

Susan Davis, for friendship, boundless enthusiasm, dozens of books, descriptions of pulling ticks off her kids – and strawberries.

Walt Hawn and Gordon Fenwick, for telling me how long is a furlong. John Ravenscroft and miscellaneous members of the UK Forum, for a riveting discussion of the RAF's underpants, circa WWII. Eve Ackerman and helpful members of the CompuServe SFLIT Forum, for the publication dates of *Conan the Barbarian*.

Barbara Raisbeck and Mary M. Robbins, for their helpful references on herbs and early pharmacology.

My anonymous library friend, for the *reams* of useful references.

Arnold Wagner and Steven Lopata, for discussions of high and low explosives and general advice on how to blow things up.

Margaret Campbell and other online residents of North Carolina, for miscellaneous descriptions of their fair state.

John L. Myers, both for telling me about his ghosts, and for generously allowing me to incorporate certain elements of his physique and persona into the formidable John Quincy Myers, Mountain Man. The hernia is fictitious.

As always, thanks also to the many members of the CompuServe Literary Forum and Writers Forum whose names have escaped my memory, for their helpful suggestions and convivial conversation, and to the AOL folderfolk for their stimulating discussions.

A special thanks to Rosana Madrid Gatti, for her labour of love in constructing and maintaining the award-winning Official Diana Gabaldon Web Page (http://www.cco.caltech.edu/~gatti/gabaldon/gabaldon.html).

And thanks to Lori Musser, Dawn Van Winkle, Kaera Hallahan, Virginia Clough, Elaine Faxon, Ellen Stanton, Elaine Smith, Cathy Kravitz, Hanneke (whose last name remains unfortunately illegible), Judith MacDonald, Susan Hunt and her sister Holly, the Boise gang, and many others, for their thoughtful gifts of wine, drawings, rosaries, chocolate, Celtic music, soap, statuary, pressed heather from Culloden, handkerchiefs with echidnas, Maori pens, English teas, garden trowels, and other miscellanea meant to boost my spirits and keep me writing far past the point of exhaustion. It worked.

And lastly to my mother, who touches me in passing.

Diana Gabaldon
76530,523@compuserve.com
[Section Leader, Research and the Craft of Writing, CompuServe Writers Forum]

PROLOGUE

I've never been afraid of ghosts. I live with them daily, after all. When I look in a mirror, my mother's eyes look back at me; my mouth curls with the smile that lured my great-grandfather to the fate that was me.

No, how should I fear the touch of those vanished hands, laid on me in love unknowing? How could I be afraid of those that molded my flesh, leaving their remnants to live long past the grave?

Still less could I be afraid of those ghosts who touch my thoughts in passing. Any library is filled with them. I can take a book from dusty shelves, and be haunted by the thoughts of one long dead, still lively as ever in their winding sheet of words.

Of course it isn't these homely and accustomed ghosts that trouble sleep and curdle wakefulness. Look back, hold a torch to light the recesses of the dark. Listen to the footsteps that echo behind, when you walk alone.

All the time the ghosts flit past and through us, hiding in the future. We look in the mirror and see the shades of other faces looking back through the years; we see the shape of memory, standing solid in an empty doorway. By blood and by choice, we make our ghosts; we haunt ourselves.

Each ghost comes unbidden from the misty grounds of dream and silence.

Our rational minds say, 'No, it isn't.'

But another part, an older part, echoes always softly in the dark, 'Yes, but it *could* be.'

We come and go from mystery and, in between, we try to forget. But a breeze passing in a still room stirs my hair now and then in soft affection. I think it is my mother.

PART ONE

O Brave New World

1

A Hanging in Eden

Charleston, June 1767

I heard the drums long before they came in sight. The beating echoed in the pit of my stomach, as though I too were hollow. The sound traveled through the crowd, a harsh military rhythm meant to be heard over speech or gunfire. I saw heads turn as the people fell silent, looking up the stretch of East Bay Street, where it ran from the half-built skeleton of the new Customs House toward White Point Gardens.

It was a hot day, even for Charleston in June. The best places were on the seawall, where the air moved; here below, it was like being roasted alive. My shift was soaked through, and the cotton bodice clung between my breasts. I wiped my face for the tenth time in as many minutes and lifted the heavy coil of my hair, hoping vainly for a cooling breeze upon my neck.

I was morbidly aware of necks at the moment. Unobtrusively, I put my hand up to the base of my throat, letting my fingers circle it. I could feel the pulse beat in my carotid arteries, along with the drums, and when I breathed, the hot wet air clogged my throat as though I were choking.

I quickly took my hand down, and drew in a breath as deep as I could manage. That was a mistake. The man in front of me hadn't bathed in a month or more; the edge of the stock about his thick neck was dark with grime and his clothes smelled sour and musty, pungent even amid the sweaty reek of the crowd. The smell of hot bread and frying pig fat from the food vendors' stalls lay heavy over a musk of rotting seagrass from the marsh, only slightly relieved by a whiff of salt-breeze from the harbor.

There were several children in front of me, craning and gawking, running out from under the oaks and palmettos to look up the street, being called back by anxious parents.

3

The girl nearest me had a neck like the white part of a grass stalk, slender and succulent.

There was a ripple of excitement through the crowd; the gallows procession was in sight at the far end of the street. The drums grew louder.

'Where is he?' Fergus muttered beside me, craning his own neck to see. 'I knew I should have gone with him!'

'He'll be here.' I wanted to stand on tiptoe, but didn't, feeling that this would be undignified. I did glance around, though, searching. I could always spot Jamie in a crowd; he stood head and shoulders above most men, and his hair caught the light in a blaze of reddish gold. There was no sign of him yet, only a bobbing sea of bonnets and tricornes, sheltering from the heat those citizens come too late to find a place in the shade.

The flags came first, fluttering above the heads of the excited crowd, the banners of Great Britain and of the Royal Colony of South Carolina. And another, bearing the family arms of the Lord Governor of the colony.

Then came the drummers, walking two by two in step, their sticks an alternate beat and blur. It was a slow march, grimly inexorable. A dead march, I thought they called that particular cadence; very suitable under the circumstances. All other noises were drowned by the rattle of the drums.

Then came the platoon of red-coated soldiers and in their midst, the prisoners.

There were three of them, hands bound before them, linked together by a chain that ran through rings on the iron collars about their necks. The first man was small and elderly, ragged and disreputable, a shambling wreck who lurched and staggered so that the dark-suited clergyman who walked beside the prisoners was obliged to grasp his arm to keep him from falling.

'Is that Gavin Hayes? He looks sick,' I murmured to Fergus.

'He's drunk.' The soft voice came from behind me, and I whirled, to find Jamie standing at my shoulder, eyes fixed on the pitiful procession.

The small man's disequilibrium was disrupting the progress of the parade, as his stumbling forced the two men

4

chained to him to zig and zag abruptly in order to keep their feet. The general impression was of three inebriates rolling home from the local tavern; grossly at odds with the solemnity of the occasion. I could hear the rustle of laughter over the drums, and shouts and jeers from the crowds on the wrought-iron balconies of the houses on East Bay Street.

'Your doing?' I spoke quietly, so as not to attract notice, but I could have shouted and waved my arms; no one had eyes for anything but the scene before us.

I felt rather than saw Jamie's shrug, as he moved forward to stand beside me.

'It was what he asked of me,' he said. 'And the best I could manage for him.'

'Brandy or whisky?' asked Fergus, evaluating Hayes's appearance with a practiced eye.

'The man's a Scot, wee Fergus.' Jamie's voice was as calm as his face, but I heard the small note of strain in it. 'Whisky's what he wanted.'

'A wise choice. With luck, he won't even notice when they hang him,' Fergus muttered. The small man had slipped from the preacher's grasp and fallen flat on his face in the sandy road, pulling one of his companions to his knees; the last prisoner, a tall young man, stayed on his feet but swayed wildly from side to side, trying desperately to keep his balance. The crowd on the point roared with glee.

The captain of the guard glowed crimson between the white of his wig and the metal of his gorget, flushed with fury as much as with sun. He barked an order as the drums continued their somber roll, and a soldier scrambled hastily to remove the chain that bound the prisoners together. Hayes was jerked unceremoniously to his feet, a soldier grasping each arm, and the procession resumed, in better order.

There was no laughter by the time they reached the gallows – a muledrawn cart placed beneath the limbs of a huge live oak. I could feel the drums beating through the soles of my feet. I felt slightly sick from the sun and the smells. The drums stopped abruptly, and my ears rang in the silence.

5

'Ye dinna need to watch it, Sassenach,' Jamie whispered to me. 'Go back to the wagon.' His own eyes were fixed unblinkingly on Hayes, who swayed and mumbled in the soldiers' grasp, looking blearily around.

The last thing I wanted was to watch. But neither could I leave Jamie to see it through alone. He had come for Gavin Hayes; I had come for him. I touched his hand.

'I'll stay.'

Jamie drew himself straighter, squaring his shoulders. He moved I pace forward, making sure that he was visible in the crowd. If Hayes was still sober enough to see anything, the last thing he saw on earth would be the face of a friend.

He could see; Hayes glared to and fro as they lifted him into the cart, twisting his neck, desperately looking.

'*Gabhainn! A charaid!*' Jamie shouted suddenly. Hayes's eyes found him at once, and he ceased struggling.

The little man stood swaying slightly as the charge was read: theft in the amount of six pounds, ten shillings. He was covered in reddish dust, and pearls of sweat clung trembling to the gray stubble of his beard. The preacher was leaning close, murmuring urgently in his ear.

Then the drums began again, in a steady roll. The hangman guided the noose over the balding head and fixed it tight, knot positioned precisely, just under the ear. The captain of the guard stood poised, saber raised.

Suddenly, the condemned man drew himself up straight. Eyes on Jamie, he opened his mouth, as though to speak.

The saber flashed in the morning sun, and the drums stopped, with a final *thunk*!

I looked at Jamie; he was white to the lips, eyes fixed wide. From the corner of my eye, I could see the twitching rope, and the faint, reflexive jerk of the dangling sack of clothes. A sharp stink of urine and feces struck through the thick air.

On my other side, Fergus watched dispassionately.

'I suppose he noticed, after all,' he murmured, with regret.

The body swung slightly, a dead weight oscillating like a

plumb-bob on its string. There was a sigh from the crowd, of awe and release. Terns squawked from the burning sky, and the harbor sounds came faint and smothered through the heavy air, but the point was wrapped in silence. From where I stood, I could hear the small *plit . . . plat . . . plit* of the drops that fell from the toe of the corpse's dangling shoe.

I hadn't known Gavin Hayes, and felt no personal grief for his death, but I was glad it had been quick. I stole a glance at him, with an odd feeling of intrusion. It was a most public way of accomplishing a most private act, and I felt vaguely embarrassed to be looking.

The hangman had known his business; there had been no undignified struggle, no staring eyes, no protruding tongue; Gavin's small round head tilted sharply to the side, neck grotesquely stretched but cleanly broken.

It was a clean break in more ways than one. The captain of the guard, satisfied that Hayes was dead, motioned with his saber for the next man to be brought to the gibbet. I saw his eyes travel down the red-clad file, and then widen in outrage.

At the same moment, there was a cry from the crowd, and a ripple of excitement that quickly spread. Heads turned and people pushed each against his neighbor, striving to see where there was nothing to be seen.

'He's gone!'

'There he goes!'

'Stop him!'

It was the third prisoner, the tall young man, who had seized the moment of Gavin's death to run for his life, sliding past the guard who should have been watching him, but who had been unable to resist the gallows' fascination.

I saw a flicker of movement behind a vendor's stall, a flash of dirty blond hair. Some of the soldiers saw it, too, and ran in that direction, but many more were rushing in other directions, and among the collisions and confusion, nothing was accomplished.

The captain of the guard was shouting, face purple, his voice barely audible over the uproar. The remaining prisoner, looking stunned, was seized and hustled back in

7

the direction of the Court of Guard as the redcoats began hastily to sort themselves back into order under the lash of their captain's voice.

Jamie snaked an arm around my waist and dragged me out of the way of an oncoming wave of humanity. The crowd fell back before the advance of squads of soldiers, who formed up and marched briskly off to quarter the area, under the grim and furious direction of their sergeant.

'We'd best find Ian,' Jamie said, fending off a group of excited apprentices. He glanced at Fergus, and jerked his head toward the gibbet and its melancholy burden. 'Claim the body, aye? We'll meet at the Willow Tree later.'

'Do you think they'll catch him?' I asked, as we pushed through the ebbing crowd, threading our way down a cobbled lane toward the merchants' wharves.

'I expect so. Where can he go?' He spoke abstractedly, a narrow line visible between his brows. Plainly the dead man was still on his mind, and he had little attention to spare for the living.

'Did Hayes have any family?' I asked. He shook his head. 'I asked him that, when I brought him the whisky. He thought he might have a brother left alive, but no notion where. The brother was transported soon after the Rising – to Virginia, Hayes thought, but he'd heard nothing since.'

Not surprising if he hadn't; an indentured laborer would have had no facilities for communicating with kin left behind in Scotland, unless the bondsman's employer was kind enough to send a letter on his behalf. And kind or not, it was unlikely that a letter would have found Gavin Hayes, who had spent ten years in Ardsmuir prison before being transported in his turn.

'Duncan!' Jamie called out, and a tall, thin man turned and raised a hand in acknowledgment. He made his way through the crowd in a cork-screw fashion, his single arm swinging in a wide arc that fended off the passersby.

'*Mac Dubh*,' he said, bobbing his head in greeting to Jamie. 'Mrs. Claire.' His long, narrow face was furrowed with sadness. He too had once been a prisoner at Ardsmuir, with Hayes and with Jamie. Only the loss of his arm to a blood infection had prevented his being transported with the others. Unfit to be sold for labor, he had instead been pardoned and set free to starve – until Jamie had found him.

'God rest poor Gavin,' Duncan said, shaking his head dolorously.

Jamie muttered something in response in Gaelic, and crossed himself. Then he straightened, casting off the oppression of the day with a visible effort.

'Aye, well. I must go to the docks and arrange about Ian's passage, and then we'll think of burying Gavin. But I must have the lad settled first.'

We struggled through the crowd toward the docks, squeezing our way between knots of excited gossipers, eluding the drays and barrows that came and went through the press with the ponderous indifference of trade.

A file of red-coated soldiers came at the quick-march from the other end of the quay, splitting the crowd like vinegar dropped on mayonnaise. The sun glittered hot on the line of bayonet points and the rhythm of their tramping beat through the noise of the crowd like a muffled drum. Even the rumbling sledges and handcarts stopped abruptly to let them pass by.

'Mind your pocket, Sassenach,' Jamie murmured in my ear, ushering me through a narrow space between a turban-clad slave clutching two small children and a street preacher perched on a box. He was shouting sin and repentance, but with only one word in three audible through the noise.

'I sewed it shut,' I assured him, nonetheless reaching to touch the small weight that swung against my thigh. 'What about yours?'

He grinned and tilted his hat forward, dark blue eyes narrowing against the bright sunlight.

'It's where my sporran would be, did I have one. So long as I dinna meet with a quick-fingered harlot, I'm safe.'

I glanced at the slightly bulging front of his breeches, and then up at him. Broad-shouldered and tall, with bold, clean features and a Highlander's proud carriage, he drew the glance of every woman he passed, even with his bright hair covered by a sober blue tricorne. The breeches, which were borrowed, were substantially too tight, and did nothing whatever to detract from the general effect – an effect enhanced by the fact that he himself was totally ignorant of it.

'You're a walking inducement to harlots,' I said. 'Stick by me; I'll protect you.'

He laughed and took my arm as we emerged into a small, clear space.

'Ian!' he shouted, catching sight of his nephew over the heads of the crowd. A moment later, a tall, stringy gawk of a boy popped out of the crowd, pushing a thatch of brown hair out of his eyes and grinning widely.

'I thought I should never find ye, Uncle!' he exclaimed. 'Christ, there are more folk here than at the Lawnmarket in Edinburgh!' He wiped a coat sleeve across his long, half-homely face, leaving a streak of grime down one cheek.

Jamie eyed his nephew askance.

'Ye're lookin' indecently cheerful, Ian, for having just seen a man go to his death.'

Ian hastily altered his expression into an attempt at decent solemnity.

'Oh, no, Uncle Jamie,' he said. 'I didna see the hanging.' Duncan raised one brow and Ian blushed slightly. 'I – I wasna afraid to see; it was only I had . . . something else I wanted to do.'

Jamie smiled slightly and patted his nephew on the back.

'Don't trouble yourself, Ian; I'd as soon not have seen it myself, only that Gavin was a friend.'

'I know, Uncle. I'm sorry for it.' A flash of sympathy showed in the boy's large brown eyes, the only feature of his face with any claim to beauty. He glanced at me. 'Was it awful, Auntie?'

'Yes,' I said. 'It's over, though.' I pulled the damp handkerchief out of my bosom and stood on tiptoe to rub away the smudge on his cheek.

Duncan Innes shook his head sorrowfully. 'Aye, poor Gavin. Still, it's a quicker death than starving, and there was little left for him but that.'

10

'Let's go,' Jamie interrupted, unwilling to spend time in useless lamenting. 'The *Bonnie Mary* should be near the far end of the quay.' I saw Ian glance at Jamie and draw himself up as though about to speak, but Jamie had already turned toward the harbor and was shoving his way through the crowd. Ian glanced at me, shrugged, and offered me an arm.

We followed Jamie behind the warehouses that lined the docks, side-stepping sailors, loaders, slaves, passengers, customers and merchants of all sorts. Charleston was a major shipping port, and business was booming, with as many as a hundred ships a month coming and going from Europe in the season.

The *Bonnie Mary* belonged to a friend of Jamie's cousin Jared Fraser, who had gone to France to make his fortune in the wine business and succeeded brilliantly. With luck, the *Bonnie Mary*'s captain might be persuaded for Jared's sake to take Ian with him back to Edinburgh, allowing the boy to work his passage as a cabin lad.

Ian was not enthused at the prospect, but Jamie was determined to ship his errant nephew back to Scotland at the earliest opportunity. It was – among other concerns – news of the *Bonnie Mary*'s presence in Charleston that had brought us here from Georgia, where we had first set foot in America – by accident – two months before.

As we passed a tavern, a slatternly barmaid came out with a bowl of slops. She caught sight of Jamie and stood, bowl braced against her hip, giving him a slanted brow and a pouting smile. He passed without a glance, intent on his goal. She tossed her head, flung the slops to the pig who slept by the step, and flounced back inside.

He paused, shading his eyes to look down the row of towering ships' masts, and I came up beside him. He twitched unconsciously at the front of his breeches, easing the fit, and I took his arm.

'Family jewels still safe, are they?' I murmured.

'Uncomfortable, but safe,' he assured me. He plucked at the lacing of his flies, grimacing. 'I would ha' done better to hide them up my bum, I think.'

'Better you than me, mate,' I said, smiling. 'I'd rather risk robbery, myself.'

The family jewels were just that. We had been driven ashore on the coast of Georgia by a hurricane, arriving soaked, ragged, and destitute – save for a handful of large and valuable gemstones.

I hoped the captain of the *Bonnie Mary* thought highly enough of Jared Fraser to accept Ian as a cabin boy, because if not, we were going to have a spot of difficulty about the passage.

In theory, Jamie's pouch and my pocket contained a sizable fortune. In practice, the stones might have been beach pebbles so far as the good they were to us. While gems were an easy, compact way of transporting wealth, the problem was changing them back into money.

Most trade in the southern colonies was conducted by means of barter – what wasn't, was handled by the exchange of scrip or bills written on a wealthy merchant or banker. And wealthy bankers were thin on the ground in Georgia; those willing to tie up their available capital in gemstones rarer still. The prosperous rice farmer with whom we had stayed in Savannah had assured us that he himself could scarcely lay his hand on two pounds sterling in cash – indeed, there was likely not ten pounds in gold and silver to be had in the whole colony.

Nor was there any chance of selling one of the stones in the endless stretches of salt marsh and pine forest through which we had passed on our journey north. Charleston was the first city we had reached of sufficient size to harbor merchants and bankers who might help to liquidate a portion of our frozen assets.

Not that anything was likely to stay frozen long in Charleston in summer, I reflected. Rivulets of sweat were running down my neck and the linen shift under my bodice was soaked and crumpled against my skin. Even so close to the harbor, there was no wind at this time of day, and the smells of hot tar, dead fish, and sweating laborers were nearly overwhelming.

Despite their protestations, Jamie had insisted on giving one of our gemstones to Mr. and Mrs. Olivier, the kindly people who had taken us in when we were shipwrecked virtually on their doorstep, as some token of thanks for their hospitality. In return, they had provided us with a wagon, two horses, fresh clothes for traveling, food for the journey north, and a small amount of money.

Of this, six shillings and threepence remained in my pocket, constituting the entirety of our disposable fortune.

'This way, Uncle Jamie,' Ian said, turning and beckoning his uncle eagerly. 'I've got something to show ye.'

'What is it?' Jamie asked, threading his way through a throng of sweating slaves, who were loading dusty bricks of dried indigo into an anchored cargo ship. 'And how did ye get whatever it is? Ye havena got any money, have you?'

'No, I won it, dicing.' Ian's voice floated back, his body invisible as he skipped around a cartload of corn.

'Dicing! Ian, for God's sake, ye canna be gambling when ye've not a penny to bless yourself with!' Holding my arm, Jamie shoved a way through the crowd to catch up to his nephew.

'You do it all the time, Uncle Jamie,' the boy pointed out, pausing to wait for us. 'Ye've been doing it in every tavern and inn where we've stayed.'

'My God, Ian, that's cards, not dice! And I know what I'm doing!'

'So do I,' said Ian, looking smug. 'I won, no?'

Jamie rolled his eyes toward heaven, imploring patience.

'Jesus, Ian, but I'm glad you're going home before ye get your head beaten in. Promise me ye willna be gambling wi' the sailors, aye? Ye canna get away from them on a ship.'

Ian was paying no attention; he had come to a half-crumbled piling, around which was tied a stout rope. Here he stopped and turned to face us, gesturing at an object by his feet.

'See? It's a dog,' Ian said proudly.

I took a quick half-step behind Jamie, grabbing his arm.

'Ian,' I said, 'that is not a dog. It's a wolf. It's a bloody *big* wolf, and I think you ought to get away from it before it takes a bite out of your arse.'

The wolf twitched one ear negligently in my direction, dismissed me, and twitched it back. It continued to sit, panting with the heat, its big yellow eyes fixed on Ian with an intensity that might have been taken for devotion by someone who hadn't met a wolf before. I had.

'Those things are dangerous,' I said. 'They'd bite you as soon as look at you.'

Disregarding this, Jamie stooped to inspect the beast.

'It's not quite a wolf, is it?' Sounding interested, he held out a loose fist to the so-called dog, inviting it to smell his knuckles. I closed my eyes, expecting the imminent amputation of his hand. Hearing no shrieks, I opened them again to find him squatting on the ground, peering up the animal's nostrils.

'He's a handsome creature, Ian,' he said, scratching the thing familiarly under the chin. The yellow eyes narrowed slightly, either in pleasure at the attention or – more likely, I thought – in anticipation of biting off Jamie's nose. 'Bigger than a wolf, though; it's broader through the head and chest, and a deal longer in the leg.'

'His mother was an Irish wolfhound,' Ian was hunkered down by Jamie eagerly explaining as he stroked the enormous gray-brown back. 'She got out in heat, into the woods, and when she came back in whelp –'

'Oh, aye, I see.' Now Jamie was crooning in Gaelic to the monster while he picked up its huge foot and fondled its hairy toes. The curved black claws were a good two inches long. The thing half closed its eyes, the faint breeze ruffling the thick fur at its neck.

I glanced at Duncan, who arched his eyebrows at me, shrugged slightly, and sighed. Duncan didn't care for dogs.

'Jamie –' I said.

'*Balach Boidheach*,' Jamie said to the wolf. 'Are ye no the bonny laddie, then?'

'What would he eat?' I asked, somewhat more loudly than necessary.

Jamie stopped caressing the beast.

'Oh,' he said. He looked at the yellow-eyed thing with some regret. 'Well.' He rose to his feet, shaking his head reluctantly.

'I'm afraid your auntie's right, Ian. How are we to feed him?'

14

'Oh, that's no trouble, Uncle Jamie,' Ian assured him. 'He hunts for himself.'

'Here?' I glanced around at the warehouses, and the stuccoed row of shops beyond. 'What does he hunt, small children?'

Ian looked mildly hurt.

'Of course not, Auntie. Fish.'

Seeing three skeptical faces surrounding him, Ian dropped to his knees and grabbed the beast's muzzle in both hands, prying his mouth open.

'He does! I swear, Uncle Jamie! Here, just smell his breath!'

Jamie cast a dubious glance at the double row of impressively gleaming fangs on display, and rubbed his chin.

'I – ah, I shall take your word for it, Ian. But even so – for Christ's sake, be careful of your fingers, lad!' Ian's grip had loosened, and the massive jaws clashed shut, spraying droplets of saliva over the stone quay.

'I'm all right, Uncle,' Ian said cheerfully, wiping his hand on his breeks. 'He wouldn't bite me, I'm sure. His name is Rollo.'

Jamie rubbed his knuckles across his upper lip.

'Mmphm. Well, whatever his name is, and whatever he eats, I dinna think the captain of the *Bonnie Mary* will take kindly to his presence in the crew's quarters.'

Ian didn't say anything, but the look of happiness on his face didn't diminish. In fact, it grew. Jamie glanced at him, caught sight of his glowing face, and stiffened.

'No,' he said, in horror. 'Oh, no.'

'Yes,' said Ian. A wide smile of delight split his bony face. 'She sailed three days ago, Uncle. We're too late.'

Jamie said something in Gaelic that I didn't understand. Duncan looked scandalized.

'Damn!' Jamie said, reverting to English. 'Bloody damn!' Jamie took off his hat and rubbed a hand over his face, hard. He looked hot, disheveled, and thoroughly disgruntled. He opened his mouth, thought better of whatever he had been going to say, closed it, and ran his fingers roughly through his hair, jerking loose the ribbon that tied it back.

15

Ian looked abashed.

'I'm sorry, Uncle. I'll try not to be a worry to ye, truly I will. And I can work; I'll earn enough for my food.'

Jamie's face softened as he looked at his nephew. He sighed deeply, and patted Ian's shoulder.

'It's not that I dinna want ye, Ian. You know I should like nothing better than to keep ye with me. But what in hell will your mother say?'

The glow returned to Ian's face.

'I dinna ken, Uncle,' he said, 'but she'll be saying it in Scotland, won't she? And we're here.' He put his arms around Rollo and hugged him. The wolf seemed mildly taken aback by the gesture, but after a moment, put out a long pink tongue and daintily licked Ian's ear. Testing him for flavor, I thought cynically.

'Besides,' the boy added, 'she kens well enough that I'm safe; you wrote from Georgia to say I was with you.'

Jamie summoned a wry smile.

'I canna say that that particular bit of knowledge will be ower-comforting to her, Ian. She's known me a long time, aye?'

He sighed and clapped the hat back on his head, and turned to me.

'I badly need a drink, Sassenach,' he said. 'Let's find that tavern.'

The Willow Tree was dark, and might have been cool, had there been fewer people in it. As it was, the benches and tables were crowded with sightseers from the hanging and sailors from the docks, and the atmosphere was like a sweatbath. I inhaled as I stepped into the taproom, then let my breath out, fast. It was like breathing through a wad of soiled laundry, soaked in beer.

Rollo at once proved his worth, parting the crowd like the Red Sea as he stalked through the taproom, lips drawn back from his teeth in a constant, inaudible growl. He was evidently no stranger to taverns. Having satisfactorily cleared out a corner bench, he curled up under the table and appeared to go to sleep.

Out of the sun, with a large pewter mug of dark ale

16

foaming gently in front of him, Jamie quickly regained his normal self-possession.

'We've the two choices,' he said, brushing back the sweat-soaked hair from his temples. 'We can stay in Charleston long enough to maybe find a buyer for one of the stones, and perhaps book passage for Ian to Scotland on another ship. Or we can make our way north to Cape Fear, and maybe find a ship for him out of Wilmington or New Bern.'

'I say north,' Duncan said, without hesitation. 'Ye've kin in Cape Fear, no? I mislike the thought of staying owerlong among strangers. And your kinsman would see we were not cheated nor robbed. Here –' He lifted one shoulder in eloquent indication of the un-Scottish – and thus patently dishonest – persons surrounding us.

'Oh, do let's go north, Uncle!' Ian said quickly, before Jamie could reply to this. He wiped away a small mustache of ale foam with his sleeve. 'The journey might be dangerous; you'll need an extra man along for protection, aye?'

Jamie buried his expression in his own cup, but I was seated close enough to feel a subterranean quiver go through him. Jamie was indeed very fond of his nephew. The fact remained that Ian was the sort of person to whom things happened. Usually through no fault of his own, but still, they happened.

The boy had been kidnapped by pirates the year before, and it was the necessity of rescuing him that had brought us by circuitous and often dangerous means to America. Nothing had happened recently, but I knew Jamie was anxious to get his fifteen-year-old nephew back to Scotland and his mother before something did.

'Ah . . . to be sure, Ian,' Jamie said, lowering his cup. He carefully avoided meeting my gaze, but I could see the corner of his mouth twitching. 'Ye'd be a great help, I'm sure, but . . .'

'We might meet with Red Indians!' Ian said, eyes wide. His face, already a rosy brown from the sun, glowed with a flush of pleasurable anticipation. 'Or wild beasts! Dr. Stern told me that the wilderness of Carolina is alive wi' fierce creatures – bears and wildcats and wicked panthers – and a great foul thing the Indians call a skunk!'

I choked on my ale.

'Are ye all right, Auntie?' Ian leaned anxiously across the table.

'Fine,' I wheezed, wiping my streaming face with my kerchief. I blotted the drops of spilled ale off my bosom, pulling the fabric of my bodice discreetly away from my flesh in hopes of admitting a little air.

Then I caught a glimpse of Jamie's face, on which the expression of suppressed amusement had given way to a small frown of concern.

'Skunks aren't dangerous,' I murmured, laying a hand on his knee. A skilled and fearless hunter in his native Highlands, Jamie was inclined to regard the unfamiliar fauna of the New World with caution.

'Mmphm.' The frown eased, but a narrow line remained between his brows. 'Maybe so, but what of the other things? I canna say I wish to be meeting a bear or a pack o' savages, wi' only this to hand.' He touched the large sheathed knife that hung from his belt.

Our lack of weapons had worried Jamie considerably on the trip from Georgia, and Ian's remarks about Indians and wild animals had brought the concern to the forefront of his mind once more. Besides Jamie's knife, Fergus bore a smaller blade, suitable for cutting rope and trimming twigs for kindling. That was the full extent of our armory – the Oliviers had had neither guns nor swords to spare.

On the journey from Georgia to Charleston, we had had the company of a group of rice and indigo farmers – all bristling with knives, pistols, and muskets – bringing their produce to the port to be shipped north to Pennsylvania and New York. If we left for Cape Fear now, we would be alone, unarmed, and essentially defenseless against anything that might emerge from the thick forests.

At the same time, there were pressing reasons to travel north, our lack of available capital being one. Cape Fear was the largest settlement of Scottish Highlanders in the American Colonies, boasting several towns whose inhabitants had emigrated from Scotland during the last twenty

18

years, following the upheaval after Culloden. And among these emigrants were Jamie's kin, who I knew would willingly offer us refuge: a roof, a bed, and time to establish ourselves in this new world.

Jamie took another drink and nodded at Duncan.

'I must say I'm of your mind, Duncan.' He leaned back against the wall of the tavern, glancing casually around the crowded room. 'D'ye no feel the eyes on your back?'

A chill ran down my own back, despite the trickle of sweat doing likewise. Duncan's eyes widened fractionally, then narrowed, but he didn't turn around.

'Ah,' he said.

'*Whose* eyes?' I asked, looking rather nervously around. I didn't see anyone taking particular notice of us, though anyone might be watching surreptitiously; the tavern was seething with alcohol-soaked humanity, and the babble of voices was loud enough to drown out all but the closest conversation.

'Anyone's, Sassenach,' Jamie answered. He glanced sideways at me, and smiled. 'Dinna look so scairt about it, aye? We're in no danger. Not here.'

'Not yet,' Innes said. He leaned forward to pour another cup of ale. '*Mac Dubh* called out to Gavin on the gallows, d'ye see? There will be those who took notice – *Mac Dubh* bein' the bittie wee fellow he is,' he added dryly.

'And the farmers who came with us from Georgia will have sold their stores by now, and be takin' their ease in places like this,' Jamie said, evidently absorbed in studying the pattern of his cup. 'All of them are honest men – but they'll talk, Sassenach. It makes a good story, no? The folk cast away by the hurricane? And what are the chances that at least one of them kens a bit about what we carry?'

'I see,' I murmured, and did. We had attracted public interest by our association with a criminal, and could no longer pass as inconspicuous travelers. If finding a buyer took some time, as was likely, we risked inviting robbery from unscrupulous persons, or scrutiny from the English authorities. Neither prospect was appealing.

Jamie lifted his cup and drank deeply, then set it down with a sigh.

'No. I think it's perhaps not wise to linger in the city.

19

We'll see Gavin buried decently, and then we'll find a safe spot in the woods outside the town to sleep. Tomorrow we can decide whether to stay or go.'

The thought of spending several more nights in the woods – with or without skunks – was not appealing. I hadn't taken my dress off in eight days, merely rinsing the outlying portions of my anatomy whenever we paused in the vicinity of a stream.

I had been looking forward to a real bed, even if flea-infested, and a chance to scrub off the grime of the last week's travel. Still, he had a point. I sighed, ruefully eyeing the hem of my sleeve, gray and grubby with wear.

The tavern door flung suddenly open at this point, distracting me from my contemplation, and four red-coated soldiers shoved their way into the crowded room. They wore full uniform, held muskets with bayonets fixed, and were obviously not in pursuit of ale or dice.

Two of the soldiers made a rapid circuit of the room, glancing under tables, while another disappeared into the kitchen beyond. The fourth remained on watch by the door, pale eyes flicking over the crowd. His gaze lighted on our table, and rested on us for a moment, full of speculation, but then passed on, restlessly seeking.

Jamie was outwardly tranquil, sipping his ale in apparent obliviousness, but I saw the hand in his lap clench slowly into a fist. Duncan, less able to control his feelings, bent his head to hide his expression. Neither man would ever feel at ease in the presence of a red coat, and for good reason.

No one else appeared much perturbed by the soldiers' presence. The little knot of singers in the chimney corner went on with an interminable version of 'Fill Every Glass', and a loud argument broke out between the barmaid and a pair of apprentices.

The soldier returned from the kitchen, having evidently found nothing. Stepping rudely through a dice game on the hearth, he rejoined his fellows by the door. As the soldiers shoved their way out of the tavern, Fergus's slight figure squeezed in, pressing against the doorjamb to avoid swinging elbows and musket butts.

I saw one soldier's eyes catch the glint of metal and

fasten with interest on the hook Fergus wore in replacement of his missing left hand. He glanced sharply at Fergus, but then shouldered his musket and hurried after his companions.

Fergus shoved through the crowd and plopped down on the bench beside Ian. He looked hot and irritated.

'Blood-sucking *salaud*,' he said, without preamble.

Jamie's brows went up.

'The priest,' Fergus elaborated. He took the mug Ian pushed in his direction and drained it, lean throat glugging until the cup was empty. He lowered it, exhaled heavily, and sat blinking, looking noticeably happier. He sighed and wiped his mouth.

'He wants ten shillings to bury the man in the churchyard,' he said. 'An Anglican church, of course; there are no Catholic churches here. Wretched usurer! He knows we have no choice about it. The body will scarcely keep till sunset, as it is.' He ran a finger inside his stock, pulling the sweat-wilted cotton away from his neck, then banged his fist several times on the table to attract the attention of the servingmaid, who was being run off her feet by the press of patrons.

'I told the super-fatted son of a pig that you would decide whether to pay or not. We could just bury him in the wood, after all. Though we should have to purchase a shovel,' he added, frowning. 'These grasping townsfolk know we are strangers; they'll take our last coin if they can.'

Last coin was perilously close to the truth. I had enough to pay for a decent meal here and to buy food for the journey north; perhaps enough to pay for a couple of nights' lodging. That was all. I saw Jamie's eyes flick round the room, assessing the possibilities of picking up a little money at hazard or loo.

Soldiers and sailors were the best prospects for gambling, but there were few of either in the taproom – likely most of the garrison was still searching the town for the fugitive. In one corner, a small group of men was being loudly convivial over several pitchers of brandywine; two of them were singing, or trying to, their attempts causing great hilarity among their comrades. Jamie gave an almost imperceptible nod at sight of them, and turned back to Fergus.

'What have ye done with Gavin for the time being?' Jamie asked. Fergus hunched one shoulder.

'Put him in the wagon. I traded the clothes he was wearing to a ragwoman for a shroud, and she agreed to wash the body as part of the bargain.' He gave Jamie a faint smile. 'Don't worry, milord; he's seemly. For now,' he added, lifting the fresh mug of ale to his lips.

'Poor Gavin.' Duncan Innes lifted his own mug in a half salute to his fallen comrade.

'*Slàinte*,' Jamie replied, and lifted his own mug in reply. He set it down and sighed.

'He wouldna like being buried in the wood,' he said.

'Why not?' I asked, curious. 'I shouldn't think it would matter to him one way or the other.'

'Oh, no, we couldna do that, Mrs. Claire.' Duncan was shaking his head emphatically. Duncan was normally a most reserved man, and I was surprised at so much apparent feeling.

'He was afraid of the dark,' Jamie said softly. I turned to stare at him, and he gave me a lopsided smile. 'I lived wi' Gavin Hayes nearly as long as I've lived with you, Sassenach – and in much closer quarters. I kent him well.'

'Aye, he was afraid of being alone in the dark,' Duncan chimed in. 'He was most mortally scairt of *tannagach* – of spirits, aye?'

His long, mournful face bore an inward look, and I knew he was seeing in memory the prison cell that he and Jamie had shared with Gavin Hayes – and with forty other men – for three long years. 'D'ye recall, *Mac Dubh*, how he told us one night of the *tannasq* he met?'

'I do, Duncan, and could wish I did not.' Jamie shuddered despite the heat. 'I kept awake myself half the night after he told us that one.'

'What was it, Uncle?' Ian was leaning over his cup of ale, round-eyed. His cheeks were flushed and streaming, and his stock crumpled with sweat.

Jamie rubbed a hand across his mouth, thinking.

'Ah. Well, it was a time in the late, cold autumn in the Highlands, just when the season turns, and the feel of the air tells ye the ground will be shivered wi' frost come dawn,' he said. He settled himself in his seat and sat back, alecup in hand. He smiled wryly, plucking at his own throat. 'Not like now, aye?

'Well, Gavin's son brought back the kine that night, but there was one beast missing – the lad had hunted up the hills and down the corries, but couldna find it anywhere. So Gavin set the lad to milk the two others, and set out himself to look for the lost cow.'

He rolled the pewter cup slowly between his hands, staring down into the dark ale as though seeing in it the bulk of the night-black Scottish peaks and the mist that floats in the autumn glens.

'He went some distance, and the cot behind him disappeared. When he looked back, he couldna see the light from the window anymore, and there was no sound but the keening of the wind. It was cold, but he went on, tramping through the mud and the heather, hearing the crackle of ice under his boots.

'He saw a small grove through the mist, and thinking the cow might have taken shelter beneath the trees, he went toward it. He said the trees were birches, standing there all leafless, but with their branches grown together so he must bend his head to squeeze beneath the boughs.

'He came into the grove and saw it was not a grove at all, but a circle of trees. There were great tall trees, spaced verra evenly, all around him, and smaller ones, saplings, grown up between to make a wall of branches. And in the center of the circle stood a cairn.'

Hot as it is in the tavern, I felt as though a sliver of ice had slid melting down my spine. I had seen ancient cairns in the Highlands myself, and found them eerie enough in the broad light of day.

Jamie took a sip of ale, and wiped away a trickle of sweat that ran down his temple.

'He felt quite queer, did Gavin. For he kent the place – everyone did, and kept well away from it. It was a strange place. And it seemed even worse in the dark and the cold, from what it did in the light of day. It was an auld cairn, the kind laid wi' slabs of rock, all heaped round with

23

stones, and he could see before him the black opening of the tomb.

'He knew it was a place no man should come, and he without a powerful charm. Gavin had naught but a wooden cross about his neck. So he crossed himself with it and turned to go.'

Jamie paused to sip his ale.

'But as Gavin went from the grove,' he said softly, 'he heard footsteps behind him.'

I saw the Adam's apple bob in Ian's throat as he swallowed. He reached mechanically for his own cup, eyes fixed on his uncle.

'He didna turn to see,' Jamie went on, 'but kept walking. And the steps kept pace wi' him, step by step, always following. And he came through the peat where the water seeps up, and it was crusted with ice, the weather bein' so cold. He could hear the peat crackle under his feet, and behind him the crack! crack! of breaking ice.

'He walked and he walked, through the cold, dark night, watching ahead for the light of his own window, where his wife had set the candle. But the light never showed, and he began to fear he had lost his way among the heather and the dark hills. And all the time, the steps kept pace with him, loud in his ears.

'At last he could bear it no more, and seizing hold of the crucifix he wore round his neck, he swung about wi' a great cry to face whatever followed.'

'What did he see?' Ian's pupils were dilated, dark with drink and wonder. Jamie glanced at the boy, and then at Duncan, nodding at him to take up the story.

'He said it was a figure like a man, but with no body,' Duncan said quietly. 'All white, like as it might have been made of the mist. But wi' great holes where its eyes should be, and empty black, fit to draw the soul from his body with dread.'

'But Gavin held up his cross before his face, and he prayed aloud to the Blessed Virgin.' Jamie took up the story, leaning forward intently, the dim firelight outlining his profile in gold. 'And the thing came no nearer, but stayed there, watching him.

'And so he began to walk backward, not daring to face

24

round again. He walked backward, stumbling and slipping, fearing every moment as he might tumble into a burn or down a cliff and break his neck, but fearing worse to turn his back on the cold thing.

'He couldna tell how long he'd walked, only that his legs were trembling wi' weariness, when at last he caught a glimpse of light through the mist, and there was his own cottage, wi' the candle in the window. He cried out in joy, and turned to his door, but the cold thing was quick, and slippit past him, to stand betwixt him and the door.

'His wife had been watching out for him, and when she heard him cry out, she came at once to the door. Gavin shouted to her not to come out, but for God's sake to fetch a charm to drive away the *tannasq*. Quick as thought, she snatched the pot from beneath her bed, and a twig of myrtle bound wi' red thread and black, that she'd made to bless the cows. She dashed the water against the doorposts, and the cold thing leapt upward, astride the lintel. Gavin rushed in beneath and barred the door, and stayed inside in his wife's arms until the dawn. They let the candle burn all the night, and Gavin Hayes never again left his house past sunset – until he went to fight for Prince *Tearlach*.'

Even Duncan, who knew the tale, sighed as Jamie finished speaking. Ian crossed himself, then looked about self-consciously, but no one seemed to have noticed.

'So, now Gavin has gone into the dark,' Jamie said softly. 'But we willna let him lie in unconsecrated ground.'

'Did they find the cow?' Fergus asked, with his usual practicality. Jamie quirked one eyebrow at Duncan, who answered.

'Oh, aye, they did. The next morning they found the poor beast, wi' her hooves all clogged wi' mud and stones, staring mad and lathered about the muzzle, and her sides heavin' fit to burst.' He glanced from me to Ian and back to Fergus. 'Gavin did say,' he said precisely, 'that she looked as though she'd been ridden to Hell and back.'

'Jesus.' Ian took a deep gulp of his ale, and I did the same. In the corner, the drinking society was making attempts on a round of 'Captain Thunder', breaking down each time in helpless laughter.

Ian put down his cup on the table.

'What happened to them?' he asked, his face troubled. 'To Gavin's wife, and his son?'.

Jamie's eyes met mine, and his hand touched my thigh. I knew, without being told, what had happened to the Hayes family. Without Jamie's own courage and intransigence, the same thing would likely have happened to me and to our daughter Brianna.

'Gavin never knew,' Jamie said quietly. 'He never heard aught of his wife – she will have been starved, maybe, or driven out to die of the cold. His son took the field beside him at Culloden. Whenever a man who had fought there came into our cell, Gavin would ask – "Have ye maybe seen a bold lad named Archie Hayes, about so tall?" ' He measured automatically, five feet from the floor, capturing Hayes's gesture. ' "A lad about fourteen," he'd say, "wi' a green plaidie and a small gilt brooch." But no one ever came who had seen him for sure – either seen him fall or seen him run away safe.'

Jamie took a sip of the ale, his eyes fixed on a pair of British officers who had come in and settled in the corner. It had grown dark outside, and they were plainly off duty. Their leather stocks were unfastened on account of the heat, and they wore only sidearms, glinting under their coats; nearly black in the dim light save where the firelight touched them with red.

'Sometimes he hoped the lad might have been captured and transported,' he said. 'Like his brother.'

'Surely that would be somewhere in the records?' I said. 'Did they – do they – keep lists?'

'They did,' Jamie said, still watching the soldiers. A small, bitter smile touched the corner of his mouth. 'It was such a list that saved me, after Culloden, when they asked my name before shooting me, so as to add it to their roll. But a man like Gavin would have no way to see the English deadlists. And if he could have found out, I think he would not.' He glanced at me. 'Would you choose to know for sure, and it was your child?'

I shook my head, and he gave me a faint smile and squeezed my hand. Our child was safe, after all. He picked

26

up his cup and drained it, then beckoned to the serving maid.

The girl brought the food, skirting the table widely in order to avoid Rollo. The beast lay motionless under the table, his head protruding into the room and his great hairy tail lying heavily across my feet, but his yellow eyes were wide open, watching everything. They followed the girl intently, and she backed nervously away, keeping an eye on him until she was safely out of biting distance.

Seeing this, Jamie cast a dubious look at the so called dog.

'Is he hungry? Must I ask for a fish for him?'

'Oh, no, Uncle,' Ian reassured him. 'Rollo catches his own fish.'

Jamie's eyebrows shot up, but he only nodded, and with a wary glance at Rollo, took a platter of roasted oysters from the tray.

'Ah, the pity of it.' Duncan Innes was quite drunk by now. He sat slumped against the wall, his armless shoulder riding higher than the other, giving him a strange, hunch-backed appearance. 'That a dear man like Gavin should come to such an end!' He shook his head lugubriously, swinging it back and forth over his alecup like the clapper of a funeral bell.

'No family left to mourn him, cast alone into a savage land – hanged as a felon, and to be buried in an unconse-crated grave. Not even a proper lament to be sung for him!' He picked up the cup, and with some difficulty, found his mouth with it. He drank deep and set it down with a muffled clang.

'Well, he *shall* have a *caithris*!' He glared belligerently from Jamie to Fergus to Ian. 'Why not?'

Jamie wasn't drunk, but he wasn't completely sober either. He grinned at Duncan and lifted his own cup in salute.

'Why not, indeed?' he said. 'Only it will have to be you singin' it, Duncan. None of the rest knew Gavin, and I'm no singer. I'll shout along wi' ye, though.'

Duncan nodded magisterially, bloodshot eyes surveying us. Without warning, he flung back his head and emitted a terrible howl. I jumped in my seat, spilling half a cup of ale into my lap. Ian and Fergus, who had evidently heard Gaelic laments before, didn't turn a hair.

All over the room, benches were shoved back, as men leapt to their feet in alarm, reaching for their pistols. The barmaid leaned out of the serving hatch, eyes big. Rollo came awake with an explosive '*Woof!*' and glared round wildly, teeth bared.

'*Tha sinn cruinn a chaoidh ar caraid, Gabhainn Hayes,*' Duncan thundered, in a ragged baritone. I had just about enough Gaelic to translate this as, 'We are met to weep and cry out to heaven for the loss of our friend, Gavin Hayes!'

'*Eisd ris!*' Jamie chimed in.

'*Rugadh e do Sheumas Immanuel Hayes agus Louisa N'ic a Liallainn an am baile Chill-Mhartainn, ann an sgire Dhun Domhnuill, anns a bhliadhnaseachd ceud deug agus a haon!*' He was born of Seaumais Emmanuel Hayes and of Louisa Maclellan, in the village of Kilmartin in the parish of Dodanil, in the year of our Lord seventeen hundred and one!

'*Eisd ris!*' This time Fergus and Ian joined in on the chorus, which I translated roughly as 'Heir him!'

Rollo appeared not to care for either verse or refrain; his ears lay flat against his skull, and his yellow eyes narrowed to slits. Ian scratched his head in reassurance, and he lay down again, muttering wolf curses under his breath.

The audience, having caught on to it that no actual violence threatened, and no doubt bored with the inferior vocal efforts of the drinking society in the corner, settled down to enjoy the show. By the time Duncan had worked his way into an accounting of the names of the sheep Gavin Hayes had owned before leaving his croft to follow his laird to Culloden, many of those at the surrounding tables were joining enthusiastically in the chorus, shouting '*Eisd ris!*' and banging their mugs on the tables, in perfect ignorance of what was being said, and a good thing too.

Duncan, drunker than ever, fixed the soldiers at the next table with a baleful glare, sweat pouring down his face.

'*A Shasunnaich na galladh, 's olc a thig e dhuibh fanaid air*

28

bàs gasgaich. Gun toireadh an diabhul fhein leis anns a bhàs sibh, direach do Fhirinn!!' Wicked Sassenach dogs, eaters of dead flesh! Ill does it become you to laugh and rejoice at the death of a gallant man! May the devil himself seize upon you in the hour of your death and take you straight to hell!

Ian blanched slightly at this, and Jamie cast Duncan a narrow look, but they stoutly shouted '*Eisd ris!*' along with the rest of the crowd.

Fergus, seized by inspiration, got up and passed his hat among the crowd, who, carried away by ale and excitement, happily flung coppers into it for the privilege of joining in their own denunciation.

I had as good a head for drink as most men, but a much smaller bladder. Head spinning from the noise and fumes as much as from alcohol, I got up and edged my way out from behind the table, through the mob, and into the fresh air of the early evening.

It was still hot and sultry, though the sun was long since down. Still, there was a lot more air out here, and a lot fewer people sharing it.

Having relieved the internal pressure, I sat down on the tavern's chopping block with my pewter mug, breathing deeply. The night was clear, with a bright half-moon peeping silver over the harbor's edge. Our wagon stood nearby, no more than its outline visible in the light from the tavern windows. Presumably, Gavin Hayes's decently shrouded body lay within. I trusted he had enjoyed his *caithris*.

Inside, Duncan's chanting had come to an end. A clear tenor voice, wobbly with drink, but sweet nonetheless, was singing a familiar tune, audible over the babble of talk.

'To Anacreon in heav'n, where he sat in full glee,
A few sons of harmony sent a petition,
That he their inspirer and patron would be!
When this answer arrived from the jolly old Grecian:
"Voice, fiddle, and flute,
    No longer be mute!
    I'll lend you my name and inspire you to boot."'

29

The singer's voice cracked painfully on 'voice, fiddle, and flute,' but he sang stoutly on, despite the laughter from his audience. I smiled wryly to myself as he hit the final couplet,

> ' "And, besides, I'll instruct you like me to entwine,
> The Myrtle of Venus with Bacchus's vine!" '

I lifted my cup in salute to the wheeled coffin, softly echoing the melody of the singer's last lines.

> 'Oh, say, does that star-spangled banner yet wave
> O'er the land of the free and the home of the brave?'

I drained my cup and sat still, waiting for the men to come out.

2

In Which We Meet a Ghost

'Ten, eleven, twelve . . . and two, and six . . . one pound, eight shillings, sixpence, two farthings!' Fergus dropped the last coin ceremoniously into the cloth pocket, pulled tight the drawstrings, and handed it to Jamie. 'And three buttons,' he added, 'but I have kept those,' and patted the side of his coat.

'Ye've settled with the landlord for our meal?' Jamie asked me, weighing the little bag.

'Yes,' I assured him. 'I have four shillings and sixpence left, plus what Fergus collected.'

Fergus smiled modestly, square white teeth gleaming in the faint light from the tavern's window.

'We have the necessary money for the burial, then,' he said. 'Will we take Monsieur Hayes to the priest now, or wait till morning?'

Jamie frowned at the wagon, standing silent at the edge of the inn yard.

'I shouldna think the priest will be awake at this hour,' he said, with a glance at the rising moon. 'Still –'

'I'd just as soon not take him with us,' I said. 'Not to be rude,' I added apologetically to the wagon. 'But if we're going to sleep out in the woods, the . . . er . . . scent . . .' It wasn't overpowering, but once away from the smoky reek of the tavern, a distinct odor was noticeable in the vicinity of the wagon. It hadn't been a gentle death, and it *had* been a hot day.

'Auntie Claire is right,' Ian said, brushing his knuckles inconspicuously under his nose. 'We dinna want to be attracting wild animals.'

'We canna be leaving Gavin here, surely!' Duncan protested, scandalized at the thought. 'What, leave him lying on the step o' the inn in his shroud, like a foundling wrapped in swaddling clothes?' He swayed alarmingly, his alcoholic intake affecting his always precarious balance.

31

I saw Jamie's wide mouth twitch with amusement, the moon shining white on the knife-edged bridge of his nose.

'No,' he said. 'We willna be leaving him here.' He tossed the little bag from hand to hand with a faint chinking sound, then, making his decision, thrust it into his coat.

'We'll bury him ourselves,' he said. 'Fergus, will ye be stepping into the stable yonder and see can ye buy a spade verra cheap?'

The short journey to the church through the quiet streets of Charleston was somewhat less dignified than the usual funeral cortege, marked as it was by Duncan's insistence on repeating the more interesting portions of his lament as a processional.

Jamie drove slowly, shouting occasional encouragement to the horses; Duncan staggered beside the team, chanting hoarsely and clutching one animal by its head-stall, while Ian held the other to prevent bolting. Fergus and I brought up the rear in staid respectability, Fergus holding his newly purchased shovel at port-arms, and muttering dire predictions as to the likelihood of us all spending the night in gaol for disturbing the peace of Charleston.

As it was, the church stood by itself in a quiet street, some distance from the nearest house. This was all to the good, in terms of avoiding notice, but it did mean that the churchyard was dauntingly dark, with no glow of torch or candle to pierce the blackness.

Great magnolia trees overhung the gate, leathery leaves drooping in the heat, and a border of pines, meant to provide shade and respite in the day, served at night to block all traces of moon and starlight, leaving the churchyard itself black as a . . . well, as a crypt.

Walking through the air felt like pushing aside curtains of black velvet, perfumed with an incense of turpentine from the sun-heated pines; endless layers of soft, pungent smothering. Nothing could have been farther from the cold purity of the Highlands than this stifling southern atmosphere. Still, faint patches of mist hung under the dark brick walls, and I could have wished not to recall Jamie's story of the *tannasq* quite so vividly.

'We'll find a place. Do you stay and hold the horses, Duncan.' Jamie slid down from the wagon's seat and took me by the arm.

'We'll find a nice wee spot by the wall, perhaps,' he said, guiding me toward the gate. 'Ian and I will dig while you hold the light, and Fergus can stand guard.'

'What about Duncan?' I asked, with a backward glance. 'Will he be all right?' The Scotsman was invisible, his tall, lanky form having faded into the larger blot comprising horses and wagon, but he was still clearly audible.

'He'll be chief mourner,' Jamie said, with a hint of a smile in his voice. 'Mind your head, Sassenach.' I ducked automatically beneath a low magnolia branch; I didn't know whether Jamie could actually see in total darkness, or merely felt things by instinct, but I had never seen him stumble, no matter how dark the surroundings.

'Don't you think someone's going to notice a fresh grave?' It was not completely black in the churchyard, after all; once out from under the magnolias, I could make out the dim forms of gravestones, looking insubstantial but sinister in the dark, a faint mist rising from the thick grass about their feet.

The soles of my own feet tingled as we picked a ginger way through the stones. I seemed to feel silent waves of reproach at this unseemly intrusion wafting up from below. I barked my shin on a tombstone and bit my lip, stifling an urge to apologize to its owner.

'I expect they might.' Jamie let go of my arm to rummage in his coat. 'But if the priest wanted money to bury Gavin, I shouldna think he'd trouble to dig him up again for nothing, aye?'

Young Ian materialized out of the darkness at my elbow, startling me.

'There's open space by the north wall, Uncle Jamie,' he said, speaking softly in spite of the obvious fact that there was no one to hear. He paused, and drew slightly closer to me.

'It's verra dark in here, no?' The boy sounded uneasy. He had had nearly as much to drink as Jamie or Fergus, but while the alcohol had imbued the older men with

33

grim humor, it had clearly had a more depressing effect on Ian's spirits.

'It is, aye. I've the bit of a candle I took from the tavern, though; wait a bit.' Faint rustlings announced Jamie's search for flint and tinderbox.

The encompassing dark made me feel disembodied, like a ghost myself. I looked upward and saw stars, so faintly visible through the thick air that they shed no light upon the ground, but only gave a feeling of immense distance and infinite remoteness.

'It's like the vigil of Easter.' Jamie's voice came softly, accompanied by the small scratching sounds of a striking flint. 'I saw the service once, at Notre Dame in Paris. Watch yourself, Ian, there's a stone just there!' A thud and a stifled grunt announced that Ian had belatedly discovered the stone for himself.

'The church was all dark,' Jamie continued, 'but the folk coming for the service would buy small tapers from the crones at the doors. It was something like this' – I felt, rather than saw, his motion at the sky above – 'a great space above, all ringing wi' the silence, and folk packed in on every side.' Hot as it was, I gave an involuntary shiver at these words, which conjured up a vision of the dead around us, crowding silently side by side, in anticipation of an imminent resurrection.

'And then, just when I thought I couldna bear the silence and the crowd, there came the priest's voice from the door. "*Lumen Christi!*" he called out, and the acolytes lit the great candle that he carried. Then from it they took the flame to their own tapers, and scampered up and down the aisles, passing the fire to the candles o' the faithful.'

I could see his hands, lit faintly by the tiny sparks from his flint.

'Then the church came alive wi' a thousand small flames, but it was that first candle that broke the dark.'

The scratching sounds ceased, and he took away the cupped hand that had shielded the newborn flame. The flame strengthened and lit his face from below, gilding the planes of high cheekbones and forehead, and shadowing the deep-set orbits of his eyes.

He lifted the candle, surveying the looming grave markers, eerie as a circle of standing stones.

'*Lumen Christi*,' he said softly, inclining his head toward a granite pillar surmounted with a cross, '*et requiescat in pace, amice.*' The half-mocking note had left his voice; he spoke with complete seriousness, and I felt at once oddly comforted, as though some watchful presence had withdrawn.

He smiled at me then, and handed me the candle.

'See can ye find a bit of wood for a torch, Sassenach,' he said. 'Ian and I will take it in turns to dig.'

I was no longer nervous, but still felt like a grave robber, standing under a pine tree with my torch, watching Young Ian and Jamie take their turns in the deepening pit, their naked backs gleaming with sweat in the torchlight.

'Medical students used to pay men to steal fresh bodies from churchyards,' I said, handing my soiled kerchief to Jamie as he hauled himself out of the hole, grunting with effort. 'That was the only way they could practice dissection.'

'Did they?' Jamie said. He wiped the sweat from his face and gave me a quick, wry glance. 'Or do they?'

Luckily, it was too dark for Ian to notice my flush, despite the torchlight. It wasn't the first slip I had made, nor was it likely to be the last, but most such inadvertencies resulted in nothing more than a quizzical glance, were they noticed at all. The truth simply was not a possibility that would occur to anyone.

'I imagine they do it now,' I admitted. I shivered slightly at the thought of confronting a freshly exhumed and unpreserved body, still smeared with the dirt of its desecrated grave. Cadavers embalmed and laid on a stainless steel surface were not particularly pleasant either, but the formality of their presentation served to keep the corruptive realities of death at some small distance.

I exhaled strongly through my nose, trying to rid myself of odors, imagined and remembered. When I breathed in, my nostrils were filled with the smell of damp earth and hot pitch from my pine torch, and the fainter, cooler echo of live scent from the pines overhead.

35

'They take paupers and criminals from the prisons, too.' Young Ian, who had evidently heard the exchange, if not understood it, took the opportunity to stop for a moment, wiping his brow as he leaned on the shovel.

'Da told me about one time he was arrested, when they took him to Edinburgh, and kept him in the Tolbooth. He was in a cell wi' three other men, and one of them a fellow with the consumption, who coughed something dreadful, keeping the rest awake all night and all day. Then one night the coughing stopped, and they kent he was dead. But Da said they were so tired, they couldna do more than say a Pater Noster for his soul, and fall asleep.'

The boy paused and rubbed an itching nose.

'Da said he woke quite sudden wi' someone clutching his legs and another someone takin' him by the arms, liftin' him up. He kicked and cried out, and the one who had his arms screeched and dropped him, so that he cracked his head on the stones. He sat up rubbin' his pate and found himself staring at a doctor from the hospital and two fellows he'd brought along to carry awa' the corpse to the dissecting room.'

Ian grinned broadly at the recollection, wiping his sweat-soaked hair out of his face.

'Da said he wasna sure who was most horrified, him or the fellows who'd got the wrong body. He did say as the doctor seemed regretful, though – said Da would have made a more interesting specimen, what wi' his leg stump and all.'

Jamie laughed, stretching his arms to ease his shoulders. With face and torso streaked with red dirt, and his hair bound back with a kerchief round his forehead, he looked disreputable as any grave robber.

'Aye, I mind that story,' he said. 'Ian did say after that as all doctors were ghouls, and wouldna have a thing to do with them.' He grinned at me; I had been a doctor – a surgeon – in my own time, but here I passed as nothing more than a wisewoman, skilled in the use of herbs.

'Fortunately, I'm no afraid of wee ghoulies, myself,' he said, and leaned down to kiss me briefly. His lips were warm, tasting of ale. I could see droplets of sweat caught in the curly hairs of his chest, and his nipples, dark buds in the dim light. A tremor that had nothing to do either with cold or with the eeriness of our surroundings ran down my spine. He saw it and his eyes met mine. He took a deep breath, and all at once I was conscious of the close fit of my bodice, and the weight of my breasts in the sweat-soaked fabric.

Jamie shifted himself slightly, plucking to ease the fit of his breeches.

'Damn,' he said softly. He lowered his eyes and turned away, mouth barely touched by a rueful smile.

I hadn't expected it, but I recognized it, all right. A sudden surge of lust was a common, if peculiar, response to the presence of death. Soldiers feel it in the lull after battle; so do healers who deal in blood and struggle. Perhaps Ian had been more right than I thought about the ghoulishness of doctors.

Jamie's hand touched my back and I started, showering sparks from the blazing torch. He took it from me and nodded toward a nearby gravestone.

'Sit down, Sassenach,' he said. 'Ye shouldna be standing so long.' I had cracked the tibia of my left leg in the shipwreck, and while it had healed quickly, the leg still ached sometimes.

'I'm all right.' Still, I moved toward the stone, brushing against him as I passed. He radiated heat, but his naked flesh was cool to the touch, the sweat evaporating on his skin. I could smell him.

I glanced at him, and saw goose bumps rise on the fair flesh where I'd touched him. I swallowed, fighting back a sudden vision of tumbling in the dark, to a fierce blind coupling amid crushed grass and raw earth.

His hand lingered on my elbow as he helped me to a seat on the stone. Rollo was lying by its side, drops of saliva gleaming in the torchlight as he panted. The slanted yellow eyes narrowed at me.

'Don't even think about it,' I said, narrowing my own eyes back at him. 'Bite me, and I'll cram my shoe down your throat so far you'll choke.'

'*Wuff!*' Rollo said, quite softly. He laid his muzzle on his paws, but the hairy ears were pricked, turned to catch the slightest sound.

37

The spade chunked softly into the earth at Ian's feet, and he straightened up, slicking sweat off his face with a palm swipe that left black smears along his jaw. He blew out a deep breath and glanced up at Jamie, miming exhaustion, tongue lolling from the corner of his mouth.

'Aye, I expect it's deep enough.' Jamie answered the wordless plea with a nod. 'I'll fetch Gavin along, then.'

Fergus frowned uneasily, his features sharp in the torchlight.

'Will you not need help to carry the corpse?' His reluctance was evident; still, he had offered. Jamie gave him a faint, wry smile.

'I'll manage well enough,' he said. 'Gavin was a wee man. Still, ye might bring the torch to see by.'

'I'll come too, Uncle!' Young Ian scrambled hastily out of the pit, skinny shoulders gleaming with sweat. 'Just in case you need help,' he added breathlessly.

'Afraid to be left in the dark?' Fergus asked sarcastically. I thought that the surroundings must be making him uneasy; though he occasionally teased Ian, whom he regarded as a younger brother, he was seldom cruel about it.

'Aye, I am,' Ian said simply. 'Aren't you?'

Fergus opened his mouth, brows arched skyward, then shut it again and turned without a word toward the black opening of the lych-gate, whence Jamie had disappeared.

'D'ye not think this is a terrible place, Auntie?' Ian murmured uneasily at my elbow, sticking close as we made our way through the looming stones, following the flicker of Fergus's torch. 'I keep thinking of that story Uncle Jamie told. And thinking now Gavin's dead, maybe the cold thing . . . I mean, do you think would it maybe . . . come for him?' There was an audible swallow punctuating this question, and I felt an icy finger touch me, just at the base of my spine.

'No,' I said, a little too loudly. I grabbed Ian's arm, less for support than for the reassurance of his solidity. 'Certainly not.'

His skin was clammy with evaporating sweat, but the skinny muscularity of the arm under my hand was comforting. His half-visible presence reminded me faintly of

Jamie; he was nearly as tall as his uncle, and very nearly as strong, though still lean and gangling with adolescence.

We emerged with gratitude into the little pool of light thrown by Fergus's torch. The flickering light shone through the wagon wheels, throwing shadows that lay like spiderwebs in the dust. It was as hot in the road as it was in the churchyard, but the air seemed somehow freer, easier to breathe, out from under the suffocating trees.

Rather to my surprise, Duncan was still awake, perched drooping on the wagon's seat like a sleepy owl, shoulders hunched about his ears. He was crooning under his breath, but stopped when he saw us. The long wait seemed to have sobered him a bit; he got down from the seat steadily enough and came round to the rear of the wagon to help Jamie.

I smothered a yawn. I would be glad to be done with this melancholy duty and on our way to rest, even if the only bed to look forward to was one of piled leaves.

'*Ifrinn an Diabhuil! A Dhia, thoir cobhair!*'

'*Sacrée Vierge!*'

My head snapped up. Everyone was shouting, and the horses, startled, were neighing and jerking frantically against their hobbles, making the wagon hop and lurch like a drunken beetle.

'*Wuff!*' Rollo said next to me.

'Jesus!' said Ian, goggling at the wagon. 'Jesus *Christ!*'

I swung in the direction he was looking, and screamed. A pale figure loomed out of the wagon bed, swaying with the wagon's jerking. I had no time to see more before all hell broke loose.

Rollo bunched his hindquarters and launched himself through the dark with a roar, to the accompaniment of shouts from Jamie and Ian, and a terrible scream from the ghost. Behind me, I could hear the sound of French cursing as Fergus ran back into the churchyard, stumbling and crashing over tombstones in the dark.

Jamie had dropped the torch; it flickered and hissed on the dusty road, threatening to go out. I fell to my knees and grabbed it, blowing on it, desperate to keep it alight.

The chorus of shouts and growling grew to a crescendo, and I rose up, torch in hand, to find Ian struggling with

39

Rollo, trying to keep him away from the dim figures wrestling together in a cloud of dust.

'*Arretes, espèce de cochon!*' Fergus galloped out of the dark, brandishing the spade he had gone to fetch. Finding his injunction disregarded, he stepped forward and brought it down one-handed on the intruder's head with a dull *clong*! Then he swung toward Ian and Rollo.

'You be quiet, too!' Fergus said to the dog, threatening him with the shovel. 'Shut up this minute, foul beast, or I brain you!'

Rollo snarled, with a show of impressive teeth that I interpreted roughly to mean 'You and who else?' but was prevented from mayhem by Ian, who wrapped his arm about the dog's throat and choked off any further remarks.

'Where did *he* come from?' Ian asked in amazement. He craned his neck, trying to get a look at the fallen figure without letting go of Rollo.

'From hell,' Fergus said briefly. 'And I invite him to go back there at once.' He was trembling with shock and exertion; the light gleamed dully from his hook as he brushed a thick lock of black hair out of his eyes.

'Not from hell; from the gallows. Do ye not know him?'

Jamie rose slowly to his feet, dusting his breeches. He was breathing heavily, and smeared with dirt, but seemed unhurt. He picked up his fallen kerchief and glanced about, wiping his face. 'Where's Duncan?'

'Here, *Mac Dubh*,' said a gruff voice from the front of the wagon. 'The beasts werena likin' Gavin much to start with, and they're proper upset to think he was a-resurrectin'. Not,' he added fairly, 'but what I was a wee bit startled myself.' He eyed the figure on the ground with disfavor, and patted one skittish horse firmly on the neck. 'Ah, it's no but a silly bugger, *luaidh*, hush your noise now, aye?'

I had handed Ian the torch and knelt to inspect the damage to our visitor This seemed to be slight; the man was already stirring. Jamie was right; it was the man who had escaped hanging earlier in the day. He was young, about thirty, muscular and powerfully built, his fair hair matted with sweat and stiff with filth. He reeked of prison,

40

and the musky-sharp smell of prolonged fear. Little wonder.

I got a hand under his arm and helped him to sit up. He grunted and put his hand to his head, squinting in the torchlight.

'Are you all right?' I asked.

'Thankin' ye kindly, ma'am, I will have been better.' He had a faint Irish accent and a soft, deep voice.

Rollo, upper lip lifted just enough to show a menacing eyetooth, shoved his nose into the visitor's armpit, sniffed, then jerked back his head and sneezed explosively. A small tremor of laughter ran round the circle, and the tension relaxed momentarily.

'How long have ye been in the wagon?' Duncan demanded.

'Since midafternoon.' The man rose awkwardly onto his knees, swaying I bit from the effects of the blow. He touched his head again and winced. 'Oh, Jaysus! I crawled in there just after the Frenchie loaded up poor old Gavin.'

'Where were you before that?' Ian asked.

'Hidin' under the gallows cart. It was the only place I thought they wouldn't be looking.' He rose laboriously to his feet, closed his eyes to get his balance, then opened them. They were a pale green in the torchlight, the color of shallow seas. I saw them flick from face to face, then settle on Jamie. The man bowed, careful of his head.

'Stephen Bonnet. Your servant, sir.' He made no move to extend a hand in greeting, nor did Jamie.

'Mr. Bonnet.' Jamie nodded back, face carefully blank. I didn't know quite how he contrived to look commanding, wearing nothing but a pair of damp and dirt-stained breeks, but he managed it. He looked the visitor over, taking in every detail of his appearance.

Bonnet was what country people called 'well set up', with a tall, powerful frame and a barrel chest, his features heavy-boned but coarsely handsome. A few inches shorter than Jamie, he stood easy, balanced on the balls of his feet, fists half closed in readiness.

No stranger to a fight, judging by the slight crookedness of his nose and a small scar by the corner of his mouth. The small imperfections did nothing to mar the overall

41

impression of animal magnetism; he was the sort of man who attracted women easily. Some women, I amended, as he cast a speculative glance at me.

'For what crime were ye condemned, Mr. Bonnet?' Jamie asked. He himself stood easy, but with a look of watchfulness that reminded me forcibly of Bonnet himself. It was the ears-back look male dogs give each other before deciding whether to fight.

'Smuggling,' Bonnet said.

Jamie didn't reply, but tilted his head slightly. One brow rose in inquiry.

'And piracy.' A muscle twitched near Bonnet's mouth; a poor attempt at a smile, or an involuntary quiver of fear?

'And will ye have killed anyone in the commission of your crimes, Mr. Bonnet?' Jamie's face was blank, save for the watchful eyes. *Think twice*, his eyes said plainly. *Or maybe three times.*

'None that were not tryin' to kill me first,' Bonnet replied. The words were easy, the tone almost flippant, but belied by the hand that closed tight into a fist by his side.

It dawned on me that Bonnet must feel he was facing judge and jury, as surely as he had faced them once before. He had no way of knowing that we were nearly as reluctant to go near the garrison soldiers as he was.

Jamie looked at Bonnet for a long moment, peering closely at him in the flickering torchlight, then nodded and took a half step back.

'Go, then,' he said quietly. 'We will not hinder ye.'

Bonnet took an audible breath; I could see the big frame relax, shoulders slumping under the cheap linen shirt.

'Thank you,' he said. He wiped a hand across his face, and took another deep breath. The green eyes darted from me to Fergus to Duncan. 'But will ye help me, maybe?'

Duncan, who had relaxed at Jamie's words, gave a grunt of surprise.

'Help you? A thief?'

Bonnet's head swivelled in Duncan's direction. The iron collar was a dark line about his neck, giving the eerie impression that his severed head floated several inches above his shoulders.

'Help me,' he repeated. 'There will be soldiers on the roads tonight – huntin' me.' He gestured toward the wagon. 'You could take me safely past them – if ye will.' He turned back to Jamie, and straightened his back, shoulders stiff. 'I am begging for your help, sir, in the name of Gavin Hayes, who was my friend as well as yours – and a thief, as I am.'

The men studied him in silence for a moment, digesting this. Fergus glanced inquiringly at Jamie; the decision was his.

But Jamie, after a long, considering look at Bonnet, turned to Duncan.

'What say ye, Duncan?' Duncan gave Bonnet the same kind of look that Jamie himself had used, and finally nodded.

'For Gavin's sake,' he said, and turned away toward the lych-gate.

'All right, then,' Jamie said. He sighed and pushed a loose lock of hair behind his ear.

'Help us to bury Gavin,' he said to our new guest, 'and then we'll go.'

An hour later, Gavin's grave was a blank rectangle of fresh-turned earth, stark among the gray hues of the surrounding grass.

'He must have his name to mark him by,' Jamie said. Painstakingly, he scratched the letters of Gavin's name and his dates upon a piece of smooth beach-stone, using the point of his knife. I rubbed soot from the torch into the incised letters, making a crude but readable grave marker, and Ian set this solidly into a small cairn of gathered pebbles. Atop the tiny monument, Jamie gently set the stub of candle that he had taken from the tavern.

Everyone stood awkwardly about the grave for a moment, not knowing how to take farewell. Jamie and Duncan stood close together, looking down. They would have taken final leave of many such comrades since Culloden, if often with less ceremony.

Finally Jamie nodded to Fergus, who took a dry pine

twig, and lighting it from my torch, bent and touched it to the candle's wick.

'*Requiem aeternam dona ei, et lux perpetua luceat ei* . . .' Jamie said quietly.

'Eternal rest grant unto him, O God – and let perpetual light shine upon him.' Young Ian echoed it softly, his face solemn in the torchlight.

Without a word, we turned and left the churchyard. Behind us, the candle burned without a flicker in the still, heavy air, like the sanctuary lamp in an empty church.

The moon was high in the sky by the time we reached the military checkpoint outside the city walls. It was only a half-moon, but shed enough light for us to see the trampled dirt track of the wagon road that ran before us, wide enough for two wagons to travel abreast.

We had encountered several such points on the road between Savannah and Charleston, mostly manned by bored soldiers who waved us through without bothering to check the passes we had obtained in Georgia. The checkpoints were mostly concerned with the interception of smuggled goods, and with the capture of the odd bond-servant or slave, escaped from his master.

Even filthy and unkempt, we passed notice for the most part; few travelers were in better case. Fergus and Duncan could not be indentured men, maimed as they were, and Jamie's presence transcended his clothes; shabby coat or not, no man would take him for a servant.

Tonight was different, though. There were eight soldiers at the checkpoint, not the usual two, and all were armed and alert. Musket barrels flashed in the moonlight as the shout of 'Halt! Your name and your business!' came from the dark. A lantern was hoisted up six inches from my face, blinding me for a moment.

'James Fraser, bound for Wilmington, with my family and servants.' Jamie's voice was calm, and his hands were steady as he handed me the reins before reaching for the passes in his coat.

I kept my head down, trying to look tired and indifferent. I was tired, all right – I could have lain down in the road and slept – but far from indifferent. What did they do to you for aiding the escape of a fugitive from the gallows? I wondered. A single drop of sweat snaked its way down the back of my neck.

'Have you seen anyone along the road as you passed, sir?' The 'sir' came a little reluctantly; the dilapidation of Jamie's coat and my gown were obvious in the pool of yellow lantern light.

'A carriage that passed us from the town; I suppose you will have seen that yourselves,' Jamie answered. The sergeant replied with a grunt, checking the passes carefully, then squinting into the dark to count and see that the attendant bodies matched.

'What goods do you carry?' He handed back the passes, motioning to one of his subordinates to search the wagon. I twitched the reins inadvertently, and the horses snorted and shook their heads. Jamie's foot nudged mine, but he didn't look at me.

'Small household goods,' he answered, still calm. 'A half of venison and a bag of salt, for provision. And a body.'

The soldier who had been reaching for the wagon covering stopped abruptly. The sergeant looked up sharply.

'A what?'

Jamie took the reins from me and wrapped them casually about his wrist. From the corner of my eye, I saw Duncan edge toward the darkness of the wood; Fergus, with his pickpocket's skill, had already faded from view.

'The corpse of the man who was hanged this afternoon. He was known to me; I asked permission of Colonel Franklin to take him to his kinsmen in the north. That is why we travel by night,' he added delicately.

'I see.' The sergeant motioned a lantern bearer closer. He gave Jamie a long, thoughtful look, eyes narrowed, and nodded. 'I remember you,' he said. 'You called out to him at the last. A friend, was he?'

'I knew him once. Some years ago,' he added. The sergeant nodded to his subordinate, not taking his eyes off Jamie.

'Have a look, Griswold.'

Griswold, who was perhaps fourteen, betrayed a notable lack of enthusiasm for the order, but dutifully lifted the canvas cover and raised his lantern to peer into the wagon bed. With an effort, I kept myself from turning to look.

The near horse snorted and tossed its head. If we did have to bolt, it would take several seconds for the horses to get the wagon moving. I heard Ian shift behind me, getting his hand on the club of hickory wood stowed behind the seat.

'Yes, sir, it's a body,' Griswold reported. 'In a shroud.' He dropped the canvas with an air of relief, and exhaled strongly through his nostrils.

'Fix your bayonet and give it a jab,' the sergeant said, eyes still on Jamie. I must have made a small noise, for the sergeant's glance shifted to me.

'You'll soil my wagon,' Jamie objected. 'The man's fair ripe, after a day in the sun, aye?'

The sergeant snorted impatiently. 'Jab it in the leg, then. Get on, Griswold!'

With a marked air of reluctance, Griswold affixed his bayonet, and standing on tiptoe, began to poke gingerly about in the wagon bed. Behind me, Ian had begun to whistle softly. A Gaelic tune whose title translated to 'In the Morn We Die', which I thought very tasteless of him.

'No, sir, he's dead all right.' Griswold dropped back on his heels, sounding relieved. 'I poked right hard, but not a twitch.'

'All right, then.' Dismissing the young soldier with a jerk of his hand, the sergeant nodded to Jamie. 'Drive on then, Mr. Fraser. But I'd advise you to choose your friends more carefully in future.'

I saw Jamie's knuckles whiten on the reins, but he only drew himself up straight and settled his hat more firmly on his head. He clicked his tongue and the horses set off sharply, leaving puffs of pale dust floating in the lantern light.

The darkness seemed engulfing after the light; despite the moon, I could see almost nothing. The night enfolded us. I felt the relief of a hunted animal that finds safe refuge, and in spite of the oppressive heat, I breathed more freely.

We covered a distance of nearly a quarter mile before anyone spoke.

'Are ye wounded, Mr. Bonnet?' Ian spoke in a loud whisper, just audible over the rattle of the wagon.

'Yes, he's pinked me in the thigh, damn the puppy.' Bonnet's voice was low, but calm. 'Thank Christ he left off before the blood soaked through the shroud. Dead men don't bleed.'

'Are you hurt badly? Shall I come back and have a look at it?' I twisted around. Bonnet had pushed back the canvas cover and was sitting up, a vague, pale shape in the darkness.

'No, I thank ye, ma'am. I've my stocking wound round it and 'twill serve well enough, I expect.' My night vision was returning; I could see the gleam of fair hair as he bent his head to his task.

'Can ye walk, do ye think?' Jamie slowed the horses to a walk, and twisted round to inspect our guest. While his tone was not inhospitable, it was clear that he would prefer to be rid of our dangerous cargo as soon as possible.

'Not easily, no. I'm that sorry, sir.' Bonnet was aware of Jamie's eagerness to be rid of him, too. With some difficulty, he hoisted himself up in the wagon bed, rising onto his good knee behind the seat. His lower half was invisible in darkness, but I could smell the blood on him, a sharper scent than the lingering faint reek of Gavin's shroud.

'A suggestion, Mr. Fraser. In three miles, we'll come to the Ferry Trail road. A mile past the crossroads, another road leads toward the coast. It's little more than a pair of ruts, but passable. That will take us to the edge of a creek with an outlet to the sea. Some associates of mine will be puttin' in to anchor there within the week; if ye would grant me some small stock of provisions, I can wait them in reasonable safety, and you can be on your way, free o' the taint of my company.'

'Associates? Ye mean pirates?' Ian's voice held a certain amount of wariness. Having been abducted from Scotland by pirates, he invested such persons with none of the romanticism normal to a fifteen-year-old.

'That would depend upon your perspective, lad.' Bonnet sounded amused. 'Certainly the governors of the Carolinas would call them so; the merchants of

Wilmington and Charleston perhaps regard them otherwise.'

Jamie gave a brief snort. 'Smugglers, aye? And what might these associates of yours be dealing in, then?'

'Whatever will fetch a price to make it worth the risk of carrying.' The amusement had not left Bonnet's voice, but was now tinged with cynicism. 'Will you be wanting some reward for your assistance? That can be managed.'

'I do not.' Jamie's voice was cold. 'I saved you for Gavin Hayes's sake, and for my own. I wouldna seek reward for such service.'

'I meant no offense to ye, sir.' Bonnet's head inclined slightly toward us.

'None taken,' Jamie answered shortly. He shook out the reins and wrapped them afresh, changing hands.

Convesation lapsed after this small clash, though Bonnet continued to ride kneeling behind us, peering over my shoulder at the dark road ahead. There were no more soldiers, though; nothing moved, not even a breath of wind in the leaves. Nothing disturbed the silence of the summer night save the occasional thin *zeek* of a passing night bird, or the hooting of an owl.

The soft rhythmic thump of the horses' hooves in the dust and the squeak and rattle of the wagon began to lull me to sleep. I tried to keep upright, watching the black shadows of the trees along the road, but found myself gradually inclining toward Jamie, my eyes falling shut despite my best efforts.

Jamie transferred the reins to his left hand, and putting his right arm around me, drew me down to rest against his shoulder. As always, I felt safe when I touched him. I went limp, cheek pressed against the dusty serge of his coat, and fell at once into that uneasy doze that is the consequence of a combination of utter exhaustion and the inability to lie down.

I opened my eyes once to see the tall, lean figure of Duncan Innes, pacing alongside the wagon with his tireless hillman's stride, head bowed as though in deep thought. Then I closed them again, and drifted into a doze in which memories of the day mingled with inchoate fragments of dreams. I dreamt of a giant skunk sleeping under a tavern's table, waking to join in a chorus of 'The Star-Spangled Banner', and then of a swinging corpse that raised its lolling head and grinned with empty eyes . . . I came awake to find Jamie gently shaking me.

'Ye'd best crawl into the back and lie down, Sassenach,' he said. 'You're craicklin' in your sleep. You'll be slippin' into the road, next thing.'

Blearily assenting, I clambered awkwardly over the seat back, changing places with Bonnet, and found a place in the wagon bed next to the slumbering form of Young Ian.

It smelt musty – and worse – in the wagon bed. Ian had his head pillowed on a packet of roughly butchered venison, wrapped in the untanned skin of the deer. Rollo had done somewhat better, his hairy muzzle resting comfortably on Ian's stomach. For myself, I took the leathern bag of salt. The smooth leather was hard under my cheek, but odorless.

The jolting boards of the wagon bed couldn't by any stretch of the imagination be called comfortable, but the relief of being able to stretch out at full length was so overwhelming that I scarcely noticed the bumps and jolts. I rolled onto my back and looked up into the hazy immensity of the southern sky, studded thick with blazing stars. *Lumen Christi*, I thought, and comforted by the thought of Gavin Hayes finding his way safe home by the lights of heaven, fell once more fast asleep.

I could not tell how long I slept, wrapped in a drugged blanket of heat and exhaustion. I woke when the pace of the wagon changed, swimming toward the surface of consciousness, drenched with sweat.

Bonnet and Jamie were talking, in the low, easy tones of men who had found their way past the early awkwardness of first acquaintance.

'You said that ye saved me for Gavin Hayes's sake – and for your own,' Bonnet was saying. His voice was soft, barely audible above the rumble of the wheels. 'What did ye mean by that, sir, and ye'll pardon my asking –?'

Jamie didn't answer at once; I nearly fell asleep again before he spoke, but at last his answer came, floating disembodied in the warm, dark air.

'Ye wilna have slept much last night, I think? Knowing what was to come to ye with the day?'

There was a low laugh from Bonnet, not entirely amused.

'Too right,' he said. 'I doubt I shall forget it in a hurry.'

'Nor will I.' Jamie said something soft in Gaelic to the horses, and they slowed in response. 'I once lived through such a night, knowing I would hang, come morning. And yet I lived, through the grace of one who risked much to save me.'

'I see,' Bonnet said softly. 'So you are an *asgina ageli*, are you?'

'Aye? And what will that be?'

There was a sound of scraping and brushing leaves against the side of the wagon, and the spicy sap-scent of the trees grew suddenly stronger. Something light touched my face – leaves, falling from above. The horses slowed, and the rhythm of the wagon changed markedly, the wheels finding an uneven surface. We had turned into the small road that led to Bonnet's creek.

'*Asgina ageli* is a term that the red savages employ – the Cherokee of the mountains; I heard it from one I had as guide one time. It means "half-ghost", one who should have died by right, but yet remains on the earth; a woman who survives a mortal illness, a man fallen into his enemies' hands who escapes. They say an *asgina ageli* has one foot on the earth and the other in the spirit world. He can talk to the spirits, and see the Nunnahee – the Little People.'

'Little People? Will that be like the faeries?' Jamie sounded surprised.

'Something of the kind.' Bonnet shifted his weight and the seat creaked as he stretched. 'The Indians do say that the Nunnahee live inside the rocks of the mountains, and come out to help their people in time of war or other evil.'

'Is that so? It will be something like the tales they tell in the Highlands of Scotland, then – of the Auld Folk.'

'Indeed.' Bonnet sounded amused. 'Well, from what I have heard of the Scotch Highlanders, there is little to choose between them and the red men for barbarous conduct.'

50

'Nonsense,' said Jamie, sounding not the least offended. 'The red savages eat the hearts of their enemies, or so I have heard. I prefer a good dish of oatmeal parritch, myself.'

Bonnet made a noise, hastily stifled.

'You are a Highlander? Well, I will say that for a barbarian, I have found ye passing civil, sir,' he assured Jamie, the laughter quivering in his voice.

'I am exceedingly obliged for your kind opinion, sir,' Jamie replied, with equal politeness.

Their voices faded into the rhythmic squeaking of the wheels, and I was asleep again before I could hear more.

The moon hung low over the trees by the time we came to a halt. I was roused by the movements of Young Ian, clambering sleepily over the wagon's edge to help Jamie tend to the horses. I poked my head up to see a broad stretch of water flowing past shelving banks of clay and silt, the stream a shiny black glittering with silver where riffles purled on the rocks near shore. Bonnet, with customary New World understatement, might call it a creek, but it would pass for a decent river among most boatmen, I thought.

The men moved to and fro in the shadows, carrying out their tasks with no more than an occasional muttered word. They moved with unaccustomed slowness, seeming to fade into the night, made insubstantial by fatigue.

'Do ye go and find a place to sleep, Sassenach,' Jamie said, pausing to steady me as I dropped down from the wagon. 'I must just see our guest provisioned and set on his way, and the beasts wiped down and put to grass.'

The temperature had dropped scarcely at all since nightfall, but the air seemed fresher here near the water, and I found myself reviving somewhat.

'I can't sleep until I've bathed,' I said, pulling the soaked bodice of my gown away from my breasts. 'I feel terrible.' My hair was pasted to my temples with sweat, and my flesh felt grimed and itchy. The dark water looked cool and inviting. Jamie cast a longing look at it, plucking at his crumpled stock.

'I canna say I blame ye. Go careful, though; Bonnet says

51

the channel in midstream is deep enough to float a ketch, and it's a tide-creek; there'll be a strong current.'

'I'll stay near the shore.' I pointed downstream, where a small point of land marked a bend in the river, its willows shining dusky silver in the moonlight. 'See that little point? There should be an eddy pool there.'

'Aye. Go careful, then,' he said again, and squeezed my elbow in farewell. As I turned to go, a large pale shape loomed up before me; our erst-while guest, one leg of his breeches stained dark with dried blood.

'Your servant, ma'am,' he said, making me a creditable bow, despite the injured leg. 'Do I bid you now adieu?' He was standing a bit closer to me than I quite liked, and I repressed the urge to step backward.

'You do,' I said, and nodded to him, brushing back a dangling lock of hair. 'Good luck, Mr. Bonnet.'

'I thank ye for your kind wishes, ma'am,' he answered softly. 'But I have found that a man most often makes his own luck. Good night to ye, ma'am.' He bowed once more and turned away, limping heavily, like the ghost of a crippled bear.

The creek's rushing masked most of the ordinary night sounds. I saw a bat blink through a patch of moonlight over the water, in pursuit of insects too small to see, and vanish into the night. If anything else lurked in the dark, it was quiet.

Jamie grunted softly to himself.

'Well, I've my doubts of the man,' he said, as though answering a question I hadn't asked. 'I must hope I've only been softhearted, and not softheaded, by helpin' him.'

'You couldn't leave him to hang, after all,' I said.

'Oh, aye, I could,' he said, surprising me. He saw me look up at him, and smiled, the wry twist of his mouth barely visible in the dark.

'The Crown doesna *always* pick the wrong man to hang, Sassenach,' he said. 'More often than not, the man on the end of a rope deserves to be there. And I shouldna like to think I've helped a villain to go free.' He shrugged, and shoved his hair back out of his face.

'Aye, well, it's done. Go and have your bath, Sassenach; I'll come to ye so soon as I may.'

I stood on tiptoe to kiss him, and felt him smile as I did so. My tongue touched his mouth in delicate invitation, and he bit my lower lip gently, in answer.

'Can ye stay awake a wee bit longer, Sassenach?'

'As long as it takes,' I assured him. 'But do hurry, won't you?'

There was a patch of thick grass edging the point below the willows. I undressed slowly, enjoying the feel of the water-borne breeze through the damp cloth of shift and stockings, and the final freedom as the last bits of clothing fell to the ground, leaving me naked to the night.

I stepped gingerly into the water. It was surprisingly cool – cold, by contrast to the hot night air. The bottom under my feet was mostly silt, but it yielded to fine sand within a yard of shore.

Though it was a tidal creek, we were far enough upstream that the water was fresh and sweet. I drank and splashed my face, washing away the dust in throat and nose.

I waded in up to mid-thigh, mindful of Jamie's cautions about channels and currents. After the staggering heat of the day and the smothering embrace of the night, the sensation of coolness on bare skin was an overwhelming relief. I cupped handfuls of cold water and splashed them on my face and breasts; the droplets ran down my stomach and tickled coldly between my legs.

I could feel the slight push of the tide coming in, shoving gently against my calves, urging me toward shore. I wasn't ready to come in yet, though. I had no soap, but knelt and rinsed my hair over and over in the clear dark water, and scrubbed my body with handfuls of fine sand, until my skin felt thin and glowing.

Finally, I climbed out onto a rocky shelf and lay languid as a mermaid in the moonlight, the heat of the air and the sun-warmed stone now a comfort to my chilled body. I combed out my thick curly hair with my fingers, scattering drops of water. The wet stone smelled like rain, dusty and tingling.

I felt very tired, but at the same time, very much alive, in that state of half consciousness where thought is slowed

53

and small physical sensations magnified. I moved my bare foot slowly over the sandstone rock, enjoying the slight friction, and ran a hand lightly down the inside of my thigh, a ripple of goose bumps rising in the wake of my touch.

My breasts rose in the moonlight, cool white domes spangled with clear droplets. I brushed one nipple and watched it slowly stiffen by itself, rising as if by magic.

Quite a magical place at that, I thought. The night was quiet and still, but with a languid atmosphere that was like floating in a warm sea. So near the coast, the sky was clear, and the stars shone overhead like diamonds, burning with a fierce, bright light.

A faint splash made me look toward the stream. Nothing moved on the surface but faint coruscations of starlight, caught like fireflies in a spider's web.

As I watched, a great head broke water in the middle of the stream, water purling back from the pointed snout. There was a fish struggling in Rollo's jaws; the flap and gleam of its scales showed briefly as he shook his head violently to break its back. The huge dog swam slowly to the shore, shook his coat briefly, and stalked away, his evening meal dangling limp and shimmering from his jaws.

He paused for a moment on the far edge of the creek, looking at me, the ruff of his hackles a dark shadow framing yellow eyes and gleaming fish. Like a primitive painting, I thought; something from Rousseau, with its contrast of utter wildness and complete stillness.

Then the dog was gone, and there was nothing on the far shore but the trees, hiding whatever might lie behind them. And what did? I wondered. More trees, answered the logical part of my mind.

'A *lot* more,' I murmured, looking into the mysterious dark. Civilization – even of the primitive kind I had grown used to – was no more than a thin crescent on the edge of the continent. Two hundred miles from the coast, you were beyond the ken of city and farm. And, past that point lay three thousand miles . . . of what? Wilderness, surely, and danger. Adventure, too – and freedom.

It was a new world, after all, free of fear and filled with

joy, for now Jamie and I were together, for all of our lives before us. Parting and sorrow lay behind us. Even the thought of Brianna caused no dreadful regret – I missed her greatly, and thought of her constantly, but I knew she was safe in her own time, and that knowledge made her absence easier to bear.

I lay back on the rock, the trapped heat of the day radiating from its surface into my body, happy only to be alive. The drops of water were drying on my breasts as I watched, vanishing to a film of moistness and then disappearing altogether.

Small clouds of gnats hovered over the water; I couldn't see them, but I knew they were there by the occasional splash of leaping fish, rising to snatch them from the air.

The bugs had been a ubiquitous plague. I inspected Jamie's skin minutely every morning, picking voracious ticks and wood fleas from his crevices, and anointed all of the men liberally with the juice of crushed pennyroyal and tobacco leaves. This kept them from being devoured alive by the clouds of mosquitoes, gnats, and carnivorous midges that hung in the suntinged shadows of the woods, but it didn't prevent the hordes of inquisitive bugs from driving them mad with a constant tickling inquiry into ears, eyes, noses, and mouths.

Oddly enough, the majority of insects left me strictly alone. Ian joked that the strong scent of herbs that hung about me must repel them, but I thought it went further than that – even when I was freshly bathed, the insects showed no desire to bother me.

I thought it might be a manifestation of the evolutionary oddity that – I surmised – protected me from colds and minor illness here. Bloodthirsty bugs, like microbes, evolved very closely with humans, and were sensitive to the subtle chemical signals of their hosts. Coming from another time, I no longer had precisely the same signals, and consequently the bugs no longer perceived me as prey.

'Or maybe Ian's right, and I just smell awful,' I said aloud. I dipped my fingers in the water and flicked a spray of drops at a dragonfly resting on my rock, no more than a transparent shadow, its colors drained by darkness.

I hoped Jamie would hurry. Riding for days on the wagon seat next to him, watching the subtle shifts of his body as he drove, seeing the changing light on the angles of his face as he talked and smiled, was enough to make my palms tingle with the urge to touch him. We had not made love in several days, owing to our hurry to reach Charleston, and my inhibitions about intimacy within earshot of a dozen men.

A breath of warm breeze slipped past me, and all the tiny down hairs on my body prickled with its passing. No hurry now, and no one to hear. I drew a hand down the soft curve of my belly and the softer skin inside my thighs, where the blood pulsed slowly to the beat of my heart. I cupped my hand, feeling the swollen moist ache of urgent desire.

I closed my eyes, rubbing lightly, enjoying the feeling of increasing urgency.

'And where the hell are *you*, Jamie Fraser?' I murmured.

'Here,' came a husky answer.

Startled, my eyes popped open. He was standing in the stream, six feet away, thigh-deep in the water, his genitals stiff and dark against the pallid glow of his body. His hair lay loose around his shoulders, framing a face white as bone, eyes unblinking and intent as those of the wolf-dog. Utter wildness, utter stillness.

Then he stirred and came toward me, still intent, but still no longer. His thighs were cold as water when he touched me, but within seconds he warmed and grew hot. Sweat sprang up at once where his hands touched my skin, and a flush of hot moisture dampened my breasts once more, making them round and slick against the hardness of his chest.

Then his mouth moved to mine and I melted – almost literally – into him. I didn't care how hot it was, or whether the dampness on my skin was my sweat or his. Even the clouds of insects faded into insignificance. I raised my hips and he slid home, slick and solid, the last faint coolness of him quenched by my heat, like the cold metal of a sword, slaked in hot blood.

My hands glided on a film of moisture over the curves of his back, and my breasts wobbled against his chest, a

56

rivulet trickling between them to oil the friction of belly and thigh.

'Christ, your mouth is slick and salty as your quim,' he muttered, and his tongue darted out to taste the tiny beads of salt on my face, butterfly wings on temple and eyelids.

I was vaguely conscious of the hard rock under me. The stored heat of the day rose up and through me, and the rough surface scraped my back and buttocks, but I didn't care.

'I can't wait,' he said in my ear, breathless.

'Don't,' I said, and wrapped my legs tight around his hips, flesh bonded to flesh in the brief madness of dissolution.

'I have heard of melting with passion,' I said, gasping slightly, 'but this is ridiculous.'

He lifted his head from my breast with a faint sticky sound as his cheek came away. He laughed and slid slowly sideways.

'God, it's hot!' he said. He pushed back the sweat-soaked hair from his forehead and blew out his breath, chest still heaving from exertion. 'How do folk do that when it's like this?'

'The same way we just did,' I pointed out. I was breathing heavily myself.

'They can't,' he said with certainty. 'Not all the time; they'd die.'

'Well, maybe they do it slower,' I said. 'Or underwater. Or wait until the autumn.'

'Autumn?' he said. 'Perhaps I dinna want to live in the south, after all. Is it hot in Boston?'

'It is at this time of year,' I assured him. 'And beastly cold in the winter. I'm sure you'll get used to the heat. And the bugs.'

He brushed a questing mosquito off his shoulder and glanced from me to the nearby creek.

'Maybe so,' he said, 'and maybe no, but for now . . .' He wrapped his arms firmly around me, and rolled. With the ponderous grace of a rolling log, we fell off the edge of the rocky shelf, and into the water.

We lay damp and cool on the rock, barely touching, the

57

last drops of water evaporating on our skins. Across the creek, the willows trailed their leaves in the water, crowns ruffled black against the setting moon. Beyond the willows lay acre upon acre and mile upon mile of the virgin forest, civilization for now no more than a foothold on the edge of the continent.

Jamie saw the direction of my glance and divined my thought.

'It will be a good bit different now than when ye last kent it, I expect?' He nodded toward the leafy dark.

'Oh, a bit.' I linked my hand with his, my thumb idly caressing his big, bony knuckles. 'The roads will be paved then; not cobbled, covered with a hard, smooth stuff – invented by a Scotsman called MacAdam, in fact.'

He grunted slightly with amusement.

'So there will be Scots in America, then? That's good.'

I ignored him and went on, staring into the wavering shadows as though I could conjure the burgeoning cities that would one day rise there.

'There will be a lot of everyone in America, then. All the land will be settled, from here to the far west coast, to a place called California. But for now' – I shivered slightly, in spite of the warm, humid air – 'it's three thousand miles of wilderness. There's nothing there at all.'

'Aye, well, nothing save thousands of bloodthirsty savages,' he said practically. 'And the odd vicious beast, to be sure.'

'Well, yes,' I agreed. 'I suppose they are.' The thought was unsettling; I had of course known, in a vague, academic way, that the woods were inhabited by Indians, bears, and other forest denizens, but this general notion had suddenly been replaced by a particular and most acute awareness that we might easily – and unexpectedly – meet any one of these denizens, face-to-face.

'What happens to them? To the wild Indians?' Jamie asked curiously, peering into the dark as I was, as though trying to divine the future among the shifting shadows. 'They'll be defeated and driven back, will they?'

Another small shiver passed over me, and my toes curled.

'Yes, they will,' I said. 'Killed, a lot of them. A good many taken prisoner, locked up.'

'Well, that's good.'

'I expect that depends a lot on your point of view,' I said, rather dryly. 'I don't suppose the Indians will think so.'

'I daresay,' he said. 'But when a bloody fiend's tryin' his best to chop off the top of my head, I'm no so much concerned with his point of view, Sassenach.'

'Well, you can't really blame them,' I protested.

'I most certainly can,' he assured me. 'If one of the brutes scalps ye, I shall blame him a great deal.'

'Ah . . . hmm,' I said. I cleared my throat and had another stab at it. 'Well, what if a bunch of strangers came round and tried to kill you and shove you off the land you'd always lived on?'

'They have,' he said, very dryly indeed. 'If they hadna, I should still be in Scotland, aye?'

'Well . . .' I said, floundering. 'But all I mean is – you'd fight, too, under those circumstances, wouldn't you?'

He drew a deep breath and exhaled strongly through his nose.

'If an English dragoon came round to my house and began to worry me,' he said precisely, 'I should certainly fight him. I would also have not the slightest hesitation in killing him. I would also *not* cut off his hair and wave it about, and I wouldna be eating his private parts, either. I am not a savage, Sassenach.'

'I didn't say you were,' I protested. 'All I said was –'

'Besides,' he added with inexorable logic, 'I dinna mean to be killing any Indians. If they keep to themselves, I shallna be worrying them a bit.'

'I'm sure they'll be relieved to know that,' I murmured, giving up for the present.

We lay cradled close together in the hollow of the rock, lightly glued with sweat, watching the stars. I felt at once shatteringly happy and mildly apprehensive. Could this state of exaltation possibly last? Once I had taken 'forever' for granted between us, but I was younger, then.

Soon, God willing, we would settle; find a place to make a home and a life. I wanted nothing more, and yet at the same time, I worried. We had known each other only a few months since my return. Each touch, each word was still at once tinged with memory and new with rediscovery. What would happen when we were thoroughly accustomed to each other, living day by day in a routine of mundane tasks?

'Will ye grow tired of me, do ye think?' he murmured. 'Once we're settled?'

'I was just wondering the same thing about you.'

'No,' he said, and I could hear the smile in his voice. 'That I willna, Sassenach.'

'How do you know?' I asked.

'I didn't,' he pointed out. 'Before. We were wed three years, and I wanted ye as much on the last day as the first. More, maybe,' he added softly, thinking, as I was, of the last time we had made love before he sent me through the stones.

I leaned down and kissed him. He tasted clean and fresh, faintly scented with the pungency of sex.

'I did, too.'

'Then dinna trouble yourself about it, Sassenach, and neither will I.' He stroked my hair, smoothing damp curls off my forehead. 'I could know ye all my life, I think, and always love you. And often as I've lain wi' you, ye still surprise me mightily sometimes, like ye did tonight.'

'I do? Why, what have I done?' I stared down at him, surprised myself.

'Oh . . . well. I didna mean . . . that is –'

He sounded suddenly shy, and there was an unaccustomed stiffness in his body.

'Mm?' I kissed the tip of his ear.

'Ah . . . when I came upon you . . . what ye were doing . . . I mean – were ye doing what I thought?'

I smiled against his shoulder in the darkness.

'I suppose that depends what you thought, doesn't it?'

He lifted up on one elbow, his skin coming away from mine with a small sucking noise. The damp spot where he had adhered was suddenly cool. He rolled onto his side and grinned at me.

'Ye ken verra well what I thought, Sassenach.'

I touched his chin, shadowed with sprouting whiskers.

'I do. And you know perfectly well what I was doing, too, so why are you asking?'

'Well, I – I didna think women did that, is all.'

The moon was bright enough for me to see his half-cocked eyebrow.

'Well, men do,' I pointed out. 'Or you do, at least. You told me so – when you were in prison, you said you –'

'That was different!' I could see his mouth twist as he tried to decide what to say. 'I – that is to say, there wasna any help for it then. After all, I couldna be –'

'Haven't you done it other times?' I sat up and fluffed out my damp hair, glancing sidelong at him over my shoulder. A blush didn't show in the moonlight, but I thought he had gone pink.

'Aye, well,' he muttered. 'I suppose I have, yes.' A sudden thought struck him and his eyes widened, looking at me. 'Do you – have ye done that – often?' The last word emerged in a croak, and he was obliged to stop and clear his throat.

'I suppose it depends on what you mean by "often",' I said, allowing a bit of acerbity to creep into my tone. 'I was widowed for two years, you know.'

He rubbed a knuckle over his lips, eyeing me with interest.

'Aye, that's so. It's only – well, I hadna thought of women doing such a thing, is all.' Growing fascination was overcoming his surprise. 'You can – finish? Without a man, I mean?'

That made me laugh out loud, and soft reverberations sounded from the trees around us, echoed by the stream.

'Yes, but it's much nicer with a man,' I assured him. I reached out and touched his chest. I could see the goose bumps ripple over his chest and shoulders, and he shivered slightly as I drew a fingertip in a gentle circle round one nipple. 'Much,' I said softly.

'Oh,' he said, sounding happy. 'Well, that's good, aye?'

He was hot – even hotter than the liquid air – and my first instinct was to draw back, but I didn't follow it. Sweat sprang up at once where his hands rested on my skin, and trickles of sweat ran down my neck.

'I've never made love to ye before like this,' he said.

61

'Like eels, aye? Wi' your body sliding through my hands, all slippery as seaweed.' Both hands passed slowly down my back, his thumbs pressing the groove of my spine, making the tiny hairs at the base of my neck prickle with pleasure.

'Mm. That's because it's too cold in Scotland to sweat like pigs,' I said. 'Though come to that, do pigs really sweat? I've always wondered.'

'I couldna say; I've never made love to a pig.' His head ducked down and his tongue touched my breast. 'But ye do taste a bit like a trout, Sassenach.'

'I taste like a *what?*'

'Fresh and sweet, wi' a bit of salt,' he explained, lifting his head for a moment. He put it back down, and resumed his downward course.

'That tickles,' I said, quivering under his tongue, but making no effort to escape.

'Well, I mean it to,' he answered, lifting his wet face for a breath before returning to his work. 'I shouldna like to think ye could do without me entirely.'

'I can't,' I assured him. 'Oh!'

'Ah?' came a thick interrogative. I lay back on the rock, my back arching as the stars spun dizzily overhead.

'I said . . . "oh",' I said faintly. And then didn't say anything coherent for some time, until he lay panting, chin resting lightly on my pubic bone. I reached down and stroked the sweat-drenched hair away from his face, and he turned his head to kiss my palm.

'I feel like Eve,' I said softly, watching the moon set behind him, over the dark of the forest. 'Just on the edge of the Garden of Eden.'

There was a small snort of laughter from the vicinity of my navel.

'Aye, and I suppose I'm Adam,' Jamie said. 'In the gateway to Paradise.' He turned his head to look wistfully across the creek toward the vast unknown, resting his cheek on the slope of my belly. 'I only wish I knew was I coming in, or going out?'

I laughed myself, startling him. I took him by both ears then, urging him gently up across the slippery expanse of my naked flesh.

'In,' I said. 'I don't see an angel with a fiery sword, after all.'

He lowered himself upon me, his own flesh heated as with fever, and I shivered under him.

'No?' he murmured. 'Aye, well, you'll no be looking close enough, I suppose.'

Then the fiery sword severed me from consciousness and set fire to my body. We blazed up together, bright as stars in the summer night, and then sank back burnt and limbless, ashes dissolved in a primordial sea of warm salt, stirring with the nascent throbbings of life.

PART TWO

Past Imperfect

3

The Minister's Cat

Boston, Massachusetts, June 1969

'Brianna?'

'Ha?' She sat bolt upright, heart pounding, the sound of her name ringing in her ear. 'Who – wha'?'

'You were asleep. Damn, I knew I'd got the time wrong! Sorry, shall I ring off?'

It was the faint hint of a burr in his voice that belatedly made the scrambled connections of her nervous system fall into place. Phone. Ringing phone. She'd snatched it by reflex, deep in her dream.

'Roger!' The rush of adrenaline from being startled awake was fading, but her heart was still beating fast. 'No, don't hang up! It's all right, I'm awake.' She scrubbed a hand over her face, trying at once to disentangle the phone cord and straighten the rumpled bedclothes.

'Aye? You're sure? What time is it there?'

'I don't know; it's too dark to see the clock,' she said, still sleep-addled. A reluctant deep chuckle answered her.

'I *am* sorry; I tried to calculate the time difference, but must've got it backward. Didn't mean to wake you.'

'That's okay, I had to wake up to answer the phone anyway,' she assured him, and laughed.

'Aye. Well . . .' She could hear the answering smile in his voice, and eased herself back against the pillows, shoving tangles of hair out of her eyes, slowly adjusting to the here and now. The feel of her dream was still with her, more real than the dark-shrouded shapes of her bedroom.

'It's good to hear your voice, Roger,' she said softly. She was surprised at just *how* good it was. His voice was far away and yet seemed much more immediate than the far-off whines of sirens, and the *whish!* of tires on wet pavement outside.

'Yours, too.' He sounded a little shy. 'Look – I've got the chance of a conference next month, in Boston. I thought

67

of coming, if – damn, there's no good way to say this. Do you want to see me?'

Her hand squeezed tight on the receiver, and her heart jumped.

'I'm sorry,' he said at once, before she could reply. 'That's putting you on the spot, isn't it? I – look – just say straight out if you'd rather not.'

'I do. Of course I want to see you!'

'Ah. You don't mind, then? Only . . . you didn't answer my letter. I thought maybe I'd done something –'

'No, you didn't. I'm sorry. It was just –'

'It's fine, I didn't mean –'

Their sentences collided, and they both stopped, stricken with shyness.

'I didn't want to push –'

'I didn't mean to be –'

It happened again, and this time he laughed, a low sound of Scottish amusement coming over the vast distance of space and time, comforting as though he'd touched her.

'It's all right, then,' he said firmly. 'I do understand, aye?'

She didn't answer, but closed her eyes, an indefinable sensation of relief sweeping over her. Roger Wakefield was likely the only person in the world who *could* understand; what she hadn't fully realized before was how important that understanding might be.

'I was dreaming,' she said. 'When the phone rang.'

'Mmphm?'

'About my father.' Her throat tightened, just a little, whenever she spoke the word. The same thing happened when she said 'mother', too. She could still smell the sun-warmed pines of her dream, and feel the crunch of pine needles under her boots.

'I couldn't see his face. I was walking with him, in the woods somewhere. I was following him up a trail, and he was talking to me, but I couldn't hear what he was saying – I kept hurrying, trying to catch up, so I could hear, but I couldn't quite umanage.'

'But you knew the man was your father?'

'Yes – but maybe I only thought so because of hiking in the mountains. I used to do that with Dad.'

'Did you? I used to do that with my dad, as well. If you come back to Scotland ever, I'll take ye Munro bagging.'

'You'll take me *what?*'

He laughed, and she had a sudden memory of him, brushing back the thick black hair that he didn't cut often enough, moss-green eyes creased half-shut by his smile. She found she was rubbing the tip of her thumb slowly across her lower lip, and stopped herself. He'd kissed her when they parted.

'A Munro is any Scottish peak more than three thousand feet. There are so many of them, it's a sport to see how many you can climb. Folk collect them, like stamps, or matchbooks.'

'Where are you now – Scotland or England?' she said, then interrupted before he could answer. 'No, let me see if I can guess. It's . . . Scotland. You're in Inverness.'

'That's right.' The surprise was evident in his voice. 'How did you know that?'

She stretched, scissoring her long legs slowly under the sheets.

'You roll your r's when you've been talking to other Scots,' she said. 'You don't when you talk to English people. I noticed when we – went to London.' There was no more than a faint catch in her voice; it was getting easier, she thought.

'And herrrrre I was beginning to think ye were psychic,' he said, and laughed.

'I wish you were here now,' she said impulsively.

'You do?' He sounded surprised, and suddenly shy. 'Oh. Well . . . that's good, isn't it?'

'Roger – why I didn't write –'

'You're not to trouble about it,' he said quickly. 'I'll be there in a month; we can talk, then. Bree, I –'

'Yes?'

She heard him draw breath, and had a vivid memory of the feel of his chest rising and falling as he breathed, warm and solid under her hand.

'I'm glad you said yes.'

She couldn't go back to sleep after hanging up; restless, she swung her feet out of bed and padded out to the kitchen of the small apartment for a glass of milk. It was only after several minutes of staring blankly into the recesses of the refrigerator that she realized she wasn't seeing ranks of ketchup bottles and half-used cans. She was seeing standing stones, black against a pale dawn sky.

She straightened up with a small exclamation of impatience, and shut the door with a slam. She shivered slightly, and rubbed her arms, chilled by the draft of the air conditioner. Impulsively, she reached up and clicked it off, then went to the window and raised the sash, letting in the warm mugginess of the rainy summer night.

She should have written. In fact, she *had* written – several times, all half-finished attempts thrown away in frustration.

She knew why, or thought she did. Explaining it coherently to Roger was something else.

Part of it was the simple instinct of a wounded animal; the urge to run away and hide from hurt. What had happened the year before was in no way Roger's fault, but he was inextricably wrapped up in it.

He'd been so tender, and so kind afterward, treating her like one freshly bereaved – which she was. But such a strange bereavement! Her mother gone for good, but certainly – she hoped – not dead. And yet it was in some ways just as it had been when her father died; like believing in a blessed afterlife, ardently hoping that your loved one was safe and happy – and being forced to suffer the pangs of loss and loneliness nonetheless.

An ambulance went by, across the park, red light pulsing in the dark, its siren muted by distance.

She crossed herself from habit, and murmured '*Miserere nobis*' under her breath. Sister Marie Romaine had told the fifth grade that the dead and dying needed their prayers; so strongly had she inculcated the notion in her class that none of the children had ever been able to pass the scene of an emergency without sending a small silent prayer upward, to succor the souls of the imminently heaven-bound.

She prayed for them every day, her mother and her

70

father – her fathers. That was the other part of it. Uncle Joe knew the truth of her paternity, too, but only Roger could truly understand what had happened; only Roger could hear the stones, too.

No one could pass through an experience like that and not be marked by it. Not him, not her. He'd wanted her to stay, after Claire had gone, but she couldn't.

There were things to do here, she'd told him, things to be attended to, her schooling to finish. That was true. More importantly, she'd had to get away – get clear away from Scotland and stone circles, back to a place where she might heal, might begin to rebuild her life.

If she'd stayed with Roger, there was no way to forget what had happened, even for a moment. And that was the last part of it, the final piece in her three-sided puzzle.

He had protected her, had cherished her. Her mother had confided her into his care, and he'd kept that trust well. But had he done it to keep his promise to Claire – or because he truly cared? Either way, it wasn't any basis for a shared future, with the crushing weight of obligation on both sides.

If there might be a future for them . . . and that was what she couldn't write to him, because how could she say it without sounding both presumptuous and idiotic?

'Go away, so you can come back and do it right,' she murmured, and made a face at the words. The rain was still pattering down, cooling the air enough to breathe comfortably. It was just before dawn, she thought, but the air was still warm enough that moisture condensed on the cool skin of her face; small beads of water formed and slid tickling down her neck one by one, dampening the cotton T-shirt she slept in.

She'd wanted to put the events of last November well behind them; make a clean break. Then, when enough time had passed, perhaps they could come to each other again. Not as supporting players in the drama of her parents' life, but this time as the actors in a play of their own choosing.

No, if anything was to happen between her and Roger Wakefield, it would definitely be by choice. It looked as though she was going to get the chance to choose now,

71

and the prospect gave her a small, excited flutter in the pit of her stomach.

She wiped a hand over her face, slicking off the rain-wet, wiping it casually through her hair to tame the floating strands. If she wasn't going to sleep, she might as well work.

She left the window open, careless of the rain puddling on the floor. She felt too restless to be sealed in, chilled by artificial air.

Clicking on the lamp on the desk, she pulled out her calculus book and opened it. One small and unexpected bonus of her change of study was her belated discovery of the soothing effects of mathematics.

When she had come back to Boston, alone, and back to school, engineering had seemed a much safer choice than history; solid, fact-bound, reassuringly immutable. Above all, controllable. She picked up a pencil, sharpened it slowly, enjoying the preparation, then bent her head and read the first problem.

Slowly, as it always did, the calm inexorable logic of the figures built its web inside her head, trapping all the random thoughts, wrapping the distracting emotions up in silken threads like so many flies. Round the central axis of the problem, logic spun her web, orderly and beautiful as an orbweaver's jeweled confection. Only the one small thought stayed free of its strands, hovering in her mind like a bright, tiny butterfly.

I'm glad you said yes, he'd said. So was she.

July 1969

'Does he talk like the Beatles? Oh, I'll just die if he sounds like John Lennon! You know how he says, "It's me grand-father?" That just knocks me out!'

'He doesn't sound anything like John Lennon, for God's sake!' Brianna hissed. She peered cautiously around a concrete pillar, but the International Arrivals gate was still empty. 'Can't you tell the difference between a Liver-pudlian and a Scot?'

'No,' her friend Gayle said blithely, fluffing out her

blond hair. 'All Englishmen sound the same to me. I could listen to them forever!'

'He's not an Englishman! I told you, he's a Scot!'

Gayle gave Brianna a look, clearly suggesting that her friend was crazed.

'Scotland's part of England; I looked on the map.'

'Scotland's part of Great Britain, not England.'

'What's the difference?' Gayle stuck her head out and craned around the pillar. 'Why are we standing back here? He'll never see us.'

Brianna ran a hand over her hair to smooth it. They were standing behind a pillar because she wasn't sure she *wanted* him to see them. Not much help for it, though; disheveled passengers were beginning to trickle through the double doors, burdened with luggage.

She let Gayle tow her out into the main reception area, still babbling. Her friend's tongue led a double life; though Gayle was capable of cool and reasoned discourse in class, her chief social skill was babbling on cue. That was why Bree had asked Gayle to come with her to the airport to pick up Roger; no chance of any awkward pauses in the conversation.

'Have you done it with him already?'

She jerked toward Gayle, startled.

'Have I done *what?*'

Gayle rolled her eyes.

'Played tiddlywinks. Honestly, Bree!'

'No. Of course not.' She felt the blood rising in her cheeks.

'Well, are you *going* to?'

'Gayle!'

'Well, I mean, you have your own apartment and everything, and nobody's going to –'

At this awkward moment, Roger Wakefield appeared. He wore a white shirt and scruffy jeans, and Brianna must have stiffened at the sight of him. Gayle's head whipped round to see where Brianna was looking.

'Ooh,' she said in delight. 'Is that him? He looks like a *pirate*!'

He did, and Brianna felt the bottom of her stomach drop another inch or two. Roger was what her mother

73

called a Black Celt, with clear olive skin and black hair, and 'eyes put in with a sooty thumb' – thick black lashes round eyes you expected to be blue but that were instead a surprising deep green. With his hair worn long enough to brush his collar, disheveled and beard-stubbled, he looked not only rakish but mildly dangerous.

Alarm tingled up her spine at the sight of him, and she wiped sweating palms on the sides of her embroidered jeans. She shouldn't have let him come.

Then he saw her, and his face lit like a candle. In spite of herself, she felt a huge, idiotic smile break out on her own face in answer, and without stopping to think of misgivings, she ran across the room, dodging stray children and luggage carts.

He met her halfway and swept her almost off her feet, hugging her hard enough to crack her ribs. He kissed her, stopped, and kissed her again, the stubble of his beard scraping her face. He smelled of soap and sweat and he tasted like Scotch whisky and she didn't want him to stop.

Then he did and let go, both of them half breathless.

'*A-hem,*' said a loud voice near Brianna's elbow. She swung away from Roger, revealing Gayle, who smiled angelically up at him under blond bangs, and waved like a child going bye-bye.

'Hell-ooo,' she said. 'You must be Roger, because if you're not, Roger's sure in for a shock when he shows up, isn't he?'

She looked him up and down with obvious approval.

'All that, and you play the guitar, too?'

Brianna hadn't even noticed the case he had dropped. He stooped and picked it up, swinging it over his shoulder.

'Well, that's my bread and butter, this trip,' he said, with a smile at Gayle, who clutched a hand to her heart in simulated ecstasy.

'Ooh, say that again!' she begged.

'Say what?' Roger looked puzzled.

'Bread and butter,' Brianna told him, hoisting one of his bags onto her shoulder. 'She wants to hear you roll the r's again. Gayle has a thing about British accents. Oh – that's Gayle.' She gestured at her friend in resignation.

'Yes, I gathered. Er . . .' He cleared his throat, fixed

Gayle with a piercing stare, and dropped his voice an octave. 'Arround the rrruggged rrrock, the rrragged rrrascals rran. That do you for a bit?'

'Would you stop that?' Brianna looked crossly at her friend, who had swooned dramatically into one of the plastic seats. 'Ignore her,' she advised Roger, turning toward the door. With a cautious glance at Gayle, he took her advice, and picking up a large box tied with string, followed her into the concourse.

'What did you mean about your bread and butter?' she asked, looking for some way to return the conversation to a sane footing.

He laughed, a little self-consciously.

'Well, the historical conference is paying the airfare, but they couldn't manage expenses. So I called round, and wangled a bit of a job to take care of that end.'

'A job playing the guitar?'

'By day, mild-mannered historian Roger Wakefield is a harmless Oxford academic. But at night, he dons his secret tartan rrregalia and becomes the dashing – Roger MacKenzie!'

'Who?'

He smiled at her surprise. 'Well, I do a bit of Scottish folk-singing, for festivals and *ceilidhs* – Highland Games and the like. I'm on to do a turn at a Celtic festival up in the mountains at the end of the week, is all.'

'Scottish singing? Do you wear a kilt when you sing?' Gayle had popped up on Roger's other side.

'I do indeed. How else would they know I was a Scotsman?'

'I just love fuzzy knees,' Gayle said dreamily. 'Now, tell me, is it true about what a Scotsman –'

'Go get the car,' Brianna ordered, hastily thrusting her keys at Gayle.

Gayle perched her chin on the windowsill of the car, watching Roger make his way into the hotel. 'Gee, I hope he doesn't shave before he meets us for dinner. I just love the way men look when they haven't shaved for a while. What do you think's in that big box?'

'His bodhran. I asked.'

'His *what?*'

'It's a Celtic war drum. He plays it with some of his songs.'

Gayle's lips formed a small circle of speculation.

'I don't suppose you want me to drive him to this festival thing, do you? I mean, you must have lots of things to do, and –'

'Ha ha. You think I'd let you anywhere around him in a kilt?'

Gayle sighed wistfully, and pulled her head in as Brianna started the car.

'Well, maybe there'd be other men there in kilts.'

'I think that's pretty likely.'

'I bet they don't have Celtic war drums, though.'

'Maybe not.'

Gayle leaned back in her seat, and glanced at her friend. 'So, are you going to do it?'

'How should I know?' But the blood bloomed under her skin, and her clothes felt too tight.

'Well, if you don't,' Gayle said positively, 'you're crazy.'

'The Minister's cat is an . . . androgynous cat.'

'The Minister's cat is an . . . alagruous cat.'

Bree gave him a lifted brow, taking her eyes briefly off the road.

'Scots again?'

'It's a Scottish game,' Roger said. 'Alagruous – "grim or woebegone". Your turn. Letter "B".'

She squinted through the windshield at the narrow mountain road. The morning sun was toward them, filling the car with light.

'The Minister's cat is a brindled cat.'

'The Minister's cat is a bonnie cat.'

'Well, that's a soft pitch for both of us. Draw. Okay, the Minister's cat is a . . .' He could see the wheels turning in her mind, then the gleam in her narrowed blue eyes as inspiration struck. ' . . . coccygodynious cat.'

Roger narrowed his own eyes, trying to work that one out.

'A cat that's a pain in the ass.'

'That's a real word, is it?'

76

'Uh-huh.' She accelerated neatly out of the turn. 'One of Mama's medical terms. Coccygodynia is a pain in the region of the tailbone. She used to call the hospital administration coccygodynians, all the time.'

'And here I thought it was one of your engineering terms. All right, then . . . the Minister's cat is a camstairy cat.' He grinned at her lifted eyebrow. 'Quarrelsome. Coccygodynians are camstairy by nature.'

'Okay, I'll call that one a draw. The Minister's cat is . . .'

'Wait,' Roger interrupted, pointing. 'There's the turn.'

Slowing, she pulled off the narrow highway and onto a still narrower road, indicated by a small red-and-white-arrowed sign that read CELTIC FESTIVAL.

'You're a love to bring to me all the way up here,' Roger said. 'I didn't realize how far it was, or I'd never have asked.'

She gave him a brief glance of amusement.

'It's not that far.'

'It's a hundred and fifty miles!'

She smiled, but with a wry edge to it.

'My father always said that was the difference between an American and an Englishman. An Englishman thinks a hundred miles is a long way; an American thinks a hundred years is a long time.'

Roger laughed, taken by surprise.

'Too right. You'll be an American, then, I suppose?'

'I suppose.' But her smile had faded.

So had the conversation; they drove in silence for a few minutes, with no sound but the rush of tires and wind. It was a beautiful hot summer's day, the mugginess of Boston left far below as they snaked their way upward, into the clearer air of the mountains.

'The Minister's cat is a distant cat,' Roger said at last, softly. 'Have I said something wrong?'

She flashed him a quick blue glance, and a half-curled mouth.

'The Minister's cat is a daydreaming cat. No, it's not you.' Her lips compressed as she slowed behind another car, then relaxed. 'No, that's not right – it *is* you, but it's not your fault.'

Roger shifted, turning in his seat to face her.

77

'The Minister's cat is an enigmatic cat.'

'The Minister's cat is an embarrassed cat – I shouldn't have said anything, sorry.'

Roger was wise enough not to press her. Instead, he leaned forward and dug under the seat for the thermos of hot tea with lemon.

'Want some?' He offered her the cup, but she made a small face and shook her head.

'No thanks. I hate tea.'

'Definitely not an Englishwoman, then,' he said, and wished he hadn't; her hands squeezed tight on the wheel. She didn't say anything, though, and he drank the tea in silence, watching her.

She didn't look English, her parentage and coloring notwithstanding. He couldn't tell whether the difference was more than a matter of clothes, but he thought so. Americans seemed so much more . . . what? Vibrant? Intense? Bigger? Just *more*. Brianna Randall was definitely more.

The traffic grew thicker, slowing to a crawling line of cars as they reached the entrance to the resort where the festival was being held.

'Look,' Brianna said abruptly. She didn't turn toward him, but stared out through the windshield at the New Jersey license plate of the car in front of them. 'I have to explain.'

'Not to me.'

She flicked one red eyebrow in brief irritation.

'To who else?' She pressed her lips together and sighed. 'Yeah, all right, me too. But I do.'

Roger could taste the acid from the tea, bitter in the back of his throat. Was this where she told him it had been a mistake for him to come? He'd thought so himself, all the way across the Atlantic, twitching and cramped in the tiny airline seat. Then he'd seen her across the airport lobby, and all doubt had vanished on the instant.

It hadn't come back during the intervening week, either; he'd seen her at least briefly every day – even managed a baseball game with her at Fenway Park on Thursday afternoon. He'd found the game itself baffling, but Brianna's enthusiasm for it enchanting. He found himself counting the hours left before he'd have to leave, and looking forward nonetheless to this – the only whole day they'd have together.

That didn't mean she felt the same. He glanced quickly over the line of cars; the gate was visible, but still a quarter-mile off. He had maybe three minutes to convince her.

'In Scotland,' she was saying, 'when all – that – happened with my mother. You were great, Roger – really wonderful.' She didn't look at him, but he could see a shimmer of moisture just above the thick auburn lashes.

'It was no great thing to do,' he said. He curled his hands into fists to keep from touching her. 'I was interested.'

She laughed shortly.

'Yeah, I bet you were.' She slowed, and turned her head to look at him, full-on. Even wide open, her eyes had a faint catlike slant to them.

'Have you been back to the stone circle? To Craigh na Dun?'

'No,' he said shortly. Then coughed and added, as if casually, 'I don't go up to Inverness all that often; it's been term time at College.'

'It isn't that the Minister's cat is a fraidycat?' she asked, but she smiled slightly when she said it.

'The Minister's cat is scared stiff of that place,' he said frankly. 'He wouldn't set foot up there if it were knee-deep in sardines.' She laughed outright, and the tension between them eased noticeably.

'Me too,' she said, and took a deep breath. 'But I remember. All the trouble you went to, to help – and then, when it – when she – when Mama went through –' Her teeth clamped savagely on her lower lip, and she hit the brake, harder than necessary.

'Do you see?' she said, in a small voice. 'I can't be around you more than half an hour, and it all comes back. I haven't talked about my parents in more than six months, and no sooner do we start playing that silly game than I've mentioned both of them in less than a minute. It's been happening all week.'

She thumbed a loose strand of red hair off her shoulder.

She went a lovely pink when she was excited or upset, and the color was burning high in her cheeks.

'I thought it might be something like that – when you didn't answer my letter.'

'It wasn't only that.' She caught her lower lip between her teeth, as though to bite back the words, but it was too late. A brilliant tide of red washed up out of the V of her white T-shirt, turning her the color of the tomato sauce she insisted on eating with chips.

He reached across the seat and gently brushed the veil of hair back from her face.

'I had a terrible crush on you,' she blurted, staring straight ahead through the windshield. 'But I didn't know whether you were just being nice to me because Mama asked you to, or whether –'

'Whether,' he interrupted, and smiled as she risked a tiny look at him. 'Definitely whether.'

'Oh.' She relaxed fractionally, loosening her stranglehold on the wheel. 'Well. Good.'

He wanted to take her hand, but didn't want to pry it off the wheel and cause an accident. Instead, he laid his arm across the back of the seat, letting his fingers brush her shoulder.

'Anyway. I didn't think – I thought – well, it was either throw myself into your arms or get the hell out of Dodge. So I did, but I couldn't figure out how to explain without looking like an idiot, and then when you wrote, it was worse – well, see, I *do* look like an idiot!'

Roger flipped open the catch of his seat belt.

'Will you drive into that car in front of us if I kiss you?'

'No.'

'Good.' He slid across the seat, took her chin in one hand, and kissed her, fast. They bumped sedately over the dirt road and into the parking lot.

She was breathing easier, and her color had receded a little. She pulled neatly into a parking slot, killed the motor, and sat for a moment, looking straight ahead. Then she opened her seat belt and turned to him.

It wasn't until they got out of the car several minutes later that it occurred to Roger that she had mentioned her parents more than once – but the real problem had likely more to do with the parent she so carefully *hadn't* mentioned.

Great, he thought, absently admiring her backside as she bent to open the trunk. *She's trying not to think of Jamie Fraser, and where the hell do* you *bring her?* He glanced at the entrance to the resort, where the Union Jack and the Saltire of Scotland snapped in the summer breeze. From the mountainside beyond came the mournful sound of bagpipes playing.

4

A Blast From the Past

Used as he was to changing in the back of someone's horse van or in the Gents' facilities of a pub, the small backstage cubicle allotted to Roger's personal use seemed remarkably luxurious. It was clean, it had hooks for his street clothes, and there were no drunken patrons snoring on the threshold. Of course, this was America, he reflected, unbuttoning his jeans and dropping them on the floor. Different standards, at least with regard to material comforts.

He yanked the bell-sleeved shirt over his head, wondering just what level of comfort Brianna was accustomed to. He was no judge of women's clothing – how expensive could blue jeans possibly be? – but he knew a bit about cars. Hers was a brand-new blue Mustang that made him itch to take the wheel.

Plainly her parents had left her enough to live on; he could trust Claire Randall to have seen to that. He only hoped it wasn't so much that she might think him interested on that account. Reminded of her parents, he glanced at the brown envelope; should he give it to her, after all?

The Minister's cat had nearly jumped out of her skin when they'd walked through the performers' entrance and come face-to-face with the 78th Fraser Highlanders' pipe-band from Canada, practicing at full blast behind the dressing rooms. She'd actually gone pale when he'd introduced her to the pipe major, an old acquaintance. Not that Bill Livingstone was intimidating on his own; it was the Fraser clan badge on his chest that had done it.

Je suis prest, it said. *I am ready.* Not nearly ready enough, Roger thought, and wanted to kick himself for bringing her.

Still, she had assured him she'd be all right exploring on her own while he dressed and got himself up for his turn.

And he'd best turn his mind to that, too, he thought, snugging the buckles of his kilt at waist and hip, and reaching for the long woolen stockings. He was on in the early afternoon, for forty-five minutes, then a shorter solo turn at the evening *ceilidh*. He had a rough lineup of songs in mind, but you always had to take the crowd into account. Lots of women, the ballads went well; more men, more of the martial – 'Killiecrankie' and 'Montrose', 'Guns and Drums'. The bawdy songs did best when the audience was well warmed up – preferably after a bit of beer.

He turned the stocking tops down neatly, and slid the antler-handled *sgian dhu* inside, tight against his right calf. He laced the buskins quickly hurrying a little. He wanted to find Brianna again, have a little time to walk round with her, get her something to eat, see she had a good seat for the performances.

He flung the plaid over one shoulder, fastened his brooch, belted on dirk and sporran, and was ready. Or not quite. He halted, halfway to the door.

The ancient olive-drab drawers were military issue, circa World War II – one of Roger's few mementos of his father. He didn't bother with pants much in the normal course, but included these with his kilt sometimes as a defensive measure against the amazing boldness of some female spectators. He'd been warned by other performers, but wouldn't have believed it, had he not experienced it first-hand. German ladies were the worst, but he'd known a few American women run them a close second for taking liberties in close quarters.

He didn't think he'd need such measures here; the crowd sounded civil, and he'd seen that the stage was safely out of reach. Besides, offstage he'd have Brianna with him, and if she should choose to take any liberties of her own . . . He dropped the pants back in his bag, on top of the brown envelope.

'Wish me luck, Dad,' he whispered, and went to find her.

'Wow!' She walked round him in a circle, goggling. 'Roger, you are *gorgeous*!' She smiled, a trifle lopsided. 'My mother always said men in kilts were irresistible. I guess she was right.'

He saw her swallow hard, and wanted to hug her for her bravery, but she had already turned away, gesturing toward the main food area.

'Are you hungry? I had a look while you were changing. We've got our choice between octopus-on-a-stick, Baja fish tacos, Polish dogs –'

He took her arm and pulled her round to face him.

'Hey,' he said softly. 'I'm sorry; I wouldn't have brought you if I'd known it would be a shock.'

'It's all right.' Her smile was better this time. 'It's – I'm glad you brought me.'

'Truly?'

'Yeah. Really. It's –' She waved helplessly at the tartan swirl of noise and color all around them. 'It's so – Scottish.'

He wanted to laugh at that; nothing could be less like Scotland than this mix of tourist claptrap and the bald-faced selling of half-faked traditions. At the same time, she was right, it *was* uniquely Scottish; an example of the Scots' age-old talent for survival – the ability to adapt to anything, and make a profit from it.

He did hug her, then. Her hair smelled clean, like fresh grass, and he could feel her heart beating through the white T-shirt she wore.

'You're Scots, too, you know,' he said in her ear, and let go. Her eyes were still bright, but with a different emotion now, he thought.

'I guess you're right,' she said, and smiled again, a good one. 'That doesn't mean I have to eat haggis, does it? I saw some over there, and I think I'd even rather try the octopus-on-a-stick.'

He'd thought she was joking, but she wasn't. The resort's sole business, it seemed, was 'ethnic fairs', as one of the food vendors explained.

'Polacks dancin' polkas, Swiss yodelers – Jeez, they musta had ten million cuckoo clocks here! Spanish, Italian, Japanese cherry blossom festivals – you wouldn't believe all the cameras them Japs have, you just wouldn't believe it.' He shook his head in bemusement, sliding across two paper plates filled with hamburgers and french fries.

'Anyways, it's something different, every two weeks. Never a dull moment. But us food vendors, we just stay in business, no matter what kinda food it is.' The man eyed Roger's kilt with some interest.

'So, you Scotch, or you just like wearing a skirt?'

Having heard several dozen variations of that pleasantry, Roger gave the man a bland look.

'Well, as my auld grand-da used to say,' he said, thickening his accent atrociously, 'when ye put on yer kilt, laddie, ye ken for sure yer a Man!'

The man doubled up appreciatively, and Brianna rolled her eyes.

'Kilt jokes,' she muttered. 'God, if you start telling kilt jokes, I'll drive off and leave you, I swear I will.'

Roger grinned at her.

'Och, now, ye wouldna do that, would ye, lass? Go off and leave a man, only because he'll tell ye what's worn under the kilt, if ye like?'

Her eyes narrowed into blue triangles.

'Oh, I'd bet nothing at all's worn under *that* kilt,' she said, with a nod at Roger's sporran. 'Why, I'll bet everything under there is in pairrrrrfect operrrating condition, no?'

Roger choked on a french fry.

'You're s'posed to say, "Give us your hand, lassie, and I'll show you," ' the food vendor prompted. 'Boy, if I've heard that one once, I've heard it a hunderd times this week.'

'If he says it now,' Brianna put in darkly, 'I'll drive off and leave him marooned on this mountain. He can stay here and eat octopus, for all I care.'

Roger took a gulp of Coca-Cola and wisely kept quiet.

There was time for a wander up and down the aisles of the vendors' stalls, selling everything from tartan ties to penny whistles, silver jewelry, clan maps of Scotland, butterscotch and shortbread, letter openers in the shape of claymores, lead Highlander figures, books, records, and every imaginable small item on which a clan badge or motto could be imprinted.

Roger attracted no more than a brief glance of curiosity; while of better quality than most, his costume was no oddity here. Still, most of the crowd were tourists, dressed in shorts and jeans, but breaking out here and there in bits of tartan, like a rash.

'Why MacKenzie?' Brianna asked, pausing by one display of clanmarked keychains. She fingered one of the silver disks that read *Luceo non uro,* the Latin motto curved around a depiction of what looked like a volcano. 'Didn't Wakefield sound Scottish enough? Or did you think the people at Oxford wouldn't like you doing – this?' She waved at the venue around them.

Roger shrugged.

'Partly that. But it's my family name, as well. Both my parents were killed during the war, and my great-uncle adopted me. He gave me his own name – but I was christened Roger Jeremiah MacKenzie.'

'Jeremiah?' She didn't laugh out loud, but the end of her nose pinkened as though she was trying not to. 'Like the Old Testament prophet?'

'Don't laugh,' he said, taking her arm. 'I was named for my father – they called him Jerry. My Mum called me Jemmy when I was small. Old family name. It could have been worse, after all; I might have been christened Ambrose or Conan.'

The laughter fizzed out of her like Coke bubbles.

'Conan?'

'Perfectly good Celtic name, before the fantasists got hold of it. Anyway, Jeremiah seems to have been the pick of the lot for good cause.'

'Why's that?'

They turned and headed slowly back toward the stage, where a gang of solemnly starched little girls were doing the Highland fling in perfect unison, every pleat and bow in place.

'Oh, it's one of the stories Dad – the Reverend, I always called him Dad – used to tell me, going down my family tree and pointing out the folk on it.'

Ambrose MacKenzie, that's your great-grandfather, Rog. He'll have been a boatwright in Dingwall. And there's Mary Oliphant – I knew your great-grandma Oliphant, did I tell you? Lived to be

86

ninety-seven, and sharp as a tack to her last breath; wonderful woman.

She was married six times – all died of natural causes, too, she assured me – but I've only put Jeremiah MacKenzie here, since he was your ancestor. The only one she had children by, I did wonder about that.

I asked her, and she closed one eye and nodded at me, and said, 'Is fhearr an giomach na 'bhi gun fear tighe.' *It's an old Gaelic proverb – 'Better a lobster than no husband.' She said some would do for marrying, but Jeremiah was the only lad bonny enough to take to her bed every night.*

'I wonder what she told the others,' Brianna said, meditatively.

'Well, she didn't say she didn't sleep with them now and then,' Roger pointed out. 'Just not every night.'

'Once is enough to get pregnant,' Brianna said. 'Or so my mother assured my high school health class. She'd draw pictures of sperm on the blackboard, all racing toward this huge egg with leers on their faces.' She'd gone pink again, but evidently from amusement rather than distressed memory.

Arm in arm, he could feel the heat of her through the thin T-shirt, and a stirring under his kilt that made him think leaving the pants off had been a mistake.

'Putting aside the question of whether sperm have faces, what has that particular subject got to do with health?'

'Health is an American euphemism for anything to do with sex,' she explained. 'They teach girls and boys separately; the girls' class is The Mysteries of Life, and Ten Ways to Say No to a Boy.'

'And the boys' class?'

'Well, I don't know for sure, because I didn't have any brothers to tell me. Some of my friends had brothers, though – one of them said they learned eighteen different synonyms for penile erection.'

'Really useful, that,' Roger said, wondering why anyone required more than one. Luckily, a sporran covered a multitude of sins.

'I suppose it might keep the conversation going – under certain circumstances.'

Her cheeks were red. He could feel the heat creeping

up his own throat, and imagined that they were beginning to attract curious glances from passersby. He hadn't let a girl embarrass him in public since he was seventeen, but she was doing nicely. She'd started it, though – let her finish it, then.

'Mmphm. I hadn't noticed much conversation, under those particular circumstances.'

'I imagine you'd know.' It wasn't quite a question. Rather late, he realized what she was up to. He tightened his arm, pulling her closer.

'If you mean have I, yes. If you mean am I, no.'

'Are you, what?' Her lips were quivering slightly, holding back the urge to laugh.

'You're asking if I've got a girl in England, right?'

'Am I?'

'I don't. Or rather I do, but nothing serious.' They were outside the door to the dressing rooms; nearly time to fetch his instruments. He stopped and turned to look at her. 'Have you? Got a bloke, I mean.'

She was tall enough to look him in the eye, and close enough that her breasts grazed his forearm when she turned to face him.

'What was it your great-grandmother said? "*Is fhearr an giomach . . .*"?'

' " *. . . na 'bhi gun fear tighe.*" '

'Uh-huh. Well, better a lobster than no boyfriend.' She lifted a hand and touched his brooch. 'So yes, there are people I go out with. But I don't have a bonny lad – yet.'

He caught her fingers and brought them to his mouth.

'Give it time, lass,' he said, and kissed them.

The audience was amazingly quiet; not at all like a rock concert. Of course, they couldn't be noisy, she thought; there weren't any electric guitars or amplifiers, only a small microphone on a stand. But then, some things didn't need amplifying. Her heart, for one, hammering in her ears.

'Here,' he'd said, appearing abruptly out of the dressing room with guitar and drum. He'd handed her a small brown envelope. 'I found these, going through my dad's old bumf in Inverness. I thought you'd maybe want them.'

88

She could tell it was photographs, but she hadn't looked at them right away. She'd sat with them burning a hole on her knee, listening to Roger's set.

He was good – even distracted, she could tell he was good. He had a surprisingly rich deep baritone voice, and he knew what to do with it. Not just in terms of tone and melody; he had the true performer's ability to pull aside the curtain between singer and audience, to look out into the crowd, meet someone's eyes, and let them see what lay behind both words and music.

He'd got them going with 'The Road to the Isles', a quick and lively clap-along song with a rousing chorus, and when they'd subsided from that, kept them going with 'The Gallowa' Hills', and a sweet slide into 'The Lewis Bridal Song', with a lovely, lilting chorus in Gaelic.

He let the last note die away on 'Vhair Me Oh', and smiled, directly at her, she thought.

'And here's one from the '45,' he said. 'This one is from the famous battle of Prestonpans, at which the Highland Army of Charles Stuart routed a much greater English force, under the command of General Jonathan Cope.'

There was an appreciative murmur from the crowd, for many of whom the song was plainly an old favorite, quickly shushed as Roger's fingers plucked out the marching line.

> *'Cope sent a challenge from Dunbar*
> *Sayin' "Charlie, meet me, and ye daur*
> *An' I'll learn ye the art o' war*
> *If ye'll meet me in the mornin'." '*

He bent his head over the strings, nodding to the crowd to join in the jeering chorus.

> *'Hey, Johnnie Cope, are ye wakin' yet?*
> *And are your drums a-beatin' yet?*
> *If ye were walkin', I would wait*
> *Tae gang tae the coals in the mornin'!'*

Brianna felt a sudden prickle at the roots of her hair that had nothing to do with singer or crowd, but with the song itself.

'When Charlie looked the letter upon,
He drew his sword the scabbard from,
Come, follow me, my merry men,
And we'll meet Johnnie Cope in the morning!'

'No,' she whispered, her fingers cold on the smooth brown envelope. *Come follow me, my merry men* . . . They'd been there – both her parents. It was her father who had charged the field at Preston, his broadsword and his targe in his hands.

' . . . For it will be a bluidie morning!'

'Hey, Johnnie Cope, are ye walkin' yet?
And are your drums a-beatin' yet? . . .'

The voices rose around her in a roar of approbation as they joined in the chorus. She had a moment of rising panic, when she would have fled away like Johnnie Cope, but it passed, leaving her buffeted by emotion as much as by the music.

'In faith, quo Johnnie, I got sic flegs,
Wi' their claymores an' philabegs,
Gin I face them again, de'il brak my legs,
So I wish you a' good morning!

Hey, Johnnie Cope, are ye walkin' yet? . . .'

Yes, he was. And he would be, as long as that song lasted. Some people tried to preserve the past; others, to escape it. And that was by far the greatest gulf between herself and Roger. Why hadn't she seen it before?

She didn't know whether Roger had seen her momentary distress, but he abandoned the dangerous territory of the Jacobites and went into 'MacPherson's Lament', sung with no more than an occasional touch of the strings. The woman next to Brianna let out a long sigh and looked doe-eyed at the stage.

'Sae rantingly, sae wantonly, sae dauntingly gaed he,

He played a tune and he danced it round . . . alow the gallows tree!'

She picked up the envelope, weighing it on her fingers. She ought to wait, maybe, until she got home. But curiosity was warring with reluctance. Roger hadn't been sure he should give it to her; she'd seen that in his eyes.

' . . . a bodhran,' Roger was saying. The drum was no more than a wooden hoop, a few inches wide, with a skin head stretched over it, some eighteen inches across. He held the drum balanced on the fingers of one hand, a small double-headed stick in the other. 'One of the oldest known instruments, this is the drum with which the Celtic tribes scared the bejesus out of Julius Caesar's troops in 52 BC.' The audience tittered, and he touched the wide drumhead with the stick, back and forth in a soft, quick rhythm like a heartbeat.

'And here's "The Sheriffmuir Fight", from the first Jacobite Rising, in 1715.'

The drumhead shifted and the beat dropped in pitch, became martial in tone, a thundering behind the words. The audience was still well-behaved, but now sat up and leaned forward, hanging on the chant that described the battle of Sheriffmuir, and all the clans who had fought in it.

' . . . *then on they rushed, and blood out-gushed, and many a puke did fall, man . . .*
They backed and hashed, while broadswords clashed . . .'

As the song ended she put her fingers inside the envelope and pulled out a set of photographs. Old snapshots, black-and-white faded to tones of brown. Her parents. Frank and Claire Randall, both looking absurdly young – and terribly happy.

They were in a garden somewhere; there were lawn chairs, and a table with drinks in a background dappled with the scattered light of tree leaves. The faces showed clearly, though – laughing, faces alight with youth, eyes only for each other.

Posing formally, arm in arm, mocking their own for-

91

mality. Laughing, Claire half bent over with hilarity at something Frank had said, holding down a wide skirt flying in the wind, her curly hair suffering no such restraint. Frank handing Claire a cup, she looking up into his face as she took it, with such a look of hope and trust that Brianna's heart squeezed tight to see it.

Then she looked at the last of the pictures, and realized what she was looking at. The two of them stood by the table, hands together on a knife, laughing as they cut into an obviously homemade cake. A wedding cake.

'And for the last, an old favorite that you'll know. This song is said to have been sent by a Jacobite prisoner, on his way to London to be hanged, to his wife in the Highlands . . .'

She spread her hands out flat on top of the pictures, as though to keep anyone from seeing them. An icy shock went through her. Wedding pictures. Snapshots of their wedding day. Of course; they'd been married in Scotland. The Reverend Wakefield wouldn't have done the ceremony, not being a Catholic priest, but he was one of her father's oldest friends; the reception must have been held at the manse.

Yes. Peeking through her fingers, she could make out familiar bits of the old house in the background. Then, reluctantly sliding her hand aside, she looked again at her mother's young face.

Eighteen. Claire had married Frank Randall at eighteen – perhaps that explained it. How could anyone know their mind so young?

'By yon bonnie banks, and by yon bonnie braes,
Where the sun shines bright on Loch Lomond,
Where me and my true love were ever wont to gae . . .'

But Claire had been sure – or she'd thought so. The broad, clear brow and delicate mouth admitted of no doubt; the big, luminous eyes were fixed on her new husband with no sign of reservation or misgiving. And yet –

92

'But me and my true love will never meet again
On the bonnie, bonnie banks of Loch Lomond.'

Oblivious of the toes she stepped on, Brianna blundered out of the row and fled, before anyone should see the tears.

'I can stay with you through part of the calling of the clans,' Roger said, 'but I've a bit to do at the end of it, so I'll have to leave you. Will you be all right?'

'Yes, of course,' she said firmly. 'I'm fine. Don't worry.'

He looked at her a little anxiously, but let it pass. Neither of them had mentioned her precipitous departure earlier; by the time he had made his way through the congratulatory well-wishers and gone to find her, she had had time to find a Ladies' and get herself under control with cold water.

They had spent the rest of the afternoon strolling through the festival, shopping a bit, going outside to watch the pipe-bands' competition, coming in half deafened to see a young man dance between two swords crossed on the ground. The photographs stayed safely out of sight in her handbag.

It was nearly dark now; people were leaving the eating area and heading for the open stands outside, at the foot of the mountain.

She had thought the families with young children would leave, and some did, but there were small bodies and sleepy heads drooping among the older people in the stands. A tiny girl lay limp, sound asleep on her father's shoulder as they made their way into one of the upper rows of the stands. There was a clear, flat space in front of the bleachers, in which a huge heap of wood had been piled.

'What's the calling of the clans?' she heard a woman ask her companion in the row ahead. The companion shrugged, and Brianna looked at Roger for enlightenment, but he only smiled.

'You'll see,' he said.

It was full dark, and the moon not risen; the bulk of the mountainside rose up as a darker black against the star-

93

flecked sky. There was an exclamation from somewhere in the crowd, a scattering of more, and then the notes of a single bagpipe came faintly through the air, silencing everything else.

A pinpoint of light appeared near the top of the mountain. As they watched, it moved down, and another sprang up behind it. The music grew stronger, and another light came over the top of the mountain. For nearly ten minutes, the anticipation grew, as the music grew louder, and the string of lights grew longer, a blazing chain down the mountainside.

Near the bottom of the slope, a trail came out from the trees above; she had seen it during her earlier exploration. Now a man stepped out of the trees into sight, holding a blazing torch above his head. Behind him was the piper, and the sound now was strong enough to drown even the oohs and ahhs of the crowd.

As the two moved down the trail and toward the cleared space in front of the bleachers, Brianna could see that there were more men behind them; a long line of men, each with a torch, all dressed in the finery of the Highland chieftains. They were barbarous and splendid, decked in grouse feathers, the silver of swords and dirks gleaming red by the torchlight, picked out amid the folds of tartan cloth.

The pipes stopped abruptly, and the first of the men strode into the clearing and stopped before the stands. He raised his torch above his head and shouted, 'The Camerons are here!'

Loud whoops of delight rang out from the stands, and he threw the torch into the kerosene-soaked wood, which went up with a roar, in a pillar of fire ten feet high.

Against the blinding sheet of flame, another man stepped out, and called, 'The MacDonalds are here!'

Screams and yelps from those in the crowd that claimed kinship with clan MacDonald, and then –

'The MacLachlans are here!'

'The MacGillivrays are here!'

She was so entranced by the spectacle that she was only dimly aware of Roger. Then another man stepped out and cried, 'The MacKenzies are here!'

94

'*Tulach Ard!*' bellowed Roger, making her jump.

'What was *that*?' she asked.

'That,' he said, grinning, 'is the war cry of clan MacKenzie.'

'Sounded like it.'

'The Campbells are here!' There must have been a lot of Campbells; the response shook the bleachers. As though that was the signal he had been waiting for, Roger stood up and flung his plaid over his shoulder.

'I'll meet you afterward by the dressing rooms, all right?' She nodded, and he bent suddenly and kissed her.

'Just in case,' he said. 'The Frasers' cry is *Caisteal Dhuni!*'

She watched him go, climbing down the bleachers like a mountain goat. The smell of woodsmoke filled the night air, mixing with the smaller fragrance of tobacco from cigarettes in the crowd.

'The MacKays are here!'

'The MacLeods are here!'

'The Farquarsons are here!'

Her chest felt tight, from the smoke and from emotion. The clans had died at Culloden – or had they? Yes, they had; this was no more than memory, than the calling up of ghosts; none of the people shouting so enthusiastically owed kinship to each other, none of them lived any longer by the claims of laird and land, but . . .

'The Frasers are here!'

Sheer panic gripped her, and her hand closed tight on the clasp of her bag.

No, she thought. *Oh, no. I'm not.*

Then the moment passed, and she could breathe again, but jolts of adrenaline still thrilled through her blood.

'The Grahams are here!'

'The Inneses are here!'

The Ogilvys, the Lindsays, the Gordons . . . and then finally, the echoes of the last shout died. Brianna held the bag on her lap, gripped tight, as though to keep its contents from escaping like the jinn from a lamp.

How could she? she thought, and then, seeing Roger come into the light, fire on his head and his bodhran in his hand, thought again, *How could she help it?*

5

Two Hundred Years From Yesterday

'You didn't wear your kilt!' Gayle's mouth turned down in disappointment.

'Wrong century,' Roger said, smiling down at her. 'Drafty for a moonwalk.'

'You have to teach me to do that.' She bounced on her toes, leaning toward him.

'Do what?'

'Roll your r's like that.' She puckered her brows and made an earnest attempt, sounding like a motorboat in low gear.

'Verra nice,' he said, trying not to laugh. 'Keep it up. Prractice makes perfect.'

'Well, did you bring your guitar, at least?' She stood on tiptoes, trying to look behind him. 'Or that groovy drum?'

'It's in the car,' Brianna said, putting away her keys as she came up beside Roger. 'We're going to the airport from here.'

'Oh, too bad; I thought we could hang around and have a hootenanny afterward, to celebrate. Do you know "This Land Is Your Land", Roger? Or are you more into protest songs? But I guess you wouldn't be, since you're English – oops, I mean Scotch. You guys don't have anything to protest about, do you?'

Brianna gave her friend a look of mild exasperation. 'Where's Uncle Joe?'

'In the living room, kicking the TV,' Gayle said. 'Shall I entertain Roger while you find him?' She linked one arm cosily through Roger's, batting her eyelashes.

'We got half the doggone MIT College of Engineering here, and nobody who can fix a doggone *television*?' Dr. Joseph Abernathy glared accusingly at the clusters of young people scattered around his living room.

'That's *electrical* engineering, Pop,' his son told him loftily. 'We're all mechanical engineers. Ask a mechanical engineer to fix your color TV, that's like asking an Ob-Gyn to look at the score on your di – ow!'

'Oh, sorry,' said his father, peering blandly over gold-rimmed glasses. 'That your foot, Lenny?'

Lenny hopped storklike around the room to general laughter, clutching one large sneaker-clad foot in exaggerated agony.

'Bree, honey!' The doctor spotted her and abandoned the television, beaming. He hugged her enthusiastically, disregarding the fact that she topped him by four inches or so, then let go and looked at Roger, his features rearranged in a look of wary cordiality.

'This the boyfriend?'

'This is Roger Wakefield,' Brianna said, narrowing her eyes slightly at the doctor. 'Roger, Joe Abernathy.'

'Dr. Abernathy.'

'Call me Joe.'

They shook hands in mutual assessment. The doctor looked him over with quick brown eyes, no less shrewd for their warmth.

'Bree, honey, you want to go lay hands on that piece of junk, see can you bring it back to life?' He jerked a thumb at the twenty-four-inch RCA sitting in mute defiance on its wire stand. 'It was working fine last night, then today . . . pffft!'

Brianna looked dubiously at the big color TV, and groped in the pocket of her jeans, coming out with a Swiss Army knife.

'Well, I can check the connections, I guess.' She flicked out the screwdriver blade. 'How much time do we have?'

'Half hour, maybe,' called a crew-cut student from the kitchen doorway. He glanced at the crowd clustered around the small black-and-white set on the table. 'We're still with Mission Control in Houston – ETA thirty-four minutes.' The muted excitement of the TV commentator came in bursts through the more vivid excitement of the spectators.

'Good, good,' said Dr. Abernathy. He laid a hand on Roger's shoulder. 'Plenty of time for a drink, then. You a Scotch man, Mr. Wakefield?'

'Call me Roger.'

97

Abernathy poured a generous measure of amber nectar and handed it over.

'Don't imagine you take water, do you, Roger?'

'No.' It was Lagavulin; astonishing to find it in Boston. He sipped appreciatively, and the doctor smiled.

'Claire gave it to me – Bree's mama. Now, there was a woman with a taste for fine whisky.' He shook his head nostalgically, and raised his glass in tribute.

'*Slàinte*,' Roger said quietly, and tipped his own glass before drinking.

Abernathy closed his eyes in silent appreciation – whether of the whisky or the woman, Roger couldn't tell.

'Water of life, huh? I do believe that particular stuff could raise the dead.' He set the bottle back in the liquor cabinet with reverent hands.

How much had Claire told Abernathy? Enough, Roger supposed. The doctor picked up his tumbler and gave him a long look of assessment.

'Since Bree's daddy is dead, I guess I get to do the honors. Reckon we got time for the third degree before they land, or shall we keep it short?'

Roger raised one eyebrow.

'Your intentions,' the doctor elaborated.

'Oh. Strictly honorable.'

'Yeah? I called Bree last night, to see if she was coming tonight. No answer.'

'We'd gone to a Celtic festival, up in the mountains.'

'Uh-huh. I called again, eleven p.m. And midnight. No answer.' The doctor's eyes were still shrewd, but a good deal less warm. He set his glass down with a small click.

'Bree's alone,' he said. 'And she's lonely. And she's lovely. I wouldn't like to see anybody take advantage of that, Mr. Wakefield.'

'Neither would I – Dr. Abernathy.' Roger drained his glass and set it down hard. Warmth burned in his cheeks, and it wasn't due to the Lagavulin. 'If you think that I –'

'THIS IS HOUSTON,' boomed the television. 'TRANQUILITY BASE, WE HAVE TOUCH-DOWN IN TWENTY MINUTES.'

The inhabitants of the kitchen came pouring out, waving Coke bottles and cheering. Brianna, flushed with her labors, was laughing and brushing off their congratulations as she put away her knife. Abernathy put a hand on Roger's arm, to keep him.

'Mind me, Mr. Wakefield,' Abernathy said, his voice low enough not to be heard over the crowd. 'I don't want to hear that you've made that girl unhappy. Ever.'

Roger carefully released his arm from the other's grip.

'D'ye think she looks unhappy?' he asked, as politely as he could.

'No-oo,' said Abernathy, rocking back on his heels and squinting hard at him. 'On the contrary. It's the way she looks tonight that makes me think I should maybe punch you in the nose, on her daddy's behalf.'

Roger couldn't help turning to look at her himself; it was true. She had dark circles under her eyes, wisps of hair were coming down from her ponytail, and her skin was glowing like the wax of a lighted candle. She looked like a woman who'd had a long night – and enjoyed it.

As though by radar, her head turned and her eyes fixed on him, over Gayle's head. She went on talking to Gayle, but her eyes spoke straight to him.

The doctor cleared his throat loudly. Roger jerked his attention away from her, to find Abernathy looking up at him, his expression thoughtful.

'Oh,' the doctor said, in a changed tone. 'Like that, is it?'

Roger's collar was unbuttoned, but he felt as though he were wearing a tie tied too tight. He met the doctor's eyes straight on.

'Yeah,' he said. 'Like that.'

Dr. Abernathy reached for the bottle of Lagavulin, and filled both glasses.

'Claire did say she liked you,' he said in resignation. He lifted one glass. 'Okay. *Slàinte.*'

'Turn it the other way – Walter Cronkite's orange!' Lenny Abernathy obligingly twirled the knob, turning the commentator green. Unaffected by his sudden change of complexion, Cronkite went on talking.

'*In approximately two minutes, Commander Neil Armstrong*

99

and the crew of the Apollo 11 will make history in the first manned landing on the moon . . .'

The living room was darkened and packed with people, everyone's attention riveted on the big TV as the footage shifted to a replay of the Apollo's launch.

'I'm impressed,' Roger said in Brianna's ear. 'How did you fix it?' He leaned against the end of a bookshelf, and pulled her snug against him, his hands on the swell of her hips, his chin on her shoulder.

Her eyes were on the television, but he felt her cheek move against his own.

'Somebody kicked the plug out of the wall,' she said. 'I just plugged it back in.'

He laughed and kissed the side of her neck. It was hot in the room, even with the air conditioner humming, and her skin tasted moist and salty.

'You've got the roundest arse in the world,' he whispered. She didn't answer, but deliberately nestled her bottom against him.

A buzz of voices from the screen and pictures of the flag the astronauts would plant on the moon.

He glanced across the room, but Joe Abernathy was as hypnotized as any of them, face rapt in the glow of the television screen. Safe in the darkness, he wrapped his arms around Brianna, and felt the soft weight of her breasts on his forearm. She sighed deeply and relaxed against him, putting her hand over his and squeezing tight.

They would both be less bold if there were any danger to it. But he was leaving in two hours; there was no chance of it going further. The night before, they had known they were playing with dynamite, and been more cautious. He wondered if Abernathy would actually have punched him, had he admitted that Brianna had spent the night in his bed?

He had driven them down the mountain, torn between trying to stay on the right side of the road, and the excitement of Brianna's soft weight, pressed against him. They'd stopped for coffee, talked long past midnight, touching constantly, hands, thighs, heads close together.

100

Driven on to Boston in the wee hours, the conversation dying, Brianna's head heavy on his shoulder.

Unable to keep awake long enough to find his way through the maze of unfamiliar streets to her apartment, he had driven to his hotel, smuggled her upstairs, and laid her on his bed, where she had fallen asleep in seconds.

He had himself spent the rest of the night on the chaste hardness of the floor, Brianna's woolly cardigan across his shoulders for warmth. With the dawn, he'd got up and sat in the chair, wrapped in her scent, silently watching the light spread across her sleeping face.

Yeah, it was like that.

'*Tranquility Base . . . the Eagle has landed.*' The silence in the room was broken by a deep collective sigh, and Roger felt the hair rise on the back of his neck.

'*One . . . small . . . step for man,*' said the tinny voice, '*one giant leap . . . for mankind.*' The picture was fuzzy, but not through any fault of the television. Heads strained forward, avid to see the bulky figure making its ginger way down the ladder, setting foot for the first time on the lunar soil. Tears gleamed on one girl's cheeks, silver in the glow.

Even Brianna had forgotten everything else; her hand had fallen from his arm and she was leaning forward, caught up in the moment.

It was a fine day to be an American.

He had a momentary qualm, seeing them all so fiercely intent, so fervently proud, and she so much a part of it. It *was* a different century, two hundred years from yesterday.

Might there be common ground for them, a historian and an engineer? He facing backward to the mysteries of the past, she to the future and its dazzling gleam?

Then the room relaxed in cheers and babbling, and she turned in his arms to kiss him hard and cling to him, and he thought perhaps it didn't matter that they faced in opposite directions – so long as they faced each other.

101

PART THREE

Pirates

6

I Encounter a Hernia

June 1767

'I hate boats,' Jamie said through clenched teeth. 'I loathe boats. I view boats with the most profound abhorrence.'

Jamie's uncle, Hector Cameron, lived on a plantation called River Run, just above Cross Creek. Cross Creek in turn lay some way upriver from Wilmington; some two hundred miles, in fact. At this time of year, we were told, the trip might take four days to a week by boat, depending on wind. If we chose rather to travel overland, the journey could take two weeks or more, depending on such things as washed-out roads, mud, and broken axles.

'Rivers do not have waves,' I said. 'And I view the notion of trudging on foot for two hundred miles through the mud with a lot more than abhorrrrence.' Ian grinned broadly, but quickly exchanged the grin for an expression of bland detachment as Jamie's glare moved in his direction.

'Besides,' I said to Jamie, 'if you get seasick, I still have my needles.' I patted the pocket where my tiny set of gold acupuncture needles rested in their ivory case.

Jamie exhaled strongly through his nose, but said no more. That little matter settled, the major problem remaining was to manage the boat-fare.

We were not rich, but did have a little money, as the result of a spot of good fortune on the road. Gypsying our way north from Charleston, and camping well off the road at night, we had discovered an abandoned homestead in the wood, its clearing nearly obliterated by new growth.

Cottonwood saplings shot like spears through the beams of the fallen roof, and a hollybush sprouted through a large crack in the hearthstone. The walls were half collapsed, black with rot and furred with green moss and rusty fungus. There was no telling how long the place had been abandoned, but it was clear that both cabin and clearing would be swallowed by the wilderness within a few years, nothing left to mark its existence save a tumbled cairn of chimney stones.

However, flourishing incongruously among the invading trees were the remains of a small peach orchard, the fruit of it burstingly ripe and swarming with bees. We had eaten as much as we could, slept in the shelter of the ruins, then risen before dawn and loaded the wagon with heaping mounds of smooth gold fruit, all juice and velvet.

We had sold it as we went, and consequently had arrived in Wilmington with sticky hands, a bag of coins – mostly pennies – and a pervasive scent of fermentation that clung to hair, clothes, and skin, as though we had all been dipped in peach brandy.

'You take this,' Jamie advised me, handing me the small leather sack containing our fortune. 'Buy what ye can for provisions – dinna buy any peaches, aye? – and perhaps a few bits and pieces so we dinna look *quite* such beggars when we come to my kinsman. A needle and thread, maybe?' He raised a brow and nodded at the large rent in Fergus's coat, incurred while falling out of a peach tree.

'Duncan and I will go about and see can we sell the wagon and horses, and inquire for a boat. And if there's such a thing as a goldsmith here, I'll maybe see what he'd offer for one of the stones.'

'Be careful, Uncle,' Ian advised, frowning at the motley crew of humanity coming and going from the harbour nearby. 'Ye dinna want to be taken advantage of, nor yet be robbed in the street.'

Jamie, gravely straight-faced, assured his nephew that he would take due precaution.

'Take Rollo,' Ian urged him. 'He'll protect ye.'

Jamie glanced down at Rollo, who was surveying the passing crowds with a look of panting alertness that suggested not so much social interest as barely restrained appetite.

'Oh, aye,' he said. 'Come along then, wee dog.' He glanced at me as he turned to go. 'Perhaps ye'd best buy a few dried fish, as well.'

Wilmington was a small town, but because of its fortuitous

situation as a seaport at the mouth of a navigable river, it boasted not only a farmer's market and a shipping dock, but several shops that stocked imported luxuries from Europe, as well as the homegrown necessities of daily life.

'Beans, all right,' Fergus said. 'I like beans, even in large quantities.' He shifted the burlap sack on his shoulder, balancing its unwieldy weight. 'And bread, of course we must have bread – and flour and salt and lard. Salt beef, dried cherries, fresh apples, all well and good. Fish, to be sure. Needles and thread I see also are certainly necessary. Even the hairbrush,' he added, with a sidelong glance at my hair, which, inspired by the humidity, was making mad efforts to escape the confinement of my broad-brimmed hat. 'And the medicines from the apothecary, naturally. But *lace*?'

'Lace,' I said firmly. I tucked the small paper packet containing three yards of Brussels lace into the large basket he was carrying. 'Likewise ribbons. One yard each of wide silk ribbon,' I told the perspiring young girl behind the counter. 'Red – that's yours, Fergus, so don't complain – green for Ian, yellow for Duncan, and the very dark blue for Jamie. And no, it isn't an extravagance; Jamie doesn't want us to look like ragamuffins when we meet his uncle and aunt.'

'What about you, Auntie?' Ian said, grinning. 'Surely ye willna let us men be dandies, and you go plain as a sparrow?'

Fergus blew air between his lips, in mingled exasperation and amusement.

'That one,' he said, pointing to a wide roll of dark pink.

'That's a color for a young girl,' I protested.

'Women are never too old to wear pink,' Fergus replied firmly. 'I have heard *les mesdames* say so, many times.' I had heard *les mesdames'* opinions before; Fergus's early life had been spent in the brothel, and judging from his reminiscences, not a little of his later life, too. I rather hoped that he could overcome the habit now that he was married to Jamie's stepdaughter, but with Marsali still in Jamaica awaiting the birth of their first child, I had my doubts. Fergus was a Frenchman born, after all.

'I suppose the Madams would know,' I said. 'All right, the pink, too.'

Burdened with baskets and bags of provisions, we made our way out into the street. It was hot and thickly humid, but there was a breeze from the river, and after the stifling confines of the shop, the air seemed sweet and refreshing. I glanced toward the harbor, where the masts of several small ships poked up, swaying gently to the rocking of the current, and saw Jamie's tall figure stride out between two buildings, Rollo pacing close behind.

Ian hallooed and waved, and Rollo came bounding down the street, tail wagging madly at sight of his master. There were few people out at this time of day; those with business in the narrow street prudently flattened themselves against the nearest wall to avoid the rapturous reunion.

'My Gawd,' said a drawling voice somewhere above me. 'That'll be the biggest dawg I believe I've *ever* seen.' I turned to see a gentleman detach himself from the front of a tavern, and lift his hat politely to me. 'Your servant, ma'am. He ain't partial to human flesh, I do sincerely hope?'

I looked up at the man addressing me – and up. I refrained from expressing the opinion that he, of all people, could scarcely find Rollo a threat.

My interlocutor was one of the tallest men I'd ever seen; taller by several inches even than Jamie. Lanky and raw-boned with it, his huge hands dangled at the level of my elbows, and the ornately beaded leather belt about his midriff came to my chest. I could have pressed my nose into his navel, had the urge struck me, which fortunately it didn't.

'No, he eats fish,' I assured my new acquaintance. Seeing me craning my neck, he courteously dropped to his haunches, his knee joints popping like rifle shots as he did so. His face thus coming into view, I found his features still obscured by a bushy black beard. An incongruous snub nose poked out of the undergrowth, surmounted by a pair of wide and gentle hazel eyes.

'Well, I'm surely obliged to hear that. Wouldn't care to have a chunk taken out my leg, so early in the day.' He removed a disreputable slouch hat with a ragged turkey feather thrust through the brim, and bowed to me, loose, snaky black locks falling forward on his shoulders. 'John Quincy Myers, your servant, ma'am.'

'Claire Fraser,' I said, offering him a hand in fascination. He squinted at it a moment, brought my fingers to his nose and sniffed them, then looked up and broke into a broad smile, nonetheless charming for missing half its teeth.

'Why, you'll maybe be a yarb-woman, won't you?'

'I will?'

He turned my hand gently over, tracing the chlorophyll stains around my cuticles.

'A green-fingered lady might just be tendin' her roses, but a lady whose hands smell of sassafras root and Jesuit bark is like to know more than how to make flowers bloom. Don't you reckon that's so?' he asked, turning a friendly gaze on Ian, who was viewing Mr. Myers with unconcealed interest.

'Oh, aye,' Ian assured him. 'Auntie Claire's a famous healer. A wisewoman!' He glanced proudly at me.

'That so, boy? Well, now.' Mr. Myers's eyes went round with interest, and swiveled back to focus on me. 'Smite me if this ain't Lucifer's own luck! And me thinkin' I'd have to wait till I come to the mountains and find me a *shaman* to take care of it.'

'Are you ill, Mr. Myers?' I asked. He didn't look it, but it was hard to tell, what with the beard, the hair, and a thin layer of greasy brown dirt that seemed to cover everything not concealed by his ragged buckskins. The sole exception was his forehead; normally protected from the sun by the black felt hat, it was now exposed to view, a wide, flat slab of purest white.

'Not to say ill, I don't reckon,' he replied. He suddenly stood up, and began to fumble up the tail of his buckskin shirt. 'It ain't the clap or the French pox, anyhow, 'cause I seen those before.' What I had thought were trousers were in fact long buckskin leggings, surmounted by a breech-clout. Still talking, Mr. Myers had hold of the leather thong holding up this latter garment, and was fumbling with the knot.

'Damnedest thing, though; all of a sudden this great big swelling come up just along behind of my balls. Purely inconvenient, as you may imagine, though it don't hurt me none to speak of, save on horseback. Might be you could take a peep and tell me what I best do for it, hm?'

'Ah . . .' I said, with a frantic glance at Fergus, who merely shifted his sack of beans and looked amused, blast him.

'Would I have the pleasure to make the acquaintance of Mr. John Mysers?' said a polite Scottish voice over my shoulder.

Mr. Myers ceased fumbling with his breechclout and glanced up inquiringly.

'Can't say whether it's a pleasure to you or not, sir,' he replied courteously. 'But be you lookin' for Myers, you've found him.'

Jamie stepped up beside me, tactfully inserting his body between me and Mr. Myers's breechclout. He bowed formally, hat under his arm.

'James Fraser, your servant, sir. I was told to offer the name of Mr. Hector Cameron by way of introduction.'

Mr. Myers looked at Jamie's red hair with interest.

'Scotch, are you? Be you one of them Highlander fellows?'

'I am a Scotsman, aye, and a Highlander.'

'Be you kin to Old Hector Cameron?'

'He is my uncle by marriage, sir, though I have not met him myself. I was told that he was well known to you, and that you might consent to guide my party to his plantation.'

The two men were frankly sizing each other up, eyes flicking head to toe as they talked, appraising bearing, dress, and armament. Jamie's eyes rested approvingly on the long sheath-knife at the woodsman's belt, while Mr. Myers's nostrils flared wide with interest.

'Comme deux chiens,' Fergus remarked softly behind me. Like two dogs. '. . . aux culs.' Next thing you know, they will be smelling each other's backside.

Mr. Myers darted a glance at Fergus, and I saw a quick flash of amusement in the hazel depths before he returned to his assessment of Jamie. Uncultured the woodsman might be, but he plainly had some working knowledge of French.

Given Mr. Myers's olfactory inclinations and lack of self-consciousness, I might not have been surprised to see him drop to all fours and perform in the manner Fergus had suggested. As it was, he contented himself with a careful inspection that took in not only Jamie but Ian, Fergus, myself, and Rollo.

'Nice dawg,' he said casually, holding out a set of massive knuckles to the latter. Rollo, thus invited, instituted his own inspection, sniffing industriously from moccasins to breechclout as the conversation went on.

'Your uncle, eh? Does he know you're coming?'

Jamie shook his head.

'I canna say. I sent a letter from Georgia, a month ago, but I've no way to tell whether he's had it yet.'

'I shouldn't think so,' Myers said thoughtfully. His eyes lingered on Jamie's face, then passed swiftly over the rest of us.

'I've met your wife. This'll be your son?' He nodded at Ian.

'My nephew, Ian. My foster son, Fergus.' Jamie made the introductions with a wave of his hand. 'And a friend, Duncan Innes, who'll be along presently.'

Myers grunted, nodding, and made up his mind.

'Well, I should reckon I can get you to Cameron's all right. Wanted to be sure you was kin, but you got the look of the widder Cameron, in the face. The boy some, too.'

Jamie's head jerked up sharply.

'The *widow* Cameron?'

A sly smile flitted through the thicket of beard.

'Old Hector caught the morbid sore throat, up and died late last winter. Don't figure they get much mail, wherever he is now.'

Abandoning the Camerons for matters of more immediate personal interest, Myers resumed his interrupted excavations.

'Big purple thing,' he explained to me, fumbling his loosened thong. 'Almost as big as one o' my balls. You don't think it might could be as I've decided sudden-like to grow an extry, do you?'

'Well, no,' I said, biting my lip. 'I really doubt it.' He moved very slowly, but had almost got the knot in his thong undone; people in the street were beginning to pause, staring.

'Please don't trouble yourself,' I said. 'I do believe I know what that is – it's an inguinal hernia.'

The wide hazel eyes got wider.

'It is?' He seemed impressed, and not at all displeased by the news.

'I'd have to look – somewhere indoors, that is,' I added hastily '– to be sure, but it sounds like it. It's quite easy to repair surgically, but . . .' I hesitated, looking up at the Colossus. 'I really couldn't – I mean, you'd need to be asleep. Unconscious,' I amplified. 'I'd have to cut you, and sew you up again, you see. Perhaps a truss – a brace – might be better, though.'

Myers scratched slowly at his jaw, meditating.

'No, I done tried that, 'twon't do. Cuttin', though . . . You folks be staying here in the town for a spell before you head up to Cameron's?'

'Not long,' Jamie interrupted firmly. 'We shall be sailing upriver to my aunt's estate, as soon as passage can be arranged.'

'Oh.' The giant pondered this for a moment, then nodded, beaming.

'I know the very man for you, sir. I'll go this minute and fetch Josh Freeman out the Sailor's Rest. Sun's still high, he'll be not too drunk to do business yet.' He swept me a bow, battered hat to his middle. 'And then could be your wife might have the kindness to meet me in yonder tavern – it's a mite more genteel than the Sailor's – and have a look at this . . . this . . .' I saw his lips try to form themselves around 'inguinal hernia', then give up the effort and relax. 'This yere obstruction.'

He clapped the hat back on his head, and with a nod to Jamie, was off.

Jamie watched the mountain man's stiff-legged retreat down the street, slowed by cordial greetings to all he passed.

'What is it about ye, Sassenach, I wonder?' he said conversationally, eyes still fixed on Myers.

112

'What is *what* about me?'

He turned then, and gave me a narrow eye.

'What it is that makes every man ye meet want to take off his breeks within five minutes of meetin' ye.'

Fergus choked slightly, and Ian went pink. I looked as demure as possible.

'Well, if you don't know, my dear,' I said, 'no one does. *I* seem to have found us a boat. And what have *you* been up to this morning?'

Industrious as always, Jamie had found us a potential gem-buyer. And not only a buyer, but an invitation to dinner with the Governor.

'Governor Tryon's in the town just now,' he explained. 'Staying at the house of a Mr. Lillington. I talked this morning wi' a merchant named MacEachern, who put me on to a man named MacLeod, who –'

'Who introduced you to MacNeil, who took you to drink with MacGregor, who told you all about his nephew Bethune, who's the second cousin half removed of the boy who cleans the Governor's boots,' I suggested, familiar by this time with the Byzantine pathways of Scottish business dealings.

Put two Highland Scots in a room together, and within ten minutes they would know each other's family histories for the last two hundred years, and have discovered a helpful number of mutual relatives and acquaintances.

Jamie grinned.

'It was the Governor's wife's secretary,' he corrected, 'and his name's Murray. That'll be your da's cousin Maggie's eldest boy from Loch Linnhe,' he added, to Ian. 'His father emigrated after the Rising.' Ian nodded casually, doubtless docketing the information in his own version of the genetic encyclopedia, stored against the day it would prove useful.

Edwin Murray, the Governor's wife's secretary, had welcomed Jamie warmly as a kinsman – if only by marriage – and had obtained an invitation for us to dine at Lillington's that night, there ostensibly to acquaint the Governor with matters of trade in the Indies. In reality, we were intending to acquaint ourselves with Baron Penzler – a

113

well-to-do German nobleman who would be dining there as well. The Baron was a man not only of wealth but of taste, with a reputation as a collector of fine objects.

'Well, it sounds a good idea,' I said dubiously. 'But I think you'd better go alone. I can't be dining with governors looking like *this*.'

'Ah, ye look f–' His voice faded as he actually looked at me. His eye roamed slowly over me, taking in my grimy, bedraggled gown, wild hair and ragged bonnet.

He frowned at me. 'No, I want ye there, Sassenach; I may need a distraction.'

'Speaking of distraction, how many pints did it take you to wangle an invitation to dinner?' I asked, mindful of our dwindling finances. Jamie didn't blink, but took my arm, turning me toward the row of shops.

'Six, but he paid half. Come along, Sassenach; dinner's at seven, and we must find ye something decent to wear.'

'But we can't afford –'

'It's an investment,' he said firmly. 'And besides, Cousin Edwin has advanced me a bit against the sale of a stone.'

The gown was two years out of fashion by the cosmopolitan standards of Jamaica but it was clean, which was the main thing so far as I was concerned.

'You're dripping, madame.' The sempstress's voice was cold. A small, spare woman of middle age, she was the preeminent dressmaker in Wilmington and – I gathered – accustomed to having her fashion dictates obeyed without question. My rejection of a frilled cap in favor of freshly washed hair had been received with bad grace and predictions of pleurisy, and the pins she held in her mouth bristled like porcupine quills at my insistence on replacing the normal heavy corsetry with light boning, scalloped at the top to lift the breasts without pinching them.

'Sorry.' I tucked up the offending wet lock inside the linen towel that wrapped my head.

The guest quarters of Mr. Lillington's great house being fully occupied by the Governor's party, I had been relegated to Cousin Edwin's tiny attic over the stable block, and the fitting of my gown was being accomplished to the accompaniment of muffled stampings and chewings from below, punctuated by the monotonous strains of the groom's whistling as he mucked out the stalls.

Still, I was not inclined to complain; Mr. Lillington's stables were a deal cleaner than the inn where Jamie and I had left our companions, and Mrs. Lillington had very graciously seen me provided with a large basin of hot water and a ball of lavender-scented soap – a consideration more important even than the fresh dress. I hoped never to see another peach.

I rose slightly on my toes, trying to see out of the window in case Jamie should be coming, but desisted at a grunt of protest from the sempstress, who was trying to adjust the hem of my skirt.

The gown itself was not at all bad; it was of cream silk, half-sleeved and very simple, but with panniers of wine-striped silk over the hips, and a ruching of claret-colored silk piping that ran in two rows from waist to bosom. With the Brussels lace I had purchased sewn around the sleeves, I thought it would do, even if the cloth was not quite of the first quality.

I had at first been surprised at the price, which was remarkably low, but now observed that the fabric of the dress was coarser than usual, with occasional slubs of thickened thread that caught the light in shimmers. Curious, I rubbed it between my fingers. I was no great judge of silk, but a Chinese acquaintance had spent most of one idle afternoon on board a ship explaining to me the lore of silkworms, and the subtle variation of their output.

'Where does this silk come from?' I asked. 'It isn't China silk; is it French?'

The sempstress looked up, her crossness temporarily relieved by interest.

'No, indeed it's not. That's made in South Carolina, that is. There's a lady, Mrs. Pinckney by name, has gone and put half her land to mulberry trees, and went to raising silkworms on 'em. The cloth's maybe not quite so fine as the China,' she acknowledged reluctantly, 'but 'tisn't but half the cost, either.'

She squinted up at me, nodding slowly.

'It'll do for fit, and the bit o' piping's good; brings out the color in your cheeks. But begging your pardon, madame, you do need something above the neck, not to look too bare. If you won't have a cap nor a wig, might be you'd have a ribbon?'

'Oh, ribbon!' I said, remembering. 'Yes, what a good idea. Do look in my basket over there, and you'll find a length that might just do.'

Between us we managed to get my hair piled up, loosely bound with the length of dark pink ribbon, damp curly tendrils coming down – I couldn't stop them – around my ears and brow.

'Not too much mutton dressed as lamb, is it?' I asked, suddenly worried. I smoothed a hand down the front of the bodice, but it fit snugly – and trimly – around my waist.

'Oh, no, madame,' the sempstress assured me. 'Quite appropriate, and I say it myself.' She frowned at me, calculating. 'Only it is a bit *bare* over the bosom, still. You haven't any jewelry, at all?'

'Just this.' We turned in surprise as Jamie ducked his head to come in the door; neither of us had heard him coming.

He had somewhere managed to have a bath and procure a clean shirt and neckcloth; beyond that, someone had combed and plaited his hair into a smooth queue, bound with the new blue silk ribbon. His serviceable coat had not only been brushed, but improved by the application of a set of silver-gilt buttons, each delicately engraved with a small flower in the center.

'Very nice,' I said, touching one.

'Rented from the goldsmith,' he said. 'But they'll do. So will this, I think.' He drew out a filthy handkerchief from his pocket, from the folds of which he produced a slender gold chain.

'He hadna time for any but the simplest mount,' he said, frowning in concentration as he fastened the chain around my neck. 'But I think that's best, don't you?'

The ruby hung glinting just above the hollow of my breasts, casting a pale rosy glow against my white skin.

'I'm glad you picked that one,' I said, touching the stone gently. It was warm from his body. 'Goes much better with the dress than the sapphire or the emerald would.' The sempstress's jaw hung slightly open. She glanced from me to Jamie, her impression of our social position evidently going up by leaps and bounds.

Jamie had finally taken time to notice the rest of my costume. His eyes traveled slowly over me from head to hem, and a smile spread across his face.

'Ye make a verra ornamental jewel box, Sassenach,' he said. 'A fine distraction, aye?'

He glanced out the window, where a pale peach color stained a hazy evening sky, then turned to me, bowed and made a leg. 'Might I claim the pleasure of your company for dinner, madame?'

7

Great Prospects Fraught With Peril

While I was familiar with the eighteenth-century willing-ness to eat anything that could be physically overpowered and dragged to the table, I did not subscribe to the mania for presenting wild dishes as though they had not in fact undergone the intermediary processes of being killed and cooked before making their appearance at dinner.

I thus viewed the large sturgeon with which I sat eyeball-to-eyeball with a marked lack of appetite. Complete not only with eyes but with scales, fins, and tail, the three-foot fish rode majestically on waves of roe in aspic, decorated with a vast quantity of tiny spiced crabs, which had been boiled whole and scattered artistically over the platter.

I took another large sip of wine and turned to my dinner companion, trying to keep my eyes off the bulging glare of the sturgeon by my elbow.

' . . . the most impertinent fellow!' Mr. Stanhope was saying, by way of describing a gentleman he had encount-ered in a post-house whilst on his way to Wilmington from his property near New Bern.

'Why, in the very midst of our refreshment, he began to speak of his piles, and what torment they caused him with the coach's continual bouncing. And then damme if the crude fellow did not pull his kerchief out of his pocket, all spotted with blood, to show the company by way of evi-dence! Quite destroyed my appetite, ma'am, I assure you,' he assured me, forking up a substantial mouthful of chicken fricassee. He chewed it slowly, regarding me with pale, bulging eyes that reminded me uncomfortably of the sturgeon's.

Across the table, Phillip Wylie's long mouth twitched with amusement.

'Take care your conversation doesn't incur a similar effect, Stanhope,' he said, with a nod at my untouched plate. 'Though a certain crudeness of company is one of the perils of public transport, I do admit.'

Stanhope sniffed, brushing crumbs from the folds of his neckcloth.

'Needn't put on airs, Wylie. It's not everyone can afford to keep a coachman, 'specially not with all these fresh taxes. New one stuck on every time one turns around, I do declare!' He waved his fork indignantly. 'Tobacco, wine, brandy, all very well, but a tax upon *newspapers*, have you heard the like? Why, my sister's oldest boy was awarded a degree from Yale University a year past' – he puffed his chest unconsciously, speaking just slightly louder than usual – 'and damned if she was not required to pay half a shilling, merely to have his diploma officially stamped!'

'But that is no longer the case at present,' Cousin Edwin said patiently. 'Since the repeal of the Stamp Act –'

Stanhope plucked one of the tiny crabs from the platter and brandished it at Edwin in accusation.

'Get rid of one tax, and another pops up in its place directly. Just like mushrooms!' He popped the crab into his mouth and was heard to mumble something indistinctly about taxing the air next, he shouldn't wonder.

'You are come but recently from the Indies, I understand, Madame Fraser?' Baron Penzler, on my other side, seized the momentary opportunity to interrupt. 'I doubt you will be familiar with such provincial matters – or interested in them,' he added, with a nod of benevolent dismissal at Stanhope.

'Oh, surely everyone is interested in taxes,' I said, turning slightly sideways so as to display my bosom to best effect. 'Or don't you believe that taxes are what we pay for a civilized society? Though having heard Mr. Stanhope's story' – I nodded to my other side – 'perhaps he would agree that the level of civilization isn't quite equal to the level of taxation?'

'Ha ha!' Stanhope choked on his bread, spewing crumbs. 'Oh, very good! Not equal to – ha ha, no, certainly not!'

Phillip Wylie gave me a look of sardonic acknowledgment.

'You must try not to be so amusing, Mrs. Fraser,' he said. 'It may be the death of poor Stanhope.'

'Er . . . what is the current rate of taxation, do you

119

think?' I asked, tactfully drawing attention away from Stanhope's spluttering.

Wylie pursed his lips, considering. A dandy, he wore the latest in modish wigs, and a small patch in the shape of a star beside his mouth. Under the powder, though, I thought I detected both a good-looking face and a very shrewd brain.

'Oh, considering all incidentals, I should say it can amount to as much as two percent of all income, if one was to include the taxes on slaves. Add taxes on lands and crops, and it amounts to a bit more, perhaps.'

'Two percent!' Stanhope choked, pounding himself on the chest. 'Iniquitous! Simply iniquitous!'

With vivid memories of the last IRS form I had signed, I agreed sympathetically that a two percent tax rate was a positive outrage, wondering to myself just what had become of the fiery spirit of American taxpayers over the intervening two hundred years.

'But perhaps we should change the subject,' I said, seeing that heads were beginning to turn in our direction from the upper end of the table. 'After all, speaking of taxes at the Governor's table is rather like talking of rope in the house of the hanged, isn't it?'

At this, Mr. Stanhope swallowed a crab whole, and choked in good earnest.

His partner on the other side pounded him helpfully on the back, and the small black boy who had been occupied in swatting flies near the open windows was sent hastily to fetch water. I marked out a sharp, slender knife by the fish platter, just in case, though I hoped I shouldn't be compelled to perform a tracheotomy on the spot; it wasn't the kind of attention I was hoping to attract.

Luckily such drastic measures weren't required; the crab was disgorged by a fortunate slap, leaving the victim empurpled and gasping, but otherwise unharmed.

'Someone had mentioned newspapers,' I said, once Mr. Stanhope had been thus rescued from his excesses. 'We've been here so short a time that I haven't seen any; is there a regular paper printed in Wilmington?'

I had ulterior motives for asking this, beyond a desire to allow Mr. Stanhope time to recover himself. Among the few worldly goods Jamie possessed was a printing press, presently in storage in Edinburgh.

Wilmington, it appeared, had two printers in residence, but only one of these gentlemen – a Mr. Jonathan Gillette – produced a regular newspaper.

'And it may soon cease to be so regular,' Stanhope said darkly. 'I hear that Mr. Gillette has received a warning from the Committee of Safety, that – ah!' He gave a brief exclamation, his plump face creased in pained surprise.

'Have you a particular interest, Mrs. Fraser?' Wylie inquired politely, darting a look under his brows at his friend. 'I had heard that your husband had some connection with the printing trade in Edinburgh.'

'Why, yes,' I said, rather surprised that he should know so much about us. 'Jamie owned a printing establishment there, though he didn't issue a newspaper – books and pamphlets and plays and the like.'

Wylie's finely arched brow twitched up.

'No political leanings, then, your husband? So often printers find their skills suborned by those whose passions seek outlet in print – but then, such passions are not necessarily shared by the printer.'

That rang numerous alarm bells; did Wylie actually know anything about Jamie's political connections in Edinburgh – most of whom had been thoroughly seditious – or was this only normal dinner-table conversation? Judging from Stanhope's remarks, newspapers and politics were evidently connected in people's minds – and little wonder, given the times.

Jamie, at the far end of the table, had caught his name and now turned his head slightly to smile at me, before returning to an earnest conversation with the Governor, at whose right hand he sat. I wasn't sure whether this placement was the work of Mr. Lillington, who sat on the Governor's left, following the conversation with the intelligent, slightly mournful expression of a basset hound, or of Cousin Edwin, consigned to the seat opposite me, between Phillip Wylie and Wylie's sister, Judith.

'Oh, a tradesman,' this lady now remarked, in a meaningful tone of voice. She smiled at me, careful not to expose her teeth. Likely decayed, I thought. 'And is this' –

121

she gave a vague wave at her head, comparing my ribbon to the towering confection of her wig – 'the style in Edinburgh, Mrs. Fraser? How . . . charming.'

Her brother gave her a narrowed eye.

'I believe I have also heard that Mr. Fraser is the nephew of Mrs. Cameron of River Run,' he said pleasantly. 'Have I been correctly informed, Mrs. Fraser?'

Cousin Edwin, who had undoubtedly been the source of this information, buttered his roll with sedulous concentration. Cousin Edwin looked very little like a secretary, being a tall and prepossessing young man with a pair of lively brown eyes – one of which now gave me the merest suggestion of a wink.

The Baron, as bored with newspapers as with taxes, perked up a bit at hearing the name Cameron.

'River Run?' he said. 'You have relations with Mrs. Jocasta Cameron?'

'She's my husband's aunt,' I replied. 'Do you know her?'

'Oh, indeed! A charming woman, most charming!' A broad smile lifted the Baron's pendulous cheeks. 'Since many years, I am the dear friend of Mrs. Cameron and her husband, unfortunately dead.'

The Baron launched into an enthusiastic recounting of the delights of River Run, and I took advantage of the lull to accept a small wedge of fish pie, full not only of fish, but of oysters and shrimps in a creamy sauce. Mr. Lillington had certainly spared no effort to impress the Governor.

As I leaned back for the footman to ladle more sauce onto my plate, I caught Judith Wylie's eyes on me, narrowed in a look of dislike that she didn't trouble to disguise. I smiled pleasantly at her, displaying my own excellent teeth, and turned back to the Baron, newly confident.

There had been no looking glass in Edwin's quarters, and while Jamie had assured me that I looked all right, his standards were rather different from those of fashion. I had received any number of admiring compliments from the gentlemen at table, true, but this might be no more than customary politeness; extravagant gallantry was common among upper-class men.

But Miss Wylie was twenty-five years my junior, fashionably gowned and jeweled, and if no great beauty, not plain, either. Her jealousy was a better reflection of my appearance, I thought, than any looking glass.

'Such a beautiful stone, Mrs. Fraser – you will permit me to look more closely?' The Baron bent toward me, pudgy fingers delicately poised above my cleavage.

'Oh, certainly,' I said with alacrity, and quickly unclasped the chain, dropping the ruby into his broad, moist palm. The Baron looked slightly disappointed not to have been allowed to examine the stone *in situ*, but lifted his hand, squinting at the glinting droplet with the air of a connoisseur – which he evidently was, for he reached into his watch pocket and withdrew a small gadget that proved to be a combination of optical lenses, including both a magnifying glass and a jeweler's loupe.

I relaxed, seeing this, and accepted a helping of something hot and savory-smelling from a glass dish being passed by the butler. What possessed people to serve hot food when the temperature in the room must be at least in the nineties?

'Beautiful,' murmured the Baron, rolling the stone gently in his palm. '*Sehr schön.*'

There were not many things about which I would have trusted Geillis Duncan, but I was sure of her taste in jewels. 'It must be a stone of the first class,' she had said to me, explaining her theory of time travel via gems, 'Large, and completely flawless.'

The ruby was large, all right; nearly the size of the pickled quail's eggs surrounding the fully plumed pheasant on the sideboard. As to its flawlessness, I felt no doubt. Geilie had trusted this stone to carry her into the future; I thought it would probably get us as far as Cross Creek. I took a bite of the food on my plate; some sort of ragout, I thought, very tender and flavorful.

'How delicious this is,' I said to Mr. Stanhope, lifting another forkful. 'What is this dish, do you know?'

'Oh, it is one of my particular favorites, ma'am,' he said, inhaling beatifically over his own plate. 'Soused hog's face. Delectable, is it not?'

I shut the door of Cousin Edwin's room behind me and

leaned against it, letting my jaw hang open in sheer relief at no longer being required to smile. Now I could take off the clinging dress, undo the tight corset, slip off the sweaty shoes.

Peace, solitude, nakedness, and silence. I couldn't think of anything else required to make my life complete for the moment, save a little fresh air. I stripped off, and attired in nothing but my shift, went to open the window.

The air outside was so thick, I thought I could have stepped out and floated down through it, like a pebble dropped in a jar of molasses. The bugs came at once to the flame of my candle, light-crazed and blood-hungry. I blew it out and sat on the window seat in the dark, letting the soft, warm air move over me.

The ruby still hung at my neck, black as a blood drop against my skin. I touched it, set it swinging gently between my breasts; the stone was warm as my own blood, too.

Outside, the guests were beginning to depart; a line of waiting carriages was drawn up on the drive. The sounds of goodbyes, conversations, and soft laughter drifted up to me in snatches.

'. . . quite clever, I thought,' came up in Phillip Wylie's cultured drawl.

'Oh, *clever*, certainly it was *clever*!' His sister's higher-pitched tones made it quite clear what she thought of cleverness as a social attribute.

'Well, cleverness in a woman can be tolerated, my dear, so long as she is also pleasant to look upon. By the same token, a woman who has beauty may perhaps dispense with wit, so long as she has sense enough to conceal the lack by keeping her mouth shut.'

Miss Wylie might not be accused of cleverness, but had certainly adequate sensibility to perceive the barb in this. She gave a rather unladylike snort.

'She is a thousand years old, at least,' she replied. 'Pleasant to look at, indeed. Though I will say it was a handsome trinket about her neck,' she added grudgingly.

'Oh, quite,' said a deeper voice that I recognized as Lloyd Stanhope's. 'Though in my own opinion, it was the setting rather than the jewel that was striking.'

'Setting?' Miss Wylie sounded blank. 'There was no setting; the jewel merely rested upon her bosom.'

'Really?' Stanhope said blandly. 'I hadn't noticed.' Wylie burst out laughing, breaking off abruptly as the door opened to release more guests.

'Well, if you didn't, old man, there were others who did,' he said with sly intonation. 'Come, here's the carriage.'

I touched the ruby again, watching the Wylies' handsome grays drive off. Yes, others had noticed. I could still feel the Baron's eyes on my bosom, knowingly avaricious. I rather thought he was a connoisseur of more than gems.

The stone was warm in my hand; it felt warmer even than my skin, though that must be illusion. I did not normally wear jewelry beyond my wedding rings; had never cared much for it. It would be a relief to be rid of at least part of our dangerous treasure. And still I sat there holding the stone, cradling it in my hand, till I almost thought I could feel it beating like a small separate heart, in time with my blood.

There was only one carriage left, its driver standing by the horses' heads. Some twenty minutes later, the occupant came out, adding to his goodbyes a good-humored '*Gute Nacht*' as he stepped into his coach. The Baron. He had waited till last, and was leaving in a good mood; that seemed a good sign.

One of the footmen, stripped of his livery coat, was extinguishing the torches at the foot of the drive. I could see the pale blur of his shirt as he walked back to the house through the dark, and the sudden flare of light onto the terrace as a door opened to admit him below. Then that too was gone, and a night silence settled on the grounds.

I had expected Jamie to come up at once, but the minutes dragged on with no sound of his step. I glanced at the bed, but felt no desire to lie down.

At last I stood up and slipped the dress back on, not bothering with shoes or stockings. I left the room, walking quietly down the hallway in my bare feet, down the stair, through the breezeway to the main house, and in through the side entrance from the garden. It was dark, save the pale squares of moonlight that came through the casements; most of the servants must have retired, along with household and guests. There was light glowing through the stairwell's banister, though; the sconces were still alight in the dining room beyond.

I could hear the murmur of masculine voices as I tiptoed past the polished stair, Jamie's deep soft Scots alternating with the Governor's English tones, in the intimate cadences of a tete-à-tete.

The candles had burnt low in their sconces. The air was sweet with melted beeswax, and low clouds of fragrant cigar smoke hung heavy outside the dining-room doors.

Moving quietly, I stopped just short of the door. From this vantage point I could see the Governor, back to me, neck stretched forward as he lit a fresh cigar from the candlestick on the table.

If Jamie saw me, he gave no hint of it. His face bore its usual expression of calm good humor, but the recent lines of strain around eyes and mouth had eased, and I could tell from the slope of his shoulders that he was relaxed and at peace. My heart lightened at once; he had been successful then.

'A place called River Run,' he was saying to the Governor. 'Well up in the hills past Cross Creek.'

'I know the place,' Governor Tryon remarked, a little surprised. 'My wife and I passed several days in Cross Creek last year; we made a tour of the colony, upon the occasion of my taking office. River Run is well up in the foothills, though, not in the town – why, it is halfway to the mountains, I believe.'

Jamie smiled and sipped his brandy.

'Aye, well,' he said, 'my family are Highlanders, sir; the mountains will be home to us.'

'Indeed.' A small puff of smoke rose over the Governor's shoulder. Then he took the cigar from his mouth and leaned confidentially toward Jamie.

'Since we are alone, Mr. Fraser, there is another matter I wished to put before you. A glass with you, sir?' He picked up the decanter without waiting for an answer, and poured more brandy.

'I thank ye, sir.'

The Governor puffed fiercely for a moment, sending up blue clouds, then having got his weed well alight, sat back, cigar fuming negligently in one hand.

'You are very newly come to the Colonies, young Edwin tells me. Are you familiar with conditions here?'

Jamie shrugged slightly.

'I have made it my business to learn what I could, sir,' he replied. 'To which conditions might ye refer?'

'North Carolina is a land of considerable richness,' the Governor answered, 'and yet it has not reached the same level of prosperity as have its neighbors – owing mostly to a lack of laborers to take advantage of its opportunities. We have no great harbor for a seaport, you see; thus slaves must be brought overland at great cost from South Carolina or Virginia – and we cannot hope to compete with Boston and Philadelphia for indentured labor.

'It has long been the policy both of the Crown and of myself, Mr. Fraser, to encourage the settlement of land in the Colony of North Carolina by intelligent, industrious and godly families, to the furtherance of the prosperity and security of all.' He lifted his cigar, took a deep lungful and exhaled slowly, pausing to cough.

'To this end, sir, there is established a system of land grants whereby a large acreage may be given to a gentleman of means, who will undertake to persuade a number of emigrants to come and settle upon a part of it under his sponsorship. This policy has been blessed with success over the last thirty years; a good many Highlanders and families from the Isles of Scotland have been induced to come and take up residence here. Why, when I arrived, I was astonished to find the banks of the Cape Fear River quite thick with MacNeills, Buchanans, Grahams, and Campbells!'

The Governor tasted his cigar again, but this time the barest nip; he was anxious to make his point.

'Yet there remains a great deal of desirable land to be settled, further inland toward the mountains. It is somewhat remote, and yet, as you say, for men accustomed to the far reaches of the Scottish Highlands –'

'I did hear mention of such grants, sir,' Jamie interrupted. 'Yet is not the wording that persons holding such

127

grants shall be white males, Protestant, and above thirty years of age? And this statement holds the force of law?'

'That is the official wording of the Act, yes.' Mr. Tryon turned so that I saw him now in profile, tapping the ash from his cigar into a small porcelain bowl. The corner of his mouth was turned up in anticipation; the face of a fisherman who feels the first twitch on his line.

'The offer is one of considerable interest,' Jamie said formally. 'I must point out, however, that I am not a Protestant, nor are most of my kinsmen.'

The Governor pursed his lips in deprecation, lifting one brow.

'You are neither a Jew nor a Negro. I may speak as one gentleman to another, may I not? In all frankness, Mr. Fraser, there is the law, and then there is what is done.' He raised his glass with a small smile, setting the hook. 'And I am convinced that you understand that as well as I do.'

'Possibly better,' Jamie murmured, with a polite smile.

The Governor shot him a sharp look, but then uttered a quick bark of laughter. He raised his brandy glass in acknowledgment, and took a sip.

'We understand each other, Mr. Fraser,' he said, nodding with satisfaction. Jamie inclined his head a fraction of an inch.

'There would be no difficulties raised, then, regarding the personal qualifications of those who might be persuaded to take up your offer?'

'None at all,' said the Governor, setting down his glass with a small thump. 'Provided only that they are able-bodied men, capable of working the land, I ask nothing more. And what is not asked need not be told, eh?' One thin brow flicked up in query.

Jamie turned the glass in his hands, as though admiring the deep color of the liquid.

'Not all who passed through the Stuart Rising were so fortunate as myself, Your Excellency,' he said. 'My foster son suffered the loss of his hand; another of my companions has but one arm. Yet they are men of good character and industry. I could not in conscience partake of a proposal which did not offer them some part.'

The Governor dismissed this with an expansive wave of the hand.

'Provided that they are able to earn their bread and will not prove a burden upon the community, they are welcome.' Then, as though fearing he had been incautious in his generosity, he sat up straight, leaving the cigar to burn, propped on the edge of the bowl.

'Since you mention Jacobites – these men will be required to swear an oath of loyalty to the Crown, if they have not already done so. If I might presume to ask, sir, as you imply you are Papist . . . you, yourself . . .'

Jamie's eyes might have narrowed only against the sting of the smoke, but I didn't think so. Neither did Governor Tryon, who was only in his thirties but no mean judge of men. He swivelled to face the table again, so that I saw only his back, but I could tell that he was gazing intently at Jamie, eyes tracing the swift movements of the trout beneath the water.

'I do not seek to remind you of past indignity,' he said quietly. 'Nor yet to offend present honor. Still, you will understand that it is my duty to ask.'

Jamie smiled, quite without humor.

'And mine to answer, I expect,' he said. 'Yes, I am a pardoned Jacobite. And aye, I have sworn the oath – like the others who paid that price for their lives.'

Quite abruptly, he set down his still-full glass and pushed back the heavy chair. He stood and bowed to the Governor.

'It grows late, Your Excellency. I must beg to take my leave.'

The Governor sat back in his chair, and lifted the cigar slowly to his lips. He drew heavily on it, making the tip glow bright, as he gazed up at Jamie. Then, he nodded, letting a thin plume of smoke drift from his pursed lips.

'Good night, Mr. Fraser. Do consider my offer, will you not?'

I didn't wait to hear the answer – I didn't need to. I skimmed down the hall in a rustle of skirts, startling a footman dozing in a dark corner.

I made it back to our borrowed room in the stable block without meeting anyone else, and collapsed. My heart was

129

pounding; not only from the dash up the stairs but from what I had heard.

Jamie would consider the Governor's offer, all right. And what an offer! To regain in one swoop all that he had lost in Scotland – and more.

Jamie had not been born a laird, but the death of his elder brother had left him heir to Lallybroch, and from the age of eight he had been raised to take responsibility for an estate, to see to the welfare of land and tenants, to place that welfare above his own. Then had come Charles Stuart, and his mad march to glory; a fiery cross leading his followers to shambles and destruction.

Jamie had never spoken bitterly of the Stuarts; had never spoken of Charles Stuart at all. Nor had he often spoken of what that venture had cost him personally.

But now . . . to have that back. New lands, cultivable and rich with game, and settled by families under his sponsorship and protection. It was rather like the Book of Job, I thought – all those sons and daughters and camels and houses, destroyed so casually, and then replaced with such extravagant largesse.

I had always viewed that bit of the Bible with some doubt, myself. One camel was much like another, but children seemed a different proposition. And while Job might have regarded the replacement of his children as simple justice, I couldn't help thinking that the dead children's mother might possibly have been of another mind about it.

Unable to sit, I went again to the window, gazing out unseeingly at the dark garden.

It wasn't simply excitement that was making my heart beat fast and my hands perspire; it was fear. With matters as they were in Scotland – as they had been since the Rising – it would be no difficult matter to find willing emigrants.

I had seen ships come into port in the Indies and in Georgia, disgorging their cargos of emigrants, so emaciated and worn by their passage that they reminded me of nothing so much as concentration camp victims – skeletal as living corpses, white as maggots from two months in the darkness below-decks.

Despite the expense and difficulty of the journey, despite the pain of parting from friends and family and homeland forever, the immigrants poured in, in hundreds and in thousands, carrying their children – those who survived the voyage – and their possessions in small, ragged bundles; fleeing poverty and hopelessness, seeking not fortune but only a small foothold on life. Only a chance.

I had spent only a short time at Lallybroch the winter before, but I knew there were tenants there who survived only by the goodwill of Ian and Young Jamie, their crofts not yielding enough to live on. While such goodwill was invariably given, it was not inexhaustible; I knew that the estate's slender resources were often stretched to the maximum.

Beyond Lallybroch, there were the smugglers Jamie had known in Edinburgh, and the illegal distillers of Highland whisky – any number of men, in fact, who had been forced to turn to lawlessness to feed their families. No, finding willing emigrants would be no problem at all for Jamie.

The problem was that in order to recruit suitable men for the purpose, he would have to go to Scotland. And in my mind was the sight of a granite gravestone in a Scottish kirkyard, on a hill high above the moors and sea.

JAMES ALEXANDER MALCOLM MACKENZIE FRASER, it read, and below that, my own name was carved – *Beloved husband of Claire.*

I would bury him in Scotland. But there had been no date on the stone when I saw it, two hundred years hence; no notion when the blow would fall.

'Not yet,' I whispered, clenching my fists in the silk of my petticoat. 'I've only had him for a little while – oh, God, please, not yet!'

As though in answer, the door swung open, and James Alexander Malcolm MacKenzie Fraser came in, carrying a candle.

He smiled at me, loosening his stock.

'You're verra light on your feet, Sassenach. I see I must teach ye to hunt one day, and you such a fine stalker.'

I made no apology for eavesdropping, but came to help him with his waistcoat buttons. In spite of the late hour and the brandy, he was clear-eyed and alert, his body tautly alive when I touched him.

'You'd best put out the candle,' I said. 'These bugs will eat you alive.' I pinched a mosquito off his neck by way of illustration, the fragile body crushed to a smear of blood between my fingers.

Among the scents of brandy and cigar smoke, I could smell the night on him, and the faint musky spice of nicotiana; he had been walking, then, amid the flowers in the garden. He did that when he was either distressed or excited – and he didn't seem distressed.

He sighed and flexed his shoulders as I took his coat; his shirt was damp with sweat underneath, and he plucked it away from his skin with a mild grunt of distaste.

'I canna tell how folk live in such heat, dressed like this. It makes the savages look quite sensible, to be goin' about in loincloths and aprons.'

'It would be a lot cheaper,' I agreed, 'if less aesthetically appealing. Imagine Baron Penzler in a loincloth, I mean.' The Baron weighed perhaps eighteen stone, with a pasty complexion.

He laughed, the sound muffled in his shirt as he pulled it over his head.

'You, on the other hand . . .' I sat down on the window seat, admiring the view as he stripped off his breeches, standing on one leg to roll down his stocking.

With the candle extinguished, it was dark in the room, but with my eyes adapted, I could still make him out, long limbs pale against the velvet night.

'And speaking of the Baron –' I prodded.

'Three hundred pounds sterling,' he replied, in tones of extreme satisfaction. He straightened up and tossed the rolled stockings onto a stool, then bent and kissed me. 'Which is in large part due to you, Sassenach.'

'For my value as an ornamental setting, you mean?' I asked dryly, recalling the Wylies' conversation.

'No,' he said, rather shortly. 'For keeping Wylie and his friends occupied at dinner, while I talked wi' the Governor. Ornamental setting . . . tcha! Stanhope nearly dropped his eyeballs into your bosom, the filthy lecher; I'd a mind to call him out for it, but –'

'Discretion is the better part of valor,' I said, standing up and kissing him back. 'Not that I've ever met a Scot who seemed to think so.'

'Aye, well, there was my grandsire, Old Simon. I suppose ye could say it was discretion that did for him, in the end.' I could hear both the smile and the edge in his voice. If he seldom spoke of the Jacobites and the events of the Rising, it didn't mean he had forgotten; his conversation with the Governor had obviously brought them close to the surface of his mind tonight.

'I'd say that discretion and deceit are not necessarily the same things. And your grandfather had been asking for it for fifty years, at least,' I replied tartly. Simon Fraser, Lord Lovat, had died by beheading on Tower Hill – at the age of seventy-eight, after a lifetime of unparalleled chicanery, both personal and political. For all of that, I quite regretted the old rogue's passing.

'Mmphm.' Jamie didn't argue with me, but moved to stand beside me at the window. He breathed in deeply, as though smelling the thick perfume of the night.

I could see his face quite clearly in the dim glow of starlight. It was calm and smooth, but with an inward look, as though his eyes didn't see what was before them, but something else entirely. The past? I wondered. Or the future?

'What did it say?' I asked suddenly. 'The oath you swore.'

I felt rather than saw the movement of his shoulders, not quite a shrug. ' "I, James Alexander Malcolm MacKenzie Fraser, do swear, and as I shall answer to God at the great day of judgment, I have not, nor shall have, in my possession any gun, sword, pistol, or arm whatsoever, and never use tartan, plaid, or any part of the Highland garb; and if I do so, may I be cursed in my undertakings, family, and property." ' He took a deep breath, and went on, speaking precisely.

' "May I never see my wife and children, father, mother or relations. May I be killed in battle as a coward, and lie without Christian burial, in a strange land, far from the graves of my forefathers and kindred; may all this come across me if I break my oath." '

133

'And did you mind a lot?' I said, after a moment.

'No,' he said softly, still looking out at the night. 'Not then. There are things worth dying or starving for – but not words.'

'Maybe not those words.'

He turned to look at me, features dim in starlight, but the hint of a smile visible on his mouth.

'Ye know of words that are?'

The gravestone had his name, but no date. I could stop him going back to Scotland, I thought. If I would.

I turned to face him, leaning back against the window frame.

'What about – "I love you"?'

He reached out a hand and touched my face. A breath of air stirred past us, and I saw the small hairs rise along his arm.

'Aye,' he whispered. 'That'll do.'

There was a bird calling somewhere close at hand. A few clear notes, succeeded by an answer; a brief twitter, and then silence. The sky outside was still thick black, but the stars were less brilliant than before.

I turned over restlessly; I was naked, covered only by a linen sheet, but even in the small hours of the night, the air was warm and smothering, and the small depression in which I lay was damp.

I had tried to sleep, and could not. Even lovemaking, which normally could relax me into a bonelessly contented stupor, had this time left me only restless and sticky. At once excited and worried by the possibilities of the future – and unable to confide my disturbed feelings – I had felt separate from Jamie; estranged and detached, despite the closeness of our bodies.

I turned again, this time toward Jamie. He lay in his usual position, on his back, the sheet crumpled about his hips, hands gently folded over a flat stomach. His head was turned slightly on the pillow, his face relaxed in sleep. With the wide mouth gentled by slumber and the dark lashes long on his cheeks, in this dim light he looked about fourteen.

I wanted to touch him, though I wasn't sure whether I

meant to caress or to poke him. While he had given me physical release, he had taken my peace of mind, and I was irrationally envious of his effortless repose.

I did neither, though, and merely turned onto my back, where I lay with my eyes shut, grimly counting sheep – who disobliged me by being Scottish sheep, cantering merrily through a kirkyard, leaping the gravestones with gay abandon.

'Is something troubling ye, Sassenach?' said a sleepy voice at my shoulder.

My eyes popped open.

'No,' I said, trying to sound equally drowsy. 'I'm fine.'

There was a faint snort and a rustling of the chaff-filled mattress as he turned over.

'You're a terrible liar, Sassenach. Ye're thinking so loudly, I can hear ye from here.'

'You can't hear people think!'

'Aye, I can. You, at least.' He chuckled and reached out a hand, which rested lazily on my thigh. 'What is it – has the spiced crab given ye flatulence?'

'It has not!' I tried to twitch my leg away, but his hand clung like a limpet.

'Oh, good. What is it, then – ye've finally thought of a witty riposte to Mr. Wylie's remarks about oysters?'

'No,' I said irritably. 'If you must know, I was thinking about the offer Governor Tryon made you. Will you let go of my leg?'

'Ah,' he said, not letting go but sounding less sleepy. 'Well, come to that, I was thinking on the matter a bit myself.'

'What *do* you think about it?' I gave up trying to detach his hand and rolled onto my elbow, facing him. The window was still dark, but the stars had dimmed visibly, faded by the distant approach of day.

'I wonder why he made it, for the one thing.'

'Really? But I thought he told you why.'

He gave a brief grunt.

'Well, he's no offering me land for the sake of my bonny blue eyes, I'll tell ye that.' He opened the eyes in question and cocked one brow at me. 'Before I make a bargain, Sassenach, I want to know what's on both sides of it, aye?'

'You don't think he's telling the truth? About Crown grants to help settle the land? But he said it's been going on for thirty years,' I protested. 'He couldn't lie about something like that, surely.'

'No, that's the truth,' he agreed. 'So far as it goes. But bees that hae honey in their mouths hae stings in their tails, aye?' He scratched at his head and smoothed the loose hair out of his face, sighing.

'Ask yourself this, Sassenach,' he said. 'Why me?'

'Well – because he wants a gentleman of substance and authority,' I said slowly. 'He needs a good leader, which Cousin Edwin has obviously told him you are, and a fairly wealthy man –'

'Which I am not.'

'He doesn't know that, though,' I protested.

'Doesn't he?' he said cynically. 'Cousin Edwin will ha' told him as much as he knows – and the Governor kens well I was a Jacobite. True, there are a few who mended their fortunes in the Indies after the Rising, and I might be one o' those – but he has nae reason to think so.'

'He knows you have *some* money,' I pointed out.

'Because of Penzler? Aye,' he said thoughtfully. 'What else does he know about me?'

'Only what you told him at dinner, so far as I know. And he can't have heard much about you from anyone else; after all, you've been in town less than a – what, you mean that's it?' My voice rose in incredulity, and he smiled, a little grimly. The light was still far off, but moving closer, and his features were clearcut in the dimness.

'Aye, that's it. I've connections to the Camerons, who are not only wealthy but well respected in the colony. But at the same time, I'm an incomer, wi' few ties and no known loyalties here.'

'Except, perhaps, to the Governor who's offering you a large tract of land,' I said slowly.

He didn't reply at once, but rolled onto his back, still keeping a grip on my leg. His eyes were fastened on the dim whiteness of the plaster ceiling above, with its clouded garlands and ghostly cupids.

'I've known a German or two in my time, Sassenach,' he said, musing. His thumb began to move slowly, back and

136

forth upon the tender flesh of my inner thigh. 'I havena found them careless wi' their money, be they Jew or Gentile. And while ye looked bonny as a white rose this evening, I canna think it was entirely your charms that made the gentleman offer me a hundred pounds more than the goldsmith did.'

He glanced at me. 'Tryon is a soldier. He'll ken me for one, too. And there was that wee bit of trouble with the Regulators two year past.'

My mind was so diverted by the possibilities intrinsic in this speech, that I was nearly unconscious of the increasing familiarity of the hand between my thighs.

'Who?'

'Oh, I forgot; ye wouldna have heard that part of the conversation – bein' otherwise occupied with your host of admirers.'

I let that one pass in favor of finding out about the Regulators. These, it appeared, were a loose association of men, mostly from the rough backcountry of the colony, who had taken offense at what they perceived as capricious and inequitable – and now and then downright illegal – behavior on the part of the Crown's appointed officials, the sheriffs, justices, tax collectors, and so on.

Feeling that their complaints were not sufficiently addressed by the Governor and Assembly, they had taken matters into their own hands. Sheriff's deputies had been assaulted, justices of the peace marched from their houses by mobs and forced to resign.

A committee of Regulators had written to the Governor, imploring him to address the iniquities under which they suffered, and Tryon – a man of action and diplomacy – had replied soothingly, going so far as to replace one or two of the most corrupt sheriffs, and issue an official letter to the court officers, regarding seizure of effects.

'Stanhope said something about a Committee of Safety,' I said, interested. 'But it sounded quite recent.'

'The trouble is damped down but not settled,' Jamie said, shrugging. 'And damp powder may smolder for a long time, Sassenach, but once it catches, it goes off with an almighty bang.'

Would Tryon think it worth the investment, to buy the

loyalty and obligation of an experienced soldier, himself in turn commanding the loyalty and service of the men under his sponsorship, all settled in a remote and troublesome area of the colony?

I would myself have called the prospect cheap, at the cost of a hundred pounds and a few measly acres of the King's land. His Majesty had quite a lot of it, after all.

'So you're thinking about it.' We were by this time facing each other, and my hand lay over his, not in restraint, but in acknowledgment.

He smiled lazily.

'I havena lived so long by believing everything I'm told, Sassenach. So perhaps I'll take up the Governor's kind offer, and perhaps I will not – but I want to know the hell of a lot more about it before I say, one way or the other.'

'Yes, it does seem a little odd – his making you such an offer on short acquaintance.'

'I should be surprised to hear I am the only gentleman he's so approached,' Jamie said. 'And it's no great risk, now, is it? Ye overheard me telling him I am a Catholic? It was no surprise to him to hear it.'

'Yes. He didn't seem to think that was a problem, though.'

'Oh, I daresay it wouldna be – unless the Governor chose to make it one.'

'My goodness.' My evaluation of Governor Tryon was rapidly changing, though I wasn't sure whether for the better or not. 'So if things didn't work out as he liked, all he would have to do is let it be known that you're a Catholic, and a court would take back the land on those grounds. Whereas if he chooses to keep quiet –'

'And if I choose to do as he likes, aye.'

'He's much sneakier than I thought,' I said, not without admiration. 'Practically Scottish.'

He laughed at that, and brushed the loose hair out of his face.

The long curtains at the window, hitherto hanging limp, suddenly puffed inward, letting in a breath of air that smelt of sandy mud, river water, and the far-off hint of fresh pines. Dawn was coming, borne on the wind.

As though this had been a signal, Jamie's hand cupped

itself, and a slight shiver communicated itself from him to me, as the coolness struck his bare back.

'I didna really do myself credit earlier,' he said softly. 'But if you're sure there's nothing troubling your mind just now . . .'

'Nothing,' I said, watching the glow from the window touch the line of his head and neck with gold. His mouth was still wide and gentle, but he didn't look fourteen any longer.

'Not a thing, just now.'

8

Man of Worth

'God, I hate boats!'

With this heart-felt valediction ringing in my ears, we swung slowly out into the waters of Wilmington harbor.

Two days of purchases and preparations found us now bound for Cross Creek. With money from the sale of the ruby in hand, there had been no need to sell the horses; Duncan had been sent with the wagon and the heavier goods, with Myers aboard to guide him, the rest of us to take a quicker, more comfortable passage with Captain Freeman, aboard the *Sally Ann*.

A craft of singular and indescribable type, the *Sally Ann* was square-beamed, long, low-sided, and blunt-prowed. She boasted a tiny cabin that measured roughly six feet square, leaving a scant two feet on either side for passage, and a somewhat greater area of deck fore and aft, this now partially obscured by bundles, bags, and barrels.

With a single sail mounted on a mast and boom above the cabin, the *Sally Ann* looked from a distance like a crab on a shingle, waving a flag of truce. The peaty brown waters of the Cape Fear lapped a scant four inches below the rail, and the boards of the bottom were perpetually damp with slow leakage.

Still, I was happy. Cramped conditions or no, it was good to be on the water, away – if only temporarily – from the Governor's siren song.

Jamie wasn't happy. He did indeed hate boats, with a profound and undying passion, and suffered from a sea-sickness so acute that watching the swirl of water in a glass could turn him green.

'It's dead calm,' I observed. 'Maybe you won't be sick.'

Jamie squinted suspiciously at the chocolate-brown water around us, then clamped his eyes shut as the wake from another boat struck the *Sally Ann* broadside, rocking her violently.

'Maybe not,' he said, in tones indicating that while the

140

suggestion was a hopeful one, he also thought the possibility remote.

'Do you want the needles? It's better if I put them in before you vomit.' Resigned, I groped in the pocket of my skirt, where I had placed the small box containing the Chinese acupuncture needles that had saved his life on our Atlantic crossing.

He shuddered briefly and opened his eyes.

'No,' he said. 'I'll maybe do. Talk to me, Sassenach – take my mind off my stomach, aye?'

'All right,' I said obligingly. 'What is your Aunt Jocasta like?'

'I havena seen her since I was two years old, so my impressions are a bit lacking,' he replied absently, eyes fixed on a large raft coming down the river, set on an apparent collision course with us. 'D'ye think that Negro can manage? Perhaps I ought to give him a bit of help.'

'Perhaps you shouldn't,' I said, eyeing the oncoming raft warily. 'He seems to know what he's doing.' Besides the captain – a disreputable old wreck who reeked of tobacco – the *Sally Ann* had a single hand, an elderly black freedman who was dealing alone with the steerage of our craft, by means of a large pole.

The man's lean muscles flexed and bulged in easy rhythm. Grizzled head bowed in effort, he took no apparent notice of the oncoming barge, but plunged and lifted in a liquid motion that made the long pole seem like a third limb.

'Let him alone. I suppose you don't know much about your aunt, then?' I added, in hopes of distracting him. The raft was moving ponderously and inexorably toward us.

Some forty feet from end to end, it rode low in the water, weighed down with barrels and stacks of hides, tied down under netting. A pungent wave of odor preceded it, of musk and blood and rancid fat, strong enough to overpower temporarily all the other smells of the river.

'No; she wed the Cameron of Errracht and left Leoch the year before my mother married my father.' He spoke abstractedly, not looking at me; his attention was all on the oncoming barge. His knuckles whitened; I could feel his urge to leap forward, snatch the pole away from the deck-

141

hand, and stave off the raft. I laid a restraining hand on his arm.

'And she never came to visit at Lallybroch?'

I could see the gleam of sun on dull iron, where it struck cleats along the edge of the raft, and the half-naked forms of the three deckhands, sweating even in the early morning. One of them waved his hat and grinned, shouting something that sounded like, 'Hah, *you!*' as they came on.

'Well, John Cameron died of a flux, and she wed his cousin, Black Hugh Cameron of Aberfeldy, and then –' He shut his eyes reflexively as the raft shot past, its hull no more than six inches from our own, amid a hail of good-natured jeers and shouts from its crew. Rollo, front paws perched on the low cabin roof, barked madly, until Ian cuffed him and told him to stop.

Jamie opened one eye, then seeing that the danger was past, opened the other and relaxed, letting go his grip on the roof.

'Aye, well, Black Hugh – they called him so for a great black wen on his knee – he was killed hunting, and so then she wed Hector Mor Cameron, of Loch Eilean –'

'She seems to have had quite a taste for Camerons,' I said, fascinated. 'Is there something special about them as a clan – beyond being accident-prone, I mean?'

'They've a way wi' words, I suppose,' he said, with a sudden wry grin. 'The Camerons are poets – and jesters. Sometimes both. Ye'll remember Lochiel, aye?'

I smiled, sharing his bittersweet recollection of Donald Cameron of Lochiel, one of the chiefs of clan Cameron at the time of the Rising. A handsome man with a soulful gaze, Lochiel's gentle-eyed demeanor and elegant manners hid a truly great talent for the creation of vulgar doggerel, with which, *sotto voce*, he had not infrequently entertained me at balls in Edinburgh, during the brief heyday of Charles Stuart's coup.

Jamie was leaning on the roof of the boat's tiny cabin, watching the river traffic with a wary eye. We had not yet cleared Wilmington's harbor, and small pirettas and sculls darted past like water bugs, whipping in and out between the larger, slower-moving craft. He was pale, but not green yet.

I leaned my elbows on the cabin roof as well, and stretched my back. Hot as it was, the heavy sunshine was comforting to the sore muscles caused by impromptu sleeping arrangements; I had spent the last night curled up on a hard oak settle in the taproom of a riverside tavern, sleeping with my head on Jamie's knee as he completed the arrangements for our passage.

I groaned and stretched.

'Was Hector Cameron a poet, or a joker?'

'Neither one at the moment,' Jamie replied, automatically gripping the back of my neck and massaging it with one hand. 'He's dead, aye?'

'That's wonderful,' I said, groaning with ecstasy as his thumb sank into a particularly tender spot. 'What you're doing, I mean, not that your uncle's dead. Ooh, don't stop. How did he get to North Carolina?'

Jamie snorted with amusement, and moved behind me so he could use both hands on my neck and shoulders. I nestled my bottom against him and sighed in bliss.

'You're a verra noisy woman, Sassenach,' he said, leaning forward to whisper in my ear. 'Ye make the same kind of sounds when I rub your neck as ye do when I –' He thrust his pelvis against me in a discreet but explicit motion that made it quite clear what he meant. 'Mm?'

'Mmmm,' I replied, and kicked him – discreetly – in the shin. 'Fine. If anyone hears me behind closed doors, they'll assume you're rubbing my neck – which is about all you're likely to do until we get off this floating plank. Now, what about your late uncle?'

'Oh, him.' His fingers dug in on either side of my backbone, rubbing slowly up and down as he unraveled yet another strand in the tangled web of his family history. At least it was keeping his mind off his stomach.

Luckier – and either more perceptive or more cynical – than his famous kinsman, Hector Mor Cameron had cannily prepared himself against the eventuality of a Stuart disaster. He had escaped Culloden unwounded and made for home, where he had promptly loaded wife, servant, and portable assets into a coach, in which they fled to Edinburgh and thence by ship to North Carolina, narrowly escaping the Crown's pursuit.

Once arrived in the New World, Hector had purchased a large tract of land, cleared the forest, built a house and a sawmill, bought slaves to work the place, planted his land in tobacco and indigo, and – no doubt worn out by so much industry – succumbed to the morbid sore throat at the ripe old age of seventy-three.

Having evidently decided that three times was enough, Jocasta MacKenzie Cameron Cameron Cameron had – so far as Myers knew – declined to wed again, but stayed on alone as mistress of River Run.

'Do you think the messenger with your letter will get there before we do?'

'He'd get there before we do if he crawled on his hands and knees,' Young Ian said, appearing suddenly beside us. He glanced in mild disgust at the patient deckhand, plunging and lifting his dripping pole. 'It will be *weeks* before we get there, at this rate. I told ye it would have been best to ride, Uncle Jamie.'

'Dinna fret yourself, Ian,' his uncle assured him, letting go of my neck. He grinned at his nephew. 'You'll have a turn at the pole yourself before long – and I expect ye'll have us in Cross Creek before nightfall, aye?'

Ian gave his uncle a dirty look and wandered off to pester Captain Freeman with questions about Red Indians and wild animals.

'I hope the Captain doesn't put Ian overboard,' I said, observing Freeman's scrawny shoulders draw defensively toward his ears as Ian approached. My own neck and shoulders glowed from the attention; so did portions further south. 'Thanks for the rub,' I said, lifting one eyebrow at him.

'I'll let ye return the favor, Sassenach – after dark.' He made an unsuccessful attempt at a leer. Unable to close one eye at a time, his ability to wink lewdly was substantially impaired, but he managed to convey his meaning nonetheless.

'Indeed,' I said. I fluttered my lashes at him. 'And just what is it you'd like rubbed after dark?'

'After dark?' Ian asked, popping up again like a jack-in-

144

the-box before his uncle could answer. 'What happens after dark?'

'That's when I drown ye and cut ye up for fish bait,' his uncle informed him. 'God's sake, can ye not settle, Ian? Ye're bumpin' about like a bumblebee in a bottle. Go and sleep in the sun, like your beast – there's a sensible dog.' He nodded at Rollo, sprawled like a rug on the cabin roof with his eyes half-closed, twitching an occasional ear against the flies.

'Sleep?' Ian looked at his uncle in amazement. '*Sleep?*'

'It's what normal people do when they're tired,' I told him, stifling a yawn. The growing heat and the boat's slow movement were highly soporific, after the short night – we had been up before dawn. Unfortunately, the narrow benches and rough deck planks of the *Sally Ann* didn't look any more inviting than the tavern's settle had been.

'Oh, I'm not a scrap tired, Auntie!' Ian assured me. 'I dinna think I'll sleep for days!'

Jamie eyed his nephew.

'We'll see if ye still think so, after a turn at the pole. In the meantime, perhaps I can find something to occupy your mind. Wait a bit –' He broke off, and ducked into the low cabin, where I heard him rootling through the baggage.

'God, it's hot!' said Ian, fanning himself. 'What's Uncle Jamie after, then?'

'God knows,' I said. Jamie had brought aboard a large crate, about the contents of which he had been most evasive. He had been playing cards when I had fallen asleep the night before, and my best guess was that he had acquired some embarrassing object in the course of gambling, which he was reluctant to expose to Ian's teasing.

Ian was right; it *was* hot. I could only hope that there would be a breeze later; for the moment, the sail above hung limp as a dishcloth, and the fabric of my shift clung damp against my legs. With a murmured word to Ian, I edged past and sidled toward the bow, where the water barrel stood.

Fergus was standing in the prow, arms crossed, giving a splendid impression of a noble figurehead, with his sternly handsome profile pointed upriver, thick, dark hair flowing back from his brow.

'Ah, milady!' He greeted me with a sudden dazzle of white teeth. 'Is this not a splendid country?'

What I could see at the moment was not particularly splendid, the landscape consisting of an extensive mudflat, reeking in the sun, and a large collection of gulls and seabirds, all raucously excited about something smelly they had found near the water's edge.

'Milord tells me that any man may enter a claim for fifty acres of land, so long as he builds a house upon it, and promises to work it for a period of ten years. Imagine – fifty acres!' He rolled the words around in his mouth, savoring them with a kind of awe. A French peasant might think himself well blessed with five.

'Well, yes,' I said, a little doubtfully. 'I think you ought to pick your fifty acres carefully, though. Some parts of this place aren't much good for farming.' I didn't hazard a guess as to how difficult Fergus might find it to carve a farm and homestead out of a howling wilderness with one hand, no matter how fertile the ground.

He wasn't paying attention in any case, his eyes shiny with dreams.

'I might perhaps have a small house built by Hogmanay,' he murmured to himself. 'Then I could send for Marsali and the child in the spring.' His hand went automatically to the vacant spot on his chest, where the greenish medal of St. Dismas had hung since his childhood.

He had come to join us in Georgia, leaving his young and pregnant wife behind in Jamaica, under the care of friends. He assured me that he had no fear for her safety, however, for he had left her also under the protection of his patron saint, with strict instructions not to remove the battered medal from around her neck until she was safely delivered.

I wouldn't myself have thought that mothers and babies fell into the sphere of influence of the patron saint of thieves, but Fergus had lived as a pickpocket for all his early life, and his trust in Dismas was absolute.

146

'Will you call the baby Dismas, if it's a boy?' I asked, joking.

'No,' he said in all seriousness. 'I shall call him Germaine. Germaine James Ian Aloysius Fraser – James Ian for Milord and Monsieur,' he explained, for so he always referred to Jamie and his brother-in-law, Ian Murray.

'Marsali liked Aloysius,' he added dismissively, making it clear that he had had nothing to do with the choice of so undistinguished a name.

'And what if it's a girl?' I asked, with a sudden vivid memory. Twenty-odd years before, Jamie had sent me back through the stones, pregnant. And the last thing he had said to me, convinced the child I carried was a boy, was, 'Name him Brian, for my father.'

'Oh.' Fergus had clearly not considered this possibility, either, for he looked vaguely disconcerted. Then his features cleared.

'Genevieve,' he said firmly. 'For Madame,' by this meaning Jenny Murray, Jamie's sister. 'Genevieve Claire, I think,' he added, with another dazzling smile.

'Oh,' I said, flustered and oddly flattered. 'Well. Thank you. Are you sure that you ought not to go back to Jamaica to be with Marsali, Fergus?' I asked, changing the subject.

He shook his head decidedly.

'Milord may have need of me,' he said. 'And I am of more use here than I should be there. Babies are women's work, and who knows what dangers we may encounter in this strange place?'

As though in answer to this rhetorical question, the gulls rose in a squawking cloud, wheeling out over the river and mudflats, revealing the object of their appetite.

A stout pine stake had been driven into the mud of the bank, the top of it a foot below the dark, weedy line that marked the upper reaches of the incoming tide. The tide was still low; it had reached no higher than halfway up the stake. Above the lapping waves of silty water hung the figure of a man, fastened to the stake by a chain around his chest. Or what had once been his chest.

I couldn't tell how long he had been there, but quite long enough, from the looks of him. A narrow gash of

147

white showed the curve of skull where skin and hair had been stripped off. Impossible to say what he had looked like; the birds had been busy.

Beside me, Fergus said something very obscene in French, softly under his breath.

'Pirate,' said Captain Freeman laconically, coming up beside me and pausing long enough to spit a brown stream of tobacco juice into the river. 'If they ain't taken to Charleston for hangin', sometimes they stake 'em out at low tide and let the river have 'em.'

'Are – are there a lot of them?' Ian had seen it, too; he was much too old to reach for my hand, but he stood close beside me, his face pale under its tan.

'Not so much, no more. The Navy does a good job keepin' 'em down. But go back a few years, why, you could see four or five pirates out here at a time. Folk would pay to come out by boat, to sit and watch 'em drown. Real pretty out here when the tide comes in at sunset,' he said, jaws moving in a slow, nostalgic rhythm. 'Turns the water red.'

'Look!' Ian, forgetting his dignity, clutched me by the arm. There was a movement near the riverbank, and we saw what had startled the birds away.

It slid into the water, a long, scaly form some five or six feet long, carving a deep groove in the soft mud of the bank. On the far side of the boat, the deckhand muttered something under his breath, but didn't stop his poling.

'It is a crocodile,' Fergus said, and made the sign of the horns in distaste.

'No, I dinna think so.' Jamie spoke behind me, and I swung around to see him peering over the cabin roof, at the still figure in the water and the V-shaped wake moving toward it. He held a book in his hand, thumb between the pages to hold his place, and now bent his head to consult the volume.

'I belive it is an alligator. They dine upon carrion, it says here, and willna eat fresh meat. When they take a man or a sheep, they pull the victim beneath the water to drown it, but then drag it to their den below ground and leave it there until it has rotted enough to suit their fancy. Of course,' he added, with a bleak glance at the bank, 'they're sometimes fortunate enough to find a meal prepared.'

The figure on the stake seemed to tremble briefly, as something bumped it from below, and Ian made a small choking noise beside me.

'Where did you get that book?' I asked, not taking my eyes off the stake. The top of the wooden pole was vibrating, as though something under the waves was worrying at it. Then the pole was still, and the V-shaped wake could be seen again, traveling back toward the river-bank. I turned away before it could emerge.

Jamie handed me the book, his eyes still fixed on the black mudflat and its cloud of screeching birds.

'The Governor gave it to me. He said he thought it might be of interest on our journey.'

I glanced down at the book. Bound in plain buckram, the title was stamped on the spine in gold leaf – *The Natural History of North Carolina.*

'Eeugh!' said Ian beside me, watching the scene on shore in horror. 'That's the most awful thing I've ever –'

'Of interest,' I echoed, eyes fixed firmly on the book. 'Yes, I expect it will be.'

Fergus, impervious to squeamishness of any kind, was watching the reptile's progress up the mudbank with interest.

'An alligator, you say. Still, it is much the same thing as a crocodile, is it not?'

'Yes,' I said, shuddering despite the heat. I turned my back on the shore. I had met a crocodile at close range in the Indies, and wasn't anxious to improve my acquaint-ance with any of its relatives.

Fergus wiped sweat from his upper lip, dark eyes intent on the gruesome thing.

'Dr. Stern once told Milord and myself about the travels of a Frenchman named Sonnini, who visited Egypt and wrote much of the sights he had witnessed and the customs he was told of. He said that in that country, the crocodiles copulate upon the muddy banks of the rivers, the female being laid upon her back, and in that position, incapable of rising without the assistance of the male.'

149

'Oh, aye?' Ian was all ears.

'Indeed. He said that some men there, hurried on by the impulses of depravity, would take advantage of this forced situation of the female, and hunt away the male, whereupon they would take his place and enjoy the inhuman embrace of the reptile, which is said to be a most powerful charm for the procurement of rank and riches.'

Ian's mouth sagged open.

'You're no serious, man?' he demanded of Fergus, incredulous. He turned to Jamie. 'Uncle?'

Jamie shrugged, amused.

'I should rather live poor but virtuous, myself.' He cocked an eyebrow at me. 'Besides, I think your auntie wouldna like it much if I was to forsake her embraces for a reptile's.'

The black man, listening to this from his position in the bow, shook his head and spoke without looking round.

'Any man what gone frig with an alligator to get rich, he's done earnt it, you ask me.'

'I rather think you're right,' I said, with a vivid memory of the Governor's charming, toothy smile. I glanced at Jamie, but he was no longer paying attention. His eyes were fixed upriver, intent on possibility, both book and alligator forgotten for the moment. At least he'd forgotten to be sick.

The tidal surge caught us a mile above Wilmington, allaying Ian's fears for our speed. The Cape Fear was a tidal river, whose daily surge carried up two-thirds of its length, nearly as far as Cross Creek.

I felt the river quicken under us, the boat rising an inch or two, then beginning slowly to pick up speed as the power of the incoming tide was funneled up the harbor and into the river's narrow channel. The slave sighed with relief and hoisted the dripping pole free of the water.

There would be no need for poling until the surge ran out, in five or six hours. Then we would either anchor for the night and catch the fresh surge of the next incoming tide, or use the sail for further progress, wind allowing. Poling, I was given to understand, was necessary only in case of sandbars or windless days.

150

A sense of peaceful somnolence settled over the craft. Fergus and Ian curled up in the bow to sleep, while Rollo kept guard on the roof above, tongue dripping as he panted, eyes half closed against the sun. The Captain and his hand – commonly addressed as 'you, Troklus', but whose name was actually Eutroclus – disappeared into the tiny cabin, from which I could hear the musical sound of liquid being poured.

Jamie was in the cabin, too, having gone to fetch something from his mysterious crate. I hoped it was drinkable; even sitting still on the stern transom with my feet dangling in the water, and with the small breeze of movement stirring the hair on my neck, I could feel sweat forming wherever skin touched skin.

There were indistinct murmurs in the cabin, and laughter. Jamie came out and turned toward the stern, stepping delicately through the piles of goods like a Clydesdale stallion in a field of frogs, a large wooden box held in his arms.

He set this gently on my lap, shucked off his shoes and stockings, and sat down beside me, putting his feet in the water with a sigh of pleasure at the coolness.

'What's this?' I ran my hand curiously over the box.

'Oh, only a wee present.' He didn't look at me, but the tips of his ears were pink. 'Open it, hm?'

It was a heavy box, both wide and deep. Carved of a dense, fine-grained dark wood, it bore the marks of heavy use – nicks and dents that had seasoned but not impaired its polished beauty. It was hasped for a lock, but there was none; the lid rose easily on oiled brass hinges, and a whiff of camphor floated out, vaporous as a jinn.

The instruments gleamed under the smoky sun, bright despite a hazing of disuse. Each had its own pocket, carefully fitted and lined in green velvet.

A small, heavy-toothed saw; scissors, three scalpels – round-bladed, straight-bladed, scoop-bladed; the silver blade of a tongue depressor, a tenaculum . . .

'Jamie!' Delighted, I lifted out a short ebony rod, to the end of which was affixed a ball of worsted, wrapped in rather moth-eaten velvet. I'd seen one before, at Versailles;

the eighteenth-century version of a reflex hammer. 'Oh, Jamie! How wonderful!'

He wiggled his feet, pleased.

'Oh, ye like it?'

'I love it! Oh, look – there's more in the lid, under this flap –' I stared for a moment at the disjointed tubes, screws, platforms and mirrors, until my mind's eye shuffled them and presented me with the neatly assembled vision. 'A microscope!' I touched it reverently. 'My God, a microscope.'

'There's more,' he pointed out, eager to show me. 'The front opens and there are wee drawers inside.'

There were – containing, among other things, a miniature balance and set of brass weights, a tile for rolling pills, and a stained marble mortar, its pestle wrapped in cloth to prevent its being cracked in transit. Inside the front, above the drawers, were row upon row of small, corked bottles made of stone or glass.

'Oh, they're beautiful!' I said, handling the small scalpel with reverence. The polished wood of the handle fit my hand as though it had been made for me, the blade weighted to an exquisite balance. 'Oh, Jamie, thank you!'

'Ye like them, then?' His ears had gone bright red with pleasure. 'I thought they'd maybe do. I've no notion what they're meant for, but I could see they were finely made.'

I had no notion what some of the pieces were meant for, but all of them were beautiful in themselves; made by or for a man who loved his tools and what they did.

'Who did they belong to, I wonder?' I breathed heavily on the rounded surface of a lenticular and brought it to a soft gleam with a fold of my skirt.

'The woman who sold it to me didna ken; he left behind his doctor's book, though, and I took that, as well – perhaps it will give his name.'

Lifting the top tray of instruments, he revealed another, shallower tray, from which he drew out a fat square-bound book, some eight inches wide, covered in scuffed black leather.

'I thought ye might be wanting a book, too, like the one ye kept in France,' he explained. 'The one where ye kept the pictures and the notes of the people ye saw at

152

L'Hopital. He's written a bit in this one, but there's a deal of blank pages left at the back.'

Perhaps a quarter of the book had been used; the pages were covered with a closely written, fine black script, interspersed with drawings that took my eye with their clinical familiarity: an ulcerated toe, a shattered kneecap, the skin neatly peeled aside; the grotesque swelling of advanced goiter, and a dissection of the calf muscles, each neatly labeled.

I turned back to the inside cover; sure enough, his name was written on the first page, adorned with a small, gentlemanly flourish: *Dr. Daniel Rawlings, Esq.*

'What happened to Dr. Rawlings, I wonder? Did the woman who had the box say?'

Jamie nodded, his brow slightly creased.

'The Doctor lodged with her for a night. He said he'd come from Virginia, where his home was, bound upon some errand, and his case with him. He was looking for a man named Garver – she thought that was the name, at least. But that night after supper he went out – and never came back.'

I stared at him.

'Never came back? Did she find out what happened to him?'

Jamie shook his head, batting away a small cloud of midges. The sun was sinking, painting the surface of the water gold and orange, and bugs were beginning to gather as the afternoon cooled into evening.

'No. She went to the sheriff, and to the justice, and the constable searched high and low – but there was nay sign of the man. They looked for a week, and then gave up. He had never told his landlady which town it was in Virginia, so they couldna trace him further.'

'How very odd.' I wiped a droplet of moisture off my chin. 'When did the Doctor disappear?'

'A year past, she said.' He looked at me, a little anxious. 'Ye dinna mind? Using his things, I mean?'

'No.' I closed the lid and stroked it gently, the dark wood warm and smooth under my fingers. 'If it were me – I'd want someone to use them.'

I remembered vividly the feel of my own doctor's bag –

cordovan leather, with my initials stamped in gilt on the handle. Originally stamped in gilt on the handle, that is; they had long since worn off, the leather gone smooth and shiny, rich with handling. Frank had given me the bag when I graduated from medical school; I had given it to my friend Joe Abernathy, wanting it to be used by someone who would treasure it as I had.

He saw the shadow drift across my face – I saw the reflection of it darken his – but I took his hand and smiled as I squeezed it.

'It's a wonderful gift. However did you find it?'

He smiled then, in return. The sun blazed low, a brilliant orange ball glimpsed briefly through dark treetops.

'I'd seen the box when I went to the goldsmith's shop – it was the goldsmith's wife who'd kept it. Then I went back yesterday, meaning to buy ye a bit of jewelry – maybe a brooch – and whilst the goodwife was showing me the gauds, we happened to speak of this and that, and she told me of the Doctor, and –' He shrugged.

'Why did you want to buy me jewelry?' I looked at him, puzzled. The sale of the ruby had left us with a bit of money, but extravagance was not at all like him, and under the circumstances –

'Oh! To make up for sending all that money to Laoghaire? I didn't mind; I said I didn't.'

He had – with some reluctance – arranged to send the bulk of the proceeds from the sale of the stone to Scotland, in payment of a promise made to Laoghaire MacKenzie – damn her eyes – Fraser, whom he had married at his sister's persuasion while under the rather logical impression that if I was not dead, I was at least not coming back. My apparent resurrection from the dead had caused any amount of complications, Laoghaire not least among them.

'Aye, ye said so,' he said, openly cynical.

'I meant it – more or less,' I said, and laughed. 'You couldn't very well let the beastly woman starve to death, appealing as the idea is.'

He smiled, faintly.

'No. I shouldna like to have that on my conscience;

there's enough without. But that's not why I wished to buy ye a present.'

'Why, then?' The box was heavy; a gracious, substantial, satisfying weight across my legs, its wood a delight under my hands. He turned his head to look full at me, then, his hair fire-struck with the setting sun, face dark in silhouette.

'Twenty-four years ago today, I married ye, Sassenach,' he said softly. 'I hope ye willna have cause yet to regret it.'

The river's edge was settled, rimmed with plantations from Wilmington to Cross Creek. Still, the banks were thickly forested, with only the occasional glimpse of fields where a break in the trees showed plantings, or every so often, a wooden dock, half-hidden in the foliage.

We proceeded slowly upriver, following the tidal surge so long as it lasted, tying up for the night when it ran out. We ate dinner by a small fire on shore, but slept on the boat, Eutroclus having casually mentioned the prevalence of water moccasins, who – he said – inhabited dens beneath the riverbank but were much inclined to come and warm their cold blood next to the bodies of unwary sleepers.

I awoke soon before dawn, stiff and sore from sleeping on boards, hearing the soft rush of a vessel passing on the river nearby, feeling the push of its wake against our hull. Jamie stirred in his sleep when he felt me move, turned over, and clasped me to his bosom.

I could feel his body curled behind mine, in its paradoxical morning state of sleep and arousal. He made a drowsy noise and moved against me in inquiry, his hand fumbling at the hem of my rumpled shift.

'Stop,' I said under my breath, batting his hand away. 'Remember where we are, for God's sake!'

I could hear the shouts and barking of Ian and Rollo, galumphing to and fro on the shore, and small stirrings in the cabin, featuring hawking and spitting noises, indicating the imminent emergence of Captain Freeman.

'Oh,' said Jamie, coming to the surface of consciousness. 'Oh, aye. A pity, that.' He reached up, squeezed my breasts with both hands, and stretched his body with voluptuous slowness against me, giving me a detailed idea of what I was missing.

'Ah, well,' he said, relaxing reluctantly, but not yet letting go. '*Foeda est in coitu*, um?'

'It what?'

' "*Foeda est in coitu et breois voluptas*," ' he recited obligingly. ' "*Et taedat Veneiis statim peractae*. Doing, a filthy pleasure is – and short. And done, we straight repent us of the sport." '

I glanced down at the stained boards under us. 'Well, perhaps "filthy" isn't altogether the wrong word,' I began, 'but –'

'It's not the filthiness that troubles me, Sassenach,' he interrupted, scowling at Ian, who was hanging over the side of the boat, shouting encouragement to Rollo as he swam. 'It's the short.'

He glanced at me, scowl changing to a look of approval as he took in my state of dishevelment. 'I mean to take my time about it, aye?'

This classical start to the day seemed to have had some lasting influence on Jamie's mind. I could hear them at it as I sat in the afternoon sun, thumbing through Daniel Rawlings's casebook – at once entertained, enlightened, and appalled at the things recorded there.

I could hear Jamie's voice in the ordered rise and fall of ancient Greek. I had heard that bit before – a passage from the *Odyssey*. He paused, with an expectant rise.

'Ah . . .' said Ian.

'What comes next, Ian?'

'Er . . .'

'Once more,' said Jamie, with a slight edge to his voice. 'Pay attention, man. I'm no talkin' for the pleasure of hearin' myself, aye?' He began again, the elegant, formal verse warming to life as he spoke.

He might not take pleasure in hearing himself, but I did. I had no Greek myself, but the rise and fall of syllables in that soft, deep voice was as soothing as the lap of water against the hull.

Reluctantly accepting his nephew's continued presence, Jamie took his guardianship of Ian with due seriousness, and had been tutoring the lad as we traveled, seizing odd moments of leisure to teach – or attempt to teach – the lad the rudiments of Greek and Latin grammar, and to improve his mathematics and conversational French.

Fortunately, Ian had the same quick grasp of mathematical principles as his uncle; the side of the small cabin beside me was covered with elegant Euclidean proofs, carried out in burnt stick. When the subject turned to languages, though, they found less common ground.

Jamie was a natural polygogue; he acquired languages and dialects with no visible effort, picking up idioms as a dog picks up foxtails in a romp through the fields. In addition, he had been schooled in the Classics at the *Université* in Paris, and – while disagreeing now and then with some of the Roman philosophers – regarded both Homer and Virgil as personal friends.

Ian spoke the Gaelic and English with which he had been raised, and a sort of low French patois acquired from Fergus, and felt this quite sufficient to his needs. True, he had an impressive repertoire of swear words in six or seven other languages – acquired from exposure to a number of disreputable influences in the recent past, not least of these being his uncle – but he had no more than a vague apprehension of the mysteries of Latin conjugation.

Still less did he have an appreciation for the necessity of learning languages that to him were not only dead, but – he clearly thought – long decayed beyond any possibility of usefulness. Homer couldn't compete with the excitement of this new country, adventure reaching out from both shores with beckoning green hands.

Jamie finished his Greek passage, and with a sigh clearly audible to me where I sat, directed Ian to take out the Latin book he had borrowed from Governor Tryon's library. With no recitation to distract me, I returned to my perusal of Dr. Rawlings's casebook.

Like myself, the Doctor had plainly had some Latin, but preferred English for the bulk of his notes, dropping into Latin only for an occasional formal entry.

Bled Mr. Beddoes of a pt. Note distinct lessening of the bilious humor, his complexion much improved of the yellowness and pustules which have afflicted him. Administered black draught to assist purifying of the blood.

'Ass,' I muttered – not for the first time. 'Can't you see the man's got liver disease?' Probably a mild cirrhosis; Rawlings had noted a slight enlargement and hardening of the liver – though he attributed this to excessive production of bile. Most likely alcohol poisoning; the pustules on face and chest were characteristic of a nutritional deficiency that I saw commonly associated with excessive alcohol consumption – and God knew, *that* was epidemic.

Beddoes, if he were still alive – a prospect I considered doubtful – was likely drinking anything up to a quart of mixed spirit daily and hadn't so much as smelled a green vegetable in months. The pustules on whose disappearance Rawlings was congratulating himself had likely diminished because he had used turnip leaves as a coloring agent in his special receipt for 'black draught'.

Absorbed in my reading, I half heard Ian's stumbling rendition of Plautus's *Vertue* from the other side of the cabin, interrupted in every other line by Jamie's deeper voice, prompting and correcting.

' "*Virtus praemium est optimus . . .*" '

'*Optimum.*'

' " . . . *est optimum. Virtus omnibus rebus*" and . . . ah . . . and . . .'

'*Anteit.*'

'Thank ye, Uncle. "*Virtus omnibus rebus anteit . . . profectus*"?'

'*Profecto.*'

'Oh, aye, *profecto.* Um . . . "*Virtus*"?'

'*Libertas.* "*Libertas salus vita res et parentes, patria et prognati . . .*" d'ye recall what is meant by "*vita*", Ian?'

'Life,' came Ian's voice, seizing gratefully on this buoyant object in a flounderous sea.

'Aye, that's good, but it's more than life. In Latin, it means not only being alive but it's also a man's substance, what he's made of. See, then it goes on, " . . . *libertas salus vita res et parentes, patria et prognati tutantur, servantur; virtus omnia in sese habet, omnia adsunt bona quem penest virtus.*" Now, what is he sayin' there, d'ye think?'

158

'Ah . . . virtue is a good thing?' Ian ventured.

There was a momentary silence, during which I could almost hear Jamie's blood pressure rising. A hiss of indrawn breath, then, as he thought better of whatever he had been about to say, a long-suffering exhalation.

'Mmphm. Look ye, Ian. "*Tutantur, servantur.*" What does he mean by using those two together, instead of putting it as . . .' My attention faded, drawn back to the book, wherein Dr. Rawlings now gave account of a duel and its consequences.

May 15. Was called from my bed at dawn to attend a gentleman staying at the Red Dog. Found him in sad case, with a wound to his hand, occasioned by the misfire of a pistol, the thumb and index fingers of the hand being blown off altogether by the explosion, the middle finger badly mangled and two-thirds of the hand so lacerated that it was scarce recognizable as a human appendage.

Determining that only prompt amputation would serve, I sent for the landlord and requested a pannikin of brandy, linen for bandages, and the help of two strong men. These being rapidly provided and the patient suitably restrained, I proceeded to take the hand – it was the right, to the misfortune of the patient – off just above the wrist. Successfully ligated two arteries, but the anterior interosseus *escaped me, being retracted into the flesh after I sawed through the bones. Was forced to loosen the tourniquet in order to find it, so bleeding was considerable – a fortunate accident, as the copious outpouring of blood rendered the patient insensible and thus put an end for the moment to his agony, as well as to his struggles, which were greatly hampering my work.*

The amputation being successfully concluded, the gentleman was put to bed, but I stayed near at hand, lest he regain consciousness abruptly and in random movement do hurt to my stitching.

This fascinating narrative was interrupted by a sudden outburst from Jamie, who had evidently reached the end of his patience.

'Ian, your Latin would disgrace a dog! And as for the

159

rest, ye havena got enough understanding of Greek to tell the difference between water and wine!'

'If they're drinkin' it, it's not water,' Ian muttered, sounding rebellious.

I closed the book and got hastily to my feet. It sounded rather as though the services of a referee might shortly be called for. Ian was making small Scottish noises of discontent as I rounded the cabin.

'Aye, mmphm, but I dinna care so much –'

'Aye, ye don't care! That's the true pity of it – that ye havena the grace even to feel shame for your ignorance!'

There was a charged silence after this, broken only by the soft splash of Troklus's pole in the bow. I peeked around the corner, to see Jamie glaring at his nephew, who looked abashed. Ian glanced at me, coughed and cleared his throat.

'Well, I'll tell ye, Uncle Jamie, if I thought shame would help, I wouldna scruple to blush.'

He looked so apologetically hangdog that I couldn't help laughing. Jamie turned, hearing me, and his scowl faded slightly.

'Ye're not a bit of help, Sassenach,' he said. 'You've the Latin, have ye not? Being a physician, ye must. Perhaps I should leave his Latin schooling to you, aye?'

I shook my head. While it was more or less true that I could read Latin – badly and laboriously – I didn't fancy trying to cram the ragbag remnants of my education into Ian's head.

'All I remember is *Arma virumque cano.*' I glanced at Ian and translated, grinning. 'My arm got bit off by a dog.'

Ian burst into giggles, and Jamie gave me a look of profound disillusion.

He sighed and ran a hand through his hair. While Jamie and Ian didn't resemble each other in any physical respect beyond height, both had thick hair and the habit of running a hand through it when agitated or thoughtful. It looked to have been a stressful lesson – both of them looked as though they'd been pulled backward through a hedgerow.

Jamie smiled wryly at me, then turned back to Ian, shaking his head.

160

'Ah, well. I'm sorry to bark at ye, Ian, truly. But ye've a fine mind, and I shouldna like to see ye waste it. God, man, at your age, I was in Paris, already starting in to study at the *Université*!'

Ian stood looking down into the water that swirled past the side of the ship in smooth brown riffles. His hands rested on the rail; big hands, broadbacked and browned by the sun.

'Aye,' he said. 'And at my age, my own father was in France, too. Fighting.'

I was a bit startled to hear this. I had known that the elder Ian had soldiered in France for a time, but not that he had gone so early for a soldier – nor stayed so long. Young Ian was just fifteen. The elder Ian had served as a foreign mercenary from that age, then, until the age of twenty-two; when a cannon blast had left him with a leg so badly shattered by grapeshot that it had been amputated just below the knee – and he had come home for good.

Jamie looked at his nephew for a moment, frowning slightly. Then he came to stand beside Ian, leaning backward, hands on the rail to balance himself.

'I ken that, aye?' Jamie said quietly. 'For I followed him, four years later, when I was outlawed.'

Ian looked up at that, startled.

'Ye were together there in France?'

There was a slight breeze caused by our movement, but it was still a hot day. Perhaps the temperature decided him that it was better to let the subject of higher learning drop for a moment, for Jamie nodded, lifting the thick tail of his hair to cool his neck.

'In Flanders. For more than a year, before Ian was wounded and sent home. We fought wi' a regiment of Scots mercenaries then – under Fergus mac Leodhas.'

Ian's eyes were alight with interest.

'Is that where Fergus – our Fergus – got his name, then?'

His uncle smiled.

'Aye, I named him for mac Leodhas; a bonny man, and a great soldier, forbye. He thought weel o' Ian. Did your Da never speak to you of him?'

Ian shook his head, his brow slightly clouded.

'He's never said a thing to me. I – I kent he'd lost his leg fighting in France – Mam told me that, when I asked – but he wouldna say a word about it, himself.'

With Dr. Rawlings's description of amputation vivid in my mind, I thought it likely that the elder Ian hadn't wanted to recall the occasion.

Jamie shrugged, plucking the sweat-damp shirt away from his chest.

'Aye, well. I suppose he meant to put that time behind him, once he'd come home and settled at Lallybroch. And then . . .' He hesitated, but Ian was insistent.

'And then what, Uncle Jamie?'

Jamie glanced at his nephew, and one side of his mouth curled up.

'Well, I think he didna want to tell too many tales of war and fighting, lest you lads get thinking on it and set yourselves to go for soldiers, too. He and your mother will ha' wanted better for you, aye?'

I thought the elder Ian had been wise; it was clear from the look on his face that the younger Ian couldn't think of a much more exciting prospect than war and fighting.

'That will ha' been my mam's doing,' Ian said, with an air of disgust. 'She'd have me wrapped in wool and tied to her apron strings, did I let her.'

Jamie grinned.

'Oh, let her, is it? And d'ye think she'd wrap ye in wool and smother ye wi' kisses if ye were home this minute?'

Ian dropped the pose of disdain.

'Well, no,' he admitted. 'I think she'd skelp me raw.'

Jamie laughed.

'Ye know a bit about women, Ian, if not so much as ye think.'

Ian glanced skeptically from his uncle to me, and back.

'And you'll ken all about them, I suppose, Uncle?'

I raised one eyebrow, inviting an answer to this, but Jamie merely laughed.

'It's a wise man who kens the limits of his knowledge, Ian.' He bent and kissed my damp forehead, then turned back to his nephew, adding, 'Though I could wish your own limits went a bit further.'

Ian shrugged, looking bored.

'I dinna mean to set up for a gentleman,' he said. 'After

all, Young Jamie and Michael dinna read Greek; they do well enough!'

Jamie rubbed his nose, considering his nephew thoughtfully.

'Young Jamie has Lallybroch. And wee Michael does well wi' Jared in Paris. They'll be settled. We did as best we might for the two o' them, but there was precious little money to pay for travel or schooling when they came to manhood. There wasna much choice for them, aye?'

He pushed himself off the rail and stood upright.

'But your parents dinna want that for you, Ian, if better might be managed. They'd have ye grow to be a man of learning and influence; *duine uasal,* perhaps.' It was a Gaelic expression I had heard before, literally 'a man of worth'. It was the term for tacksmen and lairds, the men of property and followers who ranked only below chieftains in the Highland clans.

Such a man as Jamie himself had been, before the Rising. But not now.

'Mmphm. And did ye do as your parents wanted for ye, then, Uncle Jamie?' Ian looked blandly at his uncle, with only a wary twitch of the eye to show he knew he was treading on shaky ground. Jamie had been meant to be *duine uasal,* indeed; Lallybroch had been his by right. It was only in an effort to save the property from confiscation by the Crown that he had made it over legally to Young Jamie, instead.

Jamie stared at him for a moment, then rubbed a knuckle across his upper lip before replying.

'I did say ye'd a fine mind, no?' he answered dryly. 'Though since ye ask . . . I was raised to do two things, Ian. To mind my land and people, and to care for my family. I've done those two things, as best I might – and I shall go on doing them as best I can.'

Young Ian had the grace to look abashed at this.

'Aye, well, I didna mean . . .' he mumbled, looking at his feet.

'Dinna fash, laddie,' Jamie interrupted, clapping him on the shoulder. He grinned wryly at his nephew. 'Ye'll amount to something for your mother's sake – if it kills us both. And now I think it will be my turn at the pole.'

He glanced forward, to where Troklus's shoulders gleamed like oily copper, snake-muscled with long labor. Jamie untied his breeches – unlike the other men, he would not take off his shirt for poling, but stripped his breeks for coolness and worked with his shirt knotted between his thighs, in the Highland style – and nodded to Ian.

'You think about it, laddie. Youngest son or no, your life's not meant to be wasted.'

· He smiled at me then, with a sudden heart-stopping brilliance, and handed me his shed breeks. Then, still holding my hand in his, he stood upright and, hand over heart, declaimed,

> *'Amo, amas, I love a lass,*
> *As cedar tall and slender;*
> *Sweet cowslip's grace*
> *Is her nominative case,*
> *And she's o' the feminine gender.'*

He nodded graciously to Ian, who had dissolved in giggles, and lifted my hand to his lips, blue eyes aslant with mischief.

> *'Can I decline a nymph so divine?*
> *Her voice like a flute is dulcis;*
> *Her oculus bright, her manus white*
> *And soft, when I tacto, her pulse is.*
> *O how bella, my puella*
> *I'll kiss in secula seculorum;*
> *If I've luck, sir, she's my uxor,*
> *O dies benedictorum.'*

He made a courtly leg to me, blinked solemnly in his version of a wink, and strode off in his shirt.

9

Two-thirds of a Ghost

The surface of the river gleamed like oil, the water moving gently past without a ripple. There was a single lantern hung from the starboard bow; sitting on a low stool perched on the forward deck, I could see the light below, not so much reflected in the water as trapped under it, moving slowly side by side with the boat.

The moon was a faint sickle, making its feeble sweep through the treetops. Beyond the thick trees that lined the river, the ground fell away in broad sweeps of darkness, over the rice plantations and tobacco fields. The heat of the day was sucked down into the earth, glowing with unseen energy beneath the surface of the soil, the rich, fertile flatlands simmering in black heat behind the screen of pines and sweetgum trees, working the alchemy of water and trapped sun.

To move at all was to break a sweat. The air was tangible, each tiny ripple of warmth a caress against my face and arms.

There was a soft rustle in the dark behind me, and I reached up a hand, not turning to look. Jamie's big hand closed gently over mine, squeezed and let go. Even that brief touch left my fingers damp with perspiration.

He eased himself down next to me with a sigh, plucking at the collar of his shirt.

'I dinna think I've breathed air since we left Georgia,' he said. 'Every time I take a breath, I think I'll maybe drown.'

I laughed, feeling a trickle of sweat snake down between my breasts.

'It will be cooler in Cross Creek; everyone says so.' I took a deep breath myself, just to prove I could. 'Doesn't it smell wonderful, though?' The darkness released all the pungent green scents of the trees and plants along the water's edge, mingling with the damp mud of the river-

165

bank and the scent of sun-warmed wood from the deck of the boat.

'Ye'd have made a good dog, Sassenach.' He leaned back against the wall of the cabin with a sigh. 'It's no wonder yon beast admires ye so.'

The click of toenails on deckboards announced the arrival of Rollo, who advanced cautiously toward the rail, stopped a careful foot short of it, and lowered himself gingerly to the deck. He laid his nose on his paws and sighed deeply. Rollo disapproved almost as strongly of boats as Jamie did.

'Hullo there,' I said. I extended a hand for him to sniff, and he politely condescended to let me scratch his ears. 'And where's your master, eh?'

'In the cabin, bein' taught new ways to cheat at cards,' Jamie said wryly. 'God kens best what will happen to the lad; if he's not shot or knocked on the head in some tavern, he'll likely come home wi' an ostrich he's won at faro next.'

'Surely they haven't either ostriches or faro games up in the mountains? If there aren't any towns to speak of, surely there aren't many taverns, either.'

'Well, I shouldna think so,' he admitted. 'But if a man's bound to go to the devil, he'll find a way to do it, no matter where ye set him down.'

'I'm sure Ian isn't going to the devil,' I replied soothingly. 'He's a fine boy.'

'He's a man,' Jamie corrected. He cocked an ear toward the cabin, where I could hear muffled laughter and the occasional comfortable obscenity. 'A damn young one, though, and fat-heided with it.' He looked at me, a rueful smile visible in the lantern light.

'If he were a wee lad yet, I could keep some rein on him. As it is –' He shrugged. 'He's old enough to mind his own business, and he'll not thank me for sticking my nose in.'

'He always listens to you,' I protested.

'Mmphm. Wait till I tell him something he doesna want to hear.' He leaned his head against the wall, closing his eyes. Sweat gleamed across the high cheekbones, and a small trickle ran down the side of his neck.

166

I put out a finger and delicately flicked the tiny drop away, before it further dampened his shirt.

'You've been telling him for two months that he has to go home to Scotland; he doesn't want to hear that, I don't think.'

Jamie opened one eye and surveyed me cynically.

'Is he in Scotland?'

'Well . . .'

'Mmphm,' he said, and closed the eye again.

I sat quietly for a bit, blotting the perspiration off my face with a fold of my skirt. The river had narrowed here; the near bank was no more than ten feet away. I caught a rustle of movement among the shrubs, and a pair of eyes gleamed briefly red with reflected light from our lantern.

Rollo lifted his head with a sudden low *Woof*, ears pricked to attention. Jamie opened his eyes and glanced at the bank, then sat up abruptly.

'Christ! That's the biggest rat I've ever seen!'

I laughed.

'It's not a rat; it's a possum. See the babies on her back?'

Jamie and Rollo regarded the possum with identical looks of calculation, assessing its plumpness and possible speed. Four small possums stared solemnly back, pointed noses twitching over their mother's humped, indifferent back. Obviously thinking the boat no threat, the mother possum finished lapping water, turned, and trundled slowly into the brush, the tip of her naked thick pink tail disappearing as the lantern light faded.

The two hunters let out identical sighs, and relaxed again.

'Myers did say as they're fine eating,' Jamie remarked wistfully. With a small sigh of my own, I groped in the pocket of my gown and handed him a cloth bag.

'What's this?' He peered interestedly into the bag, then poured the small, lumpy brown objects out into the palm of his hand.

'Roasted peanuts,' I said. 'They grow underground hereabouts. I found a farmer selling them for hogfood, and had the inn-wife roast some for me. You take off the shells before you eat them.' I grinned at him, enjoying

167

the novel sensation of for once knowing more about our surroundings than he did.

He gave me a mildly dirty look, and crushed a shell between thumb and forefinger, yielding three nuts.

'I'm ignorant, Sassenach,' he said. 'Not a fool. There's a difference, aye?' He put a peanut in his mouth and bit down gingerly. His skeptical look changed to one of pleased surprise, and he chewed with increasing enthusiasm, tossing the other nuts into his mouth.

'Like them?' I smiled, enjoying his pleasure. 'I'll make you peanut butter for your bread, once we're settled and I have my new mortar unpacked.'

He smiled back and swallowed before cracking another nut.

'I will say that if it's a swampish place, at least it's fine soil. I've never seen so many things grow so easily.'

He tossed another nut into his mouth.

'I have been thinking, Sassenach,' he said, looking down into the palm of his hand. 'What would ye think of maybe settling here?'

The question wasn't entirely unexpected. I had seen him eyeing the black fields and lush crops with a farmer's glittering eye, and caught his wistful expression when he admired the Governor's horses.

We couldn't go back to Scotland immediately, in any case. Young Ian, yes, but not Jamie or me, owing to certain complications – not the least of these being a complication by the name of Laoghaire MacKenzie.

'I don't know,' I said slowly. 'Indians and wild animals quite aside –'

'Och, well,' he interrupted, mildly embarrassed. 'Myers told me they were no difficulty at all, and ye keep clear of the mountains.'

I forbore from pointing out that the Governor's offer would take us into the precincts of precisely those mountains.

'Yes, but you do remember what I told you, don't you? About the Revolution? This is 1767, and you heard the conversation at the Governor's table. Nine years, Jamie, and all hell breaks loose.' We had both lived through war, and neither of us took the thought lightly. I laid a hand on his arm, forcing him to look at me.

'I was right, you know – before.' I had known what would happen at Culloden; had told him the fate of Charles Stuart and his men. And neither my knowing nor his had been enough to save us. Twenty aching years of separation, and the ghost of a daughter he would never see lay behind that knowing.

He nodded slowly, and lifted a hand to touch my cheek. The soft glow of the small lantern overhead attracted clouds of tiny gnats; they swirled suddenly, disturbed by his movement.

'Aye, ye were,' he said softly. 'But then – we thought we must change things. Or try, at the least. But here –' He turned, waving an arm at the vast land that lay unseen beyond the trees. 'I shouldna think it my business,' he said simply. 'Either to help or to hinder much.'

I waved the gnats away from my face.

'It might *be* our business, if we lived here.'

He rubbed a finger below his lower lip, thinking. His beard was sprouting, a glimmer of red stubble sparked with silver in the lantern light. He was a big man, handsome and strong in the prime of his life, but no longer a young one, and I realized that with sudden gratitude.

Highland men were bred to fight; Highland boys became men when they could lift their swords and go to battle. Jamie had never been reckless, but he had been a warrior and a soldier most of his life. As a young man in his twenties, nothing could have kept him from a fight, whether it was his own or not. Now, in his forties, sense might temper passion – or at least I hoped so.

And it was true; beyond this aunt whom he didn't know, he had no family here, no ties that might compel involvement. Perhaps, knowing what was coming, we might contrive to stay clear of the worst?

'It's a verra big place, Sassenach.' He looked out over the prow of the boat, into the vast black sweep of invisible land. 'Only since we left Georgia, we have traveled farther than the whole length of Scotland and England both.'

'That's true,' I admitted. In Scotland, even among the high crags of the Highlands, there had been no way to escape the ravages of war. Not so here; should we seek our place carefully, we might indeed escape the roving eye of Mars.

He tilted his head to one side, smiling up at me.

'I could see ye as a planter's lady, Sassenach. If the Governor will find me a buyer for the other stones, then I shall have enough, I think, to send Laoghaire all the money I promised her, and still have enough over to buy a good place – one where we might prosper.'

He took my right hand in his, his thumb gently stroking my silver wedding ring.

'Perhaps one day I shall deck ye in laces and jewels,' he said softly. 'I havena been able to give ye much, ever, save a wee silver ring, and my mother's pearls.'

'You've given me a lot more than that,' I said. I wrapped my fingers around his thumb and squeezed. 'Brianna, for one.'

He smiled faintly, looking down at the deck.

'Aye, that's true. She's maybe the real reason – for staying, I mean.'

I pulled him toward me, and he rested his head against my knee.

'This is her place, no?' he said quietly. He lifted a hand, gesturing toward the river, the trees and the sky. 'She will be born here, she'll live here.'

'That's right,' I said softly. I stroked his hair, smoothing the thick strands that were so much like Brianna's. 'This will be her country.' Hers, in a way it could never be mine or his, no matter how long we might live here.

He nodded, beard rasping gently against my skirt.

'I dinna wish to fight, or have ye ever in danger, Sassenach, but if there is a bit I can do . . . to build, maybe, to make it safe, and a good land for her . . .' He shrugged. 'It would please me,' he finished softly.

We sat silently for a bit, close together, watching the dull shine of the water and the slow progress of the sunken lantern.

'I left the pearls for her,' I said at last. 'That seemed right; they were an heirloom, after all.' I drew my ringed hand, curved, across his lips. 'And the ring is all I need.'

He took both my hands in his, then, and kissed them –

the left, which still bore the gold ring of my marriage to Frank, and then the right with his own silver ring.

'*Da mi basia mille*,' he whispered, smiling. Give me a thousand kisses. It was the inscription inside my ring, a brief quotation from a love song by Catullus. I bent and gave him one back.

'*Dein mille altera*,' I said. Then a thousand more.

It was near midnight when we tied up near a brushy grove to rest. The weather had changed; still hot and muggy, now the air held the hint of thunder, and the undergrowth stirred with small movements – random air currents, or the scurryings of tiny night things hastening for home before the storm.

We were nearly at the end of the tidal surge; from here it would be a matter of sail and pole, and Captain Freeman had hopes of catching a good breeze on the wings of a storm. It would pay us to rest while we could. I curled into our nest on the stern, but was unable to fall asleep at once, late as it was.

By the Captain's estimation, we might make Cross Creek by evening tomorrow – certainly by the day after. I was surprised to realize how eagerly I was looking forward to our arrival; two months of living hand-to-mouth on the road had given me an urgent longing for some haven, no matter how temporary.

Familiar as I was with Highland notions of hospitality and kinship, I had no fears regarding our welcome. Jamie plainly did not consider the fact that he hadn't met this particular aunt in forty-odd years to be any bar to our cordial reception, and I was quite sure he was right. At the same time, I couldn't help entertaining considerable curiosity about Jocasta Cameron.

There had been five MacKenzie siblings, the children of old Red Jacob, who had built Castle Leoch. Jamie's mother, Ellen, had been the eldest, Jocasta the youngest. Janet, the other sister, had died, like Ellen, well before I met Jamie, but I had known the two brothers, Colum and Dougal, quite well indeed, and from that knowledge, couldn't help speculating as to what this last MacKenzie of Leoch might be like.

171

Tall, I thought, with a glance at Jamie, curled up peacefully on the deck beside me. Tall, and maybe red-haired. They were all tall – even Colum, victim of a crippling degenerative disease, had been tall to begin with – fair-skinned Vikings, the lot of them, with a ruddy blaze to their coloring that shimmered from Jamie's fiery red through his uncle Dougal's deep russet. Only Colum had been truly dark.

Remembering Colum and Dougal, I felt a sudden stir of unease. Colum had died before Culloden, killed by his disease. Dougal had died on the eve of the battle – killed by Jamie. It had been a matter of self-defense – *my* self, in fact – and only one of so many deaths in that bloody April. Still, I did wonder whether Jamie had given any thoughts as to what he might say, when the greetings were past at River Run, and the casual family chat got round to 'Oh, and when did you last see So-and-so?'

Jamie sighed and stretched in his sleep. He could – and did – sleep well on any surface, accustomed as he had been to sleeping in conditions that ranged from wet heather to musty caves to the cold stone floors of prison cells. I supposed the wooden decking under us must be thoroughly comfortable by contrast.

I was neither so elastic nor so hardened, myself, but gradually weariness overwhelmed me, and even the prick of curiosity about the future was unable to keep me awake.

I woke to confusion. It was still dark, and there was noise all around, shouting and barking, and the deck beneath me trembled with the vibration of stamping feet. I jerked upright, half thinking myself aboard a sailing ship, convinced that we had been boarded by pirates.

Then my mind cleared, along with my foggy vision, and I discovered that we *had* been boarded by pirates. Strange voices shouted oaths and orders, and booted feet were heavy on the deck. Jamie was gone.

I scrabbled onto my hands and feet, taking no heed for clothes or anything else. It was near dawn; the sky was dark, but light enough that the cabin showed as a darker blotch against it. As I struggled upright, clinging to the cabin roof for support, I was nearly knocked flat by flying bodies hurling themselves across it.

172

There was a confused blur of fur and white faces, a shout and a shot and a terrible thud, and Ian was crouching ashen on the deck, over Rollo's heaving form. A strange man, hatless and disheveled, pushed himself to his feet.

'Damn! He nearly got me!' Unhinged by the near miss, the robber's hand trembled as he fumbled with the spare pistol at his belt. He pointed it at the dog, face drawing down in an ugly squint.

'Take that, arse-bite!'

A taller man appeared from nowhere, his hand knocking down the pistol before the flint could strike.

'Don't waste the shot, fool.' He gestured to Troklus and Captain Freeman – the latter volubly incensed – being herded toward me. 'How d'you mean to hold them with an empty gun?'

The shorter man cast an evil look at Rollo, but swung his pistol to bear on Freeman's midriff instead.

Rollo was making an odd noise, a low growling mixed with whimpers of pain, and I could see a wet, dark stain on the boards under his twitching body. Ian bent low over him, hands stroking his head helplessly. He looked up, and tears shone wet on his cheeks.

'Help me, Auntie,' he said. 'Please help!'

I moved impulsively, and the tall man stepped forward, thrusting out an arm to stop me.

'I want to help the dog,' I said.

'*What?*' said the short robber, in tones of outrage.

The tall man was masked – they all were, I realized, my eyes adjusting to the growing half-light. How many were there? It was impossible to tell under the mask, but I had the distinct impression that the tall man was smiling. He didn't answer, but gave a short jerk of his pistol, giving me leave.

'Hullo, old boy,' I said under my breath, dropping to my knees next to the dog. 'Don't bite, there's a good doggie. Where is he hurt, Ian, do you know?'

Ian shook his head, sniffing back the tears.

'It's under him; I can't get him to turn over.'

I wasn't about to try to heave the dog's huge carcass over either. I felt quickly for a pulse in the neck, but my fingers sank into Rollo's thick ruff, prodding uselessly. Seized by inspiration, I instead picked up a front leg and felt up its length, getting my fingers into the hollow where the leg met the body.

Sure enough, there it was; a steady pulse, throbbing reassuringly under my fingers. I began by habit to count, but quickly abandoned the effort, as I had no idea what a dog's normal pulse rate should be. It *was* steady, though; no fluttering, no arrhythmia, no weakness. That was a very good sign.

Another was that Rollo hadn't lost consciousness; the great leg I held thucked under my elbow had the tension of coiled spring, not the limp dangle of shock. The dog made a long, high-pitched noise, halfway between a whine and a howl, and began to scrabble with his claws, pulling his leg out of my grasp in an effort to right himself.

'I don't think it's very bad, Ian,' I said in relief. 'Look, he's turning over.'

Rollo stood up, swaying. He shook his head violently, shaggy coat twitching from head to tail, and a shower of blood drops flew over the deck with a sound like pattering rain. The big yellow eyes fixed on the short man with a look that was clear to the meanest intelligence.

'Here! You stop him, or I swear I'll shoot him dead!' Panic and sincerity rang out in the robber's voice, as the muzzle of the pistol drifted uncertainly between the little group of prisoners and Rollo's lip-curled snarl.

Ian, who had been frantically undoing his shirt, whipped the garment off and over Rollo's head, temporarily blinding the dog, who shook his head madly, making growling noises inside the restraint. Blood stained the yellow linen – I could see now, though, that it came from a shallow gash in the dog's shoulder; evidently, the bullet had only grazed him.

Ian hung on grimly, forcing Rollo back on his haunches, muttering orders to the dog's swaddled head.

'How many aboard?' The taller man's sharp eyes flicked toward Captain Freeman, whose mouth was pressed so tightly together, it looked no more than a purse seam in the gray fur of his face, then toward me.

I knew him; knew the voice. The knowledge must have

174

shown in my face, for he paused for a moment, then jerked his head and let the masking kerchief fall from his face.

'How many?' Stephen Bonnet asked again.

'Six,' I said. There was no reason not to answer; I could see Fergus on the shore, hands raised as a third pirate herded him at gunpoint toward the boat; Jamie had materialized out of the darkness beside me, looking grim.

'Mr. Fraser,' Bonnet said pleasantly, at sight of him. 'A pleasure to be renewing our acquaintance. But did ye not have another companion, sir? The one-armed gentleman?'

'Not here,' Jamie replied shortly.

'I'll have a look,' the short robber muttered, turning, but Bonnet stopped him with a gesture.

'Ah, now, and would ye be doubting the word of a gentleman like Mr. Fraser? No, you'll be after guarding these fine folk here, Roberts; I'll be having the look around.' With a nod to his companion, he vanished.

Looking after Rollo had distracted me momentarily from the commotion going on elsewhere on the boat. Sounds of breakage came from inside the cabin, and I leapt to my feet, reminded of my medicine box.

'Here! Where you going? Stop! I'll shoot!' The robber's voice held a desperate note, but an uncertain one, as well. I didn't stop to look at him, but dived into the cabin, cannoning into a fourth robber, who was indeed rummaging through my medicine chest.

I staggered back from the collision, then clutched his arm, with a cry of outrage. He had been carelessly opening boxes and bottles, shaking out the contents, and tossing them on the floor; a litter of bottles, many of them broken, lay amid the scattered remnants of Dr. Rawlings's selection of medicines.

'Don't you *dare* touch those!' I said, and snatching the nearest vial from the chest, I popped out the cork and flung the contents in his face.

Like most of Rawlings's mixtures, it contained a high proportion of alcohol. He gasped as the liquid hit, and reeled backward, eyes streaming.

I pressed my advantage by seizing a stone ale bottle

175

from the wreckage and hitting him on the head with it. It hit with a satisfying *thunk!* but I hadn't hit him quite hard enough; he staggered but stayed upright, lurching as he grabbed at me.

I drew back my arm for another swing, but my wrist was seized from behind by a grip like iron.

'Beggin' your pardon, Mrs. Fraser dear,' said a polite, familiar Irish voice. 'But I really cannot allow ye to crack his head. It's not very ornamental, sure, but he needs it to hold up his hat.'

'Frigging bitch! She *hit* me!' The man I had hit was clutching his head, his features screwed up in pain.

Bonnet hauled me out onto the deck, my arm twisted painfully behind my back. It was nearly light by now; the river glowed like flat silver. I stared hard at our assailants; I meant to know them again, if I saw them, masks or no masks.

Unfortunately, the improved light allowed the robbers better vision as well. The man I had hit, who seemed to be bearing a distinct grudge, seized my hand and wrenched at my ring.

'Here, let's have that!'

I yanked my hand away and made to slap him, but was stopped by a meaningful cough from Bonnet, who had stepped close to Ian and was holding his pistol an inch from the boy's left ear.

'Best hand them over, Mrs. Fraser,' he said politely. 'I fear Mr. Roberts requires some compensation for the damage ye've caused him.'

I twisted my gold ring off, hands trembling both with fear and rage. The silver one was harder; it stuck on my knuckle as though reluctant to part from me. Both rings were damp and slippery with sweat, the metal warmer than my suddenly chilled fingers.

'Give 'em up.' The man poked me roughly in the shoulder, then turned up a broad, grubby palm for the rings. I reached toward him, reluctantly, rings cupped in my hand – and then, with an impulse I didn't stop to examine, clapped my hand to my mouth instead.

My head hit the cabin wall with a thud as the man knocked me backward. His callused fingers jabbed my cheeks and poked into my mouth, probing roughly in search of the rings. I twisted and gulped hard, mouth filling with saliva and a silver taste that might have been either metal or blood.

I bit down and he jerked back with a cry; one ring must have flown out of my mouth, for I heard a faint, metallic *ping* somewhere, and then I gagged and choked, the second ring sliding into my gullet, hard and round.

'Bitch! I'll slit your friggin' throat! You'll go to hell without your rings, you cheating whore!' I saw the man's face, contorted in rage, and the sudden glitter of a knife blade drawn. Then something hit me hard and knocked me over, and I found myself crushed to the deck, flattened under Jamie's body.

I was too stunned to move, though I couldn't have moved in any case; Jamie's chest was pressing on the back of my head, squashing my face into the deck. There was a lot of shouting and confusion, muffled by the folds of damp linen around my head. There was a soft *thunk!* and I felt Jamie jerk and grunt.

Oh, God, they've stabbed him! I thought, in an agony of terror. Another *thump* and a louder grunt, though, indicated only a kick in the ribs. Jamie didn't move; just pressed himself harder against the deck, flattening me like the filling of a sandwich.

'Leave off! Roberts! I said leave him!' Bonnet's voice rang out in tones of authority, sharp enough to penetrate the muffling cloth.

'But she –' Roberts began, but his querulous whine was stopped abruptly with a sharp, meaty smack.

'Raise yourself, Mr. Fraser. Your wife is safe – not that she deserves to be.' Bonnet's husky baritone held mingled tones of amusement and irritation.

Jamie's weight lifted slowly off me, and I sat up, feeling dizzy and mildly sick from the blow on the head. Stephen Bonnet stood looking down at me, examining me with faint distaste, as though I were a mangy deerhide he'd been offered for sale. Next to him, Roberts glared malevolently, dabbing at a smear of blood at his hairline.

Bonnet blinked finally, and switched his gaze to Jamie, who had regained his feet.

177

'A foolish woman,' Bonnet said dispassionately, 'but I suppose you don't mind that.' He nodded, a faint smile showing. 'I am obliged for the opportunity to repay my debt to ye, sir. A life for a life, as the Good Book says.'

'Repay us?' Ian said angrily. 'After what we've done for ye, ye'll rob and spoil us, lay violent hands upon my aunt and my dog, and then ye'll ha' the gall to speak of repayment?'

Bonnet's pale eyes fixed on Ian's face; they were green, the color of peeled grapes. He had a deep dimple in one cheek, as though God had pressed a thumb there in his making, but the eyes were cold as river water at dawn.

'Why, were ye never after learning your Scripture, lad?' Bonnet shook his head reprovingly, with a click of the tongue. 'A virtuous woman is prized above rubies; her price is greater than pearls.'

He opened his hand, still smiling, and the lantern light glittered off three gems: emerald, sapphire, and the dark fire of a black diamond.

'I'm sure Mr. Fraser would agree, would ye not, sir?' He slipped the hand into his coat, then brought it out empty.

'And after all,' he said, cold eyes swiveling once more toward Ian, 'there are repayments of different kinds.' He smiled, not very pleasantly. 'Though I should not suppose you can be old enough to know that yet. Be glad I've no mind to give ye a lesson.'

He turned away, beckoning to his comrades.

'We have what we came for,' he said abruptly. 'Come.' He stepped up onto the rail and jumped, landing with a grunt on the muddy riverbank. His henchmen followed, Roberts casting an evil look at me before splashing awkwardly into the shallows and ashore.

The four men disappeared at once into the brush, and I heard the high-pitched greeting whinny of a horse, somewhere in the darkness. Aboard, all was silence.

The sky was the color of charcoal, and thunder grumbled faintly in the distance, sheet lightning flickering just above the far horizon.

'Bastards.'

Captain Freeman spat in valediction over the side, and turned to his mate.

'Fetch the poles, you, Troklus,' he said, and shambled toward the tiller, hitching his breeks upward as he went.

Slowly, the others stirred and came to life. Fergus, with a glance at Jamie, lit the lantern and then disappeared into the cabin, where I heard him beginning to set things to rights. Ian sat huddled on the deck, his dark head bent over Rollo as he dabbed at the dog's neck with his wadded shirt.

I didn't want to look at Jamie. I rolled onto my hands and knees and crawled slowly over to Young Ian. Rollo watched me, yellow eyes wary, but made no objection to my presence.

'How is he?' I said, rather hoarsely. I could feel the ring in my throat, an uncomfortable obstruction, and swallowed heavily several times.

Young Ian looked up at once; his face was white and set, but his eyes were alert.

'He's all right, I think,' he said softly. 'Auntie – are ye all right? Ye're no hurt, are ye?'

'No,' I said, and tried to smile reassuringly. 'I'm fine.' There was a sore spot on the back of my skull and my ears still rang slightly; the yellow halo of light around the lantern seemed to oscillate, to swell and shrink in rhythm with the beating of my heart. One cheek was scraped, I had a bruised elbow and a large splinter in one hand, but I seemed to be fundamentally sound, physically. Otherwise, I had my doubts.

I didn't look around at Jamie, some six feet behind me, but I could feel his presence, ominous as a thundercloud. Ian, who plainly *could* see him over my shoulder, looked faintly apprehensive.

There was a slight creaking of the deck, and Ian's expression eased. I heard Jamie's voice inside the cabin, outwardly casual as he asked Fergus a question, then it faded, lost in the sounds of bumping and shuffling as the men righted furniture and repiled the scattered goods. I let my breath out slowly.

'Dinna fash, Auntie,' Ian said, in an attempt at comfort. 'Uncle Jamie's no the sort to lay hands on ye, I dinna think.'

179

I wasn't at all sure of that, given the vibrations coming from Jamie's direction, but I hoped he was right.

'Is he terribly angry, do you think?' I asked in a low voice.

Ian shrugged uneasily.

'Well, last time I saw him look at *me* that way, he took me back o' the house and knocked me flat. He wouldna serve you that way, though, I'm sure,' he added hastily.

'I don't suppose so,' I said, a little bleakly. I wasn't sure I wouldn't prefer it if he did.

'It's no verra nice to get the rough side o' Uncle Jamie's tongue, either,' Ian said, shaking his head sympathetically. 'I'd rather a thrashing, myself.'

I gave Ian a quelling look and leaned over the dog.

'Sufficient to the day is the evil thereof. Has the bleeding stopped?'

It had; disregarding the blood-matted fur, there was surprisingly little damage; no more than a deep nick in the skin and muscle near the shoulder. Rollo flattened his ears and showed his teeth as I examined him, but made no audible protest.

'Good dog,' I murmured. Had I any way to numb the skin, I would have stitched the wound, but we would have to do without such niceties. 'He should have a little ointment there, to keep the flies out.'

'I'll get it, Auntie; I ken where your wee box is.' Ian gently edged Rollo's nose off his knee and got to his feet. 'It'll be the green stuff ye put on Fergus's toe?' At my nod, he disappeared into the cabin, leaving me to deal with my quivering stomach, sore head, and congested throat. I swallowed several times, but with no great result. I touched my throat gingerly, wondering which ring I still had.

Eutroclus came round the corner of the cabin, carrying a long thick pole of white wood, deeply stained at one end, the marks testifying to the frequent necessity of its use. Stabbing the pole firmly down off the side, he leaned his weight against it, heaving with a long, sustained effort.

I jumped, as Jamie came out of the shadows, a similar pole in his hand. I hadn't heard him, above the miscellaneous thumpings and shouts. He didn't look at me, but shed his shirt, and at the deckhand's indication, stabbed down his pole.

On the fourth try, I felt the vibration of the hull, a small judder as something shifted. Encouraged, Jamie and the hand shoved harder, and all of sudden, the hull slid free, with a muted *bwong!* of resonant wood that made Rollo lift his head with a startled *Wuff!*

Eutroclus nodded to Jamie, face beaming under a shiny layer of sweat, and took the pole from him. Jamie nodded back, smiling, and picking up his shirt from the deck, turned toward me.

I stiffened, and Rollo twitched his ears to full alert, but Jamie showed no immediate disposition either to berate me or to toss me overboard. Instead, he leaned down, frowning as he peered at me in the wavering lantern light.

'How d'ye feel, Sassenach? I canna tell if you're really green, or is it only the light.'

'I'm all right. A bit shaky, perhaps.' More than a bit; my hands were still clammy, and I knew my trembling knees wouldn't hold me if I tried to stand. I swallowed hard, coughed, and thumped myself on the chest.

'It's probably my imagination, but it feels like the ring is caught in my throat.'

He squinted thoughtfully at me, then turned to Fergus, who had appeared from the cabin and was hovering nearby.

'Ask the captain might I see his pipe for a moment, Fergus.' He turned away, pulling his shirt over his head, and disappeared aft himself, returning moments later with a cup of water.

I reached gratefully for it, but he held it out of my reach.

'Not just yet, Sassenach,' he said. 'Got it? Aye, thanks, Fergus. Fetch an empty bucket, now, will ye?' Taking the filthy pipe from a puzzled Fergus, he inserted his thumb into the stained bowl and began to scrape at the burnt, gummy residue that lined it.

Turning the pipe upside down, he tapped it over the cup of water, causing a small shower of brown crusts and moist crumbs of half-burnt tobacco, which he stirred into the water with his blackened thumb. Finished with these

181

preparations, he looked up at me over the rim of the cup in a distinctly sinister fashion.

'No,' I said. 'Oh, no.'

'Oh, yes,' he said. 'Come along, Sassenach; it'll cure what ails ye.'

'I'll just . . . wait,' I said. I folded my arms across my chest. 'Thanks anyway.'

Fergus had by this time reappeared with the bucket, eyebrows raised high. Jamie took it from him and plunked it on the deck next to me.

'I've done it that way, Sassenach,' he informed me, 'and it's a good deal messier than ye might think. It's also not a pleasant thing to do on a boat, in close company, aye?' He put a hand on the back of my head and pressed the cup against my lower lip. 'This will be quick. Come on, now; a wee sip is all.'

I pressed my lips tightly together; the smell from the cup was enough to make my stomach turn over, combining as it did the stale reek of tobacco, the sight of the noisome brown surface of the liquid, crusts swimming below the surface, and the memory of Captain Freeman's blobs of brown-tinged spittle sliding down the deck.

Jamie didn't bother with argument or persuasion. He simply let go of my head, pinched my nose shut, and when I opened my mouth to breathe, tipped in the foul-smelling contents of the cup.

'Mmmffff!'

'Swallow,' he said, clapping a hand tightly across my mouth and ignoring both my frenzied squirming and the muffled sounds of protest I was making. He was a lot stronger than I was, and he didn't mean to let go. It was swallow or strangle.

I swallowed.

'Good as new.' Jamie finished polishing the silver ring on his shirttail and held it up, admiring it in the glow of the lantern.

'That is somewhat better than can be said of me,' I replied coldly. I lay in a crumpled heap on the deck, which in spite of the placid current, seemed still to be heaving very slightly under me. 'You are a grade-A, double-dyed, sadistic fucking bastard, Jamie Fraser!'

He bent over me and smoothed the damp hair off my face.

'I expect so. If ye feel well enough to call me names, Sassenach, you'll do. Rest a bit, aye?' He kissed me gently on the forehead and sat back.

Excitement over and order restored to the ravaged decks, the other men had gone back to the cabin to restore themselves with the aid of a bottle of applejack that Captain Freeman had contrived to save from the pirates by dropping it into the water barrel. A small cup of this beverage rested on the deck near my head; I was still too queasy to countenance swallowing anything, but the warm, fruity smell was mildly comforting.

We were under sail; everyone was eager to get away, as though some danger still lingered over the place of the attack. We were moving faster, now; the usual small cloud of insects that hovered near the lanterns had dispersed, reduced to no more than a few lacewings resting on the beam above, their delicate green bodies casting tiny streaks of shadow. Inside the cabin, there was a small burst of laughter, and an answering growl from Rollo on the side deck – things were returning to normal.

A small, welcome breeze played across the deck, evaporating the clammy sweat on my face and lifting the ends of Jamie's hair, drifting them across his face. I could see the small vertical line between his brows and the tilt of his head that indicated deep thought.

Little wonder if he was thinking. In one stroke, we had gone from riches – potential riches, at least – to rags, our well-equipped expedition reduced to a sack of beans and a used medicine chest. So much for his desire not to appear as beggars at Jocasta Cameron's door – we were little more than that now.

My throat ached for him, pity replacing irritation. Beyond the question of his immediate pride, there was now a terrifying void in that unknown territory marked 'The Future'. The future had been well open to question before, but the sharp edges of all such questions had been buffered by the comforting knowledge that we would have money to help accomplish our aims – whatever those turned out to be.

Even our penurious trip north had felt like an adventure, with the certain knowledge that we possessed a fortune, whether it was spendable or not. I had never before considered myself a person who placed much value on money, but having the certainty of security ripped away in this violent fashion had given me a sudden and quite unexpected attack of vertigo, as though I were falling down a long, dark well, powerless to stop.

What had it done to Jamie, who felt not only his danger and mine but the crushing responsibility of so many other lives? Ian, Fergus, Marsali, Duncan, the inhabitants of Lallybroch – even that bloody nuisance Laoghaire. I wasn't sure whether to laugh or cry, thinking of the money Jamie had sent her; the vengeful creature was a good deal better off at present than we were.

At the thought of vengeance, I felt a new stab that displaced all lesser fears. While Jamie was not markedly vengeful – for a Scot – no Highlander would suffer a loss such as this with silent resignation; a loss not only of fortune but of honor. What might he feel compelled to do about it?

Jamie stared fixedly into the dark water, his mouth set; was he seeing once again the graveyard where, swayed by Duncan's intoxicated sentimentality, he had agreed to help Bonnet escape?

It belatedly occurred to me that the financial aspects of the disaster likely had not yet entered Jamie's mind – he was occupied in more bitter reflection; it was he who had helped Bonnet escape the hangman's rope, and set him free to prey on the innocent. How many besides us would suffer because of that?

'You're not to blame,' I said, touching his knee.

'Who else?' he said quietly, not looking at me. 'I kent the man for what he was. I could have left him to the fate he'd earned – but I did not. I was a fool.'

'You were kind. It's not the same thing.'

'Near enough.'

He breathed in deeply; the air was freshening with the scent of ozone; the rain was near. He reached for the cup of applejack and drank, then looked at me for the first time, holding up the cup inquiringly.

'Yes, thanks.' I struggled to sit up, but Jamie took me by the shoulders and lifted me to lean against him. He held the cup for me to drink, the blood-warm liquid sliding soft across my tongue, then taking fire as it slid down my throat, burning away the traces of sickness and tobacco, leaving in their place rum's lingering taste of burning sugarcane.

'Better?'

I nodded, and held up my right hand. He slid the ring onto my finger, the metal warm from his hand. Then, folding down my fingers, he squeezed my fist hard in his own and held it, tight.

'Had he been following us since Charleston?' I wondered aloud.

Jamie shook his head. His hair was still loose, heavy waves falling forward to hide his face.

'I dinna think so. If he'd kent we had the jewels, he would have set upon us on the road before we reached Wilmington. No, I expect he learned it from one of Lillington's servants. I thought we'd be safe enough, for we'd be away to Cross Creek before anyone heard of the gems. Someone talked, though – a footman; perhaps the sempstress who sewed your gown.'

His face was outwardly calm, but it always was, when he was hiding strong emotions. A sudden gust of hot wind shot sideways across the deck; the rain was getting closer. It whipped the loose ends of his hair across his cheek, and he wiped them back, running his fingers through the thick mass.

'I'm sorry for your other ring,' he said, after a moment.

'Oh. It's –' I started to say, 'It's all right,' but the words stuck in my throat, choked by the sudden realization of loss.

I had worn that gold ring for nearly thirty years; token of vows taken, forsaken, renewed, and at last absolved. A token of marriage, of family; of a large part of my life. And the last trace of Frank – whom, in spite of everything, I had loved.

Jamie didn't say anything, but he took my left hand in

185

his own and held it, lightly stroking my knuckles with his thumb. I didn't speak either. I sighed deeply and turned my face toward the stern; the trees along the shore were shivering in a rising wind of anticipation, leaves rustling loudly enough to drown the sound of the vessel's passage.

A small drop struck my cheek, but I didn't move. My hand lay limp and white in his, looking unaccustomedly frail; it was something of a shock to see it that way.

I was used to paying a great deal of attention to my hands, one way and another. They were my tools, my channel of touch, mingling the delicacy and strength by which I healed. They had a certain beauty, which I admired in a detached sort of way, but it was the beauty of strength and competence, the assurance of power that made its form admirable.

It was the same hand now, pale and long-fingered, the knuckles slightly bony – oddly bare without my ring, but recognizably my hand. Yet it lay in a hand so much larger and rougher that it seemed small, and fragile by comparison.

His other hand squeezed tighter, pressing the metal of the silver ring into my flesh, reminding me of what remained. I lifted his fist and pressed it hard against my heart in answer. The rain began to fall, in large, wet drops, but neither of us moved.

It came in a rush, dropping a veil over boat and shore, pattering noisily on leaves and deck and water, lending a temporary illusion of concealment. It washed cool and soft across my skin, momentary balm on the wounds of fear and loss.

I felt at once horribly vulnerable and yet completely safe. But then – I had always felt that way with Jamie Fraser.

PART FOUR

River Run

10

Jocasta

River Run stood by the edge of the Cape Fear, just above the confluence that gave Cross Creek its name. Cross Creek itself was good-sized, with a busy public wharf and several large warehouses lining the water's edge. As the *Sally Ann* made her way slowly through the shipping lane, a strong, resinous smell hung over town and river, trapped by the hot, sticky air.

'Jesus, it's like breathin' turpentine,' Ian wheezed as a fresh wave of the stultifying reek washed over us.

'You *is* breathin' turpentine, man.' Eutroclus's rare smile flashed white and disappeared. He nodded toward a barge tethered to a piling by one of the wharfs. It was stacked with barrels, some of which showed a thick black ooze through split seams. Other, larger barrels bore the brandmarks of their owners, with a large 'T' burned into the pinewood below.

''At's right,' Captain Freeman agreed. He squinted in the bright sun-light, waving one hand slowly in front of his nose, as though this might dispel the stink. 'This time o' year's when the pitch-bilers come down from the back-country. Pitch, turpentine, tar – bring it all down by barge t' Wilmington, then send it on south to the shipyards at Charleston.'

'I shouldna think it's *all* turpentine,' Jamie said. He mopped the back of his neck with a handkerchief and nodded toward the largest of the warehouses, its door flanked by red-coated soldiers. 'Smell it, Sassenach?'

I inhaled, cautiously. There was something else in the air here; a hot, familiar scent.

'Rum?' I said.

'And brandywine. And a bit of port, as well.' Jamie's long nose twitched, sensitive as a mongoose's. I looked at him in amusement.

189

'You haven't lost it, have you?' Twenty years before, he had managed his cousin Jared's wine business in Paris, and his nose and palate had been the awe of the winery tasting rooms.

He grinned.

'Oh, I expect I could still tell Moselle from horse piss, if ye held it right under my nose. But telling rum from turpentine is no great feat, is it?'

Ian drew a huge lungful of air and let it out, coughing.

'It all smells the same to me,' he said, shaking his head.

'Good,' said Jamie, 'I'll give ye turpentine next time I stand ye a drink. It'll be a good deal cheaper.'

'Turpentine's just about what I could afford now,' he added under cover of the laughter this remark caused. He straightened, brushing down the skirts of his coat. 'We'll be there soon. Do I look a terrible beggar, Sassenach?'

Seen with the sun glowing on his neatly ribboned hair, his darkened profile coin-stamped against the light, I privately thought he looked dazzling, but I had caught the faint tone of anxiety in his voice, and knew well enough what he meant. Penniless he might be, but he didn't mean to look it.

I was well aware that the notion of appearing at his aunt's door as a poor relation come a-begging stung his pride considerably. The fact that he had been forced into precisely that role didn't make it any easier to bear.

I looked him over carefully. The coat and waistcoat were not spectacular, but quite acceptable, courtesy of Cousin Edwin; a quiet gray broadcloth with a good hand and an excellent fit, buttons not silver, but not of wood or bone either – a sober pewter, like a prosperous Quaker.

Not that the rest of him bore the slightest resemblance to a Quaker, I thought. The linen shirt was rather grubby, but as long as he kept his coat on, no one would notice, and the missing button on the waistcoat was hidden by the graceful fall of his lace jabot, the sole extravagance he had permitted himself in the way of wardrobe.

The stockings were all right; pale blue silk, no visible holes. The white linen breeches were tight, but not – not quite – indecent, and reasonably clean.

The shoes were the only real flaw in his ensemble; there

had been no time to have any made. His were sound, and I had done my best to hide the scuff-marks with a mixture of soot and dripping, but they were clearly a farmer's foot-wear, not a gentleman's; thick-soled, made of rough leather, and with buckles of lowly horn. Still, I doubted that his Aunt Jocasta would be looking at his feet first thing.

I stood on tiptoe to straighten his jabot, and brushed a floating down-feather off his shoulder.

'It will be all right,' I whispered back, smiling up at him. 'You're beautiful.'

He looked startled; then the expression of grim aloof-ness relaxed into a smile.

'*You're* beautiful, Sassenach.' He leaned over and kissed me on the forehead. 'You're flushed as a wee apple; verra bonny.' He straightened up, glanced at Ian, and sighed.

'As for Ian, perhaps I can pass him off as a bondsman I've taken on to be swineherd.'

Ian was one of those people whose clothes, no matter what their original quality, immediately look as though they had been salvaged from a rubbish tip. Half his hair had escaped from its green ribbon, and one bony elbow protruded from a rip in his new shirt, whose cuffs were already noticeably gray round the wrists.

'Captain Freeman says we'll be there in no time!' he exclaimed, eyes shining with excitement as he leaned over the side, peering upriver in order to be first to sight our destination. 'What d'ye think we'll get for supper?'

Jamie surveyed his nephew with a marked lack of favor.

'I expect you'll get table scraps, wi' the dogs. Do ye not own a coat, Ian? Or a comb?'

'Oh, aye,' Ian said, glancing round vaguely, as though expecting one of these objects to materialize in front of him. 'I've a coat here. Somewhere. I think.'

The coat was finally located under one of the benches, and extracted with some difficulty from the possession of Rollo, who had made a comfortable bed of it. After a quick brush to remove at least some of the dog hairs from the garment, Ian was forcibly inserted into it, and sat firmly down to have his hair combed and plaited while Jamie gave him a quick refresher course in manners, this consisting solely of the advice to keep his mouth shut as much as possible.

Ian nodded amiably.

'Will ye tell Great-auntie Jocasta about the pirates yourself, then?' he inquired.

Jamie glanced briefly at Captain Freeman's scrawny back. It was futile to expect that such a story would not be told in every tavern in Cross Creek, as soon as they had left us. It would be a matter of days – hours perhaps – before it spread to River Run plantation.

'Aye, I'll tell her,' he said. 'But not just on the instant, Ian. Let her get accustomed to us, first.'

The mooring for River Run was some distance above Cross Creek, separated from the noise and reek of the town by several miles of tranquil tree-thick river. Having seen Jamie, Ian, and Fergus all rendered as handsome as water, comb, and ribbons could make them, I retired to the cabin, changed out of my grubby muslin, sponged myself hastily, and slipped into the cream silk I had worn to dinner with the Governor.

The soft fabric was light and cool against my skin. Perhaps a bit more formal than was usual for afternoon, but it was important to Jamie that we must look decent – especially now, after our encounter with the pirates – and my only alternatives were the filthy muslin or a clean but threadbare camlet gown that had traveled with me from Georgia.

There wasn't a great deal to be done with my hair; I gave it a cursory stab with a comb, then tied it back off my neck, letting the ends curl up as they would. I needn't trouble about jewelry, I thought ruefully, and rubbed my silver wedding ring to make it shine. I still avoided looking at my left hand, so nakedly bare; if I didn't look, I could still feel the imaginary weight of the gold upon it.

By the time I emerged from the cabin, the mooring was in sight. By contrast to the rickety fittings of most plantation moorings we had passed, River Run boasted a substantial and well-built wooden dock. A small black boy was sitting on the end of it, swinging bare legs in boredom.

When he saw the *Sally Ann's* approach, he leapt to his feet and tore off, presumably to announce our arrival.

Our homely craft bumped to a stop against the dock. From the screen of trees near the river, a brick walk swept up through a broad array of formal lawns and gardens, splitting in two to circle paired marble statues that stood in their own beds of flowers, then joining again and fanning out in a broad piazza in front of an imposing two-storied house, colonnaded and multichimneyed. At one side of the flower beds stood a miniature building, made of white marble – a mausoleum of some kind, I thought. I revised my opinions as to the suitability of the cream silk dress, and touched nervously at my hair.

I found her at once, among the people hurrying out of the house and down the walk. I would have known her for a MacKenzie, even if I hadn't known who she was. She had the bold bones, the broad Viking cheekbones and high, smooth brow of her brothers, Colum and Dougal. And like her nephew, like her great-niece, she had the extra-ordinary height that marked them all as descendants of one blood.

A head higher than the bevy of black servants who sur-rounded her, she floated down the path from the house, hand on the arm of her butler, though a woman less in need of support I had seldom seen.

She was tall and she was quick, with a firm step at odds with the white of her hair. She might once have been as red as Jamie; her hair still held a tinge of ruddiness, having gone that rich soft white that redheads do, with the buttery patina of an old gold spoon.

There was a cry from one of the little boys in the van-guard, and two of them broke loose, galloping down the path toward the mooring, where they circled us, yapping like puppies. At first I couldn't make out a word – it was only as Ian replied jocularly to them that I realized they were shouting in Gaelic.

I didn't know whether Jamie had thought what to say or to do upon this first meeting, but in the event, he simply stepped forward, went up to Jocasta MacKenzie, and embraced her, saying, 'Aunt – it's Jamie.'

It was only as he released her and stepped back that I

saw his face, with an expression I had never seen before; something between eagerness, joy, and awe. It occurred to me, with a small jolt of shock, that Jocasta MacKenzie must look very much like her elder sister – Jamie's mother.

I thought she might have his deep blue eyes, though I couldn't tell; they were blurred as she laughed through her tears, holding him by the sleeve, reaching up to touch his cheek, to smooth nonexistent strands of hair from his face.

'Jamie!' she said, over and over. 'Jamie, wee Jamie! Oh, I'm glad ye've come, lad!' She reached up once more, and touched his hair, a look of amazement on her face.

'Blessed Bride, but he's a giant! You'll be as tall as my brother Dougal was, at least!'

The expression of happiness on his face faded slightly at that, but he kept his smile, turning her with him so she faced me.

'Auntie, may I present my wife? This is Claire.'

She put out a hand at once, beaming, and I took it between my own, feeling a small pang of recognition at the long, strong fingers; though her knuckles were slightly knobbed with age, her skin was soft and the feel of her grip was unnervingly like Brianna's.

'I am so glad to meet ye, my dear,' she said, and drew me close to kiss my cheek. The scent of mint and verbena wafted strongly from her dress, and I felt oddly moved, as though I had suddenly come under the protection of some beneficent deity.

'So beautiful!' she said admiringly, long fingers stroking the sleeve of my dress.

'Thank you,' I said, but Ian and Fergus were coming up to be introduced in their turn. She greeted them both with embraces and endearments, laughing as Fergus kissed her hand in his best French manner.

'Come,' she said, breaking away at last, and wiping at her wet cheeks with the back of a hand. 'Do come in, my dearies, and take a dish of tea, and some food. Ye'll be famished, no doubt, after such a journey. Ulysses!' She turned, seeking, and her butler stepped forward, bowing low.

'Madame,' he said to me, and, 'Sir,' to Jamie. 'Everything is ready, Miss Jo,' he said softly to his mistress, and offered her his arm.

As they started up the brick walk, Fergus turned to Ian and bowed, mimicking the butler's courtly manner, then offered an arm in mockery. Ian kicked him neatly in the backside, and walked up the path, head turning from side to side to take in everything. His green ribbon had come undone, and was dangling halfway down his back.

Jamie snorted at the horseplay, but smiled nonetheless.

'Madame?' He put out an arm to me, and I took it, sweeping rather grandly up the path to the doors of River Run, flung wide to greet us.

The house was spacious and airy inside, with high ceilings and wide French doors in all the downstairs rooms. I caught a glimpse of silver and crystal as we passed a large formal dining room, and thought that on the evidence, Hector Cameron must have been a very successful planter indeed.

Jocasta led us to her private parlor, a smaller, more intimate room no less well furnished than the larger rooms, but which sported homely touches among the gleam of polished furniture and the glitter of ornaments. A large knitting basket full of yarn balls sat on a small table of polished wood, beside a glass vase spilling summer flowers and a small, ornate silver bell; a spinning wheel turned slowly by itself in the breeze from the open French doors.

The butler escorted us into the room, saw his mistress seated, then turned to a sideboard that held a collection of jugs and bottles.

'Ye'll have a dram to celebrate your coming, Jamie?' Jocasta waved a long, slim hand in the direction of the sideboard. 'I shouldna think ye'll have tasted decent whisky since ye left Scotland, aye?'

Jamie laughed, sitting down opposite her.

'Indeed not, Aunt. And how d'ye come by it here?'

She shrugged and smiled, looking complacent.

'Your uncle had the luck to lay down a good stock, some years agone. He took half a shipload of wine and liquor in trade for a warehouse of tobacco, meaning to sell it – but then the Parliament passed an Act making it illegal for any but the Crown to sell any liquor stronger than ale in the Colonies, and so we ended with two hundred bottles o' the stuff in the wine cellar!'

She stretched out her hand toward the table by her chair, not bothering to to look. She didn't need to; the butler set down a crystal tumbler softly, just where her fingers would touch it. Her hand closed around it, and she lifted it, passing it under her nose and sniffing, eyes closed in sensual delight.

'There's a good bit left of it yet. A great deal more than I can guzzle by myself, I'll tell ye!' She opened her eyes and smiled, lifting the tumbler toward us. 'To you, nephew, and your dear wife – may ye find this house home! *Slàinte!*'

'*Slàinte mhar!*' Jamie answered, and we all drank.

It *was* good whisky; smooth as buttered silk and heartening as sunshine. I could feel it hit the pit of my stomach, take root, and spread up my backbone.

It seemed to have a similar effect on Jamie; I could see the slight frown between his brows ease, as his face relaxed.

'I shall have Ulysses write this night, to tell your sister that ye've come safe here,' Jocasta was saying. 'She'll have been sair worrit for her wee laddie, I'm sure, thinking of all the misfortunes that might have beset ye along the way.'

Jamie set down his glass and cleared his throat, steeling himself for the ordeal of confession.

'As to misfortune, Aunt, I am afraid I must tell ye . . .'

I looked away, not wanting to increase his discomfort by watching as he explained concisely the dismal state of our fortunes. Jocasta listened with close attention, uttering small noises of dismay at his account of our meeting with the pirates. 'Wicked, ah, wicked!' she exclaimed. 'To repay your kindness in such fashion! The man should be hangit!'

'Well, there's none to blame save myself, Aunt,' Jamie said ruefully. 'He would have *been* hangit, if not for me. And since I did ken the man for a villain to start, I canna be much surprised to see him commit villainy at the end.'

'Mmphm.' Jocasta drew herself up taller in her seat, looking a bit over Jamie's left shoulder as she spoke.

'Be that as it may, nephew. I said ye must consider River Run as your home; I did mean it. You and yours are welcome here. And I am sure we shall contrive a way to mend your fortunes.'

'I thank ye, Aunt,' Jamie murmured, but he didn't want to meet her eyes, either. He looked down at the floor, and I could see the hand around his whisky glass clenched tight enough to leave the knuckles white.

The conversation fortunately moved on to talk of Jenny and her family at Lallybroch, and Jamie's embarrassment eased a bit. Dinner had been ordered; I could smell brief tantalizing whiffs of roasting meat from the cookhouse, borne on the evening breeze that wafted across the lawns and flower beds.

Fergus got up and tactfully excused himself, while Ian wandered around the room, picking things up and putting them down. Rollo, bored with the indoors, sniffed his way industriously along the doorsill, watched with open dislike by the fastidious butler.

The house and all its furnishings were simple but well crafted, beautiful, and arranged with something more than just taste. I realized what lay behind the elegant pro-portions and graceful arrangements, when Ian stopped abruptly by a large painting on the wall.

'Auntie Jocasta!' he exclaimed, turning eagerly to face her. 'Did you paint this? It's got your name on it.'

I thought a sudden shadow crossed her face, but then she smiled again.

'The view o' the mountains? Aye, I always loved the sight of them. I'd go with Hector, when he went up into the backcountry to trade for hides. We'd camp in the moun-tains, and set up a great blaze of a bonfire, wi' the servants keeping it going day and night, as a signal. And within a few days, the red savages would come down through the forest, and sit by the fire to talk and to drink whisky and trade – and I, I would sit by the hour wi' my sketchbook and my charcoals, drawing everything I could see.'

She turned, nodding toward the far end of the room.

'Go and look at that one in the corner, laddie. See can ye find the Indian I put in it, hiding in the trees.'

Jocasta finished her whisky and set down her glass. The

197

butler offered to refill it, but she waved him away without looking at him. He set down the decanter and vanished quietly into the hall.

'Aye, I loved the sight o' the mountains,' Jocasta said again, softly. 'They're none so black and barren as Scotland, but the sun on the rocks and the mist in the trees did remind me of Leoch, now and then.'

She shook her head then, and smiled a bit too brightly at Jamie.

'But this has been home for a long time now, nephew – and I hope ye will consider it yours as well.'

We had little other choice, but Jamie bobbed his head, murmuring something dutifully appreciative in reply. He was interrupted, though, by Rollo, who raised his head with a startled *Wuff!*

'What is it, dog?' said Ian, coming to stand by the big wolf-dog. 'D'ye smell something?' Rollo was whining, staring out into the shadowy flower border and twitching his thick ruff with unease.

Jocasta turned her head toward the open door and sniffed audibly, fine nostrils flaring.

'It's a skunk,' she said.

'A skunk!' Ian whirled to stare at her, appalled. 'They come so close to the house?'

Jamie had got up in a hurry, and gone to peer out into the evening.

'I dinna see it yet,' he said. His hand groped automatically at his belt, but of course he wasn't wearing a dirk with his good suit. He turned to Jocasta. 'Have ye any weapons in the house, Aunt?'

Jocasta's mouth hung open.

'Aye,' she said. 'Plenty. But –'

'Jamie,' I said. 'A skunk isn't –'

Before either of us could finish, there was a sudden disturbance among the snapdragons in the herbaceous border, the tall stalks waving back and forth. Rollo snarled, and the hackles stood up on his neck.

'Rollo!' Ian glanced round for a makeshift weapon, seized the poker from the fireplace, and brandishing it above his head, made for the door.

'Wait, Ian!' Jamie grabbed his nephew's upraised arm.

'Look.' A wide grin spread across his face, and he pointed to the border. The snapdragons parted, and a fine, fat skunk strolled into view, handsomely striped in black and white, and obviously feeling that all was right with his personal world.

'*That's* a skunk?' Ian asked incredulously. 'Why, that's no but a bittie wee stinkard like a polecat!' He wrinkled his nose, with a expression between amusement and disgust. 'Phew! And here I thought it was a dangerous huge beastie!'

The skunk's satisfied insouciance was too much for Rollo, who pounced forward, uttering a short, sharp bark. He feinted to and fro on the terrace, growling and making short lunges at the skunk, who looked annoyed at the racket.

'Ian,' I said, taking refuge behind Jamie. 'Call off your dog. Skunks *are* dangerous.'

'They are?' Jamie turned a look of puzzlement on me. 'But what –'

'Polecats only stink,' I explained. 'Skunks – Ian, no! Let it alone, and come inside!' Ian, curious, had reached out and prodded the skunk with his poker. The skunk, offended at this unwarranted intimacy, stamped its feet and elevated its tail.

I heard the noise of a chair sliding back, and glanced behind me. Jocasta had stood up and was looking alarmed, but made no move to come to the door.

'What is it?' she said. 'What are they doing?' To my surprise, she was staring into the room, turning her head from one side to the other, as though trying to locate someone in the dark.

Suddenly, the truth dawned on me: her hand on the butler's arm, her touching Jamie's face in greeting, the glass put ready for her grasp, and the shadow on her face when Ian talked of her painting. Jocasta Cameron was blind.

A strangled cry and a piercing yelp jerked me back to more pressing issues on the terrace. A tidal wave of acrid scent cascaded into the room, hit the floor, and boiled up around me like a mushroom cloud.

Choking and gasping, eyes watering from the reek, I

199

groped blindly for Jamie, who was making breathless remarks in Gaelic. Above the cacophony of groaning and piteous yowling outside, I barely heard the small *ting!* of Jocasta's bell behind me.

'Ulysses?' she said, sounding resigned. 'Ye'd best tell Cook the dinner will be late.'

'It was luck that it's summer, at least,' Jocasta said at breakfast next day. 'Think if it had been winter and we had to keep the doors closed!' She laughed, showing teeth in surprisingly good condition for her age.

'Oh, aye,' Ian murmured. 'Please, may I have more toast, ma'am?'

He and Rollo had been first soused in the river, then rubbed with tomatoes from the burgeoning vines that overgrew the necessary house out back. The odor-reducing properties of these fruits worked as well on skunk oil as on the lesser stinks of human waste, but in neither case was the neutralizing effect complete. Ian sat by himself at one end of the long table, next to an open French door, but I saw the maid who brought his toast to him wrinkle her nose unobtrusively as she set the plate before him.

Perhaps inspired by Ian's proximity and a desire for open air, Jocasta suggested that we might ride out to the turpentine works in the forest above River Run.

'It's a day's journey there and back, but I think the weather will keep fine.' She turned toward the open French window, where bees hummed over a herbaceous border of goldenrod and phlox. 'Hear them?' she said, turning her slightly off-kilter smile toward Jamie. 'The bees do say it will be hot and fair.'

'You have keen ears, Madame Cameron,' Fergus said politely. 'If I may be permitted to borrow a horse from your stable, though, I should prefer to go into the town, myself.' I knew he was dying to send word to Marsali in Jamaica; I had helped him to write a long letter the night before, describing our adventures and safe arrival. Rather than wait for a slave to take it with the week's mail, he would much rather post it with his own hands.

'Indeed and ye may, Mr. Fergus,' Jocasta said graciously.

She smiled round the table generally. 'As I said, ye must all consider River Run as ye would your own home.'

Jocasta plainly meant to accompany us on the ride; she came down dressed in a habit of dark green muslin, the girl named Phaedre coming behind, carrying a hat trimmed to match with velvet ribbon. She paused in the hall, but instead of putting on the hat at once, she stood while Phaedre tied a strip of white linen firmly round her head, covering her eyes.

'I can see nothing but light,' she explained. 'I canna make out objects at all. Still, the light of the sun causes me pain, so I must shield my eyes when venturing out. Are you ready, my dears?'

That answered some of my speculations concerning her blindness, though didn't entirely assuage them. Retinitis pigmentosum? I wondered with interest, as I followed her down the wide front hall. Or perhaps macular degeneration, though glaucoma was perhaps the most likely possibility. Not for the first time – or the last, I was sure – my fingers curved around the handle of an invisible ophthalmoscope, itching to see what could not be seen with eyes alone.

To my surprise, when we went out to the stable block, a mare was standing ready saddled for Jocasta, rather than the carriage I had expected. The gift of charming horses ran strong in the MacKenzie line; the mare lifted her head and whickered at sight of her mistress, and Jocasta went to the horse at once, her face alight with pleasure.

'*Ciamar a tha tu?*' she said, stroking the soft Roman nose. 'This will be my sweet Corinna. Is she not a dear lassie?' Reaching in her pocket, she pulled out a small green apple, which the horse accepted with delicate pleasure.

'And have they seen to your knee, *mo chridhe?*' Stooping, Jocasta ran a hand down the horse's shoulder and leg to just inside the knee, finding and exploring a healing scar with expert fingers. 'What say ye, nephew? Is she sound? Can she stand a day's ride?'

Jamie clicked his tongue, and Corinna obligingly took a step toward him, clearly recognizing someone who spoke her language. He took a look at her leg, took her bridle in hand and with a word or two in soft Gaelic, urged her to walk. Then he pulled her to a halt, swung into the saddle, and trotted gently twice round the stableyard, coming to a stop by the waiting Jocasta.

'Aye,' he said, stepping down. 'She's canty enough, Aunt. What did her the injury?'

'Happen as it was a snake, sir,' said the groom, a young black man who had stood back, intently watching Jamie with the horse.

'Not a snakebite, surely?' I said, surprised. 'It looks like a tear – as though she'd caught her leg on something.'

He looked at me with raised brows, but nodded with respect.

'Aye, mum, that it was. 'Twas a month past, I heard the lass let out a rare skelloch, and such a kebbie-lebbie o' bangin' and crashin', as ye'd think the whole stable was comin' doon aboot my head. When I rushed to see the trouble, I found the bloody corpse of a great poison snake lyin' crushed in the straw beneath the manger. The manger was dashit all to pieces, and the wee lassie quiverin' in the corner, the blood streamin' doon her leg from a splinter where she'd caught herself.' He glanced at the horse with obvious pride. 'Och, such a brave wee creature as ye are, lass!'

'The "great poison snake" was perhaps a foot long,' Jocasta said to me in an dry undertone. 'And a simple green gardensnake, forbye. But the foolish thing's got a morbid dread o' snakes. Let her see one, and she loses her head entirely.' She cocked her head in the direction of the young groom and smiled. 'Wee Josh is none so fond o' them, either, is he?'

The groom grinned in answer.

'No, ma'am,' he said. 'I canna thole the creatures, nay more than my lassie.'

Ian, who had been listening to this exchange, couldn't hold back his curiosity any longer.

'Where d'ye come from, man?' he asked the groom, peering at the young man in fascination.

Josh wrinkled his brow.

'Come from? I dinna come – oh, aye, I tak' your

202

meaning now. I was born upriver, on Mr. George Burnett's place. Miss Jo bought me twa year past, at Eastertide.'

'And I think we may assume that Mr. Burnett himself was conceived within crow's flight of Aberdeen,' Jamie said softly to me. 'Aye?'

River Run took in quite a large territory, including not only its prime riverfront acreage but a substantial chunk of the longleaf pine forest that covered a third of the colony. In addition, Hector Cameron had cannily acquired land containing a wide creek, one of many that flowed into Cape Fear.

Thus provided not only with the valuable commodities of timber, pitch, and turpentine but with a convenient means of getting them to market, it was little wonder that River Run had prospered, even though it produced only modest quantities of tobacco and indigo – though the fragrant fields of green tobacco through which we rode looked more than modest to me.

'There's a wee mill,' Jocasta was explaining, as we rode. 'Just above the joining of the creek and the river. The sawing and shaping are done there, and then the boards and barrels are sent downriver by barge to Wilmington. It's no great distance from the house to the mill by water, if ye choose to row upstream, but I thought to show ye a bit of the country instead.' She breathed the pine-scented air with pleasure. 'It's been a time since I was out, myself.'

It *was* pleasant country. Once in the pine forest, it was much cooler, the sun blocked out by the clustered needles overhead. Far overhead the trunks of the trees soared upward for twenty or thirty feet before branching out – no great surprise to hear that the largest part of the mill's output was masts and spars, made for the Royal Navy.

River Run did a great deal of business with the navy, it seemed, judging from Jocasta's conversation; masts, spars, laths, timbers, pitch, turpentine, and tar. Jamie rode close by her side, listening intently as she explained everything in detail, leaving me and Ian to trail behind. Evidently, she had worked closely with her husband in building River Run; I wondered how she managed the place by herself, now that he was gone.

'Look!' Ian said, pointing. 'What's that?'

I pulled up and walked my horse, along with his, to the tree he had pointed out. A great slab of bark had been taken off, exposing the inner wood for a stretch of four feet or more on one side. Within this area, the yellow-white wood was crosshatched in a sort of herringbone pattern, as though it had been slashed back and forth with a knife.

'We're near,' Jocasta said. Jamie had seen us stop, and they had ridden back to join us. 'That will be a turpentine tree you're seeing; I smell it.'

We all could; the scent of cut wood and pungent resin was so strong that even *I* could have found the tree blindfolded. Now that we had stopped, I could hear noises in the distance; the rumblings and thumps of men at work, the chunk of an ax and voices calling back and forth. Breathing in, I also caught a whiff of something burning.

Jocasta edged Corinna close to the cut tree.

'Here,' she said, touching the bottom of the cut, where a rough hollow had been chiseled out of the wood. 'We call it the box; that's where the sap and the raw turpentine drip down and collect. This one is nearly full; there'll be a slave along soon to dip it out.'

No sooner had she spoken than a man appeared through the trees; a slave dressed in no more than a loincloth, leading a large white mule with a broad strap slung across its back, a barrel suspended on either side. The mule stopped dead when he saw us, flung back his head, and brayed hysterically.

'That will be Clarence,' Jocasta said, loudly enough to be heard above the noise. 'He likes to see folk. And who is that with him? Is it you, Pompey?'

'Yah'm. S'me.' The slave gripped the mule by the upper lip and gave it a vicious twist. 'Lea'f, vassar!' As I made the mental translation of this expression into 'Leave off, you bastard!' the man turned toward us, and I saw that his slurred speech was caused by the fact that the lower left half of his jaw was gone; his face below the cheekbone simply fell away into a deep depression filled with white scar tissue.

Jocasta must have heard my gasp of shock – or only have

expected such a response – for she turned her blindfold toward me.

'It was a pitch explosion – fortunate he was not killed. Come, we're near the works.' Without waiting for her groom, she turned her horse's head expertly, and made off through the trees, toward the scent of burning.

The contrast of the turpentine works with the quiet of the forest was amazing; a large clearing full of people, all in a hum of activity. Most were slaves, dressed in the minimum of clothing, limbs and bodies smudged with charcoal.

'Is anyone at the sheds?' Jocasta turned her head toward me.

I rose in my stirrups to look; at the far side of the clearing, near a row of ramshackle sheds, I caught a flash of color; three men in the uniform of the British Navy, and another in a bottle-green coat.

'That will be my particular friend,' Jocasta said, smiling in satisfaction at my description. 'Mr. Farquard Campbell. Come, Nephew; I should like ye to meet him.'

Seen up close, Campbell proved to be a man of sixty or so, no more than middle height, but with that particular brand of leathery toughness that some Scotsmen exhibit as they age – not so much a weathering as a tanning process that results in a surface like a leather targe, capable of turning the sharpest blade.

Campbell greeted Jocasta with pleasure, bowed courteously to me, acknowledged Ian with the flick of a brow, then turned the full force of his shrewd gray eyes on Jamie.

'It's verra pleased I am that you're here, Mr. Fraser,' he said, extending his hand. 'Verra pleased, indeed. I've heard a deal about ye, ever since your aunt learned of your intentions to visit River Run.'

He appeared sincerely delighted to meet Jamie, which struck me as odd. Not that most people weren't happy to meet Jamie – he was quite a prepossessing man, if I did say so – but there was an air almost of relief in Campbell's effusive greeting, which seemed unusual for someone whose outward appearance was entirely one of reserve and taciturnity.

If Jamie noticed anything odd, he hid his puzzlement behind a facade of courtesy.

'I'm flattered that ye should have spared a moment's thought to me, Mr. Campbell.' Jamie smiled pleasantly, and bowed toward the naval officers. 'Gentlemen? I am pleased to make your acquaintance, as well.'

Thus given an opening, a chubby, frowning little person named Lieutenant Wolff and his two ensigns made their introductions, and after perfunctory bows, dismissed me and Jocasta from mind and conversation, turning their attention at once to a discussion of board feet and gallons.

Jamie lifted one eyebrow at me, with a slight nod toward Jocasta, suggesting in marital shorthand that I take his aunt and bugger off while business was conducted.

Jocasta, however, showed not the slightest inclination to remove herself.

'Do go on, my dear,' she urged me. 'Josh will show ye everything. I'll just wait in the shade whilst the gentlemen conduct their business; the heat's a bit much for me, I'm afraid.'

The men had sat down to discuss business inside an open-fronted shed that boasted a crude table with a number of stools; presumably this was where the slaves took their meals, suffering the blackflies for the sake of air. Another shed served for storage; the third, which was enclosed, I deduced must be the sleeping quarters.

Beyond the sheds, toward the center of the clearing, were two or three large fires, over which huge kettles steamed in the sunshine, suspended from tripods.

'They'll be cookin' doon the turpentine, a-boilin' it intae pitch,' Josh explained, taking me within eveshot of one of the kettles. 'Some is put intae me barrels as is' – he nodded toward the sheds, where a wagon was parked, piled high with barrels – 'but the rest is made intae pitch. The naval gentlemen will be sayin' how much they'll be needin', so as we'll know.'

A small boy of seven or eight was perched on a high, rickety stool, stirring the pot with a long stick; a taller youth stood by with an enormous ladle, with which he removed the lighter layer of purified turpentine at the top of the kettle, depositing this in a barrel to one side.

206

As I watched them, a slave came out of the forest, leading a mule, and headed for the kettle. Another man came to help, and together they unloaded the barrels – plainly heavy – from the mule, and upended them into the kettle, one at a time, with a great whoosh of pungent yellowish pinesap.

'Och, ye'll want to stand back a bit, mum,' Josh said, taking my arm to draw me away from the fire. 'The stuff does splash a bit, and happen it should take fire, ye wouldna want to be burnt.'

Having seen the man in the forest, I most certainly didn't want to be burnt. I drew away, and glanced back at the sheds. Jamie, Mr. Campbell, and the naval men were sitting on stools around a table inside one hut, sharing something from a bottle and poking at a sheaf of papers on the table.

Standing pressed against the shed wall, out of sight of the men within, was Jocasta Cameron. Having abandoned her pretense of exhaustion, she was plainly listening for all she was worth.

Josh caught the expression of surprise on my face, and turned to see what I was looking at.

'Miss Jo does hate not to have the charge o' things,' he murmured regretfully. 'I havena haird her myself, but yon lass Phaedre did say as how Mistress takes on when she canna manage something – a-rantin' dreadful, she says, and stampin' something fierce.'

'That must be quite a remarkable spectacle,' I murmured. 'What is she not able to manage, though?' From all appearances, Jocasta Cameron had her house, fields, and people well in hand, blind or not.

Now it was his turn to look surprised.

'Och, it's the bluidy Navy. Did she not say why we came today?'

Before I could go into the fascinating question of why Jocasta Cameron should wish to manage the British Navy, today or any other day, we were interrupted by a cry of alarm from the far side of the clearing. I turned to look, and was nearly trampled by several half-naked men running in panic toward the sheds.

At the far side of the clearing a peculiar sort of mound

207

rose up out of the ground; I had noticed it earlier but had had no chance to ask about it yet. While the floor of the clearing was mosty dirt, the mound was covered with grass – but grass of a peculiar, patchy sort; part was green, part gone yellow, and here and there was an oblong of grass that was stark, dead brown.

Just as I realized that this effect was the result of the mound's being covered in cut turves, the whole thing blew up. There was no sound of explosion, just a sort of muffled noise like a huge sneeze, and a faint wave of concussion in the air that brushed my cheek.

If it didn't sound like an explosion, it certainly looked like one; pieces of turf and bits of burnt wood began to rain down all over the clearing. There was a lot of shouting, and Jamie and his companions came rocketing out of the shed like a flock of startled pheasants.

'Are ye all right, Sassenach?' He grasped my arm, looking anxious.

'Yes, fine,' I said, rather confused. 'What on earth just happened?'

'Damned if I ken,' he said briefly, already looking round the clearing. 'Where's Ian?'

'I don't know. You don't think he had anything to do with this, do you?' I brushed at several floating specks of charcoal that had landed on my bosom. With black streaks ornamenting my decolletage, I followed Jamie into the small knot of slaves, all babbling in a confusing mixture of Gaelic, English, and bits of various African tongues.

We found Ian with one of the young naval ensigns. They were peering interestedly into the blackened pit that now occupied the spot where the mound had stood.

'It happens often, I understand,' the ensign was saying as we arrived. 'I hadn't seen it before, though – amazing powerful blast, wasn't it?'

'*What* happens often?' I asked, peering around Ian. The pit was filled with a crisscross jumble of blackened pine logs, all tossed higgledy-piggledy by the force of the explosion. The base of the mound was still there, rising up around the pit like the rim of a pie shell.

'A pitch explosion,' the ensign explained, turning to me. He was small and ruddy-cheeked, about Ian's age.

'They lay a charcoal fire, d'ye see, ma'am, below a great pot of pitch, and cover it all over with earth and cut turves, to keep in the heat, but allow enough air through the cracks to keep the fire burning. The pitch boils down, and flows out through a hollowed log into the tar barrel – see?' He pointed. A split log dangled over the remains of a shattered barrel oozing sticky black. The reek of burnt wood and thick tar filled the air, and I tried to breathe only through my mouth.

'The difficulty lies in regulating the flow of air,' the little ensign went on, preening himself a bit on his knowledge. 'Too little air, and the fire goes out; too much, and it burns with such energy that it cannot be contained, and is like to ignite the fumes from the pitch and burst its bonds. As you see, ma'am.' He gestured importantly toward a nearby tree, where one of the turves had been thrown with such force as to wrap itself around the trunk like some shaggy yellow fungus.

'It is a matter of the nicest adjustment,' he said, and stood on tiptoe, looking around with interest. 'Where is the slave whose task it is to manage the fire? I do hope the poor fellow has not been killed.'

He hadn't. I had been checking carefully through the crowd as we talked, looking for any injuries, but everyone seemed to have escaped intact – this time.

'Aunt!' Jamie exclaimed, suddenly recalling Jocasta. He whirled toward the sheds, but then stopped, relaxing. She was there, clearly visible in her green dress, standing rigid by the shed.

Rigid with fury, as we discovered when we reached her. Forgotten by everyone in the flurry of the explosion, she had been unable to move, sightless as she was, and was thus left to stand helpless, hearing the turmoil but unable to do anything.

I recalled what Josh had said about Jocasta's temper, but she was too much the lady to stamp and rant in public, however angry she might be. Josh himself apologized in profuse Aberdonian for not having been by her side to aid her, but she dismissed this with kind, if brusque, impatience.

'Clapper your tongue, lad; ye did as I bade ye.' She

turned her head restlessly from side to side, as though trying to see through her blindfold.

'Farquard, where are you?'

Mr. Campbell moved to her and put her hand through his arm, patting it briefly.

'There's no great harm done, my dear,' he assured her. 'No one hurt, and only the one barrel of tar destroyed.'

'Good,' she said, the tension in her tall figure relaxing slightly. 'But where is Byrnes?' she inquired. 'I do not hear his voice.'

'The overseer?' Lieutenant Wolff mopped several smuts from his sweating face with a large linen kerchief. 'I had wondered that myself. We found no one here to greet us this morning. Fortunately, Mr. Campbell arrived soon thereafter.'

Farquard Campbell made a small noise in his throat, deprecating his own involvement.

'Byrnes will be at the mill, I expect,' he said. 'One of the slaves here told me there had been some trouble wi' the main blade of the saw. Doubtless he will be attending to that.'

Wolff looked puff-faced, as though he considered defective saw blades a poor excuse for not having been appropriately received. From the tight line of Jocasta's lips, so did she.

Jamie coughed, reached over and plucked a small clump of grass out of my hair.

'I do believe that I saw a basket of luncheon packed, did I not, Aunt? Perhaps ye might help the Lieutenant to a wee bit of refreshment, whilst I tidy up matters here?'

It was the right suggestion. Jocasta's lips eased a bit, and Wolff looked distinctly happier at the mention of lunch.

'Indeed, Nephew.' She drew herself upright, her air of command restored, and nodded in the general direction of Wolff's voice. 'Lieutenant, will ye be so kind as to join me?'

Over lunch, I gathered that the Lieutenant's visit to the turpentine works was a quarterly affair, during which a contract was drawn up for the purchase and delivery of assorted naval stores. It was the Lieutenant's business to make and review similar arrangements with plantation owners from Cross Creek to the Virginia border, and Lieutenant Wolff made it plain which end of the colony he preferred.

'If there is one area of endeavor at which I will admit the Scotch excel,' the Lieutenant proclaimed rather pompously, taking a good-sized swallow of his third cup of whisky, 'it is in the production of drink.'

Farquard Campbell, who had been taking appreciative sips from his own pewter cup, gave a small, dry smile and said nothing. Jocasta sat beside him on a rickety bench. Her fingers rested lightly on his arm, sensitive as a seismograph, feeling for subterranean clues.

Wolff made an unsuccessful attempt to stifle a belch, and belatedly turned what he appeared to consider his charm on me.

'In most other respects,' he went on, leaning toward me confidentially, 'they are as a race both lazy and stubborn, a pair of traits which renders them unfit for –' At this point, the youngest ensign, red with embarrassment, knocked over a bowl of apples, creating enough of a diversion to prevent the completion of the Lieutenant's thought – though not, unfortunately, sufficient to deflect its train altogether.

The Lieutenant dabbed at the sweat leaking from under his wig, and peered at me through bloodshot eyes.

'But I collect that you are not Scotch, ma'am? Your voice is most melodious and well-bred, and I may say so. You have no trace of a barbarous accent, in spite of your associations.'

'Ah . . . thank you,' I murmured, wondering what trick of administrative incompetence had sent the Lieutenant to conduct the Navy's business in the Cape Fear River Valley, possibly the single largest collection of Scottish Highlanders to be found in the New World. I began to see what Josh had meant by, 'Och, the bluidy Navy!'

Jocasta's smile might have been stitched on. Mr. Campbell, beside her, gave me the barest flick of gray eyebrow, and looked austere. Evidently, stabbing the Lieutenant through the heart with a fruit knife wasn't on – at least not until he had signed the requisition order – so

211

I did the next best thing I could think of; I picked up the whisky bottle and refilled his cup to the brim.

'It's terribly good, isn't it? Won't you have a bit more, Lieutenant?'

It *was* good; smooth and warm. Also very expensive. I turned to the youngest ensign, smiled warmly at him, and left the Lieutenant to find his own way to the bottom of the bottle.

Conversation proceeded jerkily but without further incident, though the two ensigns kept a wary eye on the Drunkard's Progress going on across the table. No wonder; it would be their responsibility to get the Lieutenant on a horse and back to Cross Creek in one piece. I began to see why there were two of them.

'Mr. Fraser seems to be managing most creditably,' the older ensign murmured, nodding outside in a feeble attempt to restart the stalled conversation. 'Do you not think, sir?'

'Oh? Ah. No doubt.' Wolff had lost interest in anything much beyond the bottom of his cup, but it was true enough. While the rest of us sat over our lunch, Jamie – with Ian's aid – had managed to restore order to the clearing, set the pitch boilers and sap gatherers back to work, and collect the debris of the explosion. At present he was on the far side of the clearing, stripped to shirt and breeches, helping to heave half-burned logs back into the tar pit. I rather envied him; it looked to be much more pleasant work than lunching with Lieutenant Wolff.

'Aye, he's done well.' Farquard Campbell's quick eyes flicked over the clearing, then returned to the table. He assessed the Lieutenant's condition, and gave Jocasta's hand a brief squeeze. Without turning her head, she spoke to Josh, who had been lurking quietly in the corner.

'Do ye put that second bottle into the Lieutenant's saddlebag, laddie,' she said. 'I should not want it to be going to waste.' She gave the Lieutenant a charming smile, rendered the more convincing as he couldn't see her eyes.

Mr. Campbell cleared his throat.

'Since ye will so soon be leaving us, sir, perhaps we might settle the matter of your requisitions now?'

Wolff seemed vaguely surprised to hear that he had

been about to leave, but his ensigns sprang to their feet with alacrity, and began to gather up papers and saddle-bags. One snatched out a traveling inkwell and a sharpened quill and set them down in front of the Lieutenant; Mr. Campbell whipped out a folded quire of paper from his coat and laid it down, ready for signature.

Wolff frowned at the paper, and swayed a little.

'Just there, sir,' murmured the elder ensign, putting the quill into his senior's slack hand and pointing at the paper.

Wolff picked up his cup, tilted back his head, and drained the last drops. Setting the cup down with a bang, he smiled vacantly around, his eyes unfocused. The youngest ensign closed his eyes in resignation.

'Oh, why not?' the Lieutenant said recklessly, and dipped his quill.

'Will ye not wish to wash and change your clothes at once, Nephew?' Jocasta's nostrils flared delicately. 'Ye stink most dreadfully of tar and charcoal.'

I thought it just as well she couldn't see him. It went a long way beyond stinking; his hands were black, his new shirt reduced to a filthy rag, and his face so begrimed that he looked as though he had been cleaning chimneys. Such portions of him as weren't black, were red. He had left off his hat while working in the midday sun, and the bridge of his nose was the color of cooked lobster. I didn't think the color was due entirely to the sun, though.

'My ablutions can wait,' he said. 'First, I wish to know the meaning of yon wee charade.' He fixed Mr. Campbell with a dark blue look.

I am lured to the forest upon the pretext of smelling turpentine, and before I ken where I am, I'm sitting wi' the British Navy, saying aye and nay to matters I ken nothing of, wi' yon wee mannie kickin' my shins under the table like a trained monkey!'

Jocasta smiled at that.

Campbell sighed. In spite of the exertions of the day, his neat coat showed no signs of dust, and his old-fashioned peruke sat squarely on his head.

'You have my apologies, Mr. Fraser, for what must seem a monstrous imposition upon your good nature. As it is, your arrival was fortuitous in the extreme, but did not allow sufficient time for communications to be made. I was in Averasboro until last evening, and by the time I received word of your arrival, it was much too late for me to ride here to acquaint you with the circumstances.'

'Indeed? Well, as I perceive we have a bit of time at present, I invite ye to do so now,' Jamie said, with a slight click as his teeth closed on the 'now'.

'Will ye not sit down first, Nephew?' Jocasta put in, with a graceful wave of her hand. 'It will take a bit of talk to explain, and ye've had a tiring day of it, no?' Ulysses had materialized out of the ether with a linen sheet over his arm; he spread this over a chair with a flourish, and gestured to Jamie to sit down.

Jamie eyed the butler narrowly, but it *had* been a tiring day; I could see blisters amid the soot on his hands, and sweat had made clear runnels in the filth on face and neck. He sank slowly into the proffered chair, and allowed a silver cup to be put into his hand.

A similar cup appeared as if by magic in my own hand, and I smiled in gratitude at the butler; I hadn't been hoiking logs about, but the long, hot ride had worn *me* out. I took a deep, appreciative sip; a lovely, cool rough cider, that bit the tongue and slaked the thirst at once.

Jamie took a deep draught, and looked a little calmer.

'Well, then, Mr. Campbell?'

'It is a matter of the Navy,' Campbell began, and Jocasta snorted.

'A matter of Lieutenant Wolff, ye mean,' she corrected.

'For your purposes the same, Jo, and well ye know it,' Mr. Campbell said, a little sharply. He turned back to Jamie to explain.

The majority of River Run's revenues were, as Jocasta had told us, derived from the sale of its timber and turpentine products, the largest and most profitable customer being the British Navy.

'But the Navy's not what it was,' Mr. Campbell said, shaking his head regretfully. 'During the war wi' the French, they could scarce keep the fleet supplied, and any man with a working sawmill was rich. But for the last ten years, it's been peaceful, and the ships left to rot – the

Admiralty's not laid a new keel in five years.' He sighed at the unfortunate economic consequences of peace.

The Navy did still require such stores as pitch and turpentine and spars – with a leaky fleet to keep afloat, tar would always find a market. However, the market had shrunk severely, and the Navy now could pick and choose those landowners with whom they did business.

The Navy requiring dependability above all things, their covetable contracts were renewed quarterly, upon inspection and approval by a senior naval officer – in this case, Wolff. Always difficult to deal with, Wolff had nonetheless been adroitly managed by Hector Cameron, until the latter's death.

'Hector drank with him,' Jocasta put in bluntly. 'And when he left, there'd be a bottle in his saddlebag, and a bit besides.' The death of Hector Cameron, though, had severely affected the business of the estate.

'And not only because there's less for bribes,' Campbell said, with a sidelong glance at Jocasta. He cleared his throat primly.

Lieutenant Wolff, it seemed, had come to give his condolences to the widow Cameron upon the death of her husband, properly uniformed, attended by his ensigns. He had come back again the next day, alone – with a proposal of marriage.

Jamie, caught mid-swallow, choked on his drink.

'It wasna my person the man was interested in,' Jocasta said, sharply, hearing this. 'It was my land.'

Jamie wisely decided not to comment, merely eyeing his aunt with new interest.

Having heard the background, I thought she was likely right – Wolff's interest was in acquiring a profitable plantation, which could be rendered still more profitable by means of the naval contracts his influence could assure. At the same time, the person of Jocasta Cameron was no small added inducement.

Blind or not, she was a striking woman. Beyond the simple beauty of flesh and bone, though, she exuded a sensual vitality that caused even such a dry stick as Farquard Campbell to ignite when she was near.

'I suppose that explains the Lieutenant's offensive

behavior at lunch,' I said, interested. 'Hell hath no fury like a woman scorned, but the blokes don't like it, either.'

Jocasta turned her head toward me, startled – I think she had forgotten I was there – but Farquard Campbell laughed.

'Indeed they don't, Mrs. Fraser,' he assured me, eyes twinkling. 'We're fragile things, we poor men; ye trifle with our affections at your peril.'

Jocasta gave an unladylike snort at this.

'Affections, forbye!' she said. 'The man has nay affection for anything that doesna come in a bottle.'

Jamie was eyeing Mr. Campbell with a certain amount of interest.

'Since ye raise the matter of affections, Aunt,' he said, with a small edge, 'might I inquire as to the interests of your particular friend?'

Mr. Campbell returned the stare.

'I've a wife at home, sir,' he said dryly, 'and eight weans, the eldest of whom is perhaps a few years older than yourself. But I kent Hector Cameron for more than thirty years, and I'll do my best by his wife for the sake of his friendship – and hers.'

Jocasta laid a hand on his arm, and turned her head toward him. If she could no longer use her eyes for impression, she still knew the effect of downswept lashes.

'Farquard has been a great help to me, Jamie,' she said, with a touch of reproof. 'I couldna have managed, without his assistance, after poor Hector died.'

'Oh, aye,' Jamie said, with no more than a hint of skepticism. 'And I'm sure I must be as grateful to ye as is my aunt, sir. But I am still wondering just a bit where I come into this tale?'

Campbell coughed discreetly and went on with his story. Jocasta had put off the Lieutenant, feigning collapse from the stress of bereavement and had herself carried to her bedroom, from which she did not emerge until he had concluded his business in Cross Creek and left for Wilmington.

'Byrnes managed the contracts that time, and a fine mess he made of them,' Jocasta put in.

'Ah, Mr. Byrnes, the invisible overseer. And where was he this morning?'

A maid had appeared with a bowl of warm perfumed water, and a towel. Without asking, she knelt by Jamie's chair, took one of his hands, and began gently to wash the soot away. Jamie looked slightly taken aback by this attention, but was too occupied by the conversation to send her away.

A slight wry smile crossed Campbell's face.

'I'm afraid Mr. Byrnes, though usually a competent overseer, shares one small weakness wi' the Lieutenant. I sent to the sawmill for him, first thing, but the slave came back and told me Byrnes was insensible in his quarters, reekin' of drink, and could not be roused.'

Jocasta made another unladylike noise, which caused Campbell to glance at her with affection before turning back to Jamie.

'Your aunt is more than capable of managing the business of the estate with Ulysses to assist her in the documentary aspects. However, as ye will have seen yourself' – he gestured delicately at the bowl of water, which now resembled a bowl of ink – 'there are physical concerns to the running of it, as well.'

'That was the point that Lieutenant Wolff put to me,' Jocasta said, lips thinning at the memory. 'That I could not expect to manage my property alone, and me not only a woman, but sightless as well. I could not, he said, depend upon Byrnes, unable as I am to go to the forest and the mill to see what the man is doing. Or not doing.' Her mouth shut firmly on the thought.

'Which is true enough,' Campbell put in ruefully. 'It is a proverb amongst us – "Happiness is a son old enough to be factor." For when it's a matter of money or slaves, ye cannot trust anyone save your kin.'

I drew a deep breath and glanced at Jamie, who nodded. At last we'd got to it.

'And that,' I said, 'is where Jamie comes in. Am I right?'

Jocasta had already enlisted Farquard Campbell to deal with Lieutenant Wolff upon his next visit, intending that Campbell should keep Byrnes from, committing folly with the contracts. When we had so opportunely arrived, though, Jocasta had hit upon a better plan.

'I sent word to Farquard that he should inform the Lieutenant that my nephew had come to take up the management of River Run. That would cause him to go cautiously,' she explained. 'For he would not dare to press me, with a kinsman who had an interest standing by.'

'I see.' Despite himself, Jamie was beginning to look amused. 'So the Lieutenant would think his attempt at a good down-setting here was usurped by my arrival. No wonder the man seemed to take such a mislike to me. I thought it was perhaps a general disgust of Scotsmen that he had, from what he said.'

'I should imagine that he has – now,' Campbell said, dabbing his lips circumspectly with his napkin.

Jocasta reached across the table, groping, and Jamie put out his hand instinctively to hers.

'You will forgive me, Nephew?' she said. With his hand to guide her, she could look toward his face; one would not have known her blind, by the expression of pleading in her beautiful blue eyes.

'I knew nothing of your character, d'ye see, before ye came. I could not risk that you would refuse a part in the deception, did I tell ye of it first. Do say that ye hold no grudge toward me, Jamie, if only for sweet Ellen's sake.'

Jamie squeezed her hand gently, assuring her that he held no grudge. Indeed, he was pleased to have come in time to help, and his aunt might count upon his assistance, in any way she chose to call upon him.

Mr. Campbell beamed and rang the bell; Ulysses brought in the special whisky, with a tray of crystal goblets and a plate of savories, and we drank confusion to the British Navy.

Looking at that fine-boned face, so full of blind eloquence, though, I couldn't help recalling the brief synopsis Jamie had once given me of the outstanding characteristics of the members of his family.

'Frasers are stubborn as rocks,' he'd said. 'And MacKenzies are charming as larks in the field – but sly as foxes, with it.'

'And where have *you* been?' Jamie asked, giving Fergus a hard up-and-down. 'I didna think ye'd money enough for what it looks as though ye've been doing.'

Fergus smoothed his disheveled hair, and sat down, radiating offended dignity.

'I met with a pair of French fur-traders in the town. They speaking little English, and myself being fluent, I could not but agree to assist them in their transactions. If they should then choose to invite me to share a small supper at their inn . . .' He lifted one shoulder in Gallic dismissal of the matter, and turned to more immediate concerns, reaching inside his shirt for a letter.

'This had arrived in Cross Creek for you,' he said, handing it to Jamie. 'The postmaster asked me to bring it.'

It was a thick packet of paper, with a battered seal, and looked in little better condition than did Fergus. Jamie's face lighted when he saw it, though he opened it with some trepidation. Three letters fell out; one in what I recognized as his sister's writing, the other two plainly addressed by someone else.

Jamie picked up the letter from his sister, eyed it as though it might contain something explosive, and set it gently down by the fruit bowl on the table.

'I'll start wi' Ian,' he said, picking up the second letter with a grin. 'I'm not sure I want to be reading Jenny's without a glass of whisky in my hand.'

He prised off the seal with the up of the silver fruit knife, and opened the letter, scanning the first page. 'I wonder if he . . .' His voice faded off as he began to read.

Curious, I got up and stood behind his chair, looking over his shoulder. Ian Murray wrote a clear, large hand, and it was easy to read, even at a distance.

Dear Brother —

All here are well, and give thanks to God for the news of your safe arrival in the Colonies. I send this missive in care of Jocasta Cameron; should it find you in her company, Jenny bids you to give her kindest regards to her Aunt.

You will see from the enclosed that you are restored to my wife's good graces; she has quite ceased to talk of you in the

219

same breath with Auld Scratch, and I have heard no recent references to Emasculation, which may relieve your mind.

To put aside jesting – her Heart is much lightened by news of Young Ian's safety, as is my own. You will know the depth of our gratitude at his Deliverance, I think; therefore I will not Weary you with Repetitions, though in all truth, I could write a Novel upon that theme.

We manage to keep all here fed, though the barley suffered much from hail, and there is a flux abroad in the village which has claimed two children this month, to their parents' sorrow. It will be Annie Fraser and Alasdair Kirby we have lost, may God have mercy on their innocence.

On a happier note, we have had word from Michael in Paris; he continues to prosper in the wine business, and thinks of marrying soon.

I take joy in acquainting you with news of the birth of my newest grandson, Anthony Brian Montgomery Lyle. I shall content myself with this announcement, leaving a fuller description to Jenny; she is besotted of him, as are we all, he is a Dear Lad. His father, Paul – Maggie's husband – is a soldier, so Maggie and wee Anthony bide here at Lallybroch. Paul is in France at present; we pray nightly he may be left there, in relative peace; and not sent to the dangers of the Colonies nor the wilds of Canada.

We have had visitors this week; Simon, Lord Lovat, and his companions. He has come a-gathering again, seeking recruits for the Highland regiment he commands. You will perhaps hear of them in the Colonies, where I understand they have established some small reputation. Simon tells great tales of their bravery against the Indians and the wicked French, some of which are doubtless true.

Jamie grinned at this, and turned the page over.

He quite enthralled Henry and Matthew by his stories, and the girls as well. Josephine ('Kitty's eldest,' Jamie observed in an aside to me) was so inspired, indeed, as to engineer a raid upon the chicken-coop, wherefrom she and her Cousins all emerged bedecked with feathers, mud from the kail-yard being employed in lieu of war-paint.

As all wished to play Savage, Young Jamie, Kitty's husband

220

Geordie and myself were pressed into service as the Highland regiment, and obliged to suffer attack by Tomahawk (kitchen spoons and ladles) and other forms of enthusiastic assault, we essaying meanwhile a valiant defense with our broadswords (pieces of lath and willow twigs).

I put a stop to the Suggestion that the thatch of the dove-cote be set afire with flaming arrows, but was obliged in the end to submit to being Scalped. I flatter myself that I survived this Operation in better case than did the chickens.

The letter continued in this vein, giving more news of family, but dealing more often with the business of the farm, and reports of events in the district. Emigration, Ian wrote, was 'become epidemic', with virtually all of the inhabitants of the village of Shewglie having decided upon this expedient.

Jamie finished the letter and put it down. He was smiling, his eyes faintly dreamy, as though he saw the cool mists and stones of Lallybroch rather than the humid, vivid jungle that surrounded us.

The second letter was also addressed in Ian's hand, but marked *Private* below the blue wax seal.

'And what will this be, I wonder?' Jamie murmured, breaking the seal and unfolding it. It began without salutation, obviously meant as continuation to the larger letter.

Now, Brother, I have a matter of some concern to put to you, upon which I write separately, so that you might share my larger letter with Ian, without disclosing this matter.

Your last letter spoke of putting Ian aboard ship in Charleston. Should this have occurred, we will of course welcome his coming with joy. However, if by chance he has not yet quitted your company, it is our wish that he remain with you, should this obligation be not unpleasing to you and to Claire.

'Not unpleasing to me,' Jamie muttered, nostrils flaring slightly as he glanced from the page to the window. Ian and Rollo were wrestling on the grass with two young slaves, rolling over and over in a giggling tangle of limbs and cloth and wagging tail. 'Mmphm.' He turned his back to the window and resumed reading.

I mentioned Simon Fraser to you, and the cause of his presence here. The regimental levies have been a matter of concern to us for some time, though the matter has not often been pressing, our location being fortunately remote and difficult of travel.

Lovat finds little trouble in inducing lads to take the King's shilling; what is there for them here? Poverty and want, with no hope of betterment. Why should they remain here, where they have nothing to inherit, where they are forbidden the plaid or the right to carry a man's weapons? Why should they not seize the chance of reclaiming the notion of manhood – even should it mean they wear the tartan and carry a sword in the service of a German usurper?

I think sometimes this is the worst of it; not only that murder and injustice have been loosed unchecked upon us, without hope of cure or recourse – but that our young men, our hope and future, should be thus piped away, squandered for the profit of the conqueror, and paid in the small coin of their pride.

Jamie looked up at me, one brow raised.

'Ye wouldna think to look at him that Ian had such poesy in him, aye?'

There was a break in the text here. When it resumed, toward the bottom of the page, the writing, which had sprawled above into an angry scrawl with frequent blots and scratches, was once more controlled and tidy.

I must beg pardon for the passion of my words. I had not meant to say so much, but the temptation to open my heart to you as I always have is overwhelming. These are things I would not say to Jenny, though I imagine she knows them.

To the point, then; I grow garrulous. Young Jamie and Michael are well enough for the present – at least we have no fear that either of them will be tempted by a soldier's life.

The same is not true of Ian; you know the lad, and his spirit of adventure, so similar to your own. There is no real work for him here, yet he has not the mind of a scholar or a head for business. How shall he fare, in a world where he must choose between beggary and the profession of war? For there is little else.

We would have him stay with you, if you will have him. It may be that there is a greater opportunity in the New World for him than might be found here. Even if this should not be so, his mother will at least be spared the sight of her son marching away with his regiment.

I could ask no better Guardian or example for him than Yourself. I know I ask a great Favour of you in this Matter. Still, I hope the situation will not be entirely without benefit to you, beyond the presumed Great Pleasure of Ian's company.

'Not only a poet, but an ironist, too,' Jamie observed, with another glance at the boys on the lawn.

Here there was another break in the text, before the writing resumed, this time with a freshly sharpened quill, the words written carefully, reflecting the thought behind them.

I had left off writing, Brother, wishing my thoughts to be clear and unmazed by weariness before addressing this concern. I have in fact taken up my pen and put it down a dozen times, unsure whether to speak at all – I fear to offend you, in the same breath I ask your favour. And yet I must speak.

I wrote of Simon Fraser, earlier. He is a man of honour, though his father's son – but he is a bloody man. I have known him since all of us were lads (sometimes that seems but yesterday; and then again, a gulf of years), and there is a hardness in him now, a glimpse of steel at the back of his eyes, that was not there before Culloden.

What troubles me – and the knowledge you bear of my love toward you is all that emboldens me to say this – is that I have seen that steel in your own eyes, Brother.

I know too well the sights that freeze a man's heart, to harden his eyes in that fashion. I trust that you will forgive my frankness, but I have feared for your soul, many times since Culloden.

I have not spoken of the matter to Jenny, but she has seen it, too. She is a woman, forbye, and will know you in ways I cannot. It will be that fear, I think, that caused her to throw Laoghaire at your head. I did think the match ill-made, but

(here a large, deliberate blotch obscured several lines).
You are fortunate in Claire.

'Mmphm,' Jamie said at this, giving me an eye. I squeezed his shoulder, and leaned forward to read the rest.

It is late, and I ramble. I spoke of Simon – care for his men is now his sole link with humanity. He has neither wife nor child, he lives without root or hearth, his patrimony hostage to the conqueror he serves. There is a burning fire in such a man, but no heart. I hope never to say the same of you – or of Young Ian.

Thus I give you to each other, and may God's blessing – and mine – be with you both.

Write as soon as you may. We hunger for News of you, and for your accounts of the exotic precincts in which you now Abide.
Your Most Affectionate Brother,
Ian Murray

Jamie carefully folded the letter, and put it into his coat. 'Mmphm,' he said.

11

The Law of Bloodshed

July 1767

I became gradually accustomed to the rhythm of life at
River Run. The presence of the slaves disturbed me, but
there was little I could do about that, save to call upon
their services as little as I could, fetching and carrying for
myself whenever possible.

River Run boasted a 'simples' room, essentially a small
closet in which dried herbs and medicines were kept.
There was not much there – no more than a few jars of
dandelion root and willow bark, and a few patent poult-
ices, dusty from disuse. Jocasta professed herself delighted
that I should want to use the space – she had herself no
talent for medicinals, she said with a shrug, nor had any of
the slaves.

'There is a new woman who may show some skill in that
direction,' she said, long fingers drawing out the line of
wool from the spindle as the spinning wheel whirred
round.

'She is not a house slave, though; she was fresh come
from Africa only a few months past, and has neither
speech nor manners. I had thought to train her, perhaps,
but since you are here . . . ah, now the thread's grown too
thin, d'ye see?'

While I spent some time each day chatting with Jocasta
and attempting to learn from her the art of spinning wool,
Jamie spent an hour or two with the butler, Ulysses, who in
addition to serving as Jocasta's eyes and as major domo of
the house, had evidently also been managing the accounts
of the plantation since Hector Cameron's death.

'And doing a fair job of it, too,' Jamie told me privately,
after one such session. 'If he were a white man, my aunt
would have no difficulty in handling her affairs. As it is,
though –' He shrugged.

'As it is, it's lucky for her that you're here,' I said,

leaning close to sniff at him. He had spent the day in Cross Creek, arranging a complicated exchange involving indigo blocks, lumber, three pairs of mules, five tons of rice, and a warehouse receipt for a gilded clock, and as a result, a fascinating variety of scents clung to his coat and hair.

'It's the least I can do,' he said, his eyes on the boots he was brushing. His lips tightened briefly. 'Not as though I were otherwise occupied, is it?'

'A dinner party,' Jocasta declared, a few days later. 'I must have a proper festival, to introduce the two of ye to the folk of the county.'

'There's no need of it, Aunt,' Jamie said mildly, looking up from his book. 'I think I shall have met most of the county at the stock-buying last week. Or the masculine part of it, at least,' he added, smiling at me. 'Come to think on it, though, perhaps it would suit Claire to be acquainted wi' the ladies of the district.'

'I wouldn't mind knowing a few more people,' I admitted. 'Not that I don't find ample occupation here,' I assured Jocasta, 'but –'

'But not of a sort that interests you,' she answered, though with enough of a smile to take the sting out of the remark. 'Ye've no great fondness for needlework, I think.' Her hand went to the big basket of colored wools and plucked out a ball of green, to be attached to the shawl she was knitting.

The balls of wool were carefully arranged each morning by one of the maids, in a spiral spectrum, so that by counting, Jocasta could pick up a ball of the right color.

'Aye, well, not *that* sort of needlework,' Jamie put in, closing his book and smiling at me. 'It's more the stitching of severed flesh that appeals to Claire. I expect she'll be getting restless these days, wi' no more than a cracked head or a case of piles to be dealing with.'

'Ha ha,' I said tartly, but in fact he was quite right. While I was pleased to find that the inhabitants of River Run were on the whole healthy and well nourished, there was not a great deal of scope for a physician. While I certainly wished no ill to anyone, there was no denying that I *was* getting restless. So was Jamie, but I thought that was a matter better left unremarked for the moment.

'I do hope Marsali's quite well,' I said, changing the subject. Convinced at last that Jamie would not require his aid for a little while, Fergus had left the day before, bound downriver for Wilmington, thence to take ship for Jamaica. If all went well, he would return in the springtime with Marsali and – God willing – their new child.

'So do I,' said Jamie. 'I told Fergus that –'

Jocasta turned her head sharply toward the door.

'What is it, Ulysses?'

Absorbed by the conversation, I hadn't noticed foot-steps in the hallway. Not for the first time, I was struck by the acuteness of Jocasta's hearing.

'Mr. Farquard Campbell,' the butler said quietly, and stood back against the wall.

It was an indication of Farquard Campbell's familiarity with the household, I thought, that he should not have waited for Ulysses to return with an invitation for him to enter. He came into the drawing room on the butler's heels, hat carelessly thrust beneath one arm.

'Jo, Mrs. Fraser,' he said with a quick bow to Jocasta and me, and, 'Your servant, sir,' to Jamie. Mr. Campbell had been riding, and riding hard; the shirts of his coat were thick with dust, and sweat streamed down his face beneath a wig crammed on askew.

'What is it, Farquard? Has something happened?' Jocasta sat forward on the edge of her chair, her face reflecting his obvious anxiety.

'Yes,' he said abruptly. 'An accident at the sawmill. I've come to ask Mrs. Fraser –'

'Yes, of course. Let me get my box. Ulysses, will you have someone fetch a horse?' I rose hastily, searching for the slippers I had kicked off. I wasn't dressed for riding, but from Campbell's look, there wasn't time to change. 'Is it serious?'

He put out a hand to stop me, as I stooped to pull my slippers on.

'Aye, bad enough. But you needn't come, Mrs. Fraser. If your husband might fetch along some of your medicines and such, though –'

'Of course I'll come,' I said.

'No!' He spoke abruptly, and we all stared at him. His eyes sought Jamie's, and he grimaced, lips tight.

'It's not a matter for the ladies,' he said. 'But I should be most grateful for your company, Mr. Fraser.'

Jocasta was on her feet before I could protest, gripping Campbell's arm.

'What is it?' she said sharply. 'Is it one of my Negroes? Has Byrnes done something?'

She was taller than he by an inch or two; he had to look up to answer her. I could see the lines of strain in his face, and she plainly sensed it as well; her fingers tightened on the gray serge of his coat sleeve.

He glanced at Ulysses, then back at Jocasta. As though he had received a direct order, the butler turned and left the room, soft-footed as ever.

'It is a matter of bloodshed, Jo,' he said to her quietly. 'I do not know who, nor how, nor even how bad the injury may be. MacNeill's boy came for me. But for the other –' He hesitated, then shrugged. 'It is the law.'

'And you're a judge!' she burst out. 'For God's sake, can you not do something?' Her head moved jerkily, blind eyes trying to fix him, bend him to her will.

'No!' he said sharply, and then, more gently, repeated, 'No.' He lifted her hand from his sleeve and held it tightly.

'You know I cannot,' he said. 'If I could . . .'

'If you could, you would not,' she said bitterly. She pulled her hand out of his grasp and stood back, fists clenched at her sides. 'Go on, then. They've called ye to be judge; go and give them their judgment.' She whirled on her heel and left the room, her skirts rustling with angry futility.

He stared after her, then, as the sound of a slammed door came from down the passage, blew out his breath with a wry grimace and turned to Jamie.

'I hesitate to request such a favor of you, Mr. Fraser, upon such short acquaintance as we have had. But I would greatly appreciate your accompanying me upon my errand. Since Mrs. Cameron herself cannot be present, to have you there as her representative in the matter –'

'What *is* this matter, Mr. Campbell?' Jamie interrupted.

Campbell glanced at me, plainly wishing me to leave. Since I made no move to do so, he shrugged, and pulling a handkerchief from his pocket, wiped his face.

'It is the law of this colony, sir, that if a Negro shall assault a white person and in so doing, cause blood to be shed, then he shall die for his crime.' He paused, reluctant. 'Such occurrences are most thankfully rare. But when they occur –'

He stopped, lips pressed together. Then he sighed, and with a final pat of his flushed cheeks, put the handkerchief away.

'I must go. Will you come, Mr. Fraser?'

Jamie stood for a moment longer, his eyes searching Campbell's face.

'I will,' he said abruptly. He went to the sideboard and pulled open the upper drawer, where the late Hector Cameron's dueling pistols were kept.

Seeing this, I turned to Campbell.

'Is there some danger?'

'I cannot say, Mrs. Fraser.' Campbell hunched his shoulders. 'Donald MacNeill told me only that there had been an altercation of some kind at the sawmill, and that it was a matter of the law of bloodshed. He asked me to come at once to render judgment and oversee the execution, and then left to summon the other estate owners before I could obtain any particulars.'

He looked unhappy, but resigned.

'Execution? Do you mean to say you intend to execute a man without even knowing what he's done?' In my agitation, I had knocked Jocasta's basket of yarn over. Little balls of colored wool ran everywhere, bouncing on the carpet.

'I do know what he's done, Mrs. Fraser!' Campbell lifted his chin, his color high, but with an obvious effort, swallowed his impatience.

'Your pardon, ma'am. I know you are newly come here; you will find some of our ways difficult and even barbarous, but –'

'Too right I find them barbarous! What kind of law is it that condemns a man –'

'A slave –'

229

'A man! Condemns him without a trial, without even an investigation? What sort of law is that?'

'A bad one, madame!' he snapped. 'But it is still the law, and I am charged with its fulfillment. Mr. Fraser, are you ready?' He clapped the hat on his head, and turned to Jamie.

'I am.' Jamie finished stowing the pistols and ammunition in the deep pockets of his coat, and straightened, smoothing the skirts down across his thighs. 'Sassenach, will ye go and –'

I had crossed to him and grabbed him by the arm before he could finish.

'Jamie, please! Don't go; you can't be part of this!'

'Hush.' He laid his hand on mine and squeezed hard. His eyes held mine, and kept me from speaking.

'I am already part of it,' he said quietly. 'It is my aunt's property, her men involved. Mr. Campbell is right; I am her kinsman. It will be my duty to go – to see, at least. To be there.' He hesitated then, as though he might say more, but instead merely squeezed my hand again and let me go.

'Then I'm going with you.' I spoke quite calmly, with that eerie sense of detachment that comes with awareness of impending disaster.

His wide mouth twitched briefly.

'I did expect ye would, Sassenach. Go and fetch your wee box, aye? I'll have the horses brought round.'

I didn't wait to hear Mr. Campbell's expostulations, but fled toward the stillroom, my slippers pattering on the tiles like the beat of an anxious heart.

We met Andrew MacNeill on the road, resting his horse in the shade of a chestnut tree. He had been waiting for us; he stepped out of the shadows at the sound of our hoofbeats. He nodded to Campbell as we halted by him, but his eyes were on me, frowning.

'Did you not tell him, Campbell?' he said, and turned the frown on Jamie. 'It will be no affair for a woman, Mr. Fraser.'

'Ye called it a matter of bloodshed, did ye no?' Jamie said, a marked edge in his voice. 'My wife is *ban-lighiche*, she has seen war wi' me, and more. If ye wish me there, she will go with me.'

MacNeill's lips pressed tight together, but he didn't argue further. He turned abruptly and swung into his saddle.

'Acquaint us, MacNeill, with the history of this unfortunate affair.' Campbell urged his mare's nose past the withers of Jamie's horse, skillfully edging between MacNeill and Jamie. 'Mr. Fraser is newly come, as you know, and your lad said only to me that it was bloodshed. I have no particulars.'

MacNeill's burly shoulders rose slightly, shrugging toward the iron-gray pigtail that bisected his collar. His hat was jammed down on his head, set square with the shoulders, as though he had used a carpenter's level to even it. A square, blunt man, MacNeill, in words as well as appearance.

Told in brief bursts as we trotted, it was a simple story. The sawmill's overseer, Byrnes, had had an altercation with one of the turpentine slaves. This man, being armed with the large slash-knife appropriate to his occupation, had attempted to settle the matter by removing Byrnes's head. Missing his aim, he had succeeded only in depriving the overseer of an ear.

'Barked him like a pine tree,' MacNeill said, a certain grim satisfaction apparent in his voice. 'Took his lug and a wee bit o' the side of his face, as well. Not that it will ha' impaired his beauty ower-much, the ugly wee pusbag.'

I glanced toward Jamie, who lifted one eyebrow in response. Evidently Byrnes was no favorite with the local planters.

The overseer had shrieked for help, and with the assistance of two customers and several of their slaves, had succeeded in subduing his assailant. The wound stanched and the slave locked in a shed, young Donald MacNeill – who had come to have a saw blade set and found himself unexpectedly in the midst of drama – had been dispatched at once to spread the word to the plantation owners nearby.

'You'll not know,' Campbell explained, twisting in his saddle to speak to Jamie. 'When a slave must be executed, the slaves from those plantations nearby are brought to watch; a deterrent, aye? against future ill-considered action.'

'Indeed,' Jamie said politely. 'I believe that was the Crown's notion in executing my grandsire on Tower Hill after the Rising. Verra effective, too; all my relations have been quite well behaved since.'

I had lived long enough among Scots to appreciate the effects of that little jab. Jamie might have come at Campbell's request, but the grandson of the Old Fox did no man's bidding lightly – nor necessarily held English law in high regard.

MacNeill had got the message, all right; the back of his neck flushed turkey-red, but Farquard Campbell looked amused. He uttered a short, dry laugh before turning round.

'Which slave is it, d'ye know?' he asked the older man. MacNeill shook his head.

'Young Donald didna say. But ye ken as well as I do; it'll be that bugger Rufus.'

Campbell's shoulders slumped in acknowledgment.

'Jo will be sore pained to hear it,' he murmured, shaking his head regretfully.

'It's her ain fault,' MacNeill said, brutally thwacking a horsefly that had settled on his leg above the boot. 'Yon Byrnes isna fit to mind pigs, let alone run Negroes. I've told her often enough; so've you.'

'Aye, but Hector hired the man, not Jo,' Campbell protested mildly. 'And she couldna well dismiss him out of hand. What's she to do, then, come and manage the place herself?'

The answer was a grunt as MacNeill shifted his broad buttocks in the saddle. I glanced at Jamie, and found him poker-faced, eyes hidden in the shadow under the brim of his hat.

'There's little worse than a willful woman,' MacNeill said, a trifle louder than strictly necessary. 'They've none to blame save themselves if harm comes to them.'

'Whereas,' I chipped in, leaning forward and raising my own voice enough to be heard over the clop and creak of the horses, 'if harm comes to them because of some man,

232

the satisfaction of blaming him will be adequate compensation?'

Jamie snorted briefly with amusement; Campbell cackled out loud and poked MacNeill in the ribs with his crop.

'Got ye there, Andrew!' he said.

MacNeill did not reply, but his neck grew even redder. We rode in silence after that, MacNeill's shoulders hunched just under his ears.

While mildly satisfying, this exchange did nothing to settle my nerves; my stomach was knotted in dread of what might happen when we reached the mill. Despite their dislike of Byrnes and the obvious assumption that whatever had happened had likely been the overseer's fault, there wasn't the slightest suggestion that this would alter the slave's fate in any way.

'A bad law,' Campbell had called it – but the law nonetheless. Still, it was neither outrage nor horror at the thought of judicial atrocity that made my hands tremble and the leather reins slick with sweat; it was wondering what Jamie would do.

I could tell nothing from his face. He rode relaxed, left hand on the reins, the right curled loosely on his thigh, near the bulge of the pistol in his coat.

I was not even sure whether I could take comfort in the fact that he had allowed me to come with him. That might mean that he didn't expect to commit violence – but in that case, did it mean he would stand by and let the execution happen?

And if he did . . .? My mouth was dry, my nose and throat choked with the soft brown dust that rose in clouds from the horses' hooves.

I am already part of it. Part of what, though? Of clan and family, yes – but of *this*? Highlanders would fight to the death for any cause that touched their honor or stirred their blood, but they were for the most part indifferent to outside matters. Centuries of isolation in their mountain fastnesses had left them disinclined to meddle in the affairs of others – but woe to any who meddled in theirs!

Plainly Campbell and MacNeill saw this as Jamie's affair – but did he? Jamie was not an isolated Highlander, I assured myself. He was well traveled, well educated, a cultured man. And he knew damn well what *I* thought of present matters. I had the terrible feeling, though, that my opinion would count for very little in the reckoning of this day.

It was a hot and windless afternoon, with cicadas buzzing loudly in the weeds along the road, but my fingers were cold, and stiff on the reins. We had passed one or two other parties; small groups of slaves, moving on foot in the direction of the sawmill. They didn't look up as we passed, but melted aside into the bushes, making room as we cantered past.

Jamie's hat flew off, knocked by a low branch; he caught it deftly and clapped it back on his head, but not before I had caught a glimpse of his face, unguarded for a moment, the lines of it tense with anxiety. With a small shock, it occurred to me that *he* didn't know what he was going to do either. And that frightened me more than anything else so far.

We were suddenly in the pine forest; the yellow-green flicker of hickory and alder leaves gave way abruptly to the darker light of cool deep green, like moving from the surface of the ocean into the calmer depths.

I reached back to touch the wooden case strapped on behind my saddle, trying to avoid thinking of what might lie ahead, by making mental preparations for the only role I might reasonably play in this incipient disaster. I likely could not prevent damage; but I could try to repair what had happened already. Disinfection and cleansing – I had a bottle of distilled alcohol, and a wash made from pressed garlic juice and mint. Then dress the wound – yes, I had linen bandages – but surely it would need stitching first?

In the midst of wondering what had been done with Byrnes's detached ear, I stopped. The buzzing in my own ears was not from cicadas. Campbell, in the lead, reined up sharply, listening, and the rest of us halted behind him.

Voices in the distance, lots of voices, in a deep, angry buzz, like a hive of bees turned upside down and shaken. Then there was the faint sound of shouts and screams, and the sudden loud report of a shot.

We galloped down the last slope, dodging trees, and

thundered into the sawmill's clearing. The open ground was filled with people; slaves and bondsmen, women and children, milling in panic through the stacks of sawn lumber, like termites exposed by the swing of an ax.

Then I lost all consciousness of the crowd. All my attention was fixed at the side of the mill, where a crane hoist was rigged, with a huge curved hook for raising logs to the level of the saw bed.

Impaled on the hook was the body of a black man, twisting in horrid imitation of a worm. The smell of blood struck sweet and hot through the air; there was a pool of it on the platform below the hoist.

My horse stopped, fidgeting, obstructed by the crowd. The shouts had died away into moans and small, disconnected screams from women in the crowd. I saw Jamie slide off in front of me, and force his way through the press of bodies toward the platform. Campbell and MacNeill were with him, shoving grimly through the mob. MacNeill's hat fell off, unregarded, to be trampled underfoot.

I sat frozen in my saddle, unable to move. There were other men on the platform near the hoist; a small man whose head was wound grotesquely round with bandages, splotched with blood all down one side; several other men, white and mulatto, armed with clubs and muskets, making occasional threatening jabs at the crowd.

Not that there seemed any urge to rush the platform; to the contrary, there seemed a general urge to get away. The faces around me were stamped with expressions ranging from fear to shocked dismay, with only here and there a flash of anger – or satisfaction.

Farquard Campbell emerged from the press, boosted onto the platform by MacNeill's sturdy shoulder, and advanced at once on the men with clubs, waving his arms and shouting something I couldn't hear, though the screams and moans around me were dying away into the silence of shock. Jamie seized the edge of the platform and lifted himself up after Campbell, pausing to give a hand to MacNeill.

Campbell was face-to-face with Byrnes, his lean cheeks convulsed with fury.

'. . . unspeakable brutality!' he was shouting. His words came unevenly, half swallowed in the shuffle and murmur around me, but I saw him jab a finger emphatically at the hoist and its grisly burden. The slave had stopped struggling; he hung inert.

The overseer's face was invisible, but his body was stiff with outrage and defiance. One or two of his friends moved slowly toward him, plainly meaning to offer support.

I saw Jamie stand for a moment, assessing events. He drew both pistols from his coat, and coolly checked the priming. Then he stepped forward, and clapped one to Byrnes' bandaged head. The overseer went rigid with surprise.

'Bring him down,' Jamie said to the nearest thug, loudly enough to be audible over the dying grumbles of the crowd. 'Or I blow off what's left o' your friend's face. And then –' He raised the second pistol and aimed it squarely at the man's chest. The expression on Jamie's own face made further threats unnecessary.

The man moved reluctantly, narrowed eyes fixed on the pistol. He took hold of the brake-handle of the winch that controlled the hoist, and pulled it back. The hook descended slowly, its cable taut with the strain of its burden. There was a massive sigh from the spectators as the limp body touched the earth.

I had managed to urge my horse forward through the crowd, till I was within a foot or two of the end of the platform. The horse shied and stamped, tossing his head and snorting at the strong smell of blood, but was well trained enough not to bolt. I slid off, ordering a man nearby to bring my box.

The boards of the platform felt strange underfoot, heaving like the dry land does when one steps off a ship. It was no more than a few steps to where the slave lay; by the time I reached him, that cold clarity of mind that is the surgeon's chief resource had come upon me. I paid no heed to the heated arguments behind me, or to the presence of the remaining spectators.

He was alive; his chest moved in small, jerky gasps. The hook had pierced the stomach, passing through the lower

236

rib cage, emerging from the back at about the level of the kidneys. The man's skin was an unearthly shade of dark blue-gray, his lips blanched to the color of clay.

'Hush,' I said softly, though there was no sound from the slave save the small hiss of his breath. His eyes were pools of incomprehension, pupils dilated, swamped with darkness.

There was no blood from his mouth; the lungs were not punctured. The breathing was shallow, but rhythmic; the diaphragm had not been pierced. My hands moved gently over him, my mind trying to follow the path of the damage. Blood oozed from both wounds, flowed in a black slick over the ridged muscles of back and stomach, shone red as rubies on the polished steel. No spurting; they had somehow missed both abdominal aorta and the renal artery.

Behind me, a heated argument had broken out; some small, detached portion of my mind noted that Byrnes's companions were his fellow overseers from two neighboring plantations, presently being rebuked with vigor by Farquard Campbell.

'. . . blatant disregard of the law! You shall answer for it in court, gentlemen, be assured that you shall!'

'What does it matter?' came a sullen rumble from someone. 'It's bloodshed – and mutilation! Byrnes has his rights!'

'Rights no for the likes of you to decide.' MacNeill's deep growl joined in. 'Rabble, that's what ye are, no better than the –'

'And where d'you get off, old man, stickin' your long Scotch nose in where it's not wanted, eh?'

'What will ye need, Sassenach?'

I hadn't heard him come up beside me, but he was there. Jamie crouched next to me, my box open on the boards beside him. He held a loaded pistol still in one hand, his attention mostly on the group behind me.

'I don't know,' I said. I could hear the argument going on in the background, but the words blurred into meaninglessness. The only reality was under my hands.

It was slowly dawning on me that the man I touched was possibly not fatally wounded, in spite of his horrible injury.

From everything I could sense and feel, I thought that the curve of the hook had gone upward through the liver. Likely the right kidney was damaged, and the jejunum or gallbladder might be nicked – but none of those would kill him immediately.

It was shock that might do for him, if he was to die quickly. But I could see a pulse throbbing in the sweat-slick abdomen, just above the piercing steel. It was fast, but steady as a drumbeat; I could feel it echo in the tips of my fingers when I placed a hand on it. He had lost blood – the scent of it was thick, overpowering the smell of sweat and fear – but not so much as to doom him.

An unsettling thought came to me – I might be able to keep this man alive. Likely not; in the wake of the thought came a flood of all the things that could go wrong – hemorrhage when I removed the hook being only the most immediate. Internal bleeding, delayed shock, perforated intestine, peritonitis – and yet.

At Prestonpans, I had seen a man pierced through the body with a sword, the location of the wound very much like this. He had received no treatment beyond a bandage wrapped around his body – and yet he had recovered.

'Lawlessness!' Campbell was saying, his voice rising over the babble of argument. 'It cannot be tolerated, no matter the provocation. I shall have you all taken in charge, be sure of it!'

No one was paying any attention to the true object of the discussion. Only seconds had passed – but I had only seconds more to act. I placed a hand on Jamie's arm, pulling his attention away from the debate.

'If I save him, will they let him live?' I asked him, under my breath.

His eyes flicked from one to another of the men behind me, weighing the possibilities.

'No,' he said softly. His eyes met mine, dark with understanding. His shoulders straightened slightly, and he laid the pistol across his thigh. I could not help him make his choice; he could not help with mine – but he would defend me, whichever choice I made.

'Give me the third bottle from the left, top row,' I said,

with a nod at the lid of the box, where three rows of clear glass bottles, firmly corked, held a variety of medicines.

I had two bottles of pure alcohol, another of brandy. I poured a good dose of the brownish powdered root into the brandy, and shook it briskly, then crawled to the man's head and pressed it to his lips.

His eyes were glazed; I tried to look into them, to make him see me. Why? I wondered, even as I leaned close and called his name. I couldn't ask if this would be his choice – I had made it for him. And having made it, could not ask for either approval or forgiveness.

He swallowed. Once. Twice. The muscles near his blanched mouth quivered; drops of brandy ran across his skin. Once more a deep convulsive gulp, and then his straining neck relaxed, his head heavy on my arm.

I sat with my eyes closed, supporting his head, my fingers on the pulse under his ear. It jumped; skipped a beat and resumed. A shiver ran over his body, the blotched skin twitching as though a thousand ants ran over it.

The textbook description ran through my mind:

Numbness. Tingling. A sensation of the skin crawling, as though affected by insects. Nausea, epigastric pain. Labored breathing, skin cold and clammy, features bloodless. Pulse feeble and irregular, yet the mind remains clear.

None of the visible symptoms were discernible from those he already showed. Epigastric pain, forsooth.

One-fiftieth grain will kill a sparrow in a few seconds. One-tenth grain, a rabbit in five minutes. Aconite was said to be the poison in the cup Medea prepared for Theseus.

I tried to hear nothing, feel nothing, know nothing but the jerky beat beneath my fingers. I tried with all my might to shut out the voices overhead, the murmur nearby, the heat and dust and stink of blood, to forget where I was, and what I was doing.

Yet the mind remains clear.

Oh, God, I thought. It did.

12

The Return of John Quincy Myers

Deeply shaken by the events at the sawmill, Jocasta none-theless declared her intention of carrying on with the party she had planned.

'It will distract our minds from the sadness,' she said firmly. She turned to me, and reaching out, critically fingered the muslin cloth of my sleeve.

'I'll call Phaedre to begin a new gown for ye,' she said. 'The girl's a fine sempstress.'

I rather thought it would take more than a new gown and a dinner party to distract *my* mind, but I caught a warning glance from Jamie and shut my mouth hard to keep the words inside.

In the event, given the shortness of time and a lack of suitable fabric, Jocasta decided to have one of her gowns remade for me.

'How does it look, Phaedre?' Jocasta frowned in my direction, as though she could summon vision by pure will. 'Will it do?'

'Do fine,' the maid answered around a mouthful of pins. She thrust in three in quick succession, squinted at me, pinched up a fold of fabric at the waistline and stabbed in two more.

'Be just fine,' she elaborated, mouth now clear. 'She shorter than you, Miss Jo, and a bit thinner in the waist. Some bigger in the bosom, though,' Phaedre added in an undertone, grinning at me.

'Yes, I know that.' Jocasta spoke tartly, having caught the whisper. 'Slash the bodice; we can fill it with Valenciennes lace over a field of green silk – take a scrap from that old dressing gown of my husband's; it will be the right color to complement this.' She touched the sleeve, with its brilliant green striping. 'Band the slash with the green silk, too; it will show off her bosom.' The long pale fingers indicated the line of alteration, drifting across the tops of my breasts almost absentmindedly. The touch was cool, impersonal and barely felt, but I narrowly prevented myself jerking back.

'You have a most remarkable memory for color,' I said, surprised and slightly unnerved.

'Oh, I remember this dress very well,' she said. She touched the full sleeve lightly. 'A gentleman once told me I reminded him of Persephone in it; springtime incarnate, he said.' A faint smile of memory lit her face, then was erased as she lifted her head toward me.

'What color is your hair, my dear? I hadna thought to ask. You sound a bit blond, somehow, but I've no notion whether that may be actually the case. Pray, do not tell me ye're black-haired and sallow!' She smiled, but the joke sounded somehow like a command.

'It's more or less brown,' I said, touching my hair self-consciously. 'Faded a bit, though; it's gone light in streaks.'

She frowned at this, seeming to consider whether brown was quite suitable. Unable to settle the question for herself, she turned to the maid.

'How does she look, Phaedre?'

The woman took a step back and squinted at me. I realized that she must – as the other house servants were – be in the habit of giving careful descriptions to her mistress. The dark eyes passed swiftly over me, pausing on my face for a long moment of assessment. She took two pins from her mouth before replying.

'Just fine, Miss Jo,' Phaedre said. She nodded once, slowly. 'Just fine,' she said again. 'She got white skin, white as skim milk; looks real fine with that bright green.'

'Mm. But the underskirt is ivory; if she is too fair, will she not look washed out?'

I disliked being discussed as though I were an *objet d'art* – and a possibly defective one, at that – but swallowed my objections.

Phaedre was shaking her head, definitely.

'Oh, no, ma'am,' she said. 'She ain't washed out. She got them bones as makes shadows. And brown eyes, but don't be thinkin' they's mud-color. You recall that book you got, the one with the pictures of all them strange animals?'

'If you mean *Accounts of an Exploration of the Indian Sub-*

241

continent,' Jocasta said, 'yes, I recall it. Ulysses read it to me only last month. You mean that Mrs. Fraser reminds you of one of the illustrations?' She laughed, amused.

'Mm-hm.' Phaedre hadn't taken her eyes off me. 'She look like that big cat,' she said softly, staring at me. 'Like that there tiger, a-lookin' out from the leaves.'

An expression of startlement showed briefly on Jocasta's face.

'Indeed,' she said, and laughed. But she didn't touch me again.

I stood in the lower hall, smoothing the green-striped silk over my bosom. Phaedre's reputation as a sempstress was well founded; the dress fit like a glove, and the bold bands of emerald satin glowed against the paler shades of ivory and leaf.

Proud of her own thick hair, Jocasta did not wear wigs, so there was fortunately no suggestion that I adopt one. Phaedre had tried to powder my hair with rice flour instead, an attempt I had firmly resisted. Inadequately concealing her opinion of my lack of fashionable instinct, she had settled for snaring the mass of curls in a white silk ribbon and pinning them high to the back of my head.

I wasn't sure quite why I had resisted the array of baubles with which she had tried to further bedizen me; perhaps it was mere dislike of fussiness. Or perhaps it was a more subtle objection to being made an object, to be adorned and displayed to Jocasta's purpose. At any rate, I had refused. I wore no ornament save my wedding ring, a small pair of pearl earbobs, and a green velvet ribbon round the stalk of my neck.

Ulysses came down the stairs above me, impeccable in his livery. I moved, and he turned his head, catching the flicker of my skirts.

His eyes widened in a look of frank appreciation as he saw me, and I looked down, smiling a bit, as one does when being admired. Then I heard him gasp and jerked my head up to see his eyes still wide, but now with fear; his hand so tight on the banister that the knuckles shone.

'Your pardon, madame,' he said, sounding strangled, and rushed down the stairs and past me, head down, leaving the door to the cookhouse breezeway swinging in his wake.

'What on earth . . .?' I said aloud, and then I remembered where – and when – we were.

Alone for so long, in a house with a blind mistress and no master, he had grown careless. He had momentarily forgotten that most basic and essential protection – the only true protection a slave had: the blank, bland face that hid all thoughts.

No wonder he had been terrorized when he realized what he had done. If it had been any woman other than myself to have intercepted that unguarded look . . . my hands grew cold and sweaty, and I swallowed, the remembered scent of blood and turpentine sharp in my throat.

But it had been me, I reminded myself, and no one else had seen. The butler might be afraid, but he was safe. I would behave as though nothing had happened – nothing *had* – and things would be . . . well, things would be what they were. The sound of footsteps on the gallery above interrupted my thoughts. I glanced upward, and gasped, all other thoughts driven at once from my mind.

A Highlander in full regalia is an impressive sight – any Highlander, no matter how old, ill-favored, or crabbed in appearance. A tall, straight-bodied, and by no means ill-favored Highlander in the prime of his life is breathtaking.

He hadn't worn the kilt since Culloden, but his body had not forgotten the way of it.

'Oh!' I said.

He saw me then, and white teeth flashed as he made me a leg, silver shoe-buckles gleaming. He straightened and turned on his heel to set his plaid swinging, then came down slowly, eyes fixed on my face.

For a moment, I saw him as he had looked the morning I married him. The sett of his tartan was nearly the same now as then; black check on a crimson ground, plaid caught at his shoulder with a silver brooch, dipping to the calf of a neat, stockinged leg.

His linen was finer now, as was his coat; the dirk he wore at his waist had bands of gold across the haft. *Duine uasal* was what he looked, a man of worth.

But the bold face above the lace was the same, older

243

now, but wiser with it – yet the tilt of his shining head and the set of the wide, firm mouth, the slanted clear cat-eyes that looked into my own, were just the same. Here was a man who had always known his worth.

'Your servant, ma'am,' he said. And then burst into a face-splitting smile as he descended the last few stairs.

'You look wonderful,' I said, hardly able to swallow the lump in my throat.

'It's none so bad,' he agreed, with no trace of false modesty. He arranged a fold over his shoulder with care. 'Of course, that's the advantage of a plaid – there's no trouble about the fit of it.'

'It's Hector Cameron's?' I felt ridiculously shy of touching him, garbed so splendidly. Instead, I touched the hilt of the dirk; it was topped with a small knurl of gold, roughly shaped like a bird in flight.

Jamie drew a deep breath.

'It's mine, now. Ulysses brought it to me – with my aunt's compliments.' I caught an odd undertone in his voice, and glanced up at him. Despite his obvious deep pleasure at wearing the kilt again, something was troubling him. I touched his hand.

'What's wrong?'

He gave me half a smile, but his brows were drawn together in concern.

'I wouldna say anything's wrong, exactly. It's only –'

The sound of feet on the stairs interrupted him, and he drew me to one side, out of the way of a hurrying slave with a pile of linens. The house was humming with last-minute preparations; even now, I could hear the sound of wheels on the gravel at the back of the house, and savory smells floated through the air as platters were brought in at a gallop from the kitchen.

'We canna talk here,' he muttered. 'Sassenach, will ye stand ready at dinner? If I should signal to ye' – and he tugged at his earlobe – 'will ye make a diversion, right then? It doesna matter what – spill wine, swoon away, stab your dinner partner with a fork –' He grinned at me, and I took heart from that; whatever was worrying him wasn't a matter of life and death, then.

'I can do that,' I assured him. 'But what –'

244

A door opened onto the gallery above, and Jocasta's voice floated down, giving last-minute orders to Phaedre. Hearing it, Jamie stooped quickly and kissed me, then whirled away in a swirl of crimson plaid and silver shoe-buckles, disappearing neatly between two slaves bringing trays of crystal goblets toward the drawing room. I stared after him in astonishment, barely getting out of the way in time to avoid being trampled by the servants.

'Is that you, sweet Claire?' Jocasta paused on the bottom step, head turned toward me, eyes trained just over my shoulder. She was quite uncanny.

'It is,' I said, and touched her arm to let her know more precisely where I was.

'I smelt the camphor from the dress,' she said in answer to my unspoken question, tucking her hand in the crook of my elbow. 'I thought I heard Jamie's voice; is he nearby?'

'No,' I said, quite truthfully, 'I believe he's gone out to greet the guests.'

'Ah.' Her hand tightened on my arm, and she sighed, somewhere between satisfaction and impatience. 'I am not one to lament what cannot be mended, but I swear I should give one of my eyes, could the sight of the other be restored long enough to see the lad in his plaidie this night!'

She shook her head, dismissing it, and the diamonds in her ears flared with light. She wore dark blue silk, a foil to her shining white hair. The cloth was embroidered with dragonflies that seemed to dart among the folds as she moved under the lights of the wall sconces and candle-heavy chandeliers.

'Ah, well. Where is Ulysses?'

'Here, madame.' He had come back so quietly that I hadn't heard him, appearing on her other side.

'Come then,' she said, and took his arm. I didn't know if the order applied to him or me, but followed obediently in her shimmering wake, dodging to avoid two kitchen boys bearing in the centerpiece – a whole roasted boar, tusked head intact and fiercely glaring, succulent backside gleaming fatly, ready for the knife. It smelled divine.

I smoothed my hair and prepared to meet Jocasta's

guests, feeling rather as though I, too, were being presented on a silver platter, with an apple in my mouth.

The guest list would have read like the *Who's Who* of Cape Fear River gentry, had there been such a thing. Campbell, Maxwell, Buchanan, MacNeill, MacEachern . . . names from the Highlands, names from the Isles. MacNeill of Barra Meadows, MacLeod of Islay . . . many of the plantation names carried the flavor of their owners' origins, as did their speech; the high plastered ceiling echoed with the lilt of spoken Gaelic.

Several of the men came kilted, or with plaids wrapped over their coats and silk breeches, but I saw none as striking as Jamie – who was conspicuous by his absence. I heard Jocasta murmur something to Ulysses; he summoned a small serving girl with a clap of his hands and sent her zooming off into the lanterned half-dark of the gardens, presumably in search of him.

Nearly as conspicuous were the few guests who were not Scots; a broadshouldered, gently smiling Quaker by the picturesque name of Hermon Husband, a tall, rawboned gentleman named Hunter, and – much to my surprise – Phillip Wylie, immaculately suited, wigged and powdered.

'So we meet again, Mrs. Fraser,' he remarked, holding on to my hand much longer than was socially correct. 'I confess that I am ravished with enchantment to behold you again!'

'What are you doing here?' I said, rather rudely.

He grinned impudently.

'I was brought by mine host, the noble and puissant Mr. MacNeill of Barra Meadows, from whom I have just purchased an excellent pair of grays. Speaking of which, wild horses would have proved insufficient to restrain me from attendance this evening, upon my hearing that this occasion is held in your honor.' His eyes wandered slowly over me, with the detached air of a connoisseur appreciating some rare work of art.

'May I observe, ma'am, how most becoming is that shade of green?'

'I don't suppose I can stop you.'

'To say nothing of the effect of candlelight upon your

skin. "Thy neck is as a tower of ivory," ' he quoted, drawing a thumb insinuantly over my palm, ' "thine eyes like the fishpools in Heshbon." '

' "Thy nose is as the tower of Lebanon, which looketh toward Damascus," ' I said, with a pointed look at his aristocratically pronounced proboscis.

He burst out laughing, but didn't let go. I stole a glance at Jocasta, who stood only a few feet away; she seemed engrossed in conversation with a new arrival, but experience had taught me just how sharp her ears were.

'How old are you?' I asked, narrowing my eyes at him and trying to retrieve my hand without unseemly struggle.

'Five-and-twenty, ma'am,' he answered, rather surprised. He patted at the star-shaped patch near his mouth with a finger of his free hand. 'Am I looking indecently haggard?'

'No. I merely wished to be sure I was telling you the truth in informing you that I am old enough to be your mother!'

This news appeared not to distress him in the slightest. Instead he raised my hand to his lips and pressed them fervently upon it.

'I am enchanted,' he breathed. 'May I call you *Maman*?'

Ulysses stood behind Jocasta, dark eyes intent on the guests coming up the lighted walk from the river – he leaned forward now and then to whisper in her ear. I removed my hand from Wylie's grasp by main force, and used it to tap the butler on the shoulder.

'Ulysses,' I said, smiling charmingly at Wylie, 'would you be so kind as to ensure that Mr. Wylie is seated near me at dinner?'

'Indeed, madame; I will attend to it,' he assured me, and returned at once to his surveillance.

Mr. Wylie bowed extravagantly, professing undying gratitude, and allowed himself to be propelled into the house by one of the footmen. I waved pleasantly after him, thinking how much I should enjoy sticking a fork into him, when the time came.

I couldn't tell whether it was the luck of the draw, or considerate planning, but I found myself between Mr.

Wylie and the Quaker, Mr. Husband, with Mr. Hunter – the other non-Gaelic speaker – across the table from me. We formed a small island of English in the midst of a sea of swirling Scots.

Jamie had appeared at the last moment, and was now seated at the head of the table, with Jocasta at his right hand. For the dozenth time, I wondered what was going on. I kept a sharp eye on him, a clean fork by my plate, ready for action, but we had reached the third course with no untoward occurrence.

'I am surprised to find a gentleman of your persuasion in attendance at such an occasion, Mr. Husband. Does not such frivolity offend you?' Having failed to divert my attention to himself during the first two courses, Wylie now resorted to leaning across me, the action bringing his thigh casually into contact with mine.

Hermon Husband smiled. 'Even Quakers must eat, Friend Wylie. And I have had the honor to enjoy Mrs. Cameron's hospitality on many occasions; I should not think to refuse it now, only because she extends it to others.' He switched his attention back to me, resuming our interrupted conversation.

'Thou asked of the Regulators, Mrs. Fraser?' He nodded across the table. 'I should recommend thy questions to Mr. Hunter, for if the Regulators might be said to enjoy the benefits of leadership, it is to this gentleman that they look.'

Mr. Hunter bowed at the compliment. A tall, lantern-jawed individual, he was more plainly dressed than most of those in attendance, though not a Quaker. He and Mr. Husband were traveling together, both returning from Wilmington to their homes in the backcountry. With Governor Tryon's offer in mind, I wanted to find out whatever I could about matters in that area.

'We are but a loose assembly,' he said modestly, putting down his wineglass. 'In truth, I should be reluctant to claim any title whatever; it is only that I am fortunate enough to have a homestead so situated that it is a convenient meeting place.'

'One hears that the Regulators are mere rabble.' Wylie dabbed at his lips, careful not to dislodge his patch.

'Lawless, and inclined to violence against the duly author-ized deputies of the Crown.'

'Indeed we are not,' Mr. Husband put in, still mildly. I was surprised to hear him claim association with the Regulators; perhaps the movement wasn't quite so violent and lawless as Wylie implied. 'We seek only justice, and that is not a quantity that can be obtained by means of violence, for where violence enters in, justice must surely flee.'

Wylie laughed, a surprisingly deep and masculine sound, given his foppery.

'Justice apparently *should* flee! That is certainly the impression I was given by Mr. Justice Dodgson when I spoke with him last week. Or perhaps he was mistaken, sir, in his identification of the ruffians who invaded his chambers, knocked him down, and dragged him by the heels into the street?' He smiled engagingly at Hunter, who flushed dark red beneath his weathered tan. His fingers tightened about the stem of his wineglass. I glanced hopefully at Jamie. No sign of a signal.

'Mr. Justice Dodgson,' Hunter said precisely, 'is a userer, a thief, a disgrace to the profession of law, and –'

I had for some little time been hearing noises outside, but had put these down to some crisis in the cookhouse, which was separated from the main house by a breezeway. The noises became clearer now, though, and I caught a familiar voice that quite distracted me from Mr. Hunter's denunciations.

'Duncan!' I half rose from my seat, and heads nearby turned inquiringly.

There was a sudden confusion of movement out on the terrace, with shadows jerking past the open French windows, and voices calling, arguing and exhorting.

Conversation in the dining room fell silent, and everyone looked to see what was happening. I saw Jamie push back his chair, but before he could rise, an appar-ition appeared in the doorway.

It was John Quincy Myers, the mountain man, who filled the open double door from top to bottom and side to side, resplendent in the same costume in which I had first met him. He leaned heavily upon the doorframe, surveying the assemblage through bloodshot eyes. His face was flushed, his breathing stertorous, and in one hand he held a long glass bottle.

His eyes lit upon me, and his face contorted into a fearful grimace of gratification.

'THERE ye are,' he said, in tones of the deepest satisfaction. 'Said sho. Duncan wudd'n havit. Said yesh, Mishess Claire said gotter be drunk afore she cuts me. Sho I'm drunk. Drunk –' He paused, swaying dangerously, and raised his bottle high. 'As a SKUNK!' he ended triumphantly. He took a step into the room, fell flat on his face, and didn't move.

Duncan appeared in the doorway, looking a good deal the worse for wear himself. His shirt was ripped, his coat hung off his shoulder, and he had the beginnings of what looked like a black eye.

He glanced down at the prostrate form at his feet, then looked apologetically at Jamie.

'I did try to stop him, *Mac Dubh.*'

I extricated myself from my seat, and reached the body at the same time as Jamie, followed by a tidal wave of curious guests. Jamie glanced at me, eyebrows raised.

'Well, ye did say he must be unconscious,' he observed. He bent over the mountain man and thumbed back an eyelid, showing a slice of blank white eyeball. 'I'd say he's made a good job of it, myself.'

'Yes, but I didn't mean dead drunk!' I squatted by the insensible form, and put a ginger two fingers over the carotid pulse. Nice and strong. Still . . .

'Alcohol isn't a good anesthetic at all,' I said, shaking my head. 'It's a poison. It depresses the central nervous system. Put the shock of operating on top of alcohol intoxication, and it could kill him, easily.'

'No great loss,' said someone among the guests, but this caustic opinion was drowned in a flood of reproachful shushing.

'Shame to waste so much brandy,' someone else said, to general laughter. It was Phillip Wylie; I saw his powdered face loom over Jamie's shoulder, smiling wickedly.

'We've heard a great deal of your skill, Mistress Fraser.

Now's your chance of proving yourself – before witnesses!'
He waved a graceful hand at the crowd clustered round us.

'Oh, bugger off,' I said crossly.

'Ooh, hear her!' Someone murmured behind me, not
without admiration. Wylie blinked, taken aback, but then
grinned more broadly than ever.

'Your wish is my command, ma'am,' he murmured, and
bowed himself back into the crowd.

I stood up, racked with doubt. It might work. It was a
technically simple operation, and shouldn't take more
than a few minutes – if I encountered no complications. It
was a small incision – but it did involve going into the
peritoneum, with all the attendant risk of infection *that*
implied.

Still, I was unlikely to encounter better conditions than
I had here – plenty of alcohol for disinfection, plenty of
willing assistants. There was no other means of anesthesia
available, and I could under no circumstances do it with a
conscious patient. Above all, Myers had asked me to do it.

I sought Jamie's face, wanting advice. He was there,
standing beside me, and saw the question in my eyes. Well,
he'd wanted a diversion, damn it.

'Best do it, Sassenach.' Jamie eyed the prostrate form.
'He may ne'er have either the courage or the money to
get that drunk again.' I stooped and checked his pulse
again – strong and steady as a carthorse.

Jocasta's stately head appeared among the curious faces
looming over MacNeill's shoulder.

'Bring him into the salon,' she said briefly. Her head
withdrew, and the decision was made for me.

I had operated under odd conditions before, I thought,
rinsing my hands hastily in vinegar brought from the
kitchen, but none odder than this.

Relieved of his nether garb, Myers lay tastefully displayed on the mahogany table, boneless as a roasted
pheasant, and nearly as ornamental. In lieu of platter, he
lay upon a stable blanket, a gaudy centerpiece in his
quilled shirt and bear's-claw necklace, surrounded by a
garnish of bottles, rags, and bandages.

There was no time to change my own clothes; a leather
butchering apron was fetched from the smoke shed to

251

cover my dress, and Phaedre pinned up my long, frilled sleeves to leave my forearms bare.

Extra candles had been brought to give me light; candelabra blazed from sideboard and chandelier in a reckless expenditure of fragrant beeswax. Not nearly as fragrant as Myers, though; without hesitation, I took the decanter from the sideboard, and sloshed several shillings' worth of fine brandy over the curly dark-haired crotch.

'Expensive way to kill lice,' someone remarked critically behind me, observing the hasty exodus of miscellaneous small forms of life in the wake of the flood.

'Ah, but they'll die happy,' said a voice I recognized as Ian's. 'I brought your wee box, Auntie.' He set the surgical chest by my elbow, and opened it for me.

I snatched out my precious blue bottle of distilled alcohol, and the straight-edged scalpel. Holding the blade over a bowl, I poured alcohol over it, meanwhile scanning the crowd for appropriate assistants. There wouldn't be any shortage of volunteers; the spectators were boiling with suppressed laughter and murmured comment, interrupted dinner forgotten in a rush of anticipation.

Two sturdy carriage drivers were summoned from the kitchen to hold the patient's legs, Andrew MacNeill and Farquard Campbell volunteering to hold the arms, and Young Ian was set in place by my side, holding a large candlestick to cast additional light. Jamie took up his position as chief anesthetist by the patient's head, a glass full of whisky poised near the slack and snoring mouth.

I checked that my supplies and suture needles were ready, took a deep breath, and nodded to my troops.

'Let's go.'

Myers's penis, embarrassed by the attention, had already retreated, peeping shyly out of the bushes. With the patient's long legs raised and spread, Ulysses himself delicately cupping the baggy scrotum away, the hernia was clearly revealed, a smooth swelling the size of a hen's egg, its curve a deep purple where it pressed against the taut inguinal skin.

'Jesus, Lord!' said one of the drivers, eyes bulging at the sight. 'It's true – he's got three balls!'

A collective gasp and giggle ensued from the spectators,

but I was too busy to correct misapprehensions. I swabbed the perineum thoroughly with pure alcohol, dipped my scalpel in the liquid, passed the blade back and forth through the flame of a candle by way of final sterilization, and made a swift cut.

Not large, not deep. Just enough to open the skin, and see the loop of gleaming pinkish-gray intestine bulging down through the tear in the muscle layer. Blood welled, a thin, dark line, then dribbled down staining the blanket.

I extended the incision, swished my fingers thoroughly in the disinfecting bowl, then put two fingers on the loop and pushed it gently upward. Myers moved in a sudden convulsion, nearly dislodging me, and just as suddenly relaxed. He tightened again, buttocks rising, and my assistants nearly lost their grip on his legs.

'He's waking up!' I shouted to Jamie, above the various cries of alarm. 'Give him more, quick!' All my doubts about the use of alcohol as an anesthetic were being borne out, but it was too late to change my mind now.

Jamie grasped the mountain man's jaw, and squeezing open his mouth, dribbled whisky into it. Myers choked and spluttered and made noises like a drowning buffalo, but enough of the alcohol made it down his throat – the huge body relaxed. The mountain man subsided into mumbling immobility and then into long, wet, snuffling snores.

I had managed to keep my fingers in place; there was more bleeding than I would have liked, but his struggles had not brought the herniated loop back down. I snatched a clean cloth soaked in brandy and blotted the site; yes, I could see the edge of the muscle layer; scrawny as Myers was, a thin layer of yellow fat lay under the skin, separating it from the dark red fibers below.

I could feel the movement of his intestines as he breathed, the dark wet warmth of his body surrounding my gloveless fingers in that strange one-sided intimacy that is the surgeon's realm. I closed my eyes and let all sense of urgency, all consciousness of the watching crowd drop away.

I breathed in slowly, matched my rhythm to the audible snores. Above the reek of brandy and the faintly nauseating aromas of food, I could smell the earthy odors of his body; stale sweat, grimed skin, a small tang of urine and the copper scent of blood. To another, they would have been offensive, but not to me, not now.

This body *was*. No good, no bad, it simply was. I knew it, now; it was mine.

They were all mine; the unconscious body in my hands, its secrets open to me; the men who held it, their eyes on me. It didn't always happen, but when it did, the sensation was unforgettable; a synthesis of minds into a single organism. And as I took control of this organism, I became part of it, and lost myself.

Time stopped. I was acutely aware of each movement, each breath, the tug and pull of the catgut sutures as I tightened the inguinal ring, but my hands did not belong to me. My voice was high and clear, giving directions instantly obeyed, and somewhere far away, a small watcher in my brain observed the progress of the operation with a remote sense of interest.

Then it was done, and time began again. I took a step back, breaking the link, and feeling slightly dizzy at the unaccustomed solitude.

'Done,' I said, and the hum from the spectators erupted into loud applause. Still feeling intoxicated – had I caught drunkenness by osmosis from Myers? – I turned on one heel and sank into an extravagant low curtsy, facing the dinner guests.

An hour later, I was drunk on my own merits, the victim of a dozen toasts in my honor. I managed to escape briefly, on the excuse of checking on my patient, and staggered upstairs to the guest room where he lay.

I paused on the gallery, clinging to the banister while I steadied myself. There was a loud hum of conversation and laughter from below; the party was still going strong, but had dissolved into small groups scattered over the parquet of the foyer and salon. From this perspective, it looked like a honeycomb, fuzzy wigged heads and gauze-winged dresses bobbing to and fro across the six-sided tiles, buzzing busily over glasses filled with the nectar of brandywine and porter.

If Jamie had wanted a diversion, I thought muzzily, he

couldn't have asked for better. Whatever had been going to happen had been effectively forestalled. But what was it – and for how long could it be prevented? I shook my head to clear it – with indifferent results – and went in to see my patient.

Myers was still blissfully and deeply asleep, breathing in long, slow exhalations that made the cotton bed-drapes quiver. The slave Betty nodded at me, smiling.

'He's fine, Mrs. Claire,' she whispered. 'Couldn't wake that man with a gun, I don't think.'

I didn't need to check his heart; his head was turned, and I could see the huge vein that ran down the side of his neck, throbbing with a pulse slow and heavy as a hammer blow. I touched him, feeling his skin cool and damp. No fever, no signs of shock. The whole of his enormous person radiated peace and well-being.

'How is he?' Had I been less drunk, I would have been startled. As it was, I merely swayed round on my axis, to find Jamie standing behind me.

'He's fine,' I said. 'You couldn't kill him with a cannon. Like you,' I said, and found myself leaning against him, arms around his waist, my flushed face buried in the cool folds of his linen. 'Indestructible.'

He kissed the top of my head, smoothing back a few curls that had escaped from their dressing during the operation.

'Ye did well, Sassenach,' he whispered. 'Verra well, bonnie lassie.'

He smelt of wine and candlewax, of herbs and Highland wool. I slid my hands lower, feeling the curves of his buttocks, smooth and free under his kilt. He moved slightly, the length of his thigh pressing briefly against mine.

'Ye need a bit of air, Sassenach – and we must talk. Can ye leave him for a time?'

I glanced at the bed and its stertorous occupant.

'Yes. As long as Betty will keep sitting with him to be sure he doesn't vomit in his sleep and choke?' I glanced at the slave, who looked surprised that I should ask, but nodded willingly.

'Meet me by the herb garden – and take care not to fall

255

down the stairs and break your neck, aye?' Lifting my chin, he kissed me quick and deep, and left me dizzy, feeling at once more sober and more drunk than before.

13

An Examination of Conscience

Something dark landed on the path in front of us with a soft *plop!* and I stopped abruptly, clutching his arm.

'Frog,' Jamie said, unperturbed. 'D'ye hear them singing?'

'Singing' wasn't the word that would have struck me about the chorus of croaks and grunts from the reedbeds near the river. On the other hand, Jamie was tone deaf, and made no bones about it.

He extended the toe of his shoe and gently prodded the squat dark shape.

' "Brekekekex, ko-ax, ko-ax," ' he quoted. ' "Brekekekex, ko-ax!" ' The shape hopped away and disappeared into the moist plants by the path.

'I always knew you had a gift for tongues,' I said, amused. 'Didn't know you spoke frog, though.'

'Well, I'm no ways fluent,' he said modestly. 'Though I've a fine accent, and I say it myself.'

I laughed, and he squeezed my hand and let it go. The brief spark of the joke faded, failing to kindle conversation, and we walked on, physically together but miles apart in thought.

I should have been exhausted, but adrenaline was still coursing through my veins. I felt the exultation that comes with the completion of a successful bit of surgery, to say nothing of a little standard alcoholic intoxication. The effect of it all was to make me slightly wobbly on my pins, but with an acute and vivid awareness of everything around me.

There was an ornamental seat under the trees near the dock, and it was to this that Jamie led me, into the shadows. He sank onto the marble bench with a deep sigh, reminding me that I wasn't the only one for whom it had been an eventful evening.

I looked around with exaggerated attention, then sat down beside him.

'We're alone and unobserved,' I said. 'Do you want to tell me what the hell is going on now?'

'Oh, aye.' He straightened, stretching his back. 'I should have said something to ye sooner, only I didna quite expect she would do such a thing.' He reached out and found my hand in the dark.

'It's not anything wrong, exactly, as I told ye. It's only that when Ulysses brought me the plaid and dirk and the brooch, he told me that Jocasta meant to make an announcement at the dinner tonight – to tell everyone that she meant to make me heir to . . . this.'

His gesture took in the house and fields behind us – and everything else: the river mooring, the orchard, the gardens, the stables, the endless acres of resinous pines, the sawmill and the turpentine camp – and the forty slaves who worked them.

I could see the whole thing unfolding as Jocasta had no doubt envisioned it; Jamie sitting at the head of the table, dressed in Hector Cameron's tartan, wearing his blade and his brooch – that brooch with the Camerons' unsubtle clan adjuration 'Unite!' – surrounded by Hector's old colleagues and comrades, all eager to welcome their friend's younger kinsman into his place.

Let her make such an announcement, in that company of loyal Scots, well lubricated with the late Hector's fine whisky, and they would have acclaimed him on the spot as the master of River Run, anointed him with boar's fat and crowned him with beeswax candles.

It had been a thoroughly MacKenzie-like plan, I thought; audacious, dramatic – and taking no account of the wishes of the persons involved.

'And if she had,' he said, echoing my thoughts with uncanny precision, 'I should have found it verra awkward to decline the honor.'

'Yes, very.'

He sprang suddenly to his feet, too restless to stay still. Without speaking, he held out a hand to me; I rose beside him and we turned back into the orchard path, circling the formal gardens. The lanterns lit for the party had been removed, their candles thriftily snuffed for later use.

'Why did Ulysses tell you?' I wondered aloud.

'Ask yourself, Sassenach,' he said. 'Who is master now, at River Run?'

'Oh?' I said, and then, 'Oh!'

'Oh, indeed,' he said dryly. 'My aunt is blind; who has the keeping of the accounts, the running of the household? She may decide what things should be done – but who is to say whether they *are* done? Who is always at her hand to tell her aught that happens, whose words are in her ear, whose judgment does she trust above all others?'

'I see.' I stared down at the ground, thinking. 'You don't suppose he's been fiddling the accounts or anything sordid like that?' I hoped not; I liked Jocasta's butler very much, and had thought there was both fondness and respect between them; I didn't like to think of his cold-bloodedly cheating her.

Jamie shook his head.

'He is not. I've been over the ledgers and accounts, and everything is in order – verra good order indeed. I'm sure he is an honest man and a faithful servant – but he wouldna be human, to welcome giving up his place to a stranger.'

He snorted briefly.

'My aunt may be blind, but yon black man sees clear enough. He didna say a word to prevent me, or persuade me of anything: only told me what my aunt meant to do, and then left it to me what *I* should do. Or not.'

'You think he knew that you wouldn't –' I stopped there, because I wasn't sure myself that he wouldn't. Pride, caution, or both might have caused him to want to thwart Jocasta's plan, but that didn't mean he meant to reject her offer, either.

He didn't reply, and a small cold chill ran through me. I shivered, in spite of the warm summer air, and took his arm as we walked, seeking reassurance in the solid feel of his flesh beneath my fingers.

It was late July, and the scent of ripening fruit from the orchard was sweet, so heavy on the air that I could almost taste the clean, crisp tang of new apples. I thought of temptation – and the worm that lay hidden beneath a shining skin.

Temptation not only for him, but for me. For him, the

chance to be what he was made for by nature, what fate had denied him. He was born and bred to this: the stewardship of a large estate, the care of the people on it, a place of respect among men of substance, his peers. More importantly, the restoration of clan and family. *I am already part of it,* he'd said.

He cared nothing for wealth, of itself; I knew that. Neither did I think he wanted power; if he did, knowing what I knew about the future's shape, he would have chosen to go north, to seek a place among the founders of a nation.

But he had been a laird once. He had told me very little of his time in prison, but one thing he had said rang in my memory. Of the men who shared his confinement, he said – *They were mine. And the having of them kept me alive.* And I remembered what Ian had said of Simon Fraser: '*Care for his men is now his only link with humanity.*'

Yes, Jamie needed men. Men to lead, to care for, to defend and to fight with. But not to own.

Past the orchard, still in silence, and down the long walk of herbaceous borders, with the scents of lily and lavender, anemone and roses, so pungent and heady that simply to walk through the hot, heavy air was like throwing oneself headlong onto a bed of fragrant petals.

Oh, River Run was a garden of earthly delight, all right . . . but I had called a black man friend, and left my daughter in his care.

Thinking of Joe Abernathy, and Brianna, gave me a strange sense of dislocated double vision, of existing in two places at once. I could see their faces in my mind, hear their voices in my inner ear. And yet reality was the man beside me, kilt swinging with his stride, head bent in anxious thought.

And that was my temptation: Jamie. Not the inconsequentials of soft beds or gracious rooms, silk gowns or social deference. Jamie.

If he did not take Jocasta's offer, he must do something else. And 'something else' was most likely William Tryon's dangerous lure of land and men. Better than Jocasta's generous offer, in its way; what he built would be his own, the legacy he wanted to leave for Brianna. If he lived to build it.

I was still living on two planes. In this one, I could hear the whisper of his kilt where it brushed my skirt, feel the humid warmth of his body, warmer even than the heated air. I could smell the musky scent of him that made me want to pull him from his thoughts into the border, unbelt him and let the plaid fall from his shoulders, pull down my bodice and press my breasts against him, take him down half-naked and wholly roused among the damp green plants, and force him from his thoughts to mine.

But on the plane of memory, I smelled yew trees and the wind from the sea, and under my fingers was no warm man, but the cold, smooth granite of a tombstone with his name.

I didn't speak. Neither did he.

We had made a complete circle by now, and come back to the river's edge, where gray stone steps led down and disappeared under a lapping sheen of water; even so far upstream, the faint echoes of the tide could be felt.

There was a boat moored there; a small rowboat, fit for solitary fishing or a leisurely excursion.

'Will ye come for a row?'

'Yes, why not?' I thought he must feel the same desire I had – to get away from the house and Jocasta, to get enough distance in which to think clearly, without danger of interruption.

I came down, putting my hand on his arm for balance. Before I could step into the boat, though, he turned toward me. Pulling me to him, he kissed me, gently, once, then held me against his body, his chin resting on my head.

'I don't know,' he said quietly, in answer to my unspoken questions. He stepped into the boat and offered me a hand.

He was silent while we made our way out onto the river. It was a dark, moonless night, but the reflections of starlight from the surface of the river gave enough light to see, once my eyes had adapted to the shifting glimmer of water and tree-shadow.

'Ye dinna mean to say anything?' he asked abruptly, at last.

'It's not my choice to make,' I said, feeling a tightness in my chest that had nothing to do with stays.

'No?'

'She's your aunt. It's your life. It has to be your choice.'

'And you'll be a spectator, will you?' He grunted as he spoke, digging with the oars as he pulled upstream. 'Is it not *your* life? Or do ye not mean to stay with me, after all?'

'What do you mean, not stay?' I sat up, startled.

'Perhaps it will be too much for you.' His head was bent over the oars; I couldn't see his face.

'If you mean what happened at the sawmill –'

'No, not that.' He heaved back on the oars, shoulders broadening under his linen, and gave me a crooked smile. 'Death and disaster wouldna trouble ye owner-much, Sassenach. But the small things, day by day . . . I see ye flinch, when the black maid combs your hair, or when the boy takes your shoes away to clean. And the slaves who work in the turpentine camp. That troubles ye, no?'

'Yes. It does. I'm – I can't own slaves. I've told you –'

'Aye, ye have.' He rested on the oars for a moment, brushing a lock of hair out of his face. His eyes met mine squarely.

'And if I chose to do this, Sassenach . . . could ye stay by me, and watch, and do nothing – for there is nothing that could be done, until my aunt should die. Perhaps not even then.'

'What do you mean?'

'She will not free her slaves – how should she? I could not, while she lived.'

'But once you had inherited the place . . .' I hesitated. Beyond the ghoulish aspects of discussing Jocasta's death, there was the more concrete consideration that that event was unlikely to occur for some time; Jocasta was little more than sixty, and aside from her blindness, in vigorous health.

I suddenly saw what he meant; could I bring myself to live, day after day, month after month, year after year, as an owner of slaves? I could not pretend otherwise, could

262

take no refuge in the notion that I was only a guest, an outsider.

I bit my lip, in order not to cry out instant denial.

'Even then,' he said, answering my partial argument. 'Did ye not know that a slave owner cannot free his slaves without the written permission of the Assembly?'

'He what?' I stared blankly at him. 'Why ever not?'

'The plantation owners go in fear of an armed insurrection of Negroes,' he said. 'And d'ye blame them?' he added sardonically.

'Slaves are forbidden to carry weapons, save tools such as tree knives, and there are the bloodshed laws to prevent their use.' He shook his head. 'Nay, the last thing the Assembly would allow is a large group of free blacks let loose upon the countryside. Even if a man wishes to manumit one of his slaves, and is given permission to do so, the freed slave is required to leave the colony within a short time – or he may be captured and enslaved by anyone who chooses to take him.'

'You've thought about it,' I said slowly.

'Haven't you?'

I didn't answer. I trailed my hand in the water, a little wave purling up my wrist. No, I hadn't thought about the prospect. Not consciously, because I hadn't wanted to face the choice that was now being laid before me.

'I suppose it would be a great chance,' I said, my voice sounding strained and unnatural to my ears. 'You'd be in charge of everything . . .'

'My aunt is not a fool,' he interrupted, with a slight edge to his voice. 'She would make me heir, but not owner in her place. She would use me to do those things she cannot – but I would be no more than her cat's-paw. True, she would ask my opinion, listen to my advice; but nothing would be done, and she didna wish it so.'

He shook his head.

'Her husband is dead. Whether she was fond of him or no, she is mistress here now, with none to answer to. And she enjoys the taste of power too well to spit it out.'

He was plainly correct in this assessment of Jocasta Cameron's character, and therein lay the key to her plan. She needed a man; someone to go into those places she could not go, to deal with the Navy, to handle the chores of a large estate that she could not manage because of her blindness.

At the same time, she patently did *not* want a husband; someone who would usurp her power and dictate to her. Had he not been a slave, Ulysses could have acted for her – but while he could be her eyes and ears, he could not be her hands.

No, Jamie was the perfect choice; a strong, competent man, able to command respect among peers, compel obedience in subordinates. One knowledgeable in the management of land and men. Furthermore, a man bound to her by kinship and obligation, there to do her bidding – but essentially powerless. He would be held in thrall by dependence upon her bounty, and by the rich bribe of River Run itself; a debt that need not be paid until the matter was no longer of any earthly concern to Jocasta Cameron.

There was an increasing lump in my throat as I sought for words. I couldn't, I thought. I couldn't manage it. But I couldn't face the alternative, either; I couldn't urge him to reject Jocasta's offer, knowing it would send him to Scotland, to meet an unknown death.

'I can't say what you should do,' I finally said, my voice barely audible above the regular lap of the oars.

There was an eddy pool, where a large tree had fallen into the water, its branches forming a trap for all the debris that drifted downstream. Jamie made for this, backing the rowboat neatly into quiet water. He let down the oars, and wiped a sleeve across his forehead, breathing heavily from exertion.

The night was quiet around us, with little sound but the lapping of water, and the occasional scrape of submerged tree branches against the hull. At last he reached out and touched my chin.

'Your face is my heart, Sassenach,' he said softly, 'and love of you is my soul. But you're right; ye canna be my conscience.'

In spite of everything, I felt a lightening of spirit, as though some indefinable burden had dropped away.

264

'Oh, I'm glad,' I said, adding impulsively, 'it would be a terrible strain.'

'Oh, aye?' He looked mildly startled. 'Ye think me verra wicked, then?'

'You're the best man I've ever met,' I said. 'I only meant . . . it's such a strain, to try to live for two people. To try to make them fit your ideas of what's right . . . you do it for a child, of course, you have to, but even then, it's dreadfully hard work. I couldn't do it for you – it would be wrong even to try.'

I'd taken him back more than a little. He sat for some moments, his face half turned away.

'Do ye really think me a good man?' he said at last. There was a queer note in his voice, that I couldn't quite decipher.

'Yes,' I said, with no hesitation. Then added, half jokingly, 'Don't you?'

After a long pause, he said, quite seriously, 'No, I shouldna think so.'

I looked at him, speechless, no doubt with my mouth hanging open.

'I am a violent man, and I ken it well,' he said quietly. He spread his hands out on his knees; big hands, which could wield sword and dagger with ease, or choke the life from a man. 'So do you – or ye should.'

'You've never done anything you weren't forced to do!'

'No?'

'I don't think so,' I said, but even as I spoke, a shadow of doubt clouded my words. Even when done from the most urgent necessity, did such things not leave a mark on the soul?

'Ye wouldna hold me in the same estimation as, say, a man like Stephen Bonnet? He might well say he acted from necessity.'

'If you think you have the slightest thing in common with Stephen Bonnet, you're dead wrong,' I said firmly.

He shrugged, half impatient, and shifted restlessly on the narrow bench.

'There's nay much to choose between Bonnet and me, save that I have a sense of honor that he lacks. What else keeps me from turning thief?' he demanded. 'From plundering those whom I might? It is in me to do it – my one grandsire built Leoch on the gold of those he robbed in the Highland passes; the other built his fortune on the bodies of women whom he forced for their wealth and titles.'

He stretched himself, powerful shoulders rising dark against the shimmer of the water behind him. Then he suddenly took hold of the oars across his knees and flung them into the bottom of the boat, with a crash that made me jump.

'I am more than five-and-forty!' he said. 'A man should be settled at that age, no? He should have a house, and some land to grow his food, and a bit of money put away to see him through his auld age, at the least.'

He took a deep breath; I could see the white bosom of his shirt rise with his swelling chest.

'Well, I dinna have a house. Or land. Or money. Not a croft, not a tattie-plot, not a cow or a sheep or a pig or a goat! I havena got a rooftree or a bedstead, or a pot to piss in!'

He slammed his fist down on the thwart, making the wooden seat vibrate under me.

'I dinna own the clothes I stand up in!'

There was a long silence, broken only by the thin song of crickets.

'You have me,' I said, in a small voice. It didn't seem a lot.

He made a small sound in his throat that might have been either a laugh or a sob.

'Aye, I have,' he said. His voice was quivering a bit, though whether with passion or amusement, I couldn't tell. 'That's the hell of it, aye?'

'It is?'

He threw up his hand in a gesture of profound impatience.

'If it was only me, what would it matter? I could live like Myers; go to the woods, hunt and fish for my living, and when I was too old, lie down under a peaceful tree and die, and let the foxes gnaw my bones. Who would care?'

He shrugged his shoulders with irritable violence, as though his shirt was too tight.

'But it's *not* only me,' he said. 'It's you, and it's Ian and it's Duncan and it's Fergus and it's Marsali – God help me, there's even Laoghaire to think of!'

'Oh, let's don't,' I said.

'Do ye not understand?' he said, in near desperation. 'I would lay the world at your feet, Claire – and I have nothing to give ye!'

He honestly thought it mattered.

I sat looking at him, searching for words. He was half turned away, shoulders slumped in despair.

Within an hour, I had gone from anguish at the thought of losing him in Scotland, to a strong desire to bed him in the herbaceous borders, and from that to a pronounced urge to hit him on the head with an oar. Now I was back to tenderness.

At last I took one big, callused hand and slid forward so I knelt on the boards between his knees. I laid my head against his chest, and felt his breath stir my hair. I had no words, but I had made my choice.

' "Whither thou goest," ' I said, ' "I will go; and where thou lodgest, I will lodge: thy people shall be my people, and thy God my God: Where thou diest, will I die, and there will I be buried." ' Be it Scottish hill or southern forest. 'You do what you have to; I'll be there.'

The water ran fast and shallow near the middle of the creek; I could see the boulders black just beneath the glinting surface. Jamie saw them, too, and pulled strongly for the far side, bringing us to rest against a shelving gravel bank, in a pool formed by the roots of a weeping willow. I leaned out and caught a branch of the willow, and wrapped the painter round it.

I had thought we would return to River Run, but evidently this expedition had some point beyond respite. We had continued upriver instead, Jamie pulling strongly against the slow current.

Left alone with my thoughts, I could only listen to the faint hiss of his breath, and wonder what he would do. If he chose to stay . . . well, it might not be as difficult as he thought. I didn't underrate Jocasta Cameron, but neither did I underestimate Jamie Fraser. Both Colum and Dougal MacKenzie had tried to bend him to their will – and both had failed.

I had a moment's qualm at the memory of my last sight of Dougal MacKenzie, mouthing soundless curses as he drowned in his own blood, Jamie's dirk socketed at the base of his throat. *I am a violent man,* he'd said, *you know it.*

But he was still wrong; there was a difference between this man and Stephen Bonnet, I thought, watching the flex of his body on the oars, the grace and power of the sweep of his arms. He had several things beyond the honor that he claimed: kindness, courage . . . and a conscience.

I realized where we were going, as he backed with one oar, steering across the current toward the mouth of a wide creek, overhung with aspens. I had never approached by water before, but Jocasta had said it was not far.

I should not have been surprised; if he had come out tonight to confront his demons, it was a most appropriate place.

A little way above the creek mouth, the mill loomed dark and silent. There was a dim glow behind its bulk; light from the slave shanties near the woods. We were surrounded by the usual night noises, but the place seemed strangely quiet, in spite of the racket made by trees and frogs and water. Though it was night, the huge building seemed to cast a shadow – though this was plainly no more than my imagination.

'Places that are very busy in the daytime always seem particularly spooky at night,' I said, in an effort to break the mill's silence.

'Do they?' Jamie sounded abstracted. 'I didna much like that one in the daylight.'

I shuddered at the memory.

'Neither did I. I only meant –'

'Byrnes is dead.' He didn't look at me; his face was turned toward the mill, half-hidden by the willow's shadow.

I dropped the end of the tie rope.

'The overseer? When?' I said, shocked more by the abruptness than the revelation. 'And how?'

'This afternoon. Campbell's youngest lad brought the news just before sunset.'

'How?' I asked again. I gripped my knees, a double handful of ivory silk twisted in my fingers.

'It was the lockjaw.' His voice was casual, unemphatic. 'A verra nasty way to die.'

He was right about that. I had never actually seen anyone die of tetanus myself, but I knew the symptoms well enough: restlessness and difficulty swallowing, developing into a progressive stiffening as the muscles of arms and legs and neck began to spasm. The spasms increased in severity and duration until the patient's body was hard as wood, arched in an agony that came on and receded, came on again, went off, and at last came on in an endless tetany that could not be relaxed by anything save death.

'He died grinnin', Ronnie Campbell said. But I shouldna think it was a happy death, forbye.' It was a grim joke, but there was little humor in his voice.

I sat up quite straight, feeling cold all down my spine in spite of the warmth of the night.

'It isn't a quick death, either,' I said. Suspicion spread cold tentacles through my mind. 'It takes days to die of tetanus.'

'It took Davie Byrnes five days, first to last.' If there had been any trace of humor in his voice to start with, it was gone now.

'You saw him,' I said, a small flicker of anger beginning to thaw the internal chill. 'You saw him! And you didn't tell me?'

I had dressed Byrnes's injury – hideous, but not life-threatening – and had been told that he would be kept somewhere 'safe' until the disturbance over the lynching had died down. Heartsick as I was over the matter, I had made no effort to inquire further after the overseer's whereabouts or welfare; it was my own guilt at this neglect that made me angry, and I knew it – but the knowledge didn't help.

'Could ye have done anything? I thought ye told me

that the lockjaw was one of the things that couldna be helped, even in your time.' He wasn't looking at me; I could see his profile turned toward the mill, head stamped in darker black against the lighter shadow of pale leaves.

I forced myself to let go of my skirt. I smoothed the crumpled patches over my knee, thinking dimly that Phaedre would have a terrible time ironing it.

'No,' I said, with a little effort. 'No, I couldn't have saved him. But I should have seen him; I might have eased him a little.'

Now he did look at me; I saw his head turn, and felt the shifting of his weight in the boat.

'You might,' he said evenly.

'And you wouldn't let me –' I stopped, remembering his absences this past week, and his evasive replies when I had asked him where he'd been. I could imagine the scene all too well; the tiny, stifling artic room in Farquard Campbell's house where I had dressed Byrnes's injury. The racked figure on the bed, dying by inches under the cold eyes of those the law had made his unwilling allies, knowing that he died despised. The sense of cold came back, raising gooseflesh on my arms.

'No, I wouldna let Campbell send for you,' he said softly. 'There's the law, Sassenach – and there is justice. I ken the difference well enough.'

'There's such a thing as mercy, too.' And had anyone asked, I would have called Jamie Fraser a merciful man. He had been, once. But the years between now and then had been hard ones – and compassion was a soft emotion, easily eroded by circumstance. I had thought he still had his kindness, though; and felt a queer pain at the thought of its loss. *I shouldna think so, no.* Had that been no more than honesty?

The boat had drifted halfway round, so that the drooping branch hung now between us. There was a small snort from the darkness behind the leaves.

'Blessed are the merciful,' he said, 'for they shall find mercy. Byrnes wasn't, and he didn't. And as for me, once God had made his opinion of the man known, I didna think it right to interfere.'

'You think *God* gave him tetanus?'

'I canna think anyone else would have the imagination for it. Besides,' he went on, logically, 'where else would ye look for justice?'

I searched for words, and failed to find any. Giving up, I returned to the only possible point of argument. I felt a little sick.

'You ought to have told me. Even if you didn't think I could help, it wasn't your business to decide –'

'I didna want ye to go.' His voice was still quiet, but there was a note of steel in it now.

'I know you didn't! But it doesn't matter whether you thought Byrnes deserved to suffer or –'

'Not for him!' The boat rocked suddenly as he moved, and I grasped the sides to keep my balance. He spoke violently.

'I didna care a fig whether Byrnes died easy or hard, but I'm no a monster of cruelty! I didna keep you from him to make him suffer; I kept ye away to protect you.'

I was relieved to hear this, but increasingly angry as the truth of what he'd done dawned on me.

'It wasn't your business to decide that. If I'm not your conscience, it isn't up to you to be mine!' I brushed angrily at the screen of willow founds between us, trying to see him.

Suddenly a hand shot through the leaves and grabbed my wrist.

'It's up to me to keep ye safe!'

I tried to jerk away, but he had a tight grip on me, and he wasn't letting go.

'I am not a young girl who needs protection, not yet an idiot! If there's some reason for me not to do something, then tell me and I'll listen. But you can't decide what I'm to do and where I'm to go without even consulting me – I won't stand for that, and you bloody well know it!'

The boat lurched, and with a huge rustling of leaves, he popped his head through the willow, glaring.

'I am not trying to say where ye'll go!'

'You decided where I *mustn't* go, and that's just as bad!' The willow leaves slid back over his shoulders as the boat moved, jarred by his violence, and we revolved slowly, coming out of the tree's shadow.

271

He loomed in front of me, massive as the mill, his head and shoulders blotting out a good bit of the scenery behind him. The long, straight nose was in inch from mine, and his eyes had gone narrow. They were a dark enough blue to be black in this light, and looking into them at close range was most unnerving.

I blinked. He didn't.

He had let go of my wrist when he came through the leaves. Now he took hold of my upper arms. I could feel the heat of his grip through the cloth. His hands were very big and very hard, making me suddenly aware of the fragility of my own bones in contrast. *I am a violent man.*

He'd shaken me a time or two before, and I hadn't liked it. In case he had something of the sort in mind just now, I inserted a foot between his legs, and prepared to give him a swift knee where it would do most good.

'I was wrong,' he said.

Tensed for violence, I had actually started to jerk my foot up, when I heard what he had said. Before I could stop, he had clamped his legs tight together, trapping my knee between his thighs.

'I *said* I was wrong, Sassenach,' he repeated, a touch of impatience in his voice. 'D'ye mind?'

'Ah . . . no,' I said, feeling a trifle sheepish. I wiggled my knee tentatively, but he kept his thighs squeezed tight together.

'You wouldn't consider letting go of me, would you?' I said politely. My heart was still pounding.

'No, I wouldn't. Are ye going to listen to me now?'

'I suppose so,' I said, still polite. 'It doesn't look as though I'm very busy at the moment.'

I was close enough to see his mouth twitch. His thighs squeezed tighter for a moment, then relaxed.

'This is a verra foolish quarrel, and you know that as well as I do.'

'No, I don't.' My anger had faded somewhat, but I wasn't about to let him dismiss it altogether. 'It's maybe not important to you, but it is to me. It isn't foolish. And you know it, or you wouldn't be admitting you're wrong.'

The twitch was more pronounced this time. He took a deep breath, and dropped his hands from my shoulders.

272

'Well, then. I should maybe have told ye about Byrnes; I admit it. But if I had, ye would have gone to him, even if I'd said it was the lockjaw – and I kent it was, I've seen it before. Even if there was nothing ye could do, you'd still go? No?'

'Yes. Even if – yes, I would have gone.'

In fact, there was nothing I could have done for Byrnes. Myers's anesthetic wouldn't have helped a case of tetanus. Nothing short of injectable curare would ease those spasms. I could have given him nothing more than the comfort of my presence, and it was doubtful that he would have appreciated that – or even noticed it. Still, I would have felt bound to offer it.

'I would have had to go,' I said, more gently. 'I'm a doctor. Don't you see?'

'Of course I do,' he said gruffly. 'D'ye think I dinna ken ye at all, Sassenach?'

Without waiting for an answer, he went on.

'There was talk about what happened at the mill – there would be, aye? But with the man dying under your hands as he did – well, no one's said straight out that ye might have killed him on purpose . . . but it's easy to see folk thinkin' it. Not thinkin' that ye killed him, even – but only that ye might have thought to let him die on purpose, so as to save him from the rope.'

I stared at my hands, spread out on my knees, nearly as pale as the ivory satin under them.

'I did think of it.'

'I ken that fine, aye?' he said dryly. 'I saw your face, Sassenach.'

I drew a deep breath, if only to assure myself that the air was no longer thick with the smell of blood. There was nothing but the turpentine scent of the pine forest, clean and astringent in my nostrils. I had a sudden vivid memory of the hospital, of the smell of pine-scented disinfectant that hung in the air, that overlaid but could not banish the underlying smell of sickness.

I took another cleansing breath, and raised my head to look at Jamie. 'And did *you* wonder if I'd killed him?'

He looked faintly surprised.

'Ye would have done as ye thought best.' He dismissed

273

the minor question of whether I'd killed a man, in favor of the point at issue.

'But it didna seem wise for ye to preside over both deaths, if ye take my meaning.'

I did, and not for the first time I was aware of the subtle networks of which he was a part, in a way I could never be. This place in its way was as strange to him as it was to me; and yet he knew not only what people were saying – anyone could find that out, who cared to haunt tavern and market – but what they were thinking.

What was more irritating was that he knew what *I* was thinking.

'So ye see,' he said, watching me. 'I kent Byrnes was sure to die, and ye couldna help. Yet if ye knew his trouble, ye'd surely go to him. And then he would die, and folk would maybe not say how strange it was, that both men had died under your hand, so to speak – but –'

'But they'd be thinking it,' I finished for him.

The twitch grew into a crooked smile.

'Folk notice you, Sassenach.'

I bit my lip. For good or for ill, they did, and the noticing had come close to killing me more than once.

He rose, and taking hold of a branch for balance, stepped out on the gravel and pulled the plaid up over his shoulder.

'I told Mrs. Byrnes I would fetch away her husband's things from the mill,' he said. 'Ye needna come, if ye dinna wish.'

The mill loomed against the star-spattered sky. It couldn't have looked more sinister if it had tried. *Whither thou goest, I will go.*

I thought I knew now what he was doing. He had wanted to see it all, before making up his mind; see it with the knowledge that it might be his. Walking through the gardens and orchards, rowing past the acres of thick pines, visiting the mill – he was surveying the domain he was offered, weighing and evaluating, deciding what complications must be dealt with, and whether he could or would accept the challenge.

After all, I thought sourly, the Devil had insisted on showing Jesus everything He was passing up, taking Him

274

up to the top of the Temple to gaze on the cities of the world. The only difficulty was that if Jamie decided to fling himself off; there wasn't a legion of angels standing by to stop him dashing his foot – and everything else – against a slab of Scottish granite.

Only me.

'Wait,' I said, clambering out of the boat. 'I'm coming, too.'

The lumber was still stacked in the millyard; no one had moved any of it since the last time I had been here. The dark took away all sense of perspective; the stacks of fresh timber were pale rectangles that seemed to float above an invisible ground, first distant, then suddenly looming close enough to brush my skirts. The air smelt of pinesap and sawdust.

I couldn't see the ground under my own feet, for that matter, obscured as it was both by darkness and by my billowing ivory skirt. Jamie held my arm to keep me from stumbling. He never stumbled, of course. Perhaps living all his life without even the thought of light outside after sunset had given him some sort of radar, I thought; like a bat.

There was a fire burning, somewhere among the slave huts. It was very late; most would be sleeping. In the Indies, there would have been the nightlong sound of drums and keening; the slaves would have made lamentations for a fellow's death, a festival of mourning to last the week. Here, there was nothing. No sound save the pine trees' soughing, no flicker of movement save the faint light at the forest's edge.

'They are afraid,' Jamie said softly, pausing to listen to the silence, as I did.

'Little wonder,' I said, half under my breath. 'So am I.'

He made a small huffing sound that might have been amusement.

'So am I,' he muttered, 'but not of ghosts.' He took my arm and pushed open the small man-door at the side of the mill before I could ask what he *was* afraid of.

The silence inside had a body to it. At first I thought it like the eerie quiet of dead battlefields, but then I realized

275

the difference. This silence was alive. And whatever lived in the silence here, it wasn't lying quiet. I thought I could still smell the blood, thick on the air.

Then I breathed deeply and thought again, cold horror rippling up my spine. I *could* smell blood. Fresh blood.

I gripped Jamie's arm, but he had smelled it himself; his arm had gone hard under my hand, muscles tensed in wariness. Without a word, he detached himself from my grip, and vanished.

For a moment, I thought he truly *had* vanished, and nearly panicked, groping for him, my hand closing on the empty air where he'd stood. Then I realized that he had merely flung the dark plaid over his head, instantly hiding the paleness of face and linen shirt. I heard his step, quick and light on the dirt floor, and then that was gone too.

The air was hot and still, and thick with blood. A rank, sweet smell, with a metal taste on the back of the tongue. Exactly the same as it had been a week ago, conjuring hallucination. Still in the grip of a cold grue, I swung around and strained my eyes toward the far side of the cavernous room, half expecting to see the scene engraved on my memory materialize again out of darkness. The rope stretched tight from the lumber crane, the huge hook swaying with its groaning burden . . .

A groan rent the air, and I nearly bit my lip in two. My throat swelled with a swallowed scream; only the fear of drawing something to me kept me silent.

Where was Jamie? I longed to call out for him, but didn't dare. My eyes had grown enough accustomed to the dark to make out the shadow of the saw blade, an amorphous blob ten feet away, but the far side of the room was a wall of blackness. I strained my eyes to see, realizing belatedly that in my pale dress, I was undoubtedly visible to anyone in the room with me

The groan came again, and I started convulsively. My palms were sweating. *It's not!* I told myself fiercely. *It isn't, it can't be!*

I was paralyzed with fear, and it took some moments for me to realize what my ears had told me. The sound hadn't come from the blackness across the room, where the

276

crane stood with its hook. It had come from somewhere behind me.

I whirled. The door we had come through was still open, a pale rectangle in the pitch-black. Nothing showed, nothing moved between me and the door. I took a quick step toward it and stopped. Every muscle in my legs strained to run like hell – but I couldn't leave Jamie.

Again the sound, that same sobbing gasp of physical anguish; pain past the point of crying out. With it, a new thought popped into my mind; what if it was Jamie making the sound?

Shocked out of caution, I turned toward the sound and shouted his name, raising echoes from the roof high above.

'Jamie!' I cried again. 'Where *are* you?'

'Here, Sassenach.' Jamie's muffled voice came from somewhere to my left, calm but somehow urgent. 'Come to me, will ye?'

It wasn't him. Nearly shaking with relief at the sound of his voice, I blundered through the dark, not caring now what had made the sound, as long as it wasn't Jamie.

My hand struck a wooden wall, groped blindly, and finally found a door, standing open. He was inside the overseer's quarters.

I stepped through the door, and felt the change at once. The air was even closer, and much hotter, than that in the mill proper. The floor here was of wood, but there was no echo to my step; the air was dead still, suffocating. And the smell of blood was even stronger.

'Where are you?' I called again, low-voiced this time.

'Here,' came the reply, startlingly near at hand. 'By the bed. Come and help me; it's a lass.'

He was in the tiny bedroom. The small room was windowless, and lightless too. I found them by feel, Jamie kneeling on the wooden floor beside a narrow bed, and in the bed, a body.

It was a female, as he'd said; touch told me that at once. Touch told me also that she was exsanguinating. The cheek I brushed was cool and clammy. Everything else I touched was warm and wet; her clothing, the bedclothes, the mattress beneath her. I could feel wetness soaking through my skirt where I knelt on the floor.

I felt for a pulse in the throat and couldn't find it. The chest moved slightly under my hand, the only sign of life beyond the faint sigh that went with it.

'It's all right now,' I heard myself saying, and my voice was soothing, all trace of panic gone, though in truth there was more reason for it now. 'We're here, you're not alone. What's happened to you, can you tell me?'

All the time my hands were darting over head and throat and chest and stomach, pushing sodden clothes aside, searching blindly, frantically, for a wound to stanch. Nothing, no spurt of artery, no raw gash. And all the time, there was a faint but steady *pit-a-pat, pit-a-pat,* like the sound of tiny feet running.

'Tell . . .' It was not so much a word as the articulation of a sigh. Then a catch, a sobbing breath indrawn.

'Who has done this to ye, lass?' Jamie's disembodied voice came low and urgent. 'Tell me, who?'

'Tell . . .'

I touched all the places where the great vessels lie close beneath the skin and found them whole. Seized her by an unresisting arm and lifted, thrust a hand beneath to feel her back. All the heat of her body was there; the bodice was damp with sweat, but not blood-soaked.

'It will be all right,' I said again. 'You're not alone. Jamie, hold her hand.' Hopelessness came down on me; I knew what it must be.

'I already have it,' he said to me, and, 'Dinna trouble, lass,' to her. 'It will be all right, d'ye hear me?' *Pit-a-pat, pit-a-pat.* The tiny feet were slowing.

'Tell . . .'

I could not help, but nonetheless slid my hand beneath her skirt again, this time letting my fingers curve between the limp splayed things, She was still warm here, very warm. Blood flowed gently over my hand and through my fingers, hot and wet as the air around us, unstoppable as the water that flowed down the mill's sluice.

'I . . . die . . .'

'I think ye are murdered, lass,' Jamie said to her, very gently. 'Will ye not say who has killed you?'

Her breath came louder now, a soft rattle in her throat. *Pit. Pat. Pit. Pat.* The feet were tiptoeing softly now.

'Ser . . . geant. Tell . . . him . . .'

I drew my hand out from between her thighs and took her other hand in mine, heedless of the blood. It scarcely mattered now, after all.

'. . . tell . . .' came with sudden intensity, and then silence. A long silence, and then, another long, sighing breath. A silence, even longer. And a breath.

'I will,' said Jamie. His voice was no more than a whisper in the dark. 'I will do it. I promise ye.'

Pit.

Pat.

They called it the 'death drop', in the Highlands; the sound of dripping water, heard in a house when one of the inhabitants was about to die. Not water dripping here, but a sure sign, nonetheless.

There was no more sound from the darkness. I couldn't see Jamie, but felt the slight movement of the bed against my thighs as he leaned forward.

'God will forgive ye,' he whispered to the silence. 'Go in peace.'

I could hear the buzzing the moment we stepped into the overseer's quarters the next morning. In the huge, dusty silence of the mill, everything had been muffled in space and sawdust. But in this small, partitioned area the walls caught every sound and threw it back; our footsteps echoed from wooden floor to wooden ceiling. I felt like a fly sealed inside a snare drum, and suffered a moment's claustrophobia, trapped as I was in the narrow passage between the two men.

There were only two rooms, separated by a short passage that led from the outdoors into the mill proper. On our right lay the larger room that had served the Byrneses for living and cooking, and on the left, the smaller bedroom, from which the noise was coming. Jamie took a deep breath, clasped his plaid to his face, and pulled open the bedroom door.

It looked like a blanket covering the bed, a blanket of gunmetal blue sparked with green. Then Jamie took a step into the room and the flies rose buzzing from their clotted meal in a swarm of gluttonous protest.

I bit back a cry of abhorrence and ducked, flailing at them. Bloated, slow-moving bodies hit my face and arms and bounced away, circling lazily through the thick air. Farquard Campbell made a Scottish noise of overpowering disgust that sounded like 'Heuch!' then lowered his head and pushed past me, eyes slitted and lips pressed tight together, nostrils pinched to whiteness.

The tiny bedroom was hardly bigger than the coffin it had become. There were no windows, only cracks between the boards that let in a dim uncertain light. The atmosphere was hot and humid as a tropical greenhouse, thick with the rotting sweet smell of death. I could feel the sweat snaking down my sides, ticklish as flies' feet, and tried to breathe only through my mouth.

She had not been large; her body made only the slightest mound beneath the blanket we had laid over her the night before, for decency's sake. Her head seemed big by contrast to the shrunken body, like a child's stick figure with a round ball stuck on toothpick limbs.

Brushing away several flies too glutted to move, Jamie pulled back the blanket. The blanket, like everything else, was blotched and crusted, sodden at the foot. The human body, on average, contains eight pints of blood, but it seems a lot more when you spread it around.

I had seen her face briefly the night before, dead features lent an artificial glow by the light of the pine splinter Jamie held above her. Now she lay pallid and dank as a mushroom, blunt features emerging from a web of fine brown hair. It was impossible to tell her age, save that she was not old. Neither could I tell whether she had been attractive; there was no beauty of bone, but animation might have flushed the round cheeks and lent her deepset eyes a sparkle men might have found pretty. One man had, I thought. Pretty enough, anyway.

The men were murmuring together, bent over the still form. Mr. Campbell turned now to me, wearing a slight frown beneath his formal wig.

'You are reasonably sure, Mrs. Fraser, of the cause of death?'

'Yes.' Trying not to breathe the fetid air, I picked up the edge of the blanket, and turned it back, exposing the corpse's legs. The feet were faintly blue and beginning to swell.

'I drew her skirt down, but I left everything else as it was,' I explained, pulling it up again.

My stomach muscles tightened automatically as I touched her. I had seen dead bodies before, and this was far from the most gruesome, but the hot climate and closed atmosphere had prevented the body from cooling much; the flesh of her thigh was as warm as mine, but unpleasantly flaccid.

I had left it where we found it, in the bed between her legs. A kitchen skewer, more than a foot long. It was covered in dried blood as well, but clearly visible.

'I . . . um . . . found no wound on the body,' I said, putting it as delicately as possible.

'Aye, I see.' Mr. Campbell's frown seemed to lessen slightly. 'Ah, well, at least 'tis likely not a case of deliberate murder, then.'

I opened my mouth to reply, but caught a warning look from Jamie. Not noticing, Mr. Campbell went on.

'The question remains whether the poor woman will have done it herself, or met her death by the agency of another. What think ye, Mistress Fraser?'

Jamie narrowed his eyes at me over Campbell's shoulder, but the warning was unnecessary; we had discussed the matter last night, and come to our own conclusions – also to the conclusion that our opinions need not be shared with the forces of law and order in Cross Creek; not just yet. I pinched my nose slightly under pretext of the smell, in order to disguise any telltale alteration of my expression. I was a very bad liar.

'I'm sure she did it by herself,' I said firmly. 'It takes very little time to bleed to death in this manner, and as Jamie told you, she was still alive when we found her. We were outside the mill, talking, for some time before we came in; no one would have been able to leave without our seeing them.'

On the other hand, a person might quite easily have hidden in the other room, and crept out quietly in the dark while we were occupied in comforting the dying woman. If this possibility did not occur to Mr. Campbell, I saw no reason to draw it to his attention.

Jamie had rearranged his features into an expression of gravity suitable to the occasion by the time Mr. Campbell turned back to him. The older man shook his head in regret.

'Ah, poor unfortunate lass! I suppose we can but be relieved that no one else has shared her sin.'

'What about the man who fathered the child she was trying to get rid of?' I said, with a certain amount of acidity. Mr. Campbell looked startled, but pulled himself quickly back together.

'Um . . . quite so,' he said, and coughed. 'Though we do not know whether she were married –'

'So ye do not know the woman yourself, sir?' Jamie butted in before I could make any further injudicious remarks.

Campbell shook his head.

'She is not the servant of Mr. Buchanan or the MacNeills, I am sure. Nor Judge Alderdyce. Those are the only plantations near enough from which she might have walked. Though it does occur to me to wonder why she should have come to this particular place to perform such a desperate act . . .'

It had occurred to Jamie and me, too. To prevent Mr. Campbell's taking the next step in this line of inquiry, Jamie intervened again.

'She said verra little, but she did mention a "Sergeant". "Tell the Sergeant" were her words. Do ye perhaps have a thought whom she might mean by that, sir?'

'I think there is an army sergeant in charge of the guard on the royal warehouse. Yes, I am sure of it.' Mr. Campbell brightened slightly. 'Ah! Nay doubt the woman was attached in some way to the military establishment. Depend upon it, that is the explanation. Though I still wonder why she –'

'Mr. Campbell, do pardon me – I'm afraid I'm feeling a bit faint,' I interrupted, laying a hand on his sleeve. This was no lie; I hadn't slept or eaten. I felt light-headed from the heat and the smell, and I knew I must look pale.

'Will ye see my wife outside, sir?' Jamie said. He gestured toward the bed and its pathetic burden. 'I'll bring the poor lass along as I may.'

'Pray do not trouble yourself, Mr. Fraser,' Campbell protested, already turning to usher me out. 'My servant can fetch out the body.'

'It is my aunt's mill, sir, and thus my concern.' Jamie spoke politely, but firmly. 'I shall attend to it.'

Phaedre was waiting outside, by the wagon.

'I told you that place got haints,' she said, surveying me with an air of grim satisfaction. 'You white as ary sheet, ma'am.' She handed me a flask of spiced wine, wrinkling her nose delicately in my direction.

'You smellin' worse than what you was last night, and you look like you come from a pig-killin' then. Sit you down in the shade here and drink that up; fix you up peart.' She glanced over my shoulder. I looked back as well, and saw that Campbell had reached the shade of the sycamores by the creek bank, and was deep in conversation with his servant.

'Found her,' Phaedre said at once, dropping her voice. Her eyes cut sideways, toward the small cluster of slave huts, barely visible from this side of the mill.

'You're sure? You didn't have much time.' I took a mouthful of wine and held it, glad of the sharp bouquet that rose up the back of my throat, cleansing my palate of the taste of death.

Phaedre nodded, her glance moving to the men under the trees.

'Didn't need much. Walked down by them houses, saw one door hangin' open, little bits of trash scattered round like somebody done left in a hurry. I find a picanin' and ask him who livin' there, he tell me Pollyanne live there, but she gone now, he don't know where. Ask him when she leave, he say she there for supper last night, this morning she gone, nobody see her.' Her eyes met mine, dark with questions. 'Now you know, what you mean to do?'

A bloody good question, and one for which I had no

answer at all. I swallowed the wine, and along with it, a rising sense of panic.

'All the slaves here must know she's gone; how long before anyone else finds out? Whose business will it be to know such things, now that Byrnes is dead?'

Phaedre raised one shoulder in a graceful shrug.

'Anybody come askin' find out right quick. But whose business it be to ask –' She nodded toward the mill. We had left the small door to the living quarters open; Jamie was coming out, a blanket-wrapped burden cradled in his arms.

'Reckon it's his,' she said.

I am already part of it. He had known, even before the interrupted dinner party. With no formal announcement, with neither invitation nor acceptance of the role, he fit the place, the part, like a piece slipping into a jigsaw puzzle. Already he was the master of River Run – if he wanted to be.

Campbell's servant had come to help with the body; Jamie sank to one knee by the edge of the mill flume, surrendering his burden gently to the earth. I gave Phaedre back the flask, with a nod of thanks.

'Will you fetch the things from the wagon?'

Without a word, Phaedre went to get the things I had brought – a blanket, a bucket, clean rags, and a jar of herbs – while I went to join Jamie.

He was kneeling by the creek, washing his hands, a little way upstream from where the body lay. It was foolish to wash in preparation for what I was about to do, but habit was strong; I knelt beside him and dipped my hands as well, letting the cold fresh rush of water carry away the touch of clammy flesh.

'I was right,' I said to him, low-voiced. 'It was a woman called Pollyanne; she's run away in the night.'

He grimaced, rubbing his palms briskly together, and glanced over his shoulder. Campbell was standing over the corpse now, a slight frown of distaste still on his face.

Jamie scowled in concentration, gaze returning to his hands. 'Well, that'll put a cocked hat on it, aye?' He bent and splashed his face, then shook his head violently, flinging drops like a wet dog. Then he gave me a nod, and stood up, wiping his face with the end of his stained plaid.

'See to the lassie, aye, Sassenach?' He stalked purposefully toward Mr. Campbell, plaid swinging.

There was no use saving any of her clothes; I cut them off. Undressed, she looked to be in her twenties. Undernourished; ribs countable, arms and legs slender and pale as stripped branches. For all that, she was still surprisingly heavy, and the remnants of rigor mortis made her hard to handle. Phaedre and I were both sweating heavily before we finished, and strands of hair were escaping from the knot at my neck and pasting themselves to my flushed cheeks.

At least the heavy labor kept conversation to a minimum, leaving me in peace with my thoughts. Not that my thoughts were particularly peaceful.

A woman seeking to 'slip a bairn', as Jamie put it, would do it in her own room, her own bed, if she were doing it alone. The only reason for the stranger to have come to a remote place such as this was to meet the person who would do the office for her – a person who could not come to her.

We must look for a slave in the mill quarters, I had told him, one maybe with the reputation of a midwife, someone women would talk about among themselves, would recommend in whispers.

The fact that I had apparently been proved right gave me no satisfaction. The abortionist had fled, fearing that the woman would have told us who had done the deed. If she had stayed put and said nothing, Farquard Campbell might have taken my word for it that the woman must have done it herself – he could hardly prove otherwise. If anyone else found that the slave Pollyanne had run, though – and of course they would find out! – and she were caught and questioned, the whole matter would no doubt come out at once. And then what?

I shuddered, despite the heat. Did the law of bloodshed apply in this case? It certainly ought, I thought, grimly sluicing yet another bucket of water over the splayed white limbs, if quantity counted for anything.

285

Damn the woman, I thought, using irritation to cover a useless pity. I could do nothing for her now save try to tidy up the mess she had left – in every sense of the word. And perhaps try to save the other player in this tragedy; the hapless woman who had done murder unmeaning, in the guise of help, and who stood now to pay for that mistake with her own life.

Jamie had gotten the wine flask, I saw; he was passing it back and forth with Farquard Campbell, the two talking intently, occasionally turning to gesture at the mill or back toward the river or the town.

'You got anything I can comb her out with, ma'am?'

Phaedre's question pulled my attention back to the job at hand. She was squatting by the body, fingering the tangled hair critically.

'Wouldn't like to put her in the ground lookin' like this, poor child,' she said, shaking her head.

I thought Phaedre was likely not much older than the dead woman – and in any case, it scarcely mattered that the corpse should go to its grave well-groomed. Still, I groped in my pocket and came up with a small ivory comb, with which Phaedre set to work, humming under her breath.

Mr. Campbell was taking his leave. I heard the creak of his team's harness, and their small stamping of antici-pation as the groom settled himself. Mr. Campbell saw me and bowed deeply, hat held low. I sketched him a curtsy in return, and watched with relief as he drove away.

Phaedre, too, had stopped her work and was gazing after the departing carriage.

She said something under her breath, and spat in the dust. It was done without apparent malice; a charm against evil that I'd seen before. She looked up at me.

'Mister Jamie best find that Pollyanne afore sunset. Be wild animals in the piney wood, and Mister Ulysses say that woman worth two hundred pound when Miss Jocasta buy her. She don't know the woods, that Pollyanne; she be come straight from Africa, no more'n a year agone.'

Without further comment, she bent her head over her task, fingers moving dark and quick as a spider among the fine silk of our corpse's hair.

I bent to my work as well, realizing with something of a shock that the web of circumstance that enmeshed Jamie had touched me, too. I did not stand outside, as I had thought, and could not if I wanted to.

Phaedre had helped me to find Pollyanne not because she trusted or liked me – but because I was the master's wife. Pollyanne must be found and hidden. And Jamie, she thought, would of course find Pollyanne and hide her – she was his property; or Jocasta's, which in Phaedre's eyes would amount to the same thing.

At last, the stranger lay clean, on the worn linen sheet I had brought for a shroud. Phaedre had combed her hair and braided it; I took up the big stone jar of herbs. I had brought them as much from habit as from reason, but now was glad of them; not so much for aid against the progress of decomposition, but as the sole – and necessary – touch of ceremony.

It was difficult to reconcile this clumsy, reeking lump of clay with the small, cold hand that had grasped mine; with the anguished whisper that had breathed 'Tell . . .' in the smothering dark. And yet there was the memory of her, of the last of her living blood spilling hot in my hand, more vivid in my mind than this sight of her empty flesh, naked in the hands of strangers.

There was no minister nearer than Halifax; she would be buried without rites – and yet, what need had she of rites? Funeral rituals are for the comfort of the bereaved. It was unlikely that she had left anyone behind to grieve, I thought; for if she had had anyone so close to her – family, husband, or even lover – I thought she would not now be dead.

I had not known her, would not miss her – but I grieved her; her and her child. And so for myself, rather than for her, I knelt by her body and scattered herbs: fragrant and bitter, leaves of rue and hyssop flowers, rosemary, thyme and lavender. A bouquet from the living to the dead – small token of remembrance.

Phaedre watched in silence, kneeling. Then she reached out and with gentle fingers, laid the shroud across the girl's dead face. Jamie had come to watch. Without a word, he stooped and picked her up, and bore her to the wagon.

He didn't speak until I had climbed up and settled myself on the seat beside him. He snapped the reins on the horses' backs, and clicked his tongue.

'Let us go and find the Sergeant,' he said.

There were, of course, a few things to be attended to first. We returned to River Run to leave Phaedre, and Jamie disappeared to find Duncan and change his stained clothing, while I went to check on my patient and to acquaint Jocasta with the morning's events.

I needn't have troubled on either account; Farquard Campbell was sitting in the morning room sipping tea with Jocasta. John Myers, his loins swathed in a Cameron plaid, was lounging at full length upon the green velvet chaise, cheerfully munching scones. Judging from the unaccustomed cleanliness of the bare legs and feet extending from the tartan, someone had taken advantage of his temporary state of unconsciousness the night before to administer a bath.

'My dear.' Jocasta's head turned at my step, and she smiled, though I saw the twin lines of concern etched between her brows. 'Sit you down, child, and take some nourishment; ye will have had no rest last night – and a dreadful morning, it seems.'

I might ordinarily have found it either amusing or insulting to be called 'child'; under the circumstances, it was oddly comforting. I sank gratefully into an armchair, and let Ulysses pour me a cup of tea, wondering meanwhile just how much Farquard had told Jocasta – and how much he knew.

'How are you this morning?' I asked my patient. He appeared to be in amazingly good condition, considering his alcoholic intake of the night before. His color was good, and so was his appetite, judging from the quantity of crumbs on the plate by his side.

He nodded cordially at me, jaws champing, and swallowed with some effort.

'Astounding fine, ma'am, I thank ye kindly. A mite sore round the privates' – he tenderly patted the area in ques-

288

tion – 'but a sweeter job of stitchin' I've not been privileged to see. Mr. Ulysses was kind enough to fetch me a lookin' glass,' he explained. He shook his head in some awe. 'Never seen my own behind before; as much hair as I got back there, ye'd think my daddy'd bee a bear!'

He laughed heartily at this, and Farquard Campbell buried a smile in his teacup. Ulysses turned away with the tray, but I saw the corner of his mouth twitch.

Jocasta laughed out loud, blind eyes crinkling in amusement.

'They do say it's a wise bairn that kens its father, John Quincy. But I kent your mother weel, and I'll say I think it unlikely.'

Myers shook his head, but his eyes twinkled over the thick growth of beard.

'Well, my mama did admire a hairy man. Said it was a rare comfort on a cold winter's night.' He peered down the open neck of his shirt, viewing the underbrush on display with some satisfaction. 'Might be so, at that. The Indian lassies seem to like it – though it's maybe only the novelty, come to think on it. Their own men scarcely got fuzz on their balls, let alone their backsides.'

Mr. Campbell inhaled a fragment of scone, and coughed heavily into his napkin. I smiled to myself and took a deep swallow of tea. It was a strong and fragrant Indian blend, and despite the oppressive heat of the morning, more than welcome. A light dew of sweat broke out on my face as I drank, but the warmth settled comfortingly into my uneasy stomach, the perfume of the tea driving the stench of blood and excreta from my nose, even as the cheerful conversation banished the morbid scenes of the morning from my mind.

I eyed the hearth rug wistfully. I felt as though I could lie down there peacefully and sleep for a week. No rest for the weary, though.

Jamie came in, freshly shaved and combed, dressed in sober coat and clean linen. He nodded to Farquard Campbell with no apparent surprise; he must have heard his voice from the hallway.

'Auntie.' He bent and kissed Jocasta's cheek in greeting, then smiled at Myers.

'How is it, *a charaid?* Or shall I say, how are they?'

'Right as rain,' Myers assured him. He cupped a hand consideringly between his legs. 'Think I might wait a day or two before I climb back on a horse, though.'

'I would,' Jamie assured him. He turned back to Jocasta. 'Have ye maybe seen Duncan this morning, Auntie?'

'Oh, aye. He's gone a small errand for me, he and the laddie.' She smiled and reached for him; I saw her fingers wrap tight around his wrist. 'Such a dear man, Mr. Innes. So helpful. And such a quick, canny man; a real pleasure to talk to. Do ye not find him so, Nephew?'

Jamie glanced at her curiously, then his gaze flicked to Farquard Campbell. The older man avoided his eye, sipping at his tea as he affected to study the large painting that hung above the mantel.

'Indeed,' Jamie said dryly. 'A useful man, is Duncan. And Young Ian's gone with him?'

'To fetch a bittie package for me,' his aunt said placidly. 'Did ye need Duncan directly?'

'No,' Jamie said slowly, staring down at her. 'It can wait.'

Her fingers slipped free of his sleeve, and she reached for her teacup. The delicate handle was angled precisely toward her, ready for her hand.

'That's good,' she said. 'Ye'll have a bite of breakfast, then? And Farquard – another scone?'

'Ah, no, *Cha ghabh mi 'n còrr, tapa leibh.* I've business in the town, and best I be about it.' Campbell set down his cup and got to his feet, bowing to me and to Jocasta in turn. 'Your servant, ladies. Mr. Fraser,' he added, with a lift of one brow, and bowing, he followed Ulysses out.

Jamie sat down, his own brows raised, and reached for a piece of toast.

'Your errand, Aunt – Duncan's gone to find the slave woman.'

'He has.' Jocasta turned her blind eyes toward him, frowning. 'You'll not mind, Jamie? I ken Duncan's your man, but it seemed an urgent matter; and I couldna be sure when you'd come.'

'What did Campbell tell ye?' I could tell what Jamie was thinking; it seemed out of character for the upright and rigid Mr. Campbell, justice of the district, who would not

290

stir a hand to prevent a gruesome lynching, to conspire for the protection of a female slave, and an abortionist to boot. And yet – perhaps he meant it as compensation for what he had not been able to prevent before.

The handsome shoulders moved in the slightest of shrugs, and a muscle dipped near the corner of her mouth.

'I've kent Farquard Campbell these twenty years, *a mhic mo pheathar.* I hear what he doesna say better than what he does.'

Myers had been following this exchange with interest.

'Couldn't say as my own ears are that good,' he observed mildly. 'All I heard him say was how some poor woman kilt herself by accident, up to the mill, tryin' to rid herself of a burden. He said he didn't know her, himself.' He smiled blandly at me.

'And that alone tells me the lass is a stranger,' Jocasta observed. 'Farquard knows the folk on the river and in the town as well as I ken my own folk. She is no one's daughter, no one's servant.'

She set down her cup and leaned back in her chair with a sigh.

'It will be all right,' she said. 'Eat up your food, lad; ye must be starving.'

Jamie stared at her for a moment, the piece of toast uneaten in his hand. He leaned forward and dropped it back on the plate.

'I canna say I've much appetite just now, Auntie. Dead lassies curdle my wame a bit.' He stood up, brushing down the skirts of his coat.

'She's maybe no one's daughter or servant – but she's lyin' in the yard just now, drawing flies. I'd have a name for her before I bury her.' He turned on his heel and stalked out.

I drained the last of my tea and set the cup back with a faint chime of bone china.

'Sorry,' I said apologetically. 'I don't believe I'm hungry, either.'

Jocasta neither moved nor changed expression. As I left the room I saw Myers lean over from his chaise and neatly snag the last of the scones.

It was nearly noon before we reached the Crown's warehouse at the end of Hay Street. It stood on the north side of the river, with its own pier for loading, a little way above the town itself. There seemed little necessity for a guard at the moment; nothing moved in the vicinity of the building save a few sulphur butterflies who, unaffected by the smothering heat, were diligently laboring among the flowering bushes that grew thick along the shore.

'What do they keep here?' I asked Jamie, looking curiously up at the massive structure. The huge double doors were shut and bolted, the single red-coated sentry motionless as a tin soldier in front of them. A smaller building beside the warehouse sported an English flag, drooping limply in the heat; presumably this was the lair of the sergeant we were seeking.

Jamie shrugged and brushed a questing fly away from his eyebrow. We had been attracting more and more of them as the heat of the day increased, despite the movement of the wagon. I sniffed discreetly, but could smell only a faint hint of thyme.

'Whatever the Crown thinks valuable. Furs from the backcountry, naval stores – pitch and turpentine. But the guard is because of the liquor.'

While every inn brewed its own beer, and every household had its receipts for applejack and cherrywine, the more potent spirits were the province of the Crown: brandy, whisky, and rum were imported to the colony in small quantities under heavy guard, and sold at great cost under the Crown's seal.

'I should say they haven't got much in stock right now,' I said, nodding at the single guard.

'No, the shipments of liquor come upstream from Wilmington once a month, Campbell says they choose a different day each time, so as to run less risk of robbery.'

He spoke abstractedly, a small frown lingering between his eyebrows.

'Did Campbell believe us, do you think? About her doing it herself?' Without really meaning to, I cast a half glance into the wagon behind me.

Jamie made a derisory Scottish noise in the back of his throat.

'Of course not, Sassenach; the man's no a fool. But he's a good friend to my aunt; he'll not make trouble if he doesn't have to. Let's hope the woman had no one who'll make a fuss.'

'Rather a cold-blooded hope,' I said quietly. I thought you felt differently, in your aunt's drawing room. You're probably right, though; if she'd had someone, she wouldn't be dead now.'

He heard the bitterness in my voice, and looked down at me.

I dinna mean to be callous, Sassenach,' he said gently. 'But the poor lassie *is* dead. I canna do more for her than see her decently into the ground; it's the living I must take heed for, aye?'

I heaved a sigh and squeezed his arm briefly. My feelings were a good deal too complex to try to explain; I had known the girl no more than minutes before her death, and could in no way have prevented it – but she had died under my hands, and I felt the physician's futile rage in such circumstances; the feeling that somehow I had failed, had been outwitted by the Dark Angel. And beyond rage and pity, was an echo of unspoken guilt; the girl was near Brianna's age – Brianna's, who in like circumstances would also have no one.

'I know. It's only . . . I suppose I feel responsible for her, in a way.'

'So do I,' he said. 'Never fear, Sassenach; we'll see she's done rightly by.' He reined the horses in under a chestnut tree, and swung down, offering me a hand.

There were no barracks; Campbell had told Jamie that the warehouse guard's ten men were quartered in various houses in the town. Upon inquiry of the clerk laboring in the office, we were directed across the street to the sign of the Golden Goose, wherein the Sergeant might presently be found at his luncheon.

I saw the Sergeant in question at once as I entered the tavern; he was sitting at a table by the window, his white leather stock undone and his tunic unbuttoned, looking thoroughly relaxed over a mug of ale and the remains of a Cornish pasty. Jamie came in behind me, his shadow momentarily blocking the light from the open door, and the Sergeant looked up.

Dim as it was in the taproom, I could see the man's face go blank with shock. Jamie came to an abrupt halt behind me. He said something in Gaelic under his breath that I recognized as a vicious obscenity, but then he was moving forward past me, with no sign of hesitation in his manner.

'Sergeant Murchison,' he said, in tones of mild surprise, as one might greet a casual acquaintance. 'I hadna thought to lay eyes on you again – not in this world, at least.'

The Sergeant's expression strongly suggested that the feeling had been mutual. Also that any meeting this side of heaven was too soon. Blood flooded his beefy, pock-marked cheeks with red, and he shoved back his bench with a screech of wood on the sanded floor.

'You!' he said.

Jamie took off his hat and inclined his head politely.

'Your servant, sir,' he said. I could see his face now, outwardly pleasant, but with a wariness that creased the corners of his eyes. He showed it a good deal less, but the Sergeant wasn't the only one to be taken aback.

Murchison was regaining his self-possession; the look of shock was replaced by a faint sneer.

'Fraser. Oh, beg pardon, *Mr.* Fraser, it will be now, won't it?'

'It will.' Jamie kept his voice neutral, despite the insulting tone of this. Whatever past conflict lay between them, the last thing he wanted now was trouble. Not with what lay in the wagon outside. I wiped my sweaty palms surreptitiously on my skirt.

The Sergeant had begun to do up his tunic buttons, slowly, not taking his eyes off Jamie.

'I had heard there was a man called Fraser, come to leech off Mistress Cameron at River Run,' he said, with an unpleasant twist of thick lips. 'That'll be you, will it?'

The wariness in Jamie's eyes froze into a blue as cold as glacier ice, though his lips stayed curved in a pleasant smile.

'Mistress Cameron will be my kinswoman. It is on her behalf that I have come now.'

294

The Sergeant tilted back his head and scratched voluptuously at his throat. There was a deep, hard-edged red crease across the expanse of fat pale flesh, as though someone had tried unsuccessfully to garrote the man.

'Your kinswoman. Well, easy to say so, ain't it? The lady's blind as a bat, I hear. No husband, no sons; fair prey for any sharpster comes a-calling, claiming family.' The Sergeant lowered his head and smirked at me, his self-possession fully restored.

'And this'll be your doxy, will it?' It was gratuitous malice, a shot at random, the man had scarcely glanced at me.

'This will be my wife, Mistress Fraser.'

I could see the two stiff fingers of Jamie's right hand twitch once against the skirt of his coat, the only outward sign of his feelings. He tilted his head back an inch and raised his brows, considering the Sergeant with an air of dispassionate interest.

'And which one are you, sir? I beg pardon for my imperfect recollection, but I confess that I cannot tell you from your brother.'

The Sergeant stopped as though he had been shot, frozen in the act of fastening his stock.

'Damn you!' he said, choking on the words. His face had gone an unhealthy shade of plum, and I thought that he ought really to mind his blood pressure. I didn't say so, though.

At this point, the Sergeant seemed to notice that everyone in the taproom was staring at him with great interest. He glared ferociously around him, snatched up his hat, and stamped toward the door, pushing past me as he went, so that I staggered back a pace.

Jamie grabbed my arm to steady me, then ducked beneath the lintel himself. I followed, in time to see him call after the Sergeant.

'Murchison!' A word with you!'

The soldier whirled on his heel, hands fisted against the skirts of his scarlet coat. He was a good-sized man, thick through torso and shoulder, and the uniform became him. His eyes glittered with menace, but he had gained possession of himself again.

295

'A word, is it?' he said. 'And what might you have to say to me, *Mister* Fraser?'

'A word in your professional capacity, Sergeant,' Jamie said coolly. He nodded toward the wagon, which we had left beneath a nearby tree. 'We've brought ye a corpse.'

For the second time, the Sergeant's face went blank. He glanced at the wagon; flies and gnats had begun to gather in small clouds, circling lazily over the open bed.

'Indeed.' He *was* a professional; while the hostility of his manner was undiminished, the hot blood faded from his face, and the clenched fists relaxed.

'A corpse? Whose?'

'I have no idea, sir. It was my hope that you might be able to tell us. Will we look?' He nodded toward the wagon, and after a moment's hesitation, the Sergeant nodded briefly back, and strode toward the wagon.

I hurried after Jamie, and was in time to see the Sergeant's face as he drew back the corner of the makeshift shroud. He had no skill at all in hiding his feelings – perhaps in his profession it wasn't necessary. Shock flickered over his face like summer lightning.

Jamie could see the Sergeant's face as well as I.

'Ye'll know her, then?' he said.

'I – she – that is . . . yes, I know her.' The Sergeant's mouth snapped shut abruptly, as though he was afraid to let any more words out. He continued to stare at the girl's dead face, his own tightening, freezing out all feeling.

A few men had followed us out of the tavern. While they stayed at a discreet distance, two or three were craning their necks with curiosity. It wasn't going to be long before the whole district knew what had happened at the mill. I hoped Duncan and Ian were well on their way.

'What has happened to her?' the Sergeant asked, staring down at the fixed white face. His own was nearly as pale.

Jamie was watching him intently, and making no pretense otherwise.

'You'll know her, then?' he said again.

'She is – she was – a laundress. Lissa – Lissa Garver is her name.' The Sergeant spoke mechanically, still looking down into the wagon as though unable to tear his eyes away. His face was expressionless but his lips were white, and his hands were clenched into fists at his sides. 'What happened?'

'Has she people in the town? A husband, maybe?'

It was a reasonable question, but Murchison's head jerked up as though Jamie had stabbed him with it.

'None of your concern, is it?' he said. He stared at Jamie, a thin rim of white visible around the iris of his eye. He bared his teeth in what might have been politeness, but wasn't. 'Tell me what happened to her.'

Jamie's eyes met the Sergeant's without blinking.

'She meant to slip a bairn, and it went wrong,' he said quietly. 'If she has a husband, he must be told. If not – if she has no people – I will see her decently buried.'

Murchison turned his head to look down into the wagon once more.

'She has someone,' he said shortly. 'You need not trouble yourself.' He turned away, and rubbed a hand over his face, scrubbing violently as though to wipe away all feeling. 'Go to my office,' he said, voice half muffled. 'You must make a statement – see the clerk. Go!'

The office was empty, the clerk no doubt gone in search of his own luncheon. I sat down to wait, but Jamie prowled restlessly around the small room, eyes flitting from the regimental banners on the wall to the drawered cabinet in the corner behind the desk.

'Damn the luck,' he said, half to himself. 'It would have to be Murchison.'

'I take it you know the Sergeant well?'

He glanced at me with a wry quirk of the lips.

'Well enough. He was in the garrison at Ardsmuir prison.'

'I see.' No love lost between them, then. It was close in the little office; I blotted a trickle of sweat that ran down between my breasts. 'What do you suppose he's doing here?'

'That much I ken; he was sent in charge of the prisoners when they were transported to be sold. I imagine the Crown saw no good reason to bring him back to England, when there was need of soldiers here – that would have been during the war wi' the French, aye?'

'What was that business about his brother?'

He snorted, a brief, humorless sound.

'There were two o' them – twins. Wee Billy and Wee Bobby, we called them. Alike as peas, and not only in looks.'

He paused, marshaling memories. He didn't often speak of his time in Ardsmuir, and I could see the shadows of it pass across his face.

'Ye'll maybe know the sort of man is decent enough on his own, but get him wi' others like him, and they might as well be wolves?'

'Bit hard on the wolves,' I said, smiling. 'Think of Rollo. But yes, I know what you mean.'

'Pigs, then. But beasts, when they're together. There's no lack of such men in any army; it's why armies work – men will do terrible things in a mob, that they wouldna dream of on their own.'

'And the Murchisons were never on their own?' I asked slowly.

He gave me a slight nod of acknowledgment.

'Aye, that's it. There were the two of them, always. And what one might scruple at, the other would not. And of course, when it came to trouble – why, there was no saying which was to blame, was there?'

He was still prowling, restless as a caged panther. He paused by the window, looking out.

'I – the prisoners – we might complain of ill-treatment, but the officers couldna discipline both for the sins of one, and a man seldom knew which Murchison it was that had him on the ground wi' a boot in the ribs, or which it was that hung him from a hook by his fetters and left him so until he'd soil himself for the amusement of the garrison.'

His eyes were fixed on something outside, his expression unguarded. He'd spoken of beasts; I could see that the memories had roused one. His eyes caught the light from the window, gem-blue and unblinking.

'Are both of them here?' I asked, as much to break that unnerving stare as because I wanted to know.

It worked; he turned abruptly from the window.

298

No,' he said, shortly. 'This is Billy. Wee Bobby died at Ardsmuir.' His two stiff fingers twitched against the fabric of his kilt.

It had occurred to me briefly to wonder why he had worn his kilt this morning, instead of changing to breeks; the crimson tartan might be quite literally a red flag to a bull, flaunted thus before an English soldier. Now I knew.

They'd taken it from him once before, thinking to take with it pride and manhood. They had failed in that attempt, and he meant to underscore that failure, whether it was sense to do so or not. Sense had little to do with the sort of stubborn pride that could survive years of such insult – and while he had more than his share of both, I could see that pride was well in the ascendancy at present.

'From the Sergeant's reactions, I suppose we may assume it wasn't natural causes?' I asked.

'No,' he said. He sighed and shrugged his shoulders slightly, easing them inside the tight coat.

'They marched us out to the stone quarry each morning, and back again at twilight, wi' two or three guards to each wagon. One day, Wee Bobby Murchison was the sergeant in charge. He came out wi' us in the morning – but he didna come back with us at night.' He glanced once more at the window. 'There was a verra deep pool at the bottom of the quarry.'

His matter-of-fact tone was nearly as chilling as the content of this bald account. I felt a small shiver pass up my spine, in spite of the stifling heat.

'Did you –' I began, but he put a finger to his lips, jerking his head toward the door. A moment later, I heard the footsteps that his keener ears had picked up.

It was the Sergeant, not his clerk. He had been perspiring heavily; streaks of sweat ran down his face beneath his wig, and his whole countenance was the unhealthy color of fresh beef liver.

He glanced at the vacant desk, and made a small, vicious noise in his throat. I felt a qualm on behalf of the absent clerk. The Sergeant shoved aside the clutter on the desk with a sweep of his arm that sent paper cascading onto the floor.

He snatched a pewter inkwell and a sheet of foolscap from the rubble, and banged them down on the desk.

'Write it down,' he ordered. 'Where you found her, what happened.' He thrust a spattered goose-quill at Jamie. 'Sign it, date it.'

Jamie stared at him, eyes narrowed, but made no move to take the quill. I felt a sudden sinking in my belly.

Jamie was left-handed but had been taught forcibly to write with his right hand, and then had that right hand crippled. Writing, for him, was a slow, laborious business that left the pages blotted, sweat-stained, and crumpled, and the writer himself in no better case. There was no power on earth that would make him humiliate himself in that fashion before the Sergeant.

'Write. It. Down.' The Sergeant bit off the words between his teeth.

Jamie's eyes narrowed further, but before he could speak, I reached out and snatched the pen from the Sergeant's grasp.

'I was there; let me do it.'

Jamie's hand closed on mine before I could dip the quill in the inkwell. He plucked the pen from my fingers and dropped it in the center of the desk.

'Your clerk can wait upon me later, at my aunt's house,' he said briefly to Murchison. 'Come with me, Claire.'

Not waiting for an answer from the Sergeant, he grasped my elbow and all but pulled me to my feet. We were outside before I knew what had happened. The wagon still stood under the tree, but now it was empty.

'Well, she's safe for the moment, *Mac Dubh*, but what in hell shall we do with the woman?' Duncan scratched at the stubble on his chin; he and Ian had spent three days in the forest, searching, before finding the slave Pollyanne.

'She'll no be easy to move,' Ian put in, snaring a piece of bacon off the breakfast table. He broke it in half, and handed one piece to Rollo. 'The poor lady near died of terror when Rollo sniffed her out, and we had God's own time gettin' her on her feet. We couldna get her on a horse at all; I had to walk with my arm around her, to keep her from fallin' down.'

300

'We must get her clear away, somehow.' Jocasta frowned, blank eyes half hooded in thought. 'Yon Murchison was at the mill again yesterday morning, making a nuisance of himself, and last night, Farquard Campbell sent to tell me that the man has declared it was murder, and he's called for men to search the district for the slave who did it. Farquard's sae hot under his collar, I thought his head would burst into flame.'

'Do ye think she *could* have done it?' Chewing, Ian looked from Jamie to me. 'By accident, I mean?'

In spite of the hot morning, I shuddered, feeling in memory the unyielding stiffness of the metal skewer in my hand.

'You have three possibilities: accident, murder, or suicide,' I said. 'There are *lots* easier ways of committing suicide, believe me. And no motive for murder, that we know of.'

'Be that as it may,' Jamie said, neatly fielding the conversation, 'if Murchison takes the slave woman, he'll have her hanged or flogged to death within a day. He's no need of trial. No, we must take her clear out of the district. I've arranged *what* with our friend Myers.'

'You've arranged *what* with Myers?' Jocasta asked sharply, her voice cutting through the babble of exclamations and questions that greeted this announcement.

Jamie finished buttering the piece of toast that he held, and handed it to Duncan before speaking.

'We shall take the woman into the mountains,' he said. 'Myers says she'll be welcome among the Indians; he kens a good place for her, he says. And she'll be safe there from Wee Billy Murchison.'

'*We?*' I asked politely. 'And who's *we?*'

He grinned at me in reply.

'Myers and myself, Sassenach. I need to go to the backcountry to have a look before the cold weather comes, and this will be a good chance. Myers is the best guide I could have.'

He carefully refrained from noting that it might be as well for *him* to be temporarily out of Sergeant Murchison's sphere of influence, but the implication was not lost on me.

'Ye'll take me, will ye not, Uncle?' Ian brushed the matted hair out of his face, looking eager. 'Ye'll need help wi' that woman, believe me – she's the size of a molasses barrel.'

Jamie smiled at his nephew.

'Aye, Ian. I expect we can use another man along.'

'Ahem,' I said, giving him an evil stare.

'To keep an eye on your auntie, if nothing else,' Jamie continued, giving the stare back to me. 'We leave in three days, Sassenach – if Myers can sit a horse by then.'

Three days didn't allow much time, but with the assistance of Myers and Phaedre, my preparations were completed with hours to spare. I had a small traveling box of medicines and tools, and the saddlebags were packed with food, blankets, and cooking implements. The only small matter remaining was that of attire.

I recrossed the ends of the long silk strip across my chest, tied the ends in a jaunty knot between my breasts, and examined the results in the looking glass.

Not bad. I extended my arms and jiggled my torso from side to side, testing. Yes, that would do. Though perhaps if I took one more turn around my chest before crossing the ends . . .

'What, exactly, are ye doing, Sassenach? And what in the name of God are ye wearing?' Jamie, arms crossed, was leaning against the door, watching me with both brows raised.

'I am improvising a brassiere,' I said with dignity. 'I don't mean to ride sidesaddle through the mountains wearing a dress, and if I'm not wearing stays, I don't mean my breasts to be joggling all the way, either. Most uncomfortable, joggling.'

'I daresay.' He edged into the room and circled me at a cautious distance, eyeing my nether limbs with interest. 'And what are *those*?'

'Like them?' I put my hands on my hips, modeling the drawstring leather trousers that Phaedre had constructed for me – laughing hysterically as she did so – from soft buckskin provided by one of Myers's friends in Cross Creek.

'No,' he said bluntly. 'Ye canna be going about in – in –' He waved at them, speechless.

'Trousers,' I said. 'And of course I can. I wore trousers all the time, back in Boston. They're very practical.'

He looked at me in silence for a moment. Then, very slowly, he walked around me. At last, his voice came from behind me.

'Ye wore them outside?' he said, in tones of incredulity. 'Where folk could see ye?'

'I did,' I said crossly. 'So did most other women. Why not?'

'Why *not?*' he said, scandalized. 'I can see the whole shape of your buttocks, for God's sake, and the cleft between!'

'I can see yours, too,' I pointed out, turning around to face him. 'I've been looking at your backside in breeks every day for months, but only occasionally does the sight move me to make indecent advances on your person.'

His mouth twitched, undecided whether to laugh or not. Taking advantage of the indecision, I took a step forward and put my arms around his waist, firmly cupping his backside.

'Actually, it's your kilt that makes me want to fling you to the floor and commit ravishment,' I told him. 'But you don't look at all bad in your breeks.'

He did laugh then, and bending, kissed me thoroughly, his hands carefully exploring the outlines of my rear, snugly confined in buckskin. He squeezed gently, making me squirm against him.

'Take them off,' he said, pausing for air.

'But I –'

'Take them off,' he repeated firmly. He stepped back and tugged loose the lacing of his flies. 'Ye can put them back on again after, Sassenach, but if there's flinging and ravishing to be done, it'll be me that does it, aye?'

PART FIVE

Strawberry Fields Forever

14

Flee From Wrath to Come

August 1767

They had hidden the woman in a tobacco shed on the edge of Farquard Campbell's furthest fields. There was little chance of anyone noticing – other than Campbell's slaves, who already knew – but we took care to arrive just after dark, when the lavender sky had faded nearly to gray, barely outlining the dark bulk of the drying shed.

The woman slid out like a ghost, cloaked and hooded, and was hoisted onto the extra horse, bundled hastily aboard like the package of contraband she was. She drew up her legs and clung to the saddle with both hands doubled up in a ball of panic; evidently she'd never been on a horse before.

Myers tried to hand her the reins, but she paid no attention, only clung tight and moaned in a sort of melodic agony of terror. The men were becoming restive, glancing over their shoulders into the empty fields, as though expecting the imminent arrival of Sergeant Murchison and his minions.

'Let her ride with me,' I suggested. 'Maybe she'll feel safer that way.'

The woman was detached from her mount with some difficulty and set down on the horse's rump behind my saddle. She smelt strongly of fresh tobacco leaves, pungently narcotic, and something else, a little muskier. She at once flung her arms around my waist, holding on for dear life. I patted one of the hands clutched about my middle, and she squeezed tighter, but made no other move or sound.

Little wonder if she was terrified, I thought, turning my horse's head to follow Myers's. She might not know about the hullabaloo Murchison was raising in the district, but she could have no illusions about what might happen if she was caught; she had certainly been among the crowd at the sawmill two weeks earlier.

As an alternative to certain death, flight into the arms of red savages might be slightly preferable, but not by much, to judge from her trembling; the weather was far from cold, but she shook as though with chill.

She nearly squeezed the stuffings out of me when Rollo appeared, stalking out of the bushes like some demon of the forest. My horse didn't like the look of him, either, and backed up, snorting and stamping, trying to jerk the reins away from me.

I had to admit that Rollo was reasonably fearsome, even when he was in an amiable mood, which he was, at the moment – Rollo loved expeditions. Still, he undoubtedly presented a sinister aspect; all his teeth were showing in a grin of delight, his slitted eyes half closed as he whiffed the air. Add to that the way the grays and blacks of his coat faded into the shadows, and one was left with the queer and unsettling illusion that he had materialized out of the substance of the night. Appetite incarnate.

He trotted directly past us, no more than a foot away, and the woman gasped, her breath hot on my neck. I patted her hand again, and spoke to her, but she made no answer. Duncan had said she was Africa-born and spoke little English, but surely she must understand a few words.

'It will be all right,' I said again. 'Don't be afraid.'

Occupied with horse and passenger, I hadn't noticed Jamie, until he appeared suddenly by my stirrup, light-footed as Rollo.

'All right, Sassenach?' he asked softly, putting a hand on my thigh

'I think so,' I said. I nodded at the death-grip round my middle. 'If I don't die of suffocation.'

He looked, and smiled.

'Well, she's in no danger of fallin' off, at least.'

'I wish I knew something to say to her; poor thing, she's so afraid. Do you suppose she even knows where we're taking her?'

'I shouldna think so – *I* dinna ken where we're going.' He wore breeks for riding, but had his plaid belted over them, the free end slung across the shoulder of his coat.

308

The dark tartan blended into the shadows of the forest as well as it had the shades of the Scottish heather; all I could see of him was a white blotch of shirt-front and the pale oval of his face.

'Do you know any useful *taki-taki* to say to her?' I asked. 'Of course, she might not know that, either, if she wasn't brought through the Indies.'

He turned his head and looked up at my passenger, considering.

'Ah,' he said. 'Well, there's the one thing they'll all know, no matter where they've come.' He reached out and squeezed the woman's foot firmly.

'Freedom,' he said, and paused. '*Saorsa.* D'ye ken what I say?'

She didn't loosen her grip, but her breath went out in a shuddering sigh, and I thought I felt her nod.

The horses followed each other in single file, Myers in the lead. The rough track was not even a wagon trail, only a sort of flattening of undergrowth, but it did at least provide clear passage through the trees.

I doubted that Sergeant Murchison's vengeance would pursue us so far – if he pursued us at all – but the sense of escape was too strong to ignore. We shared an unspoken but pervasive sense of urgency, and with no particular discussion, agreed to ride on as far as possible.

My passenger was either losing her fear or simply becoming too tired to care anymore; after a midnight stop for refreshment she allowed Ian and Myers to boost her back on the horse without protest, and while she never released her hold on my waist, she did seem to doze now and then, her forehead pressed against my shoulder.

The fatigue of long riding crept over me, too, aided by the hypnotic soft thudding of the horses' feet, and the unending susurrus of the pines overhead. We were still in the longleaf forest, and the tall, straight trunks surrounded us like the masts of long-sunk ships.

Lines of an ancient Scottish song drifted through my mind – '*How many strawberries grow in the salt sea; how many ships sail in the forest?*' – and I wondered muzzily whether the composer had walked through a place like this, unearthly in half-moon and starlight, so dreamlike that the borders between the elements were lost; we might as well be afloat as earthbound, the heave and fall beneath me the rise of planking, and the sound of the pines the wind in our sails.

We stopped at dawn, unsaddled the horses, hobbled them, and left them to feed in the long grass of a small meadow. I found Jamie, and curled up at once into a nest of grass beside him, the horses' peaceful champing the last thing I heard.

We slept heavily through the heat of the day, and awoke near sunset, stiff, thirsty, and covered with ticks. I was profoundly thankful that the ticks seemed to share the mosquitoes' general distaste for my flesh, but I had learned on our trip north to check Jamie and the others every time we slept; there were always outriders.

'Ick,' I said, examining a particularly juicy specimen, the size of a grape, nestling amid the soft cinnamon hair of Jamie's underarm. 'Damn, I'm afraid to pull that one; it's so full it'll likely burst.'

He shrugged, busy exploring his scalp with the other hand, in search of further intruders.

'Leave it while ye deal with the rest,' he suggested. 'Perhaps it will fall off of its own accord.'

'I suppose I'd better,' I agreed reluctantly. I hadn't any objection to the tick's bursting, but not while its jaws were still embedded in Jamie's flesh. I'd seen infections caused by forcibly interrupted ticks, and they weren't anything I wanted to deal with in the middle of a forest. I had only a rudimentary medical kit with me – though this luckily included a very fine pair of small tweezer-pointed forceps from Dr. Rawlings's box.

Myers and Ian seemed to be managing all right; both stripped to the waist, Myers was crouched over the boy like a huge black baboon, fingers busy in Ian's hair.

'Here's a wee one,' Jamie said, bending over and pushing his own hair aside so I could reach the small dark bleb behind his ear. I was engaged in gently maneuvering the creature out, when I became aware of a presence near my elbow.

I had been too tired to take much notice of our fugitive

310

when we made camp, rightly assuming that she wasn't going to wander off into the wilderness by herself. She had wandered as far as a nearby stream, though, returning with a bucket of water.

She set this on the ground, dipped up a handful of water and funneled it into her mouth. She chewed vigorously for a moment, cheeks puffed out. Then she motioned me aside and, lifting a surprised Jamie's arm, spat forcefully and profusely into his armpit.

She reached into the dripping hollow, and with delicate fingers appeared to tickle the parasite. She certainly tickled Jamie, who was very sensitive in that particular region. He turned pink in the face and flinched at her touch, all the muscles in his torso quivering.

She held tight to his wrist, though, and within seconds, the bulging tick dropped off into the palm of her hand. She flicked it disdainfully away, and turned to me, with a small air of satisfaction.

I had thought she resembled a ball, muffled in her cloak. Seen without it, she still did. She was very short, no more than four feet, and nearly as wide, with a close-cropped head like a cannonball, her cheeks so round that her eyes were slanted above them.

She looked like nothing so much as one of the carved African fertility images I had seen in the Indies; massive of bosom, heavy of haunch, and the rich, burnt-coffee color of a Congolese, with skin so flawless that it looked like polished stone under its thin layer of sweat. She held out her hand to me, showing me a few small objects in her palm, the general size and shape of dried lima beans.

'Paw-paw,' she said, in a voice so deep that even Myers turned his head toward her, startled. It was a huge, rich voice, reverberant as a drum. Seeing my reaction to it, she smiled a little shyly, and said something I didn't quite understand, though I knew it was Gaelic.

'She says ye must not swallow the seeds, for they're poison,' Jamie translated, eyeing her rather warily as he wiped his armpit with the end of his plaid.

'Hau,' Pollyanne agreed, nodding vigorously. 'Poi-zin.' She stooped over the bucket for another handful of water, washed it round her mouth, and spat it at a rock with a noise like a gunshot.

'You could be dangerous with that,' I told her. I didn't know whether she understood me, but she gathered from my smile that I meant to be cordial; she smiled back, popped two more of the paw-paw seeds into her mouth, and beckoned to Myers, already chewing, the seeds making little crunching pops as she pulverized them between her teeth.

By the time we had eaten supper and were ready to leave, she was nervously willing to try riding alone. Jamie coaxed her to the horse, and showed her how to let the beast smell her. She trembled as the big nose nudged her, but then the horse snorted; she jumped, giggled in a voice like honey poured out of a jug, and allowed Jamie and Ian between them to boost her aboard.

Pollyanne remained shy of the men, but she soon gained enough confidence to talk to me, in a polyglot mixture of Gaelic, English, and her own language. I couldn't have translated it, but both her face and body were so expressive that I could often gather the sense of what she was saying, even though I understood only one word in ten. I could only regret that I was not equally fluent in body language; she didn't understand most of my questions and remarks, so I had to wait until we made camp, when I could prevail on Jamie or Ian to help me with bits of Gaelic.

Freed – at least temporarily – from the constraint of terror, and becoming cautiously secure in our company, a naturally effervescent personality emerged, and she talked with abandon as we rode side by side, regardless of my comprehension, laughing now and then with a low hooting noise like wind blowing across the mouth of a cave.

She became subdued only once: when we passed through a large clearing where the grass rose in strange undulant mounds, as though a great serpent lay buried underneath. Pollyanne went silent when she saw them, and in an effort to hurry her horse, instead succeeded only in pulling on the reins and stopping it dead. I rode back to help her.

312

'*Droch àite*,' she murmured, glancing out of the corner of her eye at the silent mounds. A bad place. '*Djudju*.' She scowled, and made a small, quick gesture with her hand, some sign against evil, I thought.

'Is it a graveyard?' I asked Myers, who had circled back to see why we had stopped. The mounds were not evenly spaced, but were distributed around the edge of the clearing in a pattern that didn't look like any natural formation. The mounds seemed too large to be graves, though – unless they were cairns, such as the ancient Scots built, or mass graves, I thought, uneasy at the memory of Culloden.

'Not to say graveyard,' he replied, pushing his hat back on his head. ''Twas a village once. Tuscarora, I expect. Those rises there' – he waved a hand – 'those are houses, fallen down. The big 'un to the side, that will have been the chief's longhouse. It be taken no time atall, the grasses come over it. From the looks, though, this 'un will have been buried a time back.'

'What happened to it?' Ian and Jamie had stopped, too, and come back to look over the small clearing.

Myers scratched thoughtfully at his beard.

'I couldn't be sayin', not for certain sure. Might be as sickness drove 'em out, might be as they were put to rout by the Cherokee or the Creek, though we be a mite north of the Cherokee land. Most likely as it happened during the war, though.' He dug fiercely into his beard, twisted, and flicked away the remnants of a lingering tick. 'Can't say as it's a place I'd tarry by choice.'

Pollyanne being plainly of the same mind, we rode on. By evening, we had passed entirely out of the pines and scrubby oakland of the foothills. We were climbing in good earnest now, and the trees began to change; small groves of chestnut trees, large patches of oak and hickory, with scattered dogwood and persimmon, chinkapin and poplar, surrounded us in waves of feathery green.

The smell and feel of the air changed, too, as we rose. The overwhelming hot resins of the pine trees gave way to lighter, more varied scents, tree leaves mingled with whiffs of the shrubs and flowers that grew from every crevice of the craggy rocks. It was still damp and humid, but not so

313

hot; the air no longer seemed a smothering blanket, but something we might breathe – and breathe with pleasure, filled as it was with the perfumes of leaf mold, sun-warmed leaves, and damp moss.

By sunset of the sixth day, we were well into the mountains, and the air was full of the sound of running water. Streams crisscrossed the valleys, spilling off ridges and trickling down the steep rock faces, trailing mist and moss like a delicate green fringe. When we rounded the side of one steep hill, I stopped in amazement; from the side of a distant mountain, a waterfall leapt into the air, arching a good eighty feet in its fall to the gorge far below.

'Will ye look at that, now?' Ian was openmouthed with awe.

''Tis right pretty,' Myers allowed, with the smug complacence of a proprietor. 'Ain't the biggest falls I've seen, but it's nice enough.'

Ian turned his head, eyes wide.

'There are bigger ones?'

Myers laughed, a mountain man's quiet laugh, no more than a breath of sound.

'Boy, you ain't seen nothin' yet.'

We camped for the night in a hollow near a good-sized creek – one big enough for trout. Jamie and Ian waded into this with enthusiasm, harrying the finny denizens with whippy rods cut from black willow. I hoped they would have some luck; our fresh provisions were running low, though we still had plenty of cornmeal left.

Pollyanne came scrambling up the bank, bringing a bucket of water with which to make a new batch of corn dodgers. These were small oblongs of rough cornmeal biscuit made for traveling; tasty when fresh and hot, and at least edible the next day. They became steadily less appetizing with time, resembling nothing so much as small chunks of cement by the fourth day. Still, they were portable, and not prone to mold, and thus were popular traveling fare, along with dried beef and salt pork.

Pollyanne's natural ebullience seemed a trifle subdued, her round face shadowed. Her eyebrows were so sketchy as to be almost nonexistent, which had the paradoxical effect of increasing the expressiveness of her face in

314

motion, and wiping all expression from it in repose. She could be as impassive as a ball bearing when she wanted to; a useful skill for a slave.

I supposed that her preoccupation was at least in part because this was the last night on which we would all be together. We had reached the backcountry, the limits of the King's land; tomorrow, Myers would turn to the north, taking her across the spine of the mountains into the Indian lands, to find what safety and what life she might there.

Her round dark head was bent over the wooden bowl, stubby fingers mixing cornmeal with water and lard. I crouched across from her, feeding small sticks to the infant fire, the black iron girdle standing ready-greased beside it. Myers had gone off to smoke a pipe; I could hear Jamie call to Ian somewhere downstream, and a faint answering laugh.

It was deep twilight by now; our hollow was ringed by brooding mountains, and darkness seemed to fill the shallow bowl, creeping up the trunks of the trees around us. I had no notion of the place she had come from, whether it might be forest or jungle, seashore or desert, but I thought it unlikely to be much like this.

What could she be thinking? She had survived the journey from Africa, and slavery; I supposed whatever lay ahead couldn't be much worse. It was an unknown future, though – going into a wilderness so vast and absolute that I felt every moment as though I might vanish into it, consumed without a trace. Our fire seemed the merest spark against the vastness of the night.

Rollo strolled into the light of the fire and shook himself, spraying water in all directions, making the fire hiss and spit. He had joined in the fishing, I saw.

'Go away, horrible dog,' I said. He didn't, of course; simply came up and nosed me rudely, to be sure I was still who he thought I was, then turned to give Pollyanne the same treatment.

With no particular expression, she turned her head and spat in his eye. He yelped, backed up, and stood shaking his head, looking thoroughly surprised. She looked up at me and grinned, her teeth very white in her face.

315

I laughed, and decided not to worry too much; anyone capable of spitting in a wolf's eye would likely cope with Indians, wilderness, and anything else that came along.

The bowl was nearly empty, a neat row of corn dodgers laid on the girdle. Pollyanne wiped her fingers on a handful of grass, watching the yellow cornmeal begin to sizzle and turn brown as the lard melted. A warm, comforting smell rose from the fire, mingled with the scent of burning wood, and my belly rumbled softly in anticipation. The fire seemed more substantial now, the scent of cooking food spreading its warmth in a wider circle, keeping the night at bay.

Had it been this way where she came from? Had fires and food held back a jungle darkness, kept away leopards instead of bears? Had light and company given comfort, and the illusion of safety? For illusion it had surely been – fire was no protection against men, or the darkness that had overtaken her. I had no words to ask.

'I have never seen such fishing, never,' Jamie repeated for the fourth time, a look of dreamy bliss on his face as he broke open a steaming trout fried in cornmeal. 'They were *swarming* in the water, were they not, Ian?'

Ian nodded, a similar look of reverence on his own homely features.

'My da would give his other leg to ha' seen it,' he said. 'They jumped on the hook, Auntie, truly!'

'The Indians don't generally bother with hook and line,' Myers put in, neatly spearing his own share of fish with his knife. 'They build snares and fish traps, or sometimes they'll put some sticks and rubbish crost the creek to prevent the fish, then stand above with a sharp stick, just spearin' them from the water.'

That was enough for Ian; any mention of Indians and their ways provoked a rash of eager questions. Having exhausted the methods of fish-catching, he asked again about the abandoned village we had seen earlier in our journey.

'Ye said it might have happened in the war,' Ian said, lifting the bones from a steaming trout, then shaking his fingers to cool them. He passed a section of the boneless flesh to Rollo, who swallowed it in a single gulp, temperature notwithstanding. 'Will that ha' been the war wi' the French, then? I didna ken there was any fighting so far south.'

Myers shook his head, chewing and swallowing before he answered.

'Oh, no. It'll be the Tuscarora War I was meanin'; that's how they call it on the white side, at least.'

The Tuscarora War, he explained, had been a short-lived but brutal conflict some forty years before, brought on by an attack upon some backcountry settlers. The then governor of the colony had sent troops into the Tuscarora villages in retaliation, and the upshot was a series of pitched battles that the colonists, much better armed, had won handily – to the devastation of the Tuscarora nation.

Myers nodded toward the darkness.

'Ain't no more than seven villages o' the Tuscarora left, now – and not above fifty or a hundred souls in any but the biggest one.' So sadly diminished, the Tuscarora would quickly have fallen prey to surrounding tribes and disappeared altogether, had they not been formally adopted by the Mohawk, and thus become part of the powerful Iroquois League.

Jamie came back to the fire with a bottle from his saddlebag. It was Scotch whisky, a parting present from Jocasta. He poured out a small cupful, then offered the half-full bottle to Myers.

'Is the Mohawk country not a verra great distance to the north?' he asked. 'How can they offer protection to their fellows here, and they with hostile tribes all round?'

Myers took a gulp of whisky and washed it pleasurably around his mouth before answering.

'Mmm. That's fine stuff, friend James. Oh, the Mohawk are a good ways off, aye. But the Nations of the Iroquois are a name to reckon with – and of all the Six Nations, the Mohawk are the fiercest. Ain't no one – red *or* white – goin' to mess with the Mohawk 'thout good cause, nossir.'

I was fascinated by this. I was also pleased to hear that the Mohawk territory was a good long way away from us.

'Why did the Mohawk want to adopt the Tuscarora,

317

then?' Jamie asked, lifting one brow. 'It doesna seem they'd be needing allies, and they so fierce as ye say.'

Myers's hazel eyes had gone to dreamy half-slits under the influence of good whisky.

'Oh, they're fierce, all right – but they're mortal,' he said, 'Indians are men o' blood, and none more than the Mohawk. They're men of honor, mind' – he raised a thick finger in admonition – 'but there's a sight of things they'll kill for, some reasonable, some not. They raid, d'ye see, amongst themselves, and they'll kill for revenge – ain't nothin' will stop a Mohawk bent on revenge, save you kill him. And even then, his brother or his son or his nephew will come after you.'

He licked his lips in slow meditation, savoring the slick of whisky on his skin.

'Sometimes Indians don't kill for any reason a man would say mattered; specially when liquor's involved.'

'Sounds very much like the Scots,' I murmured to Jamie, who gave me a cold look in return.

Myers picked up the whisky bottle and rolled it slowly between his palms.

'Any man might take a drop too much and be the worse in his actions for it, but with the Indians, the first drop's too much. I've heard of more than one massacre that might not have been, save for the men bein' mad with drink.'

He shook his head, recalling himself to his subject.

'Be so as it may, it's a hard life, and a bloody one. Some tribes are wiped out altogether, and none have men to spare. So they adopt folk into the tribe, to replace those as are killed or die of sickness. They take prisoners, sometimes – take 'em into a family, treat 'em as their own. That's what they'll do with Mrs. Polly, there.' He nodded at Pollyanne, who sat quietly by the fire, paying no attention to his speech.

'So happen back fifty years, the Mohawk took and adopted the whole tribe of the Tuscarora. Don't many tribes speak exactly the same language,' Myers explained. 'But some are closer than others. Tuscarora's more like the Mohawk than 'tis like the Creek or the Cherokee.'

'Can ye speak Mohawk yourself, Mr. Myers?' Ian's ears

318

had been flapping all through the explanation. Fascinated by every rock, tree, and bird on our journey, Ian was still more fascinated by any mention of Indians.

'Oh, a good bit.' Myers shrugged modestly. 'Any trader picks up a few words here and there. Shoo, dawg.' Rollo, who had inched his nose within sniffing distance of Myers's last trout, twitched his ears at the admonition but didn't withdraw the nose.

'Will it be the Tuscarora ye mean to take Mistress Polly to?' Jamie asked, crumbling a corn dodger into edible chunks.

Myers nodded, chewing carefully; with as few natural teeth as he had left, even fresh corn dodgers were a hazardous undertaking.

'Aye. Be four, five days' ride still,' he explained. He turned to me and gave me a reassuring smile. 'I'll see her settled fine, Mrs. Claire, you'll not be worried for her.'

'What will the Indians think of her, I wonder?' Ian asked. He glanced at Pollyanne, interested. 'Will they have seen a black woman before?'

Myers laughed at that.

'Lad, there's a many of the Tuscarora ain't seen a *white* person before. Mrs. Polly won't come as any more a shock than your auntie might.' Myers took a vast swig of water and swished it around his mouth, eyeing Pollyanne thoughtfully. She felt his eyes on her, and returned his stare, unblinking.

'I should say they'd find her handsome, though; they do like a woman as is sweetly plump.' It was moderately obvious that Myers shared this admiration; his eyes drifted over Pollyanne with an appreciation touched with innocent lasciviousness.

She saw it, and an extraordinary change came over her. She seemed scarcely to move, and yet all at once, her whole person was focused on Myers. No white showed around her eyes; they were black and fathomless, shining in the firelight. She was still short and heavy, but with only the slightest change of posture, depth of bosom and width of hip were emphasized, suddenly curved in a promise of lewd abundance.

Myers swallowed, audibly.

I glanced away from this little byplay to see Jamie watching, too, with an expression somewhere between amusement and concern. I poked him unobtrusively, and squinted hard, in an expression that said as explicitly as I could manage – 'Do something!'

He narrowed one eye.

I widened both mine and gave him a good stare, which translated to, 'I don't know, but do something!'

'Mmphm.'

Jamie cleared his throat, leaned forward, and laid a hand on Myers's arm, jarring the mountain man out of his momentary trance.

'I shouldna like to think the woman will be misused in any way,' he said, politely, but with an edge of Scottish innuendo on 'misused' that implied the possibility of unlimited impropriety. He squeezed a little. 'Will ye undertake to guarantee her safety, Mr. Myers?'

Myers shot him a look of incomprehension, which slowly cleared, cognizance coming into the bloodshot hazel eyes. The mountain man slowly pulled his arm free, then picked up his cup, gulped the last mouthful of whisky, coughed and wiped his mouth. He might have been blushing, but it was impossible to tell behind the beard.

'Oh, yes. That is, I mean to say, oh, no. No, indeed. The Mohawk and the Tuscarora both, their women choose who they bed with, even who they marry. No such thing as rape among 'em. Oh, no. No, sir; she won't be misused, I can promise that.'

'Well, and I'm glad to hear it.' Jamie sat back, at ease, and gave me an I-trust-you're-satisfied glare out of the corner of his eye. I smiled demurely.

Ian might be not quite sixteen, but he was far too observant to have missed all these exchanges. He coughed, in a meaningful Scottish manner.

'Uncle, Mr. Myers has been kind enough to invite me to go with him and Mrs. Polly, to see the Indian village. I shall be sure to see that she finds good treatment there.'

'You –' Jamie started, then broke off. He gave his

nephew a long, hard look across the fire. I could see the thoughts racing through his mind.

Ian hadn't asked permission to go; he'd announced he was going. If Jamie forbade him, he must give grounds – and he could scarcely say that it was too dangerous, as this would mean admitting both that he was willing to send the slave woman into danger and that he didn't trust Myers and his relations with the local Indians. Jamie was trapped, and very neatly too.

He breathed in strongly through his nose. Ian grinned.

I looked back across the fire. Pollyanne was still sitting as she had been, not moving. Her eyes were still fixed on Myers, but a slight smile curved her lips in invitation. One hand rose slowly, cupping a massive breast, almost absently.

Myers was staring back, dazed as a deer with a hunter's light in its eyes.

And would I do differently? I thought later, listening to the discreet rustling noises and small groans from the direction of Myers's blankets. If I knew that my life depended on a man? Would I not do anything I could to ensure he would protect me, in the face of unknown danger?

There was a snapping and crackling in the bushes, not far away. It was loud, and I stiffened. So did Jamie. He slid his hand out from under my shirt, reaching for his dirk, then relaxing, as the reassuring scent of skunk reached our nostrils.

He put his hand back under my shirt, squeezed my breast and fell back asleep, his breath warm on my neck.

No great difference at all, perhaps. Was my future any more certain than hers? And did I not depend for my life upon a man bound to me – at least in part – by desire of my body?

A faint wind breathed through the trees, and I hitched the blanket higher on my shoulder. The fire had burned to embers, and so high in the mountains, it was cool at night. The moon had set, but it was very clear; the stars blazed close, a net of light cast over the mountains' peaks.

No, there were differences. However unknown my future, it would be shared, and the bond between my man and me went much deeper than the flesh. Beyond all this was the one great difference, though – I had chosen to be there.

15

Noble Savages

We took our leave of the others in the morning, Jamie and Myers taking pains over the arrangement for a rendezvous in ten days time. Looking around me at the bewildering immensity of forest and mountain, I couldn't imagine how anyone could be sure of finding a specific place again; I could only trust in Jamie's sense of navigation.

They turned to the north, we to the southwest, making our way along the course of the stream we had camped by. It seemed very quiet at first, and strangely lonely, with only the two of us. Within a short time, though, I had grown accustomed to the solitude and began to relax, taking a keen interest in our surroundings. This might, after all, be our home.

The thought was a rather daunting one; it was a place of amazing beauty and richness, but so wild, it hardly seemed that people could live in it. I didn't voice this thought, however; only followed Jamie's horse as he led us deeper and deeper into the mountains, stopping finally in the late afternoon to make a small camp and catch fish for dinner.

The light faded slowly, retreating through the trees. The thick mossy trunks grew dense with shadow, edges still rimmed with a fugitive light that hid among the leaves, green shadows shifting with the sunset breeze.

A tiny glow lit suddenly in the grass a few feet away, cool and bright. I saw another, and another, and then the edge of the wood was full of them, lazily falling, then blinking out, cold sparks drifting in the growing dark.

'You know, I never saw fireflies until I came to live in Boston,' I said, filled with pleasure at sight of them, glowing emerald and topaz in the grass. 'They don't have fireflies in Scotland, do they?'

Jamie shook his head, reclining lazily on the grass, one arm hooked behind his head.

'Bonny wee things,' he observed, and sighed with content. 'This is my favorite time of the day, I think. When

I lived in the cave, after Culloden, I would come out near evening, and sit on a stone, waiting for the dark.'

His eyes were half closed, watching the fireflies. The shadows faded upward as night rose from the earth to the sky. A moment before, light through the oak leaves had mottled him like a fawn; now the brightness had faded, so he lay in a sort of dim green glow, the lines of his body at once solid and insubstantial.

'All the wee bugs come out just now – the moths and the midges; all the bittie things that hang about in clouds over the water. Ye see the swallows come for them, and then the bats, swooping down. And the salmon, rising to the evening hatch and making rings on the water.'

His eyes were open now, fixed on the waving sea of grass on the hillside, but I knew he saw instead the surface of the tiny loch near Lallybroch, alive with fleeting ripples.

'It's only a moment, but ye feel as though it will last forever. Strange, is it no?' he said thoughtfully. 'Ye can almost see the light go as ye watch – and yet there's no time ye can look and say, "Now! Now it's night." ' He gestured at the opening between the oak trees, and the valley below, its hollows filling with dark.

'No.' I lay back in the grass beside him, feeling the warm damp of the grass mold the buckskin to my body. The air was thick and cool under the trees, like the air in a church, dim and fragrant with remembered incense.

'Do you remember Father Anselm at the abbey?' I looked up; the color was going from the oak leaves overhead, leaving the soft silver undersides gray as mouse fur. 'He said there was always an hour in the day when time seems to stop – but that it was different for everyone. He thought it might be the hour when one was born.'

I turned my head to look at him.

'Do you know when you were born?' I asked. 'The time of day, I mean?'

He glanced at me and smiled, rolling over to face me.

'Aye, I do. Perhaps he was right, then, for I was born at suppertime – just as twilight on the first of May.' He brushed away a floating firefly and grinned at me.

'Have I never told ye that story? How my mother had put on a pot of brose to cook, and then her pains came

324

on so fast she'd no time to think of it, and no one else remembered either until they smelled the burning, and it ruined the supper and the pot as well? There was nothing else in the house to eat save a great gooseberry pie. So they all ate that, but there was a new kitchenmaid and the gooseberries were green, and all of them – except my mother and me, of course – spent the night writhing wi' the indigestion.'

He shook his head, still smiling. 'My father said it was months before he could look at me without feeling his bowels cramp.'

I laughed, and he reached to pick a last-year's leaf from my hair.

'And what hour were you born, Sassenach?'

'I don't know,' I said, with the usual pang of faint regret for my vanished family. 'It wasn't on my birth certificate, and if Uncle Lamb knew, he never told me. I know when Brianna was born, though,' I added, more cheerfully. 'She was born at three minutes past three in the morning. There was a huge clock on the wall of the delivery room, and I saw it.'

Dim as the light was, I could see his look of surprise clearly.

'You were awake? I thought ye told me women are drugged then, so as not to feel the pain.'

'They mostly were, then. I wouldn't let them give me anything, though.' I stared upward. The shadows were thick around us now, but the sky was still clear and light above, a soft, brilliant blue.

'Why the hell not?' he demanded, incredulous. 'I've never seen a woman give birth, but I've *heard* it more than once, I'll tell ye. And damned if I can see why a woman in her right mind would do it, and there was any choice about it.'

'Well . . .' I paused, not wanting to seem melodramatic. It was the truth, though. 'Well,' I said, rather defiantly, 'I thought I was going to die, and I didn't want to die in my sleep.'

He wasn't shocked. He only raised one brow, and snorted faintly with amusement.

'Would ye no?'

'No, would you?' I twisted my head to look at him. He rubbed the bridge of his nose, still amused at the question.

'Aye, well, perhaps. I've come close to death by hanging, and I didna like the waiting a bit. I've nearly been killed in battle a few times; I canna say I was much concerned about the dying then, though, bein' too busy to think of it. And then I've nearly died of wounds and fever, and that was misery enough that I was looking forward verra keenly to being dead. But on the whole, given my choice about it, I think perhaps I wouldna mind dying in my sleep, no.'

He leaned over and kissed me lightly. 'Preferably in bed, next to you. At a verra advanced age, mind.' He touched his tongue delicately to my lips, then rose to his feet, brushing dried oak leaves from his breeks.

'Best make a fire while there's light enough to strike a flint,' he said. 'Ye'll fetch the wee fish?'

I left him to deal with flints and kindling while I went down the little hill to the stream, where we had left the fresh-caught trout dangling from stringers in the icy current. As I came back up the hill it had grown dark enough that I could see him only in outline, crouched over a tiny pile of smoldering kindling. A wisp of smoke rose up like incense, pale between his hands.

I set the gutted fish down in the long grass and sat back on my heels beside him, watching as he laid fresh sticks on the fire, building it patiently, a barricade against the coming night.

'What do you think it will be like?' I asked suddenly. 'To die.'

He stared into the fire, thinking. A burning twig snapped with heat, spurting sparks into the air, which drifted down, blinking out before they touched the ground.

' "Man is like the grass that withers and is thrown into the fire; he is like the sparks that fly upward . . . and his place will know him no more," ' I quoted softly. 'Is there nothing after, do you think?'

He shook his head, looking into the fire. I saw his eyes shift beyond it, to where the cool bright sparks of the fireflies blinked in and out among the dark stems.

'I canna say,' he said at last, softly. His shoulder touched

326

mine and I leaned my head toward him. 'There's what the Church says, but –' His eyes were still fixed on the fireflies, winking through the grass stems, their light unquenchable. 'No, I canna say. But I think it will maybe be all right.'

He tilted his head, pressing his cheek against my hair for a moment, then stood up, reaching for his dirk.

'The fire's well started now.'

The heavy air of the afternoon had lifted with the coming of twilight, and a soft evening breeze blew the damp tendrils of hair off my face. I sat with my face lifted, eyes closed, enjoying the coolness after the sweaty heat of the day.

I could hear Jamie rustling around the fire, and the quick, soft *whisht* of his knife as he skinned green oak twigs for broiling the fish.

I think it will maybe be all right. I thought so, too. There was no telling what lay on the other side of life, but I had sat many times through an hour where time stops, empty of thought, soothed of soul, looking into . . . what? Into something that had neither name nor face, but which seemed good to me, and full of peace. If death lay there . . .

Jamie's hand touched my shoulder lightly in passing, and I smiled, not opening my eyes.

'Ouch!' he muttered, on the other side of the fire. 'Nicked myself, clumsy clot.'

I opened my eyes. He was a good eight feet away, head bent as he sucked a small cut on the knuckle of his thumb. A ripple of gooseflesh rose straight up my back.

'Jamie,' I said. My voice sounded peculiar, even to me. I felt a small round cold spot, centered like a target on the back of my neck.

'Aye.'

'Is there –' I swallowed, feeling the hair rise on my forearms. 'Jamie, is there . . . someone . . . behind me?'

His eyes shifted to the shadows over my shoulder, and sprang wide. I didn't wait to look round, but flung myself flat on the ground, an action that likely saved my life.

There was a loud *whuff!* and a sudden strong smell of ammonia and fish. Something struck me in the back with an impact that knocked the breath out of me, and then stepped heavily on my head, driving my face into the ground.

I jerked up, gasping for breath, shaking leaf mold out of my eyes. A large black bear, squalling like a cat, was lurching round the clearing, its feet scattering burning sticks.

For a moment, half blinded by dirt, I couldn't see Jamie at all. Then I spotted him. He was under the bear, one arm locked around its neck, his head tucked into the joint of the shoulder just under the drooling jaws.

One foot shot out from under the bear, kicking frantically, stabbing at the ground for traction. He had taken his boots and stockings off when we made camp; I gasped as one bare foot slewed through the remnants of the fire, raising showers of sparks.

His forearm was ridged with effort, half buried in thick fur. His free arm thrust and jabbed; he had kept hold of his dirk, at least. At the same time, he hauled with all his strength on the bear's neck, pulling it down.

The bear was lunging, batting with one paw, trying to shake off the clinging weight around its neck. It seemed to lose its balance, and fell heavily forward, with a loud squall of rage. I heard a muffled *whoof!* that didn't seem to come from the bear, and looked frantically around for something to use as a weapon.

The bear struggled back to its feet, shaking itself violently.

I caught a brief glimpse of Jamie's face, contorted with effort. One bulging eye widened at sight of me, and he shook his mouth clear of the bristling fur.

'Run!' he shouted. Then the bear fell on him again, and he disappeared under three hundred pounds of hair and muscle.

With vague thoughts of Mowgli and the Red Flower, I scrabbled madly over the damp earth in the clearing, finding nothing but small pieces of charred stick and glowing embers that blistered my fingers but were too small to grip.

I had always thought that bears roared when annoyed. This one was making a lot of noise, but it sounded more like a very large pig, with piercing squeals and blatting noises interspersed with hair-raising growls. Jamie was making a lot of noise, too, which was reassuring under the circumstances.

My hand fell on something cold and clammy; the fish, tossed aside at the edge of the fire clearing.

'To hell with the Red Flower,' I muttered. I seized one of the trout by the tail, ran forward, and belted the bear across the nose with it as hard as I could.

The bear shut its mouth and looked surprised. Then its head slewed toward me and it lunged, moving faster than I would have thought possible. I fell backward, landing on my bottom, and essayed a final, valiant blow with my fish before the bear charged me, Jamie still clinging to its neck like grim death.

It was like being caught in a meat grinder; a brief moment of total chaos, punctuated by random hard blows to the body and the sensation of being suffocated in a large, reeking hairy blanket. Then it was gone, leaving me lying bruised in the grass on my back, smelling strongly of bear piss and blinking up at the evening star, which was shining serenely overhead.

Things were a good deal less serene on the ground. I rolled onto all fours, shouting 'Jamie!' at the trees, where a large, amorphous mass rolled to and fro, smashing down the oak saplings and emitting a cacophony of growls and Gaelic screeches.

It was full dark on the ground by now, but there was enough light from the sky for me to make things out. The bear had fallen over again, but instead of rising and lunging, this time was rolling on its back, hind feet churning in an effort to gain a ripping purchase. One front paw landed in a heavy, rending slap and there was an explosive grunt that didn't sound like the bear's. The smell of blood was heavy on the air.

'Jamie!' I shrieked.

There was no answer, but the writhing pile rolled and tilted slowly sideways into the deeper black shadows under the trees. The mingled noises subsided to heavy grunts and gasps, punctuated by small whimpering moans.

'JAMIE!'

The thrashing and branch-cracking died away into

329

softer rustlings. Something was moving under the branches, swaying heavily from side to side, on all fours.

Very slowly, breathing in gasps with a catch and a groan, Jamie crawled out into the clearing.

Disregarding my own bruises, I ran to him, and dropped to my knees beside him.

'God, Jamie! Are you all right?'

'No,' he said shortly, and collapsed on the ground, wheezing gently.

His face was no more than a pale blotch in the starlight; the rest of his body was so dark as to be nearly invisible. I found out why as I ran my hands swiftly over him. His clothes were so soaked with blood that they stuck to his body, his hunting shirt coming away from his chest with a nasty little sucking sound as I pulled at it.

'You smell like a slaughterhouse,' I said, feeling under his chin for a pulse. It was fast – no great surprise – but strong, and a wave of relief washed over me. 'Is that your blood, or the bear's?'

'If it was mine, Sassenach, I'd be dead,' he said testily, opening his eyes. 'No credit to you that I'm not, mind.' He rolled painfully onto his side and slowly got to his hands and knees, groaning. 'What possessed ye, woman, to hit me in the heid wi' a fish whilst I was fighting for my life?'

'Hold still, for heaven's sake!' He couldn't be too badly hurt if he was trying to get away. I clutched him by the hips to stop him, and kneeling behind him, felt my way gingerly up his sides. 'Broken ribs?' I said.

'No. But if ye tickle me, Sassenach, I willna like it a bit,' he said, gasping between words.

'I won't,' I assured him. I ran my hands gently over the arch of his ribs, pressing lightly. No splintered ends protruding through the skin, no sinister depressions or soft spots; cracked maybe, but he was right, nothing broken. He yelped and twitched under my hand. 'Bad spot there?'

'It is,' he said between his teeth. He was beginning to shiver, and I hurried to fetch his plaid, which I wrapped about his shoulders.

'I'm fine, Sassenach,' he said, waving away my attempts

330

to help him to a seat. 'Go see to the horses; they'll be upset.' They were. We had hobbled the horses a little way from the clearing; they had made it a good deal farther under the impetus of terror, judging from the muffled stamping and whinnying I could hear in the distance.

There were still small wheezing groans coming from the deep shadows under the trees; the sound was so human that the hair prickled on the back of my neck. Carefully skirting the sounds, I went and found the horses, cowering in a birch grove a few hundred yards away. They whickered when they scented me, delighted to see me, bear piss and all.

By the time I had soothed the horses and coaxed them back in the direction of the clearing, the pitiful noises from the shadows had ceased. There was a small glow in the clearing; Jamie had managed to get the fire started again.

He was crouched next to the tiny blaze, still shivering under his plaid. I fed in enough sticks to make sure it wouldn't go out, then turned my attention to him once more.

'You're really not badly damaged?' I asked, still worried.

He gave me a lopsided smile.

'I'll do. It caught me a good one across the back, but I dinna think it's verra bad. Have a look?' He straightened up, wincing, and felt his side gingerly as I crossed behind him.

'What made it do that, I wonder?' he said, twisting his head toward where the bear's carcass lay. 'Myers said the black bears dinna often attack ye, without ye provoke them some way.'

'Maybe somebody else provoked it,' I suggested. 'And then had the sense to get out of the way.' I lifted the plaid, and whistled under my breath.

The back of his shirt hung in shreds, smeared with dirt and ash, splotched with blood. His blood this time, not the bear's, but luckily not much. I gently pulled the tattered pieces of the shirt apart, exposing the long bow of his back. Four long claw-marks ran from shoulder blade to armpit; deep, wicked gouges that tapered to superficial red welts.

'Ooh!' I said, in sympathy.

'Well, it's no as though my back was much to look at, anyway,' he joked feebly. 'Really, is it bad?' He twisted around, trying to see, then stopped, grunting as the movement strained his bruised ribs.

'No. Dirty, though; I'll need to wash it out.' The blood had already begun to clot; the wounds would need to be cleansed at once. I put the plaid back and set on a pan of water to boil, thinking what else I might use.

'I saw some arrowhead plant down near the stream,' I said. 'I think I can find it again from memory.' I handed him the bottle of ale I'd brought from the saddlebags, and took his dirk.

'Will you be all right?' I paused and looked at him; he was very pale, and still shivering. The fire glimmered red on his brows, throwing the lines of his face into strong relief.

'Aye, I will.' He mustered a faint grin. 'Dinna worry, Sassenach; the thought of dyin' asleep in my bed seems even better to me now than it did an hour ago.'

A sickle-moon was rising, bright over the trees, and I had little trouble finding the place I remembered. The stream ran cold and silver in the moonlight, chilling my hands and feet as I stood calf-deep in the water, groping for tubers of the arrowhead plant.

Small frogs sang all around me, and the stiff leaves of cattails rustled softly in the evening breeze. It was very, very peaceful, and all of a sudden I found myself shaking so hard that I had to sit down on the stream bank.

Anytime. It could happen anytime, and just this fast. I wasn't sure which seemed most unreal; the bear's attack, or this, the soft summer night, alive with promise.

I rested my head on my knees, letting the sickness, the residue of shock, drain away. It didn't matter, I told myself. Not only anytime, but anywhere. Disease, car wreck, random bullet. There was no true refuge for anyone, but like most people, I managed not to think of that most of the time.

I shuddered, thinking of the claw marks on Jamie's back. Had he been slower to react, not as strong . . . had the wounds been slightly deeper . . . for that matter, infection was still a major threat. But at least against that danger, I could fight.

The thought brought me back to myself, the squashed leaves and roots cool and wet in my hand. I splashed cold water over my face, and started up the hill toward the campfire, feeling somewhat better.

I could see Jamie through the thin scrim of saplings, sitting upright, outlined against the fire. Sitting bolt upright, in a way that must surely have been painful, considering his wounds.

I stopped, suddenly wary, just as he spoke.

'Claire?' He didn't turn around, and his voice was calm. He didn't wait for me to answer, but went on, voice cool and steady.

'Walk up behind me, Sassenach, and put your knife into my left hand. Then stay behind me.'

Heart hammering, I took the three steps that brought me high enough to see over his shoulder. On the far side of the clearing, just within the light of the fire, stood three Indians, heavily armed. Evidently the bear *had* been provoked.

The Indians looked us over with a lively interest that was more than returned. There were three of them; an older man, whose feathered topknot was liberally streaked with gray, and two younger, perhaps in their twenties. Father and sons, I thought – there was a certain similarity among them, more of body than of face; all three were fairly short, broad-shouldered and bow-legged, with long, powerful arms.

I eyed their weapons covertly. The older man cradled a gun in the curve of his arm; it was an ancient French wheelock, the hexagonal barrel rimed with rust. It looked as though it would explode in his face if he fired it, but I hoped he wouldn't try.

One of the younger men carried a bow to hand, arrow casually nocked. All three had sinister-looking tomahawks and skinning knives slung in their belts. Long as it was, Jamie's dirk seemed rather inadequate by comparison.

Evidently coming to the same conclusion, he leaned forward and placed the dirk carefully on the ground at his feet. Sitting back, he spread his empty hands and shrugged.

The Indians giggled. It was such an unwarlike noise that I found myself half smiling in response, even though my stomach, less easily disarmed, stayed knotted with tension.

I saw Jamie's shoulders relax their rigid line, and felt slightly reassured.

'*Bonsoir, messieurs,*' he said. '*Parlez-vous Français?*'

The Indians giggled again, glancing at each other shyly. The older man took a tentative step forward and ducked his head at us, setting the beads in his hair swinging.

'No . . . Fransh,' he said.

'English?' I said hopefully. He glanced at me with interest, but shook his head. He said something over one shoulder to one of his sons, who replied in the same unintelligible tongue. The older man turned back to Jamie and asked something, raising his brows in question.

Jamie shook his head in incomprehension, and one of the young men stepped into the firelight. Bending his knees and letting his shoulders slump, he thrust his head forward and swayed from side to side, peering nearsightedly in such perfect imitation of a bear that Jamie laughed out loud. The other Indians grinned.

The young man straightened up and pointed at the blood-soaked sleeve of Jamie's shirt, with an interrogatory noise.

'Oh, aye, it's over there,' Jamie said, gesturing toward the darkness under the trees.

Without further ado, all three men disappeared into the dark, from which excited exclamations and murmurings soon emerged.

'It's all right, Sassenach,' Jamie said. 'They willna harm us. They're only hunters.' He closed his eyes briefly, and I saw the faint sheen of sweat on his face. 'And a good thing, too, because I think I'm maybe going to swoon.'

'Don't even think about it. Don't you *dare* faint and leave me alone with them!' No matter what the savages' possible intentions, the thought of facing them alone over Jamie's unconscious body was enough to reknot my intestines with panic. I put my hand on the back of his neck and forced his head down between his knees.

334

'Breathe,' I said, squeezing cold water from my handkerchief down the back of his neck. 'You can faint later.'

'Can I puke?' he asked, his voice muffled in his kilt. I recognized the note of wry jest in it, and let my own breath out with relief.

'No,' I said. 'Sit up; they're coming back.'

They were, dragging the bear's carcass with them. Jamie sat up and mopped his face with the wet handkerchief. Warm as the night was, he was shivering slightly from shock, but he sat steadily enough.

The older man came over to us, and pointed with raised brows; first to the knife that lay at Jamie's feet, then to the dead bear. Jamie nodded modestly.

'It wasna easy, mind,' he said.

The Indian's brows rose higher. Then he ducked his head, hands spread in a gesture of respect. He beckoned to one of the younger men, who came over, untying a pouch from his belt.

Shoving me unceremoniously to one side, the younger man ripped open the throat of Jamie's shirt, pulled it off his shoulder, and squinted at the injury. He poured a handful of a lumpy, half-powdery substance into his hand, spat copiously into it, stirred it into a foul-smelling paste, and smeared it liberally over the wounds.

'Now I really am going to puke,' Jamie murmured, wincing under the ungentle ministrations. 'What is that stuff?'

'At a guess, it's dried trillium mixed with very rancid bear grease,' I said, trying not to inhale the pungent fumes. 'I don't suppose it will kill you; at least I hope not.'

'That's two of us, then,' he said under his breath. 'No, I'll do now, thank ye kindly.' He waved away further ministrations, smiling politely at his would-be doctor.

Joking or not, his lips were white, even in the dimness of the firelight. I put a hand on his good shoulder, and felt the muscles clenched tight with strain.

'Get the whisky, Sassenach. I need it badly.'

One of the Indians made a grab at the bottle as I pulled it from the bag, but I pushed him rudely away. He grunted with surprise, but didn't follow me. Instead, he picked up the bag and began rooting through it like a hog hunting truffles. I didn't try to stop him, but hurried back to Jamie with the whisky.

He took a small sip, then a larger one, shuddered once, and opened his eyes. He breathed deeply once or twice, drank again, then wiped his mouth and held out the bottle in invitation to the older man.

'Do you think that's wise?' I muttered, recalling Myers's lurid stories about massacres, and the effects of firewater on Indians.

'I can give it to them or let them take it, Sassenach,' he said, a little testily. 'There are three of them, aye?'

The older man passed the mouth of the bottle under his nose, nostrils flaring as though in appreciation of a rare bouquet. I could smell the liquor from where I stood, and was surprised that it didn't sear the lining of his nose.

A smile of beatific content spread across the man's craggy face. He said something to his sons that sounded like '*Haroo!*' and the one who had been rifling our bag came at once to join his brother, a couple of corn dodgers clutched in his fist.

The older man stood up with the bottle in his hand, but instead of drinking, took it over to where the bear's carcass lay, black as an inkblot on the ground. Without great deliberation, he poured a small amount of whisky into the palm of his hand, bent, and dribbled the liquid into the bear's half-open mouth. Then he turned slowly in a circle, shaking drops of whisky ceremoniously from his fingers. The drops flew gold and amber where they caught the light, hitting the fire with tiny, sizzling pops.

Jamie sat up straight, dizziness forgotten in his interest.

'Will ye look at that, now?' he said.

'At what?' I said, but he didn't answer, absorbed by the Indians' behavior.

One of the younger men had taken out a small beaded pouch that held tobacco. Carefully packing the bowl of a small stone pipe, he lit it with a dry twig dipped into the flames of our fire, and drew strongly on the barrel. The tobacco leaf sparked and fumed, spreading its rich aroma over the clearing.

Jamie was leaning against me, his back against my

336

thighs. I had my hand on his unwounded shoulder again, and could feel the shiver in his flesh start to ease as the warmth of the whisky began to spread in his belly. He wasn't badly hurt, but the strain of the fight and the continued effort to stay alert were taking their toll on him.

The older man took the pipe and drew several deep, leisurely mouthfuls, which he exhaled with evident pleasure. Then he knelt, and taking another deep lungful of smoke, carefully blew it up the nostrils of the dead bear. He repeated this process several times, muttering something under his breath as he exhaled.

Then he rose, with no sign of stiffness, and extended the pipe to Jamie.

Jamie smoked as the Indians had done – one or two long, ceremonious mouthfuls – and then lifted the pipe, turning to hand it to me.

I lifted the pipe and drew cautiously. Burning smoke filled my eyes and nose at once, and my throat constricted with an overwhelming urge to cough. I choked it back, and hastily gave Jamie the pipe, feeling my face turn red as the smoke curled lazily through my chest, tickling and burning as it searched its way through the channels of my lungs.

'Ye dinna *breathe* it, Sassenach,' he murmured. 'Just let it rise up the back of your nose.'

'Now . . . you . . . tell me,' I said, trying not to strangle.

The Indians watched me in round-eyed interest. The older man put his head on one side, frowning as though trying to puzzle something out. He popped up onto his feet and came round the fire, crouching to peer curiously at me, close enough for me to catch the odd, smoky scent of his skin. He wore nothing but a breechclout and a sort of short leather apron, though his chest was covered by a large, ornate necklace featuring seashells, stones, and the teeth of some large animal.

With no warning, he suddenly reached out and squeezed my breast. There was nothing even faintly lascivious about the gesture, but I jumped. So did Jamie, hand darting for his knife.

The Indian sat back calmly on his heels, waving his hand in dismissal. He clapped his hand flat on his breast, then made a cupping motion and pointed at me. He had meant nothing; he had only wanted to assure himself that I was indeed female. He pointed from me to Jamie, and raised one brow.

'Aye, she's mine.' Jamie nodded and lowered his dirk, but kept a hold on it, frowning at the Indian. 'Mind your manners, eh?'

Uninterested in this byplay, one of the younger Indians said something, and gestured impatiently at the carcass on the ground. The older man, who had paid no attention to Jamie's annoyance, replied, drawing his skinning knife from his belt as he turned.

'Here – that's mine to do.'

The Indians turned in surprise as Jamie rose to his feet. He gestured with his dirk to the bear, and then pointed the tip firmly at his own chest.

Not waiting for any response, he knelt on the ground beside the carcass, crossed himself, and said something in Gaelic, knife raised above the still body. I didn't know all the words, but I had seen him do it once before, when he had killed a deer on the road from Georgia.

It was the gralloch prayer he had been taught as a boy, learning to hunt in the Highlands of Scotland. It was old, he had told me; so old that some of the words were no longer in common use, so it sounded unfamiliar. But it must be said for any animal slain that was larger than a hare, before the throat was cut or the bellyskin split.

Without hesitation, he made a shallow slash across the chest – no need to bleed the carcass; the heart was long since still – and ripped the skin between the legs, so the pale swell of the intestines bulged up from the narrow, black-furred slit, gleaming in the light.

It took both strength and considerable skill to split and peel back the heavy skin without penetrating the mesenteric membrane that held the visceral sac enclosed. I, who had opened softer human bodies, recognized surgical competence when I saw it. So did the Indians, who were watching the proceedings with critical interest.

Jamie's skill at skinning wasn't what had fixed their attention, though – that was surely a common enough ability here. No, it was the gralloch prayer – I had seen the older man's eyes widen, and his glance at his sons as Jamie knelt over the carcass. They might not know what he was saying, but it was plain from their expressions that they knew exactly what he was doing – and were both surprised, and favorably impressed.

A small trickle of sweat ran down behind Jamie's ear, clear red in the firelight. Skinning a large animal is heavy work, and small spots of fresh blood were showing through the grimy cloth of his shirt.

Before I could offer to take the knife, though, he sat back on his heels and offered the dirk hilt-first to one of the younger Indians.

'Go ahead,' he said, gesturing at the bear's half-butchered bulk in invitation. 'Ye dinna think I'm going to eat it all myself, I hope.'

The man took the knife without hesitation, and kneeling, took over the skinning. The two others glanced at Jamie, and seeing his nod, joined in the work.

He let me sit him on the log once more and covertly clean and dress his shoulder, while he watched the Indians make quick work of the skinning and butchering.

'What was it he did with the whisky?' I asked quietly. 'Do you know?'

He nodded, eyes fixed absently on the bloody work by the fire.

'It's a charm. Ye scatter holy water to the four airs of the earth, to preserve yourself from evil. And I suppose whisky is a verra reasonable substitute for holy water, in the circumstances.'

I glanced at the Indians, stained to the elbows with the bear's blood, talking casually among themselves. One of them was building a small platform near the fire, a crude layer of sticks laid across rocks set in a square. Another was cutting chunks of meat and stringing them on a peeled green stick for cooking.

'From evil? Do you mean they're afraid of *us*?'

He smiled.

'I shouldna think we're so fearsome, Sassenach; no, from spirits.'

Frightened as I had been by the Indians' appearance, it would never have occurred to me that they might have been similarly unnerved by ours. But glancing up at Jamie now, I thought they might pardonably have been excused for nervousness.

Used to him as I was, I was seldom aware anymore of how he appeared to others. But even tired and wounded, he was formidable; straight-backed and wide-shouldered, with slanted eyes that caught the fire in a glitter as blue as the flame's heart.

He sat easily now, relaxed, big hands loose between his thighs. But it was the stillness of a great cat, eyes always watchfull behind the calm. Beyond size and quickness, there was undeniably an air of savagery about him; he was as much at home in these woods as the bear had been.

The English had always thought the Scottish Highlanders barbarians; I had never before considered the possibility that others might feel likewise. But these men had seen a ferocious savage, and approached him with due caution, arms at the ready. And Jamie, horrified beforehand at the thought of savage Red Indians, had seen their rituals – so like his own – and known them at once for fellow hunters; civilized men.

Even now, he was speaking to them quite naturally, explaining with broad gestures how the bear had come upon us and how he had killed it. They followed him with avid attention, exclaiming in appreciation in all the right places. When he picked up the remains of the mangled fish and demonstrated my role in the proceedings, they all looked at me and giggled hilariously.

I glared at all four of them.

'Dinner,' I said loudly, 'is served.'

We shared a meal of half-roasted meat, corn dodgers, and whisky, watched throughout by the head of the bear, which perched ceremonially on its platform, dead eyes gone dull and gummy.

Feeling mildly glazed, I leaned against the fallen log, listening with half an ear to the conversation. Not that I understood much that was actually said. One of the sons, an accomplished mimic, was giving a spirited rendition of Great Hunts of the Past, alternately playing the parts of hunter and prey, and doing it well enough that even I had no difficulty in telling a deer from a panther.

We had got so far in our acquaintance as an exchange of names. Mine came out in their tongue as 'Klah', which they seemed to find very funny. 'Klah,' they said, pointing at me, 'Klah-Klah-Klah-Klah-Klah!' Then they all laughed uproariously, their humor fueled by whisky. I might have been tempted to reply in kind, save that I wasn't sure I could pronounce 'Nacognaweto' once, let alone repeatedly.

They were – or so Jamie informed me – Tuscarora. With his gift of tongues, he was already pointing at objects and essaying the Indian names for them. No doubt by dawn he would be exchanging improper stories with them, I thought blearily; they were already telling him jokes.

'Here,' I said, tugging on the edge of Jamie's plaid. 'Are you all right? Because I can't stay awake to look after you. Are you going to faint and fall headfirst into the fire?'

Jamie patted me absently on the head.

'I'll be fine now, Sassenach,' he said. Restored by food and whisky, he seemed to be suffering no lingering ill effects from his battle with the bear. What he'd feel like in the morning was another question, I thought.

I was beyond worrying about that, or anything else, though; my head was spinning from the effects of adrenaline, whisky and tobacco, and I crawled off to fetch my blanket. Curled up by Jamie's feet, I drifted drowsily off to sleep, surrounded by the sacred fumes of smoke and liquor, and watched by the dull, sticky eyes of the bear.

'Know just how you feel,' I told it, and then was gone.

16

The First Law of Thermodynamics

I was awakened abruptly just after dawn by a tiny stinging sensation on top of my head. I blinked and put up a hand to investigate. The movement startled a large gray jay who had been pulling hairs out of my head, and he shot up into a nearby pine tree, screeching hysterically.

'Serve you right, mate,' I muttered, rubbing the top of my head, but couldn't help smiling. I had been told often enough that my hair looked like a bird's nest first thing in the morning; perhaps there was something to it, after all.

The Indians were gone. Luckily, the bear's head had gone with them. I felt my own head with ginger fingers, but aside from the small sting of the jay's depredations, it seemed intact. Either it had been remarkably good whisky, or my sense of intoxication had been due more to the effects of adrenaline and tobacco than to alcohol.

My comb was in the small deerskin pouch where I kept personal necessities and those few medicines. I thought might be useful on the trail. I sat up carefully, so as not to wake Jamie. He lay a short distance away on his back, hands crossed, peaceful as the carved effigy on a sarcophagus.

A lot more colorful, though. He lay in the shade, a creeping patch of sunshine sneaking up on him, barely touching the ends of his hair. In the fresh, cool light, he looked like Adam, newly touched by his Creator's hand.

Rather a battered Adam, though; on closer inspection, this was a snap taken well after the Fall. Not the fragile perfection of a child born of clay, nor yet the unused beauty of the youth God loved. No, this one was a man full-formed and powerful; each line of face and body marked with strength and struggle, made to take hold of the world he would wake to, and subdue it.

I moved very quietly, reaching for my pouch. I didn't want to wake him; the opportunity to watch him sleep came rarely. He slept like a cat, ready to spring up at any intimation of threat, and he normally rose from his bed at first light, while I was still floating on the surface of my dreams. Either he had drunk more than I thought last night, or he was in the deep sleep of healing, letting his body mend itself as he lay still.

The horn comb slid soothingly through my hair. For once, I wasn't in a hurry. There was no baby to feed, no child to rouse and dress for school, no work waiting. No patients to see, no paperwork to do.

Nothing could be farther from the sterile confines of a hospital than this place, I thought. Early birds in search of worms were making a cheerful racket in the forest, and a cool, soft breeze blew through the clearing. I smelt a faint whiff of dried blood, and the stale ashes from last night's fire.

Perhaps it was the scent of blood that had made me remember the hospital. From the moment I first walked into one, I had known it to be my sphere, my natural place. And yet I was not out of place, here in the wildwood. I thought that odd.

The ends of my hair brushed my naked shoulder blades with a pleasant, tickling feel, and the air was cool enough that the small breeze made my skin ripple with gooseflesh, my nipples standing up in tiny puckers. So I hadn't imagined it, I thought, with an inward smile. I certainly hadn't taken my own clothes off before retiring.

I pushed back the thick linen blanket, and saw the flecks of dried blood, smears on my thighs and belly. I felt dampness ooze between my legs, and drew a finger between them. Milky, with a musky scent not my own.

That was enough to bring back the shadow of the dream – or what I had thought must be one; the great bulk of the bear looming over me, darker than the night and reeking of blood, a rush of terror that kept my dream-heavy limbs from moving. My lying limp, pretending death, as he nudged and nuzzled, breath hot on my skin, fur soft on my breasts, gentleness amazing for a beast.

Then that one sharp moment of consciousness; of cold, then hot, as bare skin, not bearskin, touched my own, and then the dizzy slide back into drunken dreaming, the

343

slow and forceful coupling, climax fading into sleep . . . with a soft Scottish growling in my ear.

I looked down and saw the strawberry crescent of a bite mark on my shoulder.

'No *wonder* you're still asleep,' I said in accusation. The sun had touched the curve of his cheek, lighting the eyebrow on that side like a match touched to kindling. He didn't open his eyes, but a slow, sweet smile spread across his face in answer.

The Indians had left us a portion of the bear meat, tidily wrapped in oiled skin and hung from the branches of a nearby tree to discourage the attentions of skunks and raccoons. After breakfast and a hasty bath in the creek, Jaimie took his bearings by sun and mountain.

'That way,' he said, nodding toward a distant blue peak. 'See where it makes a notch wi' the shorter one? On the other side, it's the Indians' land; the new Treaty Line follows that ridge.'

'Someone actually *surveyed* through there?' I peered unbelievingly at the vista of saw-toothed mountain ranges rising from valleys filled with morning mist. The mountains rose ahead of us like an endless series of floating mirages, fading from black-green to blue to purple, the farthest peaks etched black and needle-sharp against a crystal sky.

'Oh, aye.' He swung up into his saddle, turning his horse's head so the sun fell over his shoulder. 'They had to, to say for sure which land could be taken for settling. I made sure of the boundary before we left Wilmington, and Myers said the same – this side of the highest ridge. I did think to ask the fellows who dined with us last night, though, only to be sure *they* thought so, too.' He grinned down at me. 'Ready, Sassenach?'

'As I'll ever be,' I assured him, and turned my horse to follow.

He had rinsed out his shirt – or what was left of it – in the stream. The stained rag of linen was spread out to dry behind his saddle, leaving him half-naked in leather riding breeks, his plaid wrapped carelessly round his waist. The long scratches left by the bear's attack were black across

344

his fair skin, but there was no visible inflammation, and from the ease with which he moved in the saddle, the wounds seemed not to trouble him.

Neither did anything else, so far as I could see. The tinge of wariness he always bore was still with him; it had been part of him since boyhood – but some weight had lifted in the night. I thought perhaps it was our meeting with the three hunters; this first encounter with savages had been vastly reassuring to us both, and seemed substantially to have eased Jamie's visions of tomahawk-wielding cannibals behind every tree.

Or it might be the trees themselves – or the mountains. His spirits had grown lighter with every foot upward from the coastal plain. I couldn't help sharing his apparent joy – but at the same time, felt a growing dread of what that joy might lead to.

By midmorning the slopes had grown too thickly forested to ride any farther. Looking up a nearly vertical rock face into a dizzying tangle of dark branches, sparked with gold and green and brown, I was inclined to think the horses were lucky to be stopping at the bottom. We hobbled them near a stream, thick with grass along its edge, and plunged in on foot, onward and upward, ever deeper into the bloody Forest Primeval.

Towering pines and hemlocks, was it? I thought, clambering over the burled knots of a fallen tree. The monstrous trunks rose so high that the lowest limbs started twenty feet above my head. Longfellow had no idea.

The air was damp, cool but fecund, and my moccasins sank soundlessly into centuries-thick black leaf mold. My own footprint in the soft mud of a stream bank seemed strange and sudden as a dinosaur's track.

We reached the top of a ridge, only to find another before us, and another beyond. I did not know what we might be looking for, or how we would know if we found it. Jamie covered miles with his tireless hill-walker's stride, taking in everything. I tagged behind, enjoying the scenery, pausing now and then to gather some fascinating plant or root, stowing my treasures in the bag at my belt.

We made our way along the back of one ridge, only to find our way blocked by a great heath bald: a patch of mountain laurel that looked from a distance like a shiny bare patch among the dark conifers, but closer to, proved to be an impenetrable thicket, its springy branches interwoven like a basket.

We backtracked, and turned downward, out from under the huge fragrant firs, across slopes of wild timothy and muhly grass that had gone bright yellow in the sun, and at last back into the soothing green of oak and hickory, on a wooded bluff that overlooked a small and nameless river.

It was cool under the trees' sudden shade, and I sighed in relief, lifting the hair off my neck to admit a breath of air. Jamie heard me and turned, smiling, holding back a limber branch so that I could follow him.

We didn't talk much; aside from the breath required for climbing, the mountain itself seemed to inhibit speech; full of secret green places, it was a vivid offspring of the ancient Scottish mountains, thick with forest, and twice the height of those barren black parental crags. Still, its air held the same injunction to silence, the same promise of enchantment.

The ground here was covered in a foot-deep layer of fallen leaves, soft and spongy underfoot, and the spaces between the trees seemed illusionary, as though to pass between those huge, lichened trunks might transport one suddenly to another dimension of reality.

Jamie's hair sparked in the occasional shafts of sunlight, a torch to follow through the shadows of the wood. It had darkened somewhat over the years, to a deep, rich auburn, but the long days of riding and walking in the sun had bleached his crown to copper fire. He had lost the thong that bound his hair; he paused, and brushed the thick damp locks back from his face, so that I saw the startling streak of white just above one temple. Normally hidden among the darker red, it showed rarely – a legacy of the bullet wound received in the cave of Abandawe.

Despite the warmth of the day, I shivered slightly in recollection. I would greatly have preferred to forget Haiti and its savage mysteries altogether, but there was little hope of that. Sometimes, on the verge of sleep, I would hear the voice of the cave-wind, and the nagging echo of the thought that came in its wake: *Where else?*

We climbed a granite ledge, thick with moss and lichen, wet with the omnipresent flow of water, then followed the path of a descending freshet, brushing aside long grass that pulled at our legs, dodging the drooping branches of mountain laurel and the thick-leaved rhododendrons.

Wonders sprang up by my feet, small orchids and brilliant fungi, trembling and shiny as jellies, shimmering red and black on fallen tree trunks. Dragonflies hung over the water, jewels immobile in the air, vanishing in mist.

I felt dazed with abundance, ravished by beauty. Jamie's face bore the dream-stunned look of a man who knows himself sleeping, but does not wish to wake. Paradoxically, the better I felt, the worse I felt, too; desperately happy – and desperately afraid. This was his place, and surely he felt it as well as I.

In early afternoon we stopped to rest and drink from a small spring at the edge of a natural clearing. The ground beneath the maple trees was covered with a thick carpet of dark green leaves, among which I caught a sudden telltale flash of red.

'Wild strawberries!' I said with delight.

The berries were dark red and tiny, about the size of my thumb joint. By the standards of modern horticulture, they would have been too tart, nearly bitter, but eaten with a meal consisting of half-cooked cold bear meat and rock-hard corn dodgers, they were delicious – fresh explosions of flavor in my mouth; pinpricks of sweetness on my tongue.

I gathered handfuls in my cloak, not caring for stains – what was a little strawberry juice among the stains of pine pitch, soot, leaf smudges and simple dirt? By the time I had finished, my fingers were sticky and pungent with juice, my stomach was comfortably full, and the inside of my mouth felt as though it had been sandpapered, from the tartly acid taste of the berries. Still, I couldn't resist reaching for just one more.

Jamie leaned his back against a sycamore, eyelids half lowered against the dazzle of afternoon sun. The little clearing held light like a cup, still and limpid.

'What d'ye think of this place, Sassenach?' he asked.

'I think it's beautiful. Don't you?'

He nodded, looking down between the trees, where a gentle slope full of wild hay and timothy fell away and rose again in a line of willows that fringed the distant river.

'I am thinking,' Jamie said, a little awkwardly. 'There is the spring here in the wood. That meadow below –' He waved a hand toward the scrim of alders that screened the ridge from the grassy slope. 'It would do for a few beasts at first, and then the land nearer the river might be cleared and put in crops. The rise of the land here is good for drainage. And here, see . . .' Caught by visions, he rose to his feet, pointing.

I looked carefully; to me, the place seemed little different from any of the steep wooded slopes and grassy coves through which we had wandered for the last couple of days. But to Jamie, with his farmer's eye, houses and stock pens and fields sprang up like fairy mushrooms in the shadows of the trees.

Happiness was sticking out all over him, like porcupine quills. My heart felt like lead in my chest.

'You're thinking we might settle here, then? Take the Governor's offer?'

He looked at me, stopping abruptly in his speculations.

'We might,' he said. 'If –'

He broke off and looked sideways at me. Sun-reddened as he was, I couldn't tell whether he was flushed with sun or shyness.

'D'ye believe in signs at all, Sassenach?'

'What sorts of signs?' I asked guardedly.

In answer, he bent, plucked a sprig from the ground, and dropped it into my hand – the dark green leaves like small round Chinese fans, a pure white flower on a slender stem, and on another a half-ripe berry, its shoulders pale with shade, blushing crimson at the tip.

'This. It's ours, d'ye see?' he said.

'Ours?'

'The Frasers', I mean,' he explained. One large, blunt finger gently prodded the berry. 'Strawberries ha' always been the emblem of the clan – it's what the name meant, to start with, when a Monsieur Fréselière came across from France wi' King William that was – and took hold of land in the Scottish mountains for his trouble.'

King William that was. William the Conqueror, that was. Perhaps not the oldest of the Highland clans, the Frasers had still a distinguished heritage.

'Warriors from the start, were you?'

'And farmers, too.' The doubt in his eyes was fading into a smile.

I didn't say what I was thinking, but I knew well enough that the thought must lie in his mind as well. There was no more of clan Fraser save scattered fragments, those who had survived by flight, by stratagem or luck. The clans had been smashed at Culloden, their chieftains slaughtered in battle or murdered by law.

Yet here he stood, tall and straight in his plaid, the dark steel of a Highland dirk by his side. Warrior and farmer both. And if the soil beneath his feet was not that of Scotland, it was free air that he breathed – and a mountain wind that stirred his hair, lifting copper strands to the summer sun.

I smiled up at him, fighting back my growing dismay.

'Fréselière, eh? Mr. Strawberry? He grew them, did he, or was he only fond of eating them?'

'Either or both,' he said dryly, 'or it was maybe only that he was redheided, aye?'

I laughed, and he hunkered down beside me, unpinning his plaid.

'It's a rare plant,' he said, touching the sprig in my open hand. 'Flowers, fruit and leaves all together at the one time. The white flowers are for honor, and red fruit for courage – and the green leaves are for constancy.'

My throat felt tight as I looked at him.

'They got that one right,' I said.

He caught my hand in his own, squeezing my fingers around the tiny stem.

'And the fruit is the shape of a heart,' he said softly, and bent to kiss me.

The tears were near the surface; at least I had a good excuse for the one that oozed free. He dabbed it away, then stood up and pulled his belt loose, letting the plaid fall in folds around his feet. Then he stripped off shirt and breeks and smiled down at me, naked.

'There's no one here,' he said. 'No one but us.'

I would have said this seemed no reason, but I felt what it was he meant. We had been for days surrounded by vastness and threat, the wilderness no farther away than the pale circle of our fire. Yet here, we were alone together, part and parcel of the place, with no need in broad daylight to hold the wilderness at bay.

'In the old days, men would do this, to give fertility to the fields,' he said, giving me a hand to rise.

'I don't see any fields.' And wasn't sure whether to hope I never would. Nonetheless, I skimmed off my buckskin shirt, and pulled loose the knot of my makeshift brassiere. He eyed me with appreciation.

'Well, no doubt I shall have to cut down a few trees first, but that can wait, aye?'

We made a bed of plaid and cloaks, and lay down upon it naked, skin to skin among the yellow grasses and the scent of balsam and wild strawberries.

We touched each other for what might have been a very long time or no time at all, together in the garden of earthly delight. I forced away the thoughts that had plagued me up the mountain, determined only to share his joy for as long as it lasted. I grasped him tight and he breathed in deep and pressed himself hard into my hand.

'And what would Eden be without a serpent?' I murmured, fingers stroking.

His eyes creased into blue triangles, so close I could see the black of his pupils.

'And will ye eat wi' me, then, *mo chridhe*? Of the fruit of the tree of the knowledge of Good and Evil?'

I put out the tip of my tongue and drew it along his lower lip in answer. He shivered under my fingers, though the air was warm and sweet.

'*Je suis prest*,' I said. '*Monsieur Fréselière.*'

His head bent and his mouth fastened on my nipple, swollen as one of the tiny ripe berries.

'*Madame Fréselière*,' he whispered back. '*Je suis à votre service.*'

And then we shared the fruit and flowers, and the green leaves covering all.

We lay tangled in drowsiness, stirring only to bat away

350

inquisitive insects, until the first shadows touched our feet. Jamie rose quietly, and covered me with a cloak, thinking me asleep. I heard the stealthy rustle as he dressed himself, and then the soft swish of his passage through the grass.

I rolled over, and saw him a little distance away, standing at the edge of the wood, looking out over the fall of land toward the river.

He wore nothing but his plaid, crumpled and blood-stained, belted round his waist. With his hair unbound and tangled round his shoulders, he looked the wild High-lander he was. What I had thought a trap for him – his family, his clan – was his strength. And what I had thought my strength – my solitude, my lack of ties – was my weakness.

Having known closeness, both its good and its bad, he had the strength to leave it, to step away from all notions of safety and venture out alone. And I – so proud of self-sufficiency at one time – could not bear the thought of loneliness again.

I had resolved to say nothing, to live in the moment, to accept whatever came. But the moment was here, and I could not accept it. I saw his head lift in decision, and at the same moment, saw his name carved in cold stone. Terror and despair washed over me.

As though he had heard the echo of my unspoken cry, he turned his head toward me. Whatever he saw in my face brought him swiftly to my side.

'What is it, Sassenach?'

There was no point in lying; not when he could see me.

'I'm afraid,' I blurted out.

He glanced quickly round for danger, one hand reaching for his knife, but I stopped him with a hand on his arm.

'Not that. Jamie – hold me. Please.'

He gathered me close against him, wrapping the cloak around me. I was shivering, though the air was still warm.

'It's all right, *a nighean donn*,' he murmured. 'I'm here. What's frightened ye, then?'

'You,' I said, and clung tight. His heart thumped just

under my ear, strong and steady. 'Here. It makes me afraid to think of you here, of us coming here –'

'Afraid?' he asked. 'Of what, Sassenach?' His arms tightened around me. 'I did say when we were wed that I would always see ye fed, no?' He pulled me closer, tucking my head into the curve of his shoulder.

'I gave ye three things that day,' he said softly. 'My name, my family, and the protection of my body. You'll have those things always, Sassenach – so long as we both shall live. No matter where we may be. I willna let ye go hungry or cold; I'll let nothing harm ye, ever.'

'I'm not afraid of any of that,' I blurted. 'I'm afraid you'll die, and I can't stand it if you do, Jamie, I really can't!'

He jerked back a little, surprised, and looked down into my face.

'Well, I'll do my best to oblige ye, Sassenach,' he said, 'but ye ken I may not have all the say in the matter.' His face was serious, but one corner of his mouth curled up irrepressibly.

The sight did me in utterly.

'Don't you laugh!' I said furiously. 'Don't you *dare* laugh!'

'Oh, I'm not,' he assured me, trying to straighten his face.

'You are!' I punched him in the chest. Now he *was* laughing. I punched him again, harder, and before I knew it, was hammering him in earnest, my fists making small dull thumps against his plaid. He grabbed for my hand, but I ducked my head and bit him on the thumb. He let out a cry and jerked his hand away.

He examined the toothmarks for a moment, then looked at me, one eyebrow raised. The humor lingered in his eyes, but at least he'd stopped laughing, the bastard.

'Sassenach, ye've seen me damn near dead a dozen times, and not turned a hair. Whyever are ye takin' on so now, and me not even ill?'

'Never turned a hair?' I gawked at him in furious amazement. 'You think I wasn't *upset*?'

He rubbed a knuckle across his upper lip, eyeing me in some amusement.

'Oh. Well, I did think ye cared, of course. But I never thought of it in just that way, I admit.'

'Of course you didn't! And if you had, it wouldn't make any difference. You – you – Scot!' It was the worst thing I could think of to call him. Finding no more words, I turned and stomped away.

Unfortunately, stomping has relatively little effect when executed in bare feet on a grassy meadow. I stepped on something sharp, uttered a small cry, and limped a few more steps before having to stop.

I had stepped on some sort of cocklebur; half a dozen vicious caltrops were stuck in my bare sole, blood drops welling from the tiny punctures. Precariously balanced on one foot, I tried to pick them out, cursing under my breath.

I wobbled and nearly fell. A strong hand caught me under the elbow and steadied me. I set my teeth and finished jerking out the spiny burs. I pulled my elbow out of his grasp and turning on my heel, walked – with a good deal more care – back to where I had left my clothing.

Dropping the cloak on the ground, I proceeded to dress, with what dignity was possible. Jamie stood, arms folded, watching me without comment.

'When God threw Adam out of Paradise, at least Eve went with him,' I said, talking to my fingers as I fastened the drawstring of my trousers.

'Aye, that's true,' he agreed, after a cautious pause. He gave me a sidelong glance, to see whether I was about to hit him again.

'Ah – ye havena been eating any o' the plants ye picked this morning, have ye, Sassenach? No, I didna think so,' he added hastily, seeing my expression. 'I only wondered. Myers says some things here give ye the nightmare something fierce.'

'I am not having nightmares,' I said, with more force than strictly necessary had I been telling the truth. I *was* having waking nightmares, though ingestion of hallucinogenic plant substances had nothing to do with it.

He sighed.

'D'ye mean to tell me straight out what ye're talkin' about, Sassenach, or do ye mean me to suffer a bit first?'

353

I glared at him, caught as usual between the urge to laugh and the urge to hit him with a blunt object. Then a wave of despair overcame both laughter and anger. My shoulders slumped in surrender.

'I'm talking about you,' I said.

'Me? Why?'

'Because you're a bloody Highlander, and you're all about honor and courage and constancy, and I know you can't help it, and I wouldn't want you to, only – only damn it, it's going to take you to Scotland and get you killed, and there's nothing I can do about it!'

He gave me a look of incredulity.

'Scotland?' he said, as though I'd said something completely mad.

'Scotland! Where your bloody grave is!'

He rubbed a hand slowly through his hair, looking down the bridge of his nose at me.

'Oh,' he said at last. 'I see, then. Ye think if I go to Scotland, I must die there, since that's where I'll be buried. Is that it?'

I nodded, too upset to speak.

'Mmphm. And just why is it ye think I'm going to Scotland?' he asked carefully.

I glared at him in exasperation, and waved an arm at the expanse of wilderness around us.

'Where the hell else are you going to get settlers for this land? Of course you're going to Scotland!'

He looked at me, exasperated in turn.

'How in the name of God d'ye think I should do that, Sassenach? I might have, when I had the gems, but now? I've maybe ten pound to my name, and that's borrowed. Shall I fly to Scotland like a bird, then? And lead folk back behind me, walkin' on the water?'

'You'll think of something,' I said miserably. 'You always do.'

He gave me a queer look, then looked away and paused for several moments before answering.

'I hadna realized ye thought I was God Almighty, Sassenach,' he said at last.

'I don't,' I said. 'Moses, maybe.' The words were facetious, but neither one of us was joking.

He walked away a bit, hands clasped behind his back.

'Watch out for the burs,' I called after him, seeing him heading for the location of my recent mishap. He altered his path in response, but said nothing. He walked to and fro across the clearing, head bent in thought. At last he came back, to stand in front of me.

'I canna do it alone,' he said quietly. 'You're right about that. But I dinna think I need go to Scotland for my settlers.'

'What else?'

'My men – the men who were wi' me in Ardsmuir,' he said. 'They're here already.'

'But you haven't any idea where they are,' I protested. 'And besides, they were transported years ago! They'll be settled; they won't want to pull up stakes and come to the ends of the bloody earth with you!'

He smiled, a little wryly.

'You did, Sassenach.'

I took a deep breath. The nagging weight of fear that had burdened my heart for the last weeks had eased. With that concern lifted, though, there was now room in my mind to contemplate the staggering difficulty of the task he was setting himself. Track down men scattered over there colonies, persuade them to come with him, and simultaneously find sufficient capital to finance the clearing of land and planting of crops. To say nothing of the sheer enormity of labor involved in carving some small foothold out of this virgin wilderness . . .

'I'll think of something,' he said, smiling slightly as he watched doubts and uncertainties flit across my face. 'I always do, aye?'

All of my breath went out in a long sigh.

'You do,' I said. 'Jamie – are you sure? Your aunt Jocasta –'

He dismissed that possibility with a flick of his hand.

'No,' he said. 'Never.'

I still hesitated, feeling guilty.

'You wouldn't – it's not just because of me? What I said about keeping slaves?'

'No,' he said. He paused, and I saw the two twisted

fingers of his right hand twitch. He saw it, too, stopped the movement abruptly.

'I have lived as a slave, Claire,' he said quietly, head bent. 'And I couldna live, knowing there was a man on earth who felt toward me as I have felt toward those who thought they owned me.'

I reached out and covered his crippled hand with my own. Tears ran down my cheeks, warm and soothing as summer rain.

'You won't leave me?' I asked at last. 'You won't die?'

He shook his head, and squeezed my hand tight.

'You are my courage, as I am your conscience,' he whispered. 'You are my heart – and I your compassion. We are neither of us whole, alone. Do ye not know that, Sassenach?'

'I do know that,' I said, and my voice shook. 'That's why I'm so afraid. I don't want to be half a person again, I can't bear it.'

He thumbed a lock of hair off my wet cheek, and pulled me into his arms, so close that I could feel the rise and fall of his chest as he breathed. He was so solid, so alive, ruddy hair curling gold against bare skin. And yet I had held him so before – and lost him.

His hand touched my cheek, warm despite the dampness of my skin.

'But do ye not see how verra small a thing is the notion of death, between us two, Claire?' he whispered.

My hands curled into fists against his chest. No, I didn't think it a small thing at all.

'All the time after ye left me, after Culloden – I was dead then, was I not?'

'I thought you were. That's why I – oh.' I took a deep, tremulous breath, and he nodded.

'Two hundred years from now, I shall most certainly *be* dead, Sassenach,' he said. He smiled crookedly. 'Be it Indians, wild beasts, a plague, the hangman's rope, or only the blessing of auld age – I will be dead.'

'Yes.'

'And while ye were there – in your own time – I *was* dead, no?'

I nodded, wordless. Even now, I could look back and see

356

the abyss of despair into which that parting had dropped me, and from which I had climbed, one painful inch at a time.

Now I stood with him again upon the summit of life, and could not contemplate descent. He reached down and plucked a stalk of grass, spreading the soft green beards between his fingers.

' "Man is like the grass of the field," ' he quoted softly, brushing the slender stem over my knuckles, where they rested against his chest. ' "Today it blooms; tomorrow it withers and is cast into the oven." '

He lifted the silky green tuft to his lips and kissed it, then touched it gently to my mouth.

'I was dead, my Sassenach – and yet all that time, I loved you.'

I closed my eyes, feeling the tickle of the grass on my lips, light as the touch of sun and air.

'I loved you, too,' I whispered. 'I always will.'

The grass fell away. Eyes still closed, I felt him lean toward me, and his mouth on mine, warm as sun, light as air.

'So long as my body lives, and yours – we are one flesh,' he whispered. His fingers touched me, hair and chin and neck and breast, and I breathed his breath and felt him solid under my hand. Then I lay with my head on his shoulder, the strength of him supporting me, the words deep and soft in his chest.

'And when my body shall cease, my soul will still be yours. Claire – I swear by my hope of heaven, I will not be parted from you.'

The wind stirred the leaves of the chestnut trees nearby, and the scents of late summer rose up rich around us; pine and grass and strawberries, sunwarmed stone and cool water, and the sharp, musky smell of his body next to mine.

'Nothing is lost, Sassenach; only changed.'

'That's the first law of thermodynamics,' I said, wiping my nose.

'No,' he said. 'That's faith.'

PART SIX

Je t'aime

17

Home for the Holidays

Inverness, Scotland, December 23, 1969

He checked the train schedule for the dozenth time, then prowled around the manse's living room, too restless to settle. An hour yet to wait.

The room was half dismantled, with piles of cartons lying higgledy-piggledy on every surface. He'd promised to have the place cleared out by the New Year, except for the pieces Fiona wanted to keep.

He wandered down the hall and into the kitchen, stood staring into the ancient refrigerator for a moment, decided he wasn't hungry and closed the door.

He wished that Mrs. Graham and the Reverend could have met Brianna, and she them. He smiled at the empty kitchen table, remembering an adolescent conversation with the two elderly people, when he, in the grip of a mad – and unrequited – lust for the tobacconist's daughter, had asked how to know if one was truly in love.

'If ye have to ask yourself if you're in love, laddie – then ye aren't.' Mrs. Graham had assured him, tapping her spoon on the edge of her mixing bowl for emphasis. 'And keep your paws off wee Mavis MacDowell, or her da will murder ye.'

'When you're in love, Rog, you'll know it with no telling,' the Reverend had chimed in, dipping a finger in the cake batter. He ducked in mock alarm as Mrs. Graham raised a threatening spoon, and laughed. 'And do mind yourself with young Mavis, lad; I'm not old enough to be a grandfather.'

Well, they'd been right. He knew, with no telling – had known since he'd met Brianna Randall. What he didn't know for sure was whether Brianna felt the same.

He couldn't wait any longer. He slapped his pocket to be sure of his keys, ran down the stair and out into the winter rain that had begun to pelt down just after breakfast. They did say a cold shower was the thing. Hadn't worked with Mavis, though.

December 24, 1969

'Now, the plum pudding's in the warming oven, and the hard sauce in the wee pan to the back,' Fiona instructed him, pulling on her fuzzy woolen hat. It was red, Fiona was short, and in it she looked like a garden gnome.

'Don't turn up the flame too high, mind. And dinna turn it out altogether, either, or you'll never get it lit again. And here, I've the directions for the birds for tomorrow all written out, they're stuffed in their pan, and I've left the veg already chopped to go along in the big yellow bowl in the fridge, and . . .' She fumbled in the pocket of her jeans and withdrew a handwritten slip of paper, which she thrust into his hand.

He patted her on the head.

'Don't worry, Fiona.' he assured her. 'We won't burn the place down. Nor starve, either.'

She frowned dubiously, hesitating at the door. Her fiancé, sitting in his car outside, revved his engine in an impatient sort of way.

'Aye, well. You're sure the two of ye won't come with us? Ernie's mam wouldna mind it a bit, and I'm sure she'd not think it right, just the two of ye left here by yourselves to keep Christmas . . .'

'Don't worry, Fiona,' he said, edging her gently backward out the door. 'We'll manage fine. You have a nice holiday with Ernie, and don't bother about us.'

She sighed, giving in reluctantly. 'Aye, I suppose you'll do.' A short irritable *beep!* from behind made her turn and glare at the car.

'Well, I'm *coming* then, aren't I?' she demanded. Turning back, she beamed suddenly at Roger, threw her arms about him, and standing on tiptoe, kissed him firmly on the lips.

She drew back and winked conspiratorially, screwing up her small, round face. '*That'll* sort our Ernie out,' she whispered. 'Happy Christmas, Rog!' she said loudly, and

362

with a gay wave, hopped off the porch and strolled in leisurely fashion toward the car, hips swinging just a bit.

Its engine roaring in protest, the car shot off with a squeal of tires before the door had quite shut behind Fiona. Roger stood on the porch waving, pleased that Ernie wasn't an especially massive bloke.

The door opened behind him and Brianna poked her head out.

'What are you doing out here with no coat on?' she inquired. 'It's freezing!'

He hesitated, tempted to tell her. After all, it had evidently worked on Ernie. But it was Christmas Eve, he reminded himself. In spite of the lowering sky and plummeting temperature, he felt warm and tingling all over. He smiled at her.

'Just seeing Fiona off,' he said, pulling back the door. 'Shall we see if we can make lunch without blowing up the kitchen?'

They managed sandwiches without incident, and returned after lunch to the study. The room was nearly empty now; only a few shelves of books remained to be sorted and packed.

On the one hand, Roger felt immense relief that the job was nearly done. On the other, it was sad to see the warm, cluttered study reduced to such a shell of its former self.

The Reverend's big desk had been emptied and removed to the garage for storage, the floor-to-ceiling shelves denuded of their huge burden of books, the cork-lined wall stripped of its many layers of fluttering papers. This process reminded Roger uncomfortably of chicken-plucking, the result being a stark and pathetic bareness that made him want to avert his eyes.

There was one square of paper still pinned to the cork. He'd take that down last.

'What about these?' Brianna waved a feather duster inquiringly at a small stack of books that sat on the table before her. An array of boxes gaped on the floor at her feet, half filled with books destined for various fates: libraries, antiquarian societies, friends of the Reverend's, Roger's personal use.

'They're autographed, but not inscribed to anybody.' she said, handing him the top one. 'You've got the set he inscribed to your father, but do you want these, too? They're first editions.'

Roger turned the book over in his hands. It was one of Frank Randall's, a lovely book, beautifully typeset and bound to match the elegance of its scholarly content.

'You should have them, shouldn't you?' he said. Without waiting for an answer, he set the book gently into a small box that rested on the seat of an armchair. 'Your dad's work, after all.'

'I've got some,' she protested. 'Tons. Boxes and boxes.'

'Not autographed, though?'

'Well, no.' She picked up another of the books and flipped it open to the flyleaf, where *Tempora mutantur nos et mutamur in illis – F. W. Randall* was written in a strong, slanting hand. She rubbed a finger gently over the signature, and her wide mouth softened.

'*The times are changing, and we with them.* You're sure you don't want them, Roger?'

'Sure,' he said, and smiled. He waved a wry hand at their book-strewn surroundings. 'Don't worry, you won't leave me short.'

She laughed and put the books in her own box, then went back to her work, dusting and wiping the stacked and sorted books before packing them. Most hadn't been cleaned in forty years, and she was liberally smudged herself by this time, long fingers grimy and the cuffs of her white shirt nearly black with filth.

'Won't you miss this place?' she asked. She wiped a strand of hair out of her eyes and gestured at the spacious room. 'You grew up here, didn't you?'

'Yes, and yes,' he answered, heaving another full carton onto the pile to be shipped to the university library. 'Not much choice, though.'

'I guess you couldn't live here,' she agreed regretfully. 'Since you have to be in Oxford most of the time. But do you have to sell it?'

'I *can't* sell it. It's not mine.' He stooped to get a grip on an extra-large carton, and rose slowly to his feet, grunting with effort. He staggered across the room and dropped it onto the stack, with a thud that raised small puffs of dust from the boxes beneath it.

'Whew!' He blew out his breath, grinning at her. 'God help the antiquarians when they pick that one up.'

'What do you mean, it's not yours?'

'What I said,' he replied matter-of-factly. 'It isn't mine. The house and land belong to the church; Dad lived here for near fifty years, but he didn't own it. It belongs to the Parish Council. The new minister doesn't want it – he's got money of his own, and a wife who likes mod cons – so the Council's putting it to let. Fiona and her Ernie are taking it, heaven help them.'

'Just the two of them?'

'It's cheap. For good reason,' he added wryly. 'She wants lots of kids, though – be room for an army of them here, I can tell you.' Designed in Victorian times for ministers with numerous families, the manse had twelve rooms – not counting one unmodernized and highly inconvenient bath.

'The wedding's in February, so that's why I've got to finish the clearing up over Christmas, to give time for the cleaners and painters to come in. Shame to make you work on your holiday, though. Maybe we'll drive down to Fort William Monday?'

Brianna picked up another book, but didn't put it in the box right away.

'So your home's gone for good,' she said, slowly. 'It doesn't seem right – though I'm glad Fiona will have it.'

Roger shrugged.

'Not as though I meant to settle in Inverness,' he said. 'And it's not as though it were an ancestral seat or anything.' He waved at the cracked linoleum, the grubby enamel paint, and the ancient glass-bowl light fixture overhead. 'Can't put it on the National Trust and charge people two quid each to tour the place.'

She smiled at that, and returned to her sorting. She seemed pensive, though, a small frown visible between her thick red brows. Finally she put the last book in the box, stretched and sighed.

'The Reverend had nearly as many books as my parents,' she said. 'Between Mama's medical books and

365

Daddy's historical stuff, they left enough to supply a whole library. It'll probably take six months to sort it all out, when I get ho– when I go back.' She bit her lip lightly, and turned to pick up a roll of packing tape, picking at it with a fingernail. 'I told the real estate agent she could list the house for sale by summer.'

'That's what's been bothering you?' he said slowly, realization dawning as he watched her face. 'Thinking about taking apart the house you grew up in – having your home gone for good?'

One shoulder lifted slightly, her eyes still fixed on the recalcitrant tape.

'If you can stand it, I guess I can. Besides,' she went on, 'it's not that bad. Mama took care of almost everything – she found a tenant and had the house leased for a year, so I could have time to decide what to do, without worrying about it just sitting there vacant. But it's silly to keep it; it's way too big for me to live in alone.'

'You might get married.' He blurted it out without thinking.

'Guess I might,' she said. She glanced at him sidelong, and the corner of her mouth twitched in what might have been amusement. 'Someday. But what if my husband didn't want to live in Boston?'

It occurred to him quite suddenly that her concern over his losing the manse might – just possibly – have been that she envisioned herself living in it.

'D'you want kids?' he asked abruptly. He hadn't thought to ask before, but hoped like hell she did.

She looked momentarily startled, but then laughed.

'Only children usually want big families, don't they?'

'Couldn't say,' he said. 'But I do.' He leaned across the boxes and kissed her suddenly.

'Me too,' she said. Her eyes went slanted when she smiled. She didn't look away, but a faint blush made her look like a spring-ripe apricot.

He wanted kids, all right; just at the moment, he wanted to do what led to kids a lot more.

'But maybe we should finish clearing up, first?'

'What?' The sense of her words penetrated only vaguely. 'Oh. Yeah. Right, guess we should.'

He bent his head and kissed her again, slowly this time. She had the most wonderful mouth; wide and full-lipped, almost too big for her face – but not quite.

He had her round the waist, his other hand tangled in silky hair. The nape of her neck was smooth and warm under his hand; he gripped it and she shivered slightly, mouth opening in a small sign of submission that made him want to lean her backward over his arm, carry her down to the hearth rug, and . . .

A brisk rapping made him jerk his head up, startled out of the embrace.

'Who's *that?*' Brianna exclaimed, hand to her heart.

The study was lined on one side by floor-to-ceiling windows – the Reverend had been a painter – and a square, whiskered face was pressed against one of these, nose nearly flattened with interest.

'That,' said Roger through his teeth, 'is the postman, MacBeth. What the hell is the old bugger doing out there?'

As though hearing this inquiry, Mr. MacBeth stepped back a pace, drew a letter out of his bag and brandished it jovially at the occupants of the study.

'A letter,' he mouthed elaborately, looking at Brianna. He cut his eyes toward Roger and beetled his brows in a knowing leer.

By the time Roger reached the front door, Mr. MacBeth was standing on the porch, holding the letter.

'Why did you not put it in the letter slot, for God's sake?' Roger demanded. 'Give it here, then.'

Mr. MacBeth held the letter out of reach and assumed an air of injured dignity, somewhat impaired by his attempts to see Brianna over Roger's shoulder.

'Thought it might be important, didn't I? From the States, i'n't it? And it's for the young lady, not you, lad.' Screwing up his face into a massive and indelicate wink, he oiled past Roger, arm extended toward Brianna.

'Ma'am,' he said, simpering through his whiskers. 'With the compliments of Her Majesty's Mail.'

'Thank you.' Brianna was still rosily flushed, but she'd smoothed her hair, and smiled at MacBeth with every evidence of self-possession. She took the letter and glanced at it, but made no move to open it. The envelope was handwritten, Roger saw, with red postal-forwarding marks, but the distance was too far to make out the return address.

'Visiting, are ye, ma'am?' MacBeth asked heartily. 'Just the two of ye here, all on your ownie-o?' He was giving Brianna a rolling eye, looking her up and down with frank interest.

'Oh, no,' Brianna said, straight-faced. She folded the letter in half and stuffed it into the back pocket of her jeans. 'Uncle Angus is staying with us; he's asleep upstairs.'

Roger bit the inside of his cheek. Uncle Angus was a moth-eaten stuffed Scottie, a remnant of his own youth, unearthed during the cleaning of the house. Brianna, charmed with him, had dusted off his plaid bonnet and placed him on her own bed in the guest room.

The postman's heavy brows rose.

'Oh,' he said, rather blankly. 'Aye, I see. He'll be an American, too, then, your Uncle Angus?'

'No, he's from Aberdeen.' Other than a slight pink-ening at the end of her nose, Brianna's face showed nothing but the most open guilelessness.

Mr. MacBeth was enchanted.

'Oh, you've a wee bit of Scots in your family, then! Well, and I should have known it, now, you wi' that hair. A bonnie, bonnie lass, and no mistake.' He shook his head in admiration, lechery replaced by a pseudoavuncular air that Roger found only slightly less objectionable.

'Yes, well.' Roger cleared his throat meaningfully. 'I'm sure we don't want to keep you from your work, MacBeth.'

'Oh, it's no trouble, no trouble at all,' the postman assured him, craning to catch a last glimpse of Brianna as he turned to go. 'Nay rest for the weary, is there, my dear?'

'That's "no rest for the *wicked*," ' Roger said, with some emphasis, opening the door. 'Good day to you, MacBeth.'

MacBeth glanced at him, the shadow of a leer back on his face.

'A good day to *you*, Mr. Wakefield.' He leaned close, dug Roger in the ribs with an elbow, and whispered hoarsely, 'And a better night, if her uncle sleeps sound!'

'Here, going to read your letter?' He plucked it from the table where she had dropped it, and held it out to her.

She flushed slightly and took it from him.

'It's not important. I'll look at it later.'

'I'll go to the kitchen, if it's private.'

The flush deepened.

'It's not. It's nothing.'

He raised one eyebrow. She shrugged impatiently, and ripped open the flap, pulling out a single sheet of paper.

'See for yourself, then. I told you, it's nothing important.'

Oh, isn't it? he thought, but didn't say anything aloud. He took the proffered sheet and glanced at it.

It was in fact nothing much; a notification forwarded from the library at her university, to the effect that a specific reference she had requested was unfortunately not obtainable via interlibrary loan, but could be viewed in the private collection of the Stuart Papers, held in the Royal Annexe of Edinburgh University.

She was watching him when he looked up, arms folded, her eyes shiny and lips tight, daring him to say something.

'You should have told me you were looking for him,' he said quietly. 'I could have helped.'

She shrugged slightly, and he saw her throat move as she swallowed.

'I know how to do historical research. I used to help my fa–' She broke off, lower lip caught between her teeth.

'Yeah, I see,' he said, and did. He took her by the arm and steered her down the hall to the kitchen, where he plunked her in a chair at the battered old table.

'I'll put the kettle on.'

'I don't like tea,' she protested.

'You *need* tea,' Roger said firmly, and lit the gas with a fiery *whoosh*. He turned to the cupboard and took down cups and saucers, and – as an afterthought – the bottle of whisky from the top shelf.

'And I *really* don't like whisky,' Brianna said, eyeing it. She started to push herself away from the table, but Roger stopped her with a hand on her arm.

'I like whisky,' he said. 'But I hate to drink alone. You'll keep me company, aye?' He smiled at her, willing her to

369

smile back. At last she did, grudgingly, and relaxed in her seat.

He sat down opposite her, and filled his cup halfway with the pungent amber liquid. He breathed in the fumes with pleasure, and sipped slowly, letting the fine strong stuff roll down his throat.

'Ah,' he breathed. 'Glen Morangie. Sure you won't join me? A wee splash in your tea, maybe?'

She shook her head silently, but when the kettle began to whistle, she got up to take it off the fire and pour the hot water into the waiting pot. Roger got up and came behind her, slipping his arms around her waist.

'It's nothing to be ashamed of,' he said softly. 'You've a right to know, if you can. Jamie Fraser was your father, after all.'

'But he wasn't – not really.' Her head was bent; he could see the neat whorl of a cowlick at her crown, an echo of the one in the center of her forehead, that lifted her hair in a soft wave off her face.

'I *had* a father,' she said, sounding a little choked. 'Daddy – Frank Randall – he *was* my father, and I love – loved him. It doesn't seem right to – to go looking for something else, like he wasn't enough, like –'

'That's not it, then, and you know it.' He turned her round and lifted her chin with a finger.

'It's nothing to do with Frank Randall or how you feel about him – aye, he *was* your father, and there's not a thing will ever change that. But it's natural to be curious, to want to know.'

'Did *you* ever want to know?' Her hand came up and brushed his away – but she clung to his fingers, holding on.

He took a deep breath, finding comfort in the whisky.

'Yeah. Yes, I did. You need to, I think.' His fingers tightened around hers, drawing her toward the table. 'Come sit down; I'll tell you.'

He knew what missing a father felt like, especially an unknown father. For a time, just after he'd started school, he'd pored obsessively over his father's medals, carried the little velvet case about in his pocket, boasted to his friends about his father's heroism.

370

'Told stories about him, all made up,' he said, looking down into the aromatic depths of his teacup. 'Got bashed for being a nuisance, got smacked at school for lying.' He looked up at her, and smiled, a little painfully.

'I had to make him real, see?'

She nodded, eyes dark with understanding.

He took another deep gulp of the whisky, not bothering to savor it.

'Luckily Dad – the Reverend – he seemed to know the trouble. He began to tell me stories about my father; the real ones. Nothing special, nothing heroic – he was a hero, all right, Jerry MacKenzie, got shot down and all, but the stories Dad told were all about what he was like as a kid – how he made a martin house, but made the hole too big and a cuckoo got in; what he liked to eat when he'd come here on holiday and they'd go into town for a treat; how he filled his pockets with winkles off the rocks and forgot about them and ruined his trousers with the stink –' He broke off, and smiled at her, his throat still tight at the memory.

'He made my father real to me. And I missed him more than ever, because then I knew a bit about what I *was* missing – but I had to know.'

'Some people would say you can't miss what you never had – that it's better not to know at all.' Brianna lifted her cup, blue eyes steady over the rim.

'Some people are fools. Or cowards.'

He poured another tot of whisky into his cup, tilted the bottle toward her with a lifted brow. She held out her cup without comment, and he splashed whisky into it. She drank from it, and set it down.

'What about your mother?' she asked.

'I had a few real memories of her; I was nearly five when she died. And there are the boxes in the garage –' He tilted his head toward the window. 'All her things, her letters. It's like Dad said, "Everybody needs a history." Mine was out there; I knew if I ever needed to, I could find out more.'

He studied her for a long moment.

'You miss her a lot?' he said. 'Claire?'

She glanced at him, nodded briefly, and drank, then held out her empty cup for more.

'I'm – I was – afraid to look,' she said, eyes fixed on the stream of whisky.

'It's not just him – it's her, too. I mean, I know his stories, Jamie Fraser's; she told me a lot about him. A lot more than I'll ever find in historical records,' she added with a feeble attempt at a smile. She took a deep breath.

'But Mama – at first I tried to pretend she was only gone, like on a trip. And then when I couldn't do that anymore, I tried to believe she was dead.'

Her nose was running, from emotion, whisky, or the heat of the tea. Roger reached for the tea towel hanging by the stove and shoved it across the table to her.

'She *isn't*, though.' She picked up the towel and wiped angrily at her nose. 'That's the trouble! I have to miss her all the time, and know that I'll never see her again, but she isn't even *dead*! How can I mourn for her, when I think – when I hope – she's happy where she is, when I *made* her go?'

She gulped the rest of her cup, choked slightly, and got her breath. She fixed Roger with a dark blue glare, as though he were to blame for the situation.

'So I want to find out, all right? I want to find her – find them. See if she's all right. But I keep thinking maybe I *don't* want to find out, because what if I find out she's not all right, what if I find out something horrible? What if I find out she's dead, or he is – well, that wouldn't matter so much, maybe, because he already is dead anyway, or he was, or – but I *have* to, I know I have to!'

She banged her cup down on the table in front of him.

'More.'

He opened his mouth to say that she'd had a good bit more than she needed already, but a glance at her face changed his mind. He shut his mouth and poured.

She didn't wait for him to add tea, but raised the cup to her mouth and took a large swallow, and another. She coughed, sputtered, and set the cup down, eyes watering.

'So I'm looking. Or I was. When I saw Daddy's books, and his handwriting, though . . . it all seemed wrong, then.

Do you think I'm wrong?' she asked, peering woefully at him through tear-clogged lashes.

'No, hen,' he said gently. 'It's not wrong. You're right, you've got to know. I'll help you.' He stood up and, taking her under the arms, hoisted her to her feet. 'But right now, I think you should maybe have a bit of a lie-down, hm?'

He got her up the stairs and halfway down the hall, when she suddenly broke free and darted into the bathroom. He leaned against the wall outside, waiting patiently until she staggered out again, her face the color of the aged plaster above the wainscoting.

'Waste of Glen Morangie, that,' he said, taking her by the shoulders and steering her into the bedroom. 'If I'd known I was dealing with a sot, I'd have given you the cheap stuff.'

She collapsed on the bed, and allowed him to take off her shoes and socks. She rolled onto her stomach, Uncle Angus cradled in the crook of her arm.

'I *told* you I didn't like tea,' she mumbled, and was asleep in seconds.

Roger worked for an hour or two by himself, sorting books and tying cartons. It was a quiet, dark afternoon, with no sound but a soft patter of rain and the occasional *whoosh* of a car's tires on the street outside. When the light began to fail, he turned on the lamps and went down the hall to the kitchen, to wash the book grime from his hands.

A huge pot of milky cock-a-leekie soup was burbling on the back of the cooker. What had Fiona said to do about that? Turn it up? Turn it off? Throw things into it? He peered dubiously into the pot and decided to leave well enough alone.

He tidied up the remains of their impromptu tea – rinsed the cups and dried them, hung them carefully from their hooks in the cupboard. They were remnants of the old willow pattern set the Reverend had had for as long as Roger could remember, the blue-and-white Chinese trees and pagodas augmented by odd bits of ill-assorted crockery acquired from jumble sales.

Fiona would have all new, of course. She'd forced them

to look at magazine pictures of china and crystal and flatware. Brianna had made suitable admiring noises; Roger's eyes had gone glassy from boredom. He supposed the old stuff would all end up at the jumble sale – at least it might still be useful to someone.

On impulse, he took down the two cups he'd washed, wrapped them in a clean tea towel, and took them to the study, where he tucked them into the box he'd set aside for himself. He felt thoroughly foolish, but at the same time, somewhat better.

He looked around the echoing study, quite bare now save for the single sheet of paper on the cork-lined wall.

So your home's gone for good. Well, he'd left home some time ago, hadn't he?

Yeah, it bothered him. A lot more than he'd let on to Brianna, in fact. That was why it had taken so bloody long to finish clearing out the manse, if he was honest about it. True, it was a monster task, true, he had his own job to do at Oxford, and true, the thousands of books had had to be sorted with care – but he could have done it faster. If he'd wanted.

With the house standing vacant, he might never have got the job finished. But with the impetus of Fiona behind, and the lure of Brianna before . . . he smiled at the thought of the two of them: little dark, curly-headed wren, and tall fire-haired Viking. Likely it took women to get men to do anything much.

Time to finish up, though.

With a sense of somber ceremony, he unpinned the corners of the yellowed sheet of paper and took it down from the cork. It was his family tree, a genealogical chart made out in the Reverend's neat round hand.

MacKenzies and more MacKenzies, generations of them. He'd thought lately of taking back the name permanently, not just for the singing. After all, with Dad gone he didn't mean to come back much more to Inverness, where folk would know him as Wakefield. That had been the point of the genealogy, after all; that Roger shouldn't forget who he was.

Dad had known a few individual stories, but no more than the names for most of the people on the list. And he hadn't known even that, for the most important one – the woman whose green eyes Roger saw each morning in the mirror. *She* was nowhere on this list, for good reason.

Roger's finger stopped near the top of the chart. There he was, the changeling – William Buccleigh MacKenzie. Given to foster parents to raise, the illegitimate offspring of the war chieftain of clan MacKenzie, and of a witch condemned to burning. Dougal MacKenzie and the witch Geillis Duncan.

Not a witch at all, of course, but something just as dangerous. He had her eyes – or so Claire said. Had he inherited something more from her as well? Was the terrifying ability to travel through the stones passed down unsuspected through generations of respectable boatwrights and herdsmen?

He thought of it each time he saw the chart now – and for that reason, tried not to look. He appreciated Brianna's ambivalence; he understood all too well the razor's edge between fear and curiosity, the pull between the need to know and the fear of finding out.

Well, he could help Brianna find out. And for himself . . .

Roger slipped the chart into a folder, and put it in the box. He closed the top of the carton, and added an 'X' of sticky tape across the flap for good measure.

'That's that, then,' he said aloud, and left the empty room.

He stopped at the head of the stairs, taken by surprise.

Brianna had been bathing, braving the ancient geyser with its cracked enamel and rumbling flame. Now she stepped into the hall, wearing nothing but a towel.

She turned down the hall, not seeing him. Roger stood very still, listening to the thud of his heart, feeling his palm slick on the polished banister.

She was modestly covered; he had seen more of her in the halters and shorts she had worn in the summer. It was the fragility of her covering that roused him; the knowledge that he could undress her with one quick tug. That, and the knowledge that they were quite alone in the house.

Dynamite.

He took a step after her, and stopped. She had heard him; she stopped, too, but it was a long moment before she turned around. Her feet were bare, high-arched and long-toed; the slender curves of her wet footprints were dark on the worn runner that covered the floor of the hallway.

She didn't say anything. Just looked at him straight-on, her eyes dark and slanting. She stood against the tall window at the end of the hall, her swaddled figure black against the pale gray light of the rainy day outside.

If he should touch her, he knew how she would feel. Her skin would be still hot from the bath, damp in the crevices of knee and thigh and elbow. He could smell her, the minglings of shampoo and soap and powder, the smell of her flesh masked by the ghosts of flowers.

Her footprints on the runner stretched before him, a fragile chain of footsteps linking them. He kicked off his sandals and planted a bare foot on one of the prints she had left; it was cool on his skin.

There were drops of water on her shoulders, matching the droplets on the windowpane behind her, as though she had stepped through it out of the rain. She lifted her head as he came toward her, and with a shake, let the towel wrapped round her head fall off.

The bronze snakes of her hair fell gleaming, brushed his cheek with wet. Not a Gorgon's beauty, but a water spirit's, changing shape from serpent-maned horse to magic woman.

'Kelpie,' he whispered against the flushed curve of her cheek. 'You look like you've come straight out of a Highland burn.' She put her arms around his neck, let go of the towel; only the pressure of their bodies held it between them.

Her back was bare. Cold air from the window raised the hair on his forearm, even as her skin warmed his palm. He wanted at once to pull the towel about her, shelter her, cover her from the cold; at the same time, to strip both her and himself, take her heat to himself and give her his own, right there in the damp and drafty hallway.

'Steam,' he whispered. 'God, you're steaming.'

376

Her mouth curved against his.

'That makes two of us, and you haven't had a bath. Roger –' Her hand was on the back of his neck, fingers cool. She opened her mouth to say something more, but he kissed her, feeling hot damp seep through the fabric of his shirt.

Her breasts rose against him and her mouth opened under his. The muffling terry cloth hid the outlines of her breasts from his hands but not his imagination; he could see them in his mind's eye, round and smooth, with that faint, enchanting wobble of full flesh.

His hand drifted lower, grasping the swell of bare buttock. She shied, lost her balance, and the two of them collapsed awkwardly, grappling with each other in an effort to stay upright.

Roger's knees hit the floor, and he dragged her down with him. She tilted and sprawled, landing laughing on her back.

'Hey!' She grabbed for her towel, then abandoned it as he lunged over her, kissing her again.

He'd been right about her breasts. The one under his hand was bare now, full and soft, the nipple hard in the center of his palm.

Dynamite, and the fuse was lit.

His other hand rested at the top of her thigh under the towel, close enough that he could feel the damp curls brush his finger. God, what color was it? Deep auburn, as he'd imagined? Copper and bronze, like the hair of her head?

Despite himself, his hand slid farther, dying to cup the soft slippery fullness he could sense, so close. With an effort that made him dizzy, he stopped.

Her hand was on his arm, pulling him back down.

'Please,' she whispered. 'Please, I want you to.'

He felt hollow as a bell; his heartbeat echoed in head and chest and painfully hard between his legs. He closed his eyes, breathing, pressing his hands against the rough fiber of the rug, trying to erase the feel of her skin, lest he grab at her again.

'No,' he said, and his voice sounded queer, hoarse to his own ear. 'No, not here, not like this.'

She was sitting up, rising out of the dark blue towel that puddled around her hips, like a mermaid from the waves. She had cooled; her flesh was pale as marble in the gray light, but goose bumps stippled the smoothness of arms and breasts and shoulders.

He touched her, rough skin and smooth, and drew his fingers over her lips, her broad mouth. The taste of her was still on his lips, clean skin and toothpaste – and a sweet, soft tongue.

'Better,' he whispered. 'I want it to be better . . . the first time.'

They knelt staring at each other, the air between them crackling with unsaid things. The fuse was still burning, but a slow match now. Roger felt rooted to the spot; perhaps it was the Gorgon, after all.

Then the smell of scorching milk rose up the stair, and both of them started up at once.

'Something's burning!' Brianna said, and made a dart toward the stair, her towel clumsily back in place.

He caught her by the arm as she passed him. She was cold to the touch, chilled by the drafty hallway.

'I'll do it,' he said. 'You go and get dressed.'

She shot him a quick blue glance and turned, disappearing into the spare bedroom. The door clicked shut behind her and he dashed down the hall, clattering down the stair toward the smell of disaster, feeling his palm burn where he had touched her.

Downstairs, Roger dealt with the spilled and scalded soup, berating himself. Where did he get off, lunging at her like a crazed salmon en route to the spawning grounds? Ripping off her towel and grappling her to the floor – Christ, she must think him next door to a rapist!

At the same time, the hot feeling that suffused his chest wasn't due either to shame or to heat from the cooker. It was the latent heat from her skin, still warming him. *I want you to*, she'd said, and she'd meant it.

He was familiar enough with the language of the body to know desire and surrender when he touched them. But what he'd felt in that brief moment when her body came alive to his went a great deal farther. The universe had

378

shifted, with a small, decisive click; he could still hear its echo in his bones.

He wanted her. He wanted all of her; not just bed, not just body. Everything, always. Suddenly the biblical injunction, *one flesh*, seemed something immediate, and very real. They'd nearly been just that, on the floor of the hallway, and stopping as he had made him feel suddenly and peculiarly vulnerable – he wasn't a whole person any longer, but only half of something not yet made.

He dumped the ruined remains of the soup into the sink. No matter; they'd have supper at the pub. Best to get out of the house and away from temptation.

Supper, casual chat, and maybe a walk by the river. She'd wanted to go to the Christmas Eve services. After that . . .

After that, he would ask her, make it formal. She would say yes, he knew. And then . . .

Why, then, they would come home, to a house dark and private. With themselves alone, on a night of sacrament and secret, with love newly come into the world. And he would lift her in his arms and carry her upstairs, on a night when virginity's sacrifice was no loss of purity, but rather the birth of everlasting joy.

Roger switched out the light and left the kitchen. Behind him, forgotten, the gas flame burned blue and yellow in the dark, ardent and steady as the fires of love.

18

Unseemly Lust

The Reverend Wakefield had been a kindly and ecumenical man, tolerant of all shades of religious opinion, and willing to entertain doctrines his flock would have found outrageous, if not downright blasphemous.

Still, a lifetime of exposure to the stern face of Scottish Presbyterianism and its abiding suspicion of anything 'Romish' had left Roger with a certain residual uneasiness upon entering a Catholic church – as though he might be seized at the door and forcibly baptized by outlandishly dressed minions of the True Cross.

No such violence offered as he followed Brianna into the small stone building. There was a boy in a long white robe visible at the far end of the nave, but he was peaceably engaged in lighting two pairs of tall white candles that decorated the altar. A faint, unfamiliar scent hung in the air. Roger inhaled, trying to be unobtrusive about it. Incense?

Beside him, Brianna stopped, rummaging in her purse. She took out a small circle of black lacy stuff, and bobby-pinned it to the top of her head.

'What's that?' he asked.

'I don't know what you call it,' she said. 'It's what you wear in church if you don't want to wear a hat or a veil. You don't really *have* to do it anymore, but I grew up doing it – it used to be that women couldn't go into a Catholic church with their heads uncovered, you know.'

'No, I didn't,' he said, interested. 'Why not?'

'Saint Paul, probably,' she said, whipping a comb from her purse to tidy the ends of her hair. 'He thought women ought to keep their hair covered all the time, so as not to be objects of unseemly lust. Cranky old crab,' she added, stuffing the comb back into the purse. 'Mama always said he was afraid of women. Thought they were dangerous,' she said, with a wide grin.

'They are.' Impulsively, he leaned forward and kissed her, ignoring the stares of the people nearby.

She looked surprised, but then rocked forward on her toes and kissed him back, soft and quick. Roger heard a faint 'Mmphm' of disapproval somewhere nearby, but paid no attention.

'In *kirk*, and on Christmas Eve, too!' came a hoarse whisper from behind.

'Well, it's no the kirk exactly, Annie, it's only the vestibule, aye?'

'And him the meenister's lad and all!'

'Well, ye ken the saying, Annie, as the cobbler's bairns go barefoot. I daresay it's a' the same wi' a preacher's lad that's gone to the deil. Come along in, now.'

The voices receded into the church, to the prim tap of Cuban heels and a man's softer shuffle accompanying. Brianna pulled back a little and looked up at him, mouth quivering with laughter.

'Have you gone to the devil?'

He smiled down at her, and touched her glowing face. She wore her grandmother's necklace, in honor of Christmas, and her skin reflected the luster of the freshwater pearls.

'If the devil will have me.'

Before she could answer, they were interrupted by a gust of foggy air as the church door opened.

'Mr. Wakefield, is it yourself?' He turned, to meet two pairs of bright, inquisitive eyes beaming up at him. A pair of elderly women, each about four foot six, stood arm in arm in their winter coats, gray hair puffed out under small felt hats, looking like a matched set of doorstops.

'Mrs. McMurdo, Mrs. Hayes! Happy Christmas to you!' He nodded to them, smiling. Mrs. McMurdo lived two doors down from the manse, and walked to church every Sunday with her friend Mrs. Hayes. Roger had known them all his life.

'Come over to Rome then, have ye, Mr. Wakefield?' Chrissie McMurdo asked. Jessie Hayes giggled at her friend's wit, the red cherries bouncing on her hat.

'Maybe not just yet awhile,' Roger said, still smiling. 'I'm only seeing a friend to the services, aye? You'll know Miss

Randall?' He brought Brianna forward and made the introductions, grinning inwardly as the two little old ladies looked her over with a frankly avid curiosity.

To Mrs. McMurdo and Mrs. Hayes, his presence here was as overt a declaration of his intentions as if he'd taken out a full-page ad in the evening newspaper. Too bad Brianna was unaware of it.

Or was she? She glanced at him with a half-hidden smile, and he felt the pressure of her fingers on his arm, just for a moment.

'Och, there's the wee laddie comin' wi' the censer!' cried Mrs. Hayes, spotting another white-robed boy emerging from the sanctuary. 'Best get in quick, Chrissie, or we'll never have a seat!'

'Such a pleasure to meet ye, my dear,' Mrs. McMurdo told Brianna, head tilted back so far that her hat was in danger of falling off. 'My, such a bonny tall lass!' She glanced at Roger, twinkling. 'Lucky to have found a lad to match ye, eh?'

'Chrissie!'

'Just coming, Jessie, just coming. Dinna fash, there's time.' Straightening her hat, trimmed with a small bunch of grouse's feathers, Mrs. McMurdo turned in leisurely fashion to join her friend.

The bell above began to clang again, and Roger took Brianna's arm. Just in front of them, he saw Jessie Hayes glance back, eyes bright with speculation, her smile half sly with knowing.

Brianna dipped her fingers in a small stone basin set in the wall by the door, and crossed herself. Roger found the gesture suddenly and oddly familiar, despite its Romanness.

Years ago, hill-walking with the Reverend, they had come upon a saint's pool, hidden in a grove. There was a flat stone standing on end beside the tiny spring, the remnants of carving on it worn nearly to smoothness, no more than the shadow of a human figure.

A sense of mystery hung about the small, dark pool; he and the Reverend had stood there for some time, not speaking. Then the Reverend had bent, scooped up a handful of water, and poured it out at the foot of the stone in silent ceremony, scooped up another and splashed it over his face. Only then had they knelt by the spring to drink the cold, sweet water.

Above the Reverend's bowed back, Roger had seen the tattered knots of fabric tied to tree branches above the spring. Pledges; reminders of prayer, left by whoever still visited the ancient shrine.

For how many thousands of years had men thus blessed themselves with water before seeking their heart's desire? Roger dabbed his fingers in the water and awkwardly touched both head and heart, with something that might have been a prayer.

They found seats in the east transept, crowded shoulder to shoulder with a murmuring family, busily engaged in settling belongings and sleepy children, passing coats and handbags and baby bottles to and fro, while a small, wheezy organ played 'O Little Town of Bethlehem' somewhere just out of sight.

Then the music stopped. There was a silence of expectation, and then it burst out once more, in a loud rendition of 'O Come, All Ye Faithful'.

Roger rose with the congregation as the procession came down the center aisle. There were several of the white-robed acolytes, one with a swinging censer that sent puffs of fragrant smoke into the crowd. Another bore a book, and a third a tall crucifix, the gruesome figure on it blatant, daubed with red paint whose bloody echoes shimmered in the priest's vestment of gold and crimson.

Despite himself, Roger felt a slight sense of shocked distaste; the mixture of barbaric pageantry and the undulations of sung Latin were quite foreign to what he subconsciously felt was proper in church.

Still, as the Mass went on, things seemed more normal; there were Bible readings, quite familiar, and then the accustomed descent into the vaguely pleasant boredom of a sermon, in which the inevitable Christmas annunciations of 'peace', 'goodwill', and 'love' rose to the surface of his mind, tranquil as white lilies floating on a pond of words.

By the time the congregation rose again, Roger had lost all sense of strangeness. Surrounded by a warm, familiar church fug composed of floor polish, damp wool, naphtha fumes, and a faint whiff of the whisky with which some worshipers had fortified themselves for the long service, he scarcely noticed the sweet, musky scent of frankincense. Breathing deeply, he thought he caught the hint of fresh grass from Brianna's hair.

It shone in the dim light of the transept, thick and soft against the dark violet of her jumper. Its copper sparks muted by the dimness, it was the deep rufous color of a red deer's pelt, and it gave him the same sense of helpless yearning he had felt when surprised by a deer on a Highland path – the strong urge to touch it, stroke the wild thing and keep it somehow with him, coupled with the sure knowledge that a finger's move would send it flying.

Whatever one thought of Saint Paul, he thought, the man had known what he was on about with respect to women's hair. Unseemly lust, was it? He had a sudden memory of the bare hallway and the steam rising from Brianna's body, the wet snakes of her hair cold on his skin. He looked away, trying to concentrate on the goings-on at the altar, where the priest was raising a large flat disk of bread, while a small boy madly shook a chime of bells.

He watched her when she went up to take Communion, and became aware with a slight start that he was praying wordlessly.

He relaxed just a bit when he realized the content of his prayer; it wasn't the ignoble 'Let me have her' he might have expected. It was the more humble – and acceptable, he hoped – 'Let me be worthy of her, let me love her rightly; let me take care of her.' He nodded toward the altar, then caught the curious eye of the man next to him, and straightened up, clearing his throat, embarrassed as though he had been surprised in private conversation.

She came back, eyes wide-open and fixed on something deep inside, a small dreaming smile on her wide sweet mouth. She knelt, and he beside her.

She had a tender look at the moment, but it was not a gentle face. Straight-nosed and severe, with thick red brows redeemed from heaviness only by the grace of their arch. The cleanness of jaw and cheek might have been cut from white marble; it was the mouth that could change in a moment, from soft generosity to the mouth of a medieval abbess, lips sealed in cool stone celibacy.

The thick Glaswegian voice beside him bawling 'We Three Kings' brought him to with a start, in time to see the priest sweep down the aisle, surrounded by his acolytes, in clouds of triumphant smoke.

' "We Three Kings of Orient Are," ' Brianna sang quietly as they made their way down River Walk, "Going to smoke a rubber cigar . . . It was loaded, and explo-oo-ded" – you *did* turn out the gas, didn't you?'

'Yes,' he assured her. 'Not to worry; between the cooker and the bathroom geyser, if the manse hasn't gone up in flames yet, it must be proof of divine protection.'

She laughed.

'Do Presbyterians believe in guardian angels?'

'Certainly not. Popish superstition, aye?'

'Well, I hope I haven't damned you to perdition by making you go to Mass with me. Or do Presbyterians believe in hell?'

'Oh, that we do,' he assured her. 'As much as heaven, if not more.'

It was even foggier, here by the river. Roger was glad they hadn't driven; you couldn't see more than five feet or so in the thick white murk.

They walked arm in arm beside the River Ness, footsteps muffled. Swaddled by the fog, the unseen city around them might not have existed. They had left the other churchgoers behind; they were alone.

Roger felt strangely exposed, chilled and vulnerable, stripped of the warmth and assurance he had felt in the church. Only nerves, he thought, and took a firmer grip of Brianna's arm. It was time. He took a deep breath, cool fog filling his chest.

'Brianna.' He had her by the arm, turned to face him before she had stopped walking, so her hair swung heavy through the dim arc from the streetlamp overhead.

Water droplets gleamed in a fine mist on her skin, glowed like pearls and diamonds in her hair, and through the padding of her jacket, he felt in memory her bare skin, cool as fog to his fingers, flesh-hot in his hand.

Her eyes were wide and dark as a loch, with secrets moving, half seen, half sensed, under rippling water. A kelpie for sure. *Each urisge*, a water horse, mane flowing, skin glowing. And the man who touches such a creature is lost, bound to it forever, taken down and drowned in the loch that gives it home.

He felt suddenly afraid, not for himself but for her; as though something might materialize from that water world to snatch her back, away from him. He grasped her by the hand, as if to prevent her. Her fingers were cold and damp, a shock against the warmth of his palm.

'I want you, Brianna,' he said softly. 'I cannot be saying it plainer than that. I love you. Will you marry me?'

She didn't say anything, but her face changed, like water when a stone is thrown into it. He could see it plainly as his own reflection in the bleakness of a tarn.

'You didn't want me to say that.' The fog had settled in his chest; he was breathing ice, crystal needles piercing heart and lungs. 'You didn't want to hear it, did you?'

She shook her head, wordless.

'Aye. Well.' With an effort, he let go her hand. 'That's all right,' he said, surprised at the calmness in his voice. 'You'll not be worried about it, aye?'

He was turning to walk on when she stopped him, hand on his sleeve.

'Roger.'

It was a great effort to turn and face her; he had no wish for empty comfort, no desire to hear a feeble offer to 'be friends'. He didn't think he could bear even to look at her, so crushing was his sense of loss. But he turned nonetheless and then she was against him, her hands cold on his ears as she gripped his head and pushed her mouth hard onto his, not so much a kiss as blind frenzy, awkward with desperation.

He gripped her hands and pulled them down, pushing her away.

'What in God's name are you playing at?' Anger was better than emptiness, and he shouted at her in the empty street.

'I'm not playing! You said you wanted me.' She gulped

air. 'I want you, too, don't you know that? Didn't I say so in the hall this afternoon?'

'I thought you did.' He stared at her. 'What in hell do you mean?'

'I mean – I mean I want to go to bed with you,' she blurted.

'But you don't want to marry me?'

She shook her head, white as a sheet. Something between sickness and fury stirred in his gut, and then erupted.

'So you'll not marry me, but you'll fuck me? How can ye say such a thing?'

'Don't use that sort of language to me!'

'Language? You can suggest such a thing, but I must not say the word? I have never been so offended, never!'

She was trembling, strands of hair sticking to her face with the damp.

'I didn't mean to insult you. I thought you wanted to – to –'

He grabbed her arms and jerked her toward him.

'If all I wanted was to fuck you, I would have had ye on your back a dozen times last summer!'

'Like hell you would!' She wrenched loose one arm and slapped him hard across the jaw, surprising him.

He grabbed her hand, pulled her toward him and kissed her, a good deal harder and a good deal longer than he ever had before. She was tall and strong and angry – but he was taller, stronger, and much angrier. She kicked and struggled, and he kissed her until he was good and ready to stop.

'The hell I would,' he said, gasping for air as he let her go. He wiped his mouth and stood back, shaking. There was blood on his hand; she'd bitten him and he hadn't felt a thing.

She was shaking, too. Her face was white, lips pressed so tight together that nothing showed in her face but dark eyes, blazing.

'But I didn't,' he said, breathing slower. 'That wasn't what I wanted; it's not what I want now.' He wiped his bloody hand against his shirt. 'But if you don't care

387

enough to marry me, then I don't care enough to have ye in my bed!'

'I do care!'

'Like hell.'

'I care too damn much to marry you, you bastard!'

'You *what*?'

'Because when I marry you – when I marry anybody – it's going to last, do you hear me? If I make a vow like that, I'll keep it, no matter what it costs me!'

Tears were running down her face. He groped in his pocket for a handkerchief and gave it to her.

'Blow your nose, wipe your face, and then tell me what the bloody hell ye think you're talking about, aye?'

She did as he said, sniffing and brushing back her damp hair with one hand. Her foolish little veil had fallen off; it was hanging by its bobby pin. He plucked it off, crumpling it in his hand.

'Your Scottish accent comes out when you get upset,' she said, with a feeble attempt at a smile as she handed back the wadded hanky.

'I shouldn't wonder,' Roger said in exasperation. 'Now tell me what you mean, and do it plainly, before ye drive me all the way to the Gaelic.'

'You can speak Gaelic?' She was gradually getting possession of herself.

'I can,' he said, 'and if you don't want to learn a good many coarse expressions right swiftly . . . talk. What d'ye mean by making me such an offer – and you a nice Catholic girl, straight out of Mass! I thought ye were a virgin.'

'I am! What does that have to do with it?'

Before he could answer this piece of outrageousness, she followed it up with another.

'Don't you tell me you haven't had girls, I know you have!'

'Aye, I have! I didn't want to marry them, and they didn't want to marry me. I didn't love them, they didn't love me. I do love you, damn it!'

She leaned against the lamppost, hands behind her, and met his eyes directly. 'I think I love you, too.'

He didn't realize he had been holding his breath until he let it out.

388

'Ah. You do.' The water had condensed in his hair, and icy trickles were running down his neck. 'Mmphm. Aye, and is the operative word there "think", then, or is it "love"?'

She relaxed, just a little, and swallowed.

'Both.'

She held up a hand as he started to speak.

'I do – I think. But – but I can't help thinking what happened to my mother. I don't want that to happen to me.'

'Your mother?' Simple astonishment was succeeded by a fresh burst of outrage. 'What? You're thinking of bloody Jamie Fraser? Ye think ye cannot be satisfied with a boring historian – ye must have a – a – great passion, as she did for him, and you think I'll maybe not measure up?'

'No! I'm not thinking of Jamie Fraser! I'm thinking of my father!' She shoved her hands deep in the pockets of her jacket, and swallowed hard. She'd stopped crying, but there were tears on her lashes, clotting them in spikes.

'She meant it when she married him – I could see it, in those pictures you gave me. She said "better or worse, richer, poorer" – and she *meant* it. And then . . . and then she met Jamie Fraser, and she didn't mean it anymore.'

Her mouth worked silently for a moment, looking for words.

'I – I don't blame her, not really, not after I thought about it. She couldn't help it, and I – when she talked about him, I could see how much she loved him – but don't you see, Roger? She loved my father, too – but then something happened. She didn't expect it, and it wasn't her fault – but it made her break her word. I won't do that, not for anything.'

She wiped a hand under her nose, and he gave her back the handkerchief, silently. She blinked back the tears and looked at him, straight.

'It's more than a year before we can be together. You can't leave Oxford; I can't leave Boston, not till I've got my degree.'

He wanted to say that he'd resign, that she should quit her schooling – but kept quiet. She was right; neither of them would be happy with such a solution.

'So what if I say yes now, and something happens? What if – if I met somebody else, or you did?' Tears welled again, and one ran down her cheek. 'I won't take the chance of hurting you. I won't.'

'But you love me now?' He touched a finger gently to her cheek. 'Bree, do ye love me?'

She took a step forward, and without speaking, reached to undo the fastenings of her coat.

'What the hell are you doing?' Blank astonishment was added to the mix of other emotions, succeeded by something else as her long pale fingers grasped the zip of his jacket and pulled it down.

The sudden whiff of cold was obliterated by the warmth of her body, pressed against his from throat to knees.

His arms went around her padded back by reflex; she was holding him tight, arms locked round him under his jacket. Her hair smelled cold and sweet, with the last traces of incense trapped in the heavy strands, blending with the fragrance of grass and jasmine flowers. He caught the gleam of a hairpin, bronze metal in the copper loops of her hair.

She didn't say a thing, nor did he. He could feel her body through the thin layers of cloth between them, and a jolt of desire shot up the backs of his legs, as though he were standing on an electric grid. He tilted up her chin, and set his mouth on hers.

' . . . see that Jackie Martin, and her with a new fur collar to her coat?'

'Och, and where's she found the money for such a thing, wi' her husband oot o' his work this six month past? I tell ye, Jessie, yon woman . . . ooh!'

The click of French-heeled shoes on the pavement halted, to be succeeded by the sound of a throat being cleared with sufficient resonance to wake the dead.

Roger tightened his grip on Brianna, and didn't move. She tightened her arms around him in response, and he felt the curve of her mouth under his.

'MMPHM!'

'Ah, now, Chrissie,' came a hissed whisper from behind him. 'Let them be, aye? Can ye not see they're getting engaged?'

'Mmphm' came again, but in a lower tone. 'Hmp. They'll be getting something else, and they go on wi' that much longer. Still . . .' A long sigh, tinged with nostalgia. 'Ah, weel, it's nice to be young, isn't it?'

The twin tap of heels came on, much slower, passed them, and faded inaudibly into the fog.

He stood for a minute, willing himself to let go of her. But once a man has touched the mane of a water horse, it's no simple matter to let go. An old kelpie-rhyme ran through his head,

> *And sit weel, Janetie*
> *And ride weel, Davie.*
> *And your first stop will be*
> *The bottom of Loch Cavie.*

'I'll wait,' he said, and let her go. He held her hands and looked into her eyes, now soft and clear as rain pools.

'Hear me, though,' he said softly. 'I will have you all – or not at all.'

Let me love her rightly, he had said in wordless prayer. And hadn't he been told often enough by Mrs. Graham – 'Be careful what ye ask for, laddie, for ye just might get it?'

He cupped her breast, soft through her jumper.

'It's not only your body that I want – though God knows, I want it badly. But I'll have you as my wife . . . or I will not have you. Your choice.'

She reached up and touched him, brushed the hair off his brow with fingers so cold, they burned like dry ice.

'I understand,' she whispered.

The wind off the river was cold, and he reached to do up the zip of her jacket. In doing so, his hand brushed his own pocket, and he felt the small package lying there. He'd meant to give it to her over supper.

'Here,' he said, handing it to her. 'Happy Christmas.'

'I bought it last summer,' he said, watching her cold fingers fumble at the holly-printed paper. 'Looks like pre-science, now, doesn't it?'

She held a silver circle, a bracelet, a flat silver band, with words etched round it. He took it from her and slipped it over her hand, onto her wrist. She turned it slowly, reading the words.

'*Je t'aime . . . un peu . . . beaucoup . . . passionnément . . . pas du tout*. I love you . . . a little . . . a lot . . . passionately . . . not at all.'

He gave the band a quarter turn more, completing the circle.

'*Je t'aime*,' he said, and then with a twist of fingers, sent it spinning on her wrist. She laid a hand on it, stopping it.

'*Moi aussi*,' she said softly, looking not at the band but at him. '*Joyeux Noël*.'

PART SEVEN

On the Mountain

19

Hearth Blessing

September 1767

Sleeping under the moon and stars in the arms of a naked lover, the two of you cradled by furs and soft leaves, lulled by the gentle murmur of the chestnut trees and the far-off rumble of a waterfall, is terribly romantic. Sleeping under a crude lean-to, squashed into a soggy mass between a large, wet husband and an equally large, equally wet nephew, listening to rain thrump on the branches overhead while fending off the advances of a immense and thoroughly saturated dog, is slightly less so.

'Air,' I said, struggling feebly into a sitting position and brushing Rollo's tail out of my face for the hundredth time. 'I can't breathe.' The smell of confined male animals was overpowering; a sort of musky, rancid smell, garnished with the scent of wet wool and fish.

I rolled onto my hands and knees and made my way out, trying not to step on anyone. Jamie grunted in his sleep, compensating for the loss of my body heat by curling himself neatly into a plaid-wrapped ball. Ian and Rollo were inextricably entangled in a mass of fur and cloth, their mingled exhalations forming a faint fog around them in the predawn chill.

It *was* chilly outside, but the air was fresh; so fresh I nearly coughed when I took a good lungful of it. The rain had stopped, but the trees were still dripping, and the air was composed of equal parts water vapor and pure oxygen, spiced with pungent green scents from every plant on the mountainside.

I had been sleeping in Jamie's spare shirt, my buckskins put away in a saddlebag to avoid soaking. I was dappled with gooseflesh and shivering by the time I pulled them on, but the stiff leather warmed enough to shape itself to my body within a few minutes.

Barefooted and cold-toed, I made my way carefully

down to the stream to wash, kettle under my arm. It wasn't yet dawn, and the forest was filled with mist and gray-blue light; crepuscle, the mysterious half-light that comes at both ends of the day, when the small secret things come out to feed.

There was an occasional tentative chirp from the canopy overhead, but nothing like the usual raucous chorus. The birds were late in starting today because of the rain; the sky was still lowering, with clouds that ranged from black in the west to a pale slate-blue in the dawning east. I felt a small rush of pleasure at the thought that I knew already the normal hour when the birds should sing, and had noticed the difference.

Jamie had been right, I thought, when he had suggested that we stay on the mountain, instead of returning to Cross Creek. It was the beginning of September; by Myers's estimation, we would have two months of good weather – relatively good weather, I amended, looking up at the clouds – before the cold made shelter imperative. Time enough – maybe – to build a small cabin, to hunt for meat, to supply ourselves for the winter ahead.

'It will be gey hard work,' Jamie had said. I stood between his knees as he sat perched high on a large rock, looking over the valley below. 'And some danger to it; we may fail if the snow is early, or if I canna hunt meat enough. I willna do it, if ye say nay, Sassenach. Would ye be afraid?'

Afraid was putting it mildly. The thought made the bottom of my stomach drop alarmingly. When I had agreed to settle on the ridge, I had thought we would return to Cross Creek to spend the winter.

We could have gathered both supplies and settlers in a leisurely manner, and returned in the spring in caravan, to clear land and raise houses communally. Instead, we would be completely alone, several days travel from the nearest tiny settlement of Europeans. Alone in a wilderness, alone through the winter.

We had virtually nothing with us in the way of tools or supplies, save a felling ax, a couple of knives, a camp kettle and girdle, and my smaller medicine box. What if something happened, if Ian or Jamie fell ill or was hurt in an accident? If we starved or froze? And while Jamie was sure that our Indian acquaintances had no objection to our intent, I wasn't so sanguine about any others who might happen along.

Yes, I bloody well *would* be afraid. On the other hand, I'd lived long enough to realize that fear wasn't usually fatal – at least not by itself. Add in the odd bear or savage, and I wasn't saying, mind.

For the first time, I looked back with some longing at River Run, at hot water and warm beds and regular food, at order, cleanliness . . . and safety.

I could see well enough why Jamie didn't want to go back; living on Jocasta's bounty for several months more would sink him that much further in obligation, make it that much harder to reject her blandishments.

He also knew – even better than I – that Jocasta Cameron was born a MacKenzie. I had seen enough of her brothers, Dougal and Colum, to have a decent wariness of that heritage; the MacKenzies of Leoch didn't give up a purpose lightly, and were certainly not above plotting and manipulation to achieve their ends. And a blind spider might weave her webs that much more surely, for depending solely on a sense of touch.

There were also really excellent reasons for staying the hell away from the vicinity of Sergeant Murchison, who seemed definitely the type to bear a grudge. And then there was Farquard Campbell and the whole waiting web of planters and Regulators, slaves and politics . . . No, I could see quite well why Jamie mightn't want to go back to such entanglement and complication, to say nothing of the looming fact of the coming war. At the same time, I was fairly sure that none of those reasons accounted for his decision.

It's not just that you don't want to go back to River Run, is it?' I leaned back against him, feeling his warmth as a contrast to the coolness of the evening breeze. The season had not yet turned; it was still late summer, and the air was rich with the sun-roused scents of leaf and berry, but so high in the mountains, the nights turned cold.

I felt the small rumble of a laugh in his chest, and warm breath brushed my ear.

'Is it so plain, then?'

'Plain enough.' I turned in his arms, and rested my forehead against his, so our eyes were inches apart. His were a very deep blue, the same color as the evening sky in the notch of the mountains.

'Owl,' I said.

He laughed, startled, and blinked as he pulled back, long auburn lashes sweeping briefly down.

'What?'

'You lose,' I explained. 'It's a game called "owl". First person to blink loses.'

'Oh.' He took hold of my ears by the lobes and drew me gently back, forehead to forehead. 'Owl, then. Ye do have eyes like an owl, have ye noticed?'

'No,' I said. 'Can't say I have.'

'All clear and gold – and verra wise.'

I didn't blink.

'Tell me then – why we're staying.'

He didn't blink either, but I felt his chest rise under my hand, as he took a deep breath.

'How shall I tell ye what it is, to feel the need of a place?' he said softly. 'The need of snow beneath my shoon. The breath of the mountains, breathing their own breath in my nostrils as God gave breath to Adam. The scrape of rock under my hand, climbing, and the sight of the lichens on it, enduring in the sun and the wind.'

His breath was gone and he breathed again, taking mine. His hands were linked behind my head, holding me, face-to-face.

'If I am to live as a man, I must have a mountain,' he said simply. His eyes were open wide, searching mine for understanding.

'Will ye trust me, Sassenach?' he said. His nose pressed against mine, but his eyes didn't blink. Neither did mine.

'With my life,' I said.

I felt his lips smile, an inch from mine.

'And with your heart?'

'Always,' I whispered, closed my eyes, and kissed him.

And so it was arranged. Myers would go back to Cross Creek, deliver Jamie's instructions to Duncan, assure

Jocasta of our welfare, and procure as much in the way of stores as the remnants of our money would finance. If there was time before the first snowfall, he would return with supplies; if not, in the spring. Ian would stay; his help would be needed to build the cabin, and to help with the hunting.

Give us this day our daily bread, I thought, pushing through the wet bushes that edged the creek, *and deliver us not into temptation.*

We were reasonably safe from temptation, though; for good or ill, we wouldn't see River Run again for at least a year. As for the daily bread, that had been coming through as dependably as manna, so far; at this time of year, there was an abundance of ripe nuts, fruits and berries, which I collected as industriously as any squirrel. In two months, though, when the trees grew bare and the streams froze, I hoped God might still hear us, above the howl of the winter wind.

The stream was noticeably swelled by the rain, the water maybe a foot higher than it had been yesterday. I knelt, groaning slightly as my back unkinked; sleeping on the ground exaggerated all the normal small morning stiffnesses. I splashed cold water on my face, swished it through my mouth, drank from cupped hands, and splashed again, blood tingling through my cheeks and fingers.

When I looked up, face dripping, I saw two deer drinking from a pool on the other side, a little way upstream from me. I stayed very still, not to disturb them, but they showed no alarm at my presence. In the shadow of the birches, they were the same soft blue as the rocks and trees, little more than shadows themselves, but each line of their bodies etched in perfect delicacy, like a Japanese painting done in ink.

Then all of a sudden, they were gone. I blinked, and blinked again. I hadn't seen them turn or run – and in spite of their ethereal beauty, I was sure I hadn't been imagining them; I could see the dark imprints of their hooves in the mud of the far bank. But they were gone.

I didn't see or hear a thing, but the hair rose suddenly on my body, instinct rippling up arms and neck like electric current. I froze, nothing moving but my eyes. Where was it, what was it?

The sun was up; the tops of the trees were visibly green, and the rocks began to glow as their colors warmed to life. But the birds were silent; nothing moved, save the water.

It was no more than six feet away from me, half visible behind a bush. The sound of its lapping was lost in the noise of the stream. Then the broad head lifted, and a tufted ear swiveled toward me, though I had made no noise. Could it hear me breathing?

The sun had reached it, lit it into tawny life, glowed in gold eyes that stared into mine with a preternatural calm. The breeze had shifted; I could smell it now; a faint acrid cat-tang, and the stronger scent of blood. Ignoring me, it lifted a dark-blotched paw and licked fastidiously, eyes slitted in hygienic preoccupation.

It rubbed the paw several times over its ear, then stretched luxuriously in the patch of new sun – my God, it must be six feet long! – and sauntered off, full belly swaying.

I hadn't consciously been afraid; pure instinct had frozen me in place, and sheer amazement – at the cat's beauty, as well as its nearness – had kept me that way. With its going, though, my central nervous system thawed out at once, and promptly went to pieces. I didn't gibber, but did shake considerably; it was several minutes before I managed to get off my knees and stand up.

My hands shook so that I dropped the kettle three times in filling it. Trust him, he'd said, did I trust him? Yes, I did – and a fat lot of good that would do, unless he happened to be standing directly in front of me next time.

But for this time – I was alive. I stood still, eyes closed, breathing in the pure morning air. I could feel every single atom of my body, blood racing to carry round the sweet fresh stuff to every cell and muscle fiber. The sun touched my face, and warmed the cold skin to a lovely glow.

I opened my eyes to a dazzle of green and yellow and blue; day had broken. All the birds were singing now.

I went up the path toward the clearing, resisting the impulse to look behind me.

Jamie and Ian had felled several tall, slender pines the day before, cut them into twelve-foot lengths, and rolled and wrestled and tumbled the logs downhill. Now they lay stacked at the edge of the small clearing, rough bark glistening black with wet.

Jamie was pacing out a line, stamping down the wet grass, when I came back with the kettle filled with water. Ian had a fire started on the top of a large flat stone – he having learned from Jamie the canny trick of keeping a handful of dry kindling always in one's sporran, along with flint and steel.

'This will be a wee shed,' Jamie was saying, frowning at the ground in concentration. 'We'll build this first, for we can sleep in it, if it should rain again, but it needna be so well built as the cabin – it'll give us something to practice on, eh, Ian?'

'What is it for – beyond practice?' I asked. He looked up and smiled at me.

'Good morning, Sassenach. Did ye sleep well?'

'Of course not,' I said. 'What's the shed for?'

'Meat,' he said. 'We'll dig a shallow pit at the back, and fill it wi' embers, to smoke what we can for keeping. And make a rack for drying – Ian's seen the Indians do it, to make what they call jerky. We must have a safe place where beasts canna get at our food.'

This seemed a sound idea; particularly in view of the sort of beasts in the area. My only doubts were regarding the smoking. I'd seen it done in Scotland, and knew that smoking meat required a certain amount of attention; someone had to be at hand to keep the fire from burning too high or going out altogether, had to turn the meat regularly, and baste it with fat to avoid scorching and drying.

I had no difficulty in seeing who was going to be nominated for this task. The only trouble was that if I didn't manage to do it right, we'd all die of ptomaine poisoning.

'Right,' I said, without enthusiasm. Jamie caught my tone and grinned at me.

'That's the first shed, Sassenach,' he said. 'The second one's yours.'

'Mine?' I perked up a bit at that.

401

'For your wee herbs and bits of plants. They do take up a bit of room, as I recall.' He pointed across the clearing, the light of builder's mania in his eye. 'And just there – that's where the cabin will be; where we'll live through the winter.'

Rather to my surprise, they had the walls of the first shed erected by the end of the second day, crudely roofed with cut branches until time should permit the cutting of shingles for a proper roof. The walls were made of slender notched logs, still with the bark on, and with noticeable chinks and gaps between them. Still, it was large enough to sleep the three of us and Rollo comfortably, and with a fire burning in a stone-lined pit at one end, it was quite cozy inside.

Enough branches had been removed from the roof to leave a smoke hole; I could see the evening stars, as I cuddled against Jamie and listened to him criticize his workmanship.

'Look at that,' he said crossly, lifting his chin at the far corner. 'I've gone and laid in a crooked pole, and it's put the whole of that line off the straight.'

'I don't imagine the deer carcasses will care,' I murmured. 'Here, let's see that hand.'

'And the rooftree's a good six inches lower at the one end than the other,' he went on, ignoring me, but letting me have his left hand. Both hands were smoothly callused, but I could feel the new roughnesses of scrapes and cuts, and so many small splinters that his palm was prickly to the touch.

'You feel like a porcupine,' I said, brushing my hand over his fingers. 'Here, move closer to the fire, so I can see to pull them out.'

He moved obligingly, crawling around Ian, who – freshly de-splintered himself – had fallen asleep with his head pillowed on Rollo's furry side. Unfortunately, the change of position exposed new weaknesses of construction to Jamie's critical eye.

'You've never built a shed out of logs before, have you?' I interrupted his denunciation of the doorway, neatly tweaking a large splinter out of his thumb with my tweezers.

402

'Ow! No, but –'

'And you built the bloody thing in two days, with nothing but a felling ax and a knife, for God's sake! There's not a nail in it! Why ought you to expect it to look like Buckingham Palace?'

'I've never seen Buckingham Palace,' he said, rather mildly. He paused. 'I do take your point, though, Sassenach.'

'Good.' I bent closely over his palm, squinting to make out the small dark streaks of splinters, trapped beneath the skin.

'I suppose it willna fall down, at least,' he said, after a longer pause.

'Shouldn't think so.' I dabbed a cloth to the neck of the brandy bottle, swabbed his hand with it, then turned my attention to his right hand.

He didn't speak for a time. The fire crackled softly to itself, flaring up now and then as a draft reached in between the logs to tickle it.

'The house is going to be on the high ridge,' he said suddenly. 'Where the strawberries grow.'

'Will it?' I murmured. 'The cabin, you mean? I thought that was going to be at the side of the clearing.' I'd taken out as many splinters as I could; those that were left were so deeply embedded that I would have to wait for them to work their way nearer the surface.

'No, not the cabin. A fine house,' he said softly. He leaned back against the rough logs, looking across the fire, out through the chinks to the darkness beyond. 'Wi' a staircase, and glass windows.'

'That will be grand.' I laid the tweezers back in their slot, and closed the box.

'Wi' high ceilings, and a doorway high enough I shall never bump my heid going in.'

'That will be lovely.' I leaned back beside him, and rested my head on his shoulder. Somewhere in the far distance, a wolf howled. Rollo lifted his head with a soft *wuff!*, listened for a moment, then lay down again with a sigh.

'With a stillroom for you, and a study for me, lined with shelves for my books.'

'Mmmm.' At the moment, he possessed one book – *The Natural History of North Carolina*, published 1733, brought along as guide and reference.

The fire was burning low again, but neither of us moved to add more wood. The embers would warm us through the night, to be rekindled with the dawn.

Jamie put an arm around my shoulders, and tilting sideways, took me with him to lie curled together on the thick layer of fallen leaves that was our couch.

'And a bed,' I said. 'You could build a bed, I expect?'

'As fine as any in Buckingham Palace,' he said.

Myers, bless his kindly heart and faithful nature, did return within the month – bringing not only three pack-mules laden with tools, small furnishing, and necessities such as salt, but also Duncan Innes.

'Here?' Innes looked interestedly over the tiny homestead that had begun to take shape on the strawberry-covered ridge. We had two sturdy sheds now, plus a split-railed penfold in which to keep the horses and any other stock we might acquire.

At the moment, our total stock consisted of a small white piglet, which Jamie had obtained from a Moravian settlement thirty miles away, exchanging for it a bag of sweet yams I had gathered and a bundle of willow-twig brooms I had made. Rather too small for the penfold, it had so far been living in the shed with us, where it had become fast friends with Rollo. I wasn't quite so fond of it myself.

'Aye. It's decent land, with plenty of water; there are springs in the wood, and the creek all through.'

Jamie guided Duncan to a spot from which the western slopes below the ridge were visible; there were natural breaks, or 'coves' in the forest, now overgrown with tangles of wild grass, but ultimately suitable for cultivation.

'D'ye see?' He gestured over the slope, which ran down gently from the ridge to a small bluff, where a line of sycamores marked the distant river's edge. 'There's room there for at least thirty homesteads, to start. We'd need to clear a deal of forest, but there's space enough to begin.

Any crofter worth his salt could feed his family from a garden plot, the soil's so rich.'

Duncan had been a fisherman, not a farmer, but he nodded obediently, eyes fixed on the vista as Jamie peopled it with future houses.

'I've paced it out,' Jamie was saying, 'though it will have to be surveyed properly as soon as may be. But I've the description of it in my head – did ye by chance bring ink and paper?'

'Aye, we did. And a few other things, as well.' Duncan smiled at me, his long, rather melancholy face transformed by the expression. 'Miss Jo's sent a feather bed, which she thought might not come amiss.'

'A feather bed? Really? How wonderful!' I immediately dismissed any ungenerous thoughts I had ever harbored about Jocasta Cameron. While Jamie had built us an excellent, sturdy bedstead framed in oakwood, with the bottom ingeniously made of laced rope, I had had nothing to lay on it save cedar branches, which were fragrant but unpleasantly lumpy.

My thoughts of luxuriant wallowing were interrupted by the emergence from the woods of Ian and Myers, the latter with a brace of squirrels hung from his belt. Ian proudly presented me with an enormous black object, which on closer inspection proved to be a turkey, fat from gorging on the autumn grains.

'Boy's got a nice eye, Mrs. Claire,' said Myers, nodding approvingly. 'Those be wily birds, turkeys. Even the Indians don't take 'em easy.'

It was early for Thanksgiving, but I was delighted with the bird, which would be the first substantial item in our larder. So was Jamie, though his pleasure lay more in the thing's tail feathers, which would provide him with a good supply of quills.

'I must write to the Governor,' he explained over dinner, 'to say that I shall be taking up his offer, and to give the particulars of the land.' He picked up a chunk of cake and bit into it absently.

'Do watch out for nutshells,' I said, a little nervously. 'You don't want to break a tooth.'

Dinner consisted of trout grilled over the fire, yams

baked in it, wild plums, and a very crude cake made of flour from hickory nuts, ground up in my mortar. We had been living mostly on fish and what edible vegetation I could scrounge, Ian and Jamie having been too busy with the building to take time to hunt. I rather hoped that Myers would see fit to stay for a bit – long enough to bag a deer or some other nice large source of protein. A winter of dried fish seemed a little daunting.

'Dinna fash, Sassenach,' Jamie murmured through a mouthful of cake, and smiled at me. 'It's good.' He turned his attention to Duncan.

'When we've done with eating, Duncan, you'll maybe walk wi' me to the river, and choose your place?'

Innes's face went blank, then flushed with a mixture of pleasure and dismay.

'My place? Land, ye mean, *Mac Dubh*?' Involuntarily, he hunched the shoulder on the side with the missing arm.

'Aye, land.' Jamie speared a hot yam with a sharpened stick, and began to peel it carefully with his fingers, not looking at Innes. 'I shall be needing you to act as my agent, Duncan – if ye will. It's only right ye should be paid. Now, what I am thinking – if ye should find it fair, mind – is that I shall make the claim for a homestead in your name, but as ye willna be here to work it, Ian and I will see to putting a bit of your land to corn, and to building a wee croft there. Then come time, you shall have a place to settle, if ye like, and a bit of corn put by. Will that suit ye, do ye think?'

Duncan's face had been going through an array of emotions as Jamie spoke, from dismay to amazement to a cautious sort of excitement. The last thing that would occurred to him was that he might own land. Penniless, and unable to work with his hands, in Scotland he would have lived as a beggar – if he had lived at all.

'Why –' he began, then stopped and swallowed, knobbly Adam's apple bobbing. 'Aye, *Mac Dubh*. That will suit fine.' A small, incredulous smile had formed on his face as Jamie spoke, and stayed there, as though Duncan were unaware of it.

'Agent.' He swallowed again, and reached for one of the

bottles of ale he had brought. 'What will ye have me to do for ye, *Mac Dubh*?'

'The two things, Duncan, and ye will. First is to find me settlers.' Jamie waved a hand at the beginnings of our new cabin, which so far consisted entirely of a fieldstone foundation, the framing of the floor, and a wide slab of dark slate selected for the hearthstone, presently leaning against the foundation.

'I canna be leaving here just at present, myself. What I want ye to do is to find as many as ye can of the men who were transported from Ardsmuir. They'll have been scattered, but they came through Wilmington; a many of them will be in North or South Carolina. Find as many as ye can, tell them what I'm about here – and bring as many as are willing here in the spring.'

Duncan was nodding slowly, lips pursed beneath his drooping mustache. Few men wore such facial adornment, but it suited him, making him look like a thin but benevolent walrus.

'Verra well,' he said. 'And the second?'

Jamie glanced at me, then at Duncan.

'My aunt,' he said. 'Will ye undertake to help her, Duncan? She's great need of an honest man, who can deal wi' the naval bastards and speak for her in business.'

Duncan had showed no hesitation in agreeing to comb several hundred miles of colony in search of settlers for our enterprise, but the notion of dealing with naval bastards struck him with profound uneasiness.

'Business? But I dinna ken aught of –'

'Dinna fash,' Jamie said, smiling at his friend, and the adjuration worked on Duncan as well as it did on me; I could see the mounting uneasiness in Duncan's eyes begin to recede. For roughly the ten-thousandth time, I wondered how he did it.

'It'll be little trouble to ye,' Jamie said soothingly. 'My aunt kens well enough what's to be done; she can tell ye what to say and what to do – it's only she needs a man for the saying and doing of it. I shall write a letter to her, for ye to take back, explaining that ye'll be pleased to act for her.'

During the latter part of this conversation, Ian had been

407

digging about in the packs that had been unloaded from the mules. Now he withdrew a flat piece of metal, and squinted at it curiously.

'What's this?' he asked, of no one in particular. He held it out for us to see; a flat piece of dark metal, pointed at one end like a knife, with rudimentary crosspieces. It looked like a small dirk that had been run over by a steamroller.

'Iron for your hearth.' Duncan reached for the piece, and handed it, handle-first, to Jamie. 'It was Miss Jo's thought.'

'Was it? That was kind.' Jamie's face was weathered to deep bronze by long days in the open, but I saw the faint flush of pink on the side of his neck. His thumb stroked the smooth surface of the iron, and then he handed it to me.

'Keep it safe, Sassenach,' he said. 'We'll bless our hearth before Duncan leaves.'

I could see that he was deeply touched by the gift, but didn't understand entirely why, until Ian had explained to me that one buries iron beneath a new hearth, to ensure blessing and prosperity on the house.

It was Jocasta's blessing on our venture; her acceptance of Jamie's decision – and forgiveness for what must have seemed his abandonment. It was more than generosity, and I folded the small piece of iron carefully into my handkerchief, and put it in my pocket for safekeeping.

We blessed the hearth two days later, standing in the wall-less cabin. Myers had removed his hat, from respect, and Ian had washed his face. Rollo was present, too, as was the small white pig, who was required to attend as the personification of our 'flocks', despite her objections; the pig saw no point in being removed from her meal of acorns to participate in a ritual so notably lacking in food.

Ignoring piercing pig-screams of annoyance, Jamie held the small iron knife upright by its tip, so that it formed a cross, and said quietly,

'God, bless the world and all that is therein.
God, bless my spouse and my children,

> *God, bless the eye that is in my head,*
> *And bless, God, the handling of my hand,*
> *What time I rise in the morning early,*
> *What time I lie down late in bed,*
> *Bless my rising in the morning early,*
> *And my lying down late in bed.'*

He reached out and touched first me, then Ian – and with a grin, Rollo and the pig – with the iron, before going on:

> *'God, protect the house, and the household,*
> *God, consecrate the children of the motherhood,*
> *God, encompass the flocks and the young,*
> *Be Thou after them and tending them,*
> *What time the flocks ascend hill and wold,*
> *What time I lie down to sleep.*
> *What time the flocks ascend hill and wold,*
> *What time I lie down in peace to sleep.*

> *'Let the fire of thy blessing burn forever upon us, O God.'*

He knelt then by the hearth and placed the iron into the small hole dug for it, covered it over, and tamped the dirt flat. Then he and I took the ends of the big hearthstone, and laid it carefully into place.

I should have felt quite ridiculous, standing in a house with no walls, attended by a wolf and a pig, surrounded by wilderness and mocked by mockingbirds, engaged in a ritual more than half pagan. I didn't.

Jamie stood in front of the new hearth, stretched out a hand to me, and drew me to stand by the hearthstone beside him. Looking down at the slate before us, I suddenly thought of the abandoned homestead we had found on our journey north; the fallen timbers of the roof, and the cracked hearthstone, from which a hollybush had sprouted. Had the unknown founders of that place thought to bless their hearth – and failed anyway? Jamie's hand tightened on mine, in unconscious reassurance.

On a flat rock outside the cabin, Duncan kindled a small fire, Myers holding the steel for him to strike. Once begun, the fire was coaxed into brightness, and a brand taken from it. Duncan held this in his one hand, and walked sunwise around the cabin's foundation, chanting in loud Gaelic. Jamie translated for me as he sang:

> 'The safeguard of Fionn mac Cumhall be yours,
> The safeguard of Cormac the shapely be yours,
> The safeguard of Conn and Cumhall be yours,
> From wolf and from bird-flock
> From wolf and from bird-flock.'

He paused in his chanting as he came to each point of the compass, and bowing to the 'four airts', swept his brand in a blazing arc before him. Rollo, plainly disapproving of these pyromaniac goings-on, growled deep in his throat, but was firmly shushed by Ian.

> 'The shield of the King of Fiann be yours,
> The shield of the king of the sun be yours,
> The shield of the king of the stars be yours,
> In jeopardy and distress
> In jeopardy and distress.'

There were a good many verses; Duncan circled the house three times. It was only as he reached the final point, next to the freshly laid hearthstone, that I realized Jamie had laid out the cabin so that the hearth lay to the north; the morning sun fell warm on my left shoulder and threw our mingled shadows to the west.

> 'The sheltering of the king of kings be yours,
> The sheltering of Jesus Christ be yours,
> The sheltering of the spirit of Healing be yours,
> From evil deed and quarrel,
> From evil dog and red dog.'

With a look down his nose at Rollo, Duncan stopped by the hearth, and gave the brand to Jamie, who stooped in turn and set alight the waiting pile of kindling. Ian gave a Gaelic whoop as the flame blazed up, and there was general applause.

Later, we saw Duncan and Myers off. They were bound not for Cross Creek but, rather, for Mount Helicon, where the Scots of the region held a yearly Gathering in the autumn, to give thanks for successful harvests, to exchange news and transact business, to celebrate marriages and christenings, to keep the far-flung elements of clan and family in touch.

Jocasta and her household would be there; so would Farquard Campbell and Andrew MacNeill. It was the best place for Duncan to begin his task of finding the scattered men of Ardsmuir; Mount Helicon was the largest of the Gatherings; Scots would come there from as far away as South Carolina and Virginia.

'I shall be here come spring, *Mac Dubh*,' Duncan promised Jamie as he mounted. 'With as many men as I can fetch to ye. And I shall hand on your letters without fail.' He patted the pouch by his saddle, and tugged his hat down to shade his eyes from the rich September sun. 'Will ye have a word for your aunt?'

Jamie paused for a moment, thinking. He had written to Jocasta already; was there anything to add?

'Tell my aunt I shall not see her at the Gathering this year, or perhaps at the next. But the one after that, I shall be there without fail – and my people with me. Godspeed, Duncan!'

He slapped Duncan's horse on the rump, and stood by me waving as the two horses dropped over the edge of the ridge and out of sight. The parting gave me an odd feeling of desolation; Duncan was our last and only link with civilization. Now we were truly alone.

Well, not quite alone, I amended. We had Ian. To say nothing of Rollo, the pig, three horses, and two mules that Duncan had left us, to manage the spring plowing. Quite a little establishment, in fact. My spirits rose in contemplation; within the month, the cabin would be finished, and we would have a solid roof over our heads. And then –

'Bad news, Auntie,' said Ian's voice in my ear. 'The pig's eaten the rest of your nutmeal.'

20

The White Raven

October 1767

' "Body, soul, and mind," ' Jamie said, translating as he
bent to seize the end of another trimmed log. ' "The body
for sensation, the soul for the springs of action, the mind
for principles. Yet the capacity for sensation belongs also
to the stalled ox; there is no wild beast or degenerate but
obeys the twitchings of impulse; and even men who deny
the gods, or betray their country, or" – careful, man!'

Ian, thus warned, stepped neatly backward over the ax
handle, and turned to the left, steering his end of the
burden carefully round the corner of the half-built log
wall.

' "– or perpetrate all manner of villainy behind locked
doors, have minds to guide them to the clear path of
duty," ' Jamie resumed Marcus Aurelius's *Meditations.*
' "Seeing then" – step up. Aye, good, that's got it – "seeing
then that all else is in common heritage of such types, the
good man's only singularity lies in his approving welcome
to every experience the looms of fate may weave for him,
his refusal to soil the divinity seated in his breast or
perturb it with disorderly impressions . . ." All right now,
one, and two, and . . . *ergh*!'

His face went scarlet with effort as they reached the
proper position and, in concert, hoisted the squared log
to shoulder height. Too occupied to go on with the meditations of Marcus Aurelius, Jamie directed his nephew's
movements with jerks of the head and breathless one-word
commands, as they maneuvered the unwieldy chunk of
wood into the notches of the crosspieces below it.

'Och, the twitchings of impulse, is it?' Ian shouldered a
lock of hair out of his sweating face. 'I feel a wee twitch in
the direction of my wame. Is that degenerate, then?'

'I believe that would be an acceptable bodily sensation
at this time o' day,' Jamie allowed, grunting slightly as they

412

maneuvered the log the last inch into place. 'A bit to the left, Ian.'

The log dropped into its notches, and both men stepped back with a shared sigh of relieved accomplishment. Ian grinned at his uncle.

'Meanin' ye're hungry yourself, aye?'

Jamie grinned back, but before he could reply, Rollo lifted his head, ears perking, and a low growl rumbled in his chest. Seeing this, Ian turned his head to look, and stopped in the act of mopping his face with his shirttail.

'Here's company, Uncle,' he said, nodding toward the forest. Jamie stiffened. Before he could turn or reach for a weapon, though, I had made out what Rollo and Ian had seen among the shifting leaf-light.

'Not to worry,' I said, amused. 'It's your erstwhile drinking companion – dressed for visiting. A little something the looms of fate have woven for your approving welcome, I expect.'

Nacognaweto waited politely in the shade of the chestnut grove until he was sure we had seen him. Then he advanced slowly out of the forest, followed this time not by his sons but by three women, two of them carrying large bundles on their backs.

One was a young girl, no more than thirteen or so, and the second, in her thirties, plainly the girl's mother. The third woman who accompanied them was much older – not the grandmother, I thought, seeing her bent form and white hair – perhaps the great-grandmother.

They had indeed come dressed for visiting; Nacognaweto was barelegged, with leather buskins on his feet, but he wore muslin breeches, loose at the knee, and a shirt of dyed-pink linen over them, belted splendidly with a girdle studded with porcupine quills and bits of white and lavender shell. Over it all he had a leather vest with beaded trim, and a sort of loose turban in blue calico over his unbound hair, with two crow's feathers dangling down beside one ear. Jewelry of shell and silver – an earring, several necklaces, a belt buckle and small ornaments tied to his hair – completed the picture.

The women were somewhat less gorgeously arrayed, but still plainly in their Sunday best, in long loose dresses

413

that reached their knees, soft boots and leather leggings showing beneath. They were girdled with deer-leather aprons decorated with painted patterns, and the two younger women wore ornamental vests as well. They advanced in single file, halfway across the clearing, then stopped.

'My God,' Jamie murmured, 'it's an ambassage.' He wiped a sleeve across his face, and nudged Ian in the ribs. 'Make my curtsies, Ian; I'll be back.'

Ian, looking a trifle bewildered, advanced to meet the Indians, waving a large hand in a ceremonial gesture of welcome. Jamie grabbed me by the arm and hustled me round the corner, into the half-built house.

'What –' I began, bewildered.

'Get dressed,' he interrupted, shoving the clothes box in my direction. 'Put on your gaudiest things, aye? It wouldna be respectful, else.'

'Gaudy' was going a bit far in the description of any item of my current wardrobe, but I did my best, hastily tying a yellow linen skirt around my waist and replacing my plain white kerchief with one Jocasta had sent me, embroidered with cherries. I thought that would do – after all, it was obviously the males of the species who were on display here.

Jamie, having flung off his breeks and belted his crimson plaid in record time, fastened it with a small bronze brooch, snatched a bottle out from under the bedframe, and was out through the open side of the house before I had finished tidying my hair. Giving up that attempt as a lost cause, I hurried out after him.

The women watched me with the same fascination I had for them, but they hung back as Jamie and Nacognaweto conducted the necessary greetings involving the ceremonial pouring and sharing of the brandy, Ian being included in this ritual. Only then did the second woman come forward at Nacognaweto's gesture, ducking her head in shy acknowledgment.

'*Bonjour, messieurs, madame,*' she said softly, looking from one to another of us. Her eyes rested on me with frank curiosity, taking in every detail of my appearance, so I felt

414

no compunction in staring at her, likewise. Mixed blood, I thought, perhaps French?

'*Je suis sa femme*,' she said, with a graceful inclination of her head toward Nacognaweto, the words verifying my guess as to her heritage. '*Je m'appelle Gabrielle.*'

'Um . . . *je m'appelle Claire*,' I said, with a slightly less graceful gesture at myself. '*S'il vous plait . . .*' I waved at the pile of waiting logs, inviting them to sit down, while mentally wondering whether there was enough of the squirrel stew to go round.

Jamie, meanwhile, was eyeing Nacognaweto with a mixture of amusement and irritation.

'Oh, "no Franch", is it?' he said. 'Not a word, I dinna suppose!' The Indian gave him a look of profound blandness, and nodded to his wife to continue with the introductions.

The elder lady was Nayawenne, not Gabrielle's grandmother as I had thought but, rather Nacognaweto's. This lady was light-boned, thin, and bent with rheumatism, but bright-eyed as the sparrow she so strongly resembled. She wore a small leather bag tied round her neck, ornamented with a rough green stone pierced through for stringing, and the spotted tail feathers of a woodpecker. She had a larger bag, this one of cloth, tied at her waist. She saw me looking at the green stains on the rough cloth, and smiled, showing two prominent yellow front teeth.

The girl was, as I had surmised, Gabrielle's daughter – but not, I thought, Nacognaweto's; she had no resemblance to him, and behaved shyly toward him. Her rather incongruous name was Berthe, and the effects of mixed blood were even more apparent in her than in her mother; her hair was dark and silky, but a deep brown rather than ebony, and her round face was ruddy, with the fresh complexion of a European, though her eyes had the Indian's epicanthic fold.

Once the official introductions were over, Nacognaweto motioned to Berthe, who obediently brought out the large bundle she had carried, and opened it at my feet, displaying a large basket of orange and green-striped squash, a string of dried fish, a smaller basket of yams, and a huge pile of Indian corn, shucked and dried on the cob.

415

'My God,' I murmured. 'The return of Squanto!'

Everyone gave me a blank look, and I hastened to smile and make exclamations – thoroughly heartfelt – of joy and pleasure over the gifts. It might not get us through the whole winter, but it was enough to augment our diet for a good two months.

Nacognaweto explained through Gabrielle that this was a small and insignificant return for Jamie's gift of the bear, which had been received with delight by his village, where Jamie's courageous exploit (here the women cut their eyes at me and tittered, having evidently heard all about the episode of the fish) had been the subject of great talk and admiration.

Jamie, thoroughly accustomed to this sort of diplomatic exchange, modestly disclaimed any pretention to prowess, dismissing the encounter as the merest accident.

While Gabrielle was employed in translation, the old lady ignored the mutual compliments, and sidled crabwise over to me. Without the least sense of offense, she patted me familiarly all over, fingering my clothes and lifting the hem of my dress to examine my shoes, keeping up a running commentary to herself in a soft, hoarse murmur.

The murmur grew louder and took on a tone of astonishment when she got to my hair. I obligingly took out the pins and shook it down over my shoulders. She pulled out a curl, drew it taut, then let it spring back, and laughed like a drain.

The men glanced in our direction, but by this time Jamie had moved on to showing Nacognaweto the construction of the house. The chimney was complete, built of fieldstone like the foundation, and the floor had been laid, but the walls, built of solid squared logs each some eight inches in diameter, rose only shoulder-high. Jamie was urging Ian to a demonstration of the debarking of logs, in which he chopped his way steadily backward as he walked along the top of the log, narrowly missing his toes with each stroke.

This form of male conversation requiring no translation, Gabrielle was left free to come and chat with me; though her French was peculiarly accented and full of

416

strange idioms, we had no trouble understanding each other.

In fairly short order, I discovered that Gabrielle was the daughter of a French fur trader and a Huron woman, and the second wife of Nacognaweto, who in turn was her second husband – the first, Berthe's father, had been a Frenchman, killed in the French and Indian War ten years before.

They lived in a village called Anna Ooka (I bit the inside of my cheek to keep a straight face; no doubt 'New Bern' would have sounded peculiar to them), some two days travel to the northwest – Gabrielle indicated the direction with a graceful inclination of her head.

While I talked with Gabrielle and Berthe, augmenting the conversation by means of hand-waving, I slowly became conscious that another sort of communication was taking place, with the old lady.

She said nothing to me directly – though she murmured now and then to Berthe, plainly demanding to know what I had said – but her bright dark eyes stayed fixed on me, and I was peculiarly aware of her regard. I had the odd feeling that she was talking to me – and I to her – without the exchange of a single spoken word.

I saw Jamie, across the clearing, offering Nacognaweto the rest of the bottle of brandy; clearly it was time to offer gifts in return. I gave Gabrielle the embroidered kerchief, and Berthe, a hairpin ornamented with paste brilliants, over which gifts they exclaimed in pleasure. For Nayawenne, though, I had something different.

I had been fortunate enough to find four large ginseng roots the week before. I fetched all four from my medicine chest and pressed them into her hands, smiling. She looked back at me, then grinned, and untying the cloth bag from her belt, thrust it at me. I didn't have to open it; I could feel the four long, lumpy shapes through the cloth.

I laughed in return; yes, we definitely spoke the same language!

Moved by curiosity, and by an impulse that I couldn't describe, I asked Gabrielle about the old lady's amulet, hoping that this wasn't an insufferable breach of good manners.

'*Grandmère est . . .*' She hesitated, looking for the right French word, but I already knew.

'*Pas docteur,*' I said, '*et pas sorcière, magicienne. Elle est . . .*' I hesitated too; there really wasn't a suitable word for it in French, after all.

'We say she is a singer,' Berthe put in shyly, in French. 'We call it *shaman*; her name, it means, "It may be; it will happen".'

The old lady said something, nodding at me, and the two younger women looked startled. Nayawenne bent her head, slipped the thong off her neck, and placed the little bag in my hand.

It was so heavy that my wrist sagged, and I nearly dropped it. Astonished, I closed my hand over it. The worn leather was warm from her body, the rounded contours fitting smoothly into my palm. For just a moment, I had the remarkable impression that something in the bag was alive.

My face must have shown my startlement, for the old lady doubled up laughing. She held out her hand and I gave her back the amulet, with a fair amount of haste. Gabrielle conveyed politely that her husband's grandmother would be pleased to show me the useful plants that grew nearby, if I would like to walk with her?

I accepted this invitation with alacrity, and the old lady set off up the path with a sure-footed spryness that belied her years. I watched her feet, tiny in soft leather boots, and hoped that when I was her age, I might be capable of walking for two days through the woods, and then wanting to go exploring.

We wandered along the stream for some way, followed at a respectful distance by Gabrielle and Berthe, who came up beside us only if summoned to interpret.

'Each of the plants holds the cure to a sickness,' the old lady explained through Gabrielle. She plucked a twig from a bush by the path and handed it to me with a wry look. 'If we only knew what they all were!'

For the most part, we managed fairly well by means of gesture, but when we reached the big pool where Jamie and Ian fished trout, Nayawenne stopped and waved, bringing Gabrielle to us again. She said something to the

418

woman, who turned to me, a faint look of surprise on her face.

'My husband's grandmother says that she had a dream about you, on the night of the full moon, two moons ago.'

'About me?'

Gabrielle nodded. Nayawenne put a hand on my arm and looked up intently into my face, as though to see the impact of Gabrielle's words.

'She told us about the dream; that she had seen a woman with –' Her lips twitched, then hastily straightened themselves, and she delicately touched the ends of her own long, straight hair. 'Three days later, my husband and his sons returned, to tell of meeting you and the Bear Killer in the forest.'

Berthe was watching me with frank interest, too, twining a lock of her own dark-brown hair around the end of an index finger.

'She who heals said at once that she must see you, and so when we heard that you were here . . .'

That gave me a small start; I had had no sensation of being watched, and yet plainly someone had taken note of our presence on the mountain, and conveyed the news to Nacognaweto.

Impatient with these irrelevancies, Nayawenne poked her granddaughter-in-law and said something, then pointed firmly at the water by our feet.

'My husband's grandmother says that when she dreamed of you, it was here.' Gabrielle gestured over the pool, and looked back at me with great seriousness.

'She met you here, at night. The moon was in the water. You became a white raven; you flew over the water and swallowed the moon.'

'Oh?' I hoped this wasn't a sinister thing for me to have done.

'The white raven flew back, and laid an egg in the palm of her hand. The egg split open, and there was a shining stone inside. My husband's grandmother knew this was great magic, that the stone could heal sickness.'

Nayawenne nodded her head several times, and taking the amulet bag from her neck, reached into it.

'On the day after the dream, my husband's grand-

419

mother went to dig *kinnea* root, and on the way, she saw something blue, sticking in the clay of the riverbank.'

Nayawenne drew out a small, lumpy object, and dropped it into my hand. It was a pebble; rough, but undeniably a gemstone. Bits of stony matrix clung to it, but the heart of the rock was a deep, soft blue.

'My goodness – it's a sapphire, isn't it?'

'Sapphire?' Gabrielle turned the word over in her mouth, tasting it. 'We call it . . .' She hesitated, looking for the proper French translation. ' . . . *pierre sans peur.*'

'*Pierre sans peur?*' A fearless stone?

Nayawenne nodded, talking again. Berthe butted in with the translation, before her mother could speak.

'My father's grandmother says a stone like this, it keeps people from being afraid, and so it makes their spirit strong, so they will be healed more easily. Already, this stone has healed two people of fever, and cured a soreness of the eyes that my younger brother had.'

'My husband's grandmother wishes to thank you for this gift.' Gabrielle neatly took back the conversation.

'Ah . . . do tell her she's quite welcome.' I nodded cordially at the old lady, and gave her back the blue stone. She popped it into the bag and drew the string tight about its neck. Then she peered closely at me, and reaching out, drew down a curl of my hair, talking as she rubbed the lock between her fingers.

'My husband's grandmother says that you have medicine now, but you will have more. When your hair is white like hers, that is when you will find your full power.'

The old lady dropped the lock of hair, and looked into my eyes for a moment. I thought I saw an expression of great sadness in the faded depths, and reached involuntarily to touch her.

She stepped back and said something else. Gabrielle looked at me queerly.

'She says you must not be troubled; sickness is sent from the gods. It won't be your fault.'

I looked at Nayawenne, startled, but she had already turned away.

'What won't be my fault?' I asked, but the old lady refused to say more.

420

21

Night on a Snowy Mountain

December 1767

The winter held off for some time, but snow began to fall in the night on November 28, and we woke to find the world transformed. Every needle on the great blue spruce behind the cabin was frosted, and ragged fringes of ice dripped from the tangle of wild raspberry canes.

The snow wasn't deep, but its coming changed the shape of daily life. I no longer foraged during the day, save for short trips to the stream for water, and for lingering bits of green cress salvaged from the icy slush along the banks. Jamie and Ian ceased their work of log felling and field clearing, and turned to roof shingling. The winter drew in on us, and we in turn withdrew from the cold, turning inward.

We had no candles; only grease lamps and rushlights, and the light of the fire that burned constantly on the hearth, blackening the roof beams. We therefore rose at first light, and lay down after supper, in the same rhythm as the creatures of the forest around us.

We had no sheep yet, and thus no wool to card or spin, no cloth to weave or dye. We had no beehives yet, and thus no wax to boil, no candles to dip. There was no stock to care for, save the horses and mules and the piglet, who had grown considerably in both size and irascibility, and in consequence been exiled to a private compartment in the corner of the crude stable Jamie had built – this itself no more than a large open-fronted shelter with a branch-covered roof.

Myers had brought a small but useful selection of tools, the iron parts clanking in a bag, to be supplied with wooden handles from the forest close at hand: a barking ax and another felling ax, a plowshare for the spring planting, augers, planes and chisels, a small grass scythe, two hammers and a handsaw, a peculiar thing called a 'twibil' that Jamie said was for cutting mortises, a 'drawk-nife' – a curved blade with handles at either end, used to smooth and taper wood – two small sharp knives, a hatchet-adze, something that looked like a medieval torture device but was really a nail-header, and a froe for splitting shingles.

Between them, Jamie and Ian had succeeded in getting a roof on the cabin before snow fell, but the sheds were less important. A block of wood sat constantly by the fire, the froe stuck through it, ready for anyone with an idle moment to strike off a few more shingles. That corner of the hearth was in fact devoted to wood carving; Ian had made a rough but serviceable stool, which sat under one of the windows for good light, and the shavings could all be tossed thriftily into the fire, which burned day and night.

Myers had brought a few woman's tools for me, as well: a huge sewing basket, well supplied with needles, pins, scissors, and balls of thread, and lengths of linen, muslin, and woven wool. While sewing was not my favorite occupation, I was nonetheless delighted to see these, since owing to Jamie and Ian's constantly lurching through thickets and crawling about on the roofs, the knees, elbows, and shoulders of all their garments were in constant disrepair.

'Another one!' Jamie sat bolt upright in bed beside me.

'Another what?' I asked sleepily, opening one eye. It was very dark in the cabin, the fire burnt to coals on the hearth.

'Another bloody leak! It hit me in the ear, damn it!' He sprang out of bed, went to the fire and thrust in a stick of wood. Once it was alight, he brought it back and stood on the bedstead, thrusting his torch upward as he glowered at the roof in search of the fiendish leak.

'Urmg?' Ian, who slept on a low trundle bed, rolled over and groaned inquiringly. Rollo, who insisted on sharing it with him, emitted a brief *'uff'*, relapsed into a heap of gray fur, and resumed his loud snoring.

'A leak,' I told Ian, keeping a narrow eye on Jamie's torch. I wasn't having my precious feather bed set alight by stray sparks.

'Oh.' Ian lay with an arm across his face. 'Has it snowed again?'

'It must have.' The windows were covered with squares of oiled deerhide, tacked down, and there was no sound from outside, but the air had the peculiar muffled quality that came with snow.

Snow came silently, and mounded on the roof, then, beginning to melt from the warmth of the shingles underneath, would drip down the slope of the roof, to leave a gleaming portcullis of icicles along the eaves. Now and then, though, the roaming water found a split in a shingle, or a join where the overlapping edges had warped, and drips poked their icy fingers through the roof.

Jamie regarded all such intrusions as a personal affront, and brooked no delay in dealing with them.

'Look!' he exclaimed. 'There it is. See it?'

I shifted my glassy gaze from the hairy ankles in front of my nose, to the roof overhead. Sure enough, the torch-light revealed the black line of a split in one shingle, with a spreading dark patch of dampness on the underside. As I watched, a clear drop formed, glistening red in the torchlight, and fell with a plop onto the pillow beside me.

'We could shift the bed a bit,' I suggested, though with no particular hope. I had been through this before. All suggestions that repair work could wait till daylight were met with astonished refusal; no proper man, I was given to understand, would countenance such a thing.

Jamie stepped down off the bedstead and prodded Ian in the ribs with his foot.

'Get up and knock at the spot where the split is, Ian. I'll deal with it on the outside.' Seizing a fresh shingle, a hammer, a hatchet, and a bag of nails, he headed for the door.

'Don't you go up on the roof in that!' I exclaimed, sitting up abruptly. 'That's your good woolen shirt!'

He halted by the door, glared briefly at me, then, with the rebuking expression of an early Christian martyr, laid down his tools, stripped off the shirt, dropped it on the floor, picked up the tools, and strode majestically out to deal with the leak, buttocks clenched with determined zeal.

I rubbed a hand over my sleep-puffed face and moaned softly to myself.

'He'll be all right, Auntie,' Ian assured me. He yawned widely, not bothering to cover his mouth, and reluctantly rolled out of his own warm bed.

Thumps on the roof that were definitely not the feet of eight tiny reindeer announced that Jamie was in place. I rolled out of the way and got up, resigned, as Ian mounted the bedstead and jabbed a stick of firewood upward into the damp patch, jarring the shingles enough for Jamie to locate the leak on the outside.

A short period of rending and banging followed, as the defective shingle was yanked loose and replaced, and the leak was summarily extinguished, leaving no more evidence of its existence than the small heap of snow that had fallen in through the hole left by the removed shingle.

Back in bed, Jamie curled his freezing body around me, clasped me to his icy bosom, and fell promptly asleep, full of the righteous satisfaction of a man who has defended hearth and home against all threat.

It was a fragile and tenuous foothold that we had upon the mountain – but a foothold, for all that. We had not much meat – there had been little time for hunting, beyond squirrel and rabbit, and those useful rodents had gone to their winter rest by now – but a fair amount of dried vegetables, from yams to squash to wild onions and garlic, plus a bushel or two of nuts, and the small stock of herbs I had managed to gather and dry. It made for a sparse diet, but with careful management, we could survive till spring.

With few chores to do outside, there was time to talk, to tell stories, and to dream. Between the useful objects like spoons and bowls, Jamie took time to carve the pieces of a wooden chess set, and spent a good deal of his time trying to inveigle me or Ian into playing with him.

Ian and Rollo, who both suffered badly from cabin fever, took to visiting Anna Ooka frequently, sometimes going on extended hunting trips with young men from the village, who were pleased to have the benefit of his and Rollo's company.

'The lad speaks the Indian tongue a great deal better

than he does Greek or Latin,' Jamie observed with some dourness, watching Ian exchanging cordial insults with an Indian companion as they left on one such excursion.

'Well, if Marcus Aurelius had written about tracking porcupines, I expect he'd have found a more eager audience,' I replied soothingly.

Dearly as I loved Ian, I was myself not displeased by his frequent absence. There were definitely times when three was a crowd.

There is nothing more delightful in life than a feather bed and an open fire – except a feather bed with a warm and tender lover in it. When Ian was gone, we would not trouble with rushlights but would go to bed with the dark, and lie curled together in shared warmth, talking late into the night, laughing and telling stories, sharing our pasts, planning our future, and somewhere in the midst of the talking, pausing to enjoy the wordless pleasures of the present.

'Tell me about Brianna.' These were Jamie's favorite stories; the tales of Brianna as a child. What she had said and worn and done; how she had looked, all her accomplishments and her tastes.

'Did I tell you about the time I was invited to her school, to talk about being a doctor?'

'No.' He shifted to make himself more comfortable, rolling onto his side and fitting himself to my shape behind. 'Why should you do that?'

'It was what they called Career Day; the schoolteachers invited a lot of people with different jobs to come and explain what they did, so the children would have some idea of what a lawyer does, for instance, or a firefighter –'

'I should think that one would be fairly obvious.'

'Hush. Or a veterinarian – that's a doctor who treats animals – or a dentist, that's a special doctor who deals only with teeth –'

'With *teeth*? What can ye do to a tooth, besides pull it?'

'You'd be surprised.' I brushed the hair out of my face and up off my neck. 'Anyway, they'd always ask me to come, because it wasn't at all common for a woman to be a doctor then.'

'Ye think it's common *now?*' He laughed, and I kicked him lightly in the shin.

'Well, it got more common rather soon after that. But at the time, it wasn't And when I'd got done speaking and asked if there were any questions, an obnoxious little boy piped up and said that *his* mother said women who worked were no better than prostitutes, and they ought to be home minding their families, instead of taking jobs away from men.'

'I shouldna think his mother can have met many prostitutes.'

'No, I don't imagine. Nor all that many women with jobs, either. But when he said that, Brianna stood up and said in a very loud voice, "Well, you'd better be glad my mama's a doctor, because you're going to *need* one!" Then she hit him on the head with her arithmetic book, and when he lost his balance and fell down, she jumped on his stomach and punched him in the mouth.'

I could feel his chest and stomach quivering against my back.

'Oh, braw lassie! Did the schoolmaster not tawse her for it, though?'

'They don't beat children in school. She had to write a letter of apology to the little beast, but then, he had to write one to *me*, and she thought that was a fair exchange. The more embarrassing part was that it turned out his father was a doctor too; one of my colleagues at the hospital.'

'I wouldna suppose you'd taken a job he'd wanted?'

'How did you guess?'

'Mmm.' His breath was warm and ticklish on the back of my neck. I reached back and stroked the length of a long, hairy thigh, enjoying the hollow and swell of the muscle.

'Ye said she was at a university, and studying history, like Frank Randall. Did she never want to be a doctor, like you?' A large hand cupped my bottom and began to knead it gently.

'Oh, she did when she was little – I used to take her to the hospital now and then, and she was fascinated by all the equipment; she loved to play with my stethoscope and the otoscope – a thing you look in ears with – but then

426

she changed her mind. She changed it a dozen times, at least; most children do.'

'They do?' This was a novel thought to him. Most children of the time would simply adopt the professions of their parents – or perhaps be apprenticed to learn one chosen for them.

'Oh, yes. Let me see . . . she wanted to be a ballerina for a while, like most little girls. That's a dancer who dances on her toes,' I explained, and he laughed in surprise. 'Then she wanted to be a garbageman – that was after our garbageman gave her a ride in his truck – and then a deep-sea diver, and a mailman, and –'

'What in God's name is a deep-sea diver? Let alone a garbageman?'

By the time I had finished a brief catalog of twentieth-century occupations, we were facing each other, our legs twined comfortably together, and I was admiring the way his nipple stiffened to a tiny bump under the ball of my thumb.

'I never was sure whether she really wanted to read history, or whether she did it mostly to please Frank. She loved him so much – and he was so proud of her.' I paused, thinking, as his hand played down the length of my back.

'She started taking history classes at the university when she was still in high school – I told you how the school system works? And then when Frank died . . . I rather think she went ahead with history because she thought he would have wanted it.'

'That's loyal.'

'Yes.' I ran my hand up through his hair, feeling the solid, rounded bones of his skull, and his scalp under my fingers. 'Can't think where she got that particular trait from.'

He snorted briefly and gathered me closer.

'Can't you?' Without waiting for an answer, he went on, 'If she goes on wi' the history – d'ye think she'll find us? Written down somewhere, I mean.'

The thought had honestly not occurred to me, and for a moment I lay quite still. Then I stretched a bit, and laid

427

my head on his shoulder with a small laugh, not altogether humorous.

'I shouldn't think so. Not unless we were to do something newsworthy.' I gestured vaguely toward the cabin wall, and the endless wilderness outside. 'Not much chance of that here, I don't imagine. And she'd have to be deliberately looking, in any case.'

'Would she?'

I was silent for a moment, breathing the musky, deep scent of him.

'I hope not,' I said quietly, at last. 'She should have her own life – not spend her time looking back.'

He didn't respond directly to this, but took my hand and eased it between us, sighing as I took hold of him.

'Ye're a verra intelligent woman, Sassenach, but short-sighted, forbye. Though perhaps it's only modesty.'

'And what makes you say that?' I asked, mildly piqued.

'The lassie's loyal, ye said. She'll have loved her father enough to shape her life to do as he would have wanted, even after he's dead. D'ye think she loved you less?'

I turned my head, and let the piled hair fall down over my face.

'No,' I said at last, voice muffled in the pillow.

'Well, then.' He took me by the hips and turned me, rolling slowly on top of me. We didn't speak anymore, then, as the melting boundaries of our bodies disappeared.

It was slow, dreamy and peaceful, his body mine as much as mine was his, so that I curled my foot round his leg and felt both smooth sole and hairy shin, felt callused palm and tender flesh, was knife and sheath together, the rhythm of our movement that of one heart beating.

The fire crackled softly to itself, casting red and yellow highlights on the wooden walls of our snug refuge, and we lay in quiet peace, not bothering to sort out whose limbs were whose. On the very verge of sleep, I felt Jamie's breath, warm on my neck.

'She'll look,' he said, with certainty.

There was a brief thaw two days later, and Jamie – suffering slightly from cabin fever himself – decided to take advantage of it to go hunting. There was still snow on the ground, but it was thin and patchy; the going would be easy enough on the slopes, he thought.

I wasn't so sure as I scooped snow into a basket for melting, later in the morning. The snow under the bushes still lay thick, though it had indeed melted on the exposed ground. I hoped he was right, though – our food supplies were low, and we had had no meat at all for more than a week; even the snares Jamie kept set had been buried under the snow.

I took my snow inside and tipped it into the large cauldron, feeling, as I always did, rather like a witch.

' "Double, double, toil and trouble," ' I muttered, watching the white clumps hiss and fade into the roiling liquid.

I had one large cauldron, filled with water, which bubbled constantly on the fire. This was not only the basic supply for washing but the means of cooking everything that could not be grilled, fried, or roasted. Stews and things to be boiled were put into hollow gourds or stone-ware jars, sealed, and lowered on strings into the bubbling depths, to be hauled out at intervals for checking. By this means, I could cook an entire meal in the one pot, and have hot water for washing afterward.

I dumped a second basket of snow into a wooden bowl and left it to melt more slowly; drinking water for the day. Then, with nothing of great urgency to do, I sat down to read Daniel Rawlings's casebook and mend stockings, my toes comfortably toasting by the fire.

At first, I didn't worry when Jamie didn't come back. That is, I did worry – I always worried when he was gone for long – but in a small and secret way that I succeeded for the most part in hiding from myself. When the shadows on the snow turned violet with the sinking sun, though, I began to listen for him with an increasing intensity.

I went about my work in constant expectation of the crunch of his footsteps, listening for a shout, ready to run out and lend a hand if he had brought back a turkey for plucking or some more or less edible thing in need of cleaning. I fed and watered the mules and horses, looking always up the mountain. As the afternoon light died around me, though, the expectation faded into hope.

It was growing chilly in the cabin, and I went out for more wood. It couldn't be much past four o'clock, I thought, and yet the shadows under the huckleberry bushes were already cold and blue. Another hour, and it would be dusk; it would be full dark in two.

The woodpile was dusted with snow, the other logs damp. By pulling a chunk of hickory from the side, though, I could reach inside and extract dry splits – being always mindful of snakes, skunks, and anything else that might have sought shelter in the hollow thus provided.

I sniffed, then bent and peered cautiously inside, and as a final precaution poked a long stick inside and stirred it briefly round. Hearing no scuffles, slitherings, or other sounds of alarm, I reached inside with confidence, and groped until my fingers encountered the deep-ridged grain of a chunk of fat pine. I wanted a hot, quick-burning fire tonight; after a full day spent hunting in snow, Jamie would be chilled through.

Fat pine for the heart of the fire, then, and three small chunks of slower-burning hickory from the wet outer layer of the woodpile. I could stack those inside the hearth to dry, while I finished the supper making; then when we went to bed, I'd smoor the fire with the damp hickory, which would burn more slowly, smoldering till morning.

The shadows went to indigo and faded into the gray winter dusk. The sky was lavender with thick cloud; snow clouds. I could breathe the cold wetness in the air; when the temperature fell after dark, so would the snow.

'Bloody man,' I said aloud. 'What have you done, shot a moose?' My voice sounded small in the muffled air, but the thought made me feel better. If he had in fact bagged something large near the end of the day, he might well have chosen to camp by the carcass; butchering a large animal was exhausting, lengthy work, and meat was too hard come by to leave it to the mercies of predators.

My vegetable stew was bubbling, and the cabin was filled with the savory scent of onions and wild garlic, but I had no appetite. I pushed the kettle on its hook to the back of the hearth – easy enough to heat again when he came. A

430

tiny flash of green caught my eye, and I stooped to look. A tiny salamander, frightened out of its winter refuge in a crack of the wood.

It was green and black, vivid as a tiny jewel; I scooped him up before he could panic and run into the fire, and carried the damp little thing outside, wriggling madly against my palm. I put him back in the woodpile, safely near the bottom.

'Watch out,' I said to him, 'you might not be so lucky next time!'

I paused before going back inside. It had gone dark now, but I could still make out the trunks of the trees around the clearing, chalk and gray against the looming black bulk of the mountain beyond. Nothing stirred among the trees, but a few fat, wet flakes of snow began to fall from the soft, pink sky, melting at once on the bare ground of the dooryard.

I barred the door, ate some supper without tasting it, smoored the fire with damp hickory, and lay down to sleep. He might have met some men from Anna Ooka and be camped with them.

The scent of hickory smoke floated in the air, wisps of white curling up over the hearth. The beams above were already black with soot, though fires had burned here for no more than two months now. Fresh resin still oozed from the timber by my head, in small gold droplets that glowed like honey and smelled of turpentine, sharp and clean. The ax strokes in the wood showed in the firelight, and I had a sudden, vivid memory of Jamie's broad back, sheened with sweat as he swung the ax, over and over in strokes like clockwork, the ax blade coming down in a flash of metal inches from his foot as he worked his way along the squared rough timber.

It was awfully easy to misjudge the stroke of an ax or hatchet. He might have cut wood for his fire and missed his stroke, caught an arm or leg. My imagination, always eager to help out, promptly supplied a crystal-clear vision of arterial blood spurting onto white snow in a crimson spray.

I flounced over onto my side. He knew how to live outdoors. He'd spent seven years in a cave, for heaven's sake!

431

In Scotland, said my imagination, cynically. Where the biggest carnivore is a wildcat the size of a house cat. Where the biggest human threat was English soldiers.

'Fiddlesticks!' I said, and rolled onto my back. 'He's a grown man and he's armed to the teeth and he certainly knows what to do if it's snowing!'

What *would* he do? I wondered. Find or make shelter, I supposed. I recalled the crude lean-to he'd built for us when we first camped on the ridge, and felt a little reassured. If he hadn't hurt himself, he probably wouldn't freeze to death.

If he hadn't hurt himself. If something else hadn't hurt him. The bears were presumably fat and fast asleep, but the wolves still hunted in winter, and the catamounts; I recalled the one I had met by the stream, and shivered in spite of the feather bed.

I rolled onto my stomach, the quilts drawn up around my shoulders. It was warm in the cabin, warmer in the bed, but my hands and feet were still icy. I longed for Jamie, in a visceral way that had nothing to do with thought or reason. To be alone with Jamie was bliss, adventure, and absorption. To be alone without him was . . . to be alone.

I could hear the whisper of snow against the oiled hide that covered the window near my head. If it kept up, his tracks would be covered by morning. And if anything *had* happened to him . . .

I flung back the quilts and got up. I dressed quickly, without thinking too much about what I was doing; I'd thought too much already. I put on my woolen cutty sark for insulation beneath my buckskins, and two pairs of stockings. I thanked God that my boots were freshly greased with otter fat; they smelt very fishy, but would keep the damp out for a good while.

He had taken the hatchet; I had to split another piece of fat pine with a mallet and wedge, cursing my slowness as I did so. Having now decided on action, every small delay seemed an unbearable irritation. The long-grained wood split easily, though; I had five decent faggots, four of which I bound with a leather strap. I thrust the end of the fifth deep into the smoky embers of the fire, and waited till the end was well caught.

Then I tied a small medicine bag about my waist, checked to be sure I had the pouch of flints and kindling, put on my cloak, took up my bundle and my torch, and set out into the falling snow.

It was not as cold as I had feared; once I began moving, I was quite warm inside my wrappings. It was very quiet; there was no wind, and the whisper of the snowfall drowned all the usual noises of the night.

He had meant to walk his trapline, that much I knew. If he came across promising sign en route, though, he would have followed it. The previous snow lay thin and patchy on the ground, but the earth was soaked, and Jamie was a big man; I was fairly sure I could follow his track, if I came across it. And if I came across *him*, denned up for the night near his kill, so much the better. Two slept much better than one in the cold.

Past the bare chestnuts that ringed our clearing to the west, I turned uphill. I had no great sense of direction, but could certainly tell up from down. Jamie had also carefully taught me to navigate using large, immutable landmarks. I glanced toward the falls, their white cascade no more than a blur in the distance. I couldn't hear them; what wind there was must be away from me.

'When you're hunting, ye want the wind toward ye,' Jamie had explained. 'So the stag or the hare wilna scent ye.'

I wondered uncomfortably what might be out in the dark, scenting *me* on the snowborne air. I wasn't armed, save for my torch. The light glittered red on the crust of packed snow, and shattered from the ice that coated every twig. If I got within a quarter-mile of him, he'd see me.

The first snare was set in a small dell no more than two hundred yards uphill from the cabin, amid a grove of spruce and hemlock. I had been with him when he set it, but that had been in daylight; even with the torch, everything looked strange and unfamiliar by night.

I cast to and fro, bending close to bring my light near the ground. It took several journeys back and forth across the little dell before I finally spotted what I was looking for – the dark indentation of a foot in a patch of snow between two spruce trees. A little more looking and I found the snare, still set. Either it had caught nothing, or he had removed the catch and reset it.

The footprints led out of the clearing and upward again, then disappeared in a bare patch of matted dead leaves. A moment's panic as I criss-crossed the patch, looking for a scuffled place that might be a footprint. Nothing showed; the leaves must be a foot thick here, spongy and resilient. But there! Yes, there was a log over-turned; I could see the dark, wet furrow where it had lain, and the scuffed moss on its side. Ian had told me that squirrels and chipmunks sometimes hibernated in the cavities under logs.

Very slowly, constantly losing the trail and having to circle and backtrack to find it again, I followed him from one snare to another. The snow was falling thicker and faster, and I felt some uneasiness. If it covered his tracks before I found him, how would I find my way back to the cabin?

I looked back, but could see nothing behind me but a long, treacherous slope of unbroken snow that fell to the dark line of an unfamiliar brook below, its rocks poking up like teeth. No sign of the cheerful plume of smoke and sparks from our chimney. I turned slowly round in a circle, but I could no longer see the falls, either.

'Fine,' I muttered to myself. 'You're lost. *Now* what?' I sternly quelled an incipient attack of panic, and stood still to think. I wasn't totally lost. I didn't know where I was, but that wasn't quite the same thing. I still had Jamie's trail to guide me – or would have, until the snow covered it. And if I could find him, he presumably could find the cabin.

My torch was burning dangerously low; I could feel the heat of it, blistering on my hand. I extracted another of the dry faggots from under my cloak, and lit it from the stub of the first, dropping the ember just before it burned my fingers.

Was I going farther from the cabin, I wondered, or walking parallel to it? I knew that the trapline described a rough circle, but had no idea precisely how many snares there were. I had found three so far, all empty and waiting.

The fourth one wasn't empty. My torch caught the glitter of ice crystals, fringing the fur of a large hare,

434

stretched out under a frozen bush. I touched it, picked it up and disentangled the noose from its neck. It was stiff, whether from cold or rigor mortis. Been dead a while, then – and what did that tell me about Jamie's whereabouts?

I tried to think logically, ignoring the increasing cold seeping through my boots and the growing numbness of face and fingers. The hare lay in snow; I could see the indentations of its pawprints, and the flurry of its death struggle. I couldn't see any of Jamie's footprints, though. All right; he hadn't visited this snare, then.

I stood still, my breath forming small white clouds around my head. I could feel ice forming inside my nostrils; it was getting colder. Somewhere between the last snare and this one, he had left his path, then. Where? And where had he gone?

Urgently, I backtracked, looking for the last footprint I was sure of. It took a long time to find; the snow had nearly covered all the bare ground with a thin dusting of glitter. My second torch was half burned through before I found it again. There it was, a featureless blur in the mud on the edge of a stream. I had found the snare with the rabbit only by going in the direction I thought this footprint pointed – but evidently it didn't. He had stepped out of the mud, and gone . . . where?

'Jamie!' I shouted. I called several times, but the snow seemed to swallow my voice. I listened, but heard nothing save the gurgle of the ice-rimmed water by my feet.

He wasn't behind me, he wasn't in front of me. Left, then, or right?

'Eeny, meeny, miney, mo,' I muttered, and turned downhill because the walking was easier, shouting now and then.

I stopped to listen. Was there an answering shout? I called again, but couldn't make out a reply. The wind was coming up, rattling the tree limbs overhead.

I took another step, landed on an icy rock, and my foot slid out from under me. I slipped and skidded, floundering down a short, muddy slope, hit a screen of dog-hobble, burst through and clutched a handful of icy twigs, heart pounding.

At my feet was the edge of a rocky outcrop, ending in thin air. Clinging to the bush to keep from slipping, I edged my way closer, and looked over.

It was not a cliff, as I'd thought; the drop was no more than five feet. It was not this that made my heart leap into my throat, though, but rather the sight that met my eyes in the leaf-filled hollow below.

There was a flurry of tossed and scuffled leaves, reminding me unpleasantly of the death marks left by the limp rabbit that hung at my belt. Something large had struggled on the ground here – and then been dragged away. A wide furrow plowed through the leaves, disappearing into the darkness beyond.

Heedless of my footing, I scrabbled my way down the side of the outcrop and rushed toward the furrow, following it under the overhanging low branches of hemlock and balsam. In the uncertain light of my flickering torch, I followed its path around a pile of rocks, through a clump of winter-green, and . . .

He was lying near the foot of a large split boulder, half covered in leaves, as though something had tried to bury him. He wasn't curled for warmth, but lay flat on his face, and deathly still. The snow lay thick on the folds of his cloak, dusted the heels of his muddy boots.

I dropped my torch and flung myself on his body with a cry of horror.

He let out a bloodcurdling groan and convulsed under me. I jerked back, torn between relief and terror. He wasn't dead, but he *was* hurt. Where, how badly?

'Where?' I demanded, wrenching at his cloak, which was tangled round his body. 'Where are you hurt? Are you bleeding, have you broken something?'

I couldn't see any large patches of blood, but I had dropped my torch, which had promptly extinguished itself in the wet leaves that covered him. The pink sky and falling snow shed a luminous glow over everything, but the light was much too dim to make out details.

He was frighteningly cold; his flesh felt chilly even to my snow-numbed hands, and he stirred sluggishly, subsiding into small moans and grunts. I thought I heard him mumble, 'Back', though, and once I got his cloak out of the way, I tore at his shirt, yanking it ruthlessly out of his breeks.

This made him groan loudly, and I thrust my hands under the cloth in a panic, looking for the bullet hole. He must have been shot in the back; the entrance would wouldn't bleed much, but where had it come out? Had the ball gone clean through? A small piece of my mind found leisure to wonder who'd shot him, and whether they were still nearby.

Nothing. I found nothing; my groping hands encountered nothing but bare, clean flesh; cold as a slab of marble and webbed with old scars, but completely unperforated. I tried again, forcing myself to slow down, feeling with mind as well as fingers, running my palms slowly over his back from nape to small. Nothing.

Lower? There were dark smudges on the seat of his breeks; I'd thought them mud. I thrust a hand under him and groped for his laces, jerked them loose and yanked down his breeches.

It *was* mud; his buttocks glowed before me, white, firm, and perfect in their roundness, unmarred beneath a silver fuzz. I clutched a handful of his flesh, unbelieving.

'Is that you, Sassenach?' he asked, rather drowsily.

'Yes, it's me! What happened to you?' I demanded, frenzy giving way to indignation. 'You said you'd been shot in the back!'

'No, I didn't. I couldna, for I haven't been,' he pointed out logically. He sounded calm and still rather sleepy, his speech slightly slurred. 'There's a verra cold wind whistlin' up my backside, Sassenach; d'ye think ye could maybe cover me?'

I jerked up his breeches, making him grunt again.

'What the hell is the matter with you?' I said.

He was waking up a bit; he twisted his head to look round at me, moving laboriously.

'Aye, well. No real matter. It's only that I canna move much.'

I stared at him.

'Why not? Have you twisted your foot? Broken your leg?'

437

'Ah . . . no.' He sounded a trifle sheepish. 'I . . . ah . . . I've put my back out of joint.'

'You *what?*'

'I've done it once before,' he assured me. 'It doesna last more than a day or two.'

'I suppose it didn't occur to you that *you* wouldn't last more than a day or two, lying out here on the ground, covered with snow?'

'It did,' he said, still drowsy, 'but there didna seem much I could do about it.'

It was rapidly dawning on me that there might not be that much *I* could do about it, either. He outweighed me by a good sixty pounds; I couldn't carry him. I couldn't even drag him very far over slopes and rocks and gullies. It was too steep for a horse; I might possibly persuade one of the mules to come up here – if I could first find my way back to the cabin in the dark, and then find my way back up the mountain, also in the dark – and in the middle of what looked like becoming a blizzard. Or perhaps I could build a toboggan of tree branches, I thought wildly, and career down the snowy slopes astride his body.

'Oh, do get a grip, Beauchamp,' I said aloud. I wiped at my running nose with a fold of cloak, and tried to think what to do next.

It was a sheltered spot, I realized; looking upward, I could see the snowflakes whirling past the top of the big rock at whose foot we crouched, but there was no wind where we sat, and only a few heavy flakes floated down onto my upturned face.

Jamie's hair and shoulders were lightly dusted with snow, and flakes were settling on the exposed backs of his legs. I pulled the hem of his cloak down, then brushed the snow away from his face. His cheek was nearly the same color as the big wet flakes, and his flesh felt stiff when I touched it.

Fresh alarm surged through me as I realized that he might be a lot closer to freezing already than I had thought. His eyes were half closed, and cold as it was, he didn't seem to be shivering much. That was *bloody* dangerous; with no movement, his muscles were generating no heat, and what warmth he had was leaching slowly from his body. His cloak was already heavy with damp; if I allowed his clothes to become soaked through, he might very well die of hypothermia right in front of me.

'Wake up!' I said, shaking him urgently by the shoulder. He opened his eyes and smiled drowsily at me.

'Move!' I said. 'Jamie, you've got to move!'

'I can't,' he said calmly. 'I told ye that.' He shut his eyes again.

I grabbed him by the ear and dug my fingernails into the tender lobe. He grunted and jerked his head away.

'Wake up,' I said peremptorily. 'Do you hear me? Wake up this moment! Move, damn you! Give me your hand.'

I didn't wait for him to comply, but dug under the cloak and seized his hand, which I chafed madly between my own. He opened his eyes again and frowned at me.

'I'm all right,' he said. 'But I'm gey tired, aye?'

'Move your arms,' I ordered, flinging the hand at him. 'Flap them, up and down. Can you move your legs at all?'

He sighed wearily, as though dragging himself out of a sticky bog, and muttered something under his breath in Gaelic, but very slowly he began to move his arms back and forth. With more prodding, he succeeded in flexing his ankles – though any further movement caused instant spasms in his back – and with great reluctance, began to waggle his feet.

He looked rather like a frog trying to fly, but I wasn't in any mood to laugh. I didn't know whether he was actually in danger of freezing or not, but I wasn't taking any chances. By dint of constant exhortation, aided by judicious pokings, I kept him at this exercise until I had got him altogether awake and shivering. In a thoroughly bad temper, too, but I didn't mind that.

'Keep moving,' I advised him. I got up with some difficulty, having grown quite stiff from crouching over him so long. 'Move, I say!' I added sharply, as he showed symptoms of flagging. 'Stop and I'll step square on your back, I swear I will!'

I glanced around, a little blearily. The snow was still falling, and it was difficult to see more than a few feet. We needed shelter – more than the rock alone could provide.

'Hemlock,' he said between his teeth. I glanced down at

him, and he jerked his head toward a clump of trees nearby. 'Take the hatchet. Big . . . branches. Six feet. C-cut four.' He was breathing heavily, and there was a tinge of color visible in his face, despite the dim light. He'd stopped moving in spite of my threats, but his teeth were clenched because they were chattering; a sign I rejoiced to see.

I stooped and groped beneath his cloak again, this time searching for the hatchet belted round his waist. I couldn't resist sliding a hand under him, inside the neck of his fringed woolen hunting shirt. Warm! Thank God, he was still warm; his chest felt superficially chilled from its contact with the wet ground, but it was still warmer than my fingers.

'Right,' I said, taking my hand away and standing up with the hatchet. 'Hemlock. Six-foot branches, do you mean?'

He nodded, shivering violently, and I set off at once for the trees he indicated.

Inside the silent grove, the fragrance of hemlock and cedar enfolded me at once in a mist of resins and turpenes, the odor cold and sharp, clean and invigorating. Many of the trees were enormous, with the lower branches well above my head, but there were smaller ones scattered here and there. I saw at once the virtues of this particular tree – no snow fell under them; the fanlike boughs caught the falling snow like umbrellas.

I hacked at the lower branches, torn between the need for haste and the very real fear of chopping off a few fingers by accident; my hands were numb and awkward with the cold.

The wood was green and elastic and it took forever to chop through the tough, springy fibers. At last, though, I had four good-sized branches, sporting multiple fans of dense needles. They looked soft and black against the new snow, like big fans of feathers; it was almost a surprise to touch them and feel the hard, cold price of the needles.

I dragged them back to the rock, and found that Jamie had managed to scoop more leaves together; he was almost invisible, submerged in a huge drift of black and gray against the foot of the rock.

440

Under his terse direction I leaned the hemlock branches fan up against the face of the rock, the chopped butt ends stuck into the earth at an angle, so as to form a small triangular refuge underneath. Then I took the hatchet again and chopped small pine and spruce branches, pulled up big clumps of dried grass, and piled it all against and over the hemlock screen. Then at last, panting with exertion, I crawled into the shelter beside him.

I nestled down in the leaves between his body and the rock, wrapped my cloak around both of us, put my arms around his body, and held on hard. Then I found the leisure to shake a bit. Not from cold – not yet – but from a mixture of relief and fear.

He felt me shivering, and reached awkwardly back to pat me in reassurance.

'It will be all right, Sassenach,' he said. 'With the two of us, it will be all right.'

'I know,' I said, and put my forehead against his shoulder blade. It was a long time before I stopped shaking, though.

'How long have you been out here?' I asked finally. 'On the ground, I mean?'

He started to shrug, then stopped abruptly, groaning.

'A good time. It was just past noon when I jumped off a wee crop of rock. It wasna more than a few feet high, but when I landed on one foot, my back went click! and next I knew, I was on my face in the dirt, feelin' as though someone had stabbed me in the spine wi' a dirk.'

It wasn't warm in our snug, by any means; the damp from the leaves was seeping in and the rock at my back seemed to radiate coldness, like some sort of reverse furnace. Still, it was noticeably less cold than it was outside. I began shivering again, for purely physical reasons.

Jamie felt me, and groped at his throat.

'Can ye get my cloak unfastened, Sassenach? Put it over ye.'

It took some maneuvering, and the cost of a few muffled oaths from Jamie as he tried to shift his weight, but I got it loose at last, and spread it over the two of us. I reached

441

down and laid a cautious hand on his back, gently rucking up his shirt to put my hand on cool, bare flesh.

'Tell me where it hurts,' I said. I hoped to hell he hadn't slipped a disc; hideous thoughts of his being permanently crippled raced through my mind, along with pragmatic considerations of how I was to get him off the mountain, even if he wasn't. Would I have to leave him here, and fetch food up to him daily until he recovered?

'Right there,' he said, with a hiss of indrawn breath. 'Aye, that's it. A wicked stab just there, and if I move, it runs straight down the back o' my leg, like a red-hot wire.'

I felt very carefully, with both hands now, probing and pressing, urging him to try to lift one leg, right, now the other knee . . . no?

'No,' he assured me. 'Dinna be worrit, though, Sassenach. It's the same as before. It gets better.'

'Yes, you said it happened before. When was that?'

He stirred briefly and settled, pressing back against my palms with a small groan.

'Och! Damn, that hurts. At the prison.'

'Pain in the same place?'

'Aye.'

I could feel a hard knot in the muscle on his right side, just below the kidney, and a bunching in the erector spinae, the long muscles near the spine. From his description of the prior occurrence, I was fairly sure it was only severe muscle spasm. For which the proper prescription was warmth, rest, and anti-inflammatory medication.

Couldn't get much further away from those conditions, I thought with some grimness.

'I suppose I could try acupuncture,' I said, thinking aloud. 'I've got Mr. Willoughby's needles in my pouch, and –'

'Sassenach,' he said, in measured tones. 'I can stand fine bein' hurt, cold, and hungry. I wilna put up wi' being stabbed in the back by my own wife. Can ye not offer a bit of sympathy and comfort instead?'

I laughed, and slid an arm around him, pressing close against his back. I let my hand slide down and rest in delicate suggestion, well below his navel.

'Er . . . what sort of comfort did you have in mind?'

He hastily grasped my hand, to prevent further intrusions.

'Not that,' he said.

'Might take your mind off the pain.' I wiggled my fingers invitingly, and he tightened his grip.

'I daresay,' he said dryly. 'Well, I'll tell ye, Sassenach; once we've got home, and I've a warm bed to lie in and a hot supper in my belly, that notion might have a good bit of appeal. As it is, the thought of – for Christ's sake, have ye not the slightest idea how cold your hands are, woman?'

I laid my cheek against his back and laughed. I could feel the quiver of his own mirth, though he couldn't laugh aloud without hurting his back.

At last we lay silent, listening to the whisper of falling snow. It was dark under the hemlock boughs, but my eyes were adapted enough to be able to see patches of the oddly glowing snow-light through the screen of needles overhead. Tiny flakes came through the open patches; I could see it in some places, as a thin cloud of white mist, and I could feel the cold tingle as it struck my face.

Jamie himself was no more than a humped dark shape in front of me, though as my eyes became accustomed to the murk, I could see the paler stalk where his neck emerged between his shirt and his queued hair. The queue itself lay cool and smooth against my face; by turning my head only a bit, I could brush it with my lips.

'What time do you think it is?' I asked. I had no idea, myself; I had left the house well after dark, and spent what seemed an eternity looking for him on the mountain.

'Late,' he said. 'It will be a long time before the dawn, though,' he added, answering my real question. 'It's just past the solstice, aye? It's one of the longest nights of the year.'

'Oh, lovely,' I said, in dismay. I wasn't warm, by any means – I still couldn't feel my toes – but I had stopped shivering. A dreadful lethargy was stealing over me, my muscles yielding to fatigue and cold. I had visions of the two of us freezing peacefully together, curled up like hedgehogs in the leaves. They did say it was a comfortable death, but that didn't make the prospect any more appealing.

Jamie's breathing was getting slower and deeper.

'Don't go to sleep!' I said urgently, poking him in the armpit.

'Agh!' He pressed his arm tight to his side, recoiling. 'Why not?'

'We mustn't sleep; we'll freeze to death.'

'No, we won't,' he said crossly. 'It's snowing outside; we'll be covered over soon.'

'I know that,' I said, rather cross in my turn. 'What's that got to do with it?'

He tried to turn his head to look at me, but couldn't, quite.

'Snow's cold if ye touch it,' he explained, striving for patience, 'but it keeps the cold out, aye? Like a blanket. It's a great deal warmer in a house that's covered wi' snow than one that's standing clean in the wind. How d'ye think bears manage? They sleep in the winter, and they dinna freeze.'

'They have layers of fat,' I protested. 'I thought that kept them warm.'

'Ha ha,' he said, and reaching back with some effort, grabbed me firmly by the bottom. 'Well, then, ye needna worry a bit, eh?'

With great deliberation I pulled down his collar, stretched my head up, and licked the back of his neck, in a lingering swipe from nape to hairline.

'Aaah!' He shuddered violently, making a sprinkle of snow fall from the branches above us. He let go of my bottom to scrub at the back of his neck.

'That was a *terrible* thing to do!' he said, reproachful. 'And me lyin' here helpless as a log!'

'Bah, humbug,' I said. I nestled closer, feeling somewhat reassured. 'You're sure we aren't going to freeze to death, then?'

'No,' he said. 'But I shouldna think it likely.'

'Hm,' I said, feeling somewhat less reassured. 'Well, perhaps we'd better stay awake for a bit, then, just in case?'

'I wilna wave my arms about anymore,' he said definitely. 'There's no room. And if ye stick your icy wee paws in my breeks, I swear I'll throttle ye, bad back or no.'

'All right, all right,' I said. 'What if I tell you a story, instead?'

Highlanders loved stories, and Jamie was no exception.

'Oh, aye,' he said, sounding much happier. 'What sort of story is it?'

'A Christmas story,' I said, settling myself along the curve of his body. 'About a miser named Ebenezer Scrooge.'

'An Englishman, I daresay?'

'Yes,' I said. 'Be quiet and listen.'

I could see my own breath as I talked, white in the dim, cold air. The snow was falling heavily outside our shelter; when I paused in the story, I could hear the whisper of flakes against the hemlock branches, and the far-off whine of wind in the trees.

I knew the story very well; it had been part of our Christmas ritual, Frank's and Brianna's and mine. From the time Bree was five or six, we had read *A Christmas Carol* every year, starting a week or two before Christmas, Frank and I taking it in turns to read to her each night before bed.

'And the specter said, "I am the Ghost of Christmas Past . . ." '

I might not be freezing to death, but the cold had a strange, hypnotic effect nonetheless. I had gone past the phase of acute discomfort and felt now slightly disembodied. I knew my hands and feet were icy, and my body chilled half through, but it didn't seem to matter anymore. I floated in a peaceful white mist, seeing the words swirl round my head like snowflakes as I spoke them.

' . . . and there was dear old Fezziwig, among the lights and music . . .'

I couldn't tell whether I was gradually thawing or becoming colder. I was conscious of an overall feeling of relaxation, and an altogether peculiar sense of déjà vu, as though I had once before been entombed, insulated in snow, snug despite desolation outside.

As Bob Cratchit bought his meager bird, I remembered. I went on talking automatically, the flow of the story coming from somewhere well below the level of consciousness, but my memory was in the front seat of a stalled 1956 Oldsmobile, its windscreen caked with snow.

We had been on our way to visit an elderly relative of Frank's, somewhere in upstate New York. The snow came on hard, halfway there, howling down across the icy roads with gusts of wind. Before we knew where we were, we had skidded off the road and halfway into a ditch, the windscreen wipers slashing futilely at the pelting snow.

There was nothing to be done but wait for morning, and rescue. We had had a picnic hamper and some old blankets; we brought Brianna up into the front seat between us, and huddled all together under coats and blankets, sipping lukewarm cocoa from the thermos and making jokes to keep her from being frightened.

As it grew later, and colder, we huddled closer, and to distract Brianna, Frank began to tell her Dickens's story from memory, counting on me to supply the missing bits. Neither of us could have done it alone, but between us, we managed well. By the time the sinister Ghost of Christmas Yet to Come had made his appearance, Brianna was snuggled sound asleep under the coats, a warm, boneless weight against my side.

There was no need to finish the story, but we did, talking to each other below the words, hands touching below the layers of blankets. I remembered Frank's hands, warm and strong on mine, thumb stroking my palm, outlining my fingers. Frank had always loved my hands.

The car had filled with the mist of our breathing, and drops of water ran down inside the white-choked windows. Frank's head had been a dark cameo, dim against the white. He had leaned toward me at the last, nose and cheeks chilled, lips warm on mine as he whispered the last words of the story.

' "God bless us, every one," ' I ended, and lay silent, a small needle of grief like an ice splinter through my heart. It was quiet inside the shelter, and seemed darker; snow had covered over all the openings.

Jamie reached back and touched my leg.

'Put your hands inside my shirt, Sassenach,' he said softly. I slid one hand up under his shirt in front, to rest

446

against his chest, the other up his back. The faded whip marks felt like threads under his skin.

He laid his hand against mine, pressing it tight against his chest. He was very warm, and his heart beat slow and strong under my fingers.

'Sleep, *a nighean donn*,' he said. 'I wilna let ye freeze.'

I woke abruptly from a chilly doze, with Jamie's hand squeezing my thigh.

'Hush,' he said softly. Our tiny shelter was still dim, but the quality of the light had changed. It was morning; we were covered over with a thick blanket of snow that blocked the daylight, but the faint otherworldly quality of the night's darkness had vanished.

The silence had vanished, too. Sounds from outside were muffled, but audible. I heard what Jamie had heard – a faint echo of voices – and jerked up in excitement.

'Hush!' he said again, in a fierce whisper, and squeezed my leg harder.

The voices were drawing closer, and it became almost possible to pick out words. Almost. Strain as I might, I could make no sense of what was being said. Then I realized that it was because they were not speaking any language I recognized.

Indians. It was an Indian tongue. But I thought the language was not Tuscarora, even though I couldn't yet make out words; the rise and fall was similar, but the rhythm was somehow different. I brushed the hair out of my eyes, feeling torn in two directions.

Here was the help we so badly needed – by the sound of it, there were several men in the party, enough to move Jamie safely. On the other hand, did we really want to attract the attention of a band of unfamiliar Indians who might be raiders?

Rather plainly we didn't, judging from Jamie's attitude. He had managed to lift himself on one elbow, and he had his knife drawn, ready in his right hand. He scratched his stubbled chin absently with the point as he tilted his head to listen more intently to the approaching voices.

A clump of snow fell from the framework of our cage, landing on my head with a little *plop!* and making me start. The movement loosened more snow, which poured inward in a glittering cascade, dusting Jamie's head and shoulders with fine white powder.

His fingers were gripping my leg hard enough to leave bruises, but I didn't move or make a sound. A patch of snow had fallen from the lattice-work of hemlock branches, leaving numerous small spaces through which I could see out between the needles, peering over Jamie's shoulder.

The ground sloped a little away from us, falling a few feet to the level of the grove where I had cut branches the night before. Everything was thick with snow; a good four inches must have fallen during the night. It was just past dawn, and the rising sun painted the black trees with coruscations of red and gold, striking white glare from the icy sweep of snow below. The wind had come up in the wake of the storm; loose snow blew off the branches in drifting clouds, like smoke.

The Indians were on the other side of the grove; I could hear the voices plainly now; arguing about something, from the sound of it. A sudden thought raised gooseflesh on my arms; if they came through the grove, they might see the hacked branches where I had chopped limbs from the hemlocks. I hadn't been neat; there would be needles and bits of bark scattered all over the ground. Would enough snow have trickled through the branches to cover my awkward spoor?

A flash of movement showed in the trees, then another, and suddenly they were there, materializing out of the hemlock grove like dragon's teeth sprung from the snow.

They were dressed for winter travel, in fur and leather, some with cloaks or cloth coats atop their leggings and soft boots. They all carried bundles of blankets and provisions, had headpieces made of fur, and most had snow-shoes slung across their shoulders; evidently the snow here was not deep enough to render them necessary.

They were armed; I could see a few muskets, and tomahawks or war clubs hung at every belt. Six, seven, eight . . . I counted silently as they came out of the trees in single file, each man treading in the prints of the one before him. One near the back called out something, half

448

laughing, and a man near the front replied over his shoulder, his words lost in the blowing veil of snow and wind.

I drew a deep breath. I could smell Jamie's scent, a sharp tinge of fresh sweat above his normal musky sleep-smell. I was sweating, too, in spite of the cold. Did they have dogs? Could they sniff us out, hidden as we were beneath the sharp reek of spruce and hemlock?

Then I realized that the wind must be toward us, carrying the sound of their voices. No, even dogs wouldn't scent us. But would they see the branches that framed our den? Even as I wondered this, a large patch of snow slid off with a rush, landing with a soft *flump!* outside.

Jamie drew in his breath sharply, and I leaned over his shoulder, staring. The last man had come out of the gap in the trees, an arm across his face to shield it from the blowing snow.

He was a Jesuit. He wore a short cape of bearskin over his habit, leather leggings and moccasins under it – but he had black skirts, kilted up for walking in the snow, and a wide, flat black priest's hat, held on with one hand against the wind. His face, when he showed it, was blond-bearded, and so fair-skinned that I could see the redness of his cheeks and nose even at such a distance.

'Call them!' I whispered, leaning close to Jamie's ear. 'They're Christians, they must be, to have a priest with them. They won't hurt us.'

He shook his head slowly, not taking his eyes off the file of men, now vanishing from our view behind a snow-topped outcropping.

'No,' he said, half under his breath. 'No. Christians they may be, but . . .' He shook his head again, more decidedly. 'No.'

There was no use arguing with him. I rolled my eyes in mingled frustration and resignation.

'How's your back?'

He stretched gingerly, and halted abruptly in mid-motion, with a strangled cry as though he'd been skewered.

'Not so good, hm?' I said, sympathy well laced with sarcasm. He gave me a dirty look, eased himself very slowly back into his bed of crushed leaves, and shut his eyes with a sigh.

'You have of course thought of some ingenious way of getting down the mountain, I imagine?' I said politely.

He opened one eye.

'No,' he said, and shut it again. He breathed quietly, his chest rising and falling gently under his fringed hunting shirt, giving a brilliant impression of a man with nothing on his mind but his hair.

It was a cold day, but a bright one, and the sun was jabbing brilliant fingers of light into our erstwhile sanctum, making little blobs of snow drop like falling sugarplums around us. I scooped up one of these and gently decanted it into the neck of his shirt.

He drew in his breath through his teeth with a sharp hiss, opened his eyes, and regarded me coldly.

'I was thinking,' he informed me.

'Oh. Sorry to interrupt, then.' I eased myself down beside him, pulling the tangled cloaks up over us. The wind was beginning to lace through the holes in our shelter, and it occurred to me that he'd been quite right about the sheltering effects of snow. Only there wasn't going to be any snow falling tonight, I didn't think.

Then there was the little matter of food to be considered. My stomach had been making subdued protests for some time, and Jamie's now voiced its much louder objections. He squinted censoriously down his long, straight nose at the offender.

'Hush,' he said reprovingly in Gaelic, and cast his eyes upward. At last he sighed and looked at me.

'Well, then,' he said. 'Ye'd best wait a bit, to be sure yon savages are well away. Then ye'll go down to the cabin –'

'I don't know where it is.'

He made a small noise of exasperation.

'How did ye find me?'

'Tracked you,' I said, with a certain amount of pride. I glanced through the needles at the blowing wilderness outside. 'I don't suppose I can do it in reverse, though.'

'Oh.' He looked mildly impressed. 'Well, that was verra resourceful of ye, Sassenach. Dinna worry, though; I can tell ye how to go, to find your way back.'

450

'Right. And then what?'

He shrugged one shoulder. The bit of snow had melted, running down his chest, dampening his shirt and leaving a tiny pool of clear water standing in the hollow of his throat.

'Bring me back a bit of food, and a blanket. I should be able to move in a few days.'

'Leave you *here?*' I glared at him, my turn to be exasperated.

'I'll be all right,' he said mildly.

'You'll be eaten by wolves!'

'Oh, I shouldna think so,' he said casually. 'They'll be busy with the elk, most likely.'

'What elk?'

He nodded toward the hemlock grove.

'The one I shot yesterday. I took it in the neck, but the shot didna quite kill it at once. It ran through there. I was following it, when I hurt myself.' He rubbed a hand over the copper and silver bristles on his chin.

'I canna think it went far. I suppose the snow must have covered the carcass, else our wee friends would have seen it, coming from that direction.'

'So you've shot an elk, which is going to draw wolves like flies, and you propose to lie here in the freezing cold waiting for them? I suppose you think by the time they get round to the second course, you'll be so numb you won't notice when they start gnawing on your feet?'

'Don't shout,' he said. 'The savages might not be so far away, yet.'

I was drawing breath for further remarks on the subject, when he stopped me, putting his hand up to caress my cheek.

'Claire,' he said gently. 'Ye canna move me. There's nothing else to do.'

'There is,' I said, repressing a quaver in my voice. 'I'll stay with you. I'll bring you blankets and food, but I'm not leaving you up here alone. I'll bring wood, and we'll make a fire.'

'There's no need. I can manage,' he insisted.

'*I* can't,' I said, between my teeth. I remembered all too well what it had been like in the cabin, during those

451

empty, suffocating hours of waiting. Freezing my arse off in the snow for several days wasn't at all an appealing prospect, but it was better than the alternative.

He saw I meant it, and smiled.

'Well, then. Ye might bring some whisky, too, if there's any left.'

'There's half a bottle,' I said, feeling happier. 'I'll bring it.'

He got an arm around me, and pulled me into the curve of his shoulder. In spite of the howling wind outside, it was actually reasonably cozy under the cloaks, snuggled tight against him. His skin smelled warm and slightly salty, and I couldn't resist raising my head and putting my lips to the damp hollow of his throat.

'Aah,' he said, shivering. 'Don't *do* that!'

'You don't like it?'

'No, I dinna like it! How could I? It makes my skin crawl!'

'Well, *I* like it,' I protested.

He looked at me in amazement.

'You do?'

'Oh, yes,' I assured him. 'I dearly love to have you nibble on my neck.'

He narrowed one eye and squinted dubiously at me. Then he reached up, took me delicately by the ear, and drew my head down, turning my face to the side. He flicked his tongue gently at the base of my throat, then lifted his head and set his teeth very softly in the tender flesh at the side of my neck.

'Eeeee,' I said, and shivered uncontrollably.

He let go, looking at me in astonishment.

'I will be damned,' he said. 'Ye *do* like it; ye've gone all gooseflesh and your nipples are hard as spring cherries.' He passed a hand lightly over my breast; I hadn't bothered with my makeshift brassiere when I dressed for my impromptu expedition.

'Told you,' I said, blushing slightly. 'I suppose one of my ancestresses was bitten by a vampire or something.'

'A what?' He looked quite blank.

There was time to kill, so I gave him a thumbnail sketch of the life and times of Count Dracula. He looked bemused and appalled, but his hand carried on with its machinations, having now moved under my buckskin shirt and found its way beneath the cutty sark as well. His fingers were chilly, but I didn't mind.

'Some people find the notion terribly erotic,' I ended.

'That's the most disgusting thing I've ever heard!'

'I don't care,' I said, stretching out at full length beside him and putting my head back, throat invitingly exposed. 'Do it some more.'

He muttered something under his breath in Gaelic, but managed to get onto one elbow and roll toward me.

His mouth was warm and soft, and whether he approved of what he was doing or not, he did it awfully well.

'Ooooh,' I said, and shuddered ecstatically as his teeth sank delicately into my earlobe.

'Oh, well, if it's like *that*,' he said in resignation, and taking my hand, pressed it firmly between his thighs.

'Gracious,' I said. 'And here I thought the cold . . .'

'It'll be warm enough soon,' he assured me. 'Get them off, aye?'

It was rather awkward, given the cramped quarters, the difficulty of staying covered in order not to suffer frostbite in any exposed portions, and the fact that Jamie was able to lend only the most basic assistance, but we managed quite satisfactorily nonetheless.

What with one thing and another, I was rather preoccupied, though, and it was only during a temporary lull in the activities that I became aware of an uneasy sensation, as though I was being watched. I lifted myself on my hands and glanced out through the screen of hemlock, but saw nothing beyond the grove and the snow-covered slope below.

Jamie gave a low groan.

'Don't stop,' he murmured, eyes half closed. 'What is it?'

'I thought I heard something,' I said, lowering myself onto his chest again.

At this, I *did* hear something; a laugh, low but distinct, directly above my head.

I rolled off in a tangle of cloaks and discarded buckskins, while Jamie cursed and snatched for his pistol.

He flung aside the branches with a swoosh, pointing the pistol upward.

From the top of the rock above, several heads peered over, all grinning. Ian, and four companions from Anna Ooka. The Indians murmured and snickered among themselves, seeming to find something immoderately funny.

Jamie laid the pistol down, scowling up at his nephew.

'And what the devil are you doin' here, Ian?'

'Why, I was on my way home to keep Christmas with ye, Uncle,' Ian said, grinning hugely.

Jamie eyed his nephew with marked disfavor.

'Christmas,' he said. 'Bah, humbug.'

The elk carcass had frozen in the night. The sight of ice crystals frosting its blank eyes made me shudder – not at the sight of death; that was quite beautiful, with the great, dark body so still, crusted with snow – but at the thought that had I not yielded to my sense of uneasiness and gone out into the night searching for Jamie, the stark, still life before my eyes might well have been entitled 'Dead Scotsman in Snow' rather than 'Frozen Elk with Arguing Indians'.

The discussion at last concluded to their satisfaction, Ian informed me that they had decided to return to Anna Ooka, but would see us safely home, in return for a share of the elk meat.

The carcass had not frozen solidly through; they eviscerated it, leaving the cooling entrails in a heap of blue-gray coils, splotched with black blood. After chopping off the head to further lessen the weight, two of the men slung the body upside down from a pole, its legs tied together. Jamie eyed them darkly, obviously suspecting that they meant to give him the same treatment, but Ian assured him that they could manage a *travois*; the men were afoot, but they had brought one sturdy pack mule to carry any skins they took.

The weather had improved; the snow had melted altogether from the exposed ground, and while the air was still crisp and cold, the sky was a blinding blue, and the forest coldly pungent with the scents of spruce and balsam fir.

It was the smell of hemlock, as we passed through one grove, that reminded me of the beginning of this hegira, and the mysterious band of Indians we had seen.

'Ian,' I said, catching up to him. 'Just before you and your friends found us on the mountainside, we saw a band of Indians, with a Jesuit priest. They weren't from Anna Ooka, I don't think – do you have any idea who they might have been?'

'Oh, aye, Auntie. I ken all about them.' He wiped a mittened hand under his red-tipped nose. 'We were following them, when we found you.'

The strange Indians, he said, were Mohawk, come from far north. The Tuscarora had been adopted by the Iroquois League some fifty years before, and there was a close association with the Mohawk, with frequent exchanges of visits between the two, both formal and informal.

The present visit held elements of both – it was a party of young Mohawk men, in search of wives. Their own village having a shortage of marriageable young women, they had determined to come south, to see if suitable mates might be found among the Tuscarora.

'See, a woman must belong to the proper clan,' Ian explained. 'If she is the wrong clan, they canna be marrit.'

'Like MacDonalds and Campbells, aye?' Jamie chimed in, interested.

'Aye, a bit,' Ian said, grinning. 'But that's why they brought the priest wi' them – if they found women, they could be married at once, and not have to sleep in a cold bed all the way home.'

'They're Christians, then?'

Ian shrugged.

'Some of them. The Jesuits have been among them for some time, and a good many of the Huron are converts. Not so many among the Mohawk, though.'

'So they'd been to Anna Ooka?' I asked, curious. 'Why were you and your friends following them?'

Ian snorted, and tightened the muffler of squirrel skins around his neck.

455

'They may be allies, Auntie, but it doesna mean Nacognaweto and his braves trust them. Even the other Nations of the Iroquois League are afraid of the Mohawk – Christian or no.'

It was near sunset when we came in sight of the cabin. I was cold and tired, but my heart lifted inexpressibly at the sight of the tiny homestead. One of the mules in the penfold, a light gray creature named Clarence, saw us and brayed enthusiastically in welcome, making the rest of the horses crowd up next to the rails, eager for food.

'The horses look fine.' Jamie, with a stockman's eye, looked first to the animals' welfare. I was rather more concerned with our own; getting inside, getting warm, and getting fed, as soon as possible.

We invited Ian's friends to stay, but they declined, unloading Jamie in the dooryard and vanishing quickly to resume their vigilance over the departing Mohawk.

'They dinna like to stay in a white person's house, Auntie,' Ian explained. 'They think we smell bad.'

'Oh, really?' I said in pique, thinking of a certain elderly gentleman I had met in Anna Ooka, who appeared to have smeared himself with bear grease and then had himself sewn into his clothes for the winter. The pot calling the kettle black, if you asked me.

Much later, Christmas properly kept with a dram – or two – of whisky all round, we lay at last in our own bed, watching the flames of the newly kindled fire, and listening to Ian's peaceful snores.

'It's good to be home again,' I said softly.

'It is.' Jamie sighed and pulled me closer, my head tucked into the curve of his shoulder. 'I did have the strangest dreams, sleeping in the cold.'

'You did?' I stretched, luxuriating in the soft yielding of the feather-stuffed mattress. 'What did you dream about?'

'All kinds of things.' He sounded a bit shy. 'I dreamt of Brianna, now and again.'

'Really?' That was a little startling; I too had dreamt of Brianna in our icy shelter – something I seldom did.

456

'I did wonder . . .' Jamie hesitated for a moment. 'Has she a birthmark, Sassenach? And if so, did ye tell me of it?'

'She does,' I said slowly, thinking. 'I don't *think* I ever told you about it, though; it isn't visible most of the time, so it's been years since I noticed it, myself. It's a –'

His hand tightening on my shoulder stopped me.

'It's a wee brown mark, shaped like a diamond,' he said. 'Just behind her left ear. Isn't it?'

'Yes, it is.' It was warm and cozy in bed, but a small coolness on the back of my neck made me shiver suddenly. 'Did you see that in your dream?'

'I kissed her there,' he said softly.

22

Spark of an Ancient Flame

Oxford, September 1970

'Oh, Jesus.' Roger stared at the page in front of him until the letters lost their meaning and became no more than curlicues. No such trick would erase the meaning of the words themselves; those were already carved into his mind.

'Oh, God, no!' he said out loud. The girl in the next carrel jerked in irritation at the noise, scraping the legs of her chair against the floor.

He leaned over the book, covering it with his forearms, eyes closed. He felt sick, and the palms of his hands were cold and sweaty.

He sat that way for several minutes, fighting the truth. It wasn't going to go away, though. Christ, it had already happened, hadn't it? A long time ago. And you couldn't change the past.

Finally he swallowed the taste of bile in the back of his throat and looked again. It was still there. A small notice from a newspaper, printed on February 13, 1776, in the American Colony of North Carolina, in the town of Wilmington.

It is with grief that the news is received of the deaths by fire of James MacKenzie Fraser and his wife, Claire Fraser, in a conflagration that destroyed their house in the settlement of Fraser's Ridge, on the night of January 21 last. Mr. Fraser, a nephew of the late Hector Cameron of River Run plantation, was born at Broch Tuarach in Scotland. He was widely known in the colony and deeply respected; he leaves no surviving children.

Except that he did.

Roger grasped for a moment at the dim hope that it wasn't them; there were, after all, any number of James

Frasers, it was a fairly common name. But not James *MacKenzie* Fraser, not with a wife named Claire. Not born in Broch Tuarach, Scotland.

No, it was them; the sick certainty filled his chest and squeezed his throat with grief. His eyes stung and the ornate eighteenth-century typeface blurred again.

So she had found him, Claire. Found her gallant Highlander, and enjoyed at least a few years with him. He hoped they had been good years. He had liked Claire Randall very much – no, that was to damn her with faint praise. If he were truthful, he had loved her, and for her own sake as well as her daughter's.

More than that. He had wanted badly for her to find her Jamie Fraser, to live happily ever after with him. The knowledge – or more accurately, the hope – that she had done so had been a small talisman to him; a witness that enduring love was possible, a love strong enough to withstand separation and hardship, strong enough to outlast time. And yet all flesh was mortal; no love could outlast that fact.

He gripped the edge of the table, trying to get himself under control. Foolish, he told himself. Thoroughly foolish. And yet he felt as bereft as he had when the Reverend had died; as though he were himself newly orphaned.

Realization came as a fresh blow. He couldn't show this to Bree, he couldn't. She'd known the risk, of course, but – no. She wouldn't have imagined anything like this.

It was the purest chance that had led him to find it. He had been looking for the lyrics of old ballads to add to his repertoire, thumbing through a book of country songs. An illustration had shown the original newspaper page on which one ballad had first been published, and Roger, idly browsing, had glanced at the archaic notices posted on the same newspaper page, his eye caught by the name 'Fraser'.

The shock was beginning to wear off a little, though grief had settled on the pit of his stomach, nagging as the pain of an ulcer. He was a scholar and the son of a scholar; he had grown up surrounded by books, imbued since childhood with the sanctity of the printed word. He felt like a murderer as he groped for his penknife and stealthily opened it, glancing around to be sure he was unobserved.

It was instinct more than reason; the instinct that leads a man to want to clear up the remains of an accident, to lay a decent covering over the bodies, to obliterate the visible traces of disaster, even though the tragedy itself remains.

With the folded page lying hidden in his pocket like a severed thumb, he left the library, to walk the rainy streets of Oxford.

The walking calmed him, made it possible to think rationally again, to force his own feelings back long enough to plan what he must do, how to protect Brianna from a grief that would be more profound and longer felt than his own.

He had checked the bibliographic information in the front of the book; published in 1906 by a small British press. It wouldn't be widely available, then; but still something Brianna might stumble over in her own researches.

It wasn't a logical place to look for information of the sort she was seeking, but the book was titled *Songs and Ballads of the Eighteenth Century.* He knew well enough that historian's curiosity that led to impulsive pokings in unlikely places; she would know enough to do that too. Still more, he knew the child's hunger for knowledge – any knowledge – that might lead her to look at anything dealing with the period, in an effort to imagine her parents' surroundings, to build a vision of lives she could neither see nor share.

Long odds, but not long enough. Someone jostled him in passing, and he realized that he had been leaning on the bridge railing for several minutes, watching raindrops patter on the surface of the river without seeing them. Slowly, he turned down the street, oblivious of the shops and the mushroom herds of umbrellas.

There was no way to ensure that she would never see a copy of that book; this might be the only copy, or there might be hundreds, lying like time bombs in libraries all over the US.

The ache in his guts was getting worse. He was soaked

through by now, and freezing. Inside, he felt a deeper cold spreading from a new thought: What might Brianna do, if she found out?

She would be devastated, grief-stricken. But then? He was himself convinced that the past could not be changed; the things Claire had told him had made him sure of it. She and Jamie Fraser had tried to avert the slaughter at Culloden, to no avail. She had tried to save her future husband, Frank, by saving his ancestor, Jack Randall – and failed, only to find that Jack had never been Frank's ancestor after all, but had married his younger brother's pregnant lover in order to legitimize the child when the brother died.

No, the past might twist on itself like a writhing snake, but it could not be changed. He wasn't at all sure that Brianna shared his conviction, though.

How do you mourn a time-traveler? she'd asked him. If he showed her the notice, she could mourn truly; she would know. The knowledge would wound her terribly, but she would heal, and could put the past behind her. If.

If it wasn't for the stones on Craigh na Dun. The stone circle and its dreadful promise of possibility.

Claire had gone through the stones of Craigh na Dun on the ancient fire feast of Samhain, on the first day of November, nearly two years before.

Roger shivered, and not from the cold. The hairs stood up on the back of his neck whenever he thought of it. It had been a clear, mild fall morning, that dawn of the Feast of All Saints, with nothing to disturb the grassy peace of the hill where the circle of stones stood sentinel. Nothing until Claire had touched the great cleft stone, and vanished into the past.

Then the earth had seemed to dissolve under his own feet, and the air had ripped away with a roar that echoed inside his head like cannon fire. He had gone blind in a blast of light and dark; only his memories of the last time had kept him from utter panic.

He'd had hold of Brianna's hand. Reflex closed his grip, even as all senses disappeared. It was like being dropped from a thousand feet into ice-cold water; terrible vertigo and a shock so intense, he could feel no sensation but the shock itself. Blind and deaf, bereft of sense and senses, he had been conscious of two last thoughts, the remnants of his consciousness flicking out like a candleflame in a hurricane. *I'm dying*, he had thought, with great calmness. And then, *Don't let go.*

The dawning sun had fallen in a bright path through the cleft stone; Claire had walked along it. When Roger stirred at last and raised his head, the sun of late afternoon glowed gold and lavender behind the great stone, leaving it black against the sky.

He was lying on Brianna, sheltering her with his body. She was unconscious but breathing, her face desperately pale against the dark red of her hair. Weak as he was, there was no question of his being able to carry her down the steep hillside to the car below; her father's daughter, she was nearly six feet tall, only a few inches shorter than Roger himself.

He had huddled over her, holding her head in his lap, stroking her face and shivering, until just before sunset. She had opened her eyes then, as dark a blue as the fading sky, and whispered, 'She's gone?'

'It's all right,' Roger had whispered back. He bent and kissed her cold forehead. 'It's all right; I'll take care of you.'

He'd meant it. But how?

It was getting dark by the time he returned to his rooms. He could hear a clatter from the dining hall as he passed, and he smelled boiled ham and baked beans, but supper was the farthest thing from his mind.

He squelched up to his rooms and dropped his wet things in a heap on the floor. He dried himself, then sat naked on the bed, towel forgotten in his hand, staring at the desk and at the wooden box that held Brianna's letters.

He would do anything to save her from grief. He would do much more to save her from the threat of the stones.

Claire had gone back – he hoped – from 1968 to 1766. And then died in 1776. Now it was 1970. A person going back now would – might – end in 1768. There would be time. That was the hell of it; there would be time.

462

Even if Brianna thought as he did – or if he could convince her – that the past could not be changed, could she live through the next seven years, knowing that the window of opportunity was closing, that her only chance ever to know her father, see her mother again, was disappearing day by day? It was one thing to let them go, not knowing where they were or what had happened to them; it was another to know explicitly, and to do nothing.

He had known Brianna for more than two years, yet been with her for only a few months of that time. And yet, they knew each other very well in some respects. How could they not, having shared such an experience? Then there had been the letters – dozens, two or three or four each week – and the rare brief holidays, spent between enchantment and frustration, that left him aching with need of her.

Yes, he knew her. She was quiet, but possessed of a fierce determination that he thought would not submit to grief without a fight. And while she was cautious, once her mind was made up, she acted with hair-raising dispatch. If she decided to risk the passage, he couldn't stop her.

His hands closed tight on the wadded towel, and his stomach dropped, remembering the chasm of the circle and the void that had nearly swallowed them. The only thing more terrifying was the thought of losing Brianna before he had ever truly had her.

He'd never lied to her. But the impact of shock and grief was slowly receding as the rudiments of a plan formed in his mind. He stood up and wrapped the towel around his waist.

One letter wouldn't do it. It would have to be slow, a process of suggestion, of gentle discouragement. He thought it wouldn't be difficult; he had found almost nothing in a year of searching in Scotland, beyond the report of the burning of Fraser's print shop in Edinburgh – he shuddered involuntarily at the thought of flames. Now he knew why, of course; they must have emigrated soon after, though he had found no trace of them on the ship's rolls he had searched.

Time to give up, he would suggest. Let the past rest – and the dead bury the dead. To keep on looking, in the

463

face of no evidence, would border on obsession. He would suggest, very subtly, that it was unhealthy, this looking back – now it was time to look forward, lest she waste her life on futile searching. Neither of her parents would have wanted that.

The room was chilly, but he barely noticed.

I'll take care of you, he'd said, and meant it. Was suppressing a dangerous truth the same as lying? Well, if it was, then he'd lie. To give consent to do wrong was a sin, he'd heard that from his early days. That was all right, he'd risk his soul for her, and willingly.

He rummaged in the drawer for a pen. Then he stopped, bent, and reached two fingers into the pocket of his sopping jeans. The paper was frayed and soggy, half disintegrating already. With steady fingers, he tore it into tiny pieces, disregarding the cold sweat that ran in trickles from his face.

23

The Skull Beneath the Skin

I had told Jamie that I didn't mind being far from civilization; wherever there were people, there would be work for a healer.

Duncan had been good as his word, returning in the spring of 1768 with eight former Ardsmuir men and their families, ready to take up homesteading on Fraser's Ridge, as the place was now known. With some thirty souls to hand, there was an immediate· call on my mildly rusty services, to stitch up wounds and treat fevers, to lance abscessed boils and scrape infected gums. Two of the women were pregnant, and it was my joy to deliver healthy children, a boy and a girl, both born in early spring.

My fame – if that's the word – as a healer soon spread outside our tiny settlement, and I found myself called farther and farther afield, to tend the ills of folk on isolated hill farms scattered over thirty miles of wild mountain terrain. In addition, I made rare visits with Ian to Anna Ooka to see Nayawenne, returning with baskets and jars of useful herbs.

At first, Jamie had insisted that he or Ian must go with me to the farther places, but it was soon apparent that neither of them could be spared; it was time for the first planting, with ground to break and harrow, corn and barley to be planted, to say nothing of the usual chores required to keep a small farm running. In addition to the horses and mules, we had acquired a small flock of chickens, a depraved-looking black boar to meet the social needs of the pig, and – luxury of luxuries – a milch goat, all of whom required to be fed and watered and generally kept from killing themselves or being eaten by bears or panthers.·

So more and more often I went alone when some stranger appeared suddenly in the dooryard, asking for healer or midwife. Daniel Rawlings's casebook began to acquire new entries, and the larder was enriched by the gifts of hams and venison haunches, bags of grain and bushels of apples, with which my patients repaid my attentions. I never asked for payment, but something was always offered – and poor as we were, anything at all was welcome.

My backcountry patients came from many places, and many spoke neither English nor French; there were German Lutherans, Quakers, Scots and Scotch-Irish, and a large settlement of Moravian brethren at Salem, who spoke a peculiar dialect of what I *thought* was Czechoslovakian. I usually managed, though; in most cases, someone could interpret for me, and at the worst, I could fall back on the language of hand and body – 'Where does it hurt?' is easy to understand in any tongue.

August 1768

I was chilled to the bone. Despite my best efforts to keep the cloak wrapped tightly round me, the wind ripped it from my body, and sent it billowing like sail canvas. It beat round the head of the boy walking next to me, and jerked me sideways in my saddle with the force of the gale. The rain drove in beneath the flapping folds like frozen needles, and I was soaked through gown and petticoats before we reached Mueller's Creek.

The creek itself was boiling past, uprooted saplings, rocks and drowned branches bubbling briefly to the surface.

Tommy Mueller peered at the torrent, shoulders hunched nearly to the brim of the slouch hat he wore pulled down over his ears. I could see doubt etched in every line of his body, and bent close to shout in his ear.

'Stay here!' I bellowed, pitching my voice below the shriek of the wind.

He shook his head, mouthing something at me, but I couldn't hear. I shook my own head vigorously, and pointed up the bank; the muddy soil was crumbly here; I could see small chunks of the black dirt melt away even as I watched.

'Get back!' I shouted.

He pointed emphatically himself – back in the direction of the farmhouse – and reached for my reins. Clearly he thought it was too dangerous; he wanted me to come back to the house, to wait out the storm.

He definitely had a point. On the other hand, I could see the stream widening, even as I watched, the ravenous water eating away the soft bank in gobbets and chunks. Wait much longer, and no one could cross – neither would it be safe for days after; floods like this kept the water high for as long as a week, as the rains from higher up the mountain trickled down to feed the torrents.

The thought of being cooped up in a four-room house for a week with all ten Muellers was enough to spur me to recklessness. Pulling the reins from Tommy's grasp, I wheeled about, the horse tossing its head against the rain, stepping carefully on the slick mud.

We reached the upper slopes of the bank, where a layer of thick dead leaves gave better footing. I turned the horse, motioned Tommy back out of the way, and leaned forward like a steeplechaser, elbows digging into the bag of barley bound over the saddle in front of me – my payment for services rendered.

The shift of my weight was enough; the horse was no more anxious to hang about here than I was. I felt the sudden thrust as the hindquarters dropped and bunched, and then we were flying down the slope like a runaway toboggan. A jolt and a moment of giddy freefall, then a resounding splash, and I was up past my thighs in freezing water.

My hands were so cold, they might as well have been welded to the reins, but I had nothing useful to offer in terms of guidance. I let my arms go slack, giving the horse his head. I could feel huge muscles moving rhythmically under my legs as it swam, and the even more powerful shove of the water rushing past us. It dragged at my skirts, threatening to pull me off into the surge.

Then came the jar and scrabble of hooves against the stream bottom, and we were out, pouring water like a colander. I turned in the saddle, to see Tommy Mueller on the other side, his jaw hanging open under his hat. I couldn't let go of the reins to wave, but bowed toward him ceremoniously, then nudged the horse with my heels and turned toward home.

The hood of my cloak had fallen back when we jumped, but it made no great difference; I couldn't get much wetter. I knuckled a wet strand of hair out of my eyes and turned the horse's head toward the upland trail, relieved to be headed home, rain or no.

I had been at the Muellers' cabin for three days, seeing eighteen-year-old Petronella through her first labor. It would be her last, too, according to Petronella. Her seventeen-year-old husband, peeking tentatively into the room in the middle of the second day, had received a burst of German invective from Petronella that sent him stumping back to the men's refuge in the barn, ears bright red with mortification.

Still, a few hours later, I had seen Freddy – looking much younger than seventeen – kneel tentatively by his wife's bedside, face whiter than her shift as he reached a hesitant, scrubbed finger to push aside the blanket covering his daughter.

He stared dumbly at the round head, furred with soft black, then looked at his wife, as though in need of prompting.

'*Ist sie nicht wunderschön?*' Petronella said softly.

He nodded, slowly, then laid his head on her lap and began to cry. The women had all smiled kindly, and gone back to fixing dinner.

It had been a good dinner, too; the food was one of the benefits of house calls to the Muellers. Even now, my stomach was comfortably distended with dumplings and fried *Blutwurst,* and the lingering taste of buttered eggs in my mouth provided some small distraction from the general discomfort of my present situation.

I hoped that Jamie and Ian had managed something adequate to eat in my absence. This being the end of summer but not yet harvest time, the pantry shelves were nowhere near the height of what I hoped would be their autumn bounty, but still there were cheeses on the shelf, a huge stoneware crock of salted fish on the floor, and sacks of flour, corn, rice, beans, barley, and oatmeal.

Jamie *could* in fact cook – at least so far as dressing game and roasting it over a fire – and I had done my best to initiate Ian into the mysteries of making oatmeal parritch, but, they being men, I suspected that they hadn't bothered, choosing instead to survive on raw onions and dried meat.

I couldn't tell whether it was simply that after a day spent in the manly pursuits of chopping down trees, plowing fields, and carrying deer carcasses over mountains, they honestly were too exhausted to think of assembling a proper meal, or whether they did it on purpose, so that I would feel necessary.

The wind had dropped, now that I was in the shelter of the ridge, but the rain was still pelting down, and the footing was treacherous, as the mud of the trail had liquified, leaving a layer of fallen leaves floating on top, deceptive as quicksand. I could feel the horse's discomfort as its hooves slipped with each step.

'Good boy,' I said soothingly. 'Keep it up, that's a good fellow.' The horse's ears pricked slightly, but he kept his head down, stepping carefully.

'Slewfoot?' I said. 'How's that?'

The horse had no name at the moment – or rather he did, but I didn't know what it was. The man from whom Jamie had bought him had called him by a German word that Jamie said was not at all suitable for a lady's horse. When I had asked him to translate the word, he had merely compressed his lips and looked Scottish, from which I deduced that it must be pretty bad. I had meant to ask old Mrs. Mueller what it meant, but had forgotten, in the haste of leaving.

In any case, Jamie's theory was that the horse would reveal his true – or at least speakable – name in the course of time, and so we were all watching the animal, in hopes of discerning its character. On the basis of a trial ride, Ian had suggested Coney, but Jamie had merely shaken his head and said, no, that wasn't it.

'Twinkletoes?' I suggested. 'Lightfoot? Damn!'

The horse had come to a full stop, for obvious reasons. A small freshet gurgled merrily down the hill, bounding from rock to rock with gay abandon. It was beautiful, the rushing water clear as crystal over dark rock and green leaves. Unfortunately, it was also bounding over the remains of the trail, which, unequal to the force of events, had slithered off the face of the hill into the valley below.

I sat still, dripping. There wasn't any way around. The hill rose nearly perpendicularly·on my right, shrubs and saplings poking out of a cracked rock face, and declined so precipitously to the left that going down would have amounted to suicide. Swearing under my breath, I backed the nameless horse and turned around.

If it hadn't been for the flooded creek, I would have gone back to the Muellers and let Jamie and Ian fend for themselves a bit longer. As it was, I had no choice; it was find another way home or stay here and drown.

Wearily, we retraced our slogging steps. Less than a quarter-mile from the washout, though, I found a spot where the hillside fell away into a small saddle, a depression between two 'horns' of granite. Such formations were common; there was a big one on a nearby mountain, which had gained it the name of Devil's Peak. If I could cross the saddle to the other side of the hill, and pick my way along it, I would in time come back to the trail where it crossed the ridge to the south.

From the saddle I had a momentary clear view of the foothills, and the blue hollow of the valley beyond. On the other side, though, clouds hid the tops of the mountains, black with rain, suffused with an occasional flicker of hidden lightning.

The wind had dropped, now that the leading edge of the storm had passed. The rain was coming down even more heavily, if such a thing was possible, and I stopped long enough to pry my cold fingers off the reins and put up the hood of my cloak.

The footing on this side of the hill was fair, the ground being rocky but not too steep. We picked our way through small groves of red-berried mountain ash and larger stands of oak. I noted the location of a huge blackberry bramble for future reference, but didn't stop. I would be lucky to get home by dark as it was.

To distract myself from the cold trickles running down my neck, I began an mental inventory of the pantry. What could I make for dinner, once I arrived?

Something quick, I thought, shivering, and something hot. Stew would take too long; so would soup. If there was squirrel or rabbit, we might have it fried, rolled in egg and cornmeal batter. Or if not that, perhaps brose with a little bacon for flavoring, and a couple of scrambled eggs with green onions.

I ducked, wincing. Despite the hood and the thickness of my hair, the raindrops were beating on my scalp like hail pellets.

Then I realized that they *were* hail pellets. Tiny white spheres pinged off the horse's back, and rattled through the oak leaves. Within seconds, the pellets were bigger, the size of marbles, and the hail had grown heavy enough that its popping sounded like machine-gun fire on the wet mats of leaves in the clearings.

The horse flung up its head, shaking its mane vigorously in an effort to escape the stinging pellets. Hastily, I reined in and guided it into the semi-shelter of a huge chestnut tree. Underneath, it was noisy, but the hail slid off the thick canopy of leaves, leaving us protected.

'Right,' I said. With some difficulty, I pried one hand off the reins and gave the horse a reassuring pat. 'Easy, then. We'll be all right, as long as we don't get struck by lightning.'

Evidently this statement had jogged someone's memory; a silent fork of dazzling light split the black sky beyond Roan Mountain. A few moments later, the dull rumble of thunder came booming up the hollow, drowning out the rasp of hail on the leaves overhead.

Sheet lightning shimmered far away, across the mountains. Then more bolts, sizzling across the sky, each succeeded by a louder roll of thunder. The hailstorm passed, and the rain resumed, pelting down as hard as ever. The valley below disappeared in cloud and mist, but the lightning lit the stark mountain ridges like bones on an X-ray.

'One hippopotamus, two hippopotamus, three hippopotamus, four hippopot–' BWOOOM! The horse jerked its head and stamped nervously.

'I know just how you feel,' I told it, peering down the valley. 'Steady, though, steady.' There it went again, a flash

471

that lit the dark ridge and left the silhouette of the horse's pricked ears imprinted on my retinas.

'One hippopotamus, two hippo–' I could have sworn the ground shook. The horse let out a high-pitched scream and reared against my pull on the reins, hooves thrashing in the leaves. The air reeked of ozone.

Flash.

'One,' I said through my teeth. 'Damn you, whoa! One hip–'

Flash.

'One–'

Flash.

'Whoa! WHOA!'

I wasn't conscious of the fall at all; nor even the landing. One moment I was sawing at the reins, a thousand pounds of panicked horse going to pieces under me, shying in all directions. The next, I was lying on my back, blinking up at a spinning black sky, trying to will my diaphragm to work.

Echoes of the shock of impact wavered through my flesh, and I tried frantically to fit myself back into my body. Then I drew breath, a painful gasp, and found myself shaking, the shock turning to the first intimations of damage.

I lay still, eyes closed, concentrating on breathing, conducting an inventory. The rain was still pounding down onto my face, puddling in my eye sockets and running down into my ears. My face and hands were numb. My arms moved. I could breathe a little easier now.

My legs. The left one hurt, but not in any threatening way; only a bruised knee. I rolled heavily onto my side, impeded by my wet, bulky garments. Still, it was the heavy clothing that had saved me from serious damage.

Above me came an uncertain whinny, audible amid the booming thunder. I looked up, dizzy, and saw the horse's head, protruding from a thicket of buckbrush some thirty feet overhead. Below the thicket, a steep, rocky slope fell away; a long scrape mark toward the bottom showed where I had struck and rolled before ending up in my present position.

We had been standing virtually on the edge of this small

precipice without my seeing it, screened as it was by the heavy growth of shrubs. The horse's panic had sent it to the edge, but evidently it had sensed the danger and caught itself before going over – not before letting me slide off into space, though.

'You bloody bugger!' I said. And wondered whether the unknown German name meant something similar. 'I could have broken my neck!' I wiped the mud from my face with a hand that still shook, and looked about me for a way back up.

There wasn't one. Behind me, the rocky cliff-face continued, merging into one of the granite horns. Before me, it ended abruptly, in a plunge straight downward into a small hollow. The slope I stood on declined into this hollow as well, rolling down through clumps of yellow-wood and sumac to the banks of a small creek some sixty feet below.

I stood quite still, trying to think. No one knew where I was. *I* didn't know exactly where I was, come to that. Worse, no one would be looking for me for some time. Jamie would think I was still at the Muellers' because of the rain. The Muellers would of course have no reason to think I hadn't made it safely home; even if they had doubts, they couldn't follow me, because of the flooded creek. And by the time anyone found the washed-out trail, any traces of my passage would long since have been obliterated by the rain.

I was uninjured, that was something. I was also afoot, alone, without food, moderately lost, and thoroughly wet. About the only certainty was that I wasn't going to die of thirst.

The lightning was still glancing to and fro like dueling pitchforks in the sky above, though the thunder had faded to a dull rumble in the distance. I had no particular fear of being struck by lightning now – not with so many better candidates standing about, in the form of gigantic trees – but finding shelter seemed a very good idea nonetheless.

It was still raining; drops rolled off the end of my nose with monotonous regularity. Limping on my bruised knee and swearing quite a bit, I made my way down the slippery slope to the edge of the stream.

473

This creek, too, was swollen by the rain; I could see the tops of drowned bushes sticking out of the water, leaves trailing limply in the rushing current. There was no bank to speak of; I fought my way through the grasping claws of holly and red-cedar toward the rocky cliff-face to the south; perhaps there would be a cave or hollow there that would offer shelter of a sort.

I found nothing but tumbled rocks, black with wet and hard to navigate. Some distance beyond, though, I saw something else that offered a small possibility of shelter.

A huge red cedar tree had fallen across the stream, its roots undermined as the water ate away the soil in which it stood. It had fallen away from me and struck the cliff, so that the thick crown sprawled into the water and over the rocks, the trunk canted across the stream at a shallow angle; on my side, I could see the huge mat of its exposed roots, a bulwark of cracked earth and small bushes heaved up about them. The cavity under them might not be complete shelter, but it looked better than standing in the open or crouching in the bushes.

I hadn't even paused to think that the shelter might have attracted bears, catamounts, or other unfriendly fauna. Fortunately, it hadn't.

It was a space about five feet long and five wide, dank, dark, and clammy. The ceiling was composed of the tree's great gnarled roots, packed with sandy earth, like the roof of a badger's sett. But it was a solid ceiling, for all that; the floor of churned earth was damp but not muddy, and for the first time in hours rain was not drumming on my skull.

Exhausted, I crawled into the farthest corner, set my wet shoes beside me, and went to sleep. The cold of my wet clothes made me dream vividly, in jumbled visions of blood and childbirth, trees and rocks and rain, and I woke frequently, in that half-conscious way of utter tiredness, falling asleep again in seconds.

I dreamt that I was giving birth. I felt no pain, but saw the emerging head as though I stood between my own thighs, midwife and mother both together. I took the naked child in my arms, still smeared with the blood that came from both of us, and gave her to her father. I gave her to Frank, but it was Jamie who took the caul from her face and said, 'She's beautiful.'

Then I woke and slept, finding my way among boulders and waterfalls, urgently seeking something I had lost. Woke and slept, pursued through woods by something fearsome and unknown. Woke and slept, a knife in my hand, red with blood – but whose, I did not know.

I woke all the way to the smell of burning, and sat bolt upright. The rain had stopped; it was the silence that wakened me, I thought. The smell of smoke was still strong in my nostrils, though – it wasn't part of the dream.

I poked my head out of my burrow like a snail cautiously emerging from its shell. The sky was a pale purple-gray, shot with streaks of orange over the mountains. The woods around me were still, and dripping. It was nearly sundown, and darkness was gathering in the hollows.

I crawled out all the way, and looked around. The creek at my back rushed past in full spate, its gurgling the only sound. The ground rose in front of me to a small ridge. At the top of this stood a large balsam poplar tree, the source of the smoke. The tree had been struck by lightning; half of it still bore green leaves, the canopy bushy against the pale sky. The other half was blackened and charred all down one side of the massive trunk. Wisps of white smoke rose from it like ghosts escaping an enchanter's bondage, and red lines of fire showed fleetingly, glowing beneath the blackened shell.

I looked about for my shoes, but couldn't find them in the shadows. Not bothering, I made my way up the ridge toward the blasted tree, panting with effort. All my muscles were stiffened with sleep and cold; I felt like a tree come awkwardly to life myself, stumping uphill on gnarled and clumsy roots.

It was warm near the tree. Blissfully, wonderfully warm. The air smelled of ash and burnt soot, but it was warm. I stood as close as I dared, spreading my cloak out wide, and stood still, steaming.

For some time I didn't even try to think; just stood there, feeling my chilled flesh thaw and soften again into something resembling humanity. But as my blood began to flow again, my bruises began to ache, and I felt the deeper ache of hunger as well; it had been a long time since breakfast.

Likely to be a lot longer time till supper, I thought grimly. The dark was creeping up from the hollow, and I was still lost. I glanced across to the opposite ridge; not a sign of the bloody horse.

'Traitor,' I muttered. 'Probably gone off to join a herd of elk or something.'

I chafed my hands together; my clothes were halfway dry, but the temperature was dropping; it would be a chilly night. Would it be better to spend the night here, in the open, near the blasted tree, or ought I to return to my burrow while I could still see to do so?

A snapping in the brush behind me decided me. The tree had cooled now; though the charred wood was still hot to the touch, the fire had burned out. It would be no deterrent to prowling night hunters. Lacking fire or weapons, my only defense was that of the hunted; lie hidden through the dark hours, like the mice and rabbits. Well, I had to go back to fetch my shoes anyway.

Reluctantly leaving the last vestiges of warmth, I made my way back down to the fallen tree. Crawling in, I saw a pale blur against the darker earth in the corner. I set my hand on it, and found not the softness of my buckskin moccasins, but something hard and smooth.

My instincts had grasped the reality of the object before my brain could retrieve the word, and I snatched my hand away. I sat for a moment, my heart pounding. Then curiosity overcame atavistic fear, and I began to scoop away the sandy loam around it.

It was indeed a skull, complete with lower jaw, though the mandible was attached only by the remnants of dried ligament. A fragment of broken vertebra rattled in the foramen magnum.

' "How long will a man lie i' the earth ere he rot?" ' I murmured, turning the skull over in my hands. The bone was cold and damp, slightly roughened by exposure to the damp. The light was too dim to see details, but I could feel the heavy ridges over the brows, and the slickness of smooth enamel on the canines. Likely a man, and not an old one; most of the teeth were present, and not unduly worn – at least insofar as I could tell with a groping thumb.

How long? Eight or nine year, the grave-digger said to Hamlet. I had no notion whether Shakespeare knew anything about forensics, but it seemed a reasonable estimate to me. Longer than nine years, then.

How had he come here? By violence, my instincts answered, though my brain was not far behind. An explorer might die of disease, hunger or exposure – I firmly suppressed that line of thought, trying to ignore my growling stomach and damp clothes – but he wouldn't end up buried under a tree.

The Cherokee and Tuscarora buried their dead, all right, but not like this, alone in a hollow. And not in fragments, either. It was that broken bit of vertebra that had told me the story at once; the edges were compressed, the broken face sheared clean, not shattered.

'Somebody took a real dislike to you, didn't they?' I said. 'Didn't stop with a scalp; they took your whole head.'

Which made me wonder – was the rest of him here, too? I rubbed a hand across my face, thinking, but after all, I had nothing better to do; I wasn't going anywhere before daylight, and the likelihood of sleep had grown remote with the discovery of my companion. I set the skull carefully to one side, and began to dig.

It was fully night by now, but even the darkest of nights outdoors is seldom completely without light. The sky was still covered with cloud, which reflected considerable light, even in my shallow burrow.

The sandy earth was soft, and easy to dig in, but after a few minutes of scratching, my knuckles and fingertips were rubbed raw, and I crawled outside, long enough to find a stick to dig with. A little more probing yielded me something hard; not bone, I thought, and not metal, either. Stone, I decided, fingering the dark oval. Just a river stone? I thought not; the surface was very smooth, but with something incised in it; a glyph of some kind, though my touch was not sufficiently sensitive to tell me what it was.

More digging yielded nothing. Either the rest of Yorick wasn't here, or it was buried so far down that I had no chance of discovering it. I put the stone in my pocket, sat back on my heels, and rubbed my sandy hands on my skirts. At least the exercise had warmed me again.

I sat down again and picked up the skull, holding it in my lap. Gruesome as it was, it was the semblance of company, some distraction from my own plight. And I was quite aware that all my actions of the last hour or so had been distractions; designed to fight off the panic that I could feel submerged below the surface of my mind, waiting to erupt like the sharp end of a drowned tree branch. It was going to be a long night.

'Right,' I said aloud to the skull. 'Read any good books lately? No, I suppose you don't get round much anymore. Poetry, maybe?' I cleared my throat and started in on Keats, warming up with 'Written in Disgust of Vulgar Superstition' and going on with 'Ode on a Grecian Urn'.

' " . . . *Forever wilt thou love, and she be fair!*" ' I declaimed. 'There's more of that one, but I forget. Not too bad, though, was it? Want to try a little Shelley? "Ode to the West Wind" is good – you'd like that one, I think.'

It occurred to me to wonder why I thought so; I had no particular reason to think Yorick was an Indian rather than a European, but I realized that I did think so – perhaps it was the stone I had found with him. Shrugging, I set in again, trusting that the repellent effect of great English poetry would be the equal of a campfire, so far as the bears and panthers were concerned.

'*Make me thy lyre, even as the forest is:*
What if my leaves are falling like its own!
The tumult of thy mighty harmonies
Will take from both a deep, autumnal tone,
Sweet though in sadness. Be thou, Spirit fierce,
My spirit! Be thou me, impetuous one!
'*Drive my dead thoughts over the universe*
Like wither'd leaves to quicken a new birth;
And, by the incantation of this verse,

'*Scatter, as from an unextinguish'd hearth*
Ashes and sparks, my words among mankind!
Be through my lips to unawaken'd earth

478

The final stanza faded on my lips. There was a light on the ridge. A small spark, growing to a flame. At first I thought it was the lightning-blasted tree, some smoldering ember come to life – but then it moved. It glided slowly down the hill toward me, floating just above the bushes.

I sprang to my feet, realizing only then that I had no shoes on. Frantically, I groped about the floor, covering the small space again and again. But it was no use. My shoes were gone.

I seized the skull and stood barefoot, turning to face the light.

I watched the light come nearer, drifting down the hill like a milkweed puff. One thought floated in my paralyzed mind – a random line of Shelley's: *Fiend, I defy thee! with a calm, fixed mind.* Somewhere in the dimmer recesses of my consciousness, something observed that Shelley had had much better nerves than I. I clutched the skull closer. It wasn't much of a weapon – but somehow I didn't think that whatever was coming would be deterred by knives or pistols, either.

It wasn't only that the wet surroundings made it seem grossly improbable that anyone was strolling through the woods with a blazing torch. The light didn't burn like a pine torch or oil lantern. It didn't flicker, but burned with a soft, steady glow.

It floated a few feet above the ground, just about where someone would hold a torch they carried before them. It drew slowly nearer, at the pace of a man walking. I could see it bob slightly, moving to the rhythm of a steady stride.

I cowered in my burrow, half hidden by the bank of earth and severed roots. I was freezing cold, but sweat ran down my sides and I could smell the reek of my own fear. My numb toes curled in the dirt, wanting to run.

I had seen St. Elmo's fire before, at sea. Eerie as that was, its liquid blue crackle didn't resemble at all the pale light approaching. This had neither spark nor color; only a spectral glow. Marsh gas, people in Cross Creek said when the mountain lights were mentioned.

Ha, I said to myself, though soundlessly. Marsh gas my left foot!

The light moved through a small thicket of alders, and out into the clearing before me. It wasn't marsh gas.

He was tall, and he was naked. Beyond a breechclout, he wore nothing but paint; long stripes of red down arms and legs and torso, and his face was solid black, from chin to forehead. His hair was greased and dressed in a crest, from which two turkey feathers stiffly pointed.

I was invisible, completely hidden in the darkness of my refuge, while the torch he held washed him in soft light, gleaming off his hairless chest and shoulders, shadowing the orbits of his eyes. But he knew I was there.

I didn't dare to move. My breath sounded painfully loud in my ears. He simply stood there, perhaps a dozen feet away, and looked straight into the dark where I was, as though it were the broadest day. And the light of his torch burned steady and soundless, pallid as a corpse candle, the wood of it not consumed.

I don't know how long I had been standing there before it occurred to me that I was no longer afraid. I was still cold, but my heart had slowed to its normal pace, and my bare toes had uncurled.

'Whatever do you want?' I said, and only then realized that we had been in some sort of communication for some time. Whatever this was, it had no words. Nothing coherent passed between us – but something passed, nonetheless.

The clouds had lifted, shredding away before a light wind, and dark streaks of starlit sky showed through rents in the racing circus. The wood was quiet, but in the usual way of a drenched night-wood; the creaks and sighs of tall trees moving, the rustle of shrubs brushed by the wind's restless edge, and in the background the constant rush of invisible water, echoing the turbulence of the air above.

I breathed deeply, feeling suddenly very much alive. The air was thick and sweet with the breath of green plants, the tang of herbs and musk of dead leaves, overlaid and interlaced with the scents of the storm – wet rock, damp earth, and rising mist, and a sharp hint of ozone, sudden as the lightning that had struck the tree.

Earth and air, I thought suddenly, and fire and water too. And here I stood with all the elements; in their midst and at their mercy.

'What do you want?' I said again, feeling helpless. 'I can't do anything for you. I know you're there; I can see you. But that's all.'

Nothing moved, no words were spoken. But quite clearly the thought formed in my mind, in a voice that was not my own.

That's enough, it said.

Without haste, he turned and walked away. By the time he had gone two dozen paces, the light of his torch disappeared, fading into nonexistence like the final glow of twilight into night.

'Oh,' I said, a little blankly. 'Goodness.' My legs were trembling, and I sat down, the skull – which I had almost forgotten – cradled in my lap.

I sat there for a long time, watching and listening, but nothing further happened. The mountains surrounded me, dark and impenetrable. Perhaps in the morning, I could find my way back to the trail, but for now, wandering about in darkness could lead to nothing but disaster.

I was no longer afraid; my fear had left me during my encounter with – whatever it was. I was still cold, though, and very, very hungry. I put down the skull and curled myself up beside it, pulling my damp cloak around me. It took a long time to fall asleep, and I lay in my chilly burrow watching the evening stars wheel overhead through rifts in the cloud.

I tried to make sense of the last half hour, but there was really nothing to make sense *of*; nothing, really, had happened. And yet it had; he had been there. The sense of him remained with me, somehow vaguely comforting, and at last I fell asleep, cheek pillowed on a clump of dead leaves.

I dreamt uneasily, because of cold and hunger; a procession of disjoint images. Lightning-blasted trees, blazing like torches. Trees uprooted from the earth, walking on their roots with a dreadful lurching gait.

Lying in the rain with my throat cut, warm blood pulsing down across my chest, a queer comfort to my

481

chilling flesh. My fingers numb, unable to move. The rain striking my skin like hail, each cold drop a hammer blow, and then the rain itself seemed warm, and soft upon my face. Buried alive, black soil showering down into open eyes.

I woke, heart pounding. Lay silent. It was deep night now; the sky stretched clear and endless overhead, and I lay in a bowl of darkness. After a time, I slept again, pursued by dreams.

Wolves howling in the distance. Fleeing panicked through a forest of white aspen that stood in snow, the trees' red sap glowing like bloody jewels on white-paper trunks. A man standing in the bleeding trees with his head plucked bald, save a standing crest of black, greased hair. He had deep eyes and a shattered smile, and the blood on his breast was brighter than the tree sap.

Wolves, much closer. Howling and barking and the scent of blood hot in my own nose, running with the pack, running from the pack. Running. Harefooted, white-toothed, and the ghost of blood a taste in my mouth, a tingle in my nose. Hunger. Chase and catch and kill and blood. Heart hammering, blood racing, sheer panic of the hunted.

I felt my armbone crack with a noise like a dry branch snapping, and tasted marrow warm and salty, slippery on my tongue.

Something brushed my face and I opened my eyes. Great yellow eyes stared into mine, from the dark ruff of a white-toothed wolf. I screamed and struck at it and the beast started back with a startled '*Woof!*'

I floundered to my knees and crouched there, gibbering. It had just gone daybreak. The dawning light was new and tender, and showed me plainly the huge black outline of . . . Rollo.

'Oh, Jesus God, what the bloody *hell* are you doing here, frigging bloody horrible . . . filthy beast!' I might eventually have gotten a grip on myself, but Jamie got one first.

Big hands pulled me up and out of my hiding place, held me tight and patted me anxiously, checking for damage. The wool of his plaid was soft against my face; it smelt of wet and lye soap and his own male scent and I breathed it in like oxygen.

'Are ye all right? For God's sake, Sassenach, are ye all right?'

'No,' I said. 'Yes,' I said, and started to cry.

It didn't last long; it was no more than the shock of relief. I tried to say as much, but Jamie wasn't listening. He scooped me up in his arms, filthy as I was, and began to carry me toward the small stream.

'Hush, then,' he said, squeezing me tightly against him. 'Hush, *mo chridhe*. It's all right now; you're safe.'

I was still fuddled with cold and dreams. Alone so long with no voice but my own, his sounded odd, unreal and hard to understand. The warm solidity of his grasp was real, though.

'Wait,' I said, tugging feebly at his shirt. 'Wait, I forgot. I have to –'

'Jesus, Uncle Jamie, look at this!'

Jamie turned, holding me. Young Ian was standing in the mouth of my refuge, framed in dangling roots, holding up the skull.

I felt Jamie's muscles tighten as he saw it.

'Holy God, Sassenach, what's that?'

'Who, you mean,' I said. 'I don't know. Nice chap, though. Don't let Rollo at him; he wouldn't like it.' Rollo was sniffing the skull with intense concentration, wet black nostrils flaring with interest.

Jamie peered down into my face, frowning slightly.

'Are ye sure you're quite all right, Sassenach?'

'No,' I said, though in fact my wits were coming back as I woke up all the way. 'I'm cold and I'm starving. You didn't happen to bring any breakfast, did you?' I asked longingly. 'I could murder a plateful of eggs.'

'No,' he said, setting me down while he groped in his sporran. 'I hadna time to trouble for food, but I've got some brandywine. Here, Sassenach; it'll do you good. And then,' he added, raising one eyebrow, 'you can tell me how the devil ye came to be out in the middle of nowhere, aye?'

I collapsed on a rock and sipped the brandywine grate-fully. The flask trembled in my hands, but the shivering

483

began to ease as the dark amber stuff made its way directly through the walls of my empty stomach and into my blood-stream.

Jamie stood behind me, his hand on my shoulder.

'How long have ye been here, Sassenach?' he asked, his voice gentle.

'All night,' I said, shivering again. 'Since just before noon yesterday, when the bloody horse – I think his name's Judas – dropped me off that ledge up there.'

I nodded at the ledge. The middle of nowhere was a good description of the place, I thought. It could have been any of a thousand anonymous hollows in these hills. A thought struck me – one that should have occurred to me long before, had I not been so chilled and groggy.

'How the hell did you find me?' I asked. 'Did one of the Muellers follow me, or – don't tell me the bloody horse led you to me, like Lassie?'

'It's a gelding, Auntie,' Ian put in reprovingly. 'No a lassie. But we havena seen your horse at all. No, Rollo led us to ye.' He beamed proudly at the dog, who contrived to look blandly dignified, as though he did this sort of thing all the time.

'But if you haven't seen the horse,' I began, bewildered, 'how did you even know I'd left the Muellers'? And how could Rollo –' I broke off, seeing the two men eyeing each other.

Ian shrugged slightly and nodded, yielding to Jamie. Jamie hunkered down on the ground beside me, and lifting the hem of my dress, took my bare feet into his big, warm hands.

'Your feet are frozen, Sassenach,' he said quietly. 'Where did ye lose your shoes?'

'Back there,' I said, with a nod toward the uprooted tree. 'They must still be there. I took them off to cross a stream, then put them down and couldn't find them in the dark.'

'They're not there, Auntie,' said Ian. He sounded so queer that I looked up at him in surprise. He was still holding the skull, turning it gingerly over in his hands.

'No, they're not.' Jamie's head was bent as he chafed my feet, and I could see the early light glint copper off his hair, which lay tumbled loose over his shoulders, disheveled as though he had just risen from his bed.

'I was in bed, asleep,' he said, echoing my thought. 'When yon beast suddenly went mad.' He jerked his chin at Rollo, without looking up. 'Barking and howling and flingin' his carcass at the door as though the Devil was outside.'

'I shouted at him, and tried to get hold of his scruff and shake him quiet,' Ian put in, 'but he wouldna stop, no matter what I did.'

'Aye, he carried on so that the spittle flew from his jaws and I was sure he'd gone truly mad. I thought he'd do us an injury, so I bade Ian unbolt the door and let him be gone.' Jamie sat back on his heels and frowned at my foot, then picked a dead leaf off my instep.

'Well, and *was* the Devil outside?' I asked flippantly.

Jamie shook his head.

'We searched the clearing, from the penfold to the spring, and didna find a thing – except these.' He reached into his sporran and drew out my shoes. He looked up into my face, his own quite expressionless.

'They were sitting on the doorstep, side by side.'

Every hair on my body rose. I lifted the flask and drained the last of the brandywine.

'Rollo tore off, bayin' like a hound,' Ian said, eagerly taking up the story. 'But then he came back a moment later, and began to sniff at your shoes and whinge and cry.'

'I felt rather like doing that myself, aye?' Jamie's mouth lifted slightly at one corner, but I could see the fear still dark in his eyes.

I swallowed, but my mouth was too dry to talk, despite the brandywine.

Jamie slipped one shoe onto my foot, and then the other. They were damp, but faintly warm from his body.

'I did think ye were maybe dead, Cinderella,' he said softly, head bent to hide his face.

Ian didn't notice, caught up in the enthusiasm of the story.

'My clever wee dog was for dashing off, the same as when he's smelt a rabbit, so we caught up our plaids and came away after him, only stopping to snatch a brand from the hearth and smoor the fire. He led us a good chase, too, did ye no, laddie?' He rubbed Rollo's ears with affectionate pride. 'And here ye were!'

The brandywine was buzzing in my ears, swaddling my wits in a warm, sweet blanket, but I had enough sense left to tell me that for Rollo to have followed a trail back to me . . . someone had walked all that way in my shoes.

I had recovered some remnants of my voice by this time, and managed to talk with only a little hoarseness.

'Did you – see anything – along the way?' I asked.

'No, Auntie,' Ian said, suddenly sober. 'Did you?'

Jamie lifted his head, and I could see how worry and exhaustion had hollowed his face, leaving the broad cheekbones sharp beneath his skin. I wasn't the only one who had had a long, hard night.

'Yes,' I said, 'but I'll tell you later. Right now, I believe I've turned into a pumpkin. Let's go home.'

Jamie had brought horses, but there was no way to get them down into the hollow; we were forced to make our way down the banks of the flooded stream, splashing through the shallows, then to clamber laboriously up a rocky slope to the ledge above, where the animals were tethered. Rubber-legged and flimsy after my ordeal, I wasn't a great deal of help in this endeavor, but Jamie and Ian coped matter-of-factly, boosting me over obstructions and handing me back and forth like a large, unwieldy package.

'You really aren't supposed to give alcohol to people suffering from hypothermia,' I said feebly as Jamie put the flask to my lips again during one pause for rest.

'I dinna care what you're suffering from, you'll feel it less with the drink in your belly,' he said. It was still chilly from the rain, but his face was flushed from the climb. 'Besides,' he added, mopping his brow with a fold of his plaid, 'if ye pass out, you'll be less trouble to hoik about. Christ, it's like hauling a newborn calf out of a bog.'

'Sorry,' I said. I lay flat on the ground and closed my eyes, hoping I wouldn't throw up. The sky was spinning in one direction, my stomach in the other.

'Away, dog!' Ian said.

I opened one eye to see what was going on, and saw Ian firmly shooing Rollo away from the skull, which I had insisted he bring with us.

Seen in daylight, it was hardly a prepossessing object. Stained and discolored by the soil in which it had been buried, from a distance it resembled a smooth stone, scooped and gouged by wind and weather. Several of the teeth had been chipped or broken, though the skull showed no other damage.

'Just what do ye mean to do wi' Prince Charming there?' Jamie asked, eyeing my acquisition rather critically. His color had faded, and he had got his breath back. He glanced down at me, reached over and smoothed the hair out of my eyes, smiling.

'All right, Sassenach?'

'Better,' I assured him, sitting up. The countryside had not quite stopped moving round me, but the brandy sloshing through my veins now gave the movement a rather pleasant quality, like the soothing rush of trees past the window of a railway carriage.

'I suppose we ought to take him home and give him Christian burial, at least?' Ian eyed the skull dubiously.

'I shouldn't think he'd appreciate it; I don't believe he was a Christian.' I fought back a vivid recollection of the man I had seen in the hollow. While it was true that some Indians had been converted by missionaries, this particular naked gentleman, with his black-painted face and feathered hair, had given me the impression that he was about as pagan as they come.

I fumbled in the pocket of my skirt, my fingers numb and stiff.

'This was buried with him.'

I drew out the flat stone I had unearthed. It was dirty brown in color, an irregular oval half the size of my palm. It was flattened on one side, rounded on the other, and smooth as though it had come from a streambed. I turned it over on my palm and gasped.

The flattened face was indeed incised with a carving, as I had thought. It was a glyph in the shape of a spiral, coiling in on itself. But it wasn't the carving that brought both Jamie and Ian to peer into my hand, heads nearly touching.

Where the smooth surface had been chipped away, the rock within glowed with a lambent fire, little flames of green and orange and red all fighting fiercely for the light.

'My God, what is it?' Ian asked, sounding awed.

'It's an opal – and a damned big one, at that,' Jamie said. He poked the stone with a large, blunt forefinger, as though checking to ensure that it was real. It was.

He rubbed a hand through his hair, thinking, then glanced at me.

'They do say that opals are unlucky stones, Sassenach.' I thought he was joking, but he looked uneasy. A widely traveled, well-educated man, still he had been born a Highlander, and I knew he had a deeply superstitious streak, though it didn't often show.

Ha, I thought to myself. You've spent the night with a ghost and you think *he's* superstitious?

'Nonsense,' I said, with rather more conviction than I felt. 'It's only a rock.'

'Well, it's no so much they're unlucky, Uncle Jamie,' Ian put in. 'My mam has a wee opal ring her mother left her – though it's nothing like this!' Ian touched the stone reverently. 'She did say as how an opal takes on something of its owner, though – so if ye had an opal that belonged to a good person before ye, then all was well, and you'd have good luck of it. But if not –' He shrugged.

'Aye, well,' Jamie said dryly. He jerked his head toward the skull, pointing with his chin. 'If it belonged to this fellow, it doesna seem as if it was ower-lucky for him.'

'At least we know nobody killed him for it,' I pointed out.

'Perhaps they didna want it because they kent it was bad luck,' Ian suggested. He was frowning at the stone, a worried line between his eyes. 'Maybe we should put it back, Auntie.'

I rubbed my nose and looked at Jamie.

'It's probably rather valuable,' I said.

'Ah.' The two of them stood in contemplation for a moment, torn between superstition and pragmatism.

'Aye well,' Jamie said finally, 'I suppose it will do no

harm to keep it for a bit.' One side of his mouth lifted in a smile. 'Let me carry it, Sassenach; if I'm struck by lightning on the way home, ye can put it back.'

I got awkwardly to my feet, holding on to Jamie's arm to keep my balance. I blinked and swayed, but stayed upright. Jamie took the stone from my hand and slipped it back into his sporran.

'I'll show it to Nayawenne,' I said. 'She might know what the carving means, at least.'

'A good thought, Sassenach,' Jamie approved. 'And if Prince Charming should be her kinsman, she can have him, with my blessing.' He nodded toward a small stand of maple trees a hundred yards away, their green barely tinged with yellow.

'The horses are tied just yonder. Can ye walk, Sassenach?'

I looked down at my feet, considering. They seemed a lot farther away than I was used to.

'I'm not sure,' I said, 'I think I'm really rather drunk.'

'Och, no, Auntie,' Ian assured me kindly. 'My da says you're never drunk, so long as ye can hold on to the floor.'

Jamie laughed at this, and threw the end of his plaid over his shoulder.

'*My* da used to say ye werena drunk, so long as ye could find your arse with both hands.' He eyed my backside with a lifted brow, but wisely thought better of whatever else he might have been going to say.

Ian choked on a giggle and coughed, recovering himself.

'Aye, well. It's no much farther, Auntie. Are ye sure ye canna walk?'

'Well, I'm no going to pick her up again, I'll tell ye,' Jamie said, not waiting for my answer. 'I dinna want to rupture my back.' He took the skull from Ian, holding it between the tips of his fingers, and placed it delicately in my lap. 'Wait here wi' your wee friend, Sassenach,' he said. 'Ian and I will fetch the horses.'

By the time we reached Fraser's Ridge, it was early afternoon. I had been cold, wet, and without food for nearly two days, and was feeling distinctly light-headed; a feeling exaggerated both by more infusions of brandywine and by my efforts to explain the events of the night before to Ian and Jamie. Viewed in the light of day, the entire night seemed unreal.

But then, almost everything seemed unreal, viewed through a haze of exhaustion, hunger, and mild drunkenness. Consequently, when we turned into the clearing, I thought at first that the smoke from the chimney was a hallucination – until the tang of burning hickory wood struck my nose.

'I thought you said you smoored the fire,' I said to Jamie. 'Lucky you didn't burn down the house.' Such accidents were common; I had heard of more than one wooden cabin burned to the ground as the result of a poorly tended hearth.

'I did smoor it,' he said briefly, swinging down from the saddle. 'Someone's here. D'ye ken the horse, Ian?'

Ian stood in his stirrups to look down into the penfold.

'Why, it's Auntie's wicked beast!' he said in surprise. 'And a big dapple with him!'

Sure enough, the newly named Judas was standing in the penfold, unsaddled, companionably switching flies head to tail with a thick-barreled gray gelding.

'Do you know who owns him?' I asked. I hadn't got down yet; small waves of dizziness had been washing over me every few minutes, forcing me to cling to the saddle. The ground under the horse seemed to be heaving gently up and down, like ocean billows.

'No, but it's a friend,' Jamie said. 'He's fed my beasts for me, and milked the goat.' He nodded from the horses' hay-filled manger to the door, where a pail of milk stood on the bench, neatly covered with a square of cloth to prevent flies falling in.

'Come along, Sassenach.' He reached up and took me by the waist. 'We'll tuck ye in bed and brew ye a dish of tea.'

Our arrival had been heard; the door of the cabin opened, and Duncan Innes looked out.

'Ah, you're there, *Mac Dubh*,' he said. 'What's amiss, then? Your goat was carryin' on fit to wake the dead, wi' her bag like to burst, when I came up the trail this

490

morning.' Then he saw me, and his long, mournful face
went blank with surprise.

'Mrs. Claire!' he said, taking in my mud-stained and
battered appearance. 'Ye'll have had an accident, then? I
was a bit worrit when I found the horse loose on the
mountainside as I came up, and your wee box on the
saddle. I looked about and called for ye, but I couldna
find any sign of ye, so I brought the beast along to the
house.'

'Yes, I had an accident,' I said, trying to stand upright by
myself and not succeeding very well. 'I'm all right,
though.' I wasn't altogether sure about that. My head felt
three times its normal size.

'Bed,' Jamie said firmly, grabbing me by the arms before
I could fall over. 'Now.'

'Bath,' I said. 'First.'

He glanced in the direction of the creek.

'You'll freeze or drown. Or both. For God's sake,
Sassenach, eat and go to bed; ye can wash tomorrow.'

'Now. Hot water. Kettle.' I hadn't the energy to waste on
prolonged argument, but I was determined. I wasn't going
to bed dirty, and I wasn't going to wash filthy sheets later.

Jamie looked at me in exasperation, then rolled his eyes
in surrender.

'Hot water, kettle, now, then,' he said. 'Ian, fetch some
wood, and then take Duncan and see to the pigs. I'm
going to scrub your auntie.'

'I can scrub myself!'

'The hell ye can.'

He was right; my fingers were so stiff, they couldn't
undo the hooks of my bodice. He undressed me as though
I were a small child, tossing the ripped skirt and mud-
caked petticoats carelessly into the corner, and stripping
off the chemise and stays, worn so long that the cloth folds
had made deep red ridges in my flesh. I groaned with a
voluptuous combination of pain and pleasure, rubbing
the red marks as blood coursed back through my constricted torso.

'Sit,' he said, pushing a stool under me as I collapsed.
He wrapped a quilt around my shoulders, put a plate containing one and a half stale bannocks in front of me, and

491

went to rootle in the cupboard after soap, washcloth, and linen towels.

'Find the green bottle, please,' I said, nibbling at the dry oatcake. 'I'll need to wash my hair.'

'Mmphm.' More clinking, and he emerged at last with his hands full of things, including a towel and the bottle full of the shampoo I had made – not wishing to wash my hair with lye soap – from soaproot, lupin oil, walnut leaves and calendula flowers. He set these on the table, along with my largest mixing bowl, and carefully filled it with hot water from the cauldron.

Leaving this to cool a bit, Jamie dipped a rag into the water, and knelt down to wash my feet.

The feeling of warmth on my sore, half-frozen feet was as close to ecstasy as I expected to get this side of heaven. Tired and half drunk as I was, I felt as though I were dissolving from the feet up, as he gently but thoroughly washed me from toe to head.

'Where did ye get this, Sassenach?' Recalled from a state as close to sleep as to waking, I glanced down muzzily at my left knee. It was swollen, and the inner side had gone the deep purplish-blue of a gentian.

'Oh . . . that happened when I fell off the horse.'

'That was verra careless,' he said sharply. 'Have I not told ye time and again to be careful, especially with a new horse? Ye canna trust them at all until ye've known them a good while. And you're not strong enough to deal with one that's headstrong or skittish.'

'It wasn't a matter of trusting him,' I said. I rather dimly admired the broad spread of his bent shoulders, flexing smoothly under his linen shirt as he sponged my bruised knee. 'The lightning scared him, and I fell off a thirty-foot ledge.'

'Ye could have broken your neck!'

'Thought I had, for a bit.' I closed my eyes, swaying slightly.

'Ye should have taken better thought, Sassenach; ye should never have been on that side of the ridge to begin with, let alone –'

'I couldn't help it,' I said, opening my eyes. 'The trail was washed out; I had to go around.'

He was glaring at me, slanted eyes narrowed into dark blue slits.

'Ye ought not to have left the Muellers' in the first place, and it raining like that! Did ye not have sense enough to know what the ground would be like?'

I straightened up with some effort, holding the quilt against my breasts. It occurred to me, with a faint sense of surprise, that he was more than slightly annoyed.

'Well . . . no,' I said, trying to marshal what wits I had. 'How could I know something like that? Besides –'

He interrupted me by slapping the washrag into the bowl, spattering water all over the table.

'Be quiet!' he said. 'I dinna mean to argue with you!'

I stared up at him.

'What the hell *do* you mean to do? And where do you get off shouting at me? I haven't done anything wrong!'

He inhaled strongly through his nose. Then he stood up, picked the rag from the bowl, and carefully wrung it out. He let out his breath, knelt down in front of me, and deftly swabbed my face clean.

'No. Ye haven't,' he agreed. One corner of his long mouth quirked wryly. 'But ye scairt hell out of me, Sassenach, and it makes me want to give ye a terrible scolding, whether ye deserve it or no.'

'Oh,' I said. I wanted at first to laugh, but felt a stab of remorse as I saw how drawn his face was. His shirt sleeve was daubed with mud, and there were burrs and foxtails in his stockings, left from a night of searching for me through the dark mountains, not knowing where I was; if I were alive or dead. I *had* scared hell out of him, whether I meant to or not.

I groped for some means of apology, finding my tongue nearly as thick as my wits. Finally I reached out and picked a fuzzy yellow catkin from his hair.

'Why don't you scold me in Gaelic?' I said. 'It will ease your feelings just as much, and I'll only understand half of what you say.'

He made a Scottish noise of derision, and shoved my head into the bowl with a firm hand on my neck. When I re-emerged, dripping, though, he dropped a towel on my head and started in, rubbing my hair with large, firm hands and speaking in the formally menacing tones of a minister denouncing sin from the pulpit.

'Silly woman,' he said in Gaelic. 'You have not the brain of a fly!' I caught the words for 'foolish', and 'clumsy', in the subsequent remarks, but quickly stopped listening. I closed my eyes and lost myself instead in the dreamy pleasure of having my hair rubbed dry and then combed out.

He had a sure and gentle touch, probably gained from handling horses' tails. I had seen him talk to horses while he groomed them, much as he was talking to me now, the Gaelic a soothing descant to the whisk of curry comb or brush. I imagined he was more complimentary to the horses, though.

His hands touched my neck, my bare back, and shoulders as he worked; fleeting touches that brought my newly thawed flesh to life. I shivered, but let the quilt fall to my lap. The fire was still burning high, flames dancing on the side of the kettle, and the room had grown quite warm.

He was now describing, in a pleasantly conversational tone, various things he would have liked to do to me, beginning with beating me black and blue with a stick, and going on from there. Gaelic is a rich language, and Jamie was far from unimaginative in matters of either violence or sex. Whether he meant it or not, I thought it was probably a good thing that I didn't understand everything he said.

I could feel the heat of the fire on my breasts; Jamie's warmth against my back. The loose fabric of his shirt brushed my skin as he leaned across to reach a bottle on the shelf, and I shivered again. He noticed this, and interrupted his tirade for a moment.

'Cold?'

'No.'

'Good.' The sharp smell of camphor stung my nose, and before I could move, one large hand had seized my shoulder, holding me in place, while the other rubbed slippery oil firmly into my chest.

'Stop! That tickles! Stop, I say!'

He didn't stop. I squirmed madly, trying to escape, but he was a lot bigger than I was.

'Be still,' he said, inexorable fingers rubbing deep between my ticklish ribs, under my collarbone, around and under my tender breasts, greasing me as thoroughly as a suckling pig bound for the spit.

'You *bastard*!' I said when he let me go, breathless from struggling and giggling. I reeked of peppermint and camphor, and my skin glowed with heat from chin to belly.

He grinned at me, revenged and thoroughly unrepentant.

'You do it to *me* when I've got an ague,' he pointed out, wiping his hands on the towel. 'Grease for the gander is grease for the goose, aye?'

'I have not got an ague! Not even a sniffle!'

'I expect ye will have, out all night and sleepin' in wet clothes.' He clicked his tongue disapprovingly, like a Scottish housewife.

'And you've never done that, have you? How many times have *you* caught cold from sleeping rough?' I demanded. 'Good heavens, you lived in a *cave* for seven years!'

'And spent three of them sneezing. Besides, I'm a man,' he added, with total illogic. 'Had ye not better put on your night rail, Sassenach? Ye havena got a stitch on.'

'I noticed. Wet clothes and being cold do not cause sickness,' I informed him, hunting about under the table for the fallen quilt.

He raised both eyebrows.

'Oh, they don't?'

'No, they don't.' I backed out from under the table, clutching the quilt. 'I've told you before, it's germs that cause sickness. If I haven't been exposed to any germs, I won't get sick.'

'Ah, gerrrrms,' he said, rolling it like a marble in his mouth. 'God, ye've got a fine, fat arse! Why do folk have more illness in the winter than the springtime, then? The germs breed in the cold, I expect?'

'Not exactly.' Feeling absurdly self-conscious, I spread the quilt, meaning to fold it around my shoulders again. Before I could wrap myself in it, though, he had grabbed me by the arm and pulled me toward him.

'Come here,' he said, unnecessarily. Before I could say anything, he had smacked my bare backside smartly, turned me around and kissed me, hard.

He let go, and I almost fell down. I flung my arms around him, and he grabbed my waist, steadying me.

'I dinna care whether it's the germs or the night air or Billy-be-damned,' he said, looking sternly down his nose. 'I willna have ye fallin' ill, and that's all about it. Now, hop yourself directly into your gown, and to bed with ye!'

He felt awfully good in my arms. The smooth linen of his shirtfront was cool against the heated glow of my greased breasts, and while the wool of his kilt was much scratchier against my naked thighs and belly, the sensation was by no means unpleasant. I rubbed myself slowly against him, like a cat against a post.

'Bed,' he said again, sounding a trifle less stern.

'Mmmm,' I said, making it reasonably obvious that I didn't mean to go there alone.

'No,' he said, squirming slightly. I supposed that he meant to get away, but since I didn't let go, the movement merely exacerbated the situation between us.

'Mm-hmm,' I said, holding on tight. Intoxicated as I was, it hadn't escaped me that Duncan would undoubtedly be spending the night on the hearth rug, Ian on the trundle. And while I was feeling somewhat uninhibited at the moment, the feeling didn't extend quite *that* far.

'My father told me never to take advantage of a woman who was the worse for drink,' he said. He had stopped squirming, but now started again, slower, as though he couldn't help himself.

'I'm not worse, I'm better,' I assured him. 'Besides –' I executed a slow, sinuous squirm of my own. 'I thought he said you weren't drunk if you could find your arse with both hands.'

He eyed me appraisingly.

'I hate to tell ye, Sassenach, but it's not your arse ye've got hold of – it's mine.'

'That's all right,' I assured him. 'We're married. Share and share alike. One flesh; the priest said so.'

'Perhaps it was a mistake to put that grease on ye,' he muttered, half to himself. 'It never does this to *me*!'

'Well, you're a man.'

He had one last gallant try.

'Should ye not eat a bit more, lass? You must be starving.'

'Mm-hm,' I said. I buried my face in his shirt and bit him, lightly. 'Ravenous.'

There is a story told of the Earl of Montrose – that after one battle, he was found lying on the field, half dead of cold and starvation, by a young woman. The young woman whipped off her shoe, mixed barley with cold water in it, and fed the resulting mess to the prostrate earl, thus saving his life.

The cup now thrust under my nose appeared to contain a portion of this same life-giving substance, with the minor difference that mine was warm.

'What is this?' I asked, eyeing the pale grains floating belly-up on the surface of a watery liquid. It looked like a cup full of drowned maggots.

'Barley crowdie,' Ian said, gazing proudly at the cup as though it were his firstborn child. 'I made it myself, from the bag ye brought from Muellers'.'

'Thank you,' I said, and took a cautious sip. I didn't *think* he had mixed it in his shoe, despite the musty aroma. 'Very good,' I said. 'How kind of you, Ian.'

He went pink with gratification.

'Och, it was nothing,' he said. 'There's plenty more, Auntie. Or shall I fetch ye a bit of cheese? I could cut the green bits off for ye.'

'No, no – this will be fine,' I said hastily. 'Ah . . . why don't you take your gun out, Ian, and see if you can bag a squirrel or a rabbit? I'm sure I'll be well enough to cook supper.'

He beamed, the smile transforming his long, bony face.

'I'm glad to hear it, Auntie,' he said. 'Ye should *see* what Uncle Jamie and I have been eatin' while ye've been gone!'

He left me lying on my pillows, wondering what to do with the cup of crowdie. I didn't want to drink it, but I felt like a puddle of warm butter – soft and creamy, nearly liquid – and the idea of getting up seemed unthinkably energetic.

Jamie, making no further protests, had taken me to bed, where he had completed the business of thawing me out with thoroughness and dispatch. I thought it was a good thing he wasn't going hunting with Ian. He reeked of camphor as much as I did; the animals would scent him a mile away.

Tucking me tenderly under the quilts, he had left me to sleep while he went to greet Duncan more formally and offer him the hospitality of the house. I could hear the deep murmur of their voices outside now; they were sitting on the bench beside the door, enjoying the last of the afternoon sunshine – long, pale beams slanted through the window, lighting a warm glow of pewter and wood within.

The sun touched the skull, too. This stood on my writing table across the room, composing a cozily domestic still life with a clay jug filled with flowers and my casebook.

It was sight of the casebook that roused me from torpor. The birth I had attended at the Muellers' farm now seemed vague and insubstantial in my mind; I thought I had better record the details while I still recalled them at all.

Thus prompted by the stirrings of professional duty, I stretched, groaned, and sat up. I still felt mildly dizzy and my ears rang from the aftereffects of brandywine. I was also faintly sore almost everywhere – more in some spots than others – but generally speaking, I was in decent working order. Beginning to be hungry, though.

I did hope Ian would come back with meat for the pot; I knew better than to gorge my shriveled stomach on cheese and salt fish, but a nice, strengthening squirrel broth, flavored with spring onions and dried mushrooms, would be just what the doctor ordered.

Speaking of broth – I slid reluctantly out of bed and stumbled across the floor to the hearth, where I poured the cold barley soup back into the pot. Ian had made enough for a regiment – always supposing the regiment to be composed of Scots. Living in a country normally barren of much that was edible, they were capable of relishing glutinous masses of cereal, untouched by any redeeming hint of spice or flavor. From a feebler race myself, I didn't feel quite up to it.

The opened bag of barley stood beside the hearth, the burlap sack still visibly damp. I would have to spread the grain to dry, or it would rot. My bruised knee protesting a bit, I went and got a large flat tray-basket made of plaited reeds, and knelt to spread the damp grain in a thin layer over it.

'Will he have a soft mouth, then, Duncan?' Jamie's voice came clearly through the window; the hide covering was rolled up, to let in air, and I caught the faint tang of tobacco from Duncan's pipe. 'He's a big, strong brute, but he's got a kind eye.'

'Oh, he's a bonny wee fellow,' Duncan said, the note of pride in his voice unmistakable. 'And a nice soft mouth, aye. Miss Jo had her stableman pick him from the market in Wilmington; said he must find a horse could be managed well wi' one hand.'

'Mmphm. Aye, well, he's a lovely creature.' The wooden bench creaked as one of the men shifted his weight. I understood the equivocation behind Jamie's compliment, and wondered whether Duncan did, as well.

Part of it was simple condescension; Jamie had been raised on horseback, and as a born horseman, would scorn the notion that hands were necessary at all; I had seen him maneuver a horse by the shifting pressure of knees and thighs alone, or set his mount at a gallop across a crowded field, the reins knotted on the horse's neck, to leave Jamie's hands free for sword and pistol.

But Duncan was neither a horseman nor a soldier; he had lived as a fisherman near Ardrossan, until the Rising had plucked him, like so many others, from his nets and his boat, and sent him to Culloden and disaster.

Jamie wouldn't be so untactful as to point up an inexperience of which Duncan was more than aware already; he *would*, though, mean to point up something else. Had Duncan caught it?

'It's you she means to help, *Mac Dubh*, and well ye ken

it, too.' Duncan's tones were very dry; he'd taken Jamie's point, all right.

'I havena said otherwise, Duncan.' Jamie's voice was even.

'Mmphm.'

I smiled, despite the air of edginess between them. Duncan was every bit as good as Jamie at the Highland art of inarticulate eloquence. This particular noise captured both mild insult at Jamie's implication that it was improper for Duncan to be accepting the gift of a horse from Jocasta, and a willingness to accept the likewise implied apology for the insult.

'Have ye thought, then?' The bench creaked as Duncan abruptly changed the subject. 'Will it be Sinclair, or Geordie Chisholm?'

Without giving Jamie time to reply, he went on, but in a way that made it clear that he had said all this before. I wondered whether he was trying to convince Jamie, or himself – or only assist them both in coming to a decision by repeating the facts of the matter.

'It's true Sinclair's a cooper, but Geordie's a good fellow; a thrifty worker, and he's the two wee sons, besides. Sinclair isna marrit, so he wouldna need so much in the way of setting up, but –'

'He'd need lathes and tools, and iron and seasoned wood,' Jamie broke in. 'He could sleep in his shop, aye, but he'll need the shop to sleep in. And it will cost verra dear, I think, to buy all that's needed for a cooperage. Geordie would need a bit of food for his family, but we can provide that from the place here; beyond that, he'll need no more to begin than a few wee tools – he'll have an ax, aye?'

'Aye, he'll have that from his indenture, but it's the planting season *now, Mac Dubh*. With the clearing –'

'I ken that weel enough,' Jamie said, a bit testily. 'It's me that put five acres in corn a month ago. *And* cleared them, first.' While Duncan had been taking his ease at River Run, chatting in taverns and breaking in his new horse. I heard it, and so did Duncan; there was a distinct silence that spoke as loud as words.

A creak from the bench, and then Duncan spoke again, mildly.

'Your auntie Jo's sent a wee gift for ye.'

'Oh, has she?' The edge in his voice was even more perceptible. I hoped Duncan had sense enough to heed it.

'A bottle of whisky.' There was a smile in Duncan's voice, answered by a reluctant laugh from Jamie.

'Oh, has she?' he said again, in quite a different tone. 'That's verra kind.'

'She means to be.' There was a substantial creak and shuffle as Duncan got to his feet. 'Come wi' me and fetch it, then, *Mac Dubh*. A wee drink wouldna do your temper any harm.'

'No, it wouldn't.' Jamie sounded rueful. 'I've not slept the night, and I'm cranky as a rutting boar. Ye'll forgive my manners, Duncan.'

'Och, dinna speak of it.' There was a soft sound, as of a hand clapping a shoulder, and I heard them walk off across the yard together. I moved to the window and watched them, Jamie's hair gleaming dark bronze in the setting sun, as he tilted his head to listen to something Duncan was telling him, the shorter man gesturing in explanation. The movements of Duncan's single arm threw off the rhythm of his stride, so he walked with jerky movements, like a large puppet.

What would have become of him, I wondered, had Jamie not found him – and found a place for him? There was no place in Scotland for a one-armed fisherman. There would have been nothing for him but beggary, surely. Starvation, perhaps. Or theft to live, and death at the end of a rope, like Gavin Hayes.

But this was the New World, and if life was chancy here, well, it meant a chance at life, at least. No wonder that Jamie should worry over who should have the best chance. Sinclair the cooper, or Chisholm the farmer?

A cooper would be valuable to have at hand; it would save the men on the ridge the long trip into Cross Creek or Averasboro to fetch the barrels needed for pitch and turpentine, for salted meat and cider. But it would be expensive to set up a cooper's shop, even with the bare rudiments the trade required. And then there was the

501

unknown Chisholm's wife and small children to be considered – how were they living now, and what might become of them without help?

Duncan had so far located thirty of the men of Ardsmuir; Gavin Hayes was the first, and we had done for him all that could be done; seen him safe into heaven's keeping. Two more were known dead, one of fever, one of drowning. Three had completed their terms of indenture, and – armed only with the ax and suit of clothes that were a bondsman's final pay – had managed to find a foothold for themselves, claiming backcountry land and carving out small homesteads there.

Of the remainder, we had brought twenty so far to settle on good land near the river, under Jamie's sponsorship. Another was feebleminded but worked for one of the others as a hired man, and so earned his keep. It had taken all of our resources to do it, using all our small quantity of cash, notes against the value of as yet non-existent crops – and one hair-raising trip into Cross Creek.

Jamie had called upon all his acquaintance there, borrowing small amounts from each, and had then taken this money to the riverside taverns, where in three sleepless nights of play, he had managed to quadruple his stake – narrowly avoiding being knifed in the process, as I learned much later.

I was speechless, looking at the long, jagged rent in the bosom of his coat.

'What –?' I croaked at last.

He shrugged briefly, looking suddenly very tired.

'It doesna matter,' he said. 'It's over.'

He had then shaved, washed, and gone round to all the plantation owners again, returning each man's money with thanks and a small payment of interest, leaving us with enough to manage seed corn for planting, an extra mule for plowing, a goat and some pigs.

I didn't ask him anything else; only mended the coat, and saw him safely into bed when he came back from repaying the money lent. I sat by him for a long time, though, watching the lines of exhaustion in his face ease a little as he slept.

Only a little. I had lifted his hand, limp and heavy with

sleep, and traced the deep lines of his smooth, callused palm, over and over. The lines of head and heart and life ran long and deep. How many lives lay in those creases now?

My own. His settlers. Fergus and Marsali, who had just arrived from Jamaica, in the custody of Germaine, a chubby blond charmer who had his besotted father in the palm of *his* fat little hand.

I glanced involuntarily through the window at the thought. Ian and Jamie had helped to build them a small cabin only a mile from our own, and sometimes Marsali would walk over in the evenings to visit, bringing the baby. I could do with seeing him, I thought wistfully. Lonely as I sometimes was for Bree, little Germaine was a substitute for the grandchild I would never hold.

I sighed, and shrugged away the thought.

Jamie and Duncan had come back with the whisky; I could hear them talking by the paddock, their voices relaxed, all tension between them eased – for the moment.

I finished spreading out a thin layer of the wet barley and set it in the corner of the hearth to dry, then went to the writing table, uncapped the inkwell, and opened my casebook. It didn't take long to record the details of the newest Mueller's arrival into the world; it had been a long labor but otherwise quite normal. The birth itself had presented no complications; the only unusual feature had been the child's caul . . .

I stopped writing and shook my head. Still distracted by thoughts of Jamie, I had let my attention wander. Petronella's child had not been born with a caul. I had a clear memory of the top of the skull crowning, the pudendum a shiny red ring stretched tight around a small patch of black hair. I had touched it, felt the tiny pulse throbbing there, just under the skin. I remembered vividly the sensation of the wet down against my fingers, like the damp skin of a new-hatched chick.

It was the dream, I thought. I had dreamed in my burrow, mingling the events of the two births together – this one, and Brianna's. It was Brianna who had been born with a caul.

503

A 'silly hoo', the Scots called it; a lucky hood. A fortunate portent, a caul offered – they said – protection from drowning in later life. And some children born with a caul were blessed with second sight – though having met one or two of those who saw with the third eye, I took leave to doubt that such a blessing was unmixed.

Whether lucky or not, Brianna had never showed any signs of that strange Celtic 'knowing', and I thought it just as well. I knew enough of my own peculiar form of second sight – the certain knowledge of things to come – not to wish its complications on anyone else.

I looked at the page before me. Only half noticing, I had sketched the rough outline of a girl's head. A curving thick line of swirling hair, the bare suggestion of a long, straight nose. Beyond that, she was faceless.

I was no artist. I had learned to make clean clinical drawings, accurate pictures of limbs and bodies, but I lacked Brianna's gift of bringing lines to life. The sketch as it stood was no more than an aide-mémoire; I could look at it and paint her face in memory. To try to do more – to conjure flesh out of the paper – would be to ruin that, and risk losing the image I held of her in my heart.

And would I conjure her in the flesh, if I could do it? No. That I would not; I would a thousand times rather think of her in the safety and comfort of her own time than wish her here amid the harshness and dangers of this one. But it didn't mean that I didn't miss her.

For the first time, I felt some small sympathy for Jocasta Cameron and her desire for an heir; someone to remain behind, to take her place; testimony that her life had not been lived in vain.

Twilight was rising beyond the window, from field and wood and river. People spoke of night falling, but it didn't, really. Darkness rose, filling first the hollows, then shadowing the slopes, creeping imperceptibly up tree trunks and fenceposts as night swallowed the ground and rose up to join the greater dark of the star-spread sky above.

I sat staring out the window, watching the light change on the horses in the paddock; not so much fading as altering, so that everything – arched necks, round rumps, even single blades of grass – stood stark and clean, reality freed for one brief moment from the day's illusions of sun and shadow.

Unseeing, I traced the line of the drawing with my finger, over and over, as the dark rose up around me and the realities of my heart stood clear in the dusky light. No, I would not wish Brianna here. But that didn't mean I didn't miss her.

I finished my notes eventually, and sat quietly for a moment. I should go and begin making supper, I knew, but the weariness of my ordeal still dragged at me, making me unwilling to move. All my muscles ached, and the bruise on my knee throbbed. All I really wanted to do was to crawl back into bed.

Instead, I picked up the skull, which I had set down next to my casebook on the table. I ran my finger gently over the rounded cranium. It was a thoroughly macabre desk ornament, I would admit that, but I felt rather attached to it, nonetheless. I had always found bones beautiful, of man or beast; stark and graceful remnants of life reduced to its foundations.

I thought suddenly of something I had not remembered in many years; a small dark closet of a room in Paris, hidden behind an apothecary's shop. The walls covered with a honeycomb of shelves, each cell holding a polished skull. Animals of many kinds, from shrews to wolves, mice to bears.

And with my hand on the head of my unknown friend, I heard Master Raymond's voice, as clear in memory as though he stood beside me.

'Sympathy?' he had said as I touched the high curve of a polished elk's skull. 'It is an unusual emotion to feel for a bone, madonna.'

But he had known what I meant. I knew he did, for when I asked him why he kept these skulls, he had smiled and said, 'They are company, of a sort.'

I knew what he meant, too; for surely the gentleman whose skull I kept had been company for me, in a very dark and lonely place. Not for the first time, I wondered whether he had in fact had anything to do with the apparition I had seen on the mountain; the Indian with his face painted black.

The ghost – if that is what he was – had not smiled or spoken aloud. I hadn't seen his teeth, which would be my only point of comparison with the skull I held – for I found that I was holding it, rubbing a thumb over the jagged edge of a cracked incisor. I lifted the skull to the light, examining it closely by the soft sunset light.

The teeth on the one side had been shattered; cracked and splintered as though he had been struck violently in the mouth, perhaps by a rock or a club – the stock of a gun? On the other side they were whole; in very good condition, actually. I was no expert but thought the skull was that of a mature man; one in his late thirties or early forties. A man of that age should show a good bit of wear to his teeth, given the Indians' diet of ground corn, which – owing to the manner of preparation, pounded between flat stones – contained quite a bit of ground stone as well.

The incisors and canine on the good side were scarcely worn at all, though. I turned the skull over, to judge the abrasion of the molars, and stopped cold.

Very cold, in spite of the fire at my back. As cold as I had been in the lost, fireless dark, alone on the mountain with a dead man's head. For the late sun now struck sparks from my hands: from the silver band of my wedding ring – and from the silver fillings in my late companion's mouth.

I sat staring for a moment, then turned the skull over and set it gently down the desk, careful as though it were made of glass.

'My God,' I said, all tiredness forgotten. 'My God,' I said, to the empty eyes and the lopsided grin. 'Who *were* you?'

'Who do ye think he can have been?' Jamie touched the skull gingerly. We had no more than moments; Duncan had gone to the privy, Ian to feed the pig. I couldn't bring myself to wait, though – I had had to tell someone at once.

'I haven't the faintest idea. Except, of course, that he has to have been someone . . . like me.' A violent shiver ran over me. Jamie glanced at me, and frowned.

506

'Ye havena take a chill, have ye, Sassenach?'

'No.' I smiled weakly up at him. 'Goose walking on my grave, I expect.'

He plucked my shawl from the hook by the door and swung it around me. His hands stayed on my shoulders, warm and comforting.

'It means the one thing else, doesn't it?' he asked quietly. 'It means there is another ... place. Perhaps nearby.'

Another stone circle – or something like it. I had thought of that, too, and the notion made me shudder once again. Jamie looked thoughtfully at the skull, then drew the handkerchief from his sleeve and draped it gently over the empty eyes.

'I'll bury him after supper,' he said.

'Oh, supper.' I pushed my hair behind my ear, trying to get my scattered thoughts to focus on food. 'Yes, I'll see if I can find some eggs. That will be quick.'

'Dinna trouble yourself, Sassenach.' Jamie peered into the pot on the hearth. 'We can eat this.'

This time, the shudder was purely one of fastidiousness.

'Ugh,' I said. Jamie grinned at me.

'Nothing wrong wi' good barley crowdie, is there?'

'Assuming there is such a thing,' I replied, looking into the pot with distaste. 'This smells more like distiller's mash.' Made with wet grain, insufficiently cooked and left standing, the cold, scummy soup was already giving off a yeasty whiff of fermentation.

'Speaking of which,' I said, giving the opened sack of damp barley a poke with my toe, 'this needs to be spread to dry, before it starts to mold, if it hasn't already.'

Jamie was staring at the disgusting soup, brows furrowed in thought.

'Aye?' he said absently, then, coming to consciousness, 'Oh, aye. I'll do it.' He twisted shut the top of the bag, and heaved it onto his shoulder. On the way out the door, he paused, looking at the shrouded skull.

'You said ye didna think him Christian,' he said, and glanced curiously at me. 'Why was that, Sassenach?'

I hesitated, but there was no time to tell him about my

dream – if that's what it had been. I could hear Duncan and Ian in conversation, coming toward the house.

'No particular reason,' I said, with a shrug.

'Aye, well,' he said. 'We'll give him the benefit o' the doubt.'

24

Letter-Writing: The Great Art o' Love

Oxford, March 1971

Roger supposed that it must rain as much in Inverness as
it did in Oxford, but somehow he had never minded the
northern rain. The cold Scottish wind sweeping in off
the Moray Firth was exhilarating and the drenching rain
both stimulation and refreshment to the spirit.

But that had been Scotland, when Brianna was with
him. Now she was in America, he in England, and Oxford
was cold and dull, all its streets and buildings gray as the
ash of dead fires. Rain pattered on the shoulders of his
scholar's gown as he dashed across the quad, shielding an
armload of papers under the poplin folds. Once in the
shelter of the porter's lodge, he stopped to shake himself,
doglike, flinging droplets over the stone passage.

'Any letters?' he asked.

'Think so, Mr. Wakefield. Just a sec.' Martin disappeared
into his inner sanctum, leaving Roger to read the names
of the College's war dead, carved on the stone tablet
inside the entry.

*George Vanlandingham, Esq. The Honorable Phillip Menzies.
Joseph William Roscoe.* Not for the first time, Roger found
himself wondering about those dead heroes and what they
had been like. Since meeting Brianna and her mother,
he'd found that the past too often wore a disturbingly
human face.

'Here you are, Mr. Wakefield.' Martin leaned beaming
across the counter, holding out a thin sheaf of letters.
'One from the States today,' he added, with a broad wink.

Roger felt an answering grin break out on his face, and
a warm glow spread at once from his chest through his
limbs dispelling the chill of the rainy day.

'Will we be seeing your young woman up soon, Mr.
Wakefield?' Martin craned his neck, peering frankly at the
letter with its US stamps. The porter had met Brianna

509

when she had come down with Roger just before Christmas, and had fallen under her spell.

'I hope so. Perhaps in the summer. Thanks!'

He turned toward his staircase, tucking the letters carefully into the sleeve of his gown while he groped for his key. He felt a mingled sense of elation and dismay at thought of the summer. She'd said she'd come in July – but July was still four months away. In some moods, he didn't think he'd last four days.

Roger folded the letter again and tucked it into his inside pocket, next to his heart. She wrote every few days, from brief notes to long screeds, and each of her letters left him with a small warm glow that lasted usually until the next arrived.

At the same time, her letters were faintly unsatisfactory these days. Still warmly affectionate, always signed 'Love,' always saying she missed him and wanted him with her. No longer the sort of thing that burned the page, though.

Perhaps it was natural; a normal progression as they knew each other longer; no one could go on writing passionate missives day after day, not with any honesty.

No doubt it was only his imagination that Brianna seemed to hold back a bit in her letters. He could do without the excesses of one friend's girl, who had clipped bits of her pubic hair and included them in a letter – though he rather admired the sentiment behind the gesture.

He took a bite of his sandwich and chewed absent-mindedly, thinking of the latest article Fiona had showed him. Now married, Fiona considered herself an expert on matters matrimonial, and took a sisterly interest in the bumpy course of Roger's love affair.

She was constantly clipping helpful tips from women's magazines and mailing them to him. The latest had been a piece from *My Weekly*, entitled 'How to Intrigue a Man'. *Sauce for the gander,* Fiona had written pointedly in the margin.

'Share his interests,' one tip advised. 'If you think football's a loss, but he's dead keen, sit down beside him and

510

ask about Arsenal's chances the week. If football's boring, *he* isn't.'

Roger smiled a little grimly. He'd been sharing Brianna's interests, all right, if tracking her bloody parents through their hair-raising history counted as a pastime. Damn little of that he could share with her, though.

'Be coy,' said another of the magazine's tips. 'Nothing piques a man's interest more than an air of reserve. Don't let him get too close, too soon.'

It occurred to Roger to wonder whether Brianna had been reading similar advice in American magazines, but he dismissed the thought. She wasn't above reading fashion magazines – he had seen her do it on occasion – but Brianna Randall was as incapable of playing that sort of silly game as he was himself.

No, she wouldn't put him off just to raise his interest in her; what would be the point? Surely she knew just how much he cared about her.

Did she, though? With a qualm of uneasiness, Roger recalled another of *My Weekly*'s tips to the lovelorn.

'Don't assume he can read your mind,' the article said. 'Give him a hint of how you feel.'

Roger took a random bite of the sandwich and chewed, oblivious to its contents. Well, he'd hinted, all right. Come out and bared his bloody soul. And she'd promptly leapt into a plane and buggered off to Boston.

'Don't be too aggressive,' he murmured, quoting Tip #14, and snorted. The woman don next to him edged slightly away.

Roger sighed and deposited the bitten sandwich distastefully on the plastic tray. He picked up the cup of what the dining hall was pleased to call coffee, but didn't drink it, merely sat with it between his hands, absorbing its meager warmth.

The trouble was that while he thought he had succeeded in deflecting Brianna's attention from the past, he had been unable to ignore it himself. Claire and that bloody Highlander of hers obsessed him, they might as well have been his own family, for the fascination they held.

'Always be honest.' Tip #3. If he had been, if he'd

helped her to find out everything, perhaps the ghost of Jamie Fraser would be laid now – and so would Roger.

'Oh, bugger!' he muttered to himself.

The woman next to him crashed her coffee cup onto her tray and stood up suddenly.

'Go bugger *yourself*!' she said crisply, and walked off.

Roger stared after her for a moment.

'No fear,' he said. 'I think maybe I already have.'

25

Enter a Serpent

October 1768

In principle, I had no objection to snakes. They ate rats, which was laudable of them, some were ornamental, and most of them were wise enough to keep out of my way. Live and let live was my basic attitude.

On the other hand, that was theory. In practice, I had any number of objections to the huge snake curled up on the seat of the privy. Beyond the fact that he was gravely discommoding me at present, he wasn't usefully eating rats and he wasn't aesthetically pleasing, either, being a sort of drab gray with darker splotches.

My major objection to him, though, was the fact that he was a rattlesnake. I supposed that in a way it was fortunate that he was; it was only the heartstopping buzz of his rattles that had prevented me sitting on him in the dawn's early light.

The first sound froze me in place, just inside the tiny privy. I extended one foot behind me, groping gingerly for the doorsill. The snake didn't like that; I froze again as the warning buzz increased in volume. I could see the vibrating tip of his tail, sticking up like a thick yellow finger, rudely pointing from the heap of coils.

My mouth had gone dry as paper; I bit the inside of my cheek, trying to summon a little saliva.

How long was he? I seemed to recall Brianna's telling me – from her Girl Scout handbook – that rattlesnakes were capable of striking at a distance up to one-third their own body length. No more than two feet separated my nightgown-covered thighs from the nasty flat head with its lidless eyes.

Was he six feet long? It was impossible to tell, but the squirm of coils looked unpleasantly massive, the rounded body thick with scaled muscle. He was a bloody big snake, and the fear of being ignominiously bitten in the crotch if I moved was enough to make me stand still.

I couldn't stand still forever, though. Other considerations aside, the shock of seeing the snake hadn't decreased the urgency of my bodily functions in the slightest.

I had some vague notion that snakes were deaf; perhaps I could shout for help. But what if they weren't? There was that Sherlock Holmes story about the snake who responded to a whistle. Perhaps the snake would find whistling inoffensive, at least. Cautiously, I pursed my lips and blew. Nothing came out but a thin stream of air.

'Claire?' said a puzzled voice behind me. 'What the hell are ye doing?'

I jumped at the sound, and so did the snake – or at least it moved suddenly, flexing its coils in what appeared to be imminent attack.

I froze to the doorframe and the snake quit moving, except for the chronic whirr of its rattles, like the annoying buzz of an alarm clock that wouldn't shut off.

'There's a fucking snake in here,' I said through my teeth, trying not to move even my lips.

'Well, why are ye standing there? Move aside and I'll pitch it out.' I could hear Jamie's footsteps, coming close.

The snake heard him too – obviously it *wasn't* deaf – and revved up its rattling.

'Ah,' Jamie said, in a different tone of voice. I heard a rustle as he stooped behind me. 'Stand still, Sassenach.'

I hadn't time to respond to this piece of gratuitous advice before a heavy stone whizzed past my hip and struck the snake amidships. It sprang into something resembling a Gordian knot, squirmed, writhed – and fell into the privy, where it landed with a nasty sort of hollow *thwuck!*

I didn't wait to congratulate the victorious warrior, but instead turned and ran for the nearest patch of woods, the dew-wet hem of my nightgown slapping round my ankles.

Returning a few minutes later in a more settled frame of mind, I found Jamie and Young Ian squeezed into the privy together – a tight fit, considering their sizes – the latter squatting on the bench with a pine-knot torch as the former bent over the hole, peering into the depths beneath.

'Can they swim?' Ian was asking, trying to see past Jamie's head without setting his uncle's hair on fire.

'I dinna ken,' Jamie replied dubiously. 'I think maybe so. What I want to know is, can they jump?'

Ian jerked back, then laughed a little nervously, not altogether sure that Jamie was joking.

'Here, I canna see a thing; hand me the light.' Jamie reached up to take the splinter of pine from Ian, and lowered it gingerly into the hole.

'If the stink doesna put the flame out, belike we'll burn down the privy,' he muttered, bending low. 'Now, then, where the devil –'

'There it is! I see it!' Ian cried.

Both heads jerked, and cracked together with the sound of splitting melons. Jamie dropped the torch, which fell into the hole and was promptly extinguished. A thin wisp of smoke drifted up from the rim of the hole, like incense.

Jamie staggered out of the privy, hands clutching his forehead, eyes squeezed shut with pain. Young Ian leaned against the inside wall, hands pressed tightly over the crown of his head, making abrupt and breathless remarks in Gaelic.

'Is it still alive?' I asked anxiously, peering toward the privy.

Jamie opened one eye and regarded me under the clutching fingers.

'Oh, my head's fine, thanks,' he said. 'I expect my ears will ha' quit ringing by next week, sometime.'

'Now, now,' I said soothingly. 'It would take a sledge-hammer to dent your skull. Let me look, though.' I pushed his fingers aside and pulled his head down, feeling gently through the thick hair. There was a small bruised spot just above the hairline, but no blood.

I kissed the spot perfunctorily and patted him on the head.

'You won't die,' I said. 'Not from that, anyway.'

'Oh, good,' he said dryly. 'I'd much rather die of snake-bite next time I sit down to my business.'

'It's a poisonous serpent, is it?' Ian asked, letting go of

515

his head and coming out of the privy. He inhaled deeply, filling his thin chest with fresh air.

'Venemous,' Jamie corrected him. 'If it bites you and makes ye sick, it's venemous; if you bite *it* and it makes ye sick, it's poisonous.'

'Oh, aye,' Ian said, dismissing this pedantry. 'It's a wicked snake, though?'

'Very wicked,' I said, with a slight shudder. 'What are you going to do about it?' I asked, turning to Jamie.

He raised one eyebrow.

'Me? Why ought I to do anything about it?' he asked.

'You can't just let him stay in there!'

'Why not?' he said, raising the other brow.

Ian scratched his head absently, winced as he encountered the lump left by his collision with Jamie, and stopped.

'Well, I dinna ken, Uncle Jamie,' he said dubiously. 'If ye want to let your balls hang over a pit wi' a deadly viper in it, that's your concern, but the notion makes my flesh creep a bit. How big's the thing?'

'Fair-sized, I'll admit.' Jamie flexed his wrist, showing his forearm by way of comparison.

'Eeugh!' said Ian.

'You don't *know* they don't jump,' I put in helpfully.

'Aye, I do.' Jamie eyed me cynically. 'Still, I grant ye, the thought's enough to make one a bit costive. How d'ye mean to get him out, though?'

'I could shoot him wi' your pistol,' Ian offered, brightening at the thought of getting his hands on Jamie's treasured pistols. 'We needn't get him out if we can kill him.'

'Is he . . . ah . . . visible?' I put in delicately.

Jamie rubbed his chin dubiously. He hadn't shaved yet, and the dark red bristles rasped under this thumb.

'Not very. There's no more than a few inches o' filth in the pit, but I shouldna think ye could see him well enough to aim, and I hate to waste the shot.'

'We could invite all of the Hansens for dinner, serve beer, and drown him,' I suggested facetiously, naming a nearby – and very numerous – Quaker family.

Ian erupted in giggles. Jamie gave me an austere sort of look, and turned toward the woods.

'I'll think of something,' he said. 'After my breakfast.'

Breakfast was luckily no great problem, as the hens had helpfully provided me with nine eggs and the bread had risen satisfactorily. The butter was still immured in the back of the pantry, under the baleful guard of the newly-farrowed sow, but Ian had managed to lean in and snatch a pot of jam from the shelf as I stood by with the broom, jabbing it into the sow's gnashing jaws as she made little darting charges at Ian's legs.

'I'll have to have a new broom,' I remarked, eyeing the tattered remains as I dished up the eggs. 'Perhaps I'll go up to the willow grove by the stream this morning.'

'Mmphm.' Jamie reached out a hand and patted absently around on the table, searching for the bread plate. His attention was wholly focused on the book he was reading, Bricknell's *Natural History of North Carolina.*

'Here it is,' he said. 'I knew I'd seen a bit about rattle-snakes.' Locating the bread by feel, he took a piece and used it to scoop a healthy portion of egg into his mouth. Having engulfed this, he read aloud, holding the book in one hand while groping over the tabletop with the other.

' "The Indians frequently pull out the snakes' Teeth, so that they never afterwards can do any Mischief by biting; this may be easily done, by trying a bit of red Wollen Cloth to the upper end of a long hollow Cane, and so provoking the Rattle-Snake to bite, and suddenly pulling it away from him, by which means the Teeth stick fast in the Cloath, which are plainly to be seen by those present." '

'Have we any red cloth, Auntie?' Ian asked, washing down his own share of the eggs with chicory coffee.

I shook my head, and speared the last of the sausages before Jamie's groping hand reached it.

'Blue, green, yellow, drab, white, and brown. No red.'

'That's a fine wee book, Uncle Jamie,' Ian said, with approval. 'Does it say more about the snakes?' He looked hungrily over the expanse of table, in search of more food. Without comment, I reached into the hutch and brought out a plate of spoonbread, which I set before him. He sighed happily and waded in, as Jamie turned the page.

'Well, here's a bit about how the rattlesnakes charm

517

squirrels and rabbits.' Jamie touched his plate, but encountered nothing save bare surface. I pushed the muffins toward him.

' "It is surprizing to observe how these Snakes will allure and charm Squirrels, Hedge-Conneys, Partridges and many other small Beasts and Birds to them, which they quickly devour. The Sympathy is so strong between these, that you shall see the Squirrel or Partridge (as they have espied this Snake) leap or fly from Bough to Bough, until at last they run or leap directly into its Mouth, not having power to avoid their Enemy, who never stirs out of the Posture or Quoil until he obtains his Prey." '

His hand, blindly groping after sustenance, encountered the muffins. He picked one up and glanced up at me. 'Damned if I've ever seen that myself D'ye think it likely?'

'No,' I said, pushing the curls back off my forehead. 'Does that book have any helpful suggestions for dealing with vicious pigs?'

He waved absently at me with the remnants of his muffin.

'Dinna fash,' he murmured. 'I'll manage the pig.' He took his eyes off the book long enough to glance over the table at the empty dishes. 'Are there no more eggs?'

'There are, but I'm taking them up to our guest at the corncrib.' I added two slices of bread to the small basket I was packing, and took up the bottle of infusion I had left steeping overnight. The brew of goldenrod, beebalm, and wild·bergamot was a blackish green, and smelled like burnt fields, but it might help. It couldn't hurt. On impulse, I picked up the tied-feather amulet old Nayawenne had given me; perhaps it would reassure the sick man. Like the medicine, it couldn't hurt.

Our impromptu guest was a stranger; a Tuscarora from a northern village. He had come to the farm several days before, as part of a hunting party from Anna Ooka, on the trail of bear.

We had offered food and drink – several of the hunters were Ian's friends – but in the course of the meal I had noticed this man gazing glassy-eyed into his cup. Close examination had showed him to be suffering from what I was convinced was measles, an alarming disease in these days.

He had insisted on leaving with his companions, but two of them had brought him back a few hours later, stumbling and delirious.

He was plainly – and alarmingly – contagious. I had made him a comfortable bed in the newly built and so-far empty corncrib, and forced his companions to go and wash in the creek, a proceeding which they plainly found senseless, but in which they humored me before departing, leaving their comrade in my hands.

The Indian was lying on his side, curled under his blanket. He didn't turn to look at me, though he must have heard my footsteps on the path. I could hear him, all right; no need for my makeshift stethoscope – the rales in his lungs were clearly audible at six paces.

'*Comment ça va?*' I said, kneeling down by him. He didn't answer; it was unnecessary, in any case. I didn't need anything beyond the rattling wheeze to diagnose pneumonia, and the look of him merely confirmed it – eyes sunken and dull, the flesh of his face fallen away, consumed to the bone by the fierce blaze of fever.

I tried to persuade him to eat – he desperately needed nourishment – but he would not even bother to turn away his face. The water bottle by his side was empty; I had brought more but didn't give it to him right away, thinking he might swallow the infusion from sheer thirst.

He did take a few mouthfuls, but then stopped swallowing, merely allowing the greenish-black liquid to run out of the corners of his mouth. I tried coaxing in French, but he was having none of it; he didn't even acknowledge my presence, just stared past my shoulder at the morning sky.

His thin body sagged with despair; plainly he thought himself abandoned, left to die in the hands of strangers. I felt a gnawing anxiety that he might be right – surely he *would* die if he would take nothing.

He would take water, at least. He drank thirstily, draining the bottle, and I went to the stream to fill it again. When I came back, I drew the amulet from my basket and held it up in front of his face. I thought I saw a flicker of surprise behind the half-closed lids – nothing so strong as to be called hope, but he did at least take conscious notice of me for the first time.

Seized by inspiration, I sank slowly down onto my knees. I had no notion at all of the proper ceremony to employ, but I had been a doctor long enough to know that while the power of suggestion was no substitute for antibiotics, it was certainly better than nothing.

I held up the raven's-feather amulet, turned my face skyward, and solemnly intoned the most sonorous thing I could remember, which happened to be Dr. Rawlings's receipt for the treatment of syphilis, rendered in Latin.

I poured a small bit of lavender oil into my hand, dipped the feather in it, and anointed his temples and throat, while singing 'Blow the Man Down', in a low, sinister voice. It might help the headache. His eyes were following the feather's movements; I felt rather like a rattlesnake charming away in its 'Quoil', waiting for a squirrel to run down my throat.

I picked up his hand, laid the oil-drabbled amulet across his palm, and closed his fingers round it. Then I took the jar of mentholated bear grease and painted mystic patterns on his chest, being careful to rub it well in with the balls of my thumbs. The reek cleared *my* sinuses; I could only hope it would help the patient's thick congestion.

I completed my ritual by solemnly blessing the bottle of infusion with '*In nomine Patri, et Filii, et Spiritu Sancti, Amen.*' and presenting it to my patient's lips. Looking mildly hypnotized, he opened his mouth and obediently drank the rest.

I drew the blanket up around his shoulders, put the food I had brought down beside him, and left him, with mixed feelings of hope and fraudulence.

I walked slowly beside the stream, eyes alert as always for anything useful. It was too early in the year for most medicinals; for medicine, the older and tougher the plant, the better; several seasons of fighting off insects ensured a higher concentration of the active principles in their roots and stems.

Also, with many plants, it was the flower, fruit, or seed

that yielded a useful substance, and while I'd spotted clumps of turtlehead and lobelia sprouting in the mud along the path, those had long since gone to seed. I marked the locations carefully in my mind for future reference, and went on hunting.

Watercress was abundant; patches of it floated among the rocks all along the margin of the stream, and a huge mat of the spicy dark green leaves lay temptingly just ahead. A nice patch of scouring rushes, too! I had come down barefoot, knowing I'd be wading before long; I tucked up my skirts and ventured cautiously out into the stream, cutting knife in hand and basket over my arm, breath sucked in against the freezing chill.

My feet lost all feeling within moments – but I didn't care. I quite forgot the snake in the privy, the pig in the pantry, and the Indian in the corncrib, absorbed in the rush of water past my legs, the wet, cold touch of stems and the breath of aromatic leaves.

Dragonflies hung in the patches of sunshine on the shallows, and minnows darted past, snatching gnats too small for me to see. A kingfisher called in a loud, dry rattle from somewhere upstream, but he was after larger prey. The minnows scattered at my intrusion but then swarmed back, gray and silver, green and gold, black marked with white, all insubstantial as the shadows from last year's leaves, floating on the water. Brownian motion, I thought, seeing puffs of silt float up and swirl around my ankles, obscuring the fish.

Everything moving, all of the time, down to the smallest molecule – but in its movement, giving the paradoxical impression of stillness, small local chaos giving way to the illusion of a greater order overall.

I moved, too, taking my part in the stream's bright dance, feeling light and shadow change across my shoulders, toes searching for footholds among the slippery, half-seen rocks. My hands and feet were numb from the water; I felt as though I were half made of wood, yet intensely alive, like the silver birch that glowed above me, or the willows that trailed wet leaves in the pool below.

Perhaps the legends of green men and the myths of transformed nymphs began this way, I thought: not with

521

trees come alive and walking, nor yet with women turned to wood – but with submersion of warm human flesh into the colder sensations of the plants, chilled to slow awareness.

I could feel my heart beat slowly, and the half-painfull throb of blood in my fingers. Sap rising. I moved with the rhythms of water and of wind, without haste or conscious thought, part of the slow and perfect order of the universe.

I had forgotten the bit about small local chaos.

Just as I came to the willows' bend, there was a loud shriek from beyond the trees. I'd heard similar noises from a variety of animals, from catamounts to hunting eagles, but I knew a human voice when I heard one.

Blundering out of the stream, I shoved my way through the tangled branches, and burst through into the clear space beyond. A boy was dancing on the bank above me, slapping madly at his legs and howling as he hopped to and fro.

'What –?' I began, and he glanced up at me, blue eyes wide with startlement at my sudden appearance.

He wasn't nearly as startled as I was. He was eleven or twelve; tall and thin as a pine sapling, with a mad tangle of thick russet hair. Slanted blue eyes stared at me from either side of a knife-bridged nose, familiar to me as the back of my own hand, though I knew I had never seen this child before.

My heart was somewhere in the vicinity of my tonsils, and the chill had shot up from my feet into the pit of my stomach. Trained to react in spite of shock, I managed to take in the rest of his appearance – shirt and breeches of good quality, though splashed with water, and long pale shins blobbed with black clots like bits of mud.

'Leeches,' I said, professional calm descending by habit over personal tumult. *It couldn't be,* I was telling myself, at the same time that I knew it damn well *was.* 'It's only leeches. They won't hurt you.'

'I know what they are!' he said. 'Get them off me!' He swatted at his calf, shuddering with dislike. 'They're vile!'

'Oh, not so terribly vile,' I said, beginning to get a grip on myself. 'They have their uses.'

'I don't care what use they are!' he bellowed, stamping in frustration. 'I hate them, get them off me!'

'Well, stop whacking at them,' I said sharply. 'Sit you down and I'll take care of it.'

He hesitated, glaring at me suspiciously, but reluctantly sat down on a rock, thrusting his leech-spattered legs out in front of him.

'Get them off *now*!' he demanded.

'In good time,' I said. 'Where did you come from?'

He stared blankly at me.

'You don't live near here,' I said, with complete certainty. 'Where did you come from?'

He made an obvious effort to collect himself.

'Ah . . . we slept in a place called Salem, three nights past. That was the last town I saw.' He wiggled his legs hard. 'Get them off, I say!'

There were assorted methods of getting leeches off, most of them somewhat more damaging than the leeches themselves. I had a look; he'd picked up four on one leg, three on the other. One of the fat little beasts was already near bloat, gone plump and shiny with stretching. I edged a thumbnail under its head and it popped off into my hand, round as a pebble and heavy with blood.

The boy stared it, pale under his tan, and shuddered.

'Don't want to waste it,' I said casually, and went to retrieve the basket I had dropped under the branches as I pushed my way through the trees.

Nearby, I saw his coat on the ground, discarded shoes and stockings with it. Simple buckles on the shoes, but silver, not pewter. Good broadcloth, not showy but cut with a deal more style than one saw anywhere north of Charleston. I hadn't really needed confirmation, but there it was.

I scooped up a handful of mud, pressed the leech gently into it and wrapped the gooey blob in wet leaves, only then noticing that my hands were trembling. The idiot! The deceitful, wicked, conniving . . . what in *hell* had made him come here? And God, what would Jamie do?

I came back to the boy, who was bent double, peering at the remaining leeches with a look of disgusted loathing.

One more was close to dropping; as I knelt in front of him, it fell off, bouncing slightly on the damp ground.

'Augh!' he said.

'Where's your stepfather?' I asked abruptly. Few things could have taken his attention off his legs, but that did. His head jerked up and he stared at me in astonishment.

It was a cool day, but a light dew of sweat shone on his face. It was narrower through cheek and temple, I thought, and the mouth was quite unlike; perhaps the resemblance was not really so pronounced as I thought.

'How do you know me?' he asked, drawing himself up with an air of hauteur that would have been extremely funny under other circumstances.

'All I know about you is that your given name is William. Am I right?' My hands curled at my sides, and I hoped I was wrong. If he *was* William, that wasn't quite all I knew about him, but it was plenty to be going on with.

A hot flush rose into his cheeks, and his eyes raked over me, his attention temporarily distracted from the leeches by being so familiarly addressed by what – I suddenly realized – appeared to be a disheveled beldame with her skirts round her thighs. Either he had good manners, or the disparity between my voice and my appearance made him cautious, because he swallowed the instant retort that came to his lips.

'Yes, it is,' he said shortly, instead. 'William, Viscount Ashness, ninth Earl of Ellesmere.'

'All that?' I said politely. 'Gracious.' I took hold of one leech between thumb and forefinger and pulled gently. The thing stretched out like a thick rubber band, but declined to let go. The boy's pale flesh pulled out, too, and he made a small choking sound.

'Let go!' he said. 'It'll break, you'll break it!'

'Could do,' I admitted. I got to my feet and shook down my skirts, putting myself in better order.

'Come along,' I said, offering him a hand. 'I'll take you to the house. If I sprinkle a bit of salt on them, they'll drop off at once.'

He refused the hand, but got to his feet, a little shakily. He glanced around, as though looking for someone.

'Papa,' he explained, seeing my expression. 'We missed

the way, and he told me to wait by the stream while he made sure of our direction. I shouldn't like him to take alarm if I am not here when he returns.'

'I shouldn't worry,' I said. 'I imagine he'll have found the house himself by this time; it isn't far.' A fair guess, as it was the only house in some distance, and at the end of a well-marked trail. Lord John had plainly left the boy while he went ahead, to find Jamie – and warn him. Very thoughtful. My lips tightened involuntarily.

'Will that be Frasers'?' the boy asked. He took a ginger step, spraddling so as not to allow his legs to rub together. 'We had come to see a James Fraser.'

'I'm Mrs. Fraser,' I said, and smiled at him. *Your step-mother,* I might have added – but didn't. 'Come along.'

He followed me through the scrim of trees toward the house, almost treading on my heels in his haste. I kept tripping over tree roots and half-buried stones, not watching where I was going, fighting the overwhelming urge to turn around and stare at him. If William, Viscount Ashness, ninth Earl of Ellesmere, was not the very last person I had ever expected to see in the backwoods of North Carolina, he was certainly next to the last – King George was a trifle less likely to turn up on the doorstep, I supposed.

What had possessed that . . . that . . . I groped about, trying to choose among several discreditable epithets to apply to Lord John Grey, and gave up the struggle, in favor of trying to think what in heaven's name to do. I gave that up, too; there wasn't a thing I *could* do.

William, Viscount Ashness, ninth Earl of Ellesmere. Or he thought he was. *And just what do you propose to do,* I thought silently and savagely toward Lord John Grey, *when he finds out that he's really the bastard son of a pardoned Scottish criminal? And more important – what's the Scottish criminal going to do? Or feel?*

I stopped, causing the boy to stumble as he tried to avoid crashing into me.

'Sorry,' I murmured. 'Thought I saw a snake,' and went on, the thought that had stopped me in my tracks still knotting my midsection like a dose of bitter apples. Could

525

Lord John have brought the boy on purpose to reveal his parentage? Did he mean to leave him here, with Jamie – with us?

Alarming as I found the notion, I couldn't reconcile it with the man I had met in Jamaica. I might have sound reasons for disliking John Grey – always difficult to feel a warm sense of goodwill toward a man with a professed homosexual passion for one's husband, after all – but I had to admit that I had seen no trace of either recklessness or cruelty in his character. On the contrary, he had struck me as a sensitive, kindly, and honorable man – or at least he had, before I'd found out about his predilections toward Jamie.

Could something have happened? Some threat to the boy that made Lord John fear for his safety? Surely no one could have found out the truth about William – no one knew, save Lord John and Jamie. And me, of course, I added as an afterthought. Without the evidence of the resemblance – again I repressed the urge to turn round and stare at him – there was no reason for anyone ever to suspect.

But see them side by side, and – well, I shortly *would* see them side by side. The thought gave me a queer hollowness beneath the breastbone, half fright and half anticipation. Was it really as strong as I thought, that resemblance?

I took a deliberate quick detour, through a clump of low-hanging dogwood, making an excuse to turn and wait for him. He came through after me, ducking awkwardly to retrieve the silver-buckled shoe he had dropped.

No, I thought, watching covertly as he straightened up, face flushed from bending. It wasn't as strong as I'd thought at first. He had the promise of Jamie's bones, but it wasn't all there yet – he had the outlines, but not yet the substance. He would be very tall – that was obvious – but now he was about my height, gawky and slender, his limbs very long, and thin enough to seem almost delicate.

He was much darker than Jamie, too; while his hair glinted red in the shafts of sunlight that came through the branches, it was a deep chestnut, nothing like Jamie's bright red-gold, and his skin had turned a soft golden brown in the sun, not at all like Jamie's half-burnt bronze.

He had the Frasers' slanted cat-eyes, though, and there was something about the set of his head, the cock of the slender shoulders, that made me think of –

Bree. It hit me with a small shock, like a spark of electricity. He did look quite a bit like Jamie, but it was my memories of Brianna that had caused that jolt of instant recognition when I saw him. Only ten years her junior, the childish outlines of his face were much more similar to hers than to Jamie's.

He had paused to disentangle a long strand of hair from a grappling dogwood branch; now he came up with me, one brow raised inquiringly.

'Is it far?' he asked. The color had come back to his face with the exertion of walking, but he still looked a trifle sick, and kept his eyes averted from his legs.

'No,' I said. I motioned toward the chestnut grove. 'Just there. Look; you can see the smoke from the chimney.'

He didn't wait to be led, but set off with dogged speed, anxious to be rid of the leeches.

I followed him quickly, not wanting him to reach the cabin ahead of me. I was prey to a mixture of the most disquieting sensations; uppermost was anxiety for Jamie, a little lower, anger at John Grey. Below that, an intense curiosity. And at the bottom, far enough down that I could almost pretend it wasn't there, was a pang of sharp longing for my daughter, whose face I had never thought to see again.

Jamie and Lord John were sitting on the bench by the door; at the sound of our steps, Jamie rose and looked toward the wood. He'd had time to prepare himself; his glance passed casually over the boy as he turned to me.

'Oh, Claire. Ye've found the other of our visitors, then. I'd sent Ian down to find ye. Ye'll recall Lord John, I expect?'

'How could I forget?' I said, giving his Lordship a particularly bright smile. His mouth twitched slightly, but he kept a straight face as he bowed deeply in my direction. How did a man stay so impeccably groomed after several days on horseback, sleeping in the woods?

'Your servant, Mrs. Fraser.' He glanced at the boy, frowning slightly at his state of undress. 'May I present my stepson, Lord Ellesmere? And William, as I see you have made the acquaintance of our gracious hostess, will you also make your compliments to our host, Captain Fraser?'

The boy was shifting from foot to foot, nearly dancing on his toes. At this prompting, though, he jerked a quick bow in Jamie's direction.

'Your servant, Captain,' he said, then cast an agonized glance at me, plainly conscious of nothing but the fact that more of his blood was being sucked out by the second.

'You'll excuse us?' I said politely, and taking the boy by the arm, led him into the cabin and shut the door firmly in the astonished faces of the men. William sat immediately on the stool I pointed out, and thrust out his legs, trembling.

'Hurry!' he said. 'Oh, please, do hurry!'

There was no salt ground; I took my digging knife and chipped a piece from the block with reckless haste, dropped it into my mortar, and smashed it into granules with a few quick jabs of the pestle. Crumbling the grains between my fingers, I scattered the salt thickly on each leech.

'Rather hard on the poor old leeches,' I said, seeing the first draw itself slowly up into a ball. 'Still, it does the trick.' The leech let go its grip and tumbled off William's leg, followed in similar fashion by its fellows, who writhed in slow-motion agony on the floor.

I scooped up the tiny bodies and flung them into the fire, then knelt in front of him, tactfully keeping my head bent while he got control of his face.

'Here, let me take care of the bites.' Tiny streams of blood ran down his legs; I dabbed them with a clean cloth, then washed the small wounds with vinegar and St.-John's-wort to stop the bleeding.

He let out a deep and tremulous sigh of relief as I dried his shins. 'It's not that I'm afraid of – of blood,' he said, in a tone of bravado that made it apparent that that was precisely what he was afraid of. 'It's only they're such filthy creatures.'

'Nasty little things,' I agreed. I stood up, took a clean

cloth, dipped it in water, and matter-of-factly wiped his smudged face. Then, without asking, I picked up my hairbrush and began to comb out the snarls of his hair.

He looked utterly startled at this familiarity, but beyond an initial stiffening of his spine, made no protest, and as I began to order his hair, he let out another small sigh, and let his shoulders slump a little.

His skin had a pleasant animal heat, and my fingers, still chilly from the stream, warmed comfortably as I ordered the soft strands of silky chestnut hair. It was very thick, and slightly wavy. On the crown of his head was a cowlick, a delicate whorl that gave me mild vertigo to see; Jamie had the same cowlick, in the same place.

'I've lost my ribbon,' he said, looking vaguely round, as though one might materialize from bread hutch or inkwell.

'That's all right; I'll lend you one.' I finished plaiting his hair and tied it with a scrap of yellow ribbon, feeling as I did so an odd sense of protectiveness.

I had learned of his existence only a few years earlier, and if I had thought of him in the meantime at all, had felt no more than a minor sense of curiosity tinged with resentment. But now something – be it his resemblance to my own child, his resemblance to Jamie, or simply the fact that I had taken care of him in some small way – had given me a strange feeling of almost proprietary concern for him.

I could hear the rumble of voices outside; the sound of a sudden laugh, and my annoyance at John Grey came back with a rush. How dare he risk both Jamie and William – and for what? Why was the bloody man *here*, in a wilderness as blatantly unsuited to someone of his sort as a –

The door opened, and Jamie poked his head in. 'Will ye be all right?' he asked. His eyes rested on the boy, an expression of polite concern on his face, but I saw his hand, curled tight as it rested on the door frame, and the line of tension that ran through leg and shoulder. He was strung like a harp; if I had touched him, he would have given off a low twanging noise.

'Quite all right,' I said pleasantly. 'Would Lord John care for some refreshment, do you think?'

I put the kettle on to boil for tea, and – with an inner sigh – took out the last loaf of bread, which I had meant to use for my next round of penicillin experiments. Feeling that the emergency justified it, I brought out the last bottle of brandy as well. Then I put the jampot on the table, explaining that the butter was unfortunately in the custody of the pig at the moment.

'Pig?' said William, looking confused.

'In the pantry,' I said, with a nod at the closed door.

'Why do you keep – ' he started, then sat up sharply and closed his mouth, having obviously been kicked under the table by his stepfather, who was smiling pleasantly over his cup.

'It is very kind of you to receive us, Mrs. Fraser,' Lord John interjected, giving his stepson a warning eye. 'I do apologize for our unexpected arrival; I hope we do not discommode you too greatly.'

'Not at all,' I said, wondering just where we were going to put them to sleep. William could go to the shed with Ian, I supposed; it was no worse than sleeping rough, as he had been doing. But the thought of sharing a bed with Jamie, with Lord John on the trundle an arm's-length away . . .

Ian, with his usual instinct for mealtimes, appeared at this delicate point in the proceedings, and was introduced all round, with such a confusion of explanations and reciprocal bowing in cramped quarters that the teapot was knocked over.

Using this minor disaster as an excuse, I sent Ian off to show William the attractions of wood and stream, with a packet of jam sandwiches and a bottle of cider to share between them. Then, free of their inhibiting presences, I filled the cups with brandy, sat down again, and fixed John Grey with a narrow eye.

'What are you doing here?' I said, without preamble.

He opened his light blue eyes very wide, then lowered his very long lashes and batted them deliberately at me.

'I did not come with the intention of seducing your husband, I assure you,' he said.

'John!' Jamie's fist struck the table with a force that

530

rattled the teacups. His cheekbones were flushed dark red, and he was scowling with embarrassed fury.

'Sorry.' Grey, by contrast, had gone white, though he remained otherwise visibly unruffled. It occurred to me for the first time that he might possibly be as unnerved as Jamie by this meeting.

'My apologies, ma'am,' he said, with a curt nod in my direction. 'That was unforgivable. I would point out, however, that you have been looking at me since we met as though you had encountered me lying in the gutter outside some notorious mollyhouse.' A light flush burned over his face now, too.

'Sorry,' I breathed. 'Give me a bit more notice next time, and I'll take care to adjust my features.'

He stood up suddenly and went to the window, where he stood with his back to the room, hands braced on the sill. There was an exceedingly awkward silence. I didn't want to look at Jamie; instead I affected great interest in a bottle of fennel seeds that stood on the table.

'My wife has died,' he said abruptly. 'On the ship between England and Jamaica. She was coming to join me there.'

'I am sorry to hear of it,' Jamie said quietly. 'The lad will have been with her?'

'Yes.' Lord John turned back, leaning against the sill, so that the spring sunlight silhouetted his neat head and gave him a gleaming halo. 'Willie was – very close to Isobel. She was the only mother he'd known since his birth.'

Willie's true mother, Geneva Dunsany, had died in giving birth to him; his presumed father, the Earl of Ellesmere, had died the same day, in an accident. So much, Jamie had already told me. Likewise, that Geneva's sister, Isobel, had taken care of the orphaned boy, and that John Grey had married Isobel when Willie was six or so – at the time Jamie had left the Dunsanys' employ.

'I'm very sorry,' I said, sincerely, and didn't mean only the death of his wife.

Grey glanced at me, and gave me the shadow of a nod in acknowledgment.

'My appointment as governor was nearly at an end; I had intended perhaps to take up residence on the island, should the climate suit my family. As it was...' He shrugged.

'Willie was grief-stricken by the loss of his mother; it seemed advisable to seek to distract his mind by whatever means I could. An opportunity presented itself almost at once; my wife's estate includes a large property in Virginia, which she had bequeathed to William. Upon her death, I received inquiries from the factor of the plantation, asking for instruction.'

He moved away from the window, coming slowly back toward the table where we sat.

'I could not well decide what to do with the property without seeing it, and evaluating the conditions that obtain here. So I determined that we should sail to Charleston, and from there, travel overland to Virginia. I trusted to the novelty of the experience to divert William from his grief – which I am pleased to observe, it seems to have done. He has been much more cheerful these past weeks.'

I opened my mouth to say that Fraser's Ridge seemed a bit out of his way, regardless, but then thought better of it.

He appeared to guess what I was thinking, for he gave me a brief wry smile. I really would have to do something about my face, I thought. Having Jamie read my thoughts was one thing, and not at all unpleasant, on the whole. Having total strangers walk in and out of my mind at will was something else.

'Where is the plantation?' Jamie asked, with somewhat more tact but the same implication.

'The nearest town of any sort is called Lynchburg – on the James River.' Lord John looked at me, still wry, but apparent good humor restored. 'It is in fact no more than a few days deviation in our journey to come here, in spite of the remoteness of your aerie.'

He switched his attention to Jamie, frowning slightly.

'I told Willie that you are an old acquaintance of mine, from my soldiering days – I trust you do not object to the deception?'

Jamie shook his head, one side of his mouth turning up a bit. 'Deception, is it? I shouldna think I could well mind

532

what ye called me, under the circumstances. And so far as that bit goes, it's true enough.'

'You don't think he'll remember you?' I asked Jamie. He had been a groom on Willie's home estate; a prisoner of war following the Jacobite Rising.

He hesitated, but then shook his head.

'I dinna think so. He was barely six when I left Helwater; that will be half a lifetime ago, to a lad – and a world away. And there's no reason he should think to recall a groom named MacKenzie, let alone connect the name wi' me.'

Willie hadn't recognized Jamie on sight, certainly, but then he had been too concerned with the leeches to take much notice of anyone. A thought struck me, and I turned to Lord John, who was fiddling with a snuffbox he had taken from his pocket.

'Tell me,' I said, moved by a sudden impulse. 'I don't mean to distress you – but . . . do you know how your wife died?'

'How?' He looked startled at the question, but collected himself at once. 'She died of a bloody flux, so her maid said.' His mouth twisted slightly. 'It was . . . not a pleasant death, I believe.' Bloody flux, eh? That was the standard description for anything from amebic dysentery to cholera.

'Was there a doctor? Someone on board who took care of her?'

'There was,' he said, a little sharply. 'What do you imply, ma'am?'

'Nothing,' I said. 'It's only that I wondered whether perhaps that was where Willie saw leeches used.'

A flicker of understanding crossed his face.

'Oh, I see. I hadn't thought –'

At this point, I noticed Ian, who was hovering in the doorway, obviously reluctant to interrupt but with a marked look of urgency on his face.

'Did you want something, Ian?' I asked, interrupting Lord John.

He shook his head, brown hair flying.

'No, I thank ye, Auntie. It's only –' He cast a helpless glance at Jamie. 'Well, I'm sorry, Uncle, I ken I shouldna ha' let him do it, but –'

'What?' Alarmed by Ian's tone of voice, Jamie was already on his feet. 'What have ye done?'

The lad twisted his big hands together, cracking his knuckles in embarrassment.

'Well, ye see, his Lordship asked for the privy, and so I told him about the snake, and that he'd best go into the wood instead. So he did, but then he wanted to see the snake, and . . . and . . .'

'He's not bitten?' Jamie asked anxiously. Lord John, who had obviously been about to ask the same thing, gave him a glance.

'Oh, no!' Ian looked surprised. 'We couldna see it to start with, because it was too dark below. So we lifted off the benchtop to get more light. We could see the serpent fine, then, and we poked at it a bit wi' a long branch, so it was lashin' to and fro like the wee book said, but it didna seem inclined to bite itself. And – and –' He darted a glance at Lord John, and swallowed audibly.

'It was my fault,' he said, nobly squaring his shoulders, the better to accept blame. 'I said as how I'd thought to shoot it earlier, but we didna want to waste the powder. And so his Lordship said as how he would fetch his papa's pistol from the saddlebag and deal with the thing at once. And so –'

'Ian,' said Jamie between his teeth. 'Stop blethering this instant and tell me straight what ye've done wi' the lad. Ye've not shot him by mistake, I hope?'

Ian looked offended at this slur upon his marksmanship.

'Of course not!' he said.

Lord John coughed politely, forestalling further recriminations.

'Perhaps you would be good enough to tell me the whereabouts of my son at this moment?'

Ian took a deep breath and visibly commended his soul to God.

'He's in the bottom of the privy,' he said. 'Have ye got a bit o' rope, Uncle Jamie?'

With an admirable economy of both words and motion, Jamie reached the door in two strides and disappeared, closely followed by Lord John.

'Is he in there *with* the snake?' I asked, hastily scrabbling through the washbasket for something to use as a tourniquet, just in case.

'Oh, no, Auntie,' Ian assured me. 'Ye dinna think I'd have left him, and the serpent was still there? Maybe I'd best go help,' he added, and disappeared as well.

I hurried after him, to find Jamie and Lord John standing shoulder to shoulder in the doorway of the privy, conversing with the depths. Standing on tiptoe to peer over Lord John's shoulder, I saw the torn butt end of a long, slender hickory branch protruding a few inches above the edge of the oblong hole. I held my breath; Lord Ellesmere's struggles had stirred up the contents of the privy, and the reek was enough to sear the cilia off my nasal membranes.

'He says he's not hurt,' Jamie assured me, turning away from the hole and unlimbering a coil of rope from his shoulder.

'Good,' I said. 'Where's the snake, though?' I peeked nervously into the outhouse, but couldn't see anything beyond the silvery cedar boards and the dark recesses of the pit.

'It went that way,' Ian said, gesturing vaguely down the path by which I had come. 'The laddie couldna quite get a clear shot, so I gave the thing a wee snoove wi' the stick, and damned if the bugger didna turn and come at me, right up the branch! It scairt me so I let out a skelloch and let go, and I bumped the lad, and – well, that's how it happened,' he ended lamely.

Trying to avoid Jamie's eye, he sidled toward the pit and, leaning over, yelled awkwardly, 'Hey! I'm glad ye didna break your neck!'

Jamie gave him a look that said rather plainly that if necks were to be broken . . . but forbore further remarks in the interests of extracting William promptly from his oubliette. This procedure was carried out without further incident, and the would-be marksman was lifted out, clinging to the rope like a caterpillar on a string.

There had luckily been enough sewage in the bottom of the pit to break his fall. From appearances, the ninth Earl of Ellesmere had landed facedown. Lord John stood for a moment on the path, wiping his hands on his breeches and surveying the encrusted object before him. He rubbed the back of a hand over his mouth, trying either to hide a smile or to stifle his sense of smell.

Then his shoulders started to shake.

'What news from the Underworld, Persephone?' he said, unable to keep the quaver of laughter out of his voice.

A pair of slanted eyes looked blue murder out of the mask of filth obscuring his Lordship's features. It was a thoroughly Fraser expression, and I felt a qualm go through me at the sight. By my side, Ian gave a sudden start. He glanced quickly from the Earl to Jamie and back, then he caught my eye and his own face went perfectly and unnaturally blank.

Jamie was saying something in Greek, to which Lord John replied in the same language, whereupon both men laughed like loons. Trying to ignore Ian, I bent an eye in Jamie's direction. Shoulders still shaking with suppressed mirth, he saw fit to enlighten me.

'Epicharmus,' he explained. 'At the Oracle of Delphi, seekers after enlightenment would throw down a dead python into the pit, and then hang about, breathing in the fumes as it decayed.'

Lord John declaimed, gesturing grandly. ' "The spirit toward the heavens, the body to the earth." '

William exhaled strongly through his nose, precisely as Jamie did when tried beyond bearing. Ian twitched beside me. Good grief, I thought, freshly unnerved. Does the boy have nothing from his mother?

'And have you attained any spiritual insights as a result of your recent m-mystical experience, William?' Lord John asked, making a poor attempt at self-control. He and Jamie were both flushed, with a laughter that I thought due as much to the release of nervous tension as to brandy or hilarity.

His Lordship, glowering, pulled off his neckcloth and flung it on the path with a soggy splat. Now Ian was giggling nervously, too, unable to help himself. My own belly muscles were quivering under the strain, but I could see that the patches of exposed flesh above William's collar were the color of the ripe tomatoes by the privy. Knowing all too well what usually happened to a Fraser who reached that particular level of incandescence, I thought the time had come to break up the party.

'Er-hem,' I said, clearing my throat. 'If you will allow me, gentlemen? Unlearned as I am in Greek philosophy, there is one small epigram I know by heart.'

I handed William the jar of lye soap I had brought in lieu of a tourniquet.

'Pindar,' I said. ' "Water is best." '

A small flash of what might have been gratitude showed through the muck. His Lordship bowed to me, with utmost correctness, then turned, gave Ian a fishy stare, and stomped off through the grass toward the creek, dripping. He seemed to have lost his shoes.

'Puir clarty bugger,' Ian said, shaking his head mournfully. 'It'll be days before he gets the stink off.'

'No doubt.' Lord John's lips were still twitching, but the urge to declaim Greek poetry seemed to have left him, replaced by less elevated concerns. 'Do you know what has become of my pistol, by the way? The one William was using before his unfortunate accident?'

'Oh.' Ian looked uncomfortable. He lifted his chin in the direction of the privy. 'I . . . ah . . . well, I'm verra much afraid –'

'I see.' Lord John rubbed his own immaculately barbered chin.

Jamie fixed Ian with a long stare.

'Ah . . .' said Ian, backing up a pace or two.

'Get it,' said Jamie, in a tone that brooked no contradiction.

'But –' said Ian.

'Now,' said his uncle, and dropped the slimy rope at his feet.

Ian's Adam's apple bobbed, once. He looked at me, wide-eyed as a rabbit.

'Take your clothes off first,' I said helpfully. 'We don't want to have to burn them, do we?'

26

Plague and Pestilence

I left the house just before sunset, to check on my patient in the corncrib. He was no better, but neither was he visibly worse; the same labored breathing and burning fever. This time, though, the sunken eyes met mine when I entered the shed, and stayed on my face as I examined him.

He still had the raven's-feather amulet, clutched in his hand. I touched it and smiled at him, then gave him a drink. He still would take no food but had a little milk, and swallowed without protest another dose of my febrifuge. He lay motionless through examination and feeding, but as I was wringing out a hot cloth to poultice his chest, he suddenly reached out a hand and grabbed my arm.

He thumped his chest with his other hand, and made an odd humming noise. This puzzled me for a moment, until I realized that he *was* humming.

'Really?' I said. I reached for the packet of poulticing herbs and folded them into the cloth. 'Well, all right then. Let me think.'

I settled on 'Onward, Christian Soldiers', which he appeared to like – I was obliged to sing it through three times before he seemed satisfied and sank back on his blanket with a small spate of coughing, wrapped in camphor fumes.

I paused outside the house, cleansing my hands carefully with the bottle of alcohol I carried. I was sure I was safe from contagion – I had had measles as a child – but wanted to take no chance of infecting anyone else.

'There was talk of an outbreak of the red measle in Cross Creek,' Lord John remarked, upon my reporting to Jamie the condition of our guest. 'Is it true, Mrs. Fraser, that the savage is congenitally less able to withstand infection than are Europeans, while African slaves are yet more hardy than their masters?'

'Depends on the infection,' I said, peering into the cauldron and giving the stew bottle a cautious poke. 'The Indians are a lot more resistant to the parasitic discases – malaria, say – caused by organisms here, and the Africans deal better with things like dengue fever – which came with them from Africa, after all. But the Indians haven't much resistance to European plagues like smallpox and syphilis, no.'

Lord John looked a bit taken aback, which gave me a small sense of satisfaction; evidently he had only asked out of courtesy – he hadn't actually expected me to know anything.

'How fascinating,' he said, though, sounding truly interested. 'You refer to organisms? Do you then subscribe to Mister Evan Hunter's theory of miasmatical creatures?'

Now it was my turn to be taken aback.

'Er ... not precisely, no,' I said, and changed the subject.

We passed a pleasant enough evening, Jamie and Lord John exchanging anecdotes of hunting and fishing, with remarks on the amazing abundance of the countryside, while I darned stockings.

Willie and Ian had a game of chess, which the latter won, to his evident satisfaction. His Lordship yawned hugely, then catching his father's minatory eye, made a belated attempt to cover his mouth. He relaxed into a sleepy smile of contentment, brought on by repletion; he and Ian between them had demolished an entire currant cake, following their huge supper.

Jamie saw it, and cocked a brow at Ian, who obligingly rose and towed his Lordship away to share his pallet in the herb shed. Two down, I thought, keeping my eyes resolutely away from the bed – and three to go.

In the event, the delicate problem of bedtime was solved by my retiring, cloaked in modesty – or at least in my nightgown – while Jamie and Lord John took over the chess table, drinking the last of the brandy by firelight.

Lord John was a much better chess player than I – or so I deduced from the fact that the game took them a good hour. Jamie could normally beat me in twenty minutes flat. The play was mostly silent, though with brief spurts of conversation.

At last Lord John made a move, sat back and stretched, as though concluding something.

'I collect you will not see much disturbance in the political way, here in your mountain refuge?' he said casually. He squinted at the board, considering.

'I do envy you, Jamie, removed from such petty difficulties as afflict the merchants and gentry of the lowlands. If your life has its hardships – as cannot help but be the case – you have the not inconsiderable consolation of knowing your struggles to be significant and heroic.'

Jamie snorted briefly.

'Oh, aye. Verra heroic, to be sure. At the moment, my most heroic struggle is like to be with the pig in my pantry.' He nodded toward the board, one eyebrow raised. 'Ye really mean to make that move?'

Grey narrowed his eyes at Jamie, then looked down, studying the board with pursed lips.

'Yes, I do,' he answered firmly.

'Damn,' said Jamie, and with a grin, reached out and tipped over his king in resignation.

Grey laughed, and reached for the brandy bottle.

'Damn!' he said in turn, finding it empty. Jamie laughed, and rising, went to the cupboard.

'Try a bit of this,' he said, and I heard the musical glug of liquid into a cup.

Grey lifted the cup to his nose, inhaled and sneezed explosively, scattering droplets over the table.

'It's not wine, John,' Jamie observed mildly. 'Ye're meant to drink it, aye? not savor the bouquet.'

'So I noticed. Christ, what is it?' Grey sniffed again, more cautiously, and essayed a trial sip. He choked, but swallowed gamely.

'Christ,' he said again. His voice was hoarse. He coughed, cleared his throat, and set the cup gingerly on the table, eyeing it as though it might explode.

'Don't tell me,' he said. 'Let me guess. It's meant to be Scotch whisky?'

'In ten years or so, it might be,' Jamie answered, pouring a small cupful for himself. He took a small sip, rolled it around his mouth and swallowed, shaking his head. 'At the moment, it's alcohol, and that's as much as I'd say for it.'

'Yes, it's that,' Grey agreed, taking another very small sip. 'Where did you get it?'

'I made it,' said Jamie, with the modest pride of a master brewer. 'I've twelve barrels of the stuff.'

Grey's fair brows shot up at that.

'Assuming that you don't mean to clean your boots with it, may I ask what you intend doing with twelve barrels of *this*?'

Jamie laughed.

'Trade it,' he said. 'Sell it, when I can. Customs tax and a license to brew spirits being one of the petty political concerns wi' which I am not afflicted, owing to our remoteness,' he added ironically.

Lord John grunted, tried another sip, and set the cup down.

'Well, you may well escape the Customs, I'll grant you – the nearest agent is in Cross Creek. But I cannot say I think it a safe practice on that account. To whom, may I ask, are you selling this remarkable concoction? Not to the savages, I trust?'

Jamie shrugged.

'Only verra small amounts – a flask or two at a time, as a gift or in trade. Never more than would make one man drunk.'

'Very wise. You'll have heard the stories, I expect. I spoke with one man who'd survived the massacre at Michilimackinac, during the war with the French. That was caused – in part, at least – by a great quantity of drink falling into the hands of a large gathering of Indians at the fort.'

'I've heard about it, too,' Jamie assured him dryly. 'But we are on good terms wi' the Indians nearby, and there are none so many of them as all that. And I'm careful, as I say.'

'Mm.' He essayed another sip, and grimaced. 'I expect you risk more by poisoning one of them than by intoxicating a mob.' He set the glass down and changed the subject.

'I have heard talk in Wilmington of an unruly group of

541

men called Regulators, who terrorize the backcountry and cause disruption by means of riot. Have you encountered anything of such nature here?'

Jamie snorted briefly.

'Terrorize what? Squirrels? There is the backcountry, John, and then there is the wilderness. Surely ye will have remarked the lack of human habitation on your journey here.'

'I did notice something of the kind,' Lord John agreed. 'And yet I had heard certain rumors regarding your presence here – that it was in part meant as a quelling influence upon the growth of lawlessness.'

Jamie laughed.

'I think it will be some time before there is much lawlessness for me to quell. Though I did go so far as to knock down an old German farmer who was abusing a young woman at the grain mill on the river. He had it in mind she had given him short weight – which she had not – and I couldna convince him otherwise. But that is my only attempt so far at maintaining public order.'

Grey laughed, and picked up the fallen king.

'I am relieved to hear it. Will you redeem your honor with another game? I cannot expect the same trick to work twice, after all.'

I rolled onto my side, facing the wall, and stared sleeplessly at the timbers. The firelight glimmered on the wing-shaped marks of the ax, running along the length of each log, regular as sand ripples on a beach.

I tried to ignore the conversation going on behind me, to lose myself instead in the memory of Jamie hewing bark and squaring logs, of sleeping in his arms under the shelter of a half-built wall, feeling the house rise up around me, enclosing me in warmth and safety, the permanent embodiment of his embrace. I always felt safe and soothed by this vision, even when I was alone on the mountain, knowing I was protected by the house he had built for me. Tonight, though, it wasn't working.

I lay still, wondering exactly what was the matter with me. Or rather, not what, but *why*. I knew by now what it was, all right; it was jealousy.

I was indeed jealous; an emotion I hadn't felt for some

years, and was appalled to feel now. I rolled onto my back and closed my eyes, trying to shut out the murmur of conversation.

Lord John had been nothing but courtesy itself to me. More than that, he had been intelligent, thoughtful – thoroughly charming, in fact. And listening to him making intelligent, thoughtful, charming conversation with Jamie knotted my insides and made me clench my hands under cover of the quilt.

You are an idiot, I told myself savagely. *What is the matter with you?* I tried to relax, breathing deeply through my nose, eyes closed.

Part of it was Willie, of course. Jamie was very careful, but I had seen his expression when he looked at the boy in unguarded moments. His whole body was suffused with shy joy, pride mingled with diffidence; and it smote me to the heart to see it.

He would never look at Brianna, his firstborn, that way. Would never see her at all. That was hardly his fault – and yet it seemed so unfair. At the same time, I could scarcely begrudge him his joy in his son – and didn't, I told myself firmly. The fact that it gave me a terrible pang of longing to look at the boy, with that bold, handsome face that mirrored his sister's, was simply my problem. Nothing to do with Jamie, or with Willie. Or with John Grey, who'd brought the boy here.

What for? That was what I'd been thinking ever since I had recovered from the first shock of their appearance, and that was still what I was thinking. What in *hell* was the man up to?

The story about the estate in Virginia might be true – or only an excuse. Even if it was true, it was a considerable detour to come to Fraser's Ridge. Why had he taken so much trouble to bring the boy here? And so much risk; Willie was clearly oblivious to the resemblance that even Ian had noticed, but what if he hadn't been? Had it been so important to Grey, to restate his claim on Jamie's obligation to him?

I rolled onto my other side and cracked an eyelid, watching them over the chessboard, redhead and fair head, bent together in absorption. Grey moved a knight and sat back, rubbing the back of his neck, smiling to himself at the effect of his move. He was a good-looking man; slight and fine-boned, but with a strong, clear-cut face and a beautiful, sensitive mouth that many a woman had no doubt envied.

Grey was even better at guarding his face than Jamie was; I hadn't yet seen an incriminating look from him. I'd seen one once, though, in Jamaica, and wasn't in any doubt about the nature of his feelings for Jamie.

On the other hand, I wasn't in any doubt about Jamie's feelings in that regard, either. The knot under my heart eased a bit, and I took a deeper breath. No matter how late they sat up over the board, drinking and talking, it would be *my* bed Jamie came to.

I unclenched my fists, and it was then, as I rubbed my palms covertly against my thighs, that I realized with a shock just why Lord John affected me so strongly.

My fingernails had dug small crescents in my palms, a small line of throbbing half-moons. For years, I had rubbed away those crescents after every dinner party, every late night when Frank had 'worked at the office'. For years, I had lain intermittently alone in a double bed, wide-awake in the darkness, nails digging into my hands, waiting for him to come back.

And he had. To his credit, he always did return before dawn. Sometimes to a back curled against him in cold reproach, sometimes to the furious challenge of a body thrust against him in demand, urging him wordlessly to deny it, to prove his innocence with his body – trial by combat. More often than not, he accepted the challenge. But it didn't help.

Yet neither of us spoke of such things in the daylight. I could not; I had no right. Frank did not; he had revenge.

Sometimes it would be months – even a year or more – between episodes, and we would live in peace together. But then it would happen again; the silent phone calls, the too-excused absences, the late nights. Never anything so overt as another woman's perfume, or lipstick on his collar – he had discretion. But I always felt the ghost of the other woman, whoever she was; some faceless, indistinguishable She.

I knew it didn't matter who it was – there were several of them. The only important thing was that She was not me. And I would lie awake and clench my fists, the marks of my nails a small crucifixion.

The murmur of conversation by the fire had mostly ceased; the only sound the small click of the chessmen as they moved.

'Do you feel yourself content?' Lord John asked suddenly.

Jamie paused for a moment.

'I have all that man could want,' he said quietly. 'A place, and honorable work. My wife at my side. The knowledge that my son is safe and well cared for.' He looked up then, at Grey. 'And a good friend.' He reached over, clasped Lord John's hand, and let it go. 'I want no more.'

I shut my eyes resolutely, and began to count sheep.

I was awakened just before dawn by Ian, crouching by my bedside.

'Auntie,' he said softly, a hand on my shoulder. 'Best ye come; the man in the corncrib's verra poorly.'

I was on my feet by reflex, wrapped in my cloak and moving bare-footed after Ian before my mind had even begun to function consciously. Not that any great diagnostic skill was needed; I could hear the deep, rattling respirations from ten feet away.

The Earl hovered by the doorway, his thin face pale and scared in the gray light.

'Go away,' I told him sharply. 'You mustn't be near him; nor you, Ian – the two of you go to the house, fetch me hot water from the cauldron, my box, and clean rags.'

Willie moved at once, eager to be away from the frightening sounds coming from the shed. Ian lingered, though, his face troubled.

'I dinna think ye can help him, Auntie,' he said quietly. His eyes met mine straight on, with an adult depth of understanding.

'Very likely not,' I said, answering him in the same terms. 'But I can't do nothing.'

He took a deep breath, nodded.

'Aye. But I think . . .' He hesitated, then went on as I

545

nodded, 'I think ye shouldna torment him wi' medicine. He's fixed to die, Auntie; we heard an owl in the night – he will have heard it, too. It is a sign of death to them.'

I glanced at the dark oblong of the door, biting my lip. The breaths were shallow and wheezing, with alarmingly long pauses between them. I looked back at Ian.

'What do the Indians do, when someone is dying? Do you know?'

'Sing,' he said promptly. 'The *shaman* puts paint upon her face, and sings the soul away to safety, so the demons dinna take it.'

I hesitated, my instincts to do *something* at war with my conviction that action would be futile. Had I any right to deprive this man of peace in his dying? Worse, to alarm him into fear that his soul would be lost by my interference?

Ian hadn't waited for the results of my dithering. He stooped and scraped up a small clot of earth, spat in it and stirred it to mud. Without comment, he dipped his forefinger into the puddle, and drew a line from my forehead down the bridge of my nose.

'Ian!'

'Shh,' he murmured, frowning in concentration. 'Like this, I think.' He added two lines across each cheekbone, and a rough zigzag down the left side of my jawbone. 'That's as near as I remember the proper way of it. I've only seen it the once, and from a distance.'

'Ian, this isn't –'

'Shhh,' he said again, laying a hand on my arm to quell protest. 'Go to him, Auntie. Ye willna frighten him; he's accustomed to ye, no?'

I rubbed away a drip from the end of my nose, feeling thoroughly idiotic. There was no time to argue, though. Ian gave me a small push, and I turned to the door. I stepped into the darkness of the corncrib, bent and laid a hand on the man. His skin was hot and dry, his hand limp as worn leather.

'Ian, can you talk to him? Say his name, tell him it's all right?'

'Ye must not say his name, Auntie; it will call demons.'

Ian cleared his throat, and said a few words in soft

546

clicking gutterals. The hand in mine twitched slightly. My eyes had adjusted now, I could see the man's face, marked with a faint look of surprise as he saw my mud paint.

'Sing, Auntie,' Ian urged, low-voiced. '*Tantum ergo*, maybe; it sounded a wee bit like that.'

There was nothing else I could do, after all. Rather helplessly, I began.

'*Tantum ergo, sacramentum . . .*'

Within a few seconds, my voice steadied, and I sat back on my bare heels, singing slowly, holding his hand. The heavy brows relaxed, and a look of what I thought might be calm came into the sunken eyes.

I had been present at a good many deaths, from accident, warfare, illness, or natural causes, and had seen men meet death in many ways, from philosophical acceptance to violent protest. But I had never seen one die quite this way.

He simply waited, eyes on mine, until I had come to the end of the song. Then he turned his face toward the door, and as the rising sun struck him, he left his body, without the twitch of a muscle or the drawing of a final breath.

I sat quite still, holding the limp hand, until it occurred to me that I was holding my breath, too.

The air around me seemed queerly still, as though time had stopped for a moment. But of course it had, I thought, and forced myself to draw breath. It had stopped for him, forever.

'What are we to do with him?'

There was nothing further to be done *for* our guest; the only question at the moment was how we might best deal with his mortal remains.

I had had a quiet word with Lord John, and he had taken Willie to gather late strawberries on the ridge. While the Indian's death had had nothing even faintly gruesome about it, I could wish Willie hadn't seen it; it wasn't a sight for a child who had seen his mother die no more than a few months before. Lord John had seemed upset himself – perhaps a little sunshine and fresh air would help both of them.

Jamie frowned and rubbed a hand over his face. He hadn't shaved yet, and the stubble made a rasping sound.

'We must give him decent burial, surely?'

'Well, I don't suppose we can leave him lying about in the corncrib, but would his people mind if we buried him here? Do you know anything about how they treat their dead, Ian?'

Ian was still a little pale, but surprisingly self-possessed. He shook his head, and took a drink of milk.

'I dinna ken a great deal, Auntie. But I have seen one man die, as I told ye. They wrapped him in a deerskin and had a procession round the village, singing, then took the body a ways into the wood and put it up on a platform, above the ground, and left it there to dry.'

Jamie seemed less than enthralled at the prospect of having mummified bodies perched in the trees near the farm. 'I should think it best maybe to wrap the body decently and carry it to the village, then, so his own folk can deal with him properly.'

'No, you can't do that.' I slid the pan of newly baked muffins out of the Dutch oven, plucked a broomtwig and stuck it into one plump brown cake. It came out clean, so I set the pan on the table, then sat down myself. I frowned abstractedly at the jug of honey, glowing gold in the late morning sun.

'The trouble is that the body is almost certainly still infectious. You didn't touch him at all, did you, Ian?' I glanced at Ian, who shook his head, looking sober.

'No, Auntie. Not after the fell sick here; before that, I dinna recall. We were all together, hunting.'

'And you haven't had measles. Drat.' I rubbed a hand through my hair. 'Have you?' I asked Jamie. To my relief, he nodded.

'Aye, when I was five or so. And you say a person canna have the same sickness twice. So it willna injure me to touch the body?'

'No, nor me either; I've had them too. The thing is, we can't take him to the village. I don't know at all how long the measles virus – that's a sort of germ – can live on clothes or in a body, but how could we explain to his people that they mustn't touch him or go near him? And we can't risk letting them be infected.'

'What troubles me,' Ian put in unexpectedly, 'is that he isna a man from Anna Ooka – he's from a village further north. If we bury him here in the usual way, his folk may hear of it and think we had done him to death in some fashion, then buried him to hide it.'

That was a sinister possibility that hadn't occurred to me, and I felt as though a cold hand had been laid on the back of my neck.

'You don't think they would, surely?'

Ian shrugged, broke open a hot muffin, and drizzled honey over the steaming insides.

'Nacognaweto's folk trust us, but Myers did say there were plenty who would not. They've reason to be suspicious, aye?'

Considering that the bulk of the Tuscarora had been exterminated in a vicious war with the North Carolina settlers no more than fifty years before, I rather thought they had a point. It didn't help with the present problem, though.

Jamie swallowed the last of his muffin and sat back with a sigh.

'Well, then. I think best we wrap the poor man in a shroud of sorts, and put him in the wee cave in the hill above the house. I've set the posts for a stable across the opening already; those will keep the beasts off. Then Ian or I should go to Anna Ooka and explain matters to Nacognaweto. Perhaps he will send someone back who can look at the body and assure the man's people that he met with no violence from us – and then we can bury him.'

Before I could reply to this suggestion, I heard footsteps, running across the dooryard. I had left the door ajar, to let in light and air. As I turned toward it, Willie's face appeared in the opening, pale and distraught.

'Mrs. Fraser! Please, will you come? Papa's ill.'

'Has he got it from the Indian?' Jamie frowned at Lord John, whom we had stripped to his shirt and put to bed. His face was by turns flushed and pale – the symptoms I had put down earlier to emotional distress.

549

'No, he can't have. The incubation period is one to two weeks. Where were you –' I turned to Willie, then shrugged, dismissing the question. They had been traveling; there was no conceivable way of telling where or when Grey had encountered the virus. Travelers normally slept several to a bed in inns, and the blankets were seldom changed; it would be easy to lie down in one and get up in the morning with the germs of anything from measles to hepatitis.

'You did say there was an epidemic of measles in Cross Creek?' I put a hand on Grey's forehead. Adept as I was at reading fevers by touch, I would have put his near a hundred and three; quite high enough.

'Yes,' he said hoarsely, and coughed. 'Have I got the measles? You must keep Willie away.'

'Ian – take Willie outside, will you, please?' I wrung out a cloth wetted with elderflower water, and wiped Grey's face and neck. There was no rash yet on his face, but when I made him open his mouth, the small whitish Koplik's spots on the lining were clear enough.

'Yes, you have got the measles,' I said. 'How long have you been feeling ill?'

'I felt somewhat light-headed when I retired last night,' he said, and coughed again. 'I woke with a bad headache, sometime in the night, but I thought it only the result of Jamie's so-called whisky.' He smiled faintly at Jamie. 'Then this morning . . .' He sneezed, and I hastily groped for a fresh handkerchief.

'Yes, quite. Well, try to rest a bit. I've put some willow bark to steep; that will help the headache.' I stood up and raised a brow at Jamie, who followed me outside.

'We can't let Willie be near him,' I said, low-voiced so as not to be overheard; Willie and Ian were by the penfold, forking hay into the horses' manger. 'Or Ian. He's very infectious.'

Jamie frowned.

'Aye. What ye said, though, about incubation –'

'Yes. Ian might have been exposed through the dead man, Willie might have been exposed to the same source as Lord John. Either one of them might have it now, but

550

show no sign yet.' I turned to look at the two boys, both of them outwardly as healthy as the horses they were feeding.

'I think,' I said, hesitating as I formed a vague plan, 'that perhaps you had better camp outside with the boys tonight – you could sleep in the herb shed, or camp in the grove. Wait a day or so; if Willie's infected – if he got it from the same source as Lord John – he'll likely be showing signs by then. If not, then he's likely all right. If he *is* all right, then you and he could go to Anna Ooka to tell Nacognaweto about the dead man. That would keep Willie safely out of danger.'

'And Ian could stay here to take care of you?' He frowned, considering, then nodded. 'Aye, I expect that will do.'

He turned to glance at Willie. Impassive as he could be when he wanted to, I knew him well enough to detect the flicker of emotion across his face.

There was worry in the tilt of his brows – concern for John Grey, and perhaps for me or Ian. But beyond that was something quite different – interest tinged with apprehension, I thought, at the prospect of spending several days alone with the boy.

'If he hasn't noticed it yet, he isn't going to,' I said softly, putting my hand on his arm.

'No,' he muttered, turning his back on the boy. 'I suppose it's safe enough.'

'They do say it's an ill wind that blows nobody good,' I said. 'You'll be able to talk to him without it seeming odd.' I paused. 'There's just the one thing, before you go.'

He put his hand over mine where it lay on his arm, and smiled down at me.

'Aye, and what's that?'

'Do get that pig out of the pantry, please.'

551

27

Trout Fishing in America

The journey began inauspiciously. It was raining, for one thing. For another, he disliked leaving Claire, especially in such difficult circumstances. For a third, he was badly worried for John; he hadn't liked the look of the man at all when he took leave of him, barely half conscious and wheezing like a grampus, his features so blotched with rash as to be unrecognizable.

And for a fourth, the ninth Earl of Ellesmere had just punched him in the jaw. He took a firm hold on the youngster's scruff and shook him, hard enough to make his teeth clack painfully together.

'Now, then,' he said, letting go. The boy staggered, and sat down suddenly as he lost his balance. He glared down at the lad, sitting in the mud by the penfold. They had been having this argument, on and off, for the last twenty-four hours, and he had had enough of it.

'I ken well enough what ye said. But what *I* said is that ye're coming with me. I've told ye why, and that's all about it.'

The boy's face drew down in a ferocious scowl. He wasn't easily cowed, but then Jamie supposed that earls weren't used to folk trying, either.

'I am *not* leaving!' the boy repeated. 'You can't make me!' He got to his feet, jaw clenched, and turned back toward the cabin.

Jamie snaked out an arm, grabbed the lad's collar, and hauled him back. Seeing the boy draw back his foot for a kick, he closed his fist and punched the boy neatly in the pit of the stomach. William's eyes bulged and he doubled over, holding his middle.

'Don't kick,' Jamie said mildly. 'It's ill-mannered. And as for makin' you, of course I can.'

The Earl's face was bright red and his mouth was opening and closing like a startled goldfish's. His hat had fallen off, and the rain was pasting strands of dark hair to his head.

'It's verra loyal of ye to want to stay by your stepfather,' Jamie went on, wiping the water out of his own face, 'but ye canna help him, and you may do yourself damage by staying. So ye're not.' From the corner of his eye, he caught a glimpse of movement as the oiled hide over the cabin's window moved aside, then fell. Claire, no doubt wondering why they were not already long gone.

Jamie took the Earl by an unresisting arm, and led him to one of the saddled horses.

'Up,' he said, and had the satisfaction of seeing the boy stick a reluctant foot in the stirrup and swing aboard. Jamie tossed the boy's hat up to him, donned his own, and mounted himself. As a precaution, though, he kept hold of both sets of reins as they set off.

'You, sir,' said a breathless, enraged voice behind him, 'are a lout!'

He was torn between irritation and an urge to laugh, but gave way to neither. He cast a look back over his shoulder, to see William also turned, and leaning perilously to the side, half off his saddle.

'Don't try it,' he advised the boy, who straightened up abruptly and glared at him. 'I wouldna like to tie your feet in your stirrups, but I'll do it, make no mistake.'

The boy's eyes narrowed into bright blue triangles, but he evidently took Jamie at his word. His jaw stayed clenched, but his shoulders slumped a little in temporary defeat.

They rode in silence for most of the morning, rain drizzling down their necks and weighting the shoulders of their cloaks. Willie might have accepted defeat, but not graciously. He was still sullen when they dismounted to eat, but did at least fetch water without protest, and pack up the remains of their meal while Jamie watered the horses.

Jamie eyed him covertly, but there was no sign of measles. The Earl's face was frowning but rashless, and while the tip of his nose was dripping, this appeared to be due solely to the effects of the weather.

'How far is it?' It was midafternoon before William's

curiosity overcame his stubbornness. Jamie had long since relinquished the boy's reins to him – there was no danger of the lad's trying to make his way back alone now.

'Two days, perhaps.' In such mountainous terrain as lay between the Ridge and Anna Ooka, they would make little better speed on horseback than on foot. Having horses, though, allowed them to bring a few small conveniences, such as a kettle, extra food, and a pair of carved fishing rods. And a number of small gifts for the Indians, including a keg of home-brewed whisky to help cushion the bad news they bore.

There was no reason to hurry, and some to delay – Claire had told him firmly not to bring Willie back for at least six days. By then, John would no longer be infectious. He would be well on the way to recovery – or dead.

Claire had been outwardly confident, assuring Willie that his stepfather would be quite all right, but he'd seen the mist of worry in her eyes. It gave him a feeling of hollowness just below the ribs. It was perhaps as well that he was leaving; he could be of no help, and sickness always left him with a helpless feeling that made him at once afraid and angry.

'These Indians – they *are* friendly?' He could hear the tone of doubt in Willie's voice.

'Yes.' He felt Willie waiting for him to add 'my lord', and took a small, perverse satisfaction in not doing it. He guided his horse's head to the side and slowed his pace, an invitation for Willie to ride up next to him. He smiled at the boy as he did so.

'We have known them more than a year, and been guests in their long-houses – aye, the people of Anna Ooka are more courteous and hospitable than most folk I've met in England.'

'You have lived in England?' The boy shot him a surprised look, and he cursed his carelessness, but luckily the lad was a great deal more interested in Red Indians than in the personal history of James Fraser, and the question passed with no more than a vague reply.

He was glad to see the boy abandon his sullen preoccupation and begin to take some interest in their surroundings. He did his best to encourage it, telling stories of the Indians and pointing out animal sign as they went, and he was glad to see the boy thaw into civility, if nothing more, as they rode.

He welcomed the distraction of conversation himself; his mind was a good deal too busy to make silence comfortable. If the worst should happen – if John should die – what then became of Willie? He would doubtless return to England and his grandmother – and Jamie would hear no more of him.

John was the only other person, besides Claire, who knew the truth of Willie's paternity without doubt. It was possible that Willie's grandmother at least suspected the truth, but she would never, under any circumstances, admit that her grandson might be the bastard of a Jacobite traitor rather than the legitimate issue of the late Earl.

He said a small prayer to Saint Bride for the welfare of John Grey, and tried to dismiss the nagging worry from his mind. In spite of his apprehensions, he was beginning to enjoy the trip. The rain had lessened to no more than a light spattering, and the forest was fragant with the scents of wet, fresh leaves and fecund dark leaf mold.

'D'ye see those scratches down the trunk of that tree?' He pointed with his chin at a large hickory whose bark hung in shreds, showing a number of long, parallel white slashes, some six feet from the ground.

'Yes.' Willie took off his hat and slapped it against his thigh to knock the water off, then leaned forward to look more closely. 'An animal did that?'

'A bear,' Jamie said. 'Fresh, too – see the sap's not dried yet in the cuts.'

'Is it nearby?' Willie glanced around, seeming more curious than alarmed.

'Not close,' Jamie said, 'or the horses would be carryin' on. But near enough, aye. Keep an eye out; we'll likely see its dung or its prints.'

No, if John died, his tenuous link with William would be broken. He had long since resigned himself to the situation, and accepted the necessity without complaint – but he would feel bereft indeed if the measles robbed him not only of his closest friend but of all connection with his son.

It had stopped raining. As they rounded the flank of a

mountain and came out above a valley, Willie gave a small exclamation of surprised delight, and sat up straight in his saddle. Against a backdrop of rain-dark clouds, a rainbow arced from the slope of a distant mountain, falling in a perfect shimmer of light to the floor of the valley far below.

'Oh, it's glorious!' Willie said. He turned a wide smile on Jamie, their differences forgotten. 'Have you ever seen such a thing before, sir?'

'Never,' said Jamie, smiling back. It occurred to him, with a small shock, that these few days in the wilderness might conceivably be the last he would see or hear of William. He hoped that he wouldn't have to hit the boy again.

He always slept lightly in the wood, and the sound woke him at once. He lay quite still for a moment, unsure what it was. Then he heard the small, choked noise, and recognized the sound of stifled weeping.

He checked his instant urge to turn and lay a hand on the boy in comfort. The lad was making every effort not to be heard; he deserved to keep his pride. He lay still, looking up into the sweep of the vast night sky above, and listening.

Not fright; William had shown no fear of sleeping in dark woods, and had there been a large animal nearby, the boy would not be keeping quiet about it. Was the lad unwell? The sounds were little more than thickened breathing, caught in the throat – perhaps the boy was in pain and too proud to say. It was that fear that decided him to speak; if the measles had caught them up, there was no time to waste; he must carry the boy back to Claire at once.

'My lord?' he said softly.

The sobbing ceased abruptly. He heard the audible sound of a swallow and the rasp of cloth on skin as the lad wiped a sleeve across his face.

'Yes?' the Earl said, with a creditable attempt at coolness, marred only by the thickness in his voice.

'Are ye unwell, my lord?' He could tell already that it wasn't that, but it would do for a pretext. 'Have ye maybe taken a touch of the cramp? Sometimes dried apples take a man amiss.'

A deep breath came from the far side of the fire, and a snuffle as an attempt was made to clear a running nose unobtrusively. The fire had burned down to nothing more than embers; still, he could see the dark shape that squirmed into a sitting position, crouched on the far side of the fire.

'I – ah – yes, I think perhaps I have got . . . something of the sort.'

Jamie sat up himself, the plaid falling away from his shoulders.

'It's no great matter,' he said, soothingly. 'I've a potion that will cure all manner of ills of the stomach. Do ye rest easy for a moment, my lord; I'll fetch water.'

He got to his feet and went away, careful not to look at the boy. By the time he came back from the stream with the kettle filled, Willie had got his nose blown and his face wiped, and was sitting with his knees drawn up, his head resting on them.

He couldn't keep himself from touching the boy's head as he passed. Familiarity be damned. The dark hair was soft to his touch, warm and slightly damp with sweat.

'A griping in your guts, is it?' he said pleasantly, kneeling and putting the kettle to boil.

'Mm-hm.' Willie's voice was muffled in the blanket over his knees.

'That passes soon enough,' he said. He reached for his sporran, and sorted through the proliferation of small items in it, coming up eventually with the small cloth bag that held the dried mixture of leaves and flowers Claire had given him. He didn't know how she'd known it would be needed, but he was long past the point of questioning anything she did in the way of healing – whether of heart or of body.

He felt a moment's passionate gratitude to her. He'd seen her look at the boy, and knew how she must feel. She'd known about the lad, of course, but seeing the flesh-and-blood proof that her husband had shared another woman's bed wasn't something a wife should be asked to

557

put up with. Little wonder if she was inclined to stick pins in John, him pushing the lad under her nose as he had.

'It willna take more than a moment to brew up,' he assured the boy, rubbing the fragrant mixture between his hands into a wooden cup, as he'd seen Claire do.

She'd not reproached him. Not with *that* at least, he thought, suddenly remembering how she'd acted when she'd found out about Laoghaire. She'd gone for him like a fiend, then, and yet when later she'd learned about Geneva Dunsany . . . perhaps it was only that the boy's mother was dead?

The realization went through him like a sword thrust. The boy's mother was dead. Not just his real mother, who'd died the same day he was born – but the woman he'd called mother all his life since. And now his father – or the man he called father, Jamie thought with an unconscious twist of his mouth – was lying sick of an illness that had killed another man before the lad's eyes no more than days before.

No, it wasn't fright that made the lad greet by himself in the dark. It was grief, and Jamie Fraser, who'd lost a mother in childhood himself, ought to have known that from the beginning.

It wasn't stubbornness, nor even loyalty, that had made Willie insist on staying at the Ridge. It was love of John Grey, and fear of his loss. And it was the same love that made the boy weep in the night, desperate with worry for his father.

An unaccustomed weed of jealousy sprang up in Jamie's heart, stinging like nettles. He stamped firmly on it; he was fortunate indeed to know that his son enjoyed a loving relationship with his stepfather. There, that was the weed stamped out. The stamping, though, seemed to have left a small bruised spot on his heart; he could feel it when he breathed.

The water was beginning to rumble in the kettle. He poured it carefully over the herb mixture, and a sweet fragrance rose up in the steam. Valerian, she'd said, and catmint. The root of a passionflower, soaked in honey and finely ground. And the sweet, half-musky smell of lavender, coming as an afterscent.

'Don't drink it yourself,' she'd said, casual in giving it to him. 'There's lavender in it.'

In fact, it didn't trouble him, if he was warned of it. It was only that now and then a whiff of lavender took him unawares, and sent a sudden surge of sickness through his wame. Claire had seen the effects on him once too often to be unwary of it.

'Here.' He leaned forward and handed the cup to the boy, wondering whether forever after, the lad too would feel troubled by the scent of lavender, or if he would find in it a memory of comfort. That, he supposed, might well depend on whether John Grey lived or died.

The respite had given Willie back his outward composure, but his face was still marked with grief. Jamie smiled at the boy, hiding his own concern. Knowing both John and Claire as he did, he was less fearful than the boy – but the dread was still there, persistent as a thorn in the sole of his foot.

'That will ease ye,' he said, nodding at the cup. 'My wife made it; she's a verra fine healer.'

'Is she?' The boy took a deep, trembling breath of the steam, and touched a cautious tongue to the hot liquid. 'I saw her – do things. With the Indian who died.' The accusation there was clear; she'd done things, and the man had died anyway.

Neither Claire nor Ian had spoken much of that, nor had he been able to ask her what had happened – she had given him a lifted brow and a brief gold look, to say that he should not speak of it before Willie, who had come back with her from the corncrib, white-faced and clammy.

'Aye?' he said curiously. 'What sort of – things?'

What the hell had she done? he wondered. Nothing to cause the man's death, surely; he would have seen that in her at once. Nor did she feel herself at fault, or helpless – he had held her in his arms more than once, comforting her as she wept for those she could not save. This time she had been quiet, subdued – as had Ian – but not deeply upset. She had seemed vaguely puzzled.

'She had mud on her face. And she sang to him. I think she was singing a Papist song; it was in Latin, and it had something to do with sacraments.'

'Indeed?' Jamie suppressed his own astonishment at this description. 'Aye, well. Perhaps she meant only to give the man a bit of comfort, if she saw she couldna save him. The Indians are much more sensible of the effects of measles, ye ken; an infection that will kill one of them wouldna cause a white man to blink twice. I've had the measle myself, as a wee lad, and took no harm from it at all.' He smiled and stretched, demonstrating his evident health.

The tense lines of the boy's face relaxed a little, and he took a cautious sip of the hot tea.

'That's what Mrs. Fraser said. She said Papa would be all right. She – she gave me her word upon it.'

'Then ye may depend upon it that he will,' Jamie said firmly. 'Mrs. Fraser is an honorable woman.' He coughed, and hitched the plaid up around his shoulders; it wasn't a cold night, but there was a breeze coming down the hill. 'Is the drink helping a bit?'

Willie looked blank, then looked down at the cup in his hand.

'Oh! Yes. Yes, thank you; it's very good. I feel very much improved. Perhaps it was not the dried apples, after all.'

'Perhaps not,' Jamie agreed, bending his head to hide a smile. 'Still, I think we'll manage better for our supper tomorrow; if luck is with us, we'll have trout.'

This attempt at distraction was successful; Willie's head popped up from his cup, an expression of deep interest on his face.

'Trout? We can fish?'

'Have ye done much fishing in England? I canna think that the trout streams would compare with these, but I know there is good fishing to be had in the Lake District – or so your father tells me.'

He held his breath. What in God's name had made him ask that? He had himself taken a five-year-old William fishing for char on the lake near Ellesmere, when he had served his indenture there. Did he *want* the boy to remember?

'Oh . . . yes. It's pleasant on the lakes, surely – but nothing like *this*.' Willie waved in the vague direction of the creek. The lines in the boy's face had smoothed themselves, and a small flicker of life had come back into his eyes. 'I have never seen such a place. It's not at all like England!'

'That it is not,' Jamie agreed, amused. 'Will ye not miss England, though?'

Willie thought about it for a moment, as he slurped the rest of his tea.

'I don't think so,' he said, with a decided shake of his head. 'I miss Grandmamma sometimes, and my horses, but nothing else. It was all tutors and dancing lessons and Latin and Greek – ugh!' He wrinkled his nose, and Jamie laughed.

'Ye dinna care for the dancing, then?'

'No. You have to do it with girls.' He shot Jamie a look under his fine, dark brows. 'Do you care for music, Mr. Fraser?'

'No,' Jamie said, smiling. 'I like the girls fine, though.' The girls were going to like this wee laddie just fine, too, he thought, covertly noting the youngster's breadth of shoulder and long shanks, and the long, dark lashes that hid his bonny blue eyes.

'Yes. Well, Mrs. Fraser is very pretty,' the Earl said politely. His mouth curled suddenly up on one side. 'Though she did look funny, with the mud on her face.'

'I daresay. Will ye have another cup, my lord?'

Claire had said the mixture was for calming; it seemed to be working. As they talked desultorily of the Indians and their strange beliefs, William's eyelids began to droop, and he yawned more than once. At last, Jamie reached over and took the empty cup from his unresisting hand.

'The night is cold, my lord,' he said. 'Will ye choose to lie next to me, that we may share our coverings?'

The night was chilly, but a long way from cold. He had guessed right, though; Willie seized the excuse with alacrity. He could not take a lord in his arms to comfort him, nor could a young earl admit to wanting such comfort. Two men could lie close together without shame, though, for the sake of warmth.

Willie fell asleep at once, nestled close against his side. Jamie lay awake for a long time, one arm laid lightly across the sleeping body of his son.

'Now the wee speckled one. Just on top, and hold it with your finger, aye?' He wrapped the thread tightly around the tiny roll of white wool, just missing Willie's finger but catching the end of the woodpecker's down feather, so the fluffy barbs rose up pertly, quivering in the light air.

'You see? It looks like a wee bug taking flight.'

Willie nodded, intent on the fly. Two tiny yellow tail feathers lay smooth under the down feather, simulating the spread wing casings of a beetle.

'I see. Is it the color that matters, or the shape?'

'Both, but more the shape, I think.' Jamie smiled at the boy. 'What matters most is how hungry the fish are. Choose your time right, and they'll strike anything – even a bare hook. Choose it wrong, and ye might as well be fishing wi' lint from your navel. Dinna tell that to a fly fisherman, though; they'll be taking all the credit, and none left to the fish.'

Willie didn't laugh – the boy didn't laugh much – but he smiled and took the willow pole with its newly tied fly.

'Is it the right time, now, do you think, Mr. Fraser?' He shaded his eyes and looked out over the water. They stood in the cool shadow of a grove of black willow, but the sun was still above the horizon, and the water of the stream glittered like metal.

'Aye, trout feed at sunset. D'ye see the prickles on the water? This pool's waking.'

The surface of the pool was restless; the water itself lay calm, but dozens of tiny ripples spread and overlapped, rings of light and shadow spreading and breaking in endless profusion.

'The rings? Yes. Is that fish?'

'Not yet. It's the hatching; midges and gnats hatch from their cases and burst through the surface to the air – the trout will see them and come to feed.'

Without warning, a silver streak shot into the air and fell back with a splash. Willie gasped.

'That's a fish,' Jamie said, unnecessarily. He quickly threaded his line through the carved guides, tied a fly to his line, and stepped forward. 'Watch now.'

He drew back his arm and rocked his wrist, back and forth, feeding more line with each circle of his forearm, until with a snap of the wrist, he sent the line sailing out in a great lazy loop, the fly floating down like a circling gnat. He felt the boy's eyes on him, and was glad the cast had been good.

He let the fly float for a moment, watching – it was hard to see, in the sparkling brightness – then began slowly to pull the line in. Quick as thought, the fly went under. The ring of its disappearance had not even begun to spread before he had jerked the line hard and felt the answering savage tug in reply.

'You've got one! You've got one!' He could hear Willie, dancing on the bank behind him with excitement, but had no attention to spare for anything save the fish.

He had no reel; only the twig that held his spare line. He pulled the tip of the rod far back, let it fall forward and gathered in the loose line with a snatch of the hand. Once more, line in, and then a desperate rush that took out all the line gained, and more.

He could see nothing amid the flashing sparks of light, but the tug and pull through his arms was as good as sight; a quiver as live as the trout itself, as though he held the thing in his hands, squirming and wriggling, fighting . . .

Free. The line went limp, and he stood for a moment, the vibrations of struggle dying away along the muscles of his arms, breathing in the air he had forgotten to take in the heat of battle.

'He got away! Oh, bad luck, sir!' Willie scampered down the bank, pole in hand, face open in sympathy.

'Good luck for the fish.' Still exhilarated from the fight, Jamie grinned and wiped a wet hand over his face. 'Will ye try, lad?' Too late, he remembered that he must call the boy 'lord,' but Willie was too eager to have noticed the omission.

Face fixed in a scowl of determination, Willie drew back his arm, squinted at the water, and snapped his wrist with a mighty jerk. The rod sailed from his fingers and flew gracefully into the pond.

The boy gaped after it, then turned an expression of utter dismay on Jamie, who made no effort at all to keep back his laughter. The young lord looked thoroughly taken aback, and not very pleased, but after a moment, one corner of his wide mouth curved up in wry acknowledgment. He gestured at the rod, floating some ten feet from the bank.

'Will it no frighten all the fish, if I go in after it?'

'I will. Take mine; I'll fetch that one back later.'

Willie licked his lips and set his jaw in concentration, taking a firm grip on the new rod, testing it with little whips and jerks. Turning to the pool, he rocked his arm back and forth, then snapped his wrist hard. He froze, the tip of the rod extended in a perfect line with his arm. The loose line wrapped itself around the rod and draped over Willie's head.

'A verra pretty cast, my lord,' Jamie said, rubbing a knuckle hard over his mouth. 'But I think we must put on a new fly first, aye?'

'Oh.' Slowly, Willie relaxed his rigid posture, and looked sheepishly at Jamie. 'I didn't think of that.'

Slightly chastened by these misadventures, the Earl allowed Jamie to fasten a fresh fly in place, and then to take him by the wrist to demonstrate the proper way of casting.

Standing behind the boy, he took Willie's right wrist in his own, marvelling both at the slenderness of the arm and at the knobby wristbones that gave promise of both size and strength to come. The boy's skin was cool with perspiration, and the feel of his arm much like the tingle of the trout on the line, live and muscular, vivid to his touch. Then Willie twisted free, and he felt a moment's confusion, and a peculiar sense of loss at the breaking of their brief contact.

'That's not right,' Willie was saying, turning to look up at him. 'You cast with the left hand. I saw you.'

'Aye, but I'm cack-handed, my lord. Most men would cast with the right.'

'Cack-handed?' Willie's mouth curved up again.

'I find my left hand more convenient to most purposes than is the right, my lord.'

'That's what I thought it meant. I'm the same.' Willie looked at once rather pleased and mildly shamefaced at this statement. 'My – my mother said it wasn't proper, and that I must learn to use the other, as a gentleman ought.

But Papa said no, and made them let me write with my left hand. He said it didn't matter so much if I should look awkward with a quill; when it came to fighting with a sword, I should be at an advantage.'

'Your father is a wise man.' His heart twisted, with something between jealousy and gratitude – but gratitude was far the uppermost.

'Papa was a soldier.' Willie drew himself up a little, straightening his shoulders with unconscious pride. 'He fought in Scotland, in the Ris– oh.' He coughed, and his face went a dull red as he caught sight of Jamie's kilt and realized that he was quite possibly talking to a defeated warrior of that particular fight. He fiddled with the rod, not knowing where to look.

'Aye, I know. That's where I met him, first.' Jamie was careful to keep any hint of amusement from his voice. He was tempted to tell the boy the circumstances of that first meeting, but that would be poor repayment to John for his priceless gift, these precious few days with his son.

'He was a verra gallant soldier, indeed,' Jamie agreed, straight-faced. 'And right about the hands, as well. Have ye begun your schooling with the sword, then?'

'Just a little.' Willie was forgetting his embarrassment in enthusiasm for the new topic. 'I've had a little whinger since I was eight, and learn feint and parry. Papa says I shall have a proper sword when we reach Virginia, now I am tall enough for the reach of tierce and longé.'

'Ah. Well, then, if ye've been handling a sword in your left hand, I think ye'll have nay great trouble in mastering a rod that way. Here, let us try again, or we'll have no supper.'

On the third try, the fly settled sweetly, to float for no more than a second before a small but hungry trout roared to the surface and engulfed it. Willie let out a shriek of excitement, and yanked the rod so hard that the astounded trout flew through the air and past his head, to land with a splat on the bank beyond.

'I did it! I did it! I caught a fish!' Willie waved his rod and ran around in little circles whooping, forgetting the dignity of both age and title.

'Indeed ye did.' Jamie picked up the trout, which

measured perhaps six inches from nose to tail, and clapped the capering Earl on the back in congratulations. 'Well done, lad! It looks as though they're biting well the e'en; let's have another cast or two, aye?'

The trout were indeed biting well. By the time the sun had sunk below the rim of the distant black mountains, and the silver water faded to dull pewter, they had each a respectable string of fish. They were also both wet to the eyebrows, exhausted, half blind from the glare, and thoroughly happy.

'I have never tasted anything half so delicious,' Willie said dreamily. 'Never.' He was naked, wrapped in a blanket, his shirt, breeches and stockings draped on a tree limb to dry. He lay back with a contented sigh, and belched slightly.

Jamie rearranged his damp plaid on a bush and laid another chunk of wood on the fire. The weather was fine, God be thanked, but it was chilly with the sun down, the night wind rising and a wet sark on his back. He stood close to the edge of the fire and let the heated air rise up under his shirt. The warmth of it ran up his thighs and touched his chest and belly, comforting as Claire's hands on the chilly flesh between his legs.

He stood quietly for a time, watching the boy without seeming to look at him. Putting vanity aside and judging fairly, he thought William a handsome child. Thinner than he should be; every rib showed – but with a wiry muscularity of limb and well formed in all his parts.

The boy had turned his head, gazing into the fire, and he could look more openly. Sap in the pinewood cracked and popped, flooding Willie's face for a moment with golden light.

Jamie stood quite still, feeling his heart beat, watching. It was one of those strange moments that came to him rarely, but never left. A moment that stamped itself on heart and brain, instantly recallable in every detail, for all of his life.

There was no telling what made these moments different from any other, though he knew them when they came. He had seen sights more gruesome and more beautiful by far, and been left with no more than a fleeting muddle of their memory. But these – the still moments, as he called them to himself – they came with no warning, to print a random image of the most common things inside his brain, indelible. They were like the photographs that Claire had brought him, save that the moments carried with them more than vision.

He had one of his father, smeared and muddy, sitting on the wall of a cow byre, a cold Scottish wind lifting his dark hair. He could call that one up and smell the dry hay and the scent of manure, feel his own fingers chilled by the wind, and his heart warmed by the light in his father's eyes.

He had such glimpses of Claire, of his sister, of Ian . . . small moments clipped out of time and perfectly preserved by some odd alchemy of memory, fixed in his mind like an insect in amber. And now he had another.

For so long as he lived, he could recall this moment. He could feel the cold wind on his face, and the crackling feel of the hair on his thighs, half singed by the fire. He could smell the rich odor of trout fried in cornmeal, and feel the tiny prick of a swallowed bone, hair-thin in his throat.

He could hear the dark quiet of the forest behind, and the soft rush of the stream nearby. And forever now he would remember the firelight golden on the sweet bold face of his son.

'*Deo gratias*,' he murmured, and realized that he had spoken aloud only when the boy turned toward him, startled.

'What?'

'Nothing.' To cover the moment, he turned away and took down his half-dry plaid from the bush. Even soaking wet, Highland wool would keep in a man's heat, and shelter him from cold.

'Ye should sleep, my lord,' he said, sitting down and arranging the damp folds of plaid around himself. 'It will be a long day tomorrow.'

'I'm not sleepy.' As though to prove it, Willie sat up and scrubbed his hands vigorously through his hair, making the thick russet mass stand out like a mane round his head.

Jamie felt a stab of alarm; he recognized the gesture

only too well as one of his. In fact, he had been just about to do precisely the same thing, and it was with an effort that he kept his hands still.

He swallowed the heart that had risen into his throat, and reached for his sporran. No. Surely the lad would never think – a boy of that age paid little heed to anything his elders said or did, let alone thought to look at them closely. Still, it had been the hell of a risk for all of them to take; the look on Claire's face had been enough to tell him just how striking the resemblance was.

He took a deep breath, and began to take out the small cloth bundles that contained his fly-trying materials. They had used all his made flies, and if he meant to fish for their breakfast, a few more should be got ready.

'Can I help?' Willie didn't wait for permission, but scooted around the fire, to sit beside him. Without comment, he pushed the small wooden box of birds' feathers toward the boy, and picked a fishhook from the piece of cork that held them.

They worked in silence for a time, stopping only to admire a completed Silver Doctor or Broom-eye, or for Jamie to lend a word of advice or help in tying. Willie soon tired of the exacting work, though, and laid down his half-done Green Whisker, asking numerous questions about fishing, hunting, the forest, the Red Indians they were going to see.

'No,' Jamie said in answer to one such. 'I've never seen a scalp in the village. They're verra kindly folk, for the most part. Do one some injury, mind, and they'll not be slow to take revenge for it.' He smiled wryly. 'They do remind me a bit of Highlanders in that regard.'

'Grandmamma says the Scots breed I–' The casually begun statement choked off abruptly. Jamie looked up to see Willie concentrating fiercely on the half-made fly between his fingers, his face redder than the firelight accounted for.

'Like rabbits?' Jamie let both irony and smile show in his voice. Willie flicked a cautious sideways glance in his direction.

'Scottish families are sometimes large, aye.' Jamie plucked a wren's down feather from the small box and laid it delicately against the shank of his hook. 'We think children a blessing.'

The bright color was fading from Willie's cheeks. He sat up a little straighter.

'I see. Have you got a lot of children yourself, Mr. Fraser?'

Jamie dropped the down feather.

'No, not a great many,' he said, eyes fixed on the mottled leaves.

'I'm sorry – I didn't think – that is . . .' Jamie glanced up to see Willie gone red again, one hand crushing the half-tied fly.

'Think what?' he said, puzzled.

Willie took a deep breath.

'Well – the . . . the . . . sickness; the measles. I didn't see any children, but I didn't think when I said that . . . I mean . . . that maybe you had some, but they . . .'

'Och, no.' Jamie smiled at him reassuringly. 'My daughter's grown; she'll be living far away in Boston this long while.'

'Oh.' Willie let out his breath, tremendously relieved. 'That's all?'

The fallen down-feather moved in a breath of wind, betraying its presence in the shadows. Jamie pinched it between thumb and forefinger and lifted it gently from the ground.

'No, I've a son, too,' he said, eyes on the hook that had somehow embedded its barb in his thumb. A tiny drop of blood welled up around the shining metal. 'A bonny lad, and I love him weel, though he's away from home just now.'

28

Heated Conversation

By evening, Ian was glassy-eyed and hot to the touch. He sat up on his pallet to greet me, but swayed alarmingly, his eyes unfocused. I didn't have the slightest doubt, but looked in his mouth for confirmation; sure enough, the small diagnostic Koplik's spots showed white against the dark pink mucous membrane. Though the skin of his neck was still fair and childlike under his hair, it showed a harmless-looking stipple of small pink spots.

'Right,' I said, resigned. 'You've got it. You'd best come up to the house so I can take care of you more easily.'

'I've got the measle? Am I going to die, then?' he asked. He seemed only mildly interested, his attention concentrated on some interior vision.

'No,' I said matter-of-factly, trusting that I was right. 'Feeling pretty bad, though, are you?'

'My head hurts a bit,' he said. I could see that it did; his brows were drawn together, and he squinted at even so dim a light as that provided by my candle.

Still, he could walk, and a good thing, too, I thought as I watched him make his unsteady way down the ladder from the loft. Scrawny and storklike as he looked, he was a good eight inches taller than I, and outweighed me by at least thirty pounds.

It was no more than twenty yards to the cabin, but Ian was trembling from exertion by the time I got him inside. Lord John sat up as we came in, and made to get out of bed, but I waved him back.

'Stay there,' I said, depositing Ian heavily on a stool. 'I can manage.'

I had been sleeping on the trundle bed; it was already made up with sheets, quilt, and pillow. I peeled Ian out of his breeks and stockings, and tucked him up at once. He was flushed and clammy-cheeked, and looked much sicker than he had done in the dimness of his loft.

The willow-bark brew I had left steeping was dark and

aromatic, ready to drink. I poured it off carefully into a cup, glancing as I did so at Lord John.

'I'd means this for you,' I said. 'But if you could stand to wait . . .'

'By all means give it to the lad,' he said, with a dismissive wave. 'I can wait easily. Can I not assist you, though?'

I thought of suggesting that if he really wanted to be helpful, he could walk to the privy rather than use the chamber pot – which I would have to empty – but I could see that he wasn't yet in any condition to be wandering round outside at night by himself. I didn't want to be explaining to young William that I had allowed his remaining parent – or what he thought was his remaining parent – to be eaten by bears, let alone take pneumonia.

So I merely shook my head politely, and knelt by the trundle to administer the brew to Ian. He felt well enough to make faces and complain about the taste, which I found reassuring. Still, the headache was obviously very bad; the line between his brows was fixed and sharp as though it had been carved there with a knife.

I sat on the trundle and took his head onto my lap, gently rubbing his temples. Then I put my thumbs just into the sockets of his eyes, pressing firmly upward on the ridge of his brows. He made a low sound of discomfort, but then relaxed, his head heavy on my thigh.

'Just breathe,' I said. 'Don't worry if it's a bit tender at first, it means I've got the right spot.'

''S all right,' he murmured, his words a little slurred. His hand drifted up and closed on my wrist, big and very warm. 'That's the Chinaman's way, no?'

'That's right. He means Yi Tien Cho – Mr. Willoughby,' I explained to Lord John, who was watching the proceedings with a puzzled frown. 'It's a way of relieving pain by putting pressure on some points of the body. This one is good for headache. The Chinaman taught me to do it.'

I felt some reluctance to mention the little Chinese to Lord John, seeing that the last time we had met, on Jamaica, Lord John had had some four hundred soldiers and sailors combing the island in pursuit of Mr. Willoughby, then suspected of a particularly atrocious murder.

571

'He didn't do it, you know,' I felt compelled to add. Lord John raised one eyebrow at me.

'That's as well,' he said dryly, 'since we never caught him.'

'Oh, I'm glad.' I looked down at Ian, and moved my thumbs a quarter of an inch outward, pressing again. His face was still tight with pain, but I thought the whiteness at the corners of his mouth was lessening a bit.

'I . . . ah . . . don't suppose you know who *did* kill Mrs. Alcott?' Lord John's voice was casual. I glanced up at him, but his face betrayed nothing beyond simple curiosity and a large number of spots.

'I do, yes,' I said hesitantly, 'but –'

'You do? A murder? Who was it? What happened, Auntie? Ooch!' Ian's eyelids popped open under my fingers, wide with interest, then snapped shut in a grimace of pain as the firelight struck them.

'You be still,' I said, and dug my thumbs into the muscles in front of his ears. 'You're ill.'

'Argk!' he said, but subsided obediently into limpness, the corn-shuck mattress rustling loudly under his thin body. 'All right, Auntie, but who? Ye canna be telling wee bits o' things like that, and expect me to sleep without knowing the rest of it. Can she, then?' He opened one eye in a slitted appeal toward Lord John, who smiled in reply.

'I bear no further responsibility in the matter,' Lord John assured me. 'However,' – he spoke more firmly to Ian – 'you might stop to think that perhaps the story incriminates someone your aunt prefers to shield. It would be discourteous to insist upon details, in that case.'

'Och, no, it's never that,' Ian assured him, eyes tight closed. 'Uncle Jamie wouldna murder anybody, save he had good reason.'

From the corner of my eye, I saw Lord John jerk, slightly startled. Plainly, it had never occurred to him that it *could* have been Jamie.

'No,' I assured him, seeing the fair brows draw together. 'It wasn't.'

'Well, and it wasna me, either,' Ian said smugly. 'And who else would Auntie be protecting?'

'You flatter yourself, Ian,' I said dryly. 'But since you insist . . .'

My hesitancy had in fact been in the interests of protecting Young Ian. No one else could be harmed by the story – the murderer was dead and, for all I knew, Mr. Willoughby, too, perished in the hidden jungles of the Jamaican hills, though I sincerely hoped not.

But the story involved someone else, as well; the woman I had first known as Geillis Duncan and known later as Geillis Abernathy, at whose behest Ian had been kidnapped from Scotland, imprisoned on Jamaica, and had suffered things that he had only lately begun to tell us.

Still, there seemed no way out of it now – Ian was fractious as a child insisting on a bedtime story, and Lord John was sitting up in bed like a chipmunk waiting for nuts, eyes bright with interest.

And so, with the macabre urge to begin with 'Once upon a time . . .' I leaned back against the wall, and with Ian's head still in my lap, began the story of Rose Hall and its mistress, the witch Geillis Duncan; of the Reverend Archibald Campbell and his strange sister, Margaret, of the Edinburgh Fiend and the Fraser prophecy; and of a night of fire and crocodile's blood, when the slaves of six plantations along the Yallahs River had risen and slain their masters, roused by the *houngan* Ishmael.

Of later events in the cave of Abandawe on Haiti, I said nothing. Ian, after all, had been there. And those happenings had nothing to do with the murder of Mina Alcott.

'A crocodile,' Ian murmured. His eyes were closed, and his face had grown more relaxed under my fingers, despite the gruesome nature of my story. 'Ye really saw it, Auntie?'

'I not only saw it, I stepped on it,' I assured him. 'Or rather, I stepped on it, and *then* I saw it. If I'd seen it first, I'd have bloody run the other way.'

There was a low laugh from the bed. Lord John scratched at his arm, smiling.

'You must find life here rather dull, Mrs. Fraser, after your adventures in the Indies.'

'I could do with a spot of dullness now and then,' I said, rather wistfully.

Involuntarily, I glanced at the bolted door, where I had propped Ian's musket, brought back from the storehouse when I had fetched him. Jamie had taken his own gun, but his pistols lay on the sideboard, loaded and primed as he had left them for me, bullet case and powder horn neatly arranged beside them.

It was cozy in the cabin, with the fire flickering gold and red on the rough-barked walls, and the air filled with the warm, lingering scents of squirrel stew and pumpkin bread, spiced with the bitter tang of willow tea. I brushed my fingers over Ian's jaw. No rash yet, but the skin was tight and hot – very hot still, in spite of the willow bark.

Talking about Jamaica had at least distracted me a bit from my worry over Ian. Headache was not an unusual symptom for someone with measles; severe and prolonged headache was. Meningitis and encephalitis were dangerous – and all too possible – complications of the disease.

'How's the head?' I asked.

'A bit better,' he said. He coughed, eyes squinching shut as the spasms jarred his head. He stopped and opened them slightly, dark slits that glowed with fever. 'I'm awfully hot, Auntie.'

I slid off the trundle and went to wring out a cloth in cool water. Ian stirred slightly as I wiped his face, his eyes closed once more.

'Mrs. Abernathy gave me amethysts to drink for the headache,' he murmured drowsily.

'Amethysts?' I was startled, but kept my voice low and soothing. 'You drank amethysts?'

'Ground up in vinegar,' he said. 'And pearls in sweet wine, but that was for the bedding, she said.' His face looked red and swollen, and he turned his cheek against the cool pillow, seeking relief. 'She was a great one for the stones, yon woman. She burned powdered emeralds in the flame of a black candle, and she rubbed my cock wi' a diamond – to keep it hard, she said.'

There was a faint sound from the bed, and I looked up to see Lord John, raised up on one elbow, eyes wide.

'And did the amethysts work?' I wiped Ian's face gently with the cloth.

'The diamond did.' He made a feeble attempt at an adolescent's bawdy laugh, but it faded into a harsh, rasping cough.

'No amethysts here, I'm afraid,' I said. 'But there's wine, if you want it.' He did, and I helped him to drink it – well diluted with water – then eased him back on the pillow, flushed and heavy-eyed.

Lord John had lain down, too, and lay watching, his thick blond hair unbound, spread out on the pillow behind him.

'That's what she wanted wi' the lads, ye ken,' Ian said. His eyes were shut tight against the light, but he could clearly see *something*, if only in the mists of memory. He licked his lips; they were beginning to dry and crack, and his nose was beginning to run.

'She said the stone grew in a lad's innards – the one she wanted. She said it must be a laddie who'd never gone wi' a lass, though, that was important. If he had, the stone wouldna be right, somehow. If he h-huh-had one.' He paused to cough, and ended breathless, nose dripping. I held a handkerchief for him to blow.

'What did she want the stone for?' Lord John's face bore a look of sympathy – he knew only too well what Ian felt like at the moment – but curiosity compelled the question. I didn't object; I wanted to know too.

Ian started to shake his head, then stopped with a groan.

'Ah! Oh, God, my head will split surely! I dinna ken, man. She didna say. Only that it was needful; she must have it to be s-sure.' He barely got out the last word before dissolving into a coughing attack that was the worst yet; he sounded like a barking dog.

'You'd better stop talk –' I began, but was interrupted by a soft thump at the door.

Instantly I froze, wet cloth still in my hand. Lord John leaned swiftly from the bed and took a pistol from inside one of his high cavalry boots on the floor. A finger to his lips to enjoin silence, he nodded toward Jamie's pistols. I moved silently to the sideboard and grasped one, reassured by the smooth, solid heft of it in my hand.

'Who is there?' Lord John called, in a surprisingly strong voice.

There was no answer save a sort of scratching, and a faint whine. I sighed and laid the pistol down, torn between irritation, relief and amusement.

'It's your blasted dog, Ian.'

'Are you sure?' Lord John spoke in a low voice, pistol still aimed unwaveringly at the door. 'It might be an Indian trick.'

Ian rolled over with an effort, facing the door.

'Rollo!' he shouted, his voice hoarse and cracking.

Hoarse or not, Rollo knew his master's voice; there was a deep, joyful 'WARF!' from outside, succeeding by frantic scratching, at a height some four feet from the ground.

'Beastly dog,' I said, hurrying to open the door. 'Stop that, or I'll make you into a rug, or a coat, or something!'

Giving this threat the attention it deserved, Rollo bounded past me into the room. Exuberant with joy, he launched his hundred and fifty pounds from the middle of the floor and landed directly on the trundle bed, making it sway dangerously, joints screeching in protest. Ignoring a strangled cry from the bed's occupant, he proceeded to lick Ian madly about the face and forearms – the latter being flung up as a wholly inadequate defense to the slobbering onslaught.

'Bad dog,' Ian said, making ineffectual efforts to push Rollo off his chest, giggling helplessly in spite of his discomfort. 'Bad dog, I say – down, sir!'

'Down, sir!' Lord John echoed sternly. Rollo, interrupted in his demonstrations of affection, rounded on Lord John, his ears laid back. He curled his lip, and gave his lordship a good look at the condition of his back teeth. Lord John started, and raised his pistol convulsively.

'Down, *a dhiobhuil*!' Ian said, prodding Rollo in the hindquarters. 'Take your hairy arse out o' my face, ye wicked beast!'

Rollo instantly dismissed Lord John from consideration, and padded around on top of the trundle, turning three times and kneading the bedding with his paws before collapsing next to his master's body. He licked Ian's ear, and with a deep sigh, laid his nose between his large muddy paws on the pillow.

'Would you like me to get him off, Ian?' I offered, eyeing the paws. I wasn't quite sure how I might move a dog of Rollo's size and temperament, bar shooting him with Jamie's pistol and dragging his carcass off the bed, so was rather relieved when Ian shook his head.

'No, let him stay, Auntie,' he said, croaking slightly. 'He's a good fellow. Are ye no, *a charaid?*' He laid a hand on the dog's neck, and turned his head so his cheek lay pillowed against Rollo's thick ruff.

'All right, then.' Moving slowly, with a wary glance at the unblinking yellow eyes, I approached the bed and smoothed Ian's hair. His forehead was still hot, but I thought the fever was a bit lower. If it broke in the night, as it well might, it was likely to be succeeded by a fit of violent shivering – when Ian might well find Rollo's warm hairy bulk a comfort.

'Sleep well.'

'*Oidhche mhath.*' He was half asleep already, drifting into the vivid dreams of fever, and his 'good-night' was barely more than a murmur.

I moved quietly about the room, tidying away the results of the day's labors; a basket of fresh-gathered peanuts to be washed, dried and stored; a pan of dried reeds laid flat and covered with a layer of bacon grease to make rush-lights. A trip to the pantry, where I stirred the beer mash fermenting in its tub, squeezed out the curds of the soft cheese a-making, and punched down the slow-rising salt bread, ready to be made into loaves and baked in the morning, when the small Dutch oven built into the side of the hearth would be heated through by the night's low fire.

Ian was sound asleep when I came back into the main room; Rollo's eyes were closed as well, though one yellow slit cracked open at my entrance. I glanced at Lord John; he was awake, but did not look round.

I sat down on the settle by the fire, and brought out the big wool basket with its green and black Indian pattern – Sun-eater, Gabrielle had called the design.

Two days since Jamie and Willie had left. Two days to the Tuscarora village. Two days back. If nothing happened to stop them.

'Nonsense,' I muttered, under my breath. Nothing would stop them. They would be home soon.

The basket was full of dyed skeins of wool and linen thread. Some I had been given by Jocasta, some I had spun myself. The difference was obvious, but even the lumpy, awkward-looking strands I produced could be used for something. Not stockings or jerseys; perhaps I could knit a tea cozy – that seemed sufficiently shapeless to disguise all my deficiencies.

Jamie had been simultaneously shocked and amused to find that I didn't know how to knit. The question had never arisen at Lallybroch, where Jenny and the female servants kept everyone in knitted goods. I had taken on the chores of stillroom and garden, and never dealt with needlework beyond the simplest mending.

'Ye canna clickit at all?' he said incredulously. 'And what did ye do for your winter stockings in Boston, then?'

'Bought them,' I said.

He had looked elaborately around the clearing where we had been sitting, admiring the half-finished cabin.

'Since I dinna see any shops about, I suppose ye'd best learn, aye?'

'I suppose so.' I dubiously eyed the knitting basket Jocasta had given me. It was well equipped, with three long circular wire needles in different sizes, and a sinister-looking set of four double-ended ivory ones, slender as stilettos, which I knew were used in some mysterious fashion to turn the heels of stockings.

'I'll ask Jocasta to show me, next time we go down to River Run. Next year perhaps.'

Jamie snorted briefly and picked up a needle and a ball of yarn.

'It's no verra difficult, Sassenach. Look – this is how ye cast up your row.' Drawing the thread out through his closed fist, he made a loop round his thumb, slipped it onto the needle, and with a quick economy of motion, cast on a long row of stitches in a matter of seconds. Then he handed me the other needle and another ball of yarn. 'There – you try.'

I looked at him in complete amazement.

'*You* can knit?'

'Well, of course I can,' he said, staring at me in puzzlement. 'I've known how to clickit wi' needles since I was seven years old. Do they not teach bairns *anything* in your time?'

'Well,' I said, feeling mildly foolish, 'they sometimes teach little girls to do needlework, but not boys.'

'They didna teach you, did they? Besides, it's no fine needlework, Sassenach, it's only plain knitting. Here, take your thumb and dip it, so . . .'

And so he and Ian – who, it turned out, could also knit and was prostrated by mirth at my lack of knowledge – had taught me the simple basics of knit and purl, explaining, between snorts of derision over my efforts, that in the Highlands all boys were routinely taught to knit, that being a useful occupation well suited to the long idle hours of herding sheep or cattle on the shielings.

'Once a man's grown and has a wife to do for him, and a lad of his own to mind the sheep, he maybe doesna make his own stockings anymore,' Ian had said, deftly executing the turn of a heel before handing me back the stocking, 'but even wee laddies ken how, Auntie.'

I cast an eye at my current project, some ten inches of a wooly shawl, which lay in a small crumpled heap at the bottom of the basket. I had learned the basics, but knitting for me was still a pitched battle with knotted thread and slippery needles, not the soothing, dreamy exercise that Jamie and Ian made of it, needles clicketing away in their big hands by the fire, comforting as the sound of crickets on the hearth.

Not tonight, I thought. I wasn't up to it. Something mindless, like winding up the balls of yarn. That I could do. I laid aside a half-finished pair of stockings Jamie was making for himself – striped, the show-off – and pulled out a heavy skein of fresh-dyed blue wool, still redolent with the heavy scents of its dyeing.

Normally I liked the smell of fresh yarn, with its faint oily whiff of sheep, the earthy smell of indigo, and the sharp tang of the vinegar used to set the dye. Tonight it seemed smothering, added as it was to woodsmoke and candle wax, to the close, acrid smells of male bodies and the reek of illness – a mingled scent of sweaty sheets and used chamber pots – all trapped together in the room's stale air.

I let the skein lie on my lap, and closed my eyes for a moment. I wanted nothing so much as to undress and sponge myself with cool water, then slip naked between the clean linen sheets of my bed and lie still, letting the fresh cool air blow through the open window across my face while I floated into oblivion.

But there was a sweating Englishman in one of my beds, and a filthy dog in the other, to say nothing of a teenage boy who was obviously in for a hard night. The sheets had not been washed in days, and when they were, it would be a backbreaking business of boiling, lifting and wringing. My bed for the night – assuming that I got to sleep in it – would be a pallet made of a folded quilt, with my pillow a sack of carded wool. I would breathe sheep all night.

Nursing is hard work, and all of a sudden I was bloody tired of it. For a moment of intense longing, I wanted them all just to go away. I opened my eyes, looking at Lord John with resentment. My little burst of self-pity faded, though, as I looked at him. He lay on his back, one arm behind his head, gazing somberly up at the ceiling. It might have been only a trick of the fire, but his face seemed marked by anxiety and grief, eyes shadowed with dark loss.

At once I felt ashamed of my ill temper. Granted, I hadn't wanted him here. I was annoyed at his intrusion into my life and the burden of obligation his illness had placed upon me. His very presence made me uneasy – to say nothing of William's. But they would go, soon. Jamie would be home, Ian would recover, and I would have back my peace, my happiness, and my clean sheets. What had happened to him was permanent.

John Grey had lost a wife – however he might have regarded her. It had taken courage of more than one kind to bring William here, and to send him off with Jamie.

580

And I didn't suppose the bloody man could help having caught the measles.

I laid the wool aside for the moment and got up to put the kettle on. A nice cup of tea all round seemed called for. As I straightened up from the hearth, I saw Lord John turn his head, my movement drawing his attention from his inward thoughts.

'Tea,' I said, embarrassed to meet his eyes after my uncharitable thoughts. I made a small, awkward gesture of interrogation toward the kettle.

He smiled faintly and nodded.

'I thank you, Mrs. Fraser.'

I took down the tea box from the cupboard, and laid out two cups and spoons, adding the sugar bowl as an afterthought; no molasses tonight.

When I had got the tea made, I sat down near the bed to drink it. We sipped in silence for a few moments, an odd air of shyness hovering between us.

At last, I set down my cup and cleared my throat.

'I'm sorry; I had meant to offer you my condolences on the loss of your wife,' I said, rather formally.

He looked surprised for a moment, then bowed his head in acknowledgment, matching my formality.

'It is a coincidence that you should say so at the moment,' he said. 'I had just been thinking of her.'

Used as I was to having other people take one look at my face and discern instantly what I was thinking, it was oddly gratifying to be able to do it to someone else.

'Do you miss her greatly – your wife?' I felt a bit hesitant about asking, but he didn't seem to find the question intrusive. I might almost have thought that he had been asking it himself, for he answered readily, if thoughtfully.

'I don't really know,' he said. He glanced at me, one eyebrow raised. 'Does that sound unfeeling?'

'I couldn't say,' I said, a little tartly. 'Surely you'd know better than I whether you had feelings for her or not.'

'I did, yes.' He let his head fall back on the pillow, his thick fair hair loose about his shoulders. 'Or I do, perhaps. That's why I came, do you see?'

'No, I can't say that I do.'

I heard Ian cough, and rose to look, but he had only

turned over in his sleep; he lay on his stomach, one long arm drooping from the trundle bed. I picked up his hand – it was still hot, but not dangerously so – and put it on the pillow near his face. His hair had fallen in his eyes; I brushed it gently back.

'You are very good with him; have you children of your own?'

Startled, I looked up to see Lord John watching me, chin propped on his fist.

'I – we – have a daughter,' I said.

His eyes widened.

'We?' he said sharply. 'The girl is Jamie's?'

'Don't call her "the girl",' I said, unreasonably irritated. 'Her name is Brianna, and yes, she's Jamie's.'

'My apologies,' he said, rather stiffly.

'I meant no offense,' he added a moment later, in a softer tone. 'I was surprised.'

I looked at him directly. I was too tired to be tactful.

'And a bit jealous, perhaps?'

He had a diplomat's face; almost anything could have been going on behind that facade of handsome amiability. I went on staring at him, though, and he let the mask drop – a flash of knowledge lit the light blue eyes, tinged with grudging humor.

'So. One more thing that we have in common.' I was startled by his acuity, though I shouldn't have been. It's always discomfiting to find that feelings you thought safely hidden are in fact sitting out in the open for anyone to look at.

'Don't tell me you didn't think of that when you decided to come here.' The tea was finished; I set the cup aside and took up my skein of wool again.

He studied me for a moment, eyes narrowed.

'I thought of it, yes,' he said finally. He let his head fall back on the pillow, eyes fixed on the low beamed ceiling. 'Still, if I was human enough – or petty enough – to consider that I might offend you by bringing William here, I would ask you to believe that such offense was not my motive in coming.'

I laid the finished ball of yarn in the basket and took up

582

another skein, stretching it across the back of a split-willow chair.

'I believe you,' I said, my eyes fixed on the skein. 'If only because it seems rather a lot of trouble to go to. What *was* your motive, though?'

I sensed the movement as he shrugged, rustling the sheets.

'The obvious – to allow Jamie to see the boy.'

'And the other obvious – to allow you to see Jamie.'

There was a marked silence from the bed. I kept my eyes on the yarn, turning the ball as I wrapped the strand, over and under, back and forth, an intricate crisscross that would in the end yield a perfect sphere.

'You are a rather remarkable woman,' he said at last, in a level tone.

'Indeed,' I said, not looking up. 'In what way?'

He leaned back; I heard the rustle of his bedding.

'You are neither circumspect nor circuitous. In fact, I don't believe I have ever met anyone more devastatingly straightforward – male *or* female.'

'Well, it's not by choice,' I said. I came to the end of the thread and tucked it neatly into the ball. 'I was born that way.'

'So was I,' he said, very softly.

I didn't answer; I didn't think he had spoken to be heard.

I rose and went to the cupboard. I took down three jars: catmint, valerian, and wild ginger. I took down the marble mortar and tipped the dried leaves and root chunks into it. A drop of water fell from the kettle, hissing into steam.

'What are you doing?' Lord John asked.

'Making an infusion for Ian,' I said, with a nod toward the trundle. 'The same I gave you four days ago.'

'Ah. We heard of you as we traveled from Wilmington,' Grey said. His voice was casual now, making conversation. 'You are well known in the countryside for your skills, it would appear.'

'Mm.' I pounded and ground, and the deep, musky smell of wild ginger filled the room.

'They say you are a conjure-woman. What is that, do you know?'

'Anything from a midwife to a physician to a caster of spells or a fortune-teller,' I said. 'Depending on who's talking.'

He made a sound that might have been a laugh, and then was silent for a bit.

'You think they will be safe.' It was a statement, but he was asking.

'Yes. Jamie wouldn't have taken the boy if he thought there'd be any danger. Surely you know that, if you know him at all?' I added, glancing at him.

'I know him,' he said.

'Do you indeed,' I said.

He was quiet for a moment, bar the sound of scratching.

'I know him well enough – or think I do – to risk sending William away with him, alone. And to be sure he will not tell William the truth.'

I poured the green and yellow powder into a small square of cotton gauze and tied it neatly into a tiny bag.

'No, he won't, you're right about that.'

'Will you?'

I looked up, startled.

'You really think I would?' He studied my face carefully for a moment, then smiled.

'No,' he said quietly. 'Thank you.'

I snorted briefly and dropped the medicine bag into the teapot. I put back the jars of herbs, and sat down with my blasted wool again.

'It was generous of you – to let Willie go with Jamie. Rather brave,' I added, somewhat grudgingly. I looked up; he was staring at the dark oblong of the hide-covered window, as though he could look beyond it to see the two figures, side by side in the forest.

'Jamie has held my life in his hands for a good many years now,' he answered softly. 'I will trust him with William's.'

'And what if Willie remembers a groom named MacKenzie better than you think? Or happens to take a good look at his own face and Jamie's?'

'Twelve-year-old boys are not remarkable for their acute perception,' Grey said dryly. 'And I think that if a boy has lived all his life in the secure belief that he is the ninth

584

Earl of Ellesmere, the notion that he might actually be the illegitimate offspring of a Scottish groom is not one that would enter his head – or be long entertained there, if it did.'

I wound wool in silence, listening to the crackle of the fire. Ian was coughing again, but didn't wake. The dog had moved, and was now curled up by his legs, a dark heap of fur.

I finished the second ball of yarn and began another. One more, and the infusion would have finished steeping. If Ian didn't need me yet, I would lie down then.

Grey had been silent for so long that I was surprised when he started to speak again. When I glanced at him, he wasn't looking at me, but was staring upward, seeking visions once again among the smoke-stained beams.

'I told you I had feelings for my wife,' he said softly. 'I did. Affection. Familiarity. Loyalty. We had known each other all her life; our fathers had been friends; I had known her brother. She might well have been my sister.'

'And was she satisfied with that – to be your sister?'

He gave me a glance somewhere between anger and interest.

'You cannot be at all a comfortable woman to live with.' He shut his mouth, but couldn't leave it there. He shrugged impatiently. 'Yes, I believe she was satisfied with the life she led. She never said that she was not.'

I didn't reply to this, though I exhaled rather strongly through my nose. He shrugged uncomfortably, and scratched his collarbone.

'I was an adequate husband to her,' he said defensively. 'That we had no children of our own – that was not my –'

'I really don't want to hear about it!'

'Oh, don't you?' His voice was still low, not to wake Ian, but it had lost the smooth modulations of diplomacy; the anger was rough in it.

'You asked me why I came; you questioned my motives; you accused me of jealousy. Perhaps you *don't* want to know, because if you did, you could not keep thinking of me as you choose to.'

'And how the hell do you know what I choose to think of you?'

His mouth twisted in an expression that might have been a sneer on a less handsome face.

'Don't I?'

I looked him full in the face for a minute, not troubling to hide anything at all.

'You did mention jealousy,' he said quietly, after a moment.

'So I did. So did you.'

He turned his head away, but continued after a moment.

'When I heard that Isobel was dead . . . it meant nothing to me. We had lived together for years, though we had not seen each other for nearly two years. We shared a bed; we shared a life, I thought. I should have cared. But I didn't.'

He took a deep breath; I saw the bedclothes stir as he settled himself.

'You mentioned generosity. It wasn't that. I came to see . . . whether I can still feel,' he said. His head was still turned away, staring at the hide-covered window, grown dark with the night. 'Whether it is my own feelings that have died, or only Isobel.'

'*Only* Isobel?' I echoed.

He lay quite still for a moment, facing away.

'I can still feel shame, at least,' he said, very softly.

I could tell by the feel of the night that it was very late; the fire had burned low, and the aching of my muscles told me that it was well past my bedtime.

Ian was getting restless; he stirred in his sleep, moaning, and Rollo got up and nuzzled him, making small whimpering noises. I went to him and wiped his face again, plumped his pillow and straightened his sheets, making comforting murmurs. He was no more than half awake; I held his head and fed him a cup of the warm infusion, sip by sip.

'You'll feel better in the morning.' There were spots visible in the open neck of his shirt – only a few as yet – but the fever was less, and the line between his brows had eased.

I wiped his face once more and eased him back on his pillow, where he turned a cheek to the cool linen and fell asleep again at once.

There was plenty of the infusion left. I poured another cup and held it out to Lord John. Surprised, he sat upright and took it from me.

'And now that you've come, and seen him – do you still have feelings?' I said.

He stared at me for a moment, eyes unblinking in the candlelight.

'I do, yes.' Hand steady as a rock, he picked up the cup and drank. 'God help me,' he added, so casual as almost to sound offhand.

Ian passed a bad night but dropped off into a fitful doze near dawn. I seized the chance of a little rest myself, and managed a few hours of delectable sleep on the floor before being roused by the loud braying of Clarence the mule.

A sociable creature, Clarence was utterly delighted by the approach of anything he regarded as a friend – this category embracing virtually anything on four legs. He gave tongue to his joy in a voice that rang off the mountainside. Rollo, affronted at being thus upstaged in the watchdog department, leapt off Ian's bed, soared over me, and out through the open window, baying like a werewolf.

Thus startled out of slumber, I staggered to my feet. Lord John, who was sitting in his shirt at the table, looked startled too, though whether at the racket or at my appearance, I couldn't tell. I went outside, running my fingers hastily through my disheveled locks, heart beating faster in the hope that it might be Jamie returning.

My heart fell as I saw that it wasn't Jamie and Willie, but my disappointment was quickly replaced by astonishment when I saw who the visitor was – Pastor Gottfried, leader of the Lutheran church in Salem. I had met the Pastor now and then, in the homes of parishioners where I had been paying medical calls, but I was more than surprised to find him so far afield.

It was nearly two days ride from Salem to the Ridge, and the nearest German Lutheran farm was at least fifteen miles away, over rough country. The Pastor was no natural horseman – I could see the mud and dust of repeated falls splashed over his black coat – and I thought that it must be a dire emergency indeed that brought him so far up the mountain.

'Down, wicked dog!' I said sharply to Rollo, who was baring his teeth and growling at the new arrival, much to the displeasure of the Pastor's horse. 'Be quiet, I say!'

Rollo gave me a yellow-eyed look and subsided with an air of offended dignity, as though to suggest that if I wished to welcome obvious malefactors onto the premises, *he* wouldn't answer for the consequences.

The Pastor was a tubby little man with a huge, curly gray beard that surrounded his face like a storm cloud, through which his normally beaming face peered like the breaking sun. He wasn't beaming this morning, though; his round cheeks were the color of suet, puffy lips pale, and his eyes red-rimmed with fatigue.

'*Meine Dame,*' he greeted me, doffing his broad-brimmed hat and bowing deeply from the waist. '*Ist Euer Mann hier?*'

I spoke no more than a few words of crude German, but could easily make out that he was looking for Jamie. I shook my head, gesturing vaguely toward the woods, to indicate Jamie's absence.

The Pastor looked even more dismayed than before, nearly wringing his hands in his distress. He said several urgent things in German, then seeing that I didn't understand him, repeated himself, speaking slower and louder, his stubby body straining for expression, trying by sheer force of will to make me understand.

I was still shaking my head helplessly when a voice spoke sharply from behind me.

'*Was ist los?*' demanded Lord John, emerging into the dooryard. '*Was habt Ihr gesagt?*' He had put on his breeches, I was glad to see, though he was still barefoot, with his fair hair streaming loose on his shoulders.

The Pastor gave me a scandalized look, plainly thinking The Worst, but this expression was wiped off his face at once by a further machine-gun rattle of German from Lord John. The Pastor bobbed in apology to me, then turned eagerly to the Englishman, waving his arms and stammering in his haste to tell his story.

'What?' I said, having failed to pluck more than a word

or two from the Teutonic flood. 'What on earth is he saying?'

Grey turned a grim face toward me.

'Do you know a family named Mueller?'

'Yes,' I said, immediate alarm flaring at the name. 'I delivered a child to Petronella Mueller, three weeks ago.'

'Ah.' Grey licked dry lips and glanced at the ground; he didn't want to tell me. 'The – the child is dead, I am afraid. So is the mother.'

'Oh, no.' I sank down on the bench by the door, swept by a feeling of absolute denial. 'No. They can't be.'

Grey rubbed a hand over his mouth, nodding as the Pastor went on, waving his small, fat hands in agitation.

'He says it was *Masern*; I think that would be what we call the measle. *Flecken, so ähnlich wie diese?*' he demanded of the Pastor, pointing at the remnants of rash still visible on his face.

The Pastor nodded emphatically, repeating '*Flecken, Masern, ja!*' and patting his own cheeks.

'But what does he want Jamie for?' I asked, bewilderment added to distress.

'Apparently he believes Jamie might be able to reason with the man – with Herr Mueller. Are they friends?'

'Not exactly, no. Jamie hit Gerhard Mueller in the mouth and knocked him down in front of the mill last spring.'

A muscle twitched in Lord John's scabbed cheek.

'I see. I suppose he's using the term "reason with" rather loosely, then.'

'Mueller can't be reasoned with by any means more sophisticated than an ax handle,' I said. 'But what is he being unreasonable about?'

Grey frowned – he didn't recognize my use of 'sophisticated', I realized, though he understood what I meant. He hesitated, then turned back to the small minister and asked something else, listening intently to the resulting torrent of *Deutsch*.

Little by little, with constant interruptions and much gesticulation, the story emerged in translation.

There was, as Lord John had told us earlier, an epidemic of measles in Cross Creek. This had evidently spread into the backcountry; several households in Salem were afflicted, but the Muellers, isolated as they were, had not suffered infection until recently.

However, the day before the first sign of measles appeared, a small band of Indians had stopped at the Mueller farm asking for food and drink. Mueller, with whose opinions of Indians I was thoroughly well acquainted, had driven them off with considerable abuse. The Indians, offended, had made – said Mueller – mysterious signs toward his house as they left.

When measles broke out among the family the next day, Mueller was positive that the disease had been brought upon them by means of a hex, placed on his house by the Indians he had rebuffed. He had at once painted anti-hexing symbols upon his walls, and summoned the Pastor from Salem to perform an exorcism . . . 'I think that is what he said,' Lord John added doubtfully. 'Though I am not sure whether he means by that . . .'

'Never mind,' I said impatiently. 'Go on!'

None of these precautions availed Mueller, though, and when Petronella and the new baby succumbed to the disease, the old man had lost what little mind he had. Vowing revenge upon the savages who had brought such devastation to his household, he had forced his sons and sons-in-law to accompany him, and ridden off into the woods.

From this expedition they had returned three days ago, the sons white-faced and silent, the old man burning with cold satisfaction.

'*Ich war dort. Ich habe ihn geschen,*' said Herr Gottfried, sweat trickling down his cheeks at the recollection. I was there. I saw.

Summoned by a hysterical message from the women, the Pastor had ridden into the stableyard, to find two long tails of dark hair hanging from the barn door, stirring gently in the wind above the crudely painted legend *Rache*.

'That means "revenge",' Lord John translated for me.

'I know,' I said, my mouth so dry I could barely speak. 'I've read Sherlock Holmes. You mean he . . .'

'Evidently so.'

The Pastor was still speaking; he seized me by the arm

and shook it, trying to communicate his urgency. Grey's look sharpened at whatever the minister was saying, and he broke in with an abrupt question, answered by frenzied noddings.

'He's coming here. Mueller.' Grey swung round to me, his face set in alarm.

Terribly upset by the scalps, the Pastor had gone in search of Herr Mueller, only to find that the patriarch had nailed his grisly trophies to the barn and then left the farm, bound – he had said – for Fraser's Ridge, to see me.

If I hadn't been sitting down already, I might have collapsed at this. I could feel the blood draining from my cheeks, and was sure I looked as pale as Pastor Gottfried.

'Why?' I said. 'Is he – he couldn't! He couldn't think I had done anything to Petronella or the baby. Could he?' I turned in appeal toward the Pastor, who pushed a pudgy, trembling hand through his gray-streaked hair, disordering its carefully larded strands.

'The clerical gentleman doesn't know what Mueller thinks, or what his purpose is in coming here,' said Lord John. He cast an interested eye over the pastor's unprepossessing form. 'Much to his credit, he set off alone, hell-for-leather after Mueller, and found him two hours later – insensible by the side of the road.'

The huge old farmer had evidently gone for days without food on his hunt for revenge. Intemperance was not a common failing among the Lutherans, but under the stimulus of fatigue and emotion, Mueller had drunk deeply upon his return, and the enormous draughts of beer he had consumed had been too much for him. Overcome, he had contrived to hobble his mule, but then had wrapped himself in his coat and fallen asleep among the trailing arbutus by the road.

The Pastor had made no attempt to rouse Mueller, being well acquainted with the man's temper and feeling it would not be improved by drink. Instead, Gottfried had mounted his own horse and ridden as quickly as he could, trusting to Providence to bring him here in time to warn us.

He had had no doubt that my *Mann* would be competent to deal with Mueller, no matter what his state or intentions, but with Jamie gone . . .

Pastor Gottfried looked helplessly from me to Lord John, and back again.

'*Vielleicht solten Sie gehen?*' he suggested, making his meaning clear with a jerk of his head toward the paddock.

'I can't leave,' I said, and gestured toward the house. '*Mein* – Christ, what's nephew? – *Mein junger Mann ist nicht gut.*'

'*Ihr Neffe ist krank,*' Lord John corrected briskly. '*Haben Sie jemals Masern gehabt?*'

The Pastor shook his head, distress altering to alarm.

'He hasn't had the measles,' Lord John said, turning to me. 'He mustn't stay here, then, or he will put himself in danger of contracting the disease, is that so?'

'Yes.' The shock was beginning to recede slightly, and I was starting to pull myself together. 'Yes, he should go at once. It's safe for him to be near you, you aren't contagious any longer. Ian is, though.' I made a vain attempt at smoothing my hair, which was standing on end – little wonder if it was, I thought. Then I thought of the scalps on Mueller's barn door and my hair actually *did* stand on end, my own scalp rippling with horror.

Lord John was speaking authoritatively to the little Pastor, urging him toward his horse by means of a grip on his sleeve. Gottfried was making protests, but increasingly weak ones. He glanced back at me, round face full of trouble.

I tried to smile reassuringly at him, though I felt as distressed as he did.

'*Danke,*' I said. 'Tell him it will be all right, will you?' I said to Lord John. 'He won't go, otherwise.' He nodded briefly.

'I have. I told him I am a soldier; that I will not let any harm come to you.'

The Pastor stood for a moment, hand on his horse's bridle, talking earnestly to Lord John. Then he dropped the bridle, turned with decision and crossed the dooryard to me. Reaching up, he laid a hand gently on my tousled head.

'*Seid gesegnet,*' he said. '*Benedicite.*'

'He said –' began Lord John.

'I understand.'

We stood silently in the dooryard, watching Gottfried make his way through the chestnut grove. It seemed incongruously peaceful out here, with a soft autumn sun warm on my shoulders, and birds going about their business overhead. I heard the far-off knocking of a woodpecker, and the liquid duet of the mockingbirds that lived in the big blue spruce. No owls, but naturally there would be no owls now; it was midmorning.

Who? I wondered, as another aspect of the tragedy belatedly occurred to me. Who had been the target of Mueller's blind revenge? The Mueller farm was several days ride from the mountain line that separated Indian territory from the settlements, but he could have reached several Tuscarora or Cherokee villages, depending on his direction.

Had he entered a village? If so, what carnage had he and his sons left behind? Worse, what carnage might ensue?

I shuddered, cold in spite of the sun. Mueller was not the only man who believed in revenge. The family, the clan, the village of whomever he had murdered – they would seek vengeance for their slain, as well; and they might not stop with the Muellers – if they even knew the identity of the killers.

And if they did not, but only knew the murderers to be white . . . I shuddered again. I had heard enough massacre stories to realize that the victims very seldom did anything to provoke their fate; they only had the misfortune of being in the wrong place at the wrong time. Fraser's Ridge lay directly between Mueller's farm and the Indian villages – which at the moment seemed distinctly the wrong place to be.

'Oh, God, I wish Jamie were here.' I wasn't aware that I had spoken aloud, until Lord John replied.

'So do I,' he said. 'Though I begin to think that William may be far safer with him than the boy might be here – and not only by reason of the illness.'

I glanced at him, realizing suddenly how weak he still was; this was the first time he had been out of bed in a week. He was white-faced under the remnants of his rash, and he was gripping the doorjamb for support, to keep from falling down.

'You shouldn't even be up!' I exclaimed, and grasped him by the arm. 'Go in and lie down at once.'

'I am quite all right,' he said irritably, but he didn't jerk away, or protest when I insisted he get back into bed.

I knelt to check Ian, who was tossing restlessly on the trundle, blazing with fever. His eyes were shut, his features swollen and disfigured with the emergent rash, the glands in his neck round and hard as eggs.

Rollo poked an inquiring nose under my elbow, nudged his master gently and whined.

'He'll be all right,' I said firmly. 'Why don't you go outside and keep an eye out for visitors, hm?'

Rollo ignored this advice, though, and instead sat patiently watching as I wrung out a rag in cool water and bathed Ian. I nudged him half awake, brushed his hair, gave him the chamber pot, and coaxed bee-balm syrup into him – all the time listening for the sound of hooves, and Clarence's joyful announcement that company was coming.

It was a long day. After several hours of starting at every sound and looking over my shoulder at every step, I finally settled into the day's work. I nursed Ian, who was feverish and miserable, fed the stock, weeded the garden, picked tender young cucumbers for pickling, and set Lord John, who was disposed to be helpful, to work shelling beans.

I looked into the woods with longing, on my way from privy to goat-pen. I would have given a lot simply to walk away into those cool green depths. It wouldn't have been the first time I'd had such an impulse. But the autumn sun beat down on the Ridge, and the hours wore on in tranquil peace, without a sign of Gerhard Mueller.

'Tell me about this Mueller,' Lord John said. His appetite was coming back; he'd finished his helping of fried mush, though he pushed aside the salad of dandelion greens and pokeweed.

I plucked a tender stalk of pokeweed from the bowl and nibbled it myself, enjoying the sharp taste.

'He's the head of a large family; German Lutherans, as you no doubt gathered. They live about fifteen miles from here, down in the river valley.'

'Yes?'

'Gerhard is big, and he's stubborn, as you no doubt gathered. Speaks a few words of English, but not much. He's old, but my God, he's strong!' I could still see the old man, shoulders corded with stringy muscle, tossing fifty-pound sacks of flour into his wagon like so many sacks of feathers.

'This fight he had with Jamie – did he appear the sort to hold a grudge?'

'He's very definitely the sort to hold a grudge, but not about that. It wasn't really a fight. It –' I shook my head, searching for a way to describe it. 'Do you know anything about mules?'

His fair brows lifted and he smiled.

'A bit, yes.'

'Well, Gerhard Mueller is a mule. He's not really bad-tempered, and he isn't precisely stupid – but he doesn't pay a great deal of attention to anything other than what's in his head, and it takes a good deal of force to switch his attention to anything else.'

I had not been present at the altercation in the mill, but had had it described to me by Ian. The old man had got it firmly stuck into his head that Felicia Woolam, one of the mill owner's three daughters, had given him short weight and owed him another sack of flour.

In vain, Felicia protested that he had brought her five bags of wheat; she had ground them, and filled four bags with the resulting flour. The difference, she insisted, was due to the chaff and hulls removed from the grain. Five bags of wheat equalled four bags of flour.

'*Fünf!*' Mueller had said, waving his open hand in her face. '*Es gibt fünf!*' He would not be persuaded otherwise, and began to curse volubly in German, glowering and backing the girl into a corner.

Ian, having tried without success to distract the old man's attention, had dashed outside to fetch Jamie from his conversation with Mr. Woolam. Both men had come hurriedly inside, but had no more success than Ian in changing Mueller's conviction that he had been cheated.

Ignoring their exhortations, he had advanced on Felicia, clearly intent on taking by force an extra bag of flour from the stack behind her.

'At that point, Jamie gave up trying to reason with him, and hit him,' I said.

He had at first been reluctant to do so, Mueller being nearly seventy, but rapidly changed his mind when his first blow bounced off Mueller's jaw as though it had been made of seasoned oakwood.

The old man had turned on him like a cornered boar, whereupon Jamie had struck him first in the stomach, and then in the mouth as hard as possible, knocking Mueller down and splitting his own knuckles on the old man's teeth.

With a word to Woolam – who was a Quaker and thus opposed to violence – he had then seized Mueller by the legs and dragged the dazed farmer outside, where one of the Mueller sons was waiting patiently in the wagon. Hauling the old man up by the collar, Jamie had pinned him against the wagon and held him there, talking pleasantly in German, until Mr. Woolam – having hastily rebagged the flour – came out and loaded *five* sacks into the wagon, under the gimlet eye of the old man.

Mueller had counted them twice, carefully, then turned to Jamie, and said with dignity, '*Danke, mein Herr.*' He had then climbed into the wagon beside his bemused son, and driven away.

Grey scratched at the remnants of his rash, smiling.

'I see. So he appeared to hold no ill will?'

I shook my head, chewing, then swallowed.

'Not at all. He was kindness itself to me, when I went to the farm to help with Petronella's baby.' My throat closed suddenly on the renewed realization that they were gone, and I choked on the bitter taste of the dandelion leaves, bile rising in my throat.

'Here.' Grey pushed the pot of ale across the table toward me.

I drank deeply, the cool sourness soothing for a moment the deeper bitterness of spirit. I set the pot down and sat for a moment, eyes closed. There was a fresh-smelling breeze from the window, but the sun was warm on the tabletop under my hands. All the tiny joys of physical existence were still mine, and I was the more acutely aware of them, for the knowledge that they had been so abruptly taken from others – from those who had barely tasted them.

'Thank you,' I said, opening my eyes.

Grey was watching me, with an expression of deep sympathy.

'You'd think it wouldn't be such a shock,' I said, needing suddenly to try to explain. 'They die here so easily. The young ones, especially. It isn't as though I haven't seen it before. And there's so seldom anything I can do.'

I felt something warm on my cheek, and was surprised to find it was a tear. He reached into his sleeve, pulled out a handkerchief and handed it to me. It wasn't especially clean, but I didn't mind.

'I did sometimes wonder what he saw in you,' he said, his tone deliberately light. 'Jamie.'

'Oh, you did? How flattering.' I sniffed, and blew my nose.

'When he began to speak of you, both of us thought you dead,' he pointed out. 'And while you are undoubtedly a handsome woman, it was never of your looks that he spoke.'

To my surprise, he picked up my hand and held it lightly.

'You have his courage,' he said.

That made me laugh, if only halfheartedly.

'If you only knew,' I said.

He didn't reply to that, but smiled faintly. His thumb ran lightly over the knuckles of my hand, his touch light and warm.

'He doesn't hold back for fear of skinned knuckles,' he said. 'Neither do you, I think.'

'I can't.' I took a deep breath and wiped my nose; the tears had stopped. 'I'm a doctor.'

'So you are,' he said quietly, and paused. 'I have not thanked you for my life.'

'It wasn't me. There isn't really anything much I can do, for something like a disease. All I can do is to . . . be there.'

'A little more than that,' he said dryly, and released my hand. 'Will you have more ale?'

I was beginning to see quite clearly what Jamie saw in John Grey.

The afternoon passed quietly. Ian tossed and moaned, but by late afternoon, the rash was fully developed, and his fever seemed to drop a little. He wouldn't be wanting food, but perhaps I could induce him to take a little milk broth. The thought reminded me that it was nearly milking time, and I stood up, with a murmured word to Lord John, and put aside my mending.

I opened the cabin door and stepped out, directly in front of Gerhard Mueller, who was standing in the dooryard.

Mueller's eyes were a reddish brown, and seemed always to be burning with an inner intensity. They burned more brightly now, for the bruised frailty of the flesh surrounding them. The deep-set eyes fixed on me, and he nodded, once, and then again.

Mueller had shrunk since I had last seen him. All his flesh had fallen away; still a huge man, he was more bone than muscle now, cadaverous and ancient. His eyes were fixed on mine, the only spark of life in a face like crumpled paper.

'Herr Mueller,' I said. My voice sounded calm to my own ears; I hoped it sounded the same to him. '*Wie geht es Euch?*'

The old man stood swaying in front of me, as though the evening breeze might knock him down. I didn't know if he had lost his mount, or left it down below the ridge, but there was no sign of horse or mule.

He took a step toward me, and I took one back, involuntarily.

'Frau Klara,' he said, and there was a note of pleading in his voice.

I stopped, wanting to call out to Lord John, but hesitant. He wouldn't call me by my first name if he meant to do me harm.

'They are dead,' he said. '*Mein Mädchen. Mein Kind.*'

Tears welled suddenly in the bloodshot eyes, and ran slowly down the weather-beaten grooves of his face. The misery in his eyes was so acute that I reached out and took his huge, work-scarred old hand in mine.

'I know,' I said. 'I'm sorry.'

He nodded again, his old mouth working. He let me lead him to the bench by the door, where he sat down quite suddenly, as though all the strength had gone out of his legs.

The door opened, and John Grey came out. He had his pistol in his hand, but when I shook my head at him, he slid it at once into his shirt. The old man had not let go of my hand; he pulled, forcing me to sit down beside him.

'*Gnädige Frau,*' he said, and suddenly turned and embraced me, hugging me tight against his filthy coat. He shook with soundless crying, and even knowing what he had done, I put my own arms around him.

He smelled dreadful, sour and reeking with old age and sorrow, with beer and sweat and filth, and somewhere under all the other odors was the fetor of dried blood. I shuddered, caught in a web of pity, horror, and revulsion, but could not pull away.

He let go, finally, and seemed suddenly to see John Grey, who was hovering nearby, not sure whether to intervene or not. The old man started at sight of him.

'*Mein Gott!*' he exclaimed, in tones of horror. '*Er hat Masern!*' The sun was sinking fast, bathing the dooryard in bloody light. It struck Grey full in the face, highlighting the darkened spots on his face, flushing his skin with red.

Mueller turned to me, and frantically seized my face between his huge, horny paws. His thumbs scraped across my cheeks, and an expression of relief came into his sunken eyes, as he saw that my skin was still clear.

'*Gott sei dank*', he said, and letting go of my face, began to rummage in his coat, saying something in German so urgent and so mumbled that I could make out no more than the occasional word.

'He says he was afraid he would be too late, and is glad that he was not,' Grey said, seeing my bewilderment. He eyed the old farmer with suspicious dislike. 'He says he's brought you something – a charm of some kind. It will ward off the curse, and keep you safe from the illness.'

The old man withdrew an object wrapped in cloth from the recesses of his coat, and laid it in my lap, still babbling in German.

'He thanks you for all your help to his family – he thinks you are a fine woman, as dear to him as one of his daughters-in-law – he says that . . .' Mueller unfolded the cloth with shaking hands, and the words died in Grey's throat.

I opened my mouth, but made no sound. I must have made some involuntary movement, for the cloth slipped suddenly to the ground, spilling out the sheaf of white-streaked hair to which a small silver ornament still clung. With it was the leather pouch, the woodpecker's feathers draggled with blood.

Mueller was still speaking, and Grey was trying to, but I was only dimly aware of their words. Inside my ears echoed the words I had heard a year before, down by the stream, in Gabrielle's soft voice, translating for Nayawenne.

Her name meant 'It may be; it will happen'. Now it had, and all that was left me for consolation was her words: 'She says you must not be troubled; sickness is sent from the gods. It won't be your fault.'

29

Charnel Houses

Jamie smelled the smoke long before the village came in sight. Willie saw him stiffen, and tensed in his own saddle, glancing warily around them.

'What?' the boy whispered. 'What is it?'

'I dinna ken.' He kept his own voice low, though there was no evidence that anyone was near enough to hear them. He swung down from his horse and handed the reins to Willie, nodding toward a vine-covered cliff face whose foot was shrouded in brush.

'Take the horses behind the cliff, lad,' he said. 'There's a deer path there, that leads up to a spruce grove. Get well in among the trees, and wait there for me.' He hesitated, not wanting to scare the boy, but there was no help for it.

'If I should not come back by dark,' he said, 'leave at once. Dinna wait for the morning; go back to the wee stream we just crossed, turn to your left, and follow it to a place where there's a waterfall – you'll hear it, even in the dark. Behind the falls there's a wee cave; the Indians use it when they're hunting.'

A small rim of white showed all the way around the lad's blue irises. Jamie took a firm grip of the boy's leg, just above the knee, to impress the directions upon him, and felt a quiver run through the long muscle of the thigh.

'Stay there till the morning,' he said, 'and if I havena caught ye up by then – go home. Keep the sun on your left in the morning, on your right after noon, and in two days give your horse his head; you'll be near enough home for him to find the way, I think.'

He took a deep breath, wondering what else to say, but there was nothing.

'God go with ye, lad.' He gave Willie as reassuring a smile as he could muster, clapped the horse on the rump to start it, and turned toward the scent of burning.

It wasn't the normal smell of village fires; not even of the

601

big ceremonial fires that Ian had told him of, when they burned whole trees in the firepit in the center of the village. Those were the size of Beltane fires, Ian said, and he knew the crackle and size of such a blaze. This was much bigger.

With great caution he made a wide circle, at last coming to a small hill from which he knew that he could gain a view of the village. As soon as he emerged from the forest's shelter, though, he saw it. Rolling plumes of gray smoke were rising from the smoldering remnants of every long-house in the village.

A thick brownish pall of smoke hung over the forest as far as he could see. He took a quick breath, coughed, and hastily drew a fold of his plaid across his nose and mouth, crossing himself with his free hand. He had smelled burning flesh before, and a sudden cold sweat bathed him at the memory of the funeral pyres of Culloden.

His soul misgave him at the sight of the desolation below, but he searched carefully, squinting through the eye-stinging haze for any sign of life among the ruins. Nothing moved save the wavering smoke, its wraiths gliding silent, wind-driven through the blackened houses. Had it been the Cherokee or the Creek, raiding up from the south? Or one of the remnant Algonkian tribes to the north, the Nanticokes or the Tuteloes?

A gust of wind smote him full in the face with the stink of charred flesh. He bent and vomited, trying to rid himself of his bone-deep knowledge of burnt crofts and murdered families. As he straightened up, wiping his mouth on his sleeve, he heard a dog bark in the distance.

He turned and went quickly downhill toward the sound, his heart beating faster. Raiders would not bring dogs. If there were survivors of the massacre, the dogs would be with them.

Still, he went as silently as possible, not daring to call out. That fire had been burning for less than a day; half the walls were still standing. Whoever had set it was still nearby, without a doubt.

It was a dog that met him; a big yellow mongrel, one that he recognized as belonging to Ian's friend Onakara. Off its normal territory, the dog neither barked nor rushed him, but stood its ground in the shadow of a pine tree, ears laid back and growling softly. He walked toward it slowly, holding out his closed fist.

'*Balach math,*' he murmured to it. 'Hold. Where are your people, then?'

The dog extended its muzzle, still growling, and sniffed at the proffered hand. Its nostrils twitched, and it relaxed a little, nosing closer in recognition.

He felt rather than saw a human presence, and looked up into the face of the dog's owner. Onakara's face was painted, with white streaks that ran from hair to chin, and behind the pale bars of paint, his eyes were dead.

'What enemy has done this?' Jamie asked, in his halting Tuscaroran. 'Does your uncle still live?'

Onakara didn't answer, but turned and went back into the forest, followed by his dog. Jamie came after them, and within a half-hour's walk emerged into a small clearing where the survivors had made a temporary camp.

As he passed through the camp, he saw faces he knew. Some of them registered awareness of his presence; others stared sightlessly into a distance he knew too well – the infinite prospect of sorrow and despair. All too many were missing.

He had seen this before, and the ghosts of war and murder dragged at his footsteps as he passed. He had seen a young woman in the Highlands, sitting on the doorstep of her smoking house with her husband's body at her feet; she had worn the same stunned look as the young Indian woman by the sycamore tree.

Slowly, though, he became aware that something was different here. Wigwam shelters dotted the clearing; bundles lay piled near the edges of the clearing, and horses and ponies were tethered among the trees. This was no hasty exodus of people plundered and fleeing for their lives – it was an orderly retreat, with most of their worldly goods neatly packed and brought along. What in God's name had happened in Anna Ooka this day?

Nacognaweto was in a wigwam at the far side of the clearing. Onakara lifted the flap and silently nodded Jamie in.

A sudden spark leapt in the older man's eyes as he

603

entered, but then died at once as Nacognaweto saw his face, with the shadow of reflected grief on it. The chieftain closed his eyes for a moment, and reopened them, composed.

'You have not met with her who heals, nor with the woman whose longhouse I dwelt in?'

Used to the Indian notion that it was rude to speak a person's name aloud save for the sake of ceremony, Jamie knew he must refer to Gabrielle and old Nayawenne. He shook his head, knowing that that gesture must destroy the last flicker of hope the other had held. It was no consolation, but he took the flask of brandy from his belt, and offered that in mute apology for his failure to bring good news.

Nacognaweto accepted it, and with a tilt of his head, summoned a woman, who dug about in one of the bundles by the hide wall and produced a gourd cup. The Indian poured a quantity of spirit that would flatten a Scotsman, and drank deeply before handing the gourd to Jamie.

He took a small sip for the sake of politeness, and handed back the gourd. It wasn't polite to come to the point of a visit at once, but he had no time for palaver and he could see that the other had no heart for it.

'What has happened?' he asked bluntly.

'Sickness,' Nacognaweto answered softly. His eyes shone wetly, watering from the fumes of brandy. 'We are cursed.'

Haltingly, the story emerged, between the swallows of brandy. Measles had broken out in the village and swept through it like fire. Within the first week, a quarter of the people lay dead; now, at the end, there were no more than a quarter left alive.

When the sickness had begun, Nayawenne had sung over the victims. When more fell sick, she had gone out into the forest in search of . . . Jamie's grasp of Tuscarora was not sufficient to interpret the words. A charm, he thought it was – some plant? Or perhaps she looked for a vision that would tell them what to do, how to make amends for whatever evil had brought the sickness on them, or the name of the enemy who had cursed them. Gabrielle and Berthe had gone with her, because she was old and should not go alone – and none of the three had come back.

Nacognaweto was swaying very slightly as he sat, the gourd cup clasped in his hands. The woman bent over him, trying to take it away, but he shrugged her aside, and she let him be.

They had searched for the women, but there was no sign. Perhaps they had been taken by raiders, perhaps they too had fallen ill, and died in the forest. But the village had no *shaman* to speak for them, and the gods had not listened.

'We are cursed.'

Nacognaweto's words were slurred, and the cup tilted dangerously in his hands. The woman knelt behind him and put her hands on his shoulders, to steady him.

'We left the dead in the houses, and set fire to them,' she said to Jamie. Her eyes were black with sadness, too, but some life still lurked within them. 'Now we will go north, to Oglanethaka.' Her hands tightened on Nacognaweto's shoulders, and she nodded to Jamie. 'You go now.'

He went, the grief of the place clinging to him like the smoke that permeated clothes and hair. And within his charred heart as he left the camp sprang a small green shoot of selfishness, relief that the grief was – for this time – not his own. His woman still lived. His children were safe.

He looked up at the sky and saw the dull glow of the sinking sun reflected in the pall of smoke. He lengthened his stride to a hill-walker's lope that ate the miles. There was not much time; night was coming fast.

PART EIGHT

Beaucoup

30

Into Thin Air

Oxford, April 1971

'No,' he said positively. Roger swung round to peer out the window at the soggy sky, holding the phone to his ear. 'Not a chance. I'm off to Scotland next week I've told you.'

'Oh, now Rog,' coaxed the Dean's voice. 'It's just your sort of thing. And it wouldn't put you off your schedule by a lot; you could be in the Hielands a-chasin' the deer this time a month – and you told me yourself your girrrl's not due till July.'

Roger gritted his teeth at the Dean's put-on Scots accent, and opened his mouth to say no again, but wasn't quite fast enough.

'It's Americans, too, Rog,' she said. 'You're so *good* with Americans. Speaking of girrls,' she added, with a brief chortle.

'Now, look, Edwina,' he said, summoning patience, 'I've things to do this holiday. And they don't include herding American tourists round the museums in London.'

'No, no,' she assured him. 'We've paid minders to do the touristy bits; all you'd need to be concerned with is the conference itself.'

'Yes, but –'

'Money, Rog,' she purred down the phone, pulling out her secret weapon. 'It's Americans, I said. You know what *that* means.' She paused pregnantly, to allow him to contemplate the fee for running a week-long conference for a gang of visiting American scholars whose official minder had fallen ill. By comparison to his normal salary, it was an astronomical sum.

'Ah . . .' He could feel himself weakening.

'I hear you're thinking of getting married one of these days, Rog. Buy an extra haggis for the wedding, wouldn't it?'

'Anyone ever tell you how subtle you are, Edwina?' he demanded.

'Never.' She chortled again briefly, then snapped into executive mode. 'Right, then, see you Monday week for the plans meeting,' she said, and hung up.

He resisted the futile impulse to slam the receiver down, and dropped it on the hook instead.

Maybe it wasn't a bad thing after all, he thought bleakly. He didn't care about the money, in all truth, but having a conference to run might keep his mind off things. He picked up the much crumpled letter that lay next to the phone, and smoothed it out, his eye traveling over the paragraphs of apology without really reading them.

So sorry, she'd said. Special invitation to engineering conference in Sri Lanka (God, did all Americans go to conferences in the summer?), valuable contacts, job interviews (job interviews? Christ, he knew it, she was never coming back!) – couldn't pass it up. Desperately sorry. See you in September. I'll write. Love.

'Yeah, right,' he said. 'Love.'

He balled up the sheet again and threw it at the dresser. It bounced off the edge of the silver picture frame and fell to the carpet.

'You could have told me straight,' he said aloud. 'So you did find someone else; you were right then, weren't you? You were wise, and me the fool. But could you not be honest, ye lying wee bitch?'

He was trying to work up a good rage; anything to fill the emptiness in the pit of his stomach. It wasn't helping.

He took the picture in its silver frame, wanting to break it to bits, wanting to clutch it to his heart. In the end, he only stood looking at it for a long time, then put it down gently, on its face.

'So sorry,' he said. 'Yeah, so am I.'

May 1971

The boxes were waiting for him at the porter's lodge when he returned to college on the last day of the conference, hot, tired, and thoroughly fed up with Americans. There were five of them, large wooden crates plastered with the bright stickers of international shipping.

'What's this?' Roger juggled the clipboard the deliveryman handed him, groping in his pocket with the other hand for a tip.

'Well, I dunno, do I?' The man, truculent and sweating from the trip through the courtyard to the porter's lodge, dropped the last crate on top of the others with a bang. 'All yours, mate.'

Roger gave the top box an experimental shove. If it wasn't books, it was lead. The push had shown him the edge of an envelope taped securely to the box below, though. With some difficulty, he pried it loose and ripped it open.

You told me once that your father said that everyone needs a history, the note inside read. *This is mine. Will you keep it with yours?* There was neither salutation nor closing; only the single letter 'B', written in bold angular strokes.

He stared at it for a moment, then folded the note and put it in his shirt pocket. Squatting carefully, he got hold of the top crate and lifted it in his arms. Christ, it must weigh sixty pounds at least!

Sweating, Roger dropped the crate on the floor of his sitting room and went through to the tiny bedroom, where he scrabbled through a drawer. Armed with a screwdriver and a bottle of beer, he came back to deal with the box. He tried to damp down his rising feelings of excitement, but couldn't. *Will you keep it with yours?* Did a girl send half her belongings to a bloke she meant to break off with?

'History, eh?' he muttered. 'Museum quality, by the way you packed it.' The contents had been double-boxed, with a layer of excelsior between, and the inner box, once opened, revealed a mysterious array of lumpy, newspaper-wrapped bundles and smaller boxes.

He picked up a sturdy shoe box and peeked inside. Photographs; old ones with scalloped edges, and newer ones, glossy and colored. The edge of large studio portrait showed, and he pulled it out.

It was Claire Randall, much as he had last seen her; amber eyes warm and startling under a tumble of brown-silk curls, a slight smile on the lush, delicate mouth. He shoved it back in the box, feeling like a murderer.

What emerged from the layers of newsprint was a very aptly named Raggedy Ann doll, its painted face so faded that only the shoe-button eyes remained, fixed in a blank and challenging stare. Its dress was torn but had been carefully mended, the soft cloth body stained but clean.

The next bundle yielded a tattered Mickey Mouse hat, with a tiny pink foam-rubber bow still fixed between its perky ears. A cheap music box, that played 'Over the Rainbow' when he opened it. A stuffed dog, synthetic fur worn away in patches. A faded red sweatshirt, a man's size Medium. It might have fit Brianna, but somehow Roger knew it had been Frank's. A ragged dressing gown in quilted maroon silk. On an impulse, he pressed it to his nose. Claire. Her scent brought her vividly to life, a faint smell of musk and green things, and he dropped the garment, shaken.

Under the layer of trivia there was more substantial treasure. The weight of the crate was caused mostly by three large flat chests at the bottom, each containing a silver dinner service, carefully wrapped in gray antitarnishing cloth. Each chest had a typewritten note tucked inside, giving the provenance and history of the silver.

A French silver-gilt service, with rope-knot borders, maker's mark DG. Acquired by William S. Randall, 1842. A George III Old English pattern, acquired 1776 Edward K. Randall, Esq. Husk Shell pattern, by Charles Boyton, acquired 1903 by Quentin Lambert Beauchamp, given as a wedding present to Franklin Randall and Claire Beauchamp. The family silver.

With a growing puzzlement, Roger went on, laying each item carefully on the floor beside him, the objects of vertu and objects of use that comprised Brianna Randall's history. History. Jesus, why had she called it that?

Alarm pricked the puzzlement as another thought occurred to him, and he grabbed the lid, checking the address label. Oxford. Yes, she *had* sent them here. Why here, when she'd known – or thought – that he meant to be in Scotland all summer? He would have been, if not for the last-minute conference – and he hadn't told her about that.

Tucked in the last corner was a jewelry box, a small but substantial container. Inside were several rings, brooches, and sets of earrings. The cairngorm brooch he had given her for her birthday was there. Necklaces and chains. Two things weren't.

The silver bracelet he had given her – and her grand-mother's pearls.

'Jesus bloody Christ.' He looked again, just to be sure, dumping out the glittering junk and spreading it on his counterpane. No pearls. Certainly no string of baroque Scottish pearls, spaced with antique gold roundels.

She couldn't be wearing them, not to an engineering conference in Sri Lanka. The pearls were an heirloom to her, not an ornament. She seldom wore them. They were her link with –

'You didn't,' he said aloud. 'God, tell me you didn't do it!'

He dropped the jewel box on the bed, and thundered down the stairs to the telephone room.

It took forever to get the international operator on the line, and a longer time yet of vague electronic poppings and buzzings, before he heard the click of connection, followed by a faint ringing. One ring, two, then a click, and his heart leapt. She was home!

'*We're sorry,*' said a woman's pleasant, impersonal voice, '*that number has been disconnected, or is no longer in service.*'

God, she *couldn't* have! Could she? Yes, she bloody could, the reckless wee coof! Where in *hell* was she?

He drummed his fingers restlessly against his thigh, fuming, as the transatlantic phone line clicked and hummed, while connections were made, while he dealt with the endless delays and stupidities of hospital switch-boards and secretaries. But at last he heard a familiar voice in his ear, deep and resonant.

'Joseph Abernathy.'

'Dr. Abernathy? This will be Roger Wakefield here. Do you know where Brianna is?' he demanded without pre-liminary.

The deep voice rose slightly in surprise.

'With you. Isn't she?'

A cold chill washed over Roger, and he gripped the receiver harder, as though he could force it to give him the answer he wanted.

'She is not,' he made himself say, as calmly as he could. 'She meant to come in the fall, after she took her degree and went to some conference.'

'No. No, that's not right. She finished her coursework the end of April – I took her to dinner to celebrate – and she said she was going straight out to Scotland, without waiting for commencement. Wait, let me think . . . yeah, that's right; my son Lenny drove her to the airport . . . when? Yeah, Tuesday . . . the 27th. You mean to say she didn't get there?' Dr. Abernathy's voice rose in agitation.

'I don't know whether she got here or not.' Roger's free hand was clenched into a fist. 'She didn't tell me she was coming.' He forced himself to take a deep breath. 'Where was she flying to – which city, do you know? London? Edinburgh?' She *might* have meant to surprise him with a sudden, unexpected arrival. He'd been surprised, all right, but he doubted that was her intention.

Visions of kidnapping, assault, IRA bombings, drifted through his mind. Almost anything might have happened to a girl traveling alone in a large city – and almost anything that could have happened would be preferable to what his gut was telling him *had* happened. *Damn* the woman!

'Inverness,' Dr. Abernathy's voice was saying in his ear. 'Boston to Edinburgh, then the train to Inverness.'

'Oh, Jesus.' It was both a curse and a prayer. If she had left Boston on Tuesday, she would likely have made Inverness sometime on the Thursday. And Friday was the thirtieth day of April – the eve of Beltane, the ancient fire feast, when the hilltops of old Scotland had blazed with the flames of purification and fertility. When – perhaps – the door to the fairies' hill of Craigh na Dun lay widest open.

Abernathy's voice quacked in his ear, urgently demanding. He forced his attention to focus on it.

614

'No,' he said, with some difficulty. 'No, she didn't. I'm still in Oxford. I had no idea.'

The empty air between them vibrated, the silence filled with dread. He had to ask. He took another breath – he seemed to be taking them one at a time, each one a conscious effort – and changed his grip on the receiver, wiping his cramped and sweaty palm on the leg of his trousers.

'Dr. Abernathy,' he said carefully. 'It's just possible that Brianna's gone to her mother – to Claire. Tell me – do you know where she is?'

The silence this time was charged with wariness.

'Ah . . . no.' Abernathy's voice came slowly, reluctant with caution. 'No, afraid I don't. Not exactly.'

Not exactly. Great way to put it. Roger rubbed a hand over his face, feeling the stubble rasp under his palm.

'Let me ask you this,' Roger said carefully. 'Have you ever heard the name Jamie Fraser?'

The line was utterly silent in his hand. Then there came a deep sigh in his ear.

'Oh, Jesus Christ on a piece of toast,' Dr. Abernathy said. 'She did it.'

Wouldn't you?

That was what Joe Abernathy had said to him, at the conclusion of their lengthy conversation, and the question lingered in his mind as he drove north, barely noticing the road signs that whizzed past, blurred by the rain.

Wouldn't you?

'I would,' Abernathy had said. 'If you didn't know your dad, never *had* known him – and all of a sudden, you found out where he was? Wouldn't you want to meet him, find out what he was really like? I'd be kind of curious, myself.'

'You don't understand,' Roger had said, rubbing a hand across his forehead in frustration. 'It's not like someone who's adopted, finding out her real father's name and then just popping up on his doorstep.'

'Seems to me that's just what it's like.' The deep voice was cool. 'Bree *was* adopted, right? I think she'd have gone before, if she hadn't felt it was disloyal to Frank.'

Roger shook his head, disregarding the fact that Abernathy couldn't see him.

'It's not that – it's the popping-up-on-the-doorstep part. That – the way through – how she went – look, did Claire tell you –?'

'Yeah, she did,' Abernathy broke in. His tone was bemused. 'Yeah, she did say it wasn't quite like walking through a revolving door.'

'To put it mildly.' The mere thought of the standing stone circle on Craigh na Dun gave Roger a cold grue.

'To put it mildly – you *know* what it's like?' The far-off voice sharpened with interest.

'Yes, damn it, I do!' He took a long, deep breath. 'Sorry. Look, it's not – I can't explain it, I don't think anyone could. Those stones . . . not everyone hears them, obviously. But Claire did. Bree does, and – and I do. And for us . . .'

Claire had gone through the stones of Craigh na Dun on the ancient fire feast of Samhain, on the first day of November, two and a half years before. Roger shivered, and not from cold. The hairs stood up on the back of his neck whenever he thought of it.

'So not everybody can go through – but you can.' Abernathy's voice was filled with curiosity – and what sounded vaguely like envy.

'I don't know.' Roger rubbed a hand through his hair. His eyes were burning, as though he'd sat up all night. 'I might.'

'The thing is . . .' He spoke slowly, trying to control his voice, and with it, his fear. 'The thing is – even if she *has* gone through, there's no way of telling whether, or where, she came out again.'

'I see.' The deep American voice had lost its jauntiness. 'And you don't know about Claire either, then. Whether she made it?'

He shook his head, his vision of Joe Abernathy so clear that he forgot again that the man couldn't see him. Dr. Abernathy was no more than average size, a thickset black man in gold-rimmed spectacles, but with such an air of authority that his simple presence gave one confidence and compelled calm. Roger was surprised to find that this presence transferred itself over the phone lines – but he was more than grateful for it.

'No,' he said aloud. Leave it at that, for now. He wasn't about to go into everything now, on the phone with a near stranger. 'She's a woman; there wasn't that much public notice of what individual women were doing, then – not unless they did something spectacular, like get burned for witchcraft, or hanged for murder. Or *be* murdered.'

'Ha ha,' said Abernathy, but he wasn't laughing. 'She did make it, though, at least once. She went – and she came back.'

'Aye, she did.' Roger had been trying to take comfort in that fact himself, but there were too many other possibilities forcing themselves upon his consciousness. 'But we don't know that Brianna went back as far – or farther. And even if she did survive the stones and come out in the right time . . . have you any idea how dangerous a place the eighteenth century *was*?'

'No,' Abernathy said dryly. 'Though I gather you do. But Claire seemed to manage all right there.'

'She survived,' Roger agreed. 'Not much of a sell for a vacation spot, is it, though – "If your luck's in, you'll come back alive?" ' Once, at least.

Abernathy did laugh at that, though with a nervous undertone. He coughed then, and cleared his throat.

'Yeah. Well. The point is – Bree's gone *someplace*. And I think you're probably right about where. I mean, if it was me, I'd have gone. Wouldn't you?'

Wouldn't you? He pulled to the left, passed a lorry with its headlights on, plodding its way through the gathering fog.

I would. Abernathy's confident voice rang in his ear.

INVERNESS, 30, read the sign, and he swung the tiny Morris abruptly to the right, skidding on wet pavement. The rain was drumming down on the tarmac, hard enough to raise a mist above the grass on the verge.

Wouldn't you? He touched the breast pocket of his shirt, where the squarish shape of Brianna's photo lay stiff over his heart. His fingers touched the small round hardness of his mother's locket, snatched at the last moment, brought along for luck.

'Yeah, maybe I would,' he muttered, squinting through the rain streaming over the windscreen. 'But I would have told you I was going to do it. In the name of God, woman – why did you not tell *me*?'

31

Return to Inverness

The fumes of furniture polish, floor wax, fresh paint, and air freshener hung in throat-clutching clouds in the hallway. Not even these olfactory evidences of Fiona's domestic zeal were able to compete with the delectable aromas floating out of the kitchen, though.

'Eat your heart out, Tom Wolfe,' Roger murmured, inhaling deeply as he set down his bag in the hall. Granted, the old manse was definitely under new management, but even its transformation from manse to bed-and-breakfast had been unable to alter its basic character.

Welcomed with enthusiasm by Fiona – and somewhat less by Ernie – he settled into his old room at the top of the stairs, and embarked at once on his job of detection. It wasn't that difficult; beyond the normal Highland inquisitiveness about strangers, a six-feet-tall woman with waist-length red hair tended to attract notice.

She'd come to Inverness from Edinburgh. He knew that much for a fact; she'd been seen at the station. Also for a fact he knew that a tall red-haired woman had hired a car and told the driver to take her out into the country. The driver had no real notion where they had gone; just that all of a sudden, the woman had said, 'Here, this is the place, let me off here.'

'Said she meant to meet her friends for a walking tour across the moors,' the driver had said, shrugging. 'She had a haversack with her, and she was dressed for walking, sure enough. A damn wet day for a walk on the moors, but ye know what loons these American tourists are.'

Well, he knew what kind of a loon *that* one was, at least. Curse her thick head and fiendish stubbornness, if she thought she had to do it, why in *hell* hadn't she told him? Because she didn't want you to know, sport, he thought grimly. And he didn't want to think about why not.

So far he had gotten. And only one way of following her any farther.

Claire had speculated that the whatever-it-was stood widest open on the ancient sun feasts and fire feasts. It seemed to work – she had herself gone through the first time on Beltane, May 1, the second time on Samhain, the first of November. And now Brianna had evidently followed in her mother's footsteps, going on Beltane.

Well, he wasn't going to wait till November – God only knew what could happen to her in five months! Beltane and Samhain were fire feasts, though; there was a sunfeast between.

Midsummer's Eve, the summer solstice; that would be next. June 20, four weeks away. He ground his teeth at the thought of waiting – his impulse was to go *now* and damn the danger – but it wouldn't help Brianna if his impulse to rush chivalrously after her killed him. He was under no illusions about the nature of the stone circle, not after what he'd seen and heard so far.

Very quietly, he began to make what preparations he could. And in the evenings, when the fog rolled in off the river, he sought distraction from his thoughts, playing draughts with Fiona, going to the pub with Ernie, and – as a last resort – having another bash at the dozens of boxes that still crammed the old garage.

The garage had an air of sinister miracle about it; the boxes seemed to multiply like the loaves and fishes – every time he opened the door, there were more of them. He'd probably finish the job of sorting his late father's effects just before being carried out feetfirst himself, he thought. Still, for the moment, the boring work was a godsend, dulling his mind enough to keep him from fretting himself to pieces in the waiting. Some nights, he even slept.

'You've got a picture on your desk.' Fiona didn't look at him, but kept her attention riveted on the dishes she was clearing.

'Lots of them.' Roger took a cautious mouthful of tea; hot and fresh, but not scalding. How did she do that? 'Is there one you want? I know there are a few snaps of your grannie – you're more than welcome, though I'd like one to keep.'

She did look up at that, mildly startled.

'Oh. Of Grannie? Aye, our da'll like to see those. But it's the big one I meant.'

'Big one?' Roger tried to think which photo she could mean; most of them were black-and-white snapshots taken with the Reverend's ancient Brownie, but there were a couple of the larger cabinet photos – one of his parents, another of the Reverend's grandmother, looking like a pterodactyl in black bombazine, taken on the occasion of that lady's hundredth birthday. Fiona couldn't possibly mean those.

'Of her that kilt her husband and went away.' Fiona's mouth compressed.

'Her that – oh.' Roger took a deep gulp of tea. 'You mean Gillian Edgars.'

'Her,' Fiona repeated stubbornly. 'Why've you got a photo of her?'

Roger set the cup down and picked up the morning paper, affecting casualness as he wondered what to say.

'Oh – someone gave it to me.'

'Who?'

Fiona was normally persistent, but seldom so direct. What was troubling her?

'Mrs. Randall – Dr. Randall, I mean. Why?'

Fiona didn't reply, but pressed her lips tight shut.

Roger had by now abandoned all interest in the paper. He laid it down carefully.

'Did you know her?' he said. 'Gillian Edgars?'

Fiona didn't answer directly, but turned aside, fiddling with the tea cozy.

'You've been up to the standing stones on Craigh na Dun; Joycie said her Albert saw ye comin' down when he was drivin' to Drumnadrochit Thursday.'

'I have, yes. No crime in that, is there?' He tried to make a joke of it, but Fiona wasn't having any.

'Ye know it's a queer place, all circles are. And don't be tellin' me ye went up there to admire the view.'

He sat back in his chair, looking up at her. Her curly dark hair was standing on end; she rumpled her hands through it when she was agitated, and agitated she surely was.

'You *do* know her. That's right; Claire said you'd met her.' The small flicker of curiosity he had felt at the mention of Gillian Edgars was growing into a clear flame of excitement.

'I canna be knowing her, now, can I? She's dead.' Fiona scooped up the empty egg cup, eyes fixed on the discarded fragments of shell. 'Isn't she?'

Roger reached out and stopped her with a hand on her arm.

'Is she?'

'It's what everyone thinks. The police havena found a trace of her.' The word came out 'polis' in her soft Highland accent.

'Perhaps they're not looking in the right place.'

All the blood drained out of her flushed, fair face. Roger tightened his grip, though she wasn't trying to pull away. She knew, dammit, she knew! But *what* did she know?

'Tell me, Fiona,' he said. 'Please – tell me. What do you know about Gillian Edgars – and the stones?'

She did pull away from him then, but didn't leave, just stood there, turning the egg cup over and over in her hands, as if it were a miniature hourglass. Roger stood up, and she shied back, glancing fearfully up at him.

'A bargain, then,' he said, trying to keep his voice calm, so as not to frighten her further. 'Tell me what you know, and I'll tell you why Dr. Randall gave me that picture – and why I was up on Craigh na Dun.'

'I've got to think.' Swiftly she bent and snatched up the tray of dirty crockery. She was out the door before he could speak a word to stop her.

Slowly he sat down again. It had been a good breakfast – all Fiona's meals were delicious – but it lay in his stomach like a bag of marbles, heavy and indigestible.

He shouldn't be so eager, he told himself. It was courting disappointment. What could Fiona know, after all? Still, any mention of the woman who had called herself Gillian – and later Geillis – was enough to rivet his attention.

He picked up his neglected teacup and swallowed, not tasting it. What if he kept the bargain, and told her everything? Not only about Claire Randall and Gillian, but about himself – and Brianna.

The thought of Bree was like a rock dropped into the pool of his heart, sending ripples of fear in all directions. *She's dead.* Fiona had said of Gillian. *Isn't she?*

Is she? he had answered, the picture of a woman vivid in his mind, green eyes wide and fair hair flying in the hot wind of a fire, poised to flee through the doors of time. No, she hadn't died.

Not then, at least, because Claire had met her – would meet her? Earlier? Later? She hadn't died, but was she dead? She must be now, mustn't she, and yet – damn this twistiness! How could he even think about it coherently?

Too unsettled to stay in one place, he got up and walked down the hall. He paused in the doorway of the kitchen. Fiona was standing at the sink, staring out of the window. She heard him and turned around, an unused dishcloth clutched in her hand.

Her face was red, but determined.

'I'm not to tell, but I will, I've got to.' She took a deep breath and squared her chin, looking like a Pekingese facing up to a lion.

'Bree's mam – that nice Dr. Randall – she asked me about my grannie. She kent Grannie'd been a – a – dancer.'

'Dancer? What, you mean in the stones?' Roger felt faintly startled. Claire had told him, when he'd first met her, but he had never quite believed it – not that the staid Mrs. Graham performed arcane ceremonies on green hilltops in the May dawn.

Fiona let out a long breath.

'So ye do know. I thought so.'

'No, I don't know. All I know is what Claire – Dr. Randall – told me. She and her husband saw women dancing in the stone circle one Beltane dawn, and your grannie was one of them.'

Fiona shook her head.

'Not just one o' them, no. Grannie was the caller.'

Roger moved into the kitchen and took the dishcloth from her unresisting hand.

'Come and sit down,' he said, leading her to the table. 'And tell me, what's a caller?'

'The one who calls down the sun.' She sat, unresisting. She had made up her mind, he saw; she was going to tell him.

'It's one of the auld tongues, the sun-song; some of the words are a bit like the Gaelic, but not all of it. First we dance, in the circle, then the caller stops and faces the split stone, and – it's no singing, really, but it's no quite talking, either; more like the minister at kirk. You've to begin at just the right moment, when the light first shows over the sea, so just as ye finish, the sun comes through the stone.'

'Do you remember any of the words?' The scholar in Roger stirred briefly, curiosity rearing its head through his confusion.

Fiona didn't much resemble her grandmother, but she gave him a look that reminded him suddenly of Mrs. Graham in its directness.

'I know them all,' she said. 'I'm the caller now.'

He realized that his mouth was hanging open, and closed it. She reached for the biscuit tin and plunked it in front of him.

'That's no what ye need to know, though,' she said matter-of-factly, 'and so I won't tell ye. You want to know about Mrs. Edgars.'

Fiona had met Gillian Edgars, all right; Gillian had been one of the dancers, though quite a new one. Gillian had asked questions of the older women, eager to learn all she could. She'd wanted to learn the sun-song, too, but that was secret; only the caller and her successor had that. Some of the older women would know some of it – those who had heard the chant every year for a long time – but not all of it, and not the secrets of when to begin and how to time the song to coincide with the rising of the sun.

Fiona paused, looking down at her folded hands.

'It's women; only women. The men havena got a part in it, and we do not tell them. Not ever.'

He laid a hand over hers.

'You're right to tell me, Fiona,' he said, very softly. 'Tell me the rest, please. I've got to know.'

624

She drew a deep, quivering breath and pulled her hand out from under his. She looked directly at him. 'D'ye know where she's gone? Brianna?'

'I think so. She's gone where Gillian went, hasn't she?'

Fiona didn't reply, but went on looking at him. The unreality of the situation swept over him all of a sudden. He couldn't be sitting here, in the comfortable, shabby kitchen he'd known since boyhood, sipping tea from a mug with the Queen's face painted on the side, discussing sacred stones and time-flight with Fiona. Not *Fiona*, for God's sake, whose interests were confined to Ernie and the domestic economy of her kitchen!

Or so he'd thought. He picked up the mug, drained it, and set it down with a soft thump.

'I have to go after her, Fiona – if I can. Can I?'

She shook her head, clearly afraid.

'I canna say. It's only women I know about; maybe it's only women who can.'

Roger's hand clenched round the saltshaker. That's what he was afraid of – or one of the things he was afraid of.

'Only one way to find out, isn't there?' he said, outwardly casual. In the back of his mind, unbidden, a tall cleft stone rose up black, stark as a threat against a soft dawn sky.

'I have her wee book,' Fiona blurted.

'What – whose? Gillian's? She wrote something?'

'Aye, she did. There's a place –' She darted a look at him, and licked her lips. 'We keep our things there, ready beforehand. She'd put the book there, and – and – I took it, after.' After Gillian's husband had been found murdered in the circle, Roger thought she meant.

'I kent the polis should maybe have it,' Fiona went on, 'but it – well, I didna like to give it to them, and yet I was thinkin' what if it's to do with the killing? And I couldna keep it back if it was to be important, and yet –' She looked up at Roger in a plea for understanding. 'It was her own book, ye see, her writing. And if she'd left it in that place . . .'

'It was secret.' Roger nodded.

Fiona nodded, and drew a deep breath.

'So I read it.'

'And that's how you know where she's gone,' Roger said softly.

Fiona let out a shuddering sigh and gave him a wan smile.

'Well, the book's no going to help the polis, that's for sure.'

'Could it help me?'

'I hope so,' she said simply, and turning to the sideboard, pulled open a drawer and withdrew a small book, bound in green cloth.

32

Grimoire

This is the grimoire of the witch, Geillis. It is a witch's name, and I take it for my own; what I was born does not matter, only what I will make of myself, only what I will become.

And what is that? I cannot yet say, for only in the making will I find what I have made. Mine is the path of power.

Absolute power corrupts absolutely, yes – and how? Why, in the assumption that power can be absolute, for it never can. For we are mortal, you and I. Watch the flesh shrink and wither on your bones, feel the lines of your skull, pushing through the skin, your teeth behind soft lips a grin of grim acknowledgment.

And yet within the bounds of flesh, many things are possible. Whether such things are possible beyond those bounds – that is the realm of others, not mine. And that is the difference between them and me, those others who have gone before to explore the Black Realm, those who seek power in magic and the summoning of demons.

I go in the body, not the soul. And by denying my soul, I give no power to any force but those I control. I do not seek favor from devil or god; I deny them. For if there is no soul, no death to contemplate, then neither god nor devil rules – their battle is of no consequence, to one who lives in the flesh alone.

We rule for a moment, and yet for all time. A fragile web woven to snare both earth and space. Only one life is given to us – and yet its years may be spent in many times – how many times?

If you will wield power, you must choose both your time and your place, for only when the shadow of the stone falls at your feet is the door of destiny truly open.

'A nutcase for sure,' Roger murmured. 'Horrible prose style, too.' The kitchen was empty; he was talking to reassure himself. It wasn't helping.

He turned the pages carefully, skimming down the lines of clear, round writing.

After the first bit, there was a section titled 'Sun Feasts and Fire Feasts', with a listing after – Imbolc, Alban Eilir, Beltane, Litha, Lughnassadh, Alban Elfed, Samhain,

Alban Arthuan – with a paragraph of notes following each name, and a series of small crosses inscribed alongside. What the hell was that for?

Samhain caught his eye, with six crosses by it.

This is the first of the feasts of the dead. Long before Christ and his Resurrection, on the night of Samhain, the souls of heroes rose from their graves. They are rare, these heroes. Who is born when the stars are right? Not all who are born to it have the courage to take hold of the power that is their right.

Even in what was plainly raving madness, she had method and organization – a queer admixture of cool observation and poetic flight. The center section of the book was labeled 'Case Studies', and if the first section had raised the hair on Roger's neck, the second was enough to freeze the blood in his veins.

It was a careful listing, by date and by place, of bodies found in the vicinity of stone circles. The appearance of each was noted, and below each description were a few words of speculation.

August 14, 1931. Sur-le-Meine, Brittany. Body of a male, unidentified. Age, mid-40s. Found near north end of standing stone circle. No evident cause of death, but deep burns on arms and legs. Clothing described only as 'rags'. No photograph.

Possible cause of failure: (1) male, (2) wrong date – 23 days from nearest sun feast.

April 2, 1650. Castlerigg, Scotland. Body of female, unidentified. Age, about 15. Found outside circle. Substantial mutilation noted, may have been dragged from circle by wolves. Clothing not described.

Possible cause of failure: (1) wrong date – 28 days prior to fire feast. (2) lack of preparation.

February 5, 1953. Callanish, Isle of Lewis. Body of male, identified as John MacLeod, lobsterman, age 26. Cause of death diagnosed as massive cerebral hemorrhage, coroner's inquest held owing to appearance of body – second-degree burns on skin of face and extremities, and scorched look of clothing.

Coroner's verdict, death by lightning – possible, but not likely. Possible cause of failure: (1) male. (2) very close to Imbolc, but perhaps not close enough? (3) improper preparation – N.B. newspaper photograph shows victim, shirt open; there is a burnt spot on the chest which appears to be in shape of Bridhe's Cross, but too indistinct to say for sure.

May 1, 1963. Tomnahurich, Scotland. Body of female, identi-fied as Mary Walker Willis. Coroner's inquest, substantial scorching of body and clothing, death due to heart failure – rupture of aorta. Inquest notes Miss Walker dressed in 'odd' clothing, details unspecified.

Failure – this one knew what she was doing, but didn't make it. Failure likely due to omission of proper sacrifice.

The list went on, chilling Roger more with each name. She had found twenty-two, altogether, reported over a period from the mid-1600s to the mid-1900s, from sites scattered over Scotland, northern England, and Brittany, all sites showing some evidence of prehistoric building. Some had been obvious accidents, he thought – people who'd walked into a circle all unsuspecting and had no notion what had hit them.

A few – only two or three – seemed to have known; they'd made some preparation of clothing. Perhaps they had passed through before, and tried again – but this time it hadn't worked. His stomach curled into a small, cold snail. Claire had been right; it wasn't like stepping through a revolving door.

Then there were the disappearances . . . these were in a separate section, neatly docketed by date, sex, and age, with as much noted of the circumstances as was recorded. Ah – that was the meaning of the crosses; how many people had disappeared near each feast. There were more of the disappeared than of the dead, but there was of necessity less data. Most bore question marks – Roger sup-posed because there was no telling whether disappearance in the vicinity of a circle was necessarily connected with it.

He turned over a page, and stopped, feeling as though he'd been punched in the stomach.

May 1, 1945. Craigh na Dun, Inverness-shire, Scotland. Claire Randall, age 27, housewife. Seen last in early morning, having declared intention to visit the circle in search of unusual plant specimens, did not return by dark. Car found parked at foot of hill. No traces in circle, no signs of foul play.

He turned the page gingerly, as though expecting it to blow up in his hand. So Claire had inadvertently given Gillian Edgars part of the evidence that had led to her own experiment. Had Geilie found the reports of Claire's return, three years later?

No, evidently not, he concluded, after flipping back and forth through those pages – or if she had, she hadn't recorded it here.

Fiona had brought him more tea and a plate of fresh ginger nut biscuits, which had sat untouched since he had begun reading. A sense of obligation rather than hunger made him pick up a biscuit and take a bite, but the sharp-flavored crumbs caught in his throat and made him cough.

The last section of the book bore the heading 'Techniques and Preparations.' It began,

Something lies here, older than man, and the stones keep its power. The old spells speak of 'the lines of the earth', and the power that flows through them. The purpose of the stones is to do with those lines, I am sure. But do the stones warp the lines of power, or are they only markers?

The bite of biscuit seemed permanently stuck in his throat, no matter how much tea he drank. He found himself reading faster, skimming, skipping pages, and finally sat back and shut the book. He would read the rest later – and more than once. But for now, he had to get out, into the fresh air. No wonder the book had upset Fiona.

He walked fast down the street, heading for the river, oblivious of the light rain falling. It was late; there was a churchbell ringing for evensong, and the evening foot traffic to the pubs was picking up across the bridges. But above bell and voice and footstep, he heard the last words he had read, chiming in his ear as though she had been speaking directly to him.

Shall I kiss you, child, shall I kiss you, man? Feel the teeth behind my lips when I do. I could kill you, as easily as I embrace you. The taste of power is the taste of blood – iron in my mouth, iron in my hand.
  Sacrifice is required.

33

Midsummer's Eve

June 20, 1971

On Midsummer's Eve in Scotland, the sun hangs in the sky with the moon. Summer solstice, the feast of Litha, Alban Eilir. Nearly midnight, and the light was dim and milky white, but light nonetheless.

He could feel the stones long before he saw them. Claire and Geillis had both been right, he thought; the date mattered. They had been eerie on his earlier visits, but silent. Now he could hear them; not with his ears but with his skin – a low buzzing hum like the drone of bagpipes.

They came over the crest of the hill and paused, thirty feet from the circle. Below was dark glen, a mystery under the rising moon. He heard a small intake of breath at his elbow, and it occurred to him that Fiona was seriously afraid.

'Look, you don't need to be here,' he told her. 'If you're afraid, you should go on down; I'll be all right.'

'It's not me I'm scairt for, fool,' she muttered, thrusting her balled fists deeper into her pockets. She turned away, lowering her head like a little bull as she faced up the path. 'Come on, then.'

The alder bush rustled near his shoulder and he shivered suddenly, feeling a cold qualm go over him, warmly as he was dressed. His dress seemed suddenly ridiculous; the long-skirted coat and the weskit in thick wool, the matching breeches and knitted stockings. A play at the college, he had told tailor who made the costume.

'Fool is right,' he muttered to himself.

Fiona went first into the circle; she would not let him come with her or watch. Obediently, he turned his back, letting her do whatever she intended. She had a plastic shopping bag, presumably containing items for her ceremonial. He had asked what was in it, and she had tersely

632

told him to mind his own business. She was nearly as nervous as he was, he thought.

The humming noise disturbed him. It wasn't in his ears but in his body – under his skin, in his bones. It made the long bones of his arms and legs thrum like plucked strings, and itched in his blood, making him want constantly to scratch. Fiona couldn't hear it; he'd asked, to be sure she was safe before letting her help him.

He hoped to God he was right; that only those who heard the stones could pass through them. He'd never forgive himself if anything happened to Fiona – though as she'd pointed out, she'd been in this circle any number of times on the fire feasts, with no ill effect. He sneaked a look over one shoulder, saw a tiny flame burning at the base of the big cleft stone, and jerked his head back around.

She was singing, in a soft, high voice. He couldn't make out the words. All the other travelers he knew of were women; would it truly work for him?

It might, he thought. If the ability to pass through the stones was genetic – something like the ability to roll one's tongue into a cylinder or color-blindness – then why not? Claire had traveled, so had Brianna. Brianna was Claire's daughter. And he was a descendant of the only other time-traveler he knew of – Geillis the witch.

He stamped both feet and shook himself like a horse with flies, trying to rid himself of the humming. God, it was like being eaten by ants! Was Fiona's chanting making it worse, or was it only his imagination?

He rubbed violently at his chest, trying to ease the irritation, and felt the small round weight of his mother's locket, taken for luck and for its garnets. He had his doubts about Geillis's speculations – he wasn't about to try blood, though Fiona seemed to be supplying fire – but after all, the gems could do no harm, and if they helped . . . Christ, would Fiona not hurry? He twisted and strained inside his clothes, trying to get out of not only his clothing but his skin.

Seeking distraction, he patted his breast pocket again, feeling the locket. If it worked . . . if he could . . . it was a notion that had come to him only lately, as the possibility

633

posed by the stones had matured into actual planning. But if it *were* possible . . . he fingered the small, round shape, seeing the face of Jerry MacKenzie on the dark surface of his mind.

Brianna had gone to find her father. Could he do the same? Jesus, Fiona! She *was* making it worse; the roots of his teeth ached, and his skin was burning. He shook his head violently, then stopped, feeling dizzy; the seams of his skull felt as though they were beginning to separate.

Then she was there, a small figure grasping his hand, saying something anxious as she led him into the circle. He couldn't hear her – the noise was much worse inside; now it was in his ears, in his head, blackening his sight, driving wedges of pain between the joints of his spine.

Gritting his teeth, he blinked back the buzzing darkness, long enough to fix his eyes on Fiona's round and fearful face.

Swiftly he bent and kissed her, full on the mouth.

'Don't tell Ernie,' he said. He turned away from her and walked through the stone.

A faint scent came to him on the summer wind; the smell of burning. He turned his head, nostrils flared to catch it. There. A flame flared and bloomed on a nearby hilltop, a rose of Midsummer's fire.

There were faint stars overhead, half shadowed by a drifting cloud. He had no urge to move, nor to think. He felt bodiless, embraced by the sky, his mind turning free, reflecting starlit images like the glass bubble of a fisher's float, adrift in the surf. There was a soft and musical hum around him – the far-off song of siren stars, and the smell of coffee.

A vague feeling of wrongness intruded on his sense of peace. Sensation prodded at his mind, rousing tiny, painful sparks of confusion. He fought back feeling, wanting only to stay afloat in starlight, but the act of resistance woke him. All of a sudden, he had a body again, and it hurt.

'ROGER!' The star's voice blared in his ear, and he jerked. Searing pain shot through his chest, and he clapped a hand to the wound. Something seized his wrist and pulled it away, but not before he had felt wetness, and the silky roughness of ash on his breast. Was he bleeding?

'Oh, ye're wakin', thank God! Aye, there, that's a good lad. Easy, aye?' It was the cloud talking, not the star. He blinked, confused, and the cloud resolved itself into the curly silhouette of Fiona's head, dark against the sky. He jerked upright, more a convulsion than a conscious movement.

His body had come back with a vengeance. He felt desperately ill, and there was a horrible smell of coffee and burnt flesh in his nostrils. He rolled onto all fours, retching, then collapsed onto the grass. It was wet, and the coolness felt good on his scorched face.

Fiona's hands were on him, soothing, wiping his face and mouth.

'Are ye all right?' she said, for what he knew must be the hundredth time. This time, he summoned enough strength to answer.

'Aye,' he whispered. 'All right. Why –?'

Her head moved back and forth, wiping out half a sky of stars.

'I don't know. Ye went – ye were gone – and then there was a burst o' fire, and ye were lyin' in the circle, wi' your coat ablaze. I had to put ye out with the thermos bottle.'

That accounted for the coffee, then, and the soggy feeling over his chest. He lifted a hand, groping, and this time she let him. There was a burnt patch on the wet cloth of his coat, maybe three inches across. The flesh of his chest was seared; he could feel the queer cushioned numbness of blisters through the hole in the cloth, and the nagging pain of a burn spread through his breast. His mother's locket was gone entirely.

'What happened, Rog?' Fiona was crouching by him, her face dim but visible; he could see the shiny tracks of tears on her face. What he had thought a Midsummer's Eve fire was the flame of her candle, burned down now to the last half inch. God, how long had he been out?

'I –' He had begun to say that he didn't know, but broke off. 'Let me think a bit, aye?' He put his head on his knees, breathing in the smell of wet grass and scorched cloth.

He concentrated on breathing, let it come back. He had

no real need to think – it was all there, distinct in his mind. But how did one describe such things? There was no sight – and yet he had the image of his father. No sound, no touch – and yet he had both heard and felt. The body seemed to make its own sense of things, translating the numinous phenomena of time into concretions.

He raised his head from his knees, and breathed deep, settling himself slowly back in his body.

'I was thinking of my father,' he said. 'When I stepped through the rock, I had just thought, if it works, could I go back and find him? And I . . . did.'

'You did? Your dad? Was he a ghost, d'ye mean?' He felt, more than saw, the flicker of her hand as she made the horns against evil.

'No. Not exactly. I – I can't explain, Fiona. But I met him; I knew him.' The feeling of peace had not left him altogether; it hovered there, fluttering gently in the back of his mind. 'Then there was – sort of an explosion, is all I can describe it as. Something hit me, here.' His fingers touched the burnt place on his chest. 'The force of it pushed me . . . out, and that's all I knew till I woke.' He touched her face gently. 'Thanks, Fee; you saved me burning.'

'Och, get on wi' ye.' She made an impatient gesture, dismissing him. She sat back on her heels, rubbing her chin as she thought.

'I'm thinking, Rog – what it said in her book, about there maybe being some protection, if ye had a gemstone with ye. There were the wee jewels in your mam's locket, no?' He could hear her swallow. 'Maybe – if ye hadn't had that – ye might not have lived. She told about the folk who didn't. They were burned – and your burn's where the locket was.'

'Yes. It could be.' Roger was beginning to feel more like himself. He glanced curiously at Fiona.

'You always say "her". Why do you never say her name?'

Fiona's curls lifted in the dawn wind as she turned to look at him. It was light enough now to see her face clearly, with its expression of disconcerting directness.

'Ye dinna call something unless ye want it to come,' she said. 'Surely ye know that, and your father a minister?'

The hairs on his forearms prickled, despite the covering of shirt and coat.

'Now that you mention it,' he said, trying for a joking tone, and failing utterly. 'I wasn't quite calling my father's name, but perhaps . . . Dr. Randall said she thought of her husband, when she came back.'

Fiona nodded, frowning. He could see her face clearly, and realized with a start that the light was growing. It was near dawn; the sky to the east was the shimmered color of a salmon's scales.

'Christ, it's almost morning! I've got to go!'

'Go?' Fiona's eyes went round with horror. 'You're no going to try it *again?*'

'I am. I've got to.' The lining of his mouth was cotton-dry, and he regretted that Fiona had used all the coffee extinguishing him. He fought down the hollow-bellied feeling and made it to his feet. His knees were wobbly, but he could walk.

'Are you mad, Rog? It'll kill ye, sure!'

He shook his head, eyes fixed on the tall cleft stone.

'No,' he said, and hoped to hell he was right. 'No, I know what went wrong. It won't happen again.'

'You can't know, nor for sure!'

'Aye, I do.' He took her hand from his sleeve and held it between his own; it was small and cold. He smiled at her, though his face felt strangely numb. 'I hope Ernie's not come home; he'll have the police looking for you. You'd best hurry back.'

She shrugged, impatient.

'Och, he's at the fishin' with his cousin Neil; he'll no be back till Tuesday. What d'ye mean, it won't happen again – why won't it?'

This was the thing that was harder to explain that the rest of it. He owned it to her to try, though.

'When I said I was thinking of my father, I was thinking of him from what I knew of him – the pictures of him in his airman's kit, or with my mother. The thing is . . . I was born by that time. Do you see?' He searched her small, round face, and saw her blink slowly, comprehending. Her breath left her in a small sigh, of fear and wonder mingled.

637

'Ye didna only meet your da, then, did ye?' she asked quietly.

He shook his head, wordless. No sight, no sound or smell or touch. There were no images at all to convey what it had been like to meet himself.

'I have to go,' he repeated softly. He squeezed her hand. 'Fiona, I cannot say enough to thank you.'

She stared at him for a moment, her soft bottom lip thrust out, eyes glistening. Then she pulled loose, and twisting off her engagement ring, put it into his hand.

'It's a wee stone, but it's a real diamond,' she said. 'It'll maybe help.'

'I can't take this!' He reached to give it back, but she took a step backward, and put her hands behind her back.

'Dinna worry, it's insured,' she said. 'Ernie's a great one for the insurance.' She tried to smile at him, though the tears were running down her face now. 'So am I.'

There was nothing more to say. He put the ring in the side pocket of his coat, and glanced at the great cleft stone, its black sides starting to glimmer as bits of mica and threads of quartz picked up the dawning light. He could hear the hum, still, though now it felt more like the pulsing of his blood; something inside him.

No words, and no need. He touched her face once lightly in farewell, and walked toward the stone, staggering slightly. He stepped into the cleft.

Fiona heard nothing, but the still, clear air of Midsummer's Day shimmered with an echoed name.

She waited for a long time, until the sun rested on top of the stone.

'*Slan leat, a charaid chòir,*' she said, softly. 'Luck to you, dear friend.' She went slowly down the hill, and didn't look back.

34

Lallybroch

The sorrel horse's name was Brutus, but luckily it didn't seem indicative of character so far. More plodder than plotter, he was strong and faithful – or if not faithful, at least resigned. He had carried her through the summer-green glens and rock-lined gorges without a slip, taking her higher and higher along the good roads made by the English general Wade fifty years before, and the bad roads beyond the General's reach, splashing through brushy burns and climbing up to the places where the roads dwindled away to nothing more than a red deer's track across the moor.

Brianna let the reins lie on Brutus's neck, letting him rest after the last climb, and sat still, surveying the small valley below. The big white-harled farmhouse sat serenely in the middle of pale green fields of oats and barley, its windows and chimneys edged in gray stone, the walled kailyard and the numerous outbuildings clustering around it like chicks round a big white hen.

She had never seen it before, but she was sure. She had heard her mother's descriptions of Lallybroch often enough. And besides, it was the only substantial house for miles; she had seen nothing else in the last three days but the tiny stone-walled crofters' cottages, many deserted and tumbled down, some no more than fire-black ruins.

Smoke was rising from a chimney below; someone was home. It was nearly midday; perhaps everyone was inside, eating dinner.

She swallowed, dry-mouthed with excitement and apprehension. Who would it be? Whom would she see first? Ian? Jenny? And how would they take her appearance, and her declaration?

She had decided simply to tell the truth, as far as who she was, and what she was doing there. Her mother had said how much she looked like her father; she would have to count on that resemblance to convince them. The Highlanders she had met so far were wary of her looks and strange speech; perhaps the Murrays wouldn't believe her. Then she remembered and touched the pocket of her coat; no, they'd believe her; she had proof, after all.

A sudden thought hollowed her breastbone. Could they possibly be here now? Jamie Fraser and her mother? The thought hadn't occurred to her before. She had been so convinced that they were in America – but that wasn't necessarily so. She only knew they *would* be in America in 1776; there was no telling where they were right now.

Brutus flung up his head and whinnied loudly. An answering neigh came from behind them, and Brianna drew up the reins as Brutus swung around. He lifted his head and nickered, nostrils flaring with interest as a handsome bay horse came round the bend of the road, carrying a tall man in brown.

The man pulled up his horse for a moment when he saw them, then twitched a heel against the bay's side and came on, slowly. He was young, she saw, and deeply tanned despite his hat; he must spend a good deal of time outdoors. The skirt of his coat was rumpled and his stockings were covered with dust and foxtails.

He came up to her warily, nodding as he came within speaking distance. Then she saw him stiffen in surprise, and smiled to herself.

He had just noticed that she was a woman. The men's clothes she wore would fool no one up close; 'boyish' was the last word one would use to describe her figure. They served their purpose well enough, though – they were comfortable for riding and, given her height, made her look like a man on horseback at a distance.

The man swept off his hat and bowed to her, surprise plain on his face. He wasn't strictly good-looking, but had a pleasant, strong sort of face, with feathery brows – presently raised high – and soft brown eyes under a thick cap of curly hair, black and glossy with good health.

'Madame,' he said. 'Might I assist ye?'

She took off her own hat and smiled at him.

'I hope so,' she said. 'Is this place Lallybroch?'

He nodded, wariness now added to his surprise as he heard her odd accent.

'It is, so. Will ye be having some business here?'

'Yes,' she said firmly. 'I will.' She drew herself up straight in the saddle and took a deep breath. 'I'm Brianna . . . Fraser.' It felt odd to say it aloud; she had never used the name before. It seemed strangely right, though.

The wariness on his face diminished, but the puzzlement didn't. He nodded cautiously.

'Your servant, ma'am. Jamie Fraser Murray,' he added formally, bowing, 'of Broch Tuarach.'

'Young Jamie!' she exclaimed, startling him with her eagerness. 'You're Young Jamie!'

'My family calls me so,' he said stiffly, managing to give her the impression that he objected to having the name used wantonly by strange women in unsuitable clothes.

'Pleased to meet you,' she said, undaunted. She extended a hand to him, leaning from her saddle. 'I'm your cousin.'

The brows, which had come down during the introductions, popped back up. He looked at her extended hand, then, incredulously, at her face.

'Jamie Fraser is my father,' she said.

His jaw dropped, and he simply goggled at her for a moment. He looked her over minutely, head to toe, peered closely at her face, and then a wide, slow smile spread across his own.

'Damned if he isn't!' he said. He seized her hand and squeezed it tight enough to grind the bones together. 'Christ, you've the look of him!'

He laughed, humor transforming his face.

'Jesus!' he said. 'My mother will have kittens!'

The great rose brier that overhung the door was newly in leaf, hundreds of tiny green buds just forming. Brianna looked up at it as she followed Young Jamie, and caught sight of the lintel over the door.

Fraser, 1716 was carved into the weathered wood. She felt a small thrill at the sight, and stood staring up at the name for a moment, the sunwarm wood of the jamb solid under her hand.

'All right, Cousin?' Young Jamie had turned to look back at her inquiringly.

'Fine.' She hurried into the house after him, automatically ducking her head, though there was no need.

'We're mostly tall, save my mam and wee Kitty,' Young Jamie said with a smile, seeing her duck. 'My grandsire – your grandsire, too – built this house for his wife, who was a verra tall woman herself. It's the only house in the Highlands where ye can go through a doorway without ducking or bashing your head, I expect.'

... *Your grandsire, too.* The casual words made her feel suddenly warm, in spite of the cool dimness of the entry hall.

Frank Randall had been an only child, as had her mother; such relatives as she had were not close – only a couple of elderly great-aunts in England, and some long-distant second cousins in Australia. She had set out thinking only to find her father; she hadn't realized that she might discover a whole new family in the process.

A *lot* of family. As she entered the hallway, with its scarred paneling, a door opened and four small children ran out, closely pursued by a tall young woman with brown curly hair.

'Ah, run for it, run for it, wee fishies!' she cried, rushing forward with outstretched hands snapping like pincers. 'The wicked crab will have ye eaten up, snap, snap!'

The children fled down the hall in a gale of giggles and shrieks, looking back over their shoulders in terrified delight. One of them, a little boy of four or so, saw Brianna and Young Jamie standing in the entry and instantly reversed his direction, charging down the hallway like a runaway locomotive, shouting, 'Daddy, Daddy, Daddy!'

The boy flung himself recklessly at Young Jamie's midriff. The latter caught him expertly, and hoisted the beaming little boy in his arms.

'Now, then, wee Matthew,' he said sternly. 'What sort of manners is this your Auntie Janet's teachin' you? What will your new cousin be thinkin', to see ye dashin' about wi' no more sense than a chicken after corn?'

The little boy giggled louder, not at all put off by the scolding. He peeked at Brianna, caught her eye, and promptly buried his face in his father's shoulder. Slowly he raised his head and peeked again, blue eyes wide.

'Da!' he said. 'Is that a lady?'

'Of course she is, I've told ye, she's your cousin.'

'But she's got on breeks!' Matthew stared at her in shock. 'Ladies dinna wear breeks!'

The young woman looked rather as though she subscribed to this opinion as well, but she interrupted firmly, moving to take the little boy from his father.

'Well, and I'm sure she's a fine reason for it, but it isna proper to be makin' remarks before people's faces. You go and get yourself washed, aye?' She set him down and turned him toward the door at the end of the hallway, giving him a gentle push. He didn't move, but turned back around to stare at Brianna.

'Where's Grannie, Matt?' his father asked.

'In the back parlor wi' Grandda and a lady and a man,' Matthew replied promptly. 'They've had two pots of coffee, a tray of scones, and a whole Dundee cake, but Mama says they're hangin' on in hopes of bein' fed dinner, too, and good luck to them because it's only brose and a bit o' hough today, and damned – oop!' – he pressed a hand over his mouth, glancing guiltily at his father – 'and drat if she'll gie them any of the gooseberry tart, no matter how long they stay.'

Young Jamie gave his son a narrow look, then glanced quizzically at his sister. 'A lady and a man?'

Janet made a faint moue of distaste.

'The Grizzler and her brother,' she said.

Young Jamie grunted, with a glance at Brianna.

'I imagine Mam will be pleased for an excuse to get away from them, then.' He nodded at Matthew. 'Go and fetch your grannie, lad. Tell her I've brought a visitor she'll like to see. And watch your language, aye?' He turned Matthew toward the back of the house and slapped him gently on the rump in dismissal.

The little boy went, but slowly, casting glances of intense fascination over his shoulder at Brianna as he went.

Young Jamie turned back to Brianna, smiling.

'That'll be my eldest,' he said. 'And this' – gesturing to

the young woman – 'is my sister, Janet Murray. Janet – Mistress Brianna Fraser.'

Brianna didn't know whether to offer to shake hands or not, and instead contented herself with a nod and a smile. 'I'm very pleased to meet you,' she said warmly.

Janet's eyes sprang wide with amazement, whether at what Brianna had said or at the accent with which she'd spoken, Brianna couldn't tell.

Young Jamie grinned at his sister's surprise.

'You'll never guess who she is, Jen,' he said. 'Never in a thousand years!'

Janet lifted one eyebrow, then narrowed her eyes at Brianna.

'Cousin,' she murmured, looking their guest frankly up and down. 'She's the look o' the MacKenzies, surely. But she's a Fraser, ye say . . .' Her eyes sprang suddenly wide.

'Oh, ye can't be,' she said to Brianna. A wide smile began to spread across her face, pointing up the family resemblance to her brother. 'You *can't* be!'

Her brother's chortle was interrupted by the swish of a swinging door and the sound of light footsteps on the boards of the hallway.

'Aye, Jamie? Mattie says we've a guest –' The soft, brisk voice died suddenly, and Brianna looked up, her heart suddenly in her throat.

Jenny Murray was very small – no more than five feet tall – and delicately boned as a sparrow. She stood staring at Brianna, mouth slightly open. Her eyes were the deep blue of gentians, made the more striking by a face gone white as paper.

'Oh, my,' she said softly. 'Oh, my.' Brianna smiled tentatively, nodding to her aunt – her mother's friend, her father's beloved only sister. *Oh, please!* she thought, suddenly suffused with a longing as intense as it was unexpected. *Please like me, please be happy I'm here!*

Young Jamie bowed elaborately to his mother, beaming.

'Mam, might I have the honor to present to ye –'

'Jamie Fraser! I kent he was back – I told ye, Jenny Murray!'

The voice rang out from the back of the hallway in tones of high-pitched accusation. Glancing up in startlement,

Brianna saw a woman emerging from the shadows, rustling with indignation.

'Amyas Kettrick *told* me he'd seen your brother riding near Balriggan! But no, ye wouldna have it, would ye, Jenny – telling me I'm a fool, telling me Amyas is blind, and Jamie in America! Liars the both of ye, you and Ian, trying to protect that wicked coward! Hobart!' she shouted, turning toward the back of the house, 'Hobart! Come out here this minute!'

'Be quiet!' said Jenny impatiently. 'Ye *are* a fool, Laoghaire!' She jerked at the woman's sleeve, urging her around. 'And as for who's blind, look at her! Are ye too far past it to tell the difference between a grown man and a lass in breeks, for heaven's sake?' Her own eyes stayed fixed on Brianna, bright with speculation.

'A *lass?*'

The other woman turned, frowning nearsightedly at Brianna. Then she blinked once, anger erased as her round face went slack with surprise. She gasped, crossing herself.

'Mary, Margaret and Bride! Who in the name of God are *you?*'

Brianna took a deep breath, looking from one woman to the other as she answered, trying to keep her voice from shaking.

'My name is Brianna. I'm Jamie Fraser's daughter.'

Both women's eyes popped wide. The woman called Laoghaire grew slowly red and seemed to swell, opening and closing her mouth in a futile search for words.

Jenny stepped forward, though, and seized Brianna's hands, looking up into her face. A soft pink bloomed in her cheeks, making her look suddenly young.

'Jamie's? You're truly Jamie's lassie?' She squeezed Brianna's hands hard between her own.

'My mother says so.'

Brianna felt the answering smile on her own face. Jenny's hands were cool, but Brianna felt a rush of warmth nonetheless, which spread through her hands and up into her chest. She caught the faint, spicy scent of baking in the folds of Jenny's gown, and something else, more earthy and pungent, that she thought must be the smell of sheep's wool.

'Does she, so?' Laoghaire had recovered both her voice and her self-possession. She stepped forward, eyes narrowed. 'Jamie Fraser's your father, aye? And just who might your mother be?'

Brianna stiffened.

'His wife,' she said. 'Who else?'

Laoghaire put back her head and laughed. It wasn't a nice laugh.

'Who else?' she said, mimicking. 'Who else indeed, lassie! And just which wife would that be, now?'

Brianna felt the blood drain from her own face, and her hands grow stiff in Jenny's as the flood of realization washed over her. You idiot, she thought. You stupid idiot. It was twenty years! Of course he would have married again. Of course. No matter how much he loved Mama.

On the heels of this thought was another, more terrible. *Did she find him? Oh, God, did she find him with a new wife, and he sent her away? Oh, God, where is she?*

She turned blindly, wanting to run, not knowing where to go, what to do, only feeling that she must get out of here at once, and find her mother.

'You'll be wanting to sit down, I expect, Cousin. Come into the parlor, aye?' Young Jamie's voice was firm in her ear, and his arm was around her, turning her, urging her down the hall and through one of the doors that opened off it.

She scarcely heard the babble of voices around her, the confusion of explanations and accusations that popped around her ears like strings of firecrackers. She glimpsed a small, neat man with a face like the White Rabbit, looking vastly surprised, and another man, much taller, who rose as she came into the parlor and came toward her, his weathered, homely face creased in concern.

It was the tall man who calmed the racket and brought everyone to order, extracting from the confused muddle of voices an explanation of her presence.

'Jamie's daughter?' He glanced at her with interest, but looked much less surprised than anyone else so far. 'What's your name, *a leannan?*'

'Brianna.' She was too upset to smile at him, but he didn't seem to mind.

'Brianna.' He eased himself down on a hassock, motioning her to a seat opposite, and she saw that he had a wooden leg that protruded stiffly to one side. He took her hand and smiled at her, the warm light in his soft brown eyes making her feel momentarily safer.

'I'm your Uncle Ian, lass. Welcome to ye.' Her own hand tightened on his involuntarily, clinging to the refuge he seemed to offer. He didn't flinch or draw back, just looked her over carefully, seeming amused by the way she was dressed.

'Been sleeping in the heather, have ye?' he said, seeing the dirt and plant stains on her clothes. 'You'll have come some way to find us, niece.'

'She *says* she's your niece,' Laoghaire said. Recovered from her shock, she peered over Ian's shoulder, her round face pinched with dislike. 'Belike she's only come to see what she can get.'

'I shouldna be callin' the kettle black, Laoghaire,' Ian said mildly. He twisted round to face her. 'Or was it not you and Hobart a half-hour past, tryin' to squeeze five hundred pounds from me?'

Her lips pressed tight together, deepening the lines that bracketed her mouth.

'That money's mine,' she snapped, 'and well ye know it! It was agreed to; you witnessed the paper.'

Ian sighed; evidently this wasn't the first he had heard of the matter today.

'I did,' he said patiently. 'And ye'll have your money – so soon as Jamie's able to send it. He's promised, and he's an honorable man. But –'

'Honorable, is it?' Laoghaire produced an unladylike snort. 'Is it honorable to commit bigamy, then? Desert his wife and children? Steal away my daughter and ruin her? Honorable!' She looked at Brianna, eyes bright and hard as fresh-rolled steel.

'I'll ask again, lass – what's your mother's name?'

Brianna simply stared at her, overwhelmed. The stock around her throat was choking her, and her hands felt icy, despite Ian's grasp.

647

'Your mother,' Laoghaire repeated, impatient. 'Who was she?'

'It doesna matter who –' Jenny began, but Laoghaire rounded on her, face flushed with fury.

'Oh, it matters! If he got her on some army whore, or some slut of a maidservant when he was in England – that's one thing. But if she's –'

'Laoghaire!'

'Sister!'

'Ye foul-tongued besom!'

Brianna put a stop to the outcry simply by standing up. She was as tall as any of the men, and towered over the women. Laoghaire took one quick step back. Every face in the room was turned to her, marked with hostility, sympathy, or merely curiosity.

With a coolness that she didn't feel, Brianna reached for the inner pocket of her coat, the secret pocket she had sewed into the seam only a week before. It seemed like a century.

'My mother's name is Claire,' she said, and dropped the necklace on the table.

There was utter silence in the room, save for the soft hissing of the peat fire, burning low on the hearth. The pearl necklace lay gleaming, the spring sun from the window picking out the gold pierced-work roundels like sparks.

It was Jenny who spoke first. Moving like a sleepwalker, she reached out a slender finger and touched one of the pearls. Freshwater pearls, the kind called baroque because of their singular, irregular, unmistakable shapes.

'Oh, my,' Jenny said softly. She lifted her head and looked Brianna in the face, the slanted blue eyes shimmering with what looked like tears. 'I am so very glad to see ye – Niece.'

'Where is my mother? Do you know?' Brianna glanced from face to face, her heart beating heavily in her ears. Laoghaire was not looking at her; her gaze was fastened to the pearls, face gone cold and frozen.

Jenny and Ian exchanged a quick glance, then Ian stood up, moving awkwardly to bring his leg under him.

'She's with your da,' he said quietly, touching Brianna's arm. 'Dinna fash yourself, lassie; they're both safe.'

Brianna resisted the impulse to collapse with relief. Instead, she let out her breath very carefully, feeling the knot of anxiety loosen slowly in her belly.

'Thank you,' she said. She tried to smile at Ian, but her face felt slack and rubbery. *Safe. And together. Oh, thank you!* she thought, in wordless gratitude.

'Those are mine, by rights.' Laoghaire nodded at the pearls. She wasn't angry now, but coldly self-possessed. Without the distortions of fury, Brianna could see that she had once been very pretty, and was still a handsome woman – tall for a Scot, and graceful in her movements. She had the kind of delicate fair coloring that fades quickly, and had thickened through the middle, but her figure was still erect and firm, and her face still showed the pride of a woman who has known herself beautiful.

'That they're not!' said Jenny, with a quick flash of temper. 'They were my mother's jewels, that my father gave to Jamie for his wife, and –'

'And his wife I am,' Laoghaire interrupted. She looked at Brianna then, a cold, gauging look.

'I am his wife,' she repeated. 'I married him in good faith, and he promised me payment for the wrong he did me.' She turned her cold gaze on Jenny. 'It's been more than a year since I've seen a penny. Am I to sell my shoes to feed my daughter – the one he's left to me?'

She lifted her chin and looked at Brianna.

'If you're his daughter, then his debts are yours as well. Tell her, Hobart!'

Hobart looked mildly embarrassed.

'Ah, now, Sister,' he said, putting a hand on her arm in an attempt to be soothing. 'I dinna think –'

'No, ye don't, and haven't since ye were born!' She shook him off in irritation, and stretched out a hand toward the pearls. 'They're mine!'

It was pure reflex; the pearls were clutched tight in Brianna's hand before she had made the decision to snatch them. The gold roundels were cool against her skin, but the pearls were warm – the sign of a genuine pearl, her mother had told her.

'You wait just one minute here.' The strength and coldness of her own voice surprised her. 'I don't know who you are, and I don't know what happened between you and my father, but –'

'I am Laoghaire MacKenzie, and your bastard of a father married me four years ago – under false pretenses, I might add.' Laoghaire's anger had not disappeared but seemed to have submerged; her face had a tight, stretched look, but she was not shouting, and the red had faded from her soft, plump cheeks.

Brianna took a deep breath, striving for calmness.

'Yes? But if my mother is with my father now –'

'He left me.'

The words were spoken without heat, but they fell with the weight of stones in still water, spreading endless ripples of pain and betrayal. Young Jamie had been opening his mouth to speak; he shut it again, watching Laoghaire.

'He said that he could not bear it longer – to dwell in the same house with me, to share my bed.' She spoke calmly, as though reciting a piece she had learned by heart, her eyes still fixed on the empty spot where the pearls had rested.

'So he left. And then he came back – with the witch. Flaunted her in my face; bedded her under my nose.' Slowly, she raised her eyes to Brianna's, studying her with quiet intensity, searching out the mysteries of her face. Slowly, she nodded.

'It was she,' she said, with a certainty that was faintly eerie in its calmness. 'She cast her spells on him from the day she came to Leoch – and on me. She made me invisible. From the day she came, he could not see me.'

Brianna felt a small shiver run up her spine, despite the hissing peat fire on the hearth.

'And then she was gone. Dead, they said. Killed in the Rising. And him come home again from England, free at long last.' She shook her head very slightly; her eyes still rested on Brianna's face, but Brianna knew Laoghaire didn't see her any longer.

'But she wasna dead at all,' Laoghaire said softly. 'And he was not free. I knew that; I always knew that. Ye canna kill a witch with steel – they must burn.' Laoghaire's pale blue eyes turned to Jenny.

'You saw her – at my wedding. Her fetch standing there, between me and him. Ye saw her, but ye didna say. I only heard it later, when ye told Maisri the seer. You should ha' told me, then.' It was a not so much an accusation as a statement of fact.

Jenny's face had gone pale again, the slanted blue eyes dark with something – perhaps fear. She licked her lips and started to reply, but Laoghaire's attention had shifted to Ian.

'Ye'd best be wary, Ian Murray,' she said, her tone now matter-of-fact. She nodded toward Brianna. 'Look at her weel, man. Is a right woman made so? Taller than most men, dressed as a man, wi' hands as broad as a dinner plate, fit to choke the life from one o' your weans, should she choose.'

Ian didn't answer, though his long, homely face looked troubled. Young Jamie's fists clenched, though, and his jaw set tight. Laoghaire saw it, and a small smile touched the corners of her mouth.

'She is a witch's child,' she said. 'And ye know it, all of you!' She glanced around the room, challenging each uncomfortable face. 'They should have burned her mother in Cranesmuir, save for the lovespell she'd put on Jamie Fraser. Aye, I say be wary of what ye've brought into your house!'

Brianna brought the flat of her hand down on the table with a thump, startling everyone.

'Hogwash,' she said loudly. She could feel the blood rushing to her face, and didn't care. All the faces were gawking, mouths open, but she had no attention to spare for anyone but Laoghaire MacKenzie.

'Hogwash,' she said again, and pointed a finger at the woman. 'If they ought to be wary of anybody, it's you, you fucking murderess!'

Laoghaire's mouth was open wider than anyone's, but no sound came out.

'You didn't tell them *all* about Cranesmuir, did you? My mother should have, but she didn't. She thought you were

651

too young to know what you were doing. You weren't, though, were you?'

'What . . .?' said Jenny, in a faint voice.

Young Jamie looked wildly at his father, who stood as though poleaxed, staring at Brianna.

'She tried to kill my mother.' Brianna was having trouble controlling her voice; it cracked and trembled, but she got the words out. 'You did, didn't you? You told her Geillis Duncan was ill and calling for her – you knew she'd go, she always went to anybody sick, she's a doctor! You knew they were going to arrest Geilie Duncan for witchcraft, and if my mother was there, they'd take her, too! You thought they'd burn her, and then you could have him – have Jamie Fraser.'

Laoghaire was white to the lips, her face set like stone. Even her eyes had no life; they were blank and dull as marbles.

'I could feel her hand on him,' she whispered. 'In our bed. Lying there between us, wi' her hand on him, so he would stiffen and cry out to her in his sleep. She *was* a witch. I always knew.'

The room was silent, save for the hissing of the fire, and the tender singing of a small bird outside the window. Hobart MacKenzie stirred at last, coming forward to take his sister by the arm.

'Come away, *a leannan*,' he said quietly. 'I'll see ye safe home now.' He nodded to Ian, who returned the nod, with a small gesture that somehow conveyed both sympathy and regret.

Laoghaire allowed her brother to lead her away, unresisting, but at the door she stopped and turned back. Brianna stood still; she didn't think she could move if she tried.

'If you're Jamie Fraser's daughter,' Laoghaire said, in a cold clear voice, 'and ye may be, given your looks – know this. Your father is a liar and a whoremaster, a cheat and a pander. I wish ye well of each other.' She gave in then to Hobart's tugging at her sleeve, and the door swung to behind her.

The rage that had filled her drained suddenly away, and Brianna leaned forward, resting her weight on the palms of her hands, the necklace hard and lumpy under her hand. Her hair had come loose, and a thick strand fell over her face.

Her eyes were closed against the dizziness that threatened to engulf her; she felt, rather than saw, the hand that touched her and tenderly smoothed the locks back from her face.

'He went on loving her,' she whispered, as much to herself as to anyone else. 'He didn't forget her.'

'Of course he didna forget her.' She opened her eyes to see Ian's long face and kind brown eyes six inches away. A broad work-worn hand rested on hers, warm and hard, a hand even larger than her own.

'Neither did we,' he said.

'Will ye no have a bit more, Cousin Brianna?' Joan, Young Jamie's wife, smiled across the table, serving spoon poised invitingly above the crumbled remains of a gigantic gooseberry tart.

'Thank you, no. I couldn't eat another bite,' Brianna said, smiling back. 'I'm stuffed!'

This made Matthew and his little brother Henry giggle loudly, but a gimlet gleam from their grandmother's eye shut them up sharply. Looking round the table, though, Brianna could see suppressed laughter blooming on all the faces; from grown-ups to toddlers, they all seemed to find her slightest remark endlessly entertaining.

It was neither her unorthodox costume nor the sheer novelty of seeing a stranger, she thought – even one stranger than most. There was something else; some current of joy that ran among the members of the family; unseen but lively as electricity.

She realized only slowly what it was; a remark from Ian brought it into focus.

'We didna think that Jamie would ever have a bairn of his own.' Ian's smile across the table was warm enough to melt ice. 'You'll never have seen him, though?'

She shook her head, swallowing the remains of the last bite, smiling back in spite of her full mouth. That was it, she thought; they were delighted with her not so much for her sake, but for Jamie's. They loved him, and they were happy not for themselves but for him.

That realization brought tears to her eyes. Laoghaire's accusations had shaken her, wild as they were, and it was a great comfort to realize that to all of these people who knew him well, Jamie Fraser was neither a liar nor a wicked man; he was indeed the man her mother thought him.

Mistaking her emotion for choking, Young Jamie pounded her helpfully on the back, making her choke in good earnest.

'Will ye have written Uncle Jamie, then, to say as ye were coming to us?' he asked, ignoring her coughing and red-faced spluttering.

'No,' she said hoarsely. 'I don't know where he is.'

Jenny's gull-winged brows went up.

'Aye, ye said that; I'd forgotten.'

'Do you know where he is now? He and my mother?' Brianna bent forward anxiously, brushing pastry crumbs from her jabot.

Jenny smiled and rose from the table.

'Aye, I do – more or less. If ye've eaten your fill, d'ye come with me, lassie. I'll fetch his last letter for ye.'

Brianna rose to follow Jenny, but stopped abruptly near the door. She had vaguely noticed some paintings on the walls of the parlor earlier, but hadn't really looked at them, in the rush of emotion and event. She looked at this one, though.

Two little boys with red-gold hair, stiffly solemn in kilts and jackets, white shirts with frills showing bright against the dark coat of a huge dog that sat beside them, tongue lolling in patient boredom.

The older boy was tall and fine-featured; he sat straight and proud, chin lifted, one hand resting on the dog's head, the other protectively on the shoulder of the small brother who stood between his knees.

It was the younger boy Brianna stared at, though. His face was round and snub-nosed, cheeks translucent and ruddy as apples. Wide blue eyes, slightly slanted, looked out under a bell of bright hair combed into an unnatural tidiness. The pose was formal, done in classic eighteenth-century style, but there was something in the robust, stocky little figure that made her smile and reach a finger to touch his face.

'Aren't you a sweetie,' she said softly.

'Jamie was a sweet laddie, but a stubborn wee fiend, forbye.' Jenny's voice by her ear startled her. 'Beat him or coax him, it made no difference; if he'd made up his mind, it stayed made up. Come wi' me; there's another picture you'll like to see, I think.'

The second portrait hung on the landing of the stairs, looking thoroughly out of place. From below she could see the ornate gilded frame, its heavy carving quite at odds with the solid, battered comfort of the house's other furnishings. It reminded her of pictures in museums; this homely setting seemed incongruous.

As she followed Jenny onto the landing the glare of light from the window disappeared, leaving the painting's surface flat and clear before her.

She gasped, and felt the hair rise on her forearms, under the linen of her shirt.

'It's remarkable, aye?' Jenny looked from the painting to Brianna and back again, her own features marked with something between pride and awe.

'Remarkable!' Brianna agreed, swallowing.

'Ye see why we kent ye at once,' her aunt went on, laying a loving hand against the carved frame.

'Yes. Yes, I can see that.'

'It will be my mother, aye? Your grandmother, Ellen MacKenzie.'

'Yes,' Brianna said. 'I know.' Dust motes stirred up by their footsteps whirled lazily through the afternoon light from the window. Brianna felt rather as though she was whirling with them, no longer anchored to reality.

Two hundred years from now, she had – I *will?* she thought wildly – stood in front of this portrait in the National Portrait Gallery, furiously denying the truth that it showed.

Ellen MacKenzie looked out at her now as she had then; long-necked and regal, slanted eyes showing a humor that did not quite touch the tender mouth. It wasn't a mirror image, by any means; Ellen's forehead was high, narrower than Brianna's, and the chin was round, not pointed, her whole face somewhat softer and less bold in its features.

But the resemblance was there, and pronounced enough to be startling; the wide cheekbones and lush red hair were the same. And around her neck was the string of pearls, gold roundels bright in the soft spring sun.

'Who painted it?' Brianna said at last, though she didn't need to hear the answer. The tag by the painting in the museum had given the artist as 'Unknown'. But having seen the portrait of the two little boys below, Brianna knew, all right. This picture was less skilled, an earlier effort – but the same hand had painted that hair and skin.

'My mother herself,' Jenny was saying, her voice filled with a wistful pride. 'She'd a great hand for drawing and painting. I often wished I had the gift.'

Brianna felt her fingers curl unconsciously, the illusion of the brush between them momentarily so vivid she could have sworn she felt smooth wood.

That's where, she thought, with a small shiver, and heard an almost audible *click!* of recognition as a tiny piece of her past dropped into place. *That's where I got it.*

Frank Randall had joked that he couldn't draw a straight line; Claire that she drew nothing else. But Brianna had the gift of line and curve, of light and shadow – and now she had the source of the gift, as well.

What else? she thought suddenly. What else did she have that had once belonged to the woman in the picture, to the boy with the stubborn tilt to his head?

'Ned Gowan brought me this from Leoch,' Jenny said, touching the frame with a certain reverence. 'He saved it, when the English battered down the castle, after the Rising.' She smiled faintly. 'He's a great one for family, Ned is. He's a Lowlander from Edinburgh, wi' no kin of his own, but he's taken the MacKenzies for his clan – even now the clan's no more.'

'No more?' Brianna blurted. 'They're all dead?' The horror in her voice made Jenny glance at her, surprised.

'Och, no. I didna mean that, lass. But Leoch's gone,' she added, in a softer tone. 'And the last chiefs with it – Colum and his brother Dougal . . . they died for the Stuarts.'

656

She had known that, of course; Claire had told her. What was surprising was the sudden rush of an unexpected grief; regret for these strangers of her newfound blood. With an effort, she swallowed the thickening in her throat and turned to follow Jenny up the stairs.

'Was Leoch a great castle?' she asked. Her aunt paused, hand on the banister.

'I dinna ken,' she said. Jenny glanced back at Ellen's picture, something like regret in her eyes.

'I never saw it – and now it's gone.'

Entering the bedroom on the second floor was like entering an undersea cavern. The room was small, as all the rooms were, with low beams smoked black from years of peat fires, but the walls were fresh and white, and the room itself was filled with a greenish, wavering light that spilled through two large windows, filtered by the leaves of the swaying rose brier.

Here and there some bright thing blinked or glowed like a reef fish in the soft gloom; a painted doll that lay on the hearthrug, abandoned by a grandchild, a Chinese basket with a pierced coin tied to its lid by way of ornament. A brass candlestick on the table, a small painting on the wall, rich colors deep against the whitewash.

Jenny went at once to the big armoire that stood at the side of the room, and stood on tiptoe to bring down a large morocco-covered box, its corners worn with age. As she put back the lid, Brianna caught the glint of metal and a small sharp flash, as of sunlight on jewels.

'Here it is.' Jenny brought out a thick, folded wad of grimy paper, much traveled and much read by the looks of it, and put it into Brianna's hand. It had been sealed; a smudge of greasy wax still clung to the end of one sheet.

'They're in the Colony of North Carolina, but they dinna live near any town,' Jenny explained. 'Jamie writes a bit in the evenings when he can, and keeps the bits all by him, till either he or Fergus takes the journey down to Cross Creek, or a traveler passes by who will carry the letter. That suits him; he doesna write easy – especially since he broke his hand that time ago.'

657

Brianna started at the casual reference, but her aunt's calm face showed no special awareness.

'Sit ye down, lassie.' She waved a hand, giving Brianna the choice of stool or bed.

'Thank you,' Brianna murmured, taking the stool. So perhaps Jenny didn't know everything about Jamie and Black Jack Randall? The notion that she might know things about this unseen man that not even his beloved sister knew was in a way unsettling. To dismiss the thought, she hurriedly opened the letter.

The scrawled words sprang out at her, black and vivid. She had seen this writing before – its cramped, difficult letters, with the big, looping tails, but that had been on a document two hundred years old, its ink brown and faded, its writing constrained by careful thought and formality. Here he had felt free – the writing rolled across the page in a bold broken scrawl, the lines tilting drunkenly up at the ends. It was untidy, but readable for all that.

Fraser's Ridge, Monday 19 September

My dearest Jenny,

All here are in Good Health and Spirits, and trust that this letter will find all in your Household likewise Content.

Your son sends his Most Affectionate Regards, and begs to be Remembered to his Father, Brothers and Sisters. He bids you tell Matthew and Henry that he sends them the Encloased Object, which is the preserved Skull of an animal called Porpentine by Reason of its Prodigious Spines (though it is not at all like the small Hedge-creepie which you will know by that name, being much Greater in Size and Dwelling in the Treetops, where it Feasts upon the tender shoots). Tell Matthew and Henry that I do not know why the Teeth are orange. No Doubt the animal finds it Decorative.

Also enclosed you will find a small Present for yourself; the Patterning is contrived by use of the Quills of this same Porpentine, which the Indians dye with the juices of several Plants, before weaving them in the Ingenious Manner you see before you.

Claire has been recently much Interested by Conversation – if the term can be used for a Communication limited mostly to

Gesticulations and the Making of Faces (she insists I note here that she does not *Make Faces, to which I reply that I am in Better Case to judge of the matter, being able to see the Face in question, which she is not) – in Conversation with an old woman of the Indians, much Esteemed in this area as a Healer, who has Given her many such plants. In consequence, her fingers are Purple at present, which I find Most Decorative.*

Tuesday, 20 Sept.
I have been much Occupied today in repair and strengthening of the penfold in which we keep our few cows, pigs, etc. at night, to protect them from the depredations of Bears, which are plentiful. In walking to the privy this morning, I espied a great Pawprint in the mud, which Measured quite the length of my own Foot. The stock appeared Nervous and disturbed, for which Condition I can scarce Blame them.

Do not, I pray you, suffer any Alarm on our account. The Black Bears of this country are wary of Humans, and Loath to approach even a Single Man. Also, our house is strongly built, and I have forbidden Ian to go Abroad after dark, save he is Well-armed.

In the matter of Armament, our situation is much Improved. Fergus has brought back from High Point both a fine Rifle of the new kind, and several excellent Knives.

Also a large boiling kettle, whose Acquisition we have Celebrated with a great quantity of tasty Stew, made with Venison, wild Onions from the wood, dried beans, and likewise some Tomatoe-fruits, dried from the Summer. None of us Died or suffered Ill-effects from Eating of this stew, so Claire is likely right, Tomatoes are not Poison.

Wednesday, 21 Sept.
The Bear has come again. I found large Prints and Scrapings on the new-turned ground of Claire's Garden today. The beast will be fattening for its Winter slumbers, and no doubt seeks to Digg for grubs in the fresh Earth.

I have Removed the Sow to our Pantry, since she is near Farrowing. Neither Claire nor the Sow was greatly pleased by this arrangement, but the Animal is valuable, having cost me three pound from Mr. Quillan.

Four Indians came today. They are of the kind called Tusca-

rora. I have met these men on several Occasions, and found them most Amiable.

The Savages having expressed a determination to hunt our particular Bear, I made them a Gift of some tobacco and a Knife, with which they seemed Pleas'd.

They sat under the eaves of the House most of the morning, Smoking and talking among themselves, but then near midday made to Depart upon their Hunt. I inquired whether, the Bear seeming Fond of our Society, it would not be best for the Hunters to lie hidden nearby, in Hopes that the animal will return here.

I was Informed – with the Kindest Condescension possible through word and sign – that the appearance of the Animal's droppings indicated beyond any Doubt that it had Quitted the area, and was Bound upon some errand to the west.

Being of no Mind to take issue with such Expert practitioners, I wished them luck and bade them a cordial Farewell. I could not accompany them, having urgent Labors still to perform here, but Ian and Rollo have gone with them, as they have done before.

I have loaded my new Rifle and left it ready to Hand, lest our friends' apprehension as to the Bear's intent be Mistaken.

Thursday, 22 Sept.

I was roused from Sleep last night by a Hideous Noise. This was a great Scraping, which reverberated thru the wooden logs of the wall, accompanied by such Thumps and loud Wails that I bolted from my Bed, convinced that the house was like to Fall about our Ears.

The Sow, observing the nearness of an Enemy, burst through the door of the Pantry (which I will say was flimsily made) and took Refuge beneath our Bed, squealing in a Manner to deafen us. Perceiving that the Bear was at Hand, I seiz'd my new Rifle and ran outside.

It was a moonlit Night, though hazy, and I could plainly see my Adversaray, a great black shape, which stretched upon its hind feet appeared near as Tall as Myself, and (to my anxious eyes) roughly three times as Wide, being at no Great Distance from me.

I fired at it, whereon it Dropped to all fours and Ran with amazing Speed toward the shelter of the nearby Wood, disappearing before I could make Shift to shoot any more.

Come Daylight, I searched the ground for sign of Blood and found none, so cannot say did my Shot find its Target. The side of the House is decorated with several long Scrapes, as might be made with a sharpened Adze or Chizl, showing white in the Wood.

We have since been at some Pains to persuade the Sow (she is a White Sow, of Prodigious Size, a most Stubborn Temper, and not lacking in Teeth) to quit our bed and repair to her Sanctuary in the pantry. She was Reluctant, but was at length persuaded by the Combination of a trail of shattered corn laid before her, and myself at her Rear, Armed with a Stout Broom.

Monday, 26th Sept.
Ian and his Red Companions have returned, their Prey having eluded them in the wood. I shewed them the Scratches upon the Side of the House, whereon they became Excited and talked among themselves at such a Rate I could not Follow their Words.

One man then detached a large tooth from his necklace of such items and presented it to me with great Ceremony, saying that it would serve to Identify me to the Bear-spirit, and thus protect me from Harm. I accepted this Token with all due Solemnity, and was then oblig'd to present him with a piece of Honeycomb in Exchange, thus the proprieties were observ'd.

Claire was called to provide the Honeycomb, and with her usual eye for such Matters, perceived that one of our guests was Unwell, being heavy-eyed, coughing, and distracted in Appearance. Claire says he is also Flushed with fever, though this is not obvious to look at him. He being too ill to continue with his Companions, we have laid him on a pallet in the corncrib.

The sow has Most Incontinently farrowed in the pantry. There are a dozen piglets, all healthy and of a Vigorous Appetite, for which God be thanked. Our own Appetites bid fair to be impoverished for the present, as the Sow viciously Attacks anyone who opens the door of the Pantry, roaring and gnashing her Teeth in Rage. I was given one egg to my supper, and informed that I shall get no more until I have Contriv'd a solution to this Difficulty.

Saturday, 1 October
A great Surprise today. Two Guests have come . . .

'It will be a wild place.'

Brianna looked up, startled. Jenny nodded at the letter, her eyes fixed on Brianna.

'Savages and bears and porpentines and such. It's no much more than a wee cot, where they live, Jamie told me. And all alone, up in the high mountains. Verra wild, it will be.' She looked at Brianna a little anxiously. 'But ye'll still wish to go?'

Brianna realized suddenly that Jenny was afraid she would not; that she would be frightened by the thought of the long journey and the savage place at the end of it. A savage place rendered suddenly real by the scrawled black words on the sheet she held – but not nearly as real as the man who had written them.

'I'm going,' she assured her aunt. 'As soon as I can.'

Jenny's face relaxed.

'Oh, good,' she said. She held out her hand, showing Brianna a small leather pouch decorated with a panel made of porcupine's quills, stained in shades of red and black, with here and there a few quills left in their natural grayish color for contrast.

'This is the present he sent me.'

Brianna took it, admiring the intricacy of the pattern, and the softness of the pale deer's hide.

'It's beautiful.'

'Aye, it is.' Jenny turned away, busying herself with unnecessary tidying of the small ornaments that stood on the bookshelf. Brianna had just turned her attention back to the letter when Jenny spoke abruptly.

'Will ye stay a bit?'

Brianna looked up, startled.

'Stay?'

'Only for a day or two.' Jenny turned around, the light from the window halo-bright behind her, shadowing her face.

'I ken ye'll wish to be gone,' she said. 'I should wish so much to talk wi' ye for a bit, though.'

Brianna looked at her, puzzled, but could read nothing

662

in the pale, even features and the slanted eyes so like her own.

'Yes,' she said slowly. 'Of course I'll stay.'

A smile touched the corner of Jenny's mouth. Her hair was deep black, streaked with white like a magpie.

'That's good,' she said softly. The smile spread slowly as she looked at her niece.

'Dear Lord, you're like my brother!'

Left alone, Brianna returned to the letter, re-reading the beginning slowly, letting the quiet room around her fade, disappearing as Jamie Fraser came to life in her hands, his voice so vivid in her inner ear that he might have stood before her, the sun from the window glinting on his red hair.

Saturday, 1 October

A great Surprise today. Two Guests have come from Cross Creek. You will recall, I think, my Telling you of Lord John Grey, whom I knew in Ardsmuir. I have not said that I had seen him since, in Jamaica, where he was Governor for the Crown.

He is perhaps the last Person one should expect to find in this Remote Place, so far Removed from all Traces of Civilization, let alone those Luxurious Offices and Trappings of Pomp to which he is Accustomed. Surely we were Most Astonish'd by his appearing at our door, though we at once made him Welcome.

It is a melancholy Event that has led him here, I am Sorry to say. His wife, embarked from England with her son, contracted a Fever on the voyage, and Died of it while on the Ocean. Fearing lest the Miasmas of the Tropics prove as Fatal to the Boy as to his Mother, Lord John determined that the lad must go to Virginia, where Lord John's family has Substantial Property, and Determined to escort him there himself, seeing that the Lad was greatly Desolated by loss of his Mother.

I Expressed Amazement, as well as Gratification, that they should chuse to make such Alteration in their Journey as required to visit this Distant Spot, but his Lordship dismisses this, saying that he would have the Boy see something of the different Colonies, so as to appreciate the Richness and Variety of this Land. The lad is most Desirous of encountering Red Indians – reminding me in this Respect of Ian, not so long ago.

He is a comely lad, tall and Well-form'd for his Years, which I believe are near Twelve. He is somewhat subject still to Melancholy from his Mother's death, but is most Pleasant in Conversation, and Mannerly, for all he is an Earl (Lord John is his stepfather, I believe; his father having been Earl of Ellesmere). His name is William.

Brianna turned the page over, expecting continuation, but the passage stopped on that abrupt note. There was a break of several days before the letter resumed, on the 4th of October.

Tuesday, 4 October

The Indian in the corncrib died early this morning, in spite of Claire's best efforts to save him. His face, body and limbs were entirely suffused with a dreadful Rash, giving him a most Grewsome and Mottled look.

Claire thinks he suffered from the Measle, and is much Concerned, this being a Vicious Disease, plaguish and quick to Spread. She would not suffer anyone to go near the Body save only herself – she says she is Safe from it, by means of some charm – but we did all Assemble near Midday, whereat I read some Scripture suitable to the Occasion, and we said a Prayer for the Repose of his soul – for I trust that even unbaptised Savages may find rest in God's Mercy.

We are in some doubt how this poor soul's Earthly Remains shall be Disposed. I would in common course send Ian to summon his Friends, that they might give him such Burial as is common among the Indians.

Claire says we must not do this, however, for the Corpse itself may Spread the Disease among the man's own People a Disaster which he would not Chuse to bring upon his Friends. She advocates burying or Burning the Corpse ourselves, and yet I am reluctant to undertake such Action, which might be easily Misunderstood by the man's Companions – they thinking that we Sought by this means to hide some Complicity in his Death.

I have said nothing of this Concern to our Guests. If Danger seems Imminent, I must send them away. Still, I am loathe to Part with their society, so isolated is our situation. For now, we have Laid the Body in a small Dry Cave in the hill above the House, wherein I had thought to build a Stable or Storehouse.

I ask your forgiveness for thus Unburdening my Mind at the cost of your own Peace. I think all will be Well in the end, but for the Moment, I confess to some Worry. Should Danger – either from Indians or Disease – seem to threaten, I will send this Letter at once in the care of our Guests, that it may be Certain of reaching you.

If all is Well, I will write quickly to tell you.

Your Most Loving Brother,
    Jamie Fraser

Brianna's mouth felt dry and she swallowed, forcing saliva. There were two sheets yet to the letter; they clung together for a moment, stubbornly resisting her efforts to separate them, and then gave way.

Postscriptum, 20 October
    We are all Safe, though the Manner of our Deliverance is most Melancholy; I will tell you of it later, having no great Heart for the matter at present.

Ian has been Sick of the Measle, as has Lord John, but they are both Recovered, and Claire bids me say that Ian does Exceeding well, you shall have no Fear for him. He writes in his own Hand, that you may know it is the Truth.

–J.

On the last sheet was writing in a different hand, this one neat and carefully schooled to an even slant, though here and there a blot defaced the page, perhaps the result either of the writer's illness or a defective pen.

Dear Mam –
    I have been Sick, but am all Right agayne. I had a Fever, with most Peculiar Dreams, full of odd things. There was a great Wolf that came and spoke to me in the Voice of a man, but Auntie Claire says this must have been Rollo, who Stayed by me all the time I was Ill, he is a very Good Dog and does not bite very often.

The Measles came out in small Bumps beneath my Skin, and

itched like Fury. I should have thought I had sat down on an Anthill, or wandered into a Hornet's nest. My head felt twice its usual Size, and I sneezd quite Ferocious.

I had three Eggs to my Breakfast today, and porridge, and have Walked to the privy alone twice, so I am quite Well, though I thought at first the Sickness had left me Blind – I could see nothing but a great Dazzle of Light when I went outside, but Auntie said this would soon be remedied, and it was.

I will write more later – Fergus is waiting to take the Letter away.

Your most Obedient and Devoted Son,
    Ian Murray

P.S. The Porpentine skull is for Henry and Mattie, I hope they will like it.

Brianna sat on the stool for some time, the whitewashed wall cool at her back, smoothing the pages of the letter and staring absently at the bookcase, with its neat row of cloth and leather bindings. *Robinson Crusoe* popped out at her, the title picked out in gold on the spine.

A savage place, Jenny had said. A dangerous place, too, where life could shift within a heartbeat from the humorous difficulty of a hog in the pantry to the instant threat of death by violence.

'And I thought *this* was primitive,' she murmured, with a glance at the peat fire on the hearth.

Not so primitive after all, she thought as she followed Ian through the barnyard and out past the outbuildings. Everything was well kept and tidy; the drystone walls and buildings all in good repair, if a little shabby. The chickens were carefully confined to their own yard, and a hovering cloud of flies behind the barn announced the presence of a discreet manure pit, well away from the house.

The only real difference between this farmyard and modern ones she had seen was the absence of rusting farm equipment; there was a shovel resting against the barn, and two or three battered plowshares in a shed that they passed, but no ramshackle tractor, no tangles of wire and scattered metal scraps.

The animals were healthy, too, if somewhat smaller than their modern counterparts. A loud 'Baaah!' announced the presence of a small herd of fat sheep in a paddock on the hillside, who trotted eagerly up to the fence as they passed, woolly backs wobbling and yellow eyes agleam in anticipation.

'Spoilt bastards,' Ian said, but with a smile. 'Think anyone's come up here has come to feed ye, don't you? My wife's,' he added, turning to Brianna. 'She gives them all the cast-off truck from the kailyard, till ye'd think they'd burst.'

The ram, a majestic creature with great coiled horns, extended his head over the fence and emitted an imperious '*Beheheh!*' that was immediately echoed by his faithful flock.

'Bugger off, Hughie,' said Ian, with tolerant scorn. 'You're no mutton yet, but the day'll come, aye?' He waved dismissively at the ram and turned up the hill, kilt swinging.

Brianna hung back a step, watching his stride in fascination. Ian wore his kilt with an air quite unlike anything she was used to; not a costume nor a uniform – with a conscious bearing, but more as though it were part of his body than an article of clothing.

In spite of that, she knew it wasn't usual for him to wear it; Jenny's eyes had opened wide when he had come down to breakfast; then she had bent her head, burying a smile in her cup. Young Jamie had flicked a dark brow at his father, got back a bland look, and settled to his sausage with a faint shrug, and one of those small subterranean noises common to Scottish males.

The plaid cloth was old – she could see the fading along the creases and the wornness at the hem – but carefully kept. It would have been hidden away after Culloden, along with the pistols and the swords, with the pipes and their pibrochs – all the symbols of pride conquered.

No, not quite conquered, she thought, with a queer small tug at her heart. She remembered Roger Wakefield, squatting beside her under a gray sky on the battlefield at Culloden, his face lean and dark, eyes shadowed with knowledge of the dead nearby.

'Scots have long memories,' he'd said, 'and they're not the most forgiving of people. There's a clan stone out there with the name of MacKenzie carved on it, and a good many of my relatives under it.' He had smiled then, but not in jest. 'I don't feel quite so personal about it as some, but I haven't forgotten either.'

No, not conquered. Not through a thousand years of strife and treachery, and not now. Defeated, scattered, but still surviving. Like Ian, maimed but upright. Like her father, exiled but still a Highlander.

With an effort she put Roger from her mind, and hurried to keep up with Ian's long, limping stride.

His lean face had lighted with pleasure when she had asked him to show her Lallybroch. It had been arranged that Young Jamie would take her to Inverness in a week's time, to see her safely aboard a ship to the Colonies, and she meant to use her time here to good advantage.

They walked – at a good pace, despite Ian's leg – over the fields toward the small foothills that rimmed the valley to the north, rising toward the pass through the black crags. It was a beautiful place, she thought. The pale green fields of oats and barley rippled with shifting light, cloud-shadows scudding through the spring sunshine, driven by the breeze that bent the stems of budding grass.

One field lay in long, dark ridges, the dirt humped and bare. At the side of the field stood a large heap of rough stones, neatly stacked.

'Is that a cairn?' she asked Ian, voice lowered in respect. Cairns were the memorials of the dead, her mother had told her – sometimes the very long dead – new rocks added to the heap by each passing visitor.

He glanced at her in surprise, caught the direction of her gaze, and grinned.

'Ah, no, lass. Those are the stones we turned up wi' the plow in the spring. Every year we take them out, and every year there come new ones. Damned if I ken where they come from,' he added, shaking his head in resignation. 'Stone fairies come and sow them in the night, I expect.'

She didn't know whether this was a joke or not. Uncertain whether to laugh, she asked a question instead.

'What will you plant here?'

'Oh, it's planted already.' Ian shaded his eyes, squinting across the long field with pride. 'This is the tattie field. The new vines will be up by the end of the month.'

'Tattie – oh, potatoes!' She looked at the field with new interest. 'Mama told me about that.'

'Aye, it was Claire's notion – and a good one, too. There's more than once the tatties have kept us from starving.' He smiled briefly but said nothing more, and moved off, heading for the wild hills beyond the fields.

It was a long walk. The day was breezy, but warm, and Brianna was sweating by the time they paused at last, halfway up a rough track through the heather. The narrow path seemed to perch precariously between a steep hillside and an even steeper fall down a sheer rock face into a small, splashing burn.

Ian stopped, wiping his brow with his sleeve, and motioned her to a seat amid the heaps of granite boulders. From this vantage point, the valley lay below them, the farmhouse seeming small and incongruous, its fields a feeble intrusion of civilization on the surrounding wilderness of crag and heather.

He brought out a stone bottle from the sack he carried, and drew the cork with his teeth.

'That'll be your mother's doing, too,' he said with a grin, handing her the bottle. 'That I've kept my teeth, I mean.' He passed the tip of his tongue meditatively over his front teeth, shaking his head.

'A great one for eatin' weeds, your mother, but who's to argue, eh? Half the men my age are eatin' naught but porridge now.'

'She was always telling me to eat up my vegetables, when I was little. And brush after every meal.' Brianna took the bottle from him and tilted it into her mouth; the ale was strong and bitter, but welcomely cool after the long walk.

'When ye were little, eh?' Amused, Ian cast an eye over her length. 'I've seldom seen a lass sae braw. I'd say your mother kent her business, aye?'

She smiled back and gave him back the bottle.

'She knew enough to marry a tall man, at least,' she said wryly.

Ian laughed and wiped the back of his hand across his mouth. He gazed affectionately at her, brown eyes warm.

'Ah, it's fine to see ye, lassie. You're verra much like him, it's true. Christ, what I wouldna give to be there when Jamie sees you!'

She looked down at the ground, biting her lip. The ground was thick with bracken, and their path up the hill showed plain, where the green fronds that had overgrown the track had been crushed and knocked aside.

'I don't know whether he knows or not,' she blurted. 'About me.' She glanced up at him. 'He didn't tell you.'

Ian rocked back a little, frowning.

'No, that's true,' he said slowly. 'But I am thinking he maybe hadna time to say, even if he knew. He'll not have been here long, that last time he came, with Claire. And then, it was such a moil, wi' all that happened –' He stopped, pursing his lips, and glanced at her.

'Your auntie's been troubled about that,' he said. 'Thinking that ye might blame her.'

'Blame her for what?' She stared at him, puzzled.

'For Laoghaire.' The brown eyes held hers, intent.

A faint chill came over Brianna at the memory of those pale eyes, cold as marbles, and the woman's hateful words. She had dismissed them as simple malice, but the echoes of 'whoremaster' and 'cheat' lingered unpleasantly in her ear.

'What did Aunt Jenny have to do with Laoghaire?'

Ian sighed, brushing back a thick lock of brown hair that fell down across his face.

'It was her doing that Jamie married the woman. She meant it well, mind,' he said warningly. 'We did think Claire was dead these many years.'

His tone held a question, but Brianna merely nodded, looking down and smoothing the fabric across her knee. This was dangerous ground; better to say nothing, if she could. After a moment, Ian went on.

'It was after he'd come home from England – he was a prisoner there for some years after the Rising –'

'I know.'

Ian's brows shot up in surprise, but he said nothing; simply shook his head.

'Aye, well. When he came back, he was – different. Well, he would be, aye?' He smiled briefly, then dropped his eyes, pleating the fabric of his kilt between his fingers.

'It was like talking to a ghost,' he said quietly. 'He would look at me, and smile, and answer – but he wasna really there.' He took a deep breath, and she could see the lines between his brows, carved deep in concentration.

'Before – after Culloden – it was different, then. He was sair wounded – and he'd lost Claire –' He glanced briefly at her, but she kept still, and he went on.

'But it was a desperate time then. A great many folk died; of the fighting, of sickness or of starving. There were English soldiers in the country, burning, killing. When it's like that, ye canna even think of dying, only because the struggle to live and keep your family takes all your time.'

A small smile touched Ian's lips, the rue of memory oddly lightened with a private amusement.

'Jamie hid,' he said, with an abrupt gesture toward the hillside above them. 'There. There's a wee cave behind that big gorse bush, halfway up. It's what I brought ye here to show ye.'

She looked where he pointed, up the tangled slope of rock and heather, the hillside a riot of tiny flowers. There was no sign of a cave, but the gorse bush stood out in a blaze of yellow blossom, brilliant as a torch.

'I came up to bring him food once, when he was sick of the ague. I told him he must come down to the house wi' me; that Jenny was scairt he'd die up here, all alone. He opened one eye, all bright with the fever, and his voice was sae hoarse I could scarcely hear him. He said Jenny needna be worrit; even though everything in the world seemed set on killin' him, he didna mean to make it easy for them. Then he closed his eye and went to sleep.'

Ian gave her a wry glance. 'I wasna so sure he had that much to say about whether he was going to die or no, so I stayed with him through the night. But he was right, after all, he's verra stubborn, ye ken?' His tone held a note of a mild apology.

Brianna nodded, but her throat felt too tight to speak.

Instead she stood up abruptly, and headed up the hill. Ian made no protest, but stayed on his rock, watching her.

It was a steep climb, and small thorny plants caught at her stockings. Near the cave, she had to scramble upward on all fours, to keep her balance on the steep granite slope.

The cave mouth was little more than a crack in the rock, the opening widening into a small triangle at the bottom. She knelt down and thrust her head and shoulders inside.

The chill was immediate, she could feel dampness condense on her cheeks. It took a moment for her sight to adapt to the dark, but enough light trickled into the cave past her shoulders for her to see.

It was perhaps eight feet long and six feet wide, a dim, dirt-floored cavity, with a ceiling so low that one could stand upright only near the entrance. To stay inside for any length of time would be like being entombed.

She pulled her head out quickly, breathing in deep-gulps of the fresh spring air. Her heart was beating heavily.

Seven years! Seven years to have lived here, in cold grime and gnawing hunger. *I wouldn't last seven days,* she thought.

Wouldn't you? said another part of her mind. And then it came again, that tiny click of recognition that she had felt when she had looked at Ellen's portrait, and felt her fingers close on an invisible brush.

She turned around slowly and sat down, the cave behind her. It was very quiet here on the mountainside, but quiet in the way of hills and forests, a quiet that was not silent at all, but composed of constant tiny sounds.

There were small buzzings in the gorse bush nearby, of bees working the yellow flowers, dusty with pollen. Far below was the rushing of the burn, a low note echoing the rush of the wind above, stirring leaves and rattling twigs, sighing past the jutting boulders.

She sat still, and listened, and thought she knew what Jamie Fraser had found here.

Not loneliness, but solitude. Not suffering, but endurance, the discovery of grim kinship with the rocks and sky. And the finding here of a harsh peace that would transcend bodily discomfort, a healing instead of the wounds of the soul.

He had perhaps found the cave not a tomb, but a refuge; drawn strength from its rocks, like Antaeus thrown to earth. For this place was part of him, who had been born here, as it was part of her, who had never seen it before.

Ian was still sitting patiently below; hands clasped about his knees, looking out over the valley. She reached up and carefully broke off a bit of the gorse bush, mindful of its spines. She laid it at the entrance of the cave, weighted with a small stone, then stood and made her way precariously down the hill.

Ian must have heard her approach, but didn't turn around. She sat down beside him.

'It's safe for you to wear that, now?' she said abruptly, with a nod at his kilt.

'Oh, aye,' he said. He glanced down, his fingers rubbing the soft, worn wool. 'It's been some years now since the soldiers last came. After all, what's left?' He gestured over the valley below.

'They carried away all they could find of value. Ruined what they couldna carry. There's no much left, save the land, is there? And I think they hadna much interest in that.' She could see he was disturbed in some way; his wasn't a face that hid its owner's feelings.

She watched him for a moment, then said quietly, 'You're still here. You and Jenny.'

His hand stilled, and lay against the plaid. His eyelids were closed, his homely, weathered face raised to the sun.

'Aye, that's true,' he said at last. He opened his eyes again, and turned to look at her. 'And so are you. We talked a bit last night, your auntie and I. When ye see Jamie, and all's well between ye – then ask him, if ye will, what would he have us do.'

'Do? About what?'

'About Lallybroch.' He waved, taking in the valley and the house below. He turned to her, eyes troubled.

'You'll maybe know – maybe not – that your father made a deed of sassine before Culloden, to give over the place to Young Jamie, should it all come to smash and he be killed or condemned as a traitor. But that would be before you were born; before he kent that he'd have a bairn of his own.'

'Yes, I did know that.' She had a sudden awareness of what he was leading up to, and put her hand on his arm, startling him with the touch.

'I didn't come for that, Uncle,' she said softly. 'Lallybroch isn't mine – and I don't want it. All I want is to see my father – and my mother.'

Ian's long face relaxed, and he put his hand over hers where it lay on his arm. He didn't say anything for a moment; then squeezed her hand gently and let it go.

'Aye, well. You'll tell him, nonetheless; if he wishes it –'

'He won't,' she interrupted firmly.

Ian looked at her, a faint smile at the back of his eyes.

'Ye ken a lot about what he'll do, for a lass that's never met him.'

She smiled at him, the spring sun warm on her shoulders.

'Maybe I do.'

The smile broke through to Ian's face.

'Aye, your mother will ha' told ye, I suppose. And she did know him, for all she was a Sassenach. But then, she was always . . . special, your mother.'

'Yes.' She hesitated for a moment, wanting to hear more about the topic of Laoghaire, but unsure how to ask. Before she could think of something, he stood, brushed down his kilt, and started down the track, forcing her to rise and follow.

'What's a fetch, Uncle Ian?' she asked the back of his head. Preoccupied with the difficulties of descent, he didn't turn, but she saw him lurch slightly, wooden leg sinking into the loose earth. At the bottom of the hill he waited for her, leaning on his stick.

'You'll be thinking of what Laoghaire said?' he asked. Without waiting for her nod, he turned and began making his way along the bottom of the hill, toward the small stream that flowed down through the rocks.

'A fetch is the sight of a person, when the person himself is far awa',' he said. 'Sometimes it will be a

674

person that's died, far from home. It's ill luck to see one, but worse luck to meet your own – for if you do, ye die.'

It was the absolute matter-of-factness of his tone that made a shiver run down her spine.

'I hope I don't,' she said. 'But she said – Laoghaire –' She stumbled on the name.

'L'heery,' Ian corrected. 'Aye, well. It was at her wedding to Jamie that Jenny saw your mother's fetch, that's true. She kent then that it was a bad match, but it was too late to be undone.'

He knelt awkwardly on his good knee, and splashed water from the burn over his face. Brianna did likewise, and gulped several handfuls of the cold, peaty-tasting water. Having no towel, she pulled her long shirttail from her breeks and wiped her face. She caught Ian's scandal-ized look at the glimpse of her bare stomach thus afforded, and dropped the shirttail abruptly, her cheeks flushing.

'You were going to tell me why my father married her,' she said, to hide her embarrassment.

Ian's cheeks had gone a dull red, and he turned hastily away, talking to cover his confusion.

'Aye. It was as I told ye – when Jamie came from England, it was like the spark had gone out o' him, and there was nothing here to kindle it again. I dinna ken what it was that happened in England, but something did, sure as I'm born.'

He shrugged, the back of his neck fading to its normal sunburnt brown.

'After Culloden, he was bad hurt, but there was fighting still to do, of a kind, and that kept him alive. When he came home from England – there wasna anything here for him, really.' He spoke quietly, eyes cast down, watching his footing on the rocky ground.

'So Jenny made the match for him, with Laoghaire.' He glanced at her, eyes bright and shrewd.

'You'll maybe be old enough to know, for all you're unwed yet. What a woman can do for a man – or he for her, I suppose. To heal him, I mean. Fill his emptiness.' He touched his maimed leg absently. 'Jamie wed

675

Laoghaire from pity, I think – and if she had truly needed him – aye, well.' He shrugged again, and smiled at her.

'It's no use to say what might have been or should be, is it? But he had left Laoghaire's house some time before your mother came back, you should know that.'

Brianna felt a small surge of relief.

'Oh. I'm glad to know that. And my mother – when she came back –'

'He was verra glad to see her,' Ian said simply. This time the smile lighted his whole face, like sunshine. 'So was I.'

35

Bon Voyage

It reminded her uncomfortably of Boston's city dog pound. A large, half-dark space whose rafters rang with yelping, and an atmosphere dense with animal smells. The big building on the market square in Inverness sheltered a great many enterprises – food vendors, cattle and swine brokers, assurance agents, ship-chandlers and Royal Navy recruiters, but it was the group of men, women and children bunched in one corner that lent most force to the illusion.

Here and there a man or a woman stood upright amid the group, chin out and shoulders set in a show of good health and spirit, putting themselves forward. But for the most part, the people who offered themselves for sale eyed the passersby warily, in darting glances whose expressions were fixed between hope and fear – much too reminiscent of the dogs in the animal shelter where her father had now and then taken her to adopt a pet.

There were several families, too, with children clinging to their mothers, or standing blank-faced beside their parents. She tried not to look at them; it was always the puppies that had broken her heart.

Young Jamie was sidling slowly around the group, hat held against his chest to save it being crushed by the crowd, eyes half closed as he considered the prospects on offer. Her uncle Ian had gone to the shipping office to arrange her passage to America, leaving her cousin Jamie to choose a servant to accompany her on the journey. In vain had she protested that she didn't need a servant; after all, she had – so far as they knew – traveled from France to Scotland by herself, in perfect safety.

The men had nodded and smiled and listened with every evidence of polite attention – and here she was, obediently following Young Jamie through the crowd like one of her aunt Jenny's sheep. She was beginning to understand exactly what her mother had meant by describing the Frasers as 'stubborn as rocks'.

Despite the hubbub around her and her annoyance at her male relatives, her heart gave a small, excited bounce at thought of her mother. It was only now, when she knew for sure that Claire was safe, that she could admit to herself how sorely she had missed her. And her father – that unknown Highlander who had come so suddenly and vividly to life for her as she read his letters. The minor fact of an intervening ocean seemed no more than a small inconvenience.

Her cousin Jamie interrupted these rosy thoughts by taking her arm and leaning close to shout in her ear.

'Yon fellow wi' the cast in one eye,' he said in a subdued bellow, indicating the gentleman in question by pointing with his chin. 'What d'ye say to him, Brianna?'

'I'd say he looks like the Boston Strangler,' she muttered, then louder, shouting into her cousin's ear, 'He looks like an ox! No!'

'He's strong, and he looks honest!'

Brianna thought the gentleman in question looked too stupid to be *dis*honest, but refrained from saying so, merely shaking her head emphatically.

Young Jamie shrugged philosophically and resumed his scrutiny of the would-be bondsmen, walking around those who took his particular interest and peering at them closely, in a way she might have thought exceedingly rude had a number of other potential employers not been doing likewise.

'Bridies! Hot bridies!' A high-pitched screech cut through the rumble and racket of the hall, and Brianna turned to see an old woman elbowing her way robustly through the crowd, a steaming tray hung round her neck and a wooden spatula in hand.

The heavenly scent of fresh hot dough and spiced meat cut through the other pungencies in the hall, noticeable as the old woman's calling. It had been a long time since breakfast, and Brianna dug in her pocket, feeling saliva fill her mouth.

Ian had taken her purse to pay for her passage, but she had two or three loose coins; she held one up and waved it to and fro. The bridie seller spotted the flash of silver and at once altered course, tacking through the chattering mob. She hove to in front of Brianna and reached up to snatch the coin.

'Mary save us, a giantess!' she said, showing strong yellow teeth in a grin as she tilted her head back to look up at Brianna. 'Ye'd best take twa, my dearie. One will never do a great lass like you!'

Heads turned, and faces grinned up at her. She stood half a head higher than most of the men nearby. Mildly embarrassed by the attention, Brianna gave the nearest offender a cold look. This seemed to entertain the young man quite a lot; he staggered back against his friend, clutching his breast and pretending to be overcome.

'My God!' he said. 'She looked at me! I'm heartstruck!'

'Och, awa' wi' ye,' his friend scoffed, shoving him upright. ''Twas me she was looking at; who'd look at *you* if they'd a choice?'

'Nothing of the sort,' his friend protested stoutly. 'It was me – wasn't it, darlin'?' He languished, making calf's eyes at Brianna and looking so ridiculous that she laughed, along with the crowd around her.

'And what would ye be doing with her, if ye got her, eh? She'd make two of ye. Now, off wi' ye, spawn,' the bridie seller said, casually smacking the young haven't. And the young woman will starve if ye dinna leave off playin' the fool and let her buy her dinner, aye?'

'She looks in fine flesh to me, grannie.' Brianna's admirer, ignoring both assault and admonition, ogled her shamelessly. 'And as for the rest – fetch me a ladder, Bobby, I'm no afraid of heights!'

Amid gales of laughter, the young man was dragged away by his friends, making loud kissing noises over his shoulder as he moved reluctantly off. Brianna took her change in coppers and retired into a corner to eat two of the hot beef pasties, her face still warm with laughter and self-consciousness.

She hadn't been so aware of her height since she had been a gawky seventh-grader, towering over all her classmates. Among her tall cousins, she had felt at home, but it was true; here she stuck out like a sore thumb, despite her

679

having abided by Jenny's insistence and changed from her men's clothes to a dress of her cousin Janet's, hastily altered and let out in the seams.

Her sense of self-consciousness was not helped by the fact that no underclothes went with the dress, beyond a shift. No one seemed to find any lack in this state of affairs, but she was intensely conscious of the unaccustomed feeling of airiness about her nether parts, and the odd feeling of her naked thighs sliding past each other as she walked, her silk stockings gartered just above the knee.

Both self-consciousness and drafts were forgotten as she bit into the first hot pastry. A bridie was a plump hot pie in a half-moon shape, filled with minced steak and suet and spiced with onion. A rush of hot, rich juice and flaky pastry filled her mouth, and she closed her eyes in bliss.

'The food was either terribly bad or terribly good,' Claire had said, describing her adventures in the past. 'That's because there's no way of keeping things; anything you eat has either been salted or preserved in lard, if it isn't half rancid – or else it's fresh off the hoof or out of the garden, in which case it can be bloody marvelous.'

The bridie was bloody marvelous, Brianna decided, even if it did keep dropping crumbs down the top of her bodice. She brushed at her bosom, trying to be unobtrusive, but the crowd's attention had turned – no one was looking at her now.

Or almost no one. A slight, fair man in a shabby coat had materialized by her elbow, making small nervous movements as though he wanted to pluck her sleeve but hadn't quite got up the nerve. Not sure whether he was a beggar or another importunate suitor, she looked suspiciously down her nose at him.

'Yes?'

'You – you are requiring a servant, ma'am?'

She dropped her aloofness, realizing that he must be one of the crowd of indentures.

'Oh. Well, I wouldn't say I require one, exactly, but it looks as though I'm going to get one anyway.' She glanced at Young Jamie, who was now interrogating a squat, beetle-browed individual with shoulders like the Village Black-smith. Young Jamie's notion of the ideal servant seemed to

680

be limited to muscle. She looked back at the small man in front of her; he wasn't much by Young Jamie's standards, but by hers . . .

'Are you interested?' she asked.

The expression of haggard nervousness didn't leave his face, but a fugitive gleam of hope showed in his eyes.

'It – I – that is – not me, no. But will you think – perhaps consider – will you take my daughter?' he said abruptly. 'Please!'

'Your daughter?' Brianna looked down at him, startled, her half-eaten bridie forgotten.

'I beg you, ma'am!' To her surprise, tears stood in the man's eyes. 'Ye cannot think how urgently I pray you, or what gratitude I must bear ye!'

'But – ah –' Brianna brushed crumbs from the corner of her mouth, feeling desperately awkward.

'She is a strong girl in spite of her appearance, and most willing! She will be content to do any service whatever for ye, ma'am, and ye'll buy her contract!'

'But why should – look, what's the trouble?' she said, moved past awkwardness by curiosity and pity for his obvious distress. She took him by the arm and drew him into the shelter of a corner, where the racket was slightly diminished.

'Now, why are you so anxious that I should hire your daughter?'

She could see the muscles move in his throat as he swallowed convulsively.

'There is a man. He – he desires her. Not as a servant. As a – as a – concubine.' The words came out in a hoarse whisper, and a flood of ugly crimson stained his face.

'Mmphm,' said Brianna, discovering all at once the utility of this ambiguous expression. 'I see. But you needn't let your daughter go to him, surely?'

'I have no choice.' His agony was patent. 'Her contract has been bought by Mr. Ransom – the broker.' He jerked his head backward, indicating a tough-looking gentleman in a tie-wig, who was talking to Young Jamie. 'He can dispose of it to whom he will – and he will sell her without a moment's hesitation to this . . . this . . .' He choked, overcome by despair.

'Here, take this.' She hastily untucked the wide kerchief from her bodice, took it off her neck, and handed it to him. It left her slightly less than modest, but this seemed like an emergency.

Clearly it was, to him. He swabbed blindly at his face, then dropped the cloth and seized her free hand in both of his.

'He is a drover; he has gone to the cattle market to sell his beasts. When he has done so, he will return with the money for her contract, and take her away to his house in Aberdeen. When I heard him say so to Ransom, I was thrown into the most violent despair. I prayed most urgently to the Lord for her deliverance. And then –' He gulped.

'I saw you – so proud and noble and kind-seeming – and it did come to me as my prayers were answered. Oh, ma'am, I pray ye, do not disdain a father's plea. Take her!'

'But I'm going to America! You'd never –' She bit her lip. 'I mean, you wouldn't see her – for a very long time.'

The desperate father went quite white at this. He closed his eyes, and seemed to sway slightly, giving at the knees.

'The Colonies?' he whispered. Then he opened his eyes once more and set his jaw.

'Better she should be gone from me forever to a wild place, than to meet dishonor before my eyes.'

Brianna had no idea what to say to this. She glanced helplessly over the man's head at the sea of bobbing heads.

'Er . . . your daughter . . . which one . . .?'

The flicker of hope in his eyes sprang into sudden flame, shocking in its intensity.

'Bless ye, lady! I will fetch her to ye directly!'

He pressed her hand fervently, then darted away into the crowd, leaving her staring after him. After a moment, she shrugged helplessly, and bent to pick up her fallen kerchief. How had *this* happened? And what in the name of goodness would her uncle and her cousin say, if she –

'This is Elizabeth,' a voice announced breathlessly. 'Do your duty to the lady, Lizzie.'

Brianna looked down and found the decision made for her.

'Oh, dear,' she murmured, seeing the neat white parting down the middle of the small head that bent in a deep curtsy before her. 'A puppy.'

The head bobbed upright, presenting her with a thin, starved-looking face, in which scared gray eyes occupied most of the available space.

'Your servant, mum,' said the small, white-lipped mouth. Or at least that's what it looked like it said; the girl spoke so softly, she couldn't be heard above the surrounding racket.

'She will serve ye well, ma'am, aye, indeed she will!' The father's anxious voice was more audible. She glanced at him; there was a strong resemblance between father and daughter, both with the same flyaway fair hair, the same thin, anxious faces. They were nearly the same height, though the girl was so frail, she seemed like her father's shadow.

'Er . . . hello.' She smiled at the girl, trying to seem reassuring. The girl's head tilted fearfully back, looking up. She swallowed visibly, and licked her lips.

'Ah . . . how old are you, Lizzie? May I call you Lizzie?'

The small head bobbed on a neck that looked like a wild mushroom's stalk; long, colorless, and infinitely fragile. The girl whispered something that Brianna didn't catch; she looked at the father, who answered eagerly.

'Fourteen, ma'am. But she's a rare hand with cooking and sewing, clean in her person and ye'll never find a soul more biddable and willing!'

He stood behind his daughter, hands on her shoulders, gripped tight enough to show his knuckles white. His eyes met Brianna's. They were pale blue, pleading. His lips moved – without sound, but she heard him clearly.

'Please,' he said.

Beyond him, Brianna could see her uncle, who had come into the hall. He was talking to Young Jamie, smooth head and curly bent together in close conversation. In a moment they would be looking for her.

She took a deep breath and drew herself up to her full height. Well, and if you came right down to it, she thought, she was as much a Fraser as her cousin. Let them find out just how stubborn a rock could be.

She smiled at the girl and held out a hand, offering the second, uneaten bridie.

'It's a bargain, Lizzie. Will you have a bite to seal it?'

'She's eaten my food,' Brianna said, with as much assurance as she could conjure up. 'She's mine.'

Rather to her surprise, this statement finally put a stop to the argument. Her cousin looked as though he meant to go on remonstrating, but her uncle put a hand on Young Jamie's arm to silence him. The look of surprise on Ian's face turned to a sort of amused respect.

'Has she, now?' He looked at Lizzie, cowering behind Brianna, and his lips twitched. 'Mmphm. Well, then, not much more to be said, is there?'

Young Jamie evidently didn't share his father's assessment of this point; he could think of quite a lot more to be said.

'But a wee lassie like that – she's useless!' He waved a dismissive hand at Lizzie, frowning. 'Why, she isna big enough even to carry baggage, let alone –'

'I'm big enough to carry my own bags, thanks,' Brianna put in. She lowered her brows and gave her cousin back scowl for scowl, straightening up to emphasize her height.

He lifted an eyebrow in acknowledgment, but didn't give up.

'A woman shouldna be traveling alone –'

'I won't be alone, I'll have Lizzie.'

'– and certainly not to a place like America! Why, it's –'

'You'd think it was the ends of the earth to hear you talk, and you haven't even seen it!' Brianna said in exasperation. 'I was *born* in America, for heaven's sake!'

Uncle and cousin gaped at her, identical expressions of shock on their faces. She seized the opportunity to press her advantage.

'It's my money, and my servant, and my journey. I've given my word, and I'll keep it!'

Ian rubbed a knuckle across his upper lip, suppressing a grin. He shook his head.

'They say it's a wise bairn that kens its father, but I dinna

684

think there's much doubt who yours is, lass. Ye might have had the lang nebbit and red locks from anyone, but ye didna get the stubbornness from any man but Jamie Fraser.'

A self-conscious flush rose to her cheeks, but Brianna felt an odd flutter of something like pleasure.

His feathers ruffled from the argument. Young Jamie made one last attempt.

'It's verra unseemly for a woman to be givin' her opinions sae free, and her with menfolk to look after her,' he said stiffly.

'You don't think women ought to have opinions?' Brianna asked sweetly.

'No, I don't!'

Ian gave his son a long look.

'And you'll have been marrit what, eight years?' He shook his head. 'Aye, well, your Joan's a tactful woman.' Ignoring Young Jamie's black look, he turned back to Lizzie.

'Verra well, then. Go and take farewell of your father, lassie. I'll see to the papers.' He watched Lizzie scurry away, thin shoulders hunched against the crowd. He shook his head a little doubtfully, and turned back to Brianna.

'Well, she'll maybe be better company for ye than a manservant, lass, but your cousin's right about the one thing – she'll be no protection. It'll be you lookin' out for her, likely.'

Brianna straightened her shoulders and thrust out her chin, summoning up as much self-confidence as she could, in spite of the sudden hollow feeling that assailed her.

'I can manage,' she said.

She kept her hand curled tight, holding on to the stone in her palm. It was something to cling to, as the Moray Firth widened into the sea, and the cradling shore of Scotland fell away to either side.

Why ought she to feel so strongly for a place she hardly knew? Lizzie, born and raised in Scotland, had spared no glance for the receding land but had gone below at once, to lay claim to their space and arrange the few belongings they had brought aboard.

Brianna had never thought of herself as Scottish – had not *known* she was Scottish until quite recently – yet she had scarcely felt more bereft by her mother's leaving or her father's death than by this parting from people and places she had known for so short a time.

Perhaps it was only the contagious emotion of the other passengers. Many of them were standing at the rail as she was, several weeping openly. Or fear of the long journey ahead. But she knew quite well it was none of those things.

'That's that, I expect.' It was Lizzie, appearing at her elbow after all, to see the last sight of the land fade away. Her small pale face was expressionless, but Brianna didn't mistake lack of expression for lack of feeling.

'Yes, we're on our way.' Moved by impulse, Brianna put out a hand and drew the girl to stand in front of her at the rail, sheltered alike from freshening wind and from jostling passengers and seamen. Lizzie was a good foot shorter than Brianna, and fine-boned as the delicate sooty terns that circled the masts, squawking overhead.

The sun did not really set at this time of year but hung low above the dark hills, and the air had grown quite cold in the Firth. The girl was thinly dressed; she shivered, and pressed quite unselfconsciously against Brianna for warmth. Brianna had a blue woolen *arisaid* provided by Jenny; she wrapped her arms and the shawl ends around the younger girl, finding as much comfort in the embrace as she gave.

'It will be all right,' she said, to herself as much as to Lizzie.

The pale blond head bobbed briefly under her chin; she couldn't tell whether it was a nod, or only Lizzie's attempt to get the wind-whipped strands of hair out of her eyes. Elf-locks snatched from her own thick plait fluttered in the stiff salt breeze, echoing the pull of the huge sails above. Despite her misgivings, she felt her spirits start to rise with the wind. She had survived a good many partings so far; she would survive this. That was what made this leaving hard, she thought. She had already lost father, mother, lover, home, and friends. She was alone by

686

necessity, and also by choice. But then to find both home and family again so unexpectedly at Lallybroch had caught her unaware. She would have given almost anything to stay – just a little longer.

But there were promises to keep, losses to be made good. Then she could come back. To Scotland. And to Roger.

She shifted her arm, feeling his thin silver band warm on her wrist under the shawl, the metal heated by her own flesh. *Un peu ... beaucoup ...* Her other hand gripped the cloth together, exposed to the wind and damp with sea spray. If it hadn't been so cold, she might not have noticed the sudden warmth of the drop that fell on the back of her hand.

Lizzie stood stiff as a stick, her arms hugged tight around herself. Her ears were large and transparent, her hair fine and thin, sleek to her skull. Her ears poked out like a mouse's, tender and fragile in the soft deep light of the low night sun.

Brianna reached up and wiped away the tears by touch. Her own eyes were dry, and her mouth set firm as she looked out at the land over Lizzie's head, but the cold face and quivering lips against her hand might as well have been her own.

They stood for some time silently, until the last of the land was gone.

36

You Can't Go Home Again

Inverness, July 1769

Roger walked slowly through the town, looking around him with a mixture of fascination and delight. Inverness had changed a bit in two hundred-odd years, no doubt of it, and yet it was recognizably the same town; a good deal smaller, to be sure, with half its muddy streets unpaved, and yet he *knew* this street he was walking down, had walked down it a hundred times before.

It was Huntly Street, and while most of the small shops and buildings were unfamiliar, across the river stood the Old High Church – not so Old, now – its stubby steeple blunt as ever. Surely if he went inside, Mrs. Dunvegan, the minister's wife, would be setting out flowers in the chancel, ready for the Sunday service. But she wouldn't – Mrs. Dunvegan hadn't happened yet, with her thick wool sweaters and the terrible pot pies with which she tormented the sick of her husband's parish. Yet the small stone kirk stood solid and familiar, in the charge of a stranger.

His father's own church wasn't here; it had been – would be? – built in 1837. Likewise the manse, which had always seemed so elderly and decrepit, had not been built until the early 1900s. He had passed the site on his way; there was nothing there now save a tangle of cinquefoil and sweet broom, and a single small rowan sapling that sprouted from the underbrush, leaves fluttering in the light wind.

There was the same damp coolness to the air, tingling with freshness – but the overlying stink of motor exhaust was gone, replaced by a distant reek of sewage. The most striking absence was the churches; where both banks of the river would one day sport a noble profusion of steeples and spires, now there was nothing save a scatter of small buildings.

There was only the one stone footbridge, but the River Ness itself was naturally much the same. The river was low and the same gulls sat in the riffles, squawking companionably to one another as they picked small fish from among the stones just under the water's surface.

'Luck to you, mate,' he said to a fat gull who sat on the bridge, and crossed the river into the town.

Here and there, a gracious residence sat comfortably insulated by its wide grounds, a grand lady spreading her skirts, ignoring the presence of the hoi polloi nearby. There was Mountgerald in the distance, the big house looking precisely as he had always known it, save that the great copper beeches that would in future surround the house had not yet been planted; instead, a row of spindly Italian cypresses leaned dismally against the garden wall, looking homesick for their sunny birthplace.

For all its elegance, Mountgerald was reputed to have been built in the oldest of the old ways – with the foundation laid over the body of a human sacrifice. By report, a workman had been lured into the hole of the cellar, and a great stone dropped onto him from the top of the newly built wall, crushing him to death. He had – so local history said – been buried there in the cellar, his blood a propitiation to the hungry spirits of the earth, who thus satisfied, had allowed the edifice to stand prosperous and untroubled through the years.

The house could be no more than twenty or thirty years old now, Roger thought. There might easily be people in the town who had worked on its building; who knew exactly what had happened in that cellar, to whom, and why.

But he had other things to do; Mountgerald and its ghost would have to keep their secrets. With a mild pang of regret, he left the big house behind, and turned his scholar's nose into the road that led to the docks downriver.

With a feeling of what could only be called déjà vu, he pushed open the door of a pub. The half-timbered entry, with its stone flags, was as he had seen it a week before – and two hundred years hence – and the familiar smell of hops and yeast in the air was a comfort to his spirit. The name had changed, but not the smell of beer.

Roger took a deep gulp from his wooden cup and nearly choked. 'All right, man?' The barman paused, a bucket of sand in his hand, to peer at Roger.

'Fine,' Roger said hoarsely. 'Just fine.'

The barman nodded and went back to scattering sand, but kept a practiced eye on Roger in case he looked like vomiting on the freshly swept and sanded floor.

Roger coughed and cleared his throat, then essayed a further cautious sip. The flavor was fine; very good, in fact. It was the alcohol content that was unexpected; this stuff packed a wallop far greater than any modern beer Roger had ever encountered. Claire had said that alcoholism was endemic to the time, and Roger could easily see why. Still, if drunkenness were the greatest hazard he faced, he could deal with that.

He sat quietly by the hearth and drank, savoring the dark, bitter brew as he watched and listened.

It was a port pub, and a busy one. So near the docks on the Moray Firth, it hosted sea captains and merchants, as well as sailors from the ships in port and longshoremen and laborers from the nearby warehouses. A great deal of business of one kind and another was being transacted over the beer-stained surfaces of its many small tables.

With half an ear Roger could hear a contract being arranged for the shipping of three hundred bolts of cheap drugget cloth from Aberdeen, bound for the Colonies, with an exchange to be made for a cargo of rice and indigo from the Carolinas. A hundred head of Galloway cattle, six hundred-weight of rolled copper, casks of sulfur, molasses, and wine. Quantities and prices, delivery dates and conditions floated through the babble and beer fumes of the pub like the thick blue clouds of tobacco smoke that floated near the low ceiling-beams.

Not only goods were being bargained for. In one corner sat a ship's captain, marked by the cut of his long, full-skirted coat and the fine black tricorne that lay on the table by his elbow. He was attended by a clerk, a ledger and a money box on the table before him, interviewing a

690

steady stream of people, emigrants seeking passage to the Colonies for themselves and their families.

Roger watched the proceedings covertly. The ship was bound for Virginia, and after listening for some time he deduced that the cost of passage for a male passenger – for a gentleman, that is – was ten pounds, eight shillings. Those willing to travel in the steerage, packed like casks and cattle in the lower holds, might ship aboard for four pounds, two shillings each, bringing their own food for a six-weeks voyage. Fresh water, he gathered, was provided.

For those desiring passage but lacking funds, there were other means available.

'Indenturement for yourself, your wife, and your two elder sons?' The captain tilted his head appraisingly, looking over the family that stood before him. A small, wiry man, who might be in his early thirties but looked much older, shabby and bowed with labor. His wife, perhaps a little younger, standing behind her husband, eyes glued to the floor, tightly grasping the hands of two little girls. One of the girls held on to her baby brother, a lad of three or four. The elder boys stood by their father, trying to look manly. Roger thought they might be ten and twelve, allowing for the puny stature caused by malnutrition.

'Yourself and the boys, aye, that'll do,' the captain said. He frowned at the woman, who didn't look up. 'No one will buy a woman with so many young ones – she might keep one, perhaps. You'll have to sell the girls, though.'

The man glanced back at his family. His wife kept her head down, unmoving, not looking at anything. One of the girls twitched and jerked, though, complaining in an undertone that her hand was being crushed. The man turned back.

'All right,' he said, low-voiced. 'Can they – might they – go together?'

The captain rubbed a hand across his mouth, and nodded indifferently.

'Likely enough.'

Roger didn't wait to witness the details of the transaction. He got up abruptly and left the pub; the dark beer had lost its taste.

He paused in the street outside, fingering the coins in his pocket. It was all he had been able to collect of suitable money, in the time he'd had. He had thought that it would be enough, though; he was good-sized and had a fair amount of confidence in his own abilities. Still, the little scene he had witnessed in the pub had shaken him.

He had grown up with the history of the Highlands. He knew well enough the sorts of things that drove families to such a pitch of desperation that they would accept permanent separation and semislavery as the price of survival.

He knew all about the sale of lands that forced small crofters off the lands their families had tended for hundreds of years, all about the dreadful conditions of penury and starvation in the cities, the simple insupportableness of life in Scotland in these days. And not all his years of reading and study had prepared him for the look of that woman's face, her eyes fixed on the fresh-sanded floor, her daughters' hands clutched hard in her own.

Ten pounds, eight shillings. Or four pounds, two. Plus whatever it might cost for food. He had exactly fourteen shillings, threepence in his pocket, together with a handful of copper doits and a couple of farthings.

He walked slowly down the lane that led along the seaside, glancing at the collection of ships that lay moored by the wooden docks. Fishing ketches, for the most part, small galleys and brigs that plied their trade up and down the Firth, or at most ran across the Channel, carrying cargo and passengers to France. Only three large ships lay at anchor in the Firth, those of a size to brave the winds of the Atlantic crossing.

He could cross to France, of course, and take ship from there. Or travel overland to Edinburgh, a much larger port than Inverness. But it would be late in the year then, for sailing. Brianna was six weeks before him already; he could waste no time in finding her – God knew what could happen to a woman alone here.

Four pounds, two shillings. Well, he could work, certainly. With neither children nor wife to support, he could save most of his earnings. But given that the average clerk earned something like twelve pounds per year, and that he was much more likely to find work shoveling stables than keeping accounts, the chances of his saving up passage money in any reasonable time were fairly slim.

'First things first,' he muttered. 'Be sure where she's gone, before you trouble about getting there yourself.'

Taking his hand out of his pocket, he turned right between two warehouses, and into a narrow lane. His high spirits of the morning had largely evaporated, but they lifted slightly, nonetheless, when he saw that he had been right in his guess; the harbormaster's office was where he had known it must be – in the same squat stone building where it still would be, two hundred years hence. Roger smiled with wry humour; Scots were not inclined to make changes purely for the sake of change.

It was crowded and busy inside, with four harried clerks behind a battered wooden counter, scribbling and stamping, carrying bundles of paper to and fro, taking money and conveying it carefully into an inner office, from which they issued moments later, bearing receipts on japanned tin trays.

A crush of impatient men pressed against the counter, each endeavoring to signal by means of voice and posture that his business was much more urgent than that of the fellow standing next him. Once Roger had succeeded in capturing the attention of one of the clerks, though, there turned out to be no great difficulty in seeing the registers of the ships that had sailed from Inverness within the last few months.

'Here, wait,' he said to the young man who pushed a large, leather-bound book across the counter to him.

'Aye?' The clerk was flushed with hurry, and had a smut of ink on his nose, but paused politely, arrested in flight.

'How much d'ye get paid for working here?' Roger asked.

The clerk's fair eyebrows lifted, but he was in too much hurry either to ask questions or to take offense at the inquiry.

'Six shillings the week,' he said briefly, and promptly disappeared in response to an irritable shout of 'Munro!' from the office beyond the counter.

'Mmphm.' Roger pushed back through the crowd and

took the book of registers away to a small table by the window, out of the main stream of traffic.

Having seen the conditions under which the clerks worked, Roger was impressed at the legibility of the hand-written registers. He was well accustomed to archaic spelling and eccentric punctuation, though those he was used to seeing were always yellowed and fragile, on the verge of disintegration. It gave him an odd little historian's thrill to see the page before him fresh and white, and just beyond, the clerk who sat at a high table, copying as fast as quill could write, shoulders hunched against the hubbub in the room.

You're shilly-shallying, said a cold little voice in the middle of his brain. *She's here or she's not; being afraid to look won't change it. Get on!*

Roger took a deep breath and flipped open the big ledger book. The ships' names were neatly lettered at the tops of pages, followed by the names of their masters and mates, their main cargoes and dates of sailing. *Arianna. Polyphemus. Merry Widow. Tiburon.* Despite his apprehensions, he couldn't help admiring the names of the ships as he thumbed through the pages.

Half an hour later, he had ceased to marvel over both poetry and picturesqueness, barely noting each ship's name as he ran his finger down the pages in increasing desperation. Not here, she wasn't here!

But she had to be, he argued with himself. She *had* to have taken a ship to the Colonies, where else could she bloody be? Unless she hadn't found the notice, after all . . . but the sick feeling under his ribs assured him that she had; nothing else would have made her risk the stones.

He took a deep breath and closed his eyes, which were starting to feel the strain of the handwritten pages. Then he opened his eyes, turned back to the first relevant register, and began to read again, doggedly muttering each name beneath his breath, to be sure of not missing one out.

Mr. Phineas Forbes, gentleman.
Mrs. Wilhelmina Forbes.
Master Joshua Forbes.

694

Mrs. Josephine Forbes.
Mrs. Eglantine Forbes.
Mrs. Charlotte Forbes . . .

He smiled to himself at the thought of Mr. Phineas Forbes, surrounded by his womenfolk. Even knowing that 'Mrs.' here was sometimes merely the abbreviated form of 'Mistress', and thus used for both married and unmarried women – rather than the 'Miss' for little girls – he found himself with an irresistible mental picture of Phineas marching stoutly aboard at the head of a train of four wives, Master Joshua no doubt bringing up the rear.

Mr. William Talbot, merchant.
Mr. Peter Talbot, merchant.
Mr. Jonathan Bicknell, physician.
Mr. Robert MacLeod, farmer.
Mr. Gordon MacLeod, farmer.
Mr. Martin MacLeod. . .

No Randalls this time through, either. Not for the *Persephone*, the *Queen's Revenge*, or the *Phoebe*. He rubbed his aching eyes, and began on the register of the *Phillip Alonzo*. A Spanish name, but it was listed under Scottish registry. Sailing from Inverness, under the command of Captain Patrick O'Brian.

He hadn't given up, but had already begun to think what to do next, if she should not be listed in the registers. Lallybroch, of course. He had been there once, in his own time, to the abandoned remains of the estate; could he find it now, without the guidance of roads and signposts?

His thoughts stopped with a jolt as his gliding finger came to a halt, near the bottom of a page. Not Brianna Randall, not the name he'd been looking for, but a name that rang bells of recognition in his mind. *Fraser,* read the slanted, crisp black writing. *Mr. Brian Fraser.* No, not Brian. And not Mr., either. He bent closer, squinting at the cramped black lettering.

He closed his eyes, feeling his heart thump hard in his chest, and relief flowed through him, intoxicating as the pub's special dark beer. *Mrs.,* not Mr. And what had first

695

seemed merely an exuberant tail on the 'n' of Brian was on closer inspection almost surely instead a careless 'a'.

Her, it was her, it had to be! It was an unusual first name – he had seen no other Briannas or Brianas anywhere in the massive register. And even Fraser made sense, of a sort; embarked on a quixotic quest to find her father, she had taken his name, the name she was entitled to by right of birth.

He slammed the register closed, as though to keep her from escaping from the pages, and sat for a moment, breathing. Got her! He saw the fair-haired clerk eyeing him curiously from the counter and, flushing, opened the book again.

The *Phillip Alonzo*. Sailed from Inverness on the fourth of July, Anno Domini 1769. For Charleston, South Carolina.

He frowned at the name, suddenly uncertain. South Carolina. Was that her real destination, or only as close as she could get? A quick glance at the rest of the registers showed no ships in July for North Carolina. Perhaps she had simply taken the first ship for the southern colonies, intending to journey overland.

Or maybe he was wrong. A chill gripped him that had nothing to do with the river wind seeping through the cracks of the window next to him. He looked at the page again, and was reassured. No, there was no profession given, as there was for all the men. It was certainly 'Mrs.' and therefore it must be 'Briana' as well. And if 'Briana' it was, then Brianna it was, too, he knew it.

He rose and handed the book across the counter to his fair-haired acquaintance.

'Thanks, man,' he said, relaxing into his own soft accent. 'Can ye be tellin' me, is there a ship in port bound for the American Colonies soon, now?'

'Oh, aye,' the clerk said, deftly stowing the register with one hand and accepting a bill of lading from a customer with the other. 'Happen it will be *Gloriana*; she sails day after tomorrow for the Carolinas.' He looked Roger up and down. 'Emigrant or seaman?' he asked.

'Seaman,' Roger said promptly. Ignoring the other's

696

raised eyebrow, he waved toward the forest of masts visible through the paned windows. 'Where do I go to sign on?'

Both eyebrows high, the clerk nodded in the direction of the door.

'Her master works from the Friars when he's in port. Likely he'll be there now – Captain Bonnet.' He forbore adding what was obvious from his skeptical expression; if Roger was a seaman, he, the clerk, was an African parrot.

'Right, *mo ghille.* Thanks.' Sketching a salute, Roger turned away, but turned back at the door to find the clerk still watching him, ignoring the press of impatient customers.

'Wish me luck!' Roger called, with a grin.

The clerk's answering grin was tinged with something that might have been either admiration or wistfulness.

'Luck to ye, man!' he called, and waved in farewell. By the time the door swung shut, he was deep in conversation with the next customer, quill pen poised in readiness.

He found Captain Bonnet in the pub, as advertised, settled in a corner under a thick blue haze of smoke, to which the Captain's own cigar was adding.

'Your name?'

'MacKenzie,' Roger said on sudden impulse. If Brianna could do it, so could he.

'MacKenzie. Any experience, Mr. MacKenzie?'

A bar of sunlight cut across the Captain's face, making him squint. Bonnet drew back into the shadow of the settle, and the lines around his eyes relaxed, leaving Roger exposed to a gaze of uncomfortable penetration.

'It is myself has fished the herring now and then, in the Minch.'

It was no lie, at that; he'd had several teenage summers as hand on a herring boat captained by an acquaintance of the Reverend's. The experience had left him with a useful layer of muscle, an ear for the singsong cadence of the Isles, and a fixed dislike of herring. But he knew the feel of a rope in his hands, at least.

'Ah, ye're a good-sized lad. But a fisherman will not be the same as a sailor, sure.' The man's soft Irish lilt left it

697

open whether this was question, statement – or provocation.

'I shouldna have thought it an occupation requiring great skill.' For no reason he could name, Captain Bonnet raised the hairs on the back of his neck.

The green eyes sharpened.

'Perhaps more than ye think – but sure it's nothing a willing man can't learn. But what would it be, now, that makes a fellow of your sort crave the sea of a sudden?'

The eyes flickered in the tavern's shadows, taking him in. *Of your sort.* What was it? Roger wondered. Not his speech – he had taken care to suppress any hint of the Oxford scholar, by taking on the 'teuchter' cant of the Isles. Was he too well dressed for a would-be sailor? Or was it the singed collar and the burn mark on the breast of his coat?

'That will be none of your business, I am thinking,' he answered evenly. With a minor effort, he kept his hands relaxed at his sides.

The pale green eyes studied him dispassionately, unblinking. Like a leopard watching a passing wildebeest, Roger thought, wondering whether it would be worth the chase.

The heavy lids dropped; not worth it – for the moment.

'You'll be aboard by sundown,' Bonnet said. 'Five shillings the month, meat three days in the week, plum duff on Sundays. You'll have a hammock, but find your own clothes. You will be free to leave the ship once the cargo is unloaded, not until that time. We are agreed, sir?'

'It is agreed,' Roger said, suddenly dry-mouthed. He would have given a lot for a pint, but not now, not here, under that pale green gaze.

'Ask for Mr. Dixon when yez come aboard. He's paymaster.' Bonnet leaned back, took a small leather-bound book from his pocket and flipped it open. Audience concluded.

Roger turned smartly and went out, without a backward glance. There was a small cold spot at the base of his skull. If he looked back, he knew, he would see that lucent green gaze fixed unwaveringly over the edge of the unread book, taking note of every weakness.

The cold spot, he thought, was where the teeth would meet.

37

Gloriana

•

Before shipping with the *Gloriana*, Roger had assumed himself to be in reasonably good condition. In fact, compared to most of the obviously malnourished and wizened specimens of humanity who constituted the rest of the crew, he considered himself well endowed, indeed. It took precisely fourteen hours – the length of one day's work – to disabuse him of this notion.

Blisters he had bargained for, and sore muscles; heaving crates, lifting spars, and hauling ropes was familiar labor, though he hadn't done it for some time.

What he had forgotten was the bone-deep fatigue that sprang as much from the constant chill of damp clothes as from the work. He welcomed the heavy labor in the cargo hold, because it warmed him temporarily, even though he knew the warmth would be succeeded by a fine, constant shiver as soon as he emerged on deck, where the wind could resume its icy probe of his sweat-soaked clothes.

Hands roughened and scraped by wet hemp were painful, but expected; by the end of his first day, his palms were black with tar, and the skin of his fingers cracked and bled at the joints, scraped raw. But the gnawing ache of hunger had been something of a surprise. He hadn't thought it possible to be as hungry as he was.

The knobbled lump of humanity working beside him – one Duff by name – was similarly damp, but seemed unfazed by the condition. The long, pointed nose that quested, ferret-like, from the upturned collar of a ragged jacket was blue at the tip and dripped regularly as a stalactite, but the pale eyes were and the mouth beneath grinned wide, displaying teeth the color of the water in the Firth.

'Take hairt, man. Grub in twa bells.' Duff gave him a companionable elbow in the ribs and disappeared nimbly down a hatchway, from whose cavernous recesses echoed blasphemous shouts and loud bangings.

Roger resumed his unloading of the cargo net, heartened indeed at the prospect of supper.

The after hold has already been half filled. The water casks were loaded; there upon tier of wooden hogsheads, squatting in the shadowy gloom, each hundred-gallon cask weighing more than seven hundred pounds. But the forward hold still gaped empty, and a constant procession of loaders and quaymen streamed like ants across the dock, piling up such a heap of boxes and barrels, rolls and bundles, that it seemed inconceivable that the mass should ever be condensed sufficiently to fit within the ship.

It took two days to finish the loading: barrels of salt, bolts of cloth, huge crates of ironmongery that had to be lowered with rope slings because of their weight. It was here that Roger's size proved of benefit. At the end of a rope belayed round the capstan, he leaned back against the weight of a crate suspended at the other end and, muscles popping with the strain, lowered it slowly enough that the two men below could catch and guide it into place in the increasingly crowded hold.

The passengers came aboard in the late afternoon, a straggling line of emigrants, burdened with bags, bundles, caged chickens, and children. These were the cargo of the steerage – a space created by erection of a bulkhead across the forward hold – and as profitable in their way as the harder goods aft.

'Bondsmen and redemptioners,' Duff had told him, looking over the incomers with a practised eye. 'Worth fifteen pund each on the hoof in the plantations, weans three or four. Bairns at the teat go free wi' their mithers.'

The seaman coughed, a deep, rattling noise like an ancient motor starting up, and hawked a glob of phlegm, narrowly missing the side rail as he spat. He shook his head as he looked the shuffling line over.

'Happen some can pay their way, but no many in this lot. They'll have had a job to come up wi' twa pund a family for their feed on the voyage.'

'The Captain doesn't feed them, then?'

'Oh, aye.' Duff rumbled in his chest again, coughed and

701

spat. 'For a price.' He grinned at Roger, wiped his mouth, and jerked his head toward the gangplank. 'Go and lend a hand, laddie. We wouldna want the Captain's profit to be fallin' intae the water, now, would we?'

Surprised by the padded feel of a little girl as he swung her aboard, Roger looked closer and saw that the stout build of many of the women was illusion, occasioned by their wearing several layers of clothes; all they owned in the world, apparently, beyond small bundles of personal possessions, boxes of food put by for the journey – and the scrawny children for whose sake they took this desperate step.

Roger squatted, smiling at a reluctant toddler who clung to his mother's skirts. He was no more than two, still in smocks, with a riot of soft blond curls, his fat little mouth drawn down in fearful disapproval of everything around him.

'Come on, man,' Roger said softly, putting out a hand in invitation. It was no longer an effort to control his accent; his usual clipped Oxbridge had elided to the gentler Highland speech with which he had grown up, and he used it now without conscious thought. 'Your mam can't be pickin' ye up now; you come with me.'

Grossly mistrustful, the boy snuffled and glowered at him, but suffered him to peel the grubby little fingers away from his mother's skirts. Roger carried the little boy across the deck, the woman following him silently. She looked up at him as he handed her down the ladder, her eyes fixed on his; her face disappeared in the darkness like a white rock dropped down a well, and he turned away with a feeling of unease, as though he had abandoned someone to drowning.

As he turned back to his work, he saw a young woman, just coming down above the quay. She was the sort of girl called 'bonny' – not beautiful, but lively and nicely made, with something about her that took the eye.

Perhaps it was only her posture; straight as a lily stem among the hunched and drooping backs around her. Or her face, which showed apprehension and uncertainty, but had still about it the brightness of curiosity. A darer, that one, he thought, and his heart – oppressed by so many

702

downcast faces among the emigrants – lightened at the sight of her.

She hesitated at sight of the ship and the crowd around it. A tall fair-haired young man was with her, a baby in his arms. He touched her shoulder in reassurance, and she glanced up at him, an answering smile lighting her face like the striking of a match. Watching them, Roger felt a mild pang of something that might have been envy.

'You, MacKenzie!' The bosun's shout pulled him from his contemplation. The bosun jerked his head aft. 'There's cargo a-waitin' – it's no goin' to walk aboard by itself!'

Once embarked and under sail, the voyage went smoothly for some weeks. The stormy weather that accompanied their exodus from Scotland quickly diminished into good winds and rolling seas, and while the immediate effect of this on the passengers was to make the majority of them seasick, this ailment also faded in time. The smell of vomit from the steerage subsided, becoming only a minor note in the symphony of stinks aboard the *Gloriana*.

Roger had been born with an acute sense of smell, an attribute he was finding a marked liability in close quarters. Still, even the keenest nose grew accustomed in time, and within a day or so he had ceased to note any but the most novel stenches.

He was fortunately not subject to seasickness himself, though his experiences with the herring fishers had been enough to give him a keen appreciation of the weather, with the sailor's unsettling knowledge that his life might depend on whether the sun was shining that day.

His new shipmates were not friendly, but neither were they hostile. Whether it was his 'teuchter' accent from the Isles – for most of the *Gloriana*'s hands were English-speakers from Dingwall or Peterhead – the occasional odd things that he said, or simply his size, they regarded him with a certain watchful distance. No overt antagonism – his size prevented that – but distance nonetheless.

Roger wasn't disturbed by the coolness. He was pleased enough to be left to his thoughts, his mind ranging free while his body dealt with the daily round of shipboard duties. There was plenty to think about.

He had taken no heed to the reputation of the *Gloriana* or her captain before signing on; he would have sailed with Captain Ahab, provided only that gentleman was bound for North Carolina. Still, from the talk he heard among the crew, he gathered that Stephen Bonnet was known as a good captain; hard but fair, and a man whose voyages always turned a profit. To the seamen, many of whom sailed on shares rather than wages, this latter quality plainly more than compensated for any small defects of character or address.

Not that Roger had seen open evidence of such defects. But he did see that Bonnet stood always as though an invisible circle had been drawn around him, a circle that few were bold enough to enter. Only the first mate and the bosun spoke directly to the Captain; the crewmen kept their heads down as he passed. Roger remembered the cool green leopard-eyes that had looked him over; little wonder that no one wanted to attract their notice.

He was more interested in the passengers, though, than in either crew or captain. Little was seen of them normally, but they were allowed on deck briefly twice each day, to take a bit of air, to empty their slop jars over the side – for the ship's heads were woefully inadequate for so many – and to carry down again the small amounts of water carefully rationed to each family. Roger looked forward to these brief appearances, and tried to see to it that he was employed as often as possible near the end of the deck where they took their fleeting exercise.

His interest was both professional and personal; his historian's instincts were roused by their presence, and his loneliness soothed by the homeliness of their talk. Here were the seeds of the new country, the legacy of the old. What these poor emigrants knew and valued, was what would endure to be passed on.

If one were handpicking the repository of Scottish culture, he thought, it might not contain such things as the recipe for warts about which an elderly woman was berating her long-suffering daughter-in-law ('I did tell ye, Katie Mac, and why ye chose tae leave my nice dried toadie behind, when ye could find room to bring all yon rubbish that we be squattin' on and pickin' oot from under our hurdies day and night . . .'), but that would last too, right along with the folksongs and prayers, with the woven wool and the Celtic patterns of their art.

He glanced at his own hand; he vividly remembered Mrs. Graham rubbing a large wart on his third finger with what she *said* was a dried toad. He grinned, rubbing a thumb across the spot. Must have worked; he'd never had another.

'Sir,' said a small voice by his side. 'Sir, may we go and touch the iron?'

He glanced down and smiled at the tiny girl, holding two tinier brothers by their hands.

'Aye, *a leannan*,' he said. 'Get on; yourself will be minding the men, though.'

She nodded and the three of them pattered off, looking anxiously up and down to be sure they were not in the way, before scrambling up to touch the horseshoe nailed to the mast for luck. Iron was protection and healing; the mothers often sent the little ones who were ailing to touch it.

They could have used iron to better effect internally, Roger thought, seeing the rash on the pasty white faces, and hearing the high-pitched complaints of itching boils, of loose teeth and fever. He resumed his job, measuring out water by the dipperful into the buckets and dishes the emigrants held out to him. They were living on oatmeal, the lot of them – that, with dried peas now and then and a bit of hard biscuit, was the sum total of the 'provisions' supplied them for the voyage.

At that, he'd heard no complaint; the water was clean, the biscuit was not moldy, and if the allowance of 'corn' was not generous, neither was it niggardly. The crew was fed better, but still on meat and starch, with only the occasional onion for relief. He ran his tongue round his teeth, testing, as he did every few days. The faint taste of iron was nearly always in his mouth now; his gums were beginning to bleed from the lack of fresh vegetables.

Still, his teeth were strongly rooted, and he had no sign of the swollen joints or bruised nails that several .of the other crewmen showed. He'd looked it up, during his weeks of waiting; a normal adult male in good health should be able to endure from three to six months of prolonged vitamin deficiency before suffering any real symptoms. If the good weather held, they'd be across in only two.

'It will be good weather tomorrow, aye?' His attention recalled by this apparent reading of his thoughts, he looked down to find that it was the bonny brown-haired girl he'd admired on the quay in Inverness. Morag, her friends called her.

'I am hoping it may be,' he said, taking her bucket with an answering smile. 'Why do ye say so?'

She nodded, pointing over his shoulder with a small sharp chin. 'There's the new moon in the arms o' the old; if that means fine weather on the land, I should think it is the same on the sea, no?'

He glanced back to see the pale clean curve of a silver moon, holding a glowing orb in its cup. It rode high and perfect in an endless evening sky of pale violet, its reflection swallowed by the indigo sea.

'Dinna be wasting time chattering, lass – go on and ask him!' He turned back in time to hear this hissed over Morag's shoulder by the middle-aged woman behind her. Morag glared back.

'Will ye hush?' she hissed back. 'I'll not, I said I won't!'

'Ye're a stubborn lass, Morag,' the older woman declared, stepping boldly forward, 'and if ye willna be asking for yourself, I shall do it for ye!'

The good-lady laid a broad hand on Roger's arm and gave him a charming smile.

'And what might your name be, lad?'

'MacKenzie, is it! Well, there, ye see, Morag, and belike he'll be some kinsman of your man's, and happy to do ye a service, at that!' The woman turned triumphantly to the girl, then swung back to let Roger have the full force of her personality.

'She's suckling a wean, and dyin' o' thirst in the doin' of it. A woman needs to drink when she's giving suck, or her milk dries; everyone kens that weel enough. But the silly lass cannae bring herself to ask ye for a bittie more water.

There's nane here grudge it to her – is there?' she demanded rhetorically, turning round to glare at the other women in line. Not surprisingly, all the heads shook back and forth like clockwork toys.

It was getting dark, but Morag's face was visibly pink. Lips pressed tight together, she accepted the brimming bucket of water with a brief bob of her head.

'I thank ye, Mr. MacKenzie,' she murmured. She didn't look up until she had reached the hatchway – but then she stopped, and looked back over her shoulder at him, with a smile of such gratitude that he felt himself grow warm, in spite of the sharp evening wind that blew through his shirt and jacket.

He was sorry to see the water line finish and the emigrants go below, the hatch battened down over them for the night watches. He knew they told stories and sang songs to pass the time, and would have given much to hear them. Not only from curiosity, but from longing – what moved him was neither pity for their poverty nor thought of their uncertain future; it was envy of the sense of connection among them.

But the Captain, the crew, the passengers, even the all-important weather, occupied no more than a fragment of Roger's thoughts. What he thought about, day and night, wet or dry, hungry or fed, was Brianna.

He went down to the mess when the signal came for supper, and ate without much noticing the contents of his trencher. His was the second watch; he went to his hammock after eating, choosing solitude and rest over the possibility of companionship on the forecastle.

Solitude was an illusion, of course. Swinging gently in his hammock, he could feel each twitch and turn of the man next to him, the sweating heat of sleeping flesh clammy against his own through the thick cotton mesh. Each man had eighteen inches of sleeping space to call his own, and Roger was uncomfortably aware that when he lay upon his back, his shoulders exceeded that allowance by a good two inches on either side.

After two nights of sleep interrupted by the bumps and muttered insults of his shipmates, he had swapped places and ended in the space next the bulkhead, where he would have only one companion to discommode. He learned to lie on one side, his face an inch or two from the wooden partition, back turned to his companions, and tune his ears to the sounds of the ship, blocking out the noises of the men around him.

A very musical thing was a ship – lines and hawsers singing in the wind, the timber knees creaking with each rise and fall, the faint thumps and murmurs on the far side of the bulkhead, in the dark recesses of the passengers' hold in the steerage. He stared at the dark wood, lit by the shadows of the swinging lantern overhead, and began to re-create her, the lines of face and hair and body all vivid in the dark. Too vivid.

He could conjure her face without difficulty. What lay behind it was a good deal harder.

Rest was also an illusion. When she had gone through the stones, she had taken with her all peace of mind. He lived in a mixture of fear and anger, spiced with the hurt of betrayal, rubbed like pepper into the wounds. The same questions ran round and round inside his mind without answers, a snake chasing its tail.

Why had she gone?
What was she doing?
Why didn't she tell him?

It was the effort to come up with an answer to the first of these that kept him going over and over it, as though the answer might afford him the key to the whole mystery of Brianna.

Yeah, he'd been lonely. Knew bloody well what it felt like to have no one in the world who belonged to you, or you to them. But surely that was one reason why they had reached out to each other – he and Brianna.

Claire knew, too, he thought suddenly. She'd been orphaned, lost her uncle – of course, she'd been married then. But she'd been separated from her husband during the war . . . yes, she knew a lot about being alone. And that was why she'd taken care not to leave Bree alone, to assure herself that her daughter was loved.

Well, he'd tried to love her properly – was still trying, he thought grimly, twisting uncomfortably in his hammock. During the day, the demands of work suppressed the growing needs of his body. At night, though ... she was a deal too vivid, the Brianna of his memory.

He hadn't hesitated; he'd known from the first moment of realization that he must follow her. Sometimes, though, he was not sure whether he had come to save her or to savage her – anything, so long as it was settled once and for all between them. He'd said he'd wait – but he'd waited long enough.

The worst of it was not the loneliness, he thought, flinging restlessly over again, but the doubt. Doubt of her feelings, and of his. Panic that he did not truly know her.

For the first time since his passage through the stones, he realized what she had meant in refusing him, and knew her hesitance for wisdom. But *was* it wisdom, and not only fear?

If she had not gone through the stones – would she have turned to him at last, wholeheartedly? Or turned away, always looking for something else?

It was a leap of faith – to throw one's heart across a gulf, and trust another to catch it. His own was still in flight across the void, with no certainty of landing. But still in flight.

The sounds on the other side of the bulkhead had faded to silence, but now they started up again, in a stealthy, rhythmic fashion with which he was thoroughly familiar. They were at it again, whoever they were.

They did it almost every night, when the others had gone to sleep. At first the sounds had made him feel only his isolation, alone with the burning ghost of Brianna. There seemed no possibility of true human warmth, no joining of heart or mind, no more than the animal consolation of a body to cling to in the dark. Was there really any more for a man than this?

But then he began to hear something else in the sounds, half-caught words of tenderness, small furtive sounds of affirmation, that made him in some way not a voyeur, but a participant in their joining.

He couldn't tell, of course. It might have been any of the couples, or a random pairing of lust – and yet he put faces to them, this unknown pair; in his mind, he saw the tall, fair-haired young man, the brown-haired lass with the open face, saw them look at each other as they had on the quay, and would have sold his soul to know such certainty.

38

For Those in Peril on the Sea

A sudden hard squall kept the passengers belowdecks for three days, and the sailors at their posts with no more than scant minutes snatched for rest or food. At the end of it, when the *Gloriana* rode high on the dying storm-swell and the dawn sky was filled with racing mare's-tails, Roger staggered down to his hammock, too exhausted even to shuck his wet clothes.

Crumpled, damp, crusted with salt and feeling fit for nothing but a hot bath and another week's sleep, he answered the bosun's whistle for the afternoon watch after four hours rest, and staggered through his duties.

He was so tired by sunset that his muscles quivered as he helped to heave up a fresh water barrel from the hold. He caved in the top with a hatchet, thinking that he might just manage the exertion of ladling out water rations without falling headfirst into the barrel. Then again, he might not. He splashed a cool handful of the fresh water into his face, in hopes of soothing his burning eyes, and gulped down a whole dipperful, ignoring for once the strictures imposed by that constant contradiction of the sea – always both too much water, and too little.

The folk bringing up their jars and buckets to be filled looked as though they felt even worse than he did; green-gilled as mushrooms, bruised from being pitched to and fro in the hold like billiard balls, reeking of renewed sea-sickness and overflowing chamber pots.

In marked contrast to the general air of pallid malaise, one of his old acquaintances was skipping in rings around him, singing in a monotonous chant that grated on his ears.

> *'Seven herrings are a salmon's fill,*
> *Seven salmon are a seal's fill,*
> *Seven seals are a whale's full,*
> *And seven whales the fill of a Cirein Croin!'*

Bubbling with the freedom of release from the hold, the little girl hopped around like a demented chickadee, making Roger smile in spite of his tiredness. She hopped to the rail, then stood on tiptoe, and peeked cautiously over.

'D'ye think 'twas a Cirein Croin caused the storming. Mr. MacKenzie? Grandda says it was, like enough. They lash their great huge tails about ye ken,' she informed him. 'That's what makes the waves go sae big.'

'I shouldna be thinking such a thing, myself. Where's your brothers, then, *a leannan*?'

'Fevered,' the girl answered, indifferently. It was nothing out of the way; half the emigrants in line were coughing and sneezing, three days in darkness and damp clothes having done nothing for their precarious state of health.

'Have ye seen a Cirein Croin, then?' she asked, leaning far over the rail, a hand shading her eyes. 'Are they really big enough to swallow the boat?'

'Myself has not seen one.' Roger dropped his dipper and grabbed her by the apron sash, pulling her firmly off the rail. 'Have a care, aye? It would take no more than a spratling to swallow *you*, lassie!'

'Look!' she shrieked, leaning farther over in spite of his grasp. 'Look it is, it *is*!'

Drawn as much by the terror in her voice as what she said, Roger leaned over the rail involuntarily. A dark shape hovered just below the surface, smooth and black, graceful as a bullet – and half the length of the ship. It kept pace for a few moments with the racing vessel, then was outdistanced and left behind.

'Shark,' Roger said, shaken in spite of himself. He gave the girl a small shake, to stop her steam-whistle screeches. 'It's no but a shark, hear? Ye ken what's a shark, do ye not? We ate one, only last week!'

She had quit shrieking, but was still white-faced and wide-eyed, tender mouth quivering.

'You're sure?' she said. 'It – it wasna a Cirein Croin?'

'No,' Roger said gently, and gave her a dipper of water to drink, by herself. 'Only a shark.' The biggest shark he had ever seen, with an air of blind ferocity that raised the hair on his forearms to see – but only a shark. They hung about the ship whenever her speed slowed, eager for the garbage and slops tossed overboard.

'Isobeàil!' An indignant cry summoned his erstwhile companion to come and lend a hand with the family chores. With dragging step and out-thrust lip, Isobeàil slouched off to help her mother with the water buckets, leaving Roger to finish his job without further distraction.

No further distraction than his thoughts, at least. For the most part, he succeeded in forgetting that the *Gloriana* had nothing below her save leagues of empty water; that the ship was not, in fact, the small and solid island that it seemed, but instead no more than a fragile shell, at the mercy of forces that could crush her in moments – and everyone aboard.

Had the *Phillip Alonzo* reached port in safety? he wondered. Ships did sink, and fairly often; he'd read enough accounts of it. Having lived through the last three days, he could only be amazed that more of them *didn't* sink. Well, and there was precisely nothing he could do about that prospect, except pray.

For those in peril on the deep, Lord, have mercy.

With sudden vividness, he understood exactly what the maker of that line had meant.

Finished, he dropped the dipper into the barrel and reached for a board to cover the open top; rats tended to fall in and drown otherwise. One of the women clutched him by the arm as he turned away. She gestured at the little boy she held, fussing against his mother's neck.

'Mr. MacKenzie, might the Captain gie us a wee rub wi' his ring? Our Gibbie has a touch o' sore eyes from bein' in the dark sae long.'

Roger hesitated, but then ridiculed himself. He, like the rest of the crew, tended to steer clear of Bonnet, but there was no reason to refuse the woman's request; the Captain had obliged before with a rub of his gold ring, this being a popular remedy for sore eyes and inflammations.

'Yeah, sure,' he said, forgetting himself for a moment. 'Come on.' The woman blinked in surprise, but followed him obediently. The Captain was on his quarterdeck, engaged in close conversation with the mate; Roger

713

motioned to the woman to wait for a bit, and she nodded, shrinking, estly behind him.

The Captain looked as tired as any of them, the lines of dissipation carved deeper in his face. Lucifer after a week of running Hell, and finding it no picnic, Roger thought, sourly amused.

' . . . damage to the tea chests?' Bonnet was saying to the mate.

'Only two, and not soaked through,' Dixon replied. 'We can salvage a bit; maybe get rid of it upriver in Cross Creek.'

'Aye, they're more particular in Edenton and New Bern. We'll get the best prices there, though; we'll get rid of what we can before we go to Wilmington.'

Bonnet turned slightly and caught sight of Roger. His expression hardened, but relaxed again when he heard the request. Without comment, he reached down and rubbed the gold ring he wore on his little finger gently over little Gilbert's closed eyes. A plain wide band, Roger saw; it almost looked like a wedding ring, though smaller – a woman's ring, maybe. The formidable Bonnet with a love token? Could be, Roger supposed; some women might find the Captain's air of subdued violence attractive.

'The wean's ailing,' Dixon remarked. He pointed, there was a prickle of red bumps behind the boy's ears, and his pale cheeks bloomed with fever.

'No but milk fever,' the woman said, pulling her child defensively against her bosom. 'He's a new tooth coming, likely.'

The Captain nodded indifferently and turned away. Roger escorted the woman to the galley to beg a bit of hard biscuit for the child to gnaw on, then sent her back to the forward hold with the others.

He had little thought for Gilbert's gums, though; as he climbed the ladderway to the deck, his mind was occupied by the conversation he had overhead.

Stops in New Bern and Edenton, before Wilmington. And plainly Bonnet was in no rush; he'd be looking for good prices for his cargo, and taking the time to broker the indentures of his passengers – Christ, it could be weeks before they made Wilmington!

It wouldn't do, Roger thought. God knew where Brianna could get to – or what sort of thing happen to her. The *Gloriana* had made swift passage, in spite of the squall – God willing, they'd make North Carolina in only eight weeks, if the winds held. He didn't want to sacrifice the valuable time so gained to lallygagging in the northern Carolina ports, mooching their way south.

He'd be off the *Gloriana* in the first port they touched, he resolved, and make his way south as best he could. True, he'd given his word to stay with the ship until the cargo was disposed of, but then, he wouldn't be taking his wages, either, so the exchange seemed fair enough.

The fresh, cold air above decks did a little bit to rouse him. His head still felt stuffed with damp cotton wool, though, and the back of his throat was raspy with salt. Three hours more to go on his watch; he made his way forward for another dipper of water, hoping it would help him stay on his feet.

Dixon had left the Captain, and was strolling through the clusters of passengers, nodding to the men, stopping to say something to a woman with children. Odd, Roger thought. The mate wasn't a sociable man with the crew, let alone with the passengers, whom he regarded as nothing more than an unusually inconvenient form of cargo.

Something stirred in his mind at the mention of cargo, something uncomfortable, but he couldn't bring it to the forefront of recognition. It hung in the shadows of exhaustion, just out of sight, nearly close enough to smell. Yes, that was it, it had to do with a smell. But what –

'MacKenzie!' One of the seamen was calling from the afterdeck, waving for him to come and help with the mending of sails torn by the storm; huge stacks of folded canvas lay like dirty snowdrifts on the boards, their upper layers billowing in the wind.

Roger groaned, and stretched his aching muscles. No matter what happened in North Carolina, he would be very glad to get off this ship.

Two nights later, Roger was deep in dreams when the shouting roused him. His feet hit the deck and he was running for the companionway, heart pumping at full

715

bore, before his mind had grasped the fact that he was awake. He sprang for the ladder, only to be knocked sprawling by a blow to his chest.

'Stay where ye are, fool!' Dixon's voice growled from the rungs above. He could see the mate's head, outlined against the starry square of the hatchway overhead.

'What is it? What's happening?' He shook off the confusion of his dreams, to find no less confusion in the waking.

There were others in the dark near him, he could feel bodies stumble over him as he struggled to his feet. All the noise was up above, though; a thunder of feet on the deck and a shouting and shrieking like nothing he had ever heard.

'Murderers!' A woman's voice cut through the racket, shrill as a fife. 'Wicked *mur*–' The voice cut off abruptly, with a heavy thump on the deck above.

'What is it?' On his feet again, Roger shoved his way through the men by the ladder, shouting up to Dixon, 'What? Are we boarded?' His words were drowned by the shouting above; the steam-whistle shrieks of women and children, cutting through men's bellowing and curses.

Red light flickered somewhere above. Was the ship afire? He shoved through the press of men and grabbed the ladder, reached up and seized Dixon's foot.

'Gerrof!' The foot jerked free, aimed a kick at his head. 'Stay down there! Christ, man, ye want to catch pox?'

'Pox? What the *hell* is going on up there?' Eyes accustomed to the dark by now, Roger grabbed the stabbing foot and gave it a vicious twist, jerked downward. Unprepared for assault, Dixon lost his grip on the ladder and fell heavily, sliding over Roger's head and into the men below.

Roger ignored the cries of rage and surprise behind him and clambered out onto the deck. There was a group of men clustered thick about the forward hatchway. Lanterns hung above in the rigging, shooting beams of red and white and yellow light that caught the gleam of blades.

He looked quickly for another ship, but the ocean was black and empty on all sides. No boarders, no pirates; all the struggle was taking place near the hatchway, where half the crew was gathered in a knot, armed with knives and clubs.

Mutiny? he thought, and dismissed it, even as he pushed forward; Bonnet's head showed above the crowd, hatless, fair hair gleaming in the flash of lantern light. Roger shoved his way into the mob, ruthlessly shouldering smaller seamen aside.

Shrieks and shouts echoed from the hold, and a flicker of light showed below. A bundle of rags was handed up, passed rapidly from hand to hand, disappeared behind the shifting mass of limbs and clubs. There was a heavy splash to port, and then another.

'What is it, what's happening?' He bellowed in the ear of the bosun, who stood near the hatchway, holding a lantern. The man jerked round and glared at him.

'You've not had pox, have you? Get below!' Hutchinson's attention had already gone back to the open hatchway.

'Yes, I have! What's that got to –'

The bosun swung back, surprised.

'You've had pox? You're not marked. Ach, let it go – get you down, then, we need all hands!'

'For what?' Roger leaned forward, to make himself heard above the noise from below.

'Smallpox!' the bosun bellowed back. He gestured at the open hatchway, as one of the seamen appeared at the top of the ladder, a child under one arm, feebly kicking. Hands clawed and beat at the man's hunched back, and a woman's voice rose high above the other noises, shrill with terror.

She got a grip on the seaman's blouse, and as Roger watched, she began to climb the man's body, dragging him backward as she struggled to reach the child, screaming as she clawed the man's back, digging handfuls of cloth and flesh.

The man roared and swatted at her, trying to dislodge her. The ladder was fixed, but the seaman, one-handed and pulled off balance, swayed wildly, his look of rage turning to alarm as his feet slipped on the rung.

Reflex alone made Roger lunge forward, grabbing the child like a rugger ball as the seaman threw his arms out in a last effort to save himself. Entangled like lovers, man and woman fell backward together into the open maw of the hatchway. There was a crash and more screams from below, then the sudden, momentary silence of shock. Then the outcries began again, below, and a muttering babble around him.

Roger righted the child, trying to stop its whimpering with awkward pats. It seemed curiously loose-jointed in his arms, and it felt hot, even through its layers of clothes. Light flashed over Roger as the bosun lifted his lantern high, looking at the child with distaste.

'Hope you *have* had the pox, MacKenzie,' he said.

It was wee Gilbert, the lad with sore eyes – but two days had made such a change that Roger scarcely recognized him. The boy was thin as a wraith, the round face gone so thin that the skullbones showed. The fair, dirt-smudged skin had gone, too, submerged under a mass of suppurating pustules so thick that the eyes were mere slits in the lolling head.

He had barely time to register the sight before hands plucked the small, burning body from him. Before he could grasp the sudden emptiness in his arms, there was another splash to port.

He swung toward the rail in vain reflex, hands curled in fists of shock, but then turned back as a new roar came from the hatchway behind.

The passengers had recovered from the surprise of the attack. A rush of men boiled up the ladder, armed with anything they could seize, and fell upon the seamen at the top, bearing them down with sheer frenzy.

Someone cannoned into Roger and he fell, rolling to the side as a stool leg thudded into the deck near his head. He got to his hands and knees, was kicked in the ribs, shied and was pushed, heaved back against obstruction, and with a moment's opportunity, threw himself blindly at a pair of legs, having no idea whether he fought crew or passengers, fighting only for room to stand up and breathe.

The stink of sickness rolled out of the hold, a sweet, rotting smell that overlaid the usual harsh reek of ripe bodies and sewage. The lanterns swung with the wind, and light and shadow cut the scene to pieces, so that here showed a face, wild-eyed and shouting, there an arm upraised, here a naked foot, only to vanish in the darkness and be replaced at once by elbows and knives and thrusting knees, so the deck seemed awash in dismembered bodies.

So strong was the confusion that Roger felt dismembered himself; he glanced down, feeling numbness in his left arm, half expecting to find the limb struck off. It was there, though, and he raised it by reflex, fending off an unseen blow that jarred through bone.

Someone grasped his hair; he jerked free and swung round, elbowed someone hard in the ribs and swung again, hitting air. He found himself momentarily standing clear of the fight, gasping for breath. Two figures crouched before him, in the shadow of the rail; as he shook his head to clear it, the taller stood up and launched itself at him.

He reeled backward under the impact, clutching his attacker. They struck the foremast and fell together, then rolled over and over, hammering each other in blind earnest. Caught in the web of noise and blows, he paid no mind to the disjointed words that panted in his ear.

Then a boot struck him, and another, and as he loosed his hold on his opponent, two crewmen kicked them apart. Someone seized the other man and pulled him upright, and Roger saw the flash of the bosun's lantern held high, revealing the face of the tall fair-haired passenger – Morag MacKenzie's husband, green eyes dark and wild with fury.

MacKenzie was the worse for wear – so was Roger, as he discovered when he passed a hand across his face and felt his split lip – but his skin was clear of pustules.

'Good enough,' said Hutchinson briefly, and the man was thrust unceremoniously toward the hatchway.

His comrades gave Roger a rough hand up, and then left him swaying, dazed and ignored, as they finished their work. The resistance had been short-lived; though armed with the fury of despair, the passengers were weakened by six weeks under hatches, by sickness and scanty food. The

719

stronger had been clubbed into submission, the weaker forced back, and those sick of pox –

Roger looked out at the rail and the path of the moon's aisle, serene on the water. He grabbed the rail and vomited, retching till no more than bile came up, burning the back of nose and throat. The water below was black, and empty.

Drained and shaking from exertion, he made his way slowly across the deck. Those seamen he passed were silent, but from the battened forward hatchway, a single thin wail rose up, and up, an endless keen that drew no breath and knew no respite.

He nearly fell down the companionway into the crew's quarters, went to his hammock, ignoring all questions, and wrapped his blanket over his head, trying to shut out the sound of the wailing – to shut out everything.

But there was no oblivion to be found in the suffocating woolen folds, and he jerked the blanket off, heart pounding, with a sensation of drowning so strong in his chest that he gulped air, again and again until he felt dizzy, and still breathed deep, as though he must breathe for those who could not.

'It's for the best, lad,' Hutchinson had said to him with gruff sympathy, passing by as he puked his guts out over the rail. 'Pox spreads like wildfire; none in that hold would live to make landfall, did we not take out the sick.'

And was this better than the slower death of scabs and fever? Not for those left behind; the wail went on and on, lancing the silence, piercing wood and heart alike.

Maimed pictures flashed in his mind, truncated scenes caught by the popping of invisible flashbulbs: the sailor's contorted face as he fell into the hold; the little boy's half-open mouth, the inside scabbed with pustules. Bonnet standing above the fray, with his face of a fallen angel, watching. And the dark hungry water, empty under the moon.

Something bumped softly, sliding past the hull, and he rolled into a shivering ball, oblivious alike to the sweltering heat in the hold, and the sleepy complaint of the man next to him. No, not empty. He had heard the seamen say that sharks never sleep.

'Oh, God,' he said aloud. 'Oh, God!' He should have been praying for the dead, but could not.

He rolled again, squirming, trying to escape, and in the echo of the futile prayer found memory – the misplaced hearing of those few frantic words, panted in his ear during those moments of unthinking frenzy.

For the love of God, man, the fair-haired man had said. *For the love of God, let her go!*

He straightened and lay stiff, bathed in cold sweat.

Two figures in the shadow. And the open hatchway to the stores hold some twenty feet away.

'Oh, God,' he said again, but this time, it *was* a prayer.

It was the middle of the dogwatch next day before Roger found an opportunity to go down to the hold. He made no effort to avoid being seen; watching his shipmates had taught him quickly that in close quarters, nothing drew attention faster than furtiveness.

If anyone asked, he had heard a bumping noise, and thought perhaps the load had shifted. Close enough to the truth, at that.

He hung from the edge of the hatch by his hands; less chance of being followed if he didn't put down the ladder. He dropped into the dark and landed hard, jarring his bones. Anyone down here would have heard that – and by the same token, if anyone followed him, he would be warned.

He took a moment to recover from the shock of landing, then began to move cautiously through the looming dim bulks of the stacked cargo. Everything seemed blurred round the edges. It wasn't only the faint light, he thought; everything in the hold was vibrating very slightly, thrumming to the shiver of the hull beneath. He could hear it, if he listened closely; the lowest note in the ship's song.

Through the narrow aisles between the ranks of crates, past the huge bellies of the serried water casks. He breathed in; the air was full of the smell of wet wood, overlaid by the faint perfume of tea. There were rustlings and creakings, plenty of odd noises – but no sign of any human presence. Still, he was sure that someone was here.

721

And why are you here, mate? he thought. What if one of the steerage passengers *had* taken refuge here? If someone lay hidden here, chances were good that they had the pox; Roger could do nothing for them – why bother to look?

Because he couldn't not look, was the answer. He didn't reproach himself for failing to save the pox-stricken passengers; nothing could have helped them in any case, and perhaps a quick death by drowning was not in fact more terrible than the slow agony of the disease. He'd like to believe that.

But he hadn't slept; the events of the night filled him with such a sense of horror and sick futility that he could find no rest. Whether he could do anything now, or not, he must do *something*. He had to look.

Something small moved in the deep shadows of the hold. *Rat*, he thought, and turned reflexively to stamp on it. The movement saved him; a heavy object whizzed past his head and landed with a splash in the bilges below.

He put his head down and lunged in the direction of the movement, shoulders hunched against an expected blow. There was nowhere to run, and not much place to hide. He saw it again, lunged, and grabbed cloth. Jerked hard, and got flesh. A quick scuffle in the dark, and a cry of alarm, and he found himself pressing a body hard against a bulkhead, clutching the skinny wrist of Morag MacKenzie.

'What the *hell*?' She kicked at him, and tried to bite, but he ignored this. He got a good grip on the scruff of her neck and hauled her out of the shadows, into the dim brown light of the hold. 'What are you doing here?'

'Nothing! Let go! Let me go, please! Please, I beg ye, sir –' Force not availing to free herself – she weighed perhaps half what he did – she turned to pleading, words pouring out in a half-whispered stream of desperation. 'For the sake of your own mother, sir! Ye canna do it, please ye cannot let them kill him *please*!'

'I'm not going to kill anyone. For God's sake, hush yourself!' he said, and gave her a small shake.

From the blackest shadows behind the anchor chain came the high, thin wail of a fretful baby.

She gave a small gasp and looked up at him, frantic.

722

'They'll hear him! God, man, let me go to him!' Such was her desperation that she succeeded in wrenching herself free, and fled toward the sound, clambering over the great rusted links of the anchor chain, heedless of filth.

He followed, more slowly; she couldn't get away – there was nowhere for her to go. He found them in the darkest spot, crouched against one of the ship's knees, the huge angled timbers that framed the hull. There was barely a foot of clearance between the rough wood of the hull and the piled mass of the anchor chain; she was no more than a darker blot on the stygian blackness.

'I will not hurt you,' he said softly. The shadow seemed to shrink away from him, but she didn't answer.

His eyes were slowly growing accustomed to the dark; even back here, a faint light seeped through from the distant hatch. A patch of white – her breast was bared, giving suck to the child. He could hear the small wet noises as it fed.

'What the hell are you doing here?' he asked, though he knew well enough. His stomach clenched tight, and not just because of the foul smell of the bilges. He squatted next to her, barely able to fit in the tiny space.

'I'm hiding!' she said fiercely. 'Surely to goodness ye see that?'

'Is the child sick?'

'No!' She hunched herself over the baby, squirming as far away from him as she could get.

'Then –'

'It's no but a wee rash! All bairns get them, my mither said so!' He could hear the fear in her voice, underneath the furious denial.

'Are you sure?' he said, as gently as he could. He reached a tentative hand toward the dark blotch she held.

She struck at him, awkwardly one-handed, and he jerked back with a hiss of pain.

'Jesus! Ye stabbed me!'

'Stay back! I've my husband's dirk,' she warned. 'I won't let ye take him, I'll kill ye first, I swear I will!'

He believed her. Hand to his mouth, he could taste his own blood, sweet and salt on his tongue. It was no more than a scratch, but he believed her. She'd kill him – or die herself, which was a great deal more likely if one of the crew found her.

But no, he thought. She was worth money. Bonnet wouldn't kill her – only have her dragged on deck and forced to watch as her child was torn out of her arms and thrown into the sea. He remembered the dark shadows that dogged the ship, and shuddered with a cold that had nothing to do with the dank surroundings.

'I won't take him. But if it's the pox –'

'It's not! I swear to Bride, it's not!' A small hand shot out of the shadows and gripped him by the sleeve. 'It's as I tell ye, it's no but a milk rash, I've seen it, man – a hundred times before! I'm the eldest o' nine, I ken weel enough when a bairn's sick and when he's but teething!'

He hesitated, then made up his mind abruptly. If she was wrong, and the child had smallpox, she was likely already infected; to return her to the hold would be only to spread the disease. And if she was right – he knew as well as she that it didn't matter; any rash would condemn the child on sight.

He could feel her quivering, on the brink of hysteria. He wanted to touch her in reassurance, but thought better of it. She wouldn't trust him, and no wonder.

'I won't give you away,' he whispered.

He was met by suspicious silence.

'You need food, don't you? And fresh water. You'll have no milk soon, without it, and then what of the bairn?'

He could hear her breathing, ragged and phlegmy. She was ill, but it needn't be pox; all the hold passengers coughed and wheezed – the damp had got into their lungs early on.

'Show him to me.'

'No!' Her eyes shone in the dark, fearful as a cornered rat's, and the edge of her lip lifted over small white teeth.

'I swear I will not take him from you. I need to see, though.'

'What will ye swear on?'

He groped his memory for a suitable Celtic oath, then gave up and said what was in his mind.

724

'On my own woman's life,' he said, 'and on the heads of my unborn sons.'

He could feel doubt, and then a small easing of the tension in her; the round knee pressed against his leg moved slightly as she relaxed. There was a stealthy rustling in the chains nearby. Real rats this time.

'I canna leave him here alone while I steal food.' He saw the faint tilt of her head toward the noise. 'They'll eat him alive; they've bitten me in my sleep already, the filthy vermin.'

He reached out his hands, conscious all the time of the sounds from the deck above. It wasn't likely that anyone would come down here, but how long before he was missed above?

She still hesitated, but at last reached a finger toward her breast, and freed the child's mouth with a tiny *pop!* It made a small sound of protest, and wriggled slightly as he took it.

He hadn't held babies very often; the feel of the dirty little bundle was startling – inert but lively, soft yet firm.

'Mind his head!'

'I've got it.' Cradling the warm round skull in one careful palm, he duck-walked backward a step or two, bringing the child's face into dim light.

The cheeks were splotched with reddish pustules, topped with white – they looked for all the world like pox to Roger, and he felt a tremor of revulsion in the palms of his hands. Immunity or not, it took courage to touch contagion and not flinch.

He squinted at the child, then carefully undid its wrappings, ignoring the mother's hissed protest. He slid a hand under its dress, feeling first the soggy clout that hung between its chubby legs, and then the smooth, silky skin of chest and stomach.

The child didn't really seem so sick; his eyes were clear, not gummy. And while the tiny boy seemed feverish, it wasn't the searing heat he had felt the night before. The baby whined and squirmed, true, but he kicked with a fretful strength in the tiny limbs, not the weak spasms of a dying child.

The very young go quickly, Claire had said. *You have no*

notion how fast disease moves, when there's nothing to fight it with. He had some notion, after last night.

'All right,' he whispered at last. 'I think you're maybe right.' He felt, rather than saw, the easing of her arm – she had held her dagger ready.

He gingerly handed back the child, with a mingled sense of relief and reluctance. And the terrifying realization of the responsibility he had accepted.

Morag was cooing to the boy, cuddling him against her breast as she hastily rewrapped him.

'Sweet Jemmy, aye, that's a good laddie. Hush, bittie, hush now, it'll be all right, Mammy's here for ye.'

'How long?' Roger whispered, laying a hand on her arm. 'How long will the rash last, if it's milk rash?'

'Maybe four days, maybe five,' she whispered back. 'But it's no but maybe twa more, and the rash will be different – less. Anyone can see then that it's not the pox. I can come out, then.'

Two days. If it was pox, the child would be dead in two days. But if not – he might just manage. And so might she.

'Can you keep awake that long? The rats –'

'Aye, I can,' she said fiercely. 'I can do what I must. Will ye help me, then?'

He drew a deep breath, ignoring the stench.

'Aye, I will.' He stood up, and gave her his hand. After a moment's hesitation, she took it, and stood too. She was small, she barely reached his shoulder, and her hand in his was the size of a child's – in the shadows, she looked like a young girl cradling her doll.

'How old are you?' he asked suddenly.

He caught the gleam of her eyes, surprised, and then the flash of teeth.

'Yesterday I was two-and-twenty,' she said dryly. 'Today, I'm maybe a hundred.'

The small damp hand pulled free of his, and she melted back into the darkness.

39

A Gambling Man

The fog gathered through the night. By dawn the ship rode in a cloud so thick that the sea below could not be seen from the rail, and only the susurrus of the hull's passage indicatcd that the *Gloriana* still floated on water, not air.

There was no sun, and little wind; the sails hung limp, shuddering now and then with a passing air. Oppressed by the dimness, men walked the decks like ghosts, appearing out of the murk with a suddenness that startled one another.

This obscurity served Roger well; he was able to pass almost unseen through the ship, and slip unobserved into the hold, the small store of food he had kept back from his own meals concealed in his shirt.

The fog had gotten into the hold as well; clammy white tendrils touched his face, drifting out between the looming water casks, and hovered near his feet. It was darker than ever here below, gone from dusty-gold dimness to the black-brown of cold, wet wood.

The child was asleep; Roger saw no more than the curve of its cheek, still spattered with red pustules. They looked angry and inflamed. Morag saw his look of doubt and said nothing, but took his hand in her own and pressed it to the baby's neck.

The tiny pulse went bump-bump-bump under his finger, and the soft creased skin was warm but damp. Reassured, he smiled at Morag, and she gave him back a tiny glimmer.

A month in steerage had left her thin and grimy; the last two days had stamped her face with permanent lines of fear. Her hair straggled lank around her face, caked with grease and thick with lice. Her eyes were bruised with tiredness, and she smelled of feces and urine, sour milk and stale sweat. Her lips were tight and pale as the rest of her face. Roger took her very gently by the shoulders, bent, and kissed her mouth.

At the top of the ladder, he looked back. She was still standing there looking up at him, the child in her arms.

The deck was quiet save for the murmur of helmsman and bosun, invisible at the wheel. Roger eased the hatch cover back in place, his heart beginning to slow again, the touch of her still warming his hands. Two days. Maybe three. Perhaps they would make it; Roger at least was convinced she was right, the child did not have pox.

There should be no occasion for anyone to go into the hold soon – a fresh water-cask had been brought up only the day before. He could contrive to feed her – if only she could stay awake long enough . . . the sharp *ting* of the ship's bell pierced the fog, a reminder of time that no longer seemed to exist, its passage unmarked by any change of light or dark.

It was as Roger crossed toward the stern that he heard it; a sudden loud *whoosh* in the mist off the rail, very near at hand. The next instant, the ship trembled slightly underfoot, her boards brushed by something huge.

'Whale!' came a cry from aloft. He could see two men near the mainmast, dimly outlined in the fog. At the cry, they froze, and he realized that he, too, was standing rigid, listening.

There was another *whoosh* nearby, another farther off. The crew of the *Gloriana* stood silent, each man charting in his head the great exhalations, marking an invisible map on which the ship drifted through moving shoals, mountains of silent, intelligent flesh.

How big were they? Roger wondered. Big enough to damage the ship? He strained his eyes, vainly trying to see anything at all through the fog.

It came again, a thump hard enough to jar the rail under his hands, followed by a long, grating rasp that shuddered through the boards. There were muffled cries of fear from below; to those in the steerage, it would be right next to them, no more than the planks of the hull between them and rupture – a sudden smash and the frightful inrush of the sea. Three-inch oak planks seemed no more substantial than tissue paper against the great beasts that floated nearby, breathing unseen in the fog.

'Barnacles,' said a soft Irish voice from the mist behind

him. Despite himself, Roger jumped, and a low chuckle materialized into Bonnet's shadowed bulk. The Captain held a cheroot between his teeth, a spill from the galley fire illumining the lines and planes of his face, dissolute in red light. The rasping shudder came again through the boards.

'They scratch themselves to rid their skins of parasites,' Bonnet said casually. 'We are no more to them than a floating stone.' He drew heavily to start the flame, blew flagrant smoke, and tossed the burning paper overboard. It vanished in the mist like a falling star.

Roger let out a breath only slightly less noisy than the whales'. How close had Bonnet been? Had the Captain seen him coming out of the hold?

'They will not damage the ship, then?' he said, matching the Captain's casual tone.

Bonnet smoked for a moment in silence, concentrating on the draw of his cigar. Without the illumination of the open flame, he was once more a shadow, marked only by the glowing coal of the tip.

'Who knows?' he said at last, small spurts of smoke puffing out between his teeth as he spoke. 'Any one of the beasts might sink us, should he have a mind in him for mischief. I saw a ship once – or what was left of it – battered to pieces by an angry whale. Three feet of board, and a bit of spar left floating – sunk with all hands, two hundred souls.'

'You don't seem troubled by the possibility.'

There was a long sound of exhalation, a faint echo of the whales' sighing, as Bonnet blew smoke between pursed lips.

''Twould be a waste of strength to worry myself. A wise man leaves those things beyond his power to the gods – and prays that Danu will be with him.' The edge of the Captain's hat turned toward him. 'Ye'll know of Danu, will ye, MacKenzie?'

'Danu?' Roger said stupidly, and then the penny dropped, an old chant coming back to him from the mists of childhood – something Mrs. Graham had taught him to say. 'Come to me, Danu, change my luck. Make me bold. Give me wealth – and love to hold.'

729

There was an amused grunt behind the coal.

'Ah, and you not even an Irishman. But sure I knew you from the first for a man of learning, MacKenzie.'

'I know Danu the Luck-Giver,' Roger said, hoping against hope that that particular Celtic goddess was both a good sailor and on his side. He took a step backward, meaning to go, but a hand descended on his wrist, holding tight.

'A man of learning,' Bonnet repeated softly, all levity gone from his voice, 'but no wisdom. And are you a praying man at all, MacKenzie?'

He tensed, but felt the force of Bonnet's grip and did not pull away. Strength gathered in his limbs, his body knowing before he did that the fight had come.

'I said a wise man does not trouble himself with things beyond his power – but on this ship, MacKenzie, everything is in my power.' The grip on his wrist tightened. 'And everyone.'

Roger jerked his wrist sideways, breaking the grip. He stood alone, knowing there was neither help nor escape. There was no world beyond the ship, and within it, Bonnet was right – all were in the Captain's power. If he died, it would not help Morag – but that choice was made already.

'Why?' said Bonnet, sounding only mildly interested. 'The woman's no looker, sure. And a man of such learning, too; would you risk my ship and my venture, then, only for the sake of a warm body?'

'No risk.' The words came out hoarse, forced through a tight throat. *Come at me,* he thought, and his hands curled at his sides. *Come at me, and give me a chance to take you with me.* 'The child doesn't have pox – a harmless rash.'

'You will forgive my putting my ignorant opinion above your own, Mr. MacKenzie, but I am Captain here.' The voice was still soft, but the venom was clear.

'It is a child, for God's sake!'

'It is – and of no value.'

'No value to you, perhaps!'

There was a moment's silence, broken only by a distant *whoosh* in the empty white.

'And what value to you?' the voice asked, implacable. 'Why?'

For the sake of a warm body. Yes, for that. For the touch of humanity, the memory of tenderness, for the feeling of life stubborn in the face of death.

'For pity,' he said. 'She is poor; there was no one to help her.'

The rich perfume of tobacco reached him, narcotic, enchanting. He breathed it in, taking strength from it.

Bonnet moved, and he moved, too, settling himself in preparation. But there was no blow forthcoming; the shadow dug in a pocket, held out a ghostly hand in which he caught a magpie glitter from the diffuse lantern light – coins and bits of rubbish and what might have been a jewel's quick gleam. Then the Captain plucked out a silver shilling, and thrust the rest back into his pocket.

'Ah, pity,' he said. 'And did yez say you were a gambling man at all, MacKenzie?'

He held out the shilling, dropped it. Roger caught it, only by reflex.

'For the suckling's life, then,' Bonnet said, and the tone of light amusement was back. 'A gentleman's wager, shall we call it? Heads it lives, and tails it dies.'

The coin was warm and solid in his palm, an alien thing in this world of drifting chill. His hands were slick with sweat, and yet his mind had gone cold and sharp, focused to an ice pick's point.

Heads he lives, and tails he dies, he thought quite calmly, and did not mean the child below. He marked throat and crotch on the other man; grip and lunge, a blow and heave – the rail was no more than a foot away, the empty realm of the whales beyond.

There was no room beyond his calculations for any sense of fear. He saw the coin spin up as though it were thrown by another hand, then fall to the deck. His muscles bunched themselves, slowly.

'It seems Danu is with ye the night, sir.' Bonnet's soft Irish voice seemed to come to him from a great way off, as the Captain bent and picked up the coin.

Realization was only beginning to bloom in his chest, when the Captain gripped his shoulder, turning him down the deck.

'You'll walk with me awhile, MacKenzie.'

731

Something had happened to his knees; he felt as though he would sink down with every step, and yet somehow stayed upright, keeping pace with the shadow. The ship was silent, the deck under his feet a mile away; but the sea beyond was a live thing, breathing. He felt the breath in his own lungs rise and fall with the shifting deck, and felt as though there were no boundaries to his body. It might have been wood under his feet, or water, for all he could feel.

It was some time before he made sense of Bonnet's words, and realized, with a vague sense of amazement, that the man seemed to be recounting the story of his life, in a quiet, matter-of-fact sort of way.

Orphaned in Sligo at an early age, he had learned quickly to fend for himself; he said, working as a cabin boy aboard trading ships. But one winter, with ships scarce, he had found work ashore in Inverness, digging the foundation for a grand house that was building near the town.

'I was just seventeen,' he said. 'The youngest of the crew of workmen. I could not say why it was they hated me. Mayhap it was my manner, for that was rough enough – or jealousy for my size and strength; they were an unchancy, whey-faced lot. Or maybe that the lasses smiled on me. Or maybe 'twas only that I was a stranger.

'Still, I knew well enough I was unpopular with them – little did I know quite *how* unpopular, though, until the day the cellar was finished and the foundation ready to be laid.'

Bonnet paused to draw on his cigar, lest it go out. He let out puffs of smoke from the corners of his mouth, white wisps that curled past his head into the greater white of the fog.

'The trenches were dug,' he went on, the cigar clenched between his teeth, 'and the walls started; the great block of the cornerstone standin' ready. I had gone to my supper, and was just walkin' back to the place where I slept, when to my surprise I was caught up by a pair of the lads with whom I worked.

'They'd a bottle; they sat down on a wall and urged me to drink with them. I should've known better, for they were friendly, which they'd never been before. But I did

drink, and drink again, and in no time at all I was reelin'
drunk, for I'd no head for liquor, havin' never the money
to buy strong drink. I was well fuddled by the time 'twas
full dark, and scarcely thought to pull away when they
took me by the arms and hastened me down the lane.
Then they seized me, tossed me over a half-built wall, and
to my surprise, I found myself lyin' in the damp dirt of the
cellar I'd helped dig.

'All of them were there, the workmen. Another man was
with them, too; one o' them had a lantern, and when he
held it up, I could see the man was Daft Joey. Daft Joey was
a beggarman that lived beneath the bridge – he had nay
teeth, and he ate rotten fish and floating dung from the
river, and he stank worse than a blackbirder's hold.

'I was so dazed with the whisky and the fall that I lay
where I was, only half hearin' them as they talked – or
argued, rather, for the chief o' the gang was angry that the
two had brought me. The daftie would do, he said; a
mercy to him, at that. But them that brought me said no,
better me. Someone might miss the beggarman, they said.
Then someone laughed and said aye, and they would not
have to pay me my last week's wages, and 'twas then I
began to know they meant to kill me.

'They'd talked before, while we worked. A sacrifice, they
said, for the foundation, lest the earth tremble and the
walls collapse. But I had not listened – and if I had, would
not have guessed that they meant any more than to chop
the head off a cockerel and bury it, as was usual.'

He had not looked at Roger through this recital, his
eyes instead fixed on the mist, as though the events he
described were happening again, somewhere just beyond
the white curtain of fog.

Roger's clothing hung on him, clinging, wringing wet
with mist and cold sweat. His stomach clenched, and the
cesspool smell of the steerage might have been the stink
of Daft Joey in the cellar.

'So they palavered for a bit,' Bonnet went on, 'and the
beggarman began to make noise, for he wanted more
drink. And at last the chief said it was not worth so much
talk, he would throw for the choice. Then he took a coin

from his pocket and he said to me, laughin', 'Will ye take heads or tails, then, man?'

'I was too sick to say a word; the sky was black and whirling round and bits of light kept flickering at the edges of my eyes, like fallin' stars. So he said it for me; by Geordie's head should I live, and by his arse I should die, and he threw the shilling up in the air. It came down in the dirt by my head, but I had nay strength to turn and look.

'He bent to see and gave a grunt, then he stood up and took nay more notice of me.'

They had reached the stern in their quiet pacing. Bonnet stopped there, hands on the rail, smoking silently. Then he took the cigar from his mouth.

'They pulled the daftie to the wall that was built, and made him sit down on the ground at its foot. I do remember his foolish face,' he said softly. 'He took a drink and he laughed wi' them, and his mouth was open – slack and wet as a old whore's cunt. The next moment, the stone came down from the top of the wall, and crushed his head.'

Drops of moisture had gathered on the spikes of hair at the back of Roger's neck; he could feel them run down, one at a time, trickling cold down the crease of his back.

'They rolled me on my face and hit me,' Bonnet continued matter-of-factly. 'When I came to myself again, I was in the bottom of a fishing boat. The fisherman left me on the shore near Peterhead and said he would advise me to find a new ship – he could see, he said, I was not meant for the land.'

He held up the cigar and tapped it gently with a finger to loosen the ash.

'At that,' he said, 'they did give me my wages; when I came to look, the shilling was in my pocket. Ah, they were honest men, sure.'

Roger leaned against the rail, gripping its wood as the single solid thing in a world gone soft and nebulous.

'And did you go back to the land?' he asked, and heard his own voice, preternaturally calm, as though it belonged to someone else.

'Did I find them, ye mean.' Bonnet turned and leaned

back against the rail, half facing Roger. 'Oh, yes. Years later. One at a time. But I found them all.' He opened the hand that held the coin, and held it cupped thoughtfully before him, tilting it back and forth so the silver gleamed in the lantern light.

'Heads you live, and tails you die. A fair chance, would yez say, MacKenzie?'

'For them?'

'For you.'

The soft Irish voice was as unemphatic as it might be were it making observations of the weather.

As in a dream, Roger felt the weight of the shilling drop once more into his hands. He heard the suck and hiss of the water on the hull, the blowing of the whales – and the suck and hiss of Bonnet's breath as he drew on his cigar. *Seven whales the fill of a Cirein Croin.*

'A fair chance,' Bonnet said. 'Luck was with you before, MacKenzie. See will Danu come for you again – or will it be the Soul-Eater this time?'

The fog had closed over the deck. There was nothing visible save the glowing coal of Bonnet's cigar, a burning cyclops in the mist. The man might be a devil indeed, one eye closed to human misery, one eye open to the dark. And here Roger stood quite literally between the devil and the deep blue sea, with his fate shining silver in the palm of his hand.

'It is my life; I'll make the call,' he said, and was surprised to hear his voice calm and steady. 'Tails – tails is mine.' He threw, and caught, clapped his one hand hard against the back of the other, trapped the coin and its unknown sentence.

He closed his eyes and thought just once of Brianna. *I'm sorry,* he said silently to her, and lifted his hand.

A warm breath passed over his skin, and then he felt a spot of coolness on the back of his hand as the coin was picked up, but he didn't move, didn't open his eyes.

It was some time before he realized that he stood alone.

PART NINE

Passionnément

40

Virgin Sacrifice

Wilmington, the Colony of North Carolina, September 1, 1769

This was the third attack, of whatever Lizzie's sickness was. She had seemed to recover after the first bad fever, and after a day spent regaining her strength, had insisted she was able to travel. They had got no more than a day's ride north of Charleston, though, before the fever struck again.

Brianna had hobbled the horses, and made a hasty camp near a small creek, then made trip after trip through the night, scrabbling up and down a muddy bank in the dark, carrying water in a small canteen to dribble down Lizzie's throat and over her steaming body. She wasn't afraid of dark woods or lurking animals, but the thought of Lizzie dying in the wilderness, miles from any sort of help, was terrifying enough to make her want to head straight back to Charleston as soon as Lizzie could sit a horse.

By morning, however, the fever had broken, and though Lizzie was weak and pale, she had been able to ride. Brianna had hesitated, but finally decided to press on toward Wilmington, rather than turn back. The urge that had driven her all this way now had a sharper spur; she *had* to find her mother, for Lizzie's sake as well as her own.

Brianna hadn't appreciated her size for most of a life spent looming in the back row of class pictures, but she had begun to feel the advantages of height and strength as she grew older. And the longer she spent in this miserable place, the more advantageous they seemed.

She braced one arm against the bed frame as she eased the chamber pot out from under Lizzie's frail white buttocks with the other hand. Lizzie was scrawny but surprisingly heavy, and no more than half conscious; she moaned and twitched restlessly, the twitch suddenly springing into the full-fledged convulsion of a chill.

The shivering was beginning to ease a little now, though Lizzie's teeth were still clenched hard enough to make the sharp bones of her jaws stand out like struts beneath her skin.

Malaria, Brianna thought, for the dozenth time. It must be, to keep coming back like this. A number of small pink welts showed on Lizzie's neck, reminders of the mosquitoes that had plagued them ever since the *Phillip Alonzo* drew within sight of land. They had made landfall too far south, and wasted three weeks in meandering through the shallow coastal waters to Charleston, gnawed incessantly by bloodsucking bugs.

'There now. Feeling a little better?'

Lizzie nodded feebly, and tried to smile, succeeding only in looking like a white mouse that had taken poisoned bait.

'Water, honey. Try a little, just a sip.' Brianna held the cup to Lizzie's mouth, coaxing. She felt a strange sense of déjà vu and realized that her voice was the echo of her mother's, both in words and tone. The realization was oddly comforting, as though her mother somehow stood behind her, speaking through her.

If it were her mother speaking, though, next would have come the orange-flavored St. Joseph's aspirin, a tiny pill to be sucked and savored, as much treat as medicine, the aches and fever seeming to subside as quickly as the sweet tart pill dissolved on her tongue. Brianna cast a bleak glance at her saddlebags, bulging in the corner. No aspirin there; Jenny had sent a small bundle of what she called 'simples', but the chamomile and peppermint tea had only made Lizzie vomit.

Quinine was what you gave people for malaria; that's what she needed. But she had no idea whether it was even *called* quinine here, or how it was administered. Malaria was an old disease, though, and quinine came from plants – surely a doctor would have some, whatever it was called?

Only the hope of finding medical help had kept her going through Lizzie's second bout. Afraid to stop on the road again, she had taken Lizzie up in front of her, cradling the girl's body against her as they rode, leading Lizzie's horse. Lizzie had alternately blazed with heat and shaken with chill, and both of them had arrived in Wilmington limp with exhaustion.

But here they were, in the midst of Wilmington, and as far from real help as they had ever been. Bree glanced at the bedside table, lips tight. A wadded cloth lay there, dabbled with blood.

The landlady had taken one look at Lizzie and sent for an apothecary. Despite what her mother had said about the primitive state of medicine and its practitioners here, Brianna had felt a sudden instinctive surge of relief at sight of the man.

The apothecary was a decently dressed young man with a kindly air and reasonably clean hands. No matter what his state of medical knowledge, he was likely to know as much about fevers as she herself did. More important, she could feel that she wasn't alone in caring for Lizzie.

Modesty prompted her to step outside when the apothecary drew down the linen sheet to make his examination, and it was not until she heard a small cry of distress that she flung open the door, to find the young apothecary, fleam in hand, and Lizzie, her face white as chalk, red blood streaming from a cut in the crook of her elbow.

'But it is to draw the humors, miss!' the apothecary had pleaded, trying to shield both himself and the body of his patient. 'Do you not understand? You must draw the humors! If it is not done, hot bile will toxify within her organs and fill her body entirely, to her certain detriment!'

'It will be to *your* certain detriment if you don't leave,' Brianna had informed him, through clenched teeth. 'Get out of here this minute!'

Medical zeal disappearing in favor of self-preservation, the young man had picked up his case and left with what dignity he could, pausing at the foot of the stairs to shout dire warnings up at her.

The warnings kept echoing in her ears, between trips downstairs to fill the basin from the kitchen copper. Most of the apothecary's words were simple ignorance – ranting

741

about humors and bad blood – but there were some that came back with uncomfortable force.

'If you will not take heedful advice, miss, you may well condemn your maid to death!' he had called, indignant face upturned in the darkness of the stairwell. 'You do not know how to care for her yourself!'

She didn't. She didn't even know for sure what Lizzie's sickness was; the apothecary had called it an 'ague', and the landlady had talked of 'seasoning'. It was quite common for new immigrants to fall ill repeatedly, exposed as they were to an unfamiliar array of new germs. From the landlady's unguarded remarks, it seemed apparent that it was also quite common for such immigrants not to survive this seasoning process.

The basin tilted, sloping hot water over her wrists. Water was the only thing she had. God knew whether the well behind the inn was sanitary or not; better to use the boiling water from the copper and let it cool, even if it took longer. There was cool water in the pitcher; she dribbled a little between Lizzie's dry, cracked lips, then eased the girl down on the bed. She washed Lizzie's face and neck, pulled back the quilt and soaked the linen nightdress again, the tiny nipples showing as dark pink points beneath.

Lizzie managed a small smile, eyelids drooping, then sank back with a tiny sigh and fell asleep, loose joints relaxing like a rag doll's.

Brianna felt as though her own stuffing had been removed as well. She dragged the single stool over to the window and collapsed on it, leaning on the sill in a vain effort to get a breath of fresh air. The atmosphere had lain on them like a thick blanket all the way from Charleston – little wonder that poor Lizzie had crumpled under its weight.

She scratched uneasily at a bite on her own thigh; the bugs were not nearly as fond of her as they were of Lizzie, but she had suffered a few bites. Malaria wasn't a danger; she had had the shots for that, as well as for typhoid, cholera, and anything else she could think of. But there was no vaccine for things like dengue fever, or any of a dozen other diseases that haunted the thick air like malevolent spirits. How many of those were spread by biting insects?

She closed her eyes and leaned her head against the wooden frame, blotting trickles of sweat from her breast-bone with the folds of her shirt. She could smell herself; how long had she been wearing these clothes? It didn't matter; she had been awake for most of two days and two nights, and was too tired to undress, let alone make the effort to wash.

Lizzie's fever seemed to have broken – but for how long? If it kept coming back, it was sure to kill the little maid-servant; she had already lost all the weight she had gained on the voyage, and her fair skin was beginning to show a yellow tinge in sunlight.

There was no help to be found in Wilmington. Brianna sat up straight, stretching and feeling the bones of her back pop into place. Tired or not, there was only one thing to do. She had to find her mother, and as quickly as possible.

She would sell the horses and find a boat to take them up the river. Even if the fever came back, she could take care of Lizzie as well on a boat as she could in this hot, smelly little room – and they would still be traveling toward their goal.

She got up and splashed a little water on her face, twisting her sweat-soaked hair up out of the way. She loos-ened the crumpled breeches and stepped out of them, making plans in a dreamy, disconnected sort of way.

A boat, on the river. Surely it would be cooler on the river. No more riding; her thigh muscles ached from four days in the saddle. They would sail to Cross Creek, find Jocasta MacKenzie.

'Aunt,' she murmured, swaying slightly as she reached for the oil-dip lamp. 'Great-aunt Jocasta.' She imagined a kindly white-haired old lady who would greet her with the same joy she had found at Lallybroch. Family. It would be so good to have family again. Roger drifted into her thoughts, as he did so often. She resolutely pushed him out again; time enough to think of him when her mission was accomplished.

A tiny cloud of gnats hovered over the flame, and the-wall nearby was spattered with the arrowed shapes of moths and lacewings, taking respite from their quest. She pinched out the flame, scarcely hotter than the air in the room, and pulled the shirt off over her head in darkness.

Jocasta would know exactly where Jamie Fraser and her mother were – would help her get to them. For the first time since stepping through the stones, she thought of Jamie Fraser with neither curiosity nor trepidation. Nothing mattered but finding her mother. Her mother would know what to do for Lizzie; her mother would know how to take care of everything.

She spread a folded quilt on the floor and lay down naked on it. She was asleep in moments, dreaming of the mountains, and clean white snow.

By the next evening, things looked better. The fever *had* broken, just as before, leaving Lizzie spent and weak, but clearheaded, and as cool as the climate allowed. Restored by a night's rest, Brianna had washed her hair and sponge-bathed in the basin, then had paid the landlady to keep an eye on Lizzie while she, dressed in breeches and coat, went about her business.

It had taken most of the day – and the suffering of a good many widened eyes and gaping mouths as men realized her sex – to sell the horses at what she hoped was an honest price. She had heard of a man named Viorst, who took passengers between Wilmington and Cross Creek in his canoe for a price. She hadn't found Viorst before dark, though – and wasn't about to hang around the docks at night, breeches or no breeches. Morning would be time enough.

Still more heartening, Lizzie had been downstairs when she returned to the inn toward sunset, being cosseted by the landlady and fed morsels of corn pudding and chicken fricassee.

'You're better!' Brianna exclaimed. Lizzie nodded, beaming, and gulped her mouthful.

'I am, so,' she said. 'I feel quite myself again, and Mrs. Smoots has been so kind as to let me wash all of our things. Oh, it's so nice to feel clean again!' she said fervently, laying a pale hand on her kerchief, which looked freshly ironed.

'You shouldn't be washing and ironing,' Brianna scolded, sliding into the bench beside her maid. 'You'll wear yourself out, and get sick again.'

Lizzie looked down her thin nose, a prim smile perched at the corners of her mouth.

'Well, I didna think ye'd be wanting to meet your da in clothes all spotted wi' filth. Not but what even a clarty gown would be better than what ye've got on.' The little maid's eyes passed reprovingly over Brianna's breeches; she didn't approve at all of her mistress's penchant for male costume.

'Meet my da? What do you – Lizzie, have you heard something?' A flare of hope shot up inside her, a sudden bright puff like the lighting of a gas stove.

Lizzie looked smug.

'I have that. And 'twas all because of the washin', too – my da did always say as how virtue brings its reward.'

'I'm sure it does,' Brianna said dryly. 'What did you find out, and how?'

'Well, I was just after hanging out your petticoat – the nice one, aye, wi' the lace about the hem –'

Brianna picked up a small jug of milk, and held it menacingly over her maid's head. Lizzie squeaked and ducked away, giggling.

'All right! I'm telling! I'm telling!'

In the middle of her washing, one of the tavern's patrons had come out into the yard to smoke a pipe, the day being fine. He had admired Lizzie's domestic skills and taken up a pleasant conversation, in the course of which it was revealed that this gentleman – one Andrew MacNeill by name – had not only heard of James Fraser but was well acquainted with him.

'He is? What did he say? Is this MacNeill still here?'

Lizzie put out a hand and made small quelling motions.

'I'm sayin' it as quick as I can. No, he's not here; I did try to make him stay, but he was bound for New Bern by the packet boat, and couldna bide.' She was nearly as excited as Brianna; her cheeks were still pale and sallow, but the tip of her nose had gone pink.

745

'Mr. MacNeill knows your da, and your great-auntie Cameron as well – she's a great lady, he says, verra rich, with a tremendous great house, and lots of slaves, and –'

'Never mind about that now, what did he say about my father? Did he mention my mother?'

'Claire,' Lizzie said triumphantly. 'Ye did say that was your mam's name? I asked, and he said yes, Mrs. Fraser's name was Claire. And he said she was a most amazing healer – did ye not say as your mother was a fine physician? He said as he had seen her do a desperate operation on a man, laid him smack in the middle of the dinner table and cut off his ballocks and then stitched them back on, right there on the spot, wi' all the dinner party lookin' on!'

'That's my mother, all right.' There were tears of what might have been laughter in the corners of her eyes. 'Are they well? Had he seen them lately?'

'Och, that's the best of it!' Lizzie leaned forward, eyes big with the importance of her news. 'He's in Cross Creek – your da, Mr. Fraser! A man he knows is on trial there for assault, and your da's come down to be witness for him.' She patted her handkerchief against her temple, mopping up tiny beads of sweat.

'Mr. MacNeill says the court willna sit again till Monday week because the judge fell ill, and another is coming from Edenton, and the trial canna go on until he arrives.'

Brianna brushed back a lock of hair and blew out her breath, hardly daring to believe their luck.

'A week from Monday . . . and it's Saturday now. God, I wonder how long it will take to get upriver?'

Lizzie crossed herself hastily in atonement for her mistress's casual blasphemy, but shared in her excitement.

'I dinna ken, but Mrs. Smoots did say as her son's made the trip once before – we could ask him.'

Brianna swung round on her bench, looking over the room. Men and boys had begun coming in as darkness fell, stopping for a drink or a supper on their way from work to bed, and now there were fifteen or twenty people crammed into the small space.

'Which one is Junior Smoots?' Brianna asked, craning her neck to see through the press of bodies.

'Yonder – the laddie wi' the sweet brown eyes. I'll fetch

him to ye, shall I?' Emboldened by excitement, Lizzie slipped out of her seat and pushed way into the throng.

Brianna was still holding the jug of milk, but made no move to pour into her cup. Her throat was too asked with excitement to swallow. Little more than a week!

Wilmington was a small town, Roger thought. How many places could she be? If she was here at all. He thought there was a good chance of it; inquiries in the dockside taverns in New Bern had given him the valuable information that the *Phillip Alonzo* had reached Charleston safely – and only ten days before the *Gloriana* had docked in Edenton.

It might have taken Brianna anything from two days to two weeks to make her way from Charleston to Wilmington – assuming that she was indeed headed there.

'She's here,' he muttered. 'Damn it, I *know* she's here!' Whether this conviction was the result of deduction, intuition, hope, or merely stubbornness, he clung to it like a drowning sailor to a spar.

He had managed the journey from Edenton to Wilmington with a fair amount of ease, himself. Put to work unloading cargo from the *Gloriana's* hold, he had carried a chest of tea into a warehouse, set it down, walked back to the door, and busied himself in retying the sweat-soaked kerchief round his head. As soon as the next man had passed him, he stepped out onto the dock, turned right instead of left, and within seconds was headed up the narrow cobbled lane that led from docks to town. By the next morning he'd found a berth as loader on a small cargo boat, transporting naval stores from Edenton to the main depot at Wilmington, there to be transferred to a larger ship for transport to England.

He jumped ship again in Wilmington, without a moment's compunction. He hadn't time to waste; there was Brianna to be found.

He knew she was here. Fraser's Ridge was in the mountains; she'd need a guide, and Wilmington was the most likely port in which to find one. And if she was here, someone would have noticed her; he'd bet money on that.

He could only hope the wrong sort of person hadn't noticed her already.

A quick reconnoiter of the main street and the harbor gave him a count of twenty-three taverns. Christ, these people drank like fish! There was the chance she'd taken a room in a private house, but the taverns were the place to start.

By evening he'd covered ten of the taverns, slowed by the necessity of avoiding any of his erstwhile shipmates. Being in the presence of so much drink, and he without an extra penny to spend, had given him a raging thirst. He hadn't eaten all day, either, which didn't help matters.

At the same time, he scarcely noticed the physical discomfort. A man in the fifth tavern had seen her, so had a woman in the seventh. 'A tall *man* wi' red hair,' the man had said, but, 'A great huge girl, dressed in men's breeches,' the woman had said, clicking her tongue in shock. 'Walkin' down the street, plain as you please, with her coat over her arm and her backside in view of everyone!'

Let Roger get that particular backside in *his* view, he thought with some grimness, and he'd know what to do with it. He begged a cup of water from a kindhearted landlady, and set off with renewed determination.

By the time it was full dark, he had covered another five taverns. The taprooms were full now, and he discovered that the tall redheaded girl in men's clothing had been causing public comment for nearly a week. The quality of some of this comment caused the blood to throb in his cheeks with outrage, and only the fear of being arrested kept him from outright assault.

As it was, he left the fifteenth tavern after an ugly exchange of words with two drunkards, boiling with fury. Christ, had the woman no sense at all? Did she have no notion what men were capable of?

He stopped in the street and wiped a sleeve across his sweating face. He breathed heavily, wondering what to do next. Keep on, he supposed, though if he didn't find something to eat soon, he was going to fall flat on his face in the road.

The Blue Bull, he decided. He'd glanced into the shed

there as he passed earlier, and seen a good pile of clean straw. He'd spend a penny or two for dinner, and perhaps the owner would let him sleep in the stable for the sake of Christian kindness.

Turning, his eye caught sight of a sign on the house across the road.

WILMINGTON GAZETTEER, JNO. GILLETTE. PROP., it read. Wilmington's newspaper; one of few in the Colony of North Carolina. One too many, if you asked Roger. He fought the urge to pick up a rock and hurl it through Jno. Gillette's window. Instead, he yanked the sodden band off his head and, making an effort to tidy himself into some semblance of decency, turned toward the river and the Blue Bull.

She was there.

She was sitting by the hearth, her tailed hair sparking in the firelight, engaged in conversation with a young man whose smile Roger wanted to wipe off forcibly. Instead, he slammed the door behind him with a crash and started toward her. She turned startled, and stared blankly at the bearded stranger. Recognition flashed in her eyes, then joy, and a huge smile spread across her face.

'Oh,' she said. 'It's you.' Then her eyes changed, as realization flared up like a brushfire. She screamed. It was a good full-bodied scream, and every head in the tavern snapped round at the sound of it.

'Damn you!' He lunged across the table, and got her by the arm. 'What the devil do you think you're doing?'

Her face had gone dead white, her eyes round and dark with shock. She jerked away, trying to free herself.

'Let go!'

'That I won't! You'll come with me, and ye'll do it this moment!'

Sidling round the table, he got hold of her other arm, jerked her up, whirled her around and pushed her in front of him toward the door.

'MacKenzie!' Damn, it was one of the seamen from the cargo boat. Roger glowered at the man, willing him to keep out of it. Luckily the man was both smaller and older than Roger; he hesitated, but then took courage from the company and lifted his chin pugnaciously.

'What you doing to the lass, MacKenzie? Leave her be!' There was a stir among the crowd, men turning from their drinks, attracted by the up-roar. He had to get out of here *now*, or he wouldn't get out at all.

'Tell them it's all right, tell them you know me!' he whispered into Brianna's ear.

'It's all right.' Brianna spoke, voice husky with shock, but loud enough to be heard over the growing hubbub. 'It's all right. I – I know him.' The seaman dropped back a little, still dubious. A scrawny young girl in the inglenook had gotten to her feet; she looked frightened to death, but bravely clutched a stone ale bottle in one fist, evidently intending to hit Roger with it, if necessary. Her high-pitched voice rang out above the suspicious grumble of voices.

'Miss Bree! Ye'll not go wi' yon black villain, surely?'

Brianna made a sound that might have been laughter, choked by hysteria. Reaching up, she dug her nails hard into the back of his hand. Startled by the pain, he loosened his grip and she yanked her arm out of his grasp.

'It's all right,' she repeated, more firmly to the room at large. 'I know him.' She made a small shooing gesture at the girl. 'Lizzie, go on up to bed. I'll – I'll be back later.' She whirled on her bootheel and headed for the door, walking fast. Roger gave the taproom a menacing glare, to discourage anyone who thought of interfering, and followed her.

She was waiting right outside the door; her fingers sank into his arm with a fierceness that might have been gratifying were it prompted solely by joy at seeing him. He doubted it.

'What are you *doing* here?' she asked.

He detached her fingers and gripped them firmly.

'Not here,' he snapped. He took her arm and dragged her a little way down the road, to the shelter of a big horse-chestnut tree. The sky still glowed with the remnants of twilight, but the drooping branches reached nearly to the ground, and it was dark enough underneath to hide them from any curious souls who thought of venturing after them.

She whirled on him the instant they reached its shadows.

'What are you doing here, for God's sake?'

'Looking for you, ye wee fool! And what in the name of all holy are *you* doing here? And dressed like *that*, God damn you!' He'd had the briefest look at her in her breeches and shirt, but it was enough.

In her own time, the clothes would have been so baggy as to be sexless. After months of seeing women in long skirts and *arisaids*, though, the blatant division of her legs, the sheer bloody length of thigh and curve of calf, seemed so outrageous that he wanted to wrap a sheet around her.

'Bloody woman! You might as well walk down the street naked!'

'Don't be an idiot! What are you doing here?'

'I told you – looking for you.'

He took her by the shoulders, then, and kissed her, hard. Fear, anger, and the sheer relief of finding her were fused at once into a solid bolt of desire, and he found he was shaking with it. So was she. She was clinging to him, shaking in his arms.

'It's all right,' he whispered to her. He buried his mouth in her hair. 'It's all right, I'm here. I'll take care of you.'

She jerked upright, out of his arms.

'All *right?*' she cried. 'How can you say that? For God's sake, you're *here!*'

There was no mistaking the horror in her voice. He grabbed her by the arm.

'And where the hell else should I be, with you tearing off into fucking nowhere and risking your bloody neck, and – why the hell did you do it?!'

'I'm looking for my parents. What *else* would I be doing here?'

'I know that, for God's sake! I mean why in *hell* did you not tell me what you meant to do?'

She jerked her arm out of his grasp and gave him a healthy shove in the chest that all but sent him staggering.

'Because you wouldn't have let me go, that's why! You'd have tried to stop me, and –'

'Damn right I would! God, I'd have locked you in a

room, or tied you hand and foot! Of all the flea-brained notions –'

She hit him, a full-palmed slap that caught him hard across the cheekbone.

'Shut up!'

'Bloody woman! D'ye expect me to let you go off into – into *nothing*, and I sit at home twiddling my thumbs while you're having your womb paraded on a pike in the market-place? What sort of man d'ye think I am?'

He felt her movement rather than saw it, and grabbed her wrist before she could slap him again.

'I'm in no mood for that, girl! Hit me once more, and by Christ, I will do you violence!'

She folded her other hand into a fist and punched him in the belly, quick as a striking snake.

He wanted to hit her back. Instead, he grabbed her, and with a handful of her hair wrapped round his fist, kissed her as hard as he could.

She squirmed and struggled against him, making strangled noises, but he didn't stop. Then she was kissing him back, and they sank to their knees together. Her arms came round his neck as he bore her down beneath him to the leaf-matted ground beneath the tree. Then she was crying in his arms, choking and gasping, tears running down her face as she clutched him.

'Why?' she sobbed. 'Why did you have to follow me? Didn't you realize? Now what are we going to do!'

'Do? Do about what?' He couldn't tell whether she was crying from anger or fear – both, he thought.

She stared up at him through strands of tangled hair.

'Getting back! You have to have somebody to go to – somebody you care for. You're the only person I love at that end – or you were! How am I going to get back, if you're *here*? And how will you get back, if *I'm* here?'

He stopped dead, fear and anger both forgotten, and his hands clamped tight on her wrists to stop her hitting him again.

'That's why? That's why you wouldn't tell me? Because you *love* me? Jesus Christ!'

He let go of her wrists and lay on top of her instead. He grabbed her face with both hands and tried to kiss her again. She gave a sudden snap of her hips, swung her legs up on either side, and scissored him neatly across the back, crushing his ribs.

He rolled, breaking the hold, and brought her with him, ending on his back, with her on top. He got a hand in her hair and drew her face down to his, panting.

'Stop,' he said. 'Christ, what is this, a wrestling match?'

'Let go of my hair.' She shook her head, trying to dislodge his grip. 'I *hate* having my hair pulled.'

He let go of her hair, and slid his hand up the length of her neck, fingers curled round the slender nape, a thumb resting on the pulse in her throat. It was going like a trip-hammer; so was his.

'Right, how are ye on being choked?'

'Don't like it.'

'Neither do I. Get your arm off my neck, aye?'

Very slowly, her weight eased back. He still felt short of breath, but not from being choked. He didn't want to let go of her neck. Not from fear of her cutting loose again, but because he couldn't bear to lose the feel of her. It had been too long.

She reached up and took hold of his wrist, but didn't pull his hand away. He felt her swallow.

'Right,' he whispered. 'Say it. I want to hear it.'

'I . . . love . . . you,' she said, between her teeth. 'Got it?'

'Aye, I've got it.' He took her face between his hands, very gently, and drew her down. She came, arms trembling and giving way beneath her.

'You're sure?' he said.

'Yes. What are we going to *do*?' she said, and began to cry.

'*We.*' She'd said *we*. She'd said she was sure.

Roger lay in the dust of the road, bruised, filthy, and starving, with a woman trembling and weeping against his chest, now and then giving him a small thump with her fist. He had never felt happier in his life.

'Hush,' he whispered, half rocking her. 'It's all right; there's another way. We'll get back; I know how. Don't worry, I'll take care of you.'

Finally, she wore herself out, and lay still in the crook of his arm, sniffling and hiccuping. There was a large wet spot on the front of his shirt. The crickets in the tree, startled into silence by the uproar, cautiously resumed their songs overhead.

She freed herself and sat up, fumbling in the dark.

'I have to blow my dose,' she said thickly. 'Do you have a hanky?'

He gave her the damp rag he used to tie back his hair. She made whooshing noises, and he smiled in the dark.

'You sound like a can of shaving cream.'

'And when was the last time you saw one of those?' She lay down on him again, head tucked into the curve of his shoulder, and reached up to touch his jaw. He'd shaved two days ago; there had been neither time nor opportunity since.

Her hair still smelled faintly of grass, though no longer of artificial flowers. It must be her natural scent.

She sighed deeply, tightened her arm around him.

'I'm sorry,' she said. 'I didn't want you to come after me. But . . . Roger, I'm awfully glad you're here!'

He kissed her temple; she was damp and salty with sweat and tears.

'So am I,' he said, and for the moment all the trials and dangers of the past two months seemed insignificant. All but one.

'How long have you been planning this?' he asked. He thought he could have told her, to the day. Since her letters had begun to change.

'Oh . . . about six months,' she said, confirming his guess. 'It was when I went to Jamaica during last Easter vacation.'

'Aye?' To Jamaica, instead of to Scotland. She'd asked him to join her, and he'd refused, foolishly hurt that she hadn't planned to come to him automatically.

She took a deep breath and let it out, blotting the neck of her shirt against her skin.

'I kept dreaming,' she said. 'About my father. Fathers. Both of them.'

The dreams were little more than fragments; vivid glimpses of Frank Randall's face, longer stretches now and then, in which she saw her mother. And now and then a

754

tall, red-haired man whom she knew to be the father she had never seen.

'There was one dream in particular...' It had been night in the dream, somewhere tropical, with fields of tall green plants that might have been sugarcane, and fires burning in the distance.

'There were drums beating, and I knew something was hiding, waiting in the canes; something horrible,' she said. 'My mother was there, drinking tea with a crocodile.' Roger grunted, and her voice grew sharper. 'It was a dream, all right?

'Then he stepped out of the canes. I couldn't see his face very well, because it was dark, but I could see that he had red hair; there were copper glints when he turned his head.'

'Was he the dreadful thing in the canes?' Roger asked.

'No.' He could hear the susurrus of her hair as she shook her head. It had gone quite dark by now, and she was little more than a comforting weight on his chest, a soft voice beside him, speaking from the shadows.

'He was standing between my mother and the awful thing. I couldn't see it, but I knew it was there, waiting.' She gave a small, involuntary shudder and Roger tightened his hold on her.

'Then I knew my mother was going to stand up and walk right toward it. I tried to stop her, but I couldn't make her hear me or see me. So I turned to him, and I called to him to go with her – to save her from whatever it was. And he saw me!' The hand on his arm squeezed tight. 'He did, he saw me, and he heard me. And then I woke up.'

'Aye?' Roger said skeptically. 'And this made you go to Jamaica, and –'

'It made me think,' she said sharply. 'You'd looked; you couldn't find them anywhere in Scotland after 1766, and you couldn't find them on any of the emigration rolls to the Colonies. That was when you said you thought we should give up; that there wasn't any more we could find out.'

Roger was glad of the darkness that hid his guilt. He kissed the top of her head, quickly.

'But I wondered; the place I saw them in the dream was in the tropics. What if they were in the Indies?'

'I looked,' Roger said. 'I checked the passenger rolls of every ship that left Edinburgh or London in the late 1760s and '70s – headed for anyplace. I did tell you,' he added, an edge in his voice.

'I know that,' she said, with a matching edge. 'But what if they weren't passengers? Why did people *go* to the Indies then – now, I mean?' She caught herself, voice cracking a little in realization.

'For trade, mostly.'

'Right. So what if they went on a cargo ship? They wouldn't show up on the passenger rolls.'

'Okay,' he said slowly. 'Right, they wouldn't. But then how would you look for them?'

'Warehouse registers, plantation account books, port manifests. I spent the whole vacation in libraries and museums. And – and I found them,' she said, with a small catch in her voice.

Christ, she'd seen the notice.

'Aye?' he said, striving for calmness.

She laughed, a little tremulously.

'A Captain James Fraser, of a ship named *Artemis*, sold five tons of bat guano to a planter. Montego Bay on April 2, 1767.'

Roger couldn't help a grunt of amusement, but at the same time, couldn't help objecting.

'Aye, but a ship's captain? After all your mother said about the man's seasickness? And not to be discouraging, but there must be literally hundreds of James Frasers; how could you possibly know –'

'There might; but on April the first, a woman named Claire Fraser bought a slave from the slave market in Kingston.'

'She *what*?'

'I don't know why,' Brianna said firmly, 'but I'm sure she had a good reason.'

'Well, sure, but –'

'The papers gave the slave's name as "Temeraire", and described him as having one arm. Makes him stand out, doesn't it? Anyway, I started looking through collections of old newspapers; not just from the Indies, from all the southern colonies, looking for that name – my mother wouldn't keep a slave; if she bought him, she'd free him somehow, and the notices of manumission were sometimes printed in the local papers. I thought I could maybe find where the slave was freed.'

'And did you?'

'No.' She was quiet for a minute. 'I – I found something else. A notice of their . . . deaths. My parents.'

Even knowing that she must have found it, to hear it from her lips was still a shock. He pulled her tight against him, wrapping his arms around her.

'Where?' he said softly. 'How?'

He should have known better. He wasn't listening to her half-choked explanation; he was too busy cursing himself. He should have known she was too stubborn to be dissuaded. All he'd done with his fatheaded interference was to drive her into secrecy. And it had been he who'd paid for that – in months of worry.

'But we're in time,' she said. 'It said 1776; we've got time to find them.' She sighed hugely. 'I'm so glad you're here. I was so worried you'd find out before I could get back and I didn't know what you'd do.'

'What I *did* do : . . You know,' he said conversationally, 'I have a friend with a two-year-old child. He says that he'd never in life condone child abuse – but by God, he understands what makes people do it. I feel very much the same about wife beating just now.'

There was a small quiver of laughter from the heavy weight on his chest.

'What do you mean by that?'

He slid a hand down her back and got a firm grip on one round buttock. She wore no underclothes beneath the loose breeches.

'I mean that were I a man of this time, instead of my own, nothing would give me greater pleasure than to lay my belt across your arse a dozen times or so.'

She didn't seem to consider this a serious threat. In fact, he thought she was laughing.

'So since you're not from this time, you wouldn't do it? Or you would, but you wouldn't enjoy it?'

'Oh, I'd enjoy it,' he assured her. 'There's nothing I'd like better than to take a stick to you.'

She *was* laughing.

Suddenly furious, he shoved her off and sat up.

'What's the matter with you?'

'I thought you'd found someone else! Your letters, the last few months . . . and then that last one. I was sure of it. It's that I want to beat you for – not for lying to me or going off without telling me – for making me think I'd lost you!'

She was silent for a moment. Her hand came out of darkness and touched his face, very softly.

'I'm sorry,' she said quietly. 'I never meant for you to think that. I only wanted to keep you from finding out, until it was too late.' Her head turned toward him, silhouetted by the faint light from the road outside their refuge. 'How *did* you find out?'

'Your boxes. They came to the college.'

'What? But I told them not to send those until the end of May, when you'd be in Scotland!'

'I would have been; only for a last-minute conference that kept me in Oxford. They came the day before I left.'

There was a sudden spill of light and noise as the door of the tavern opened, disgorging a knot of patrons into the road. Voices and footsteps passed by their refuge, startlingly close. Neither of them spoke until the sounds had disappeared. In the renewed silence, he heard the sound of a conker falling through the leaves, to bounce on the leaves nearby.

Brianna's voice was oddly husky.

'You thought I'd found somebody else . . . and you still came after me?'

He sighed, anger gone as suddenly as it had come, and wiped the damp hair off his face.

'I'd have come if you were married to the King of Siam. Bloody woman.'

She was no more than a pale blur in the darkness; he saw the brief movement as she leaned to pick up the fallen conker, and sat toying with it. Finally, she drew a very deep breath and let it out slowly.

'You said *wife* beating.'

He paused. The crickets had stopped again.

'You said you were sure. Did you mean it?'

There was a silence, long enough to fill a heartbeat, long enough to fill forever.

'Yes,' she said softly.

'In Inverness, I said –'

'You said you'd have me all – or not at all. And I said I understood. I'm sure.'

Her shirt had pulled free of her breeches in their struggle, and billowed loose around her in the faint hot breeze. He reached under the floating hem and touched bare skin, which rippled into gooseflesh at his touch. He pulled her close, ran his hands over bare back and bare shoulders under the cloth, buried his face in her hair, her neck, exploring, asking with his hands – did she mean it?

She gripped his shoulders and leaned back, urging him. Yes, she did. He answered, wordless, opening the front of her shirt, spreading it apart. Her breasts were white and soft.

'Please,' she said. Her hand was at the back of his head, pulling him toward her. 'Please!'

'If I take you now, it's for always,' he whispered.

She scarcely breathed, but stood stock-still, letting his hands go where they would.

'Yes,' she said.

The tavern door opened again, startling them apart. He let her go and stood up, reaching down a hand to help her, then stood with her hand in his, waiting while the voices receded into distance.

'Come on,' he said, and ducked under the drooping branches.

The shed was some distance from the tavern, dark and quiet. They stopped outside, waiting, but there was no sound from the back of the inn; all the windows on the upper floor were dark.

'I hope Lizzie's gone to bed.'

He wondered dimly who Lizzie was, but didn't care. At this distance he could see her face clearly, though the night washed all color from her skin. She looked like a harlequin, he thought, white cheek planes slashed by leaf shadows, framed by the dark of her hair, her eyes black triangles set above a dash of vivid mouth.

He took her hand in his, palm to palm.

'D'ye know what handfasting is?'

'Not exactly. Sort of a temporary marriage?'

'A bit. In the Isles and the remoter parts of the Highlands, where folk were a long way from the nearest minister, a man and a woman now would be handfast; vowed to each other for a year and a day. At the end of it, they find a minister and wed more permanently – or they go their own ways.'

Her hand tightened in his.

'I don't want anything temporary.'

'Neither do I. But I don't think we'll find a minister easily. There are no churches here yet; the nearest minister is likely in New Bern.' He lifted their linked hands. 'I did say I wanted it all, and if ye did not care enough to wed me . . .'

Her hand tightened, hard.

'I do.'

'All right.'

He took a deep breath and began.

'I, Roger Jeremiah, do take thee, Brianna Ellen, to be my lawful wedded wife. With my goods I thee endow, with my body I thee worship . . .' Her hand twitched in his, and his balls tightened. Whoever had worded this vow had understood, all right.

'. . . in sickness and in health, in richness and in poverty, so-long as we both shall live.'

If I make a vow like that, I'll keep it – no matter what it costs me. Was she thinking of that now?

She brought their linked hands down together, and spoke with great deliberation.

'I, Brianna Ellen, take thee, Roger Jeremiah . . .' Her voice was scarcely louder than the beating of his own heart, but he heard every word. A breeze came through the tree, rattling the leaves, lifting her hair.

'. . . as long as we both shall live.'

The phrase meant a good bit more to each of them now, he thought, than it would have even a few months before.

760

The passage through the stones was enough to impress anyone with the fragility of life.

There was a moment's silence, broken only by the rustle of leaves overhead and a distant murmur of voices from the tavern's taproom. He raised her hand to his mouth and kissed it, on the knuckle of her fourth finger, where one day – God willing – her ring would be.

It was more of a large shed than a barn, though some beast – a horse or mule – stirred in its stall at one end. There was a strong, clean tang of hops in the air, enough to overpower the milder scents of hay and manure; the Blue Bull brewed its own ale. Roger felt drunk, but not from alcohol.

The shed was very dark, and undressing her was both frustration and delight.

'And I thought it took blind people years to develop a keen sense of touch,' he murmured.

The warm breath of her laugh brushed his neck, making the tiny hairs at his nape stir and prickle.

'You're sure it's not like the poem about the five blind men and the elephant?' she said. Her own hand groped, found the opening of his shirt, and slid inside.

' "No, the beast is like a wall," ' she quoted. Her fingers curved and flattened, curiously exploring the sensitive flesh around his nipple. 'A wall with hair. Goodness, a wall with goose bumps, too.'

She laughed again, and he bent his head, finding her mouth on the first try, sightless and unerring as a bat snatching a moth from the air.

'Amphora,' he murmured against the wide, sweet curve of her lips. His hands slid over the wide, sweet curve of her hips, cupping smoothness cool and solid, timeless and graceful as the swell of ancient pottery, promising abundance. 'Like a Grecian vase. God, you've got the most beautiful arse!'

'Jug-butt, huh?'

She vibrated against him, the quiver of laughter passing from her lips to his and into his bloodstream like infection. Her hand slid down his own hip, and up, long fingers fumbling loose the flap of his breeches, groping hesitantly and then more surely, gradually rucking his shirt up to disentangle him from the layers of fabric.

' "No, the beast is like a rope" . . . oops . . .'

'Stop laughing, damn you.'

' . . . like a snake . . . no . . . well, maybe a cobra . . . gosh, what would you call *that*?'

'I had a friend once who called it "Mr. Happy",' Roger said, feeling light-headed, 'but that's a bit whimsical for my tastes.' He grabbed her by the arms and kissed her again, long enough to put a stop to any further comparisons.

She was still quivering, but he didn't *think* it was laughter. He slid his arms around her and pulled her closely against him, amazed as always by the sheer size of her – a good deal more amazed now that she was naked, those complex planes of bone and muscle transformed to immediate sensation in his arms.

He paused for breath. He wasn't sure whether the sensation was more akin to drowning or to mountain climbing, but whatever it was, there wasn't much oxygen left between them.

'I've never been able to kiss a girl without stooping before,' he said, making conversation in hopes of getting his breath back.

'Oh, good; we wouldn't want you to have a stiff *neck*.' The quiver was back in her voice, and it definitely was laughter, though he thought it stemmed as much from nervousness as humor.

'Ha, ha,' he said, and grabbed her again, oxygen be damned. Her breasts were high and round, pressed against his chest with that unique mixture of softness and firmness that so intrigued him whenever he touched her. One of her hands slid hesitantly between them, groping, then withdrew.

He couldn't bring himself to stop kissing her long enough to finish undressing, but arched his back to let her push the breeches down over his hips. They were loose enough to fall in a puddle around his feet, and he stepped free of them, still holding her, only making a small noise in his throat when her hand came back between them.

She had eaten onions with her dinner. Blindness sharpened not only touch, but taste and smell as well. He tasted roast meat, and sour ale, and bread. And a faint sweet taste that he couldn't identify, that reminded him somehow of green meadows full of waving grass. Did he taste it, or smell it in her hair? He couldn't tell; he seemed to be losing track of his senses as he lost the boundaries between them, breathing her breath, feeling her heart beat as though it lay in his own chest.

She was grasping him a trifle too tightly for comfort, and he broke the kiss at last, breathing heavily.

'Would you consider letting go for a moment? I grant you, it's an effective handle, but it's got better uses.'

Instead of letting go, she dropped to her knees.

Roger made a slight move back, startled.

'Christ, are you sure you want to do that?' He wasn't sure whether he hoped she did or not. Her hair tickled against his thighs, and his cock was quivering, desperate for engulfment. At the same time, he didn't want to frighten or repulse her.

'Don't you want me to?' Her hands moved up the backs of his thighs, tentative and ticklish. He could feel every hair on his body spring erect, from knees to waist. It made him feel like a satyr, goat-legged and reeking.

'Well . . . yes. But I haven't bathed in days,' he said, rather awkwardly trying to detach himself.

Deliberately, she brushed her nose over his stomach and down, inhaling deeply. His skin pebbled with gooseflesh, the shiver having nothing to do with the temperature of the room.

'You smell good,' she whispered. 'Like some kind of big male animal.'

He grasped her head hard, fingers twisted in the thick, silky hair.

'Too right about that,' he whispered. Her hand rested on his wrist, light and warm – God, she was warm.

Without his actually intending it, his grip loosened; he felt the fall of her hair brush his thighs and then stopped thinking anything coherent, as all of the blood left his brain, heading south at a high rate of speed.

'Mi oing i' i'?'

763

'What?' He came out of his daze a few moments later as she drew back, brushing the hair away from her face.

'I said, am I doing it right?'

'Oh. Ah . . . I think so.'

'You *think* so? You don't know for sure?' Brianna seemed to have been regaining her composure as fast as Roger had been losing his; he could hear the suppressed laughter in her voice.

'Well . . . no,' he said. 'I mean, I haven't . . . that is, no one's . . . yeah, I think so.' He had hold of her head again, urging her gently forward.

He thought she was making a low humming noise, somewhere deep in her throat. It might be his own blood, though, thrumming through distended veins, purling in violent eddies like the trapped water of the ocean, seething through the rocks. Another minute, and he was going off like a waterspout.

He pulled away and before she could protest, lifted her to her feet, then urged her down, onto the heap of straw where he had thrown her clothes.

His eyes had adjusted to the dark, but the starlight from the window was still so faint that he could see no more of her than shapes and outlines, white as marble. Not cold, though; not cold at all.

He approached his own duty with mingled excitement and caution; he had tried this exactly once, only to be met with a faceful of a feminine hygiene product that smelled like the flowers in his father's church on Sunday – an off-putting idea if ever there was one.

Brianna was not hygienic. The scent of her was enough to make him want to dispense with any preliminaries and throw himself on her in a pure abandonment of lust.

Instead, he breathed deeply, and kissed her just above the dark smudge of curls.

'Damn,' he said.

'What is it?' She sounded faintly alarmed. 'Do I smell terrible?'

He closed his eyes and breathed. His head was spinning slightly, and he felt giddy with a combination of lust and laughter.

'No. It's only that I've been wondering for more than a

year what color your hair is here.' He tugged gently on the curls. 'Now here I am face-to-face with it, and I still can't tell.'

She giggled, the vibration making her belly shake gently under his hand.

'Do you want me to tell you?'

'No, let me be surprised in the morning.' He bent his head to his work, surprised now by the amazing variety of textures, all in such a small space – a smoothness like glass, tickling roughness, a yielding rubberiness, and that sudden slippery slickness, musk and tang and salt together.

After a few moments, he felt her hands come to rest gently on his head, as though in benediction. He hoped the stubble of his beard wasn't hurting her, but she didn't seem to mind. A subterranean quiver ran through the warm flesh of her thighs and she made a small sound that made a similar quiver dart through his belly.

'Am I doing it right?' he inquired half jokingly, lifting his head.

'Oh, yeah,' she said softly. 'You sure are.' Her hands tightened in his hair.

He had started to lower his head again, but jerked it up at this, staring up across the dim white reaches of her body toward the pale oval of her face.

'And just how the hell do you know *that*?' he asked. His only answer was a deep, gurgling laugh. Then he was beside her, with no real notion how he'd got there, his mouth on her mouth, the length of his body pressed to hers, aware only of the heat of her, burning like fever.

She tasted of him, and he of her, and God help him, he wasn't going to be able to go slowly.

He did, though. She was eager, but awkward, trying to lift her hips to him, touching him too quickly, too lightly. He took her hands, one at a time, and placed them flat against his chest. Her palms were hot, and his nipples tightened.

'Feel my heart,' he said. His voice sounded thick to his own ears. 'Tell me if it stops.'

He hadn't actually meant to be funny, and was faintly surprised when she gave a nervous laugh. The laugh disappeared as he touched her. Her hands tightened on his chest; then he felt her relax, opening her legs to him.

'I love you,' he murmured. 'Oh, Bree, I do love you.'

She didn't answer, but a hand floated up from the dark and lay along his cheek, gentle as a tendril of seaweed. She kept it there while he took her, laid open in trust, while her other hand held his beating heart.

He felt more drunk than before. Not groggy or sleepy, though; alive to everything. He could smell his own sweat; he could smell hers, smell the faint tang of fear that tinged her desire.

He closed his eyes and breathed. Tightened his grip on her shoulders. Pressed slowly. Slid in. Felt her tear and bit his own lip, hard-enough to draw blood.

Her fingernails dug into his chest.

'Go on!' she whispered.

One sharp hard thrust, and he possessed her.

He stayed that way, eyes closed, breathing. Balanced on an edge of pleasure sharp enough to cause him pain. Dimly he wondered if the pain he felt was hers.

'Roger?'

'Ah?'

'Are you . . . really big, do you think?' Her voice was slightly tremulous.

'Ah . . .' He groped for remnants of coherence. 'About the usual.' A flash of concern penetrated the feelings of drunkenness. 'Am I hurting you a lot?'

'N-no, not exactly. Just . . . can you not move for a minute?'

'A minute, an hour. All my life, if you want.' He thought it would kill him not to move, and would have died gladly.

Her hands moved slowly down his back, touching his buttocks. He shivered and ducked his head, eyes closed, painting her face before his mind's eye with a dozen small and mindless kisses.

'Okay.' She whispered in his ear, and like an automaton he began to move, as slowly as he could, restrained as he went by the pressure of her hand on his back.

She stiffened very slightly and relaxed, stiffened and relaxed, he knew he was hurting her, did it again, he ought to stop, she lifted up against him, taking him, and there was a deep and bestial noise that he must have made, now, it had to be now, he had to . . .

Shaking and gasping like a landed fish, he jerked free of her body and lay on her, feeling her breasts crushed against him as he jerked and moaned.

Then he lay still, no longer drunk but wrapped in guilty peace, and felt her arms around him and the warm breath of the whisper in his ear.

'I love you,' she said, her voice husky in the hop-scented air. 'Stay with me.'

'All my life,' he said, and wrapped his arms around her.

They lay peacefully together, welded with the sweat of their efforts, listening to each other breathe. Roger stirred at last, lifting his face from her hair, his limbs at once weightless and heavy as lead.

'All right, love?' he whispered. 'Have I hurt you?'

'Yes, but I didn't mind.' Her hand passed lightly down the length of his back, making him shiver despite the heat. 'Was it all right? Did I do it right?' She sounded faintly anxious.

'Oh, God!' He bent his head and kissed her, long and lingering. She tensed a little, but then her mouth relaxed under his.

'It was all right, then?'

'Oh, Jesus!'

'You certainly swear a lot, for a minister's son,' she said, with a faint note of accusation. 'Maybe those old ladies in Inverness were right; you *have* gone to the devil.'

'Not blasphemy,' he said. He put his forehead against her shoulder, breathing in the deep, ripe scent of her, of them. 'Prayers of thanksgiving.'

That made her laugh.

'Oh, it *was* all right, then,' she said, with an unmistakable note of relief.

He lifted his head.

'Christ, yes,' he said, making her laugh again. 'How could you possibly think otherwise?'

'Well, you didn't say anything. You just lay there like somebody's hit you over the head; I thought maybe you were disappointed.'

Now it was his turn to laugh, his face half buried in the smooth damps of her neck.

'No,' he said finally, coming up for air. 'Behaving as though your spinal column's been removed is a fair indication of male satisfaction. No very gentleman-like, maybe, but honest.'

'Oh, okay.' She seemed satisfied with that. 'The book didn't say anything about that, but then it wouldn't; it didn't bother with what happens afterward.'

'What book is this?' He moved cautiously, their skins separating with a noise like two strips of flypaper being parted. 'Sorry about the mess.' He groped for his wadded shirt and handed it to her.

'*The Sensuous Man.*' She took the shirt and dabbed fastidiously. 'There was a lot of stuff about ice cubes and whipped cream that I thought was pretty extreme, but it was good about how to do things like fellatio, and –'

'You learned that from a *book*?' Roger felt as scandalized as one of the ladies of his father's congregation.

'Well, you don't think I go around doing that with people I go out with!' She sounded truly shocked in turn.

'They write books telling young women how to – that's terrible!'

'What's terrible about it?' she said, rather huffy. 'How else would I know what to do?'

Roger rubbed a hand over his face, at a loss for words. If asked an hour before, he would have stoutly claimed to be in favor of sexual equality. Under the veneer of modernity, though, there was apparently enough of the Presbyterian minister's son left to feel that a nice young woman really ought to be an ignoramus on her wedding night.

Manfully suppressing this Victorian notion, Roger brought a hand up over the smooth white curves of hip and flank, and cupped a soft full breast.

'Not a thing,' he said. 'Only,' he said, and dipped his head to touch his lips to hers, 'there's a bit more to it,' and lightly nipped her lower lip, 'than ye read in books, aye?'

She moved suddenly, turning to bring all that long white heat against his bare skin, and he shuddered at the shock of it.

'Show me,' she whispered, and bit the lobe of his ear.

A rooster crowed, somewhere nearby. Brianna woke from a light doze, berating herself for sleeping. She felt disoriented, tired enough from emotion and exertion to feel light-headed, as though she were floating a foot or two off the ground. At the same time, she didn't want to miss a moment.

Roger stirred by her side, feeling her move. He groped, put an arm around her, and rolled her over, curving himself to fit behind her, knees to knees, belly to buttocks. He brushed the tangles of her hair away from his face, making little *pfft!* noises that made her want to laugh.

He'd made love to her three times. She was very sore, and very happy. She'd imagined it a thousand times, and been wrong every time. There wasn't any way to imagine the sheer terrifying immediacy of being taken like that – stretched suddenly beyond the limits of flesh, penetrated, rent, *entered.* Nor was there any way she could have imagined the sense of power in it.

She had expected to be helpless, the object of desire. Instead, she had held him, felt him quiver with need, all his strength leashed for fear of hurting her – hers to unleash as she would. Hers, to touch and rouse, to call to her, to command.

Nor had she ever thought such tenderness existed as when he cried out and shuddered in her arms, pressing his forehead hard against her own, trusting her with that moment when his strength turned so suddenly to helplessness.

'I'm sorry,' he said softly in her ear.

'For what?' She reached back, stroked his thigh. She could do that, now. She could touch him anywhere, delighting in the textures and tastes of his body. She couldn't wait for the daylight, to see him naked.

'For this.' He made a small movement with his hand, encompassing the dark around them, the hard straw under them. 'I should have waited. I wanted it to be . . . good for you.'

'It was very good for me,' she said softly. There was a shallow groove down the side of his thigh, where the muscle was indented.

He laughed, a little ruefully.

'I wanted you to have a proper wedding night. Soft bed, clean sheets . . . it should have been better, for your first time.'

'I've had soft beds and clean sheets,' she said. 'But not this.' She turned in his arms, reached down and cupped him, that fascinating mass of changeability between his *legs*. He stiffened for a second in surprise, then relaxed, letting her handle him as she liked. 'It couldn't have been better,' she said softly, and kissed him.

He kissed her back, slow and lazy, exploring all the depths and hollows of her mouth, letting her have his. He moaned a little, far back in his throat, and reached down to take her hand away.

'Oh, God, you're going to kill me, Bree.'

'I'm sorry,' she said, anxious. 'Did I squeeze too hard? I didn't mean to hurt you.'

He laughed at that.

'Not that. But give the poor thing a wee rest, hm?' With a firm hand, he turned her over again, nuzzling her shoulder.

'Roger?'

'Mm?'

'I don't think I've ever been so happy.'

'Aye? Well, that's good, then.' He sounded drowsy.

'Even if – if we don't get back, as long as we're together, I don't mind.'

'We'll get back.' His hand cupped her breast, gentle as seaweed coming to rest round a rock. 'I told you, there's another way.'

'There is?'

'I think so.' He told her about the grimoire, the mixture of careful notes and crazed rambling – and about his own passage through the stones of Craigh na Dun.

'The second time, I thought of you,' he said softly, and traced her features with a finger in the dark. 'I lived. And I did come to the right time. But the diamond Fiona gave me was no more than a smear of lampblack in my pocket.'

'So it might be possible to – to steer, somehow?' Brianna couldn't keep a hint of hope from her voice.

'There might be.' He hesitated. 'There was a – I suppose

it must have been a poem, or maybe meant to be a spell –
in the book.' His hand fell away as he recited it.

> '*I raise my athame to the North*
>   *Where is the home of my power,*
> *To the West*
>   *Where is the hearth of my soul,*
> *To the South*
>   *Where is the seat of friendship and refuge,*
> *To the East*
>   *From whence rises the Sun.*
>
> '*Then lay I my blade on the altar I have made.*
>   *I sit down amid three flames.*
>
> '*Three points define a plane, and I am fixed.*
> *Four points box the earth and mine is the fullness thereof.*
> *Five is the number of protection; let no demon hinder me.*
> *My left hand is wreathed in gold*
>   *And holds the power of the sun.*
> *My right hand is sheathed in silver*
>   *And the moon reigns serene.*
>
> '*I begin.*
> *Garnets rest in love about my neck.*
>   *I will be faithful.*'

Brianna sat up, arms wrapped around her knees. She
was silent for moment.

'That's *nuts*,' she said, finally.

'Being certifiably insane is unfortunately no guarantee
that someone is likewise wrong,' Roger said dryly. He
stretched, groaning, and sat up cross-legged on the straw.

'Part of it is traditional ritual, I think – given that the
tradition is ancient Celt. The bits about the directions;
those are the "four airts", which you'll find running
through Celtic legend for some way back. As for the blade,
the altar, and the flames, it's straight witchcraft.'

'She stabbed her husband through the heart and set
him on fire.' She still remembered as well as he did the
stink of petrol and burning flesh in the circle of Craigh na
Dun, and shivered, though it was warm in the shed.

'I hope we won't be forced to find someone for a human sacrifice,' Roger said, trying and failing to make a joke of it. 'The metal, though, and the gems . . . were you wearing any jewelry when you came through, Bree?'

She nodded in reply.

'Your bracelet,' she said softly. 'And I had my grand-mother's pearl necklace in my pocket. The pearls weren't hurt, though; they came through fine.'

'Pearls aren't gemstones,' he reminded her. 'They're organic – like people.' He rubbed a hand across his face; it had been a long day, and his head was starting to throb. 'Silver and gold, though; you had the silver bracelet, and the necklace has gold, as well as the pearls. Ah – and your mother; she wore both silver and gold, too, didn't she? Her wedding rings.'

'Uh-huh. But "Three points define a plane, Four points box the earth, Five is the number of protection . . ." ' Brianna murmured under her breath. 'Could she mean that you need gemstones to – to do whatever she was trying to do? Are those the "points"?'

'Could be. She had drawings of triangles and penta-grams, and lists of different gemstones, with the supposed "magickal" properties listed alongside. She wasn't laying out her theories in any great detail – didn't need to, since she was talking to herself – but the general notion seemed to be that there are lines of force – "ley lines", she called them – running through the earth. Every now and again, the lines run close to each other, and sort of curl up into knots; and wherever you get such a knot, you've got a place where time essentially doesn't exist.'

'So if you step into one, you might step out again . . . anytime.'

'Same place, different time. And if you believe that gem-stones have a force of their own, which might warp the lines a bit . . .'

'Would any gemstone do?'

'God knows,' Roger said. 'But it's the best chance we have, aye?'

'Yes,' Brianna agreed, after a pause. 'But where are we going to find any?' She waved an arm toward the town and its harbor. 'I haven't seen anything like that anywhere – in

Inverness or here. I think you'd need to go to a large city – London, or maybe Boston or Philadelphia. And then – how much money do you have, Roger? I managed to get twenty pounds, and I still have most of it, but that wouldn't be nearly enough for –'

'That's the point,' he interrupted. 'I was thinking of that, while you were sleeping. I know – I think I know – where I might lay hands on one stone, at least. The thing is –' He hesitated. 'I'll have to go at once, to find it. The man who has it is in New Bern right now, but he won't be there for long. If I take a bit of your money, I can get a boat in the morning and be in New Bern by the next day. I think it's best you stay here, though. Then –'

'I can't stay here!'

'Why not?' He reached for her, groping in the dark. 'I don't want you with me. Or rather I do,' he corrected himself, 'but I think it's a lot safer for you here.'

'I don't mean I want to come with you; I mean I can't stay here,' she repeated, though she grasped his groping hand. She had nearly forgotten, but now all the excitement of discovery flooded back again. 'Roger, I found him – I found Jamie Fraser!'

'Fraser? Where? Here?' He turned toward the door, startled.

'No, he's in Cross Creek, and I know where he'll be on Monday. I have to go, Roger. Don't you understand? He's so close – and I've come so far.' She wanted suddenly and irrationally to weep, with the thought of seeing her mother again.

'Aye, I see.' Roger sounded faintly anxious. 'But could you not wait a few days? It's only a day or so by sea to New Bern, the same back – and I think I can manage what I have to do within a day or two.'

'No,' she said. 'I can't. There's Lizzie.'

'Who's Lizzie?'

'My maid – you saw her. She was going to hit you with a bottle.' Brianna grinned at the memory. 'Lizzie's very brave.'

'Aye, I daresay,' Roger said dryly. 'Be that as it may –'

'But she's sick,' Brianna interrupted him. 'Didn't you see how pale she is? I think it's malaria; she has horrible

fevers and chills that last for a day or so and then stop –
and then a few days later, they're back again. I have to find
my mother as soon as I can. I *have* to.'

She could feel him struggling, choking back arguments.
She reached out in the darkness and stroked his face.

'I have to,' she repeated softly, and felt him surrender.

'All right,' he said. 'All right! I'll come to join you, as
soon as may be. Do me the one favor, though, aye? Wear a
bloody dress!'

'You don't like my breeches?' Laughter fizzed up like
the bubbles in carbonated soda – then stopped abruptly,
as something occurred to her.

'Roger,' she said. 'What you're going to do – are you
going to steal this stone?'

'Yes,' he said simply.

She was quiet for a minute, her long thumb rubbing
slowly over the palm of his hand.

'Don't,' she said at last, very quietly. 'Don't do it, Roger.'

'Don't trouble yourself over the man who's got it.'
Roger reached for her, trying to reassure her. 'It's odds-on
he stole it from someone else.'

'It's not him I'm worried about – it's you!'

'Oh, I'll be all right,' he assured her, with casual
bravado.

'Roger, they *hang* people in this time for stealing!'

'I won't be caught.' His hand sought hers in the darkness, found it, and squeezed. 'I'll be with you before ye
know it.'

'But it isn't –'

'It will be all right,' he said firmly. 'I said I would take
care of you, aye? I will.'

'But –'

He rose up on one elbow and silenced her with his
mouth. Very slowly, he brought her hand toward him,
pressed it between his legs.

She swallowed, the hairs on her arms rising suddenly
with anticipation.

'Mm?' he murmured, against her mouth, and without
waiting for an answer, pulled her down on the straw, and
rolled onto her, nudging her legs apart with his knee.

She gasped and bit his shoulder when he took her, but he made no sound.

'D'ye know,' Roger said sleepily, some time later, 'I think I've just married my great-aunt six times removed? I've only just thought.'

'You *what?*'

'Don't worry, it's nowhere close enough to be incest,' he assured her.

'Oh, good,' she said, with a certain amount of sarcasm. 'I was really worried about that. How can I be your great-aunt, for heaven's sake?'

'Well, as I said, I just thought; I hadn't realized it before. But your father's uncle was Dougal MacKenzie – and it was him that caused all the trouble by getting a child on Geilie Duncan, aye?'

It was the unsatisfactory method of contraception he had been forced to adopt that had caused him to think of it, in fact, but he thought it more tactful not to mention that. Neither shirt was fit to be worn by now. All things considered, he supposed it was just as well that Dougal. MacKenzie hadn't had his sense of conscientiousness, since that would effectively have prevented Roger's own existence.

'Well, I don't think it was all *his* fault.' Brianna sounded pleasantly drowsy as well. It couldn't be much off dawn; birds were already making noises outside, and the air had changed, growing fresher as the wind came in off the harbor.

'So if Dougal is my great-uncle, and your six-times great-grandfather . . . no, you're wrong. I'm about your sixth or seventh cousin, not your aunt.'

'No, that would be right if we were in the same generation of descent but we're not; you're up about five – on your father's side, at least.'

Brianna was silent, trying to work this out in her head. Then giving up, she rolled over with a faint groan, nestling her bottom snugly into the hollow of his thighs.

'The hell with it,' she said. 'As long as you're sure it's not incest.'

He clasped her to his bosom, but his sleepy brain had grasped the point and wouldn't let it go.

'I really hadn't thought of it,' he marveled. 'You know what it means, though? I'm related to your father, too – in fact, I suppose he's my *only* living relation, besides you!' Roger felt thoroughly nonplussed by this discovery, and rather moved. He had long since reconciled himself to having no close family at all – not that a seven-times great-uncle was all that close, but –

'No, he isn't,' Brianna mumbled.

'What?'

'Not the only one. Jenny, too. And her kids. And grand-kids. My aunt Jenny's your – hm, maybe you're right, after all. 'Cause if she's my aunt, she's your umpty-great aunt, so maybe *I'm* your . . . gahh.' She let her head loll back against Roger's shoulder, the spill of her hair soft against his chest. 'Who'd you tell them you were?'

'Who?'

'Jenny and Ian.' She shifted, stretching. 'When you went to Lallybroch.'

'Never been there.' He shifted, too, fitting his body to hers. His hand settled in the dip of her waist, and he sank back into drowsiness, giving up the abstract complexities of genealogical calculation for more immediate sensations.

'No? But then . . .' her voice did away. Fogged with sleep and the exhaustion of pleasure, Roger paid no attention, only snuggling closer with a luxurious moan. A moment later, her voice sliced through his personal fog like a knife through butter.

'How did you know where I was?' she said.

'Hm?'

She twisted suddenly, leaving him with empty arms, and a pair of dark eyes a few inches from his own, slanted with suspicion.

'How did you know where I was?' she repeated slowly, each word a splinter of ice. 'How did you know I'd gone to the Colonies?'

'Ah . . . I . . . why . . .' Much too late, he woke to the realization of his danger.

'You didn't have any way of knowing I'd left Scotland,'

she said, 'unless you went to Lallybroch, and they told you where I was going. But you've never been to Lallybroch.'

'I . . .' He groped frantically for an explanation – any explanation – but there was none, other than the truth. And from the stiffening of her body, she had deduced that too.

'You knew,' she said. Her voice wasn't much above a whisper, but the effect was as great as if she'd shouted in his ear. 'You *knew*, didn't you?'

She was sitting up now, looming over him like one of the Erinyes.

'You *saw* that death notice! You already knew, you knew all the time, didn't you?'

'No,' he said, trying to gather his scattered wits. 'I mean yes, but –'

'How long have you known? Why didn't you *tell* me?' she cried. She stood up and snatched at the pile of clothes under them.

'Wait,' he pleaded. 'Bree – let me explain –'

'Yeah, explain! I want to hear you explain!' Her voice was ragged with fury, but she did stop her rummaging for a moment, waiting to hear.

'Look.' He was up himself by now. 'I did find it. Last spring. But I –' He took a deep breath, searching desperately for words that might make her understand.

'I knew it would hurt you. I didn't want to show it to you because I knew there was nothing you could do – there was no point in you breaking your heart for the sake of –'

'What do you mean there's nothing I could do?' She jerked a shirt over her head, and glared toward him, fists clenched.

'You can't change things, Bree! Don't you know that? Your parents tried – they knew about Culloden, and they did everything they possibly could have, to stop Charles Stuart – but they couldn't, could they? They failed! Geillis Duncan tried to make Stuart a king. She failed! They all failed!' He risked a hand on her arm; she was stiff as a statue.

'You can't help them, Bree,' he said, more quietly. 'It's part of history, it's part of the past – you're not from this time; you can't change what's going to happen.'

'You don't know that.' She was still rigid, but he thought he heard a hint of doubt in her voice.

'I do!' He wiped a bead of sweat from his jaw. 'Listen – if I'd thought there was the slightest chance – but I didn't. I – God, Bree, I couldn't stand the thought of you being hurt!'

She stood still, breathing heavily through her nose. If she'd had choice, he was sure it would have been fire and brimstone rather than air.

'It wasn't your business to make up my mind for me,' she said, speaking through clenched teeth. 'No matter what you thought. And about something so important – Roger, how could you *do* something like that?'

The tone of betrayal in her voice was too much.

'Damn it, I was afraid if I told you, ye'd do just what you did!' he burst out. 'You'd leave me! You'd try to go through the stones by yourself. And now look what you've done – here's the both of us in this godforsaken –'

'You're trying to blame *me* for you being here? When I did everything I possibly could to keep you from being such an idiot as to follow me?'

Months of toil and terror, days of worry and fruitless searching caught up with Roger in a scorching blast.

'An idiot? That's the thanks I get for killing myself to find you? For risking my fucking *life* to try to protect you?' He rose from the straw, meaning to get hold of her, not sure if he meant to shake her or bed her again. He had the chance to do neither; a hard shove caught him off balance, square in the chest, and he went sprawling into the hay.

She was hopping on one foot, cursing incoherently as she struggled into her breeches.

'You – bloody – arrogant – damn you, Roger! – *damn* you!' She jerked up the breeches and, leaning down, snatched up her shoes and stockings.

'Go!' she said. 'Damn you, go! Go and get hanged if you want to! I'm going to find my parents! And I'm going to save them, too!'

She whirled away, reached the door and jerked it open before he could reach her. She stood for a moment, silhouetted in the paler square of the doorway, dark strands

778

of hair afloat in the wind, live as the strands of Medusa's mane.

'I'm going. Come, or don't come, I don't care. Go back to Scotland – go back through the stones by yourself, for all I care! But by God, you can't stop me!'

And then she was gone.

Lizzie's eyes shot wide as the door banged open against the wall. She hadn't been asleep – how could she sleep? – but had been lying with her eyes closed. She struggled up out of the bedclothes and fumbled for the tinderbox.

'Are ye all right, Miss Bree?'

It didn't sound like it; Brianna was stamping to and fro, hissing through her teeth like a snake, stopping to kick the wardrobe with a resounding thud. There were two more thuds in succession; by the wavering light of the newly lit candle, Lizzie could see that these were caused by Brianna's shoes, which had hit the wall and fallen to the floor.

'Are ye all right?' she repeated, uncertainly.

'Fine!' said Brianna.

From the black air beyond the window a voice roared, 'Brianna! I shall come for you! Do ye hear me! I will *come*!'

Her mistress made no answer, but strode to the window, seized the shutters and crashed them shut with a bang that made the room echo. Then she turned like a panther striking, and dashed the candlestick to the floor, plunging the room in suffocating dark.

Lizzie eased herself back into bed and lay frozen, afraid to move or speak. She could hear Brianna tearing off her clothes in silent frenzy, the hiss of indrawn breath punctuating the rustle of cloth and the stamp of bare feet on the wooden floor. Through the shutter, she heard outside the muffled sound of cursing, then nothing.

She had seen Brianna's face for a moment in the light; white as paper and hard as bone, with the eyes black holes. Her gentle, kindly mistress had vanished like smoke, taken over by a *deamhan*, a she-devil. Lizzie was a town lass, born long after Culloden. She had never seen the wild clansmen of the glens, or a Highlander in the grip of blood fury – but she'd heard the auld stories, and now she knew them true. A person who looked like that might do anything at all.

She tried to breathe as though she were sleeping, but the air came through her mouth in strangled gasps. Brianna seemed not to notice, though; she walked about the room in quick, hard steps, poured water in the bowl and splashed it on her face, then slid between the quilts and lay flat, rigid as a board.

Summoning all her courage, she turned her head toward her mistress.

'Are ye . . . all right, *a bann-sielbheadair*?' she asked, in a voice so low that her mistress could pretend not to have heard it if she wanted.

· For a moment she thought that Brianna meant to ignore her. Then, 'Yes' came the answer, in a voice so flat and expressionless, it didn't sound like Brianna's at all. 'Go to sleep.'

She didn't, of course. A body didn't sleep, lying next to someone who might turn into a *ursiq* next thing. Her eyes had adjusted to the dark again, but she was afraid to look, in case the red hair lying on the pillow next to her should suddenly be a mane, and the delicate straight nose changed to a curved, soft muzzle, over teeth that would rend and devour.

It was a few moments before Lizzie realized that her mistress was trembling. Not weeping; there was no sound – but shaking hard enough to make the bedclothes rustle.

Fool, she scolded herself. *It's no but your friend and your lady, with something terrible that's happened to her – and you lyin' here sniveling over fancies!*

On impulse she rolled toward Brianna, reaching for the other girl's hand.

'Bree,' she said softly. 'Can I be helpin' ye at all, then?'

Brianna's hand curled round hers and squeezed, quick and hard, then let go.

'No,' Brianna said, very softly. 'Go to sleep, Lizzie; everything will be all right.'

Lizzie took leave to doubt that, but said no more, lying back down and breathing quietly. It was a very long time, but at last Brianna's long body shuddered gently and relaxed into sleep. Lizzie couldn't sleep – with the fever gone again, she was alert and restless. The single quilt lay heavy and damp on her, and with the shutters closed, the air in the tiny room was like breathing hot molasses.

Finally, unable to stand it any longer, Lizzie slid quietly out of bed. Keeping an ear out for any sound from the bed, she crept to the window and eased open the shutters.

The air was still hot and muggy outside, but it had begun to move a little; the dawn breeze was coming, with the turn of the air from sea to land. It was still dark, but the sky had begun to lighten as well; she could make out the line of the road below, blessedly empty.

Not knowing what else to do, she did what she always did when troubled or confused; set about to make things tidy. Moving quietly about the room, she picked up the clothes Brianna had so violently discarded, and shook them out.

They were filthy; covered with streaks of leaf stain and dirt, riddled with bits of straw; she could see it even in the dim light from the window. What had Brianna been doing, rolling about on the ground? The instant the thought came into her head, she saw it in her mind, so plain that the notion froze her with shock – Brianna pinned to the ground, struggling with the black devil who had taken her away.

Her mistress was a fine big woman, but yon MacKenzie was a great tall brute of a man; he could have – she stopped herself abruptly, not wanting to imagine. She couldn't help it, though; her mind had gone too far already.

With great reluctance, she brought the shirt to her nose and sniffed. Yes, there it was, the reek of a man, strong and sour as the smell of a rutting goat. The thought of the wicked creature with his body pressed to Brianna's, rubbing against her, leaving his scent on her like a dog who marks his ground – she shuddered in revulsion.

Trembling, she snatched up the breeches and stockings, and bore all the clothes to the basin. She would wash them out, rinse away the reminder of MacKenzie with the dirt and the grass stains. And if the clothes were too wet for her mistress to wear in the morning . . . well, so much the better for that.

She still had the pot of soft yellow lye soap the landlady had given her for laundering; that would take care of it. She plunged the breeks into the water, added a finger's dollop of the soap, and began to work it into a scummy lather, pressing it through and through the fabric.

The window's square was lightening. She cast a stealthy glance over her shoulder at her mistress, but Brianna's breath came slow and steady; good, she wouldn't wake for a time yet.

She looked back to her work, and froze, feeling a chill colder than those that came with her fevers. The thin suds that covered her hands were dark, and small black eddies spread through the water like the ink stains of a cuttlefish.

She didn't want to look, but it was too late to pretend she hadn't seen. She turned back the wet fabric carefully, and there it was; a large, dark blotch, discoloring the cloth just where the seams crossed in the crotch of the breeks.

The rising sun oozed a sullen red through the hazy sky, turning the water in the basin, the air in the room, the whole spinning world, the color of fresh blood.

41

Journey's End

Brianna thought she might scream. Instead, she patted Lizzie's back and spoke softly.

'Don't worry, it'll be all right. Mr. Viorst says he'll wait for us. As soon as you feel better, we'll leave. But for now, don't worry about anything, just rest.'

Lizzie nodded, but couldn't answer; her teeth were chattering too hard, in spite of the three blankets over her and the hot brick at her feet.

'I'll go and get your drink, honey. Just rest,' Brianna repeated, and with a final pat, rose and left the room.

It wasn't Lizzie's fault, of course, Brianna thought, but she could scarcely have picked a worse moment to have another attack of fever. Brianna had slept late and restlessly after the dreadful scene with Roger, waking to find her clothes washed and hung to dry, her shoes polished, her stockings folded, the room ruthlessly swept and tidied – and Lizzie collapsed in a shivering heap on the empty hearth.

For the thousandth time, she counted the days. Eight days until Monday. If Lizzie's attack followed its usual pattern, she might be able to travel the day after tomorrow. Six days. And according to Junior Smoots and Hans Viorst, five to six days to make the trip upriver at this time of year.

She couldn't miss Jamie Fraser, she couldn't! She had to be in Cross Creek by Monday, come hell or high water. Who knew how long the trial might take, or whether he would leave as soon as it was over? She would have given anything to be able to go at once.

The burning ache to move, to go, was so intense it obliterated all the other aches and burnings of her body – even the deep heart-burning of Roger's betrayal – but there was nothing to be done. She could go nowhere until Lizzie was better.

The taproom was full; two new ships had come into the

harbor during the day, and now at evening the benches were full of seamen, with a game of cards loud and lively at the table in the corner. Brianna edged through the blue clouds of tobacco smoke, ignoring the whistles and ribald remarks. Roger had wanted her to wear a dress, had he? Damn him. Her breeches normally kept men at a safe distance, but Lizzie had washed them, and they were still too damp to wear.

She gave one man who reached for her buttocks a glare fit to sear his eyebrows. He stopped in mid-grab, startled, and she slid by him, through the door to the kitchen breezeway.

On the way back, with the jug of steaming catmint tea wrapped in a cloth to keep from burning her, she made a detour around the edge of the room to avoid her would-be assailant. If he touched her, she would pour boiling water in his lap. And while that would be no more than he deserved, and some palliative to her own volcanic feelings, it would waste the tea, which Lizzie badly needed.

She stepped carefully sideways, squeezing between the raucous cardplayers and the wall. The table was scattered with coins and other small valuables: silver and gilt and pewter buttons, a snuffbox, a silver penknife, and scrib-bled scraps of paper – IOUs, she supposed, or the eighteenth-century equivalent. Then one of the men moved, and beyond his shoulder she caught the gleam of gold.

She glanced down, looked away, then looked back, startled. It was a ring, a plain gold band, but wider than most. It wasn't the gold alone that had caught her eye, though. The ring was no more than a foot away, and while the light in the taproom was more than dim, a candlestick sat on the cardplayers' table, shedding its light in the inner curve of the golden band.

She couldn't quite read the letters engraved there, but she knew the pattern so well that the legend sprang into her mind, unbidden.

She laid a hand on the shoulder of the man who had the ring, interrupting him in mid-jest. He turned, half frowning, the frown clearing as he saw who had touched him.

'Aye, sweetheart, and have ye come to change my luck, then?' He was a big man, with a heavy-boned, handsome face, a broad mouth and a broken nose, and a pair of light green eyes that moved over her with quick appraisal.

She forced her lips to smile at him.

'I hope so,' she said. 'Shall I give your ring a rub for luck?' Without waiting for permission, she snatched the ring from the table and gave it a brisk rub on her sleeve. Then holding it up to admire the shine, she could see plainly the words written inside.

From F. to C. with love. Always.

Her hand was trembling as she gave it back.

'It's very pretty,' she said. 'Where did you get it?'

He looked startled, then wary, and she hastened to add, 'It's too small for you – won't your wife be angry if you lose her ring?' *How?* she thought wildly. *How did he get it? And what's happened to my mother?*

The full lips curved in a charming smile.

'And if I had a wife, sweetheart, sure I'd leave her for you.' He looked her over more closely, long lashes dropping to hide his gaze. He touched her waist in a casual gesture of invitation.

'I'm busy just now, sweetheart, but later . . . eh?'

The jug was burning through the cloth, but her fingers felt cold. Her heart had congealed into a small lump of terror.

'Tomorrow,' she said. 'In the daylight.'

He looked at her, startled, then threw his head back and laughed.

'Well, I've heard men say I'm not a one to be met in the dark, poppet, but the women seem to prefer it.' He ran a thick finger down her forearm in play; the red-gold hairs rose at his touch.

'In the daylight, then, if ye like. Come to my ship – *Gloriana,* near the naval yard.'

'Gracious, you vill not how long haf eaten?' Miss Viorst peered at Brianna's empty bowl with good-willed incredulity. About the same age as Brianna herself, she was a broad-built, placid-tempered Dutchwoman whose motherly manner made her seem a good deal older.

'Day before yesterday, I think.' Brianna gratefully accepted a second helping of dumplings and broth, and yet another thick slab of salt-rising bread slathered with curls of fresh white butter. 'Oh, thank you!' The food did something to fill the hollow space that yawned inside her, a small warm comfort around which to center herself.

Lizzie's fever had come on again, two days upriver. This time the attack was longer and more severe, and Brianna had been seriously afraid that Lizzie would die, right there in the middle of the Cape Fear River.

She had sat in mid-canoe for all of a day and a night, while Viorst and his partner paddled like maniacs, she alternately pouring handfuls of water over Lizzie's head and wrapping her in all the coats and blankets available, all the time praying to see the girl's small bosom rise with the next breath.

'If I die, will ye tell my father?' Lizzie had whispered to her in the rushing dark.

'I will, but you won't, so dinna fash yourself,' Brianna said firmly. It was successful; Lizzie's frail back quivered with laughter at Brianna's attempted Scots, and a small bony hand reached up to hers, holding on until sleep loosened its grip and the fleshless fingers slipped free.

Viorst, alarmed at Lizzie's state, had taken them to the house he shared with his sister a little way below Cross Creek, carrying Lizzie's blanket-wrapped body up the dusty trail from the river to a small framed cottage. The girl's stubborn spirit had brought her through once more, but Brianna thought that the fragile flesh might not be equal to many more such demands.

She cut a dumpling in half and ate it slowly, savoring the rich warm juices of chicken and onion. She was grubby, travel-worn, starved, and exhausted, every bone in her body aching. They had made it, though. They were in Cross Creek, and tomorrow was Monday. Somewhere nearby was Jamie Fraser – and God willing, Claire as well.

She touched the leg of her breeches, and the secret pocket sewn into the seam. It was still there, the small round hardness of the talisman. Her mother was still alive. That was all that mattered.

After eating, she went once more to check on Lizzie.

Hanneke Viorst was sitting by the bed darning socks. She nodded to Brianna, smiling.

'She is *gut*.'

Looking down at the wasted, sleeping face, Brianna wouldn't have said that much. Still, the fever was gone; a hand on Lizzie's brow came away cool and damp, and a half-empty bowl on the table nearby showed that she had managed a little nourishment.

'You vill rest, too?' Hanneke half rose, gesturing toward the trundle bed pulled out in readiness.

Brianna cast a glance of longing at the clean quilts and puffy bolster, but shook her head.

'Not yet, thank you. What I'd really like is to borrow your mule, if I might.'

There was no telling where Jamie Fraser was now. Viorst had told her that River Run was a good distance from the town; he might be there, or he might be staying somewhere in Cross Creek, for convenience. She couldn't leave Lizzie long enough to ride all the way to River Run, but she did want to go into town and find the courthouse where the trial would be held tomorrow. She was taking no chance of missing him by not knowing where to go.

The mule was large and elderly, but not averse to ambling along the riverbank road. He walked somewhat slower than she could have done herself, but that didn't matter; she was in no hurry, now.

Despite her tiredness, she began to feel better as she rode, her bruised, stiff body relaxing into the easy rhythm of the mule's slow gait. It was a hot, humid day, but the sky was clear and blue, and great elms and hickory trees overhung the road, cool leaves filtering the sun.

Torn between Lizzie's illness and her own painful memories, she had noticed nothing of the second half of their voyage, taken no notice of change in the countryside they passed. Now it was like being magically transported during sleep, waking up in a different place. She put everything else aside, determined to forget the last few days and everything in them. She was going to find Jamie Fraser.

The sandy roads, scrub-pine forests, and marshy swamps of the coast were gone, replaced by thickets of cool green, by tall, thick-trunked, canopied trees, and a soft orange dirt that darkened to black mold where the dead leaves lay matted at the edge of the road. The shrieks of gulls and terns were gone, replaced by the muted chatter of a jay, and the soft liquid song of a whippoorwill, far back in the forest.

How would it be? she wondered. She had wondered the same thing a hundred times, and a hundred times imagined different scenes: what she would say, what he would say – would he be glad to see her? She hoped so; and yet he would be a stranger. Likely he would bear no resemblance at all to the man of her imagination. With some difficulty, she fought back the memory of Laoghaire's voice: *A liar and a cheat* . . . Her mother hadn't thought so.

' "Sufficient unto the day is the evil thereof," ' she murmured to herself. She had come into the town of Cross Creek itself; the scattered houses thickened, and the dirt track widened into a cobbled street, lined with shops and larger houses. There were people about, but it was the hottest part of the afternoon, when the air lay still and heavy on the town. Those who could be, were inside in the shade.

The road curved out, following the riverbank. A small sawmill stood by itself on a point of land, and near it, a tavern. She'd ask there, she decided. Hot as it was, she could use something to drink.

She patted the pocket of her coat, to be sure she had money. She felt instead the prickly outline of a horse chestnut's hull, and pulled her hand away as though she'd been burned.

She felt hollow again, in spite of the food she'd eaten. Lips pressed tight together, she tethered the mule and ducked into the dark refuge of the tavern.

The room was empty save for the landlord, perched in somnolence on his stool. He roused himself at her step, and after the usual goggle of surprise at her appearance, served her beer and gave her courteous directions to the courthouse.

'Thank you.' She wiped the sweat from her forehead with a coat sleeve – even inside, the heat was stifling.

'You'll have come for the trial, then?' the landlord ventured, still looking at her curiously.

'Yes – well, not really. Whose trial is it?' she asked, belatedly realizing that she had no idea.

'Oh, it'll be Fergus Fraser,' the man said, as though assuming that naturally everyone knew who Fergus Fraser was. 'Assault on an officer of the Crown is the charge. He'll be acquitted, though,' the landlord went on matter-of-factly. 'Jamie Fraser's come down from the mountain for him.'

Brianna choked on her beer.

'You *know* Jamie Fraser?' she asked breathlessly, swabbing at the spilled foam on her sleeve.

The landlord's brows went up.

'Wait but a moment and you'll know him, too.' He nodded at a pewter tankard full of beer, sitting on the nearby table. She hadn't noticed it when she came in. 'He went out the back, just as you came in. He – hey!' He fell back with a cry of surprise as she dropped her own tankard on the floor, and shot out the back door like a bat out of hell.

The light outside was dazzling after the taproom's gloom. Brianna blinked, eyes tearing at the shafts of sun that stabbed through the shifting greens of a screen of maples. Then a movement caught her eye, below the flickering leaves.

He stood in the shade of the maples, half turned away from her, head bent in absorption. A tall man, long-legged, lean and graceful, with his shoulders broad under a white shirt. He wore a faded kilt in pale greens and browns, casually rucked up in front as he urinated against a tree.

He finished and, letting the kilt fall, turned toward the post house. He saw her then, standing there staring at him, and tensed slightly, hands half curling. Then he saw past her men's clothes, and the look of wary suspicion changed at once to surprise as he realized that she was a woman.

There was no doubt in her mind, from the first glimpse. She was at once surprised and not surprised at all; he was not quite what she had imagined – he seemed smaller, only man-sized – but his face had the lines of her own; the long, straight nose and stubborn jaw, and the slanted cat-eyes, set in a frame of solid bone.

He moved toward her out of the maples' shadow, and the sun struck his hair with a spray of copper sparks. Half consciously she raised a hand and pushed a strand of hair back from her face, seeing from the corner of her eye the matching gleam of thick red-gold.

'What d'ye want here, lassie?' he asked. Sharp, but not unkind. His voice was deeper than she had imagined; the Highland burr slight but distinct.

'You,' she blurted. Her heart seemed to have wedged itself in her throat; she had trouble forcing any words past it.

He was close enough that she caught the faint whiff of his sweat and the fresh smell of sawn wood; there was a golden scatter of sawdust caught in the rolled sleeves of his linen shirt. His eyes narrowed with amusement as he looked her up and down, taking in her costume. One reddish eyebrow rose, and he shook his head.

'Sorry, lass,' he said, with a half-smile. 'I'm a marrit man.'

He made to pass by, and she made a small incoherent sound, putting out a hand to stop him, but not quite daring to touch his sleeve. He stopped and looked at her more closely.

'No, I meant it; I've a wife at home, and home's not far,' he said, evidently wishing to be courteous. 'But –' He stopped, close enough now to take in the grubbiness of her clothes, the hole in the sleeve of her coat and the tattered ends of her stock.

'Och,' he said in a different tone, and reached for the small leather purse he wore tied at his waist. 'Will ye be starved, then, lass? I've money, if you must eat.'

She could scarcely breathe. His eyes were dark blue, soft with kindness. Her eyes fixed on the open collar of his shirt, where the curly hairs showed, bleached gold against his sunburnt skin.

'Are you – you're Jamie Fraser, aren't you?'

He glanced sharply at her face.

'I am,' he said. The wariness had returned to his

face; his eyes narrowed against the sun. He glanced quickly behind him, toward the tavern, but nothing stirred in the open doorway. He took a step closer to her.

'Who asks?' he said softly. 'Have you a message for me, lass?'

She felt an absurd desire to laugh welling up in her throat. Did she have a message?

'My name is Brianna,' she said. He frowned, uncertain, and something flickered in his eyes. He knew it! He'd heard the name and it meant something to him. She swallowed hard, feeling her cheeks blaze as though they'd been seared by a candle flame.

'I'm your daughter,' she said, her voice sounding choked to her own ears. 'Brianna.'

He stood stock-still, not changing expression in the slightest. He had heard her, though; he went pale, and then a deep, painful red washed up his throat and into his face, sudden as a brushfire, matching her own vivid color.

She felt a deep flash of joy at the sight, a rush through her midsection that echoed that blaze of blood, recognition of their fair-skinned kinship. Did it trouble him to blush so strongly? she wondered suddenly. Had he schooled his face to immobility, as she had learned to do, to mask that telltale surge?

Her own face felt stiff, but she gave him a tentative smile.

He blinked, and his eyes moved at last from her face, slowly taking in her appearance, and – with what seemed to her a new and horrified awareness – her height.

'My God,' he croaked. 'You're *huge.*'

Her own blush had subsided, but now came back with a vengeance.

'And whose fault is *that*, do you think?' she snapped. She drew herself up straight and squared her shoulders, glaring. So close, at her full height, she could look him right in the eye, and did.

He jerked back, and his face did change then, mask shattering in surprise. Without it, he looked younger; underneath were shock, surprise, and a dawning expression of half-painful eagerness.

'Och, no, lassie!' he exclaimed. 'I didna mean it that

way, at all! It's only –' He broke off, staring at her in fascination. His hand lifted, as though despite himself, and traced the air, outlining her cheek, her jaw and neck and shoulder, afraid to touch her directly.

'It's true?' he whispered. 'It is you, Brianna?' He spoke her name with a queer accent – *Bree*anah – and she shivered at the sound.

'It's me,' she said, a little huskily. She made another attempt at a smile. 'Can't you tell?'

His mouth was wide and full-lipped, but not like hers; wider, a bolder shape, that seemed to hide a smile in the corners of it, even in repose. It was twitching now, not certain what to do.

'Aye,' he said. 'Aye, I can.'

He did touch her then, his fingers drawing lightly down her face, brushing back the waves of ruddy hair from temple and ear, tracing the delicate line of her jaw. She shivered again, though his touch was noticeably warm; she could feel the heat of his palm against her cheek.

'I hadna thought of you as grown,' he said, letting his hand fall reluctantly away. 'I saw the pictures, but still – I had ye in my mind somehow as a wee bairn always – as my babe. I never expected . . .' His voice trailed off as he stared at her, the eyes like her own, deep blue and thick-lashed, wide in fascination.

'Pictures,' she said, feeling breathless with happiness. 'You've seen pictures of me? Mama found you, didn't she? When you said you had a wife at home –'

'Claire,' he interrupted. The wide mouth had made its decision; it split into a smile that lit his eyes like the sun in the dancing tree leaves. He grabbed her arms, tight enough to startle her.

'You'll not have seen her, then? Christ, she'll be mad wi' joy!'

The thought of her mother was overwhelming. Her face cracked, and the tears she had been holding back for days spilled down her cheeks in a flood of relief, half choking her as she laughed and cried together.

'Here, lassie, dinna weep!' he exclaimed in alarm. He let go of her arm and snatched a large, crumpled handkerchief from his sleeve. He patted tentatively at her cheeks, looking worried.

'Dinna weep, *a leannan*, dinna be troubled,' he murmured. 'It's all right, *m' annsachd*; it's all right.'

'I'm all right; everything's all right. I'm just – happy,' she said. She took the handkerchief, wiped her eyes and blew her nose. 'What does that mean – *a leannan*? And the other thing you said?'

'You'll not have the Gaelic, then?' he asked, and shook his head. 'No, of course she wouldna have been taught,' he murmured, as though to himself.

'I'll learn,' she said firmly, giving her nose a last wipe. '*A leannan*?'

A slight smile reappeared on his face as he looked at her.

'It means "darling",' he said softly. '*M' annsachd* – my blessing.'

The words hung in the air between them, shimmering like the leaves. They stood still, both stricken suddenly with shyness by the endearment, unable to look away from each other, unable to find more words.

'Fa–' Brianna started to speak, then stopped, suddenly seized with doubt. What should she call him? Not Daddy. Frank Randall had been Daddy to her all her life; it would be a betrayal to use that name to another man – any other man. Jamie? No, she couldn't possibly; rattled as he was by her appearance, he had still a formidable dignity that forbade such casual use. 'Father' seemed remote and stern – and whatever Jamie Fraser might be, he wasn't that; not to her.

He saw her hesitate and flush, and recognized her trouble.

'You can . . . call me Da,' he said. His voice was husky; he stopped and cleared his throat. 'If – if ye want to, I mean,' he added diffidently.

'Da,' she said, and felt the smile bloom easily this time, unmarred by tears. 'Da. Is that Gaelic?'

He smiled back, the corners of his mouth trembling slightly.

'No. It's only . . . simple.'

And suddenly it was all simple. He held out his arms to

her. She stepped into them and found that she had been wrong; he *was* as big as she'd imagined – and his arms were as strong about her as she had ever dared to hope.

Everything after that seemed to happen in a daze. Overcome by emotion and fatigue, Brianna was conscious of events more as a series of images, sharp as stop-frame photos, than as a moving flow of life.

Lizzie, gray eyes blinking in the sudden light, tiny and pale in the arms of a sturdy black groom with an improbable Scottish accent. A wagon piled with glass and fragrant wood. The polished rumps of horses, and the jolt and creak of wooden wheels. Her father's voice, deep and warm in her ear, describing a house to be built, high on a mountain ridge, explaining that the windows were a surprise for her mother.

'But no such a surprise as you, lassie!' And a laugh of deep joy that seemed to echo in her bones.

A long ride down dusty roads, and sleeping with her head on her father's shoulder, his free arm around her as he drove, breathing the unfamiliar scent of his skin, his strange long hair brushing her face when he turned his head.

Then the cool luxury of the big, breezy house, filled with the scent of beeswax and flowers. A tall woman with white hair and Brianna's face, and a blue-eyed gaze that looked disconcertingly beyond her. Long, cool hands that touched her face and stroked her hair with abstract curiosity.

'Lizzie,' she said, and a pretty woman bent over Lizzie, murmuring, 'Jesuit bark,' her black hands beautiful against the yellow porcelain of Lizzie's face.

Hands – so many hands. Everything was done as if by magic, with soft murmurs as they passed her from hand to hand. She was stripped and bathed before she could protest, scented water poured over her, firm, gentle fingers that massaged her scalp as lavender soap was sluiced from her hair. Linen towels and a small black girl who dried her feet and sprinkled them with rice powder.

A fresh cotton gown and floating barefoot over polished floors, to see her father's eyes light at sight of her. Food –

794

cakes and trifles and jellies and scones – and hot, sweet tea that seemed to replace the blood in her veins.

A pretty blond girl with a frown on her face, who seemed peculiarly familiar; her father called her Marsali. Lizzie, washed and wrapped in a blanket, both frail hands round a mug of pungent liquid, looking like a stepped-on flower newly watered.

Talk, and people coming, and more talk, with only the occasional phrase penetrating through her growing fog.

'... Farquard Campbell has more sense ...'

'Fergus, Da, did ye see him? Is he all right?'

Da? she thought, half puzzled, faintly indignant that someone else should call him that, because ... because ...

Her aunt's voice, coming from a great distance, saying, 'The poor child is asleep where she sits; I can hear her snoring. Ulysses, take her up to bed.'

And then strong arms that lifted her with no sense of strain, but not the candlewax smell of the black butler; the sawdust and linen scent of her father. She gave up the struggle and fell asleep, her head on his chest.

Fergus Fraser might sound like a Scottish clansman; he looked like a French noble. A French noble on his way to the guillotine, Brianna silently amended her first impression.

Handsomely dark, slightly built, and not very tall, he sauntered into the dock, and turned to face the room, long nose lifted an inch above the usual. The shabby clothes, the unshaven jaw, and the large purple bruise over one eye subtracted nothing from his air of aristocratic disdain. Even the curved metal hook that he wore in replacement of a missing hand only added to his impression of disreputable glamour.

Marsali gave a small sigh at sight of him, and her lips grew tight. She leaned across to Brianna to whisper to Jamie.

'What have they done to him, the bastards?'

'Nothing that matters.' He made a small motion, gesturing her back, and she subsided into her seat, glowering at bailiff and sheriff in turn.

They had been lucky to procure seats; every space in the small building was filled, and people were jostling and muttering at the back of the room, kept in order only by the presence of the red-coated soldiers who guarded the doors. Two more soldiers stood to attention at the front of the room, beside the Justice's bench, an officer of some sort lurking in the corner behind them.

Brianna saw the officer catch Jamie Fraser's eye, and a look of malign satisfaction crept over the man's broad features, a look almost of gloating. It made the small hairs rise on the back of her neck, but her father met the man's gaze squarely, then turned away, indifferent.

The Justice arrived and took his place, and the ceremonies of justice being duly performed, the trial began. Evidently, it was not intended to be a trial by jury, since no such body was present; only the Justice and his minions.

Brianna had made out little from the conversation the evening before, though over breakfast she had managed to disentangle the confusion of persons. The young black woman's name was Phaedre, one of Jocasta's slaves, and the tall homely boy with the charming smile was Jamie's nephew, Ian – her cousin, she thought, with the same small thrill of discovered kinship she had felt at Lallybroch. The lovely blond Marsali was Fergus's wife, and Fergus, of course, was the French orphan whom Jamie had informally adopted in Paris, before the Stuart Rising.

Mr. Justice Conant, a tidy gentleman of middle age, settled his wig, arranged his coat, and called for the charges to be read. These were, to wit, that one Fergus Claudel Fraser, resident of Rowan County, had on August 4 of this year of our Lord 1769, feloniously assaulted the person of one Hugh Berowne, a deputy sheriff of said county, and stolen from him Crown property, then lawfully in the deputy's custody.

The said Hugh, being called to the stand, proved to be a gangling fellow of some thirty years and a nervous disposition. He twitched and stammered through his testimony, averring that he had encountered the defendant on the Buffalo Trail Road, while he, Berowne, was in pursuit of his lawful duties. He had been roughly abused by the defendant in the French tongue, and upon his endeavoring to leave, had been pursued by the defendant, who had apprehended him, struck him in the face, and taken away the property of the Crown in Berowne's custody, to wit, one horse, with bridle and saddle.

Upon the invitation of the court, the witness here pulled back the right side of his mouth in a grimace, disclosing a broken tooth, suffered in the assault.

Mr. Justice Conant peered interestedly at the shattered remains of the tooth, and turned to the prisoner.

'Indeed. And now, Mr. Fraser, might we hear your account of this unfortunate event?'

Fergus lowered his nose half an inch, awarding the justice the same regard he might have bestowed on a cockroach.

'This loathsome wad of dung,' he began in measured tones, 'had –'

'The prisoner will refrain from insult,' Justice Conant said coldly.

'The deputy,' Fergus resumed, without turning a hair, 'had come upon my wife as she returned from the flour mill, with my infant son upon her saddle. This – the deputy – hailed her, and without ceremony dragged her from the saddle, informed her that he was taking the horse and its equipment in payment of tax, and left her and the child on foot, five miles from my home, in the blazing sun!' He glared ferociously at Berowne, who narrowed his own gaze in reply. Next to Brianna, Marsali exhaled strongly through her nose.

'What tax did the deputy claim was owed?'

A dark flush had mantled Fergus's cheeks.

'I owe nothing! It was his claim that my land is subject to an annual rent of three shillings, but it is not! My land is exempt from this tax, by virtue of the terms of a land grant made to James Fraser by Governor Tryon. I told the stinking *salaud* as much, when he visited my home to try to collect the money.'

'I heard nothing of such a grant,' Berowne said sulkily. 'These folks will tell you any tale at all, to put off paying. Lallygags and cheats, the lot of them.'

'*Oreilles en feuille de chou!*'

A small ripple of laughter ran through the room, nearly

797

drowning out the Justice's rebuke. Brianna's high-school French was just about adequate to translate this as 'Cauliflower ears!' and she joined in the general smile.

The Justice lifted his head and peered into the courtroom.

'Is James Fraser present?'

Jamie rose and bowed respectfully.

'Here, milord.'

'Swear the witness, Bailiff.'

Jamie, having been duly sworn, attested to the facts that he was in fact the proprietor of a grant of land, that said grant had been made and its terms agreed to by Governor Tryon, that said terms did include a quitment of land rent to the Crown for a period of ten years, such period to expire some nine years hence, and finally, that Fergus Fraser did maintain a house upon and farm crops within the boundaries of the granted territory, under license from himself, James Alexander Malcolm MacKenzie Fraser.

Brianna's attention had at first been fixed upon her father; she could scarcely get enough of looking at him. He was the tallest man in the courtroom, and by far the most striking, attired in snowy linen and a coat of deep blue that set off his slanted eyes and fiery hair.

A movement in the corner attracted her eye, though, and she looked to see the officer she had noticed before. He was no longer looking at her father, but had fixed Hugh Berowne with a penetrating stare. Berowne gave the shadow of a nod, and sat back to await the end of Fraser's testimony.

'It would appear that Mr. Fraser's claim of exemption holds true, Mr. Berowne,' the Justice said mildly. 'I must therefore hold him acquitted of the charge of –'

'He cannot prove it!' Berowne blurted out. He glanced at the officer, as though for moral support, and stiffened his long chin. 'There is no documentary proof, only James Fraser's word.'

Another stir went through the courtroom; this one uglier in tone. Brianna had no trouble hearing the shock and outrage that her father's word had been called in question, and felt an unexpected pride.

Her father showed no anger, though, he rose again, and bowed to the Justice.

'And your Lordship will permit me.' He reached into his coat and removed a folded sheet of parchment, with a blob of red sealing wax affixed.

'Your Lordship will be familiar with the Governor's seal, I am sure,' he said, laying it on the table before Mr. Conant. The Justice raised one eyebrow, but looked carefully at the seal, then broke it open, examined the document within, and laid it down.

'This is a duly witnessed copy of the original grant of land,' he announced, 'signed by His Excellency William Tryon.'

'How did you get that?' Berowne blurted. 'There wasn't time to get to New Bern and back!' Then all the blood drained from his face. Brianna looked at the officer; his pudgy face seemed to have acquired all the blood Berowne had lost.

The Justice cast him a sharp glance, but merely said, 'Given that documentary proof *is* now entered in evidence, we find that the defendant is plainly not guilty of the charge of theft since the property in question was his own. On the matter of assault, however –' At this point he noticed that Jamie had not sat down, but was still standing in front of the bench.

'Yes, Mr. Fraser? Had you something else to tell the court?' Justice Conant dabbed at a trickle of sweat that ran down from under his wig; with so many bodies packed into the small room, it was like a sweatbath.

'I beg the court might gratify my curiosity, your Lordship. Does Mr. Berowne's original charge describe more fully the attack upon him?'

The Justice raised both eyebrows, but shuffled quickly through the papers on the table before him, then handed one to the bailiff, pointing to a spot on the page.

'Complainant stated that one Fergus Fraser struck him in the face with his fist, causing complainant to fall stunned upon the ground, whereat the defendant seized the bridle of the horse, leapt upon it, and rode away, calling out remarks of an abusive nature in the French tongue. Complainant –'

A loud cough from the dock pulled all eyes to the defendant, who smiled charmingly at Mr. Justice Conant, plucked a handkerchief from his pocket and elaborately wiped his face – using the hook at the end of his left arm.

'Oh!' said the Justice, and swiveled cold eyes toward the witness chair, where Berowne squirmed in hot-faced agony.

'And would you care to explain, sir, how you have sustained injury upon the right side of your face, when struck by the left fist of a man who does not have one?'

'Yes, *crottin*,' Fergus said cheerfully. 'Explain that one.'

Perhaps feeling that Berowne's attempts at explanation were best conducted in privacy, Justice Conant mopped his neck and put a summary end to the trial, dismissing Fergus Fraser with no stain upon his character.

'It was me,' Marsali said proudly, clinging to the arm of her husband at the celebratory feast that followed the trial.

'You?' Jamie gave her an amused glance. 'That fisted yon deputy in the face, ye mean?'

'Not my fist, my foot,' she corrected. 'When the wicked *salaud* tried to drag me off the horse, I kicked him in the jaw. He'd never ha' got me down,' she added, glowering at the memory, 'save he snatched Germaine from me, so of course I had to go and get him.'

She petted the sleek blond head of the toddler who clung to her skirts, a piece of biscuit clutched in one grubby fist.

'I don't quite understand,' Brianna said. 'Did Mr. Berowne not want to admit that a woman hit him?'

'Ah, no,' Jamie said, pouring another cup of ale and handing it to her. 'It was only Sergeant Murchison making a nuisance of himself.'

'Sergeant Murchison? That would be the army officer who was at the trial?' she asked. She took a small sip of the ale, for politeness' sake. 'The one who looks like a half-roasted pig?'

Her father grinned at this characterization.

'Aye, that'll be the man. He's a mislike of me,' he

explained. 'This wilna be the first time – or the last – that he's tried such a trick to cripple me.'

'He could not hope to succeed with such a ridiculous charge,' Jocasta chimed in, leaning forward and reaching out a hand. Ulysses, standing by, moved the plate of bannocks the necessary inch. She took one, unerringly, and turned her disconcerting blind eyes toward Jamie.

'Was it really necessary for you to subvert Farquard Campbell?' she asked, disapproving.

'Aye, it was,' Jamie answered. Seeing Brianna's confusion, he explained.

'Farquard Campbell is the usual justice of this district. If he hadna fallen ill so conveniently' – and here he grinned again, mischief dancing in his eyes – 'the trial would have been held last week. That was their plan, aye? Murchison and Berowne. They meant to bring the charge, arrest Fergus, and force me down from the mountain in the midst of the harvest – and they succeeded in that much, damn them,' he added ruefully.

'But they counted on my not being able to obtain a copy of the grant from New Bern before the trial – as indeed I could not, had it been last week.' He gave Ian a smile, and the boy, who had ridden hellbent to New Bern to procure the document, blushed pink and buried his face in a bowl of punch.

'Farquard Campbell is a friend, Auntie,' Jamie said to Jocasta, 'but ye ken as well as that he's a man of the law; it wouldna make a bit of difference that he knows the terms of my grant as well as I do; if I couldna produce the proof in court, he would feel himself forced to rule against me.

'And if he had,' he went on, returning to Brianna, 'I should have been forced to appeal the verdict, which would mean Fergus being taken to prison in New Bern, and a new trial scheduled there. The end of it would have been the same – but it would have taken both Fergus and myself off the land for most of the harvest season, and cost me more in fees than the harvest will bring.'

He looked at Brianna over the rim of his cup, blue eyes suddenly serious.

'You'll no be thinking me rich, I hope?' he asked.

'I hadn't thought of it at all,' she replied, startled, and he smiled.

'That's as well,' he said, 'for while I've a good bit of land, there's little of it under cultivation as yet; we've enough – barely – to seed the fields and feed ourselves, wi' a bit left over for the cattle. And capable as your mother is' – the smile widened – 'she canna bring in thirty acres of corn and barley by herself.' He set down his empty cup and stood up.

'Ian, will ye see to the supplies and drive up the wagon with Fergus and Marsali? The lass and I will go ahead, I think.' He glanced down at Brianna questioningly.

·'Jocasta will care for your wee maid here. Ye dinna mind going so soon?'

'No,' she said, putting down her cup and standing up too. 'Can we go today?'

I took down the bottles from the cupboard, one by one, uncorking one now and then to sniff at the contents. If not thoroughly dry before storage, fleshy-leaved herbs would rot in the bottle; seeds would grow exotic molds.

The thought of molds made me think once more of my penicillin plantation. Or what I hoped might one day be one, were I lucky enough, and observant enough to know my luck. Of the hundreds of molds that grew easily on stale, damp bread, *Penicillium* was only one. What were the odds of a stray spore of that one precious mold taking root on the slices of bread I laid out weekly? What were the odds of an exposed slice of bread surviving long enough for *any* spores to find it? And lastly, what were the odds that I would recognize it if I saw it?

I had been trying for more than a year, with no success so far.

Even with the marigolds and yarrow I scattered for repellency, it was impossible to keep the vermin away. Mice and rats, ants and cockroaches; one day I had even found a party of burglarious squirrels in the pantry, holding riot over scattered corn and the gnawed ruins of half my seed potatoes.

The only recourse was to lock all edibles in the big hutch Jamie had built – that, or keep them in thick wooden casks or lidded jars, resistent to the efforts of tooth and claw. But to seal food away from four-footed thieves was also to seal it away from the air – and the air was the only messenger that might one day bring me a real weapon against disease.

Each of the plants carries an antidote to some illness – if we only knew what it was. I felt a renewed pang of loss when I thought of Nayawenne; not only for herself but for her knowledge. She had taught me only a fraction of the things she knew, and I regretted that most bitterly – though not as bitterly as the loss of my friend.

Still, I knew one thing she had not – the manifold virtues of that smallest of plants, the lowly bread mold. To find it would be difficult, to recognize it, and to use it, even more so. But I never doubted it was worth the search.

To leave bread exposed in the house was to draw the mice and rats inside. I had tried setting it on the sideboard – Ian had absentmindedly consumed half of my budding antibiotic incubator, and mice and ants made short work of the rest while I was away from the house.

It was simply impossible, in summer, spring, or autumn, either to leave bread exposed and unguarded or to stay inside to look after it. There were too many urgent chores to be done outside, too many calls to attend births or illness, too much opportunity for foraging.

In the winter, of course, the vermin went away, to lay their eggs against the spring, and hibernate under a blanket of dead leaves, secure from the cold. But the air was cold, too; too cold to bring me living spores. The bread I laid out either curled and dried, or went soggy, depending on its distance from the fire; in either case, sporting nothing but the occasional orange or pink crust: the molds that lived in the crevices of the human body.

I would try again in the spring, I thought, sniffing at a bottle of dried marjoram. It was good; musky as incense, smelling of dreams. The new house on the ridge was already rising, foundation laid and rooms marked out. I could see the skeletal framework from the cabin door, black against the clear September sky on the ridge.

By the spring, it would be finished. I would have plastered walls and laid oak floors, glass windows with stout frames that kept out mice and ants – and a nice snug, sunny surgery in which to conduct my medical practice.

My glowing visions were interrupted by a raucous bellow from the penfold; Clarence announcing an arrival. I could hear voices in the distance, in between Clarence's shrieks of ecstasy, and I hastily began to tidy away the scatter of corks and bottles. It must be Jamie returning with Fergus and Marsali – or at least I hoped so.

Jamie had been confident of the trial's outcome, but I worried nonetheless. Raised to believe that British law in the abstract was one of the great achievements of civilization, I had seen a good deal too many of its concrete applications to have much faith in its avatars. On the other hand, I had quite a bit of faith in Jamie.

Clarence's vocalizations had dropped to the wheezing gargle he used for intimate converse, but the voices had stopped. That was odd. Perhaps things had gone wrong after all?

I thrust the last of the bottles back into the cupboard and went to the door. The dooryard was empty. Clarence hee-hawed enthusiastically at my appearance, but nothing else moved. Someone had come, though – the chickens had scattered, fleeing into the bushes.

A brisk chill ran up my spine and I whirled, trying to look in front of me and over my shoulder at the same time. Nothing. The chestnut trees behind the house sighed in the breeze, a shimmer of sun filtered through their yellowing leaves.

I knew beyond the shadow of a doubt that I wasn't alone. Damn, and I'd left my knife on the table inside!

'Sassenach.' My heart nearly stopped at the sound of Jamie's voice. I spun toward it, relief being rapidly overcome by annoyance. What did he think he –

For a split second, I thought I was seeing double. They were sitting on the bench outside the door, side by side, the afternoon sun igniting their hair like matchheads.

My eyes focused on Jamie's face, alight with joy – then shifted right.

'Mama.' It was the same expression; eagerness and joy and longing all together. I had no time even to think before she was in my arms, and I was in the air, knocked off my feet both literally and figuratively.

'Mama!'

I hadn't any breath; what hadn't been taken away by shock was being squeezed out by a rib-crushing hug.

'Bree!' I managed to gasp, and she put me down, though she didn't let go. I looked disbelievingly up, but she was real. I looked for Jamie, and found him standing beside her. He said nothing, but gave me an face-splitting grin, his cars bright pink with delight.

'I, ah, I wasn't expecting –' I said idiotically.

Brianna gave me a grin to match her father's, eyes bright as stars and damp with happiness.

'Nobody expects the Spanish Inquisition!'

'What?' said Jamie blankly.

PART TEN

Impaired Relations

42

Moonlight

September 1769

She woke from a dreamless sleep, a hand on her shoulder. She jerked and started up on one elbow, blinking. Jamie's face was barely distinguishable above her in the gloom; the fire had burned down to nothing more than a glow, and it was nearly pitch-black in the cabin.

'I shall be hunting up the mountain, lass; will ye come wi' me?' he whispered.

She rubbed her eyes, trying to reassemble her sleep-scattered thoughts, and nodded.

'Good. Wear your breeks.' He rose silently and went out, letting in a breath of piercing-sweet cold air as the door opened.

By the time she had pulled on breeks and stockings, he was back, moving just as silently, despite the armload of firewood he carried. He nodded to her and knelt to rekindle the fire; she thrust her arms into her coat and went out herself, in search of the privy.

The world outside was black and dreamlike; if not for the chill, she might have thought herself still asleep. Stars burned coldly bright, but seemed to hang low, as though they might fall from the sky any minute and be extinguished, sizzling, in the mist-damp trees on the ridges beyond.

What time was it? she wondered, shivering at the touch of damp wood on her sleep-warmed thighs. Somewhere in the small hours; surely it was a long time until dawn. Everything was hushed; no insects hummed yet in her mother's garden, and there were no rustlings, even from the dry corn-stooks propped in the field.

When she pushed open the door of the cabin, the air inside seemed almost solid; a block of stale smoke, fried food, and the smell of sleeping bodies. By contrast, the air outside was sweet but thin – she kept taking large gulps, to get enough.

He was ready; a leather bag was tied at his belt with ax and powder horn, a bigger canvas sack slung over his shoulder. She didn't come in, but stood in the doorway watching as he bent quickly and kissed her mother in the bed.

He knew she was there, of course – and it was no more than a light kiss on the forehead – but she felt like an intruder, a voyeur. The more so when Claire's long, pale hand floated up from the quilts and touched his face with a tenderness that squeezed her heart. Claire murmured something, but Brianna didn't hear it.

She turned away quickly, face hot in spite of the chilly air, and was standing by the edge of the clearing when he came out. He shut the door behind him, waiting for the *clunk* within as it was barred. He had a gun, a long-barreled thing that seemed nearly as tall as she was.

He didn't speak, but smiled at her and cocked his head toward the wood. She followed, keeping up easily as he took a faint trail that led through groves of spruce and chestnut. His feet knocked the dew from clumps of grass, and left a dark trail through tussocks of shimmering silver.

The trail wound to and fro, nearly level for a long time, but then began to head uphill. She felt the shift, rather than saw it. It was still very dark, but suddenly the silence was gone. In the next breath, a bird began to call from the wood nearby.

Then the whole mountainside was alive with birdsong, screeches and trills and whirrs. Under the calling was a sense of movement, of fluttering and scratching just below the threshold of hearing. He stopped, listening.

She stopped, too, looking at him. The light had changed so slowly that she was scarcely aware of it; her eyes adapted to the dark, she could see easily by the starlight, and knew the change to daylight only when she glanced from the ground and saw the vivid color of her father's hair.

He had food in his bag; they sat on a log and shared apples and bread. Then she drank from a trickle that dropped from a ledge, filling her hands with cold crystal.

Looking back, she could no longer see any trace of the small settlement; houses and fields were gone, as though the mountain had silently drawn her forests together, swallowing them up.

She wiped her hands on the skirts of her coat; feeling the prickly shape of the conker in her pocket. No horse chestnuts on these wooded slopes; that was an English tree, planted by some expatriate in the hope of creating a memory of home; a living link to another life. She curled her hand around it briefly, wondering whether her own links had been severed for good, then let it go, and turned to follow her father uphill.

At first her heart had pounded and her thigh muscles strained at the unaccustomed labor of climbing, but then her body had found the rhythm of the ground. With the coming of light, she no longer stumbled. By the time they emerged at the top of a steep slope, her feet trod so lightly on the spongy leaves that she felt she might float off into the sky that seemed so near, cut free of the earth.

For a single moment, she wished that she could. But the links still held in the chain that bound her to the earth – her mother, her father, Lizzie . . . and Roger. The morning sun was rising, a great ball of flame above the mountains. She had to shut her eyes for a moment, not to be blinded.

Here it was; the place he had meant to bring her. At the foot of a towering escarpment, part of the rock had fallen into a loose tumble, overgrown by moss and lichen, small saplings jutting drunkenly from cracks in the rock. He tilted his head, gesturing her to follow him. There was a way through the huge boulders, hard to see, but there. He felt her hesitate behind him, and looked back.

She smiled and waved a hand at the rock. A huge piece of limestone had fallen and split in two; he stood between the pieces.

'It's all right,' she said softly. 'It just reminded me.'

That reminded *him*, and raised the hairs on his forearms. He had to stop and watch as she stepped through, only to be sure. But it was fine; she stepped through carefully, and joined him. He felt the need to touch her, though, only to be sure; he held out a hand, and felt reassured by the solid clasp of his fingers around hers.

He had judged it right; the sun was just coming over the farthest ridge as they came out into the open space at the top of the slope. Below them spread ridges and valleys, so full of mist that it looked like smoke boiling through the hollows. From the mountain opposite, the waterfall arched out and down in a thin white plume, falling into the mist.

'Here,' he said, stopping at a place where the rocks lay scattered, surrounded by thick grass. 'Let's rest for a bit.' Chilly as the early mornings were, the climb had heated him; he sat on a flat rock, legs stretched out to let the air come under his kilt, and pushed the plaid off his shoulders.

'It feels so different here,' she said, brushing back a lock of the soft red hair whose flames warmed him more than the sun. She glanced back at him, smiling. 'Do you know what I mean? I rode from Inverness to Lallybroch, through the Great Glen, and that was wild enough' – she shivered slightly at the recollection – 'but it wasn't like this at all.'

'No,' he said. He knew exactly what she meant; the wildness of the glens and the moors was inhabited, in a way that this place of forests and rushing waters was not.

'I think –' he began, then stopped. Would she think him daft? But she was looking up at him, wanting him to say. 'The spirits that live there,' he said, a little awkwardly. 'They are auld, and they've seen men for thousands on thousands of years; they ken us weel, and they're none so wary of showing themselves. What lives here' – he laid a hand on the trunk of a chestnut tree that rose a hundred feet above them, whose girth measured more than thirty feet around – 'they havena seen our like before.'

She nodded, seeming not at all taken back.

'They're curious, though, aren't they,' she said, 'some of them?' and tipped back her head to look up into the dizzy spiral of the branches overhead. 'Don't you feel them watching, now and then?'

'Now and then.'

He sat on the rock beside her and watched the light

spread, spilling over the edge of the mountain, lighting the distant falls the way kindling catches from a spark, filling the mist with a glow like pearls, then burning it away altogether. Together they saw the slope of the mountain come to the light of day, and he said a quiet word to the spirit of this place, in thanks. If it had no Gaelic, still it might catch his meaning.

She stretched her long legs, breathing in the scent of the morning.

'You didn't really mind, did you?' Her voice was soft, and she kept her eyes on the valley below, careful not to look at him. 'Living in the cave near Broch Mhorda.'

'No,' he said. The sun was warm on his breast and face, and filled him with a sense of peace. 'No, I didna mind it.'

'Only hearing about it – I thought it must have been terrible. Cold and dirty and lonely, I mean.' She did look at him then, and the morning sky lived in her eyes.

'It was,' he said, and smiled a little.

'Ian – Uncle Ian – took me there to show me.'

'Did he, then? It's none so bleak, in the summertime, when the yellow's on the broom.'

'No. But even when it was –' She hesitated.

'No, I didna mind it.' He closed his eyes and let the sun heat his eyelids.

At first he had thought the loneliness would kill him, but once he had learned it would not, he came to value the solitude of the mountainside. He could see the sun clear, though his eyes were closed; a great red ball, flaming round the edges. Was that how Jocasta saw it behind her blind eyes?

She was silent for a long time, and so was he, content to listen. There were wee birds working in the spruce nearby, hanging upside down from the branches, hunting the bugs that they ate and talking to themselves about what they found.

'Roger –' she said suddenly, and his heart was struck by a dart of jealousy, the more painful for being unexpected. Was he not to have her to himself, even for so short a time? He opened his eyes and did his best to look interested.

'I tried to tell him, once, about being alone. That I

thought it maybe wasn't a bad thing.' She sighed, the heavy brows drawn down. 'I don't think he understood.'

He made a noncommittal sound in his throat.

'I thought –' She hesitated, glanced at him, then away. 'I thought maybe that was why it's – why you and Mama . . .' Her skin was so clear, he could see the blood bloom under it. She took a deep breath, hands braced on the rock.

'She's like that too. She doesn't mind being alone.'

He glanced at her, wanting badly to know what made her say so. What had Claire's life been in their years apart to give her that knowledge? It was so; Claire knew the flavor of solitude. It was cold as spring water, and not all could drink it; for some it was not refreshment, but mortal chill. But she had lived daily with a husband; how had she drunk deep enough of loneliness to know?

Brianna could maybe tell him, but he wouldn't ask; the last name he wished to hear spoken in this place was Frank Randall's.

He coughed instead.

'Well, it's maybe true,' he agreed cautiously. 'I've seen women – and men too, sometimes – as canna bear the sound of their own thoughts, and they maybe dinna make such good matches with those who can.'

'No,' she said, brooding. 'Maybe they don't.'

The small pang of jealousy eased. So she had doubts about this Wakefield, did she? She'd told him and Claire everything, about her search, the death notice, the journey from Scotland, the visit to Lallybroch – damn Laoghaire! – and about the man Wakefield, who'd come after her. She wasn't telling everything there, he thought, but that was as well; he didn't want to hear it. He was less bothered at the prospect of a distant death by fire than by the more imminent interruption of his idyll with his long-lost daughter.

He drew up his knees and sat quiet. Much as he wanted to recapture his sense of tranquility, he could not free his mind from the thought of Randall.

He had won. Claire was his; so was this glorious child – this young woman, he corrected himself, looking at her. But Randall had had the keeping of them for twenty years;

there was no doubt he had set his mark on them. But what mark had it been?

'Look.' Brianna's hand squeezed his arm as she breathed the word.

He followed her gaze and saw them; two does, standing just under the shadow of the trees, not twenty feet away. He didn't move, but breathed quietly. He could feel Brianna beside him, enchanted into stillness too.

The deer saw them; delicate heads upraised, dark, moist nostrils flaring for scent. After a moment, though, one doe stepped out, dainty, nervous footsteps leaving streaks in the dew-wet grass. The other followed, cautious, and they grazed along the grassy strips between the rocks, turning now and then to lift their head and cast tranquil eyes on the strange but harmless creatures on the ledge.

He couldn't have come within a mile of a Scottish red deer that had his scent. The red stags kent weel what a man was.

He watched the deer graze, with the innocence of perfect wildness, and felt the sun's benediction on his head. This was a new place, and he was content to be alone here with his daughter.

'What are we hunting, Da?' He was standing still, eyes squinted as he scanned the horizon, but she was reasonably sure he wasn't looking at an animal; she could speak without scaring the game.

They'd seen a good many animals in the course of the day; the two deer at dawn, a red fox that sat watching on a rock, licking dainty black paws until they came too close, then vanishing like a blown-out flame. Squirrels – dozens of them – chattering through the treetops, playing hide-and-seek past the tree boles. Even a flock of wild turkey, with two males strutting, chests puffed and tail fans spread for the edification of a gobbling harem.

None of these were the chosen prey, for which she was glad. She had no objection to killing for food, but would have been sorry to have the beauty of the day soiled by blood.

'Bees,' he said.

'*Bees?* How do you hunt bees?'

815

He picked up his gun and smiled at her, nodding down-hill toward a brilliant patch of yellow.

'Look for flowers.'

There were certainly bees in the flowers; close enough, and she could hear the hum. There were several different kinds: huge black bumblebees, a smaller kind, striped with black and yellow fuzz, and the smooth lethal shapes of wasps, bellies pointed as daggers.

'What ye want to do,' her father told her, slowly circling the patch, 'is to watch and see which direction the honey-bees go. And not get stung.'

A dozen times, they lost sight of the tiny messengers they followed, lost in the broken light over a stream, dis-appearing into brush too thick to follow. Each time, Jamie cast to and fro, finding another patch of flowers.

'There's some!' she cried, pointing to a flash of brilliant red in the distance.

He squinted at them and smiled, shaking his head.

'Nay, not red,' he said. 'The wee hummingbirds like the red ones, but bees like yellow and white – yellow's best.' He plucked a small white daisy from the grass near her feet and handed it to her – the petals were streaked with pollen, fallen from the delicate stamens in the round yellow center of the bloom. Looking closer, she saw a tiny beetle the size of a pinhead crawl out of the center, its shiny black armor dusted with gold.

'The hummingbirds drink from the long-throated flowers,' he explained. 'But the bees canna get all the way inside. They like the broad, flat flowers like this, and the ones that grow in heavy bunches. They light on them and wallow, till they're covered over wi' the yellow.'

They hunted up and down the mountainside, laughing as they dodged the bomber assaults of enraged bumble-bees, hunting telltale patches of yellow and white. The bees liked the mountain laurel, but too many of those patches were too high to see over, too dense to pass through.

It was late afternoon before they found what they were looking for. A snag, the remnants of a good-sized tree, its branches reduced to stumps, bark worn away to show weathered silver wood beneath – and a wide split in the wood, through which the bees were crowding, hanging in a veil around it.

'Oh, good,' Jamie said, with satisfaction at the sight. 'Sometimes they hive in the rocks, and then there's little ye can do.' He unslung the ax at his belt, and his bags, and gestured to Brianna to sit down on a nearby rock.

'It's best to wait till dark,' he explained. 'For then all the swarm will be inside the hive. Meanwhile, will ye have a bite to eat?'

They shared the rest of the food, and talked sporadically, watching the light fade from the nearby mountains. He let her fire the long musket when she asked, showing her how to load a new round: swab the barrel, patch the ball, ram home ball, patch, and wadding with a charge of powder from the cartridge; pour the rest of the powder into the priming pan of the flintlock.

'You're no a bad shot at all, lass,' he said, surprised. He bent and picked up a small chunk of wood, setting it on top of a large boulder as a target. 'Try again.'

She did, and again, and again, growing used to the awkward weight of the weapon, finding the lovely balancing point of its length and its natural seat in the curve of her shoulder. It kicked less than she'd expected; black powder hadn't the force of modern cartridges. Twice chips flew from the boulder; the third time the chunk of wood disappeared in a shower of fragments.

'Verra nice,' he said, one eyebrow raised. 'And where in God's name did ye learn to shoot?'

'My father was a target shooter.' She lowered the gun, cheeks flushed with pleasure. 'He taught me to shoot with a pistol or a rifle. A shotgun, too.' Then her cheeks flushed a deeper hue, remembering. 'Um. You wouldn't have seen a shotgun.'

'No, I dinna suppose I have,' was all he said, his face a careful blank.

'How will you move the hive?' she asked, wanting to cover the awkward moment. He shrugged.

'Oh, once the bees have gone to their rest, I shall blow a bit o' smoke into the hive, to keep them stunned. Then chop free the part of the trunk that's got the combs in it, slide a bit of flat wood beneath it, and wrap it in my plaid.

Once at the house, I'll nail a bit of wood top and bottom, to make a bee gum.' He smiled at her. 'Come morning, the bees will come out, look around, and venture out for the nearest flowers.'

'Won't they realize they aren't in their proper place?'

He shrugged again.

'And what will they do about it, if they do? They've no means to find their way back, and they'll have no home left here to come to. Nay, they'll be content in the new place.' He reached for the gun. 'Here, let me clean it; the light's too bad for shooting.'

Conversation died, and they sat in silence for half an hour or so, watching darkness fill the hollows below, an invisible tide that crept higher by the minute, engulfing the trunks of the trees so that the green canopies seemed to float on a lake of darkness.

At last she cleared her throat, feeling that she must say *something*.

'Won't Mama be worried about us, coming back so late?'

He shook his head, but didn't answer; only sat, a grass blade drooping idle in his hand. The moon was edging its way above the trees, big and golden, lopsided as a smudged teardrop.

'Your mother did tell me once that men meant to fly to the moon,' he said abruptly. 'They hadna done it yet, that she knew, but they meant to. Will ye know about that?'

She nodded, eyes fixed on the rising moon.

'They did. They will, I mean. She smiled faintly. '*Apollo*, they called it – the rocket ship that took them.'

She could see his smile in answer; the moon was high enough to shed its radiance on the clearing. He tilted his face up, considering.

'Aye? And what did they say of it, the men who went?'

'They didn't need to say anything – they sent back pictures. I told you about the television?'

He looked a little startled, and she knew that like most things she had told him from her time, he had no real grasp of the reality of moving, talking pictures, let alone the notion that such things could be sent through thin air.

'Aye?' he said, a little unsurely. 'You've seen these pictures, then?'

'Yes.' She rocked back a little, hands clasped around her knees, looking up at the misshapen globe above them. There was a faint nimbus of light around it, and farther out in the starlit sky, a perfect, hazy ring, as though it were a big yellow stone dropped into a black pond, frozen in place as the first ripple formed.

'Fair weather tomorrow,' he said, looking up at it.

'Will it be?' She could see everything around them, almost as clearly as in the daylight, but the color had fled now; everything was black and gray – like the pictures she described.

'It took hours, waiting. No one could say exactly how long it would take them to land and get out in their space suits – you know there isn't any air on the moon?' She raised a questioning brow, and he nodded, attentive as a schoolboy.

'Claire told me so,' he murmured.

'The camera – the thing that made the pictures – was looking out of the side of the ship, so we could see the foot of the ship itself, settled in the dust, and the dust rising up over it like a horse's hoof when it puts its foot down.

'It was flat where the ship came down; covered with a soft, powdery kind of dust, with little rocks scattered on it here and there. Then the camera moved – or maybe another one started sending pictures – and you could see that there were rocky cliffs off in the distance. It's barren – no plants, no water, no air – but sort of beautiful, in an eerie kind of way.'

'It sounds like Scotland,' he said. She laughed at the joke, but thought she heard under the humor his longing for those barren mountains.

Wanting to distract him, she waved upward at the stars, beginning to burn brighter in the velvet sky.

'The stars are really suns, like ours. It's only that they're so far away from us, they look tiny. They're so far away that it may take years and years for their light to reach us; in fact, sometimes a star has died and we still see its light.'

'Claire told me that, long ago,' he said softly. He sat a moment, then got up with an air of decision.

'Come then,' he said. 'Let's take the hive, and be off home.'

The night was warm enough that we had left the hide window-covering unpinned and rolled aside. Occasional moths and June bugs blundered in to drown themselves in the cauldron or commit fiery suicide on the hearth, but the cool leaf-scented air that washed over us was worth it.

On the first night, Ian had gallantly given Brianna the trundle bed and gone off to sleep with Rollo on a pallet in the herb shed, assuring her that he liked the privacy. Leaving, his quilt over one arm, he had clapped Jamie solidly on the back and squeezed his shoulder in a surprisingly adult gesture of congratulation that made me smile.

Jamie had smiled, too; in fact, he had scarcely stopped smiling in several days. He wasn't smiling now, though his face bore a tender, inward look. There was a half-full moon riding the sky, and enough light came through the window for me to see him clearly as he lay on his back beside me.

I was surprised that he wasn't asleep yet. He had risen well before dawn and spent the day with Brianna on the mountain, returning long after dark with a plaid full of smoke-stunned bees, who were likely to be more than irritated when they woke in the morning and discovered the trick perpetrated on them. I made a mental note to keep away from the end of the garden where the row of bee gums sat; newly moved bees were inclined to sting first and ask questions afterward.

Jamie gave a massive sigh, and I rolled toward him, curving myself to fit against him. The night wasn't cold, but he wore a shirt to bed, in deference to Brianna's modesty.

'Can't sleep?' I asked softly. 'Does the moonlight bother you?'

'No.' He was looking out at the moon, though; it rode high above the ridge, not yet full, but a luminous white that flooded the sky.

'If it's not the moon, it's something.' I rubbed his stomach lightly, and let my fingers curve around the wide arch of his ribs.

820

He sighed again, and squeezed my hand.

'Och, it's no more than a foolish regret, Sassenach.' He turned his head toward the trundle bed, where the dark spill of Brianna's hair fell in a moon-polished mass across the pillow. 'I am only sorry that we must lose her.'

'Mm.' I let my hand rest flat on his chest. I had known it would come – both the realization and the parting itself – but I hadn't wanted to speak of it, and break the temporary spell that had bound the three of us so closely.

'You can't really lose a child,' I said softly, one finger tracing the small, smooth hollow in the center of his chest.

'She must go back, Sassenach – ye know it as well as I do.' He stirred impatiently but didn't move away. 'Look at her. She's like Louis's camel, no?'

Despite my own regrets, I smiled at the thought. Louis of France kept a fine menagerie at Versailles, and on good days the keepers would exercise certain of the animals, leading them through the spreading gardens, to the edification of startled passersby.

We had been walking in the gardens one day, and turned a corner to find the Bactrian camel advancing toward us down the path, splendid and stately in its gold and silver harness, towering in calm disdain above a crowd of gawking spectators – strikingly exotic, and utterly out of place among the formalized white statues.

'Yes,' I said, though with a reluctance that squeezed my heart. 'Yes, of course she'll have to go back. She belongs there.'

'I ken that well enough.' He put his own hand over mine, but kept his face turned away, looking at Brianna. 'I shouldna grieve for it – but I do.'

'So do I.' I put my forehead against his shoulder, breathing in the clean male scent of him. 'It's true, though – what I said. You can't truly lose a child. Do you – do you remember Faith?'

My voice trembled slightly as I asked it; we had not spoken in years of our first daughter, stillborn in France.

His arm curled around me, pulling me against him.

'Of course I do,' he said softly. 'D'ye think I would ever forget?'

'No.' The tears were flowing down my face, but I was

not truly weeping; it was no more than the overflow of feeling. 'That's what I mean. I never told you — when we were in Paris, to see Jared — I went to the Hopital des Anges; I saw her grave there. I — I brought her a pink tulip.'

He was quiet for a moment.

'I took her violets,' he said, so softly I almost didn't hear him.

I was quite still for a moment, tears forgotten.

'You didn't tell me.'

'Neither did you.' His fingers traced the bumps of my spine, brushing softly up and down the line of my back.

'I was afraid you'd feel . . .' My voice trailed off. I had been afraid he would feel guilty, worry that I blamed him — I once had — for the loss. We were newly reunited, then; I had no wish to jeopardize the tender link between us.

'So was I.'

'I'm sorry that you never saw her,' I said at last, and felt him sigh. He turned toward me and put his arms around me, his lips brushing my forehead.

'It doesna matter, does it? Aye, it's true, what ye say, Sassenach. She was — and we will have her, always. And Brianna. If — when she goes — she will still be with us.'

'Yes. It doesn't matter what happens; no matter where a child goes — how far or how long. Even if it's forever. You never lose them. You can't.'

He didn't answer, but his arms tightened round me, and he sighed once more. The breeze stirred the air above us with the sound of angels' wings, and we fell slowly asleep together, as the moonlight bathed us in its ageless peace.

43

Whisky in the Jar

I didn't like Ronnie Sinclair, I never *had* liked him. I didn't like his half-handsome face, his foxy smile, or the way his eyes met mine: so direct, so openly honest, that you *knew* he was hiding something even when he wasn't. I particularly didn't like the way he was looking at my daughter.

I cleared my throat loudly, making him jump. He turned a sharptoothed smile on me, idly turning a truss ring in his hands.

'Jamie says he'll need a dozen more of the small whisky casks by the end of the month, and I'll need a large barrel of hickory wood for the smoked meat, as soon as you can manage.'

He nodded and made a number of cryptic marks on a slab of pine that hung on the wall. Oddly for a Scot, Sinclair couldn't write but had some sort of private shorthand that enabled him to keep track of orders and accounts.

'Right, Missus Fraser. Anything else?'

I paused, trying to reckon up all the possible necessities for cooperage that might spring up before snowfall. There would be fish and meat to salt down, but those did better in stoneware jars; wooden casks left them tasting of turpentine. I had a good seasoned barrel for apples and another for squash already; the potatoes would be stored on shelves to keep from rotting.

'No,' I decided. 'That will be all.'

'Aye, missus.' He hesitated, twirling the cask band faster. 'Will Himself be coming down before the casks are ready?'

'No; he has the barley to get in, and the slaughtering to do, as well as the distilling. Everything's late, because of the trial.' I raised an eyebrow at him. 'Why, though? Do you have a message for him?'

Sited at the foot of the cove nearest the wagon road, the cooper's shop was the first building most visitors encount-

823

ered, and thus a reception point for most gossip that came from outside Fraser's Ridge.

Sinclair tilted his gingery head, considering.

'Och, likely it's nothing. Only that I've heard of a stranger in the district, asking questions about Jamie Fraser.'

From the corner of my eye, I saw Brianna's head snap round, distracted at once from her inspection of the spokeshavers, mallets, saws, and axes on the wall. She turned, skirt rustling in the wood shavings that littered the shop, ankle-deep.

'Do you know the stranger's name?' she asked anxiously. 'Or what he looks like?'

Sinclair shot her a look of surprise. He was oddly proportioned, with slender shoulders but muscular arms, and hands so huge that they might have belonged to a man twice his height. He looked at her, and his broad thumb unconsciously stroked the metal of the ring, slowly, over and over again.

'Why, I couldna speak to his appearance, mistress,' he said, politely enough, but with a hungry look in his eyes that made me want to take the truss ring away from him and wrap it around his neck. 'He gave his name as Hodgepile, though.'

Brianna's face lost its look of hope, though the muscle at the edge of her mouth curved slightly at the name.

'I don't suppose *that* could be Roger,' she murmured to me.

'Likely not,' I agreed. 'He wouldn't have any reason to use a false name, anyway.' I turned back to Sinclair.

'You won't have heard of a man called Wakefield, will you? Roger Wakefield?'

Sinclair shook his head decisively.

'No, missus. Himself has put word about that if such a one should come, he's to be taken to the Ridge at once. If yon Wakefield sets foot within the county, you'll hear of it as soon as I do.'

Brianna sighed, and I heard her swallow her disappointment. It was mid-October, and while she said nothing, she was clearly growing more anxious by the day. She wasn't the only one, either; she had told us what Roger was trying to do, and the thought of the variety of disasters that might have befallen him in the attempt was enough to keep me wakeful at night.

'– about the whisky,' Sinclair was saying, jerking my attention back to him.

'The whisky? Hodgepile was asking about Jamie and whisky?'

Sinclair nodded, and set down the truss ring.

'In Cross Creek. No one would say a word to him, o' course. But the one who told me did say as the one who spoke to the man thought him a soldier.' He grimaced briefly. 'Hard for a lobsterback to wash the flour from his hair.'

'He wasn't dressed as a soldier, surely?' Foot soldiers wore their hair in a tight folded queue, wrapped round a core of lamb's wool and powdered with rice flour – which, in this climate, rapidly turned to paste as the flour mixed with sweat. Still, I imagined Sinclair meant the man's attitude rather than his appearance.

'Och, no; he did claim to be a fur trader – but he walked wi' a ramrod up his arse, and ye could hear the leather creak when he talked. So Geordie McClintock said.'

'Likely one of Murchison's men. I'll tell Jamie – thank you.'

I left the cooper's shop with Brianna, wondering just how much trouble this Hodgepile might prove to be. Likely not much; the sheer distance from civilization and the inaccessibility of the Ridge was protection against most intrusions; one of Jamie's purposes in choosing it. The multiple inconveniences of remoteness would be outweighed by its benefits, when it came to war. No battle would be fought on Fraser's Ridge, I was sure of that.

And no matter how virulent Murchison's grudge might be, or how good his spies, I couldn't see his superiors allowing him to mount an armed expedition more than a hundred miles into the mountains, for the sole purpose of extirpating an illegal distillery whose total output was less than a hundred gallons a year.

Lizzie and Ian were waiting for us outside, occupied in gathering kindling from Sinclair's rubbish heap. A cooper's work generated immense quantities of shavings, splinters, and discarded chunks of wood and bark, and it was worth the labor of picking them up to save splitting kindling by hand at home.

'Can you and Ian load the barrels, honey?' I asked Brianna. 'I want a look at Lizzie in the sunlight.'

Brianna nodded, still looking abstracted, and went to help Ian heave the half-dozen small kegs outside the shop into the wagon. They were small, but heavy.

It was the skill that went into these particular barrels that had earned Ronnie Sinclair his land and shop, in spite of his less than prepossessing personality; not every cooper knew the trick of charring the inside of an oak barrel so as to lend a beautiful amber color and deep smoky flavor to the whisky aging gently inside.

'Come here, sweetie. Let me see your eyes.' Lizzie obediently widened her eyes, and let me pull down the lower lid to see the white sclera of the eyeball.

The girl was still shockingly thin, but the nasty yellow tinge of jaundice was fading from her skin, and her eyes were nearly white again. I cupped my fingers gently under her jaw; lymph glands only slightly swollen – that was better, too.

'Feeling all right?' I asked. She smiled shyly, and nodded. It was the first time she had been outside the cabin since her arrival with Ian three weeks before; she was still wobbly as a new calf. Frequent infusions of Jesuit bark had helped, though; she had had no fresh attacks of fever in the last week, and I had hopes of clearing up the liver involvement in short order.

'Mrs. Fraser?' she said, and I jumped, startled to hear her talk. She was so shy that she could seldom bring herself to say anything to me or to Jamie directly; she murmured her needs to Brianna, who conveyed them to me.

'Yes, dear?'

'I – I couldna help hearing what yon cooper said – about how Mr. Fraser's asked word of Miss Brianna's man. I did wonder –' Her words trailed off in a spasm of shyness, and a faint rose-pink blush showed in her transparent cheeks.

'Yes?'

'Could he ask for my father, do ye think?' The words came out in a rush, and she blushed still harder.

'Oh, Lizzie! I'm sorry.' Brianna, finished with the barrels, came and hugged her little maid. 'I hadn't forgotten, but I hadn't thought, either. Just a minute, I'll go and tell Mr. Sinclair.' With a whiff of skirts, she vanished into the cool dimness of the cooper's shop.

'Your father?' I asked. 'Have you lost him?'

The girl nodded, pressing her lips together to prevent their quivering.

'He'll ha' gone as a bondsman, but I dinna ken where; only it would be to the southern colonies.'

Well, that limited the search to several hundred thousand square miles, I thought. Still, it could do no harm to ask Ronnie Sinclair to put out word. Newspapers and other printed matter were scarce in the South; most real news still passed by word of mouth, handed on in shops and taverns, or carried by slaves and servants between far-flung plantations.

The thought of newspapers gave me a small nasty jolt of remembrance. Still, seven years seemed comfortingly far away – and Brianna must be right; whether the house was doomed to burn on January 21 or not, surely it would be possible for us not to be in it on that date?

Brianna appeared, rather red in the face, swung aboard the wagon, and picked up the reins, waiting impatiently for the rest of us.

Ian, seeing her flushed face, frowned and glanced toward the cooper's shop.

'What is it, Coz? Did yon wee mannie say aught amiss to ye?' He flexed his hands, nearly as large as Sinclair's.

'No,' she said tersely. 'Not a word. Are we ready to go?'

Ian picked Lizzie up and swung her into the wagon bed, then put out a hand and helped me up on the seat by Brianna. He glanced at the reins in Brianna's hands; he had taught her to drive the mules, and took professional pride in her skill.

'Watch the bugger on the gee side,' he advised her. 'He'll no be pullin' his share o' the load, unless ye touch him up now and again wi' a slap across the rump.'

He subsided into the wagon bed with Lizzie as we set off

up the road. I could hear him telling her outlandish stories, and her faint giggle in reply. The baby of his own family, Ian was charmed by Lizzie and treated her like a younger sister, by turns nuisance and pet.

I glanced over my shoulder at the receding cooper's shop, then at Brianna.

'What did he do?' I asked, quietly.

'Nothing. I interrupted him?' The flush across her wide cheekbones grew deeper.

'What on earth was he doing?'

'Drawing pictures on a piece of wood,' she said, and bit the inside of her cheek. 'Of naked women.'

I laughed, as much from shock as from amusement.

'Well, he hasn't got a wife, and not likely to get one soon; women are very scarce in the colony generally, and even more so up here. I suppose one can't blame him.'

I felt an unexpected pang of sympathy for Ronnie Sinclair. He'd been alone for a very long time, after all. His wife had died in the terrible days after Culloden, and he himself had spent more than ten years in prison before being transported to the Colonies. If he had made connections here, they had not endured; he was a solitary man, and suddenly I saw his avid questing for gossip, his stealthy watching – even his use of Brianna for artistic inspiration – in a different light. I knew what it was like to be lonely.

Brianna's embarrassment had faded, and she was whistling softly under her breath, hunched casually over the reins – a Beatles' tune, I thought, though I never could keep pop groups straight.

The idle thought floated insidiously through my mind; if Roger didn't come, she wouldn't be left alone for long, either here or when she returned to the future. But that was ridiculous. He *would* come. And if not . . .

A thought I had been trying to keep at bay sneaked past my defenses and appeared in my mind, full blown. *What if he had chosen not to come?* I knew they had had some sort of argument, though Brianna had been tight-lipped about it. Had he been so infuriated that he would go back without her?

I rather thought the possibility had occurred to her, too; she had stopped speaking much of Roger, but I saw the anxious light spring up in her eyes whenever Clarence announced a visitor, and saw it die each time the visitor proved to be one of Jamie's tenants, or some of Ian's Tuscaroran friends.

'Hurry up, you blighter,' I muttered under my breath. Brianna caught it, and smartly snapped the reins over the left mule's rump.

'Gee up!' she shouted, and the wagon rattled faster, jolting over the narrow track toward home.

'It's a far cry from the still-cellar at Leoch,' Jamie said, ruefully poking at the makeshift pot still at the edge of the small clearing. 'It does make whisky, though – of a sort.'

In spite of his diffidence, Brianna could see that he was proud of his infant distillery. It was nearly two miles from the cabin, located – as he explained – close to Fergus's place, so that Marsali could come up several times a day to keep an eye on the operation. In return for this service, she and Fergus had a slightly larger share in the resulting whisky than did the other farmers on the Ridge, who supplied the raw barley and helped in the distribution of the liquor.

'No, darlin', ye dinna want to be eating that nasty wee thing,' Marsali said firmly. She grasped her son's wrist and began prying open his fingers, one by one, in an effort to free the large and madly wriggling insect that – in open contradiction of his mother's adjuration – he very obviously *did* want to be eating.

'Feh!' Marsali dropped the cockroach on the ground and stamped on it.

Germaine, a stoic, stubby child, didn't cry at the loss of his treat, but glowered balefully under his blond fringe. The cockroach, nothing daunted by rough treatment, rose out of the leaf mold and walked off, staggering only slightly.

'Oh, I shouldna think it would do him harm,' Ian said, amused. 'I've eaten them, now and again, wi' the Indians. The locusts are better, though – especially the smoked ones.'

Marsali and Brianna both made gagging noises, causing Ian to grin even wider. He picked up another bag of barley and poured a thick layer into a flat rush basket. Two more roaches, suddenly exposed to the light of day, skittered madly over the side of the basket, fell to the ground and dashed away, disappearing under the edge of the crudely built malting floor.

'No, I said!' Marsali kept a tight hold on Germaine's collar, preventing his determined attempts to follow them. 'Stay, ye wee fiend, d'ye want to be smoked, too?' Small wisps of transparent smoke rose up through the cracks of the wooden platform, permeating the small clearing with the breakfastlike scent of roasting grain. Brianna felt her stomach gurgle; it was nearly suppertime.

'Maybe you should leave them in,' she suggested, joking. 'Smoked roaches might add a nice flavor to the whisky.'

'I doubt they'd harm it any,' her father agreed, coming up beside her. He wiped his face with a handkerchief, looked at it, and made a slight face at the sooty smudges on it before tucking it back up his sleeve. 'All right, Ian?'

'Aye, it'll do. It's only the one bag that's spoilt all through, Uncle Jamie.' Ian rose with his tray of raw barley, and kicked negligently at a split bag, where the soft green of mold and black tinge of rot showed the ill effects of seeping damp. Two more opened bags, with the spoiled top layer scooped off, sat by the edge of the malting floor.

'Let's finish, then,' Jamie said. 'I'm starved.' He and Ian each seized a burlap bag and scattered the fresh barley in a thick layer over the clear space on the platform, using a flat wooden spade to flatten and turn the grain.

'How long does it all take?' Brianna poked her nose over the edge of the mash tub, where Marsali was stirring the fermenting grain of the last smoking. The mash had only begun to work; there was no more than a faint whiff of alcohol in the air.

'Oh, it will depend on the weather, a bit.' Marsali cast an experienced eye skyward. It was late afternoon, and the sky had begun to darken into a clear deep blue, with no more than streaks of white cloud floating over the horizon. 'Clear as it is, I should say – Germaine!' Germaine's bottom was the only part of him, visible, the top half having disappeared under a log.

'I'll get him.' Brianna took three quick strides across the clearing, and scooped him up. Germaine made a deep sound of protest at this unwarranted interference, and began to kick, hammering his sturdy heels against her legs.

'Ow!' Brianna set him on the ground, rubbing her thigh with one hand.

Marsali made a sound of exasperation and dropped her ladle. '*Now* what have ye got, ye wicked thing?' Germaine, having learned from experience, popped his latest acquisition into his mouth and swallowed convulsively. He immediately turned purple and began to choke.

With a cry of alarm, Marsali dropped to her knees and tried to pry his mouth open. Germaine gagged, wheezed, and staggered backward, shaking his head. His blue eyes bulged, and a thin line of drool snaked down his chin.

'Here!' Brianna grabbed the little boy, by the arm, pulled his back against her, and with both hands fisted into his stomach, jerked them sharply back.

Germaine made a loud whooping noise, and something small and round shot out of his mouth. He gurgled, gasped for air, got a good lungful and started to howl, his face going from dusky purple to a healthy red within seconds.

'Is he all right?' Jamie peered anxiously at the little boy, who was crying in his mother's arms, then, satisfied, glanced at Brianna. 'That was verra quick, lass. A good job.'

'Thanks. I – thanks. I'm glad it worked.'

Brianna felt a little shaky. Seconds. It hadn't taken more than a few seconds. Life to death and back again, in nothing flat. Jamie touched her arm, giving her a brief squeeze, and she felt a little better.

'Best take the laddie down to the house,' he told Marsali. 'Give him his supper and put him to bed. We'll finish here.'

Marsali nodded, looking shaken herself. She brushed a strand of pale hair out of her eyes, and gave Brianna a poor attempt at a smile.

'I thank ye, good-sister?'

Brianna felt a surprising small glow of pleasure at the title. She gave Marsali back the smile.

'I'm glad he's all right.'

Marsali picked up her bag from the ground, and with a nod to Jamie, turned and made her way carefully down the steep path, toddler in her arms, Germaine's chubby fists twined tightly in her hair.

'That was pretty work, Coz.' Ian had finished the spreading, and jumped down from the platform to congratulate her. 'Where did ye learn a thing like that?'

'From my mother.'

Ian nodded, looking impressed. Jamie bent over, searching the ground nearby.

'What is it the laddie swallowed, I wonder?'

'This.' Brianna spotted the object, half buried under fallen leaves, and plucked it out. 'It looks like a button.' The object was a lopsided circle, crudely carved from wood, but indisputably a button, with a long shank and holes bored for thread.

'Let me see.' Jamie held out a hand, and she dropped the button into it.

'You'll no be missing any buttons, will ye, Ian?' he asked, frowning at the small object in his palm.

Ian peered over Jamie's shoulder, and shook his head. 'Maybe Fergus?' he suggested.

'Maybe, but I dinna think so. Our Fergus is too much the dandy to be wearin' something like this. All the buttons on his coat are made of polished horn.' He shook his head slowly, still frowning, then shrugged. Picking up his sporran, he put the button into it before fastening it about his waist.

'Ah, well. I'll ask about. Will ye finish here, Ian? There's no much left to do.' He smiled at Brianna and cocked his head toward the path. 'Come then, lass; we'll ask at Lindseys', on our way home.'

In the event, Kenny Lindsey was not at home.

'Duncan Innes came to fetch him, not an hour since,' Mrs. Lindsey said, shading her eyes against the late sun as she stood in the doorway of her house. 'I make nay doubt they'll be to your house the noo. Will ye and your lassie no step in, *Mac Dubh*, and have a taste of something?'

'Ah, no, I thank ye, Mrs. Kenny. My wife will be having the supper ready for us. But perhaps ye could be tellin' me whether this wee bawbee is from Kenny's coat?'

Mrs. Lindsey peered at the button in his hand, then shook her head.

'No, indeed. Have I not just finished sewing on a whole fresh set of buttons for him, that's he's carved from the bone of a deer? The bonniest things ye ever saw, too,' she declared, with pride in her husband's craftsmanship. 'Each one has got a wee face on it, grinnin' like an imp, and each one different!'

Her eye ran speculatively over Brianna.

'There's Kenny's brother, now,' she said. 'With a fine wee place near Cross Creek – twenty acres in tobacco, and a good creek through it. He'll be at the Gathering at Mount Helicon; perhaps you'll be going, *Mac Dubh?*'

Jamie shook his head, smiling at the bald hint. There were few available women in the colony, and even though Jamie had given it out that Brianna was promised elsewhere, this had not by any means put a stop to the matchmaking attempts.

'I fear not this year, Mrs. Kenny. Perhaps the next, but I canna spare the time just now.'

They took their leave politely, and turned toward home, the sinking sun at their backs casting long shadows on the path ahead of them.

'Do you think the button's important?' Brianna asked curiously.

Jamie shrugged slightly. A light breeze lifted the hair on the crown of his head, and tugged at the leather thong that held it back.

'I canna say. It could be nothing – but it could be something, too. Your mother told me what Ronnie Sinclair said, about the man in Cross Creek, asking about the whisky.'

'Hodgepile?' Brianna couldn't help smiling at the name. Jamie returned the smile briefly, then became serious again.

'Aye. If the button belongs to someone on the Ridge – they ken well enough where the still is, and they might stop to look and no harm done. But if it was to be a stranger . . .' He glanced at her and shrugged again.

'It's none so easy for a man to pass unnoticed here – unless he should be hiding a-purpose. A man come for any innocent reason would stop at a house for a bit of food and drink, and I'd hear of it the same day. But there's been nothing of the sort. Nor would it be an Indian; they dinna use such things in their clothing.'

A gust of wind whirred across the path in a swirl of brown and yellow leaves, and they turned uphill, toward the cabin. They walked in near silence, affected by the growing quiet of the woods; the birds were still singing twilight songs, but the shadows were lengthening under the trees. The northern slope of the mountain across the valley had already gone dark and silent, as the sun edged behind it.

The cabin's clearing was still filled with sunlight, though, filtered through a yellow blaze of chestnut trees. Claire was in the palisaded garden, a basin on one hip, snapping beans from poled vines. Her slender figure was silhouetted dark against the sun, her hair a great aureole of curly gold.

'Innisfree,' Brianna said involuntarily, stopping dead at the sight.

'Innisfree?' Jamie glanced at her, bewildered.

She hesitated, but there was no way out of explaining.

'It's a poem, or part of one. Daddy always used to say it, when he'd come home and find Mama puttering in her garden – he said she'd live out there if she could. He used to joke that she – that she'd leave us someday, and go find a place where she could live by herself, with nothing but her plants.'

'Ah.' Jamie's face was calm, its broad planes ruddy in the dying light. 'How does the poem go, then?'

She was conscious of a small tightness round her heart as she said it.

> *'I will arise and go now, and go to Innisfree,*
> *And a small cabin build there, of clay and wattles made:*
> *Nine bean-rows will I have there, a hive for the honey-bee.*
> *And live alone in the bee-loud glade.'*

The thick red brows drew together slightly, sparking in the sun.

'A poem, is it? And where is Innisfree?'

'Ireland, maybe. He was Irish,' Brianna said in explanation. 'The poet.' The row of bee gums stood squat on their stones at the edge of the wood.

'Oh.'

Tiny motes of gold and black drifted past them through honeyed air – bees homing from the fields. Her father made no move to go forward, but stood silent by her side, watching her mother pick beans, black and gold among the leaves.

Not alone, after all, she thought. But the small tightness stayed in her chest, not quite an ache.

Kenny Lindsey took a sip of whisky, closed his eyes, and rolled the liquor round his tongue like a professional wine taster. He paused, frowning in concentration, then swallowed with a convulsive gulp.

'Hoo!' He drew breath, shuddering all over.

'Christ,' he said hoarsely. 'That'll strip your tripes!'

Jamie grinned at the compliment, and poured another small measure, shoving it toward Duncan.

'Aye, it's better than the last,' he agreed, with a cautious sniff before essaying his own drink. 'This one doesna take the hide off your tongue – quite.'

Lindsay wiped his mouth with the back of his hand, nodding in agreement.

'Weel, it'll find a good home. Woolam wants a cask – that'll last him a year, the way yon Quakers dole it out.'

'Ye've agreed a price?'

Lindsay nodded, sniffing appreciatively at the platter of bannocks and savories that Lizzie set in front of him.

'A hundredweight of barley for the cask; another, if ye'll go halves wi' him in the whisky from it.'

'That's fair.' Jamie took a bannock and chewed absently for a moment. Then he raised one brow at Duncan, seated across the table.

'Will ye ask MacLeod on Naylor's Creek will he make us the same bargain? You'll pass that way going home, aye?'

Duncan nodded, chewing, and Jamie lifted his cup to

me in a silent toast of celebration – Woolam's offer made a total of eight hundred pounds of barley, scraped together by barter and promise. More than the surplus output of every field on the Ridge; the raw material for next year's whisky.

'A cask each to the houses on the Ridge, two to Fergus –' Jamie pulled absently at his earlobe, calculating. 'Two, maybe, to Nacognaweto, one kept back to age – aye, we can spare maybe a dozen casks for the Gathering, Duncan.'

Duncan's coming was opportune. While Jamie had managed to barter the first year's crop of raw whisky to the Moravians in Salem for the tools, cloth, and other things we so urgently needed, there was no doubt that the wealthy Scottish planters of the Cape Fear would make a better market.

We couldn't possibly spare time away from the homestead for long enough to make the week-long journey to Mount Helicon, but if Duncan could take the whisky down and sell it . . . I was already making lists in my head. Everyone brought things to sell, at a Gathering. Wool, cloth, tools, food, animals . . . I urgently needed a small copper kettle, and six lengths of fresh muslin for shifts, and . . .

'Do you think you should give alcohol to the Indians?' Brianna's question pulled me from my greedy reverie.

'Why not?' Lindsey asked, a little disapproving of her intrusion. 'After all, we're no going to *give* it to them, lass. They've little silver, but they pay in hides – and they pay well.'

Brianna glanced at me for support, then at Jamie.

'But Indians don't – I mean I've heard that they can't handle alcohol.'

All three men looked at her uncomprehendingly, and Duncan looked at his cup, turning it round in his hand.

'Handle it?'

The corner of her mouth quirked inward.

'They get drunk easily, I mean.'

Lindsey peered into his cup, then looked at her, rubbing a hand over the balding crown of his head.

'Ye've a point, lass?' he said, more or less politely.

Brianna's full mouth compressed itself, then relaxed.

'I *mean*,' she said, 'it seems wrong to encourage people to drink, who can't stop drinking if they start.' She looked at me, a little helplessly. I shook my head.

'Alcoholic' isn't a noun yet,' I said. 'It's not a disease now – just weak character.'

Jamie glanced up at her quizzically.

'Well, I'll tell ye, lass,' he said, 'I've seen many a drunkard in my day, but I've yet to see a bottle leap off a table and pour itself down anyone's throat.'

There were general grunts of agreement with this, and another small round to accompany the change of subject.

'Hodgepile? No, I've not seen the man, though I do believe I've heard the name.' Duncan swilled the rest of his drink and set down his cup, wheezing gently. 'You'll want me to ask at the Gathering?'

Jamie nodded, and took another bannock. 'Aye, if ye will, Duncan.'

Lizzie was bent over the fire, stirring the stew for supper. I saw her shoulders tighten, but she was too shy to speak before so many men. Brianna suffered no such inhibitions.

'I have someone to ask after, too, Mr. Innes.' She leaned over the table toward him, eyes fixed on him in earnest entreaty. 'Will you ask for a man named Roger Wakefield? Please?'

'Och, indeed. Indeed I will.' Duncan went pink at the proximity of Brianna's bosom, and in confusion drank down the rest of Kenny's whisky. 'Is there aught else I can do?'

'Yes,' I said, putting down a fresh cup in front of the disgruntled Lindsey. 'While you're asking after Hodgepile and Bree's young man, would you also ask for a man named Joseph Wemyss? He'll be a bondsman.' From the corner of my eye, I saw Lizzie's thin shoulders slump in relief.

Duncan nodded, his composure restored as Brianna disappeared into the pantry to fetch butter. Kenny Lindsey looked after her, interested.

'Bree? Is that the name ye call your daughter?' he asked.

'Yes,' I said. 'Why?'

A smile showed briefly on Lindsey's face. Then he glanced at Jamie, coughed, and buried the smile in his cup.

'It's a Scots word, Sassenach,' Jamie said, a rather wry smile appearing on his own face. 'A *bree* is a great disturbance.'

44

Three-Cornered Conversation

October 1769

The shock of impact juddered through his arms. With a rhythm born of long practice, Jamie jerked the axhead free, swung it back and brought it down in a *tchunk!* of splintered bark and yellow wood chips. He shifted his foot on the log and struck again, the ax blow judged to a nicety, sharp metal embedded in the wood a scant two inches from his toes.

He could have told Ian off to do the chopping, and gone himself to fetch the flour from the tiny mill at Woolam's Point, but the lad deserved the treat of a visit with the three unmarried Woolam daughters who worked with their father in the mill. They were Quaker girls, dressed drab as sparrows, but lively of wit and fair of face, and they made a pet of Ian, vying with each other to offer him small beer and meat pies when he came.

A good deal better the lad should spend his time flirting with virtuous Quakers than with the bold-eyed Indian lassies over the ridge, he thought, with a little grimness. He hadn't forgotten what Myers had said about Indian women taking men to their beds as they liked.

He had sent the wee bondmaid with Ian as well, thinking the brisk fall air might bring a bit of color to the lassie's face. The wean was white-skinned as Claire, but with the sickly blue-white cast of skimmed milk, not Claire's pale glow, rich and grainless as the silk-white heartwood of a poplar tree.

The log was nearly split; one more blow, and a twist of the ax, and two good chunks lay ready for the hearth, smelling clean and sharp with resin. He stacked them neatly on the growing woodpile next to the pantry, and rolled another half log into place beneath his foot.

The truth of it was that he liked chopping wood. Quite different from the damp, backbreaking, foot-freezing job of cutting peats, but with that same feeling of soul-deep satisfaction at seeing a good stock of fuel laid by, which only those who have spent winters shivering in thin clothes can know. The woodpile reached nearly to the eaves of the house by now, dry split chunks of pine and oak, hickory and maple, the sight of them warming his heart as much as the wood itself would warm his flesh.

Speak of warmth; it was a warm day for late October, and his shirt was clinging to his shoulders already. He wiped a sleeve across his face and examined the damp patch critically.

If he got wringing, Brianna would insist on washing it again, protest as he might that sweat was clean enough. 'Phew,' she would say, with a disapproving nostril-flare, wrinkling her long nose up like a possum. He had laughed out loud when he first saw her do it; as much from surprise as from amusement.

His mother had died long ago, in his childhood, and while the odd memory of her came now and then in dreams, he had mostly replaced her presence with static pictures, frozen images in his mind. But she had said 'Phew!' to him when he came in mucky, and wrinkled up her long nose in just that way – it had come back with a flash when he saw Brianna do it.

What a mystery blood was – how did a tiny gesture, a tone of voice, endure through generations like the harder verities of flesh? He had seen it again and again, watching his nieces and nephews grow, and accepted without thought the echoes of parent and grandparent that appeared for brief moments, the shadow of a face looking back through the years – that vanished again into the face that was now.

Yet now that he saw it in Brianna . . . he could watch her for hours, he thought, and was reminded of his sister, bending close over each of her newborn bairns in fascination. Perhaps that was why parents watched their weans in such enchantment, he thought; finding out all the tiny links between them, that bound the chains of life, one generation to the next.

He shrugged, and pulled the shirt off. It was his own place, after all; there was no one to see the marks on his

840

back, and no one whose business it would be to care if they did. The air was chill and sudden on his damp skin, but a few swings of the ax brought the warm blood pulsing back again.

He loved all Jenny's children deeply – especially Ian, the wee gowk whose mixture of foolishness and pigheaded courage reminded him so much of himself at that age. They were his blood, after all. But Brianna . . .

Brianna was his blood, and his flesh as well. An unspoken promise kept to his own parents; his gift to Claire, and hers to him.

Not for the first time, he found himself wondering about Frank Randall. And what had Randall thought, holding the child of another man – and a man he had no cause to love?

Perhaps Randall had been the better man, come to that – to harbor a child for her mother's sake, and not his own; to search her face with joy only in its beauty, and not because he saw himself reflected there. He felt vaguely ashamed, and struck down with greater force to exorcise the feeling.

His mind was concerned entirely with its thoughts, and not at all with his actions. While he used it, though, the ax was as much a part of his body as the arms that swung it. Just as a twinge in wrist or elbow would have warned him instantly of damage, some faint vibration, some subtle shift in weight arrested him in midswing, so that the loosened axhead flew harmlessly across the clearing, rather than slamming into his vulnerable foot.

'Deo gratias,' he muttered, with rather less thankfulness than the words indicated. He crossed himself perfunctorily and went to pick up the slab of metal. Damn the dry weather; it hadn't rained in nearly a month, and the shrunken haft of his ax was less worrying than the drooping heads of the plants in Claire's garden near the house.

He cast a glance at the half-dug well, shrugging in irritation. Another thing that must be done, which there wasn't time to do. It would have to wait a bit; they could haul water from the creek or melt snow, but without wood to burn they would starve or freeze, or both.

841

The door opened and Claire came out, cloak on against the chill of autumn shadows, her basket over her arm. Brianna was behind her, and at sight of them he forgot his annoyance.

'What have you done?' Claire said at once, seeing him with the axhead in one hand. Her eyes flicked over him quickly, looking for blood.

'Nay, I'm whole,' he assured her. 'It's only I've got to mend the handle. You'll be foraging?' He nodded at Claire's basket.

'I thought we'd try up the stream, for wood ears.'

'Ah? Dinna go too far, aye? There are Indians hunting the far mountain. I smelt them on the ridge this morning.'

'You smelled them?' Brianna asked.

One red brow went up in inquiry. He saw Claire glance from Brianna to him and smile slightly, to herself; it was one of his own gestures, then. He lifted one brow, looking at Claire, and saw her smile grow wider.

'It's autumn, and they're dryin' venison,' he explained to Brianna. 'Ye can smell the smoking fires a great ways away, if the wind sets right.'

'We won't go far,' Claire assured him. 'Just above the trout pool.'

'Aye, well. I daresay it's safe enough.' He felt some reluctance at letting the women go, but he could scarcely keep them mewed up in the house only because there were savages nearby – the Indians were no doubt peacefully employed as he was himself, in making winter preparations.

If he knew for sure it was Nacognaweto's folk, he wouldn't worry, but as it was, the hunting parties often roamed far afield and it could as easily be Cherokee, or the odd small tribe that called themselves the Dog People. There was only one village of them left, and they were deeply suspicious of white strangers – not without reason.

Brianna's eyes rested on his bare chest for a moment, at the tiny knot of puckered scar tissue, but she showed no sign of disgust or curiosity – nor did she when she laid her hand briefly on his shoulder, kissing his cheek in goodbye, though he knew she must feel the healed welts beneath her fingers.

842

Claire would have told her, he supposed – all about Jack Randall, and the days before the Rising. Or perhaps not quite all. A small shiver that had nothing to do with cold ran up the crease of his spine, and he stepped back, away from her touch, though he still smiled at her.

'There's bread in the hutch, and a little stew left in the kettle for you and Ian and Lizzie.' Claire reached up and flicked a stray wood chip from his hair. 'Don't eat the pudding in the pantry; that's for supper.'

He caught her fingers in his and kissed her knuckles lightly. She looked surprised, and then a faint warm glow came up under her skin. She came up a-tiptoe and kissed his mouth, then hurried after Brianna, already at the edge of the clearing.

'Be careful!' he called after them. They waved, and disappeared into the woods, leaving him with their kisses soft on his face.

'*Deo gratias,*' he murmured again, watching them, and this time spoke with heartfelt gratitude. He waited until the last flicker of Brianna's cloak had vanished, before returning to his work.

He sat on the chopping block, a handful of square-headed nails on the ground beside him, carefully driving them one at a time into the end of the ax handle with a small mallet. The dry wood split and spread, but held by the iron enclosure of the axhead, could not splinter.

He twisted the head, then finding it firm, stood up and brought the ax down in a mighty blow on the chopping block, by way of test. It held.

He was chilled now, from sitting, and pulled his shirt back on. He was hungry, too, but he would wait a bit for the young ones. Not but what they had likely stuffed themselves already, he thought cynically. He could almost smell the meat pies Sarah Woolam made, the rich scent twining in his memory through the actual autumn smells of dead leaves and damp earth.

The thought of meat pies lingered in his mind as he went on with his work, along with the thought of winter. The Indians said it would be hard, this winter, not like the last. How would it be, hunting in deep snow? It snowed in

Scotland, of course, but often enough it lay light on the ground, and the trodden paths of the red deer showed black on the steep, bare mountainsides.

Last winter had been like that. But this wilderness was given to extremes. He had heard stories of snowfalls that lay six feet deep, valleys where a man might sink to his oxters, and ice that froze so thick on the creeks that a bear could walk across. He smiled a little grimly, thinking of bears. Well, and that would be eating for the whole winter if he could kill another, and the skin would not come amiss, either.

His thoughts drifted slowly into the rhythm of his work, one part of his mind dimly occupied with the words to 'Daddy's Gone A-Hunting', while the other was taken up with a intriguingly vivid picture of Claire's white skin, pale and intoxicant as Rhenish wine against the glossy black of a bearskin.

'Daddy's gone to fetch a skin / To wrap his baby bunting in,' he murmured tunelessly under his breath.

He wondered just how much Claire *had* told Brianna. It was odd, though pleasant, their three-cornered way of talking; he and the lassie were a bit shy yet with each other – inclined to say personal things to Claire instead, confident that she would pass on their essence; their interpreter in this new and awkward language of the heart.

Thankful though he was for the miracle of his daughter, he wanted to make love to his wife in his bed again. It was getting overchilly to be having at it in the herb shed or the forest – though he would admit that floundering naked in the huge drifts of yellow chestnut leaves had a certain charm, even if it lacked dignity.

'Aye, well,' he muttered, smiling slightly to himself. 'And when did a man ever worry for his dignity, doin' *that?*'

He glanced thoughtfully at the pile of long, straight pine logs that lay at the side of the clearing, then at the sun. If Ian was quick enough returning, they might shape and notch a dozen or so before sunset.

Setting down the ax for a moment, he crossed to the house and began to pace out the dimensions of the new room he planned, to make do while the big house was a-building. She was a grown woman, Brianna – she should have a wee place of her own, to be private in, she and the maid. And if that restored his own privacy with Claire, well, so much the better, aye?

He heard the small crackling noises among the dried leaves in the yard, but didn't turn round. There was a tiny cough behind him, like a squirrel sneezing.

'Mrs. Lizzie,' he said, eyes still on the ground. 'And did ye enjoy your ride? I trust ye found all the Woolams well.' Where was Ian and the wagon? he wondered. He hadn't heard it on the road below.

She didn't speak, but made an inarticulate noise that made him swing round in surprise to look at her.

She was pale and pinch-faced and looked like a scared white mouse. This was not unusual; he knew he frightened her with his size and deep voice, and so he spoke gently to her, slowly, as he would have done to a mistreated dog.

'Have ye had an accident, lass? Has something come amiss wi' the wagon or the horses?'

She shook her head, still wordless. Her eyes were nearly round, gray as the hem of her washed-out gown, and the tip of her nose had gone bright pink.

'Is Ian all right?' He didn't want to upset her further, but she was beginning to alarm him. *Something* had happened, that was sure.

'I'm fine, Uncle. So are the horses.' Quiet as an Indian, Ian appeared round the corner of the cabin. He moved to Lizzie's side, offering her the support of his presence, and she took his arm as though by reflex.

He glanced from one to the other; Ian was outwardly calm, but his inner agitation was plain to see.

'What's happened?' he asked, more sharply than he'd intended. The lassie flinched.

'Ye'd better tell him,' Ian said. 'There might not be much time.' He touched her shoulder in encouragement, and she seemed to take strength from his hand; she stood up straighter and bobbed her head.

'I – there was – I saw a man. At the mill, sir.'

She tried to speak further, but her nerve had dried up; the tip of her tongue protruded between her teeth with effort, but no words came out.

'She kent him, Uncle,' Ian said. He looked disturbed, but not afraid; excited, rather, in an unfamiliar way. 'She'd seen him before – with Brianna.'

'Aye?' He tried to speak encouragingly, but the hair on the back of his neck was rising with premonition.

'At Wilmington,' Lizzie got out. 'MacKenzie was his name; I heard a sailor call him so.'

Jamie glanced quickly at Ian, who shook his head.

'He didna give his place, but I dinna ken any from Leoch like him. I saw him and heard him speak; he's maybe a Highlander, but schooled in the south, I'd say – an educated man.'

'And did this Mr. MacKenzie seem to know my daughter?' he asked. Lizzie nodded, frowning in concentration.

'Oh, aye, sir! And she kent him, too – she was afraid of him.'

'Afraid? Why?' He spoke sharply, and she blanched, but she was well started now, and the words came out, tripping and stumbling, but still coming.

'I dinna ken, sir. But she turned white when she saw him, sir, and let out a wee skelloch. Then she went red and white and red again – oh, she was fair upset, anyone could see it!'

'What did he do?'

'Why – why – nothing, then. He came close to her, and held her by the arms, and said to her that she must come awa' with him. Everyone in the taproom was looking. She pulled herself away, white as my shift, but she said to me as it was all right, I was to wait, and she would come back. And – and then she went out with him.'

Lizzie drew in a quick breath and wiped the end of her nose, which had begun to drip.

'And ye let her go?'

The little bondmaid shrank back, cowering.

'Ooh, I should have gone after her, I ken weel I should, sir!' she cried, face twisted with misery. 'But I was afraid, sir, and may God forgive me!'

With an effort, Jamie smoothed the frown from his face and spoke as patiently as he might.

'Aye, well. And what happened, then?'

'Oh, I went upstairs as she told me, and I lay in the bed, sir, prayin' for all I was worth!'

'Well, that was verra helpful, I'm sure!'

'Uncle –' Ian's voice was soft but not at all tentative, and his brown eyes were steady on Jamie's. 'She's no but a wee lassie, Uncle; she did her best.'

Jamie rubbed his hand hard over his scalp.

'Aye,' he said. 'Aye, I'm sorry, lass; I didna mean to bite your head off. But will ye no get on wi' it?'

A hot pink spot had begun to burn on each of Lizzie's cheeks.

'She – she didna come back till nearly dawn. And – and –'

Jamie had very little patience left, and no doubt it showed on his face.

'I could smell him on her,' she whispered, voice dropping almost to inaudibility. 'His . . . seed.'

The surge of rage took him unaware, like a white-hot bolt of lightning through chest and belly. He felt half choked with it, but clamped it down tight, hoarding it like coals in a hearth.

'He bedded her, then; you're sure of that?'

Thoroughly mortified at this bluntness, the little bond-maid could do no more than nod.

Lizzie was twisting her hands in the stuff of her gown, leaving her skirt all bunched and crumpled. Her paleness was replaced with a hot flush; she looked like one of Claire's tomatoes. She couldn't look at him, but hung her head, staring at the ground.

'Oh, sir. She's wi' child, can ye not see? It must be him – she was virgin when he took her. He's come after her – and she's afraid of him.'

Quite suddenly, he *could* see it, and felt the hairs rise all up his arms and shoulders. The autumn breeze struck cold through shirt and skin, and the rage turned to sickness. All the small things he had half seen and half thought, not allowing them to rise to the surface of his mind, came together at once in a logical pattern.

The look of her, and the way she acted; one moment lively and another lost in troubled thought. And the glow in her face that was not all from the sun. He knew the look of a woman breeding well enough; if he had known her before, he would have seen the change; but as it was . . .

Claire. Claire knew. The thought came to him, cold in its certainty. She knew her daughter, and she was a physician. She must know – and hadn't told him.

'Are ye sure of this?' The coldness froze his rage. He could feel it stuck in his chest – a dangerous, jagged object that seemed to point in every direction.

Lizzie nodded, wordless, and blushed deeper, if such a thing were possible.

'I am her maid, sir,' she whispered, eyes on the ground.

'She means Brianna hasna had her courses in two months,' Ian provided matter-of-factly. The youngest of a family containing several older sisters, he was not constrained by Lizzie's delicacy. 'She's sure.'

'I – I wouldna have said anything at all, sir,' the girl went on wretchedly. 'Only, when I saw the man . . .'

'D'ye think he's come to claim her, Uncle?' Ian interrupted. 'We must stop him, aye?' The look of angry excitement was clear now, flushing the lad's lean cheeks with feeling.

Jamie took a deep breath, only then realizing that he had been holding it.

'I dinna ken,' he said, surprised at the calmness of his own tone. He had barely had time to take in the news, let alone to draw conclusions, but the lad was right, there was a danger to be dealt with.

If this MacKenzie wished it, he might claim Brianna as his wife by right of common law, with the coming bairn as evidence of his claim. A court of law would not necessarily force a woman to wed a rapist, but any magistrate would uphold the right of a man to his wife and child – regardless of the wife's feelings in the matter.

His own parents had wed by such device: fleeing and hiding among the Highland crags until his mother was well with child, so that her brothers were forced to accept the unwelcome marriage. A child was a permanent, undeniable bond between man and woman, and he had cause to know it.

He glanced toward the path that came up through the lower wood.

'Will he not be here on your heels? The Woolams will have told him the way.'

'Nooo,' said Ian thoughtfully. 'I shouldna think so. We took his horse, aye?' He grinned suddenly at Lizzie, who giggled faintly in reply.

'Aye? And what's to stop him taking the wagon, or one of the wagon mules?'

The grin widened substantially on Ian's face.

'I left Rollo in the wagon bed,' he said. 'I think he'll walk it, Uncle Jamie.'

Jamie was forced to a grudging smile in return.

'That was quick of ye, Ian.'

Ian shrugged modestly.

'Well, I didna want the bastard to take us unawares. And though I've not heard Cousin Brianna talk about her laddie lately – yon Wakefield, aye?' He paused delicately. 'I didna think she'd want to see this MacKenzie. Especially if –'

'I should say Mr. Wakefield has left his coming ower-long,' Jamie said. 'Especially if.' It was no wonder she had stopped looking forward to Wakefield's coming – once she'd realized. After all, how would a woman explain a swelling belly to a man who'd left her virgin?

He slowly and consciously unclenched his fists. There would be time enough for all that later. For the moment, there was the one thing to be dealt with.

'Fetch my pistols from the house,' he said, turning to Ian. 'And you, lassie –' He gave Lizzie something intended for a smile, and reached for the coat he'd hung on the edge of the woodpile.

'Bide ye here, and wait for your mistress. Tell my wife – tell her I've gone to give Fergus a hand with his chimney. And dinna speak a word about this to my wife or daughter – or I'll have your guts for garters.' This last threat was spoken half in jest, but the girl went white as though he'd meant it literally.

Lizzie sank down on the chopping block, her knees wobbling beneath her. She fumbled for the tiny medallion at her neck, seeking reassurance from the cold metal. She watched Mr. Fraser stride down the path, menacing as a great red wolf. His shadow stretched out black before him, and the late autumn sun touched him with fire.

The medal in her hand was cold as ice.

'O dear Mother,' she murmured, over and over. 'O Blessed Mother, what have I done?'

45

Fifty-Fifty

The oak leaves were dry and crackling underfoot. There was a constant fall of leaves from the chestnut trees that towered overhead, a slow yellow rain that mocked the dryness of the ground.

'Is it true that Indians can move through the woods without making a sound, or is that just something they tell you in Girl Scouts?' Brianna kicked at a small drift of oak leaves, sending them flying. Dressed in wide skirts and petticoats that caught at leaves and twigs, we sounded like a herd of elephants ourselves.

'Well, they can't do it in dry weather like this, unless they swing through the trees like chimpanzees. In a wet spring, it's another story – even *I* could walk through here quietly then; the ground is like a sponge.'

I drew in my skirts to keep them away from a big elderberry bush, and stooped to look at the fruit. It was dark red, but not yet showing the blackish tinge of true ripeness.

'Two more days,' I said. 'If we were going to use them for medicine, we'd pick them now. I want them for wine, though, and to dry like raisins – and for that, you want them to have a lot of sugar, so you wait until they're nearly ready to drop from their stems.'

'Right. What landmark is it?' Brianna glanced around, and smiled. 'No, don't tell me – it's that big rock that looks like an Easter Island head.'

'Very good,' I said approvingly. 'Right, because it won't change with the seasons.'

Reaching the edge of a small stream, we separated, working our way slowly down the banks. I had set Brianna to collect cress, while I poked about the trees in search of wood ears and other edible fungi.

I watched her covertly as I hunted, one eye on the ground, one on her. She was knee-deep in the stream with her skirts kilted up, showing an amazing stretch of long, muscular thigh as she waded slowly, eyes on the rippling water.

There was something wrong; had been for days. At first I had assumed her air of tension was due to the obvious stresses of the new situation in which she found herself. But over the past weeks she and Jamie had settled into a relationship that, while still marked by shyness on both sides, was increasingly warm. They delighted each other – and I was delighted to see them together.

Still, there was something troubling her. It had been three years since I had left her – four since she had left me, to live on her own, and she had changed; had grown entirely into a woman now. I could no longer read her as easily as I once had. She had Jamie's trick of hiding strong feeling behind a mask of calmness – I knew it well in both of them.

In part, I had arranged this foraging expedition as an excuse to talk to her alone; with Jamie, Ian, and Lizzie in the house, and the constant traffic of tenants and visitors come to see Jamie, private conversation there was impossible. And if what I suspected was true, this wasn't a conversation I wished to have where anyone could hear.

By the time I had my basket half filled with thick, fleshy orange wood ears, Brianna had emerged dripping from the stream, her own basket overflowing with clumps of wet green cress and bunches of jointed horsetail reeds to make into tapers.

She wiped her feet on the hem of her petticoat, and came to join me under one of the huge chestnut trees. I handed her the canteen of cider, and waited till she had had a drink.

'Is it Roger?' I said then, without preliminary.

She glanced at me, a flash of startlement visible in her eyes, and then I saw the tense line of her shoulder ease.

'I wondered whether you could still do that,' she said.

'Do what?'

'Read my mind. I sort of hoped you could.' Her wide mouth quirked awkwardly, trying to smile.

'I expect I'm a bit out of practice,' I said. 'But give me a moment.' I reached up and smoothed the hair off her face. She looked at me, but beyond me, too shy to meet my eyes. A whippoorwill called in the far green shadows.

'It's all right, baby,' I said quietly. 'How far gone are you?'

The breath left her in a huge sigh. Her face went slack with relief.

'Two months.'

Now she met my eyes, and I felt a small shock of difference, the kind I had been getting since her arrival. Once, her relief would have been a child's; a fear confided, and half-eased already by the knowledge that I would somehow deal with it. But now it was only the relief of sharing an unbearable secret; she was not expecting me to remedy things. The knowledge that I *couldn't* do anything in any case didn't stop my irrational feeling of loss.

She squeezed my hand, as though reassuring *me*, and then sat down with her back against a tree trunk, stretching out her legs in front of her, long feet bare.

'Did you know already?'

I sat down next to her, less gracefully.

'I expect so; but I didn't know I knew, if that makes sense.' Looking at her now, it was plain to see; the faint pallor of her skin and tiny alterations in her color, the fleeting look of inwardness. I had noticed, but had put the changes down to unfamiliarity and strain – to the flurry of emotions over finding me, meeting Jamie, to worry over Lizzie's sickness, worry over Roger.

That particular worry now took on a sudden new dimension.

'Oh, Jesus. Roger!'

She nodded, pale in the filtered yellow shade of the chestnut leaves overhead. She looked jaundiced, and no wonder.

'It's been nearly two months. He should have been here – unless something happened.'

My mind was busy calculating.

'Two months, and now it's nearly November.' The leaves under us lay thick and soft, yellow and brown, fresh-fallen from the hickory and chestnut trees. My heart dropped suddenly in my chest. 'Bree – you've got to go back.'

'What?' Her head jerked up. 'Go back where?'

'To the stones.' I waved a hand in agitation. 'To Scotland, and right away!'

She stared at me, thick brows drawn down.

'*Now?* What for?'

I took a deep breath, feeling a dozen different emotions collide. Concern for Bree, fear for Roger, a terrible sorrow for Jamie, who would have to give her up again, so soon. And for myself.

'You can go through, pregnant. We know that much, because I did it, with you. But honey – you can't take a baby through that . . . that . . . you can't,' I ended, helpless. 'You know what it's like.' It had been three years since I came through the stones, but I recalled the experience vividly.

Her eyes went black as the little blood remaining in her face drained away.

'You can't take a child through,' I repeated, trying to get myself under control, think logically. 'It would be like jumping off Niagara Falls with the baby in your arms. You'll have to go back before it's born, or –' I broke off, making calculations.

'It's almost November. Ships won't make the passage between late November and March. And you can't wait till March – that would mean making a two-month trip across the Atlantic, six or seven months pregnant. If you didn't deliver on the ship – which would likely kill you or the baby or both – you'd still have to ride thirty miles to the circle, and then make the passage, find your way to help on the other side . . . Brianna, you can't do it! You have to go now, as soon as we can manage.'

'And if I do go now – how will I make sure I end up in the right time?'

She spoke quietly, but her fingers were pleating the fabric of her skirt.

'You – I think – well, *I* did,' I said, my initial panic beginning to subside into rational thought.

'You had Daddy at the other end.' She glanced up at me sharply. 'Whether you wanted to go to him or not, you had strong feelings for him – he would have pulled you. Or me. But he isn't there anymore.' Her face tightened, then relaxed.

'Roger knew – knows – how,' she corrected herself. 'Geillis Duncan's book said you could use gems to travel – for protection and navigation.'

'But you and Roger are both only guessing!' I argued. 'And so was bloody Geilie Duncan! You might not need either gemstones *or* a strong attachment. In the old fairy tales, when people go inside a fairy's dun and then return, it's always two hundred years. If that's the usual pattern, then –'

'Would you risk finding out it's not? And it's not – Geilie Duncan went *farther* than two hundred years.'

It occurred to me, a little belatedly, that she had thought all this out herself. Nothing I was saying came as any surprise. And that meant she had also reached her own conclusion – which did not involve taking ship back to Scotland.

I rubbed a hand between my brows, making an effort to match her calmness. The mention of Geillis had called to mind another memory – though one I had tried to forget.

'There's another way,' I said, fighting for calm. 'Another passage, I mean. It's on Haiti – they call it Hispaniola now. In the jungle, there are standing stones on a hill, but the crack, the passage, is underneath, in a cave.'

The forest air was cool, but it wasn't the shadows that made my skin ripple into gooseflesh. I rubbed my fore-arms, trying to erase the chill. I would willingly have erased all memory of the cave of Abandawe as well – I'd tried – but it wasn't a place easily forgotten.

'You've been there?' She leaned forward, intent.

'Yes. It's a horrible place. But the Indies are a good deal closer than Scotland is, and ships sail between Charleston and Jamaica nearly all year.' I took a deep breath, feeling a little better. 'It wouldn't be easy to go through the jungle – but it would give you a little longer – long enough for us to find Roger.' If he could still be found, I thought, but didn't say so. That particular fear could be dealt with later.

One of the chestnut leaves spiraled down onto Brianna's lap, vivid yellow against the soft brown home-spun, and she picked it off, smoothing the waxy surface absently with her thumb. She looked at me, blue eyes intent.

'Does this place work like the other one?'

'I don't know how any of them work! It sounded different, a bell sound instead of a buzzing noise. But it was a passage, all right.'

'You've been there,' she said slowly, looking at me under her brows.

'Why? Did you want to go back? After you'd found – him?' There was still a slight hesitation in her voice; she couldn't quite bring herself to refer to Jamie as 'my father'.

'No. It was to do with Geillis Duncan. She found it.'

Brianna's eyes sprang wide.

'She's *here*?'

'No. She's dead.'

I took a deep breath, feeling the remembered shock and tingle of an ax blow run up my arm. Sometimes I thought of her, of Geillis, when I was alone in the forest. Sometimes I thought I heard her voice behind me, and turned around swiftly, but saw no more than the hemlock branches, soughing in the wind. But now and then I felt her eyes on me, green and bright as the springtime wood.

'Quite dead,' I said firmly, and changed the subject. 'How did this happen, anyway?'

There wasn't any pretence of not knowing what I was talking about. She gave me a straight look, one eyebrow raised.

'You're the doctor. How many ways *are* there?'

I gave her back the look, with interest.

'Didn't you even think of taking any precautions?'

She glowered, thick brows drawn down.

'I wasn't *planning* to have sex here!'

I clutched my head, digging my fingers into my scalp in exasperation.

'You think people *plan* it? Good God, how many times did I come to that school of yours and give talks about –'

'All the time! Every year! My mother the sex encyclopedia! Do you have any idea how mortifying it is to have your own mother standing up in front of everybody, drawing pictures of *penises*?'

Her face went the color of the scarlet maples, flushed with the memory.

'I must not have done it all that well,' I said tartly, 'since you seem not to have recognized one when you saw it.'

Her face jerked toward me, blood in her eye, but then relaxed when she saw that I was joking – or trying to.

'Right,' she said. 'Well, they look different in 3-D.'

Taken unawares, I laughed. After a moment's hesitation, she joined me, a hesitant giggle.

'You know what I mean. I gave you that prescription before I left.'

She looked down her long, straight nose at me.

'Yes, and I was never so shocked in my life! You thought I'd run right out and have sex with everybody in sight the minute you left?'

'You're implying that it was only my presence stopping you?' The corner of her wide mouth twitched.

'Well, not *only* that,' she conceded. 'But you had something to do with it, you and Daddy. I mean, I – I wouldn't have wanted to disappoint you.' The twitch had turned to a quiver in an instant, and I hugged her hard, her smooth bright hair against my cheek.

'You couldn't, baby,' I murmured, rocking her slightly. 'We'd never be disappointed in you, never.'

I felt both tension and worry ebb as I held her. Finally, she took a deep breath and let go of me.

'Maybe not you or Daddy,' she said. 'But what about –?' She tilted her head toward the now invisible house.

'He won't –' I began, but then stopped. The truth was that I didn't know *what* Jamie would do. On the one hand, he was strongly inclined to think that Brianna hung the moon. On the other hand, he had opinions regarding sexual honor that could only be described – for obvious reasons – as old-fashioned, and no inhibitions at all about expressing them.

He was worldly, well educated, tolerant, and compassionate. This did not in any way, shape, or form mean that he shared or understood modern sensibilities; I knew quite well he didn't. And I couldn't think that his attitude toward Roger would be tolerant in the slightest.

'Well,' I said dubiously, 'I shouldn't wonder if he didn't

want to punch Roger in the nose or something. But don't worry,' I added, seeing her look of alarm. 'He loves you,' I said, and smoothed the tumbled hair off her flushed face. 'He won't stop.'

I got up, brushing yellow leaves from my skirt.

'We'll have a bit of time, then, but none to waste. Jamie can send word downriver, to keep an eye out for Roger. Speaking of Roger . . .' I hesitated, picking a bit of dried fern from my sleeve. 'I don't suppose he knows about this, does he?'

Brianna took a deep breath, and her fist closed tight on the leaf in her hand, crushing it.

'Well, see, there's a problem about that,' she said. She looked up at me, and suddenly she was my little girl again. 'It isn't Roger's.'

'What?' I said stupidly.

'It. Isn't. Roger's. Baby,' she said, between clenched teeth.

I sank down beside her once more. Her worry over Roger suddenly took on new dimensions.

'Who?' I said. 'Here, or there?' Even as I spoke, I was calculating – it had to be someone here, in the past. If it had been a man in her own time, she'd be farther along than two months. Not only in the past, then, but here, in the Colonies.

I wasn't planning to have sex, she'd said. No, of course not. She hadn't told Roger, for fear he would follow her – he was her anchor, her key to the future. But in that case –

'Here,' she said, confirming my calculations. She dug in the pocket of her skirt, and came out with something. She reached toward me, and I held out my hand automatically.

'Jesus H. Roosevelt Christ.' The worn gold wedding band sparked in the sun, and my hand closed reflexively over it. It was warm from being carried next to her skin, but I felt a deep coldness seep into my fingers.

'Bonnet?' I said. 'Stephen *Bonnet?*'

Her throat moved convulsively, and she swallowed, head jerking in a brief nod.

'I wasn't going to tell you – I couldn't; not after Ian told me about what happened on the river. At first I didn't

858

know what Da would do; I was afraid he'd blame me. And then when I knew him a little better – I knew he'd try to find Bonnet – that's what Daddy would have done. I couldn't let him do that. You met that man, you know what he's like.' She was sitting in the sun, but a shudder passed over her, and she rubbed her arms as though she was cold.

'I do,' I said. My lips were stiff. Her words were ringing in my ears.

I wasn't planning to have sex. I couldn't tell . . . I was afraid he'd blame me.

'What did he do to you?' I asked, and was surprised that my voice sounded calm. 'Did he hurt you, baby?'

She grimaced, and pulled her knees up to her chest, hugging them against herself.

'Don't call me that, okay? Not right now.'

I reached to touch her, but she huddled closer into herself, and I dropped my hand.

'Do you want to tell me?' I didn't want to know; I wanted to pretend it hadn't happened, too.

She looked up at me, lips tightened to a straight white line.

'No,' she said. 'No, I don't want to. But I think I'd better.'

She had stepped aboard the *Gloriana* in broad daylight, cautious, but feeling safe by reason of the number of people around; loaders, seamen, merchants, servants – the docks bustled with life. She had told a seaman on the deck what she wanted; he had vanished into the recesses of the ship, and a moment later, Stephen Bonnet had appeared.

He had on the same clothes as the night before; in the daylight, she could see that they were of fine quality, but stained and badly crumpled. Greasy candle wax had dripped on the silk cuff of his coat, and his jabot had crumbs in it.

Bonnet himself showed fewer marks of wear than did his clothes; he was fresh-shaven, and his green eyes were pale and alert. They passed over her quickly, lighting with interest.

'I did think ye comely last night by candlelight,' he said,

taking her hand and raising it to his lips. 'But a-many seem so when the drink is flowin'. It's a good deal more rare to find a woman fairer in the sun than she is by the moon.'

Brianna tried to extract her hand from his grasp, giving him a polite smile.

'Thank you. Do you still have the ring?' Her heart beat fast in her throat. He could still tell her about the ring – about her mother – even if he had lost it gambling. But she wanted very badly to have it in her hands. She suppressed the fear that had haunted her all night; that the ring might be all that was left of the mother. It couldn't be, not if the newspaper clipping was right, but –

'Oh, indeed. The luck of Danu herself was with me the night – and still is, by the looks of it.' He gave her a charming smile, still keeping hold of her hand.

'I – ah, I wondered if you would sell it to me.' She had brought nearly all the money she had with her, but had no idea what the cost of a gold ring might be.

'Why?' The blunt question took her unawares, and she fumbled for an answer.

'It – it looks like one my mother had,' she answered, unable to invent an answer better than the truth. 'Where did you get it?'

Something moved behind his eyes, though he still smiled at her. He gestured toward the dark companionway, and tucked her hand in the crook of his elbow. He was taller than she, a big man. She pulled, cautiously, but he held her hand fast.

'So ye want the ring? Come down to my cabin, my dear, and we shall see if an accommodation might be reached.'

Below, he poured her brandy; she took the barest sip, but he drank deeply, draining one glass and pouring another.

'Where?' he said carefully, in answer to her persistent questions. 'Ah – well, a gentlemen should not be tellin' tales of his ladies, should he?' He winked at her. 'A love token,' he whispered.

The smile on her own face felt stiff, and the sip of a brandy she had taken burned in her stomach.

'The lady who – gave it to you,' she said. 'Is she in good health?'

He gaped at her, lower jaw fallen slightly open.

'Luck,' she said hastily. 'It's bad luck to wear jewelry that belongs to someone who's – who's dead.'

'Is it?' The smile returned. 'I cannot say I have noticed that effect myself.' He set down the glass and gave a slight, pleasurable belch.

'Still, I can assure ye, the lady from whom I had that ring was both alive and well when I left her.'

The burning sensation in her stomach eased slightly.

'Oh. I'm glad to hear that. Will you sell it to me, then?'

He rocked back in his chair, eyeing her a small smile on his lips.

'Sell it. And what will ye offer me, sweetheart?'

'Fifteen pounds sterling.' Her heart began to beat faster again, as he stood up. He was going to agree! Where did he keep it?

He stood up, took her hand, and pulled her up out of her chair.

'I've enough money, sweetheart,' he said. 'What color's the hair between your legs?'

She jerked her hand out of his grasp, and backed up as quickly as she could, slamming into the wall of the cabin within a few steps.

'You've mistaken me,' she said. 'I didn't mean –'

'Maybe not,' he said, and the edges of his teeth showed in his smile. 'But I do. And I do think perhaps you've mistaken *me*, sweetheart.'

He took a step toward her. She snatched the brandy bottle from the table, and swung it at his head. He ducked adroitly, plucked the bottle from her hand, and slapped her hard across the face.

She staggered, half blinded by the sudden pain. He grasped her by the shoulders, and forced her to her knees. His fingers twisted tight in her hair, close to the scalp, and jerked her head, hard. He held her, head canted at an awkward angle, while he fumbled with the other hand at the front of his breeches. He grunted slightly with satisfaction and took a half step closer, thrusting his hips forward.

'Meet Leroi,' he said.

Leroi was both uncircumcised and unwashed, and gave off a powerful smell of stale urine. She felt a bolus of vomit

861

rise in her throat, and tried to turn her head away. The answer to that was a vicious yank on her hair that brought her back, stifling a cry of pain.

'Put out that little pink tongue and give us a kiss, sweetheart.' Bonnet sounded cheerful and unconcerned, his grip on her hair tight as ever. She lifted her hands toward him in unspoken protest; he saw it and tightened his grip, making tears start in her eyes. She put out her tongue.

'Not bad, not bad,' he said, judiciously. 'All right, open your mouth.' He let go of her hair quite suddenly and her head snapped back. Before she could jerk away, he had seized her by one ear, twisting slightly.

'Bite me, sweetheart, and I'll mash your nose flat. Eh?' He brushed his closed fist lightly under her nose, nudging the tip with a massive knuckle. Then he took a firm grip on her other ear, holding her head immobile between his big hands.

She concentrated on the taste of the blood from her cut lip, the taste and the pain of it. With her eyes closed, she could see the taste, salt and metal, a burnished copper, shining pure in the dark inside her eyes.

If she vomited, she would choke. She would choke, and he would not notice. She would strangle and die, and he wouldn't stop. She put her hands on his thighs to brace herself, and dug her fingers into the heavy muscle, pushing back as hard as she could, to resist the battering. He was humming, deep in his throat. *From Ushant to Scilly is thirty-five leagues.* Wiry hairs brushed her lips.

Then Leroi was gone. He let go of her ears and stepped back; unbalanced, she fell forward on hands and knees, gagging and coughing, the strings of saliva from her mouth tinged pink with blood. She coughed and spat, and spat again, trying to clear her mouth of foulness. Her lips were swollen, and throbbing with her heartbeat.

He lifted her effortlessly, hands under her arms, and kissed her, tongue thrusting, one palm cupping the back of her head to keep her from pulling away. He tasted overpoweringly of brandy, with a faint nastiness of decaying teeth. The other hand, at her waist, roamed slowly downward, kneading her buttocks.

862

'Mmm,' he said, sighing pleasurably. 'Bedtime, eh, sweetheart?'

She lowered her head and butted him in the face. Her forehead struck hard against bone, and he uttered a sharp cry of surprise and loosened his grip. She wrenched free and ran. Her flying skirt caught on the doorlatch and tore, disregarded as she hurled herself out into the dark companionway.

The sailors were at supper; twenty men sat at a long table in the mess at the end of the companionway, twenty faces turned toward her in expressions ranging from startlement to lascivious interest. It was the cook who tripped her, sticking out a foot as she dashed past the galley. Her knees hit the deck with numbing force.

'Like games, do you, sweetheart?' It was Bonnet's voice in her ear, jovial as ever, as a pair of hands scooped her up with disconcerting ease. He whirled her to face him, and smiled. She had hit him in the nose; a thick trickle of blood flowed down from one nostril. It ran over his upper lip, and followed the grooves of his smile, thin lines of red showing between his teeth, and dark drops dripping slowly from his chin.

His grip on her arms tightened, but the merry glint shone as ever in his light green eyes.

'That's all right, sweetheart,' he said. 'Leroi likes games. Don't you, Leroi?' He glanced down, and she followed his gaze. He had shed his breeches in the cabin, and stood half naked, Leroi brushing against her skirts, quivering with eagerness.

He took her by one elbow, and bowing gallantly, gestured toward the cabin. Numbly, she stepped forward, and he took his place beside her, arm in arm, nonchalantly exposing the white cheeks of his buttocks to the stares of his gaping crew.

'After that . . . it wasn't so bad.' She could hear her own voice, unnaturally calm, as though it belonged to someone else. 'I didn't – didn't fight him anymore.'

He hadn't bothered to make her undress, merely untucked her kerchief. Her dress was made in the usual fashion, with a low, square neckline, and her breasts were high and round; it took no more than a casual downward yank to bare them, popping them up over the edge of the bodice like a pair of apples.

He mauled them idly for a moment, pinching her nipples between a large thumb and forefinger to make them stand up, then pushed her toward his tumbled bed.

The sheets were stained with spilled liquor and stank of perfume and wine, and overwhelmingly of the rank, heavy odor of Bonnet himself. He shoved up her skirt and arranged her legs to suit him, humming all the while beneath his breath. *Farewell to you all, ye fine Spanish ladies . . .*

In her mind's eye, she could see herself thrusting him away, flinging herself off the bed and running for the door, skimming light as a gull down the dark companionway and bursting up through the grated deck to freedom. She could feel the wooden boards under her bare feet, and the glare of the hot summer sun in her dark-blind eyes. Almost. She lay in the dim cabin, wooden as a figurehead, tasting blood in her mouth.

There was a blind, insistent prodding between her thighs and she convulsed in panic, scissoring her legs. Still humming, he thrust a muscular leg between her own, brutally nudging her thighs apart. Naked from the waist downward, he still wore his shirt and stock. The long tails drooped around Leroi's pale stalk as he rose up on his knees above her.

He stopped humming long enough to spit copiously into his palm. Rubbing roughly and thoroughly, he eased the path and then set to business. With one hand clutched firmly on her breast, he guided himself with the other to an inescapable berth, making a jovial remark about the snugness of the accommodation, and then loosed Leroi on his mindless – and mercifully brief – gallop to pleasure.

Two minutes, maybe three. And then it was over, and Bonnet lay heavily collapsed upon her, sweat crumpling his linen stock, one hand still crushing her breast. His lank fair hair fell soft against her cheek and his exhalations purled hot and damp on her neck. At least he'd stopped humming.

She lay frozen for endless long minutes, staring up at the ceiling, where the reflections from the water danced across the polished beams. He sighed at last, and rolled slowly off her onto his side. He smiled at her, dreamily scratching one bared and hairy hip.

'Not bad, sweetheart, though I've had livelier rides. Move your arse more next time, hm?' He sat up, yawned, and began to straighten his attire. She edged toward the side of the bed, then, sure that he didn't mean to restrain her, rolled abruptly off and onto her feet. She felt light-headed and desperately short of air, as though his bulk still pressed upon her.

Moving in a daze, she went to the door. It was bolted. As she struggled to lift the bolt, her hands shaking, she heard him say something behind her, and swung around in amazement.

'*What* did you say?'

'I said the ring's on the desk,' he said, straightening up from retrieving his stockings. He sat down on the bed and began to pull them on, waving casually at the desk that stood against the wall. 'There's money, too. Take what you want.'

The top of the desk was a magpie's nest, littered with inkpots, trinkets, bits of jewelry, bills of lading, tattered quills, silver buttons, ragged bits of paper and crumpled clothing, and a scatter of coins in silver and bronze, copper and gold, currency of several colonies, several countries.

'You're offering me *money*?'

He looked up quizzically, fair brows arched.

'I pay for my pleasures,' he said. 'Did you think I wouldn't?'

Everything in the cabin seemed unnaturally vivid, detailed and individual as the objects in a dream, which would vanish with waking.

'I didn't think anything,' she said, her voice sounding very clear, but distant, someone speaking from far away. Her kerchief lay on the floor where he had thrown it, by the desk. She walked there, carefully, trying not to think of the warm slipperiness that streaked down her thighs.

'I'm an honest man – for a pirate,' he said behind her,

865

and laughed. He stamped once on the deck to settle his foot in its shoe, then brushed past her and lifted the bolt easily with one hand.

'Help yourself, sweetheart,' he said, with another casual wave toward the desk as he went out. 'You were worth it.'

She heard his footsteps going away down the companionway, a burst of laughter and a muffled remark as he met someone, then a shift of his voice, suddenly clear and harsh, shouting orders to someone above, and the tramp and scurry of feet overhead, rushing to obey. Back to business.

It was sitting in a bowl made of cowhorn, jumbled with a collection of bone buttons, string, and other bits of rubbish. Like him, she thought, with a cold clarity. Acquisition for its own sake; a reckless and savage delight in the taking, with no knowledge at all of the value of what he stole.

Her hand was shaking; she saw it with a vague sense of surprise. She tried to grasp the ring, failed, gave up. She scooped up the bowl and emptied its contents into her pocket. She walked down the dark companionway, her fist wrapped tight around the pocket, holding it like a talisman. There were seamen all around, too busy about their tasks to spare her more than a glance of lewd speculation. Her shoes were perched on the end of the mess table, bows perky in a shaft of light from the grating overhead.

She put them on, and with an even tread walked up the ladder, across the deck and gangplank, onto the dock. Tasting blood.

'I thought at first I could just pretend it didn't happen.' She took a deep breath, and looked at me. Her hands folded over her stomach, as though to hide it. 'But I guess that won't work, will it?'

I was silent for a moment, thinking. It was no time for delicacy.

'When?' I said. 'How long after . . . um, after Roger?'

'Two days.'

My eyebrows lifted at that.

'Why are you so sure it isn't Roger's, then? You weren't

using pills, obviously, and I'll bet my life Roger didn't use what passes for condoms in these times.'

She half smiled at that, and a small flush rose in her cheeks.

'No. He . . . um . . . he . . . ah . . .'

'Oh, coitus interruptus?'

She nodded.

I took a deep breath and blew it out through pursed lips.

'There is a word,' I said, 'for people who depend on that particular method of birth control.'

'What's that?' she asked, looking wary.

'Parents,' I said.

46

Comes a Stranger

Roger bent his head and drank from cupped hands. A piece of luck, that flash of green, pointed out by a finger of sunlight stabbing down through the trees. Without it, he would never have seen the spring, so far off the trail as it was.

A clear trickle bubbled through a crack in the rock, cooling his hands and face. The rock itself was a smooth blackish green, and the ground all round was boggy, rumpled by tree roots and furred with a moss that grew brilliant as emeralds in the fleeting patch of sun.

The knowledge that he would see Brianna shortly – perhaps within the hour – soothed his annoyance as effectively as the cool water eased his dry throat. If he'd had to have his horse stolen, it was some consolation that he'd been close enough to reach his destination on foot.

The horse itself had been an ancient nag, barely worth stealing. At least he'd had the sense to keep his valuables on his person, not in the saddlebags. He clapped a hand against the side seam of his breeches, reassured to feel the small hardness snuggled against his thigh.

Beyond the horse itself, he hadn't lost much more than a pistol – nearly as ancient as the horse and not half so reliable – a bit of food, and a leather water flask. The loss of the flask had troubled him for the last few miles of hot, dusty walking, but now that minor inconvenience was remedied.

His feet sank into the damp ground as he stood up, leaving dark streaks in the emerald moss. He stepped back and wiped the mud from his shoe soles on the carpet of dry leaves and crusted needles. Then he dusted down the skirts of his coat as well as he could, and straightened the grimy stock at his throat. His knuckles rasped the stubble on his jaw; his razor had been in the saddlebag.

He looked a right villain, he thought ruefully. No way to meet your in-laws. In truth, though, he wasn't much concerned with what Claire and Jamie Fraser might think of him. His thoughts were all on Brianna.

She'd found her parents now; he could only hope that the reunion had been so satisfactory that she'd be in a mood to forgive his betrayal. Christ, he'd been stupid!

He made his way back toward the path, feet sinking in the soft leaf-layer. Stupid in underestimating her stubbornness, stupid not to have been honest with her, he amended. Stupid to have bullied her into secrecy. Trying to keep her safely in the future – no, that hadn't been stupid at all, he thought, with a grimace at the things he'd seen and heard in the last few months.

He pushed aside an overhanging limb of loblolly pine, then ducked with an exclamation of alarm, as something black shot past his head.

A hoarse *craawk!* announced that his assailant was a raven. Similar cries gave notice of the arrival of reinforcements in the trees nearby, and within seconds, another black missile whizzed past, within inches of his ear.

'Hey, bugger off!' he exclaimed, ducking away from yet another croaking buzz bomb. He was plainly near a nest, and the ravens didn't like it.

The first raven sailed back for another try. This pass knocked his hat into the dirt. The mobbing was unnerving, the sense of hostility out of all proportion to the size of his adversaries. Another came in, zooming low, and struck him a glancing blow as its claws ripped at the shoulder of his coat. Roger snatched up his hat and ran.

A hundred yards up the trail, he slowed to a walk and looked round. The birds were nowhere in sight; he'd passed their nesting place, then.

'And where's Alfred Hitchcock when you need him?' he muttered to himself, trying to shake off the sense of danger.

His voice was damped at once by the thick vegetation; it was like talking into a pillow. He was breathing heavily, and his face felt flushed. All at once, it seemed very quiet in the forest. With the ceasing of the ravens' racket, all the other birds seemed to have stopped as well. It was no wonder the old Scots thought ravens birds of bad omen; spend much longer here, and all the old ways that had been no more than curiosities would be flourishing away in his mind.

Dangerous, dirty, and uncomfortable as it was, he had to admit the fascination of being here – of experiencing at firsthand things he'd read about, seeing objects he knew as museum artifacts being casually used in daily life. If it wasn't for Brianna, he might not regret the adventure, in spite of Stephen Bonnet and the things he had seen aboard the *Gloriana*.

Once more his hand went to his thigh. He had been luckier than he'd dared hope; Bonnet had had not one gemstone, but two. Would they really work? He ducked again, having to walk half crouched for several steps before the branches opened up again. Hard to believe that people lived up here, save that someone had cut this trail, and it must lead somewhere.

'You can't miss it,' the girl at the mill had assured him, and he could see why. There wasn't anyplace else to go.

He shaded his eyes, looking up the trail, but the drooping branches of pine and maple hid everything, presenting only a shadowy, mysterious tunnel through the trees. No telling how far it might be to the top of the ridge.

'You'll make it by sundown, easy,' the girl had told him, and it was late midafternoon now. But that had been when he had a horse. Not wanting to be caught on the mountainside in the dark, he picked up his pace, straining his eyes for sunlight ahead that would show him the openness of the ridge at the end of the trail.

As he walked, his thoughts ran inevitably ahead of him, quick with speculation.

And how had it gone, Brianna's reunion with her parents? What had she thought of Jamie Fraser? Was he the man she'd been imagining for the last year, or only a pale reflection of the image she had built up from her mother's stories?

At least she had a father to know, he thought, with a queer little pang at the memory of Midsummer's Eve, and that burst of light in the passage through the stones.

There it was! A lightening of the dense green shadow ahead; a brightening as tongues of sun struck autumn leaves in a flare of orange and yellow.

870

The sun dazzled him for a moment as he came out of the tunnel of greenery. He blinked once, and found himself not on the ridge, as he had expected, but in a small natural clearing, edged with scarlet maples and yellow scrub oak. It held the sunlight like a cup, dark forest spreading beyond on all sides.

As he turned about, searching for the continuation of the trail, he heard a horse's whicker and whirled to find his own elderly mount, jerking its head against the pull of a rein tied to a tree at the edge of the clearing.

'Well, I'll be buggered!' he exclaimed in astonishment. 'How the hell did you get up here?'

'The same way you did,' a voice answered him. A tall young man emerged from the wood beside the horse, and stood pointing a pistol at Roger; his own, he saw, with a sense of outrage as well as apprehension. He took a deep breath and choked down his fear.

'You've got my horse and my gun,' Roger said coolly. 'What else d'you want? My hat?' He held out the battered tricorne in invitation. The robber couldn't possibly know what else he carried; he hadn't shown them to anyone.

The young man – couldn't be more than in his teens, in spite of his size, Roger thought – didn't smile.

'A bit more than that, I expect.' For the first time, the young man took his eyes off Roger, shifting his glance to one side. Following the direction of his gaze, Roger felt a jolt like an electric shock.

He hadn't seen the man at the edge of the clearing, though he must have been there all the time, standing motionless. He wore a faded hunting kilt whose browns and greens blended into the grass and brush, as his flaming hair blended with the brilliant leaves. He looked as if he'd grown out of the forest.

Beyond the sheer unexpectedness of his appearance, it was his looks that stunned Roger into speechlessness. It was one thing to have been told that Jamie Fraser resembled his daughter. It was another to see Brianna's bold features transmuted into power by the stamp of years, and fronting a personality not only thoroughly masculine, but fierce in aspect.

It was like lifting his hand from the fur of a handsome

ginger cat, only to find himself staring into the unblinking gaze of a tiger. Roger barely kept himself from taking an involuntary step backward, thinking as he did so that Claire had not exaggerated a single thing in her description of Jamie Fraser.

'You'll be Mr. MacKenzie,' the man said. It wasn't a question. The voice was deep but not loud, barely lifted above the sound of the rustling leaves, but Roger had no difficulty hearing him.

'I am,' he said, taking a step forward. 'And you'll be . . . ah . . . Jamie Fraser?' He stretched out a hand, but quickly let it drop. Two pairs of eyes rested coldly on him.

'I am,' said the red-haired man. 'You'll know me?' The tone of the question was distinctly unfriendly.

Roger took a deep breath, cursing his own dishevelment. He didn't know how Brianna might have described him to her father, but Fraser had evidently expected something a good deal more prepossessing.

'Well, you – look quite a bit like your daughter.'

The young man gave a loud snort, but Fraser didn't look around.

'And what business have ye wi' my daughter?' Fraser moved for the first time, stepping out from the shadow of the trees. No, Claire hadn't exaggerated. He *was* big, even an inch or two taller than Roger himself.

Roger felt a stab of alarm, mingled with his confusion. What the hell had Brianna told him? Surely she couldn't have been so angry that – well, he'd sort that out when he saw her.

'I've come to claim my wife,' he said boldly.

Something changed in Fraser's eyes. Roger didn't know what it was, but it made him drop his hat, and half raise his hands in reflex.

'Oh, no, ye're not.' It was the boy who had spoken, in an odd tone of satisfaction.

Roger glanced at him, and was still more alarmed to see the lad's big, bony knuckles white on the pistol's grip.

'Here be careful! You don't want that to go off by accident,' he said. The young man's lip lifted in a sneer.

'If it goes off, it'll be no accident.'

'Ian.' Fraser's voice stayed level, but the pistol lowered,

reluctantly. The big man took another step forward. His eyes were fixed on Roger's, deep blue and slanted; unnervingly like Brianna's.

'I'll ask only the once, and I mean to hear the truth,' he said, quite mildly. 'Have ye taken my daughter's maidenheid?'

Roger felt his face grow hot as a flood of warmth washed up from chest to hairline. Christ, what had she told her father? And for God's sake, *why*? The last thing he had expected to meet was an infuriated father, bent on avenging his daughter's virtue.

'It's . . . ah . . . well, it's not what you think,' he blurted. 'I mean, we . . . that is . . . we meant to . . .'

'Did ye or no?' Fraser's face was no more than a foot away, completely expressionless, save for whatever it was that burned, far back in his eyes.

'Look – I – damn it, yes! She wanted to –'

Fraser hit him, just under the ribs.

Roger doubled and staggered back, gasping from the blow. It didn't hurt – yet – but he'd felt the force of it all the way to his spine. His principal feeling was one of amazement, tinged with anger.

'Stop,' he said, trying to get enough breath to talk. 'Stop! For God's sake, I said –'

Fraser hit him again, this time on the side of the jaw. That one hurt, a glancing blow that scraped the skin and left his jawbone throbbing. Roger jerked back, fear turning rapidly to fury. The bloody sod was trying to kill him!

Fraser swung at him again, but missed as Roger ducked and whirled. Well, to fuck with good family relations, then!

He took a giant step backward, shrugging out of his coat. To his surprise, Fraser didn't come after him, but stood there, fists at his sides, waiting.

The blood was drumming in Roger's ears, and he had no eyes for anyone but Fraser. If it was a fight the bugger wanted, that's what he'd get, then.

Roger crouched, hands up and ready. He'd been taken by surprise, but he wouldn't be caught that way again. No brawler, still he'd been in his share of pub fights. They

873

were well matched for height and reach, and he had more than fifteen years' advantage on the man.

He saw Fraser's right, ducked and countered, felt his fist brush linen as it passed Fraser's side and then the left he hadn't seen took him in the eye. Bloody stars and streaks of light exploded through the side of his head, and tears ran down his cheek as he launched himself at Fraser, roaring.

He hit the man; he could feel his fists strike flesh, but it seemed to make no difference. Through his one sound eye, he could see that broad-boned face, set in eerie calm, like a Viking berserker. He swung, and it disappeared, bobbed up again; he swung, grazing an ear. A blow struck him in the shoulder; he swung half around with it, recovered, and launched himself headfirst.

'She's . . . mine,' Roger gritted between clenched teeth. He had his arms wrapped around Fraser's body, felt the deep-sprung ribs give as he squeezed. He'd crack the bastard like a nut. 'Mine . . . hear?'

Fraser rabbit-punched him in the back of the neck, a glancing blow, but hard enough to numb his left arm and shoulder. He let go his grip, hunched and drove his right shoulder hard into Fraser's chest, trying to drive the older man off his feet.

Fraser took a short step back and hooked him hard, but the blow struck his ribs, not the soft flesh below. Still, it was hard enough to make him grunt and jerk back, crouching to protect himself.

Fraser lowered his head and butted him, straight on; he flew backward and landed hard. Blood from his nose ran down his mouth and chin; with a sense of remoteness, he watched the spatter of dark red drops grow and run together into a splotch on his shirt.

He rolled to one side to avoid the kick he saw coming, but not far enough. As he rolled frantically the other way, it occurred to him, in a detached sort of way, that while he might be fifteen years younger than his opponent, Jamie Fraser had likely spent every one of those fifteen years engaged in physical combat.

He had got momentarily out of range. Gulping air, he rolled up onto his hands and knees. Blood gurgled through smashed cartilage with each breath; he could taste it in the back of his throat, a taste like sheared metal.

''Nuff,' he panted. 'No. 'Nuff!'

A hand grabbed his hair and jerked back his head. Blue eyes glittered six inches away, and he felt the man's breath hot on his face

'Not nearly enough,' Fraser said, and kneed him in the mouth. He fell over and rolled once, then struggled to his feet. The clearing blurred in a throb of orange and yellow; only instinct got him up and moving.

He was fighting for his life, and knew it. He hurled himself blindly at the weaving figure, got a grip of Fraser's shirt and drove a punch at the man's belly, as hard as he could. Fabric tore and his fist struck bone. Fraser shifted like a snake and shot a hand down between them. He grabbed Roger's testicles and squeezed with all his strength.

Roger stood stock-still, then dropped as though his spinal cord had been severed. There was a split second, before the pain hit, when Roger was conscious of one last thought, cold and clear as a shard of ice. *My God*, he thought, *I'm going to die before I've been born.*

47

A Father's Song

It was well after dark before Jamie came in, and my nerves were thoroughly on edge from the waiting; I could only imagine Brianna's. We had eaten supper – or I should say, supper had been served. None of us had any appetite, either for food or conversation; even Lizzie's normal voracity was noticeably impaired. I hoped the girl wasn't ill; pale and silent, she had pled a headache and gone to bed in the herb shed. Still, it was fortunate in the circumstances; it saved me having to invent an excuse to get rid of her once Jamie did arrive.

The candles had been lit for over an hour when I finally heard the goats bleat in greeting at his step on the path. Brianna looked up at once at the sound, her face pale in the yellow light.

'It'll be all right,' I said. She heard the confidence in my voice and nodded, slightly reassured. The confidence was authentic, but not unalloyed. I thought everything *would* be all right eventually – but God knew, it wasn't going to be a jolly family evening. Well as I knew Jamie, there were still a good many circumstances in which I had no idea how he would react – and hearing that his daughter was pregnant by a rapist was certainly one of them.

In the hours since Brianna had made my suspicions a certainty, I had envisioned virtually every possible response he *might* make, several of them involving shouting or the putting of his fists through solid objects, behavior which I always found upsetting. So might Bree, and I knew rather better what *she* might do when upset.

She was under a tight control for the moment, but I knew how precarious her calm demeanor was. Let him say a bruising word to her, and she would flare like a striking match. Beyond red hair and arresting height, she had from Jamie both a passionate nature and a perfect readiness to speak her mind.

So unfamiliar and so anxious to please each other, they

had both so far stepped delicately – but there seemed no delicate way of handling this. Unsure whether I should prepare myself to be advocate, interpreter, or referee, it was with rather a hollow feeling that I lifted the latch to let him in.

He had washed at the creek; his hair was damp at the temples, and he had wiped his face on his shirttail, judging by the moist patches on it.

'You're very late; where were you?' I asked, standing on tiptoe to give him a kiss. 'And where's Ian?'

'Fergus came and asked could we give him a hand wi' his chimney stones, as he couldna manage verra well by himself. Ian's stayed ower, to help finish the job.' He dropped an absent kiss on top of my head, and patted my bottom. He'd been working hard, I thought; he was warm to my touch and smelled pungently of sweat, though the skin of his face was cool and fresh from washing.

'Did Marsali feed you supper?' I peered at him in the gloom. Something seemed different about him, though I couldn't think what.

'No. I dropped a stone and I've maybe broken my blasted finger again; I thought I'd best come home and have ye tend to it.' That was it, I thought; he'd patted me with his left hand instead of his right.

'Come into the light and let me see.' I drew him to the fire, and made him sit to down on one of the oak settles. Brianna was on the other, her sewing spread around her. She got up and came to look over my shoulder.

'Your poor hands, Da!' she said, seeing the swollen knuckles and scraped skin.

'Och, it's no great matter,' he said, glancing dismissively at them. 'Save for the bloody finger. Ow!'

I felt my way gently over the fourth finger of his right hand, from base to nail, disregarding his small grunt of pain. It was reddened and slightly swollen, but not visibly dislocated.

It always troubled me slightly to examine this hand. I had set a number of broken bones in it long ago, before I knew anything of formal surgery, and working under far from ideal conditions. I had managed; I had saved the hand from amputation, and he had good use of it, but

877

there were small awkwardnesses; slight twistings and thickenings that I was aware of whenever I felt it closely. Still, at the moment, I blessed the opportunity for delay.

I closed my eyes, feeling the fire's warm flicker on my lids as I concentrated. The fourth finger was always stiff; the middle joint had been crushed, and healed frozen. I could see the bone in my mind; not the polished dry surface of a laboratory specimen, but the faintly luminous matte glow of living bone, all the tiny osteoblasts busily laying down their crystal matrix, and the hidden pulse of the blood that fed them.

Once more, I drew my own finger down the length of his, then took it gently between my thumb and index finger, just below the distal joint. I could feel the crack in my mind, a thin dark line of pain.

'There?' I asked, opening my eyes.

He nodded, a faint smile on his lips as he looked at me.

'Just there. I like the way ye look when ye do that, Sassenach.'

'What way is that?' I asked, a bit startled to hear that I looked any way in particular.

'I canna describe it, exactly,' he said, head tilted to one side as he examined me. 'It's maybe like –'

'Madame Lazonga with her crystal ball,' Brianna said, sounding amused.

I glanced up, taken aback to find Brianna gazing down at me, head cocked at the same angle, with the same appraising look. She switched her gaze to Jamie. 'A fortune-teller, I mean. A seer.'

He laughed.

'Aye, I think you're maybe right, a *nighean*. Though it was a priest I was thinking of; the way they look saying Mass, when they look past the bread and see the flesh of Christ instead. Not that I should think to compare my measly finger wi' the Body of Our Lord, mind,' he added, with a modest nod toward the offending digit.

Brianna laughed, and a smile curved his mouth on one side, as he looked up at her, his eyes soft despite the lines of tiredness round them. He'd had a long day, I thought. And likely to be a lot longer. I would have given anything to hold that fleeting moment of connection between them, but it had passed already.

'*I* think you are both ridiculous,' I said I touched his finger lightly at the spot I'd had. 'The bone is cracked, just there below the joint. It's not bad, though; no more than a hairline fracture. I'll splint it, just in case.'

I got up and went to rummage through my medical chest for a linen bandage and one of the long, flat wood chips I used as tongue depressors. I glanced covertly over the raised lid, watching him. Something was definitely odd about him this evening, though I still couldn't put my finger on it.

I had sensed it from the first, even through my own agitation, and it even more strongly when I held his hand to examine it; a sort of pulsed through him, as though he were excited or upset, though he gave no outward sign of it. He was bloody good at hiding things when he wanted to; what the hell had happened at Fergus's house?

Brianna said something to Jamie, too low for me to catch, and then turned away without waiting for an answer, and came to join me by the open chest.

'Do you have some ointment, for his hands?' she asked. Then, leaning close on pretext of looking into the chest, said in a low voice, 'Should I tell him tonight? He's tired and he's hurt. Hadn't I better let him rest?'

I glanced at Jamie. He was leaning back against the settle, eyes wide open as he watched the flames, hands resting flat on his thighs. He wasn't relaxed, though; whatever strange current was flowing through him, it had him strung like a telegraph wire.

'He might rest better not knowing, but you won't,' I said, equally low-voiced. 'Go ahead and tell him. You might let him eat first, though,' I added practically. I was a strong believer in meeting bad news on a full stomach.

I splinted Jamie's finger while Brianna sat down beside him and dabbed gentian ointment onto the abraded knuckles of his other hand. Her face was quite calm; no one would ever guess what was going on behind it.

'You've torn your shirt,' I said, finishing off the last bandage with a small square knot. 'Give it to me after supper and I'll mend it. How's that, then?'

'Verra nice, Madame Lazonga,' he said, gingerly wiggling his freshly splinted finger. 'I shall be getting quite spoilt, wi' so much attention paid me.'

'When I start to chew your food for you, you can worry,' I said tartly.

He laughed, and gave the splinted hand to Bree for anointing.

I went to the cupboard to fetch a plate for him. As I turned back toward the hearth, I saw him watching her intently. She kept her head bent, eyes on the large, callused hand she held between her own. I could imagine her search for words with which to begin, and my heart ached for her. Perhaps I should have told him privately myself, I thought; not let him near her until the first rush of feeling was safely past and he had himself in hand again.

'*Ciamar a tha tu, mo chridhe?*' he said suddenly. It was his customary greeting to her, the beginning of their evening Gaelic lesson, but his voice was different tonight; soft, and very gentle. *How are you, darling?* His hand turned and covered hers, cradling her long fingers.

'*Tha mi gle mhath, athair,*' she replied, looking a bit surprised. *I am well, Father.* Normally he began the lesson after dinner.

Slowly he reached out with his other hand and rested it gently on her stomach.

'*An e 'n fhirinn a th'agad?*' he asked. *Do you tell me true?* I closed my eyes and let out a breath I didn't realized I'd been holding. No need to break *all* the news, after all. And now I knew the reason for his taut-strung strangeness; he knew, and whatever the knowledge cost him to hold, hold it he would, and treat her gently.

She didn't know enough Gaelic yet to tell what he'd asked, but she knew well enough what he meant. She stared at him for a moment, frozen, then lifted his sound hand to her cheek and bent her head over it, the loose hair hiding her face.

'Oh, Da,' she said, very quietly. 'I'm sorry.'

She sat quite still, holding to his hand as though it were a lifeline.

'Ah, now, *m' annsachd,*' he said softly, 'it will be all right.'

'No, it won't,' she said, her voice small but clear. 'It can't ever be right. You know that.'

He glanced at me out of habit, but only briefly. I couldn't tell him what to do, now. He drew a deep breath, took her by the shoulder and gave her a gentle shake.

'All I know,' he said softly, 'is that I'm here by ye, and your mother, too. We willna see ye shamed or hurt. Not ever. D'ye hear me?'

She didn't answer or look up, but kept her eyes on her lap, her face hidden by the rich fall of her hair. A maiden's hair, thick and unbound. His hand traced the shining curve of her head, then his fingers trailed along her jaw and lifted her chin so her eyes looked into his.

'Lizzie's right?' he asked gently. 'It was rape?'

She pulled her chin away and looked down at her knotted hands, the gesture as much an admission as her nod.

'I didn't think she knew. I didn't tell her.'

'She guessed. But it's no your fault, and dinna ever think so,' he said firmly. 'Come here to me, *a leannan*.' He reached for her, and gathered her awkwardly onto his knee.

The oakwood creaked alarmingly under their combined weight, but Jamie had built it after his usual sturdy fashion; it could have held six of him. Tall as Brianna was, she looked almost small cradled in his arms, her head tucked into the curve of his shoulder. He stroked her hair gently, and murmured small things to her, half in Gaelic.

'I'll see ye safe marrit, and your bairn wi' a good father,' he murmured to her. 'I swear it to ye, *a nighean*.'

'I can't marry anybody,' she said, sounding choked. 'It wouldn't be right. I can't take somebody else when I love Roger. And Roger won't want me now. When he finds out –'

'It'll make no difference to him,' Jamie said, grasping her harder, almost fiercely, as though he could make things right by pure force of will. 'If he's a decent man, it'll make no difference. And if it does – well, then he doesna deserve ye, and I shall beat him into pulp and stamp on the pieces, and then go and find ye a better man.'

881

She gave a small laugh that turned into a sob, and buried her head in the cloth of his shoulder. He patted her, rocking and murmuring as though she were a tiny girl with a skinned knee, and his eyes met mine over her head.

I hadn't wept when she had told me; mothers are strong. But now she couldn't see me, and Jamie had taken the burden of strength from my shoulders for the moment.

She hadn't cried when she told me, either. But now she clung to him and wept, as much from relief, I thought, as from grief. He simply held her and let her cry, stroking her hair again and again, his eyes on my face.

I blotted my eyes on my sleeve, and he smiled at me, faintly. Brianna had subsided into long, sighing breaths, and he patted her gently on the back.

'I'm hungry, Sassenach,' he said. 'And I should imagine a wee drop wouldna come amiss for any of us, aye?'

'Right,' I said, and cleared my throat. 'I'll go and fetch some milk from the shed.'

'That's no what I meant by drink!' he called after me in mock outrage.

Ignoring both this and Brianna's choked laugh, I pushed open the door.

The night outside was cold and bright, the autumn stars bright sparks overhead. I wasn't dressed to be outdoors – my face and hands were already beginning to tingle – but I stood quite still nonetheless, letting the cold wind sweep past me, taking with it the tension of the last quarter hour.

Everything was quiet; the crickets and cicadas had long since died or gone underground with the rustling mice, the skunks and possums who left off their endless search for food and went to dream their winter dreams, the rich fat of their efforts wrapped warm about their bones. Only wolves hunted in the cold, starry nights of late autumn, and they went silent, fur-footed on the frozen ground.

'What are we going to do?' I said softly, addressing the question to the overwhelming depths of the vast dark sky overhead.

I heard no sound but the rush of wind in the pine trees; no answer, save the form of my own question – the faint echo of 'we' that rang in my ears. That much was true at least; whatever happened, none of us need face things alone. And I supposed that was after all as much answer as I needed, for now.

They were still on the settle when I came back in, red heads close together, haloed by the fire. The smell of gentian ointment mingled with the pungent scent of burning pine and the mouth-watering aroma of the venison stew – quite suddenly, I was hungry.

I let the door close quietly behind me, and slid to the heavy bolt. I went to poke the fire and lay a new supper, fetching down a fresh loaf of bread from the shelf, then went to get sweet butter from the crock in the pantry. I stayed a moment there, glancing over the loaded shelves.

'Put your trust in God, and pray for guidance. And when in doubt, eat.' A Franciscan monk had once given me that advice, and on the whole, I had found it useful. I picked out a jar of black currant jam, a small round goat cheese, and a bottle of elderflower wine, to go with the meal.

Jamie was talking quietly when I came back. I finished my preparations, letting the deep lilt of his voice soothe me, as well as Brianna.

'I used to think of you, when ye were small,' Jamie was saying to Bree, his voice very soft. 'When I lived in the cave; I would imagine that I held ye in my arms, a wee babe. I would hold ye so, against my heart, and sing to ye there, watching the stars go by overhead.'

'What would you sing?' Brianna's voice was low, too, barely audible above the crackle of the fire. I could see her hand, resting on his shoulder. Her index finger touched a long, bright strand of his hair, tentatively stroking its softness.

'Old songs. Lullabies I could remember, that my mother sang to me, the same that my sister Jenny would sing to her bairns.'

She sighed, a long, slow sound.

'Sing to me now, please, Da.'

He hesitated, but then tilted his head toward hers and began to chant softly, an odd tuneless song in Gaelic. Jamie was tone-deaf; the song wavered oddly up and down, bearing no resemblance to music, but the rhythm of the words was a comfort to the ear.

I caught most of the words; a fisher's song, naming the fish of loch and sea, telling the child what he would bring home to her for food. A hunter's song, naming birds and beasts of prey, feathers for beauty and furs for warmth, meat to last the winter. It was a father's song – a soft litany of providence and protection.

I moved quietly around the room, taking down the pewter plates and wooden bowls for supper, coming back to cut bread and spread it with butter.

'Do you know something, Da?' Bree asked softly.

'What's that?' he said, momentarily suspending his song.

'You can't sing.'

There was a soft exhalation of laughter and the rustle of cloth as he shifted to make them both more comfortable.

'Aye, that's true. Shall I stop, then?'

'No.' She snuggled closer, tucking her head into the curve of his shoulder.

He resumed his tuneless crooning, only to interrupt himself a few moments later.

'D'ye ken something yourself, *a leannan?*'

Her eyes were closed, her lashes casting deep shadows on her cheeks, but I saw her lips curve in a smile.

'What's that, Da?'

'Ye weigh as much as a full-grown deer.'

'Shall I get off, then?' she asked, not moving.

'Of course not.'

She reached up and touched his cheek.

'*Mi gradhaich a thu, athair,*' she whispered. *My love to you, Father.*

He gathered her tightly against him, bent his head and kissed her forehead. The fire struck a knot of pitch and blazed up suddenly behind the settle, limning their faces in gold and black. His features were harsh-cut and bold; hers, a more delicate echo of his heavy, clean-edged bones. Both stubborn, both strong. And both, thank God, mine.

Brianna fell asleep after supper, worn out from emotion. I was feeling rather limp, myself, but not yet in any mood to sleep. I was at once exhausted and jittery, with that horrible battlefield feeling, of being in the midst of events beyond my ability to control, but which must be dealt with anyway.

I didn't want to deal with anything. What I wanted was to push away all thought of both present and future, and go back to the peace of the night before.

I wanted to crawl into bed with Jamie, and lie warm against him, the two of us sealed safe beneath the quilts against the growing chill of the room. Watch the embers fade as we talked softly, colloquy changing from the gossip and small jokes of the day to the language of the night. Let our talk go from words to touch, from breath to the small movements of the body that were in themselves question and answer; the completion of our conversation come at last to silence in the unity of sleep.

But trouble lay on the house tonight, and there was no peace between

He roamed the house like a caged wolf, picking things up and putting them down. I tidied away the things from dinner, watching him from the corners of my eyes. I wanted nothing more than to talk to him – and at the same time, dreaded it. I had promised Bree not to tell him about Bonnet. But I was a bad enough liar at any time – and he knew my face so well.

I filled a bucket of hot water from the big cauldron, and took the pewter plates outside to rinse clean.

I came back to find Jamie standing by the small shelf where he kept his inkhorn, quills and paper. He had not undressed for bed, but he made no move to take them down and begin the usual evening's work. But of course – he couldn't write, with his damaged hand.

'Do you want me to write something for you?' I asked, seeing him pick up a quill and put it down again.

He turned away with a restless gesture.

'No. I must write to Jenny, of course – and there are other things that must be done – but I canna bear to sit down and think just now.'

'I know how you feel,' I said sympathetically. He looked at me, a trifle startled.

'I canna tell quite how I feel myself, Sassenach,' he said, with a queer laugh. 'If ye think ye know, tell me.'

'Tired,' I said, and laid a hand on his arm. 'Angry. Worried.' I glanced at Brianna asleep in the trundle. 'Heartbroken, maybe,' I added softly.

'All of that,' he said. 'And a good bit more.' He wore no stock, but plucked at the collar of his shirt, as though it choked him.

'I canna stay in here,' he said. He glanced at me; I was still dressed in my day clothes; skirt, shift, and bodice. 'Will ye come out and walk wi' me a bit?'

I went at once to fetch my cloak. It was dark outside; he wouldn't be able to watch my face.

We paced slowly together, across the dooryard and past the sheds, down to the penfold and the field beyond. I held his arm, feeling it tense and stiff under my fingers.

I had no notion how to begin, what to say. Perhaps I should simply keep quiet, I thought. Both of us were still upset, though we had done our best to be calm for Brianna.

I could feel the rage boiling just under his skin. Very understandable, but anger is as volatile as kerosene – bottled under pressure, with no target on which to unleash it. An unwary word of mine might be enough to trigger an explosion. And if he exploded at me, I might either cry or go for his throat – my own mood was far from certain.

We walked for quite a long time, through the trees to the dead cornfield, all round the edge and back, moving all the time soft-footed through a minefield of silence.

'Jamie,' I said at last, as we reached the edge of the field, 'what have you been doing with your hands?'

'What?' He swung toward me, startled.

'Your hands.' I caught one of them, held it between my own. 'You didn't do that kind of damage stacking chimney stones.'

'Ah.' He stood still, letting me touch the swollen knuckles of his hand.

'Brianna,' he said. 'She – she didna tell ye anything about the man? Did she tell ye his name?'

I hesitated – and was lost. He knew me very well.

'She did tell ye, no?' His voice was thick with danger.

'She made me promise not to tell you,' I blurted. 'I told

886

her you'd know I was keeping something from you; but Jamie, I did promise – don't make me tell you, please!'

He snorted again, in half-amused disgust.

'Aye, I ken ye well, Sassenach; ye couldna keep a secret from anyone who knows ye in the slightest. Even wee Ian can read ye like a book.'

He flapped a hand in dismissal.

'Dinna trouble your conscience. Let her tell me herself, when she will. I can wait.' His bruised hand curled slowly against his kilt, and a small shiver ran up my back.

'Your hands,' I said again.

He took a deep breath and held them out before him, backs up. He flexed them, slowly.

'D'ye recall, Sassenach, once when we were first acquent? Dougal deviled me to where I thought I must pound him, and yet I couldna do it, then. You told me, "Hit something, you'll feel better." ' He gave me a wry, lopsided smile. 'And I hit a tree. It hurt, but you were right, no? I did feel better, at least for a bit.'

'Oh.' I let out my breath, relieved that he didn't mean to press the matter. Let him wait, then; I doubted that he quite realized yet that his daughter could be as stubborn as he was himself.

'Did she – did she tell ye what happened?' I couldn't see his face, but the hesitation in his speech was noticeable. 'I mean –' He drew in his breath with a deep hiss. 'Did the man hurt her?'

'No, not physically.'

I hesitated myself, imagining that I could feel the weight of the ring in my pocket, though of course I couldn't. Brianna had not asked me to keep anything to myself, other than Bonnet's name, but I would not tell Jamie any of the details she had told me, unless he asked. And I did not think he would ask; it was the last thing he would want to know.

He didn't ask; only muttered something under his breath in Gaelic and walked on, head bent.

The silence once broken, I found that I could not bear it any longer. Better to explode than suffocate. I took my hand from his arm.

'What are you thinking?'

'I am wondering – if it is as terrible to be – to be violated . . . if it is – is not . . . if there is not . . . damage.' He shifted his shoulders restlessly, half shrugging as though his coat were too tight.

I knew very well what was in his mind. Wentworth prison, and the faint scars that webbed his back, a net of dreadful memory.

'Bad enough, I suppose,' I said. 'Though I expect you're right, it would be easier to stand if there were no physical reminder of it. But then, there *is* a physical reminder of it,' I felt obliged to add. 'And a bloody noticeable one, come to that!' His left hand curled at his side, clenching involuntarily.

'Aye, that's so,' he muttered. He glanced uncertainly at me, the halfmoon's light gilding the planes of his face. 'But still – he didna hurt her, that's something. If he had . . . killing would be too good for him,' he finished abruptly.

'There is the very minor detail that you don't precisely "recover" from pregnancy,' I said with a marked edge to my voice. 'If he'd broken her bones or shed her blood, she'd heal. As it is – she isn't ever going to forget it, you know.'

'I know!'

I flinched slightly, and he saw it. He made a sketchy gesture of apology.

'I didna mean to shout.'

I gave him back a brief nod of acknowledgment, and we walked on, side by side, but not touching.

'It –' he began, and then broke off, glancing at me. He grimaced, impatient with himself.

'I do know,' he said, more quietly. 'Ye'll forgive me, Sassenach, but I ken the hell of a lot more about the matter than you do.'

'I wasn't arguing with you. But you haven't borne a child; you can't know what that's like. It's –'

'You *are* arguing wi' me, Sassenach. Don't.' He squeezed my arm, hard, and let it go. There was a touch of humor in his voice, but he was dead serious overall.

'I am trying to tell ye what *I* know.' He stood still for a minute, gathering himself.

'I havena put myself in mind of Jack Randall for some good time,' he said at last. 'I dinna want to do it now. But there it is.' He shrugged again, and rubbed a hand hard down one cheek.

'There is body, and there is soul, Sassenach,' he said, speaking slowly, ordering his ideas with his words. 'You're a physician; ye'll ken the one well. But the other is more important.'

I opened my mouth to say that I knew that as well as he did, if not better – but then shut it without saying anything. He didn't notice; he wasn't seeing the dark cornfield, or the maple wood with its leaves gone silver with moonlight. His eyes were fixed on a small room with thick stone walls, furnished with a table and stools and a lamp. And a bed.

'Randall,' he said, and his voice was meditative. 'The most of what he did to me – I could have stood it.' He spread out the fingers of his right hand; the dressing on the cracked finger shone white.

'I would have been afraid, been hurt; I would have meant to kill him for doing it. But I could have lived, after, and not felt his touch always on my skin, felt filthy in myself – were it not that he wasna satisfied with my body. He wanted my soul – and he had it.' The white bandage vanished as his fist folded.

'Aye, well – ye ken all that.' He turned away abruptly and began to walk. I had to scurry to catch him up.

'What I am saying, I suppose, is – was this man a stranger to her, who only took her for a moment's pleasure? If it was only her body that he wanted . . . then I think she will heal.'

He took a deep breath and let it out again; I saw the faint white mist surround his head for a moment, the steam of his anger made visible.

'But if he knew her – was close enough to want *her*, and not just any woman – then perhaps it might be that he could touch her soul, and do real damage –'

'You don't think he did real damage?' My voice rose, despite myself. 'Whether he knew her or not –'

'It is different, I tell ye!'

'No, it's not. I know what you mean –'

'You don't!'

'I do! But why –'

'Because it is not your body that matters when I take you,' he said. 'And ye ken that well enough, Sassenach!'

He turned and kissed me fiercely, taking me completely by surprise. He crushed my lips against my teeth, then took my whole mouth with his, half biting, demanding.

I knew what he wanted of me; the same thing I wanted so desperately of him – reassurance. But neither of us had it to give, tonight.

His fingers dug into my shoulders, slid upward and grasped my neck. The hairs rose up on my arms as he pressed me to him – and then he stopped.

'I can't,' he said. He squeezed my neck hard, and then let go. His breath came raggedly. 'I can't.'

He stepped back and turned away from me, groping for the fence rail before him as though blind. He grasped the wood hard with both hands, and stood there, eyes closed.

I was shaking, my legs gone watery. I wrapped my arms around myself under my cloak and sat down at his feet. And waited, my heart beating painfully loud in my ears. The night wind moved through the trees on the ridge, murmuring through the pines. Somewhere, far away in the dark hills, a panther screamed, sounding like a woman.

'It's not that I dinna want ye,' he said at last, and I caught the faint rustle of his coat as he turned toward me. He stood for a moment, head bowed, his bound hair gleaming in the moonlight, face hidden by the darkness, with the moon behind him. At last he leaned down and took my hand in his bruised one, lifting me to my feet.

'I want ye maybe more than I ever have,' he said quietly. 'And Christ! I do need ye, Claire. But I canna bear even to think of myself as a man just now. I cannot touch you, and think of what he – I can't.'

I touched his arm.

'I do understand,' I said, and did. I was glad that he hadn't asked for the details; I wished I didn't know them. How would it be, to make love with him, envisioning all the time an act identical in its motions, but utterly different in its essence?

'I understand, Jamie,' I said again.

He opened his eyes and looked at me.

'Aye, ye do, don't you? And that's what I mean.' He took my arm and drew me close to him.

'You could tear me limb from limb, Claire, without touching me,' he whispered, 'for ye know me.' His fingers touched the side of my face. They were cold, and stiff. 'And I could do the same to you.'

'You could,' I said, feeling a little faint. 'But I really wish you wouldn't.'

He smiled a little at that, bent and kissed me, very gently. We stood together, barely touching save our lips, breathing each other's breath.

Yes, we said silently to each other. *Yes, I am still here.* It was not rescue, but at least a tiny lifeline, stretched across the gulf that lay between us. I did know what he meant, about the difference between damage to body or soul; what I couldn't explain to him was the link between the two that centered in the womb. At last I stepped back, looking up at him.

'Bree's a very strong person,' I said quietly. 'Like you.'

'Like me?' He gave a small snort. 'God help her, then.'

He sighed, then turned and began to walk slowly along the line of the fence. I followed, hurrying a little to catch up.

'This man, this Roger she speaks of. Will he stand by her?' he asked abruptly.

I took a deep breath and let it out slowly, not knowing how to answer. I'd known Roger only a few months. I liked him; was very fond of him, in fact. From everything I knew of him, he was a thoroughly decent, honorable young man – but how could I even pretend to know what he might think, do, or feel, upon finding that Brianna had been raped? Even worse, that she might well carry the rapist's child?

The best of men might not be able to deal with such a situation; in my years as a doctor, I had seen even well-established marriages shatter under the strain of smaller things. And those that did not shatter, but were crippled by mistrust . . . involuntarily, I pressed a hand against my

891

leg, feeling the tiny hardness of the gold circle in my pocket. *From F. to C. with love. Always.*

'Would you do it?' I said at last. 'If it were me?'

He glanced at me sharply, and opened his mouth as though to speak. Then he closed it and looked at me, searching my face, his brows knotted with· troubled thought.

'I meant to say, "Aye, of course!" ' he said slowly, at last. 'But I did promise ye honesty once, did I not?'

'You did,' I said, and felt my heart sink beneath its guilty burden. How could I force him to honesty when I couldn't give it him back? And yet he had asked.

He struck the fencepost a light blow with his fist.

'*Ifrinn!* Yes, damn it – I would. You would be mine, even if the child was not. And if you – yes. I would,' he repeated firmly. 'I should take you, and the child with ye, and damn the whole world!'

'And never think about it afterward?' I asked. 'Never let it come into your mind when you came to my bed? Never see the father when you looked at the child? Never throw it back at me or let it make a difference between us?'

He opened his mouth to reply, but closed it without speaking. Then I saw a change come over his features, a sudden shock of sick realization.

'Oh, Christ,' he said. 'Frank. Not me. It's Frank ye mean.'

I nodded, and he gripped my shoulders.

'What did he do to ye?' he demanded. 'What? Tell me, Claire!'

'He stood by me,' I said, sounding choked even to my own ears. 'I tried make him go, but he wouldn't. And when the baby – when Brianna came – he loved her, Jamie. He wasn't sure, he didn't think he could – neither did I – but he truly did. I'm sorry,' I added.

He took a deep breath and let go of my shoulders.

'Dinna be sorry for that, Sassenach,' he said gruffly. 'Never.' He rubbed a hand across his face, and I could hear the faint rasp of his evening stubble.

'And what about you, Sassenach?' he said. 'What ye said – when he came to your bed. Did he think –' He broke off abruptly, leaving all the questions hanging in the air between us, unstated, but asked nonetheless.

'It might have been me – my fault, I mean,' I said at last, into the silence. 'I couldn't forget, you see. If I could . . . it might have been different.' I should have stopped there, but I couldn't; the words that had been dammed up all evening rushed out in a flood.

'It might have been easier – better – for him if it *had* been rape. That's what they told him, you know – the doctors; that I had been raped and abused, and was having delusions. That's what everyone believed, but I kept saying to him, no it wasn't that way, I insisted on telling him the truth. And after a time – he believed me, at least halfway. And that was the trouble; not that I'd had another man's child – but that I'd loved you. And I wouldn't stop. I couldn't,' I added, in a softer tone. 'He was better than me, Frank was. He could put the past away, at least for Bree's sake. But for me –' The words caught in my throat and I stopped.

He turned then, and looked at me for a long time, his face quite expressionless, eyes hidden by the shadows of his brows.

'And so ye lived twenty years with a man who couldna forgive ye for what was never your fault? I did that to ye, no?' he said. 'I am sorry, too, Sassenach.'

A small breath escaped me, not quite a sob.

'You said you could tear me limb from limb without touching me,' I said. 'You were right, damn you.'

'I am sorry,' he whispered again, but this time he reached for me, and held me tight against him.

'That I loved you? Don't be sorry for that,' I said, my voice half muffled in his shirt. 'Not ever.'

He didn't answer, but bent his head and pressed his cheek against my hair. It was quiet; I could hear his heart beating, over and under the wind in the trees. My skin was cold; the tears on my cheeks chilled instantly.

At last I let my arms drop from around him and stepped back.

'We'd better go back to the house,' I said, trying for a normal tone. 'It's getting awfully late.'

'Aye, I suppose so.' He offered me his arm, and I took

it. We passed in an easier silence down the path to the edge of the gorge above the stream. It was cold enough that tiny ice crystals glinted among the rocks where the starlight struck them, but the creek was far from frozen. Its gurgle and rush filled the air, and kept us from being too quiet.

'Aye, well,' he said, as we turned up the path past the pigsty. 'I hope Roger Wakefield is a better man than the two of us – Frank and I.' He glanced at me. 'Mind ye, if he's not, I shall beat him to a pudding.'

Despite myself I laughed.

'That will be a *great* help to the situation, I'm sure.'

He snorted briefly and walked on. At the bottom of the hill, we turned without speaking, and came back in the direction of the house. Just short of the path that led to the door, I stopped him.

'Jamie,' I said hesitantly. 'Do you believe I love you?'

He turned his head and looked down at me for a long moment before replying. The moon shone on his face, picking out his features as though they had been chiseled in marble.

'Well, if ye don't, Sassenach,' he said at last, 'ye've picked a verra poor time to tell me so.'

I let out my breath in the ghost of a laugh.

'No, it's not that,' I assured him. 'But –' My throat tightened, and I swallowed hastily, needing to get the words out.

'I – I don't say it often. Perhaps it's only that I wasn't raised to say such things; I lived with my uncle, and he was affectionate, but not – well, I didn't know how married people –'

He put his hand lightly over my mouth, a faint smile touching his lips. After a moment, he took it away.

I took a deep breath, steadying my voice.

'Look, what I mean to say is – if I don't say it, how do you *know* I love you?'

He stood still, looking at me, then nodded in acknowledgment.

'I know because ye're here, Sassenach,' he said quietly. 'And that's what ye mean, aye? That he came after her – this Roger. And so perhaps he will love her enough?'

'It's not a thing you'd do, just for friendship's sake.'

He nodded again, but I hesitated, wanting to tell him more, to impress him with the significance of it.

'I haven't told you a great deal about it, because – there aren't words for it. But one thing about it I could tell you. Jamie –' I shivered involuntarily, and not from the cold. 'Not everyone who goes through the stones comes out again.'

His look sharpened.

'How d'ye ken that, Sassenach?'

'I can – I could – hear them. Screaming.'

I was shaking outright by this time, from a mixture of cold and memory, and he caught my hands between his own and drew me close. The autumn wind rattled the branches of the willows by the stream, a sound like dry, bare bones. He held me until the shivering stopped, then let me go.

'It's cold, Sassenach. Come inside.' He turned toward the house, but I laid my hand on his shoulder to stop him again.

'Jamie?'

'Aye?'

'Should I – would you – do you need me to say it?'

He turned around and looked down at me. With the light behind him, he was haloed in moonlight, but his features were once more dark.

'I dinna need it, no.' His voice was soft. 'But I wouldna mind if ye wanted to say it. Now and again. Not too often, mind; I wouldna want to lose the novelty of it.' I could hear the smile in his voice, and couldn't help smiling in return, whether he could see it or not.

'Once in a while wouldn't hurt, though?'

'No.'

I stepped close to him and put my hands on his shoulders.

'I love you.'

He looked down at me for a long moment.

'I'm glad of it, Claire,' he said quietly, and touched my face. 'Verra glad. Come to bed now; I'll warm ye.'

48

Away in a Manger

The tiny stable was in a shallow cave under a rocky over-hang, walled in along the front with a stockade of unpeeled cedar logs, sunk two feet deep in packed earth, stout enough to deter the most resolute bear. Light spilled out through the open upper half of the stable door, and ruddy, light-filled smoke shimmered up the face of the cliff above, rippling like bright water over the stone.

'Why a double door?' she had asked. It seemed excessive labor; an unnecessary refinement for such a crude structure.

'Ye must give the beasts a place to look out,' her father had explained, showing her where to smooth the leather strap hinges tight around the curve of the wood. He picked up the hammer to tack down the leather and smiled at her, kneeling over the half-made gate. 'Keeps them happy, aye?'

She didn't know if the animals were happy in the stable, but *she* was; cool and shadowy, smelling pungently of cut straw and the droppings of grass-fed animals, it was a peaceful refuge during the day, when its inhabitants were out grazing in the meadow. In bad weather or at night, the little stockade was a pocket of coziness; once she had passed near enough after dark to see the soft, misty exhalations of the animals drifting through the gap between wood and rock, as though the earth itself were breathing through pursed lips, warmly asleep in the autumn cold.

It was cold tonight, the stars sharp as needle points in the hard, clear air. It was only five minutes' walk from the house, but Brianna was shivering under her cloak by the time she reached the stable. The light spilling out came not only from a hanging lantern, she saw, but also from a small makeshift brazier in the corner, providing head and light for the vigil within.

Her father lay curled up on a bed of straw, his plaid drawn over him, within arm's reach of the small brindled cow. The heifer lay on her chest, feet tucked to the side, grunting now and then, a look of mild concentration on her broad white face.

His head lifted abruptly at the sound of her step on the gravel, and his hand went by reflex to his belt, under his plaid.

'It's me,' she said, and saw him relax as she came into the light. He swung his feet to the side and sat up, rubbing a hand over his face as she came in, carefully latching the lower gate behind her.

'Your mother's not back yet?' She was clearly alone, but he glanced briefly over her shoulder as though hoping to see Claire materialize out of the darkness.

Brianna shook her head. Claire had gone with Lizzie as escort to attend a birth at one of the farms at the far side of the cove; if the child hadn't arrived before sunset, they would stay the night at the Lachlans'.

'No. She said if she wasn't back, I was to bring you up some supper, though.' She knelt and began to unpack the small basket she had brought, laying out small loaves of bread stuffed with cheese and tomato-pickle, a dried-apple tart, and two stone bottles – one of hot vegetable broth, the other of cider.

'That's kind, lassie.' He smiled at her and picked up one of the bottles. 'Will ye have eaten yet, yourself?'

'Oh, yes,' she assured him. 'Plenty.' She *had* eaten, but couldn't resist a quick look of longing at the fresh rolls; the early faint sense of malaise had left her, replaced by an appetite mildly alarming in its intensity.

He saw her glance, and with a smile, drew his dirk and sliced one of the rolls in half, handing her the bigger piece.

They munched companionably for a few moments, sitting side by side on the straw, the silence broken only by soft snuffles and grunts from the stable's other inhabitants. The far end of the stable was fenced off to provide a pen for the gigantic sow and her new brood of piglets; Brianna could just make them out in the gloom – a row of plump bodies packed in the straw, prophetically sausage-shaped.

The rest of the small space was divided into three rough

stalls. One belonged to the red cow, Magdalen, who lay in the straw peacefully chewing her cud, her month-old calf curled in sleep against her massive chest. The second stall was empty, filled with fresh straw, ready for the brindled cow and her tardy calf. The third stall held Ian's mare, sides glossy and bulging with the weight of an impending foal.

'It looks like a maternity ward in here,' Brianna said, nodding toward Magdalen as she brushed crumbs off her skirt. Jamie smiled and raised a brow, as he always did when she said something he didn't understand.

'Oh, aye?'

'That's a special part of a hospital, where they put the new mothers and their babies,' she explained. 'Mama would take me to work with her sometimes, and let me go look at the nursery while she did her rounds.'

She had a sudden memory of the smell of the hospital corridor, faintly acrid with the scent of disinfectant and floor polish, the babies lying bundled, plump as piglets in their bassinets, their blankets coded pink and blue. She always spent a long time going up and down the row, trying to pick which one she would take home with her, if she could keep one.

Pink or blue? For the first time, she wondered what the one she *would* now keep might wear. The thought of 'it' as male or female was strangely upsetting, and she pushed the thought away with words.

'They put the babies all behind a glass wall, so you could look at them, but not breathe germs on them,' she said, with a glance at Magdalen, contentedly oblivious to the strings of green saliva that dripped from her placidly moving jaws onto the head of her calf.

'Germs,' he said thoughtfully. 'Aye, I've heard about the germs. Dangerous wee beasties, are they not?'

'They can be.' She had a vivid memory of her mother checking her box of medical supplies for the visit to Lachlans', carefully refilling the large glass bottle of distilled alcohol from the barrel in the pantry. And a more distant but equally vivid memory, of her mother explaining the past to Roger Wakefield.

'Childbirth was the most dangerous thing a woman

could do,' Claire had said, frowning in memory of the sights she had seen. 'Infection, ruptured placenta, abnormal presentation, miscarriage, hemorrhage, puerperal fever – in most places, surviving birth was roughly a fifty-fifty proposition.'

Brianna's fingers felt cold, in spite of the hissing pine chunks in the brazier, and her ravenous appetite seemed suddenly to have deserted her. She set the rest of her roll down on the straw, swallowing hard, feeling as though a bite of the thick bread had wedged itself in her throat.

Her father's broad hand touched her knee, warm even through the wool of her skirt.

'Your mother willna let ye come to harm,' he said gruffly. 'She's fought the germs before; I've seen her. She didna let them have the better of me, and she willna let them trouble you, either. She's a verra stubborn person, aye?'

She laughed, and the choking feeling eased.

'She'd say it takes one to know one.'

'I expect she's right about that.' He rose and walked around the brindled heifer, squatting down and squinting at her tail. He stood up, shaking his head, and came to sit down again. He settled comfortably back and picked up the discarded part of Brianna's roll.

'Is she doing all right?' Brianna bent and scooped up a twist of straw, holding it invitingly under the heifer's nose. The cow breathed heavily on her knuckles, but otherwise ignored the attention, the long-lashed brown eyes rolling restlessly to and fro. Now and then the bulging brindled sides rippled, the cow's thick winter coat rough but shining in the light of the hanging lantern.

Jamie frowned slightly.

'Aye, I think she'll maybe do all right. It's her first calf, though, and she's small for it. She's no much more than a yearling herself; she shouldna have been bred so early, but . . .' He shrugged, and took another bite of roll.

Brianna wiped the sticky moisture from her hand with a fold of her skirt. Feeling suddenly restless, she stood up and walked over to the pigpen.

The vast curve of the sow's belly rose up out of the hay like a swollen balloon, pink flesh visible beneath the soft, sparse white hair. The sow lay in stuporous dignity, breathing slow and deep, ignoring the squirms and squeaks of the hungry brood that scrabbled at her underside. One piglet was nudged too roughly by a fellow and momentarily lost his hold; there was a high-pitched shriek of protest, and a jet of milk spurted from the suddenly released nipple, hissing softly into the hay.

Brianna felt a slight tingle in her own breasts; they seemed suddenly heavier than usual, resting on her folded forearms as she leaned on the fence.

It wasn't a particularly aesthetic picture of motherhood – not exactly Madonna and Child – but there was something vaguely reassuring about the sow's nonchalant maternal torpor, nonetheless – a sort of careless confidence, a blind trust in natural processes.

Jamie had another look at the brindled cow, and came to stand beside Brianna by the pigpen.

'That's a good wee lass,' he said approvingly, with a nod at the sow. As though in reply, the sow released a long, rumbling fart, and shifted a bit, stretching out in the straw with a voluptuous sigh.

'Well, she does look as though she knows what she's doing,' Brianna agreed, biting her lip.

'That she does. She's a wicked temper, but she's an able mother, forbye. This will be her fourth litter, and not one lost or a runt weaned yet.' He nodded approvingly at the sow, then glanced at the brindled heifer. 'I could hope that one does half so well.'

She took a deep breath.

'What if she doesn't?'

He didn't answer at once, but stood leaning on the fence, looking down at the gently squirming litter. Then his shoulders rose slightly.

'If she canna bring forth the calf alone, and I canna pull it for her, then I shall have to slaughter her,' he said, matter-of-factly. 'If I can save the calf, I can maybe foster it on Magdalen.'

Her insides clenched tight, making lumps and knots of the food she'd eaten. She'd seen the dirk at his belt, of course, but it was so much a part of his normal costume, she hadn't thought to question its presence in this pastoral setting. The small round presence in her belly lay still and heavy, like a time bomb waiting.

He crouched beside the brindled heifer, and ran a light hand over the bulging flank. Evidently satisfied for the moment, he scratched the cow between the ears, muttering in Gaelic.

How could he murmur endearments to it, she thought, knowing that within hours he might be slicing into its living flesh? It seemed cold-blooded; did a butcher whisper 'Sweet lass' to his victims? A small icy doubt dropped into her stomach, to join the other cold weights that lay there, like a collection of ball bearings.

He stood up and stretched himself, groaning as his spine crackled. He shifted his shoulders, settled, blinked, and smiled at her.

'Will I walk ye to the house, lassie? It will be some time before aught happens here.'

She looked up at him, hesitating, but then made up her mind.

'No, I'll wait with you a little while. If you don't mind?'

Now, she decided on impulse. She would ask now. She had been waiting for days for the right time, but when could a time possibly *be* right for something like this? At least they would be alone now, with no chance of disturbance.

'As ye like. I shall be glad of the company.'

Not for long, she thought, as he turned away to rummage in the basket she had brought. She would much have preferred darkness. It would have been a lot easier to ask what she needed to know, on the dark trail to the house. But words wouldn't be enough; she had to see his face.

Her mouth was dry; she accepted gratefully when he offered her a cup of cider. It was strong and rich, and the slight buzz of alcohol seemed to lighten the weight in her belly a little.

She gave him the cup but didn't wait for him to drink, afraid the momentary heartening effect of the cider would desert her before she could get the words out.

'Da –'

'Aye, lass?' He was pouring more cider, his eyes fixed on the cloudy golden stream.

901

'I need to ask you something.'

'Mm?'

She took a deep breath and got it out in a rush.

'Did you kill Jack Randall?'

He froze for a moment, the jug still tilted over the cup. Then he turned the jug carefully upright, and set it down on the floor.

'And where will ye have heard that name?' he asked. He looked at her straight on, his voice as level as his eyes. 'From your father, maybe? From Frank Randall?'

'Mother told me about him.'

A muscle twitched near the corner of his mouth, the only outward indication of shock.

'Did she.'

It wasn't a question, but she answered it anyway.

'She told me what – what happened. What he d-did to you. At Wentworth.'

Her small spurt of courage was exhausted, but it didn't matter; she was in too deep to go back now. He simply sat and looked at her, the gourd cup forgotten in his hand. She longed to take it and drain it herself, but didn't dare.

It occurred to her, much too late, that he might think it a betrayal that Claire had told anyone, let alone her. She rushed ahead, babbling in her nervousness.

'It wasn't now; it was before – I didn't know you – she thought I'd never meet you. I mean – I don't think – I know she didn't mean to –' He raised one eyebrow at her.

'Be still, aye?'

She was only too glad to stop talking. She couldn't look at him, but sat staring down at her lap, her fingers pleating the russet cloth of her skirt. The silence lengthened, broken only by the shiftings and muffled squeals of the piglets, and an occasional digestive rumbling from Magdalen.

Why hadn't she found some other way? she wondered, in an agony of embarrassment. *Thou shalt not uncover they father's nakedness.* To invoke Jack Randall's name was to invoke the images of what he had done – and that was not something she could bear even to think about. She should have asked her mother, let Claire ask him . . . but no.

There hadn't been any choice, not really. She had to find out from him . . .

Her racing thoughts were interrupted by his words, calmly spoken.

'Why are ye asking, lass?'

She jerked her head up, to find him watching her over his undrunk cider. He didn't look upset, and the jelly in her backbone stiffened a little. She clenched her fists on her knees to steady herself, and met his eyes, straight on.

'I need to know whether it will help. I want to kill . . . him. The man who –' She made a vague gesture at her belly, and swallowed hard. 'But if I do, and it doesn't help –' She couldn't go on.

He didn't seem shocked; abstracted, rather. He raised the cup to his mouth and took a sip, slowly.

'Mmphm. And will ye have killed a man before?' He phrased it as a question, but she knew it wasn't. The muscle quivered near his mouth again – with amusement, she thought, not shock – and she felt a quick spurt of anger.

'You think I can't, don't you? I can. You'd better believe me, I can!'

Her hands spread out, gripping her knees, broad and capable. She thought she could do it; though her image of how it might happen wavered. In cold blood, shooting seemed the best, perhaps the only certain way. But trying to imagine this, she had realized vividly the truth of the old saying 'Shooting's too good for him.'

It might be too good for Bonnet; it wouldn't be nearly good enough for *her*. In the night when she flung off her blankets, unable to bear even this slight weight and its reminder of restraint, she didn't just want him dead – she wanted to *kill* him, purely and passionately – kill him with her hands, taking back by the flesh what had been taken from her by that means.

And yet . . . what good would it be to murder him, if he would still haunt her? There was no way to know – unless her father could tell her.

'Will you tell me?' she blurted. 'Did you kill him, finally – and did it help?'

903

He seemed to be thinking it over, his eyes traveling slowly over her, narrowed in assessment.

'And what would be helped by your doing murder?' he asked. 'It willna take the child from your belly – or give ye back your maidenheid.'

'I know that!' She felt her face flush hot, and turned away, irritated both with him and herself. They spoke of rape and murder, and she was embarrassed to have him mention her lost virginity? She forced herself to look back at him.

'Mama said you tried to kill Jack Randall in Paris, in a duel. What did *you* think you'd get back?'

He rubbed his chin hard, then drew in his breath through his nose and let it out slowly, eyes fixed on the stained rock of the ceiling.

'I meant to take back my manhood,' he said softly. 'My honor.'

'You think my honor isn't worth taking back? Or do you figure it's the same thing as my *maidenheid?*' She mocked his accent nastily.

Sharp blue eyes swung back to hers.

'Is it the same thing to *you?*'

'No, it is not,' she said, through clenched teeth.

'Good,' he said, shortly.

'Then answer me, damn it!' She struck a fist on the straw, finding no satisfaction in the soundless blow. 'Did killing him give you back your honor? Did it help? Tell me the truth!'

She stopped, breathing heavily. She glared at him, and he met her eyes with a cold stare. Then he raised the cup abruptly to his mouth, swallowed the cider in one gulp, and set the cup down on the hay beside him.

'The truth? The truth is that I dinna ken whether I killed him or no.'

Her mouth dropped open in surprise.

'You don't *know* whether you killed him?'

'I said so.' A slight jerk of the shoulders betrayed his impatience. He stood up abruptly, as if unable to sit any longer.

'He died at Culloden, and I was there. I woke on the moor after the battle, with Randall's corpse on top of me.

904

I ken that much – and not much more.' He paused as though thinking, then, mind made up, he thrust one knee forward, pulled up his kilt and nodded downward. 'Look.'

It was an old scar, but no less impressive for its age. It ran up the inner side of his thigh, nearly a foot in length, its lower end starred and knotted like the head of a mace, the rest of it a cleaner line, though thick and twisted.

'A bayonet, I expect,' he said, looking at it dispassionately. He dropped the kilt, hiding the scar once more.

'I remember the feel of the blade strikin' bone, and no more. Not what came after – or before.'

He took a deep, audible breath, and for the first time she realized that his apparent calmness was taking a good deal of effort to maintain.

'I thought it a blessing – that I couldna remember,' he said at last. He wasn't looking at her, but into the shadows at the end of the stable. 'There were gallant men who died there; men I loved well. If I didna know their deaths; if I couldna recall them or see them in my mind – then I didna have to think of them as dead. Maybe that was cowardice, maybe not. Perhaps I chose not to remember that day; perhaps I cannot if I would.' He looked down at her, his eyes gone softer, but then turned away, plaid swinging, not waiting for an answer.

'Afterward – aye, well. Vengeance didna seem important, then. There were a thousand dead men on that field, and I thought I should be one of them in hours. Jack Randall . . .' He made an odd, impatient gesture, brushing aside the thought of Jack Randall as he might a biting deerfly. 'He *was* one of them. I thought I could leave him to God. Then.'

She took a deep breath, trying to keep her feelings under control. Curiosity and sympathy struggled with an overwhelming feeling of frustration.

'You're . . . all right, though. I mean – in spite of what he – did to you?'

He gave her a look of exasperation, understanding mingled with half-angry amusement.

'Not many die of it, lass. Not me. And not you.'

'Not *yet.*' Involuntarily, she put a hand over her belly.

905

She stared up at him. 'I guess we'll see in six months if I die of it.'

That rattled him; she could see it. He blew out his breath and scowled at her.

'Ye'll do fine,' he said curtly. 'Ye're wider through the hip than yon wee heifer.'

'Like your mother? Everybody says how much I'm like her. I guess she was wide through the hip, too, but it didn't save *her*, did it?'

He flinched. Quick and sharp as though she'd slapped him across the face with a stinging nettle. Perversely, seeing it filled her with panic, rather than the satisfaction she'd expected.

She understood then that his promise of protection was in good part illusion. He would kill for her, yes. Or willingly die himself, she had no doubt. He would – if she let him – avenge her honor, destroy her enemies. But he could not defend her from her own child; he was as powerless to save her from that threat as if she had never found him.

'I'll die,' she said, cold certainty filling her belly like frozen mercury. 'I know I will.'

'Ye won't!' He rounded on her fiercely, and she felt his hands bite into her upper arms. 'I will not let you!'

She would have given anything to believe him. Her lips were numb and stiff, rage giving way to a cold despair.

'You can't help,' she said. 'You can't do anything!'

'Your mother can,' he said, but sounded only half convinced. His grip slackened, and she wrenched herself free.

'No, she can't – not without a hospital, without drugs and things. If it – if it goes wrong, all she can do is try to save the b-baby.' Despite herself, her gaze flickered to his dirk, blade gleaming cold against the straw where he had left it.

Her knees felt watery, and she sat down suddenly. He snatched up the jug and slopped cider into a cup, pushing it under her nose.

'Drink it,' he said. 'Drink up, lass, you're pale as my sark.' His hand was on the back of her head, urging her. She took a sip, but choked and drew back, waving him off. She drew a sleeve across her wet chin, wiping off the spilled cider.

'You know what's the worst? You said it wasn't my fault, but it is.'

'It is not!'

She flapped a hand at him, bidding him be quiet.

'You talked about cowardice; you know what it is. Well, I was a coward. I should have fought, I shouldn't have let him . . . but I was scared of him. If I'd been brave enough, this wouldn't have happened, but I wasn't, I was scared! And now I'm even more scared,' she said, voice breaking. She took a deep breath to steady herself, bracing her hands on the straw.

'You can't help, and neither can Mama, and I can't do anything either. And Roger –' Her voice did crack then, and she bit her lip hard, forcing back tears.

'Brianna – a *leannan* . . .' He made a move to comfort her, but she drew back, arms folded tight across her stomach.

'I keep thinking – if I kill him, that's something I can do. It's the *only* thing I can do. If I – if I have to die, at least I'll take him with me, and if I don't – then maybe I can forget, if he's dead.'

'Ye willna forget.' The words were blunt and uncompromising as a blow to the stomach. He was still holding the cup of cider. Now he tilted back his head and drank, quite deliberately.

'It doesna matter, though,' he said, setting down the cup with an air of businesslike finality. 'We shall find you a husband, and once the babe's born, ye willna have much time to fret.'

'What?' She gaped at him. 'What do you mean, find me a husband?'

'You'll need one, aye?' he said, in tones of mild surprise. 'The bairn must have a father. And if ye willna tell me the name of the man who's given ye a swollen belly, so that I might make him do his duty by ye –'

'You think I'd *marry* the man who did this?' Her voice cracked again, this time with astonishment.

His voice sharpened slightly.

'Well, I'm thinkin' – are ye maybe playin' wi' the truth a

907

bit, lass? Perhaps it wasna rape at all; perhaps it was that ye took a mislike to the man, and ran – and made up the story later. Ye were not marked, after all. Hard to think a man could force a lass of your size, if ye were unwilling altogether.'

'You think I'm *lying*?'

He raised one brow in cynicism. Furious, she swung a hand at him, but he caught her by the wrist.

'Ah, now,' he said, reprovingly. 'Ye're no the first lass to make a slip and try to hide it, but –' He caught the other wrist as she struck at him, and pulled them both up sharply.

'Ye dinna need to make such a fuss,' he said. 'Or is it that ye wanted the man and he threw ye over? Is that it?'

She swiveled in his grip, used her weight to swing aside, brought her knee up hard. He turned only slightly, and her knee collided with his thigh, not the vulnerable flesh between his legs she had been aiming for.

The blow must have bruised him, but didn't lessen his grip on her wrists in the least. She twisted, kicking, cursing her skirts. She hit his shin dead-on at least twice, but he only chuckled, as though finding her struggles funny.

'Is that all ye can do, lassie?' He broke his grip then, but only to shift both her wrists to one hand. The other prodded her playfully in the ribs.

> *'There was a man*
> *In Muir of Skene,*
> *He had dirks*
> *And I had none;*
> *But I fell on him*
> *With my thumbs,*
> *And wot you how,*
> *I dirkit him,*
> *Dirkit him,*
> *Dirkit him?'*

With each repetition, he dug a thumb hard between her ribs.

'You fucking *bastard*!' she screamed. She braced her feet and yanked down on his arm as hard as she could, bringing it into biting range. She lunged at his wrist, but before she could sink her teeth in his flesh, she found herself jerked off her feet and whirled through the air.

She ended hard on her knees, one arm twisted up behind her back so tightly that her shoulder joint cracked. The strain on her elbow hurt; she writhed, trying to turn into the hold, but couldn't budge. An arm like an iron bar clamped across her shoulders, forcing her head down. And farther down.

Her chin drove into her chest; she couldn't breathe. And still he forced her head down. Her knees slid apart, her thighs forced wide by the downward pressure.

'Stop!' she grunted. It hurt to force sound through her constricted windpipe. 'Gd's sk, stp!'

The relentless pressure paused, but did not ease. She could feel him there behind her, an inexorable, inexplicable force. She reached back with her free hand, groping for something to claw, something to hit or bend, but there was nothing.

'I could break your neck,' he said, very quietly. The weight of his arm left her shoulders, though the twisted arm still held her bent forward, hair loose and tumbled, nearly touching the floor. A hand settled on her neck. She could feel thumb and index fingers on either side, pressing lightly on her arteries. He squeezed, and black spots danced before her eyes.

'I could kill you, so.'

The hand left her neck, and touched her, deliberately, knee and shoulder, cheek and chin, emphasizing her helplessness. She jerked her head away, not letting him touch the wetness, not wanting him to feel her tears of rage. Then the hand pressed sudden and brutal on the small of her back. She made a small, choked sound and arched her back to keep her arm from breaking, thrusting out her hips backward, legs spread to keep her balance.

'I could use ye as I would,' he said, and there was a coldness in his voice. 'Could you stop me, Brianna?'

She felt as though she would suffocate with rage and shame.

'Answer me.' The hand took her by the neck again, and squeezed.

'No!'

She was free. So suddenly released, she pitched forward onto her face, barely getting one hand down in time to save herself.

She lay on the straw, panting and sobbing. There was a loud whuffle near her head – Magdalen, roused by the noise, leaning out of her stall to investigate. Slowly, painfully, she raised herself to a sitting position.

He was standing over her, arms folded.

'Damn you!' she gasped. She slammed a hand down in the hay. 'God, I want to kill you!'

He stood quite still, looking down at her.

'Aye,' he said quietly. 'But ye can't, can you?'

She stared up at him, not understanding. His eyes were intent on hers, not angry, not mocking. Waiting.

'You *can't*,' he repeated, with emphasis.

And then realization came, flooding down her aching arms to her bruised fists.

'Oh, God,' she said. 'No. I can't. I couldn't. Even if I'd fought him . . . I *couldn't*.'

Quite suddenly she began to cry, the knots inside her slipping loose, the weights shifting, lifting, as a blessed relief spread through her body. It hadn't been her fault. If she had fought with all her strength – as she had fought just now –

'Couldn't,' she said, and swallowed hard, gasping for air. 'I couldn't have stopped him. I kept thinking, if only I'd fought harder . . . but it wouldn't have mattered. I couldn't have stopped him.'

A hand touched her face, big and very gentle.

'You're a fine, braw lassie,' he whispered. 'But a lassie, nonetheless. Would ye fret your heart out and think yourself a coward because ye couldna fight off a lion wi' your bare hands? It's the same. Dinna be daft, now.'

She wiped the back of her hand under her nose, and sniffed deeply.

He put a hand under her elbow and helped her up, his strength no longer either threat or mockery, but unutterable comfort. Her knees stung, where she had scraped them on the ground. Her legs wobbled, but she made it to the haypile, where he let her sit down.

'You could just have *told* me, you know,' she said. 'That it wasn't my fault.'

He smiled faintly.

'I did. Ye couldna believe me, though, unless ye knew for yourself.'

'No. I guess not.' A profound but peaceful weariness had settled on her like a blanket. This time she had no urge to tear it off.

She watched, feeling too limp to move, as he wetted a cloth from the trough and wiped her face, straightened her twisted skirts, and poured out a drink for her.

When he handed her the freshly filled cup of cider, though, she laid a hand on his arm. Bone and muscle were solid, warm under her hand.

'You could have fought back. But you didn't.'

He laid a big hand over hers, squeezed and let it go.

'No, I didna fight,' he said quietly. 'I gave my word – for your mother's life.' His eyes met hers squarely, neither ice nor sapphire now, but clear as water. 'I dinna regret it.'

He took her by the shoulders, and eased her down onto the piled hay.

'Do ye rest a bit, *a leannan.*'

She lay down, but reached up to touch him as he knelt by her.

'Is it true – that I won't forget?'

He paused for a moment, hand on her hair.

'Aye, that's true,' he said softly. 'But it's true, too, that it willna matter after a time.'

'Won't it?' She was too tired even to wonder what he might mean by this. She felt almost weightless; strangely remote, as though she no longer inhabited her troublesome body. 'Even if I'm not strong enough to kill him?'

A clear cold draft from the open door cut through the warm fog of smoke, making all the animals stir. The brindled cow shifted her weight in sudden irritation and let out a low-throated *mwaaah*, not of distress so much as of querulous complaint.

She felt her father glance at the cow before turning back to her.

'You're a verra strong woman, *a bheanachd,*' he said at last, very softly.

911

'I'm not strong. You just proved I'm not –'

His hand on her shoulder stopped her.

'That's not what I mean.' He stopped, thinking, his hand smoothing her hair, over and over.

'She was ten when our mother died, Jenny was,' he said at last. 'It was the day after the funeral when I came into the kitchen and found her kneeling on a stool, to be tall enough to stir the bowl on the table.

'She was wearing my mother's apron,' he said softly, 'folded up under the arms, and the strings wrapped twice about her waist. I could see she'd been weepin', like I had, for her face was all stained and her eyes red. But she just went on stirring, staring down into the bowl, and she said to me, "Go and wash, Jamie; I'll have supper for you and Da directly." '

His eyes closed altogether, and he swallowed once. Then he opened them, and looked down at her again.

'Aye, I ken fine how strong women are,' he said quietly. 'And you're strong enough for what must be done, *m'annsachd* – believe me.'

He stood up then, and went to the cow. It had risen to its feet and was moving restlessly in a small circle, swaying and shuffling on its tether. He caught it by the tether rope, gentled it with hands and words, made his way behind the heifer, frowning in concentration. She saw him turn his head and look, to check his dirk, then turn back, murmuring.

Not a loving butcher, no. A surgeon in his way, like her mother. From this odd plateau of remoteness, she could see how much her parents – so wildly different in temperament and manner – were alike in this one respect; that odd ability to mingle compassion with sheer ruthlessness.

But they were different even in that, she thought; Claire could hold life and death together in her hands, and yet preserve herself, hold aloof; a doctor must go on living, for the sake of her patients, if not for her own sake. Jamie would be ruthless toward himself, as much as – or more than – he would be to anyone else.

He had thrown off his plaid; now he unfastened his shirt, with no haste but neither with any wasted motion. He pulled the pale linen over his head and laid it neatly

912

aside, returning to his watching post at the heifer's tail, ready to assist.

A long ripple ran down the cow's rounded side, and the torchlight glimmered white on the tiny knot of a scar over his heart. Uncover his nakedness? He would strip himself to the bone, if he thought it necessary. And – a much less comforting thought – if he thought it necessary, he would do the same to her, without a moment's hesitation.

He had a hand at the base of the cow's tail, speaking to it in Gaelic, soothing, encouraging. She felt as though she could almost grasp the sense of his words – but not quite.

All might be well, or it might not. But whatever happened, Jamie Fraser would be there, fighting. It was a comfort.

Jamie paused by the upper fence of the cowpen, on the rise above the house. It was late, and he was more than tired, but his mind kept him wakeful. The calving completed, he had carried Brianna down to the cabin – she sleeping sound as a babe in his arms – and then gone out again, to seek relief in the solitude of the night.

His shins ached where she had kicked him, and there were deep bruises on his thighs; she was amazingly powerful for a woman. None of that troubled him in the least; in fact, he felt an odd and unexpected pride in this evidence of her strength. *She will be all right*, he thought. Surely she will.

There was more hope than confidence behind this thought. Yet it was on his own account that he was wakeful, and he felt at once troubled and foolish at the knowledge. He had thought himself thoroughly healed, old hurts so far behind him that they could safely be dismissed from mind. He had been wrong about that, and it unsettled him to find just how close to the surface the buried memories lay.

If he were to find rest tonight, they would have to be exhumed; the ghosts raised in order to lay them. Well, he had told the lass it took strength. He stopped, gripping the fence.

The rustle of night sounds faded slowly from his mind as he waited, listening for the voice. He had not heard it

913

for years, had thought never to hear it again – but he had already heard its echo once tonight; seen the blaze of anger's phantom in his daughter's eyes, and felt its flames singe his own heart.

Better to call it forth and face it boldly than let it lie in ambush. If he could not face his own demons, he could not conquer hers. He touched a bruise on his thigh, finding an odd comfort in the soreness.

No one dies of it, he'd said. *Not you; not me.*

The voice did not come at first; for a moment he hoped it would not – perhaps it *had* been long enough . . . but then it was there again, whispering in his ear as though it had never left, its insinuations a caress that burned his memory as once they had burned his skin.

'Gently at first,' it breathed. 'Softly. Tender as though you were my infant son. Gently, but for so long you will forget there was a time I did not own your body.'

The night stood still around him, paused as time had paused so long before, poised on the edge of a gulf of dread, waiting. Waiting for the next words, known before-hand and expected, but nonetheless . . .

'And then,' the voice said, loving, 'then I'll hurt you very badly. And you will thank me, and ask for more.'

He stood quite still, face turned upward to the stars. Fought back the surge of fury as it murmured in his ear, the pulse of memory in his blood. Then made himself surrender, let it come. He trembled with remembered helplessness, and clenched his teeth in rage – but stared unblinking at the brightness of heaven overhead, invoking the names of the stars as the words of a prayer, aban-doning himself to the vastness overhead as he sought to lose himself below.

Betelgeuse. Sirius. Orion. Antares. The sky is very large, and you are very small. Let the words wash through him, the voice and its memories pass over him, shivering his skin like the touch of a ghost, vanishing into darkness.

The Pleiades. Cassiopeia. Taurus. Heaven is wide, and you are very small. Dead, but none the less powerful for being dead. He spread his hands wide, gripping the fence – those were powerful, too. Enough to beat a man to death, enough to choke out a life. But even death was not enough to loose the bands of rage.

With great effort, he let go. Turned his hands palm upward, in gesture of surrender. He reached beyond the stars, searching. The words formed themselves quietly in his mind, by habit, so quietly he was not aware of them until he found them echoed in a whisper on his lips.

' " . . . *Forgive us our trespasses as we forgive those who trespass against us.*" '

He breathed slowly, deeply. Seeking, struggling; struggling to let go. ' "*Lead us not into temptation, but deliver us from evil.*" '

Waited, in emptiness, in faith. And then grace came; the necessary vision; the memory of Jack Randall's face in Edinburgh, stricken to bare bone by the knowledge of his brother's death. And he felt once more the gift of pity, calm in its descent as the landing of a dove.

He closed his eyes, feeling the wounds bleed clean again as the succubus drew its claws from his heart.

He sighed, and turned his hands over, the rough wood of the fence comforting and solid under his palms. The demon was gone. He had been a man, Jack Randall; nothing more. And in the recognition of that common frail humanity, all power of past fear and pain vanished like smoke.

His shoulders slumped, relieved of their burden.

'Go in peace,' he whispered, to the dead man and himself. 'You are forgiven.'

The night sounds had returned; the cry of a hunting cat rose sharp on the air, and rotting leaves crunched soft underfoot as he made his way back toward the house. The oiled hide that covered the window glowed golden in the dark, with the flame of the candle he had left burning in the hope of Claire's return. His sanctuary.

He thought that he should perhaps have told Brianna all this, too – but no. She couldn't understand what he *had* told her; he had had to show her, instead. How to tell her in words, then, what he had learned himself by pain and grace? That only by forgiveness could she forget – and that forgiveness was not a single act, but a matter of constant practice.

Perhaps she would find such grace herself; perhaps this unknown Roger Wakefield could be her sanctuary, as Claire had been his. He found his natural jealousy of the man dissolved in a passionate wish that Wakefield could indeed give her what he himself could not. Pray God he would come soon; pray God he would prove a decent man.

In the meantime, there were other matters to be dealt with. He walked slowly down the hill, oblivious to the wind that blew the kilt about his knees and billowed through his shirt and plaid. Things must be done here; winter was coming, and he could not leave his women here alone with only Ian to hunt for them and defend them. He couldn't leave to search for Wakefield.

But if Wakefield did not come? Well, there were other ways; he would see Brianna and the child protected, one way or another. And at least his daughter was safe from the man who had harmed her. Permanently safe. He rubbed a hand across his face, smelling blood still on his skin from the calving.

Forgive us our trespasses as we forgive those who trespass against us. Yes, but what of those who trespass against the ones we love? He could not forgive on another's behalf – and would not, if he could. But if not . . . how should he expect forgiveness in return?

Educated in the universities of Paris, confidant of kings and friend to philosophers, still he was a Highlander, born to blood and honor. The body of a warrior and the mind of a gentleman – and the soul of a barbarian, he thought wryly, to whom neither God's nor mortal law stood more sacred than the ties of blood.

Yes, there was forgiveness; she must find a way to forgive the man, for her own sake. But he was a different matter.

' "*Vengeance is mine, sayeth the Lord.*" ' He whispered it to himself. Then he looked up, away from the safe small glow of hearth and home, to the flaming glory of the stars above.

'The hell it is,' he said, aloud, shamed but defiant. It was ungrateful, he knew. And wrong, forbye. But there it was, and no use to lie either to God or to himself about it.

'The hell it is,' he repeated, louder. 'And if I am

damned for what I've done – then let it be! She is my daughter.'

He stood still for a moment, looking up, but there was no answer from the stars. He nodded once, as though in reply, and went on down the hill, the wind cold behind him.

49

Choices

I opened Daniel Rawlings's box, and stared at the rows of bottles filled with the soft greens and browns of powdered root and leaf, the clear gold of distillations. There was nothing among the bottles to help. Very slowly, I lifted the covering that lay over the top compartment, over the blades.

I lifted out the scalpel with the curved edge, tasting cold metal in the back of my throat. It was a beautiful tool, sharp and sturdy, well balanced, part of my hand when I chose it to be. I balanced it on the end of my finger, letting it tilt gently back and forth.

I set it down, and picked up the long, thick root that lay on the table. Part of the stem was still attached, the remnants of leaves hanging limp and yellow. Only one. I had searched the woods for nearly two weeks, but it was so late in the year that the leaves of the smaller herbs had yellowed and fallen; it was impossible to recognize plants that were no more than brown sticks. I had found this one in a sheltered spot, a few of the distinctive fruits still clinging to its stalk. Blue cohosh, I was sure. But only one. It wasn't enough.

I had none of the European herbs, no hellebore, no wormwood. I could perhaps get wormwood, though with some difficulty; it was used to flavor absinthe.

'And who makes absinthe in the backwoods of North Carolina?' I said aloud, picking up the scalpel again.

'No one that I know of.'

I jumped, and the blade jabbed deep into the side of my thumb. Blood spattered across the tabletop, and I snatched the corner of my apron, wadding the cloth hard against the wound in reflex.

'Christ, Sassenach! Are ye all right? I didna mean to startle ye.'

It didn't hurt a great deal yet, but the shock of sudden injury made me bite my lower lip. Looking worried, Jamie took my wrist and lifted the edge of the wadded cloth. Blood promptly welled from the cut and ran down my hand, and he clamped the cloth back in place, squeezing tight.

'It's all right; just a cut. Where did you come from? I thought you were up at the still.' I felt surprisingly shaky, perhaps from the shock.

'I was. The mash isna ready for distilling yet. You're bleeding like a pig, Sassenach. Are ye sure you're all right?' I *was* bleeding badly; besides the splashes of blood across the table, the corner of my apron was soaked with dark red.

'Yes. I probably severed a tiny vein. It's not an artery, though; it will stop. Hold my hand up, will you?' I fumbled one-handed with the strings of my apron, seeking to free it. Jamie undid it with a quick yank, wrapped the apron round my hand, and held the whole clumsy bundle up over my head.

'What were ye doing with your wee knife?' he asked, eyeing the dropped scalpel, where it lay alongside the twisted cohosh root.

'Ah . . . I was going to slice up that root,' I said, waving weakly at it.

He gave me a sharp look, glanced across to the sideboard, where my paring knife lay in plain sight, then looked back at me with raised brows.

'Aye? I've never seen ye use one of these' – he nodded at the open array of scalpels and surgical blades – 'save on people.'

My hand twitched slightly in his, and he tightened his grip on my thumb, squeezing hard enough to make me catch my breath in pain. He loosened his grip, then looked intently into my face, frowning.

'What in heaven's name are ye about, Sassenach? Ye look as though I'd surprised ye about to commit murder.'

My lips felt stiff and bloodless. I pulled my thumb out of his grasp and sat down, holding the wounded digit against my bosom with my other hand.

'I was . . . deciding,' I said, with great reluctance. It was

919

no good to lie; he would have to know, sooner or later, if Bree –

'Deciding what?'

'About Bree. What was the best way to do it.'

'To do it?' His eyebrows shot up. He glanced at the open medicine case, then at the scalpel, and a look of sudden shocked comprehension washed over his face.

'You mean to –'

'If she wants me to.' I touched the knife, its small blade stained with my own blood. 'There are herbs – or this. There are awful risks to using herbs – convulsions, brain damage, hemorrhage – but it doesn't matter; I don't have enough of the right kind.'

'Claire – have you done it before?'

I looked up, to see him looking down at me with something I had never seen in his eyes before – horror. I pressed my hands flat on the table, to stop them trembling. I didn't do as well with my voice.

'Would it make a difference to you if I had?'

He stared at me for a moment, then eased himself down on the bench opposite, slowly, as though afraid he might break something.

'Ye havena done it,' he said softly. 'I know it.'

'No,' I said. I stared down at his hand, covering mine. 'No, I haven't.'

I could feel the tension go out of his hand; it relaxed, curling over mine, enfolding it. But my own lay limp in his grasp.

'I knew ye couldna do murder,' he said.

'I could. I have.' I didn't look up at him, but spoke to the tabletop. 'I killed a man, a patient in my care. I told you about Graham Menzies.'

He was silent for a moment, but held on to my hand, squeezing slightly.

'I think it isna the same,' he said at last. 'To ease a doomed man to a death he wishes . . . it seems to me that that is mercy, not murder. And duty, too, perhaps.'

'Duty?' That did make me look at him, startled. The look of shock had faded from his eyes, though he was still solemn.

'Do ye not recall Falkirk Hill, and the night Rupert died in the chapel there?'

I nodded. It wasn't something easily forgotten – the cold dark of the tiny church, the eerie sounds of pipes and battle far outside. Inside the black air thick with the sweat of frightened men, and Rupert dying slowly on the floor at my feet, choking on his blood. He had asked Dougal MacKenzie, as his friend and his chief, to hasten him . . . and Dougal had.

'It will be a doctor's duty, too, I think,' Jamie said gently. 'If you are sworn to heal – but cannot – and to save men pain – and can?'

'Yes.' I took a deep breath and curled my hand around the scalpel. 'I *am* sworn – and by more than a doctor's oath. Jamie, she's my daughter. I would rather do anything in the world but this – anything.' I looked up at him and blinked, holding back tears.

'Don't you think I haven't thought about it? That I don't know what the risks are? Jamie, I could kill her!' I pulled the cloth off my wounded thumb; the cut was still oozing.

'Look – it shouldn't bleed like that, it's a deep cut but not a bad one. But it does! I hit a vein. I could do the same to Bree and never know it, until she began to bleed – and if so . . . Jamie, I couldn't stop it! She'd bleed to death under my hand, and there isn't a thing I could do about it, not a thing!'

He looked at me, eyes dark with shock.

'How could ye think of doing such a thing, knowing that?' His voice was soft with disbelief.

I drew a deep, trembling breath, and felt despair wash over me. There was no way to make him understand, no way.

'Because I know other things,' I said at last, very softly, not looking at him. 'I know what it is to bear a child. I know what it is to have your body and your mind and your soul taken from you and changed without your will. I know what it is to be ripped out of the place you thought was yours, to have choice taken from you. *I know what it is,* do you hear me? and it isn't something anyone should do without being willing.' I looked up at him, and my fist clenched hard on my wounded thumb.

921

'And you – for God's sake – *you* know what I don't; what it's like to live with the knowledge of violation. Do you mean to tell me that if I could have cut that from you after Wentworth, that you wouldn't have had me do it, no matter what the risks? Jamie, that may be a rapist's child!'

'Aye, I know,' he began, and had to stop, too choked to finish. 'I *know*,' he began again, and his jaw muscles bulged as he forced the words. 'But I know the one thing else – if I dinna ken his father, I ken his grandsire well enough. Claire, that is a child of my blood!'

'*Your* blood?' I echoed. I stared at him, the truth dawning on me. 'You want a grandchild badly enough to sacrifice your daughter?'

'Sacrifice? It isna me that's meaning to commit slaughter in cold blood!'

'You didn't mind the angel-makers at the Hopital des Anges; you had pity for the women they helped, you said so.'

'Those women had nay choice!' Too agitated to sit, he got up and paced restlessly back and forth in front of me. 'They had no one to protect them, no way to feed a child – what else could they do, poor creatures? But it isna so, for Brianna! I will never let her be hungry or cold, never let aught harm her or the bairn, never!'

'That isn't all there is to it!'

He stared at me, brows drawn down in stubborn incomprehension.

'If she bears a child here, she won't leave,' I said unsteadily. 'She can't – not without tearing herself apart.'

'So *you* mean to tear her apart?' I flinched, as though he'd struck me.

'You want her to stay,' I said, striking back. 'You don't care that she has a life somewhere else, that she *wants* to go back. If she'll stay – and better yet, if she'll give you a grandchild – then you bloody don't care what it does to her, do you?'

It was his turn to flinch, but he turned on me squarely.

'Aye, I care! That doesna mean I think it right for you to force her into –'

'What do you mean, force her?' The blood was burning hot in my cheeks. 'For God's sake, you think I want to do this? No! But, by God, she'll have the choice if she wants it!'

I had to press my hands together to stop them shaking. The apron had fallen to the floor, stained with blood, reminding me much too vividly of operating theaters and battlefields – and of the terrible limits of my own skill.

I could feel his eyes on me, narrowed and burning. I knew that he was as torn in the matter as I was. He did indeed care desperately for Bree – but now I had spoken the truth, we both recognized it; deprived of his own children, living for so long as an exile, there was nothing he wanted more in life than a child of his blood.

But he couldn't stop me, and he knew it. He wasn't used to feeling helpless, and he didn't like it. He turned abruptly and went to the sideboard, where he stood, fists resting on top of it.

I had never felt so desolate, so in need of his under- standing. Did he not realize how horrible the prospect was for me, as well as him? Worse, because it was my hand that must do the damage.

I came up behind him, and laid a hand on his back. He stood unmoving, and I stroked him lightly, taking some comfort from the simple fact of his presence, of the solid strength of him.

'Jamie.' My thumb left a slight smear of red on the linen of his shirt. 'It will be all right. I'm sure it will.' I was talking to convince myself, as much as him. He didn't move, and I ventured to put my arm around his waist, laying my cheek against the curve of his back. I wanted him to turn and take me in his arms, to assure me that it would indeed somehow be all right – or at the least, that he would not blame me for whatever happened.

He moved abruptly, dislodging my hand.

'Ye've a high opinion of your power, have ye no?' He spoke coldly, turning to face me.

'What do you mean by that?'

He grasped my wrist in one hand, pinning it to the wall above my head. I could feel the tickle of blood down my wrist, flowing from my wounded thumb. His fingers wrapped around my hand, squeezing tight.

'Ye think it's yours alone to say? That life and death is

yours?' I could feel the small bones of my hand grind together, and I stiffened, trying to pull free.

'It's not mine to say! But if *she* says – then yes, it's my power. And yes, I'll use it. Just like you would – like you *have*, when you've had to.' I shut my eyes, fighting down fear. He wouldn't hurt me . . . surely? It occurred to me with a small shock that he could indeed stop me. If he broke my hand . . .

Very slowly, he bent his head and rested his forehead against mine.

'Look at me, Claire,' he said, very quietly.

Slowly, I opened my eyes and looked. His eyes were no more than an inch away; I could see the tiny gold flecks near the center of his iris, the black ring surrounding it. My fingers in his were slippery with blood.

He let go of my hand, and touched my breast lightly, cupping it for a moment.

'Please,' he whispered, and then was gone.

I stood quite still against the wall, and then slowly slid to the floor in a bloom of skirts, the cut on my thumb throbbing with my heartbeat.

I was so shaken by the quarrel with Jamie that I couldn't settle to anything. At last, I put on my cloak and went out, walking up the ridge. I avoided the path that led across the Ridge toward Fergus's cabin, and down toward the road. I didn't want to risk meeting anyone at all.

It was cold and cloudy, with a light rain sputtering intermittently among the leaf-bare branches. The air was heavy with cold moisture; let the temperature drop a few degrees more, and it would snow. If not tonight, tomorrow – or next week. Within a month at the most, the Ridge would be cut off from the lowlands.

Ought I to take Brianna to Cross Creek? Whether she decided to bear the child or not, might she be safer there?

I shuffled through layers of wet, yellow leaves. No. My impulse was to think that civilization must offer some advantage, but not in this case. There was nothing Cross Creek could offer that would truly be of help in case of any obstetrical emergency; in fact, she might well be in active danger from the medical practitioners of the time.

No, whatever she decided, she was better off here, with me. I wrapped my arms about myself under my cloak, and flexed my fingers, trying to work some warmth and suppleness into them, to feel some sense of surety in touch.

Please, he'd said. Please what? Please don't ask her, please don't do it if she asks? But I had to. *I swear by Apollo the physician . . . not to cut for the stone, nor to procure abortion . . .* Well, and Hippocrates was neither a surgeon, a woman . . . nor a mother. As I'd told Jamie, I'd sworn by something a lot older than Apollo the physician – and that oath was in blood.

I never had done an abortion though I had had some experience as a resident, in the post-care of miscarriage. On the rare occasions a patient had asked it of me, I had referred them to a colleague. I had no absolute objection; I had seen too many women killed in body or spirit by untimely children. If it was killing – and it was – then I thought it not murder, but a justifiable homicide, undertaken in desperate self-defense.

At the same time, I could not bring myself to do it. The surgeon's sense that gave me knowledge of the flesh under my hands gave me also an acute awareness for the living contents of the womb. I could touch a pregnant woman's belly, and feel in my fingertips the second beating heart; could trace unseeing the curve of limb and head, and the snakelike curl of the umbilicus with its rush of blood, all red and blue.

I could not bring myself to destroy it. Not until now; when it was a matter of killing my own flesh and blood.

How? It would have to be surgical. Dr. Rawlings had evidently not done such procedures; he had no uterine 'spoon' for scraping the womb, nor any of the slender rods for dilation of the cervix. I could manage, though. One of the ivory knitting needles, its point blunted; the scalpel, bent to a shallow curve, its deadly edge sanded down for the delicate – but no less deadly – job of scraping.

When? Now. She was already three months gone; if it was to be done, it must be as soon as possible. Neither could I bear to be in the same room with Jamie while the

925

matter was unresolved, feeling his anguish added to my own.

Brianna had taken Lizzie to Fergus's house. Lizzie was to stay and help Marsali, who had her hands full with the distillery, little Germaine, and the farm work that Fergus couldn't manage single-handed. It was a terrible load for an eighteen-year-old girl to be carrying, but she managed, with tenacity and style. Lizzie could at least help with the household chores, and mind the little fiend long enough to let his mother rest now and then.

Brianna would come back before suppertime. Ian was away, hunting with Rollo. Jamie . . . without being told, I knew that Jamie would not be back for some time. We would have a little while alone.

Would it be a suitable moment to ask her such a question, though – fresh from seeing Germaine's cherubic face? Though on reflection, exposure to a two-year-old boy was probably the best possible object lesson in the dangers of motherhood, I thought wryly.

Vaguely lightened by the faint whiff of humor, I turned back, drawing my cloak around me against the increasing wind. As I came down the hill I saw Brianna's horse in the penfold; she was home. My stomach clenched in dread, I went to lay the choice before her.

'I thought of it,' she said, with a deep breath. 'As soon as I realized. I wondered if you could do – something like that, here.'

'It wouldn't be easy. It would be dangerous – and it would hurt. I don't even have any laudanum; only whisky. But yes, I can do it – if you want me to.' I forced myself to sit still, watching her pace slowly back and forth before the hearth, hands folded behind her in thought.

'It would have to be surgical,' I said, unable to keep quiet. 'I don't have the right herbs – and they aren't always reliable, in any case. At least surgery is . . . certain.' I laid the scalpel on the table; she should not be under any illusions as to what I was suggesting. She nodded at my words, but didn't stop her pacing. Like Jamie, she always thought better while moving.

A trickle of sweat ran down my back, and I shivered. The

fire was warm enough, but my fingers were still cold as ice. Christ, if she wanted it, would I even be able to do it? My hands had begun to tremble, with the strain of waiting.

She turned at last to look at me, eyes clear and appraising under thick, ruddy brows.

'Would you have done it? If you could?'

'If I could –?'

'You said once that you hated me, when you were pregnant. If you could have not been –'

'God, not you!' I blurted, horror-stricken. 'Not you, ever. It –' I knotted my hands together, to still their trembling. 'No,' I said, as positively as I could. 'Never.'

'You did say so,' she said, looking at me intently. 'When you told me about Da.'

I rubbed a hand across my face, trying to focus my thoughts. Yes, I *had* told her that. Idiot.

'It was a horrible time. Terrible. We were starving, it was war – the world was coming apart at the seams.' Wasn't hers? 'At the time, it seemed as though there was no hope; I had to leave Jamie, and the thought drove almost everything else out of my mind. But there was one other thing,' I said.

'What was that?'

'It wasn't rape,' I said softly, meeting her eyes. 'I loved your father.'

She nodded, her face a little pale.

'Yes. But it *might* be Roger's. You did say that, didn't you?'

'Yes. It might. Is the possibility enough for you?'

She laid a hand over her stomach, long fingers gently curved.

'Yeah. Well. It isn't an it, to me. I don't know who it is, but –' She stopped suddenly and glanced at me, looking suddenly shy.

'I don't know if this sounds – well . . .' She shrugged abruptly, dismissing doubt. 'I had this sharp pain that woke me up in the middle of the night, a few days . . . after. Quick, like somebody had stabbed me with a hatpin, but deep.' Her fingers curled inward, her fist pressing just above her pubic bone, on the right side.

'Implantation,' I said softly. 'When the zygote takes root

in the womb.' When that first, eternal link is formed between mother and child. When the small blind entity, unique in its union of egg and sperm, comes to anchor from the perilous voyage of beginning, home from its brief, free-floating existence in the body, and settles to its busy work of division, drawing sustenance from the flesh in which it embeds itself, in a connection that belongs to neither side, but to both. That link, which cannot be severed, either by birth or by death.

She nodded. 'It was the strangest feeling. I was still half asleep, but I . . . well, I just knew all of a sudden that I wasn't alone.' Her lips curved in a faint smile, reminiscent of wonder. 'And I said to . . . it . . .' Her eyes rested on mine, still lit by the smile, 'I said, "Oh, it's you." And then I went back to sleep.'

Her other hand crossed the first, a barricade across her belly.

'I thought it was a dream. That was a long time before I knew. But I remember. It *wasn't* a dream. I remember.'

I remembered, too.

I looked down and saw beneath my hands not the wooden tabletop nor gleaming blade, but the opal skin and perfect sleeping face of my first child, Faith, with slanted eyes that never opened on the light of earth.

Looked up into the same eyes, open now and filled with knowledge. I saw that baby, too, my second daughter, filled with bloody life, pink and crumpled, flushed with fury at the indignities of birth, so different from the calm stillness of the first – and just as magnificent in her perfection.

Two miracles I had been given, carried beneath my heart, born of my body, held in my arms, separated from me and part of me forever. I knew much too well that neither death nor time nor distance ever altered such a bond – because I had been altered by it, once and forever changed by that mysterious connection.

'Yes, I understand,' I said. And then said, 'Oh, but Bree!' as the knowledge of what her decision would mean to her flooded in on me anew.

She was watching me, brows drawn down, lines of trouble in her face, and it occurred to me belatedly that

928

she might take my exhortations as the expression of my own regrets.

Appalled at the thought that she might think I had not wanted her, or had ever wished she had not been, I dropped the blade and reached out across the table to her.

'Bree,' I said, seized with panic at the thought. 'Brianna. I love you. Do you believe I love you?'

She nodded without speaking, and stretched out a hand toward me. I grasped it like a lifeline, like the cord that had once joined us.

She closed her eyes, and for the first time I saw the glitter of tears that clung to the delicate, thick curve of her lashes.

'I've always known that, Mama,' she whispered. Her fingers tightened around mine; I saw her other hand press flat against her stomach. 'From the beginning.'

50

In Which All is Revealed

By late November, the days as well as the nights were cold, and the rain clouds began to hang lower on the slopes above us.The weather had an unfortunate effect on people's tempers; everyone was increasingly edgy, and for obvious reason: There was still no word of Roger Wakefield.

Brianna was still silent about the cause of their argument; in fact, she almost never referred to Roger anymore. She had made her decision; there was nothing to do but to wait, and let Roger make his – if he hadn't already. Still, I could see fear warring with anger when she left her face unguarded – and doubt hung over everyone like the clouds over the mountains.

Where was he? And what would happen when – or if – he finally appeared?

I took some despite from the prevailing mood of edginess by taking stock of the pantry. Winter was nearly here; the foraging was over, the garden harvested, the preserving done. The pantry shelves bulged with sacks of nuts, heaps of squash, rows of potatoes, jars of dried tomatoes, peaches, and apricots, bowls of dried mushrooms, wheels of cheese, and baskets of apples. Braids of onions and garlic and strings of dried fish hung from the ceiling; bags of flour and beans, barrels of salt beef and salt fish, and stone jars of sauerkraut stood on the floor.

I counted over my hoard like a squirrel reckoning nuts, and felt soothed by our abundance. No matter what else happened, we would neither starve nor go hungry.

Emerging from the pantry with a wedge of cheese in one hand and a bowl of dry beans in the other, I heard a tap on the door. Before I could call out, it opened and Ian's head poked in, cautiously surveying the room.

'Brianna's no here?' he asked. As she clearly wasn't, he didn't wait for an answer but stepped in, trying to smooth back his hair.

'Have ye a bit o' looking glass, Auntie?' he asked. 'And maybe a comb?'

'Yes, of course,' I said. I set down the food, got my small mirror and the tortoiseshell comb from the drawer of the sideboy and handed them to him, peering upward at his gangling form.

His face seemed abnormally shiny, his lean cheeks blotched with red, as though he had not only shaved but had scrubbed the skin to the point of rawness. His hair, normally a thick, stubborn sheaf of soft brown, was now slicked straight back on the sides of his head with some kind of grease. Liberally pomaded with the same substance, it erupted in an untidy quiff over his forehead, making him look like a deranged porcupine.

'What have you got on your hair, Ian?' I asked. I sniffed at him and recoiled slightly at the result.

'Bear fat,' he said. 'But it stank a bit, so I mixed in a wee scoop of incense soap to make it smell better.' He peered critically at himself in the mirror and made small jabs at his coiffure with the comb, which seemed pitifully inadequate to the task.

He was wearing his good coat, with a clean shirt and – unheard of touch for a workday – a clean, starched stock wrapped about his throat, looking tight enough to strangle him.

'You look very nice, Ian,' I said, biting the inside of my cheek. 'Um . . . are you going somewhere special?'

'Aye, well,' he said awkwardly. 'It's just if I'm meant to be courting, like, I thought I must try to look decent.'

Courting? I wondered at his haste. While he was certainly interested in girls – and there were a few girls in the district who made no secret of returning his interest – he was barely seventeen. Men did marry that young, of course, and Ian had both his own land and a share in the whisky making, but I hadn't thought his affections so strongly engaged yet.

'I see,' I said. 'Ah . . . is the young lady anyone I know?' He rubbed at his jaw, raising a red flush along the bone.

'Aye, well. It's – it's Brianna.' He wouldn't meet my eyes, but the flush rose slowly over his face.

'What?' I said incredulously. I set down the slice of

bread I was holding and stared at him. 'Did you say *Brianna*?'

His eyes were fixed on the floor, but his jaw was set stubbornly.

'Brianna,' he repeated. 'I've come to make her a proposal of marriage.'

'Ian, you can't possibly mean that.'

'I do,' he said, sticking out his long, square chin in a determined manner. He glanced toward the window, and shuffled his feet. 'Will she – is she comin' in soon, d'ye think?'

The sharp scent of nervous perspiration reached me, mingled with soap and bear fat, and I saw that his hands were clenched in fists, tight enough to make the knobby knuckles stand out white against his tanned skin.

'Ian,' I said, torn between exasperation and tenderness, 'are you doing this because of Brianna's baby?'

The whites of his eyes flashed as he glanced at me, startled. He nodded, shifting his shoulders uncomfortably inside the stiff coat.

'Aye, of course,' he said, as though surprised that I should ask.

'Then you're not in love with her?' I knew the answer quite well, but thought we had better have it all out.

'Well . . . no,' he said, the painful blush renewing itself. 'But I'm no promised to anyone else,' he hastened to add. 'So that's all right.'

'It is not all right,' I said firmly. 'Ian, that's a very, very kind notion of yours, but –'

'Oh, it's not mine,' he interrupted, looking surprised. 'Uncle Jamie thought of it.'

'He *what*?' A loud, incredulous voice spoke behind me, and I whirled to find Brianna standing in the doorway, staring at Ian. She advanced slowly into the room, hands fisted at her sides. Just as slowly, Ian retreated, fetching up with a bump against the table.

'Cousin,' he said, with a bob of his head that dislodged a spike of greased hair. He brushed at it, but it stuck out, hanging disreputably over one eye. 'I . . . ah . . . I . . .' He saw the look on Brianna's face and promptly shut his eyes.

'I-have-come-to-express-my-desire-to-ask-for-your-hand-

932

in-the-blessed-sacrament-of-matrimony,' he said in one breath. He took in another, with an audible gasp. 'I –'

'Shut up!'

Ian, his mouth opened to continue, immediately shut it. He opened one eye in a cautious slit, like one viewing a bomb momentarily expected to go off.

Bree glared from Ian to me. Even in the dim room, I could see the tight look of her mouth and the crimson rising in her cheeks. The tip of her nose was red, whether from the nippy air outside or from annoyance, I couldn't tell.

'Did you know about this?' she demanded of me.

'Of course not!' I said. 'For heaven's sake, Bree –' Before I could finish, she had whirled on her heel and run out of the door. I could see the quick flash of her rusty skirts as she hurried up the slope leading to the stable.

I pulled off my apron and flung it hastily over the chair. 'I'd better go after her.'

'I'll go, too,' Ian offered, and I didn't stop him. Reinforcements might be needed.

'What do you think she'll do?' he asked, panting in my wake as I hastened up the steep slope.

'God knows,' I said. 'But I'm afraid we're going to find out.' I was entirely too familiar with the look of a Fraser roused to fury. Neither Bree nor Jamie lost their temper easily, but when they did, they lost it thoroughly.

'I'm glad she didna strike me,' Ian said thankfully. 'I thought for a moment she was going to.' He pulled even with me, his long legs outstripping mine, hurrying though I was. I could hear uplifted voices from the open half-door of the stable.

'Why on earth would you put poor little Ian up to such a thing?' Brianna was saying, her voice high with indignation. 'I've never heard of such a high-handed, arrogant –'

'Poor little Ian?' Ian said, vastly affronted. 'What does she –'

'Oh, high-handed, am I?' Jamie's voice interrupted. He sounded both impatient and irritable, though not yet angry. Perhaps I was in time to avert full-scale hostilities. I peeked through the stable door, to see them face-to-face, glaring at each other over a large pile of half-dried manure.

'And what better choice could I make, will ye tell me that?' he demanded. 'Let me tell ye, lassie, I thought of every bachelor in fifty miles before I settled on Ian. I wouldna have ye wed to a cruel man or a drunkard, nor yet a poor man – nor one auld enough to be your grandsire, either.'

He shoved a hand through his hair, sure sign of mental agitation, but made a masterful effort to calm himself. He lowered his voice a bit, trying to be conciliatory.

'Why, I even put aside Tammas McDonald, for while he's a fine stretch of land and a good temper, and he's an age for you, he's a bittie wee fellow forbye, and I thought ye wouldna care to stand up side by side with him before a priest. Believe me, Brianna, I've done my best to see ye well wed.'

Bree wasn't having any; her own hair had come loose during her dash up the hill, and was floating round her face like the flames of a vengeful archangel.

'And what makes you think I want to be married to anybody at all?' His mouth dropped open.

'Want?' he said incredulously. 'And what has *want* to do with it?'

'Everything!' She stamped her foot.

'Now there you're wrong, lassie,' he advised her, turning to pick up his fork. He eyed her stomach with a nod. 'You've a bairn coming, who needs a name. Your time to be choosy is long since past, aye?'

He dug his fork into the pile of manure and heaved the load into the waiting barrow, then dug again, with a smooth economy of motion born of years of labor.

'Now, Ian's a sweet-tempered lad, and a hard worker,' he said, eyes on his task. 'He's got his own land; he'll have mine, too, in time, and that will –'

'I am not going to marry anybody!' Brianna drew herself up to her full height, fists balled at her sides, and spoke in a voice loud enough to disturb the bats in the corners of the ceiling. One small dark form detached itself from the shadows and flittered out into the gathering dusk, ignored by the combatants underneath.

'Well, then, make your own choice,' Jamie said shortly. 'And I wish ye well of it!'

'You . . . are . . . not . . . listening!' Brianna said, grinding each word between her teeth. 'I've made my choice. I said I won't . . . marry . . . *anyone*!' She punctuated this with another stamp of her foot.

Jamie thrust the fork into the pile with a thump. He straightened up and eyed Brianna, rubbing his fist across his jaw.

'Aye, well. I seem to recall hearin' a verra similar opinion expressed by your mother – the night before our wedding. I havena asked her lately does she regret bein' forced to wed me or not, but I flatter myself she's maybe not been miserable altogether. Perhaps ye should go and have a word wi' her?'

'It's not the same thing at all!' Brianna snapped.

'No, it's not,' Jamie agreed, keeping a firm grip on his temper. The sun was low behind the hills, flooding the stable with a golden light in which the creeping tide of red in his skin was nonetheless quite visible. Still, he was making every attempt to be reasonable.

'Your mother wed me to save her life – and mine. It was a brave thing she did, and generous, too. I'll grant it's no a matter of life or death, but – have ye no idea what it is to live branded as a wanton – or as a fatherless bastard, come to that?'

Seeing her expression falter slightly at this, he pressed his advantage, stretching out a hand to her and speaking kindly.

'Come, lassie. Can ye not bring yourself to do it for the bairn's sake?'

Her face tightened again and she stepped back.

'No,' she said, sounding strangled. 'No. I can't.'

He dropped his hand. I could see them both, despite the fading light, and saw the danger signs all too clearly, in the narrowing of his eyes and the set of his shoulders, squared for battle. 'Is that how Frank Randall raised ye, lass, to have no regard for what's right or wrong?'

Brianna was trembling all over, like a horse that's run too far.

'My father always did what was right for me! And he

would never have tried to pull something like this!' she said. 'Never! *He* cared about me!'

At this, Jamie finally lost his temper, which went off with a bang.

'And I don't?' he said. 'I am not trying my best to do what's right for ye? In spite of your being –'

'Jamie –' I turned toward him, saw his eyes gone black with anger, and turned toward her. 'Bree – I know he didn't – you have to understand –'

'Of all the reckless, thoughtless, selfish ways in which to behave!'

'You self-righteous, insensitive bastard!'

'Bastard! Ye'll call *me* a bastard, and your belly swellin' like a pumpkin with a child that ye mean to doom to finger-pointing and calumny for all its days, and –'

'Anybody points a finger at my child, and I'll break it off and stuff it down their throat!'

'Ye senseless wee besom! Have ye no the faintest notion o' how things are? Ye'll be a scandal and a hissing! Folk will call ye whore to your face!'

'Let them try it!'

'Oh, let them try it? And ye mean me to stand by and listen, I suppose?'

'It's not your job to defend me!'

He was so furious that his face went white as fresh-bleached muslin.

'Not my job to defend you? For Christ's sake, woman, who *else* is meant to do it?'

Ian tugged gently on my arm, drawing me back.

'Ye've only the twa choices now, Auntie,' he murmured in my ear. 'Douse them both wi' a pan o' cold water, or come away with me and leave them to it. I've seen Uncle Jamie and my mam go at it before. Believe me, ye dinna want to step between two Frasers wi' their dander up. My Da said he's tried once or twice, and got the scars to prove it.'

I took a final glance at the situation and gave up. He was right; they were nose to nose, red hair bristling and eyes slitted like a couple of bobcats, circling, spitting and snarling. I could have set the hay on fire, and neither one would have spared an instant's notice.

It seemed remarkably quiet and peaceful outside. A whippoorwill sang in the aspen grove, and the wind was in the east, carrying the faint sounds of the waterfall to us. By the time we reached the dooryard, we couldn't hear the shouting anymore.

'Dinna be worrit, Auntie,' Ian said comfortingly. 'They'll get hungry, sooner or later.'

In the event, it was unnecessary to starve them out; Jamie stamped down the hill a few minutes later and without a word, fetched his horse from the paddock, bridled him, mounted, and rode bareback at a gallop down the track toward Fergus's cabin. As I watched his departing form, Brianna stalked out of the stable, puffing like a steam engine, and made for the house.

'What does *nighean na galladh* mean?' she demanded, seeing me at the door.

'I don't know,' I said. I did, but thought it much more prudent not to say. 'I'm sure he didn't mean it,' I added. 'Er . . . whatever it means.'

'Ha,' she said, and with an angry snort, stomped into the house, reappearing moments later with the egg basket over her arm. Without a word, she disappeared into the bushes, making a rustling noise like a hurricane.

I took several deep breaths and went in to start supper, cursing Roger Wakefield.

Physical exertion seemed to have dissipated at least some of the negative energy in the household. Brianna spent an hour in the bushes, and returned with sixteen eggs and a calmer face. There were leaves and stickers in her hair, and from the look of her shoes, she had been kicking trees.

I didn't know what Jamie had been ˙doing, but he returned at suppertime, sweaty and windblown but outwardly calm. They pointedly ignored each other, a reasonably difficult feat for two large persons confined in a twenty-foot-square log cabin. I glanced at Ian, who rolled his eyes skyward and came to help carry the big serving bowl to the table.

Conversation over supper was limited to requests to pass the salt, and afterward, Brianna cleared the dishes, then went to sit at the spinning wheel, working the foot treadle with unnecessary emphasis.

Jamie gave her back a glare, then jerked his head at me and went out. He was waiting on the path to the privy when I followed him a moment later.

'What am I to do?' he demanded, without preamble.

'Apologize,' I said.

'Apologize?' His hair seemed to be standing on end, though it was likely only the effects of the wind. 'But I havena done anything wrong!'

'Well, what difference does that make?' I said, exasperated. 'You asked me what you should do, and I told you.'

He exhaled strongly through his nose, hesitated a moment, then turned and stalked back into the house, shoulders set for martyrdom or battle.

'I apologize,' he said, looming up in front of her.

Surprised, she nearly dropped the yarn, but caught it adeptly.

'Oh,' she said, and flushed. She took her foot off the treadle, and the great wheel creaked and slowed.

'I was wrong,' he said, with a quick look at me. I nodded encouragingly, and he cleared his throat. 'I shouldna have –'

'It's all right.' She spoke quickly, eager to meet him. 'You didn't – I mean, you were only trying to help.' She looked down at the thread, slowing as it ran through her fingers. 'I'm sorry too – I shouldn't have been mad at you.'

He closed his eyes briefly and sighed, then opened them and lifted one eyebrow at me. I smiled faintly and turned back to my work, pounding fennel seeds in the mortar.

He pulled up a stool and sat down beside her, and she turned toward him, putting one hand on the wheel to stop it.

'I know you meant well,' she said. 'You and Ian both. But don't you see, Da? I have to wait for Roger.'

'But if something has happened to the man – if he's met with an accident of some kind . . .'

'He isn't dead. I *know* he isn't.' She spoke with the fervency of someone who means to bend reality to her will.

'He'll come back. And how would it be if he did, and found me married to Ian?'

Ian looked up, hearing his name. He sat on the floor by the fire, Rollo's great head resting on his knee, his yellow wolf-eyes mere slits of pleasure as Ian methodically combed through the thick pelt, pulling out ticks and burs as he found them.

Jamie ran his fingers through his hair in a gesture of frustration.

'I have had word out since ye told me of him, *a nighean*. I sent Ian to Cross Creek to leave word at River Run, and with Captain Freeman to pass to the other rivermen. I've sent Duncan wi' word, all through the Cape Fear valley and as far north as Edenton and New Bern, and wi' the packet boats that run from Virginia to Charleston.'

He looked at me, pleading for understanding. 'What more can I do? The man is nowhere to be found. If I thought there were the slightest chance –' He stopped, teeth set in his lip.

Brianna dropped her gaze to the yarn in her hand, and with a quick, sharp gesture, snapped it. Leaving the loose end to flap from the spindle, she got up and crossed the room, sitting down at the table with her back to us.

'I'm sorry, lass,' Jamie said, more quietly. He reached out and laid a hand on her shoulder, gingerly, as though she might bite him.

She stiffened slightly, but didn't pull away. After a moment, she reached up and took his hand, squeezing it lightly, then putting it aside.

'I see,' she said. 'Thank you, Da.' She sat, eyes fixed on the flames, her face and figure utterly still, but managing to radiate complete desolation. I put my hands on her shoulders, rubbing gently, but she felt like a wax manikin under my fingers – not resisting but not acknowledging the touch.

Jamie studied her for a moment, frowning, and glanced at me. Then, with an air of decision, he got up, reached to the shelf, brought down his inkhorn and quill jar, and set them on the table with a clank.

'Here's a thought,' he said firmly. 'Let us draw up a broadsheet, here, and I will take it to Gillette in

Wilmington. He can print it up, and Ian and the Lindsey lads will take the copies up and down the coast, from Charleston to Jamestown. It may be that someone's not kent Wakefield, not hearing his name, but they'll maybe know him by his looks.'

He shook ink powder made of iron and oak gall into the stained half-gourd he used as a well, and poured a little water from the pitcher, using the shaft of a quill to stir the ink. He smiled at Brianna, and took a sheet of paper from the drawer.

'Now, then, lass, how is this man of yours to look at?'

The suggestion of action had brought a spark of life back to Brianna's face. She sat up straighter, and a current of energy flowed up her spine, into my fingers.

'Tall,' she said. 'Nearly as tall as you, Da. People *would* notice; they always look at you. He has black hair, and green eyes – bright green; it's one of the first things you notice about him, isn't it, Mama?'

Ian gave a small start, and looked up from his grooming.

'Yes,' I said, sitting down on the bench next to Brianna. 'But you can maybe do better than just the written description. Bree's a good hand with a likeness,' I explained to Jamie. 'Can you draw Roger from memory, do you think, Bree?'

'Yes!' She reached for the quill, eager to try. 'Yes, I'm sure I can – I've drawn him before.'

Jamie surrendered the quill and paper, the vertical lines between his brows showing in a slight frown.

'Can the printer work from an ink sketch?' I asked, seeing it.

'Oh – aye, I expect so. It's no great matter to make a woodblock, if the lines are clear.' He spoke abstractedly, eyes fixed on the paper in front of Brianna.

Ian pushed Rollo's head off his knee and came to stand by the table, looking over Bree's shoulder in what seemed a rather exaggerated curiosity.

Lower lip fixed between her teeth, she drew clean and swiftly. High forehead, with a thick lock of black hair that rose from an invisible cowlick, then dipped almost to the strongly marked black brows. She drew him in profile; a bold nose, not quite beaky, a clean-lined, sensitive mouth

940

and a wide, slanted jaw. Thick-lashed eyes, deepset, with lines of good humor marking a strong, appealing face. She added a neat, flat ear, then turned her attention to the elegant curve of the skull, drawing thick, wavy dark hair pulled back in a short tail.

Ian made a small, strangled noise in his throat.

'Are you all right, Ian?' I looked up at him, but he wasn't looking at the drawing – he was looking across the table, at Jamie. He was wearing a glazed sort of expression, like a pig on a spit.

I turned, to find precisely the same expression on Jamie's face.

'What on earth is the matter?' I asked.

'Oh . . . nothing.' The muscles of his throat moved in a convulsive swallow. The corner of his mouth twitched, and twitched again, as though he couldn't control it.

'Like hell it is!' Alarmed, I leaned across the table, seizing his wrist and groping for his pulse. 'Jamie, what is it? Are you having chest pains? Do you feel ill?'

'*I* do.' Ian was leaning over the table, looking as though he might be going to throw up any minute. 'Coz – d'ye mean honestly to tell me that . . . *this*' – he gestured feebly at the sketch – 'is Roger Wakefield?'

'Yes,' she said, looking up at him in puzzlement. 'Ian, are you all right? Did you eat something funny?'

He didn't answer, but dropped heavily onto the bench beside her, put his head in his hands, and groaned.

Jamie gently detached his hand from my grip. Even in the red of the firelight, I could see that he was white and strained. The hand on the table curled around the quill jar, as though seeking support.

'Mr. Wakefield,' he said carefully to Brianna. 'Has he by any chance . . . another name?'

'Yes,' Brianna and I said in unison. I stopped and let her explain as I rose and went hurriedly to fetch a bottle of brandy from the pantry. I didn't know what was going on, but had the horrible feeling that it was about to be called for.

'– adopted. MacKenzie was his own family name,' she was saying as I emerged with the bottle in hand. She glanced from father to cousin, frowning. 'Why? You haven't heard of a Roger MacKenzie, have you?'

Jamie and Ian exchanged an appalled glance. Ian cleared his throat. So did Jamie.

'What?' Brianna demanded, leaning forward, glancing anxiously from one to the other. 'What is it? Have you seen him? Where?'

I saw Jamie's jaw tighten as he summoned up words.

'Aye,' he said carefully. 'We have. On the mountain.'

'What – here? On *this* mountain?' She stood up, pushing back the bench. Alarm and excitement played over her face like flames. 'Where is he? What happened?'

'Well,' Ian said defensively, 'he *did* say as he'd taken your maidenheid, after all.'

'He WHAT?' Brianna's eyes sprang open so far that a rim of white showed all around the iris.

'Well, your da asked him, just to be sure, and he admitted that he'd –'

'You *what?*' Brianna rounded on Jamie, clenched fists on the table.

'Aye, well. It – was a mistake,' Jamie said. He looked utterly wretched.

'You bet it was! What in the name of – what have you done?' Her own cheeks had blanched, and blue sparks glinted in her eyes, hot as the heart of a flame.

Jamie took a deep breath. He looked up, straight into her face, and set his jaw.

'The wee lassie,' he said. 'Lizzie. She told me that ye were with child, and that the man who'd got it on ye was a wicked brute called MacKenzie.'

Brianna's mouth opened and shut, but no words came out. Jamie looked at her steadily.

'Ye did say to me that ye'd been violated, did ye no?'

She nodded, jerky as a badly sprung puppet.

'So, then. Ian and the lassie were at the mill, when MacKenzie came askin' for ye. They rode to fetch me, and Ian and I met him in the clearing just above the green spring.'

Brianna had got her voice working, though only barely.

'What did you do to him?' she asked hoarsely. 'What?'

'It was a fair fight,' Ian said, still defensive. 'I wanted to shoot him on sight, but Uncle Jamie said no, he meant to have his hands on the – the man.'

'You *hit* him?'

'Aye, I did!' Jamie said, stung at last. 'For God's sake, woman, what would ye have me do to the man who'd used ye that way? It was you wanting to do murder, aye?'

'Besides, he hit Uncle Jamie, too,' Ian put in helpfully. 'It was a fair fight. I said.'

'Be quiet, Ian, there's a good lad,' I said. I poured two fingers, neat, and pushed the cup in front of Jamie.

'But it was – he *wasn't* –' Brianna was sputtering, like a firecracker with a short fuse lit. Then she caught fire, and slammed one fist on the table, going off like a rocket.

'WHAT HAVE YOU DONE WITH HIM?' she screamed.

Jamie blinked and Ian flinched. They exchanged haunted glances.

I put a hand on Jamie's arm, squeezing tight. I couldn't keep the quaver out of my own voice as I asked the necessary question.

'Jamie – did you kill him?'

He glanced at me, and the tension in his face relaxed, if only marginally.

'Ah . . . no,' he said. 'I gave him to the Iroquois.'

'Och, now, Coz, it could have been worse.' Ian patted Brianna tentatively on the back. 'We didna kill him, after all.'

Brianna made a small choking sound, and pulled her head up off her knees. Her face was white and damp as the inside of an oyster shell, her hair in a tangle round it. She hadn't vomited or fainted, but looked as though she still might do either.

'We did mean to,' Ian went on, looking at her a little nervously. 'I'd my pistol pressed behind his ear, but then I thought it was really Uncle Jamie's right to blow his brains out, but then he –'

Brianna choked again, and I hastily placed an ashet on the table in front of her, just in case.

'Ian, I really think she doesn't need to hear this just now,' I said, narrowing my eyes at him.

'Yes, I do.' Brianna pushed herself upright, hands gripping the edge of the table. 'I have to hear it all, I have to.' She turned her head slowly, as though her neck was stiff, toward Jamie.

'Why?' she said. 'WHY?'

He was as white and ill-looking as she was. He had pushed away from the table and gone to the chimney corner, as though trying to get as far away as possible from the drawing, with its damning likeness of Roger MacKenzie Wakefield.

He looked as though he would have done anything rather than answer, but answer he did, his eyes steady on hers.

'I meant to kill him. I stopped Ian because shooting the prick seemed too easy a death – too quick for what he'd done.' He took a deep breath, and I could see that the hand gripping his writing shelf was clenched so tight that the knuckles stood out white against his skin.

'I stopped to think, how it should be; what I must do. I left Ian with him, and I walked away.' He swallowed; I could see the muscles move in his throat, but he didn't look away.

'I walked into the forest a wee way, and leaned my back against a tree to let my heart slow. It seemed best he should be awake, to know – but I didna think I could bear to hear him speak again. He'd said too much already. But then I began to hear it, over again, what he'd said.'

'What? What did he say?' Even her lips were white.

So were Jamie's.

'He said . . . that ye'd asked him to your bed. That you –' He stopped and bit his lip, savagely.

'He said ye wanted him; that ye'd asked him to take your maidenheid,' Ian said. He spoke coolly, his eyes on Brianna.

She drew in breath with a ragged sound, like paper being torn.

'I did.'

I glanced involuntarily at Jamie. His eyes were closed, his teeth fixed in his lip.

Ian made a shocked sound, and Brianna drew back a hand like lightning and slapped him across the face.

He jerked back, lost his balance, and half fell off the

944

bench. He grabbed the edge of the table and staggered to his feet.

'How?' he shouted, his face contorted in sudden anger. 'How could ye do such a thing? I told Uncle Jamie that ye'd never play the whore, never! But it's true, isn't it?'

She was on her feet like a leopard, her cheeks gone from white to blazing fury in a second.

'Well, damn you for a self-righteous prig, Ian! Who gave you the right to call me a whore?'

'Right?' He sputtered for a moment, at a loss for words. 'I – you – he –'

Before I could intervene, she drew back a fist and punched him hard in the pit of the stomach. With a look of intense surprise, he sat down hard on the floor, mouth open like a suckling pig.

I moved, but Jamie was faster. In less than a second he was beside her, gripping her arm. She whirled, meaning to hit him, too, I think, but then froze. Her mouth was working soundlessly, tears of shock and fury running down her cheeks.

'Be still,' he said, and his voice was very cold. I saw his fingers dig into her flesh, and I made a small sound of protest. He paid no attention, too intent on Brianna.

'I didna want to believe it,' he said, in a voice like ice. 'I told myself he was only saying so to save himself, it wasna true. But if it was –' He seemed to become aware at last that he was hurting her. He let go of her arm.

'I couldna take the man's life, without being sure,' he said, and paused, his eyes searching her face. For regret? I wondered. Or remorse? Whatever he might be looking for, all he found was a smoldering rage. Her face was the echo of his own, her blue eyes hot as his.

His own face changed, and he looked away.

'I did regret it,' he said, very quietly. 'When I came that night, and saw ye, I was sorry then that I hadna killed him. I held ye in my arms – and I felt my heart go sma' wi' shame, that I should doubt my daughter's virtue.' He looked down, and I could see the mark where he had bitten his lip.

'Now my heart is shrunk altogether. Not only that ye should be impure but that ye should lie to me.'

'Lie to you?' Her voice was no more than whisper. '*Lie* to you?'

'Aye, lie to me!' With sudden violence, he turned back to her. 'That ye should bed a man from lust, and cry rape when ye find ye're with child! Do ye not realize that it's only chance I have not the sin of murder on my soul, and you the cause of it?'

She was too furious to speak; I saw her throat swell with words, and knew I had to do something, at once, before either of them had the opportunity to say more.

I couldn't speak, either. Blindly, I fumbled in the pocket of my gown, feeling for the ring. I found it, pulled it out, and dropped it on the table. It chimed against the wood; spun, and rattled to a stop, the gold of the tiny circlet gleaming red in the firelight.

From F. to C. with love. Always.

Jamie looked at it, his face gone completely blank. Brianna drew in her breath with a sob.

'That's your ring, Auntie,' Ian said. He sounded dazed, and bent close to look, as though he couldn't believe his eyes. 'Your gold ring. The one that Bonnet took from ye, on the river.'

'Yes,' I said. My knees felt weak. I sat down at the table, and laid my hand over the telltale ring as though to take it back, deny its presence.

Jamie took my wrist and lifted it. Like a man handling a dangerous insect, he picked the ring up gingerly between thumb and forefinger.

'Where did ye get this?' he asked, his voice almost casual. He looked at me, and a bolt of terror shot through me at the look in his eyes.

'I brought it to her.' Brianna's tears had dried, evaporated by the heat of her fury. She stood behind me and gripped me by the shoulders. 'Don't you look at her that way, don't you dare!'

He shifted the look to her, but she didn't flinch; only held on to me harder, her fingers digging into my shoulders.

'Where did ye get it?' he asked again, his voice no more than a whisper. 'Where?'

'From him. From Stephen Bonnet.' Her voice was

shaking, but from rage, not fear. 'When ... he ... raped ... me.'

Jamie's face cracked suddenly, as though some explosion had burst him from within. I made an incoherent sound of distress, and reached out for him, but he whirled away and stood rigid, back turned to us, in the middle of the room.

I felt Brianna draw herself upright, heard Ian say, rather stupidly, '*Bonnet?*' I heard the ticking of the clock on the sideboard, felt the draft from the door. I was dimly aware of all these things, but had no eyes for anything but Jamie.

I pushed back the bench, stumbled to my feet. He stood as though rooted into the floor, fists clenched into his belly like a man gut-shot, trying to hold back the inevitable fatal spill of his insides.

I should be able to do something, to say something. I should be able to help them, to take care of them. But I could do nothing. I could not help one without betraying the other – had already betrayed them both. I had sold Jamie's honor to keep him safe, and the doing of it had taken Roger and destroyed Bree's happiness.

I could go to neither of them now. All I could do was to stand there, feeling my heart crumble into small, jagged chunks.

Bree left me, and walked quietly around the table, across the room, around Jamie. She stood in front of him, looking up into his face, her own set like marble, cold as a saint's.

'Damn you,' she said, scarcely audible. 'Damn you very much, you bastard. I'm sorry I ever saw you.'

PART ELEVEN

Pas du Tout

51

Betrayal

October 1769

Roger opened his eyes and threw up. Or rather, down. It didn't matter; The burning rush of bile through his nose and the trickle of vomitus that ran into his hair were unimportant by comparison with the agony in head and groin.

A thumping swerve of movement jarred him, shooting kaleidoscopic colors from crotch to brain. A damp smell of canvas filled his nose. Then a voice spoke somewhere near, and formless panic took sudden, jagged shape among the colors.

Glorianna! They'd got him! He lurched in reflex, brought up short by a searing jolt through his temples – but brought up a split-second earlier by something round his wrists. Tied, he was tied up in the hold.

The shape of panic blew up bold and black against his mind. Bonnet. They'd caught him, taken back the stones. And now they'd kill him.

He jerked convulsively, yanking at his wrists, teeth clenched against the pain. The deck dropped beneath him with a startled snort, and he slammed down hard.

He vomited again, but his stomach was empty. He retched, ribs grating with each spasm against the canvas-wrapped bundles he lay across. Not sails; not a hold. Not the *Glorianna*, not a ship at all. A horse. He was tied hand and foot, belly down across a fucking horse!

The horse jolted on a few more steps, then stopped. Voices muttered, hands fumbled at him, then pulled him off roughly and dropped on his feet. He fell down at once, unable either to stand or to break his fall. He lay doubled on the ground, concentrating on breathing. Without the jouncing, it was easier. Nobody troubled him, and gradually he began to be aware of his surroundings.

Awareness didn't help much. There were damp leaves under his cheek, cool and smelling of sweet rot. He

951

cracked a cautious eye. Sky above, and impossible deep color, between blue and purple. The sound of trees, the rush of nearby water.

Everything seemed to be revolving slowly around him, painfully vivid. He closed his eyes and pressed his hands flat against the ground.

Jesus, where am I? The voices were talking casually, words half lost in the stamping and whickering of nearby horses. He listened intently but couldn't make out the words. He felt a moment's panic at the inability; he couldn't even put a name to the language.

There was a large, tender lump behind one ear, another on the back of his head, and a pain that made his temples throb; he'd been hit hard – but when? Had the blows ruptured vessels in his brain, deprived him of language? He opened his eyes all the way, and – with infinite caution – rolled onto his back.

A square brown face glanced down at him, with no particular expression of interest, then looked back to the horse the man was tending.

Indians. The shock was so great that he forgot momentarily about his pain, and sat up abruptly. He gasped and put his face on his knees, eyes closed as he fought to keep from passing out again, blood pounding through a splitting head.

Where was he? He bit his knee, grinding the cloth savagely between his teeth, fighting for memory. Fragments of images came back to him, in mocking bits that stubbornly refused to fit together into sense.

The creak of boards and the smell of bilges. Blinding sun through panes of glass. Bonnet's face, and the breathing of whales in the mist, and a little boy named . . . named . . .

Hands clasped in dark and the tang of hops. *I thee wed, with my body I thee worship* . . .

Bree. Brianna. Cold sweat rolled down his cheek and his jaw muscles ached with clenching. The images hopped around in his mind like fleas. Her face, her face, he must not let it go!

Not gentle, not a gentle face. A nose dead straight and cold blue eyes . . . no, not cold . . .

A hand on his shoulder yanked him from the tortured pursuit of memory into the all too immediate present. It was an Indian, knife in hand. Numb with confusion, Roger simply looked at the man.

The Indian, a middle-aged man with a bone in his roached hair, and an air of no-nonsense about him, took Roger by his own hair and tilted his head back and forth with a critical air. Confusion evaporated, as it occurred to Roger that he was about to be scalped as he sat there.

He flung himself backward and lashed out with his feet, catching the Indian in the knees. The man went down with a cry of surprise, and Roger rolled, lurching and stumbling to his feet, running for his life.

He ran like a drunken spider, spraddle-legged, staggering toward the trees. Shadows, refuge. There were shouts behind him, and the sound of quick feet scattering leaves. Then something jerked his feet from under him and he fell headlong with a bone-shaking thud.

They had him on his feet before he had his breath back. No good to struggle; there were four of them, including the one Roger had knocked down. That one came toward them, limping, still holding the knife.

'Not hurt you!' he said crossly. He slapped Roger briskly across the face, then leaned over and sawed through the leather thong that bound Roger's wrists. With a loud snort, he turned on his heel and went back to the horses.

The two men holding Roger promptly let go of him and walked off, too, leaving him swaying like a sapling in a high wind.

Great, he thought blankly, *I'm not dead. What the bloody hell?*

No answer to this presenting itself, he rubbed a hand gingerly over his face, discovering several bruises he'd missed earlier, and looked around.

He stood in a small clearing, surrounded by huge oaks and half-shed hickory trees; the ground was thick with brown and yellow leaves, and the squirrels had left heaps of acorn caps and nut hulls scattered over the ground. He stood on a mountain; the slope of the ground told him that, as the chill air and jewel-deep sky told him the time was near sunset.

The Indians – there were four, all men – ignored him completely, going about the business of camp-building without a glance in Roger's direction. He licked dry lips and took a cautious step toward the small stream that burbled over algae-furred rocks a few yards away.

He drank his fill, though the cold water made his teeth ache; nearly all the teeth were loose on one side of his mouth, and the lining of his cheek was badly cut. He rinsed his face gingerly, with a feeling of déjà vu. Some-time earlier, he had washed and drunk like this, cold water running over emerald rocks . . .

Fraser's Ridge. He sat back on his heels, memory dropping back in place, in large, ugly chunks.

Brianna, and Claire . . . and Jamie Fraser. Suddenly the confusing image he had sought so desperately came back unbidden; Brianna's face, with its broad, clean bones, blue eyes set slantwise above a long, straight nose. But Brianna's face grown older, weathered to bronze, rough-cut and toughened by masculinity and experience, blue eyes gone black with a murderous rage. Jamie Fraser.

'You bloody sod,' Roger said softly. 'You bloody, fucking *sod.* You tried to kill me.'

His initial feeling was one of astonishment – but anger wasn't far behind.

He remembered everything now; the meeting in the clearing, the autumn leaves like fire and honey and the blazing man among them; the brown-haired youth – and who the hell was *he?* The fight – he touched a sore spot under his ribs with a grimace – and the end of it, lying flat in the leaves, sure that he was about to be killed.

Well, he hadn't been. He had a dim memory of hearing the man and the boy arguing somewhere over him – one of them had been for killing him on the spot, the other said no – but damned if he knew which one. Then one of them had hit him again, and he remembered nothing more until now.

And now – he glanced around. The Indians had a fire going, and a clay pot sitting by it. None of them paid him the least attention, though he was sure they were all aware of him.

Perhaps they had taken him from Fraser and the boy –

why, though? More likely, Fraser had given him to the Indians. The man with the knife had said they didn't mean to hurt him. What *did* they mean to do with him?

He looked around. It would be night, soon; already, the distant shadows under the oaks had thickened.

So what, sport? If you slope off after dark, where're you going to? The only direction you know is down. The Indians were apparently ignoring him because they were confident that he wasn't going anywhere.

Dismissing the uncomfortable truth of this observation, he stood up. First things first. It was the last thing he wanted to do at the moment, but his bladder was bursting. His fingers were slow and clumsy, congested with blood, but he managed to fumble loose the lacing of his breeches.

His first feeling was one of relief; it wasn't as bad as it felt. Very sore, but ginger prodding seemed to indicate that he was basically intact and unruptured.

It was only as he turned back toward the fire that simple relief was succeeded by a burst of rage so pure and blinding as to burn away both pain and fear. On his right wrist was a smudged black oval – a thumbprint, clear and mocking as a signature.

'Christ,' he said, very softly. Fury burned hot and thick in the pit of his belly. He could taste it, sour in his mouth. He looked down the mountainside behind him, not knowing whether he faced Fraser's Ridge or not.

'Wait for me, bugger,' he said, under his breath. '*Both* of you – wait for me. I'm coming back.'

Not right away, though. The Indians allowed him to share the food – a sort of stew, which they scooped up with their hands in spite of its near-boiling temperature – but were otherwise indifferent to him. He tried them in English, French – even the small bits of German that he knew, but got no response.

They did tie him when they lay down to sleep; his ankles were bound and a noose put round his neck, tied to the wrist of one of his captors. Whether from indifference or because there wasn't one, they didn't give him a blanket, and he spent the night shivering, huddled as close to the dwindling fire as he could get without choking himself.

He hadn't thought he could sleep, but did, exhausted with pain. It was a restless sleep, though, filled with violent, fragmentary dreams and broken by the constant illusion of being strangled.

In the morning, they set off again. No question of riding this time, he walked, and as fast as he could; the noose was left around his neck, hanging loose, but a short length of rope bound his wrists to the harness leathers of one of the horses. He stumbled and fell several times, but managed to scramble to his feet, in spite of bruises and aching muscles. He had the distinct impression that they would allow him to be dragged without compunction if he didn't.

They were heading roughly north; he could tell as much by the sun. Not that that helped a lot, since he had no notion where they had started from. Still, they could be no great distance from Fraser's Ridge; he couldn't have been unconscious for more than a few hours. He looked at the churning hooves of the horse beside him, trying to estimate its speed. No more than two or three miles per hour; he was managing to keep up without great strain.

Landmarks. There was no telling where they meant to take him – or why – but if he was ever to get back, he had to memorize the shape of the terrain through which they passed.

A cliff, forty feet high and overgrown with shaggy plants, a twisted persimmon tree protruding from a crack in the rock like a jack-in-the-box popping out, covered in bright orange bobbles.

They emerged onto the crest of a ridge, to a breathtaking view of distant mountains; three sharp peaks, clustered together against a blazing sky, the left one higher than the other two. He could remember that. A stream – a river? – that fell through a small gorge; they drove the horses through a shallow ford, soaking Roger to the waist in icy water.

The routine of travel lasted for days, moving ever northward. His captors did not talk to him, and by the fourth day he realized that he was beginning to lose track of time, falling into a dreamlike trance, overcome by fatigue and the silence of the mountains. He pulled a long thread from the hem of his coat and began to knot it, one knot for each day, both as some small hold on reality, and as a crude method of estimating the distance traveled.

He was going back. Whatever it took, he was going back to Fraser's Ridge.

It was on the eighth day that he found his chance. They were high in the mountains by now. They had crossed through one pass the day before, and come down a steep slope, the ponies grunting, slowing to brace each careful step as the loads on their saddles creaked and shifted.

Now they were headed up again, and the ponies slowed their pace still further as the ground sloped sharply upward. Roger was able to gain a little ground, to pull even with the pony's side and cling to the harness leather, letting the tough little beast pull him along.

The Indians had dismounted, walking and leading the ponies. He kept a narrow eye on the long black scalp lock hanging down the back of the brave leading the pony he clung to. He held on with one hand; the other was busy under cover of a hanging flap of canvas, picking at the knot that bound him to the harness.

Strand by strand, the hemp came free, until no more than a single thread of rope held him to the pony. He waited, sweat streaming down his ribs from fear and the effort of the climb, rejecting one opportunity after another, worrying from moment to moment that he had left it too late, that they would stop to make camp, that the brave who led his pony would turn and see him, would think to check.

But they didn't stop, and the brave didn't turn. *There*, he thought, and his heart beat fast, seeing the first pony in the string step out along a narrow deer trail cut into the hillside. The ground fell away sharply below the trail, then leveled out about six feet down. Below was a thickly wooded slope, ideal for concealment.

One pony, then another, negotiated the narrow stretch of trail, putting down their feet with finicking care. A third, and then it was Roger's turn. He squeezed in close to the pony's side, smelling the sweet, pungent foam of its sweat. One step, then another, and they were on the narrow trail.

He jerked the rope loose and jumped. He hit with a jolt and sank halfway to his knees, sprang up and ran downhill. His shoes came off and he left them behind. He splashed across a tiny creek, scrabbled up its bank on hands and knees, and clambered to his feet, running before he'd got upright.

He heard calls behind him, then silence, but knew he was pursued. He had no breath to waste; neither would they.

The landscape slid past in a blur of leaves and rocks as he swung his head from side to side, looking for which way to go, someplace to hide. He chose a grove of birch, burst through and into a sloping meadow, careened down across the slippery grass, bare feet stubbing on roots and rocks. At the far side, he took a second to glance back. Two of them; he saw the round dark heads among the leaves.

On into another copse, out again, zigzagging madly through a field of broken rocks, breath coming hard in his throat. One thing the bloody past had done for him, he thought grimly; improved his wind. Then there was no room for any thought – nothing but the blind instincts of flight.

And down again, a scrambling drop down the wet, cracked face of a twenty-foot cliff, grabbing at the plants as he half fell past them, roots ripping, hands sinking into pockets of mud, blunting his fingers on unseen rocks. He landed hard at the bottom, bent over, gasping.

One of them was right behind him, coming backward down the cliff. He snatched off the noose still around his neck, and whipped it hard at the Indian's hands. The man's hold slipped; he let go and slithered down, landing askew. Roger flung the noose over the man's head, gave it a vicious yank, and fled, leaving the man on his knees, choking and clawing at the rope round his neck.

Trees. He needed cover. He vaulted a fallen log, stumbled and rolled, was up again running. Up, a spruce thicket up a little way. Heart laboring, he jabbed his feet down hard, bounding up the slope.

He flung himself into the spruces, fighting through the pricks of a million needles, blind, eyes shut against the lashing twigs. Then the ground gave way underneath him and he fell in a blur of sky and branches.

He hit, half curled, his breath knocked out; had barely sense to curl up further and keep on rolling, bashing off rocks and saplings, setting off showers of dirt and fallen needles, bouncing and smashing his way to the bottom.

He fetched up with a crash amid a tangle of woody stems, hung a moment, then slid down, to end with a thud. Dazed and bleeding, he lay still for a moment, then rolled painfully onto his side, wiping dirt and blood from his face.

He looked up, searching. There they were. The two of them, at the top of the slope, coming carefully down beside the ledge he had fallen from.

On hands and knees, he dived between the woody stems, and crawled for his life. Twigs bent, sharp ends jabbed him, and cascades of dust, dead leaves and insects fell from the higher branches above as he heaved his way forward, forcing a passage through the close-grown stems, twisting and turning, following such openings as he found.

Hell was his first coherent thought. Then he realized that it was as much description as curse. He was in a rhododendron hell. With that belated realization, he slowed his flight – if crawling at roughly ten feet per hour could be called 'flight'.

The tunnel-like opening in which he found himself was too narrow to allow him to turn around, but he managed to see behind him by thrusting his head to one side and craning his neck. There was nothing there; nothing but damp and musty darkness, illumined by a faint scatter of light, swirling with dust motes. Nothing was visible but the stems and limber branches of the rhododendron thicket.

His shaking limbs gave way, and he collapsed. He lay for a moment, curled up between the stems, breathing the musk of rotting leaves and damp earth.

'You wanted cover, mate,' he murmured to himself. Things were beginning to hurt. He was ripped and bleeding in a dozen places. Even in the dim light, the ends of his fingers looked like raw meat.

He took a slow inventory of the damage, listening all the while for sounds of pursuit. Not surprisingly, there were none. He had heard talk about rhododendron hells in the taverns in Cross Creek; half-boasting stories of hunting dogs who had chased a squirrel into one of the huge tangles and become hopelessly lost, never to be seen again.

Roger hoped there was a fair amount of exaggeration to these stories, though a good look around wasn't reassuring. What light there was had no direction. Any way he looked, looked the same. Drooping clusters of cool, leathery leaves, thick stems and slender branches laced together in a nearly impenetrable snarl.

With a slight feeling of panic, he realized that he had no idea from which direction he had come.

He put his head on his knees and breathed deeply, trying to think. All right, first things first. His right foot was bleeding freely from a deep gash on the edge of the sole. He took off his tattered stockings and used one to bind his foot. Nothing else seemed bad enough to need a bandage, save the shallow gouge in his scalp; that was still seeping blood, wet and sticky to his touch.

His hands were shaking; it was hard to tie the stocking round his head. Still, the small action made him feel better. Now, then. He'd climbed countless Munros in Scotland, those endless craggy peaks, and more than once had helped to find day-trippers lost among the rocks and heather.

If you were lost in the wilderness, the usual caution was to stay put; wait for someone to find you. That would seem not to apply, he thought, if the only people looking for you were ones you didn't want to be found by.

He looked upward, through the snarl of branches. He could see small patches of sky, but the rhododendrons rose nearly twelve feet over his head. There was no way to stand up; he could barely sit upright under the interlacing branches.

There was no way of telling how big this particular hell was; on their journey through the mountains, he had seen entire slopes covered with heath balds, valleys filled with the deep green of rhododendron, only a few ambitious trees protruding above the waving sea of leaves. Then again, they had detoured round small tangles of the stuff, no more than a hundred feet square. He knew he was fairly close to one edge of the thing, but that knowledge was useless, with no idea in which direction the edge lay.

He became aware that he was very cold, his hands still shaking. *Shock*, he thought dimly. What did you do for shock? Hot liquids, blankets. Brandy. Yeah, right. Elevate the feet. That much, he could do.

He scooped a shallow, awkward little depression and eased himself into it, scraping the clammy, half-rotted leaves over his chest and shoulders. He propped his heels in the fork of a stem and closed his eyes, shivering.

They wouldn't come in after him. Why should they? A lot better to wait, if they were in no hurry. He'd have to come out eventually – if he still could.

Any movement here below would shake the leaves above, and pinpoint his movements to the watchers. That was a cold thought; they undoubtedly knew where he was now, and were simply waiting for his next move. The patches of sky were the deep blue of sapphires; it was still afternoon. He would wait till dark before he moved, then.

Hands clasped together on his chest, he willed himself to rest, to think of something beyond his present situation. Brianna. Let him think of her. Without the rage or bewilderment, now; there was no time for that.

Let him pretend that all was still between them as it had been on that night, their night. Warm against him in the dark. Her hands, so frank and curious, eager on his body. The generosity of her nakedness, freely given. And his momentary, mistaken conviction that all was forever right with the world. Gradually, the shivering eased, and he slept.

He woke sometime after moonrise; he could see bright-ness suffusing the sky, though not the moon itself. He was stiff and cold, and very sore. Hungry, too, and with a desperate thirst. Well, if he got himself out of this bloody tangle, at least he could find water; streams were every-

961

where in these mountains. Feeling awkward as a turtle on its back, he turned slowly over.

One direction was as good as another. On hands and knees, he started off, pushing through crevices, breaking branches, trying his best to go in a straight line. One fear haunted him more than thought of the Indians; he could so easily lose his bearings, moving blindly through this maze. He could end by going in endless circles, trapped forever. The stories of the hunting dogs had lost any element of exaggeration.

Some small animal ran over his hand and he jerked, hitting his head on the branches overhead. He gritted his teeth and kept on, a few inches at a time. Crickets chirped all around him, and countless small rustlings let him know that the inhabitants of this particular hell didn't appreciate his intrusion. He couldn't see anything at all; it was almost pitch-black here below. There was the one good thing, though: The constant effort heated him; sweat stung the gouge in his scalp and dripped from his chin.

Whenever he had to stop for breath, he listened for some clue – to either his location or his pursuers' – but he heard nothing beyond the occasional night bird's call and the rustle of the leaves all around. He wiped his sweating face on his sleeve and pushed on.

He didn't know how long he had been going when he found the rock. Or not so much found it as ran headfirst into it. He reeled back, clutching his head and gritting his teeth to keep from crying out.

Blinking from the pain, he put out a hand and found what he had struck. Not a boulder; a flat-faced rock. A tall one, too; the hard surface extended up as high as he could reach.

He groped to the side, and made his way around the rock. There was a thick stem growing near it; his shoulders stuck in the narrow space between. He wrenched and heaved, squirming, and finally shot forward, losing his balance and landing on his face.

Doggedly, he rose up onto his hands again – and realized that he could *see* his hands. He looked up, and around, in complete amazement.

His head and shoulders protruded into a clear space.

Not merely clear, but *empty*. Eagerly, he wriggled forward, out of the claustrophobic grip of the rhododendrons.

He was standing in an open space, facing a cliff wall that rose on the far side of a small clearing. It really was a clearing, too; nothing at all grew in the soft dirt beneath his feet. Astonished, he turned slowly round, gulping great lungfuls of cold, sharp air.

'My God in heaven,' he said softly, aloud. The clearing was roughly oval in shape, ringed by standing stones, with one end of the oval closed by the cliff face. The stones were evenly spaced around the ring, a few of them fallen, a couple more dislodged from their places by the press of roots and stems behind them. He could see the dense black mass of the rhododendrons, showing between and above the stones – but not one plant grew within the perimeter of the ring.

Feeling gooseflesh ripple over his body, he walked softly toward the center of the ring. It couldn't be – but it was. And why not, after all? If Geillis Duncan had been right . . . he turned and saw in the moonlight the scratchings on the cliff face.

He walked closer to look at them. There were several petroglyphs, some the size of his hand, others nearly as tall as he was; spiral shapes, and what might be a bent man, dancing – or dying. A nearly closed circle, that looked like a snake chasing its tail. Warning signs.

He shuddered again, and his hand went to the seam of his breeches. They were still there: the two gems he had risked his life to get, tiny passports to safety – he hoped – for him and for Brianna.

He could hear nothing; no humming, no buzzing. The autumn air was cold, a light wind stirring the rhododendron leaves. Damn, what was the date? He didn't know, had lost track long since. He thought it had been near the beginning of September, though, when he left Brianna in Wilmington. It had taken much longer than he'd thought, to track Bonnet and find an opportunity to steal the gems. It must be nearly the end of October now – the feast of Samhain, the Eve of All Hallows, was nearly come, or only recently past.

Would this ring follow the same dates, though? He supposed that it would; if the Earth's lines of force shifted with its revolution around the sun, then all the passages should stand open or closed with the shift.

He stepped closer to the cliff and saw it; an opening near the base of the cliff, a split in the rock, perhaps a cave. A chill ran over him that had nothing to do with the cold night wind. His fingers closed tightly over the small round hardness of the gems. He heard nothing; was it open? If so . . .

Escape. It would be that. Escape to when, though? And how? The words of Geilie's spell chanted in his mind. *Garnets rest in love about my neck; I will be faithful.*

Faithful. To try that avenue of escape was to abandon Brianna. *And hasn't she abandoned you?*

'No, I'm damned if she has!' he whispered to himself. There was some reason for what she'd done, he knew it.

She's found her parents; she'll be safe enough. 'And for this reason, a woman shall leave her parents, and cleave to her husband.' Safety wasn't what mattered; love was. If he'd cared for safety, he wouldn't have crossed that desperate void to begin with.

His hands were sweating; he could feel the damp grain of the rough cloth under his fingers, and his torn fingertips burned and throbbed. He took one more step toward the split in the cliff face, his eyes fixed on the pitch-black inside. If he didn't step inside . . . there were only two things to do. Go back to the suffocating grip of the rhododendrons, or try to scale the cliff before him.

He tilted his head back to gauge its height. A face was looking down at him, featureless in the dark, silhouetted against the moon-bright sky. He hadn't time to move or think before the rope noose settled gently over his head and tightened, pressing his arms against his body.

52

Desertion

River Run, December 1769

It had been raining, and soon would be again. Drops of water hung trembling under the petals of the marble Jacobite roses on Hector Cameron's tomb, and the brick walk was dark with wet.

Semper Fidelis, it said, beneath his name and dates. Semper Fi. She had dated a Marine cadet once; he'd had it carved on the ring he had tried to give her. Always faithful. And who had Hector Cameron been faithful to? His wife? His prince?

She hadn't spoken to Jamie Fraser since that night. Nor he to her. Not since the final moment, when in a fury of fear and outrage, she had screamed at him, 'My father would never have said such a thing!'

She could still see what his face had looked like when she spoke her final words to him; she wished she could forget. He had turned without a word and left the cabin. Ian had risen, and quietly gone after him; neither of them had come back that night.

Her mother had stayed with her, comforting, petting, stroking her head and murmuring small soothing things as she alternately raged and sobbed. But even as her mother held Brianna's head in her lap and wiped her face with cool cloths, Bree could feel a part of her yearning toward that man, wanting to follow him, wanting to comfort *him.* And she blamed him for that as well.

Her head throbbed with the effort of staying stone-faced. She didn't dare relax the muscles of eyes and jaw until she was sure they had left; it would be too easy to break down.

She hadn't; not since that night. Once she had pulled herself together, she had assured her mother that she was all right, insisted that Claire go to bed. She had herself sat up till dawn, eyes burning from rage and woodsmoke, with the drawing of Roger on the table before her.

He had come back at dawn, called her mother to him, not looking at Brianna. Murmured a bit in the dooryard, and sent her mother back, face hollow-eyed with worry, to pack her things.

He had brought her here, down the mountain to River Run. She had wanted to go with them, had wanted to go at once to find Roger, without a moment's delay. But he had been obdurate, and so had her mother.

It was late December, and the winter snows lay thick on the mountainside. She was nearly four months gone; the taut curve of her belly was tightly rounded now. There was no telling how long the journey might take, and she was reluctantly compelled to admit that she didn't want to give birth on a raw mountainside. She might have over-ridden her mother's opinion, but not when it was buttressed by *his* stubbornness.

She leaned her forehead against the cool marble of the mausoleum; it was a cold day, spitting rain, but her face felt hot and swollen, as though she were coming down with a fever.

She couldn't stop hearing him, seeing him. His face, congested with rage, sharp-edged as a devil's mask. His voice, rough with fury and contempt, reproaching her – reproaching *her*! – for the loss of his bloody honor!

'*Your* honor?' she had said incredulously. 'Your *honor*? Your fucking notion of honor is what's caused all the trouble in the first place!'

'Ye willna use that sort of language to me! Though if it's fucking we're speaking of –'

'I'll fucking well say anything I want!' she bellowed, and slammed a fist on the table, rattling the dishes.

She had, too. So had he. Her mother had tried once or twice to stop them – Brianna flinched at the belated memory of the distress in Claire's deep golden eyes – but neither of them had paid a moment's notice, too intent on the savagery of their mutual betrayal.

Her mother had told her once that she had a Scottish temper – slowfused, but long-burning. Now she knew where it came from, but the knowing didn't help.

She put her folded arms against the tomb and rested her face on them, breathing in the faint sheep-smell of the wool. It reminded her of the handknit sweaters her father – her *real* father, she thought, with a fresh burst of desolation – had liked to wear.

'Why did you have to die?' she whispered to the hollow of damp wool. 'Oh, why?' If Frank Randall hadn't died, none of this would have happened. He and Claire would still be there, in the house in Boston, her family and her life would be intact.

But her father was gone, replaced by a violent stranger; a man who had her face, but could not understand her heart, a man who had taken both family and home from her, and not satisfied with that, had taken love and safety, too, leaving her bereft in this strange, harsh land.

She pulled the shawl closer around her shoulders, shivering at the wind that cut through the loose weave. She should have brought a cloak. She had kissed her white-lipped mother goodbye and then left, running through the dead garden, not looking at him. She'd wait here until she was sure they were gone, no matter if she froze.

She heard a step on the brick path above her and stiffened, though she didn't turn around. Perhaps it was a servant, or Jocasta come to persuade her inside.

But it was a stride too long and a footfall too strong for any but one man. She blinked hard, and gritted her teeth. She wouldn't turn around, she wouldn't.

'Brianna,' he said quietly behind her. She didn't answer, didn't move.

He made a small snorting noise – anger, impatience?

'I have a thing to say to ye.'

'Say it,' she said, and the words hurt her throat, as though she'd swallowed some jagged object.

It was beginning to rain again; fresh spatters slicked the marble in front of her, and she could feel the icy *pat!* of drops that struck through her hair.

'I will bring him home to you,' Jamie Fraser said, still quiet, 'or I will not come back myself.'

She couldn't bring herself to turn around. There was a small sound, a click on the pavement behind her, and then the sound of his footsteps, going away. Before her tear-blurred eyes, the drops on the marble roses gathered weight and began to fall.

When at last she turned around, the brick-lined walk was empty. At her feet was a folded paper, damp with rain, weighted with a stone. She picked it up, and held it crumpled in her hand, afraid to open it.

February 1770

In spite of worry and anger, she found herself easily absorbed into the flow of daily life at River Run. Her great-aunt, delighted at her company, encouraged her to find distraction; finding that she had some skill in drawing, Jocasta had brought out her own painting equipment, urging Brianna to make use of it.

By comparison with the cabin on the ridge, life at River Run was so luxurious as to be almost decadent. Still, Brianna woke at dawn, out of habit. She stretched langourously, wallowing in the physical delight of a feather bed that embraced and yielded to her every move – a definite contrast to lumpy quilts spread over a chilly straw tick.

There was a fire burning on the hearth, and a large copper can on the washstand, its burnished sides glowing. Hot water for washing; she could see the tiny shimmers of heat wavering over the metal. There was still a chill in the room, and the light outside was winter-blue with cold; the servant who had come and gone in silence must have risen in the black predawn and broken ice to get the water.

She ought to feel guilty at being waited on by slaves, she thought drowsily. She must remember to, later. There were a lot of things she didn't mean to think about until later; one more wouldn't hurt.

For now, she was warm. Far away, she could hear small noises in the house; a comforting scuffle of domesticity. The room itself was wrapped in silence, the occasional pop of kindling from the fire the only sound.

She rolled onto her back and, mind still half afloat in sleep, began to reacquaint herself with her body. This was a morning ritual; something she had begun to do half consciously as a teenager, and found necessary to do on purpose now – to find and make peace with the small changes of the night, lest she look suddenly during the day and find herself a stranger in her own body.

One stranger in her body was enough, she thought. She pushed the bedclothes down, running her hands slowly over the dormant swell of her stomach. A tiny ripple ran across her flesh as the inhabitant stretched, turning slowly as she had turned in the bed a few minutes before, enclosed and embraced.

'Hi, there,' she said softly. The bulge flexed briefly against her hand and then fell still, the occupant returned to its mysterious dreams.

Slowly, she ruffled up the nightgown – it was Jocasta's, warm soft flannel – registering the smooth long muscle at the top of each thigh, the soft hollow curving in at the top. Then up and down and over, bare skin to bare skin, palms to legs and belly and breasts. Smooth and soft, round and hard; muscle and bone . . . but now not all *her* muscle and bone.

Her skin felt different in the morning, like a snake's skin, newly shed, all tender and light-lucent. Later, when she rose, when the air got at it, it would be harder, a duller but more serviceable envelope.

She lay back against the pillow, watching the light fill the room. The house was awake beyond her. She could hear the myriad faint noises of people at work, and felt soothed. When she was small, she would wake on summer mornings to hear the chatter of her father's lawnmower underneath her window; his voice calling out in greeting to a neighbor. She had felt safe, protected, knowing he was there.

More recently, she had waked at dawn and heard Jamie Fraser's voice, speaking in soft Gaelic to his horses outside, and had felt that same feeling return with a rush. No more, though.

It had been true, what her mother said. She was removed, changed, altered without consent or knowledge, learning only after the fact. She threw aside the quilts and got up. She couldn't lie in bed mourning what was lost; it was no longer anyone's job to protect her. The job of protector was hers, now.

The baby was a constant presence – and, oddly enough, a constant reassurance. For the first time she felt blessing in it, and an odd reconciliation; her body had known this long before her mind. So that was true, too – her mother had said it often – 'Listen to your body.'

She leaned against the window frame, looking out on the patchy snow that lay on the kitchen garden. A slave, muffled in cloak and scarf, was kneeling on the path, digging overwintered carrots from one of the beds. Tall elms bordered the walled garden; somewhere beyond those stark bare branches lay the mountains.

She stayed still, listening to the rhythms of her body. The intruder in her flesh stirred a little, the tides of its movement merging with the pulsing of her blood – their blood. In the beating of her heart, she thought she heard the echo of that other, smaller heart, and in the sound found at last the courage to think clearly, with the assurance that if the worst happened – she pressed hard against the window frame, and felt it creak under the force of her urgency – if the worst happened, still she would not be totally alone.

53

Blame

Jamie spoke barely a word to anyone, between our departure from Fraser's Ridge, and our arrival at the Tuscaroran village of Tennago. I rode in a state of misery, torn between guilt at leaving Brianna, fear for Roger, and pain at Jamie's silence. He was short with Ian, and had said no more than absolutely necessary to Jocasta at Cross Creek. To me, he said nothing.

Plainly, he blamed me for not telling him at once about Stephen Bonnet. In retrospect, I blamed myself bitterly, seeing what had come of it. He had kept the gold ring I had thrown at him; I had no idea what he had done with it.

The weather was intermittently bad, the clouds hanging so low to the mountains that on the higher ridges, we traveled for days on end through a thick, cold fog, water droplets condensing on the horses' coats, so that a constant rain dripped from their manes and moisture shone on their flanks. We slept at night in whatever shelter we could find, each rolled in a damp cocoon of blankets, lying separately around a smoldering fire.

Some of the Indians who had known us at Anna Ooka made us welcome when we reached Tennago. I saw several men eye the casks of whisky as we unloaded our pack mules, but no one made any move to molest them. There were two mule-loads of whisky; a dozen small casks, all of the Fraser share of the year's distilling – most of our income for the year. A king's ransom, in terms of trade. Enough to ransom one young Scotsman, I hoped.

It was the best – and the only – thing we had to trade with, but it was also a dangerous one. Jamie presented one cask to the *sachem* of the village, and he and Ian disappeared into one of the longhouses to confer. Ian had given Roger to some of his friends among the Tuscarora, but did not know where they had taken him. I hoped against hope that it was Tennago. If so, we could be back at River Run within a month.

This was a faint hope, though. In the midst of the bitter quarrel with Brianna, Jamie had admitted telling Ian to make sure that Roger didn't come back again. Tennago was about ten days journey from the Ridge; much too close for the purposes of an enraged father.

I wanted to ask the women who entertained me about Roger, but no one in the house had any French or English, and I had only enough words of Tuscaroran to allow for basic politeness. Better to let Ian and Jamie handle the diplomatic negotiations. Jamie, with his gift for languages, was competent in Tuscaroran; Ian, who spent half his time hunting with the Indians, was thoroughly fluent.

One of the women offered me a platter containing steaming mounds of grain cooked with fish. I leaned to scoop up a bit with the flat piece of wood provided for the purpose, and felt the amulet swing forward under my shirt, its small weight both a reminder of grief and a comfort to it.

I had brought both Nayawenne's amulet, and the carved opal I had found under the red cedar tree. I had brought the former, intending to give it back – to whom, I had no idea. The latter might augment the whisky, if additional bargaining power was needed. For the same reason, Jamie had brought every small valuable he possessed – not many – with the exception of his father's ruby ring, which Brianna had brought to him from Scotland.

We had left the ruby with Brianna, just in case we did not return – the possibility had to be faced. There was no telling whether Geillis Duncan had been right or wrong in her theories regarding the use of gemstones, but at least Brianna would have one.

She had hugged me fiercely and kissed me when we left River Run. I hadn't wanted to go. Nor had I wanted to stay. I was torn between them once more; between the necessity to stay and look after Brianna, and the equally urgent necessity to go with Jamie.

'You have to go,' Brianna had said firmly. 'I'll be fine; you said yourself I'm healthy as a horse. You'll be back a long time before I need you.'

She had glanced at her father's back; he stood in the

stableyard, supervising the loading of the horses and mules. She turned back to me, expressionless.

'You have to go, Mama. I trust you to find Roger.' There was an uncomfortable emphasis on the *you*, and I hoped very much that Jamie couldn't hear her.

'Surely you don't think Jamie would –'

'I don't know,' she interrupted. 'I don't know what he'd do.' Her jaw was set in a way I recognized all too well. Argument was futile, but I tried anyway.

'Well, *I* know,' I said firmly. 'He'd do anything for you, Brianna. Anything. And even if it weren't you, he'd do everything he possibly could to get Roger back. His sense of honor –' Her face shut up like a trap, and I realized my mistake.

'His honor,' she said flatly. 'That's what matters. I guess it's all right, though; as long as it makes him get Roger back.' She turned away, bending her head against the wind.

'Brianna!' I said, but she only hunched her shoulders, pulling the shawl tight around them.

'Auntie Claire? We're ready now.' Ian had appeared nearby, glancing from me to Brianna, his face troubled. I looked from him to Brianna, hesitating, not wanting to leave her like this.

'Bree?' I said again.

Then she had turned back in a flurry of wool and embraced me, her cheek cold against mine.

'Come back!' she whispered. 'Oh, Mama – come back safe!'

'I can't leave you, Bree, I can't!' I held her tight, all strong bone and tender flesh, the child I had left, the child I had regained – and the woman who now put my arms away from her and stood straight, alone.

'You have to go,' she whispered. The mask of indifference had fallen and her cheeks were wet. She glanced over my shoulder at the archway to the stableyard. 'Bring him back. You're the only one who can bring him back.'

She kissed me quickly, turned and ran, the sound of her steps ringing on the brick path.

Jamie came through the stable arch and saw her, flying

through the stormy light like a banshee. He stood still, looking after her, his face expressionless.

'You can't leave her like this,' I said. I wiped my own wet cheeks with the corner of my shawl. 'Jamie, go after her. Please, go and say goodbye, at least.'

He stood still for a moment, and I thought he was going to pretend he hadn't heard me. But then he turned and walked slowly down the path. The first drops of rain were beginning to fall, splatting on the dusty brick, and the wind belled his cloak as he went.

'Auntie?' Ian's hand was under my arm, gently urging. I went with him, and let him give me a hand under my foot to mount. Within a few minutes Jamie was back. He had mounted, not looking at me, and, with a signal to Ian, ridden out of the stableyard without looking back. *I* had looked back, but there was no sign of Brianna.

Night had long since fallen, and Jamie was still in the longhouse with Nacognaweto and the *sachem* of the village. I looked up whenever anyone came into the house, but it was never him. At length, though, the hide flap over the doorway lifted, and Ian came in, a small, round figure behind him.

'I've a surprise for ye, Auntie,' he said, beaming, and stepped aside to show me the smiling round face of the slavewoman Pollyanne.

Or rather, the ex-slave. For here, of course, she was free. She sat down beside me, grinning like a jack-o'-lantern, and turned back the deerskin mantle she wore to show me the little boy in the crook of her arm, his face as round and beaming as her own.

With Ian as interpreter, her own bits of English and Gaelic, and the odd bit of female sign language, we were soon deep in conversation. She had, as Myers surmised, been welcomed by the Tuscarorans and adopted into the tribe, where her skills at healing were valued. She had taken as husband a man who had been widowed in the measles epidemic, and had presented him with this new addition to the family a few months before.

I was delighted that she had found both freedom and happiness, and congratulated her warmly. I was reassured, too; if the Tuscarorans had treated her so kindly, perhaps Roger had not fared as badly as I feared.

A thought struck me, and I pulled Nayawenne's amulet from the neck of my buckskin shirt.

'Ian – will you ask if she knows who I should give this to?'

He spoke to her in Tuscaroran, and she leaned forward, fingering the amulet curiously as he spoke. At last she shook her head and sat back, replying in her curious deep voice.

'She says they will not want it, Auntie,' Ian translated. 'It is the medicine bundle of a *shaman*, and it is dangerous. It should have been buried with the person to whom it belonged; no one here will touch it, for fear of attracting the *shaman*'s ghost.'

I hesitated, holding the leather pouch in my hand. The strange sense of holding something alive had not recurred since Nayawenne's death. Surely it was no more than imagination that seemed to stir against my palm.

'Ask her – what if the *shaman* wasn't buried? If the body couldn't be found?'

Pollyanne's round face was solemn, listening. She shook her head when Ian had finished and replied.

'She says that in that case the ghost walks with you, Auntie. She says you should not show it to anyone here – they will be frightened.'

'She isn't frightened, is she?' Pollyanne caught that on her own; she shook her head, and touched her massive bosom.

'Indian now,' she said simply. 'Not always.' She turned to Ian, and explained through him that her own people revered the spirits of the dead; in fact, it was not unusual for a man to keep by him the head or some other part of his grandfather or other ancestor, for protection or advice. No, the thought of a ghost walking with me did not trouble her.

Nor did the notion trouble me. In fact, I found the thought of Nayawenne walking with me to be rather a comfort, under the circumstances. I put the amulet back in my shirt. It brushed soft and warm against my skin, like the touch of a friend.

We talked for some time, until long after the others in the longhouse had gone to their separate cubicles, and the sound of snoring filled the smoky air. We were surprised, in fact, by Jamie's arrival, which let in a draft of cold air.

It was as Pollyanne made her farewells that she hesitated, trying to decide whether to tell me something. She glanced at Jamie, then shrugged her massive shoulders and made up her mind. She leaned close to Ian, murmured something that sounded like honey trickling over rocks, putting both hands to her face, fingertips against the skin. She then embraced me quickly and left.

Ian stared after her in astonishment.

'What did she say, Ian?'

He turned back to me, his sketchy brows drawn together in concern.

'She says I should tell Uncle Jamie, that the night the woman died in the sawmill, she saw a man.'

'What man?'

He shook his head, still frowning.

'She didna ken him. Only that he was a white man, heavy and square, not so tall as Uncle or I. She saw him come out of the mill, and walk fast into the forest. She was sitting in the door to her hut, in the dark, so she thinks he didna see her – but he passed close enough to the fire that she saw his face. She says he was pockmarked' – here he put his fingertips against his face, as she had – 'with a face like a pig.'

'Murchison?' My heart skipped a beat.

'Did the man wear a uniform?' Jamie asked, frowning.

'No. But she was curious to know what he had been doing there; he wasna one of the plantation owners, nor yet a hand or an overseer. So she crept to the mill to see, but when she put her head inside, she knew something evil had happened. She said she smelt blood, and then she heard voices, so she didna go in.'

So it had been murder, and Jamie and I had missed preventing it by a matter of moments. It was warm in the longhouse, but I felt cold at the memory of the thick, bloody air in the sawmill, and the hardness of a kitchen skewer in my hand.

Jamie's hand settled on my shoulder. Without thinking, I reached up and took it. It felt very good in mine, and I realized that we had not purposely touched each other in nearly a month.

'The dead lass was an army laundress,' he said quietly. 'Murchison has a wife in England; I suppose he might have found a pregnant mistress to be an encumbrance.'

'No wonder he was making such a fuss of hunting for whoever was responsible – and then seizin' on yon poor woman who couldna even speak for herself.' Ian's face was flushed with indignation. 'If he could have got her hanged for it, he'd ha' thought himself safe, I daresay, the wicked wee scut.'

'Perhaps I will pay a call on the Sergeant, when we return,' Jamie said. 'Privately.'

The thought made my blood run cold. His voice was soft and even, and his face calm when I turned to look, but I seemed to see the surface of a dark Scottish pool reflected in his eyes, the water ruffled as though something heavy had just sunk below.

'Don't you think you've enough vengeance to keep you occupied for the moment?'

I spoke more sharply than I intended, and his hand slipped abruptly out of mine.

'I expect so,' he said, both face and voice without expression. He turned to Ian.

'Wakefield – or MacKenzie, or whatever the man's name is – is a good way to the north. They sold him to the Mohawk; a small village below the river. Your friend Onakara has agreed to guide us; we'll leave at first light.'

He rose and walked away, toward the far end of the house. Everyone else had already retired for the night. Five hearths burned, down the length of the house, each with its own smokehole, and the far wall was divided into cubicles, one for each couple or family, with a low, wide shelf for sleeping and space beneath for storage.

Jamie stopped at the cubicle assigned for our use, where I had left our cloaks and bundles. He slipped off his boots, unbelted the plaid he wore over breeches and shirt, and disappeared into the darkness of the sleeping space without a backward glance.

I scrambled to my feet, meaning to follow him, but Ian stopped me with a hand on my arm.

'Auntie,' he said hesitantly. 'Will ye not forgive him?'

'Forgive *him*?' I stared at him. 'For what? For Roger?'

He grimaced.

'No. It was a grievous mistake, but we would do the same again, thinking matters as we did. No – for Bonnet.'

'For Stephen Bonnet? How can he possibly think I blame him for that? I've never said such a thing to him!' And I had been too busy thinking that he blamed *me*, to even consider it.

Ian scratched a hand through his hair.

'Well . . . do ye not see, Auntie? He blames himself for it. He has, ever since the man robbed us on the river; and now wi' what he's done to my cousin . . .' He shrugged, looking mildly embarrassed. 'He's fair eaten up with it, and knowing that you're angry wi' him –'

'But I'm not angry with him! I thought he was angry with me, because I didn't tell him Bonnet's name right away.'

'Och.' Ian looked as though he didn't know whether to laugh or look distressed. 'Well, I daresay it would ha' saved us a bit of trouble if ye had, but no, I'm sure it's not that, Auntie. After all, by the time Cousin Brianna told ye, we'd already met yon MacKenzie on the mountainside and done him a bit of no good.'

I took in a deep breath and blew it out again.

'But you think he thinks I'm angry at him?'

'Oh, anyone could see ye are, Auntie,' he assured me earnestly. 'Ye dinna look at him or speak to him save for what ye must – and,' he said, clearing his throat delicately, 'I havena seen ye go to his bed, anytime this month past.'

'Well, he hasn't come to mine, either!' I said hotly, before reflecting that this was scarcely a suitable conversation to be having with a seventeen-year-old boy.

Ian hunched his shoulders and gave me an owlish look.

'Well, he's his pride, hasn't he?'

'God knows he has,' I said, rubbing a hand over my face. 'I – look, Ian, thank you for saying something to me.'

He gave me one of the rare sweet smiles that transformed his long, homely face.

'Well, I do hate to see him suffer. I'm fond of Uncle Jamie, aye?'

'So am I,' I said, and swallowed the small lump in my throat. 'Good night, Ian.'

I walked softly down the length of the house, past cubicles in which whole families slept together, the sound of their mingled breathing a peaceful descant to the anxious beating of my heart. It was raining outside; water dripped from the smokeholes, sizzling in the embers.

Why had I not seen what Ian had? That was easy to answer; it wasn't anger, but my own sense of guilt that had blinded me. I had kept back my knowledge of Bonnet's involvement as much because of the gold wedding ring as because Brianna had asked me to; I could have persuaded her to tell Jamie, had I tried.

She was right; he would undoubtedly go after Stephen Bonnet sooner or later. I had somewhat more confidence in Jamie's success than she did, though. No, it had been the ring that had made me keep silence.

And why should I feel guilty over that? There was no sensible answer; it had been instinct, not conscious thought, to hide the ring. I had not wanted to show it to Jamie, to put it back on my finger in front of him. And yet I had wanted – needed – to keep it.

My heart squeezed small, thinking of the past few weeks, of Jamie, going grimly about the necessities of reparation in loneliness and guilt. That was why I had come with him, after all – because I was afraid that if he went alone, he might not come back. Spurred by guilt and courage, he might go to reckless lengths; with me to consider, I knew he would be careful. And all the time he had thought himself not only alone but bitterly reproached by the one person who could – and should – have offered him comfort.

'Eaten up with it' indeed.

I paused by the cubicle. The shelf was some eight feet wide, and he lay well back; I could see little more of him than a humped shape under a blanket made of rabbit skins. He lay very still, but I knew he wasn't asleep.

I climbed onto the platform, and once safe within the shadows of the cubicle, slipped out of my clothes. It was fairly warm in the longhouse, but my bare skin prickled and my nipples tightened. My eyes had grown accustomed to the dimness; I could see that he lay on his side facing me. I caught the shine of his eyes in the dark, open and watching me.

I knelt down and slid under the blanket, the fur soft against my skin. Without stopping to think too much, I rolled to face him, pressing my nakedness against him, face buried in his shoulder.

'Jamie,' I whispered to him. 'I'm cold. Come and warm me. Please?'

He turned to me, wordless, with a quiet ferocity that I might have thought the hunger of desire long stifled – but knew now for simple desperation. I sought no pleasure for myself; I wanted only to give him comfort. But opening to him, urging him, some deep wellspring opened too, and I cleaved to him in a sudden need as blind and desperate as his own.

We clung tight together, shuddering, heads buried in each other's hair, unable to look at each other, unable to let go. Slowly, as the spasms died away, I became aware of things outside our own small mortal coil, and realized that we lay in the midst of strangers, naked and helpless, shielded only by darkness.

And yet we were alone, completely. We had the privacy of Babel; there was a conversation going on at the far end of the longhouse, but its words held no meaning. It might as well have been the hum of bees.

Smoke from the banked fire wavered up outside the sanctuary of our bed, fragrant and insubstantial as incense. It was dark as a confessional inside the cubicle; I could see no more of Jamie than the faint curve of light that rimmed his shoulder, a transient gleam in the locks of his hair.

'Jamie, I'm sorry,' I said softly. 'It wasn't your fault.'

'Who else?' he said, with some bleakness.

'Everyone. No one. Stephen Bonnet, himself. But not you.'

'Bonnet?' His voice was blank with surprise. 'What has he to do with it?'

'Well . . . everything,' I said, taken aback. 'Er . . . doesn't he?'

He rolled halfway off me, brushing hair out of his face.

'Stephen Bonnet is a wicked creature,' he said precisely, 'and I shall kill him at the first opportunity I have. But I dinna see how I can blame him for my own failings as a man.'

'What on earth are you talking about? What failings?'

He didn't answer right away, but bent his head, a humped shadow in the dark. His legs were still entangled with mine; I could feel the tension of his body, knotted in his joints, rigid in the hollows of his thighs.

'I hadna thought ever to be so jealous of a dead man,' he whispered at last. 'I shouldna have thought it possible.'

'Of a dead man?' My own voice rose slightly, with astonishment, as it finally dawned on me. 'Of *Frank*?'

He lay still, half on top of me. His hand touched the bones of my face, hesitant.

'Who else? I have been worm-eaten wi' it, all these days of riding. I see his face in my mind, waking and sleeping. Ye did say he looked like Jack Randall, no?'

I gathered him tight against myself, pressing his head down so that his ear was near my mouth. Thank God I hadn't mentioned the ring to him – but had my face, my traitorous, transparent face, somehow given away that I thought of it?

'How?' I whispered to him, squeezing hard. 'How could you think of such a thing?'

He broke loose, rising on one elbow, his hair falling down over my face in a mass of flaming shadows, the firelight sparking gold and crimson through it.

'How could I not?' he demanded. 'Ye heard her, Claire; ye ken well what she said to me!'

'Brianna?'

'She said she would gladly see me in hell, and sell her own soul to have her father back – her real father.' He swallowed; I heard the sound of it, above the murmur of distant voices.

'I keep thinking he would not have made such a

mistake. He would have trusted her; he would have known that she . . . I keep thinking that Frank Randall was a better man than I am. She thinks so.' His hand faltered, then settled on my shoulder, squeezing tight. 'I thought . . . perhaps ye felt the same, Sassenach.'

'Fool,' I whispered, and didn't mean him. I ran my hands down the long slope of his back, digging my fingers into the firmness of his buttocks. 'Wee idiot. Come here.'

He dropped his head, and made a small sound against my shoulder that might have been a laugh.

'Aye, I am. Ye dinna mind it so much, though?'

'No.' His hair smelt of smoke and pinesap. There were still bits of needles caught in it; one pricked smooth and sharp against my lips.

'She didn't mean it,' I said.

'Aye, she did,' he said, and I felt him swallow the thickness in his throat. 'I heard her.'

'I heard you both.' I rubbed slowly between his shoulder blades, feeling the faint traces of the old scars, the thicker, more recent welts left by the bear's claws. 'She's just like you; she'll say things in a temper she'd never say in cold blood. You didn't mean all the things you said to her, did you?'

'No.' I could feel the tightness in him lessening, the joints of his body loosening, yielding reluctantly to the persuasion of my fingers. 'No, I didna mean it. Not all of it.'

'Neither did she.'

I waited a moment, stroking him as I had stroked Brianna, when she was small, and afraid.

'You can believe me,' I whispered. 'I love you both.'

He sighed, deeply, and was quiet for a moment.

'If I can find the man and bring him back to her. If I do – d'ye think she'll forgive me one day?'

'Yes,' I said. 'I know it.'

On the other side of the partition, I heard the small sounds of love-making begin; the shift and sigh, the murmured words that have no language.

'*You have to go.*' Brianna had said to me. '*You're the only one who can bring him back.*'

982

It occurred to me for the first time that perhaps she hadn't been speaking of Roger.

It was a long trek through the mountains, made longer by the winter weather. There were days when it was impossible to travel; when we crouched all day under rocky overhangs or in the shelter of a grove of trees, huddled against the wind.

Once we were through the mountains, the traveling was somewhat easier, though the temperatures grew colder as we headed north. Some nights we ate cold food, unable to keep a fire alight in snow and wind. But each night I lay with Jamie, closely huddled together within a single cocoon of furs and blankets, sharing our warmth.

I kept close count of the days, marking them by means of a length of knotted twine. We had left River Run in early January; it was mid-February before Onakara pointed out to us the smoke rising in the distance that marked the Mohawk village where he and his companions had taken Roger Wakefield. 'Snake-town,' he said it was called.

Six weeks, and Brianna would be nearly six months gone. If we could get Roger back quickly – and if he was capable of travel, I added grimly to myself – we should be back well before the child was due. If Roger wasn't here, though – if the Mohawk had sold him elsewhere . . . or if he was dead – said a small cold voice inside my head, we would return without delay.

Onakara declined to accompany us into the village, which did absolutely nothing to increase my confidence in our prospects. Jamie thanked him and saw him off, with one of the horses, a good knife, and a flask of whisky in payment for his services.

We buried the rest of the whisky, hiding it carefully some distance outside the village.

'Will they understand what we want?' I asked, as we remounted. 'Is Tuscarora close enough to Mohawk for us to talk to them?'

'It's no quite the same, Auntie, but close,' Ian said. It was snowing lightly, and the flakes clung melting to his eyelashes. 'Like the differences between Italian and Spanish, maybe. But Onakara says that the *sachem* and a few others have a bit of English, though they mostly dinna choose to use it. But the Mohawk fought with the English against the French; there will be some who ken it.'

'Well, then.' Jamie smiled at us and laid his musket across the saddle in front of him. 'Let's go and try our luck.'

54

Captivity I

February 1770

He had been in the Mohawk village nearly three months, by the reckoning of his knotted string. At first he had not known who they were; only that they were a different kind of Indian than his captors – and that his captors were afraid of them.

He had stood numb with exhaustion while the men who had brought him talked and pointed. The new Indians were different; they were dressed for the cold, in fur and leather, and many of the men's faces were tattooed.

One of them prodded him with the point of a knife, and made him undress. He was forced to stand naked in the middle of a long wooden house while several men – and women – poked and jeered at him. His right foot was badly swollen; the deep cut had become infected. He could still walk, but each step sent jabs of pain through his leg, and he burned intermittently with fever.

They shoved him, pushing him to the door of the house. There was a lot of noise outside. He recognized the gauntlet; a double row of shouting savages, all armed with sticks and clubs. Someone behind poked him in the buttock with the point of a knife, and he felt a warm trickle of blood run down his leg. '*Cours!*' they said. Run.

The ground was trampled, snow packed into grimy ice. It burned his feet as a shove in his back sent him staggering into pandemonium.

He stayed upright most of the way, lurching one way, then another, as the clubs struck him to and fro and sticks lashed at his legs and back. There was no way to avoid the blows. All he could do was keep going, as fast as possible.

Close to the end, a club swung straight and took him hard across the belly; he doubled over and another swatted him behind the ear. He rolled bonelessly into the snow, barely feeling the cold on his broken skin.

A switch stung his legs, then lashed him hard just under the balls. He jerked his legs up in reflex, rolled again, and found himself on hands and knees, still somehow going, the blood from his nose and mouth mixing with the frozen mud.

He reached the end, and with the last blows still stinging on his back, grasped the poles of a longhouse and pulled himself slowly to his feet. He turned to face them, holding on to the poles to keep from falling. They liked that; they were laughing, with high-pitched yips that made them sound like a pack of dogs. He bowed low, and straightened up, head whirling. They laughed harder. He'd always known how to please a crowd.

They took him inside then, gave him water to wash with, some food. They gave him back his ragged shirt and filthy breeches, but not his coat or shoes. It was warm in the house; there were several fires burning at intervals down the length of the long structure, each with its own open smokehole above. He crawled into a corner and fell asleep, his hand on the lumpy seam of his breeches.

After this reception, the Mohawk treated him with general indifference but no great cruelty. He was the slave of the longhouse, at the use of anyone who lived there. If he did not understand an order, they would show him – once. If he refused or pretended not to understand, they beat him, and he refused no more. Still, he shared equally in their food and was given a decent place to sleep, at the end of the house.

As it was winter, the main work was in gathering wood and fetching water, though now and then a hunting party would take him along to help in butchering and carrying meat. The Indians made no great effort to communicate with him, but by careful listening he acquired a little of the language.

He began, with great caution, to try a few words. He chose a young girl to begin with, feeling her less dangerous. She stared at him, then laughed, delighted as if she had heard a crow talk. She called a friend to come and hear, and another, and the three of them crouched in front of him, laughing softly behind their hands and looking sideways at him from the corners of their eyes. He

986

said all the words he knew, pointing at the objects – fire, pot, blanket, corn – then pointed at a string of dried fish overhead and raised his eyebrows.

'*Yona'kensyonk*,' said his new friend promptly, and giggled when he repeated it. Over the next days and weeks, the girls taught him a great deal; it was from them that he finally learned where he was. Or not where, precisely, but in whose hands.

They were *Kahnyen'kehaka*, they told him proudly, with looks of surprise that he did not know that. Mohawk. Keepers of the Eastern Gate of the Iroquois League. He, on the other hand, was *Kakonhoaerhas*. It took a certain amount of discussion to determine the exact meaning of this term; he finally discovered, when one of the girls dragged in a mongrel in illustration, that it meant 'dogface'.

'Thanks,' he said, fingering the thick growth of his beard. He bared his teeth at them and growled, and they shrieked with laughter.

One of the girls' mothers became interested; seeing that his foot was still swollen, she brought ointment and bathed it, bandaging it for him with lichen and corn husks. The women began to speak to him when he brought them wood or water.

He made no attempt at escape; not yet. Winter kept its grip on the village, with frequent snows and bitter wind. He wouldn't get far, unarmed, lame, and with no protection from the weather. He bided his time. And he dreamed at night of lost worlds, waking often in the dawn to the smell of fresh grass, with the ache of his need spilled warm on his belly.

The edges of the river were still frozen when the Jesuit came.

Roger had the run of the village; he was outside when the dogs began to bark and yelps from the sentries signaled the arrival of visitors. People began to gather, and he went with them, curious.

The new arrivals were a large group of Mohawk, men and women both, all on foot, burdened with the usual bundles of traveling gear. That seemed odd; such visitors as had come to the village before were small hunting parties. What was odder was that the visitors had with them a white man – the pale winter sun gleamed on the man's fair hair.

Roger moved closer, eager to see, but was shoved back by some of the villagers. Not before seeing that the man was a priest, though; the tattered remnants of a long black robe showed beneath a bearskin cape, over leather leggings and moccasins.

The priest didn't act like a prisoner, nor was he bound. And yet Roger had the feeling that he traveled under compulsion; there were lines of strain in an otherwise young face. The priest and several of his companions disappeared into the longhouse where the *sachem* held council; Roger had never been inside, but had heard the women talk.

One of the older women from his own longhouse saw him loitering in the crowd, and ordered him sharply to fetch more wood. He went, and didn't see the priest again, though the faces of the new arrivals showed in the village, scattered among the longhouses to share the hospitality of their hearths.

Something was happening in the village; he could feel the currents of it eddying around him but did not understand them. The men sat later by the fires in the evenings, talking, and the women murmured to each other as they worked, but the discussion was far beyond the grasp of Roger's rudimentary comprehension. He asked one of the little girls about the new visitors; she could tell him only that they came from a village to the north – why they had come, she did not know, save it had to do with the Black Robe, the *Kahontsi'yatawi*.

It was more than a week later that Roger went out with a hunting party. The weather was cold but clear, and they traveled far, eventually finding and killing a moose. Roger was stunned, not only by the size of the thing but by its stupidity. He could understand the attitude of the hunters: There was no honor in killing such a thing; it was only meat.

It was a *lot* of meat. He was burdened like a pack mule, and the extra weight bore hard on his lame foot; by the

988

time they returned to the village, he was limping so badly that he couldn't keep up with the hunting party, but lagged far behind, desperately trying to keep them in view lest he be lost in the forest.

To his surprise, several men were waiting for him when he finally limped into view of the village palisades. They grabbed him, relieved him of the burden of meat, and hustled him into the village. They didn't take him to his own longhouse, but to a small hut that stood at the far end of the central clearing.

He hadn't enough Mohawk to ask questions, and didn't think they would be answered in any case. They shoved him inside the hut, and left him.

There was a small fire burning, but the interior was so dark after the brightness of the day outside that he was momentarily blinded.

'Who are you?' said a startled voice in French.

Roger blinked several times, and made out a slight figure rising from its seat beside the fire. The priest.

'Roger MacKenzie,' he said. '*Et vous?*' He experienced a sudden and unexpected flood of happiness at the simple speaking of his name. The Indians didn't care what his name was; they called him dogface when they wanted him.

'Alexandre.' The priest came forward, looking both pleased and incredulous. 'Père Alexandre Ferigault. *Vous etes anglais?*'

'Scots,' said Roger, and sat down suddenly, his lame leg giving way.

'A Scotsman? How do you come here? You are a soldier?'

'A prisoner.'

The priest squatted by him, looking him over curiously. He *was* fairly young – in his late twenties or early thirties, though his fair skin was chapped and weathered by the cold.

'You will eat with me?' He gestured to a small collection of clay pots and baskets that held food and water.

Speaking in his own language seemed to be as much a relief for the priest as speaking freely was for Roger. By the time the meal was concluded, they had gleaned a cautious knowledge of each other's basic past – if no explanation as yet for their present situation.

'Why have they put me here with you?' Roger asked, wiping grease from his mouth. He didn't think it was to provide the priest with company. Thoughtfulness was not an outstanding Mohawk characteristic, so far as he'd noticed.

'I cannot say. I was in fact astonished to see another white man.'

Roger glanced at the door of the hut. It moved slightly; there was someone outside.

'Are you a prisoner?' he asked, in some surprise. The priest hesitated, then shrugged, with a small smile.

'I cannot say that, either. With the Mohawk, one is *Kahn-yen'kehaka* or one is – other. And if one is other, the line between guest and prisoner can alter in a moment. Leave it that I have lived among them for several years – but I have not been adopted into the tribe. I am still "other".' He coughed and changed the subject. 'How did you come to be taken captive?'

Roger hesitated, not really knowing how to answer.

'I was betrayed,' he said at last. 'Sold.'

The priest nodded sympathetically.

'Is there anyone who might ransom you? They will take care to keep you alive if they have some hope of ransom.'

Roger shook his head, feeling hollow as a drum.

'There's no one.'

Conversation ceased as the light from the smokehole dimmed into dusk, leaving them in darkness below. There was a firepit, but no wood; the fire died out. The hut seemed to have been abandoned; there was a bed frame built of poles, but nothing else in the hut save a couple of tattered deerskins and a small heap of domestic debris in one corner.

'Have you been here – in this hut – long?' Roger asked at last, breaking the silence. He could barely see the other man, though the last remnants of twilight were visible through the smokehole.

'No. They brought me here today – shortly before you

came.' The priest coughed, shifting uneasily on the packed dirt floor.

That seemed sinister, but Roger thought it more tactful – and less frightening – not to mention it. It was no doubt as obvious to the priest as to himself that the line between 'guest' and 'prisoner' had been crossed. What had the man done?

'You are a Christian?' Alexandre broke the silence abruptly.

'Yes. My father was a minister.'

'Ah. May I ask – if they take me away, will you pray for me?'

Roger felt a sudden chill that had nothing to do with the cheerless surroundings.

'Yes,' he said awkwardly. 'Of course. If you like.'

The priest rose and began to walk restlessly about the confines of the hut, unable to keep still.

'It may be all right,' he said, but it was the voice of a man trying to convince himself. 'They are still deciding.'

'Deciding what?'

He felt rather than saw the priest's shrug.

'Whether I live.'

There seemed no good response to that, and they fell once more into silence. Roger sat huddled by the cold firepit, resting his lame foot, while the priest paced to and fro, finally settling beside him. Without comment, the two moved close together, pooling their warmth; it was going to be a cold night.

Roger had dozed off, one of the deerskins pulled over him, when there was a sudden noise at the door. He sat up, blinking, to a blaze of fire.

There were four Mohawk warriors in the hut; one dumped a load of wood into the firepit and thrust the brand he held into the pile. Ignoring Roger, the others pulled Père Ferigault to his feet and roughly stripped him of his clothes.

Roger moved instinctively, half rising, and was knocked flat. The priest gave him a quick, open-eyed look that begged him not to interfere.

One of the warriors held his own brand close to Père Ferigault's face. He said something that sounded like a

991

question, then, receiving no answer, passed his brand downward, so close to the priest's body that the white skin glowed red.

Sweat stood out on Alexandre's face as the fire hovered near his genitals, but his face remained carefully blank. The warrior with the brand poked it suddenly at the priest, who could not keep from flinching. The Indians laughed, and did it again. This time he was prepared; Roger smelled singed hair, but the priest didn't move.

Tiring of this sport, two of the warriors seized the priest by the arms, and dragged him out of the hut.

If they take me away – pray for me. Roger sat up slowly, the hairs on his body prickling with dread. He could hear the voices of the Indians, talking among themselves, receding in the distance; no sound from the priest.

Alexandre's discarded clothes were flung around the hut; Roger picked them up, carefully beating the dust from them and folding them. His hands were shaking.

He tried to pray, but found it hard to focus his mind upon devotion. Over and around the words of his prayer, he could hear a small, cold voice, saying, *And when they come to take me away – who will pray for me?*

They had left him a fire; he tried to believe that meant that they did not mean to kill him right away. The granting of comforts to a condemned prisoner was not the Mohawk way, either. After a time he lay down under the deerskins, curled on his side, and watched the flames until he fell asleep, worn out by terror.

He was roused from uneasy sleep by the shuffle of feet and many voices. He sprang awake, rolled away from the fire and crouched, looking frantically for some means of defense.

The door flap lifted, and the naked body of the priest fell into the hut. The noises outside moved away.

Alexandre stirred and moaned. Roger came quickly and knelt by him. He could smell fresh blood, a hot-copper smell he recognized from the slaughtering of the moose.

'Are you hurt? What have they done?'

The answer to that was quick in coming. He turned the half-conscious priest over, to see blood streaming over face and neck in a shiny red glaze. He snatched the priest's discarded robe to staunch the wound, pushed back the matted blond hair, and found that the priest's right ear was missing. Something sharp had taken a patch of skin some three inches square from just behind the jaw, removing both ear and a section of scalp.

Roger clenched his stomach muscles and pressed the cloth tight against the raw wound. Holding it in place, he dragged the limp body to the fire, and piled the remnants of clothes and both deerskins on top of Père Ferigault.

The man was moaning now. Roger washed his face, made him drink a little water.

'It's all right,' he muttered, over and over, though he was uncertain whether the other could hear him. 'It's all right, they didn't kill you.' He couldn't help wondering whether it might have been better if they had; did they mean this only as a warning to the priest, or was it only the preliminary to greater tortures?

The fire had burned itself to coals; in the reddish light, the seeping blood was black.

Father Alexandre moved constantly in small jerks, the restlessness of his body at once caused and constrained by the pain of his wound. He could not by any means settle to sleep, and consequently neither could Roger, nearly as aware as the priest of each interminably passing minute.

Roger cursed himself for helplessness; he would have given anything to assuage the other man's pain, even for a moment. It wasn't merely sympathy, and he knew it; Father Alexandre's small, breathless sounds kept the knowledge of the mutilation fresh in Roger's mind, and terror alive in his blood. If the priest could only sleep, the sounds would stop – and perhaps in the darkness, the horror would recede a bit.

For the first time, he thought he understood what it was that made Claire Randall tick; made her walk onto battlefields, to lay her hands on wounded men. To ease pain and death in another was to soothe the fear of it in oneself – and to soothe his own fear, he would do almost anything.

At last, unable to bear the whispered prayers and stifled

993

whimpering any longer, he lay down beside the priest, and took Alexandre in his arms.

'Hush,' he said, his lips close to Père Alexandre's head. He hoped he had the side with the ear. 'Be still now. *Reposez-vous.*'

The priest's lean body quivered against his own, the muscles knotted with cold and agony. Roger rubbed the man's back briskly, chafed his palms over the chilled limbs, and pulled both tattered deerskins over them.

'You'll be all right.' Roger spoke in English, aware that it didn't matter what he said, only that he said something. 'Here now, it's all right. Yes, go on, then.' He talked as much to distract himself as the other man; the feel of Alexandre's naked body was vaguely shocking – as much because it didn't feel unnatural as because it did.

The priest clung to him, head pressed into his shoulder. He said nothing, but Roger could feel the wetness of tears against his skin. He made himself hug the priest tightly, rubbing up and down the spine with its small lumps of knobby bone, forcing himself to think only of stopping the terrible shaking.

'You could be a dog,' Roger said. 'A mistreated stray of some kind. I'd do it if you were a dog, of course I would. No, I wouldn't,' he muttered to himself. 'Call the ruddy RSPCA, I expect.'

He patted Alexandre's head, careful where his fingers went, cold with gooseflesh at the thought of touching that raw, bloody patch by inadvertence. The hair at the priest's nape was lank with sweat, though the flesh of his neck and shoulders was like ice. His lower body was warmer, but not by much.

'Nobody'd treat a dog like this,' he muttered. 'Fucking savages. Set the police onto them. Put their bloody pictures in *The Times*. Complain to my MP.'

A small ripple of something too frightened to be called laughter went through him. He gripped the priest fiercely, and rocked him to and fro in darkness.

'*Reposez-vous, mon ami. C'est bien, là, c'est bien.*'

55

Captivity II

Brianna rolled the wet brush along the edge of the palette, squeezing out the excess turps to form a good point. She touched the point briefly to the viridian-cobalt mix and added a fine line of shadow to the river's edge.

There were footsteps on the path behind her, coming from the house. She recognized the arrythmic double step; it was the Deadly Duo. She tensed slightly, fighting the urge to snatch the wet canvas and put it out of sight behind Hector Cameron's mausoleum. She didn't mind Jocasta, who often came to sit with her while she painted in the mornings, to discuss techniques of painting, grinding pigments, and the like. In fact, she welcomed her great-aunt's company and treasured the older woman's stories of her girlhood in Scotland, of Brianna's grandmother, and of the other MacKenzies of Leoch. But when Jocasta brought her faithful Seeing-eye Dog along, it was a different matter.

'Good morning, Niece! Is it not too cold for you the morn?'

Jocasta halted, her own cloak drawn around her, and smiled at Brianna. If she hadn't known better, she wouldn't have realized her aunt's blindness.

'No, it's fine here; the . . . er . . . tomb blocks the wind. I'm finished for now, though.' She wasn't, but stabbed her brush into the turpentine jar and began to scrape the palette. Damned if she'd paint with Ulysses describing her every brushstroke out loud.

'Ah? Well, leave your things, then; Ulysses will take them up for you.'

Reluctantly abandoning her easel, Brianna picked up her private sketch-book and tucked it under one arm, giving her other to Jocasta. She wasn't leaving *that* for Mr. Sees-all, Tells-all to flip through.

'We have company today,' Jocasta said, turning back toward the house. 'Judge Alderdyce, from Cross Creek, and his mother. I thought perhaps ye'd wish time to change, before luncheon.' Brianna bit the inside of her cheek, to prevent any rejoinder to this less than subtle hint. More visitors.

Under the circumstances, she could scarcely refuse to meet her aunt's guests – or even to change clothes for them – but she could have wished that Jocasta were a good deal less sociable. There was a constant stream of visitors; for luncheon, for tea, for supper, overnight, for breakfast, come to buy horses, sell cows, trade lumber, borrow books, bring gifts, play music. They came from neighboring plantations, from Cross Creek, and from as far away as Edenton and New Bern.

The array of Jocasta's acquaintance was staggering. Still, Brianna had noticed an increasing tendency of late for the callers to be men. Single men.

Phaedre verified Brianna's suspicions, voiced as the maid dug in the wardrobe for a fresh morning gown.

'There ain't a lot of single women in the colony,' Phaedre observed, when Brianna mentioned the peculiar coincidence that most of the recent visitors appeared to be bachelors. Phaedre cast an eye at Brianna's midsection, which was bulging noticeably under the loose muslin shift. ''Specially not young ones. To say nothing of women who's got River Run a-coming to them.'

'Who's got *what?*' Brianna said. She stopped, hair half pinned, and stared at the maid.

Phaedre laid one graceful hand across her mouth, eyes wide above it.

'Your auntie ain't told you yet? Thought sure you knew, or I'd not've said.'

'Well, now you've said that much, go on saying. What do you mean?' Phaedre, a born gossip, took little coaxing.

'Your daddy and them hadn't been gone but a week, before Miss Jo sent for Lawyer Forbes and had her will changed. When Miss Jo dies, they's some little bits of money goes to your daddy, and some personal things to Mr. Farquard and some of her other friends – but everything else, that's yours. The plantation, the timber, the sawmill . . .'

'But I don't want it!'

Phaedre's elegantly lifted eyebrow expressed profound doubt, then dropped, dismissing it.

'Well, it ain't what you want, I reckon. Miss Jo is kind of inclined to get what *she* wants.'

Brianna laid the hairbrush down, slowly.

'And just what *does* she want?' she asked. 'Do you happen to know that, too?'

'Ain't any big secret. She wants River Run to last longer than she does – and to belong to somebody from her blood. Seems sense to me; she got no children, no grandchildren. Who else is there to carry on after her?'

'Well . . . there's my father.'

Phaedre laid the fresh dress across the bed and frowned at it appraisingly, glancing back at Brianna's middle.

'This one going to last no more than another couple weeks, the way that belly's growing. Oh, yes, there's your daddy. She done tried to make him her heir, but the way I hears it, he wasn't havin' none of it.' She pursed her lips in amusement.

'Now there's a stubborn man for you. Go off into the mountains and live like a red man, just to keep from doing what Miss Jo want him to do. But Mr. Ulysses reckons your daddy had the right of it, at that. Be him and Miss Jo buttin' heads day and night, if he'd a-stayed.'

Brianna slowly twisted up the other side of her hair, but the hairpin slipped out again, letting it fall.

'Here, you be lettin' me do that, Miss Bree.' Phaedre slid behind her, pulled out the slipshod pinning, and began deftly to braid the sides of her hair.

'And all these visitors – these men –'

'Miss Jo out to pick you a good one,' Phaedre assured her. 'You can't run the place alone, no more than Miss Jo can. That Mr. Duncan, he's a godsend; don't know what she'd do without him.'

Sheer astonishment was giving way to outrage.

'She's trying to pick a husband for me? She's showing me off like – like some prize heifer?'

'Uh-huh.' Phaedre appeared to see nothing wrong with

997

this. She frowned, drawing a straying lock skillfully into the main braid.

'But she knows about Roger – about Mr. Wakefield! How can she be trying to marry me off to –'

Phaedre sighed, not without sympathy.

'I don't reckon she thinks they're going to find the man, tell you true. Miss Jo, she knows a bit about the Indians; we've all heard Mr. Myers tell about the Iroquois.'

It was chilly in the room, but prickles of sweat broke out along Brianna's hairline and jaw.

'Besides,' Phaedre went on, weaving a blue silk ribbon into the braid, 'Miss Jo don't know this Wakefield. Might be he'd not be a good manager. Better – she thinks – to get you married to a man she knows will take good care of her place; add it to his own, maybe, make a truly grand place for you.'

'I don't *want* a grand place! I don't want *this* place!' Outrage in turn was giving way to panic.

Phaedre tied the end of the ribbon with a small flourish.

'Well, like I say – it ain't so much what you want. It's what Miss Jo wants. Now, let's try this dress.'

There was a sound in the hallway, and Brianna hastily flipped the page of her sketchbook over, to a half-finished charcoal drawing of the river and its trees. The steps went by, though, and she relaxed, turning back the page.

She wasn't working; the drawing was complete. She only wanted to look at it.

She'd drawn him in three-quarter profile, head turned to listen as he tuned his guitar strings. It was no more than a sketch, but it caught the line of head and body with a rightness that memory confirmed. She could look at this and conjure him, bring him close enough almost to touch.

There were others; some botched messes, some that came close. A few that were good drawings in themselves, but that failed to capture the man behind the lines. One or two, like this one, that she could use to comfort herself in the late gray afternoons, when the light began to fail and the fires burned low.

The light was fading over the river now, the water dimming from bright silver to the gentler glow of pewter.

There were others; sketches of Jamie Fraser, of her mother, of Ian. She had begun to draw them out of loneliness, and looked at them now with fear, hoping against hope that these fragments of paper were not the only remnants of the family she had known so briefly.

Tell you true, I don't reckon Miss Jo thinks they going to find the man . . . Miss Jo knows about Indians.

Her hands were damp; the charcoal smeared at the corner of a page. A soft step sounded just outside the parlor door, and she closed her book at once.

Ulysses came in, a lighted taper in his hand, and began to light the branches of the great candelabrum.

'You don't need to light all those for me.' Brianna spoke as much from a desire not to disturb the quiet melancholy of the room as from modesty. 'I don't mind the dark.'

The butler smiled gently and went on with his work. He touched each wick precisely, and the tiny flames sprang up at once, jinni called up by a magician's wand.

'Miss Jo will be down soon,' he said. 'She can see the lights – and the fire – so she knows where she is in the room.'

He finished and blew out the taper, then moved about the room in his usual soft-footed way, tidying the small disorder left by the afternoon guests, adding wood to the fire, puffing it into crackling life with the bellows.

She watched him; the small, precise movements of the well-kept hands, his complete absorption in the correct placement of the whisky decanter and its glasses. How many times had he straightened this room? Put back each piece of furniture, each tiny ornament precisely in its place, so that its mistress's hand would fall upon it without groping?

A whole life devoted to the needs of someone else. Ulysses could read and write both French and English; could reckon numbers, could sing and play the harpsichord. All that skill and learning – used only for the entertainment of an autocratic old lady.

To say to one, 'Come,' and he cometh, to say to another 'Go,' and he goeth. Yes, that was Jocasta's way.

And if Jocasta had her way . . . she would own this man.

The thought was unconscionable. Worse, it was ridiculous! She shifted impatiently in her seat, trying to push it away. He caught the slight movement, and turned inquiringly, to see if anything was wanted.

'Ulysses,' she blurted. 'Do you want to be free?'

The moment the words were out, she bit her tongue, and felt her cheeks go red with mortification.

'I'm sorry,' she said at once, and looked down at her hands, twisted in her lap. 'That was a terribly rude question. Please forgive me.'

The tall butler didn't say anything, but regarded her quizzically for a moment. Then he touched his wig lightly, as though to settle it in place, and turned back to his work, picking up the scattered sketches on the table and tapping them neatly into a stack.

'I was born free,' he said at last, so quietly that she wasn't sure she'd heard him. His head was bent, eyes on the long black fingers that plucked the ivory counters from the game table and placed each one neatly in its box.

'My father had a tiny farm, not too far from here. But he died of a snake's bite, when I was six or so. My mother could not manage to keep us – she was not strong enough for farming – and so she sold herself, putting the money with a carpenter for my apprenticeship once I should come of age, that I might learn a useful trade.'

He set the ivory box in its slot in the game table, and wiped away a crumb of tea cake that had fallen on the cribbage board.

'But then she died,' he went on matter-of-factly. 'And the carpenter, instead of taking me as an apprentice, claimed that as I was the child of a slave, I was by law a slave myself. And so he sold me.'

'But that's not right!'

He looked at her in patient amusement, but didn't speak. And what had right ever had to do with it? his dark eyes said.

'I was fortunate,' he said. 'I was sold – cheaply, for I was very small and puny – to a schoolmaster, whom several plantation owners on the Cape Fear had hired to teach their children. He would ride from one house to another, staying in each for a week or a month, and I would go with him, perched behind him on the horse's rump, tending the horse when we stopped, and doing such small services as he required.

'And because the journeys were long and tedious, he would talk to me as we rode. He sang – he loved to sing, that man, and he had a most delightful voice –' To Brianna's surprise, Ulysses looked faintly nostalgic, but then he shook his head, recalling himself, and took out a cloth from his pocket, with which he wiped the sideboard.

'It was the schoolmaster who gave me the name Ulysses,' he said, back turned to her. 'He knew some Greek, and some Latin as well, and for his own amusement, he taught me to read, on the nights when darkness befell us and we were forced to encamp on the road.'

The straight, lean shoulders rose in the faintest of shrugs.

'When the schoolmaster died as well, I was a young man of twenty or so. Hector Cameron bought me, and discovered my talents. Not all masters would value such endowments in a slave, but Mr. Cameron was not a common man.' Ulysses smiled faintly.

'He taught me to play chess, and would wager upon my success, playing against his friends. He had me taught to sing, and to play the harpsichord, that I might provide entertainment for his guests. And when Miss Jocasta began to lose her sight, he gave me to her, to be her eyes.'

'What was your name? Your real name?'

He paused, thinking, then gave her a smile that did not reach his eyes. 'I am not sure that I remember,' he said politely, and went out.

56

Confessions of the Flesh

He woke a little before dawn. It was still black dark, but the air had changed; the embers had burned to staleness and the forest's breath moved past his face.

Alexandre was gone. He lay alone under the tattered deerskin, very cold. 'Alexandre?' he whispered hoarsely. 'Père Ferigault?'

'I am here.' The young priest's voice was soft, somehow remote, though he sat no more than a yard away.

Roger rose up on one elbow, squinting. Once the sleep had left his eyes, he could see dimly. Alexandre was sitting cross-legged, his back very straight, his face turned up to the square of the smokehole overhead.

'Are you all right?' One side of the priest's neck was stained dark with blood, though his face – what Roger could see of it – seemed serene.

'They will kill me soon. Perhaps today.'

Roger sat up, clutching the deerskin to his chest. He was already cold; the calm tone of this froze him.

'No,' he said, and had to cough to clear his throat of soot. 'No, they won't.'

Alexandre didn't bother contradicting him. Didn't move. He sat naked, oblivious of the cold morning air, looking up. At last he lowered his gaze, and turned his head toward Roger.

'Will you hear my confession?'

'I'm not a priest.' Roger scrambled to his knees and scuffled across the floor, the skin held awkwardly before him. 'Here, you'll freeze. Get under this.'

'It does not matter.'

Roger wasn't sure whether he meant being cold didn't matter, or whether Roger's not being a priest didn't matter. He laid a hand on Alexandre's bare shoulder. Whether it mattered or not, the man was cold as ice.

Roger sat down next to Alexandre, as close as could be managed, and spread the skin over them both. Roger could feel his own skin ripple into gooseflesh where the other man's icy skin touched him, but it didn't trouble him; he leaned closer, wanting urgently to give Alexandre some of his own warmth.

'Your father,' Alexandre said. He had turned his head; his breath touched Roger's face, and his eyes were dark holes in his face. 'You told me he was a priest.'

'A minister. Yes, but I'm not.'

He sensed, rather than saw, the other's small gesture of dismissal.

'In time of need, any man may do the office of a priest,' Alexandre said. Cold fingers touched Roger's thigh, briefly. 'Will you hear my confession?'

'If that's – yes, if you like.' He felt awkward, but it couldn't hurt, and if it helped the other at all . . . The hut, and the village outside, were quiet around them. There was no sound but the wind in the pine trees.

He cleared his throat. Did Alexandre mean to begin, or was he to say something first?

As though the sound had been a signal, the Frenchman turned to face him, bowing his head so the soft light smoothed the gold hair of his crown.

'Bless me, brother, for I have sinned,' Alexandre said in a low voice. And with his head bowed, hands folded in his lap, he made confession.

Sent out from Detroit with an escort of Hurons, he had ventured down the river as far as the settlement of Ste. Berthe de Ronvalle, to relieve the elderly priest in charge of the mission, whose health had broken down.

'I was happy there,' Alexandre said, in the half-dreaming voice that men use for events that have taken place decades ago. 'It was a wild place, but I was very young, and ardent in my faith. I welcomed hardship.'

Young? The priest couldn't be much older than himself.

Alexandre shrugged, dismissing the past.

'I spent two years with the Huron, and converted many. Then I went with a group of them to Ft. Stanwix, where there was a great gathering of the tribes of the region. There I met Kennyanisi-t'ago, a war chief of the Mohawk. He heard me preach, and being moved of the Holy Spirit, invited me to return with him to his village.'

The Mohawk were notoriously wary of conversion; it had seemed a heaven-sent chance. So Père Ferigault had traveled down the river by canoe, in company with Kennyanisi-t'ago and his warriors.

'That was my first sin,' he said quietly. 'Pride.' He lifted one finger to Roger, as though suggesting that he keep count. 'Still, God was with me.' The Mohawk had sided with the English during the recent French and Indian War, and were more than suspicious of the young French priest. He had persevered, learning the Mohawk language, that he might preach to them in their own tongue.

He had succeeded in converting a number of the village, though by no means all. However, among his converts was the war chief, so he was protected from interference. Unfortunately, the *sachem* of the village opposed his influence, and there was continued uneasiness between Christian and non-Christian in the village.

The priest licked dry lips, then picked up the water jar and drank.

'And then,' he said, taking a deep breath, 'then I committed my second sin.'

He had fallen in love with one of his own converts.

'Had you had women, before –?' Roger choked off the question, but Alexandre answered quite simply, without hesitation.

'No, never.' There was a breath there, not quite a laugh, of bitter self-mockery. 'I had thought I was immune to *that* temptation. But man is frail in the face of Satan's fleshly lures.'

He had lived in the girl's longhouse for some months. Then, one morning, he had risen early, and going to the stream to wash, had seen his own reflection in the water.

'There was a sudden disturbance in the water, and the surface broke. A huge and gaping mouth rose through the surface, shattering the reflection of my face.'

It had been no more than a rising trout, leaping for a dragonfly, but the priest, shaken by the experience, had seen it as a sign from God that his soul was in danger of being swallowed by the mouth of Hell. He had gone at once to the longhouse and removed his things, going to

1004

live alone in a shelter outside the village. However, he had left his lover pregnant.

'Was that what caused the trouble that brought you here?' Roger asked.

'No, not in itself. They do not see matters of marriage and morality as we do,' Alexandre explained. 'Women take men as they will, and marriage is an agreement that endures so long as the partners are in amity; if they should fall out, then the woman may expel the man from her house – or he may leave. The children, if there are children, stay with the mother.'

'But then –'

'The difficulty was that I had always, as a priest, refused to baptize infants unless both parents were Christian and in a state of grace. This is necessary, you understand, if the child is to be raised in faith – for the Indians are inclined otherwise to view the sacrament of baptism as no more than one of their pagan rituals.'

Alexandre drew a deep breath.

'And of course I could not baptize this child. This offended and horrified Kennyanisi-t'ago, who insisted that I must do so. Upon my refusing, he ordered me to be tortured. My – the girl – interceded for me, and was abetted in this by her mother and several other influential persons.'

Consequently the village had been torn by controversy and schism, and at last the *sachem* had decreed that they must take Père Alexandre to Onyarekenata, where an impartial council might judge what must be done to restore the harmony amongst them.

Roger scratched at his beard; perhaps the Indian dislike of hairy Europeans was the association with lice.

'I am afraid I don't quite understand,' he said carefully. 'You refused to baptize your own child because the mother was not a good Christian?'

Alexandre looked surprised.

'Ah, *non*! She retains her faith – though she would have every excuse if she did not,' he added ruefully. He sighed. 'No. I cannot baptize the child, not because of its mother – but because its father is not in a state of grace.'

Roger rubbed his forehead, hoping his face didn't betray his astonishment.

'Ah. Is this why you wished to make confession to me? That you might be restored to a state of grace, and thus able to –'

The priest stopped him with a small gesture. He sat quietly for a moment, slender shoulders slumped. He must have brushed his wound accidentally; the clotted mass had cracked, and blood was once more seeping slowly down his neck.

'Forgive me,' Alexandre said. 'I should not have asked you; it was only that I was so grateful to be able to speak in my own language; I could not resist the temptation to ease my soul by telling you. But it is no good; there can be no absolution for me.'

The man's despair was so plain, Roger laid a hand on the priest's forearm, wanting urgently to assuage it.

'Are you sure? You said that in time of need –'

'It is not that.' He laid his hand on top of Roger's, squeezing tight, as though he might draw strength from the other's grip.

Roger said nothing. After a moment, Alexandre's head rose and the priest looked him in the face. The light outside had changed; there was a faint glow, a brightness in the air just short of light. His own breath rose white from his mouth, like smoke rising toward the hole above.

'Even though I confess, I will not be forgiven. There must be true repentance in order to obtain absolution; I must reject my sin. And that I cannot do.'

He fell silent. Roger didn't know whether to speak, or what to say. A priest, he supposed, would have said something like 'Yes, my son?' but he couldn't. Instead, he took Alexandre's other hand in his, and held it tightly.

'My sin was to love her,' Alexandre said, very softly, 'and that I cannot stop.'

57

A Shattered Smile

Two Spears is agreeable. The matter must be spoken of before the Council, and accepted, but I think it will be done.' Jamie slouched against a pine tree, slumping a little in exhaustion. We had been in the village for a week; he had been with the *sachem* of the village for the greater part of the last three days. I had barely seen him or Ian, but had been entertained by the women, who were polite but distant. I kept my amulet carefully out of sight.

'Then they do have him?' I asked, and felt the knot of anxiety that had traveled with me for so long begin to loosen. 'Roger's really here?' So far, the Mohawks had been unwilling to admit either to Roger's continued existence – or the alternative.

'Aye, well, as to that, the auld bugger's no admitting it – for fear I should try to steal him away, I suppose – but either he's here or he's not far off. If the Council approves the bargain, we'll exchange the whisky for the man in three days time – and be off.' He glanced at the heavy-laden clouds that hid the distant mountains. 'God, I hope that's rain coming, and not snow.'

'Do you think there's any chance the Council won't agree?'

He sighed deeply and ran a hand through his hair. It was unbound and fell rumpled over his shoulders; evidently the negotiations had been difficult.

'Aye, there's a chance. They want the whisky, but they're wary of it. Some of the older men will be against the bargain, for fear of the damage liquor might do to the folk; the younger men are all for it. Some in the middle say aye, take it; they can use the liquor in trade if they're fearful of using it.'

'Wakatihsnore told you all that?' I was surprised. The *sachem*, Acts Fast, seemed much too cool and wily a customer for such openness.

'Not him: wee Ian.' Jamie smiled briefly. 'The lad shows

great promise as a spy, I will say. He's eaten at every hearth in the village, and he's found a lassie who's taken a great liking to him. She tells Ian what the Council of Mothers is thinking.'

I hunched my shoulders and pulled my cloak tight around them; our perch on the rocks outside the village made us safe from interruption, but the price of visibility was exposure to the bitter wind.

'And what does the Council of Mothers say?' A week spent in a longhouse had given me some idea of the importance of the women's opinions in the scheme of things; though they didn't make direct decisions about general affairs, very little would be done without their approval.

'They could wish I offered some ransom other than whisky, and they're none so sure about giving up the man; more than one lady has a small fancy for him. They wouldna mind adopting him into the tribe.' Jamie's mouth twisted at that, and I laughed despite my worry.

'Roger's a nice-looking lad,' I said.

'I've seen him,' Jamie said shortly. 'Most of the men think he's an ugly, hairy bastard. Of course, they think that of me, too.' One side of his mouth lifted reluctantly, as he brushed a hand over his jaw; knowing the Indians' dislike of facial hair, he was careful to shave every morning.

'As it is, that may be what makes the difference.'

'What, Roger's looks? Or yours?'

'The fact that more than one lady wants the bugger. Ian says his lassie says her aunt thinks it will make trouble to keep him; she's thinking better to give him back to us than to have ill-feeling amongst the women over him.'

I rubbed my cold-reddened knuckles over my lips, trying to keep from laughing.

'Has the men's Council any idea that some of the women are interested in Roger?'

'I dinna ken. Why?'

'Because if they knew, they'd give him to you for free.'

Jamie snorted at that, but gave me a reluctant lift of one eyebrow.

'Aye, maybe. I'll have Ian mention the matter among the young men. It canna hurt.'

'You said the women wished you would offer something instead of whisky. Did you mention the opal to Acts Fast?'

He sat up straight at that, interested.

'Aye, I did. They couldna have been taken more aback had I pulled a snake from my sporran. They got verra excited – angry and fearful both, and I think they might well have done me harm, save I'd already mentioned the whisky.'

He reached into the breast of his coat and drew out the opal, dropping it into my hand.

'Best you take it, Sassenach. But I think you'll maybe not want to show it to anyone.'

'How odd.' I looked down at the stone, its spiral petroglyph shimmering with color. 'So it did mean something to them.'

'Oh, that it did,' he assured me. 'I couldna say what, but whatever it was, they didna like it a bit. The war chief demanded to know where I'd got it, and I told them ye'd found it. That made them back off a bit, but they were like a kettle on the boil over it.'

'Why are you wanting me to take it?' The stone was warm from his body, and felt smooth and comfortable in my hand. Instinctively, my thumb ran round and round the spiraled carving.

'They were shocked when they saw it, as I said – and then angry. One or two of them made as though to strike me, but they held back. I watched for a bit, wi' the stone in my hand, and I realized that they were afraid of it; they wouldna touch me while I held it.'

He reached out and closed my fist around the stone.

'Keep it by ye. If there should be danger, bring it out.'

'You're more likely to be in danger than I am,' I protested, trying to hand it back.

He shook his head, though, the ends of his hair lifting in the wind.

'No, not now they ken about the whisky. They'd not harm me until they've heard where it is.'

'But why should I be in any danger?' The thought was disquieting; the women had been cautious but not hostile, and the men of the village had largely ignored me.

He frowned, and looked down toward the village. From

here, little was visible save the outer palisades, with trails of smoke drifting above them from the unseen longhouses beyond.

'I canna say, Sassenach. Only that I have been a hunter – and I have been hunted. Ye ken how when something strange is near, the birds stop singing, and there is a stillness in the wood?'

He nodded toward the village, eyes fixed on the swirl of smoke as though some shape might emerge from it.

'There is a stillness there. Something is happening that I canna see. I dinna think it is to do with us – and yet . . . I am uneasy,' he said abruptly. 'And I have lived too long to dismiss such a feeling.'

Ian, who joined us shortly at the rendezvous, seconded this opinion.

'Aye, it's like holding the edge of a fishing net that's underwater,' he said, frowning. 'Ye can feel the wriggling through your hands, and ye ken there's fish there – but ye canna see where.' The wind ruffled his thick brown hair; as usual, it was half plaited, with strands coming loose. He thumbed one absently behind an ear.

'There's something happening among the people; some disagreement, I think. And *something* happened last night, in the Council house. Emily willna answer me when I ask about it; she only looks away and tells me it's naught to do with us. But I think it is, somehow.'

'Emily?' Jamie lifted one eyebrow, and Ian grinned.

'It's what I call her for short,' he said. 'Her own name's Wakyo'teyehsnonhsa; it means Works with Her Hands. She's a rare carver, is wee Emily. See what she's made for me?' He reached into his pouch and proudly displayed a tiny otter carved in white soapstone. The animal stood alert, head up and ready for mischief; just to look at it made me smile.

'Verra nice.' Jamie examined the carving with approval, stroking the sinuous curve of the body. 'The lassie must like ye fine, Ian.'

'Aye, well, I like her too, Uncle.' Ian was very casual, but his lean cheeks were slightly redder than the cold wind

1010

could account for. He coughed and changed the subject slightly.

'She said to me that she thinks the Council might be swayed a bit in our favor, if ye were to give some of them a taste of the whisky, Uncle Jamie. If it's all right wi' you, I'll fetch up a cask and we'll have a wee *ceilidh* tonight. Emily will manage it.'

Jamie lifted both eyebrows at that, but nodded after a moment.

'I'll trust your judgment, Ian,' he said. 'In the Council House?'

Ian shook his head.

'Nay. Emily says it will be better if it's done at the long-house of her aunt – auld Tewaktenyonh is the Pretty Woman.'

'Is what?' I asked, startled.

'The Pretty Woman,' he explained, wiping his running nose on his sleeve. 'One woman of influence in the village has it in her power to decide what's done wi' captives; they call her the Pretty Woman, no matter what she looks like. So ye ken, it's to our advantage if Tewaktenyonh can be convinced the bargain we offer is a good one.'

'I suppose to a captive that's been freed, the woman would seem beautiful, regardless,' Jamie said wryly. 'Aye, I see. Go ahead then; can ye fetch the whisky by yourself?'

Ian nodded and turned to go.

'Wait a minute, Ian,' I said, and held out the opal as he turned back to me. 'Could you ask Emily if she knows anything about this?'

'Aye, Auntie Claire, I'll mention it. Rollo!' He whistled sharply through his teeth, and Rollo, who had been nosing suspiciously under a rock shelf, left off and bounded after his master. Jamie watched them go, a slight frown between his eyebrows.

'D'ye ken where Ian's spending his nights, Sassenach?'

'If you mean in which longhouse, yes. If you mean in whose bed, no. I could guess, though.'

'Mmphm.' He stretched and shook his hair back. 'Come on, Sassenach, I'll see ye back to the village.'

Ian's *ceilidh* got underway soon after dark; the invited

guests included the most prominent members of the Council, who came one at a time to Tewaktenyonh's longhouse, paying their respects to the *sachem*, Two Spears, who sat at the main hearth with Jamie and Ian flanking him. A slight, pretty girl, who I assumed must be Ian's Emily, sat quietly behind him, on the keg of whisky.

With the exception of Emily, women were not involved in the whisky-tasting. I had come along, though, to watch, and sat at one of the smaller hearths, keeping an eye on the proceedings while helping two of the women to braid onions, exchanging occasional politenesses in a halting mixture of Tuscarora, English, and French.

The woman at whose hearth I sat offered me a gourd of spruce beer and some kind of cornmeal mush as refreshment. I did my best to accept with cordiality, but my stomach was knotted too tightly to make more than a token attempt at eating.

Too much depended on this impromptu party. Roger was here; somewhere in the village, I knew it. He was alive; I could only hope he was well – well enough to travel, at least. I glanced at the far end of the longhouse, at the largest hearth. I could see no more of Tewaktenyonh than the curve of a white-streaked head; a queer jolt went through me at the sight, and I touched the small lump of Nayawenne's amulet, where it hung beneath my shirt.

Once the guests were assembled, a rough circle was formed around the hearth, and the opened keg of whisky brought into the center of it. To my surprise, the girl also came into the circle, and took a place beside the keg, a dipping gourd in her hand.

After some words from Two Spears, the festivities commenced, with the girl measuring out portions of the whisky. She did this not by pouring the whisky into the cups, but by taking mouthfuls from the gourd, carefully spitting three mouthfuls into each cup before passing it to one of the men in the circle. I glanced at Jamie, who looked momentarily taken aback, but who politely accepted his cup and drank without hesitation.

I rather wondered just how much whisky the girl was absorbing through the lining of her mouth. Not nearly as much as the men, though I thought it might take quite a

1012

bit to lubricate Two Spears, who was a taciturn old bastard with a face like a dyspeptic prune. Before the party had got well underway, though, I was distracted by the arrival of a young boy, the offspring of one of my companions. He came in silently and sat down by his mother, leaning heavily against her. She looked sharply at him, then set down her onions and rose with an exclamation of concern.

The firelight fell on the boy, and I could see at once the peculiar hunched way he sat. I rose hastily to my knees, pushing aside the basket of onions. I knelt forward and took him by the other arm, turning him toward me. His left shoulder had been slightly dislocated; he was sweating, his lips pressed tightly together in pain.

I gestured to his mother, who hesitated, frowning at me. The boy made a small, whimpering noise, and she pulled him away, holding him tight. With sudden inspiration, I pulled Nayawenne's amulet from my shirt; she wouldn't know whose it was but might recognize *what* it was. She did; her eyes widened at the sight of the tiny leather bag.

The boy made no more noise, but I could see the sweat run down his chest, clear in the firelight. I fumbled at the thong that held the pouch shut, digging inside for the rough blue stone. *Pierre sans peur*, Gabrielle had called it. The fearless stone. I took the boy's good hand and pressed the stone firmly into his palm, folding his fingers around it.

'*Je suis une sorciere*,' I said softly. '*C'est medecine, la.*' Trust me, I thought. Don't be afraid. I smiled at him.

The boy stared round-eyed at me; the two women at the hearth exchanged a look, then as one, looked toward the distant hearth where the old woman sat.

There was talk from the *ceilidh*; someone was telling an old story – I recognized the rise and fall of the formal rhythms. I had heard Highlanders tell their stories and legends in Gaelic, in just that way; it sounded much the same.

The mother nodded; her sister went quickly down the length of the house. I didn't turn, but felt the stir of interest behind me as she passed the other hearths; heads were turning, looking toward us. I kept my eyes on the boy's face, smiling, holding his hand tightly in my own.

The sister's footsteps came softly behind me. The boy's mother reluctantly released her hold on him, leaving him to me. Permission had been received.

It was a simple matter to put back the joint; he was a small boy and the injury was minor. His bones were light under my hand. I smiled at him as I felt the joint, assessing damage. Then a quick bending of the arm, rotation of the elbow, whipping the arm upward – and it was done.

The boy looked intensely surprised. It was a most satisfactory operation, in that pain was relieved almost instantly. He felt his shoulder, then smiled shyly back at me. Very slowly, he opened his hand and held out the stone to me.

The minor sensation created by this occupied my attention for some time, with the women crowding close, touching the boy and peering at him, summoning their friends to stare at the murky sapphire. By the time I had attention to spare for the whisky party at the far hearth, the festivities were well advanced. Ian was singing in Gaelic, very off-key, accompanied in a haphazard way by one or two of the other men, who chimed in with the weird, high-pitched *Haihai!* that I had heard now and then among Nayawenne's people.

As though my thought had conjured her, I felt eyes on my back, and turned, to see Tewaktenyonh watching me steadily from her own hearth at the end of the longhouse. I met her eyes and nodded to her. She leaned across to say something to one of the young women at her hearth, who rose and came toward me, stepping carefully around a couple of toddlers playing under their family bed-cubicle.

'My grandmother asks if you will come to her.' The young woman squatted beside me, speaking quietly in English. I was surprised, though not astonished, to hear it. Onakara had been right, some of the Mohawk had some English. They would not use it, though, except from necessity, preferring their own language.

I rose and accompanied her to Tewaktenyonh's hearth, wondering what necessity impelled the Pretty Woman. I had my own necessities; the thought of Roger, and of Brianna.

The old woman nodded to me, inviting me to sit down, and spoke to the girl, not taking her eyes off me.

'My grandmother asks if she may see your medicine.'

'Of course.' I could see the old lady's eyes on my amulet, watching curiously as I took out the sapphire. I had added to Nayawenne's woodpecker feather two of my own; a raven's stiff black wing quills.

'You are the wife of Bear Killer?'

'Yes. The Tuscarora call me White Raven,' I said, and the girl jerked, startled. She translated quickly for her grandmother. The old lady's eyes flew wide and she glanced at me in consternation. Evidently this was not the most auspicious name she'd ever heard. I smiled at her, keeping my mouth closed; the Indians usually bared their teeth only when laughing.

The old lady handed me back the stone, very gingerly. She studied me narrowly, then spoke to her grand-daughter, not taking her eyes off me.

'My grandmother has heard that your man bears a bright stone also,' the girl said, interpreting. 'She would hear more of this; what it is like, and how you came to have it.'

'She's welcome to see it.' The girl's eyes widened in surprise as I reached into the pouch at my waist and drew out the stone. I held out the opal to the old woman; she bent and peered closely at it, but made no move to take it from me.

Tewaktenyonh's arms were brown and hairless, wrinkled and smooth as weathered satinwood to the eye. But as I watched I saw the prick of gooseflesh rising, raising vanished hairs in vain defense. *She's seen it*, I thought. *Or at least she knows what it is.*

I didn't need the interpreter's words; her eyes met mine directly and I heard the question clearly, for all that the words were strange.

'How did this come to you?' she said, and the girl echoed it faithfully.

I let my hand lie open; the opal fit snugly in my palm, its

weight belied by its colors, glimmering like a soap bubble in my hand.

'It came to me in a dream,' I said at last, not knowing how else to explain.

The old woman's breath went out in a sigh. The fear didn't quite leave her eyes, but was overlaid with something else – curiosity, perhaps? She said something, and one of the women at the hearth rose, digging in a basket under the bed frame at her back. She came back and bent by the old lady, handing her something.

The old lady began to sing, quietly, in a voice cracked with age, but still strong. She rubbed her hands together over the fire, and a shower of small brown particles rained down, only to rise up again at once as smoke, thick with the scent of tobacco.

It was a quiet night; I could hear the rise and fall of voices and loud laughter from the far hearth, where the men were drinking. I could pick out the odd word in Jamie's voice – he was speaking French. Was Roger perhaps close enough to hear it too?

I took a deep breath. The smoke rose straight up from the fire in a thin white pillar, and the strong sweet scent of tobacco mingled with the smell of cold air, triggering incongruous memories of Brianna's high school football games; cozy scents of wool blankets and thermoses of cocoa, wisps of cigarette smoke drifting from the crowd. Farther back were other, harsher memories, of young men in uniform, in the shattered light of airfields, crushing out glowing fag ends and running to their battles, leaving no more of themselves behind than the smell of smoke on winter air.

Tewaktenyonh spoke, her eyes still on me, and the girl's soft voice chimed in.

'Tell me this dream.'

Was it truly a dream I would tell her, or a memory like these, brought to life on the wings of smoke from a burning tree? It didn't matter; here, all my memories were dreams.

I told her what I could. The memory – of the storm and my refuge among the red cedar's roots, the skull buried with the stone – and the dream; the light on the mountain

1016

and the man with his face painted black – making no distinction between them.

The old lady leaned forward, the astonishment on her features mirroring that of her granddaughter.

'You have seen the Fire-Carrier?' the girl blurted. 'You have seen his *face*?' She shrank away from me, as though I might be dangerous.

The old lady said something peremptory; her startlement had faded into a piercing gaze of interest. She poked the girl, and repeated her question impatiently.

'My grandmother says, can you say what he looked like; what did he wear?'

'Nothing. A breech-clout, I mean. And he was painted.'

'Painted. How?' the girl asked, in response to her grandmother's sharp question.

I described the body paint of the man I had seen, as carefully as I could. This wasn't difficult; if I closed my eyes, I could see him, as clearly as he had appeared to me on the mountainside.

'And his face was black, from forehead to chin,' I ended, opening my eyes.

When I described the man, the interpreter became visibly upset; her lips trembled, and she glanced fearfully from me to her grandmother. The old woman listened intently, though, her eyes searching, straining to discern meaning from my face before the slower words could reach her ears.

When I finished, she sat silent, dark eyes still fastened on my own. At last she nodded, reached up a wrinkled hand and took hold of the purple wampum strings that lay across her shoulder. Myers had told me enough so that I recognized the gesture. The wampum was her family record, badge of her office; speech made while holding it was tantamount to testimony made upon the Bible.

'At the feast of Green Corn, this many years ago' – the interpreter's fingers flashed four times – 'a man came among us from the north. His speech was strange, but we could understand him; he spoke like Canienga, or maybe Onondaga, but he would not tell us his tribe or village – only his clan, which was the Turtle.

'He was a wild man, but a brave one. He was a good

hunter, and a warrior. Oh, a fine man; all the women liked to look at him, but we were afraid to come too close.' Tewaktenyonh paused a moment, a far-off look in her eye that made me count back; she would have been a full-grown woman then, but perhaps young enough still to have been impressed by the frightening, intriguing stranger.

'The men were not so careful; men aren't.' She gave a brief, sardonic glance at the *ceilidh*, growing louder by the minute. 'So they would sit and smoke with him, and drink spruce beer and listen. He would talk from midday till the dark, and then again in the night by the fires. His face was always fierce, because he talked of war.'

She sighed, fingers curling over the purple shell strands.

'Always war. Not against the frog-eaters of the next village, or the ones who eat moose dung. No, we must lift our tomahawks against the *O'seronni*. Kill them all, he said, from the oldest to the youngest, from the Treaty Line to the big water. Go to the Cayuga, send messengers to the Seneca, let the League of the Iroquois go forth as one. Go before it is too late, he said.'

One frail shoulder lifted, fell.

' "Too late for what?" the men asked. 'And why shall we make war for no cause? We need nothing this season; there is no war treaty' – this was before the Time of the French, you understand.

' "It is our last chance," he said to them. "Already it may be too late. They seduce us with their metal, bring us close to them in the hope of knives and guns, and destroy us for the sake of cooking pots. Turn back, brothers! You have left the ways of years too great to count. Go back, I say – or you will be no more. Your stories will be forgotten. Kill them now or they will eat you."

'And my brother – he was *sachem* then, and my other brother war chief – said that this was foolishness. Destroy us with tools? Eat us? The whites do not consume the hearts of their enemies, even in battle.

'The young men listened; they listen to anyone with a loud voice. But the older ones looked at the stranger with a narrow eye, and said nothing.

'He knew,' she said, and the old lady nodded emphatically, speaking almost faster than her granddaughter could translate. 'He knew what would happen – that the British and the French would fight with each other, and would seek our help, each against the other. He said that that would be the time; when they fought each other, then we must rise up against them both and cast them out.

'Tawineonawira – Otter-Tooth – that was his name – said to me, "You live in the moment. You know the past, but you don't look to the future. Your men say, 'We need nothing this season,' and so they will not move. Your women think it is easier to cook in a iron kettle than to make clay pots. You don't see what will happen because of your laziness, your greed."

' "It's not true," I said to him. "We are not lazy. We scrape hides, we dry the meat and the corn, we press the oil from sunflowers and put it in jars; we take heed for the next season – always. If we didn't, we would die. And what have pots and kettles to do with it?"

'He laughed at that, but his eyes were sad. He was not always fierce with me, you see.' The young woman's eyes slid toward her grandmother at this, but then she looked away, eyes once more on her lap.

' "A woman's heed," he said, and shook his head. "You think of things to eat, what to wear. None of this matters. Men can't think of such things."

' "You can be *Hodeenosaunee* and think this?" I said. "Where do you come from that you don't take heed of what the women think?"

'He shook his head again and said, "You cannot see far enough." I asked him how far then did *he* see, but he would not answer me.'

I knew the answer to that, and my skin prickled with gooseflesh, too, in spite of the fire. I knew too bloody well how far he'd seen – and how dangerous the view was from that particular precipice.

'But nothing I said was any use,' the old lady continued, 'nor what my brothers said. Otter-Tooth grew more angry. One day he came out and danced the war dance. He was painted – his arms and legs were striped with red – and he sang and shouted through the village. Everyone came out to watch, to see who would follow him, and when he drove

1019

his tomahawk into the war tree and shouted that he went to gain horses and plunder from the Shawnee, a number of the young men followed him.

'They were gone for the rising and setting of a moon, and came back with horses, and with scalps. White scalps, and my brothers were angry. It would bring soldiers from the fort, they said – or revenge parties from the Treaty Line settlements, where they had taken the scalps.

'Otter-Tooth answered boldly that he hoped this was so; then we would be forced to fight. And he said plainly that he would lead such raids again – again and again, until the whole land was roused and we saw that it was as he said; that we must kill the *O'seronni* or die ourselves.

'No one could stop him doing what he said, and there were a few of the young men whose blood was hot; they would follow him, no matter what anyone said. My brother the *sachem* made his medicine tent, and called the Great Turtle to counsel with him. He stayed in the tent for a day and a night. The tent shook and heaved, and voices came out of it, and the people were afraid.

'When my brother came out of the tent, he said that Otter-Tooth must leave the village. He would do what he would do, but we would not let him bring destruction to us. He caused disharmony among the people; he must go.

'Otter-Tooth became more angry then than we had ever seen him. He stood up in the center of the village and he shouted until the veins stood out in his neck and his eyes were red with rage.' The girl's voice dropped. 'He shouted terrible things.

'Then he became very quiet, and we were afraid. He said things that took the hearts from our bodies. Even those who had followed him were afraid of him, then.

'He didn't sleep or eat. For all of a day, and all of a night, and all of the next day, he went on talking, walking round and round the village, stopping at the doors of the houses and talking, until the people in the house drove him away. And then he left.

'But he came back again. And again. He would go away, and hide in the forest, but then he would be back again, by the fires at night, thin and hungry, with his eyes glowing like a fox's, always talking. His voice filled the village at night, and no one could sleep.

'We began to know that he had an evil spirit in him; perhaps it was Atatarho, from whose head Hiawatha combed the snakes; perhaps the snakes had come to this man, looking for a home. Finally, my brother the war chief said that it must stop; he must leave or we would kill him.'

Tewaktenyonh paused. Her fingers, which had stroked the wampum continuously, as though she drew strength from it for her story, were now still.

'He was a stranger,' she said softly. 'But he didn't know he was a stranger. I think he never understood.'

At the other end of the longhouse the drinking party was growing riotous; all the men were laughing, rocking to and fro with mirth. I could hear the girl Emily's voice, higher, laughing with them. Tewaktenyonh glanced that way, frowning slightly.

Mice were creeping briskly up and down my spine. A stranger. An Indian, by his face, by his speech; his slightly strange speech. An Indian – with silver fillings in his teeth. No, he hadn't understood. He had thought they were his people, after all. Knowing what their future held, he had come to try to save them. How could he believe that they meant to do him harm?

But they *had* meant it. They stripped him, said Tewaktenyonh, her face remote. They tied him to a pole in the center of the village, and painted his face with an ink made from soot and oak galls.

'Black is for death; prisoners who are to be killed are always painted so,' the girl said. One eyebrow lifted slightly. 'You knew this when you met the man on the mountain?'

I shook my head, mute. The opal had grown warm in my palm, slick with sweat.

They had tortured him for a time; prodding his naked body with sharpened sticks, and then with hot embers, so that blisters rose up and burst, and his skin hung in tatters. He stood this well, not crying out, and this pleased them. He seemed still strong, so they left him overnight, still tied to the pole.

'In the morning, he was gone.' The old woman's face

1021

was smooth with secrets. If she had been pleased, or relieved, or distressed by the escape, no one would ever have known.

'I said that they should not follow him, but my brother said it was no good; he would only come back again, if we did not finish the matter.'

So a party of warriors left the village, on Otter-Tooth's track. Bloody as he was, it was not difficult to follow.

'They chased him to the south. They thought to catch him, time after time, but he was strong. He ran on. For four days, they followed him, and finally they caught him, in a grove of aspens, leafless in the snow and their branches white as finger bones.'

She saw the question in my eyes at this, and nodded.

'My brother the war chief was there. He told me, afterward.

'He was alone, and unarmed. He had no chance, and knew it. But he faced them nonetheless – and he talked. Even after one of the men had struck him in the mouth with a war club, he talked through the blood, spitting out words with his broken teeth.

'He was a brave man,' she said, reflectively. 'He didn't beg. He told them the same things he had said before, but my brother said this time it was different. Before, he had been hot as fire; dying, he was cold as snow – and because they were so cold, his words terrified the warriors.

'Even when the stranger lay dead in the snow, his words seemed to go on ringing in the warriors' ears. They lay down to sleep, but his voice talked to them in their dreams, and kept them from sleeping. *You will be forgotten,* he said. *The Nations of the Iroquois will be no more. No one will tell your stories. Everything you are and have been will be lost.*

'They turned toward home, but his voice followed them. At night, they could not sleep for the evil words in their ears. In the day, they heard cries and whispers from the trees along their trail. Some of them said it was only ravens calling, but others said no, they heard him plainly.

'At last, my brother said it was clear this man was a sorcerer.'

The old lady glanced sharply at me. *Je suis une sorciere,*

I'd said. I swallowed, and my hand went to the amulet at my neck.

'The thing to do, my brother said, was to cut off his head, and then he would talk no more. So they went back, and they cut off his head, and tied it in the branches of a spruce. But when they slept that night, they still heard his voice, and they woke with shriveled hearts. The ravens had picked out his eyes, but the head still spoke.

'One man, very brave, said he would take the head, and bury it far away.' She smiled briefly. 'This brave man was my husband. He wrapped the head in a piece of deerskin, and he ran with it, far to the south, and the head still talking under his arm all the time, so he had to put plugs of beeswax in his ears. At last he saw a very big red cedar tree, and he knew this was the place, because the red cedar has a strong spirit for healing.

'So he buried the head under the tree's roots, and when he took the beeswax from his ears, he could hear nothing but the wind and water. So he came home, and no one has spoken the name of Otter-Tooth in this village, from that day until this one.'

The girl finished this, eyes on her grandmother. Evidently this was true; she had never heard this story.

I swallowed, and tried to get a clear breath. The smoke had ceased to rise as she talked; it had gathered instead in a low cloud overhead, and the air was thick with narcotic perfume.

The hilarity from the drinking circle had lessened. One of the men got up and, stumbling, went outside. Two more lay on their sides by the fire, half asleep.

'And this?' I said, holding out the opal. 'You've seen it? It was his?'

Tewaktenyonh reached out as though to touch the stone, but then drew back.

'There is a legend,' the girl said softly, not taking her eyes from the opal. 'Magic snakes carry stones in their heads. If you kill such a snake and take the stone, it will give you great power.' She shifted uneasily, and I had no trouble imagining with her the size of the snake that might have carried a stone like this.

The old lady spoke suddenly, nodding at the stone. The girl jumped, but repeated the words obediently.

'It was his,' she said. 'He called it his *tika-ba.*'

I looked at the interpreter, but she shook her head. '*Tika-ba,*' she said, enunciating clearly. 'This is not an English word?'

I shook my head.

Her story finished, the old woman sat back in her furs, watching me with deep speculation. Her eyes rested on the amulet around my neck.

'Why did he speak to you? Why has he given you that?' She nodded at my hand, and my fingers closed over the opal's curve in reflex.

'I don't know,' I said – but she had taken me unaware; I had had no time to prepare my face.

She fixed me with a piercing look. She knew I was lying, all right – and yet how could I tell her the truth? Tell her what Otter-Tooth – whatever his real name – had been? Much less that his prophecies were true.

'I think perhaps he was a part of my . . . family,' I said at last, thinking of what Pollyanne had told me about the ghosts of one's ancestors. There was no telling from where – or when – he had come; he must, I supposed, be an ancestor or a descendant. If not of me, then of someone like me.

Tewaktenyonh sat up very straight at that, and looked at me in astonishment. Slowly the look faded, and she nodded.

'He has sent you to me to hear this. He was wrong,' she declared, with confidence. 'My brother said that we must not speak of him; we must let him be forgotten. But a man is not forgotten, as long as there are two people left under the sky. One, to tell the story; the other, to hear it. So.'

She reached out and touched my hand, careful not to touch the stone. The glitter of moisture in her black eyes might have been from the tobacco smoke.

'I am one. You are the other. He is not forgotten.'

She motioned to the girl, who rose silently and brought us food and drink.

When I rose finally to go back to the longhouse where we were lodged, I glanced toward the drinking party. The ground was littered with snoring bodies, and the keg lay empty on its side. Two Spears lay peacefully on his back, a beatific smile creasing the wrinkles of his face. The girl, Ian, and Jamie were gone.

Jamie was outside, waiting for me. His breath rose white in the night air, and the scents of whisky and tobacco wafted from his plaid.

'You seemed to be having fun,' I said, taking his arm. 'Any progress, do you think?'

'I think so.' We walked side by side across the big central clearing to the longhouse where we were lodged. 'It went well. Ian was right, bless him; now they've seen this wee *ceilidh* did no harm, I think they'll maybe be disposed to make the bargain.'

I glanced at the row of longhouses with their floating clouds of smoke, and the glow of firelight from smoke-holes and doorways. Was Roger in one of them now? I counted automatically, as I did every day – seven months. The ground was thawing; if we traveled partway by river, we could perhaps make the trip in a month – six weeks at the most. Yes, if we left soon, we would be in time.

'And you, Sassenach? Ye seemed to be having a most earnest discussion wi' the auld lady. Did she ken aught of that stone?'

'Yes. Come inside and I'll tell you about it.'

He lifted the skin over the doorway, and I walked inside, the opal a solid weight in my hand. They hadn't known what he had called it, but I did. The man called Otter-Tooth, who had come to raise a war, to save a nation – with silver fillings in his teeth. Yes, I knew what it was, the *tika-ba*.

His unused ticket back. My legacy.

58

Lord John Returns

River Run, March 1770

Phaedre had brought a dress, one of Jocasta's, yellow silk, very full in the skirt.

'We got better company tonight than ol' Mr. Cooper or Lawyer Forbes,' Phaedre said with satisfaction. 'We got us a real live *lord*, how 'bout *that*?'

She let down a huge armload of fabric on the bed and began to pull bits and pieces from the frothing billows, issuing instructions like a drill sergeant.

'Here, you strip off and put on these yere stays. You need somethin' strong, keep that belly pushed down. Ain't nobody but backcountry trash goes 'thout stays. Your auntie wasn't blind as a bat, she'd 'a had you fitted out proper long since – *long* since. Then put on the stockins and garters – ain't those pretty? I always did like that pair with the little bitty leaves on 'em – then we'll tie on the petticoats, and then –'

'What lord?' Brianna took the proferred stays and frowned at them. 'My God, what's this made of, whalebones?'

'Uh-huh. Ain't no cheap tin or iron for Miss Jo, surely not.' Phaedre burrowed like a terrier, frowning and muttering to herself. 'Where that garter gone to?'

'I don't need these. And what lord is it that's coming?'

Phaedre straightened up, staring at Brianna over the folds of yellow silk.

'Don't need 'em?' she said censoriously. 'And you with a six-month belly? What you thinking of, girl, come into dinner all pooched out, and a lordship sittin' by the soup a-gogglin' at you through his eyeglass?'

Brianna couldn't help smiling at this description, but replied with considerable dryness nonetheless.

'What difference would it make? The whole county knows by now that I'm having a baby. I wouldn't be surprised if that circuit rider – Mr. Urmstone, is it? didn't preach a sermon about me up on the Buttes.'

Phaedre uttered a short laugh.

'He did,' she said. 'Two Sundays back. Mickey and Drusus was there – they thought it was right funny, but your auntie didn't. She set Lawyer Forbes on to law him for the slander, but ol' Reverend Urmstone, he said 'twasn't slander if it was the truth.'

Brianna stared back at the maid.

'And just what did he say about me?'

Phaedre shook her head and resumed her rummaging.

'You don' want to know,' she said darkly. 'But be that as it might, whether the county knows ain't the same thing as you flauntin' your belly through the dining room and leavin' his lordship in no doubt, so you put on them stays.'

Her authoritative tone left no room for argument. Brianna struggled resentfully into the stiff garment, and suffered Phaedre to lace it tight. Her waist was still slender, and the remaining bulge in front would be easily disguised by the full skirt and petticoats.

She stared at herself in the mirror, Phaedre's dark head bobbing near her thighs as the maid adjusted the green silk stockings to her own satisfaction. She couldn't breathe, and being squeezed like that *couldn't* be good for the baby. The stays laced in front; as soon as Phaedre left, she'd undo them. The hell with his Lordship, whoever he was.

'And who *is* this lord we're having for dinner?' she asked for the third time, stepping obediently into the billow of starched white linen the maid held for her.

'This be Lord John William Grey, of Mount Josiah plantation in Virginia.' Phaedre rolled out the syllables with great ceremony, though seeming rather disappointed by the unfortunately brief and simple names of the lord. She would, Brianna knew, have preferred a Lord FitzGerald Vanlandingham Walthamstead if she could have got one.

'He a friend of your daddy's, or so Miss Jo says,' the maid added, more prosaically. 'There, that's good. Lucky you got nice bosoms, this dress is made for 'em.'

Brianna hoped this didn't mean the dress wasn't going to cover her breasts; the stays ended just beneath, pushing

1027

them up so that they swelled startlingly high, like something bubbling over the rim of a pot. Her nipples stared at her in the mirror, gone a rich dark color, like raspberry wine.

It wasn't worry over which bulges she was exposing that made her oblivious to the rest of Phaedre's brisk ministrations, though; it was the maid's casual *He a friend of your daddy's.*

It was not a crowd; Jocasta seldom had crowds. Dependent on her ears for the nuances of social byplay, she would not risk commotion. Still, there were more people here in the drawing room than was usual; Lawyer Forbes, of course, with his spinster sister; Mr. MacNeill and his son, Judge Alderdyce and his mother, a couple of Farquard Campbell's unmarried sons. No one, though, resembling Phaedre's lordship.

Brianna smiled sourly to herself. 'Let 'em look, then,' she murmured, straightening her back so that her bulge swelled proudly before her, glistening under the silk. She gave it an encouraging pat. 'Come on, Osbert, let's be social.'

Her entrance was greeted by a general outcry of cordiality that made her mildly ashamed of her cynicism. They were kind men and women, including Jocasta; and the situation, after all, was none of *their* doing.

Still, she did enjoy the expression of mild shock that the Judge tried to hide, and the too-sweet smile on his mother's face, as her beady little parrot eyes registered the blatant fact of Osbert's unbound presence. Jocasta might propose, but the Judge's mother would dispose, no doubt of that. Brianna met Mrs. Alderdyce's eye with a sweet smile of her own.

Mr. MacNeill's weatherbeaten face twitched slightly with amusement, but he bowed gravely and asked after her health with no sign of embarrassment. As for Lawyer Forbes, if he noticed anything amiss in her appearance, he drew the veil of his professional discretion over it and greeted her with his customary suavity.

'Ah, Miss Fraser!' he said. 'Precisely whom we were wanting. Mrs. Alderdyce and myself have just been engaged in amiable dispute concerning a question of aesthetics. You, with your instinct for loveliness, would have a most valuable opinion, should you be willing to oblige me by giving it.' Taking her arm, he drew her smoothly to his side – away from MacNeill, who twitched a bushy brow at her but made no move to interfere.

He led her to the hearthside, where four small wooden boxes sat on the table. Ceremoniously removing the lids of these, the lawyer displayed in turn four jewels, each the size of a marrow-fat pea, each nestled in a pad of dark blue velvet, the better to set off its brilliance.

'I think of purchasing one of these stones,' Forbes explained. 'To have made into a ring. I had them sent from Boston.' He smirked at Brianna, plainly feeling that he had stolen a march on the competition – and judging from the faint glower on MacNeill's face, he had.

'Tell me, my dear – which do you prefer? The sapphire, the emerald, the topaz or the diamond?' He rocked back on his heels, waistcoat swelling with his own cleverness.

For the first time in her pregnancy, Brianna felt a sudden qualm of nausea. Her head felt light and giddy, and her fingertips tingled with numbness.

Sapphire, emerald, topaz, diamond. And her father's ring held a ruby. Five stones of power, the points of a traveler's pentagram, the guarantors of safe passage. For how many? Without thinking, she spread a hand protectively over her belly.

She realized the trap Forbes thought he was luring her toward. Let her make a choice and he would present her with the unmounted stone on the spot, a public proposal that would – he thought – force her either to accept him at once, or cause an unpleasant scene by rejecting him outright. Gerald Forbes really knew nothing about women, she thought.

'I – ah – I should not like to venture my own opinion without first hearing Mrs. Alderdyce's choice,' she said, forcing a cordial smile and a nod toward the Judge's mother, who looked both surprised and gratified by being so deferred to.

Brianna's stomach clenched, and she surreptitiously wiped sweaty hands on her skirt. There they were, all

1029

together and in one place – the four stones she had thought it would take a lifetime to find.

Mrs. Alderdyce was jabbing an arthritic finger at the emerald, explaining the virtues of her choice, but Brianna paid no attention to what the woman said. She glanced at Lawyer Forbes, his round face still reflecting smugness. A sudden wild impulse filled her.

If she said yes, now, tonight, while he still had all four stones . . . could she bring herself to that? Inveigle him, kiss him, lull him into complacency – and then steal the stones?

Yes, she could – and then what? Run off into the mountains with them? Leave Jocasta disgraced and the county in an uproar, run and hide like a common thief? And how would she get to the Indies before the baby came? She counted in her head, knowing it was insanity, but still – it could be done.

The stones glittered and winked, temptation and salvation. Everyone had come to look, heads bent over the table, murmuring their admiration, herself temporarily overlooked.

She could hide, she thought, the steps of the plan unfolding inevitably before her mind's eye, quite without her willing it. Steal a horse, head up the Yadkin valley into the backcountry. Despite the nearness of the fire, she shivered, feeling cold at the thought of flight through the winter snows. But her mind ran on.

She could hide in the mountains, at her parents' cabin, and wait for them to come back with Roger. If they came back. If Roger was with them. Yes, and what if the baby came first, and she was there on the mountain, all alone with no one at hand, and nothing to help but a handful of stolen brightness?

Or should she ride at once for Wilmington and find a ship to the Indies? If Jocasta was right, Roger was never coming back. Was she sacrificing her only chance at return to wait for a man who was dead – or who, if not dead, might reject her and her child?

'Miss Fraser?'

Lawyer Forbes was waiting, swollen with expectation.

She took a deep breath, feeling sweat trickle down between her breasts, beneath the loosened stays.

'They're all very lovely,' she said, surprised at how coolly she was able to speak. 'I could not possibly choose among them – but then, I have no particular liking for gems. I have very simple tastes, I'm afraid.'

She caught the flicker of a smile on Mr. MacNeill's face, and the deep flush of Forbes's round cheeks, but turned her back on the stones with a polite word.

'I think we will not wait dinner,' Jocasta murmured in her ear. 'If his Lordship should be delayed . . .'

On cue, Ulysses appeared in the doorway, elegant in full livery, to announce dinner. Instead, in a mellifluous voice that carried easily over the chatter, he said, 'Lord John Grey, ma'am,' and stepped aside.

Jocasta breathed a sigh of satisfaction, and urged Brianna forward, toward the slight figure that stood in the doorway.

'Good. You shall be his partner at dinner, my dear.'

Brianna glanced back at the table by the hearth, but the stones were gone.

Lord John Grey was a surprise. She had heard her mother speak of John Grey – soldier, diplomat, nobleman – and expected someone tall and imposing. Instead, he was six inches shorter than she was, fine-boned and slight, with large, beautiful eyes, and a fair-skinned handsomeness that was saved from girlishness only by the firm set of mouth and jaw.

He had looked startled upon seeing her; many people did, taken aback by her size – but then had set himself to exercise his considerable charm, telling her amusing anecdotes of his travel, admiring the two paintings that Jocasta had hung upon the wall, and regaling the table at large with news of the political situation in Virginia.

What he did not mention was her father, and for that she was grateful.

Brianna listened to Miss Forbes's descriptions of her brother's importance with an absent smile. She felt more and more as though she were drowning in a sea of kind intentions. Could they not leave her alone? Could Jocasta not even have the decency to wait a few months?

' . . . and then there's the wee sawmill he's just bought, up to Averasboro. Heavens, how the man manages, I couldna tell you!'

No, they couldn't, she thought, with a kind of despair. They couldn't leave her alone. They were Scots, kindly but practical, and with an iron conviction of their own rightness – the same conviction that had got half of them killed or exiled after Culloden.

Jocasta was fond of her, but clearly had made up her mind that it would be foolish to wait. Why sacrifice the chance of a good, solid, respectable marriage, to a will-o'-the-wisp hope of love?

The horrible thing was that she knew herself it was foolish to wait. Of all the things she had been trying not to think of for weeks, this was the worst – and here it was, rising up in her mind like the shadow of a dead tree, stark against snow.

If. If they came back – if, if, *IF*. If her parents came back at all, Roger would not be with them. She knew it. They wouldn't find the Indians who had taken him – how could they, in a trackless wilderness of snow and mud? Or they would find the Indians, only to learn that Roger was dead – of injuries, disease, torture.

Or he would be found, alive, and refuse to come back, not wanting to see her ever again. Or he would come back, with that maddening sense of Scottish honor, determined to take her, but hating her for it. Or he would come back, see the baby, and . . .

Or none of them would come back at all. *I will bring him home to you – or I will not come home myself.* And she would live here alone forever, drowned in the waves of her own guilt, her body bobbing in the swirl of good intentions, anchored by a rotting umbilical cord to the child whose dead weight had pulled her under.

'Miss Fraser! Miss Fraser, are ye quite weel, then?'

'Not very, no,' she said. 'I think I'm going to faint.' And did, shaking the table with a crash as she fell forward into a whirling sea of china and white linen.

The tide had turned again, she thought. She was buoyed up on a flood of kindness as people bustled to and fro, fetching warm drinks and a brick to her feet, seeing her tucked up warmly on the sofa in the little parlor, with a pillow to her head and salts to her nose, a thick shawl round her knees.

At last they were gone. She could be alone. And now that the truth was out in her own mind, she could cry for all her losses – for father and lover, family and mother, for the loss of time and place and all that she should have been and would never be.

Except that she couldn't.

She tried. She tried to summon up the sense of terror she had felt in the drawing room, alone among the crowd. But now that she truly *was* alone, paradoxically she wasn't afraid anymore. One of the house slaves popped a head in, but she waved a hand, sending the girl away again.

Well, she was Scottish, too – 'Well, half,' she muttered, cupping a hand over her belly – and entitled to her own stubbornness. They *were* coming back. All of them; mother, father, Roger. If it felt as though that conviction were made of feathers rather than iron . . . still it was hers. And she was hanging on to it like a raft, until they pried her fingers off and let her sink.

The door to the small parlor opened, silhouetting the tall, spare figure of Jocasta against the lighted hall.

'Brianna?' The pale oval face turned unerringly toward the sofa; did she only guess where they had put her, or could she hear Brianna breathing?

'I'm here, Aunt.'

Jocasta came into the room, followed by Lord John, with Ulysses bringing up the rear with a tea tray.

'How are you, child? Had I best send for Dr. Fentiman?' She frowned, laying a long hand across Brianna's forehead.

'No!' Brianna had met Dr. Fentiman, a small, damp-handed golliwog of a man with a strong faith in lye and leeches; the sight of him made her shudder. 'Er . . . no. Thank you, but I'm quite all right; I was just taken queer for a moment.'

'Ah, good.' Jocasta turned blind eyes toward Lord John.

'His Lordship will be going on to Wilmington in the morning; he wished to pay you his regards, if you are well enough.'

'Yes, of course.' She sat up, swinging her feet to the floor. So the lord wasn't going to linger; that would be a disappointment to Jocasta, if not to her. Still, she could be polite for a little while.

Ulysses set down the tray, and soft-footed out the door behind her aunt, leaving them alone.

He drew up an embroidered footstool and sat down, not waiting for invitation.

'Are you truly well, Miss Fraser? I have no desire to see you prostrate among the teacups.' A smile pulled at the corner of his mouth, and she flushed.

'I'm fine,' she said shortly. 'Did you have something to say to me?'

He wasn't taken aback by her abruptness.

'Yes, but I thought perhaps you would prefer that I not mention it in the midst of the company. I understand that you are interested in the whereabouts of a man named Roger Wakefield?'

She had been feeling fine; at this, the wave of faintness threatened to return.

'Yes. How do you – do you know where he is?'

'No.' He saw her face change, and took her hand between his. 'No, I am sorry. Your father had written to me, some three months ago, asking me to assist him in finding this man. It had occurred to him that if Mr. Wakefield was anywhere in the ports, he might have been taken up by a pressgang, and thus be now at sea in one of His Majesty's ships. He asked if I would make use of my acquaintance in naval circles to determine whether such a fate had in fact befallen Mr. Wakefield.'

Another wave of faintness passed over her, this one tinged with remorse, as she realized the lengths her father had gone to, in attempting to find Roger for her.

'He isn't on a ship.'

He looked surprised at her tone of certainty.

'I have found no evidence that he was impressed anywhere between Jamestown and Charleston. Still, there is the possibility that he was taken up on the eve of sailing, in

1034

which case his presence on the crew would not be registered until the ship reached port. That is why I travel tomorrow to Wilmington, to make inquiries –'

'You don't need to. I know where he is.' In as few words as possible, she acquainted him with the basic facts.

'Jamie – your father – that is, your parents – have gone to rescue this man from the Iroquois?' Looking shaken, he turned and poured two cups of tea, handing her one without asking if she wanted it.

She held it between her hands, finding a small comfort in the warmth; a greater comfort in being able to speak frankly to Lord John.

'Yes. I wanted to go with them, but –'

'Yes, I see.' He glanced at her bulge and coughed. 'I collect there is some urgency in finding Mr. Wakefield?'

She laughed, unhappily.

'I can wait. Can you tell me something, Lord John? Have you ever heard of handfasting?'

His fair brows drew together momentarily.

'Yes,' he said slowly. 'A Scottish custom of temporary marriage, is it not?'

'Yes. What I want to know is, is it legal here?'

He rubbed his jaw, thinking. Either he'd shaved recently or he had a light beard; late as it was, he showed no sign of stubble.

'I don't know,' he said finally. 'I have never seen the question addressed in law. Still, any couple who dwells together as man and wife are considered married, by common law. I should think handfasting would fall into that class, would it not?'

'It might, except that we're rather obviously not dwelling together,' Brianna said. She sighed. '*I* think I'm married – but my aunt doesn't. She keeps insisting that Roger won't come back, or that if he does, I'm still not legally bound to him. Even by the Scots custom, I'm not bound beyond a year and a day. She wants to pick a husband for me – and God, she's trying! I thought you were the newest candidate, when you showed up.'

Lord John looked amused at the idea.

'Oh. That would explain the oddly assorted company at dinner. I did notice that the rather florid gentleman –

1035

Alderdyce? A judge? – seemed inclined to pay you attention beyond the normal limits of gallantry.'

'Much good it will do him.' Brianna snorted briefly. 'You should have seen the looks Mrs. Alderdyce kept giving me, all through dinner. She's not going to have her ewe lamb – God, he must be forty, if he's a day – marry the local whore of Babylon. I'd be surprised if she ever lets him set foot over the doorstep again.' She patted her small bulge. 'I think I've seen to that.'

One brow rose, and Grey smiled wryly at her. He set down his teacup and reached for the sherry decanter and a glass.

'Ah? Well, while I admire the boldness of your strategy, Miss Fraser – may I call you "my dear"? – I regret to inform you that your tactics do not suit the terrain upon which you've chosen to employ them.'

'What do you mean by that?'

He leaned back in his chair, glass in hand, surveying her kindly.

'Mrs. Alderdyce. Not being blind – though by no means as astute as your aunt – I did indeed observe her observing you. But you mistake the nature of her observations, I'm afraid.' He shook his head, looking at her over the rim of his glass as he sipped.

'Not the look of outraged respectability, by any means. It's granny lust.'

Brianna sat up straight.

'It's *what?*'

'Granny lust,' he repeated. He sat up himself and topped his glass, pouring the golden liquid carefully. 'You know; an elderly woman's urgent desire for grandchildren to dandle upon her knee, spoil with sweetmeats, and generally corrupt.' He raised his glass to his nose and reverently breathed in the vapors. 'Oh, ambrosia. I haven't had a decent sherry in two years, at least.'

'What – you mean Mrs. Alderdyce thinks that I – I mean, because I've shown I'm – that I can have children, then she's sure to get grandchildren out of me later on? That's ridiculous! The Judge could pick any healthy girl – of good character,' she added bitterly, 'and be fairly sure of having children by her.'

1036

He took a drink, let it drift across his tongue, and swallowed, relishing the final ghost of the taste before answering. 'Well. No. I rather think that she realizes he could not. Or would not; it makes no difference.' He looked at her directly, pale blue eyes unblinking.

'You said it yourself – he is forty and unmarried.'

'You mean he – but he's a judge!' The moment her horrified exclamation came out, she realized the idiocy of it, and clapped a hand over her mouth, blushing furiously. Lord John laughed, though with a wry edge to it.

'The more certainty therefore,' he said. 'You are quite right; he could have his choice of any girl in the county. If he has not so chosen . . .' He paused delicately, then lifted his glass to her in ironic toast. 'I rather think that Mrs. Alderdyce has realized that her son's marriage to you is her best – possibly her only – expectation of having the grandchild she so ardently desires.'

'Damn!' She couldn't make a move right, she thought with despair. 'It doesn't matter what I do. I'm doomed. They'll have me married off to *somebody*, no matter what I do!'

'You must give me leave to doubt that,' he said. His smile quirked sideways, a little painfully. 'From what I have seen of you, you have your mother's bluntness and your father's sense of honor. Either would be sufficient to preserve you from such entrapment.'

'Don't talk to me about my father's honor,' she said sharply. 'He's who got me into this mess!'

His eyes dropped to her waistline, frankly ironical.

'You shock me,' he said politely, seeming not shocked at all.

She felt the blood surge up in her face once more, hotter than before.

'You know perfectly well that's not what I mean!'

He hid a smile in his sherry cup, eyes crinkling at her.

'My apologies, Miss Fraser. What did you mean, then?'

She took a deep sip of tea to cover her confusion, and felt the comforting heat run down her throat and into her chest.

'I mean,' she said through her teeth, '*this* particular mess; being put on show like a piece of bloodstock with doubtful lines. Being held up by the scruff of the neck like an orphaned kitten, in hopes somebody will take me in! Being – being left alone here in the first place,' she ended, her voice trembling unexpectedly.

'Why are you alone here?' Lord John asked, quite gently. 'I should have thought that your mother might have –'

'She wanted to. I wouldn't let her. Because she had to – that is, he – oh, it's all such a fucking *mess!*' She dropped her head into her hands and stared wretchedly at the tabletop; not crying, but not far from it, either.

'I can see that.' Lord John leaned forward and put his empty glass back on the tray. 'It's very late, my dear, and if you will pardon my observing it, you are in need of rest.' He stood up and laid a hand lightly on her shoulder; oddly, it seemed only friendly, and not condescending, as another man's might.

'As it seems my journey to Wilmington is unnecessary, I think I will accept your aunt's kind invitation to remain here for a little. We will speak again, and see whether perhaps there is at least some palliative for your situation.'

59

Blackmail

The commode was magnificent, a beautiful piece of smooth carved walnut that mingled appeal with convenience. Particularly convenient on a rainy, cold night like this. She fumbled sleepily with the lid in the dark, lit by lightning flashes from the window, then sat down, sighing with relief as the pressure on her bladder eased.

Evidently pleased with the additional internal space thus provided, Osbert performed a series of lazy somersaults, making her belly undulate in ghostly waves beneath her white flannel nightgown. She stood up slowly – she did almost everything slowly these days – feeling pleasantly drugged with sleep.

She paused by the rumpled bed, looking out at the stark beauty of the hills and the rain-lashed trees. The glass of the window was icy to the touch, and the clouds rolled down from the mountains, black-bellied and growling with thunder. It wasn't snowing, but it was a nasty night and no mistake.

And what was it like in the high mountains now? Had they reached a village that would shelter them? Had they found Roger? She shivered involuntarily, though the embers still glowed red in the hearth and the room was warm. She felt the irresistible pull of her bed, promising warmth and, even more, the lure of dreams in which she might escape the chronic nag of fear and guilt.

She turned to the door, though, and pulled her cloak from the peg behind it. The urgency of pregnancy might necessitate her using the commode in her room, but she was resolved that no slave would ever carry a chamber pot for her – not as long as she could walk. She wrapped the cloak tightly around her, took the lidded pewter receptacle from its cabinet, and stepped quietly into the corridor.

It was very late; all the candles had been put out, and the stale smell of dead fires lay in the stairwell, but she could see clearly enough by the flicker of the lightning as she made her way downstairs. The kitchen door was unbolted, a piece of carelessness for which she blessed the cook; no need to make noise struggling one-handed with the heavy bolt.

Freezing rain struck her face and whooshed up beneath the hem of her nightgown, making her gasp. Once past the first shock of cold, though, she enjoyed it; the violence of it was exhilarating, the wind strong enough to lift her cloak in billowing surges that made her feel light on her feet for the first time in months.

She swept in a flurry to the necessary house, rinsed out the pot in the drench of rain that poured from its gutters, then stood in the paved yard, letting the fresh wind sweep into her face and slash her cheeks with rain. She wasn't sure if this was expiation or exultation – a need to share the discomfort her parents might be facing, or some more pagan rite – a need to lose herself by joining in the ferocity of the elements. Either or both, it didn't matter; she stepped deliberately under the spout of the gutter, letting the water pound against her scalp and soak her hair and shoulders.

Gasping and shaking water from her hair like a dog, she stepped back – and stopped, her eye caught by a sudden flash of light. Not lightning; a steady beam that shone for a moment, then vanished.

A door in the slave quarters opened for a moment, then closed. Was someone coming? Someone was; she could hear footsteps on the gravel, and took another step back into the shadows – the last thing she wanted was to explain what she was doing out here.

The lightning showed him clearly as he passed, and she felt a jar of recognition. Lord John Grey, hurrying shirt sleeved and bareheaded, his fair hair unbound and blowing in the wind, evidently oblivious to the cold and rain. He passed without seeing her, and vanished under the overhang of the kitchen porch.

Realizing that she was in danger of being locked out, she ran after him, awkward but still fast. He was just closing the door when she hit it with her shoulder. She burst into the kitchen and stood dripping, Lord John goggling at her in disbelief.

'Nice night for a walk,' she said, half breathless. 'Isn't it?' She wiped back her wet hair, and with a cordial nod slipped past him, out, and up the stairs, her bare feet leaving wet half-moon prints on the dark, polished wood. She listened, but heard no steps behind her as she reached her room.

She left cloak and gown spread out before the fire to dry, and having toweled her hair and face, climbed naked into bed. She was shivering, but the feel of the cotton sheets on her bare skin was wonderful. She stretched, wiggling her toes, then rolled on her side, curling tightly around her center of gravity, letting the constant heat from within tendril outward, gradually reaching her skin, forming a small cocoon of warmth around her.

She replayed the scene on the footpath once more in memory, and very gradually, the shadowy thoughts that had been rattling around in her mind for days fell together into a rational shape.

Lord John treated her always with attention and respect – often with amusement or admiration – but there was something missing. She had not been able to identify it – for some time had not even been aware of it – but now she knew what it was, without doubt.

She was accustomed, as are most striking women, to the open admiration of men, and this she had from Lord John as well. But below such admiration was usually a deeper awareness, more subtle than glance or gesture, a vibration like the distant chime of a bell, a visceral acknowledgment of herself as female. She had thought she felt it from Lord John when they met – but it had been gone on subsequent meetings, and she had concluded that she had mistaken it at first.

She should have guessed before, she thought; she'd encountered that inner indifference once before, in the roommate of a casual boyfriend. But then, Lord John hid it very well; she might never have guessed, were it not for that chance encounter in the yard. No, he didn't chime for her. But when he came out of the servants' quarters, he had been ringing like a firebell.

She wondered briefly if her father knew, but dismissed the possibility. After his experiences in Wentworth Prison, he couldn't possibly hold a man with that preference in such warm regard as she knew he felt for Lord John.

She rolled onto her back. The polished cotton of the sheet slid across the bare skin of breasts and thighs, caressing. She half noticed the feeling, and as her nipple hardened she raised a hand to cup her breast in reflex, felt Roger's large warm hand in memory, and a sudden surge of wanting. Then in memory she felt the sudden grasp of rougher hands, pinching and mauling, and wanting changed at once to sickened fury. She flipped onto her stomach, arms crossed beneath her breasts and face buried in her pillow, legs clenched and teeth gritted in futile defense.

The baby was a large, uncomfortable lump; impossible to lie that way now. With a small half-spoken curse, she rolled over and jerked out of bed, out from under the betraying, seductive sheets.

She walked naked through the half-lit room, and stood again by the window, looking out at the pounding rain. Her hair hung damp down her back, and cold was coming through the glass, pebbling the white flesh of arms and thighs and belly. She made no move either to cover herself or to go back to bed, but only stood there, one hand on the gently squirming bulge, looking out.

It would be too late soon. She had known when they left that it was already too late – so had her mother. Neither of them had wanted to admit it to the other, though; they had both pretended that Roger would come back in time, that he and she would sail to Hispaniola, and find their way back through the stones – together.

She laid her other hand against the glass; at once, a mist of condensation sprang up, outlining her fingers. It was early March; maybe three months left, maybe less. It would take a week, maybe two, to travel to the coast. No ship would risk the treacherous Outer Banks in March, though. Early April, at the soonest, before a journey could be undertaken. How long to the West Indies? Two weeks, three?

The end of April, then. And a few days to make their

way inland, find the cave; it would be slow, fighting through the jungle, more than eight months pregnant. And dangerous, though that didn't matter much, considering.

That would be if Roger were here now. But he wasn't. He might never come, though that was a possibility she fought hard against envisioning. If she didn't think about all the ways he could die, then he wouldn't die; it was one article of her stubborn faith; the others were that he wasn't dead yet, and that her mother would come back before the child was born. As to her father – rage boiled up again, as it did whenever she thought of him – him or Bonnet – so she tried to think of either of them as little as possible.

She prayed, of course, as hard as she could, but she wasn't constituted for praying and waiting; she was made for action. If only she could have gone with them, to find Roger!

She hadn't had a choice about that, though. Her jaw tightened, and her hand splayed flat against her belly. She hadn't had a choice about a lot of things. But she had made one choice – to keep her child – and now she'd have to live with the consequences of it.

She was beginning to shiver. Abruptly she turned away from the storm, and went to the fire. A small tongue of flame played along the blackened back of a red-crackled log, the heart of the embers glowing gold and white.

She sank down on the hearth rug, closing her eyes as the heat of the fire sent waves of comfort over her cold skin, caressing as the stroke of a hand. This time she kept all thought of Bonnet at bay, refusing him entrance to her mind, concentrating fiercely instead on the few precious memories she had of Roger.

. . . *put your hand on my heart. Tell me if it stops* . . . She could hear him, half breathless, half choked between laughter and passion.

How the hell do you know that? The rough feel of curly hairs under her palms, the smooth hard curves of his shoulders, the throb of the pulse in the side of his throat when she'd pulled him down to her and put her mouth on him, wanting in her urgency to bite him, to taste him, to breathe the salt and dust of his skin.

The dark and secret places of him, that she knew only by feel, recalled as soft weight, rolling and vulnerable in her palm, a complexity of curve and depth that yielded reluctantly to her probing fingertips (*Oh, God, don't stop, but careful, aye? Oh!*), the strange wrinkled silk that grew taut and smooth, filled her hand rising, silent and incredible as the stalk of a night-blooming flower that opens as you watch.

His gentleness as he touched her (*Christ, I wish I could see your face, to know how it is for you, am I doing well by ye. Is it good, just here? Tell me, Bree, talk to me . . .*), as she explored him, and then the moment when she had pushed him too far, her mouth on his nipple. She felt again the sudden amazing surge of power in him, as he lost all sense of restraint and seized her, lifting her as though she weighed nothing, rolled her back against the straw and took her, half hesitating as he remembered her freshly riven flesh, then answering the demand of her nails in his back to come to her fiercely, forcing her past the fear of impalement, into acceptance, and welcome, and finally into a frenzy that matched his own, rupturing the last membrane of reticence between them, joining them forever in a flood of sweat and musk and blood and semen.

She moaned out loud, shuddered and lay still, too weak even to move her hand away. Her heart was thumping, very slowly. Her belly was tight as a drum, the last of the spasms slowly relaxing its grip on her swollen womb. One half of her body blazed with heat, the other was cool and dark.

After a moment she rolled onto her hands and knees, and crawled away from the fire. She hauled herself onto the bed like a wounded beast, and lay half stunned, ignoring the currents of heat and cold that played over her.

At last she stirred, pulled a single quilt over her, and lay staring at the wall, hands crossed in protection above her baby. Yes, it was too late. Sensation and yearning must be put aside, along with love and anger. She must resist the mindless pull of both body and emotion. There were decisions to be made.

It took three days to convince herself of the virtue of her

plan, to overcome her own scruples, and, at last, to find a suitable time and place in which to catch him alone. But she was thorough and she was patient; she had all the time in the world – nearly three months of it.

On Tuesday, her opportunity came at last. Jocasta was closeted in her study with Duncan Innes and the account books, Ulysses – with a brief, inscrutable look at the closed door of the study – had gone to the kitchen to superintend the preparations for yet another lavish dinner in his Lordship's honor, and she had gotten rid of Phaedre by sending her on horseback to Barra Meadows to fetch a book Jenny Ban Campbell had promised her.

With a fresh blue camlet gown that matched her eyes, and a heart beating in her chest like a trip-hammer, she set out to stalk her victim. She found him in the library, reading the *Meditations* of Marcus Aurelius by the French windows, the morning sun streaming over his shoulder making his smooth fair hair gleam like buttered toffee.

He looked up from his book when she came in – a hippopotamus could have made a more graceful entrance, she thought crossly, catching her skirt on the corner of a bric-a-brac table in her nervousness – then graciously laid it aside, springing to his feet to bow over her hand.

'No, I don't want to sit down, thank you.' She shook her head at the seat he was offering her. 'I wondered – that is, I thought I'd go for a walk. Would you like to come with me?'

There was frost on the lower panes of the French door, a stiff breeze whining past the house, and soft chairs, brandy, and blazing fire within. But Lord John was a gentleman.

'There is nothing I should like better,' he gallantly assured her, and abandoned Marcus Aurelius without a backward glance.

It was a bright day, but very cold. Muffled in thick cloaks, they turned into the kitchen garden, where the high walls gave them some shelter from the wind. They exchanged small, breathless comments on the brightness of the day, assured each other that they were not cold at all, and came through a small archway into the brick-

1045

walled herbary. Brianna glanced around them; they were quite alone, and she would be able to see anyone coming along the walk. Best not waste time, then.

'I have a proposal to make to you,' she said.

'I am sure any notion of yours must necessarily be delightful, my dear,' he said, smiling slightly.

'Well, I don't know about that,' she said, and took a deep breath. 'But here goes. I want you to marry me.'

He kept smiling, evidently waiting for the punch line.

'I mean it,' she said.

The smile didn't altogether go away, but it altered. She wasn't sure whether he was dismayed at her gaucherie or just trying not to laugh, but she suspected the latter.

'I don't want any of your money,' she assured him. 'I'll sign a paper saying so. And you don't need to live with me, either, though it's probably a good idea for me to go to Virginia with you, at least for a little while. As for what I could do for you . . .' She hesitated, knowing that hers was the weaker side of the bargain. 'I'm strong, but that doesn't mean much to you, since you have servants. I'm a good manager, though – I can keep accounts, and I think I know how to run a farm. I *do* know how to build things. I could manage your property in Virginia while you were in England. And . . . you have a young son, don't you? I'll look after him; I'd be a good mother to him.'

Lord John had stopped dead in the path during this speech. Now he leaned slowly back against the brick wall, casting his eyes up in a silent prayer for understanding.

'Dear God in heaven,' he said. 'That I should live to hear an offer like that!' Then he lowered his head and gave her a direct and piercing look.

'Are you out of your mind?'

'No,' she said, with an attempt at keeping her own composure. 'It's a perfectly reasonable suggestion.'

'I have heard,' he said, rather cautiously, with an eye to her belly, 'that women in an expectant condition are somewhat . . . excitable, in consequence of their state. I confess, though, that my experience is distressingly limited with respect to . . . that is – perhaps I should send for Dr. Fentiman?'

She drew herself up to her full height, put a hand on

the wall and leaned toward him, deliberately looking down on him, menacing him with her size.

'No, you should not,' she said, in measured tones. 'Listen to me, Lord John. I'm not crazy, I'm not frivolous, and I don't mean it to be an inconvenience to you in any way – but I'm dead serious.'

The cold had reddened his fair skin, and there was a drop of moisture glistening on the tip of his nose. He wiped it on a fold of his cloak, eyeing her with something between interest and horror. At least he'd stopped laughing.

She felt mildly sick, but she'd have to do it. She'd hoped it could be avoided, but there seemed no other way.

'If you don't agree to marry me,' she said, 'I'll expose you.'

'You'll do what?' His usual mask of urbanity had disappeared, leaving puzzlement and the beginnings of wariness in its stead.

She was wearing woolen mittens, but her fingers felt frozen. So did everything else, except the warm lump of her slumbering child.

'I know what you were doing – the other night, at the slave quarters. I'll tell everyone; my aunt, Mr. Campbell, the sheriff. I'll write letters,' she said, her lips feeling numb even as she uttered the ridiculous threat. 'To the Governor, and the Governor of Virginia. They put p-pederasts in the pillory here; Mr. Campbell told me so.'

A frown drew his brows together; they were so fair that they scarcely showed against his skin when he stood in strong light. They reminded her of Lizzie's.

'Stop looming over me, if you please.'

He took hold of her wrist and pulled it down with a force that surprised her. He was small but much stronger than she had supposed, and for the first time, she was slightly afraid of what she was doing.

He took her firmly by the elbow and propelled her into motion, away from the house. The thought struck her that perhaps he meant to take her down to the river, out of sight, and try to drown her. She thought it unlikely, but still resisted the direction of his urging, and turned back into the square-laid paths of the kitchen garden instead.

He made no demur, but went with her, though it meant walking headon into the wind. He didn't speak until they had turned once more, and reached a sheltered corner by the onion bed.

'I am halfway tempted to submit to your outrageous proposal,' he said at last, the corner of his mouth twitching – whether with fury or amusement, she couldn't tell.

'It would certainly please your aunt. It would outrage your mother. And it would teach *you* to play with fire, I do assure you.' She caught a gleam in his eye that gave her a sudden surge of doubt about her conclusions as to his preferences. She drew back from him a bit.

'Oh. I hadn't thought of that – that you might . . . men and women both, I mean.'

'I *was* married,' he pointed out, with some sarcasm.

'Yes, but I thought that was probably the same kind of thing I'm suggesting now – just a formal arrangement, I mean. That's what made me think of it in the first place, once I realized that you – ' She broke off with an impatient gesture. 'Are you telling me that you *do* like to go to bed with women?'

He raised one eyebrow.

'Would that make a substantial difference to your plans?'

'Well . . .' she said uncertainly. 'Yes. Yes, it would. If I'd known that, I wouldn't have suggested it.'

' "Suggested," she says,' he muttered. 'Public denunciation? The pillory? *Suggested?*'

The blood burned so hotly in her cheeks, she was surprised not to see the cold air turn to steam around her face.

'I'm sorry,' she said. 'I wouldn't have done it. You have to believe me, I really wouldn't have said a word to anybody. It's only when you laughed, I thought – anyway, it doesn't matter. If you did want to sleep with me, I couldn't marry you – it wouldn't be right.'

He closed his eyes very tight and held them squinched shut for a minute. Then he opened one light blue eye and looked at her.

'Why not?' he asked.

'Because of Roger,' she said, and was infuriated to hear

her voice break on the name. Still more infuriated to feel a hot tear escape to run down her cheek.

'Damn it!' she said. 'Damn it to hell! I wasn't even going to *think* about him!'

She swiped the tear angrily away, and clenched her teeth.

'Maybe you're right,' she said. 'Maybe it is being pregnant. I cry all the time, over nothing.'

'I rather doubt it is nothing,' he said dryly.

She took a deep breath, the cold air hollowing her chest. There was one last card to play, then.

'If you do like women . . . I couldn't – I mean, I don't want to sleep with you regularly. And I wouldn't mind your sleeping with anybody else – male or female –'

'Thank you for that,' he muttered, but she ignored him, bent only on the need to get it all out.

'But I can see that you might want a child of your own. It wouldn't be right for me to keep you from having one. I can give you that, I think.' She glanced down at herself, arms clasped across the round of her belly. 'Everyone says I'm made for childbearing,' she went on steadily, eyes on her feet. 'I'd – just until I got pregnant again, though. You'd have to put that in the contract, too – Mr. Campbell could draw it up.'

Lord John massaged his forehead, evidently suffering the onslaught of a massive headache. Then he dropped his hand and took her by the arm.

'Come and sit down, child,' he said quietly. 'You'd best tell me what the devil you're up to.'

She took a deep, savage breath to steady her voice.

'I am not a child,' she said. He glanced up at her and seemed to change his mind about something.

'No, you're not – God help us both. But before you startle Farquard Campbell into an apoplexy with your notion of a suitable marriage contract, I beg you to sit with me for a moment and share the processes of your most remarkable brain.' He motioned her through the archway into the ornamental garden, where they would be invisible from the house.

The garden was bleak, but orderly; all the dead stalks of the year before had been pulled out, the dry stems chopped and scattered as mulch over the beds. Only in the circular bed around the dry fountain were there signs of life; green crocus spikes poked up like tiny battering rams, vivid and intransigent.

They sat, but she couldn't sit. Not and face him. He got up with her, and walked beside her, not touching her but keeping pace, the wind whipping strands of blond hair across his face, not saying a word, but listening, listening as she told him almost everything.

'So I've been thinking, and thinking,' she ended wretchedly. 'And I never get anywhere. Do you see? Mother and – and Da, they're out there somewhere –' She waved an arm toward the distant mountains. 'Anything could happen to them – anything might have happened to Roger already. And here I sit, getting bigger and bigger, and there's nothing I can *do*!'

She glanced down at him and drew the back of a mittened hand under her dripping nose.

'I'm not crying,' she assured him, though she was.

'Of course not,' he said. He took her hand and drew it through his arm.

'Round and round,' he murmured, eyes on the path of crazy paving as they circled the fountain.

'Yes, round and round the mulberry bush,' she agreed. 'And it'll be Pop! goes the weasel in three months or so. I have to do *something*,' she ended, miserably.

'Believe it or not, in your case waiting *is* doing something, though I admit it may not seem so,' he answered dryly. 'Why is it that you will not wait to see whether your father's quest is successful? Is it that your sense of honor will not allow you to bear a fatherless child? Or –'

'It's not my honor,' she said. 'It's his. Roger's. He's – he followed me. He gave up – everything – and came after me, when I came here to find my father. I knew he would, and he did.

'When he finds out about this –' She grimaced, cupping a hand to the swell of her stomach. 'He'll marry me; he'll feel as though he has to. And I can't let him do that.'

'Why not?'

'Because I love him. I don't want him to marry me out of obligation. And I –' She clamped her lips tight on the

1050

rest of it. 'I won't,' she ended firmly. 'I've made up my mind, and I won't.'

Lord John pulled his cloak tighter as a fresh blast of wind came rocketing in off the river. It smelled of ice and dead leaves, but there was a hint of freshness in it; spring was coming.

'I see,' he said. 'Well, I quite agree with your aunt that you require a husband. Why me, though?' He raised one pale brow. 'Is it my title or my wealth?'

'Neither one. It was because I was sure that you didn't like women,' she said, giving him one of those candid blue looks.

'I do like women,' he said, exasperated. 'I admire and honor them, and for several of the sex I feel considerable affection – your mother among them, though I doubt the sentiment is reciprocated. I do not, however, seek pleasure in their beds. Do I speak plainly enough?'

'Yes,' she said, the small lines between her eyes vanishing like magic. 'That's what I thought. See, it wouldn't be right for me to marry Mr. MacNeill or Barton McLachlan or any of those men, because I'd be promising something I couldn't give them. But you don't want that anyway, so there isn't any reason why I can't marry you.'

He repressed a strong urge to bang his head against the wall.

'There most assuredly is.'

'What?'

'To name only the most obvious, your father would undoubtedly break my neck!'

'What for?' she demanded, frowning. 'He likes you; he says you're one of his best friends.'

'I am honored to be the recipient of his esteem,' he said shortly. 'However, that esteem would very shortly cease to exist, upon Jamie Fraser's discovering that his daughter was serving as consort and brood mare to a degenerate sodomite.'

'And how would he discover that?' she demanded. '*I* wouldn't tell him.' Then she flushed and, meeting his outraged eye, suddenly dissolved into laughter, in which he helplessly joined.

'Well, I'm sorry, but *you* said it,' she gasped at last, sitting up and wiping her streaming eyes with the hem of her cloak.

'Oh, Christ. Yes, I did.' Distracted, he thumbed a strand of hair out of his mouth, and wiped his running nose on his sleeve again. 'Damn, why haven't I a handkerchief? I said it because it's true. As for your father finding out, he's well aware of the fact.'

'He is?' She seemed disproportionately surprised. 'But I thought he'd never –'

A flash of yellow apron interrupted her; one of the kitchen maids was in the adjoining garden. Without comment, Lord John stood up and gave her a hand; she got ponderously to her feet and they sailed out onto the dry brown scurf of the dead lawn, cloaks billowing like sails around them.

The stone bench under the willow tree was devoid of its usual charm at this time of year, but it was at least sheltered from the icy blasts off the river. Lord John saw her seated, sat down himself, and sneezed explosively. She opened her cloak and dug in the bosom of her dress, finally coming out with a crumpled handkerchief, which she handed to him with apologies.

It was warm and smelled of her – a disconcerting odor of girl-flesh, spiced with cloves and lavender.

'What you said about teaching me to play with fire,' she said. 'Just what did you mean by that?'

'Nothing,' he said, but now it was his turn to flush.

'Nothing, hm?' she said, and gave him the ghost of an ironic smile. 'That was a threat if I ever heard one.'

He sighed, and wiped his face once more with her handkerchief.

'You have been frank with me,' he said. 'To the point of embarrassment and well beyond. So yes, I suppose I – no, it *was* a threat.' He made a small gesture of surrender. 'You look like your father, don't you see?'

She frowned at him, his words obviously meaning nothing. Then realization flickered, sprang to full life. She sat bolt upright, staring down at him.

'Not you – not Da! He wouldn't!'

'No,' Lord John said, very dryly. 'He wouldn't. Though your shock is scarcely flattering. And for what the statement is worth, I would under no circumstances take advantage of your likeness to him – that was as much an idle threat as was your menacing me with exposure.'

'Where did you . . . meet my father?' she asked carefully, her own troubles superseded for the moment by curiosity.

'In prison. You knew he was imprisoned, after the Rising?'

She nodded, frowning slightly.

'Yes. Well. Leave it as said that I harbor feelings of particular affection for Jamie Fraser, and have for some years.' He shook his head, sighing.

'And here you come offering me your innocent body, with its echoes of his flesh – and add to that the promise of giving me a child who would mingle my blood with his – and all this, because your honor will not let you wed a man you love, or love a man you wed.' He broke off and sank his head in his hands.

'Child, you would make an angel weep, and God knows I am no angel!'

'My mother thinks you are.'

He glanced up at her, startled.

'She thinks *what?*'

'Maybe she wouldn't go quite *that* far,' she amended, still frowning. 'She says you're a good man, though. I think she likes you, but she doesn't want to. Of course, I understand that now; I suppose she must know – how you . . . er . . . feel about . . .' She coughed, hiding her blushes in a fold of her cloak.

'Hell,' he muttered. 'Oh, hell and thundering damnation. I ought never to have come out with you. Yes, she does. Though in all truth, I am not sure why she regards me with suspicion. It cannot be jealousy, surely.'

Brianna shook her head, chewing thoughtfully on her lower lip.

'I think it's because she's afraid you'll hurt him, somehow. She's afraid for him, you know.'

He glanced up at her, startled.

'Hurt him? How? Does she think I will overpower him and commit depraved indignities upon his person?'

He spoke lightly, but a flicker in her eyes froze the words in his throat. He tightened his grip on her arm. She bit her lip, then gently detached his hand, laying it on his knee.

'Have you ever seen my father with his shirt off?'

'Do you mean the scars on his back?'

She nodded.

He drummed his fingers restlessly on his knees, soundless on the fine broadcloth.

'Yes, I've seen them. I did that.'

Her head jerked back, eyes wide. The end of her nose was cherry-red, but the rest of her skin so pale that her hair and eyebrows seemed to have leached all the life from it.

'Not all of it,' he said, staring off into a bed of dead hollyhocks. 'He'd been flogged before, which made it all the worse – that he knew what he was doing, when he did it.'

'Did . . . what?' she asked. Slowly, she rearranged herself on the bench, not so much turning toward him as flowing in her garments, like a cloud changing shape in the wind.

'I was the commander at Ardsmuir prison; did he tell you? No, I thought not.' He made an impatient gesture, brushing back the strands of fair hair that whipped across his face.

'He was an officer, a gentleman. The only officer there. He spoke for the Jacobite prisoners. We dined together, in my quarters. We played chess, we spoke of books. We had interests in common. We . . . became friends. And then . . . we were not.'

He stopped speaking.

She drew away from him a bit, distaste in her eyes.

'You mean – you had him flogged because he wouldn't –'

'No, damn it, I did not!' He snatched the handkerchief and scrubbed angrily at his nose. He flung it down on the seat between them and glared at her. 'How dare you suggest such a thing!'

'But you said yourself you did it!'

'*He* did it.'

'You can't flog yourself!'

He started to reply, then snorted. He raised one brow at her, still angry, but with his feelings coming back under control.

'The hell you can't. You've been doing it for months, according to what you've told me.'

'We aren't talking about me.'

'Of course we are!'

'No, we're not!' She leaned toward him, heavy brows drawn down. 'What the hell do you mean, he did it?'

The wind was blowing from behind her, into his face. It made his eyes sting and water, and he looked away.

'What am I doing here?' he muttered to himself. 'I must be mad to be talking with you in this manner!'

'I don't care if you're mad or not,' she said, and gripped him by the sleeve. 'You tell me what happened!'

He pressed his lips tight together, and for a moment, she thought he wouldn't. But he had already said too much to stop, and he knew it. His shoulders rose under his cloak and dropped, slumping in surrender.

'We were friends. Then . . . he discovered my feeling for him. We were no longer friends, by his choice. But that was not enough for him; he wished a final severance. And so he deliberately brought about an occasion so drastic that it must alter our relation irrevocably and prevent any chance of friendship between us. So he lied. During a search of the prisoners' quarters, he claimed a piece of tartan publicly as his own. Possession was against the law, then – it still is, in Scotland.'

He drew a deep breath and let it out. He wouldn't look at her, but kept his eyes focused on the ragged fringe of bare trees across the river, raw against the pale spring sky.

'I was the governor, charged with execution of the law. I was obliged to have him flogged. As he damn well knew I would be.'

He tilted his head back, resting it against the carved stone back of the bench. His eyes were closed against the wind.

'I could forgive his not wanting me,' he said, with quiet bitterness. 'But I couldn't forgive him for making me use him in that fashion. Not forcing me merely to hurt him, but to degrade him. He could not merely refuse to acknowledge my feeling; he must destroy it. It was too much.'

Bits of debris boiled past on the flood; storm-cracked

twigs and branches, a broken board from the hull of a boat, wrecked somewhere up-stream. Her hand covered his where it rested on his knee. It was slightly larger than his own, and warm from sheltering in her cloak.

'There was a reason. It wasn't you. But it's for him to tell you, if he wants to. You did forgive him, though,' she said quietly. 'Why?'

He sat up then, and shrugged, but didn't put away her hand.

'I had to.' He glanced at her, eyes straight and level. 'I hated him for as long as I could. But then I realized that loving him . . . that was part of me, and one of the best parts. It didn't matter that he couldn't love me, that had nothing to do with it. But if I could not forgive him, then I could not love him, and that part of me was gone. And I found eventually that I wanted it back.' He smiled, faintly. 'So you see, it was really entirely selfish.'

He squeezed her hand then, stood up, and pulled her to her feet.

'Come, my dear. We shall both freeze solid if we sit here any longer.'

They walked back toward the house, not talking, but walking close together, arm in arm. As they came back through the gardens he spoke abruptly.

'You're right, I think. To live with someone you love, knowing that they tolerate the relation only for the sake of obligation – no, I wouldn't do it, either. Were it only a matter of convenience and respect on both sides, then yes; such a marriage is one of honor. As long as both parties are honest – ' His mouth twisted briefly as he glanced in the direction of the servants' quarters. 'There is no need for shame on either side.'

She looked down at him, brushing a strand of wind-blown copper hair out of her eyes with her free hand.

'Then you'll accept my proposal?' The hollow feeling in her chest didn't feel like the relief she had expected.

'No,' he said bluntly. 'I may have forgiven Jamie Fraser for what he did in the past – but he would never forgive *me* for marrying you.' He smiled at her, and patted the hand he held tucked in the curve of his arm.

'I can give you some respite from both your suitors and

your aunt, though.' He glanced at the house, whose curtains hung unstirring against the glass.

'Do you suppose anyone's watching?'

'I'd say you can bet on it,' she said, a little grimly.

'Good.' Pulling off the sapphire ring he wore, he turned to face her and took her hand. He pulled off her mitten and ceremoniously slid the ring onto her little finger – the only one it would fit. Then he rose smoothly on his toes and kissed her on the lips. Leaving her no time to recover from surprise, he clasped her hand in his, and turned once more toward the house, his expression bland.

'Come along, my dear,' he said. 'Let us announce our engagement.'

60

Trial by Fire

They were left alone all day. The fire was dead, and there was no food left. It didn't matter; neither man could eat, and no fire would have reached Roger's soul-deep chill.

The Indians came back in late afternoon. Several warriors, escorting an elderly man, dressed in a flowing lace shirt and a woven mantle, his face painted with red and ocher – the *sachem*, bearing a small clay pot in his hand, filled with black liquid.

Alexandre had put on his clothes; he stood when the *sachem* approached him, but neither spoke nor moved. The *sachem* began to sing in a cracked old voice, and as he sang, dipped a rabbit's foot into the pot and painted the priest's face in black, from forehead to chin.

The Indians left, and the priest sat down on the ground, his eyes closed. Roger tried to speak to him, to offer him water, or at least the knowledge of company, but Alexandre made no response, sitting as though he had been carved of stone.

In the last of the twilight, he spoke, finally.

'There is not much time,' he said softly. 'I asked you once before to pray for me. I did not know then what I would have you pray for – for the preservation of my life, or my soul. Now I know that neither is possible.'

Roger moved to speak, but the priest twitched a hand, stopping him.

'There is only the only thing I can ask for. Pray for me, brother – that I might die well. Pray that I may die in silence.' He looked at Roger for the first time, then, his eyes glinting with moisture. 'I would not shame her by crying out.'

It was some time after dark that the drums began. Roger had not heard them in his time in the village. Impossible to say how many there were; the sound seemed to come from everywhere. He felt it in the marrow of his bones and the soles of his feet.

The Mohawks returned. When they came in, the priest stood up at once. He undressed himself, and walked out, naked, without a backward glance.

Roger sat staring at the hide-covered doorway, praying – and listening. He knew what a drum could do; had done it himself – evoked awe and fury with the beating of a stretched hide, calling to the deep and hidden instincts of the listener. Knowing what was happening, though, didn't make it any less frightening.

He could not have said how long he sat there listening to the drums, hearing other sounds – voices, footsteps, the noises of a large assembly – trying not to listen for Alexandre's voice.

Suddenly the drumming stopped. It started again, no more than a few tentative thumps, and then quit altogether. There were shouts, and then a sudden cacophony of yells. Roger started up, and hobbled toward the door. The guard was still there, though; he thrust his head through the flap and gestured menacingly, one hand on his war club.

Roger stopped, but couldn't return to the fire. He stood in the half-dark, sweat rolling down his ribs, listening to the sounds outside.

It sounded like all the devils in hell had been let loose. What in God's name was going on out there? A terrific fight, obviously. But who, and why?

After the first salvo of shrieks, the vocal part of it had lessened, but there were still individual high-pitched yelps and ululations from every part of the central clearing. There were thuds, too; moans, and other noises indicative of violent combat. Something struck the wall of the longhouse; the wall shivered and a bark panel cracked down the middle.

Roger glanced at the door flap; no, the guard wasn't looking. He dashed across to the panel and tore at it with his fingers. No good; the wood fibers shredded away beneath his nails and wouldn't give him purchase. In desperation, he pressed his eye to the hole he had made, trying to see what was happening outside.

No more than a narrow slice of the central clearing was

visible. He could see the longhouse opposite, a strip of churned earth between, and over everything, the flickering light of an enormous fire. Red and yellow shadows fought with black ones, peopling the air with fiery demons.

Some of the demons were real; two dark figures reeled past and out of sight, locked in violent embrace. More figures streaked across his line of sight, running toward the fire.

Then he stiffened, pressing his face against the wood. Among the incomprehensible Mohawk yells, he could have sworn he had heard someone bellowing in *Gaelic*.

He had.

'*Caisteal Dhuni!*' somebody shouted nearby, followed by a hair-raising screech. Scots – white men! He had to get to them! Roger smashed his fists on the shattered wood in a frenzy, trying to batter his way through the panel by main force. The Gaelic voice broke loose again.

'*Caisteal Dhuni!*' No, wait – God, it was *another* voice! And the first one, answering. '*Do mi! Do mi!*' To me! To me! And then a fresh wave of Mohawk shrieks rose up and drowned the voices – women, it was women screaming now, their voices even louder than the men's.

Roger flung himself at the panel, shoulder first; it cracked and splintered further, but would not give way. He tried again, and a third time, with no result. There was nothing in the longhouse that could be used as a weapon, nothing. In desperation he seized the lashings of one of the bed cubicles and tore at it with hands and teeth, ripping until he had loosened part of the frame.

He grabbed the wood, heaved; shook it and heaved again, until with a rending crack it came free in his hands, leaving him panting, holding a six-foot pole with a shattered, sharpened end. He tucked the butt end under his arm and charged the doorway, pointed end aimed like a spear at the hide flap.

He shot out into dark and flame, cold air and smoke, into noise that singed his blood. He saw a figure ahead of him, and charged it. The man danced aside, and raised a war club. Roger couldn't stop, couldn't turn, but threw

1060

himself flat, and the club smashed down inches from his head.

He rolled to the side and swung his pole wildly. It crashed against the Indian's head, and the man stumbled and went down, falling over Roger.

Whisky. The man reeked of whisky. Not stopping to wonder, Roger wriggled out from under the squirming body, staggering to his feet, pole still in his hand.

A scream came from behind him and he whirled, stabbing with all his strength as he pivoted on the ball of his foot. The shock of impact shuddered up his arms and through his chest. The man he had struck was clawing at the pole; it jerked and quivered, then was wrenched from his grasp as the man fell over.

He staggered, caught himself, then whirled toward the fire. It was an immense pyre; flames billowing in a wall of pure and ardent scarlet, vivid against the night. Through the bobbing heads of the watchers, he saw the black figure in the heart of the flame, arms spread in a gesture of benediction, lashed to the pole from which he hung. Long hair fluttered up, strands catching fire with a burst of flame, surrounding the head with a halo of gold, like Christ in a missal. Then something crashed down on Roger's head, and he dropped like a rock.

He didn't quite lose consciousness. He couldn't see or move, but he could still hear, dimly. There were voices near him. The yelling was still there, but fainter, almost a background noise, like the roar of the ocean.

He felt himself rise in the air, and the crackle of the flames got louder, it matched the roar in his ears . . . Christ, they were going to throw him into the fire! His head spun with effort and light blazed behind his shut lids, but his stubborn body wouldn't move.

The roar diminished, but paradoxically he felt warm air brush his face. He struck the ground, half bounced, and rolled, ending up on his face, his arms flung out. Cool earth was under his fingers.

He breathed. Mechanically, one breath at a time. Very slowly, the spinning sensation began to ebb.

There was noise, a long way away, but he couldn't hear anything near him but his own loud breathing. Very slowly, he opened one eye. Firelight flickered on poles and bark panels, a dim echo of the brilliance outside. Longhouse. He was inside again.

His breathing was loud and ragged in his ears. He tried to hold his breath, but couldn't. Then he realized that he *was* holding his breath; the gasping noise was coming from someone else.

It was behind him. With immense effort, he got his hands under him, and rose onto hands and knees, swaying, eyes squinted against the pain in his head.

'Jesus Christ,' he muttered to himself. He rubbed a hand hard over his face and blinked, but the man was still there, six feet away.

Jamie Fraser. He was lying on his side in a huddle of limbs, a crimson plaid tangled round his body. Half his face was obscured with blood, but there wasn't any mistaking him.

For a moment, Roger just looked at him blankly. For months the greater part of his waking moments had been devoted to imagining a meeting with this man. Now it had happened, and it seemed simply impossible. There was room for no feeling beyond a sort of dull amazement.

He rubbed his face again, harder, forcing aside the fog of fear and adrenaline. What . . . *what* was Fraser doing here?

When thought and feeling connected again, his first recognizable feeling was neither fury nor alarm, but an absurd burst of joyful relief.

'She didn't,' he muttered, and the words sounded queer and hoarse to his ears, after so long without spoken English. 'Oh, God, she didn't do it!'

Jamie Fraser could be here for only one reason – to rescue him. And if that was so, it was because Brianna had made her father come. Whether it was misunderstanding or malevolence that had put him through the hell of the last few months, it had not been hers.

'Didn't,' he said again. 'She didn't.' He shuddered, both with nausea from the blow and with relief.

He had thought he would be hollow forever, but suddenly there was something there; something small, but very solid. Something he could hold in the cup of his heart. *Brianna.* He had her back.

There was another set of high-pitched screams from just outside; ululations that went on and on, sticking into his flesh like a thousand pins. He jerked, and shuddered again, all other feelings subsumed in renewed realization.

Dying with the reassurance that Brianna loved him was better than dying without it – but he hadn't wanted to die in the first place. He remembered what he had seen outside, felt his gorge rise, and choked it down.

With a trembling hand he began the unfamiliar sign of the Cross. 'In the name of the Father,' he whispered, and then the words failed him. 'Please,' he whispered instead. 'Please, don't let him have been right.'

He crawled shakily to Fraser's body, hoping that the man was still alive. He was; blood was flowing from a gash on Fraser's temple, and when he thrust his fingers under the man's jaw, he could feel the steady bump of a pulse.

There was water in one of the pots under the shattered bed frame; luckily it hadn't spilled. He dipped the end of the plaid in water and used it to mop Fraser's face. After a few minutes of this ministration, the man's eyelids began to flutter.

Fraser coughed, gagged heavily, turned his head to one side, and threw up. Then his eyes shot open, and before Roger could speak or move, Fraser had rolled up onto one knee, his hand on the *sgian dhu* in his stocking.

Blue eyes glared at him, and Roger raised an arm in instinctive defense. Then Fraser blinked, shook his head, groaned, and sat down heavily on the earthen floor.

'Oh, it's you,' he said. He closed his eyes and groaned again. Then his head snapped up, eyes blue and piercing, but this time with alarm rather than fury.

'Claire!' he exclaimed. 'My wife, where is she?'

Roger felt his jaw drop.

'Claire? You brought her *here*? You brought a woman into *this*?'

Fraser gave him a glance of extreme dislike, but wasted no words. Palming the knife from his stocking, he glanced at the doorway. The flap was down; no one was visible. The noise outside had died down, though the rumble of voices was still audible. Now and then one stood out, shouting or raised in exhortation.

'There's a guard,' Roger said.

Fraser glanced at him and rose to his feet, smooth as a panther. Blood was still running down the side of his face, but it didn't seem to trouble him. Silently, he flattened himself along the wall, glided to the edge of the door flap, and eased the flap aside with the tip of the tiny dagger.

Fraser grimaced at whatever he saw. Letting the flap swing back in place, he returned and sat down, putting the knife away in his stocking.

'A good dozen of them just outside. Is that water?' He put out a hand, and Roger silently scooped a gourdful of water and handed it to him. He drank deeply, splashed water in his face, then poured the rest of it over his head.

Fraser wiped a hand over his battered face, then opened bloodshot eyes and looked at Roger.

'Wakefield, is it?'

'I go by my own name, these days. MacKenzie.'

Fraser gave a brief, humorless snort.

'So I've heard.' He had a wide, expressive mouth – like Bree's. His lips compressed briefly, then relaxed.

'I've done wrong to ye, MacKenzie, as ye'll know. I've come to put it right, so far as may be, but it may be as I'll not have the chance.' He gestured briefly toward the door. 'For now, you've my apology. For what satisfaction ye may want of me later – I'll bide your will. But I'd ask ye to let it wait until we're safe out of this.'

Roger stared at him for a moment. Satisfaction for the last months of torment and uncertainty seemed as far-fetched a notion as the thought of safety. He nodded.

'Done,' he said.

They sat in silence for several moments. The fire in the hut was burning low, but the wood to feed it was outside; the guards kept charge of anything that might be used as a weapon.

'What happened?' Roger asked at last. He nodded toward the door. 'Out there?'

Fraser took a deep breath and let it out in a sigh. For the first time, Roger noticed that he held the elbow of his

1064

right arm cradled in his left palm, the arm itself held close to the body.

'I will be damned if I know,' he said.

'They did burn the priest? He's dead?' There could be no doubt of it after what he'd seen, but still Roger felt compelled to ask.

'He was a priest?' Thick reddish brows rose in surprise, then fell. 'Aye, he's dead. And not only him.' An involuntary shudder went over the Highlander's big frame.

Fraser hadn't known what they meant to do when the drums began to sound, and everyone went out to gather by the great fire. There was plenty of talk, but his knowledge of the Mohawk tongue was insufficient to make out what was happening, and his nephew, who spoke the tongue, was nowhere to be found.

The whites had not been invited, but no one made any move to keep them away. And so it was that he and Claire had come to be standing on the edge of the crowd, curious onlookers, when the *sachem* and the Council came out and the old man began to speak. Another man had spoken, too, very angrily.

'Then they brought the man out, naked as a tadpole, bound him to a stake, and started in upon him.' He paused, eyes shadowed, and glanced at Roger.

'I'll tell ye, man, I've seen French executioners keep a man alive who wished he weren't. It wasna worse than that – but no a great deal better.' Fraser drank again, thirstily, and lowered the cup.

'I tried to take Claire away – I didna ken but what they meant to attack us next.' The crowd was pressed so tight around them, though, that movement was impossible; there was no choice but to go on watching.

Roger's mouth felt dry, and he reached for the cup. He didn't want to ask, but he felt a perverse need to know – whether for Alexandre's sake or for his own.

'Did he – cry out at all?'

Fraser gave him another glance of surprise, then something like understanding crossed his face.

'No,' he said slowly. 'He died verra well – by their lights. Ye will have been knowing the man?'

Roger nodded, wordless. It was difficult to believe

Alexandre was gone, even hearing this. And *where* had he gone? Surely he could not have been right. *I will not be forgiven.* Surely not. No just God –

Roger shook his head hard, pushing the thought away. It was plain that Fraser had no more than half his mind on his story, horrific as it was. He kept glancing at the door, a look of anxious expectation on his face. Was he expecting rescue?

'How many men did you bring with you?'

The blue eyes flashed, surprised.

'My nephew Ian.'

'That's all?' Roger tried to keep the stunned disbelief out of his voice, but patently failed.

'Ye were expecting the 78th Hieland regiment?' Fraser asked sarcastically. He got to his feet, swaying slightly, arm pressed to his side. 'I brought whisky.'

'Whisky? Did that have anything to do with the fighting?' Remembering the reek of the man who had fallen over him, Roger nodded toward the wall of the longhouse.

'It may have.'

Fraser went to the wall with the cracked panel, and pressed an eye against the opening, staring out at the clearing for some time before returning to the dwindling fire. Things had gone quiet outside.

The big Highlander was looking more than unwell. His face was white and sheened with sweat under the streaks of dried blood. Roger silently poured more water; it was as silently accepted. He knew well enough what was wrong with Fraser, and it wasn't the effects of injury.

'When you last saw her –'

'When the fighting broke out.' Unable to stay seated, Fraser set down the cup and got to his feet again, prowling the confines of the longhouse like a restless bear. He paused, glancing at Roger.

'Will ye maybe ken a bit what happened there?'

'I could guess.' He acquainted Fraser with the priest's story, finding some small respite from worry in the telling.

'They wouldn't have harmed her,' he said, trying to reassure himself as much as Fraser. 'She'd nothing to do with it.'

1066

Fraser gave a derisory snort.

'Aye, she did.' Without warning, he smashed a fist against the ground, in a muffled thump of fury. 'Damn the woman!'

'She'll be all right,' Roger repeated stubbornly. He couldn't bear to think otherwise, but he knew what Fraser plainly knew as well – if Claire Fraser was alive, unhurt, and free, nothing could have kept her from her husband's side. And as for the unknown nephew . . .

'I heard your nephew – in the fight. I heard him call out to you. He sounded all right.' Even as he offered this bit of information, he knew how feeble it was as reassurance. Fraser nodded, though, head bent on his knees.

'He's a good lad, Ian,' he murmured. 'And he has friends among the Mohawk. God send they will protect him.'

Roger's curiosity was coming back, as the shock of the evening began to fade.

'Your wife,' he said. 'What did she do? How could she possibly have been involved in this?'

Fraser sighed. He scrubbed his good hand over his face and through his hair, rubbing until the loose red locks stood up in knots and snarls.

'I shouldna have said so,' he said. 'It wasna her fault in the least. It's only – she'll not be killed, but God, if they've harmed her . . .'

'They won't,' Roger said firmly. 'What happened?'

Fraser shrugged and closed his eyes. Head tilted back, he described the scene as though he could still see it, engraved on the inside of his eyelids. Perhaps he could.

'I didna take heed of the girl, in such a crowd. I couldna even say what she looked like. It was only at the last that I saw her.'

Claire had been by his side, white-faced and rigid in the press of shouting, swaying bodies. When the Indians had nearly finished with the priest, they untied him from the stake and fastened his hands instead to a long pole, held above his head, from which to suspend him in the flames.

Fraser glanced at him, wiping the back of a hand across his lips.

'I've seen a man's heart pulled beating from his chest

before,' he said. 'But I hadna seen it eaten before his eyes.' He spoke almost shyly, as though apologizing for his squeamishness. Shocked, he had looked to Claire. It was then that he had seen the Indian girl standing on Claire's other side, with a cradleboard in her arms.

With great calmness, the girl had handed the board to Claire, then turned and slipped through the crowd.

'She didna look to left or right, but walked straight into the fire.'

'What?' Roger's throat closed with shock, the exclamation emerging in a strangled croak.

The flames had embraced the girl in moments. A head taller than the folk near him, Jamie had seen everything clearly.

'Her clothes caught, and then her hair. By the time she reached him, she was burning like a torch.' Still, he had seen the dark silhouette of her arms, raised to embrace the empty body of the priest. Within moments, it was no longer possible to distinguish man or woman; there was only the one figure, black amid the towering flames.

'It was then everything went mad.' Fraser's wide shoulders slumped a little, and he touched the gash in his temple. 'All I ken is one woman set up a howl, and then there was the hell of a screech, and of a sudden, everyone was either fleeing or fighting.'

He had himself tried to do both, shielding Claire and her burden while fighting his way out of the thrashing press of bodies. There were too many of them, though. Unable to escape, he had pushed Claire against the wall of a longhouse, seized a stick of wood with which to defend them, and shouted for Ian, while wielding his makeshift club on anyone reckless enough to come near.

'Then a wee fiend leapt out o' the smoke, and struck me with his club.' He shrugged, one-shouldered. 'I turned to fight him off, and then there were three of them on me.' Something had caught him in the temple, and he had known no more till waking in the longhouse with Roger.

'I havena seen Claire since. Nor Ian.'

The fire had burned itself to coals, and it was growing cold in the longhouse. Jamie unfastened his brooch and pulled the plaid around his shoulders as well as he could, one-handed, and leaned gingerly back against the wall.

His right arm might be broken; he'd taken a blow from one of the war clubs just below the shoulder, and the stricken spot went from numbness to blinding pain with no warning. That was of no moment, though, compared with his worry for Claire and wee Ian.

It was very late. If Claire hadn't been hurt in the fighting, she was likely safe enough, he told himself. The old woman wouldn't countenance harm done to her. As for Ian, though – he felt a moment's pride in the lad, in spite of his fear. Ian was a bonny fighter, and a credit to the uncle who'd taught him.

If he should have been overcome, though . . . there had been so many of the savages, and with the fighting so hot . . .

He shifted restlessly, trying not to think of facing his sister with ill news of her youngest boy. Christ, he'd rather have his own heart torn from his breast and eaten before his eyes; it would feel much the same.

Seeking distraction – any distraction – from his fears, he shifted again, taking random stock of the shadowy insides of the house. Bare as a Skyeman's cupboard, for the most part. A jug of water, a broken bed frame, and one or two tattered skins for bedding lying crumpled on the earthen floor.

MacKenzie was sitting hunched across the fire, heedless of the growing chill. His arms were wrapped about his knees, head bent in thought. He was half turned away, unaware of Jamie's eye on him.

He grudged to admit it, but the man was decently made. Long shanks and a good breadth through the shoulders; he'd have a fair reach with a sword. He was tall as the MacKenzies of Leoch – and why not? he thought suddenly. The man was Dougal's get, if a few generations onward.

He found that notion both disturbing and oddly comforting. He'd killed men when he must, and mostly their ghosts let him sleep at night with no great rattling of bones. Dougal's death, though, was one that he had lived

1069

through more than once, and woke from sweating, with the sound of those last silent words of Dougal's ringing in his ears; words mouthed in blood.

There'd been not the slightest choice; it was kill or be killed, and a near thing either way. And yet . . . Dougal MacKenzie had been his foster father, and if he was honest, a part of him had loved the man.

Yes, it was some comfort to know that a small part of Dougal was left. The other part of this MacKenzie's heritage was a wee bit more troubling. He'd seen the man's eyes first thing when he woke, bright green and intent, and for one second his wame had shriveled up into a ball, thinking of Geillis Duncan.

Did he much want his daughter linked with a witch's spawn? He eyed the man covertly. Perhaps it was as well if Brianna's child was not of this man's blood.

'Brianna,' MacKenzie said, lifting his head suddenly from his knees. 'Where is she?'

Jamie jerked, and a hot knife-blade seared his arm, leaving him sweating.

'Where?' he said. 'At River Run, with her aunt. She's safe.' His heart was thundering in his ears. Christ, was the man able to read thoughts? Or had he the Sight?

The green eyes were steady, dark in the dim light.

'Why did you bring Claire, and not Brianna? Why did she not come with you?'

Jamie returned the man's cool look. They'd see if it was a matter of mind reading or not. If not, the last thing he meant to tell MacKenzie now was the truth; time enough for that when – if – they were safely away.

'I should have left Claire as well, if I thought I could. She's a stubborn wee besom. Short of tying her hand and foot, I couldna prevent her coming.'

Something dark flickered in MacKenzie's eyes – doubt, or pain?

'I should not have thought Brianna the kind of lass to mind her father's word overmuch,' he said. His voice had an edge to it – yes, pain, and a sort of jealousy.

Jamie relaxed slightly. No mind reading.

1070

'Did ye no? Well, and perhaps ye dinna ken her so well as all that,' he said. Pleasantly enough, but with a jeering undertone that would make one sort of man go for his throat.

MacKenzie wasn't that sort. He sat up straight, and drew a deep breath.

'I know her well,' he said levelly. 'She is my wife.'

Jamie sat up straight in turn, and clenched his teeth on a hiss of pain.

'The hell she is.'

MacKenzie's black brows drew down at that.

'We are handfast, she and I. Did she not tell you that?'

She hadn't – but he hadn't given her much chance to tell him, either. Too furious at the thought of her willing to bed a man, stung at thinking she'd made a fool of him, proud as Lucifer and suffering the Devil's pains for it, in wishing her perfect and finding her only as human as himself.

'When?' Jamie asked.

'Early September, in Wilmington. When I – just before I left her.' The admission came unwillingly, and through the black veil of his own guilt he saw a reflection of it on MacKenzie's face. As well deserved as his own, he thought viciously. If the coward had not left her . . .

'She didna tell me.'

He saw the doubt and the pain in MacKenzie's eyes quite clearly now. The man worried that Brianna did not want him – for if she did, she would have come. He knew well enough that no power on earth or below it would keep Claire from *his* side if she thought him in danger – and felt a jolt of fear renewed at that thought; for where was she?

'I suppose she thought you wouldn't see handfasting as a legal form of marriage,' MacKenzie said quietly.

'Or perhaps she didna see it so herself,' Jamie suggested cruelly. He could relieve the man's mind by telling him a part of the truth – that Brianna had not come because she was with child – but he was in no charitable mood.

It was getting quite dark, but even so he could see

MacKenzie's face flush at that, and his hands clench on the ragged deerskin.

'I saw it so,' was all he said.

Jamie closed his eyes, and said no more. The last coals in the fire died slowly, leaving them in darkness.

61

The Office of a Priest

The smell of burnt things hung in the air. We passed close by the pit and I couldn't help seeing from the corner of my eye the heap of charred fragments, shattered ends frosted white with ash. I hoped it was wood. I was afraid to look directly.

I stumbled on the frozen ground, and my escort caught me by the arm. Pulled me up without comment and pushed me toward a longhouse where two men stood on guard, huddled against a cold wind that filled the air with drifting ashes.

I had not slept and had not eaten, though food was offered. My feet and my fingers were cold. There was keening from a longhouse at the far end of the village, and over it the louder formal chant of a death song. Was it for the girl that they sang, or someone else? I shivered.

The guards glanced at me and stood aside. I lifted the hide flap at the door and went in.

It was dark, the fire inside as dead as the one outside. Gray light from the smokehole gave me enough illumination to see an untidy heap of skins and cloth on the floor, though. A patch of red tartan showed amid the jumble, and I felt a surge of relief.

'Jamie!'

The pile heaved and came apart. Jamie's rumpled head popped up, alert but looking a good deal the worse for wear. Next to him was a dark, bearded man who seemed oddly familiar. Then he moved into the light, and I caught the flash of green eyes above the shrubbery.

'Roger!' I exclaimed.

Without a word he rose out of the blankets and clasped me in his arms. He held so tight, I could hardly breathe.

He was terribly thin; I could feel every one of his ribs. Not starved, though; he stank, but with the normal scents of dirt and stale sweat, not the yeasty effluvium of starvation.

'Roger, are you all right?' He let go, and I looked him up and down, searching for any signs of injury.

'Yes,' he said. His voice was husky, from sleep and emotion. 'Bree? She's all right?'

'She's fine,' I assured him. 'What's happened to your foot?' He wore nothing but a tattered shirt and a stained rag wrapped around one foot.

'A cut. Nothing. Where is she?' He clutched my arm, anxious.

'At a place called River Run, with her great-aunt. Didn't Jamie tell you? She's –'

I was interrupted by Jamie clutching my other arm.

'Are ye all right, Sassenach?'

'Yes, of course I – my God, what happened to you?' My attention was momentarily distracted from Roger by the sight of Jamie. It wasn't the nasty contusion on his temple or the dried blood on his shirt that struck my notice, so much as the unnatural way he held his right arm.

'My arm's maybe broken,' he said. 'Hurts like a bugger. Will ye come and tend to it?'

Without waiting for an answer he turned and walked away, sitting down heavily near the broken bed frame. I gave Roger a brief pat and went after him, wondering what the hell. Jamie wouldn't admit to being in pain in front of Roger Wakefield, if splintered raw bone were sticking out of his flesh.

'What are you up to?' I muttered, kneeling beside him. I felt the arm gingerly through his shirt – no compound fractures. I rolled it carefully up for a better look.

'I havena told him about Brianna,' he said, very softly. 'And I think it better you do not.'

I stared at him.

'We can't do that! He has to know.'

'Keep your voice down. Aye, he maybe should know about the bairn – but not the other, not Bonnet.'

I bit my lip, feeling gingerly down the swell of his biceps. He had one of the worst bruises I had ever seen; a huge mottled splotch of purple-blue – but I was fairly sure the arm wasn't broken.

I wasn't so sure about his suggestion.

1074

He could see the doubt on my face; he squeezed my hand hard.

'Not yet; not here. Let it wait, at least until we're safe away.'

I thought for a moment, as I ripped the sleeve of his shirt and used it to make a rough sling. Learning that Brianna was pregnant was going to be a shock by itself. Perhaps Jamie was right; there was no telling how Roger would react to the news of the rape, and we were a long way from being home free yet. Better he should have his head clear. At last I nodded, reluctantly.

'All right,' I said aloud, getting up. 'I don't think it's broken, but the sling will help.'

I left Jamie sitting on the ground and went to Roger, feeling like a Ping-Pong ball.

'How's the foot?' I knelt to unwrap the unsanitary-looking rag around it, but he stopped me with an urgent hand on my shoulder.

'Brianna. I know there's something wrong. Is she –'

'She's pregnant.'

Whatever possibilities he had been turning over in his mind, that hadn't been among them. It isn't possible to mistake sheer amazement. He blinked, looking as though I'd hit him on the head with an ax.

'Are you sure?'

'She'll be seven months gone by now; it's noticeable.' Jamie had come up so quietly that neither of us had heard him. He spoke coldly, and looked even colder, but Roger was well beyond noticing subtleties.

Excitement brightened his eyes, and his shocked face came alive beneath the black whiskers.

'Pregnant. My God, but how?'

Jamie made a derisive noise in the back of his throat. Roger glanced at him, then quickly away.

'That is, I never thought –'

'*How?* Aye, ye didna think, and it's my daughter left to pay the price of your pleasure!'

Roger's head snapped round at that, and he glared at Jamie.

'She is not left, in any way! I told you she is my wife!'

'She is?' I said, startled in the midst of my unwrapping.

1075

'They're handfast,' Jamie said, very grudgingly. 'Why could the lass not have told us, though?'

I thought I could answer that one – in more than one way. The second answer wasn't one I could suggest in front of Roger, though.

She hadn't said, because she was with child, and thought it was Bonnet's. Believing that, she might have thought it better not to reveal their handfasting, so as to leave Roger an escape – if he wanted it.

'Most likely because she thought you wouldn't see that as a true marriage,' I said. 'I'd told her about our wedding; about the contract and how you insisted on marrying me in church, with a priest. She wouldn't want to tell you anything she thought you might not approve of – she wanted so badly to please you.'

Jamie had the grace to look abashed at this, but Roger ignored the argument.

'Is she well?' he asked, leaning forward and grasping my arm.

'Yes, she's fine,' I assured him, hoping it was still true. 'She wanted to come with us, but of course we couldn't let her do that.'

'She wanted to come?' His face lighted up, joy and relief plain to see, even through the hair and filth. 'Then she didn't – ' He stopped abruptly, and glanced from me to Jamie and back. 'When I met . . . Mr. Fraser on the mountainside, he seemed to think that she – er – had said –'

'A terrible misunderstanding,' I put in hastily. 'She hadn't told us about the handfasting, so when she turned up pregnant, we, er . . . assumed . . .' Jamie was brooding, looking at Roger with no particular favor, but jerked into awareness when I nudged him sharply.

'Oh, aye,' he said, a little grudgingly. 'A mistake. I've given Mr. Wakefield my apologies and told him I shall do my best to see it right. But we've other things to think of now. Have ye seen Ian, Sassenach?'

'No.' I became aware for the first time that Ian was not with them, and felt a small lurch of fear in the pit of my stomach. Jamie looked grim.

'Where have ye been all night, Sassenach?'

'I was with – oh, Jesus!'

I ignored his question for a moment, caught up in the sight of Roger's foot. The flesh was swollen and reddened over half his foot, with a severe ulceration on the outer margin of the sole. I pressed firmly, a little way in, and felt the nasty give of small pockets of pus under the skin.

'What happened here?'

'I cut it, trying to get away. They bound it and put things on it, but it's been infected on and off. It gets better, and then it gets worse.' He shrugged; his attention wasn't on his foot, ugly as it was. He looked up at Jamie, evidently having come to a decision.

'Brianna didn't send you to meet me, then? She didn't ask you to – get rid of me?'

'No,' Jamie said, taken by surprise. He smiled briefly, his features suffused with sudden charm. 'That was my own notion.'

Roger drew a deep breath and closed his eyes briefly.

'Thank God,' he said, and opened them. 'I thought perhaps she'd – we'd had a terrible argument, just before I left her, and I thought maybe that was why she hadn't told you about the handfasting; that she'd decided she didn't want to be married to me.' There was sweat on his forehead, either from the news or from my handling of his foot. He smiled, a little painfully. 'Having me beaten to death or sold into slavery seemed a trifle extreme, though, even for a woman with her temper.'

'Mmphm.' Jamie was slightly flushed. 'I did say I was sorry for it.'

'I know.' Roger looked at him for a minute, evidently making up his mind about something. He took a deep breath, then bent down and put my hand gently away from his foot. He straightened up and met Jamie's eyes, dead-on.

'I've something to tell you. What we fought over. Has she told you what brought her here – to find you?'

'The death notice? Aye, she's told us. Ye dinna think I'd allow Claire to come with me otherwise?'

'What?' Puzzled wariness showed in Roger's eyes.

'Ye canna have it both ways. If she and I are to die at Fraser's Ridge six years from now, we canna very well be killed by the Iroquois any time before that, now can we?'

I stared at him; that particular implication had escaped me. Rather staggering; practical immortality – for a time. But that was assuming –

'That's assuming that you can't change the past – that *we* can't, I mean. Do you believe that?' Roger leaned forward a little, intent.

'I will be damned if I know. Do *you* think so?'

'Yes,' Roger said flatly. 'I do think the past can't be changed. That's why I did it.'

'Did what?'

He licked his lips, but went doggedly on.

'I found that death notice long before Brianna did. I thought, though, that it would be useless to try to change things. So I – I kept it from her.' He looked from me to Jamie. 'So now you know. I didn't want her to come; I did everything I could to keep her away from you. I thought it was too dangerous. And – I was afraid of losing her,' he ended simply.

To my surprise, Jamie was looking at Roger with sudden approval.

'Ye tried to keep her safe, then? To protect her?'

Roger nodded, a certain relief lessening the tension in his shoulders.

'So you understand?'

'Aye, I do. That's the first thing I've heard that gives me a good opinion of ye, sir.'

It wasn't an opinion I shared at the moment.

'You found that thing – and didn't tell her?' I could feel the blood climbing into my cheeks.

Roger saw the look on my face, and looked away.

'No. She . . . um . . . she saw it your way, I'm afraid. She thought – well, she said I'd betrayed her, and –'

'And you did! Her and us both! Of all the – Roger, how could you *do* such a thing?'

'He did right,' Jamie said. 'After all –' I turned on him fiercely, interrupting.

'He did *not*! He deliberately kept it from her, and tried to keep her from – don't you realize, if he'd succeeded, you'd never have seen her?'

'Aye, I do. And what's happened to her would not have

1078

happened.' His eyes were deep blue, steady on mine. 'I would it had been so.'

I swallowed down my grief and anger, until I thought I could speak again without choking.

'I don't think *she* would have had it so,' I said softly. 'And it was hers to say.'

Roger jumped in, before Jamie could reply.

'You said what's happened to her wouldn't have – you mean, being pregnant?' He didn't wait for a reply; he had plainly recovered from the shock of the news sufficiently to begin thinking, and was rapidly reaching the same unpleasant conclusions Brianna had come to, some months earlier. He swung his head toward me, eyes wide with shock.

'She's seven months along, you said. Jesus! She can't go back!'

'Not *now,*' I said, with bitter emphasis. 'She might have, when we first found out. I tried to make her go back to Scotland, or at least to the Indies – there's another . . . opening, there. But she wouldn't do it. She wouldn't go without finding out what happened to you.'

'What happened to me,' he repeated, and glanced at Jamie. Jamie's shoulders tensed, and he set his jaw.

'Aye,' he said. 'It's my fault, and no remedy for it. She's trapped here. And I can do nothing for her – save bring ye back to her.' And that, I realized, was why he had not wanted to tell Roger anything; for fear that when he realized Brianna was trapped in the past, Roger would refuse to come back with us. Following her into the past was one thing; staying there forever with her was something else again. Neither was it guilt over Bonnet alone that had eaten Jamie up on our journey here; the Spartan boy with the fox gnawing at his vitals would have recognized a kindred soul on the spot, I thought, looking at him with exasperated tenderness.

Roger gazed at him, completely at a loss for words.

Before he could find any, a noise of shuffling footsteps approached the door of the hut. The flap lifted, and a large number of Mohawks came in, one after the other.

We looked at them in astonishment; there were about fifteen of them, men and women and children, all dressed for traveling, in leggings and furs. One of the older women held a cradleboard, and without hesitation she walked up to Roger and pressed it into his arms, saying something in Mohawk.

He frowned at her, not understanding. Jamie, suddenly alert, leaned toward her and said a few halting words. She repeated what she had said, impatiently, then looked behind her and motioned to a young man.

'You are . . . priest,' he said haltingly to Roger. He pointed at the cradleboard. 'Water.'

'I'm not a priest.' Roger tried to give the board back to the woman, but she refused to take it.

'Prees,' she said definitely. 'Babtize.' She motioned to one of the younger women, who stepped forward, holding a small bowl made of horn, filled with water.

'Father Alexandre – he say you priest, son of priest,' said the young man. I saw Roger's face go pale beneath the beard.

Jamie had stepped aside, murmuring in French patois to a man he recognized among the crowd. Now he pushed his way back to us.

'These are what is left of the priest's flock,' he said softly. 'The council has told them to leave. They mean to travel to the Huron mission at Ste. Berthe, but they would have the child baptized, lest it die on the journey.' He glanced at Roger. 'They think ye are a priest?'

'Evidently.' Roger looked down at the child in his arms.

Jamie hesitated, glancing at the waiting Indians. They stood patiently, their faces calm. I could only guess what lay behind them. Fire and death, exile – what else? There were marks of sorrow on the face of the old woman who brought the baby; she would be its grandmother, I thought.

'In case of need,' Jamie said quietly to Roger, 'any man may do the office of a priest.'

I wouldn't have thought it was possible for Roger to go any whiter, but he did. He swayed briefly, and the old lady, alarmed, reached out a hand to steady the cradleboard.

He caught himself, though, and nodded to the young woman with the water, to come closer.

'*Parlez-vous français?*' he asked, and heads nodded, some with certainty, some with less.

'*C'est bien,*' he said, and taking a deep breath, lifted the cradleboard, showing the child to the congregation. The baby, a round-faced charmer with soft brown curls and a golden skin, blinked sleepily at the change of perspective.

'Hear the words of our Lord Jesus Christ,' he said clearly in French. 'Obeying the word of our Lord Jesus, and sure of his presence with us, we baptize those whom he has called to be his own.'

Of course, I thought, watching him. He *was* the son of a priest, so to speak; he would often enough have seen the Reverend administer the sacrament of baptism. If he didn't recall the entire service, he seemed to know the general form of it.

He had the baby passed from hand to hand among the congregation – for so his agreement had made them – following and asking questions of each person there, in a low voice.

'*Qui est votre Seigneur, votre Sauveur?*' Who is your Lord and Savior?

'*Voulez-vous placer votre foi en Lui?*' Do you have faith in Him?

'Do you promise to tell this child the good news of the gospel, and all that Christ commands, and by your fellowship, to strength his family ties with the household of God?'

Head after head bobbed in reply.

'*Oui, certainement. Je le promets. Nous le ferons.*' Yes, of course. I promise. We will.

At last Roger turned and gave the child to Jamie.

'Who is your Lord and Savior?'

'Jesus Christ,' he answered without hesitation, and the baby was handed on to me.

'Do you trust in him?'

I looked down into the face of innocence, and answered for it. 'I do.'

He took the cradleboard, gave it to the grandmother, then dipping a sprig of juniper into the bowl of water, sprinkled water on the baby's head.

'I baptize you –' he began, and stopped, with a sudden panicked glance at me.

'It's a girl,' I murmured, and he nodded, lifting the sprig of juniper again.

'I baptize you, Alexandra, in the name of the Father and of the Son and of the Holy Spirit, Amen.'

After the small band of Christians had left, there were no more visitors. A warrior brought us wood for the fire, and some food, but he ignored Jamie's questions and left, saying nothing.

'Do you think they'll kill us?' Roger asked suddenly, after a period of silence. His mouth twitched in an attempted smile. 'Kill me, I suppose I mean. Presumably the two of you are safe.'

He didn't sound worried. Looking at the deep shadows and lines in his face, I thought that he was simply too exhausted to be afraid anymore.

'They won't kill us,' I said, and pushed a hand through the tangle of my hair. I dimly realized that I, too, was exhausted; I had been without sleep for more than thirty-six hours.

'I started out to tell you. I spent last night in Tewaktenyonh's house. The Council of Mothers met there.'

They hadn't told me everything; they never would. But at the end of the long hours of ceremony and discussion, the girl who spoke English had told me as much as they wanted me to know, before they sent me back to Jamie.

'Some of the young men found the whisky cache,' I said. 'They brought it back to the village yesterday, and started to drink. The women thought they didn't mean anything dishonest, that they thought the bargain was already made. But then some argument started among them, just before they lit the fire to – to execute the priest. A fight broke out, and some of the men ran into the crowd, and – one thing led to another.' I rubbed a hand hard over my face, trying to keep my thoughts clear enough to speak.

'A man was killed in the fighting.' I glanced at Roger. 'They think you killed him; did you?'

He shook his head, shoulders slumping with tiredness.

'I don't know. I – probably. What will they do about it?'

1082

'Well, it took them a long time to decide, and it isn't settled yet; they've sent word to the main Council, but the *sachem* hasn't made a decision yet.' I took a deep breath.

'They won't kill you, because the whisky was taken, and that was offered as the price of your life. But since they've decided not to kill us in revenge for their dead, what they usually do instead is to adopt an enemy into the tribe, in replacement of the dead man.'

That shook Roger out of his numbness.

'Adopt me? They want to keep me?'

'One of us. One of you. I don't suppose I'd be a suitable replacement, since I'm not a man.' I tried to smile, but failed completely. All the muscles of my face had gone numb.

'Then it must be me,' Jamie said quietly.

Roger's head jerked up, startled.

'You've said yourself; if the past canna be changed, then nothing will happen to me. Leave me, and as soon as it can be managed, I will escape and come home.'

He laid a hand on my arm before I could protest.

'You and Ian will take MacKenzie back to Brianna.' He looked at Roger, his face inscrutable. 'After all,' he said quietly, 'it's the two of you she needs.'

Roger started in at once to argue, but I butted in.

'May the Lord deliver me from stubborn Scotsmen!' I said. I glared at the two of them. 'They haven't decided yet. That's only what the Council of Mothers says. So there's no sense in arguing about it until we know for sure. And speaking of knowing things for sure,' I said, in hopes of distracting them, 'where's Ian?'

· Jamie stared at me.

'I don't know,' he said, and I saw his throat ripple as he swallowed. 'But I hope to God he's safe in that girl's bed.'

No one came. The night passed quietly, though none of us slept well. I dozed fitfully, through sheer exhaustion, waking every time there was a sound outside, my dreams a vivid crazy-quilt of blood and fire and water.

It was midday before we heard the sound of voices approaching. My heart leapt as I recognized one of them, and Jamie was on his feet before the door flap lifted.

1083

'Ian? Is that you?'

'Aye, Uncle. It's me.'

His voice sounded odd; breathless and uncertain. He stepped into the light from the smokehole and I gasped, feeling as though I had been punched in the stomach.

The hair had been plucked from the sides of his skull; what was left stood up in a thick crest from his scalp, a long tail hanging down his back. One ear had been freshly pierced and sported a silver earring.

His face had been tattooed. Double crescent lines of small dark spots, most still scabbed with dried blood, ran across each cheekbone, to meet at the bridge of his nose.

'I – canna stay long, Uncle,' Ian said. He looked pale, under the lines of tattooing, but stood erect. 'I said they must let me come to say goodbye.'

Jamie had gone white to the lips.

'Jesus, Ian,' he whispered.

'The naming ceremony is tonight,' Ian said, trying not to look at us. 'They say that after that I will be Indian, and I must not speak any tongue but the *Kahnyen'kehaka*; I canna speak again in English, or the Gaelic.' He smiled painfully. 'And I ken ye didna have much Mohawk.'

'Ian, ye canna be doing this!'

'I've done it, Uncle Jamie,' Ian said softly. He looked at me then.

'Auntie. Will ye say to my mother that I willna forget her? My da will know, I think.'

'Oh, Ian!' I hugged him hard, and his arms went gently around me.

'Ye can leave in the morning,' he said to Jamie. 'They willna prevent ye.'

I let him go, and he crossed the hut to where Roger stood, looking stunned. Ian offered him a hand.

'I am sorry for what we did to ye,' he said quietly. 'Ye'll take good care of my cousin and the bairn?'

Roger took his hand and shook it. He cleared his throat and found his voice.

'I will,' he said. 'I promise.'

Then Ian turned to Jamie.

'No, Ian,' he said. 'God, no, lad. Let it be me!'

Ian smiled, though his eyes were full of tears. 'Ye said to

1084

me once, that my life wasna meant to be wasted,' he said. 'It won't be.' He held out his arms. 'I willna forget you, either, Uncle Jamie.'

They took Ian to the bank of the river, just before sunset. He stripped and waded into the freezing water, accompanied by three women, who ducked and pummeled him, laughing and scrubbing him with handfuls of sand. Rollo ran up and down the bank, barking madly, then plunged into the river and joined in what he plainly saw as fun and games, coming close to drowning Ian in the process.

All of the spectators who lined the bank found it hilarious – save the three whites.

Once the white blood had been thus ceremonially scrubbed from Ian's body, more women dried him, dressed him in fresh clothing, and took him to the Council longhouse for the naming ceremony.

Everyone crowded inside; all of the village was there. Jamie, Roger, and I stood silently in a corner, watching as the *sachem* sang and spoke over him, as the drums beat, as the pipe was lit and passed from hand to hand. The girl he called Emily stood near him, eyes shining as she looked at him. I saw him look back at her, and the light that sprang up in his own eyes did a little to ease the soreness of my heart.

They called him Wolf's Brother. His brother wolf sat panting at Jamie's feet, viewing the proceedings with interest.

At the end of the ceremony a small hush fell on the crowd, and at that moment Jamie stepped out of the corner. All heads turned as he crossed to Ian, and I saw more than one warrior tense in disapproval.

He unpinned the brooch from his plaid, unbelted it, and laid the length of bloodstained crimson tartan across his nephew's shoulder.

'*Cuimhnich*,' he said softly, and stepped back. *Remember.*

All of us were quiet as we made our way down the narrow trail that led away from the village next morning. Ian had taken a formal, white-faced farewell of us as he stood with his new family. I hadn't been so stalwart, though, and seeing my tears made Ian bite his lip to hold back his own emotion. Jamie had embraced him, kissed his mouth and left him, without speaking a word.

Jamie went about the business of setting camp that night with his usual efficiency, but I could tell that his mind was somewhere else. And no wonder if it was; my own was divided in worry between Ian behind us and Brianna ahead of us, with very little attention to spare for present circumstances.

Roger dumped an armload of wood beside the fire and sat down next to me.

'I've been thinking,' he said quietly. 'About Brianna.'

'Have you? So have I.' I was so tired, I thought I might tumble headfirst into the flames before I got the water boiling.

'You said there was another circle – opening, whatever it is – in the Indies?'

'Yes.' I thought briefly of telling him all about Geilie Duncan and the cave at Abandawe, and dismissed it. I hadn't the energy. Another time. Then I jerked out of my mental fog, catching what he was saying.

'Another one? Here?' I looked wildly around, as though expecting to see a menhir standing menacingly at my back.

'Not *here*,' he said. 'Somewhere between here and Fraser's Ridge, though.'

'Oh.' I tried to gather my scattered thoughts. 'Yes, I know there is, but –' Then it penetrated, and I grabbed his arm. 'You mean you *know* where it is?'

'You knew about it?' He stared at me in astonishment.

'Yes, I – here, look . . .' I scrabbled in my pouch and came up with the opal. He grabbed it from me before I could explain.

'Look! It's the same; this same symbol – it's carved on the rock in the circle. Where the hell did you get this?'

'It's a long story,' I said. 'I'll tell you later. But for now – do you know where this circle is? You've actually seen it?'

Jamie, attracted by our excitement, had come to see what was going on.

'A circle?'

'A time-circle, an opening, a – a –'

'I've been there,' Roger said, interrupting my stuttering explanations. 'I found it by accident while I was trying to escape.'

'Could you find it again? How far is it from River Run?' My mind was making frantic calculations. A little more than seven months. If it took six weeks to return, Brianna would be eight and a half months gone. Could we possibly take her into the mountains in time? And if we could – what would be the greater risk, to travel through a time-passage on the verge of delivery, or to stay in the past permanently?

Roger dug in the waistband of his ragged breeches and brought out a strand of thread, grimy and knotted. 'Here,' he said, grasping a double knot. 'It was eight days past the day that they took me. Eight days from Fraser's Ridge.'

'And a week, at least, from River Run to the Ridge.' I let myself breathe again, not sure whether I felt disappoint-ment or relief. 'We'd never make it.'

'But the weather is turning,' Jamie said. He nodded toward a big blue spruce, its needles wet and dripping. 'When we came, that tree was cased in ice.' He looked at me. 'The traveling may be easier; we may make better time – or not.'

'Or not.' I shook my head reluctantly. 'You know as well as I do that spring means mud. And mud is worse to travel in than snow.' I felt my heart begin to slow down, accepting it. 'No, it's too late, too risky. She'll have to stay.'

Jamie was gazing at Roger, over the fire.

'He doesn't,' he said.

Roger looked at him, startled.

'I –' he began, then firmed his jaw and started over. 'I do. You don't think I'd leave her? And my child?'

I opened my mouth, and felt Jamie stiffen beside me in warning.

'No,' I said sharply. 'No. We have to tell him. Brianna will. Better he should know now. If it makes a difference to him, then it's better he knows before he sees her.'

Jamie's lips pressed tight together, but he nodded.

'Aye,' he said. 'Tell him, then.'

'Tell me what?' Roger's dark hair was loose, rising

1087

around his head in the evening wind. He looked more alive than he had since we had found him, alarmed and excited at once. I bit the bullet.

'It may not be your child,' I said.

His expression didn't change for a moment; then the words fell into place. He grabbed me by the arms, so suddenly that I yelped with alarm.

'What do you mean? What's happened?'

Jamie moved like a striking snake. He caught Roger a short, sharp blow under the chin that loosened his grip and sent him sprawling backward on the ground.

'She means that when ye left my daughter to her own devices, she was raped,' he said roughly. 'Two days past the time ye lay with her. So maybe the wean's yours, and maybe it's not.'

He glared down at Roger.

'So. D'ye mean to stand by her, or no?'

Roger shook his head, trying to clear it, and got slowly back to his feet.

'Raped. Who? Where?'

'In Wilmington. A man named Stephen Bonnet. He –'

'*Bonnet?*' It was only too clear from Roger's expression that the name was familiar. He stared wildly from me to Jamie and back. 'Brianna was raped by Stephen Bonnet?'

'So I said.' Suddenly all the rage Jamie had been holding since our exit from the village broke loose. He seized Roger by the throat and slammed him into a tree trunk.

'And where were you when it was done, ye coward? She was angry with ye, and so ye ran away and left her! If ye thought ye must go, why did ye not see her safe into my keeping first?'

I grabbed Jamie's arm and yanked.

'Let go of him!'

He did, and whirled away, breathing hard. Roger, shaken and almost as furious as Jamie, shook down his ruffled clothing.

'I didn't leave because we argued! I left to find this!' He snatched a handful of his loose breeches, and ripped at the cloth. A spark of green brightness glowed in the palm of his hand.

1088

'I risked my life to get that, to see her safe back through the stones! Do you know where I went to get it, who I got it from? Stephen Bonnet! That's why it took me so long to come to Fraser's Ridge; he wasn't where I expected him to be; I had to ride up and down the coast to find him.'

Jamie was frozen, staring at the gemstone. So was I.

'I shipped with Stephen Bonnet, from Scotland.' Roger was growing a little calmer. 'He is a – a –'

'I ken what he is.' Jamie stirred, breaking his trance. 'But what he also may be, is the father of my daughter's child.' He gave Roger a long, cold look. 'So I'm askin' ye, MacKenzie; can ye go back to her, and live with her, knowing that it's likely Bonnet's child she bears? For if ye canna do it – then say so now, for I swear, if ye come to her and treat her badly . . . I will kill ye without a second thought.'

'For God's sake!' I burst out. 'Give him a moment to think, Jamie! Can't you see that he hasn't had a chance even to take it in, yet?'

Roger's fist closed tight over the jewel, then opened. I could hear him breathing, harsh and ragged.

'I don't know,' he said. 'I don't know!'

Jamie stooped and picked up the stone, where Roger had dropped it. He flung it hard between Roger's feet.

'Then go!' he said. 'Take yon cursed stone and find your wicked circle. Get ye gone – for my daughter doesna need a coward!'

He had not yet unsaddled the horses; he seized his saddlebags and heaved them across the horse's back. He untied both his horse and mine, and mounted in one fluid motion.

'Come,' he said to me. I looked helplessly at Roger. He was staring up at Jamie, green eyes glinting with firelight, bright as the emerald in his hand.

'Go,' he said softly to me, not taking his eyes off Jamie. 'If I can – then I'll come.'

My hands and feet seemed not to belong to me; they moved smoothly, without my direction. I walked to my horse, put my foot in the stirrup, and was up.

When I looked back, even the light of the fire had disappeared. There was nothing behind us but the dark.

62

Three-thirds of a Ghost

River Run, April 1770

'They have captured Stephen Bonnet.'

Brianna dropped the game box on the floor. Ivory counters exploded in every direction, and rolled off under the
furniture. Speechless, she stood staring at Lord John, who
set down his glass of brandy and came hastily to her side.

'Are you all right? Do you require to sit down? I apologize most profoundly. I should not have –'

'Yes, you should. No, not the sofa, I'll never get out of
it.' She waved away his offered hand, and made her way
slowly toward a plain wooden chair near the windows.
Once solidly on it, she gave him a long, level look.

'Where?' she said. 'How?'

He didn't trouble asking whether he ought to send for
wine or burnt feathers; she plainly wasn't going to swoon.

He drew up a stool beside her, but then thought better,
and went to the parlor door. He glanced out into the dark
hallway; sure enough, one of the maids was dozing on a
stool in the curve of the staircase, available in case they
should want anything. The woman's head snapped up at
his step, eyes showing white in the dimness.

'Go to bed,' he said. 'We shall not require anything
further this evening.'

The slave nodded and shuffled off, relief in the droop
of her shoulders; she would have been awake since dawn,
and it was near midnight now. He was desperately tired
himself, after the long ride from Edenton, but it wasn't
news that could wait. He had arrived in the early evening,
but this had been his first opportunity to make an excuse
to see Brianna alone.

He closed the double doors and placed a footstool in
front of them, to prevent any interruptions.

'He was taken here, in Cross Creek,' he said without
preamble, sitting down beside her. 'As to how, I could

not say. The charge brought was smuggling. Once they discovered his identity, of course, there were others added.'

'Smuggling what?'

'Tea and brandy. At least this time.' He rubbed the back of his neck, trying to relieve the stiffness caused by hours in the saddle. 'I heard of it in Edenton; evidently the man is notorious. His reputation extends from Charleston to Jamestown.'

He looked closely at her; she was pale, but not ghastly.

'He is condemned,' he said quietly. 'He will hang next week, in Wilmington. I thought you would wish to know.'

She took a deep breath, and let it out slowly, but said nothing. He stole a closer look at her, not wanting to stare, but amazed at the sheer size of her. By God, she was immense! In the two months since their engagement, she had doubled in size, at least.

One side of her enormous abdomen bulged suddenly out, startling him. He was having second thoughts about the wisdom of having told her; if the shock of his news brought on her confinement prematurely, he would never forgive himself. Jamie wouldn't forgive him, either.

She was staring off into space, her brow wrinkled in concentration. He'd seen broodmares in foal look that way; thoroughly absorbed in inward matters. It had been a mistake to send the slave away. He got his feet under him, meaning to go and fetch assistance, but the movement brought her out of her trance.

'Thank you,' she said. The frown was still there, but her eyes had lost that distant look; they were fixed on him with a disconcerting blue directness – the more disconcerting for being so familiar.

'When will they hang him?' She leaned forward a little, hand pressed against her side. Another swell rippled across her belly in apparent response to the pressure.

He sat back, eyeing her stomach uneasily.

'Friday week.'

'Is he in Wilmington now?'

Slightly reassured by her calm demeanor, he reached for his abandoned glass. He took a sip and shook his head, feeling the comfort of the warm liquor spread through his chest.

'No. He is still here; there was no need for trial, as he had been previously convicted.'

'So they'll move him to Wilmington for the execution? When?'

'I have no idea.' The distant look was back; with deep misgiving, he recognized it this time – not motherly abstraction; calculation.

'I want to see him.'

Very deliberately, he swallowed the rest of the brandy.

'No,' he said definitely, setting down the glass. 'Even if your state allowed of travel to Wilmington – which it assuredly does not,' he added, glancing sidelong at her dangerous-looking abdomen – 'attendance at an execution could not but have the worst effects upon your child. Now, I am in complete sympathy with your feelings, my dear, but –'

'No you aren't. You don't know what my feelings are.' She spoke without heat, but with complete conviction. He stared at her for a moment, then got up and went to fetch the decanter.

She watched the amber liquid purl up in the glass and waited for him to pick it up before she went on.

'I don't want to watch him die,' she said.

'Thank God for that,' he muttered, and took a mouthful of brandy.

'I want to talk to him.'

The mouthful went down the wrong way and he choked, spluttering brandy over the frills of his shirt.

'Maybe you should sit down,' she said, squinting at him. 'You don't look so good.'

'I can't think why.' Nonetheless, he sat down, and groped for a kerchief to wipe his face.

'Now, I know what you're going to say,' she said firmly, 'so don't bother. Can you arrange for me to see him, before they take him to Wilmington? And before you say no, certainly not, ask yourself what I'll do if you *do* say that.'

Having opened his mouth to say 'No, certainly not,'

Lord John shut it and contemplated her in silence for a moment.

'I don't suppose you are intending to threaten me again, are you?' he asked conversationally. 'Because if you are . . .'

'Of course not.' She had the grace to blush slightly at that.

'Well, then, I confess I do not see quite what you –'

'I'll tell my aunt that Stephen Bonnet fathered my baby. And I'll tell Farquard Campbell. And Gerald Forbes. And Judge Alderdyce. And then I'll go down to the garrison headquarters – that must be where he is – and I'll tell Sergeant Murchison. If he won't let me in, I'll go to Mr. Campbell for a writ to make him admit me. I have a right to see him.'

He looked at her narrowly, but he could see it was no idle threat. She sat there, solid and immobile as a piece of marble statuary, and just as susceptible of persuasion.

'You do not shrink from creating a monstrous scandal?' It was a rhetorical question; he sought only to buy himself a moment to think.

'No,' she said calmly. 'What have I got to lose?' She lifted one eyebrow in a half-humorous quirk.

'I suppose you'd have to break our engagement. But if the whole county knows who the baby's father is, I think that would have the same effect as the engagement, in terms of keeping men from wanting to marry me.'

'Your reputation –' he began, knowing it was hopeless.

'Is not real hot to start with. Though come to that, why should it be worse for me to be pregnant because I was raped by a pirate than because I was wanton, as my father so charmingly put it?' There was a small note of bitterness in her voice that stopped him from saying any more.

'Anyway, Aunt Jocasta isn't likely to throw me out, just because I'm scandalous. I won't starve; neither will the baby. And I can't say I care whether the Misses MacNeill call on me or not.'

He took up his glass and drank again, carefully this time, with an eye on her to prevent further shocks. He was curious to know what had passed between her and her father – but not reckless enough to ask. Instead he put down the glass and asked, 'Why?'

'Why?'

'Why do you feel you must speak with Bonnet? You say I do not know your feelings, which is undeniably true.' He allowed a tinge of wryness to creep into his voice. 'Whatever they are, though, they must be exigent, to cause you to contemplate such drastic expedients.'

A slow smile grew on her lips, spreading into her eyes.

'I really like the way you talk,' she said.

'I am exceeding flattered. However, if you would contemplate answering my question . . .'

She sighed, deeply enough to make the flame of the candle flicker. She stood up, moving ponderously, and groped in the seam of her gown. She had evidently had a pocket sewn into it, for she extracted a small piece of paper, folded and worn with much handling.

'Read that,' she said, handing it to him. She turned away, and went to the far end of the room, where her paints and easel stood in a corner by the hearth.

The black letters struck him with a small jolt of familiarity. He had seen Jamie Fraser's hand only once before, but once was enough; it was a distinctive scrawl.

Daughter –

I cannot say if I shall see you again. My fervent hope is that it shall be so, and that all may be mended between us, but that event must rest in the Hand of God. I write now in the event that He may will otherwise.

You asked me once whether it was right to kill in revenge of the great Wrong done you. I tell you that you must not. For the sake of your Soul, for the sake of your own Life, you must find the grace of forgiveness. Freedom is hardwon, but it is not the fruit of Murder.

Do not Fear that he will escape Vengeance. Such a man carries with him the seeds of his own Destruction. If he does not Die at my Hand, it will be by another. But it must not be your Hand that strikes him down.

Hear me, for the sake of the Love I bear you.

Below the text of the letter, he had written Your most

affectionate and loving Father, James Fraser. This was scratched out, and below it was written simply, *Da.*

'I never said goodbye to him.'

Lord John looked up, startled. Her back was turned to him; she was staring at the half-finished landscape on the easel as though it were a window.

He crossed the carpet to stand beside her. The fire had burned down in the hearth, and it was growing cold in the room. She turned to face him, clutching her elbows against the chill.

'I want to be free,' she said quietly. 'Whether Roger comes back or not. Whatever happens.'

The child was restless; he could see it kicking and squirming below her crossed arms, like a cat in a sack. He drew a deep breath, feeling chilled and apprehensive.

'You are sure you must see Bonnet?'

She gave him another of those long blue looks.

'I have to find a way to forgive him, Da says. I've been trying, ever since they left, but I can't do it. Maybe if I see him, I can. I have to try.'

'All right.' He let his breath out in a long sigh, shoulders slumping in capitulation.

A small light – relief? – showed in her eyes, and he tried to smile back.

'You'll do it?'

'Yes. God knows how, but I'll do it.'

He put out all the candles save one, keeping that to light their way to bed. He gave her his arm and they walked in silence through the empty hall, the unpeopled quiet wrapping them in peace. At the foot of the stair, he paused, letting her go ahead of him.

'Brianna.'

She turned, questioning, on the stair above him. He stood hesitant, not knowing how to ask for what he suddenly wanted so badly. He reached out a hand, lightly poised.

'May I – I?'

Without speaking, she took his hand and pressed it against her belly. It was warm and very firm. They stood quite still for a moment, her hand locked over his. Then it

1095

came, a small hard push against his hand, which sent a thrill through his heart.

'My God,' he said, in soft delight. 'He's real.'

Her eyes met his in rueful amusement.

'Yes,' she said. 'I know.'

It was well past dark when they drove up beside the garrison headquarters. It was a small, unprepossessing little building, dwarfed by the loom of the warehouse behind it, and Brianna eyed it askance.

'They have him in there?' Her hands felt cold, in spite of being muffled under her cloak.

'No.' Lord John glanced around, as he got down to tie the horses. A light burned in the window, but the small dirt yard was empty, the narrow street silent and deserted. There were no houses or shops nearby, and the warehousemen had long since gone home to their suppers and their beds.

He reached up both hands to help her down; alighting from a wagon was easier than getting out of a carriage, but still no small task.

'He's in the cellar below the warehouse,' he told her, his voice pitched low. 'I've bribed the soldier on duty to admit us.'

'Not *us*,' she said, her voice pitched as low as his, but no less firm for that. 'Me. I'll see him alone.'

She saw his lips compress tightly for a moment, then relax as he nodded.

'Private Hodgepile assures me he is in chains, or I would not countenance such a suggestion. As it is . . .' He shrugged, half irritably, and took her arm to guide her over the rutted ground.

'Hodgepile?'

'Private Arvin Hodgepile. Why? Are you acquainted?'

She shook her head, holding her skirts out of the way with her free hand.

'No. I've heard the name, but –'

The door of the building opened, spilling light into the yard.

'That'll be you, will it, my lord?' A soldier looked out

warily. Hodgepile was slight and narrow-faced, tight-jointed as a marionette. He jerked, startled, as he saw her.

'Oh! I didn't realize –'

'You needn't.' Lord John's voice was cool. 'Show us the way, if you please.'

With an apprehensive glance at Brianna's looming bulk, the private brought out a lantern, and led them to a small side door into the warehouse.

Hodgepile was short as well as slight, but held himself more erect than usual in compensation. *He walks with a ramrod up his arse.* Yes, she thought, watching him with interest as he marched ahead of them. It had to be the man Ronnie Sinclair had described to her mother. How many Hodgepiles could there be, after all? Perhaps she could talk to him when she'd finished with – her thoughts stopped abruptly as Hodgepile unlocked the warehouse door.

The April night was cool and fresh, but the air inside was thick with the reek of pitch and turpentine. Brianna felt suffocated. She could almost feel the tiny molecules of resin floating in the air, sticking to her skin. The sudden illusion of being trapped in a block of solidifying amber was so oppressive that she moved suddenly forward, almost dragging Lord John with her.

The warehouse was nearly full, its vast space crowded with bulky shapes. Kegs of pitch bled sticky black in the farthest shadows, while wooden racks near the huge double doors at the front held piles of barrels; brandy and rum, ready to roll down the ramps and out onto the dock, to barges waiting in the river below.

Private Hodgepile's shadow stretched and shrank by turns as he passed between the towering ranks of casks and boxes, his steps muffled by the thick layer of sawdust on the floor.

'. . . must be careful of fire . . .' His high, thin voice floated back to her, and she saw his puppet shadow wave an etiolated hand. 'You will be careful where you set the lantern, won't you? Though there should be no danger, no danger at all down below . . .'

The warehouse was built out over the river, to facilitate loading, and the front part of the floor was wood; the back half of the building was brick-floored. Brianna heard the echo of their footsteps change as they crossed the boundary. Hodgepile paused by a trapdoor set into the bricks.

'You won't be long, my lord?'

'No longer than we can help,' Lord John replied tersely. He took the lantern and waited in silence as Hodgepile heaved up the door and propped it. Brianna's heart was beating heavily; she could feel each separate thump, like a blow to the chest.

A flight of redbrick stairs ran down into darkness. Hodgepile took out his ring of keys and counted them over in the pool of lantern light, making sure of the right one before descending. He squinted dubiously at Brianna, then motioned them to follow him.

'It's a good thing they made the stairs wide enough for rum casks,' she murmured to Lord John, holding on to his arm as she edged herself down, one step at a time.

She could see at once why Private Hodgepile wasn't worried about fire down here; the air was so damp, she wouldn't have been surprised to see mushrooms sprouting from the walls. There was a sound of dripping water somewhere, and the light of the lantern shone off wet brick. Cockroaches scattered in panic from the light, and the air smelled of mold and mildew.

She thought briefly of her mother's penicillin farm, less briefly of her mother, and her throat closed tight. Then they were there, and she could no longer distract herself from the realization of what she was doing.

Hodgepile struggled with the key, and the panic she had been suppressing all day swept over her. She had no idea what to say, what to do. What was she *doing* here?

Lord John squeezed her arm in encouragement. She took a deep breath of the dank wet air, ducked her head, and stepped inside.

He sat on a bench at the far side of the cell, eyes fixed on the door. He'd clearly been expecting someone – he'd heard the footsteps outside – but it wasn't her. He jerked in startlement, and his eyes flashed briefly green as the light swept over him.

She heard a faint metallic clink; of course, they'd said

he was in chains. The thought gave her a little courage. She took the lantern from Hodgepile, and shut the door behind her.

She leaned against the wooden door, studying him in silence. He seemed smaller than she remembered. Perhaps it was only that she was now so much bigger.

'Do you know who I am?' It was a tiny cell, low-ceilinged, with no echo. Her voice sounded small, but clear.

He cocked his head to one side, considering. His eyes traveled slowly over her.

'I don't think ye were after tellin' me your name, sweetheart.'

'Don't call me that!' The spurt of rage took her by surprise, and she choked it back, clenching her fists behind her. If she had come here to administer forgiveness, it wasn't a good start.

He shrugged, good-natured but cool.

'As ye will. No, I don't know who you are. I'll know your face – and a few other things' – his teeth gleamed briefly in the blond stubble of his beard – 'but not your name. I suppose you'll mean to tell me, though?'

'You do recognize me?'

He drew in air and blew it out through pursed lips, looking her over carefully. He was a good bit the worse for wear, but it hadn't impaired his assurance.

'Oh, indeed I do.' He seemed amused, and she wanted to cross the room and slap him, hard. Instead, she took a deep breath. That was a mistake – she could smell him.

Without warning, her gorge rose suddenly and violently. She hadn't been sick before, but the stench of him brought up everything in her. She had barely time to turn away before the flood of bile and half-digested food came hurtling up, splattering the damp brick floor.

She leaned her forehead against the wall, waves of hot and cold running over her. Finally, she wiped her mouth and turned around.

He was still sitting there, watching her. She'd set the lantern on the floor. It threw a yellow flicker upward, carving his face from the shadows behind him. He might have a been a beast, chained in its den; only wariness showed in the pale green eyes.

'My name is Brianna Fraser.'

He nodded, repeating it.

'Brianna Fraser. A lovely name, sure.' He smiled briefly, lips together. 'And?'

'My parents are James and Claire Fraser. They saved your life, and you robbed them.'

'Yes.'

He said it with complete matter-of-factness, and she stared at him. He stared back.

She felt a wild urge to laugh, as unexpected as the surge of nausea had been. What had she expected? Remorse? Excuses? From a man who took things because he wanted them?

'If ye've come in the hopes of getting back the jewels, I'm afraid you've left it too late,' he said pleasantly. 'I sold the first to buy a ship, and the other two were stolen from me. Perhaps you'll find that justice; I should think it cold comfort, myself.'

She swallowed, tasting bile.

'Stolen. When?'

Don't trouble yourself over the man who's got it, Roger had said. *It's oddson he stole it from someone else.*

Bonnet shifted on the wooden bench and shrugged.

'Some four months gone. Why?'

'No reason.' So Roger had made it; had got them – the gems that might have been safe transport for them both. Cold comfort.

'I recall there was a trinket, too – a ring, was it? But you got that back.' He smiled, showing his teeth this time.

'I paid for it.' One hand went unthinking to her belly, gone round and tight as a basketball under her cloak.

His gaze stayed on her face, mildly curious.

'Have we business still to do then, darlin'?'

She took a deep breath – through her mouth, this time.

'They told me you're going to hang.'

'They told me the same thing.' He shifted again on the hard wooden bench. He stretched his head to one side, to ease the muscles of his neck, and peered up sidelong at her. 'You'll not have come from pity, though, I shouldn't think.'

1100

'No,' she said, watching him thoughtfully. 'To be honest, I'll rest a lot easier once you're dead.'

He stared at her for a moment, then burst out laughing. He laughed hard enough that tears came to his eyes; he wiped them carelessly, bending his head to swipe his face against a shrugged shoulder, then straightened up, the marks of his laughter still on his face.

'What is it you want from me, then?'

She opened her mouth to reply, and quite suddenly, the link between them dissolved. She had not moved, but felt as though she had taken one step across an impassable abyss. She stood now safe on the other side, alone. Blessedly alone. He could no longer touch her.

'Nothing,' she said, her voice clear in her own ears. 'I don't want anything at all from you. I came to give you something.'

She opened her cloak, and ran her hands over the swell of her abdomen. The small inhabitant stretched and rolled, its touch a blind caress of hand and womb, both intimate and abstract.

'Yours,' she said.

He looked at the bulge, and then at her.

'I've had whores try to foist their spawn on me before,' he said. But he spoke without viciousness, and she thought there was a new stillness behind the wary eyes.

'Do you think I'm a whore?' She didn't care if he did or not, though she doubted he did. 'I've no reason to lie. I already told you, I don't want anything from you.'

She drew the cloak back together, covering herself. She drew herself up then, feeling the ache in her back ease with the movement. It was done. She was ready to go.

'You're going to die,' she said to him, and she who had not come for pity's sake was surprised to find she had some. 'If it makes the dying easier for you, to know there's something of you left on earth – then you're welcome to the knowledge. But I've finished with you, now.'

She turned to pick up the lantern, and was surprised to see the door half cracked ajar. She had no time to feel anger at Lord John for eavesdropping, when the door swung fully open.

'Well, 'twas a gracious speech, ma'am,' Sergeant

1101

Murchison said judiciously. He smiled broadly then, and brought the butt of his musket up even with her belly. 'But I can't say I've finished, quite, with you.'

She took a quick step back, and swung the lantern at his head in a reflex of defense. He ducked with a yelp of alarm, and a grip of iron seized her wrist before she could dash the lamp at him again.

'Christ, that was close! You're fast, girl, if not quite so fast as the good Sergeant.' Bonnet took the lantern from her and released her wrist.

'You're not chained after all,' she said stupidly, staring at him. Then her wits caught up with the situation, and she whirled, plunging for the door. Murchison shoved his musket in front of her, blocking her way, but not before she had seen the darkened corridor through the doorway – and the dim form sprawled facedown on the bricks outside.

'You've killed him,' she whispered. Her lips were numb with shock, and a dread deeper than nausea sickened her to the bone. 'Oh, God, you've killed him.'

'Killed who?' Bonnet held the lantern up, peering at the spill of butter-yellow hair, blotched with blood. 'Who the hell is that?'

'A busybody,' Murchison snapped. 'Hurry, man! There's no time to waste. I've taken care of Hodgepile and the fuses are lit.'

'Wait!' Bonnet glanced from the Sergeant to Brianna, frowning.

'There's no time, I said.' The Sergeant brought up his gun and checked the priming. 'Don't worry; no one will find them.'

Brianna could smell the brimstone scent of the gunpowder in the priming pan. The Sergeant swung the stock of the gun to his shoulder, and turned toward her, but the quarters were too cramped; with her belly in the way, there was no room to raise the long muzzle.

The Sergeant grunted with irritation, reversed the gun, and raised it high, to club her with the butt.

Her hand was clenched around the barrel before she knew she had reached for it. Everything seemed to be moving very slowly, Murchison and Bonnet both standing frozen. She herself felt quite detached, as though she stood to one side, watching.

She plucked the musket from Murchison's grip as though it were a broomstraw, swung it high, and smashed it down. The jolt of it vibrated up her arms, into her body, her whole body charged as though someone had thrown a switch and sent a white-hot current pulsing through her.

She saw so clearly the man's face hanging drop-jawed in the air before her, eyes passing from astonishment through horror to the dullness of unconsciousness, so slowly that she saw the change. Had time to see the vivid colors in his face. A plum lip caught on a yellow tooth, half lifted in a sneer. Slow tiny blossoms of brilliant red unfolding in a graceful curve across his temple, Japanese water flowers blooming on a field of fresh-bruised blue.

She was entirely calm, no more than a conduit for the ancient savagery that men call motherhood, who mistake its tenderness for weakness. She saw her own hands, knuckles stark and tendons etched, felt the surge of power up her legs and back, through wrists and arms and shoulders, swung again, so slowly, it seemed so slowly, and yet the man was still falling, had not quite reached the floor when the gun butt struck again.

A voice was calling her name. Dimly, it penetrated through the crystal hum around her.

'Stop, for God's sake! Woman – Brianna – stop!'

There were hands on her shoulders, dragging, shaking. She pulled free of the grip and turned, the gun still in hand.

'Don't touch me,' she said, and he took a quick step back, his eyes filled with surprise and wariness – perhaps a touch of fear. Afraid of her? Why would anyone be afraid of her? she thought dimly. He was talking; she saw his mouth moving, but she couldn't catch the words, it was just noise. The current in her was dying, making her dizzy.

Then time readjusted itself, began to move normally again. Her muscles quivered, all their fibers turned to jelly. She set the stained butt of the gun against the floor to balance herself.

'What did you say?'

Impatience flickered across his face.

'I said, it's no time we have to be wasting! Did ye not hear your man sayin' that the fuses are lit?'

'What fuses? Why?' She saw his eyes flick toward the door behind her. Before he could move, she stepped back into the doorway, bringing up the muzzle of the gun. He backed away from her instinctively, hitting the bench with the backs of his legs. He fell back, and struck the chains fastened to the wall; empty manacles chimed against the brick.

Shock was beginning to steal over her, but the memory of the white-hot current still burned through her spine, keeping her upright.

'You do not mean to kill me, surely?' He tried to smile, and failed; couldn't keep the panic from his eyes. She *had* said she would rest easier with him dead.

Freedom is hard-won, but is not the fruit of Murder. She had her hard-won freedom now, and would not give it back to him.

'No,' she said, and took a firmer hold on the gun, the butt snugged solid into her shoulder. 'But I will by God shoot you through the knees and leave you here, if you don't tell me right this minute what the *hell* is going on!'

He shifted his weight, big body hovering, pale eyes on her, judging. She blocked the door entirely, her bulk filling it from side to side. She saw the doubt in his posture, the shift of his shoulders as he thought to rush her, and cocked the gun with a single loud *click!*

He stood six feet from the muzzle's end; too far to lunge and grab it from her. One move, one pull of her trigger finger. She couldn't miss, and he knew it.

His shoulders slumped.

'The warehouse above is laid with gunpowder and fuses,' he said, speaking quick and sharp, anxious to get it done. 'I can't say how long, but it's goin' up with an almighty bang. For God's sake, let me out of here!'

'Why?' Her hands were sweating, but solid on the gun. The baby stirred, a reminder that she had no time to waste, either. She would risk one minute to know, though. She had to know, with John Grey's body limp on the floor behind her. 'You've killed a good man here, and I want to know *why*!'

1104

He made a gesture of frustration.

'The smuggling!' he said. 'We were partners, the Sergeant and I. I'd bring him in cheap contraband, he'd stamp it with the Crown's mark. He'd steal the licensed stuff, I'd sell it for a good price and split with him.'

'Keep talking.'

He was nearly dancing with impatience.

'A soldier – Hodgepile – he was on to it, asking questions. Murchison couldn't say if he'd told anyone, but it wasn't wise to wait and see, not once I was taken. The Sergeant moved the last of the liquor from the warehouse, substituted barrels of turpentine, and laid the fuses. It all goes up, no one can say it wasn't brandy burning – no evidence of theft. That's it, that's all. Now let me go!'

'All right.' She lowered the musket a few inches, but didn't yet uncock it. 'What about him?' She nodded toward the fallen Sergeant, who was beginning to snort and mumble.

He stared at her blankly.

'What about him?'

'Aren't you going to take him with you?'

'No.' He sidled to one side, looking for a way past her. 'For Christ's sweet sake, woman, let me go, and leave yourself! There's twelve hundred-weight of pitch and turpentine overhead. It'll go off like a bomb!'

'But he's still alive! We can't leave him here!'

Bonnet gave her a look of sheer exasperation, then crossed the room in two strides. He bent, jerked the dagger from the Sergeant's belt, and drew it hard across the fat throat, just above the leather stock. A thick spray of blood soaked Bonnet's shirt, and whipped against the wall.

'There,' he said, straightening up. 'He's not alive. Leave him.'

He dropped the dagger, pushed her aside, and lunged out into the corridor. She could hear his footsteps going away, quick and ringing on the brick.

Trembling all over with the shock of action and reaction, she stood still for a second, staring down at John Grey's body. Grief ripped through her, and her womb clenched hard. There was no pain, but every fiber had contracted; her stomach bulged as though she'd swallowed a basketball. She felt breathless, unable to move.

No, she thought quite clearly, to the child inside. *I am not in labor, I absolutely, positively am not. I won't have it. Stay put. I haven't got time right now.*

She took two steps down the black corridor, then stopped. No, she had to check, at least, make sure. She turned back, and knelt by John Grey's body. He had looked dead when she first saw him lying there, and still did; he hadn't moved or even twitched since she had first seen his body.

She leaned forward but couldn't reach easily over the bulge of her belly. She grasped his arm instead, and pulled at him, trying to turn him over. A small, fine-boned man, he was still heavy. His body tilted up, rolled boneless toward her, head lolling, and her heart sank anew, seeing his half-closed eyes and slack mouth. But she reached beneath the angle of his jaw, feeling frantically for a pulse point.

Where the hell was it? She'd seen her mother do it in emergencies; faster to find than a wrist pulse, she'd said. She couldn't find one. How long had it been, how long were the fuses set to burn?

She wiped a fold of her cloak across her clammy face, trying to think. She looked back, judging the distance to the stairs. Jesus, could she risk it, even alone? The thought of popping out into the warehouse above, just as everything went off – She cast one look upward, then bent to her work and tried again, pushing his head far back. There! She could see the damn vein under his skin – that's where the pulse should be, shouldn't it?

For a moment, she wasn't sure she felt it; it might be only the hammering of her own heart, beating in her fingertips. But no, it was – a different rhythm, faint and fluttering. He might be close to dead, but not quite.

'Close,' she muttered, 'but no cigar.' She felt too frightened to be greatly relieved; now she'd have to get him out, too. She scrambled to her feet, and reached down to get hold of his arms, to drag him. But then she stopped, a memory of what she had seen a moment before penetrating her panic.

1106

She turned and lumbered hastily back into the cell. Averting her eyes from the sodden red mound on the floor, she snatched up the lantern and brought it back to the corridor. She held it high, casting light on the low brick ceiling. Yes, she'd been right!

The bricks curved up from the floor in groynes, making arches all along both sides of the corridors. Storage alcoves and cells. Above the groynes, though, ran sturdy beams made of eight-inch pine. Over that, thick planking – and above the planks, the layer of bricks that formed the floor of the warehouse.

Going up like a bomb, Bonnet had said – but was he right? Turpentine burned, so did pitch; yes, they'd likely explode if they burned under pressure, but not like a bomb, no. Fuses. Fuses, in the plural. Long fuses, plainly, and likely running to small caches of gunpowder; that was the only true explosive Murchison would have; there were no high explosives now.

So the gunpowder would explode in several places, and ignite the barrels nearby. But the barrels would burn slowly; she'd seen Sinclair make barrels like those; the staves were half an inch thick, watertight. She remembered the reek as they walked through the warehouse; yes, Murchison would likely have opened the bungs of a few barrels, let the turpentine flow out, to help the fire along.

So the barrels would burn, but likely they wouldn't explode – or if they did, not all at once. Her breathing eased a little, making calculations. Not a bomb; a string of firecrackers, maybe.

So. She took a deep breath – as deep a breath as she could manage, with Osbert in the way. She put her hands across her stomach, feeling her racing heart begin to slow.

Even if some of the barrels did explode, the force of the explosion would be out, and up, through the thin plank walls and the roof. Very little force would be deflected down. And what was – she reached up a hand and pushed against a beam, reassuring herself of its strength.

She sat down quite suddenly on the floor, skirts puffed out around her.

'I think it'll be all right,' she whispered, not sure if she was talking to John, to the baby, or to herself.

1107

She sat huddled for a moment, shaking with relief, then rolled awkwardly onto her knees again, and began with fumbling fingers to administer first aid.

She was still struggling to tear a strip from the hem of her petticoat when she heard the footsteps. Coming fast, almost running. She turned sharply toward the stairs, but no – the footsteps came from the other way, behind her.

She whirled around, to see the form of Stephen Bonnet looming out of the darkness.

'Run!' he shouted at her. 'For Christ's sweet sake, why have ye not gone?'

'Because it's safe here,' she said. She had laid the musket down on the floor beside Grey's body; she stooped and picked it up, lifted it to her shoulder. 'Go away.'

He stared at her, mouth half open in the gloom.

'Safe? Woman, you're an eedjit! Did ye not hear –'

'I heard, but you're wrong. It's not going to explode. And if it did, it would still be safe down here.'

'The hell it is! Sweet bleeding Jesus! Even if the cellar doesn't go, what happens when the fire burns through the floor?'

'It can't, it's brick.' She jerked her chin upward, not taking her eyes off him.

'Back here it is – up front, by the river, it's wood, like the wharf. It'll burn through, then collapse. And what happens back here then, eh? Do ye no good for the ceiling to hold, when the smoke comes rolling back to smother ye!'

She felt a wave of sickness roil up from her depths.

'It's open? The cellar isn't sealed? The other end of the corridor's open?' Knowing even as she spoke that of course it was – he had run that way, heading for the river, not for the stairs.

'Yes! Now come!' He lunged forward, reaching for her arm, but she jerked away, back against the wall, the muzzle of the gun trained on him.

'I'm not going without him.' She licked dry lips, nodding at the floor. 'The man's dead!'

'He's not! Pick him up!'

An extraordinary mixture of emotions crossed Bonnet's face; fury and astonishment preeminent among them.

'Pick him up!' she repeated fiercely. He stood still, staring at her. Then, very slowly, he squatted, and gathering John Grey's limp form into his arms, got the point of his shoulder into Grey's abdomen and heaved him up.

'Come on, then,' he said, and without another glance at her started off into the dark. She hesitated for a second, then seized the lantern and followed him.

Within fifty feet, she smelled smoke. The brick corridor wasn't straight; it branched and turned, encompassing the many partitions of the cellar. But all the time it slanted down, heading toward the riverbank. As they descended through the multiple turnings, the scent of smoke thickened; a layer of acrid haze swirled lazily around them, visible in the lantern light.

Brianna held her breath, trying not to breathe. Bonnet was moving fast, despite Grey's weight. She could barely keep up, burdened with gun and lantern, but she didn't mean to give up either one, just yet. Her belly tightened again, another of those breathless moments.

'Not *yet*, I said!' she muttered through gritted teeth.

She had had to stop for a moment; Bonnet had disappeared into the haze ahead. Evidently he'd noticed the fading of the lantern light, though – she heard him bellow, from somewhere up ahead.

'Woman! Brianna!'

'I'm coming!' she called, and hurried as fast as she could, waddling, discarding any pretense of grace. The smoke was much thicker, and she could hear a faint crackle, somewhere in the distance – overhead? Before them?

She was breathing heavily, in spite of the smoke. She drew in a ragged gulp of air, and smelled water. Damp and mud, dead leaves and fresh air, slicing through the smoky murk like a knife.

A faint glow shone through the smoke and grew as they hurried toward it, dwarfing the light of her lantern. Then a dark square loomed ahead. Bonnet turned and seized her arm, dragging her out into the air.

They were under the wharf, she realized; dark water lapped ahead of them, brightness dancing on it. Reflection; the brightness came from up above, and so did the crackle of flame. Bonnet didn't stop or let go of her arm; he pulled her to one side, into the long, dank grass and mud of the bank. He let go within a few steps, but she followed, gasping for breath, slipping and sliding, tripping on the soggy edges of her skirts.

At last he stopped, in the shadow of the trees. He bent, and let Grey's body slide to the ground. He stayed bent for a moment, chest heaving, trying to get his breath back.

Brianna realized that she could see both men plainly; could see every bud on the twigs of the tree. She turned and looked back, to see the warehouse lighted like a jack-o'-lantern, flames licking through cracks in the wooden walls. The huge double doors had been left ajar; as she watched, the blast hot air forced one open, and small tongues of fire began to creep across the dock, deceptively small and playful-looking.

She felt a hand on her shoulder, and whirled, looking up into Bonnet's face.

'I've a ship waiting,' he said. 'A little way upriver. Will you come with me, then?'

She shook her head. She still held the gun, but didn't need it now. He was no threat to her.

Still he didn't go, but lingered, staring down at her, a small frown between his brows. His face was gaunt, hollowed and shadowed by the distant fire. The surface of the river was aflame now, small tongues of fire flickering from the dark water as a slick of turpentine spread across it.

'Is it true?' he asked abruptly. He asked no permission, but set his hands on her belly. It tightened at his touch, rounding in another of those breathless, painless squeezes, and a look of astonishment crossed his face.

She jerked away from his touch, pulling her cloak together, and nodded, unable to speak.

He seized her chin in his hand and peered into her face – assessing her truthfulness, perhaps? Then he let go, and stuck a finger into his mouth, groping in the recesses of his cheek.

He took her hand, and put something wet and hard in her palm.

'For his maintenance, then,' he said, and grinned at her. 'Take care of him, sweetheart!'

And then he was gone, bounding long-legged up the riverbank, silhouetted like a demon in the flickering light. The turpentine flowing into the water had caught fire, and roiling billows of scarlet light shot upward, floating pillars of fire that lit the riverbank bright as day.

She half raised the musket, finger on the trigger. He was no more than twenty yards away, a perfect shot. *Not by your hand.* She lowered the gun, and let him go.

The warehouse was fully ablaze by now; the heat from it beat against her cheeks and blew the hair back from her face.

'I have a ship upriver,' he'd said. She squinted into the glare. The fire had nearly filled the river, a great floating slick that bloomed from bank to bank in a fiery garden of unfolding flames. Nothing could come through that blinding wall of light.

Her other fist was still closed around the object he had given her. She opened her hand and looked down at the wet black diamond that gleamed in her palm, the fire glowing red and bloody in its facets.

PART TWELVE

Je t'aime

63

Forgiveness

River Run, May 1770

'That is the most stubborn woman I have ever met!' Brianna huffed into the room like a ship in full sail, and subsided onto the love seat by the bed, billowing.

Lord John Grey opened one eye, bloodshot under his turban of bandages.

'Your aunt?'

'Who else?'

'You have a looking glass in your room, do you not?' His mouth curved, and after a reluctant moment, so did hers.

'It's her bloody will. I *told* her I don't want River Run, I can't own slaves – but she won't change it! She just smiles as though I were a six-year-old having a tantrum and says by the time it happens, I'll be glad of it. Glad of it!' She snorted and flounced into a more comfortable position. 'What am I going to do?'

'Nothing.'

'Nothing?' She turned the force of her displeasure on him. 'How can I do nothing?'

'To begin with, I should be extremely surprised if your aunt were not immortal; several of that particular race of Scots seem to be. However,' – he waved a hand in dismissal – 'should this prove untrue, and should she persist in her delusions that you would prove a good mistress to River Run –'

'What makes you think I wouldn't?' she said, pride stung.

'You cannot run a plantation of this size without slaves, and you decline to own them for reasons of conscience, or so I was given to understand. Though a less likely Quaker I have never seen.' He narrowed his open eye, indicating the immense tent of purple-striped muslin in which she was swathed. 'Returning to the point at issue – or one of them – should you find yourself the unwilling recipient

1115

of a number of slaves, arrangements can undoubtedly be made to free them.'

'Not in North Carolina. The Assembly –'

'No, not in North Carolina,' he agreed patiently. 'If the occasion should arise, and you find yourself in possession of slaves, you will simply sell them to me.'

'But that's –'

'And I will take them to Virginia, where manumission is much less stringently controlled. Once they are freed, you will return my money. At this point, you will be totally destitute and lacking in property, which appears to be your chief desire, second only to preventing any possibility of personal happiness by ensuring that you cannot marry the man you love.'

She pleated a handful of muslin between her fingers, frowning at the big sapphire that shone on her hand.

'I promised I'd listen to him first.' She cast a narrow eye at Lord John. 'Though I still say it's emotional blackmail.'

She'd ignored this.

'And I only more effective than any other kind,' he agreed. 'Almost worthy a cracked pate, to finally hold the whip hand on a Fraser.'

She ignored this.

'And I only said I'd listen. I still think when he knows everything, he'll – he can't.' She put a hand on her enormous belly. 'You couldn't, could you? Care – really care, I mean – for a child that wasn't yours?'

He moved higher on the pillow, grimacing slightly.

'For the sake of its parent? I expect I could.' He opened both eyes and looked at her, smiling. 'Indeed, I was under the impression that I had been doing so for some time.'

She looked momentarily blank, before a tide of pink flowed up from the scooped neck of her bodice. She was charming when she blushed.

'You mean me? Well, yes, but – I mean – I'm not a baby, and you're not having to claim me as your own.' She gave him a direct blue look, at odds with the lingering pinkness of her cheeks. 'And I did hope it wasn't *all* for my father's sake.'

He was quiet for a moment, then reached out and squeezed her hand.

'No, it wasn't,' he said gruffly. He let go, and lay back with a small groan.

'Are you feeling worse?' she asked anxiously. 'Shall I get you something? Some tea? A poultice?'

'No, it's only the blasted headache,' he said. 'The light makes it throb.' He shut his eyes again.

'Tell me,' he said without opening them, 'why is it that you seem so convinced that a man could not care for a child unless it were the fruit of his loins? As it is, my dear, I did *not* mean to refer to you when I said I had been doing such a thing myself. My son – my stepson – is in fact the son of my late wife's sister. By tragic accident, both of his parents died within a day of each other, and my wife Isobel and her parents raised him from babyhood. I married Isobel when Willie was six or so. So you see, there is no blood between us at all – and yet were any man to impugn my affection for him, or to say he is not my son, I would call him out on the instant for it.'

'I see,' she said, after a moment. 'I didn't know that.' He cracked an eyelid; she was still twisting her ring, looking pensive.

'I think . . .' she began, and glanced at him. 'I think I'm not so worried about Roger and the baby. If I'm honest –'

'Heaven forfend you should be otherwise,' he murmured.

'If I'm honest,' she went on, glowering at him, 'I think I'm worried more about how it would be between us – between Roger and me.' She hesitated, then took the plunge.

'I didn't know Jamie Fraser was my father,' she said. 'Not all the time I was growing up. After the Rising, my parents were separated; they each thought the other was dead. And so my mother married again. I thought Frank Randall was my father. I didn't find out otherwise until after he died.'

'Ah.' He viewed her with increased interest. 'And was this Randall cruel to you?'

'No! He was . . . wonderful.' Her voice broke slightly, and she cleared her throat, embarrassed. 'No. He was the best father I could have had. It's just that I thought my parents had a good marriage. They cared for each other, they respected each other, they – well, I thought everything was fine.'

Lord John scratched at his bandages. The doctor had shaved his head, a condition which, in addition to affronting his vanity, itched abominably.

'I fail to see the difficulty, as applied to your present situation.'

She heaved a huge sigh.

'Then my father died, and . . . we found out that Jamie Fraser was still alive. My mother went to join him, and then I came. And – it was different. I saw how they looked at each other. I never saw her look at Frank Randall that way – or him at her.'

'Ah, yes.' A small gust of bleakness swept through him. He'd seen that look once or twice; the first time, he had wanted desperately to put a knife through Claire Randall's heart.

'Do you know how rare such a thing is?' he asked quietly. 'That peculiar sort of mutual passion?' The one-sided kind was common enough.

'Yes.' She had half turned, her arm along the back of the love seat, and was looking out through the French doors, over the burgeoning spread of the spring flower beds below.

'The thing is – I think I had it,' she said, even more quietly. 'For a little while. A very little while.' She turned her head and looked at him, with eyes that let him see clear through her.

'If I've lost it – then I have. I can live with that – or without it. But I won't live with an imitation of it. I couldn't stand that.'

'It looks like you may get me by default.' Brianna put the breakfast tray over his lap and collapsed heavily into the love seat, making the joints groan.

'Don't riddle with a sick man,' he said, picking up a piece of toast. 'What do you mean?'

'Drusus just came racing into the cookhouse, saying he saw two riders coming down through Campbell's fields. He said he was sure one of them was my father – he said it

1118

was a big man with red hair; God knows there aren't that many like him.'

'Not many, no.' He smiled briefly, his eyes traveling over her. 'So, two riders?'

'It must be Da and my mother. So they haven't found Roger. Or they did, and he – didn't want to come back.' She twisted the big sapphire on her finger. 'Good thing I have a fallback, isn't it?'

Lord John blinked, and made haste to swallow his mouthful of toast.

'If by that extraordinary metaphor, you mean that you intend to marry me after all, I assure you –'

'No.' She gave him a halfhearted smile. 'Just teasing.'

'Oh, good.' He took a gulp of tea, closing his eyes to enjoy the fragrant steam. 'Two riders. Did your cousin not go with them?'

'Yes, he did,' she said slowly. 'God, I hope nothing's happened to Ian.'

'It might be that they experienced any variety of disasters on the journey, which obliged your cousin and your mother to travel behind your father and Mr. MacKenzie. Or your cousin and MacKenzie behind your parents.' He waved a hand, indicating innumerable possibilities.

'I guess you're right.' She still looked peaked, and Lord John suspected she had cause. Comforting possibilities were all very well for the short term, but the colder probabilities were inclined to triumph over the longer course – and whoever accompanied Jamie Fraser, they would be arriving shortly, with the answers to all questions.

He pushed back the unfinished breakfast and leaned back against his pillows.

'Tell me – how far does your remorse extend for having nearly gotten me killed?'

She colored and looked uncomfortable.

'What do you mean?'

'If I ask you to do something you do not wish to, will your sense of guilt and obligation compel you to do it nonetheless?'

'Oh, more blackmail. What is it?' she asked warily.

'Forgive your father. Whatever has happened.'

Pregnancy had made her complexion more delicate; all

her emotions ebbed and flowed just under the surface of that apricot skin. A touch would bruise her.

He reached out and laid a hand very gently along her cheek.

'For your sake, as well as his,' he said.

'I already have.' Her lashes covered her eyes as she looked down; her hands lay still in her lap, the blue fire of his sapphire glowing on her finger.

The sound of hooves came clearly through the open French doors, rattling on the gravel drive.

'Then I think you had better go down and tell him so, my dear.'

She pursed her lips, and nodded. Without a word, she stood up and floated out the door, disappearing like a storm cloud over the horizon.

'When we heard that there were two riders coming, and one of them Jamie, we feared lest something had happened to your nephew, or MacKenzie. Somehow, it occurred to neither of us to think that anything had happened to *you*.'

'I'm immortal,' she murmured, peering alternately into his eyes. 'Didn't you know?' The pressure of her thumbs lifted from his eyelids and he blinked, still feeling her touch.

'You have a slight enlargement of one pupil, but very small. Grip my fingers and squeeze as hard as you can.' She held out her index fingers and he obliged, annoyed to feel the weakness of his grip.

'Did you find MacKenzie?' He was further annoyed not to be able to control his curiosity.

She gave him a quick, wary glance from those sherry-colored eyes, and returned her gaze to his hands.

'Yes. He'll be coming along. A little later.'

'Will he?' She caught the tone of his question and hesitated, then looked at him directly.

'How much do you know?'

'Everything,' he said, and had the momentary satisfaction of seeing her startled. Then one side of her mouth curved up.

'Everything?'

'Enough,' he amended sardonically. 'Enough to ask whether your statement of Mr. MacKenzie's return is knowledge on your part or wishful thinking.'

'Call it faith.' Without so much as a by-your-leave, she tugged loose the strings of his nightshirt and spread it open, exposing his chest. Rolling a sheet of parchment deftly into a tube, she applied one end of it to his breast, putting her ear to the other end.

'I beg your pardon, madame!'

'Hush, I can't hear,' she said, making small shushing motions with one hand. She proceeded to move her tube to different parts of his chest, pausing now and then to thump experimentally or prod him in the liver.

'Have you moved your bowels yet today?' she inquired, poking him familiarly in the abdomen.

'I decline to say,' he said, pulling his nightshirt back together with dignity.

She looked more outrageous even than usual. The woman must be forty at least, yet she showed no more sign of age than a fine webbing of lines at the corners of her eyes, and threadings of silver in that ridiculous mass of hair.

She was thinner than he remembered, though it was hard to judge of her figure, dressed as she was in a barbaric leather shirt and trouserings. She'd plainly been in the sun and weather for some time; her face and hands had baked a delicate soft brown, that made the big golden eyes that much more startling when they turned full on one – which they now did.

'Brianna says that Dr. Fentiman trephined your skull.'

He shifted uncomfortably under the sheets.

'I am told that he did. I am afraid I was not aware of it at the time.'

Her mouth quirked slightly.

'Just as well. Would you mind if I look at it? It's only curiosity,' she went on, with unaccustomed delicacy. 'Not medical necessity. It's only that I've never seen a trepanation.'

He closed his eyes, giving up.

'Beyond the state of my bowels, I have no secrets from you, madame.' He tilted his head, indicating the location

1121

of the hole in his head, and felt her cool fingers slide under the bandage, lifting the gauze and allowing a breath of air to soothe his hot head.

'Brianna is with her father?' he asked, eyes still closed.

'Yes.' Her voice was softer. 'She told me – us – a little of what you'd done for her. Thank you.'

The fingers left his skin and he opened his eyes.

'It was my pleasure to be of service to her. Perforated skull and all.'

She smiled faintly.

'Jamie will be up to see you in a bit. He's . . . talking to Brianna in the garden.'

He felt a small stab of anxiety.

'Are they – in accord?'

'See for yourself.' She put an arm behind him, and with amazing strength for a woman with such fine bones, levered him upright. Just beyond the balustrade he could see the two figures at the bottom of the garden, heads close together. As he watched, they embraced, then broke apart, laughing at the awkwardness caused by Brianna's shape.

'I think we got here just in time,' Claire murmured, looking at her daughter with a practiced eye. 'It isn't going to be much longer.'

'I confess to some gratitude at your prompt arrival,' he said, letting her ease him back onto the pillows and smooth his bedding. 'I have barely survived the experience of being your daughter's nursemaid; I fear serving as her midwife would finish me completely.'

'Oh, I nearly forgot.' Claire reached into a nasty-looking leather pouch around her neck. 'Brianna said to give this back to you – she won't need it anymore.'

He held out his hand, and a tiny spark of brilliant blue fell into his palm.

'Jilted, by God!' he said, and grinned.

64

Bottom of the Ninth

'It's like baseball,' I assured her. 'Long stretches of boredom, punctuated by short periods of intense activity.'

She laughed, then stopped abruptly, grimacing.

'Ugh. Intense, yeah. Whew.' She smiled, a little lopsidedly. 'At least at baseball games you get to drink beer and eat hot dogs in the boring parts.'

Jamie, grasping at the only part of this conversation that made sense, leaned forward.

'There's a crock of small beer, cool in the pantry,' he said, peering anxiously at Brianna. 'Will I fetch it in?'

'No,' I said. 'Not unless you want some; alcohol wouldn't be good for the baby.'

'Ah. What about the hot dog?' He stood up and flexed his hands, obviously preparing to dash out and shoot one.

'It's a sort of sausage in a roll,' I said, rubbing my upper lip in an effort not to laugh. I glanced at Brianna. 'I don't think she wants one.' Small beads of sweat had popped out quite suddenly on her wide brow, and she was looking white around the eye sockets.

'Oh, barf,' she said faintly.

Correctly interpreting this remark from the look on her face, Jamie hastily applied the damp cloth to her face and neck.

'Put your head between your knees, lass.'

She glared at him ferociously.

'I can't get . . . my head . . . *near* my knees!' she said, teeth clenched. Then the spasm relaxed and she took a deep breath, the color coming back into her face.

Jamie glanced from her to me, frowning worriedly. He took a hesitant step toward the door.

'I expect I'd best go, then, if you –'

'Don't leave me!'

'But it's – I mean, you've your mother, and –'

'Don't leave me!' she repeated. Agitated, she leaned

over and grabbed his arm, shaking it for emphasis. 'You can't!'

'You said I wouldn't die.' She was staring intently into his face. 'If you stay, it will be all right. I won't die.' She spoke with such intensity that I felt a sudden spasm of fear clutch my own innards, hard as the pain of labor.

She was a big girl, strong and healthy. She should have no great trouble delivering. But I was large enough, healthy as well – and twenty-five years before, I had lost a stillborn child at six months, and nearly died myself. I might be able to protect her from childbed fever, but there was no defense against a sudden hemorrhage; the best I could do under such circumstances would be to try to save her child via Caesarian section. I resolutely kept my eyes off the chest in which the sterile blade lay ready, just in case.

'You're not going to die, Bree,' I said. I spoke as soothingly as I could, and put a hand on her shoulder, but she must have felt the fear under my professional facade. Her face twisted, and she grabbed my hand, clinging so tightly the bones rubbed together. She closed her eyes and breathed through her nose, but didn't cry out.

She opened her eyes and looked straight at me, her pupils dilated so that she seemed to be looking past me, into a future that only she could see.

'If I do . . .' she said, putting a hand to her swollen belly. Her mouth worked, but whatever she'd been meaning to say couldn't force its way out.

She struggled to her feet, then, and leaned heavily on Jamie, her face muffled in his shoulder, repeating, 'Da, don't leave me, don't.'

'I willna leave ye, *a leannan*. Dinna be afraid, I'll stay wi' ye.' He put an arm around her, looking helplessly over her head at me.

'Walk her,' I said to Jamie, seeing her restlessness. 'Like a horse with colic,' I added, as he looked blank.

That made her laugh. With the ginger air of a man approaching an armed bomb, he put an arm around her waist and towed her slowly around the room. Given their respective sizes, it sounded a lot like someone leading a horse, too.

1124

'All right?' I heard him ask anxiously, on one circuit.

'I'll tell you when I'm not,' she assured him.

It was warm for mid-May; I opened the windows wide, and the scents of phlox and columbine flowed in, mixed with cool, damp air from the river.

The house was filled with an air of expectation: eagerness, with a hint of fear beneath. Jocasta walked up and down the terrace below, too nervous to stay put. Betty put her head in every few minutes to ask if anything was needed; Phaedre came up from the pantry with a jug of fresh buttermilk, just in case. Brianna, her eyes focused inwardly, merely shook her head at it; I sipped a glass myself, mentally checking off the preparations.

The fact was that there wasn't a hell of a lot you needed to do for a normal birth, and not the hell of a lot you *could* do if it wasn't. The bed was stripped and old quilts laid to protect the mattress; there was a stack of clean cloths to hand, and a can of hot water, renewed every half hour or so from the kitchen copper. Cool water for sipping and brow-mopping, a small vial of oil for rubbing, my suture kit to hand, just in case – and beyond that, everything was up to Brianna.

After nearly an hour's walking, she stopped dead in the middle of the floor, gripping Jamie's arm and breathing through her nose like a horse at the end of a twenty-furlong race.

'I want to lie down,' she said.

Phaedre and I got her gown off, and got her safely onto the bed in her shift. I laid my hands on the huge mound of her belly, marveling at the sheer impossibility of what had happened already, and what was about to happen next.

The rigidity of the contraction passed off, and I could clearly feel the curves of the child below the thin rubbery covering of skin and muscle. It was large, I could tell that, but it seemed to be lying well, head down and fully engaged.

Normally, babies about to be born were fairly quiet, intimidated by the upheaval of their surroundings. This one was stirring; I felt a small, distinct surge against my hand as an elbow poked out.

'Daddy!' Brianna reached out blindly, flailing as a contraction took her unaware. Jamie lunged forward and caught her hand, squeezing tight.

'I'm here, *a bheanachd*, I'm here.'

She breathed heavily, face bright red, then relaxed, and swallowed.

'How long?' she asked. She was facing me but not looking at me; she wasn't looking at anything outside.

'I don't know. Not an awfully long time, I don't think.' The contractions were roughly five minutes apart, but I knew they could continue like that for a long time, or speed up abruptly; there was simply no telling.

There was a light breeze from the window, but she was sweating. I wiped her face and neck again, and rubbed her shoulders.

'You're doing fine, lovey,' I murmured to her. 'Just fine.' I glanced up at Jamie, and smiled. 'So are you.'

He made a game try at returning the smile; he was sweating, too, but his face was white, not red.

'Talk to me, Da,' she said suddenly.

'Och?' He looked at me, frantic. 'What shall I say?'

'It doesn't matter,' I said. 'Tell her stories; anything to take her mind off things.'

'Oh. Ah . . . will ye have heard the one about . . . Habetrot the spinstress?'

Brianna grunted in reply. Jamie looked apprehensive, but started in nonetheless.

'Aye, well. It happened that in an old farmhouse that stood by the river, there lived a fair maid called Maisie. She'd red hair and blue een, and was the bonniest maid in all the valley. But she had no husband, because . . .' He stopped, appalled. I glared at him.

He coughed and went on, plainly not knowing what else to do. 'Ah . . . because in those days men were sensible, and instead of looking for lovely lasses to be their brides, they looked out for girls who could cook and spin, who might make notable housewives. But Maisie . . .'

Brianna made a deep inhuman noise. Jamie clenched his teeth for a moment, but went on, holding tight to both her hands.

'But Maisie loved the light in the fields and the birds of the glen . . .'

The light faded gradually from the room, and the smell of sun-warmed flowers was replaced by the damp green smell of the willows by the river, and the faint scent of woodsmoke from the cookhouse.

Brianna's shift was wet through, and stuck to her skin. I dug my thumbs into her back, just above the hips, and she squirmed hard against me, trying to ease the ache. Jamie sat with his head down, clinging doggedly to her hands, still talking soothingly, telling stories of silkies and seal catchers, of pipers and elves, of the great giants of Fingal's Cave, and the Devil's black horse that passes through the air faster than the thought between a man and a maid.

The pains were very close together. I motioned to Phaedre, who ran away and came back with a lighted taper, to light the candles in the sconces.

It was cool and dim in the room, the walls lit with flickering shadows. Jamie's voice was hoarse; Brianna's was nearly gone.

Suddenly she let go of him and sat up, grabbing at her knees, face dark red with effort, pushing.

'Now, then,' I said. I stacked pillows quickly behind her, made her lean back against the bedstead, called Phaedre to hold the candlestick for me.

I oiled my fingers, reached under her shift, and touched flesh I had not touched since she was a baby herself. I rubbed slowly, gently, talking to her, knowing it made no great difference what I said.

I felt the strain, the sudden change under my fingers. A relaxation, then once more. There was a sudden gush of amniotic fluid, that splashed across the bed and dripped on the floor, filling the room with the scent of fecund rivers. I rubbed and eased, praying that it would not come too fast, not tear her.

The ring of flesh opened suddenly, and my fingers touched something wet and hard. Relaxation, and it moved back, away, leaving the ends of my fingers tingling with the knowledge that I had touched someone entirely new. Once more the great pressure, the stretching came, and once more eased slowly back. I pushed back the edge

1127

of the shift, and with the next push the ring stretched to impossible size, and a head like a Chinese gargoyle popped out, with a flood of amniotic fluid and blood.

I found myself nose to nose with a waxy-white head with a face like a fist, that grimaced at me in utter fury.

'What is it? Is it a boy?' Jamie's hoarse question cut through my startlement.

'I hope so,' I said, hastily thumbing mucus from nose and mouth. 'It's the ugliest thing I've ever seen; God help it if it's a girl.'

Brianna made a noise that might have started as a laugh, and turned into an enormous grunt of effort. I barely had time to get my fingers in and turn the wide shoulders slightly to help. There was an audible *pop*, and a long, wet form slithered out onto the soggy quilt, wriggling like a landed trout.

I seized a clean linen towel and wrapped him – it was him, the scrotal sac swelled up round and purple between fat thighs – checking quickly for his Apgar signs: breathing, color, activity . . . all good. He was making thin, angry noises, short explosions of breath, not really crying, and punching the air with clenched tiny fists.

I laid him on the bed, one hand on the bundle as I checked Brianna. Her thighs were smeared with blood, but there was no sign of hemorrhage. The cord was still pulsing, a thick wet snake of connection between them.

She was panting, lying back on the crushed pillows, hair plastered wetly to her temples, an enormous smile of relief and triumph on her face. I laid a hand on her belly, suddenly flaccid. Deep inside, I felt the placenta give way, as her body surrendered its last physical link with her son.

'Once more, honey,' I said softly to her. The last contraction shivered over her belly, and the afterbirth slid out. I tied off the cord and cut it, and placed the solid little bundle of her child in her arms.

'He's beautiful,' I whispered.

I left him to her, and turned my attention to immediate matters, kneading her belly firmly with my fists, to encourage the uterus to contract and stop the bleeding. I could hear the babble of excitement spreading through the house as Phaedre rushed downstairs to spread the news. I glanced upward once, to see Brianna glowing, still smiling from ear to ear. Jamie was behind her, also smiling, his cheeks wet with tears. He said something to her in husky Gaelic, and brushing the hair away from her neck, leaned forward and kissed her gently, just behind the ear.

'Is he hungry?' Brianna's voice was deep and cracked, and she tried to clear her throat. 'Shall I feed him?'

'Try him and see. Sometimes they're sleepy right afterward, but sometimes they want to nurse.'

She fumbled at the neck of her shift and pulled loose the ribbon, baring one high, full breast. The bundle made small *growf* noises as she turned it awkwardly toward her, and her eyes sprang open in surprise as the mouth fastened on her nipple with sudden ferocity.

'Strong, isn't he?' I said, and realized that I was crying only when I tasted the salt of my tears running into the corners of my smile.

Sometime later, with mother and child cleaned up and made comfortable, food and drink brought for Brianna, and a last check assuring that all was well, I walked out into the deep shadows of the upper gallery. I felt pleasantly detached from reality, as though I were walking a foot or so off the ground.

Jamie had gone down to tell John; he was waiting for me at the foot of the stairs. He drew me into his arms without a word and kissed me; as he let me go I saw the deep red crescents of Brianna's nailmarks on his hands, not yet faded.

'Ye did brawly too,' he whispered to me. Then the joy in his eyes bloomed bright and flowered in a face-splitting grin. 'Grannie!'

'Is he dark or fair?' Jamie asked suddenly, rising on one elbow beside me in bed. 'I counted his fingers, and I didna even think to look.'

'You can't really tell yet,' I said drowsily. I'd counted his toes, and I'd thought of it. 'He's sort of reddish-purple, and he's still got the vernix – the white stuff – all over him. It will probably be a day or two before his skin fades into a natural color. He's got just a bit of dark hair, but it's the sort that rubs off soon after birth.' I stretched, enjoying the pleasant ache in legs and back; labor was hard work, even for the midwife. 'It wouldn't prove anything, even if he were fair, since Brianna is; he could be, either way.'

'Aye . . . but if he were dark, we'd know for sure.'

'Maybe not. Your father was dark; so was mine. He could have recessive genes and come out dark even if –'

'He could have *what?*'

I tried without success to think whether Gregor Mendel had yet started messing about with his pea plants, but gave up the effort, too sleepy to concentrate. Whether he had or not, Jamie evidently hadn't heard of him.

'He could be any color, and we wouldn't know for sure,' I said. I yawned widely. 'We won't know until he gets old enough to start resembling . . . somebody. And even then . . .' I trailed off. Did it matter a great deal who his father had been, if he wasn't going to have one?

Jamie rolled toward me and scooped me into a spooned embrace. We slept naked, and the hair on his body brushed against my skin. He kissed me softly on the back of the neck and sighed, his breath warm and tickling on my ear.

I hovered on the edge of sleep, too happy to fall completely over into dreams. Somewhere nearby, I heard a small stifled squawk, and the murmur of voices.

'Aye, well,' Jamie's voice roused me, some moments later. He sounded defiant. 'If I dinna ken his father, at least I'm sure who his grandsire is.'

I reached back and patted his leg.

'So am I – Grandpa. Hush up and go to sleep. "Sufficient unto the day is the evil thereof." '

He snorted, but his arms relaxed around me, hand curved on my breast, and in moments, he was asleep.

I lay wide-eyed, watching stars through the open window. Why had I said that? It was Frank's favorite quotation, one he always used to soothe Brianna or me when we worried over things: *Sufficient unto the day is the evil thereof.*

The air in the room was live; a light breeze stirred the curtains, and coolness touched my cheek.

'Do you know?' I whispered, soundless. 'Do you know she has a son?'

There was no answer, but peace came gradually over me in the quiet of the night, and I fell at last over the edge of dreams.

65

Return to Fraser's Ridge

Jocasta was loath to part with her newest relative, but the spring planting was already very late, and the homestead sadly neglected; we needed to return to the Ridge without delay, and Brianna would not hear of staying behind. Which was a good thing, as it would have taken dynamite to separate Jamie from his grandson.

Lord John was well enough to travel; he came with us as far as the Great Buffalo Trail Road, where he kissed Brianna and the baby, embraced Jamie and – to my shock – me, before turning north toward Virginia and Willie.

'I'll trust you to take care of them,' he said quietly to me, with a nod toward the wagon, where two bright heads bent together in mutual absorption over the bundle in Brianna's lap.

'You may,' I said, and pressed his hand. 'I'll trust you, too.' He lifted my hand to his lips, briefly, smiled at me, and rode away without looking back.

A week later, we bumped over the grass-choked ruts to the ridge where the wild strawberries grew, green and white and red together, constancy and courage, sweetness and bitterness mingled in the shadows of the trees.

The cabin was dirty and uncared for, its sheds empty and full of dead leaves. The garden was a tangle of old dried stalks and random shoots, the paddock an empty shell. The framework of the new house stood black and skeletal, reproachful on the Ridge. The place looked barely habitable, a ruin.

I had never felt such joy in any homecoming, ever.

Name, I wrote, and paused. God knew, I thought. His last name was open to question; his Christian name not yet even considered.

I called him 'sweetie' or 'darling', Lizzie called him 'dear lad', Jamie addressed him with Gaelic formality either as 'grandson' or '*a Ruaidh*', the Red One – his dark infant fuzz and dusky skin having given way to a blazing fair ruddiness that made it clear to the most casual observer just who his grandsire was – whoever his father might have been.

'When?' Lizzie had asked, but Brianna didn't answer. I knew when; when Roger came.

'And if he doesna come,' said Jamie privately to me, 'I expect the poor wee lad will go to his grave wi' no name at all. Christ, that lass is stubborn!'

'She trusts Roger,' I said evenly. 'You might try to do the same.'

He gave me a sharp look.

'There is a difference between trust and hope, Sassenach, and ye ken that as well as I do.'

'Well, have a stab at hope, then, why don't you?' I snapped, and turned my back on him, dipping my quill and shaking it elaborately. Little Query Mark had a rash on his bottom, that had kept him – and everyone else in the house – awake all night. I was grainy-eyed and cross, and not inclined to tolerate any show of bad faith.

Jamie walked deliberately around the table and sat down opposite me, resting his chin on his folded arms, so that I was forced to look at him.

'I would,' he said, a shadow of humor in his eyes. 'If I could decide whether to hope he comes or hope he does not.'

I smiled, then reached across and ran the feathered tip of my quill down the bridge of his nose in token of forgiveness, before returning to my work. He wrinkled his nose and sneezed, then sat up straight, peering at the paper.

'What's that you're doing, Sassenach?'

'Making out little Gizmo's birth certificate – so far as I can,' I added.

'Gizmo?' he said doubtfully. 'That will be a saint's name?'

'I shouldn't think so, though you never know, what with people named Pantaleon and Onuphrius. Or Ferreolus.'

'Ferreolus? I dinna think I ken that one.' He leaned back, hands linked over his knee.

'One of my favorites,' I told him, carefully filling in the

birthdate and time of birth – even that was an estimate, poor thing. There were precisely two bits of unequivocal information on this birth certificate – the date and the name of the doctor who'd delivered him.

'Ferreolus,' I went on with some enjoyment, 'is the patron saint of sick poultry. Christian martyr. He was a Roman tribune and a secret Christian. Having been found out, he was chained up in the prison cesspool to await trial – I suppose the cells must have been full. Sounds rather a dare-devil; he slipped his chains and escaped through the sewer. They caught up with him, though, dragged him back and beheaded him.'

Jamie looked blank.

'What has that got to do wi' chickens?'

'I haven't the faintest idea. Take it up with the Vatican,' I advised him.

'Mmphm. Aye, well, I've always been fond of Saint Guignole, myself.' I could see the glint in his eye, but couldn't resist.

'And what's he the patron of?'

'He's invoked against impotence.' The glint got stronger. 'I saw a statue of him in Brest once; they did say it had been there for a thousand years. 'Twas a miraculous statue – it had a cock like a gun muzzle, and –'

'A *what*?'

'Well, the size wasna the miraculous bit,' he said, waving me to silence. 'Or not quite. The townsfolk say that for a thousand years, folk have whittled away bits of it as holy relics, and yet the cock is still as big as ever.' He grinned at me. 'They do say that a man wi' a bit of St. Guignole in his pocket can last a night and a day without tiring.'

'Not with the same woman, I don't imagine,' I said dryly. 'It does rather make you wonder what he did to merit sainthood, though, doesn't it?'

He laughed.

'Any man who's had his prayer answered could tell ye that, Sassenach.' He swiveled on his stool, looking out the open door. Brianna and Lizzie sat on the grass, skirts blooming around them, watching the baby, who lay naked on an old shawl on his stomach, red-arsed as a baboon.

Brianna Ellen, I wrote neatly, then paused.

1134

'Brianna Ellen Randall, do you think?' I asked. 'Or Fraser? Or both?'

He didn't turn around, but his shoulder moved in the faintest of shrugs.

'Does it matter?'

'It might.' I blew across the page, watching the shiny black letters go dull as the ink dried. 'If Roger comes back – whether he stays or not – if he chooses to acknowledge little Anonymous, I suppose his name will be MacKenzie. If he doesn't or won't, then I imagine the baby takes his mother's name.'

He was silent for a moment, watching the two girls. They had washed their hair in the creek that morning; Lizzie was combing out Brianna's mane, the long strands shimmering like red silk in the summer sun.

'She calls herself Fraser,' he said softly. 'Or she did.'

I put down my quill and reached across the table to lay a hand on his arm.

'She's forgiven you,' I said. 'You know she has.'

His shoulders moved; not quite a shrug, but the unconscious attempt to ease some inner tightness.

'For now,' he said. 'But if the man doesna come?'

I hesitated. He was quite right; Brianna had forgiven him for his original mistake. Still, if Roger did not appear soon, she would be bound to blame Jamie for it – not without reason, I was forced to admit.

'Use both,' he said abruptly. 'Let her choose.' I didn't think he meant last names.

'He'll come,' I said firmly, 'and it will be all right.'

I picked up the quill, and added, not quite under my breath. 'I hope.'

He stooped to drink, the water splashing over dark green rock. It was a warm day; spring now, not autumn, but the moss was still emerald-green underfoot.

The memory of a razor was far behind him; his beard was thick and his hair hung past his shoulders. He'd bathed in a creek the night before, and done his best to wash himself and his clothes, but he had no illusions about his appearance. Neither did he care, he told himself. What he looked like didn't matter.

He turned toward the path where he had left his horse, limping. His foot ached, but that didn't matter either.

He rode slowly through the clearing where he had first met Jamie Fraser. The leaves were new and green, and in the distance he could hear the raucous calling of the ravens. Nothing stirred among the trees but the wild grasses. He breathed deep and felt a stab of memory, a broken remnant from a past life, a sharp as glass.

He turned his horse's head toward the top of the Ridge and urged it on, kicking gently with his good foot. Soon now. He had no idea what his reception might be, but that didn't matter.

Nothing mattered now save the fact that he was here.

66

Child of My Blood

Some enterprising rabbit had dug its way under the stakes of my garden again. One voracious rabbit could eat a cabbage down to the roots, and from the looks of things, he'd brought friends. I sighed and squatted to repair the damage, packing rocks and earth back into the hole. The loss of Ian was a constant ache; at such moments as this, I missed his horrible dog as well.

I had brought a large collection of cuttings and seeds from River Run, most of which had survived the journey. It was mid-June, still time – barely – to put in a fresh crop of carrots. The small patch of potato vines was all right, so were the peanut bushes; rabbits wouldn't touch those, and didn't care for the aromatic herbs either, except the fennel, which they gobbled like licorice.

I wanted cabbages, though, to preserve as sauerkraut; come midwinter, we would want food with some taste to it, as well as some vitamin C. I had enough seed left, and could raise a couple of decent crops before the weather turned cold, if I could keep the bloody rabbits off. I drummed my fingers on the handle of my basket, thinking. The Indians scattered clippings of their hair around the edges of the fields, but that was more protection against deer than rabbits.

Jamie was the best repellent, I decided. Nayawenne had told me that the scent of carnivore urine would keep rabbits away – and a man who ate meat was nearly as good as a mountain lion, to say nothing of being more biddable. Yes, that would do; he'd shot a deer only two days ago; it was still hanging. I should brew a fresh bucket of spruce beer to go with the roast venison, though . . .

As I wandered toward the herb shed to see if I had any maypop fruits for flavoring, my eye caught a movement at the far edge of the clearing. Thinking it was Jamie, I turned to go and inform him of his new duty, only to be stopped dead in my tracks when I saw who it was.

He looked worse than he had the last time I'd seen him, which was saying quite a bit. He was hatless, hair and beard a glossy black tangle, and his clothes hung on him in tatters. He was barefoot, one foot wrapped in a bundle of filthy rags, and he limped badly.

He saw me at once, and stopped while I came up to him.

'I'm glad it's you,' he said. 'I wondered who I'd meet first.' His voice sounded soft and rusty, and I wondered whether he had spoken to a living soul since we had left him in the mountains.

'Your foot, Roger –'

'It doesn't matter.' He gripped my arm. 'Are they all right? The baby? And Brianna?'

'They're fine. Everybody's in the house.' His head turned toward the cabin, and I added, 'You have a son.'

He jerked sharply back toward me, green eyes wide with startlement.

'He's mine? *I* have a son?'

'I suppose you do,' I said. 'You're here, aren't you?' The look of startlement – and hope, I realized – faded slowly. He looked into my eyes and seemed to see how I felt, for he smiled – not easily, no more than a painful lifting of the corner of his mouth – but he smiled.

'I'm here,' he said, and turned toward the cabin and its open doorway.

Jamie sat in his rolled-up shirt sleeves at the table, shoulder to shoulder with Brianna, frowning at a set of house drawings as she pointed with her quill. Both of them were liberally covered with ink, being inclined to enthusiasm when discussing architecture. The baby snored peacefully in his cradle nearby; Brianna was rocking it absently with one foot. Lizzie was spinning by the window, humming softly under her breath as the great wheel went round.

'Very domestic,' Roger said under his breath, stopping in the dooryard. 'Seems a shame to disturb them.'

'Do you have a choice?' I said.

'Aye, I do,' he replied. 'But I've made it already.' He walked purposefully up to the open door and stepped inside.

Jamie reacted instantly to this unfamiliar darkening of

his door; he pushed Brianna off the bench and lunged for his pistols on the wall. He had one leveled at Roger's chest before he realized what – or whom – he was looking at, and lowered it with a small exclamation of disgust.

'Oh, it's you,' he said.

The baby, rudely wakened by the crash of the overturned bench, was shrieking like a fire engine. Brianna scooped him out of his cradle and clasped him to her breast, looking wild-eyed at the apparition in the door.

I had forgotten that she hadn't had the benefit of seeing him even as recently as I had; he must be substantially changed from the young history professor who'd left her in Wilmington nearly a year before.

Roger took a step toward her; instinctively, she took a step back. He stood quite still, looking at the child. She sat down on the nursing stool, fumbling at her bodice, bending protectively over the baby. She pulled a shawl across her shoulder and gave him a breast in its shelter, and he stopped squawking at once.

I saw Roger's eyes shift from the baby to Jamie. Jamie stood beside Brianna with that utter stillness that so frightened me – straight and still as a stick of dynamite, with a lit match laid a hairsbreadth from the fuse.

The flame of Brianna's head moved slightly, looking from one to the other, and I saw what she saw; the echo of Jamie's dangerous stillness in Roger. It was both unexpected and shocking; I had never seen any resemblance between them at all – and yet at the moment they might have been day and dark, images of fire and night, each mirroring the other.

MacKenzie, I thought suddenly. Viking beasts, bloody-minded and big. And saw the third echo of that flaming heritage blaze up in Brianna's eyes, the only thing alive in her face.

I should say something, do something, to break the awful stillness. But my mouth was dry, and there was nothing I could say in any case.

Roger's reached his hand toward Jamie, palm up, and the gesture held no hint of supplication.

'I don't imagine it pleases you any more than it does me,' he said, in his rusty voice, 'but you are my nearest kinsman. Cut me. I've come to swear an oath in our shared blood.'

I couldn't tell whether Jamie hesitated or not; time seemed to have stopped, the air in the room crystallized around us. Then I watched Jamie's dirk cut the air, honed edge draw swift across the thin, tanned wrist, and blood well red and sudden in its path.

To my surprise, Roger didn't look at Brianna, or reach for her hand. Instead, he swiped his thumb across his bleeding wrist, and stepped close to her, eyes on the baby. She pulled back instinctively, but Jamie's hand came down on her shoulder.

She stilled at once under its weight, at once a promise of restraint and protection, but she held the child tight, cradled against her breast. Roger knelt in front of her, and reaching out, pushed the shawl aside and smeared a broad red cross upon the downy curve of the baby's forehead.

'You are blood of my blood,' he said softly, 'and bone of my bone. I claim thee as my son before all men, from this day forever.' He looked up at Jamie, challenging. After a long moment, Jamie gave the slightest nod of acknowledgment, and stepped back, letting his hand fall from Brianna's shoulder.

Roger's gaze shifted to Brianna.

'What do you call him?'

'Nothing – yet.' Her eyes rested on him, questioning. It was only too clear that the man who had come back was not the man who'd left her.

Roger's eyes were fixed on hers as he stood. Blood was still dripping from his wrist. With a small shock, I realized that she was as changed to him as he to her.

'He's my son,' Roger said quietly, nodding at the baby. 'Are you my wife?'

Brianna had gone pale to the lips.

'I don't know.'

'This man says that you are handfast.' Jamie took a step closer to her, watching Roger. 'Is that true?'

'We – we were.'

'We still are.' Roger took a deep breath, and I realized suddenly that he was about to fall over, whether from hunger, exhaustion, or the shock of being cut. I took his

1140

arm, made him sit down, sent Lizzie to the dairy shed for milk, and fetched down my small medical box to bind his wrist.

This small bustle of normality seemed to break the tension a little. Meaning to help things along in that direction, I broke out a bottle of brandy from River Run, pouring a cup for Jamie, and putting a good-sized dollop in Roger's milk. Jamie gave me a wry look, but sat back on the replaced bench and sipped his drink.

'Verra well, then,' he said, calling the meeting to order. 'If you're handfast, Brianna, then you're married and this man is your husband.'

Brianna's flush deepened, but she looked at Roger, not Jamie.

'You said handfasting was good for a year and a day.'

'And you said ye did not want anything temporary.'

She flinched at that, but then set her lips firmly.

'I didn't. But I didn't know what was going to happen.' She glanced at me and Jamie, then back at Roger. 'They told you – that the baby isn't yours?'

Roger raised his eyebrows.

'Oh, but he is mine. Mm?' He lifted his bandaged wrist in illustration.

Brianna's face had lost its frostbitten look; she was pink around the edges.

'You know what I mean.'

He met her eyes straight on.

'I know what you mean,' he said softly. 'I am sorry for it.'

'It wasn't your fault.'

Roger glanced at Jamie.

'Aye, it was,' he said quietly. 'I should have stayed with you; seen you safe.'

Brianna's brows drew together.

'I told you to go, and I meant it.' She twitched her shoulders impatiently. 'But it doesn't matter now.' She took a firmer hold on the baby and sat up straight.

'I just want to know one thing,' she said, her voice trembling only a little. 'I want to know why you came back.'

He set his empty cup down deliberately.

'Did ye not want me to come back?'

'Never mind what I wanted. What I want now is to know.

Did you come back because you wanted to – or because you thought you should?'

He looked at her for a long moment, then down at his hands, still clasped around the cup.

'Perhaps both. Perhaps neither. I don't know,' he said very softly. 'That's God's truth; I don't know.'

'Did you go to the stone circle?' she asked. He nodded, not looking at her. He fumbled in his pocket, and laid the big opal stone on the table.

'I went there. That's why I was long in coming; it took me a long time to find it.'

She was silent for a moment, then nodded.

'You didn't go back. But you can. Maybe you should.' She looked at him straight on, her gaze the twin of her father's.

'I don't want to live with you, if you came back for duty,' she said. She looked at me then, her eyes soft with pain. 'I've seen a marriage made from obligation – and I've seen one made for love. If I hadn't – ' She stopped and swallowed, then went on, looking at Roger. 'If I hadn't seen both, I could have lived with obligation. But I *have* seen both – and I won't.'

I felt as though someone had struck me in the breast-bone. *My* marriages, she meant. I looked for Jamie, and found him looking at me with the same expression of shock I knew was on my own face. He coughed to break the silence, and cleared his throat, turning to Roger.

'When were ye handfast?'

'September the second,' Roger answered promptly.

'And now it is mid-June.' Jamie glanced from one to the other, frowning.

'Well, *mo nighean*, if you are handfast with this man, then you are bound to him; there's no question.' He turned and gave Roger a dark blue stare. 'So you'll live here, as her husband. And on September the third, she will choose whether she'll wed ye by priest and book – or whether ye'll leave and trouble her no more. Ye've that long to decide why you're here – and convince her of it.'

Roger and Brianna both started to speak, to protest, but he stopped them, picking up the dirk he had left on the table. He lowered the blade gently, until it touched the cloth over Roger's chest.

'Ye'll live here as her husband, I said. But if ye touch her unwilling, I'll cut your heart out and feed it to the pig. Ye understand me?'

Roger stared down at the gleaming blade for a long moment, no expression visible beneath the thick beard, then lifted his head to meet Jamie's eyes.

'You think I'd trouble a woman who didn't want me?'

A rather awkward question, given that Jamie had beaten him to pulp under precisely that mistaken assumption. Roger put a hand on Jamie's and shoved the dirk point-first into the table. He pushed back his stool abruptly and stood up, turned on his heel, and left.

Just as quickly, Jamie stood and went after him, sheathing his dirk as he went.

Brianna looked at me helplessly.

'What do you think he'll –'

She was interrupted by a loud thud and an equally loud grunt, as a heavy body struck the wall outside.

'Treat her badly and I'll rip your balls off and cram them down your throat,' Jamie's voice said softly, in Gaelic.

I glanced at Brianna, and saw that her mastery of Gaelic was sufficient to have appreciated the gist of this. Her mouth opened, but she didn't get a word out.

There was the sound of a quick scuffle outside, ending in an even louder thump, as of a head striking logs.

Roger didn't have Jamie's air of quiet menace, but his voice rang with sincerity. 'Lay hands on me once more, you fucking sod, and I'll stuff your head back up your arse where it came from!'

There was a moment's silence, and then the sound of feet moving off. A moment later, Jamie made a Scottish noise deep in his throat, and moved off too.

Brianna's eyes were round as she looked at me.

'Testosterone poisoning,' I said, with a shrug.

'Can you do anything about it?' she asked. The corner of her mouth twitched, though I couldn't tell whether with laughter or incipient hysteria.

I pushed a hand through my hair, considering.

'Well,' I said finally, 'there are only two things they do with it, and one of them is try to kill each other.'

Brianna rubbed her nose.

'Uh-huh,' she said. 'And the other . . .' Our eyes met with a perfect understanding.

'I'll take care of your father,' I said. 'But Roger's up to you.'

Life on the mountain was a trifle tense, with Brianna and Roger behaving respectively like a trapped hare and a cornered badger, Jamie fixing Roger with brooding looks of Gaelic disapproval over the supper table, Lizzie falling over her feet to apologize to everyone in sight, and the baby deciding that the time was ripe to have nightly attacks of screaming colic.

It was probably the colic that spurred Jamie into a frenzy of activity on the new house. Fergus and some of the tenants had kindly put in a small planting for us, so that while we would have no extra corn this year to sell, at least we would eat. Freed of the need to tend a large acreage, Jamie instead spent every free moment on the ridge, hammering and sawing.

Roger was doing his best to assist with the other farm chores, though hampered by his lame foot. He had several times brushed off my attempts to treat it, but now I refused to be put off any longer. A few days after his arrival, I made my preparations and informed him firmly that I meant to deal with it first thing in the morning.

The time come, I made him lie down, and unwrapped the layers of rags wound around his foot. The sweet-rotten smell of deep infection tickled my nose, but I thanked God to see neither the red streaks of blood poisoning nor the black tinges of incipient gangrene. It was bad enough, for all that.

'You've got chronic abscesses, deep in the tissue,' I said, probing firmly with my thumbs. I could feel the squishy yielding of pockets of pus, and as I squeezed harder, the half-healed wounds broke open and a nasty yellow-gray slime oozed from an inflamed crack at the edge of the sole.

Roger went white under his tan, and his hands clenched

on the wooden frame of the bed, but he didn't make a sound.

'You're lucky,' I said, still working his foot back and forth, flexing the tiny joints of the metacarpals. 'You've been breaking open the abscesses and partially draining them by walking on it. They re-form, of course, but the movement's kept the infection from moving much deeper, and it's kept your foot flexible.'

'Oh, good,' he said faintly.

'Bree, I need you to help,' I said, turning casually toward the far end of the room, where the two girls sat, taking turns between baby and spinning wheel.

'I could; let me do it.' Lizzie sprang up, eager to help. Remorseful over her part in Roger's ordeal, she had been trying to make amends in any way possible, constantly bringing him bits of food, offering to mend his clothes, and driving him mad generally with her expressions of contrition.

I smiled at her.

'Yes, you can help. Take the baby so Brianna can come here. Why don't you take him outside for a little air?'

With a dubious glance, Lizzie did as I said, scooping little Gizmo into her arms and murmuring endearments to him as they went out. Brianna came to stand beside me, carefully keeping her eyes off Roger's face.

'I'm going to open this up and drain it the best I can,' I said, indicating the long black-crusted slit. 'Then we'll have to debride the dead tissue, disinfect it, and hope for the best.'

'And what exactly does "debride" mean?' Roger asked. I let go of his foot and his body relaxed, very slightly.

'Cleansing of a wound by the surgical or nonsurgical removal of dead tissue or bone,' I said. I touched his foot. 'Luckily, I don't think the bone's been affected, though there may be a bit of damage in the cartilage between the metacarpals. Don't worry,' I said, patting his leg. 'The debridement isn't going to hurt.'

'It isn't?'

'No. It's the draining and disinfecting that will hurt.' I glanced up at Bree. 'Go take hold of his hands, please.'

She hesitated no more than a second, then moved to

the head of the couch and held out her hands to him. He took them, his eyes on her. It was the first time they had touched each other in nearly a year.

'Hold on tight,' I instructed them. 'This is the nasty part.'

I didn't look up, but worked quickly, opening the half-healed wounds cleanly with a scalpel, pressing out as much pus and dead matter as I could. I could feel the tension quivering in his leg muscles, and the slight arching of his body as the pain lifted and bent him, but he didn't say a word.

'Do you want something to bite down on, Roger?' I asked, taking out my bottle of dilute alcohol-water mixture for irrigating. 'It's going to sting a bit, now.'

He didn't answer; Brianna did.

'He's all right,' she said steadily. 'Go ahead.'

He made a muffled noise when I began to wash out the wounds, and rolled halfway onto his side, his leg convulsing. I kept tight hold of his foot and finished the job as quickly as possible. When I let go and recorked the bottle, I looked up toward the head of the bed. She was sitting on the bed, her arms locked tight around his shoulders. His face was buried in her lap, his arms around her waist. Her face was white, but she gave me a strained smile.

'Is it over?'

'The bad part is. Just a little more to do,' I assured them. I had made my preparations two days before; at this time of year, there was no difficulty. I went outside to the smoking shed. The venison carcass hung in the shadows, bathing in clouds of protectively fragrant hickory smoke. My goal was less thoroughly preserved meat, though.

Good, it had been out long enough. I picked up the small saucer from its place near the door and carried it back to the house.

'Phew!' Brianna wrinkled her nose as I came in. 'What's that? It smells like rotten meat.'

'That's what it is.' The partial remains of a snare-killed rabbit, to be exact, retrieved from the edge of the garden and set out to wait for visitors.

She was still holding his hands. I smiled to myself and

resumed my place, picking up the wounded foot and reaching for my long-nosed forceps.

'Mama! What are you *doing*?'

'It won't hurt,' I said. I squeezed the foot slightly, spreading one of my surgical incisions. I picked one of the small white grubs out of the stinking scraps of rabbit meat and inserted it deftly into the gaping slit.

Roger's eyes had been closed, his forehead sheened with sweat.

'What?' he said, lifting his head and squinting over his shoulder in an effort to see what I was doing. 'What are you doing?'

'Putting maggots in the wounds,' I said, intent on my work. 'I learned it from an old Indian lady I used to know.'

Twin sounds indicative of shock and nausea came from the bedhead, but I kept a tight hold on his foot and went on with it.

'It works,' I said, frowning slightly as I opened another incision and deposited three of the wriggling white larvae. 'Much better than the usual means of debridement; for that, I'd have to open up your foot much more extensively, and physically scrape out as much dead tissue as I could reach – which would not only hurt like the dickens, it would likely cripple you permanently. Our little friends here eat dead tissue, though; they can get into tiny places where I couldn't reach, and do a nice, thorough job.'

'Our friends the maggots,' Brianna muttered. 'God, Mama!'

'What, exactly, is going to stop them eating my entire leg?' Roger asked with a thoroughly spurious attempt at detachment. 'They . . . um . . . they *spread*, don't they?'

'Oh, no,' I assured him cheerfully. 'Maggots are larval forms; they don't breed. They also don't eat live tissue – only the nasty dead stuff. If there's enough to get them through their pupal cycle, they'll develop into tiny flies and fly off – if not, when the food's exhausted, they'll simply crawl out, searching for more.'

Both faces were a pale green by now. Finished with the work, I wrapped the foot loosely in gauze bandages, and patted Roger's leg.

'There now,' I said. 'Don't worry, I've seen it before.

One brave told me that they tickle a bit, gnawing, but it doesn't hurt at all.'

I picked up the saucer and took it outside to wash. At the edge of the dooryard I met Jamie, coming down from the new house, Ruaidh in his arms.

'There's Grannie,' he informed the baby, removing his thumb from Ruaidh's mouth and wiping saliva from it against the side of his kilt. 'Is she no a bonny woman?'

'Gleh,' said Ruaidh, focusing a slightly cross-eyed look on his grandfather's shirt button, which he began to mouth in a meditative fashion.

'Don't let him swallow that,' I said, standing on tiptoe and kissing first Jamie, then the baby. 'Where's Lizzie?'

'I found the lassie sitting on a stump, greetin',' he said. 'So I took the lad and sent her off to be by herself for a bit.'

'She was crying? What's the matter?'

A small shadow crossed Jamie's face.

'She'll be grieving for Ian, won't she?' Putting that and his own grief aside, he took my arm and turned back toward the trail up the ridge.

'Come up wi' me, Sassenach, and see what I've done the day. I've laid the floor for your surgery; all that's needed now is a bit of a temporary roof, and it'll do for sleeping.' He glanced back toward the cabin. 'I was thinking that MacKenzie might be put there – for the time being.'

'Good idea.' Even with the additional small room to the cabin that he had built for Brianna and Lizzie, conditions were more than crowded. And if Roger was to be bedridden for several days, I would as soon not have him lying in the middle of the cabin.

'How are they faring?' he asked, with assumed casualness.

'Who? Brianna and Roger, you mean?'

'Who else?' he asked, dropping the casualness. 'Is it well between them?'

'Oh, I think so. They're getting used to each other again.'

'They are?'

'Yes,' I said, with a glance back at the cabin. 'He's just thrown up in her lap.'

1148

67

The Toss of a Coin

Roger rolled onto his side and sat up. There was no glass in the windows as yet – none needed, so long as the summer weather kept fine – and the surgery was at the front of the new house, facing the slope. If he craned his neck to one side, he could watch Brianna most of the way down to the cabin, before the chestnut trees hid her from view.

A last flick of rusty homespun, and she was gone. She'd come without the baby this evening; he didn't know whether that was progress or the reverse. They'd been able to talk without the incessant interruptions of wet diapers, squawking, fussing, feeding, and spitting up; that was a rare luxury.

She hadn't stayed as long as usual, though – he could feel the presence of the child pulling her away, as though she were tethered to it by a rubber band. He did not resent the little bugger, he told himself grimly. It was only that . . . well, only that he resented the little bugger. Didn't mean he didn't *like* him.

He hadn't eaten yet; hadn't wanted to waste any of their rare solitude. He uncovered the basket she'd brought and inhaled the warm, rich scent of squirrel stew and salt-rising bread with fresh butter. Apple tart, too.

His foot still throbbed, and it took considerable effort not to think of the helpful maggots, but in spite of that, his appetite had returned with a vengeance. He ate slowly, savoring both the food and the quiet dusk creeping over the mountainside below.

Fraser had known what he was about when he'd chosen the site of this house. It commanded the entire slope of the mountain, with a view that ran to the distant river and beyond, with mist-filled valleys in the distance and dark peaks that touched a star-strewn sky. It was one of the most solitary, magnificent, heart-wrenchingly romantic spots he had ever seen.

And Brianna was down below, nursing a small bald parasite, while he was here – alone with a few dozen of his own.

He put the empty basket on the floor, hopped to the slop jar in the corner, then back to his lonely bed on the new surgery table. Why in hell had he told her he didn't know, when she'd asked why he'd come back?

Well, because just then, he *hadn't* known. He'd been wandering in the bloody wilderness for months, half starved and off his head with solitude and pain. He hadn't seen her in nearly a year – a year in which he'd gone through hell and back. He'd sat on the cliff above that bloody stone circle for three solid days without food or fire, thinking things over, trying to decide. And in the end he'd simply gotten up and begun walking, knowing that it was the only possible choice.

Obligation? Love? How in hell could you have love *without* obligation?

He turned restlessly onto his other side, turning his back on the glorious night of scent and sun-warmed winds. The trouble with being restored to health was that some parts of him were getting a damn sight too healthy for comfort, given that the chance of their having any proper exercise was something below nil.

He couldn't even suggest such a thing to Brianna. One, she might think he'd come back solely for *that*, and two, the bloody Great Scot had not been joking about the pig.

He knew now. He'd come back because he couldn't live on the other side. If it were guilt over abandoning them – or the simple knowledge that he would die without her . . . either or both, take your choice. He knew what he was giving up, and none of it bloody mattered; he had to be here, that was all.

He flopped onto his back, staring up at the dim paleness of the pine boards that roofed his shelter. Thumps and skitterings announced the nightly visitation of squirrels from the nearby hickory tree, who found it a convenient shortcut.

How to tell her that, so she would believe it? Christ, she was so jumpy that she'd barely let him touch her. A brush of lips, a touch of hands, and she was sidling away. Except for the day when she'd held him while Claire had tortured his foot. Then, she'd been truly there for him, hanging on with all her strength. He could still feel her arms around him, and the memory gave him a small thump of satisfaction in the pit of his stomach.

Thinking on that, he wondered a bit. True, the doctoring had hurt like buggery, but it was nothing he couldn't have stood with a little tooth-gritting, and Claire, with her battlefield experience, would certainly have known that.

Done it on purpose, had she? Given Bree a chance to touch him without feeling pressured or pursued? Given him a chance to remember just how strong the pull between them was? He rolled again, onto his stomach this time, and lay with his chin on his folded arms, looking out into the soft dark outside.

She could have the other foot, if she'd do it again.

Claire looked in on him once or twice each day, but he waited until the end of the week, when she came to remove the bandages, the maggots having presumably done their dirty work and – he hoped to God – cleared out.

'Oh, lovely,' she said, poking his foot with a surgeon's ghoulish delight. 'Granulating beautifully; almost no inflammation left.'

'Great,' he said. 'Are they gone?'

'The maggots? Oh, yes,' she assured him. 'They pupate within a few days. Did a nice job, didn't they?' She ran a delicate thumbnail along the side of his foot, which tickled.

'I'll take your word for it. I'm clear to walk on it, then?' He flexed the foot experimentally. It hurt a bit, but nothing compared to what it had before.

'Yes. Don't wear shoes for a few more days, though. And for God's sake, don't step on anything sharp.'

She began to put away her things, humming to herself. She looked happy but tired; there were shadows under her eyes.

'Kid still howling at night?' he asked.

'Yes, poor thing. Can you hear him up here?'

'No. You just look tired.'

'I'm not surprised. Nobody's had a good night's sleep all week, especially poor Bree, since she's the only one who can feed him.' She yawned briefly and shook her head, blinking. 'Jamie's got the back bedroom here nearly floored; he wants to move up here as soon as it's ready – give Bree and the baby more room, and, not incidentally, have a little peace and quiet ourselves.'

'Good idea. Ah – speaking of Bree . . .'

'Mm?'

No use dragging it out; better say it straight.

'Look – I'm trying all I can. I love her, and I want to show her that, but – she sheers off. She comes and we talk, and it's great, but then I go to put an arm around her or kiss her, and suddenly she's across the room, picking leaves off the floor. Is there something wrong, something I should do?'

She gave him one of those disconcerting yellow looks of hers; straightforward and ruthless as a hawk.

'You were her first, weren't you? The first man she slept with, I mean.'

He felt the blood rising his cheeks.

'I – ah – yes.'

'Well, then. So far her entire experience of what one might call the delights of sex consists of being deflowered – and I don't care how gentle you were about it, it tends to hurt – being raped two days later, then giving birth. You think this is calculated to make her fall swooning into your arms in anticipation of your reclaiming your marital rights?'

You asked for it, he thought, *and you got it. Right between the eyes.* His cheeks burned hotter than they ever had with fever.

'I never thought of that,' he muttered to the wall.

'Well, naturally not,' she said, sounding torn between exasperation and amusement. 'You're a bloody *man*. That's why I'm telling you.'

He took a deep breath, and reluctantly turned back to face her.

'And just what *are* you telling me?'

'That she's afraid,' she said. She cocked her head to one

side, evaluating him. 'Though it's not you she's afraid of, by the way.'

'It's not?'

'No,' she said bluntly. 'She may have convinced herself that she has to know why you came back, but that's not it – a regiment of blind men could see that. It's that she's afraid she won't be able to – mmphm.' She raised one brow at him, encompassing a wealth of indelicate suggestion.

'I see,' he said, taking a deep breath. 'And just what do you suggest I do about it?'

She picked up her basket and put it over her arm.

'I don't know,' she said, giving him another yellow look. 'But I think you should be careful.'

He had just about recovered his equanimity after this unsettling consultation, when another visitor darkened his door. Jamie Fraser, bearing gifts.

'I've brought ye a razor,' Fraser said, looking critically at him. 'And some hot water.'

Claire had clipped his beard short with her surgical scissors a few days earlier, but he had felt too shaky then to attempt shaving with what was called a 'cutthroat' razor for good reason.

'Thanks.'

Fraser had brought a small looking glass and a pot of shaving soap as well. Very thoughtful. He could have wished that Fraser might have left him alone, rather than leaning against the doorframe, lending a critical eye to the proceedings, but under the circumstances Roger could scarcely ask him to leave.

Even with the unwelcome spectator, it was a sublime relief to get rid of the beard. It itched like a fiend, and he hadn't seen his own face in months.

'Work going well?' He tried for a bit of polite conversation, rinsing the blade between strokes. 'I heard you hammering in the back this morning.'

'Oh, aye.' Fraser's eyes followed his every move with interest – sizing him up, he thought. 'I've got the floor laid, and a bit of roof on. Claire and I will sleep up here tonight, I think.'

1153

'Ah.' Roger stretched his neck, negotiating the turn of his jaw. 'Claire's told me I can walk again; let me know which chores I can take over.'

Jamie nodded, arms crossed.

'Are ye handy wi' tools?'

'Haven't done a lot of building,' Roger admitted. A birdhouse done in school didn't count, he suspected.

'I dinna suppose you'll be much hand wi' a plow, or a farrowing hog?' There was a definite glimmer of amusement in Fraser's eyes.

Roger lifted his chin, clearing the last of the stubble from his neck. He'd thought about it, the last few days. Not much call for the skills of either a historian or a folk singer, on an eighteenth-century hill farm.

'No,' he said evenly, putting down the razor. 'Nor do I know how to milk a cow, build a chimney, split shingles, drive horses, shoot bears, gut deer, or spit someone with a sword.'

'No?' Overt amusement.

Roger splashed water on his face and toweled it dry, then turned to face Fraser.

'No. What I've got is a strong back. That do you?'

'Oh, aye. Couldna ask better, could I?' One side of Fraser's mouth curled up. 'Know one end of a shovel from the other, do ye?'

'That much I know.'

'Then ye'll do fine.' Fraser shoved himself away from the doorframe. 'Claire's garden needs spading, there's barley to be turned at the still, and there's an almighty heap of manure waitin' in the stable. After that, I'll show ye how to milk a cow.'

'Thanks.' He wiped the razor, put it back in the bag, and handed the lot over.

'Claire and I are going to Fergus's place the eve,' Fraser said casually, accepting it. 'Takin' the wee maid to help Marsali for a bit.'

'Ah? Well . . . enjoy yourselves.'

'Oh, I expect we will.' Fraser paused in the doorway. 'Brianna thought she'd stay; the bairn's settled a bit, and she doesna want to upset him wi' the walk.'

Roger stared hard at the other man. You could read anything – or nothing – in those slanted blue eyes.

'Oh, aye?' he said. 'So you're telling me they'll be alone? I'll keep an eye on them, then.'

One ruddy brow lifted an inch.

'I'm sure ye will.' Fraser's hand reached out and opened over the empty basin. There was a small metallic clink and a red spark glowed against the pewter. 'Ye'll mind I told ye, MacKenzie – my daughter doesna need a coward.'

Before he could reply, the brow dropped, and Fraser gave him a level blue look.

'Ye've cost me a lad I loved, and I'm no inclined to like ye for it.' He glanced down at Roger's foot, then up. 'But I've maybe cost ye more than that. I'll call the score settled – or not – at your word.'

Astonished, Roger nodded, then found his voice.

'Done.'

Fraser nodded, and disappeared as quickly as he'd come, leaving Roger staring at the empty doorway.

He lifted the latch and pushed gently on the cabin's door. It was bolted. So much for the notion of waking Sleeping Beauty with a kiss. He lifted a fist to knock, then stopped. Wrong heroine. Sleeping Beauty hadn't had an irascible dwarf in bed with her, ready to yell the house down at any disturbance.

He circled the small cabin, checking the windows, names like Sneezy and Grumpy drifting through the back of his mind. What would they call this one? Noisy? Smelly?

The house was snug as a drum, oiled skins nailed over the windows. He could punch one loose, but the last thing he wanted was to scare her by breaking in on her.

Slowly, he circled the house once more. The sensible thing was to go back to the surgery and wait till morning. He could talk to her then. Better than waking her out of a sound sleep, waking the kid.

Yes, that was plainly the thing to do. Claire would take the little bas – the baby, if he asked her. They could talk calmly, without fear of interruption, walk in the wood, get things settled between them. Right. That was it, then.

Ten minutes later he had circled the house twice more,

and was standing in the grass at the back, looking at the faint glow of the window.

'What the hell do you think you are?' he muttered to himself. 'A bloody moth?'

The creak of boards prevented his answering himself. He shot around the end of the house in time to see a white-gowned figure float ghostlike down the path toward the privy.

'Brianna?'

The figure whirled, with a small yelp of fright.

'It's me,' he said, and saw the dark blotch of her hand press against the white of her nightdress, over her heart.

'What's the matter with you, sneaking up on me like that?' she demanded furiously.

'I want to talk to you.'

She didn't answer, but whipped round and made off down the path.

'I said, I want to talk to you,' he repeated more loudly, following.

'*I* want to go to the bathroom,' she said. 'Go away.' She shut the door of the privy with a decisive slam.

He retreated a short distance up the path and waited for her to emerge. Her step slowed when she saw him, but there was no way around him without stepping into the long, wet grass.

'You shouldn't be up walking on that foot,' she said.

'The foot's fine.'

'I think you should go back to bed.'

'All right,' he said, and moved solidly into the center of the path in front of her, 'Where?'

'Where?' She froze, but made no pretense of not understanding.

'Up there?' He jerked a thumb at the ridge. 'Or here?'

'I – ah –'

Be careful, her mother said, and *my daughter doesna need a coward,* said her father. He could flip a bloody coin, but for the moment he was taking Jamie Fraser's advice, and damn the torpedoes.

'You said you'd seen a marriage of obligation and one of love. And do the one cuts out the other? Look – I spent three days in that godforsaken circle, thinking. And by

God, I thought. I thought of staying, and I though of going. And I stayed.'

'So far. You don't know what you'd be giving up, if you stay for good.'

'I do! And even if I did not, I know bloody well what I'd be giving up by going.' He gripped her shoulder, the light gauze of her shift coarse under his hand. She was very warm.

'I could not go, and live with myself, thinking I'd left behind a child who might be mine – who *is* mine.' His voice dropped a little. 'And I could not go, and live without you.'

She hesitated, drawing back, trying to escape his hand.

'My father – my fathers –'

'Look, I'm neither one of your bloody fathers! Give me credit for my own sins, at least!'

'You haven't committed any sins,' she said, her voice sounding choked.

'No, and neither have you.'

She looked up at him, and he caught the gleam of a dark, slanted eye.

'If I hadn't – ' she began.

'And if I hadn't,' he interrupted roughly. 'Drop it, aye? It doesn't matter what you've done – or I. I said I was neither of your fathers, and I meant it. But there they are, the two of them, and you know them well – far better than I.

'Did Frank Randall not love you as his own? Take you as the child of his heart, *knowing* you were the blood of another man, and one he'd good reason to hate?'

He took her other shoulder and gave her a little shake.

'Did that redheaded bastard not love your mother more than life? And love you enough to sacrifice even that love to save you?'

She made a small, choked noise, and a pang went through him at the sound, but he would not release her.

'If you believe it of them,' he said, his voice little more than a whisper, 'then by God you must believe it of me. For I am a man like them, and by all I hold holy, I do love you.'

1157

Slowly her head rose, and her breath was warm on his face.

'We have time,' he said softly, and knew suddenly why it had been so important to talk to her now, here in the dark. He reached for her hand, clasped it flat against his breast.

'Do you feel it? Do you feel my heart beat?'

'Yes,' she whispered, and slowly brought their linked hands to her own breast, pressing his palm against the thin white gauze.

'This is our time,' he said. 'Until that shall stop – for one of us, for both – it is our time. *Now.* Will ye waste it, Brianna, because you are afraid?'

'No,' she said, and her voice was thick, but clear. 'I won't.'

There was a sudden thin wail from the house, and a surprising gush of moist heat against his palm.

'I have to go,' she said, pulling away. She took two steps, then turned. 'Come in,' she said, and ran up the path in front of him, fleet and white as the ghost of a deer.

By the time he reached the door, she had already fetched the baby from his cradle. She had been in bed; the quilt was thrown back and the hollow of her body was printed on the feather bed. Looking self-conscious, she sidled past him and lay down.

'I usually feed him in bed at night. He stays asleep longer if he's next to me.'

Roger made some murmur of assent, and drew up the low nursing chair before the fire. It was very warm in the room, and the air was thick with smells of cooking, used diapers – and Brianna. Her scent was slightly different these days; the tang of wild grass tempered with a light, sweet smell that he thought must be milk.

Her head was bent, loose red hair falling over her shoulders in a cascade of sparks and shadows. The front of her gown was open to her waist, and the full round curve of one breast showed plainly, only the nipple obscured by the roundness of the baby's head. There was a faint sound of sucking.

As though feeling his eyes on her, she raised her head.

'I'm sorry,' he said softly, not to disturb the baby. 'I cannot pretend not to be looking.'

He couldn't tell if she flushed; the fire cast a red glow over face and breasts alike. She glanced down, though, as if she was embarrassed.

'Go ahead,' she said. 'Nothing much worth looking at.'

Without a word, he stood up and began to undress.

'What are you doing?' Her voice was low, but shocked.

'Not fair for me to sit here gawking at you, is it? It's much less worth looking at, I expect, but . . .' He paused, frowning at a knot in the lacing of his breeches. 'But at least you'll not feel you're on display.'

'Oh.' He didn't look up to see, but he thought that had made her smile. He'd got his shirt off; the fire felt good on his bare back. Feeling unspeakably self-conscious, he stood up and eased his breeches halfway down before stopping.

'Is this a striptease?' Brianna's mouth quivered as she tried to keep from laughing out loud, joggling the baby.

'I couldn't decide whether to turn my back or not.' He paused. 'Have you got a preference?'

'Turn your back,' she said softly. 'For now.'

He did, and got the breeches off without falling into the fire.

'Stay that way for a minute,' she said. 'Please. I like to look at you.'

He straightened up and stood still, looking into the fire. The heat played over him, uncomfortably warm, and he took a step back, a sudden memory of Father Alexandre vivid in his mind. Christ, and why would he think of that now?

'You have marks on your back, Roger,' Brianna said, her voice softer than ever. 'Who hurt you?'

'The Indians. It doesn't matter. Not now.' He hadn't bound or cut his hair; it fell over his shoulders, tickling the bare skin of his back. He could imagine the tickle of her eyes, going lower, over back and arse and thighs and calves.

'I'm going to turn around now. All right?'

'I won't be shocked,' she assured him. 'I've seen pictures.'

She had her father's trick of hiding her expressions when she wanted to. He couldn't tell a thing from the soft, wide mouth or the slanted cat-eyes. Was she shocked, frightened, amused? Why ought she to be any of those things? She had touched everything she was now looking at; had caressed and handled him with such intimacy that he had lost himself in her hands, yielded himself to her without reservation – and she to him.

But that had been a lifetime ago, in the freedom and frenzy of hot darkness. Now he stood before her for the first time naked in the light, and she sat there watching him with a baby in her arms. Which of them had changed more, since their wedding night?

She looked at him carefully, head on one side, then smiled, her eyes rising to meet his. She sat up, shifting the child easily to the other breast, leaving her gown open, the one breast bared.

He couldn't stand there any longer; the fire was singeing the hair on his arse. He moved to the side of the hearth and sat down again, watching her.

'What does that feel like?' he asked, partly from a need to break the silence before it got too heavy, partly from a deep curiosity.

'It feels good,' she answered softly, head bent over the child. 'Sort of a pulling. It tingles. When he starts to feed, something happens, and there's a rushing feeling, like everything in me is surging toward him.'

'It's not – you don't feel drained? I should have thought it would feel like your substance being taken, somehow.'

'Oh, no, not like that at all. Here, look.' She put a finger in the infant's mouth and detached it with a soft *pop!* She lowered the small body for an instant, and Roger saw the nipple drawn up taut, milk jetting out in a thin stream of incredible force. Before the child could start to wail, she put him back, but not before Roger had felt the spray of tiny droplets, warm and then suddenly cool against the skin of his chest.

'My God,' he said, half shocked. 'I didn't know it did that! It's like a squirt gun.'

'Neither did I.' She smiled again, her hand cupping the

1160

tiny head. Then the smile faded. 'There are lots of things I couldn't have imagined before they happened to me.'

'Bree.' He sat forward, forgetting his nakedness in the need to touch her. 'Bree, I know you're scared. So am I. I don't want you to be afraid of me – but Bree, I do want ye so.'

His hand rested on the round of her knee. After a moment, her free hand came down on his, light as a landing bird.

'I want you, too,' she whispered. They sat frozen together for what seemed a long time; he had no notion what to do next, only that he must not go too fast, not frighten her. *Be careful.*

The tiny sucking sounds had ceased and the bundle had gone limp and heavy in the curve of her arm.

'He's asleep,' she whispered. Moving as cautiously as one holding a vial of nitroglycerine, she scooted to the edge of the bed and stood up.

She might have meant to lay the child in its cradle, but Roger lifted his hands instinctively. She hesitated for no more than a second, then bent to lay the child in his arms. Her breasts hung full and heavy in the shadow of her open gown, and he smelled the deep musk of her body as she brushed him.

The baby was surprisingly heavy; dense, for the size of the bundle. He was amazingly warm, too; warmer even than his mother's body.

Roger boosted the tiny body cautiously, cuddling it against him; the small, curved buttocks fit in the palm of his hand. It – *he* – wasn't quite bald, after all. There was a soft red-blond fuzz all over the head. Tiny ears. Almost transparent; the one he could see was red and crumpled from being pressed against his mother's arm.

'You can't tell by looking.' Brianna's voice jerked him out of his contemplation. 'I've tried.' She was standing across the room, one drawer of the sideboard open. He thought it might be regret on her face, but the shadows were too deep to tell.

'That wasn't what I was looking for.' He lowered the baby carefully to his lap. 'It's only – this is the first time

1161

I've had a proper look at my son.' The words sounded peculiar, stiff to his tongue. She relaxed a little, though.

'Oh. Well, he's all there.' There was a small note of pride in her voice that caught at his heart, and made him look closer. The little fists were curled up tight as snail shells; he picked one up and gently stroked it with his thumb. Slowly as an octopus moving, the hand opened, enough for him to insert the tip of his index finger. The fist closed again in reflex, astonishing in the strength of its grip.

He could hear a rhythmic *whish* across the room, and realized that she was brushing her hair. He would have liked to watch her, but was too fascinated to look up.

The body had feet like a frog's; wide at the toes, narrow at the heel. Roger stroked one with a fingertip, and smiled as the tiny toes sprang wide apart. Not webbed, at least.

My son, he thought, and wasn't sure what he felt at the thought. It would take time to get used to.

But he could be, came the next thought. Not just Brianna's child, to be loved for her sake – but his own flesh and blood. That thought was even more foreign. He tried to push it from his mind, but it kept coming back. That coupling in the dark, that bittersweet mix of pain and joy – had he started this, in the midst of that?

He hadn't meant to – but he hoped like hell he had.

The child was wearing some long thing made of white gauzy stuff; he lifted it, looking at the sagging diaper and the perfect oval of the tiny navel just above. Moved by a curiosity he didn't think to question, he hooked a finger in the edge of the clout and pulled it down.

'I told you he was all there.' Brianna was standing at his elbow.

'Well, it's there,' Roger said dubiously. 'But isn't it a bit . . . small?'

She laughed.

'It'll grow,' she assured him. 'It's not like he needs it for much yet.'

His own penis, gone flaccid between his thighs, gave a small twitch at that reminder.

'Shall I take him?' She reached for the baby, but he shook his head and picked up the child again.

'Not just yet.' It – he – smelled of milk and something sweetly putrid. Something else, his own indefinable smell, like nothing else Roger had ever encountered.

'Eau de baby, Mama calls it.' She sat on the bed, a faint smile on her face. 'She says it's a natural protective device; one of the things babies use to keep their parents from killing them.'

'Killing him? But he's a sweet wee lad,' Roger protested.

One eyebrow quirked up in derision.

'You haven't been living with the little fiend for the last month. This is the first night he hasn't had colic in three weeks. I would have exposed him on a hillside if he wasn't mine.'

If he wasn't mine. That certainty was a mother's reward, he supposed. She'd always know – had always known. For a brief, surprising moment, he envied her.

The baby stirred and made a small, faint *yawp!* noise against his neck. Before he could move, she was up and had the child back in her arms, patting the rounded little back. There was a soft belch, and he subsided into limpness once more.

Brianna set him on his stomach in the cradle, carefully, as if he were wired to a stick of dynamite. He could see the faint outline of her body through the gauze, highlighted by the fire behind her. When she turned around, he was ready.

'You could have gone back, once you knew. There would have been time.' He held her eyes, not letting her look away. 'So it's my turn to ask, then, isn't it? What made you wait for me? Love – or obligation?'

'Both,' she said, her eyes nearly black. 'Neither. I – just couldn't go without you.'

He breathed deeply, feeling the last small doubt in the pit of his stomach melt away.

'Then you do know.'

'Yes.' She lifted her shoulders and let them fall, and the loose gown fell too, leaving her as naked as he was. It *was* red, by God. More than red; she was gold and amber, ivory and cinnabar, and he wanted her with a longing that went beyond flesh.

'You said that you loved me, by all you hold holy,' she whispered. 'What is it that's holy to you, Roger?'

He stood and reached for her, gently, carefully. Held her against his heart, and remembered the stinking hold of the *Gloriana* and a thin, ragged woman who smelled of milk and ordure. Of fire and drums and blood, and an orphan baptized with the name of the father who had sacrificed himself for fear of the power of love.

'You,' he said, against her hair. 'Him. Us. There isn't anything else, is there?'

68

Domestic Bliss

It was a peaceful morning. The baby had slept all night, for which feat he was the recipient of general praise. Two hens had obligingly laid eggs in their coop rather than scattering them round the landscape, so I was not required to crawl through the blackberry bushes in search of breakfast before cooking it.

The bread had risen to a perfect snowy mound in its bowl, been molded into loaves by Lizzie, and – the new Dutch oven sharing the general mood of cooperation – had been baked into a delicate brown fragrance that suffused the house with contentment. Spiced ham and turkey hash sizzled pleasantly on the griddle, adding their aromas to the softer morning scents of damp grass and summer flowers that came through the open window.

These things all helped, but the general atmosphere of drowsy well-being owed more to the night before than to the events of the morning.

It had been a perfect moon-drenched night. Jamie had put out the candle and gone to bolt the door, but instead he stood, arms braced on the doorframe, looking down the valley.

'What is it?' I asked.

'Nothing,' he said softly. 'Come and see.'

Everything seemed to be floating, deprived of depth by the eerie light. Far off, the spurt of the falls seemed frozen, suspended in air. The wind was toward us, though, and I could hear the faint rumble of tons of falling water.

The night air was scented with grass and water, and the breath of pine and spruce blew down cool from the mountaintops. I shivered in my shift, and drew closer to him for warmth. His shirttails were split at the side, open nearly to his waist. I slid my hand inside the opening nearest me, and cupped one round, warm buttock. The muscles tensed under my grip, then flexed as he turned.

He hadn't pulled away; only stepped back in order to yank the shirt off over his head. He stood on the porch naked, and held out a hand to me.

He was furred with silver and the moonlight carved his body from the night. I could see every small detail of him, long toes to flowing hair, clear as the clean black canes of the blackberry bushes at the bottom of the yard. Yet like them he was dimensionless; he might have been within hand's touch or a mile away.

I shrugged the shift from my shoulders and let it fall from my body, left it puddled by the door and took his hand. Without a word we had floated through the grass, walked wet-legged and cool-skinned into the forest, turned wordless toward each other's warmth and stepped together into the empty air beyond the ridge.

We had wakened in the dark after moonset, leaf-spattered, twig-strewn, bug-bitten, and stiff with cold. We had said not a word to each other, but laughing and staggering drunkenly, stumbling over roots and stones, had helped each other through the moonless wood and made our way back to bed for an hour's brief sleep before dawn.

I leaned over his shoulder now and deposited a bowl of oatmeal in front of him, pausing to pluck an oak leaf from his hair. I laid it on the table beside his bowl.

He turned his head, a smile hiding in his eyes, caught my hand and kissed it lightly. He let me go, and went back to his parritch. I touched the back of his neck, and saw the smile spread to his mouth.

I looked up, smiling myself, and found Brianna watching. One corner of her mouth turned up, and her eyes were warm with understanding. Then I saw her gaze shift to Roger, who was spooning in his parritch in a absent-minded sort of way, his gaze intent on her.

The picture of domestic bliss was broken by the stentorian tones of Clarence, announcing a visitor. I missed Rollo, I reflected, going to the door to see, but at least Clarence didn't leap on visitors and knock them flat or chase them round the dooryard.

The visitor was Duncan Innes, who had come bearing an invitation.

'Your aunt asks if perhaps ye will be coming to the Gathering at Mount Helicon this autumn. She says ye did give her your word, twa year past.'

Jamie shoved the platter of eggs in front of Duncan.

'I hadna thought of it,' he said, frowning a little. 'There's the devil of a lot to do, and I'm to have a roof on this place before snowfall.' He gestured upward with his chin, indicating the slats and branches that were temporarily shielding us from the vagaries of weather.

'There's a priest coming, down from Baltimore,' Duncan said, carefully avoiding looking at Roger or Brianna. 'Miss Jo did think as how ye might be wishing to have the wean baptized.'

'Oh.' Jamie sat back, lips pursed in thought. 'Aye, that's a thought. Perhaps we will go, then, Duncan.'

'That's fine; your auntie will be pleased.' Something appeared to be caught in Duncan's throat; he was turning slowly red as I watched. Jamie squinted at him and pushed a jug of cider in his direction.

'Ye've something in your throat, man?'

'Ah . . . no.' Everyone had stopped eating by now, viewing the changes to Duncan's complexion in fascination. He had gone a sort of puce by the time he managed to squeeze out the next words.

'I – errr – wish to ask your consent, *an fhearr Mac Dubh*, to the marriage of Mistress Jocasta Cameron and . . . and –'

'And who?' Jamie asked, the corner of his mouth twitching. 'The governor of the colony?'

'And myself!' Duncan seized the cup of cider and buried his face in it with the relief of a drowning man seeing a life raft float past.

Jamie burst out laughing, which seemed to be no great solace to Duncan's embarrassment.

'My consent? D'ye not think my aunt's of an age, Duncan? Or you, come to that?'

Duncan was breathing a little easier now, though the purple tinge hadn't yet begun to fade from his cheeks.

'I thought it only proper,' he said, a little stiffly. 'Seeing as how ye're her nearest kinsman.' He swallowed, and unbent a bit. 'And . . . it didna seem entirely right, *Mac Dubh*, that I should be takin' what might be yours.'

Jamie smiled and shook his head.

'I've no claim on any of my aunt's property, Duncan – and wouldna take it when she offered. You'll be married at the Gathering? Tell her we'll come, then, and dance at the wedding.'

69

Jeremiah

October 1770

Roger rode with Claire and Fergus, close to the wagon. Jamie, not trusting Brianna to drive a vehicle containing his grandson, insisted on driving, with Lizzie and Marsali in the wagon bed and Brianna on the seat beside him.

From his saddle Roger caught snatches of the discussion that had been going on ever since his arrival.

'John, for sure,' Brianna was saying, frowning down at her son, who was burrowing energetically under her shawl. 'But I don't know if it should be his first name. And if it was – should it maybe be Ian? That's "John" in Gaelic – and I'd like to name him that, but would it be too confusing, with Uncle Ian and our Ian, too?'

'Since neither one of them is here, I think it wouldna be too troublesome,' Marsali put in. She glanced up at her stepfather's back. 'Did ye not say ye wanted to use one of Da's names, as well?'

'Yes, but which one?' Brianna twisted around to talk to Marsali. 'Not James, that *would* be confusing. And I don't think I like Malcolm much. He'll already have MacKenzie, of course, so maybe – ' She caught Roger's eye and smiled up at him.

'What about Jeremiah?'

'John Jeremiah Alexander Fraser MacKenzie?' Marsali frowned, saying the names over to taste them.

'I rather like Jeremiah,' Claire chipped in. 'Very Old Testament. It's one of your names, isn't it, Roger?' She smiled at him and drew closer to the wagon, leaning over to talk to Brianna.

'Besides, if Jeremiah seems too formal, you can call him Jemmy,' she said. 'Or is that too much like Jamie?'

Roger felt a small chill prickle down his spine, at the sudden recollection of another child whose mother had

1169

called him Jemmy – a child whose father was fair-haired, with eyes as green as Roger's own.

He waited until Brianna had turned to rummage through her bag for a fresh diaper, handing the fussing baby to Lizzie to mind. He kneed his horse, urging it up close to Claire's mare.

'Do you recall something?' he asked in a low voice. 'When you first came to call on me in Inverness, with Brianna – you'd had my genealogy researched beforehand.'

'Yes?' She quirked a brow at him.

'It's been some time, and you likely wouldn't have noticed in any case . . .' He hesitated, but he had to know, if it could be known. 'You pointed out the place on my family tree where the substitution was made; where Geilie Duncan's child by Dougal was adopted in place of another child who'd died, and given his name.'

'William Buccleigh MacKenzie,' she said promptly, and smiled at his look of surprise. 'I went over that genealogy at some length,' she said dryly. 'I could probably tell you every name on it.'

He took a deep breath, uneasiness curling at the back of his neck.

'Can you? What I'm wondering – do you know the name of the changeling's wife – my six-times great-grand-mother? Her name wasn't listed on my own family tree; only William Buccleigh.'

Soft lashes dropped over the golden eyes as she thought, lips pursed.

'Yes,' she said at last, and looked at him. 'Morag. Her name was Morag Gunn. Why?'

He only shook his head, too shaken to reply. He glanced at Brianna; the baby lay half naked in her lap, the soggy diaper in a heap on the seat beside her – and remembered the smooth damp skin and soggy clout of the little boy named Jemmy.

'And their son's name was Jeremiah,' he said at last, so softly that Claire had to lean close to hear it.

'Yes.' She watched him curiously, then turned her head to look down the twisting road ahead, disappearing between the dark pines.

'I asked Geilie,' Claire said suddenly. 'I asked her why. Why we can do it.'

'And did she have an answer?' Roger stared at a deerfly on his wrist without seeing it.

'She said – "To change things." ' Claire smiled at him, her mouth curled wryly. 'I don't know whether that's an answer or not.'

70

The Gathering

It had been nearly thirty years since the last Gathering I had seen; the Gathering at Leoch, and the oath-taking of clan MacKenzie. Colum MacKenzie was dead now, and his brother Dougal – and all the clans with them. Leoch lay in ruins, and there would be no more Gatherings of the clans in Scotland.

Yet here were the plaids and the pipes, and the remnants of the Highlanders themselves undiminished in fierce pride, among the the new mountains they claimed for their own. MacNeills and Campbells, Buchanans and Lindseys, MacLeods and MacDonalds; families, slaves and servants, indentured men and lairds.

I looked out over the stir and bustle of the dozens of encampments to see if I could find Jamie, and spotted instead a familiar tall form, striding loose-jointed through the scattered throng. I stood up and waved, calling out to him.

'Myers! Mr. Myers!'

John Quincy Myers spotted me and, beaming, made his way up the slope to our encampment.

'Mrs. Claire!' he exclaimed, sweeping off his disreputable hat and bowing over my hand with his usual courtliness. 'I'm right uplifted to see ye.'

'The feeling is mutual,' I assured him, smiling. 'I didn't expect to see you here.'

'Oh, I usually reckon to come to a Gathering,' he said, straightening up and beaming down at me. 'If I'm down from the mountains in time. Fine place to sell my hides; any little bits of things I have to get rid of. Speakin' of which . . .' He began a slow, methodical rummage through the contents of his big buckskin pouch.

'Will you have been far to the north, Mr. Myers?'

'Oh, 'deed I have, 'deed I have, Mrs. Claire. Halfway up the Mohawk River, to the place they call the Upper Castle.'

'The Mohawk?' My heart began to beat faster.

'Mm.' He withdrew something from his bag, squinted at it, put it back, and rummaged further. 'Imagine my surprise, Mrs. Claire, when I stopped at a Mohawk village to the south, to see a familiar face.'

'Ian! You've seen Ian? Is he all right?' I was so excited, I grasped him by the arm.

'Oh, aye,' he assured me. 'Fine-lookin' boy – though I will say it did give me a right turn to see him rigged out like a brave, and his face burnt dark enough that I might ha' taken him for one, did he not hail me by name.'

At last he found what he was looking for, and handed me a small package wrapped in thin leather and tied with a strip of buckskin – a woodpecker's feather thrust through the knot.

'He trusted me with that, ma'am, to bring to you and your goodman.' He smiled kindly. 'Reckon as you'll want to read that right promptly; I'll meet up with ye a mite later, Mrs. Claire.' He bowed with solemn formality, and walked away, hailing acquaintances as he passed.

I wouldn't read it without waiting for Jamie; luckily, he appeared no more than a few minutes later. The letter was written on what seemed to be the torn-out flyleaf of a book, its ink the pale brown of oak-galls, but legible enough. *Ian salutat avunculus Jacobus*, the note began, and a grin broke out on Jamie's face.

Ave! That exhausting my Remembrance of the Latin tongue, I must now lapse into Plain English, of which I recall much more. I am well, Uncle, and Happy – I ask you to believe it. I have been married, after the custom of the Mohawk, and live in the house of my Wife. You will remember Emily, who carves so cleverly. Rollo has sired a Great many puppies; the village is littered with small wolfish Replicas. I cannot hope to claim the same profligacy of Procreation – yet I hope you will write to my Mother with the wish that she has not yet so many Grandchildren that she will overlook the addition of one more. The birth will be in spring; I will send Word of its outcome so soon as I may. In the meantime, you will oblige me by Remembering me to all at Lallybroch, at River Run, and Fraser's Ridge. I remember them all most Fondly, and will, so long as I shall live. My love to Auntie Claire, to Cousin Brianna, and most of all to yourself. Your most affectionate nephew, Ian Murray. Vale, avunculus.

Jamie blinked once or twice, and folding the torn page carefully, tucked it in his sporran.

'It's *avuncule*, ye wee idiot,' he said softly. 'A greeting takes the vocative case.'

Looking over the dotted campfires that evening, I would have said that every Scottish family between Philadelphia and Charleston had come – and yet more arrived with the dawn next day, and kept coming.

It was on the second day, while Lizzie, Brianna, and I were comparing babies with two of Farquard Campbell's daughters, that Jamie made his way through a mass of women and children, a wide smile on his face.

'Mrs. Lizzie,' he said. 'I've a wee surprise for ye. Fergus!'

Fergus, likewise beaming, came from behind a wagon, ushering a slight man with windblown, thin fair hair.

'Da!' Lizzie shrieked, and flung herself into his arms. Jamie put a finger in his ear and wiggled it, looking amazed.

'I dinna think I've ever heard her make a noise that loud before,' he said. He grinned at me and handed me two pieces of paper; originally part of one document, they had been carefully torn apart so that the notched edge of one fitted the jagged edge of the other.

'That'll be Mr. Wemyss's indenture,' he said. 'Put it away for now, Sassenach; we'll burn it at the bonfire tonight.'

Then he vanished back into the crowd, summoned by a wave and a shout of *Mac Dubh*! from across the clearing.

By the third day of the Gathering, I had heard so much news, gossip, and general chatter that my ears rang with the sound of Gaelic. Those who were not talking were singing; Roger was in his element, wandering through the grounds and listening. He was hoarse from singing himself; he had been up most of the night before, strumming a borrowed guitar and singing to a crowd of enchanted listeners while Brianna sat curled by his feet, looking smug.

1174

'Is he any good?' Jamie had murmured to me, squinting dubiously at his putative son-in-law.

'Better than good,' I assured him.

He lifted one eyebrow and shrugged, then leaned down to take the baby from me.

'Aye, well, I'll take your word for it. I think wee Ruaidh and I will go and find a game of dice.'

'You're going gambling with a baby?'

'Of course,' he said, and grinned at me. 'He's never too young to learn an honest trade, in case he canna sing for his supper like his da.'

'When you make bashed neeps,' I said, 'be sure to boil the tops along with the turnips. Then save the pot liquor and give it to the children; you take some too – it's good for your milk.'

Maisri Buchanan pressed her smallest child to her breast and nodded solemnly, committing my advice to memory. I could not persuade most of the new immigrants either to eat fresh greens or to feed them to their families, but now and then I found opportunity to introduce a bit of vitamin C surreptitiously into their usual diet – which consisted for the most part of oatmeal and venison.

I had tried the expedient of making Jamie eat a plate of sliced tomatoes in public view, in hopes that the sight of him would ease some of the new immigrants' fears. This had not been successful; most of them regarded him with a half-superstitious awe, and I was given to understand that Himself could naturally survive the eating of things that would kill a normal person dead on the spot.

I dismissed Maisri, and welcomed the next visitor to my impromptu clinic, a woman with two little girls, covered with an eczematous rash that I at first thought evidence of more nutritional deficiency, but which fortunately proved to be only poison ivy.

I became aware of a stir in the crowd, and paused in my ministrations, turning to see who had arrived. Sunlight glinted from metal near the edge of the clearing, and Jamie's was not the only hand to go to gun or knife hilt.

They came into the sun in marchstep, though their drums were muffled, with no more than a soft *tap-tap!* of stick on rim to guide them. Muskets pointing skyward, broadswords waggling like scorpion tails, they emerged from the grove in small bursts of scarlet, two by two, green kilts aswish around their knees.

Four, and six, and eight, and ten . . . I was counting silently, with everyone else. Forty men came on, eyes straight ahead beneath their bearskin caps, looking neither to left nor to right, with no sound but the shuffle of feet and the tap of their drum.

Across the clearing, I saw MacNeill of Barra rise from his seat and straighten up; there was a subtle stir around him, a few steps bringing his men to stand near him. I didn't need to look around to sense the same thing happening behind me; felt, rather than saw, the eddies of similar small rallyings around the mountain's foot, each group with one eye on the intruders, one eye on its chief for direction.

I looked for Brianna and was startled, if not surprised, to find her just behind me, the baby in her arms, watching intently over my shoulder.

'Who are they?' she asked, low-voiced, and I could hear the echo of the question running through the Gathering like ripples in water.

'A Highland regiment,' I said.

'I see that,' she said tartly. 'Friend or foe?'

That was plainly the question – were they here as Scots, or as soldiers? But I didn't have an answer, nor did anyone else, judging from the shiftings and mutterings among the crowd. There were incidents of troops coming to disperse unruly groups, of course. But surely not a peaceable gathering like this, which had no political purpose?

At one time, though, the mere presence of a number of Scots in one place was a political declaration, and most of those present remembered those times. The murmuring got louder, Gaelic spoken with the muffled sibilance of vehemence, sighing round the mountain like the wind before a storm.

There were forty soldiers coming up the road with guns and swords. There were two hundred Scotsmen here, most of them armed, many with slaves and servants. But also with their wives and children.

I thought of the days after Culloden, and without looking round, said to Brianna, 'If anything happens – anything at all – take the baby up into the rocks.'

Roger appeared suddenly in front of me, his attention focused on the soldiers. He didn't look at Jamie but moved silently so they stood, shoulder to shoulder, a bulwark before us. All over the clearing, the same thing was happening; the women gave not an inch, but their men stepped out before them. Anyone coming into the clearing would think that the women had melted into invisibility, leaving an implacable phalanx of Scotsmen staring down the glen.

Then two men rode out from the shelter of the trees; an officer on horseback, his aide by his side, regimental banner flying. Spurring up, they rode past the column of soldiers into the edge of the crowd. I saw the aide lean down from his horse to ask a question, saw the officer's head turn toward us in acknowledgment of the answer.

The officer barked an order and the soldiers stood to rest, muskets planted in the dust, their checkered legs apart. The officer turned his horse into the crowd, slowly nosing his way among the throng, who gave way reluctantly before him.

He was coming toward us; I saw his eyes fix on Jamie from a distance, so conspicuous by his height and his hair, bright as scarlet maple leaves.

The man drew up before us, and took off his feathered cap. He slid off his horse, took two steps toward Jamie, and bowed, rigidly correct. He was a short man, but solid, maybe thirty, with dark eyes that glittered bright as the gorget at his throat. Closer now, I saw what I had missed before, the smaller bit of metal pinned to the shoulder of his red coat; a battered brooch of tarnished gilt.

'Ma name is Airchie Hayes,' he said in broad Scots. His eyes were fixed on Jamie's face, dark with hope. 'They say ye kent my faither.'

1177

71

Circle's Close

'I have a thing to say to you,' Roger said. He'd waited for some time to catch Jamie Fraser alone. Fraser was much in demand; everyone wanted his ear for a moment. For this moment, though, he was by himself, sitting on the fallen log from which he held court. He looked up at Roger, brows raised, but nodded toward a seat on the log.

Roger sat down. He had the baby with him; Brianna and Lizzie were making the dinner, and Claire had gone to visit with the Camerons of Isle Fleur, whose fire was nearby. The night air was thick with the scent of woodsmoke rather than peat fires, but in many ways it might be Scotland, he thought.

Jamie's eye lighted on the curve of little Jemmy's skull, dusted with copper fuzz that shone in the firelight. He held out his arms, and with only the slightest hesitation, Roger carefully passed the sleeping baby to him.

'*Balach Boidheach,*' Jamie murmured as the baby stirred against him. 'There now, it's fine.' He looked across at Roger. 'You've a thing to say to me, you said.'

Roger nodded.

'I have, though not on my own account. You might say it is a message to be passed on for someone else.'

Jamie lifted one quizzical brow, in a gesture so reminiscent of Brianna that Roger felt a small internal start. To cover it, he coughed.

'I – ah – when Brianna went to the stones on Craigh na Dun, I was forced to wait a few weeks until I could follow after her.'

'Aye?' Jamie looked wary, as he always did at any mention of stone circles.

'I went to Inverness,' Roger continued, keeping his eyes on his father-in-law. 'I stayed at the house that my father had lived in, and I spent part of the time in sorting through his papers; he was a great saver of letters and bits of old rubbish.'

Jamie nodded, evidently wondering what Roger was on about, but too polite to interrupt him.

'I found a letter.' Roger took a deep breath, feeling his heart thump in his chest. 'I committed it to memory, thinking that if I found Claire, I would tell her of it. But then when I found her' – he shrugged – 'I was not sure whether I should tell her or not – or tell Brianna.'

'And you are asking me if you should tell them?' Fraser's brows rose, and ruddy, showing his puzzlement.

'Perhaps I am. But thinking on it, it occurred to me that the letter was perhaps of more concern to you than to them.' Now that the moment was at hand, Roger found himself feeling some sympathy for Fraser.

'You'll know my father was a minister? The letter was to him. I suppose it was written under the seal of confession, in a way – but I imagine death has dissolved this particular seal.'

Roger took a deep breath and closed his eyes, seeing the black letters slanting across the page, in the neat, angular handwriting. He'd read it over more than a hundred times; he was sure of every word.

Dear Reg (the letter said);

I've something the matter with my heart. Besides Claire, I mean (says he with irony). The doctor says it might be years yet, with care, and I hope it is – but there's the odd chance. The nuns at Bree's school used to scare the kids into fits about the horrible fate in store for sinners who died unconfessed and unforgiven; damned (if you'll pardon the expression) if I'm afraid of whatever comes after – if anything. But again – there's the odd chance, isn't there?

Not a thing I could say to my parish priest, for obvious reasons. I doubt he'd see the sin in it, even if he didn't slip out to telephone discreetly for psychiatric help!

But you're a priest, Reg, if not a Catholic – and more importantly, you're my friend. You needn't reply to this; I don't suppose a reply is possible. But you can listen. One of your great gifts, listening. Had I told you that before?

I'm delaying, though I don't know why I shouldn't. Best have it out.

You'll recall the favor I asked you a few years ago – about the gravestones at St. Kilda's? Kind friend that you are, you never asked, but it's time I should tell you why.

God knows why old Black Jack Randall should have been left out there on a Scottish hill instead of taken home to Sussex for burial. Perhaps no one cared enough to bring him home. Sad to think of; I rather hope it wasn't that.

There he is, though. If Bree's ever interested in her history – in my history – she'll look, and she'll find him there; the location of his grave is mentioned in the family papers. That's why I asked you to have the other stone put up nearby. It will stand out – all the other stones in that kirkyard are crumbling away with age.

Claire will take her to Scotland one day; I'm sure of that much. If she goes to St. Kilda's, she'll see it – no one goes into an old churchyard and doesn't have a browse round the stones. If she wonders, if she cares to look further – if she asks Claire – well, that's as far as I'm prepared to go. I've made the gesture; I shall leave it to chance what happens when I've gone.

You know all the rubbish Claire talked when she came back. I did all I could to get it out of her head, but she wouldn't be budged; God, she is a stubborn woman!

You'll not credit this, perhaps, but when I came last to visit you, I hired a car and went to that damned hill – to Craigh na Dun. I told you about the witches dancing in the circle, just before Claire disappeared. With that eerie sight in mind, standing there in the early light among those stones – I could almost believe her. I touched one. Nothing happened, of course.

And yet I looked. Looked for the man – for Fraser. And perhaps I found him. At least I found a man of that name, and what I could dredge up of his connections matched what Claire told me of him. Whether she was telling the truth, or whether she had grafted some delusion onto real experience . . . well, there was a man, I'm sure of that!

You'll scarcely credit this, but I stood there with my hand on that bloody stone, and wanted nothing more than that it should open, and put me face-to-face with James Fraser. Whoever he was, whenever he was, I wanted nothing more in life than to see him – and to kill him.

I have never seen him – I don't know that he existed! – and yet I hate this man as I have never hated anyone else. If what Claire said and what I found was true – then I've taken her from him, and kept her by me through these years by a lie. Maybe only a lie of omission, but nonetheless a lie for that. I could call that revenge, I suppose.

Priests and poets call revenge a two-edged sword; and the other edge of it is that I'll never know — if I gave her the choice, would she have stayed with me? Or if I told her that her Jamie survived Culloden, would she have been off to Scotland like a shot?

I cannot think Claire would leave her daughter. I hope she'd not leave me, either . . . but . . . if I had any certainty of it, I swear I'd have told her, but I haven't, and that's the truth of it.

Fraser — shall I curse him for stealing my wife, or bless him for giving me my daughter? I think these things, and then I stop, appalled that I should be giving a moment's credence to such a preposterous theory. And yet . . . I have the oddest sense of James Fraser, almost a memory, as though I must have seen him somewhere. Though likely this is just the product of jealousy and imagination — I know what the bastard looks like, well enough; I see his face on my daughter, day by day!

That's the queer side of it, though — a sense of obligation. Not just to Bree, though I do think she's a right to know — later. I told you I had a sense of the bastard? Funny thing is, it's stayed with me. I can almost feel him, sometimes, looking over my shoulder, standing across the room.

Hadn't thought of this before — do you suppose I'll meet him in the sweet by-and-by, if there is one? Funny to think of it. Should we meet as friends, I wonder, with the sins of the flesh behind us? Or end forever locked in some Celtic hell, with our hands wrapped round each other's throat?

I treated Claire badly — well, depending how one looks at it. I won't go into the sordid details; leave it that I'm sorry.

So there it is, Reg. Hate, jealousy, lying, stealing, unfaithfulness, the lot. Not much to balance it save love. I do love her — love them. My women. Maybe it's not the right kind of love, or not enough. But it's all I've got.

Still, I won't die unshriven — and I'll trust you for a conditional absolution. I raised Bree as a Catholic; do you suppose there's some forlorn hope that she'll pray for me?

'It was signed, "Frank", of course,' Roger said.

'Of course,' Jamie echoed softly. He sat quite still, his face unreadable.

Roger didn't need to read it; he knew well enough the thoughts that were going through the other's mind. The same thoughts he'd wrestled with, during those weeks between Beltane and Midsummer's Eve, during the search for Brianna across the ocean, during his captivity – and at the last, in the circle in the rhododendron hell, hearing the song of the standing stones.

If Frank Randall had chosen to keep secret what he'd found, had never placed that stone at St. Kilda's – would Claire have learned the truth anyway? Perhaps; perhaps not. But it had been the sight of that spurious grave that had led her to tell her daughter the story of Jamie Fraser, and to set Roger on the path of discovery that had led them all to this place, this time.

It had been the stone that had at once sent Claire back to the arms of her Scottish lover – and possibly to her death in those arms. That had given Frank Randall's daughter back to her father, and simultaneously condemned her to live in a time not her own; that had resulted in the birth of a red-haired boy who might otherwise not have been – the continuance of Jamie Fraser's blood. Interest on the debt owed? Roger wondered.

And then there were Roger's private thoughts, of another boy who might not have been, save for that cryptic stone hint, left by Frank Randall for the sake of forgiveness. Morag and William MacKenzie were not at the Gathering; Roger was unsure whether to be disappointed or relieved.

Jamie Fraser stirred at last, though his eyes stayed fixed on the fire.

'Englishman,' he said softly, and it was a conjuration. The hair rose very slightly on the back of Roger's neck; he could believe he saw something move in the flames.

Jamie's big hands spread, cradling his grandson. His face was remote, the flames catching sparks from hair and brows.

'Englishman,' he said, speaking to whatever he saw beyond the flames. 'I could wish that we shall meet one day. And I could hope that we shall not.'

Roger waited, hands loose on his knees. Fraser's eyes were shadowed, his face masked by the flicker of the dancing fire. At last, something like a shudder seemed to go over the big frame; he shook his head as though to clear it, and seemed to realize for the first time that Roger was still there.

'Do I tell her?' Roger said. 'Claire?'

The big Highlander's eyes sharpened.

'Will ye have told Brianna?'

'Not yet; but I will.' He gave back Fraser's stare, eye for eye. 'She is my wife.'

'For now.'

'Forever – if she will.'

Fraser looked toward the Camerons' fire. Claire's lithe shape was visible, dark against the brightness.

'I did promise her honesty,' he said at last, very quietly. 'Aye, tell her.'

By the fourth day, the slopes of the mountain were filled with new arrivals. Just before dusk, the men began to bring wood, piling it in the burnt space at the foot of the mountain. Each family had its campfire, but here was the great fire, around which everyone gathered each night to see who had come during the day.

As the dark came on, the fires bloomed on the mountainside, dotted here and there among the shallow ledges and sandy pockets. For a moment, I had a vision of the MacKenzie clan badge – a 'burning mountain' – and realized suddenly what it was. Not a volcano, as I had thought. No, it was the image of a Gathering like this one, the fires of families burning in the dark, a signal to all that the clan was present – and together. And for the first time, I understood the motto that went with the image: *Luceo non uro; I shine, not burn.*

Soon the mountainside was alive with fires. Here and there were smaller, moving flames, as the head of each family or plantation thrust a brand into his fire and brought it down the hill, to add to the blazing pyre at the foot. From our perch high on the mountainside, the figures of the men showed small and dark in silhouette against the huge fire.

A dozen families had declared themselves before Jamie finished his conversation with Gerald Forbes, and rose himself. He handed me the baby, who was sleeping soundly in spite of all the racket around him, and bent to light a brand from our fire. The shouts came from far below, thin but audible on the clear autumn air.

'The MacNeills of Barra are here!'

'The Lachlans of Glen Linnhe are here!'

And after a little, Jamie's voice, loud and strong on the dark air.

'The Frasers of the Ridge are here!' There was a brief spatter of applause from those around me – whoops and yelps from the tenants who had come with us, just as there had been from the followers of the other heads of families.

I sat quietly, enjoying the feel of the limp, heavy little body in my arms. He slept with the abandonment of total trust, tiny pink mouth half open, his breath warm and humid on the slope of my breast.

Jamie came back smelling of woodsmoke and whisky, and sat down on the log behind me. He took me by the shoulders and I leaned back against him, enjoying the feeling of him behind me. Across the fire, Brianna and Roger were talking earnestly, their heads close together. Their faces shone in the firelight, each reflecting the other.

'Ye dinna suppose they're going to change his name again, do you?' Jamie said, frowning slightly at them.

'I don't think so,' I said. 'There are other things ministers do besides christenings, you know.'

'Oh, aye?'

'It's well past the third of September,' I said, tilting back my head to look at him. 'You did tell her to choose by then.'

'So I did.' A lopsided moon floated low in the sky, shedding a soft light over his face. He leaned forward and kissed my forehead.

Then he reached down and took my free hand in his own.

'And will ye choose, too?' he asked softly. He opened his hand, and I saw the glint of gold. 'Do ye want it back?'

I paused, looking up into his face, searching it for

doubt. I saw none there, but something else; a waiting, a deep curiosity as to what I might say.

'And a long time,' he said. 'I am a jealous man, but not a vengeful one. I would take you from him, my Sassenach – but I wouldna take him from you.'

He paused for a moment, the fire glinting softly from the ring in his hand. 'It was your life, no?'

And he asked again, 'Do you want it back?'

I held up my hand in answer and he slid the gold ring on my finger, the metal warm from his body.

From F. to C. with love. Always.

'What did you say?' I asked. He had murmured something in Gaelic above me, too low for me to catch.

'I said, "Go in peace," ' he answered. 'I wasna talking to you, though, Sassenach.'

Across the fire, something winked red. I glanced across in time to see Roger lift Brianna's hand to his lips; Jamie's ruby shone dark on her finger, catching the light of moon and fire.

'I see she's chosen, then,' Jamie said softly.

Brianna smiled, her eyes on Roger's face, and leaned to kiss him. Then she stood up, brushing sand from her skirts and bent to pick up a brand from the campfire. She turned and held it out to him, speaking in a voice loud enough to carry to us where we sat across the fire.

'Go down,' she said, 'and tell them the MacKenzies are here.'

THE FIFTH NOVEL IN THE BESTSELLING OUTLANDER SERIES

The Fiery Cross

America 1771: the Colony of North Carolina stands in an uneasy balance, with the rich, colonial aristocracy on one side and the struggling pioneers of the backcountry on the other.

Between them stands Jamie Fraser, a man of honour, a man of worth. By his side his extraordinary wife, Claire, a woman blessed with the uneasy gift of the knowledge of what is to come. In the past, that knowledge has brought danger and deliverance to them both.

Now it could be a flickering torch that will light their way through the perilous years ahead – or might ignite a conflagration that will leave their lives in ashes.

arrow books

The multimillion bestselling

OUTLANDER series